Lionel Booth

Shakespeare

A reprint of his collected work as put forth in 1623

Lionel Booth

Shakespeare

A reprint of his collected work as put forth in 1623

ISBN/EAN: 9783742867070

Manufactured in Europe, USA, Canada, Australia, Japa

Cover: Foto ©Andreas Hilbeck / pixelio.de

Manufactured and distributed by brebook publishing software
(www.brebook.com)

Lionel Booth

Shakespeare

SHAKESPEARE

A REPRINT

of his

COLLECTED WORKS

As put forth in 1623

PART I CONTAINING

THE COMEDIES

LONDON
Printed for Lionel Booth 307 Regent Street   1862

LONDON:

Printed by *J. Strangeways* and *H. S. Walden*, 28 Caſtle Street,
Leiceſter Square.

SHAKESPEARE.

Collation of the Edition of 1623.

THE COMEDIES.

*** *This Collation is given, "not from an unkind wish to show infallibility at fault, but," that similar errors to those perpetrated by the "Athenæum" literary Newspaper of January 25, 1862, may be avoided.*

M R. WILLIAM SHAKESPEARES Comedies, Histories, & Tragedies. Published according to the true Originall Copies. London Printed by Isaac Iaggard, and Edward Blount. 1623*. Folio.

Title as above, on which there is a Portrait of Shakespeare engraved by Martin Droeshout; opposite to this there is a leaf containing on its reverse *ten* lines, headed, "To the Reader"—signed, "B. I." *i.e.* Ben Jonson.

Dedication to "William Earle of Pembroke, &c." and "Philip Earle of Montgomery" —signed "Iohn Heminge" and "Henry Condell"—*one* leaf.

"To the great Variety of Readers"—signed "*Iohn Heminge*" and "*Henrie Condell*"— *one* leaf.

"To the memory of my beloued, the Avthor Mr. William Shakespeare :" &c.—*two* pages of verses, signed "Ben: Ionson"—*one* leaf.

"Vpon the Lines and Life of the Famous Scenicke Poet, Master William Shakespeare"— *fourteen* lines, signed "Hvgh Holland"—*one* leaf.

"To the Memorie of the deceased Authour Maister W. Shakespeare"—*twenty-two* lines, signed "L. Digges"—"To the memorie of M. W. Shake-speare"—*eight* lines, signed "I. M."—*one* leaf.

"The Workes of William Shakespeare," &c. "The Names of the Principall Actors," &c. —*one* leaf.

"A Catalogve of the feuerall Comedies, Histories, and Tragedies," &c.—*one* leaf.

* *This general Title-page will be delivered with Part III.; the one prefixed to this portion of the Reprint being only for Part I.*

The Tempeſt—pages 1 to 19.

The Two Gentlemen of Verona—pages 20 to 38—(the head-lines of pages 37, 38 are, in error, "The Merry Wiues of Windſor.")

The Merry Wiues of Windſor—pages 39 to 60—(pages 50 & 59 are miſprinted 58 & 51).

Meaſvre, for Meaſure—pages 61 to 84.

The Comedie of Errors—pages 85 to 100—(page 86 is miſprinted 88).

Much adoe about Nothing—pages 101 to 121.

Loues Labour's loſt—pages 122 to 144.

A Midſommer Nights Dreame—pages 145 to 162—(pages 153 and 161 are miſprinted 151 and 163).

The Merchant of Venice—pages 163 to 184—(pages 164 and 165 are miſprinted 162 and 163).

As you Like it—pages 185 to 207—(page 189 is miſprinted 187).

The Taming of the Shrew—pages 208 to 229 : in ſome copies page 214 is printed 212 ; *this affords one of the evidences that copies of the firſt edition vary, and that correċtions were effeċted during the progreſs of the work through the preſs;* and it may alſo be noted that ſignature V in many copies is indicated by Vv.

All's Well, that Ends Well—pages 230 to 254—(page 237 in ſome copies is miſprinted 233, pages 249, 250 are miſprinted 251, 252).

Twelfe Night, Or what you will—pages 255 to 275—(page 265 is miſprinted 273, page 276 is *blank*).

The Winters Tale—pages 277 to 303, page 304 being *blank*.

⁎ *A ſimilar Collation will be given with its reſpeċtive Part.*

As copies are known to vary, any ſuch variations, not noticed above, being communicated will greatly oblige; as will alſo any information that will tend to render thoroughly complete the Collation of the whole work, which it is purpoſed to iſſue with the "Corrigenda." It will be obſerved that this reprint has a diſtinċt pagination; alſo, a diſtinċt ſet of ſignatures—in fours; theſe, to facilitate preciſe reference, will be continuous throughout the volume. It may be here remarked, that wherever type may be ſeen in the book out of gear, in any way defeċtive or irregular, it has been ſo permitted in accordance with a preſcribed plan—no departure from the Original: the faċt of ſuch trifles being attended to, it is hoped, may be regarded as proof that aught of importance has not been, will not be, negleċted.

SHAKESPEARE;

A REPRINT OF THE "FAMOUS FOLIO OF 1623."

ADVERTISEMENT.

IN this reproduction of the firſt edition of the collected Works of Shakeſpeare, the prime object has been to ſecure its entire identity with the Original. It is well known that there exiſts in the Original a great variety of errors; but not one of theſe has here been corrected. Whatever the defects of the Volume, it was felt that if reproduced at all it muſt be reproduced intact as it was firſt put forth in 1623, and that if the leaſt "licenſe of ink" were aſſumed, all reliance upon its identity would be deſtroyed. Notwithſtanding its defects, it ſhould not be forgotten that the Folio of 1623 is the moſt important edition extant; for, as Mr. Howard Staunton has well obſerved, it is "the only authority we poſſeſs for above one-half of Shakeſpeare's plays, and a very important one for thoſe which had been publiſhed before its appearance." Yet while, for the reaſons given, the blemiſhes muſt be allowed to remain, they have not been unheeded. On the hint of Horne Tooke (*Diverſions of Purley*, part ii. p. 52, edit. 1805), they have all been noted with a view to a comprehenſive liſt of corrigenda.

After accuracy, the next object is to place within eaſy attainment of the many a book the poſſeſſion of which has hitherto been reſtricted to the very fortunate few. Henceforth for leſs than two pounds may be ſecured, in a perfect ſtate, the coveted of all Engliſh book-collectors,—a Volume which in the Original, and in a condition more or leſs of defacement and repair, would be conſidered cheap at a hundred; and this in form and condition more pleaſing to the eye—a "cheerful ſemblance" of its prototype—and much more convenient for ufe. The Folio of 1623, although fo important for the authority of its Text, from its rarity may almoſt be regarded as a fealed book; and it is hoped that the opportunity now afforded of a more extended knowledge of its contents, will lead to a correfponding elucidation of the many perplexities which yet remain, but which poffibly are not " perplex'd beyond felf-explication." A recent writer, doing good battle for the Text of the Firſt Edition, with reference to a paffage in *Anthony and Cleopatra*, obferves, " I am inclined to think the original reading the right one, and the emendation impoffible;" poffibly, this remark may be found to have a juſt application in numerous other inſtances.

The chances of error in the paffing of an elaborate work through the prefs are mul-tifarious—occafionally their origin is moſt myſterious and unaccountable; experience, not lefs than inclination, precludes the leaſt pretenfion to infallibility, and though not fearing the complaints made againſt the laſt reprint of this book, they are not out of memory; therefore, the communication of any—the moſt trifling—departure from the Original which may be difcovered will be moſt thankfully acknowledged, and the required correction effected by a cancel.

307 REGENT STREET,
  December 18*th*, 1861.

To the Reader.

This Figure, that thou here feeſt put,
    It was for gentle Shakeſpeare cut;
Wherein the Grauer had a ſtrife
    with Nature, to out-doo the life :
O, could he but haue drawne his wit
    As well in braſſe, as he hath hit
His face; the Print would then ſurpaſſe
    All, that vvas euer vvrit in braſſe.
But, ſince he cannot, Reader, looke
    Not on his Picture, but his Booke.

                                    B. I.

Mr. WILLIAM

SHAKESPEARES

COMEDIES.

Publiſhed according to the True Originall Copies.

L O N D O N

Printed by Isaac Iaggard, and Ed. Blount, 1623; and Re-Printed
for Lionel Booth, 307 Regent Street, 1862.

T ⋯neral T ⋯ ⋯ ⋯ ⋯ret F⋯ ⋯ ⋯ f th Or.⋯ ⋯ P ⋯ III
⋯tain th ⋯⋯ f the *Tragedie*; P⋯ II.⋯ ⋯ pr⋯ in H. P
⋯will be pr⋯⋯ d ⋯with all good ſpe⋯⋯

Mr. WILLIAM

SHAKESPEARES

COMEDIES.

Publifhed according to the True Originall Copies.

L O N D O N
Printed by Isaac Iaggard, and Ed. Blount, 1623 ; and Re-Printed
for Lionel Booth, 307 Regent Street, 1862.

The general Title page, an accurate Fac-fimile of the Original, will be given with Part III., which will
contain the whole of the Tragedies; Part II., comprifing the Hiftor: Plays, is in preparation, and
will be produced " with all good fpeed."

LONDON:
Printed by *J. Strangeways* and *H. S. Walden*, 28 Caftle Street,
Leicefter Square.

TO THE MOST NOBLE

And

INCOMPARABLE PAIRE
OF BRETHREN.

VVILLIAM
Earle of Pembroke, &c. Lord Chamberlaine to the
Kings most Excellent Maiesty.

AND

PHILIP

Earle of Montgomery,&c. Gentleman of his Maiesties
Bed-Chamber. Both Knights of the most Noble Order
of the Garter, and our singular good
LORDS.

Right Honourable,

Hilst we studie to be thankful in our particular, for
the many fauors we haue receiued from your L.L
we are falne vpon the ill fortune, to mingle
two the most diuerse things that can bee, feare,
and rashnesse; rashnesse in the enterprize, and
feare of the successe. For, when we valew the places your H.H.
sustaine, we cannot but know their dignity greater, then to descend to
the reading of these trifles: and, vvhile we name them trifles, we haue
depriu'd our selues of the defence of our Dedication. But since your
L.L. haue beene pleas'd to thinke these trifles some-thing, heereto-
fore; and haue prosequuted both them, and their Authour liuing,
vvith so much fauour: we hope, that (they out-liuing him, and he not
hauing the fate, common with some, to be exequutor to his owne writings) you will vse the like indulgence toward them, you haue done
A 2   vnto

The Epiftle Dedicatorie.

vnto their parent. There is a great difference, vvhether any Booke choofe his Patrones, or finde them : This hath done both. For, fo much were your L L. likings of the feuerall parts, vvhen they were acted, as before they vvere publifhed, the Volume ask'd to be yours. We haue but collected them, and done an office to the dead, to procure his Orphanes, Guardians; vvithout ambition ei_ ther of felfe-profit, or fame : onely to keepe the memory of fo worthy a Friend, & Fellow aliue, as was our S H A K E S P E A R E , by hum_ ble offer of his playes, to your moft noble patronage. Wherein, as we haue iuftly obferued, no man to come neere your L.L. but vvith a kind of religious addreffe ; it hath bin the height of our care, vvho are the Prefenters, to make the prefent worthy of your H.H. by the perfection. But, there we muft alfo craue our abilities to be confiderd, my Lords. We cannot go beyond our owne powers. Country hands reach foorth milke, creame, fruites, or what they haue : and many Nations (we haue heard) that had not gummes & incenfe , obtai_ ned their requefts with a leauened Cake. It vvas no fault to approch their Gods, by what meanes they could : And the moft , though meaneft, of things are made more precious, when they are dedicated to Temples. In that name therefore, we moft humbly confecrate to your H.H. thefe remaines of your feruant Shakefpeare ; that what delight is in them, may be euer your L.L. the reputation his, & the faults ours, if any be committed, by a payre fo carefull to fhew their gratitude both to the liuing, and the dead, as is

Your Lordfhippes moft bounden,

I OHN H E M I N G E.
H E N R Y C O N D E L L.

To the great Variety of Readers.

Rom the moſt able, to him that can but ſpell : There you are number'd. We had rather you were weighd. Eſpecially, when the fate of all Bookes depends vp-on your capacities : and not of your heads alone, but of your purſes. Well ! it is now publique, & you wil ſtand for your priuiledges wee know : to read, and cenſure. Do ſo, but buy it firſt. That doth beſt commend a Booke, the Stationer ſaies. Then, how odde ſoeuer your braines be, or your wiſedomes, make your licence the ſame, and ſpare not. Iudge your ſixe-pen'orth, your ſhillings worth, your fiue ſhil-lings worth at a time, or higher, ſo you riſe to the juſt rates, and wel-come. But, what euer you do, Buy. Cenſure will not driue a Trade, or make the Iacke go. And though you be a Magiſtrate of wit, and ſit on the Stage at *Black-Friers*, or the *Cock-pit*, to arraigne Playes dailie, know, theſe Playes haue had their triall alreadie, and ſtood out all Ap-peales; and do now come forth quitted rather by a Decree of Court, then any purchas'd Letters of commendation.

It had bene a thing, we confeſſe, worthie to haue bene wiſhed, that the Author himſelfe had liu'd to haue ſet forth, and ouerſeen his owne writings; But ſince it hath bin ordain'd otherwiſe, and he by death de-parted from that right, we pray you do not envie his Friends, the office of their care, and paine, to haue collected & publiſh'd them; and ſo to haue publiſh'd them, as wherc (before) you were abus'd with diuerſe ſtolne, and ſurreptitious copies, maimed, and deformed by the frauds and ſtealthes of iniurious impoſtors, that expos'd them : euen thoſe, are now offer'd to your view cur'd, and perfect of their limbes; and all the reſt, abſolute in their numbers, as he conceiued thẽ. Who, as he was a happie imitator of Nature, was a moſt gentle expreſſer of it. His mind and hand went together: And what he thought, he vttered with that eaſineſſe, that wee haue ſcarſe receiued from him a blot in his papers. But it is not our prouince, who onely gather his works, and giue them you, to praiſe him. It is yours that reade him. And there we hope, to your diuers capacities, you will finde enough, both to draw, and hold you : for his wit can no more lie hid, then it could be loſt. Reade him, therefore.; and againe, and againe : And if then you doe not like him, ſurely you are in ſome manifeſt danger, not to vnderſtand him. And ſo we leaue you to other of his Friends, whom if you need, can bee your guides : if you neede them not, you can leade your ſelues, and others . And ſuch Readers we wiſh him.

A 3

Iohn Heminge.
Henrie Condell.

To the memory of my beloued,
The AVTHOR
Mr. William Shakespeare:
AND
what he hath left vs.

To draw no enuy (Shakeſpeare) on thy name,
  Am I thus ample to thy Booke, and Fame :
While I confeſſe thy writings to be ſuch,
  As neither Man, nor Muſe, can praiſe too much.
'Tis true, and all mens ſuffrage. But theſe wayes
  Were not the paths I meant vnto thy praiſe :
For ſeelieſt Ignorance on theſe may light,
  Which, when it ſounds at beſt, but eccho's right ;
Or blinde Affeƈtion, which doth ne're aduance
  The truth, but gropes, and vrgeth all by chance ;
Or crafty Malice, might pretend this praiſe,
  And thinke to ruine, where it ſeem'd to raiſe.
Theſe are, as ſome infamous Baud, or Whore,
  Should praiſe a Matron. What could hurt her more ?
But thou art proofe againſt them, and indeed
  Aboue th' ill fortune of them, or the need.
I, therefore will begin.   Soule of the Age !
  The applauſe ! delight ! the wonder of our Stage !
My Shakeſpeare, riſe ; I will not lodge thee by
  Chaucer, or Spenſer, or bid Beaumont lye
A little further, to make thee a roome :
  Thou art a Moniment, without a tombe,
And art aliue ſtill, while thy Booke doth liue,
  And we haue wits to read, and praiſe to giue.
That I not mixe thee ſo, my braine excuſes ;
  I meane with great, but diſproportion'd Muſes :
For, if I thought my iudgement were of yeeres,
  I ſhould commit thee ſurely with thy peeres,
And tell, how farre thou didſtſt our Lily out-ſhine,
  Or ſporting Kid, or Marlowes mighty line.
And though thou hadſt ſmall Latine, and leſſe Greeke,
  From thence to honour thee, I would not ſeeke
For names ; but call forth thund'ring Æſchilus,
  Euripides, and Sophocles to vs,
Paccuuius, Accius, him of Cordoua dead,
  To life againe, to heare thy Buskin tread,
And ſhake a Stage : Or, when thy Sockes were on,
  Leaue thee alone, for the compariſon

Of

Of all, that insolent Greece, *or haughtie* Rome
  sent forth, or since did from their ashes come.
Triümph, my Britaine, *thou hast one to showe,*
  To whom all Scenes of Europe *homage owe.*
He was not of an age, but for all time!
  And all the Muses still were in their prime,
When like Apollo *he came forth to warme*
  Our eares, or like a Mercury *to charme!*
Nature her selfe was proud of his designes,
  And ioy'd to weare the dressing of his lines!
Which were so richly spun, and wouen so fit,
  As, since, she will vouchsafe no other Wit.
The merry Greeke, *tart* Aristophanes,
  Neat Terence, *witty* Plautus, *now not please;*
But antiquated, and deserted lye
  As they were not of Natures family.
Yet must I not giue Nature all: Thy Art,
  My gentle Shakespeare, *must enioy a part.*
For though the Poets matter, Nature be,
  His Art doth giue the fashion. And, that he,
Who casts to write a liuing line, must sweat,
  (such as thine are) and strike the second heat
Vpon the Muses anuile: turne the same,
  (And himselfe with it) that he thinkes to frame;
Or for the lawrell, he may gaine a scorne,
  For a good Poet's made, as well as borne.
And such wert thou. Looke how the fathers face
  Liues in his issue, euen so, the race
Of Shakespeares *minde, and manners brightly shines*
  In his well torned, and true-filed lines:
In each of which, he seemes to shake a Lance,
  As brandish't at the eyes of Ignorance.
Sweet Swan of Auon! *what a sight it were*
  To see thee in our waters yet appeare,
And make those flights vpon the bankes of Thames,
  That so did take Eliza, *and our* Iames!
But stay, I see thee in the Hemisphere
  Aduanc'd, and made a Constellation there!
Shine forth, thou Starre of Poets, *and with rage,*
  Or influence, chide, or cheere the drooping Stage;
Which, since thy flight frŏ hence, hath mourn'd like night,
  And despaires day, but for thy Volumes light.

B E N: I O N S O N.

Vpon the Lines and Life of the Famous
Scenicke Poet, Maſter VVILLIAM
SHAKESPEARE.

Hoſe hands, which you ſo clapt, go now, and wring
You *Britaines* braue ; for done are *Shakeſpeares* dayes :
His dayes are done, that made the dainty Playes,
Which made the Globe of heau'n and earth to ring.
　Dry'de is that veine, dry'd is the *Theſpian* Spring,
Turn'd all to teares, and *Phœbus* clouds his rayes :
That corp's, that coffin now beſticke thoſe bayes,
Which crown'd him *Poet* firſt, then *Poets* King.
If *Tragedies* might any *Prologue* haue,
All thoſe he made, would ſcarſe make one to this :
Where *Fame*, now that he gone is to the graue
(Deaths publique tyring-houſe) the *Nuncius* is.
　　For though his line of life went ſoone about,
　　The life yet of his lines ſhall neuer out.

HVGH HOLLAND.

TO THE MEMORIE
of the deceafed Authour Maifter
W. SHAKESPEARE.

Hake-fpeare, *at length thy pious fellowes giue*
The world thy Workes : thy Workes, by which, out-liue
Thy Tombe, thy name muft : when that ftone is rent,
And Time diffolues thy Stratford Moniment,
Here we aliue fhall view thee ftill. This Booke,
When Braffe and Marble fade, fhall make thee looke
Frefh to all Ages : when Pofteritie
Shall loath what's new, thinke all is prodegie
That is not Shake-fpeares ; eu'ry Line, each Verfe
Here fhall reuiue, redeeme thee from thy Herfe.
Nor Fire, nor cankring Age, as Nafo faid,
Of his, thy wit-fraught Booke fhall once inuade.
Nor fhall I e're beleeue, or thinke thee dead
(Though mift) vntill our bankrout Stage be fped
(Jmpofsible) with fome new ftraine t'out-do
Pafsions of Iuliet, and her Romeo ;
Or till J heare a Scene more nobly take,
Then when thy half-Sword parlying Romans fpake.
Till thefe, till any of thy Volumes reft
Shall with more fire, more feeling be expreft,
Be fure, our Shake-fpeare, thou canft neuer dye,
But crown'd with Lawrell, liue eternally.

L. Digges.

To the memorie of M. *W. Shake-fpeare*.

VVEE *wondred* (Shake-fpeare) *that thou went'ft fo foone*
From the Worlds-Stage, to the Graues-Tyring-roome.
Wee thought thee dead, but this thy printed worth,
Tels thy Spectators, that thou went'ft but forth
To enter with applaufe.   An Actors Art,
Can dye, and liue, to acte a fecond part.
That's but an Exit of Mortalitie ;
This, a Re-entrance to a Plaudite.

I. M.

The Workes of William Shakefpeare,

containing all his Comedies, Hiftories, and

Tragedies : Truely fet forth, according to their firft
ORJGJNALL.

The Names of the Principall Actors
in all thefe Playes.

Illiam Shakefpeare.

Richard Burbadge.

John Hemmings.

Auguftine Phillips.

William Kempt.

Thomas Poope.

George Bryan.

Henry Condell.

William Slye.

Richard Cowly.

John Lowine.

Samuell Croffe.

Alexander Cooke.

Samuel Gilburne.

Robert Armin.

William Oftler.

Nathan Field.

John Underwood.

Nicholas Tooley.

William Eccleftone.

Joseph Taylor.

Robert Benfield.

Robert Goughe.

Richard Robinfon.

Iohn Shancke.

Iohn Rice.

A CATALOGVE

of the feuerall Comedies, Hiftories, and Tragedies contained in this Volume.

THE
TEMPEST.

Actus primus, Scena prima.

A tempestuous noise of Thunder and Lightning heard: Enter a Ship-master, and a Botesvaine.

Master.
Ote-swaine.

Botes. Heere Master: What cheere?

Mast. Good : Speake to th'Mariners : fall too't, yarely, or we run our selues a ground, bestirre, bestirre. *Exit.*

Enter Mariners.

Botes. Heigh my hearts, cheerely, cheerely my harts: yare, yare : Take in the toppe-sale : Tend to th'Masters whistle : Blow till thou burst thy winde, if roome enough.

Enter Alonso, Sebastian, Anthonio, Ferdinando, Gonzalo, and others.

Alon. Good Botesvaine haue care : where's the Master? Play the men.

Botes. I pray now keepe below.

Anth. Where is the Master, Boson?

Botes. Do you not heare him? you marre our labour, Keepe your Cabines : you do assist the storme.

Gonz. Nay, good be patient.

Botes. When the Sea is : hence, what cares these roarers for the name of King? to Cabine; silence : trouble vs not.

Gon. Good, yet remember whom thou hast aboord.

Botes. None that I more loue then my selfe. You are a Counsellor, if you can command these Elements to silence, and worke the peace of the present, wee will not hand a rope more, vse your authoritie : If you cannot, giue thankes you haue liu'd so long, and make your selfe readie in your Cabine for the mischance of the houre, if it so hap. Cheerely good hearts : out of our way I say. *Exit.*

Gon. I haue great comfort from this fellow : methinks he hath no drowning marke vpon him, his complexion is perfect Gallowes : stand fast good Fate to his hanging, make the rope of his destiny our cable, for our owne doth little aduantage: If he be not borne to bee hang'd, our case is miserable. *Exit.*

Enter Botesvaine.

Botes. Downe with the top-Mast : yare, lower, lower, bring her to Try with Maine-course. A plague———
A cry within. Enter Sebastian, Anthonio & Gonzalo.

vpon this howling : they are lowder then the weather, or our office : yet againe? What do you heere? Shal we giue ore and drowne, haue you a minde to sinke?

Sebas. A poxe o'your throat, you bawling, blasphemous incharitable Dog.

Botes. Worke you then.

Anth. Hang cur, hang, you whoreson insolent Noysemaker, we are lesse afraid to be drownde, then thou art.

Gonz. I'le warrant him for drowning, though the Ship were no stronger then a Nutt-shell, and as leaky as an vnstanched wench.

Botes. Lay her a hold, a hold, set her two courses off to Sea againe, lay her off.

Enter Mariners wet.

Mari. All lost, to prayers, to prayers, all lost.

Botes. What must our mouths be cold?

Gonz. The King and Prince, at prayers, let's assist them, for our case is as theirs.

Sebas. I'am out of patience.

An. We are meerly cheated of our liues by drunkards, This wide-chopt-rascall, would thou mightst lye drowning the washing of ten Tides.

Gonz. Hee'l be hang'd yet,
Though euery drop of water sweare against it,
And gape at widst to glut him. *A confused noyse within.*
Mercy on vs.
We split, we split, Farewell my wife, and children,
Farewell brother: we split, we split, we split.

Anth. Let's all sinke with' King

Seb. Let's take leaue of him. *Exit.*

Gonz. Now would I giue a thousand furlongs of Sea, for an Acre of barren ground : Long heath, Browne firrs, any thing; the wills aboue be done, but I would faine dye a dry death. *Exit.*

Scena Secunda.

Enter Prospero and Miranda.

Mira. If by your Art (my deerest father) you haue Put the wild waters in this Rore; alay them:
The skye it seemes would powre down stinking pitch,
But that the Sea, mounting to th' welkins cheeke,
Dashes the fire out. Oh! I haue suffered
With those that I saw suffer: A braue vessell

A   (Who

(Who had no doubt ſome noble creature in her)
Daſh'd all to peeces : O the cry did knocke
Againſt my very heart : poore ſoules, they periſh'd.
Had I byn any God of power, I would
Haue ſuncke the Sea within the Earth, or ere
It ſhould the good Ship ſo haue ſwallow'd, and
The fraughting Soules within her.

   Proſ. Be collected,
No more amazement : Tell your pitteous heart
there's no harme done.

   Mira. O woe, the day.

   Proſ. No harme :
I haue done nothing, but in care of thee
(Of thee my deere one ; thee my daughter) who
Art ignorant of what thou art . naught knowing
Of whence I am : nor that I am more better
Then *Proſpero*, Maſter of a full poore cell,
And thy no greater Father.

   Mira. More to know
Did neuer medle with my thoughts.

   Proſ. 'Tis time
I ſhould informe thee farther : Lend thy hand
And plucke my Magick garment from me : So,
Lye there my Art : wipe thou thine eyes, haue comfort,
The direfull ſpectacle of the wracke which touch'd
The very vertue of compaſſion in thee :
I haue with ſuch prouiſion in mine Art
So ſafely ordered, that there is no ſoule
No not ſo much perdition as an hayre
Betid to any creature in the veſſell
Which thou heardſt cry, which thou ſaw'ſt ſinke : Sit
For thou muſt now know farther.   [downe,

   Mira. You haue often
Begun to tell me what I am, but ſtopt
And left me to a booteleſſe Inquiſition,
Concluding, ſtay : not yet.

   Proſ. The how'r's now come
The very minute byds thee ope thine eare,
Obey, and be attentiue. Canſt thou remember
A time before we came vnto this Cell ?
I doe not thinke thou canſt, for then thou was't not
Out three yeeres old.

   Mira. Certainely Sir, I can.

   Proſ. By what ? by any other houſe, or perſon ?
Of any thing the Image, tell me, that
Hath kept with thy remembrance.

   Mira. 'Tis farre off :
And rather like a dreame, then an aſſurance
That my remembrance warrants : Had I not
Fowre, or fiue women once, that tended me ?

   Proſ. Thou hadſt ; and more *Miranda :* But how is it
That this liues in thy minde ? What ſeeſt thou els
In the dark-backward and Abiſme of Time ?
Yf thou remembreſt ought ere thou cam'ſt here,
How thou cam'ſt here thou maiſt.

   Mira. But that I doe not.

   Proſ. Twelue yere ſince (*Miranda*) twelue yere ſince,
Thy father was the Duke of *Millaine* and
A Prince of power :

   Mira. Sir, are not you my Father ?

   Proſ. Thy Mother was a peece of vertue, and
She ſaid thou waſt my daughter ; and thy father
Was Duke of *Millaine*, and his onely heire,
And Princeſſe ; no worſe Iſſued.

   Mira. O the heauens,
What fowle play had we, that we came from thence ?

Or bleſſed was't we did ?

   Proſ. Both, both my Girle.
By fowle-play (as thou ſaiſt) were we heau'd thence,
But bleſſedly holpe hither.

   Mira. O my heart bleedes
To thinke oth' teene that I haue turn'd you to,
Which is from my remembrance, pleaſe you, farther;

   Proſ. My brother and thy vncle, call'd *Antbonio* :
I pray thee marke me, that a brother ſhould
Be ſo perfidious : he, whom next thy ſelfe
Of all the world I lou'd, and to him put
The mannage of my ſtate, as at that time
Through all the ſignories it was the firſt,
And *Proſpero*, the prime Duke, being ſo reputed
In dignity ; and for the liberall Artes,
Without a parrell ; thoſe being all my ſtudie,
The Gouernment I caſt vpon my brother,
And to my State grew ſtranger, being tranſported
And rapt in ſecret ſtudies, thy falſe vncle
(Do'ſt thou attend me ?)

   Mira. Sir, moſt heedefully.

   Proſ. Being once perfected how to graunt ſuites,
how to deny them : who t'aduance, and who
To traſh for ouer-topping ; new created
The creatures that were mine, I ſay, or chang'd 'em,
Or els new form'd 'em ; hauing both the key,
Of Officer, and office, ſet all hearts i'th ſtate
To what tune pleas'd his eare, that now he was
The Iuy which had hid my princely Trunck,
And ſuckt my verdure out on't : Thou attend'ſt not ?

   Mira. O good Sir, I doe.

   Proſ. I pray thee marke me :
I thus neglecting worldly ends, all dedicated
To cloſenes, and the bettering of my mind
with that, which but by being ſo retir'd
Ore-priz'd all popular rate : in my falſe brother
Awak'd an euill nature, and my truſt
Like a good parent, did beget of him
A falſehood in it's contrarie, as great
As my truſt was, which had indeede no limit,
A confidence ſans bound. He being thus Lorded,
Not onely with what my reuenew yeelded,
But what my power might els exact. Like one
Who hauing into truth, by telling of it,
Made ſuch a ſynner of his memorie
To credite his owne lie, he did beleeue
He was indeed the Duke, out o'th' Subſtitution
And executing th'outward face of Roialtie
With all prerogatiue : hence his Ambition growing :
Do'ſtthou heare ?

   Mira. Your tale, Sir, would cure deafeneſſe.

   Proſ. To haue no Schreene between this part he plaid,
And him he plaid it for, he needes will be
Abſolute *Millaine*, Me (poore man) my Librarie
Was Dukedome large enough : of temporall roalties
He thinks me now incapable. Confederates
(ſo drie he was for Sway) with King of *Naples*
To giue him Annuall tribute, doe him homage
Subiect his Coronet, to his Crowne and bend
The Dukedom yet vnbow'd (alas poore *Millaine*)
To moſt ignoble ſtooping.

   Mira. Oh the heauens :

   Proſ. Marke his condition, and th'euent, then tell me
If this might be a brother.

   Mira. I ſhould ſinne
To thinke but Noblie of my Grand-mother,

                              Good

Good wombes haue borne bad ſonnes.
  Pro. Now the Condition.
This King of *Naples* being an Enemy
To me inueterate, hearkens my Brothers ſuit,
Which was, That he in lieu o'th' premiſes,
Of homage, and I know not how much Tribute,
Should preſently extirpate me and mine
Out of the Dukedome, and confer faire *Millaine*
With all the Honors, on my brother: Whereon
A treacherous Armie leuied, one mid-night
Fated to th' purpoſe, did *Anthonio* open
The gates of *Millaine*, and ith' dead of darkeneſſe
The miniſters for th' purpoſe hurried thence
Me, and thy crying ſelfe.
  Mir. Alack, for pitty:
I not remembring how I cride out then
Will cry it ore againe: it is a hint
That wrings mine eyes too't.
  Pro. Heare a little further,
And then I'le bring thee to the preſent buſineſſe
Which now's vpon's: without the which, this Story
Were moſt impertinent.
  Mir. Wherefore did they not
That howre deſtroy vs?
  Pro. Well demanded, wench:
My Tale prouokes that queſtion: Deare, they durſt not,
So deare the loue my people bore me: nor ſet
A marke ſo bloudy on the buſineſſe; but
With colours fairer, painted their foule ends.
In few, they hurried vs a-boord a Barke,
Bore vs ſome Leagues to Sea, where they prepared
A rotten carkaſſe of a Butt, not rigg'd,
Nor tackle, ſayle, nor maſt, the very rats
Inſtinctiuely haue quit it: There they hoyſt vs
To cry to th' Sea, that roard to vs; to ſigh
To th' windes, whoſe pitty ſighing backe againe
Did vs but louing wrong.
  Mir. Alack, what trouble
Was I then to you?
  Pro. O, a Cherubin
Thou was't that did preſerue me; Thou didſt ſmile,
Infuſed with a fortitude from heauen,
When I haue deck'd the ſea with drops full ſalt,
Vnder my burthen groan'd, which rais'd in me
An vndergoing ſtomacke, to beare vp
Againſt what ſhould enſue.
  Mir. How came we a ſhore?
  Pro. By prouidence diuine,
Some food, we had, and ſome freſh water, that
A noble *Neopolitan Gonzalo*
Out of his Charity, (who being then appointed
Maſter of this deſigne) did giue vs, with
Rich garments, linnens, ſtuffs, and neceſſaries
Which ſince haue ſteeded much, ſo of his gentleneſſe
Knowing I lou'd my bookes, he furniſhd me
From mine owne Library, with volumes, that
I prize aboue my Dukedome.
  Mir. Would I might
But euer ſee that man.
  Pro. Now I ariſe,
Sit ſtill, and heare the laſt of our ſea-ſorrow:
Heere in this Iland we arriu'd, and heere
Haue I, thy Schoolemaſter, made thee more profit
Then other Princeſſe can, that haue more time
For vainer howres; and Tutors, not ſo carefull.
  Mir. Heuens thank you for't. And now I pray you Sir,

For ſtill 'tis beating in my minde; your reaſon
For rayſing this Sea-ſtorme?
  Pro. Know thus far forth,
By accident moſt ſtrange, bountifull *Fortune*
(Now my deere Lady) hath mine enemies
Brought to this ſhore: And by my preſcience
I finde my *Zenith* doth depend vpon
A moſt auſpitious ſtarre, whoſe influence
If now I court not, but omit; my fortunes
Will euer after droope: Heare ceaſe more queſtions,
Thou art inclinde to ſleepe: 'tis a good dulneſſe,
And giue it way: I know thou canſt not chuſe:
Come away, Seruant, come; I am ready now,
Approach my *Ariel*. Come.   *Enter Ariel.*
  Ari. All haile, great Maſter, graue Sir, haile: I come
To anſwer thy beſt pleaſure; be't to fly,
To ſwim, to diue into the fire: to ride
On the curld clowds: to thy ſtrong bidding, taske
Ariel, and all his Qualitie.
  Pro. Haſt thou, Spirit,
Performd to point, the Tempeſt that I bad thee.
  Ar. To euery Article.
I boorded the Kings ſhip: now on the Beake,
Now in the Waſte, the Decke, in euery Cabyn,
I flam'd amazement, ſometime I'ld diuide
And burne in many places; on the Top-maſt,
The Yards and Bore-ſpritt, would I flame diſtinctly,
Then meete, and ioyne. *Ioues* Lightning, the precurſers
O'th dreadfull Thunder-claps more momentarie
And ſight out-running were not; the fire, and cracks
Of ſulphurous roaring, the moſt mighty *Neptune*
Seeme to beſiege, and make his bold waues tremble,
Yea, his dread Trident ſhake.
  Pro. My braue Spirit,
Who was ſo firme, ſo conſtant, that this coyle
Would not infect his reaſon?
  Ar. Not a ſoule
But felt a Feauer of the madde, and plaid
Some tricks of deſperation; all but Mariners
Plung'd in the foaming bryne, and quit the veſſell;
Then all a fire with me the Kings ſonne *Ferdinand*
With haire vp-ſtaring (then like reeds, not haire)
Was the firſt man that leapt; cride hell is empty,
And all the Diuels are heere.
  Pro. Why that's my ſpirit:
But was not this nye ſhore?
  Ar. Cloſe by, my Maſter.
  Pro. But are they (*Ariell*) ſafe?
  Ar. Not a haire periſhd:
On their ſuſtaining garments not a blemiſh,
But freſher then before: and as thou badſt me,
In troops I haue diſperſd them 'bout the Iſle:
The Kings ſonne haue I landed by himſelfe,
Whom I left cooling of the Ayre with ſighes,
In an odde Angle of the Iſle, and ſitting
His armes in this ſad knot.
  Pro. Of the Kings ſhip,
The Marriners, ſay how thou haſt diſpoſd,
And all the reſt o'th'Fleete?
  Ar. Safely in harbour
Is the Kings ſhippe, in the deepe Nooke, where once
Thou calldſt me vp at midnight to fetch dewe
From the ſtill-vext *Bermoothes*, there ſhe's hid;
The Marriners all vnder hatches ſtowed,
Who, with a Charme ioynd to their ſuffred labour
I haue left aſleepe: and for the reſt o'th' Fleet
               A 2   Which

(Which I diſpers'd) they all haue met againe,
And are vpon the *Mediterranian* Flote
Bound ſadly home for *Naples*,
Suppoſing that they ſaw the Kings ſhip wrackt,
And his great perſon periſh.
  Pro. Ariel, thy charge
Exactly is perform'd; but there's more worke:
What is the time o'th'day?
  Ar. Paſt the mid ſeaſon.
  Pro. At leaſt two Glaſſes: the time 'twixt ſix & now
Muſt by vs both be ſpent moſt preciouſly.
  Ar. Is there more toyle? Since ẙ doſt giue me pains,
Let me remember thee what thou haſt promis'd,
Which is not yet perform'd me.
  Pro. How now? moodie?
What is't thou canſt demand?
  Ar. My Libertie.
  Pro. Before the time be out? no more:
  Ar. I prethee,
Remember I haue done thee worthy ſeruice,
Told thee no lyes, made thee no miſtakings, ſerv'd
Without or grudge, or grumblings; thou did promiſe
To bate me a full yeere.
  Pro. Do'ſt thou forget
From what a torment I did free thee?   *Ar.* No.
  Pro. Thou do'ſt: & thinkſt it much to tread ẙ Ooze
Of the ſalt deepe;
To run vpon the ſharpe winde of the North,
To doe me buſineſſe in the veines o'th' earth
When it is bak'd with froſt.
  Ar. I doe not Sir.
  Pro. Thou lieſt, malignant Thing: haſt thou forgot
The fowle Witch *Sycorax*, who with Age and Enuy
Was growne into a hoope? haſt thou forgot her?
  Ar. No Sir.
  Pro. Thou haſt: where was ſhe born? ſpeak: tell me:
  Ar. Sir, in *Argier*.
  Pro. Oh, was ſhe ſo: I muſt
Once in a moneth recount what thou haſt bin,
Which thou forgetſt. This damn'd Witch *Sycorax*
For miſchiefes manifold, and ſorceries terrible
To enter humane hearing, from *Argier*
Thou know'ſt was baniſh'd: for one thing ſhe did
They wold not take her life: Is not this true?   *Ar.* I, Sir.
  Pro. This blew ey'd hag, was hither brought with
And here was left by th'Saylors; thou my ſlaue,   (child,
As thou reportſt thy ſelfe, was then her ſeruant,
And for thou waſt a Spirit too delicate
To act her earthy, and abhord commands,
Refuſing her grand heſts, ſhe did confine thee
By helpe of her more potent Miniſters,
And in her moſt vnmittigable rage,
Into a clouen Pyne, within which rift
Impriſon'd, thou didſt painefully remaine
A dozen yeeres: within which ſpace ſhe di'd,
And left thee there: where thou didſt vent thy groanes
As faſt as Mill-wheeles ſtrike: Then was this Iſland
(Saue for the Son, that he did littour heere,
A frekelld whelpe, hag-borne) not honour'd with
A humane ſhape.
  Ar. Yes: *Caliban* her ſonne.
  Pro. Dull thing, I ſay ſo: he, that *Caliban*
Whom now I keepe in ſeruice, thou beſt know'ſt
What torment I did finde thee in; thy grones
Did make wolues howle, and penetrate the breaſts
Of euer-angry Beares; it was a torment

To lay vpon the damn'd, which *Sycorax*
Could not againe vndoe: it was mine Art,
When I arriu'd, and heard thee, that made gape
The Pyne, and let thee out.
  Ar. I thanke thee Maſter.
  Pro. If thou more murmur'ſt, I will rend an Oake
And peg-thee in his knotty entrailes, till
Thou haſt howl'd away twelue winters.
  Ar. Pardon, Maſter,
I will be correſpondent to command
And doe my ſpryting, gently.
  Pro. Doe ſo: and after two daies
I will diſcharge thee.
  Ar. That's my noble Maſter:
What ſhall I doe? ſay what? what ſhall I doe?
  Pro. Goe make thy ſelfe like a Nymph o'th' Sea,
Be ſubiect to no ſight but thine, and mine: inuiſible
To euery eye-ball elſe: goe take this ſhape
And hither come in't: goe: hence
With diligence.   *Exit.*
  Pro. Awake, deere hart awake, thou haſt ſlept well,
Awake.
  Mir. The ſtrangenes of your ſtory, put
Heauineſſe in me.
  Pro. Shake it off: Come on,
Wee'll viſit *Caliban*, my ſlaue, who neuer
Yeelds vs kinde anſwere.
  Mir. 'Tis a villaine Sir, I doe not loue to looke on.
  Pro. But as 'tis
We cannot miſſe him: he do's make our fire,
Fetch in our wood, and ſerues in Offices
That profit vs: What hoa: ſlaue: *Caliban*:
Thou Earth, thou: ſpeake.
  Cal. within. There's wood enough within.
  Pro. Come forth I ſay, there's other buſines for thee:
Come thou Tortoys, when?   *Enter Ariel like a water*
Fine appariſon: my queint *Ariel*,   *Nymph.*
Hearke in thine eare.
  Ar. My Lord, it ſhall be done.   *Exit.*
  Pro. Thou poyſonous ſlaue, got by ẙ diuell himſelfe
Vpon thy wicked Dam; come forth.   *Enter Caliban.*
  Cal. As wicked dewe, as ere my mother bruſh'd
With Rauens feather from vnwholeſome Fen
Drop on you both: A Southweſt blow on yee,
And bliſter you all ore.
  Pro. For this be ſure, to night thou ſhalt haue cramps,
Side-ſtitches, that ſhall pen thy breath vp, Vrchins
Shall for that vaſt of night, that they may worke
All exerciſe on thee: thou ſhalt be pinch'd
As thicke as hony-combe, each pinch more ſtinging
Then Bees that made 'em.
  Cal. I muſt eat my dinner:
This Iſland's mine by *Sycorax* my mother,
Which thou tak'ſt from me: when thou cam'ſt firſt
Thou ſtroakſt me, & made much of me: wouldſt giue me
Water with berries in't: and teach me how
To name the bigger Light, and how the leſſe
That burne by day, and night: and then I lou'd thee
And ſhew'd thee all the qualities o'th' Iſle,
The freſh Springs, Brine-pits; barren place and fertill,
Curs'd be I that did ſo: All the Charmes
Of *Sycorax*: Toades, Beetles, Batts light on you:
For I am all the Subiects that you haue,
Which firſt was min owne King: and here you ſty-me
In this hard Rocke, whiles you doe keepe from me
The reſt o'th' Iſland.
                        Pro. Thou

Pro. Thou moſt lying ſlaue,
Whom ſtripes may moue, not kindnes: I haue vs'd thee
(Filth as thou art) with humane care, and lodg'd thee
In mine owne Cell, till thou didſt ſeeke to violate
The honor of my childe.

Cal. Oh ho, oh ho, would't had bene done:
Thou didſt preuent me, I had peopel'd elſe
This Iſle with *Calibans.*

Mira. Abhorred Slaue,
Which any print of goodneſſe wilt not take,
Being capable of all ill: I pittied thee,
Took pains to make thee ſpeak, taught thee each houre
One thing or other: when thou didſt not (Sauage)
Know thine owne meaning; but wouldſt gabble, like
A thing moſt brutiſh, I endow'd thy purpoſes
With words that made them knowne: But thy vild race
(Tho thou didſt learn) had that in't, which good natures
Could not abide to be with; therefore waſt thou
Deſeruedly confin'd into this Rocke, who hadſt
Deſeru'd more then a priſon.

Cal. You taught me Language, and my profit on't
Is, I know how to curſe: the red-plague rid you
For learning me your language.

Proſ. Hag-ſeed, hence:
Fetch vs in Fewell, and be quicke thou'rt beſt
To anſwer other buſineſſe: ſhrug'ſt thou (Malice)
If thou neglecſt, or doſt vnwillingly
What I command, Ile racke thee with old Crampes,
Fill all thy bones with Aches, make thee rore,
That beaſts ſhall tremble at thy dyn.

Cal. No, 'pray thee.
I muſt obey, his Art is of ſuch pow'r,
It would controll my Dams god *Setebos,*
And make a vaſſaile of him.

Pro. So ſlaue, hence.   *Exit Cal.*
Enter Ferdinand & Ariel, inuiſible playing & ſinging.

*Ariel Song. Come vnto theſe yellow ſands,
and then take hands:
Curtſied when you haue, and kiſt
the wilde waues whiſt:
Foote it featly heere, and there, and ſweete Sprights beare
the burthen.*   Burthen diſperſedly.
*Harke, harke, bowgh wawgh: the watch-Dogges barke,
bowgh-wawgh.*

Ar. Hark, bark, I heare, the ſtraine of ſtrutting Chanticlere
cry cockadidle-dowe.

Fer. Where ſhold this Muſick be? I'th aire, or th'earth?
It ſounds no more: and ſure it waytes vpon
Some God 'oth'Iland, ſitting on a banke,
Weeping againe the King my Fathers wracke.
This Muſicke crept by me vpon the waters,
Allaying both their fury, and my paſſion
With it's ſweet ayre: thence I haue follow'd it
(Or it hath drawne me rather) but 'tis gone.
No, it begins againe.

*Ariell Song. Full fadom fiue thy Father lies,
Of his bones are Corrall made:
Thoſe are pearles that were his eies,
Nothing of him that doth fade,
But doth ſuffer a Sea-change
Into ſomething rich, & ſtrange:
Sea-Nimphs hourly ring his knell.*
    Burthen: ding dong.
Harke now I heare them, ding-dong bell.

Fer. The Ditty do's remember my drown'd father,
This is no mortall buſines, nor no ſound

That the earth owes: I heare it now aboue me.

Pro. The fringed Curtaines of thine eye aduance,
And ſay what thou ſee'ſt yond.

Mira. What is't a Spirit?
Lord, how it lookes about: Beleeue me ſir,
It carries a braue forme. But 'tis a ſpirit.

Pro. No wench, it eats, and ſleeps, & hath ſuch ſenſes
As we haue: ſuch. This Gallant which thou ſeeſt
Was in the wracke: and but hee's ſomething ſtain'd
With greefe (that's beauties canker) y̆ might'ſt call him
A goodly perſon: he hath loſt his fellowes,
And ſtrayes about to finde 'em.

Mir. I might call him
A thing diuine, for nothing naturall
I euer ſaw ſo Noble.

Pro. It goes on I ſee
As my ſoule prompts it: Spirit, fine ſpirit, Ile free thee
Within two dayes for this.

Fer. Moſt ſure the Goddeſſe
On whom theſe ayres attend: Vouchſafe my pray'r
May know if you remaine vpon this Iſland,
And that you will ſome good inſtruction giue
How I may beare me heere: my prime requeſt
(Which I do laſt pronounce) is (O you wonder)
If you be Mayd, or no?

Mir. No wonder Sir,
But certainly a Mayd.

Fer. My Language? Heauens:
I am the beſt of them that ſpeake this ſpeech,
Were I but where 'tis ſpoken.

Pro. How? the beſt?
What wer't thou if the King of *Naples* heard thee?

Fer. A ſingle thing, as I am now, that wonders
To heare thee ſpeake of *Naples:* he do's heare me,
And that he do's, I weepe: my ſelfe am *Naples,*
Who, with mine eyes (neuer ſince at ebbe) beheld
The King my Father wrack't.

Mir. Alacke, for mercy.

Fer. Yes faith, & all his Lords, the Duke of *Millaine*
And his braue ſonne, being twaine.

Pro. The Duke of *Millaine*
And his more brauer daughter, could controll thee
If now 'twere fit to do't: At the firſt ſight
They haue chang'd eyes: Delicate *Ariel,*
Ile ſet thee free for this. A word good Sir,
I feare you haue done your ſelfe ſome wrong: A word.

Mir. Why ſpeakes my father ſo vngently? This
Is the third man that ere I ſaw: the firſt
That ere I ſigh'd for: pitty moue my father
To be enclin'd my way.

Fer. O, if a Virgin,
And your affection not gone forth, Ile make you
The Queene of *Naples.*

Pro. Soft ſir, one word more.
They are both in eythers pow'rs: But this ſwift buſinẽs
I muſt vneaſie make, leaſt too light winning
Make the prize light. One word more: I charge thee
That thou attend me: Thou do'ſt heere vſurpe
The name thou ow'ſt not, and haſt put thy ſelfe
Vpon this Iſland, as a ſpy, to win it
From me, the Lord on't.

Fer. No, as I am a man.

Mir. Ther's nothing ill, can dwell in ſuch a Temple,
If the ill-ſpirit haue ſo fayre a houſe,
Good things will ſtriue to dwell with't.

Pro. Follow me.

     A 3   *Pro.*

Prof. Speake not you for him : hee's a Traitor : come,
Ile manacle thy necke and feete together :
Sea water fhalt thou drinke : thy food fhall be
The frefh-brooke Muffels, wither'd roots, and huskes
Wherein the Acorne cradled . Follow.
Fer. No,
I will refift fuch entertainment, till
Mine enemy ha's more pow'r.

He drawes, and is charmed from mouing.

Mira. O deere Father,
Make not too rafh a triall of him, for
Hee's gentle, and not fearfull.
Prof. What I fay,
My foote my Tutor ? Put thy fword vp Traitor,
Who mak'ft a fhew, but dar'ft not ftrike : thy confcience
Is fo poffeft with guilt : Come, from thy ward,
For I can heere difarme thee with this fticke,
And make thy weapon drop.
Mira. Befeech you Father.
Prof. Hence : hang not on my garments.
Mira. Sir haue pity,
Ile be his furety.
Prof. Silence : One word more
Shall make me chide thee, if not hate thee : What,
An aduocate for an Impoftor ? Hufh :
Thou think'ft there is no more fuch fhapes as he,
(Hauing feene but him and *Caliban* :) Foolifh wench,
To th'moft of men, this is a *Caliban*,
And they to him are Angels.
Mira. My affections
Are then moft humble : I haue no ambition
To fee a goodlier man.
Prof. Come on, obey :
Thy Nerues are in their infancy againe.
And haue no vigour in them.
Fer. So they are :
My fpirits, as in a dreame, are all bound vp :
My Fathers loffe, the weakneffe which I feele,
The wracke of all my friends, nor this mans threats,
To whom I am fubdude, are but light to me,
Might I but through my prifon once a day
Behold this Mayd : all corners elfe o'th'Earth
Let liberty make vfe of : fpace enough
Haue I in fuch a prifon.
Prof. It workes : Come on.
Thou haft done well, fine *Ariell* : follow me,
Harke what thou elfe fhalt do mee.
Mira. Be of comfort,
My Fathers of a better nature (Sir)
Then he appeares by fpeech : this is vnwonted
Which now came from him.
Prof. Thou fhalt be as free
As mountaine windes ; but then exactly do
All points of my command.
Ariell. To th'fyllable.
Prof. Come follow : fpeake not for him. *Exeunt.*

Actus Secundus. Scœna Prima.

*Enter Alonfo, Sebaftian, Anthonio, Gonzalo, Adrian,
Francifco, and others.*
Gonz. Befeech you Sir, be merry ; you haue caufe,
(So haue we all) of Ioy ; for our efcape

Is much beyond our loffe ; our hint of woe
Is common, euery day, fome Saylors wife,
The Mafters of fome Merchant, and the Merchant
Haue iuft our Theame of woe : But for the miracle,
(I meane our preferuation) few in millions
Can fpeake like vs : then wifely (good Sir) weigh
Our forrow, with our comfort.
Alonf. Prethee peace.
Seb. He receiues comfort like cold porredge.
Ant. The Vifitor will not giue him ore fo.
Seb. Looke, hee's winding vp the watch of his wit,
By and by it will ftrike.
Gon. Sir.
Seb. One : Tell.
Gon. When euery greefe is entertaind,
That's offer'd comes to th'entertainer.
Seb. A dollor.
Gon. Dolour comes to him indeed, you haue fpoken
truer then you purpos'd.
Seb. You haue taken it wifelier then I meant you
fhould.
Gon. Therefore my Lord.
Ant. Fie, what a fpend-thrift is he of his tongue.
Alon. I pre-thee fpare.
Gon. Well, I haue done : But yet
Seb. He will be talking.
Ant. Which, of he, or Adrian, for a good wager,
Firft begins to crow ?
Seb. The old Cocke.
Ant. The Cockrell.
Seb. Done : The wager ?
Ant. A Laughter.
Seb. A match.
Adr. Though this Ifland feeme to be defert.
Seb. Ha, ha, ha.
Ant. So : you'r paid.
Adr. Vninhabitable, and almoft inacceffible.
Seb. Yet
Adr. Yet
Ant. He could not miffe't.
Adr. It muft needs be of fubtle, tender, and delicate
temperance.
Ant. Temperance was a delicate wench.
Seb. I, and a fubtle, as he moft learnedly deliuer'd.
Adr. The ayre breathes vpon vs here moft fweetly.
Seb. As if it had Lungs, and rotten ones.
Ant. Or, as 'twere perfum'd by a Fen.
Gon. Heere is euery thing aduantageous to life.
Ant. True, faue meanes to liue.
Seb. Of that there's none, or little.
Gon. How lufh and lufty the graffe lookes ?
How greene ?
Ant. The ground indeed is tawny.
Seb. With an eye of greene in't.
Ant. He miffes not much.
Seb. No : he doth but miftake the truth totally.
Gon. But the rariety of it is, which is indeed almoft
beyond credit.
Seb. As many voucht rarieties are.
Gon. That our Garments being (as they were) drencht
in the Sea, hold notwithstanding their frefhneffe and
gloffes, being rather new dy'de then ftain'd with falte
water.
Ant. If but one of his pockets could fpeake, would
it not fay he lyes?
Seb. I, or very falfely pocket vp his report.

Gon.

Gon. Me thinkes our garments are now as freſh as
when we put them on firſt in Affricke, at the marriage
of the kings faire daughter *Claribel* to the king of *Tunis*.

Seb. 'Twas a ſweet marriage, and we proſper well in
our returne.

Adri. *Tunis* was neuer grac'd before with ſuch a Paragon to their Queene.

Gon. Not ſince widdow *Dido's* time.

Ant. Widow? A pox o'that: how came that Widdow in? Widdow *Dido*!

Seb. What if he had ſaid Widdower *Æneas* too?
Good Lord, how you take it?

Adri. Widdow *Dido* ſaid you? You make me ſtudy
of that: She was of *Carthage*, not of *Tunis*.

Gon. This *Tunis* Sir was *Carthage*.

Adri. *Carthage*? *Gon.* I aſſure you *Carthage*.

Ant. His word is more then the miraculous Harpe.

Seb. He hath rais'd the wall, and houſes too.

Ant. What impoſſible matter wil he make eaſy next?

Seb. I thinke hee will carry this Iſland home in his
pocket, and giue it his ſonne for an Apple.

Ant. And ſowing the kernels of it in the Sea, bring
forth more Iſlands.

Gon. I. *Ant.* Why in good time.

Gon. Sir, we were talking, that our garments ſeeme
now as freſh as when we were at *Tunis* at the marriage
of your daughter, who is now Queene.

Ant. And the rareſt that ere came there.

Seb. Bate (I beſeech you) widdow *Dido*.

Ant. O Widdow *Dido*? I, Widdow *Dido*.

Gon. Is not Sir my doublet as freſh as the firſt day I
wore it? I meane in a ſort.

Ant. That ſort was well fiſh'd for.

Gon. When I wore it at your daughters marriage.

Alon. You cram theſe words into mine eares, againſt
the ſtomacke of my ſenſe: would I had neuer
Married my daughter there: For comming thence
My ſonne is loſt, and (in my rate) ſhe too,
Who is ſo farre from *Italy* remoued,
I ne're againe ſhall ſee her: O thou mine heire
Of *Naples* and of *Millaine*, what ſtrange fiſh
Hath made his meale on thee?

Fran. Sir he may liue,
I ſaw him beate the ſurges vnder him,
And ride vpon their backes; he trod the water
Whoſe enmity he flung aſide: and breſted
The ſurge moſt ſwolne that met him: his bold head
'Boue the contentious waues he kept. and oared
Himſelfe with his good armes in luſty ſtroke
To th'ſhore; that ore his waue-worne baſis bowed
As ſtooping to releeue him: I not doubt
He came aliue to Land.

Alon. No, no, hee's gone.

Seb. Sir you may thank your ſelfe for this great loſſe,
That would not bleſſe our Europe with your daughter,
But rather looſe her to an Affrican,
Where ſhe at leaſt, is baniſh'd from your eye,
Who hath cauſe to wet the greefe on't.

Alon. Pre-thee peace.

Seb. You were kneel'd too, & importun'd otherwiſe
By all of vs: and the faire ſoule her ſelfe
Waigh'd betweene loathneſſe, and obedience, at
Which end o'th'beame ſhould bow: we haue loſt your
I feare for euer: *Millaine* and *Naples* haue (ſon,
Mo widdowes in them of this buſineſſe making,
Then we bring men to comfort them:

The faults your owne.

Alon. So is the deer'ſt oth'loſſe.

Gon. My Lord *Sebaſtian*,
The truth you ſpeake doth lacke ſome gentleneſſe,
And time to ſpeake it in: you rub the ſore,
When you ſhould bring the plaiſter.

Seb. Very well. *Ant.* And moſt Chirurgeonly.

Gon. It is foule weather in vs all, good Sir,
When you are cloudy.

Seb. Fowle weather? *Ant.* Very foule.

Gon. Had I plantation of this Iſle my Lord.

Ant. Hee'd ſow't vvith Nettle-ſeed.

Seb. Or dockes, or Mallowes.

Gon. And were the King on't, what vvould I do?

Seb. Scape being drunke, for want of Wine.

Gon. I'th'Commonwealth I vvould (by contraries)
Execute all things: For no kinde of Trafficke
Would I admit: No name of Magiſtrate:
Letters ſhould not be knowne: Riches, pouerty,
And vſe of ſeruice, none: Contract, Succeſsion,
Borne, bound of Land, Tilth, Vineyard none:
No vſe of Mettall, Corne, or Wine, or Oyle:
No occupation, all men idle, all:
And Women too, but innocent and pure:
No Soueraignty.

Seb. Yet he vvould be King on't.

Ant. The latter end of his Common wealth forgets
the beginning.

Gon. All things in common Nature ſhould produce
Without ſweat or endeuour: Treaſon, fellony,
Sword, Pike, Knife, Gun, or neede of any Engine
Would I not haue: but Nature ſhould bring forth
Of it owne kinde, all foyzon, all abundance
To feed my innocent people.

Seb. No marrying 'mong his ſubiects?

Ant. None (man) all idle; Whores and knaues,

Gon. I vvould vvith ſuch perfection gouerne Sir:
T'Excell the Golden Age.

Seb. 'Saue his Maieſty. *Ant.* Long liue *Gonzalo*.

Gon. And do you marke me, Sir? (me.

Alon. Pre-thee no more: thou doſt talke nothing to
Gon. I do vvell beleeue your Highneſſe, and did it
to miniſter occaſion to theſe Gentlemen, who are of
ſuch ſenſible and nimble Lungs, that they alwayes vſe
to laugh at nothing.

Ant. 'Twas you vve laugh'd at.

Gon. Who, in this kind of merry fooling am nothing
to you: ſo you may continue, and laugh at nothing ſtill.

Ant. What a blow vvas there giuen?

Seb. And it had not falne flat-long.

Gon. You are Gentlemen of braue mettal: you would
lift the Moone out of her ſpheare, if ſhe would continue
in it fiue weekes vvithout changing.

Enter Ariell playing ſolemne Muſicke.

Seb. We vvould ſo, and then go a Bat-fowling.

Ant. Nay good my Lord, be not angry.

Gon. No I warrant you, I vvill not aduenture my
diſcretion ſo weakly: Will you laugh me aſleepe, for I
am very heauy.

Ant. Go ſleepe, and heare vs.

Alon. What, all ſo ſoone aſleepe? I wiſh mine eyes
Would (with themſelues) ſhut vp my thoughts,
I finde they are inclin'd to do ſo.

Seb. Pleaſe you Sir,
Do not omit the heauy offer of it:
It ſildome viſits ſorrow, when it doth, it is a Comforter.

Ant.

Ant. We two my Lord, will guard your perſon,
While you take yo'r reſt, and watch your ſafety.
Alon. Thanke you : Wondrous heauy.
Seb. What a ſtrange drowſines poſſeſſes them ?
Ant. It is the quality o'th'Clymate.
Seb. Why
Doth it not then our eye-lids ſinke ? I finde
Not my ſelfe diſpos'd to ſleep.
 Ant. Nor I, my ſpirits are nimble :
They fell together all, as by conſent
They dropt, as by a Thunder-ſtroke : what might
Worthy *Sebaſtian?* O, what might ? no more :
And yet, me thinkes I ſee it in thy face,
What thou ſhould'ſt be : th'occaſion ſpeaks thee, and
My ſtrong imagination ſee's a Crowne
Dropping vpon thy head.
 Seb. What? art thou waking ?
 Ant. Do you not heare me ſpeake ?
 Seb. I do, and ſurely
It is a ſleepy Language ; and thou ſpeak'ſt
Out of thy ſleepe : What is it thou didſt ſay ?
This is a ſtrange repoſe, to be aſleepe
With eyes wide open : ſtanding, ſpeaking, mouing :
And yet ſo faſt aſleepe.
 Ant. Noble *Sebaſtian,*
Thou let'ſt thy fortune ſleepe : die rather : wink'ſt
Whiles thou art waking.
 Seb. Thou do'ſt ſnore diſtinctly,
There's meaning in thy ſnores.
 Ant. I am more ſerious then my cuſtome : you
Muſt be ſo too, if heed me : which to do,
Trebbles thee o're.
 Seb. Well : I am ſtanding water.
 Ant. Ile teach you how to flow.
 Seb. Do ſo : to ebbe
Hereditary Sloth inſtructs me.
 Ant. O !
If you but knew how you the purpoſe cheriſh
Whiles thus you mocke it : how in ſtripping it
You more inueſt it : ebbing men, indeed
(Moſt often) do ſo neere the bottome run
By their owne feare, or ſloth.
 Seb. 'Pre-thee ſay on,
The ſetting of thine eye, and cheeke proclaime
A matter from thee ; and a birth, indeed,
Which throwes thee much to yeeld.
 Ant. Thus Sir :
Although this Lord of weake remembrance; this
Who ſhall be of as little memory
When he is earth'd, hath here almoſt perſwaded
(For hee's a Spirit of perſwaſion, onely
Profeſſes to perſwade) the King his ſonne's aliue,
'Tis as impoſsible that hee's vndrown'd,
As he that ſleepes heere, ſwims.
 Seb. I haue no hope
That hee's vndrown'd.
 Ant. O, out of that no hope,
What great hope haue you? No hope that way, Is
Another way ſo high a hope, that euen
Ambition cannot pierce a winke beyond
But doubt diſcouery there. Will you grant with me
That *Ferdinand* is drown'd.
 Seb. He's gone.
 Ant. Then tell me, who's the next heire of *Naples* ?
 Seb. *Claribell.*
 Ant. She that is Queene of *Tunis* : ſhe that dwels

Ten leagues beyond mans life : ſhe that from *Naples*
Can haue no note, vnleſſe the Sun were poſt :
The Man i'th Moone's too ſlow, till new-borne chinnes
Be rough, and Razor-able : She that from whom
We all were ſea-ſwallow'd, though ſome caſt againe,
(And by that deſtiny) to performe an act
Whereof, what's paſt is Prologue ; what to come
In yours, and my diſcharge.
 Seb. What ſtuffe is this ? How ſay you ?
'Tis true my brothers daughter's Queene of *Tunis*,
So is ſhe heyre of *Naples*, 'twixt which Regions
There is ſome ſpace.
 Ant. A ſpace, whoſe eu'ry cubit
Seemes to cry out, how ſhall that *Claribell*
Meaſure vs backe to *Naples* ? keepe in *Tunis*,
And let *Sebaſtian* wake. Say, this were death
That now hath ſeiz'd them, why they were no worſe
Then now they are : There be that can rule *Naples*
As well as he that ſleepes : Lords, that can prate
As amply, and vnneceſſarily
As this *Gonzallo* : I my ſelfe could make
A Chough of as deepe chat : O, that you bore
The minde that I do ; what a ſleepe were this
For your aduancement ? Do you vnderſtand me ?
 Seb. Me thinkes I do.
 Ant. And how do's your content
Tender your owne good fortune ?
 Seb. I remember
You did ſupplant your Brother *Proſpero.*
 Ant. True :
And looke how well my Garments fit vpon me,
Much feater then before : My Brothers ſeruants
Were then my fellowes, now they are my men.
 Seb. But for your conſcience.
 Ant. I Sir : where lies that ? If 'twere a kybe
'Twould put me to my ſlipper : But I feele not
This Deity in my boſome : 'Twentie conſciences
That ſtand 'twixt me, and *Millaine,* candied be they,
And melt ere they molleſt : Heere lies your Brother,
No better then the earth he lies vpon,
If he were that which now hee's like (that's dead)
Whom I with this obedient ſteele (three inches of it)
Can lay to bed for euer : whiles you doing thus,
To the perpetuall winke for aye might put
This ancient morſell : this Sir Prudence, who
Should not vpbraid our courſe : for all the reſt
They'l take ſuggeſtion, as a Cat laps milke,
They'l tell the clocke, to any buſineſſe that
We ſay befits the houre.
 Seb. Thy caſe, deere Friend
Shall be my preſident : As thou got'ſt *Millaine,*
I'le come by *Naples* : Draw thy ſword, one ſtroke
Shall free thee from the tribute which thou paieſt,
And I the King ſhall loue thee.
 Ant. Draw together :
And when I reare my hand, do you the like
To fall it on *Gonzalo.*
 Seb. O, but one word.

   Enter Ariell with Muſicke *and Song.*
 Ariel. My Maſter through his Art foreſees the danger
That you (his friend)are in, and ſends me forth
(For elſe his proiect dies) to keepe them liuing.
         Sings in Gonzaloes *eare.*
  While you here do ſnoaring lie,
  Open-ey'd Conſpiracie
  His time doth take :

If

8

If of Life you keepe a care ,
Shake off ſlumber and beware.
Awake, awake.

Ant. Then let vs both be ſodaine.

Gon. Now, good Angels preſerue the King.

Alo. Why how now hoa ; awake ? why are you drawn ?
Wherefore this ghaſtly looking ?

Gon. What's the matter ?

Seb. Whiles we ſtood here ſecuring your repoſe,
(Euen now) we heard a hollow burſt of bellowing
Like Buls, or rather Lyons, did't not wake you ?
It ſtrooke mine eare moſt terribly.

Alo. I heard nothing.

Ant. O, 'twas a din to fright a Monſters eare ;
To make an earthquake : ſure it was the roare
Of a whole heard of Lyons.

Alo. Heard you this Gonzalo ?

Gon. Vpon mine honour, Sir, I heard a humming,
(And that a ſtrange one too) which did awake me :
I ſhak'd you Sir, and cride : as mine eyes opend,
I ſaw their weapons drawne : there was a noyſe,
That's verily : 'tis beſt we ſtand vpon our guard ;
Or that we quit this place : let's draw our weapons.

Alo. Lead off this ground & let's make further ſearch
For my poore ſonne.

Gon. Heauens keepe him from theſe Beaſts :
For he is ſure i'th Iſland.

Alo. Lead away.   (done.

Ariell. Proſpero my Lord, ſhall know what I haue
So (King) goe ſafely on to ſeeke thy Son.   *Exeunt.*

Scæna Secunda.

Enter Caliban, with a burthen of Wood (a noyſe of
Thunder heard.)

Cal. All the infections that the Sunne ſuckes vp
From Bogs, Fens, Flats, on *Proſper* fall, and make him
By ynch-meale a diſeaſe : his Spirits heare me,
And yet I needes muſt curſe. But they'll nor pinch,
Fright me with Vrchyn-ſhewes, pitch me i'th mire,
Nor lead me like a fire-brand, in the darke
Out of my way, vnleſſe he bid 'em ; but
For euery trifle, are they ſet vpon me,
Sometime like Apes, that moe and chatter at me,
And after bite me : then like Hedg-hogs, which
Lye tumbling in my bare-foote way, and mount
Their pricks at my foot-fall : ſometime am I
All wound with Adders, who with clouen tongues
Doe hiſſe me into madneſſe : Lo, now Lo,   *Enter*
Here comes a Spirit of his, and to torment me   *Trinculo.*
For bringing wood in ſlowly : I'le fall flat,
Perchance he will not minde me.

Tri. Here's neither buſh, nor ſhrub to beare off any
weather at all : and another Storme brewing, I heare it
ſing ith' winde : yond ſame blacke cloud, yond huge
one, lookes like a foule bumbard that would ſhed his
licquor : if it ſhould thunder, as it did before, I know
not where to hide my head : yond ſame cloud cannot
chooſe but fall by paile-fuls. What haue we here, a man,
or a fiſh ? dead or aliue ? a fiſh, hee ſmels like a fiſh : a
very ancient and fiſh-like ſmell : a kinde of, not of the

neweſt poore-Iohn : a ſtrange fiſh : were I in *England*
now (as once I was) and had but this fiſh painted ; not
a holiday-foole there but would giue a peece of ſiluer :
there, would this Monſter, make a man : any ſtrange
beaſt there, makes a man : when they will not giue a
doit to relieue a lame Begger, they will lay out ten to ſee
a dead *Indian* : Leg'd like a man ; and his Finnes like
Armes : warme o'my troth : I doe now let looſe my o-
pinion ; hold it no longer ; this is no fiſh, but an Iſlan-
der, that hath lately ſuffered by a Thunderbolt : Alas,
the ſtorme is come againe : my beſt way is to creepe vnder his Gaberdine : there is no other ſhelter herea-
bout : Miſery acquaints a man with ſtrange bedfel-
lowes : I will here ſhrowd till the dregges of the ſtorme
be paſt.

Enter Stephano ſinging.

Ste. *I ſhall no more to ſea, to ſea, here ſhall I dye aſhore.*
This is a very ſcuruy tune to ſing at a mans
Funerall : well, here's my comfort.   *Drinkes.*

Sings. *The Maſter, the Swabber, the Boate-ſwaine & I ;*
The Gunner, and his Mate
Lou'd Mall, Meg, and Marrian, and Margerie,
But none of vs car'd for Kate.
For ſhe had a tongue with a tang ,
Would cry to a Sailor goe hang :
She lou'd not the ſauour of Tar nor of Pitch,
Yet a Tailor might ſcratch her where ere ſhe did itch.
Then to Sea Boyes, and let her goe hang.

This is a ſcuruy tune too :
But here's my comfort.   *drinks.*

Cal. Doe not torment me : oh.

Ste. What's the matter ?
Haue we diuels here ?
Doe you put trickes vpon's with Saluages, and Men of
Inde ? ha ? I haue not ſcap'd drowning , to be afeard
now of your foure legges : for it hath bin ſaid ; as proper a man as euer went on foure legs, cannot make him
giue ground : and it ſhall be ſaid ſo againe, while *Ste-*
phano breathes at' noſtrils.

Cal. The Spirit torments me : oh.

Ste. This is ſome Monſter of the Iſle, with foure legs ;
who hath got (as I take it) an Ague : where the diuell
ſhould he learne our language ? I will giue him ſome reliefe if it be but for that : if I can recouer him, and keepe
him tame , and get to *Naples* with him, he's a Preſent for any Emperour that euer trod on Neates-lea-
ther.

Cal. Doe not torment me 'prethee : I'le bring my
wood home faſter.

Ste. He's in his fit now ; and doe's not talke after the
wiſeſt ; hee ſhall taſte of my Bottle : if hee haue neuer
drunke wine afore, it will goe neere to remoue his Fit :
if I can recouer him, and keepe him tame, I will not take
too much for him ; hee ſhall pay for him that hath him,
and that ſoundly.

Cal. Thou do'ſt me yet but little hurt ; thou wilt a-
non, I know it by thy trembling : Now *Proſper* workes
vpon thee.

Ste. Come on your wayes : open your mouth : here
is that which will giue language to you Cat ; open your
mouth ; this will ſhake your ſhaking, I can tell you, and
that ſoundly : you cannot tell who's your friend ; open
your chaps againe.

Tri. I ſhould know that voyce :
It ſhould be,

          But

But hee is dround; and theſe are diuels; O defend me.

Ste. Foure legges and two voyces; a moſt delicate
Monſter: his forward voyce now is to ſpeake well of
his friend; his backward voice, is to vtter foule ſpeeches,
and to detract: If all the wine in my bottle will recouer
him, I will helpe his Ague: Come: Amen, I will
poure ſome in thy other mouth.

Tri. Stephano.

Ste. Doth thy other mouth call me? Mercy, mercy:
This is a diuell, and no Monſter: I will leaue him, I
haue no long Spoone.

Tri. Stephano: if thou beeſt *Stephano*, touch me, and
ſpeake to me: for I am *Trinculo*; be not afeard, thy
good friend *Trinculo.*

Ste. If thou bee'ſt *Trinculo*: come foorth: I'le pull
thee by the leſſer legges: if any be *Trinculo's* legges,
theſe are they: Thou art very *Trinculo* indeede: how
cam'ſt thou to be the ſiege of this Moone-calfe? Can
he vent *Trinculo's*?

Tri. I tooke him to be kil'd with a thunder-ſtrok; but
art thou not dround *Stephano*: I hope now thou art
not dround: Is the Storme ouer-blowne? I hid mee
vnder the dead Moone-Calfes Gaberdine, for feare of
the Storme: And art thou liuing *Stephano*? O *Stephano*,
two *Neapolitanes* ſcap'd?

Ste. 'Prethee doe not turne me about, my ſtomacke
is not conſtant.

Cal. Theſe be fine things, and if they be not ſprights:
that's a braue God, and beares Celeſtiall liquor: I will
kneele to him.

Ste. How did'ſt thou ſcape?
How cam'ſt thou hither?
Sweare by this Bottle how thou cam'ſt hither: I eſcap'd
vpon a But of Sacke, which the Saylors heaued o're-
boord, by this Bottle which I made of the barke of
a Tree, with mine owne hands, ſince I was caſt a'-
ſhore.

Cal. I'le ſweare vpon that Bottle, to be thy true ſub-
ject, for the liquor is not earthly.

St. Heere: ſweare then how thou eſcap'dſt.

Tri. Swom aſhore (man) like a Ducke: I can ſwim
like a Ducke i'le be ſworne.

Ste. Here, kiſſe the Booke.
Though thou canſt ſwim like a Ducke, thou art made
like a Gooſe.

Tri. O *Stephano*, ha'ſt any more of this?

Ste. The whole But (man) my Cellar is in a rocke
by th'ſea-ſide, where my Wine is hid:
How now Moone-Calfe, how do's thine Ague?

Cal. Ha'ſt thou not dropt from heauen?

Ste. Out o'th Moone I doe aſſure thee. I was the
Man ith' Moone, when time was.

Cal. I haue ſeene thee in her: and I doe adore thee:
My Miſtris ſhew'd me thee, and thy Dog, and thy Buſh.

Ste. Come, ſweare to that: kiſſe the Booke: I will
furniſh it anon with new Contents: Sweare.

Tri. By this good light, this is a very ſhallow Mon-
ſter: I afeard of him? a very weake Monſter:
The Man ith' Moone?
A moſt poore creadulous Monſter:
Well drawne Monſter, in good ſooth.

Cal. I'le ſhew thee euery fertill ynch 'oth Iſland: and
I will kiſſe thy foote: I prethee be my god.

Tri. By this light, a moſt perfidious, and drunken
Monſter, when's god's a ſleepe he'll rob his Bottle.

Cal. Ile kiſſe thy foot. Ile ſweare my ſelfe thy Subiect.

Ste. Come on then: downe and ſweare.

Tri. I ſhall laugh my ſelfe to death at this puppi-hea-
ded Monſter: a moſt ſcuruie Monſter: I could finde in
my heart to beate him.

Ste. Come, kiſſe.

Tri. But that the poore Monſter's in drinke:
An abhominable Monſter.

Cal. I'le ſhew thee the beſt Springs: I'le plucke thee
Berries: I'le fiſh for thee; and get thee wood enough.
A plague vpon the Tyrant that I ſerue;
I'le beare him no more Stickes, but follow thee, thou
wondrous man.

Tri. A moſt rediculous Monſter, to make a wonder of
a poore drunkard.

Cal. I 'prethee let me bring thee where Crabs grow;
and I with my long nayles will digge thee pig-nuts;
ſhow thee a Iayes neſt, and inſtruct thee how to ſnare
the nimble Marmazet: I'le bring thee to cluſtring
Philbirts, and ſometimes I'le get thee young Scamels
from the Rocke: Wilt thou goe with me?

Ste. I pre'thee now lead the way without any more
talking. *Trinculo*, the King, and all our company elſe
being dround, wee will inherit here: Here; beare my
Bottle: Fellow *Trinculo*; we'll fill him by and by a-
gaine.

    Caliban Sings drunkenly.
Farewell Maſter; farewell, farewell.

Tri. A howling Monſter: a drunken Monſter.

    Cal. No more dams I'le make for fiſh,
    Nor fetch in firing, at requiring,
    Nor ſcrape trenchering, nor waſh diſh,
    'Ban' ban' Cacalyban
    Has a new Maſter, get a new Man.
Freedome, high-day, high-day freedome, freedome high-
day, freedome.

Ste. O braue Monſter; lead the way.   *Exeunt.*

Actus Tertius. Scœna Prima.

    Enter Ferdinand (bearing a Log.)

Fer. There be ſome Sports are painfull; & their labor
Delight in them ſet off: Some kindes of baſeneſſe
Are nobly vndergon; and moſt poore matters
Point to rich ends: this my meane Taske
Would be as heauy to me, as odious, but
The Miſtris which I ſerue, quickens what's dead,
And makes my labours, pleaſures: O She is
Ten times more gentle, then her Father's crabbed;
And he's compos'd of harſhneſſe. I muſt remoue
Some thouſands of theſe Logs, and pile them vp,
Vpon a ſore iniunction; my ſweet Miſtris
Weepes when ſhe ſees me worke, & ſaies, ſuch baſenes
Had neuer like Executor: I forget:
But theſe ſweet thoughts, doe euen refreſh my labours,
Moſt buſie leſt, when I doe it.   *Enter Miranda*

Mir. Alas, now pray you   *and Proſpero.*
Worke not ſo hard: I would the lightning had
Burnt vp thoſe Logs that you are enioynd to pile:
Pray ſet it downe, and reſt you: when this burnes
'Twill weepe for hauing wearied you: my Father
Is hard at ſtudy; pray now reſt your ſelfe,

                    He's

Hee's fafe for thefe three houres.

Fer. O moft deere Miftris,
The Sun will fet before I fhall difcharge
What I muft ftriue to do.

Mir. If you'l fit downe
Ile beare your Logges the while : pray giue me that,
Ile carry it to the pile.

Fer. No precious Creature,
I had rather cracke my finewes, breake my backe,
Then you fhould fuch difhonor vndergoe,
While I fit lazy by.

Mir. It would become me
As well as it do's you ; and I fhould do it
With much more eafe : for my good will is to it,
And yours it is againft.

Pro. Poore worme thou art infected,
This vifitation fhewes it.

Mir. You looke wearily.

Fer. No, noble Miftris, 'tis frefh morning with me
When you are by at night : I do befeech you
Cheefely, that I might fet it in my prayers,
What is your name ?

Mir. Miranda, O my Father,
I haue broke your heft to fay fo.

Fer. Admir'd *Miranda*,
Indeede the top of Admiration, worth
What's deereft to the world : full many a Lady
I haue ey'd with beft regard, and many a time
Th'harmony of their tongues, hath into bondage
Brought my too diligent eare : for feuerall vertues
Haue I lik'd feuerall women, neuer any
VVith fo full foule, but fome defect in her
Did quarrell with the nobleft grace fhe ow'd,
And put it to the foile. But you, O you,
So perfect, and fo peetieffe, are created
Of euerie Creatures beft.

Mir. I do not know
One of my fexe ; no womans face remember,
Saue from my glaffe, mine owne : Nor haue I feene
More that I may call men, then you good friend,
And my deere Father : how features are abroad
I am skilleffe of ; but by my modeftie
(The iewell in my dower) I would not wifh
Any Companion in the world but you :
Nor can imagination forme a fhape
Befides your felfe, to like of : but I prattle
Something too wildely, and my Fathers precepts
I therein do forget.

Fer. I am, in my condition
A Prince (*Miranda*) I do thinke a King
(I would not fo) and would no more endure
This wodden flauerie, then to fuffer
The flefh-flie blow my mouth : heare my foule fpeake.
The verie inftant that I faw you, did
My heart flie to your feruice, there refides
To make me flaue to it, and for your fake
Am I this patient Logge-man.

Mir. Do you loue me ?

Fer. O heauen ; O earth, beare witnes to this found,
And crowne what I profeffe with kinde euent
If I fpeake true : if hollowly, inuert
VVhat beft is boaded me, to mifchiefe : I,
Beyond all limit of what elfe i'th world
Do loue, prize, honor you.

Mir. I am a foole
To weepe at what I am glad of.

Pro. Faire encounter
Of two moft rare affections : heauens raine grace
On that which breeds betweene 'em.

Fer. VVherefore weepe you ?

Mir : At mine vnworthineffe, that dare not offer
VVhat I defire to giue ; and much leffe take
VVhat I fhall die to want : But this is trifling,
And all the more it feekes to hide it felfe,
The bigger bulke it fhewes. Hence bafhfull cunning,
And prompt me plaine and holy innocence.
I am your wife, if you will marrie me ;
If not, Ile die your maid : to be your fellow
You may denie me, but Ile be your feruant
VVhether you will or no.

Fer. My Miftris (deereft)
And I thus humble euer.

Mir. My husband then ?

Fer. I, with a heart as willing
As bondage ere of freedome : heere's my hand.

Mir. And mine, with my heart in't ; and now farewel
Till halfe an houre hence.

Fer. A thoufand, thoufand.   *Exeunt.*

Pro. So glad of this as they I cannot be,
VVho are furpriz'd with all ; but my reioycing
At nothing can be more : Ile to my booke,
For yet ere fupper time, muft I performe
Much bufineffe appertaining.   *Exit.*

Scæna Secunda.

Enter Caliban, Stephano, and Trinculo.

Ste. Tell not me, when the But is out we will drinke
water, not a drop before ; therefore beare vp, & boord
em' Seruant Monfter, drinke to me.

Trin. Seruant Monfter ? the folly of this Iland, they
fay there's but fiue vpon this Ifle ; we are three of them,
if th'other two be brain'd like vs, the State totters.

Ste. Drinke feruant Monfter when I bid thee, thy
eies are almoft fet in thy head.

Trin. VVhere fhould they bee fet elfe ? hee were a
braue Monfter indeede if they were fet in his taile.

Ste. My man-Monfter hath drown'd his tongue in
facke : for my part the Sea cannot drowne mee, I fwam
ere I could recouer the fhore, fiue and thirtie Leagues
off and on, by this light thou fhalt bee my Lieutenant
Monfter, or my Standard.

Trin. Your Lieutenant if you lift, hee's no ftandard.

Ste. VVeel not run Monfieur Monfter.

Trin. Nor go neither : but you·l lie like dogs, and yet
fay nothing neither.

Ste. Moone-calfe, fpeak once in thy life, if thou beeft
a good Moone-calfe.

Cal. How does thy honour ? Let me licke thy fhooe ?
Ile not ferue him, he is not valiant.

Trin. Thou lieft moft ignorant Monfter, I am in cafe
to iuftle a Conftable : why, thou debofh'd Fifh thou,
was there euer man a Coward, that hath drunk fo much
Sacke as I to day ? wilt thou tell a monftrous lie, being
but halfe a Fifh, and halfe a Monfter ?

Cal. Loe, how he mockes me, wilt thou let him my
Lord ?

                                   Cal.

Trin. Lord, quoth he? that a Monſter ſhould be ſuch a Naturall?

Cal. Loe, loe againe: bite him to death I prethee.

Ste. Trinculo, keepe a good tongue in your head: If you proue a mutineere, the next Tree: the poore Mon-ſter's my ſubiect, and he ſhall not ſuffer indignity.

Cal. I thanke my noble Lord. Wilt thou be pleas'd to hearken once againe to the ſuite I made to thee?

Ste. Marry will I: kneele, and repeate it, I will ſtand, and ſo ſhall *Trinculo.*

Enter *Ariell inuiſible.*

Cal. As I told thee before, I am ſubiect to a Tirant, A Sorcerer, that by his cunning hath cheated me Of the Iſland.

Ariell. Thou lyeſt.

Cal. Thou lyeſt, thou ieſting Monkey thou: I would my valiant Maſter would deſtroy thee. I do not lye.

Ste. Trinculo, if you trouble him any more in's tale, By this hand, I will ſupplant ſome of your teeth.

Trin. Why, I ſaid nothing.

Ste. Mum then, and no more: proceed.

Cal. I ſay by Sorcery he got this Iſle From me, he got it. If thy Greatneſſe will Reuenge it on him, (for I know thou dar'ſt) But this Thing dare not.

Ste. That's moſt certaine.

Cal. Thou ſhalt be Lord of it, and Ile ſerue thee.

Ste. How now ſhall this be compaſt? Canſt thou bring me to the party?

Cal. Yea, yea my Lord, Ile yeeld him thee aſleepe, Where thou maiſt knocke a naile into his head.

Ariell. Thou lieſt, thou canſt not.

Cal. What a py'de Ninnie's this? Thou ſcuruy patch: I do beſeech thy Greatneſſe giue him blowes, And take his bottle from him: When that's gone, He ſhall drinke nought but brine, for Ile not ſhew him Where the quicke Freſhes are.

Ste. Trinculo, run into no further danger: Interrupt the Monſter one word further, and by this hand, Ile turne my mercie out o'doores, and make a Stockfiſh of thee.

Trin. Why, what did I? I did nothing: Ile go farther off.

Ste. Didſt thou not ſay he lyed?

Ariell. Thou lieſt.

Ste. Do I ſo? Take thou that, As you like this, giue me the lye another time.

Trin. I did not giue the lie: Out o'your wittes, and hearing too? A pox o'your bottle, this can Sacke and drinking doo: A murren on your Monſter, and the diuell take your fingers.

Cal. Ha, ha, ha.

Ste. Now forward with your Tale: prethee ſtand further off.

Cal. Beate him enough: after a little time Ile beate him too.

Ste. Stand farther: Come proceede.

Cal. Why, as I told thee, 'tis a cuſtome with him I'th afternoone to ſleepe: there thou maiſt braine him, Hauing firſt ſeiz'd his bookes: Or with a logge Batter his skull, or paunch him with a ſtake, Or cut his wezand with thy knife. Remember Firſt to poſſeſſe his Bookes; for without them

Hee's but a Sot, as I am; nor hath not One Spirit to command: they all do hate him As rootedly as I. Burne but his Bookes, He ha's braue Vtenſils (for ſo he calles them) Which when he ha's a houſe, hee'l decke withall. And that moſt deeply to conſider, is The beautie of his daughter: he himſelfe Cals her a non-pareill: I neuer ſaw a woman But onely *Sycorax* my Dam, and ſhe; But ſhe as farre ſurpaſſeth *Sycorax,* As great'ſt do's leaſt.

Ste. Is it ſo braue a Laſſe?

Cal. I Lord, ſhe will become thy bed, I warrant, And bring thee forth braue brood.

Ste. Monſter, I will kill this man: his daughter and I will be King and Queene, ſaue our Graces: and *Trin-culo* and thy ſelfe ſhall be Vice-royes: Doſt thou like the plot *Trinculo?*

Trin. Excellent.

Ste. Giue me thy hand, I am ſorry I beate thee: But while thou liu'ſt keepe a good tongue in thy head.

Cal. Within this halfe houre will he be aſleepe, Wilt thou deſtroy him then?

Ste. I on mine honour.

Ariell. This will I tell my Maſter.

Cal. Thou mak'ſt me merry: I am full of pleaſure, Let vs be iocond. Will you troule the Catch You taught me but whileare?

Ste. At thy requeſt Monſter, I will do reaſon, Any reaſon: Come on *Trinculo,* let vs ſing.

Sings.

Flout 'em, and cout 'em: and skowt 'em, and flout 'em,
    Thought is free.

Cal. That's not the tune.

    Ariell plaies the tune on a Tabor and Pipe.

Ste. What is this ſame?

Trin. This is the tune of our Catch, plaid by the pic-ture of No-body.

Ste. If thou beeſt a man, ſhew thy ſelfe in thy likenes: If thou beeſt a diuell, take't as thou liſt.

Trin. O forgiue me my ſinnes.

Ste. He that dies payes all debts: I defie thee; Mercy vpon vs.

Cal. Art thou affeard?

Ste. No Monſter, not I.

Cal. Be not affeard, the Iſle is full of noyſes, Sounds, and ſweet aires, that giue delight and hurt not: Sometimes a thouſand twangling Inſtruments Will hum about mine eares; and ſometime voices, That if I then had wak'd after long ſleepe, Will make me ſleepe againe, and then in dreaming, The clouds methought would open, and ſhew riches Ready to drop vpon me, that when I wak'd I cri'de to dreame againe.

Ste. This will proue a braue kingdome to me, Where I ſhall haue my Muſicke for nothing.

Cal. When *Proſpero* is deſtroy'd.

Ste. That ſhall be by and by:

I remember the ſtorie.

Trin. The ſound is going away, Lets follow it, and after do our worke.

Ste. Leade Monſter,

Wee'l follow: I would I could ſee this Taborer, He layes it on.

Trin. Wilt come?

Ile follow *Stephano.*   *Exeunt.*
                 Scœna

Scena Tertia.

Enter Alonso, Sebastian, Anthonio, Gonzallo,
Adrian, Francisco, &c.

Gon. By'r lakin, I can goe no further, Sir,
My old bones akes: here's a maze trod indeede
Through fourth rights, & Meanders: by your patience,
I needes muſt reſt me.

Al. Old Lord, I cannot blame thee,
Who, am my ſelfe attach'd with wearineſſe
To th'dulling of my ſpirits: Sit downe, and reſt:
Euen here I will put off my hope, and keepe it
No longer for my Flatterer: he is droun'd
Whom thus we ſtray to finde, and the Sea mocks
Our fruſtrate ſearch on land: well, let him goe.

Ant. I am right glad, that he's ſo out of hope:
Doe not for one repulſe forgoe the purpoſe
That you reſolu'd t'effect.

Seb. The next aduantage will we take throughly.

Ant. Let it be to night,
For now they are oppreſs'd with trauaile, they
Will not, nor cannot vſe ſuch vigilance
As when they are freſh.

Solemne and ſtrange Muſicke: and Proſper on the top (inui-
ſible) Enter ſeuerall ſtrange ſhapes, bringing in a Banket;
and dance about it with gentle actions of ſalutations, and
inuiting the King, &c. to eate, they depart.

Seb. I ſay to night: no more.

Al. What harmony is this? my good friends, harke.

Gon. Maruellous ſweet Muſicke.

Alo. Giue vs kind keepers, heaues: what were theſe?

Seb. A liuing *Drolerie*: now I will beleeue
That there are Vnicornes: that in *Arabia*
There is one Tree, the Phœnix throne, one Phœnix
At this houre reigning there.

Ant. Ile beleeue both:
And what do's elſe want credit, come to me
And Ile beſworne 'tis true: Trauellers nere did lye,
Though fooles at home condemne 'em.

Gon. If in *Naples*
I ſhould report this now, would they beleeue me?
If I ſhould ſay I ſaw ſuch Iſlands;
(For certes, theſe are people of the Iſland)
Who though they are of monſtrous ſhape, yet note
Their manners are more gentle, kinde, then of
Our humaine generation you ſhall finde
Many, nay almoſt any.

Pro. Honeſt Lord,
Thou haſt ſaid well: for ſome of you there preſent;
Are worſe then diuels.

Al. I cannot too much muſe
Such ſhapes, ſuch geſture, and ſuch ſound expreſſing
(Although they want the vſe of tongue) a kinde
Of excellent dumbe diſcourſe.

Pro. Praiſe in departing.

Fr. They vaniſh'd ſtrangely.

Seb. No matter, ſince   (macks.
They haue left their Viands behinde; for wee haue ſto-
Wilt pleaſe you taſte of what is here?

Alo. Not I.   (Boyes

Gon. Faith Sir, you neede not feare: when wee were
Who would beleeue that there were Mountayneeres,
Dew-lapt, like Buls, whoſe throats had hanging at'em
Wallets of fleſh? or that there were ſuch men

Whoſe heads ſtood in their breſts? which now we finde
Each putter out of fiue for one, will bring vs
Good warrant of.

Al. I will ſtand to, and feede,
Although my laſt, no matter, ſince I feele
The beſt is paſt: brother: my Lord, the Duke,
Stand too, and doe as we.

Thunder and Lightning. Enter Ariell (like a Harpey) claps
his wings vpon the Table, and with a quient deuice the
Banquet vaniſhes.

Ar. You are three men of ſinne, whom deſtiny
That hath to inſtrument this lower world,
And what is in't: the neuer ſurfeited Sea,
Hath caus'd to belch vp you; and on this Iſland,
Where man doth not inhabit, you 'mongſt men,
Being moſt vnfit to liue: I haue made you mad;
And euen with ſuch like valour, men hang, and drowne
Their proper ſelues: you fooles, I and my fellowes
Are miniſters of Fate, the Elements
Of whom your ſwords are temper'd, may as well
Wound the loud windes, or with bemockt-at-Stabs
Kill the ſtill cloſing waters, as diminiſh
One dowle that's in my plumbe: My fellow miniſters
Are like-inuulnerable: if you could hurt,
Your ſwords are now too maſſie for your ſtrengths,
And will not be vplifted: but remember
(For that's my buſineſſe to you) that you three
From *Millaine* did ſupplant good *Proſpero*,
Expos'd vnto the Sea (which hath requit it)
Him, and his innocent childe: for which foule deed,
The Powres, delaying (not forgetting) haue
Incens'd the Seas, and Shores; yea, all the Creatures
Againſt your peace: Thee of thy Sonne, *Alonſo*
They haue bereft; and doe pronounce by me
Lingring perdition (worſe then any death
Can be at once) ſhall ſtep, by ſtep attend
You, and your wayes, whoſe wraths to guard you from,
Which here, in this moſt deſolate Iſle, elſe fals
Vpon your heads, is nothing but hearts-ſorrow,
And a cleere life enſuing.

He vaniſhes in Thunder: then (to ſoft Muſicke.) Enter the
ſhapes againe, and daunce (with mockes and mowes) and
carrying out the Table.

Pro. Brauely the figure of this *Harpie*, haſt thou
Perform'd (my *Ariell*) a grace it had deuouring:
Of my Inſtruction, haſt thou nothing bated
In what thou had'ſt to ſay: ſo with good life,
And obſeruation ſtrange, my meaner miniſters
Their ſeuerall kindes haue done: my high charmes work,
And theſe (mine enemies) are all knit vp
In their diſtractions: they now are in my powre;
And in theſe fits, I leaue them, while I viſit
Yong *Ferdinand* (whom they ſuppoſe is droun'd)
And his, and mine lou'd darling.

Gon. I'th name of ſomething holy, Sir, why ſtand you
In this ſtrange ſtare?

Al. O, it is monſtrous: monſtrous:
Me thought the billowes ſpoke, and told me of it,
The windes did ſing it to me: and the Thunder
(That deepe and dreadfull Organ-Pipe) pronounc'd
The name of *Proſper*: it did baſe my Treſpaſſe,
Therefore my Sonne i'th Ooze is bedded; and
I'le ſeeke him deeper then ere plummet ſounded,
And with him there lye mudded.   *Exit.*

Seb. But one feend at a time,
Ile fight their Legions ore.   *Ant.*

B

Ant. Ile be thy Second. *Exeunt.*

Gon. All three of them are deſperate : their great guilt
(Like poyſon giuen to worke a great time after)
Now gins to bite the ſpirits : I doe beſeech you
(That are of ſuppler ioynts) follow them ſwiftly,
And hinder them from what this extaſie
May now prouoke them to.

Ad. Follow, I pray you. *Exeunt omnes.*

Actus Quartus. Scena Prima.

Enter Proſpero, Ferdinand, and Miranda.

Pro. If I haue too auſterely puniſh'd you,
Your compenſation makes amends, for I
Haue giuen you here, a third of mine owne life,
Or that for which I liue : who, once againe
I tender to thy hand : All thy vexations
Were but my trials of thy loue, and thou
Haſt ſtrangely ſtood the teſt : here, afore heauen
I ratifie this my rich guift : O *Ferdinand,*
Doe not ſmile at me, that I boaſt her of,
For thou ſhalt finde ſhe will out-ſtrip all praiſe
And make it halt, behinde her.

Fer. I doe beleeue it
Againſt an Oracle.

Pro. Then, as my gueſt, and thine owne acquiſition
Worthily purchas'd, take my daughter : But
If thou do'ſt breake her Virgin-knot, before
All ſanctimonious ceremonies may
With full and holy right, be miniſtred,
No ſweet aſperſion ſhall the heauens let fall
To make this contract grow ; but barraine hate,
Sower-ey'd diſdaine, and diſcord ſhall beſtrew
The vnion of your bed, with weedes ſo loathly
That you ſhall hate it both : Therefore take heede,
As Hymens Lamps ſhall light you.

Fer. As I hope
For quiet dayes, faire Iſſue, and long life,
With ſuch loue, as 'tis now the murkieſt den,
The moſt opportune place, the ſtrongſt ſuggeſtion,
Our worſer *Genius* can, ſhall neuer melt
Mine honor into luſt, to take away
The edge of that dayes celebration,
When I ſhall thinke, or *Phœbus* Steeds are founderd,
Or Night kept chain'd below.

Pro. Fairely ſpoke ;
Sit then, and talke with her, ſhe is thine owne ;
What *Ariell* ; my induſtrious ſeruāt *Ariell. Enter Ariell.*

Ar. What would my potent maſter ? here I am.

Pro. Thou, and thy meaner fellowes, your laſt ſeruice
Did worthily performe : and I muſt vſe you
In ſuch another tricke : goe bring the rabble
(Ore whom I giue thee powre) here, to this place :
Incite them to quicke motion, for I muſt
Beſtow vpon the eyes of this yong couple
Some vanity of mine Art : it is my promiſe,
And they expect it from me.

Ar. Preſently ?

Pro. I : with a twincke.

Ar. Before you can ſay come, and goe,
And breathe twice ; and cry, ſo, ſo :
Each one tripping on his Toe,
Will be here with mop, and mowe.
Doe you loue me Maſter ? no ?

Pro. Dearely, my delicate *Ariell :* doe not approach
Till thou do'ſt heare me call.

Ar. Well : I conceiue. *Exit.*

Pro. Looke thou be true : doe not giue dalliance
Too much the raigne : the ſtrongeſt oathes, are ſtraw
To th'fire ith' blood : be more abſtenious,
Or elſe good night your vow.

Fer. I warrant you, Sir,
The white cold virgin Snow, vpon my heart
Abates the ardour of my Liuer.

Pro. Well.
Now come my *Ariell,* bring a Corolary,
Rather then want a Spirit ; appear, & pertly. *Soft muſick.*
No tongue : all eyes : be ſilent. *Enter Iris.*

Ir. *Ceres,* moſt bounteous Lady, thy rich Leas
Of Wheate, Rye, Barley, Fetches, Oates and Peaſe ;
Thy Turphie-Mountaines, where liue nibling Sheepe,
And flat Medes thetchd with Stouer, them to keepe :
Thy bankes with pioned, and twilled brims
Which ſpungie *Aprill,* at thy heſt betrims ;
To make cold Nymphes chaſt crownes ; & thy broome-
Whoſe ſhadow the diſmiſſed Batchelor loues, (groues;
Being laſſe-lorne : thy pole-clipt vineyard,
And thy Sea-marge ſtirrile, and rockey-hard,
Where thou thy ſelfe do'ſt ayre, the Queene o'th Skie,
Whoſe watry Arch, and meſſenger, am I.
Bids thee leaue theſe, & with her ſoueraigne grace, *Iuno*
Here on this graſſe-plot, in this very place *deſcends.*
To come, and ſport : here Peacocks flye amaine :
Approach, rich *Ceres,* her to entertaine. *Enter Ceres.*

Cer. Haile, many-coloured Meſſenger, that nere
Do'ſt diſobey the wife of *Iupiter :*
Who, with thy ſaffron wings, vpon my flowres
Diffuſeſt hony drops, refreſhing ſhowres,
And with each end of thy blew bowe do'ſt crowne
My boskie acres, and my vnſhrubd downe,
Rich ſcarph to my proud earth : why hath thy Queene
Summond me hither, to this ſhort gras'd Greene ?

Ir. A contract of true Loue, to celebrate,
And ſome donation freely to eſtate
On the bles'd Louers.

Cer. Tell me heauenly Bowe,
If *Venus* or her Sonne, as thou do'ſt know,
Doe now attend the Queene ? ſince they did plot
The meanes, that duskie *Dis,* my daughter got,
Her, and her blind-Boyes ſcandald company,
I haue forſworne.

Ir. Of her ſocietie
Be not afraid : I met her deitie
Cutting the clouds towards *Paphos :* and her Son
Doue-drawn with her : here thought they to haue done
Some wanton charme, vpon this Man and Maide,
Whoſe vowes are, that no bed-right ſhall be paid
Till *Hymens* Torch be lighted : but in vaine,
Marſes hot Minion is returnd againe,
Her waſpiſh headed ſonne, has broke his arrowes,
Swears he will ſhoote no more, but play with Sparrows,
And be a Boy right out.

Cer. Higheſt Queene of State,
Great *Iuno* comes, I know her by her gate.

Iu. How do's my bounteous ſiſter? goe with me
To bleſſe this twaine, that they may proſperous be,
And honourd in their Iſſue. *They Sing.*

   Iu. Honor, riches, marriage, bleſſing,
   Long continuance, and encreaſing,
   Hourſly ioyes, be ſtill vpon you,

Iuno

Iuno ſings her bleſſings on you.
Earths increaſe, foyzon plentie,
Barnes, and Garners, neuer empty.
Vines, with cluſtring bunches growing,
Plants, with goodly burthen bowing:
Spring come to you at the fartheſt,
In the very end of Harueſt.
Scarcity and want ſhall ſhun you,
Ceres bleſſing ſo is on you.

Fer. This is a moſt maieſticke viſion, and
Harmonious charmingly : may I be bold
To thinke theſe ſpirits ?

Pro. Spirits, which by mine Art
I haue from their confines call'd to enact
My preſent fancies.

Fer. Let me liue here euer,
So rare a wondred Father, and a wiſe
Makes this place Paradiſe.

Pro. Sweet now, ſilence :
Iuno and *Ceres* whiſper ſeriouſly,
There's ſomething elſe to doe : huſh, and be mute
Or elſe our ſpell is mar'd.

Iuno and Ceres *whiſper, and ſend* Iris *on employment.*

Iris. You Nimphs cald *Nayades* of ỹ windring brooks,
With your ſedg'd crownes, and euer-harmeleſſe lookes,
Leaue your criſpe channels, and on this greene-Land
Anſwere your ſummons, *Iuno* do's command.
Come temperate *Nimphes,* and helpe to celebrate
A Contract of true Loue : be not too late.

Enter Certaine Nimphes.

You Sun-burn'd Sicklemen of Auguſt weary,
Come hether from the furrow, and be merry,
Make holly day : your Rye-ſtraw hats put on,
And theſe freſh Nimphes encounter euery one
In Country footing.

Enter certaine Reapers (properly habited:) they ioyne with
the Nimphes, in a gracefull dance, towards the end where-
of, Proſpero ſtarts ſodainly and ſpeakes, after which to a
ſtrange hollow and confuſed noyſe, they heauily vaniſh.

Pro. I had forgot that foule conſpiracy
Of the beaſt *Calliban,* and his confederates
Againſt my life : the minute of their plot
Is almoſt come : Well done, auoid : no more.

Fer. This is ſtrange : your fathers in ſome paſſion
That workes him ſtrongly.

Mir. Neuer till this day
Saw I him touch'd with anger, ſo diſtemper'd.

Pro. You doe looke (my ſon) in a mou'd ſort,
As if you were diſmaid : be cheerefull Sir,
Our Reuels now are ended : Theſe our actors,
(As I foretold you) were all Spirits, and
Are melted into Ayre, into thin Ayre,
And like the baſeleſſe fabricke of this viſion
The Clowd-capt Towres, the gorgeous Pallaces,
The ſolemne Temples, the great Globe it ſelfe,
Yea, all which it inherit, ſhall diſſolue,
And like this inſubſtantiall Pageant faded
Leaue not a racke behinde : we are ſuch ſtuffe
As dreames are made on ; and our little life
Is rounded with a ſleepe : Sir, I am vext,
Beare with my weakeneſſe, my old braine is troubled :
Be not diſturb'd with my infirmitie,
If you be pleas'd, retire into my Cell,
And there repoſe, a turne or two, Ile walke
To ſtill my beating minde.

Fer. Mir. We wiſh your peace. *Exit.*

Pro. Come with a thought ; I thank thee *Ariell* : come.

Enter Ariell.

Ar. Thy thoughts I cleaue to, what's thy pleaſure ?

Pro. Spirit : We muſt prepare to meet with *Caliban.*

Ar. I my Commander, when I preſented *Ceres*
I thought to haue told thee of it, but I fear'd
Leaſt, I might anger thee.

Pro. Say again, where didſt thou leaue theſe varlots ?

Ar. I told you Sir, they were red-hot with drinking,
So full of valour, that they ſmote the ayre
For breathing in their faces : beate the ground
For kiſſing of their feete ; yet alwaies bending
Towards their proiect : then I beate my Tabor,
At which like vnback't colts they prickt their eares,
Aduanc'd their eye-lids, lifted vp their noſes
As they ſmelt muſicke, ſo I charm'd their eares
That Calfe-like, they my lowing follow'd, through
Tooth'd briars, ſharpe firzes, pricking goſſe, & thorns,
Which entred their fraile ſhins : at laſt I left them
I'th' filthy mantled poole beyond your Cell,
There dancing vp to th'chins, that the fowle Lake
Ore-ſtunck their feet.

Pro. This was well done (my bird)
Thy ſhape inuiſible retaine thou ſtill :
The trumpery in my houſe, goe bring it hither
For ſtale to catch theſe theeues. *Ar.* I go, I goe. *Exit.*

Pro. A Deuill, a borne-Deuill, on whoſe nature
Nurture can neuer ſticke : on whom my paines
Humanely taken, all, all loſt, quite loſt,
And, as with age, his body ouglier growes,
So his minde cankers : I will plague them all ,
Euen to roaring : Come, hang on them this line.

Enter Ariell, loaden with gliſtering apparell, &c. Enter
Caliban, Stephano, and Trinculo, all wet.

Cal. Pray you tread ſoftly, that the blinde Mole may
not heare a foot fall : we now are neere his Cell.

St. Monſter, your Fairy, w̃ you ſay is a harmles Fairy,
Has done little better then plaid the Iacke with vs.

Trin. Monſter, I do ſmell all horſe-piſſe, at which
My noſe is in great indignation.

Ste. So is mine. Do you heare Monſter : If I ſhould
Take a diſpleaſure againſt you : Looke you.

Trin. Thou wert but a loſt Monſter.

Cal. Good my Lord, giue me thy fauour ſtil,
Be patient, for the prize Ile bring thee too
Shall hudwinke this miſchance : therefore ſpeake ſoftly,
All's huſht as midnight yet.

Trin. I, but to looſe our bottles in the Poole.

Ste. There is not onely diſgrace and diſhonor in that
Monſter, but an infinite loſſe.

Tr. That's more to me then my wetting :
Yet this is your harmleſſe Fairy, Monſter.

Ste. I will fetch off my bottle,
Though I be o're eares for my labour.

Cal. Pre-thee (my King) be quiet. Seeſt thou heere
This is the mouth o'th Cell : no noiſe, and enter :
Do that good miſcheefe, which may make this Iſland
Thine owne for euer, and I thy *Caliban*
For aye thy foot-licker.

Ste. Giue me thy hand,
I do begin to haue bloody thoughts.

Trin. O King *Stephano,* O Peere : O worthy *Stephano,*
Looke what a wardrobe heere is for thee.

Cal. Let it alone thou foole, it is but traſh.

Tri. Oh, ho, Monſter : wee know what belongs to a
frippery, O King *Stephano.*

Ste. Put off that gowne (*Trinculo*) by this hand Ile haue that gowne.

Tri. Thy grace ſhall haue it.   (meane

Cal. The dropſie drowne this foole , what doe you To doate thus on ſuch luggage ? let's alone And doe the murther firſt : If he awake , From toe to crowne hee'l fill our ſkins with pinches, Make vs ſtrange ſtuffe.

Ste. Be you quiet (Monſter) Miſtris line, is not this my Ierkin ? now is the Ierkin vnder the line : now Ierkin you are like to loſe your haire, & proue a bald Ierkin.

Trin. Doe, doe; we ſteale by lyne and leuell , and't like your grace.

Ste. I thank thee for that ieſt ; heer's a garment for't : Wit ſhall not goe vn-rewarded while I am King of this Country : Steale by line and leuell, is an excellent paſſe of pate : there's another garment for't.

Tri. Monſter , come put ſome Lime vpon your fingers, and away with the reſt.

Cal. I will haue none on't : we ſhall looſe our time, And all be turn'd to Barnacles, or to Apes With foreheads villanous low.

Ste. Monſter, lay to your fingers : helpe to beare this away, where my hogſhead of wine is, or Ile turne you out of my kingdome : goe to, carry this.

Tri. And this.

Ste. I , and this.

A noyſe of Hunters heard. Enter diuers Spirits in ſhape of Dogs and Hounds, hunting them about : Proſpero and Ariel ſetting them on.

Pro. Hey *Mountaine,* hey.

Ari. Siluer : there it goes, Siluer.

Pro. Fury, Fury : there Tyrant, there : harke, harke.

Goe, charge my Goblins that they grinde their ioynts With dry Convulſions, ſhorten vp their ſinewes With aged Cramps, & more pinch-ſpotted make them, Then Pard, or Cat o'Mountaine.

Ari. Harke, they rore.

Pro. Let them be hunted ſoundly : At this houre Lies at my mercy all mine enemies : Shortly ſhall all my labours end, and thou Shalt haue the ayre at freedome : for a little Follow, and doe me ſeruice.   *Exeunt.*

Actus quintus: Scæna Prima.

Enter Proſpero (in his Magicke robes) and Ariel.

Pro. Now do's my Proiect gather to a head : My charmes cracke not : my Spirits obey, and Time Goes vpright with his carriage : how's the day ?

Ar. On the ſixt hower, at which time, my Lord You ſaid our worke ſhould ceaſe.

Pro. I did ſay ſo, When firſt I rais'd the Tempeſt : ſay my Spirit, How fares the King, and 's followers ?

Ar. Confin'd together In the ſame faſhion, as you gaue in charge, Iuſt as you left them ; all priſoners Sir In the *Line-groue* which weather-fends your Cell, They cannot boudge till your releaſe : The King, His Brother, and yours, abide all three diſtracted, And the remainder mourning ouer them, Brim full of ſorrow, and diſmay : but chiefly

Him that you term'd Sir, the good old Lord *Gonzallo,* His teares runs downe his beard like winters drops From eaues of reeds : your charm ſo ſtrongly works 'em That if you now beheld them, your affections Would become tender.

Pro. Doſt thou thinke ſo, Spirit?

Ar. Mine would , Sir, were I humane.

Pro. And mine ſhall.

Haſt thou (which art but aire) a touch, a feeling Of their afflictions, and ſhall not my ſelfe, One of their kinde, that relliſh all as ſharpely, Paſſion as they, be kindlier mou'd then thou art? Thogh with their high wrongs I am ſtrook to th' quick, Yet, with my nobler reaſon, gainſt my furie Doe I take part : the rarer Action In vertue, then in vengeance : they, being penitent, The ſole drift of my purpoſe doth extend Not a frowne further : Goe, releaſe them *Ariell,* My Charmes Ile breake, their ſences Ile reſtore, And they ſhall be themſelues.

Ar. Ile fetch them, Sir.   *Exit.*

Pro. Ye Elues of hils, brooks, ſtäding lakes & groues, And ye, that on the ſands with printleſſe foote Doe chaſe the ebbing-*Neptune,* and doe flie him When he comes backe : you demy-Puppets, that By Moone-ſhine doe the greene ſowre Ringlets make, Whereof the Ewe not bites : and you, whoſe paſtime Is to make midnight-Muſhrumps, that reioyce To heare the ſolemne Curfewe, by whoſe ayde (Weake Maſters though ye be) I haue bedymn'd The Noone-tide Sun, call'd forth the mutenous windes, And twixt the greene Sea, and the azur'd vault Set roaring warre : To the dread ratling Thunder Haue I giuen fire, and rifted *Ioues* ſtowt Oke With his owne Bolt : The ſtrong baſs'd promontorie Haue I made ſhake, and by the ſpurs pluckt vp The Pyne, and Cedar. Graues at my command Haue wak'd their ſleepers, op'd, and let 'em forth By my ſo potent Art. But this rough Magicke I heere abiure : and when I haue requir'd Some heauenly Muſicke (which euen now I do) To worke mine end vpon their Sences, that This Ayrie-charme is for, I'le breake my ſtaffe, Bury it certaine fadomes in the earth , And deeper then did euer Plummet ſound Ile drowne my booke.   *Solemne muſicke.*

Heere enters Ariel *before : Then* Alonſo *with a franticke geſture, attended by* Gonzalo. Sebaſtian *and* Anthonio *in like manner attended by* Adrian *and* Franciſco : *They all enter the circle which* Proſpero *had made, and there ſtand charm'd : which* Proſpero *obſeruing, ſpeakes.*

A ſolemne Ayre, and the beſt comforter, To an vnſetled fancie, Cure thy braines (Now vſeleſſe) boile within thy ſkull : there ſtand For you are Spell-ſtopt. Holy *Gonzallo,* Honourable man, Mine eyes ev'n ſociable to the ſhew of thine Fall fellowly drops : The charme diſſolues apace, And as the morning ſteales vpon the night (Melting the darkeneſſe) ſo their riſing ſences Begin to chace the ignorant fumes that mantle Their cleerer reaſon. O good *Gonzallo* My true preſeruer, and a loyall Sir, To him thou follow'ſt ; I will pay thy graces Home both in word, and deede : Moſt cruelly

Didſt

Did thou *Alonſo*, vſe me, and my daughter:
Thy brother was a furtherer in the Act,
Thou art pinch'd for't now *Sebaſtian*. Fleſh, and bloud,
You, brother mine, that entertaine ambition,
Expelld remorſe, and nature, whom, with *Sebaſtian*
(Whoſe inward pinches therefore are moſt ſtrong)
Would heere haue kill'd your King: I do forgiue thee,
Vnnaturall though thou art: Their vnderſtanding
Begins to ſwell, and the approching tide
Will ſhortly fill the reaſonable ſhore
That now ly foule, and muddy: not one of them
That yet lookes on me, or would know me: *Ariell*,
Fetch me the Hat, and Rapier in my Cell,
I will diſcaſe me, and my ſelfe preſent
As I was ſometime *Millaine*: quickly Spirit,
Thou ſhalt ere long be free.

   Ariell ſings, and helps to attire him.
   Where the Bee ſucks, there ſuck I,
   In a Cowſlips bell, I lie,
   There I cowch when Owles doe crie,
   On the Batts backe I doe flie
     after Sommer merrily.
   Merrily, merrily, ſhall I liue now,
   Vnder the bloſſom that hangs on the Bow.

Pro. Why that's my dainty *Ariell*: I ſhall miſſe
Thee, but yet thou ſhalt haue freedome: ſo, ſo, ſo.
To the Kings ſhip, inuiſible as thou art,
There ſhalt thou finde the Marriners aſleepe
Vnder the Hatches: the Maſter and the Boat-ſwaine
Being awake, enforce them to this place;
And preſently, I pre'thee.

Ar. I drinke the aire before me, and returne
Or ere your pulſe twice beate.   *Exit.*

Gon. All torment, trouble, wonder, and amazement
Inhabits heere: ſome heauenly power guide vs
Out of this fearefull Country.

Pro. Behold Sir King
The wronged Duke of *Millaine*, *Proſpero*:
For more aſſurance that a liuing Prince
Do's now ſpeake to thee, I embrace thy body,
And to thee, and thy Company, I bid
A hearty welcome.

Alo. Where thou bee'ſt he or no,
Or ſome inchanted triſle to abuſe me,
(As late I haue beene) I not know: thy Pulſe
Beats as of fleſh, and blood: and ſince I ſaw thee,
Th'affliction of my minde amends, with which
I feare a madneſſe held me: this muſt craue
(And if this be at all) a moſt ſtrange ſtory.
Thy Dukedome I reſigne, and doe entreat
Thou pardon me my wrongs: But how ſhold *Proſpero*
Be liuing, and be heere?

Pro. Firſt, noble Frend,
Let me embrace thine age, whoſe honor cannot
Be meaſur'd, or confin'd.

Gonz. Whether this be,
Or be not, I'le not ſweare.

Pro. You doe yet taſte
Some ſubtleties o'th'Iſle, that will nor let you
Beleeue things certaine: Wellcome, my friends all,
But you, my brace of Lords, were I ſo minded
I heere could plucke his Highneſſe frowne vpon you
And iuſtifie you Traitors: at this time
I will tell no tales.

Seb. The Diuell ſpeakes in him:

Pro. No:

For you (moſt wicked Sir) whom to call brother
Would euen infect my mouth, I do forgiue
Thy rankeſt fault; all of them: and require
My Dukedome of thee, which, perforce I know
Thou muſt reſtore.

Alo. If thou beeſt *Proſpero*
Giue vs particulars of thy preſeruation,
How thou haſt met vs heere, whom three howres ſince
Were wrackt vpon this ſhore? where I haue loſt
(How ſharp the point of this remembrance is)
My deere ſonne *Ferdinand*.

Pro. I am woe for't, Sir.

Alo. Irreparable is the loſſe, and patience
Saies, it is paſt her cure.

Pro. I rather thinke
You haue not ſought her helpe, of whoſe ſoft grace
For the like loſſe, I haue her ſoueraigne aid,
And reſt my ſelfe content.

Alo. You the like loſſe?

Pro. As great to me, as late, and ſupportable
To make the deere loſſe, haue I meanes much weaker
Then you may call to comfort you; for I
Haue loſt my daughter.

Alo. A daughter?
Oh heauens, that they were liuing both in *Naples*
The King and Queene there, that they were, I wiſh
My ſelfe were mudded in that oo-zie bed
Where my ſonne lies: when did you loſe your daughter?

Pro. In this laſt Tempeſt. I perceiue theſe Lords
At this encounter doe ſo much admire,
That they deuoure their reaſon, and ſcarce thinke
Their eies doe offices of Truth: Their words
Are naturall breath: but howſoeu'r you haue
Beene iuſtled from your ſences, know for certain
That I am *Proſpero*, and that very Duke
Which was thruſt forth of *Millaine*, who moſt ſtrangely
Vpon this ſhore (where you were wrackt) was landed
To be the Lord on't: No more yet of this,
For 'tis a Chronicle of day by day,
Not a relation for a break-faſt, nor
Befitting this firſt meeting: Welcome, Sir;
This Cell's my Court: heere haue I few attendants,
And Subiects none abroad: pray you looke in:
My Dukedome ſince you haue giuen me againe,
I will requite you with as good a thing,
At leaſt bring forth a wonder, to content ye
As much, as me my Dukedome.

   Here Proſpero diſcouers Ferdinand and Miranda, play-
    ing at Cheſſe.

Mir. Sweet Lord, you play me falſe.

Fer. No my deareſt loue,
I would not for the world.   (wrangle,

Mir. Yes, for a ſcore of Kingdomes, you ſhould
And I would call it faire play.

Alo. If this proue
A viſion of the Iſland, one deere Sonne
Shall I twice looſe.

Seb. A moſt high miracle.

Fer. Though the Seas threaten they are mercifull,
I haue curs'd them without cauſe.

Alo. Now all the bleſſings
Of a glad father, compaſſe thee about:
Ariſe, and ſay how thou cam'ſt heere.

Mir. O wonder!
How many goodly creatures are there heere?
How beauteous mankinde is? O braue new world

B 3   That

That has ſuch people in't.

Pro. 'Tis new to thee.   (play?

Alo. What is this Maid, with whom thou was't at
Your eld'ſt acquaintance cannot be three houres :
Is ſhe the goddeſſe that hath ſeuer'd vs,
And brought vs thus together ?

Fer. Sir, ſhe is mortall ;
But by immortall prouidence, ſhe's mine ;
I choſe her when I could not aske my Father
For his aduiſe : nor thought I had one : She
Is daughter to this famous Duke of *Millaine,*
Of whom, ſo often I haue heard renowne,
But neuer ſaw before : of whom I haue
Receiu'd a ſecond life ; and ſecond Father
This Lady makes him to me.

Alo. I am hers.
But O, how odly will it ſound, that I
Muſt aske my childe forgiueneſſe ?

Pro. There Sir ſtop,
Let vs not b urthen our remembrances, with
A heauineſſe that's gon.

Gon. I haue inly wept,
Or ſhould haue ſpoke ere this : looke downe you gods
And on this couple drop a bleſſed crowne ;
For it is you, that haue chalk'd forth the way
Which brought vs hither.

Alo. I ſay Amen, *Gonzallo.*

Gon. Was *Millaine* thruſt from *Millaine,* that his Iſſue
Should become Kings of *Naples* ? O reioyce
Beyond a common ioy, and ſet it downe
With gold on laſting Pillers : In one voyage
Did *Claribell* her husband finde at *Tunis,*
And *Ferdinand* her brother , found a wife,
Where he himſelfe was loſt : *Proſpero,* his Dukedome
In a poore Iſle : and all of vs, our ſelues,
When no man was his owne.

Alo. Giue me your hands :
Let griefe and ſorrow ſtill embrace his heart,
That doth not wiſh you ioy.

Gon. Be it ſo, Amen.

*Enter Ariell, with the Maſter and Boatſwaine
amazedly following.*

O looke Sir, looke Sir, here is more of vs :
I propheſi'd, if a Gallowes were on Land
This fellow could not drowne : Now blaſphemy,
That ſwear'ſt Grace ore-boord, not an oath on ſhore,
Haſt thou no mouth by land ?
What is the newes ?

Bot. The beſt newes is, that we haue ſafely found
Our King, and company : The next : our Ship,
Which but three glaſſes ſince, we gaue vp ſplit,
Is tyte, and yare, and brauely rig'd, as when
We firſt put out to Sea.

Ar. Sir, all this ſeruice
Haue I done ſince I went.

Pro. My trickſey Spirit.

Alo. Theſe are not naturall euents, they ſtrengthen
From ſtrange, to ſtranger : ſay, how came you hither ?

Bot. If I did thinke, Sir, I were well awake,
I'ld ſtriue to tell you : we were dead of ſleepe,
And (how we know not) all clapt vnder hatches,
Where, but euen now, with ſtrange, and ſeuerall noyſes
Of roring, ſhreeking, howling, gingling chaines,
And mo diuerſitie of ſounds, all horrible.
We were awak'd : ſtraight way, at liberty;
Where we, in all our trim, freſhly beheld

Our royall, good, and gallant Ship : our Maſter
Capring to eye her : on a trice, ſo pleaſe you,
Euen in a dreame, were we diuided from them,
And were brought moaping hither.

Ar. Was't well done ?

Pro. Brauely (my diligence) thou ſhalt be free.

Alo. This is as ſtrange a Maze, as ere men trod,
And there is in this buſineſſe, more then nature
Was euer conduct of : ſome Oracle
Muſt rectifie our knowledge.

Pro. Sir, my Leige,
Doe not infeſt your minde, with beating on
The ſtrangeneſſe of this buſineſſe, at pickt leiſure
(Which ſhall be ſhortly ſingle) I'le reſolue you,
(Which to you ſhall ſeeme probable) of euery
Theſe happend accidents : till when, be cheerefull
And thinke of each thing well : Come hither Spirit,
Set *Caliban,* and his companions free :
Vntye the Spell : How fares my gracious Sir ?
There are yet miſſing of your Companie
Some few odde Lads, that you remember not.

*Enter Ariell, driuing in Caliban, Stephano, and
Trinculo in their ſtolne Apparell.*

Ste. Euery man ſhift for all the reſt, and let
No man take care for himſelfe ; for all is
But fortune : *Coragio* Bully-Monſter *Coraſio.*

Tri. If theſe be true ſpies which I weare in my head,
here's a goodly ſight.

Cal. O *Setebos,* theſe be braue Spirits indeede :
How fine my Maſter is ? I am afraid
He will chaſtiſe me.

Seb. Ha, ha :
What things are theſe, my Lord *Anthonio?*
Will money buy em ?

Ant. Very like : one of them
Is a plaine Fiſh, and no doubt marketable.

Pro. Marke but the badges of theſe men, my Lords,
Then ſay if they be true : This miſhapen knaue ;
His Mother was a Witch, and one ſo ſtrong
That could controle the Moone ; make flowes, and ebs,
And deale in her command, without her power :
Theſe three haue robd me, and this demy-diuell ;
(For he's a baſtard one) had plotted with them
To take my life : two of theſe Fellowes, you
Muſt know, and owne, this Thing of darkeneſſe, I
Acknowledge mine.

Cal. I ſhall be pincht to death.

Alo. Is not this *Stephano,* my drunken Butler ?

Seb. He is drunke now ;
Where had he wine ?

Alo. And *Trinculo* is reeling ripe : where ſhould they
Finde this grand Liquor that hath gilded 'em ?
How cam'ſt thou in this pickle ?

Tri. I haue bin in ſuch a pickle ſince I ſaw you laſt,
That I feare me will neuer out of my bones :
I ſhall not feare fly-blowing.

Seb. Why how now *Stephano* ?

Ste. O touch not me, I am not *Stephano,* but a Cramp.

Pro. You'ld be King o'the Iſle, Sirha ?

Ste. I ſhould haue bin a ſore one then.

Alo. This is a ſtrange thing as ere I look'd on.

Pro. He is as diſproportion'd in his Manners
As in his ſhape : Goe Sirha, to my Cell,
Take with you your Companions : as you looke
To haue my pardon, trim it handſomely.

Cal. I that I will : and Ile be wiſe hereafter,

                        And

And ſeeke for grace : what a thrice double Aſſe
Was I to take this drunkard for a god ?
And worſhip this dull foole ?

Pro. Goe to, away. (found it.

Alo. Hence , and beſtow your luggage where you
Seb. Or ſtole it rather.

Pro. Sir, I inuite your Highneſſe, and your traine
To my poore Cell : where you ſhall take your reſt
For this one night, which part of it, Ile waſte
With ſuch diſcourſe, as I not doubt, ſhall make it
Goe quicke away : The ſtory of my life,
And the particular accidents, gon by
Since I came to this Iſle : And in the morne
I'le bring you to your ſhip, and ſo to *Naples*,

Where I haue hope to ſee the nuptiall
Of theſe our deere-belou'd, ſolemnized,
And thence retire me to my *Millaine*, where
Euery third thought ſhall be my graue.

Alo. I long
To heare the ſtory of your life ; which muſt
Take the eare ſtarngely.

Pro. I'le deliuer all,
And promiſe you calme Seas, auſpicious gales,
And ſaile, ſo expeditious, that ſhall catch
Your Royall fleete farre off : My *Ariel* ; chicke
That is thy charge : Then to the Elements
Be free, and fare thou well : pleaſe you draw neere.

Exeunt omnes.

EPILOGVE,

ſpoken by *Proſpero.*

NOw my *Charmes* are all ore-throwne,
  And what ſtrength I haue's mine owne.
Which is moſt faint : now 'tis true
I muſt be heere confinde by you,
Or ſent to Naples, *Let me not*
Since I haue my Dukedome got ,
And pardon'd the deceiuer , dwell
In this bare Iſland, by your Spell,
But releaſe me from my bands
With the helpe of your good hands :
Gentle breath of yours, my Sailes
Muſt fill, or elſe my proiect failes,
Which was to pleaſe : Now I want
Spirits to enforce : Art to inchant,
And my ending is deſpaire,
Vnleſſe I be relieu'd by praier
Which pierces ſo, that it aſſaults
Mercy it ſelfe, and frees all faults.
  As you from crimes would pardon'd be,
  Let your Indulgence ſet me free. Exit.

The Scene,an vn-inhabited Iſland

Names of the Actors.

Alonſo, K. of Naples :
Sebaſtian his Brother.
Proſpero, the right Duke of Millaine.
Anthonio his brother,the vſurping Duke of Millaine.
Ferdinand, Son to the King of Naples.
Gonzalo, an honeſt old Councellor.
Adrian, & Franciſco, Lords.
Caliban, a ſaluage and deformed ſlaue.
Trinculo, a Ieſter.
Stephano, a drunken Butler.
Maſter of a Ship.
Boate-Swaine.
Morriners.
Miranda, daughter to Proſpero.
Ariell, an ayrie ſpirit.
Iris
Ceres
Iuno   } *Spirits.*
Nymphes
Reapers

FINIS.

THE

THE
Two Gentlemen of Verona.

Actus primus, Scena prima.

Valentine : Protheus, and *Speed.*

Valentine.

Eafe to perfwade, my louing *Protheus*;
Home-keeping-youth, haue euer homely wits,
Wer't not affeɗion chaines thy tender dayes
To the fweet glaunces of thy honour'd Loue,
I rather would entreat thy company,
To fee the wonders of the world abroad,
Then (liuing dully fluggardiz'd at home)
Weare out thy youth with fhapeleffe idleneffe.
But fince thou lou'ft; loue ftill, and thriue therein,
Euen as I would, when I to loue begin.
  Pro. Wilt thou be gone ? Sweet *Valentine* ad ew,
Thinke on thy *Protheus*, when thou (hap'ly) feeft
Some rare note-worthy obieɗ in thy trauaile.
Wifh me partaker in thy happineffe,
When thou do'ft meet good hap ; and in thy danger,
(If euer danger doe enuiron thee)
Commend thy grieuance to my holy prayers,
For I will be thy beadef-man, *Valentine.*
  Val. And on a loue-booke pray for my fucceffe ?
  Pro. Vpon fome booke I loue, I'le pray for thee.
  Val. That's on fome fhallow Storie of deepe loue,
How yong *Leander* croft the *Hellefpont.*
  Pro. That's a deepe Storie, of a deeper loue,
For he was more then ouer-fhooes in loue.
  Val. 'Tis true ; for you are ouer-bootes in loue,
And yet you neuer fwom the *Hellefpont.*
  Pro. Ouer the Bootes ? nay giue me not the Boots.
  Val. No, I will not ; for it boots thee not.
  Pro. What ?   (grones :
  Val. To be in loue ; where fcorne is bought with
Coy looks, with hart-fore fighes : one fading moments
With twenty watchfull, weary, tedious nights ;   (mirth,
If hap'ly won, perhaps a hapleffe gaine ;
If loft, why then a grieuous labour won ;
How euer : but a folly bought with wit,
Or elfe a wit, by folly vanquifhed.
  Pro. So, by your circumftance, you call me foole.
  Val. So, by your circumftance, I feare you'll proue.
  Pro. 'Tis Loue you cauill at, I am not Loue.
  Val. Loue is your mafter, for he mafters you ;
And he that is fo yoked by a foole,
Me thinkes fhould not be chronicled for wife.
  Pro. Yet Writers fay ; as in the fweeteft Bud,
The eating Canker dwels ; fo eating Loue
Inhabits in the fineft wits of all.
  Val. And Writers fay ; as the moft forward Bud

Is eaten by the Canker ere it blow,
Euen fo by Loue, the yong, and tender wit
Is turn'd to folly, blafting in the Bud,
Loofing his verdure, euen in the prime,
And all the faire effeɗs of future hopes.
But wherefore wafte I time to counfaile thee
That art a votary to fond defire ?
Once more adieu : my Father at the Road
Expeɗs my comming, there to fee me fhip'd.
  Pro. And thither will I bring thee *Valentine.*
  Val. Sweet *Protheus*, no : Now let vs take our leaue :
To *Millaine* let me heare from thee by Letters
Of thy fucceffe in loue ; and what newes elfe
Betideth here in abfence of thy Friend :
And I likewife will vifite thee with mine.
  Pro. All happineffe bechance to thee in *Millaine.*
  Val. As much to you at home : and fo farewell. *Exit.*
  Pro. He after Honour hunts, I after Loue ;
He leaues his friends, to dignifie them more ;
I loue my felfe, my friends, and all for loue :
Thou *Iulia* thou haft metamorphis'd me :
Made me negleɗ my Studies, loofe my time ;
Warre with good counfaile ; fet the world at nought ;
Made Wit with mufing, weake ; hart fick with thought.
  Sp. Sir *Protheus* : 'faue you : faw you my Mafter ?
  Pro. But now he parted hence to embarque for *Millain.*
  Sp. Twenty to one then, he is fhip'd already,
And I haue plaid the Sheepe in loofing him.
  Pro. Indeede a Sheepe doth very often ftray,
And if the Shepheard be awhile away.
  Sp. You conclude that my Mafter is a Shepheard then,
and I Sheepe ?
  Pro. I doe.
  Sp. Why then my hornes are his hornes, whether I
wake or fleepe.
  Pro. A filly anfwere, and fitting well a Sheepe.
  Sp. This proues me ftill a Sheepe.
  Pro. True : and thy Mafter a Shepheard.
  Sp. Nay, that I can deny by a circumftance.
  Pro. It fhall goe hard but ile proue it by another.
  Sp. The Shepheard feekes the Sheepe, and not the
Sheepe the Shepheard ; but I feeke my Mafter, and my
Mafter feekes not me : therefore I am no Sheepe.
  Pro. The Sheepe for fodder follow the Shepheard,
the Shepheard for foode followes not the Sheepe : thou
for wages followeft thy Mafter, thy Mafter for wages
followes not thee : therefore thou art a Sheepe.
  Sp. Such another proofe will make me cry baá.
  Pro. But do'ft thou heare : gau'ft thou my Letter
to *Iulia* ?

Sp. I Sir: I (a loſt-Mutton) gaue your Letter to her (a lac'd-Mutton) and ſhe (a lac'd-Mutton) gaue mee (a loſt-Mutton) nothing for my labour.

Pro. Here's too ſmall a Paſture for ſuch ſtore of Muttons.

Sp. If the ground be ouer-charg'd, you were beſt ſticke her.

Pro. Nay, in that you are aſtray : 'twere beſt pound you.

Sp. Nay Sir, leſſe then a pound ſhall ſerue me for carrying your Letter.

Pro. You miſtake ; I meane the pound, a Pinfold.

Sp. From a pound to a pin? fold it ouer and ouer, 'Tis threefold too little for carrying a letter to your louer

Pro. But what ſaid ſhe ?

Sp. I.

Pro. Nod-I, why that's noddy.

Sp. You miſtooke Sir: I ſay ſhe did nod ; And you aske me if ſhe did nod, and I ſay I.

Pro. And that ſet together is noddy.

Sp. Now you haue taken the paines to ſet it together, take it for your paines.

Pro. No, no, you ſhall haue it for bearing the letter.

Sp. Well, I perceiue I muſt be faine to beare with you.

Pro. Why Sir, how doe you beare with me ?

Sp. Marry Sir, the letter very orderly, Hauing nothing but the word noddy for my paines.

Pro. Beſhrew me, but you haue a quicke wit.

Sp. And yet it cannot ouer-take your ſlow purſe.

Pro. Come, come, open the matter in briefe ; what ſaid ſhe.

Sp. Open your purſe, that the money, and the matter may be both at once deliuered.

Pro. Well Sir : here is for your paines: what ſaid ſhe ?

Sp. Truely Sir, I thinke you'll hardly win her.

Pro. Why? could'ſt thou perceiue ſo much from her ?

Sp. Sir, I could perceiue nothing at all from her ; No, not ſo much as a ducket for deliuering your letter : And being ſo hard to me, that brought your minde ; I feare ſhe'll proue as hard to you in telling your minde. Giue her no token but ſtones, for ſhe's as hard as ſteele.

Pro. What ſaid ſhe, nothing ?

Sp. No, not ſo much as take this for thy pains: (me ; To teſtifie your bounty, I thank you, you haue ceſtern'd In requital whereof, henceforth, carry your letters your ſelfe ; And ſo Sir, I'le commend you to my Maſter.

Pro. Go, go, be gone, to ſaue your Ship from wrack, Which cannot periſh hauing thee aboarde, Being deſtin'd to a drier death on ſhore : I muſt goe ſend ſome better Meſſenger, I feare my *Iulia* would not daigne my lines, Receiuing them from ſuch a worthleſſe poſt.   *Exit.*

Scæna Secunda.

Enter Iulia and Lucetta.

Iul. But ſay *Lucetta* (now we are alone) Would'ſt thou then counſaile me to fall in loue ?

Luc. I Madam, ſo you ſtumble not vnheedfully.

Iul. Of all the faire reſort of Gentlemen, That euery day with par'le encounter me,

In thy opinion which is worthieſt loue ?

Lu. Pleaſe you repeat their names, ile ſhew my minde, According to my ſhallow ſimple skill.

Iu. What thinkſt thou of the faire ſir *Eglamoure* ?

Lu. As of a Knight, well-ſpoken, neat, and fine ; But were I you, he neuer ſhould be mine.

Iu. What think'ſt thou of the rich *Mercatio* ?

Lu. Well of his wealth ; but of himſelfe, ſo, ſo.

Iu. What think'ſt thou of the gentle *Protheus* ?

Lu. Lord, Lord : to ſee what folly raignes in vs.

Iu. How now ? what meanes this paſſion at his name ?

Lu. Pardon deare Madam, 'tis a paſſing ſhame, That I (vnworthy body as I am) Should cenſure thus on louely Gentlemen.

Iu. Why not on *Protheus*, as of all the reſt ?

Lu. Then thus : of many good, I thinke him beſt.

Iul. Your reaſon ?

Lu. I haue no other but a womans reaſon : I thinke him ſo, becauſe I thinke him ſo.

Iul. And would'ſt thou haue me caſt my loue on him ?

Lu. I : if you thought your loue not caſt away.

Iul. Why he, of all the reſt, hath neuer mou'd me.

Lu. Yet he, of all the reſt, I thinke beſt loues ye.

Iul. His little ſpeaking, ſhewes his loue but ſmall.

Lu. Fire that's cloſeſt kept, burnes moſt of all.

Iul. They doe not loue, that doe not ſhew their loue.

Lu. Oh, they loue leaſt, that let men know their loue.

Iul. I would I knew his minde.

Lu. Peruſe this paper Madam.

Iul. To *Iulia* : ſay, from whom ?

Lu. That the Contents will ſhew.

Iul. Say, ſay ; who gaue it thee ?

Lu. Sir *Valentines* page : & ſent I think from *Protheus* ; He would haue giuen it you, but I being in the way, Did in your name receiue it : pardon the fault I pray.

Iul. Now (by my modeſty) a goodly Broker : Dare you preſume to harbour wanton lines ? To whiſper, and conſpire againſt my youth ? Now truſt me, 'tis an office of great worth, And you an officer fit for the place : There : take the paper : ſee it be return'd, Or elſe returne no more into my ſight.

Lu. To plead for loue, deſerues more fee, then hate.

Iul. Will ye be gon ?

Lu. That you may ruminate.   *Exit.*

Iul. And yet I would I had ore-look'd the Letter ; It were a ſhame to call her backe againe, And pray her to a fault, for which I chid her. What 'foole is ſhe, that knowes I am a Maid, And would not force the letter to my view ? Since Maides, in modeſty, ſay no, to that, Which they would haue the profferer conſtrue, I. Fie, fie : how way-ward is this fooliſh loue ; That (like a teſtie Babe) will ſcratch the Nurſe, And preſently, all humbled kiſſe the Rod ? How churliſhly, I chid *Lucetta* hence, When willingly, I would haue had her here ? How angerly I taught my brow to frowne, When inward ioy enforc'd my heart to ſmile ? My pennance is, to call *Lucetta* backe And aske remiſſion, for my folly paſt. What hoe : *Lucetta*.

Lu. What would your Ladiſhip ?

Iul. Is't neere dinner time ?

Lu. I would it were, That you might kill your ſtomacke on your meat,

And

And not vpon your Maid.

Iu. What is't that you
Tooke vp fo gingerly?

Lu. Nothing.

Iu. Why didft thou ftoope then?

Lu. To take a paper vp, that I let fall.

Iul. And is that paper nothing?

Lu. Nothing concerning me.

Iul. Then let it lye, for thofe that it concernes.

Lu. Madam, it will not lye where it concernes,
Vnleffe it haue a falfe Interpreter.

Iul. Some loue (although I) hath writ to you in Rime.

Lu. That I might fing it (Madam) to a tune:
Giue me a Note, your Ladiſhip can fet

Iul. As little by fuch toyes, as may be poffible:
Beft fing it to the tune of *Light O, Loue.*

Lu. It is too heauy for fo light a tune.

Iu. Heauy? belike it hath fome burden then?

Lu. I: and melodious were it, would you fing it,

Iu. And why not you?

Lu. I cannot reach fo high.

Iu. Let's fee your Song:
How now Minion?

Lu. Keepe tune there ftill; fo you will fing it out:
And yet me thinkes I do not like this tune.

Iu. You doe not?

Lu. No (Madam) tis too ſharpe.

Iu. You (Minion) are too faucie.

Lu. Nay, now you are too flat;
And marre the concord, with too harſh a defcant:
There wanteth but a Meane to fill your Song.

Iu. The meane is drownd with you vnruly bafe.

Lu. Indeede I bid the bafe for *Protheus.*

Iu. This babble ſhall not henceforth trouble me;
Here is a coile with proteftation:
Goe, get you gone: and let the papers lye;
You would be fingring them, to anger me.

Lu. She makes it ftrãge, but ſhe would be beft pleas'd
To be fo angred with another Letter.

Iu. Nay, would I were fo angred with the fame:
Oh hatefull hands, to teare fuch louing words;
Iniurious Wafpes, to feede on fuch fweet hony,
And kill the Bees that yeelde it, with your ftings;
Ile kiffe each feuerall paper, for amends:
Looke, here is writ, kinde *Iulia*: vnkinde *Iulia*,
As in reuenge of thy ingratitude,
I throw thy name againſt the bruzing-ftones,
Trampling contemptuouſly on thy difdaine.
And here is writ, *Loue wounded Protheus.*
Poore wounded name: my bofome, as a bed,
Shall lodge thee till thy wound be throughly heal'd;
And thus I fearch it with a foueraigne kiffe.
But twice, or thrice, was *Protheus* written downe:
Be calme (good winde) blow not a word away,
Till I haue found each letter, in the Letter,
Except mine own name: That, fome whirle-winde beare
Vnto a ragged, fearefull, hanging Rocke,
And throw it thence into the raging Sea.
Loe, here in one line is his name twice writ:
Poore forlorne Protheus, paffionate Protheus:
To the fweet Iulia: that ile teare away:
And yet I will not, fith fo prettily
He couples it, to his complaining Names;
Thus will I fold them, one vpon another;
Now kiffe, embrace, contend, doe what you will.

Lu. Madam: dinner is ready: and your father ftaies.

Iu. Well, let vs goe.

Lu. What, ſhall thefe papers lye, like Tel-tales here?

Iu. If you refpect them; beft to take them vp.

Lu. Nay, I was taken vp, for laying them downe.
Yet here they ſhall not lye, for catching cold.

Iu. I fee you haue a months minde to them.

Lu. I (Madam) you may fay what fights you fee;
I fee things too, although you iudge I winke.

Iu. Come, come, wilt pleafe you goe.   *Exeunt.*

Scæna Tertia.

Enter Antonio and Panthino. Protheus.

Ant. Tell me *Panthino*, what fad talke was that,
Wherewith my brother held you in the Cloyfter?

Pan. 'Twas of his Nephew *Protheus*, your Sonne.

Ant. Why? what of him?

Pan. He wondred that your Lordſhip
Would fuffer him, to fpend his youth at home,
While other men, of ſlender reputation
Put forth their Sonnes, to feeke preferment out.
Some to the warres, to try their fortune there;
Some, to difcouer Iflands farre away:
Some, to the ftudious Vniuerfities;
For any, or for all thefe exercifes,
He faid, that *Protheus*, your fonne, was meet;
And did requeft me, to importune you
To let him fpend his time no more at home;
Which would be great impeachment to his age,
In hauing knowne no trauaile in his youth.

Ant. Nor need'ſt thou much importune me to that
Whereon, this month I haue bin hamering.
I haue confider'd well, his loffe of time,
And how he cannot be a perfect man,
Not being tryed, and tutord in the world:
Experience is by induftry atchieu'd,
And perfected by the fwift courfe of time:
Then tell me, whether were I beft to fend him?

Pan. I thinke your Lordſhip is not ignorant
How his companion, youthfull *Valentine*,
Attends the Emperour in his royall Court.

Ant. I know it well.

Pan. 'Twere good, I thinke, your Lordſhip fent him (thither,
There ſhall he practife Tilts, and Turnaments;
Heare fweet difcourfe, conuerfe with Noble-men,
And be in eye of euery Exercife
Worthy his youth, and nobleneffe of birth.

Ant. I like thy counfaile: well haft thou aduis'd:
And that thou maiſt perceiue how well I like it,
The execution of it ſhall make knowne;
Euen with the fpeedieft expedition,
I will difpatch him to the Emperors Court.

Pan. To morrow, may it pleafe you, *Don Alphonfo*,
With other Gentlemen of good efteeme
Are iournying, to falute the *Emperor*,
And to commend their feruice to his will.

Ant. Good company: with them ſhall *Protheus* go:
And in good time: now will we breake with him.

Pro. Sweet Loue, fweet lines, fweet life,
Here is her hand, the agent of her heart;
Here is her oath for loue, her honors pawne;

O that our Fathers would applaud our loues
To feale our happineffe with their confents.
Pro. Oh heauenly *Iulia.*
Ant. How now? What Letter are you reading there?
Pro. May't pleafe your Lordfhip, 'tis a word or two
Of commendations fent from *Valentine*;
Deliuer'd by a friend, that came from him.
Ant. Lend me the Letter: Let me fee what newes.
Pro. There is no newes (my Lord) but that he writes
How happily he liues, how well-belou'd,
And daily graced by the Emperor;
Wifhing me with him, partner of his fortune.
Ant. And how ftand you affected to his wifh?
Pro. As one relying on your Lordfhips will,
And not depending on his friendly wifh.
Ant. My will is fomething forted with his wifh:
Mufe not that I thus fodainly proceed;
For what I will, I will, and there an end:
I am refolu'd, that thou fhalt fpend fome time
With *Valentinus*, in the Emperors Court:
What maintenance he from his friends receiues,
Like exhibition thou fhalt haue from me,
To morrow be in readineffe, to goe,
Excufe it not: for I am peremptory.
Pro. My Lord I cannot be fo foone prouided,
Pleafe you deliberate a day or two.
Ant. Look what thou want'ft fhalbe fent after thee:
No more of ftay: to morrow thou muft goe;
Come on *Panthino*; you fhall be imployd,
To haften on his Expedition.
Pro. Thus haue I fhund the fire, for feare of burning,
And drench'd me in the fea, where I am drown'd.
I fear'd to fhew my Father *Iulias* Letter,
Leaft he fhould take exceptions to my loue,
And with the vantage of mine owne excufe
Hath he excepted moft againft my loue.
Oh, how this fpring of loue refembleth
The vncertaine glory of an Aprill day,
Which now fhewes all the beauty of the Sun,
And by and by a clowd takes all away.
Pan. Sir *Protheus*, your Fathers call's for you,
He is in haft, therefore I pray you go.
Pro. Why this it is: my heart accords thereto,
And yet a thoufand times it anfwer's no.
                              Exeunt.   Finis.

Actus fecundus: Scæna Prima.

Enter Valentine, Speed, Siluia.

Speed. Sir, your Gloue.
Valen. Not mine: my Gloues are on.
Sp. Why then this may be yours: for this is but one.
Val. Ha? Let me fee: I, giue it me, it's mine:
Sweet Ornament, that deckes a thing diuine,
Ah *Siluia, Siluia.*
Speed. Madam *Siluia*: Madam *Siluia.*
Val. How now Sirha?
Speed. Shee is not within hearing Sir.
Val. Why fir, who bad you call her?
Speed. Your worfhip fir, or elfe I miftooke.
Val. Well: you'll ftill be too forward.
Speed. And yet I was laft chidden for being too flow.

Val. Goe to, fir, tell me: do you know Madam *Siluia*?
Speed. Shee that your worfhip loues?
Val. Why, how know you that I am in loue?
Speed. Marry by thefe fpeciall markes: firft, you haue
learn'd (like Sir *Protheus*) to wreath your Armes like a
Male-content: to rellifh a Loue-fong, like a *Robin*-red-
breaft: to walke alone like one that had the peftilence:
to figh, like a Schoole-boy that had loft his *A. B. C.* to
weep like a yong wench that had buried her Grandam:
to faft, like one that takes diet: to watch, like one that
feares robbing: to fpeake puling, like a beggar at Hal-
low-Maffe: You were wont, when you laughed, to crow
like a cocke; when you walk'd, to walke like one of the
Lions: when you fafted, it was prefently after dinner:
when you look'd fadly, it was for want of money: And
now you are Metamorphis'd with a Miftris, that when I
looke on you, I can hardly thinke you my Mafter.
Val. Are all thefe things perceiu'd in me?
Speed. They are all perceiu'd without ye.
Val. Without me? they cannot.
Speed. Without you? nay, that's certaine: for without you were fo fimple, none elfe would: but you are
fo without thefe follies, that thefe follies are within you,
and fhine through you like the water in an Vrinall: that
not an eye that fees you, but is a Phyfician to comment
on your Malady.
Val. But tell me: do'ft thou know my Lady *Siluia*?
Speed. Shee that you gaze on fo, as fhe fits at fupper?
Val. Haft thou obferu'd that? euen fhe I meane.
Speed. Why fir, I know her not.
Val. Do'ft thou know her by my gazing on her, and
yet know'ft her not?
Speed. Is fhe not hard-fauour'd, fir?
Val. Not fo faire (boy) as well fauour'd.
Speed. Sir, I know that well enough.
Val. What doft thou know?
Speed. That fhee is not fo faire, as (of you) well-fa-
uourd?
Val. I meane that her beauty is exquifite,
But her fauour infinite.
Speed. That's becaufe the one is painted, and the o-
ther out of all count.
Val. How painted? and how out of count?
Speed. Marry fir, fo painted to make her faire, that no
man counts of her beauty.
Val. How efteem'ft thou me? I account of her beauty.
Speed. You neuer faw her fince fhe was deform'd.
Val. How long hath fhe beene deform'd?
Speed. Euer fince you lou'd her.
Val. I haue lou'd her euer fince I faw her,
And ftill I fee her beautifull.
Speed. If you loue her, you cannot fee her.
Val. Why?
Speed. Becaufe Loue is blinde: O that you had mine
eyes, or your owne eyes had the lights they were wont
to haue, when you chidde at Sir *Protheus*, for going vn-
garter'd.
Val. What fhould I fee then?
Speed. Your owne prefent folly, and her paffing de-
formitie: for hee beeing in loue, could not fee to garter
his hofe; and you, beeing in loue, cannot fee to put on
your hofe.   (ning
Val. Belike (boy) then you are in loue, for laft mor-
You could not fee to wipe my fhooes.
Speed. True fir: I was in loue with my bed, I thanke
you, you fwing'd me for my loue, which makes mee the
                                                   bolder

bolder to chide you, for yours.

Val. In conclusion, I stand affected to her.

Speed. I would you were set, so your affection would cease.

Val. Last night she enioyn'd me ,
To write some lines to one she loues.

Speed. And haue you ?

Val. I haue.

Speed. Are they not lamely writt?

Val. No (Boy) but as well as I can do them :
Peace, here she comes.

Speed. Oh excellent motion ; oh exceeding Puppet :
Now will he interpret to her.

Val. Madam & Mistres, a thousand good-morrows.

Speed. Oh, 'giue ye-good-ev'n : heer's a million of manners.

Sil. Sir *Valentine,* and seruant, to you two thousand.

Speed. He should giue her interest : & she giues it him.

Val. As you inioyed me ; I haue writ your Letter
Vnto the secret, nameles friend of yours :
Which I was much vnwilling to proceed in,
But for my duty to your Ladiship.   (done.

Sil. I thanke you (gentle Seruant) 'tis very Clerkly-

Val. Now trust me (Madam) it came hardly-off :
For being ignorant to whom it goes,
I writ at randome, very doubtfully.

Sil. Perchance you think too much of so much pains ?

Val. No (Madam) so it steed you ; I will write
(Please you command) a thousand times as much :
And yet ——

Sil. A pretty period : well : I ghesse the sequell ;
And yet I will not name it : and yet I care not.
And yet, take this againe : and yet I thanke you :
Meaning henceforth to trouble you no more.

Speed. And yet you will : and yet, another yet.

Val. What meanes your Ladiship ?
Doe you not like it ?

Sil. Yes, yes : the lines are very queintly writ ,
But (since vnwillingly) take them againe.
Nay, take them.

Val. Madam, they are for you.

Silu. I, I : you writ them Sir, at my request,
But I will none of them : they are for you :
I would haue had them writ more mouingly :

Val. Please you, Ile write your Ladiship another.

Sil. And when it's writ : for my sake read it ouer,
And if it please, so : if not : why so :

Val. If it please me, (Madam ?) what then ?

Sil. Why if it please you, take it for your labour;
And so good-morrow Seruant.   *Exit. Sil.*

Speed. Oh Iest vnseene : inscrutible : inuisible,
As a nose on a mans face, or a Wethercocke on a steeple:
My Master sues to her : and she hath taught her Sutor,
He being her Pupill, to become her Tutor.
Oh excellent deuise, was there euer heard a better ?
That my master being scribe,
To himselfe should write the Letter ?

Val. How now Sir ?
What are you reasoning with your selfe ?

Speed. Nay : I riming : 'tis you y̆ haue the reason.

Val. To doe what ?

Speed. To be a Spokes-man from Madam *Siluia.*

Val. To whom ?

Speed. To your selfe : why, she woes you by a figure.

Val. What figure ?

Speed. By a Letter, I should say.

Val. Why she hath not writ to me ?

Speed. What need she,
When shee hath made you write to your selfe ?
Why, doe you not perceiue the Iest?

Val. No, beleeue me.

Speed. No beleeuing you indeed sir :
But did you perceiue her earnest ?

Val. She gaue me none, except an angry word.

Speed. Why she hath giuen you a Letter.

Val. That's the Letter I writ to her friend.

Speed. And y̆ letter hath she deliuer'd, & there an end.

Val. I would it were no worse.

Speed. Ile warrant you, 'tis as well :
For often haue you writ to her : and she in modesty,
Or else for want of idle time, could not againe reply,
Or fearing els some messeger, y̆ might her mind discouer
Her self hath taught her Loue himself, to write vnto her
All this I speak in print, for in print I found it.   (louer.
Why muse you sir, 'tis dinner time.

Val. I haue dyn'd.

Speed. I, but hearken sir : though the Cameleon Loue
can feed on the ayre, I am one that am nourish'd by my
victuals ; and would faine haue meate : oh bee not like
your Mistresse, be moued, be moued.   *Exeunt.*

Scæna secunda.

Enter Protheus, Iulia, Panthion.

Pro. Haue patience, gentle *Iulia :*

Iul I must where is no remedy.

Pro. When possibly I can, I will returne.

Iul. If you turne not : you will return the sooner :
Keepe this remembrance for thy *Iulia's* sake.

Pro. Why then wee'll make exchange ;
Here, take you this.

Iul. And seale the bargaine with a holy kisse.

Pro. Here is my hand, for my true constancie :
And when that howre ore-slips me in the day,
Wherein I sigh not (*Iulia*) for thy sake,
The next ensuing howre, some foule mischance
Torment me for my Loues forgetfulnesse :
My father staies my comming : answere not :
The tide is now ; nay, not thy tide of teares,
That tide will stay me longer then I should,
Iulia, farewell : what, gon without a word ?
I, so true loue should doe : it cannot speake,
For truth hath better deeds, then words to grace it.

Panth. Sir *Protheus :* you are staid for.

Pro. Goe : I come, I come :
Alas, this parting strikes poore Louers dumbe.

                                            Exeunt.

Scæna Tertia.

Enter Launce, Panthion.

Launce. Nay, 'twill bee this howre ere I haue done
weeping : all the kinde of the *Launces,* haue this very
fault : I haue receiu'd my proportion, like the prodigious
                                                    sonne,

Sonne, and am going with Sir *Protheus* to the Imperialls
Court : I thinke *Crab* my dog, be the fowreſt natured
dogge that liues : My Mother weeping : my Father
wayling : my Siſter crying : our Maid howling : our
Catte wringing her hands, and all our houſe in a great
perplexitie, yet did not this cruell-hearted Curre ſhedde
one teare : he is a ſtone, a very pibble ſtone, and has no
more pitty in him then a dogge : a Iew would haue wept
to haue ſeene our parting : why my Grandam hauing
no eyes, looke you, wept her ſelfe blinde at my parting :
nay, Ile ſhew you the manner of it. This ſhooe is my father : no, this left ſhooe is my father ; no, no, this left
ſhooe is my mother : nay, that cannot bee ſo neyther :
yes ; it is ſo, it is ſo : it hath the worſer ſole : this ſhooe
with the hole in it, is my mother : and this my father :
a veng'ance on't, there 'tis : Now ſir, this ſtaffe is my ſiſter : for, looke you, ſhe is as white as a lilly, and as
ſmall as a wand : this hat is *Nan* our maid : I am the
dogge : no, the dogge is himſelfe, and I am the dogge :
oh, the dogge is me, and I am my ſelfe : I ; ſo, ſo : now
come I to my Father ; Father, your bleſſing : now
ſhould not the ſhooe ſpeake a word for weeping :
now ſhould I kiſſe my Father ; well, hee weepes on :
Now come I to my Mother : Oh that ſhe could ſpeake
now, like a would-woman : well, I kiſſe her : why
there 'tis ; heere's my mothers breath vp and downe :
Now come I to my ſiſter ; marke the moane ſhe makes :
now the dogge all this while ſheds not a teare : nor
ſpeakes a word : but ſee how I lay the duſt with my
teares.

Panth. *Launce*, away, away : a Boord : thy Maſter is
ſhip'd, and thou art to poſt after with oares ; what's the
matter ? why weep'ſt thou man ? away aſſe, you'l looſe
the Tide, if you tarry any longer.

Laun. It is no matter if the tide were loſt, for it is the
vnkindeſt Tide, that euer any man tide.

Panth. What's the vnkindeſt tide ?

Lau. Why, he that's tide here, *Crab* my dog.

Pant. Tut, man : I meane thou'lt looſe the flood, and
in looſing the flood, looſe thy voyage, and in looſing thy
voyage, looſe thy Maſter, and in looſing thy Maſter,
looſe thy ſeruice, and in looſing thy ſeruice : —— why
doſt thou ſtop my mouth ?

Laun. For feare thou ſhouldſt looſe thy tongue.

Panth. Where ſhould I looſe my tongue ?

Laun. In thy Tale.

Pauth. In thy Taile.

Laun. Looſe the Tide, and the voyage, and the Maſter, and the Seruice, and the tide : why man, if the Riuer
were drie, I am able to fill it with my teares : if the winde
were downe, I could driue the boate with my ſighes.

Panth. Come : come away man, I was ſent to call
thee.

Lau. Sir : call me what thou dar'ſt.

Pant. Wilt thou goe ?

Laun. Well, I will goe.   *Exeunt.*

Scena Quarta.

Enter Valentine, Siluia, Thurio, Speed, Duke, Protheus.

Sil. Seruant.

Val. Miſtris.

Spee. Maſter, Sir *Thurio* frownes on you.

Val. I Boy, it's for loue.

Spee. Not of you.

Val. Of my Miſtreſſe then.

Spee. 'Twere good you knockt him.

Sil. Seruant, you are ſad.

Val. Indeed, Madam, I ſeeme ſo.

Thu. Seeme you that you are not ?

Thu. So doe Counterfeyts.

Val. So doe you.

Thu. What ſeeme I that I am not ?

Val. Wiſe.

Thu. What inſtance of the contrary ?

Val. Your folly.

Thu. And how quoat you my folly ?

Val. I quoat it in your Ierkin.

Thu. My Ierkin is a doublet.

Val. Well then, Ile double your folly.

Thu. How ?

Sil. What, angry, Sir *Thurio*, do you change colour ?

Val. Giue him leaue, Madam, he is a kind of *Camelion*.

Thu. That hath more minde to feed on your bloud,
then liue in your ayre.

Val. You haue ſaid Sir.

Thu. I Sir, and done too for this time.

Val. I know it wel ſir, you alwaies end ere you begin.

Sil. A fine volly of words, gentlemē, & quickly ſhot off

Val. 'Tis indeed, Madam, we thanke the giuer.

Sil. Who is that Seruant ?

Val. Your ſelfe (ſweet Lady) for you gaue the fire,
Sir *Thurio* borrows his wit from your Ladiſhips lookes,
And ſpends what he borrowes kindly in your company.

Thu. Sir, if you ſpend word for word with me, I ſhall
make your wit bankrupt.   (words,

Val. I know it well ſir : you haue an Exchequer of
And I thinke, no other treaſure to giue your followers :
For it appeares by their bare Liueries
That they liue by your bare words.

Sil. No more, gentlemen, no more :
Here comes my father.

Duk. Now, daughter *Siluia*, you are hard beſet.
Sir *Valentine*, your father is in good health,
What ſay you to a Letter from your friends
Of much good newes ?

Val. My Lord, I will be thankfull,
To any happy meſſenger from thence.

Duk. Know ye, *Don Antonio*, your Countriman ?

Val. I, my good Lord, I know the Gentleman
To be of worth, and worthy eſtimation,
And not without deſert ſo well reputed.

Duk. Hath he not a Sonne ?

Val. I, my good Lord, a Son, that well deſerues
The honor, and regard of ſuch a father.

Duk. You know him well ?

Val. I knew him as my ſelfe : for from our Infancie
We haue conuerſt, and ſpent our howres together,
And though my ſelfe haue beene an idle Trewant,
Omitting the ſweet benefit of time
To cloath mine age with Angel-like perfection :
Yet hath Sir *Protheus* (for that's his name)
Made vſe, and faire aduantage of his daies :
His yeares but yong, but his experience old :
His head vn-mellowed, but his Iudgement ripe ;
And in a word (for far behinde his worth
Comes all the praiſes that I now beſtow.)

C   He

He is compleat in feature, and in minde,
With all good grace, to grace a Gentleman.
  Duk. Beſhrew me fir, but if he make this good
He is as worthy for an Empreſſe loue,
As meet to be an Emperors Councellor :
Well, Sir : this Gentleman is come to me
With Commendation from great Potentates,
And heere he meanes to ſpend his time a while,
I thinke 'tis no vn-welcome newes to you.
  Val. Should I haue wiſh'd a thing, it had beene he.
  Duk. Welcome him then according to his worth :
Siluia, I ſpeake to you, and you Sir *Thurio,*
For *Valentine,* I need not cite him to it,
I will ſend him hither to you preſently.
  Val. This is the Gentleman I told your Ladiſhip
Had come along with me, but that his Miſtreſſe
Did hold his eyes, lockt in her Chriſtall lookes.
  Sil. Be-like that now ſhe hath enfranchis'd them
Vpon ſome other pawne for fealty.
  Val. Nay ſure, I thinke ſhe holds them priſoners ſtil.
  Sil. Nay then he ſhould be blind, and being blind
How could he ſee his way to ſeeke out you ?
  Val. Why Lady, Loue hath twenty paire of eyes.
  Thur. They ſay that Loue hath not an eye at all.
  Val. To ſee ſuch Louers, *Thurio,* as your ſelfe,
Vpon a homely obiect, Loue can winke.
  Sil. Haue done, haue done : here comesʒ gentleman.
  Val. Welcome, deer *Protheus* : Miſtris, I beſeech you
Confirme his welcome, with ſome ſpeciall fauor.
  Sil. His worth is warrant for his welcome hether,
If this be he you oft haue wiſh'd to heare from.
  Val. Miſtris, it is : ſweet Lady, entertaine him
To be my fellow-ſeruant to your Ladiſhip.
  Sil. Too low a Miſtres for ſo high a ſeruant.
  Pro. Not ſo, ſweet Lady, but too meane a ſeruant
To haue a looke of ſuch a worthy a Miſtreſſe.
  Val. Leaue off diſcourſe of diſabilitie :
Sweet Lady, entertaine him for your Seruant.
  Pro. My dutie will I boaſt of, nothing elſe.
  Sil. And dutie neuer yet did want his meed.
Seruant, you are welcome to a worthleſſe Miſtreſſe.
  Pro. Ile die on him that ſaies ſo but your ſelfe.
  Sil. That you are welcome?
  Pro. That you are worthleſſe.　　　　　(you.
  Thur. Madam, my Lord your father wold ſpeak with
  Sil. I wait vpon his pleaſure : Come Sir *Thurio,*
Goe with me : once more, new Seruant welcome ;
Ile leaue you to confer of home affaires,
When you haue done, we looke too heare from you.
  Pro. Wee'll both attend vpon your Ladiſhip.
  Val. Now tell me : how do al from whence you came ?
  Pro. Your frends are wel, & haue the̅ much co̅mended.
  Val. And how doe yours ?
  Pro. I left them all in health.
  Val. How does your Lady ? & how thriues your loue ?
  Pro. My tales of Loue were wont to weary you,
I know you ioy not in a Loue-diſcourſe.
  Val. I *Protheus,* but that life is alter'd now,
I haue done pennance for contemning Loue,
Whoſe high emperious thoughts haue puniſh'd me
With bitter faſts, with penitentiall grones,
With nightly teares, and daily hart-ſore ſighes,
For in reuenge of my contempt of loue,
Loue hath chas'd ſleepe from my enthralled eyes,
And made them watchers of mine owne hearts ſorrow,
O gentle *Protheus,* Loue's a mighty Lord,

And hath ſo humbled me, as I confeſſe
There is no woe to his correction,
Nor to his Seruice, no ſuch ioy on earth :
Now, no diſcourſe, except it be of loue :
Now can I breake my faſt, dine, ſup, and ſleepe,
Vpon the very naked name of Loue.
  Pro. Enough ; I read your fortune in your eye :
Was this the Idoll, that you worſhip ſo?
  Val. Euen She ; and is ſhe not a heauenly Saint ?
  Pro. No ; But ſhe is an earthly Paragon.
  Val. Call her diuine.
  Pro. I will not flatter her.
  Val. O flatter me : for Loue delights in praiſes.
  Pro. When I was ſick, you gaue me bitter pils,
And I muſt miniſter the like to you.
  Val. Then ſpeake the truth by her ; if not diuine,
Yet let her be a principalitie,
Soueraigne to all the Creatures on the earth.
  Pro. Except my Miſtreſſe.
  Val. Sweet : except not any,
Except thou wilt except againſt my Loue.
  Pro. Haue I not reaſon to prefer mine owne ?
  Val. And I will help thee to prefer her to :
Shee ſhall be dignified with this high honour,
To beare my Ladies traine, left the baſe earth
Should from her veſture chance to ſteale a kiſſe,
And of ſo great a fauor growing proud,
Diſdaine to roote the Sommer-ſwelling flowre,
And make rough winter euerlaſtingly.
  Pro. Why *Valentine,* what Bragadiſme is this ?
  Val. Pardon me (*Protheus*) all I can is nothing,
To her, whoſe worth, make other worthies nothing ;
Shee is alone.
  Pro. Then let her alone.
  Val. Not for the world : why man, ſhe is mine owne,
And I as rich in hauing ſuch a Iewell
As twenty Seas, if all their ſand were pearle,
The water, Nectar, and the Rocks pure gold.
Forgiue me that I doe not dreame on thee,
Becauſe thou ſeeſt me doate vpon my loue :
My fooliſh Riuall that her Father likes
(Onely for his poſſeſſions are ſo huge)
Is gone with her along, and I muſt after,
For Loue (thou know'ſt is full of iealouſie.)
  Pro. But ſhe loues you ?　　　　　(howre,
  Val. I, and we are betroathd : nay more, our mariage
With all the cunning manner of our flight
Determin'd of : how I muſt climbe her window,
The Ladder made of Cords, and all the means
Plotted, and 'greed on for my happineſſe.
Good *Protheus* goe with me to my chamber,
In theſe affaires to aid me with thy counſaile.
  Pro. Goe on before : I ſhall enquire you forth:
I muſt vnto the Road, to diſ-embarque
Some neceſſaries, that I needs muſt vſe,
And then Ile preſently attend you.
  Val. Will you make haſte ?　　　　　*Exit.*
  Pro. I will.
Euen as one heate, another heate expels,
Or as one naile, by ſtrength driues out another.
So the remembrance of my former Loue
Is by a newer obiect quite forgotten ,
It is mine, or *Valentines* praiſe ?
Her true perfection, or my falſe tranſgreſſion ?
That makes me reaſonleſſe, to reaſon thus ?
Shee is faire : and ſo is *Iulia* that I loue,

　　　　　　　　　　　　　　　　　　(That

(That I did loue, for now my loue is thaw'd,
Which like a waxen Image 'gainſt a fire
Beares no impreſſion of the thing it was.)
Me thinkes my zeale to *Valentine* is cold,
And that I loue him not as I was wont:
O, but I loue his Lady too-too much,
And that's the reaſon I loue him ſo little.
How ſhall I doate on her with more aduice,
That thus without aduice begin to loue her?
'Tis but her picture I haue yet beheld,
And that hath dazel'd my reaſons light:
But when I looke on her perfections,
There is no reaſon, but I ſhall be blinde.
If I can checke my erring loue, I will,
If not, to compaſſe her Ile vſe my skill.

Exeunt.

Scena Quinta.

Enter Speed and Launce.

Speed. *Launce*, by mine honeſty welcome to *Padua*.
Laun. Forſweare not thy ſelfe, ſweet youth, for I am
not welcome. I reckon this alwaies, that a man is neuer
vndon till hee be hang'd, nor neuer welcome to a place,
till ſome certaine ſhot be paid, and the Hoſteſſe ſay wel-
come.
Speed. Come-on you mad-cap : Ile to the Ale-houſe
with you preſently ; where, for one ſhot of fiue pence,
thou ſhalt haue fiue thouſand welcomes : But ſirha, how
did thy Maſter part with Madam *Iulia* ?
Lau. Marry after they cloas'd in earneſt, they parted
very fairely in ieſt.
Spee. But ſhall ſhe marry him ?
Lau. No.
Spee. How then ? ſhall he marry her ?
Lau. No, neither.
Spee. What, are they broken ?
Lau. No ; they are both as whole as a fiſh.
Spee. Why then, how ſtands the matter with them ?
Lau. Marry thus, when it ſtands well with him, it
ſtands well with her.
Spee. What an aſſe art thou, I vnderſtand thee not.
Lau. What a blocke art thou, that thou canſt not ?
My ſtaffe vnderſtands me.
Spee. What thou ſaiſt ?
Lau. I, and what I do too : looke thee, Ile but leane,
and my ſtaffe vnderſtands me.
Spee. It ſtands vnder thee indeed.
Lau. Why, ſtand-vnder: and vnder-ſtand is all one.
Spee. But tell me true, wil't be a match ?
Lau. Aske my dogge, if he ſay I, it will : if hee ſay
no, it will : if hee ſhake his taile, and ſay nothing, it
will.
Spee. The concluſion is then, that it will.
Lau. Thou ſhalt neuer get ſuch a ſecret from me, but
by a parable.
Spee. 'Tis well that I get it ſo : but *Launce*, how ſaiſt
thou that that my maſter is become a notable Louer ?
Lau. I neuer knew him otherwiſe.
Spee. Then how ?
Lau. A notable Lubber : as thou reporteſt him to
bee.

Spee. Why, thou whorſon Aſſe, thou miſtak'ſt me,
Lau. Why Foole , I meant not thee , I meant thy
Maſter.
Spee. I tell thee, my Maſter is become a hot Louer.
Lau. Why, I tell thee, I care not, though hee burne
himſelfe in Loue. If thou wilt goe with me to the Ale-
houſe : if not, thou art an Hebrew, a Iew, and not worth
the name of a Chriſtian.
Spee. Why?
Lau. Becauſe thou haſt not ſo much charity in thee as
to goe to the Ale with a Chriſtian : Wilt thou goe ?
Spee. At thy ſeruice.

Exeunt.

Scæna Sexta.

Enter Protheus ſolus.

Pro. To leaue my *Iulia*; ſhall I be forſworne?
To loue faire *Siluia*; ſhall I be forſworne ?
To wrong my friend, I ſhall be much forſworne,
And ev'n that Powre which gaue me firſt my oath
Prouokes me to this three-fold periurie.
Loue bad mee ſweare, and Loue bids me for-ſweare ;
O ſweet-ſuggeſting Loue, if thou haſt ſin'd,
Teach me (thy tempted ſubiect) to excuſe it.
At firſt I did adore a twinkling Starre,
But now I worſhip a celeſtiall Sunne :
Vn-heedfull vowes may heedfully be broken,
And he wants wit, that wants reſolued will,
To learne his wit, t'exchange the bad for better ;
Fie, fie, vnreuerend tongue, to call her bad,
Whoſe ſoueraignty ſo oft thou haſt preferd,
With twenty thouſand ſoule-confirming oathes.
I cannot leaue to loue ; and yet I doe :
But there I leaue to loue, where I ſhould loue.
Iulia I looſe, and *Valentine* I looſe,
If I keepe them, I needs muſt looſe my ſelfe :
If I looſe them, thus finde I by their loſſe,
For *Valentine*, my ſelfe : for *Iulia*, *Siluia*.
I to my ſelfe am deerer then a friend,
For Loue is ſtill moſt precious in it ſelfe,
And *Siluia* (witneſſe heauen that made her faire)
Shewes *Iulia* but a ſwarthy Ethlope.
I will forget that *Iulia* is aliue,
Remembring that my Loue to her is dead.
And *Valentine* Ile hold an Enemie,
Ayming at *Siluia* as a ſweeter friend.
I cannot now proue conſtant to my ſelfe,
Without ſome treachery vs'd to *Valentine*.
This night he meaneth with a Corded-ladder
To climbe celeſtiall *Siluia's* chamber window,
My ſelfe in counſaile his competitor.
Now preſently Ile giue her father notice
Of their diſguiſing and pretended flight :
Who (all inrag'd) will baniſh *Valentine*:
For *Thurio* he intends ſhall wed his daughter,
But *Valentine* being gon, Ile quickely croſſe
By ſome ſlie tricke, blunt *Thurio's* dull proceeding.
Loue lend me wings, to make my purpoſe ſwift
As thou haſt lent me wit, to plot this drift.

Exit.

Scœna feptima.

Enter Iulia *and* Lucetta.

Iul. Counfaile, *Lucetta,* gentle girle aſſiſt me,
And eu'n in kinde loue, I doe coniure thee,
Who art the Table wherein all my thoughts
Are viſibly Charaĉter'd, and engrau'd,
To leſſon me, and tell me ſome good meane
How with my honour I may vndertake
A iourney to my louing *Protheus.*

Luc. Alas, the way is wearifome and long.

Iul. A true-deuoted Pilgrime is not weary
To meaſure Kingdomes with his feeble ſteps,
Much leſſe ſhall ſhe that hath Loues wings to flie,
And when the flight is made to one ſo deere,
Of ſuch diuine perfeĉtion as Sir *Protheus.*

Luc. Better forbeare, till *Protheus* make returne.

Iuli Oh, know'ſt ỹ not, his looks are my ſoules food ?
Pitty the dearth that I haue pined in,
By longing for that food ſo long a time.
Didſt thou but know the inly touch of Loue ,
Thou wouldſt as ſoone goe kindle fire with ſnow
As feeke to quench the fire of Loue with words.

Luc. I doe not feeke to quench your Loues hot fire,
But qualifie the fires extreame rage ,
Leſt it ſhould burne aboue the bounds of reaſon.

Iul. The more thou dam'ſt it vp, the more it burnes :
The Current that with gentle murmure glides
(Thou know'ſt) being ſtop'd, impatiently doth rage :
But when his faire courſe is not hindered,
He makes ſweet muſicke with th'enameld ſtones,
Giuing a gentle kiſſe to euery ſedge
He ouer-taketh in his pilgrimage.
And ſo by many winding nookes he ſtraies
With willing ſport to the wilde Ocean.
Then let me goe, and hinder not my courſe :
Ile be as patient as a gentle ſtreame,
And make a paſtime of each weary ſtep,
Till the laſt ſtep haue brought me to my Loue,
And there Ile reſt, as after much turmoile
A bleſſed foule doth in *Eliʒium.*

Luc. But in what habit will you goe along ?

Iul. Not like a woman, for I would preuent
The loofe encounters of lafciuious men :
Gentle *Lucetta,* fit me with ſuch weedes
As may befeeme ſome well reputed Page.

Luc. Why then your Ladiſhip muſt cut your haire.

Iul. No girle, Ile knit it vp in ſilken ſtrings,
With twentie od-conceited true-loue knots :
To be fantaſtique, may become a youth
Of greater time then I ſhall ſhew to be.   (ches?

Luc. What faſhion (Madam) ſhall I make your bree-

Iul. That fits as well, as tell me (good my Lord) (dam)
What compaſſe will you weare your Farthingale ?

Why eu'n what faſhion thou beſt likes (*Lucetta.*)

Luc. You muſt needs haue thē with a cod-peece (Ma-

Iul. Out, out, (*Lucetta*) that wilbe illfauourd.

Luc. A round hofe (Madam) now's not worth a pin
Vnleſſe you haue a cod-peece to ſtick pins on.

Iul. *Lucetta,* as thou lou'ſt me let me haue
What thou think'ſt meet, and is moſt mannerly.
But tell me (wench) how will the world repute me
For vndertaking ſo vnſtaid a iourney ?

I feare me it will make me ſcandaliʒ'd.

Luc. If you thinke ſo, then ſtay at home, and go not.

Iul. Nay, that I will not.

Luc. Then neuer dreame on Infamy, but go :
If *Protheus* like your iourney, when you come,
No matter who's difpleas'd, when you are gone :
I feare me he will ſcarce be pleas'd with all.

Iul. That is the leaſt (*Lucetta*) of my feare :
A thouſand oathes, an Ocean of his teares,
And inſtances of infinite of Loue,
Warrant me welcome to my *Protheus.*

Luc. All theſe are feruants to deceitfull men.

Iul. Bafe men, that vfe them to ſo bafe effeĉt ;
But truer ſtarres did gouerne *Protheus* birth,
His words are bonds, his oathes are oracles,
His loue ſincere, his thoughts immaculate,
His teares, pure meſſengers, ſent from his heart,
His heart, as far from fraud, as heauen from earth.

Luc. Pray heau'n he proue ſo when you come to him.

Iul. Now, as thou lou'ſt me, do him not that wrong,
To beare a hard opinion of his truth:
Onely deferue my loue, by louing him,
And prefently goe with me to my chamber
To take a note of what I ſtand in need of,
To furnifh me vpon my longing iourney :
All that is mine I leaue at thy difpofe ,
My goods, my Lands, my reputation ,
Onely, in lieu thereof, difpatch me hence :
Come ; anfwere not : but to it prefently,
I am impatient of my tarriance.   *Exeunt.*

Aĉtus Tertius, Scena Prima.

Enter Duke, Thurio, Protheus, Valentine,
Launce, Speed.

Duke. Sir *Thurio,* giue vs leaue (I pray) a while,
We haue ſome ſecrets to confer about.
Now tell me *Protheus,* what's your will with me ?

Pro. My gracious Lord, that which I wold difcouer,
The Law of friendſhip bids me to conceale,
But when I call to minde yonr gracious fauours
Done to me (vndeferuing as I am)
My dutie pricks me on to vtter that
Which elfe, no worldly good ſhould draw from me:
Know (worthy Prince) Sir *Valentine* my friend
This night intends to ſteale away your daughter :
My ſelfe am one made priuy to the plot.
I know you haue determin'd to beſtow her
On *Thurio,* whom your gentle daughter hates,
And ſhould ſhe thus be ſtolne away from you,
It would be much vexation to your age.
Thus (for my duties fake) I rather chofe
To croſſe my friend in his intended drift,
Then (by concealing it) heap on your head
A pack of forrowes, which would preſſe you downe
(Being vnpreuented) to your timeleſſe graue.

Duke. *Protheus,* I thank thee for thine honeſt care,
Which to requite, command me while I liue.
This loue of theirs, my ſelfe haue often feene,
Haply when they haue iudg'd me faſt aſleepe,
And oftentimes haue purpos'd to forbid

Sir *Valentine* her companie, and my Court.
But fearing leſt my iealous ayme might erre,
And ſo (vnworthily) diſgrace the man
(A raſhneſſe that I euer yet haue ſhun'd)
I gaue him gentle lookes, thereby to finde
That which thy ſelfe haſt now diſclos'd to me.
And that thou maiſt perceiue my feare of this,
Knowing that tender youth is ſoone ſuggeſted,
I nightly lodge her in an vpper Towre,
The key whereof, my ſelfe haue euer kept:
And thence ſhe cannot be conuay'd away.

  Pro. Know (noble Lord) they haue deuis'd a meane
How he her chamber-window will aſcend,
And with a Corded-ladder fetch her downe:
For which, the youthfull Louer now is gone,
And this way comes he with it preſently.
Where (if it pleaſe you) you may intercept him.
But (good my Lord) doe it ſo cunningly
That my diſcouery be not aimed at:
For, loue of you, not hate vnto my friend,
Hath made me publiſher of this pretence.

  Duke. Vpon mine Honor, he ſhall neuer know
That I had any light from thee of this.

  Pro. Adiew, my Lord, Sir *Valentine* is comming.

  Duk. Sir *Valentine*, whether away ſo faſt?

  Val. Pleaſe it your Grace, there is a Meſſenger
That ſtayes to beare my Letters to my friends,
And I am going to deliuer them.

  Duk. Be they of much import?

  Val. The tenure of them doth but ſignifie
My health, and happy being at your Court.

  Duk. Nay then no matter: ſtay with me a while,
I am to breake with thee of ſome affaires
That touch me neere: wherein thou muſt be ſecret.
'Tis not vnknown to thee, that I haue ſought
To match my friend Sir *Thurio*, to my daughter.

  Val. I know it well (my Lord) and ſure the Match
Were rich and honourable: beſides, the gentleman
Is full of Vertue, Bounty, Worth, and Qualities
Beſeeming ſuch a Wife, as your faire daughter:
Cannot your Grace win her to fancie him?

  Duk. No, truſt me, She is peeuiſh, ſullen, froward,
Prowd, diſobedient, ſtubborne, lacking duty,
Neither regarding that ſhe is my childe,
Nor fearing me, as if I were her father:
And may I ſay to thee, this pride of hers
(Vpon aduice) hath drawne my loue from her,
And where I thought the remnant of mine age
Should haue beene cheriſh'd by her child-like dutie,
I now am full reſolu'd to take a wife,
And turne her out, to who will take her in:
Then let her beauty be her wedding dowre:
For me, and my poſſeſſions ſhe eſteemes not.

  Val. What would your Grace haue me to do in this?

  Duk. There is a Lady in *Verona* heere
Whom I affect: but ſhe is nice, and coy,
And naught eſteemes my aged eloquence.
Now therefore would I haue thee to my Tutor
(For long agone I haue forgot to court,)
Beſides the faſhion of the time is chang'd)
How, and which way I may beſtow my ſelfe
To be regarded in her ſun-bright eye.

  Val. Win her with gifts, if ſhe reſpect not words,
Dumbe Iewels often in their ſilent kinde
More then quicke words, doe moue a womans minde.

  Duk. But ſhe did ſcorne a preſent that I ſent her,

  Val. A woman ſomtime ſcorns what beſt cōtents her.
Send her another: neuer giue her ore,
For ſcorne at firſt, makes after-loue the more.
If ſhe doe frowne, 'tis not in hate of you,
But rather to beget more loue in you.
If ſhe doe chide, 'tis not to haue you gone,
For why, the fooles are mad, if left alone.
Take no repulſe, what euer ſhe doth ſay,
For, get you gon, ſhe doth not meane away.
Flatter, and praiſe, commend, extoll their graces:
Though nere ſo blacke, ſay they haue Angells faces,
That man that hath a tongue, I ſay is no man,
If with his tongue he cannot win a woman.

  Duk. But ſhe I meane, is promis'd by her friends
Vnto a youthfull Gentleman of worth,
And kept ſeuerely from reſort of men,
That no man hath acceſſe by day to her.

  Val. Why then I would reſort to her by night.

  Duk. I, but the doores be lockt, and keyes kept ſafe,
That no man hath recourſe to her by night.

  Val. What letts but one may enter at her window?

  Duk. Her chamber is aloft, far from the ground,
And built ſo ſheluing, that one cannot climbe it
Without apparant hazard of his life.

  Val. Why then a Ladder quaintly made of Cords
To caſt vp, with a paire of anchoring hookes,
Would ſerue to ſcale another *Hero's* towre,
So bold *Leander* would aduenture it.

  Duk. Now as thou art a Gentleman of blood
Aduiſe me, where I may haue ſuch a Ladder.

  Val. When would you vſe it? pray ſir, tell me that.

  Duk. This very night; for Loue is like a childe
That longs for euery thing that he can come by.

  Val. By ſeauen a clock, ile get you ſuch a Ladder.

  Duk. But harke thee: I will goe to her alone,
How ſhall I beſt conuey the Ladder thither?

  Val. It will be light (my Lord) that you may beare it
Vnder a cloake, that is of any length.

  Duk. A cloake as long as thine will ſerue the turne?

  Val. I my good Lord.

  Duk. Then let me ſee thy cloake,
Ile get me one of ſuch another length.

  Val. Why any cloake will ſerue the turn (my Lord)

  Duk. How ſhall I faſhion me to weare a cloake?
I pray thee let me feele thy cloake vpon me.
What Letter is this ſame? what's here? to *Siluia*?
And heere an Engine fit for my proceeding,
Ile be ſo bold to breake the ſeale for once.

My thoughts do harbour with my Siluia *nightly,
And ſlaues they are to me, that ſend them flying.
Oh, could their Maſter come, and goe as lightly,
Himſelfe would lodge, where (ſenceles) they are lying.
My Herald Thoughts, in thy pure boſome reſt-them,
While I (their King) that thither them importune
Doe curſe the grace, that with ſuch grace hath bleſt them,
Becauſe my ſelfe doe want my ſeruants fortune.
I curſe my ſelfe, for they are ſent by me,
That they ſhould harbour where their Lord ſhould be.*

What's here? *Siluia*, this night I will enfranchiſe thee.
'Tis ſo: and heere's the Ladder for the purpoſe.
Why *Phaeton* (for thou art *Merops* ſonne)
Wilt thou aſpire to guide the heauenly Car?
And with thy daring folly burne the world?
Wilt thou reach ſtars, becauſe they ſhine on thee?

                                        C 3   Goe

Goe bafe Intruder, ouer-weening Slaue,
Beftow thy fawning fmiles on equall mates,
And thinke my patience, (more then thy defert)
Is priuiledge for thy departure hence.
Thanke me for this, more then for all the fauors
Which (all too-much) I haue beftowed on thee.
But if thou linger in my Territories
Longer then fwifteft expedition
Will giue thee time to leaue our royall Court,
By heauen, my wrath fhall farre exceed the loue
I euer bore my daughter, or thy felfe.
Be gone, I will not heare thy vaine excufe,
But as thou lou'ft thy life, make fpeed from hence.
  Val. And why not death, rather then liuing torment?
To die, is to be banifht from my felfe,
And *Siluia* is my felfe : banifh'd from her
Is felfe from felfe. A deadly banifhment :
What light, is light, if *Siluia* be not feene?
What ioy is ioy, if *Siluia* be not by?
Vnleffe it be to thinke that fhe is by
And feed vpon the fhadow of perfection.
Except I be by *Siluia* in the night,
There is no muficke in the Nightingale.
Vnleffe I looke on *Siluia* in the day,
There is no day for me to looke vpon.
Shee is my effence, and I leaue to be;
If I be not by her faire influence
Fofter'd, illumin'd, cherifh'd, kept aliue.
I flie not death, to flie his deadly doome,
Tarry I heere, I but attend on death,
But flie I hence, I flie away from life.
  Pro. Run (boy) run, run, and feeke him out.
  Lau. So-hough, Soa hough ――――
  Pro. What feeft thou?
  Lau. Him we goe to finde,
There's not a haire on's head, but t'is a *Valentine.*
  Pro. *Valentine?*
  Val. No.
  Pro. Who then? his Spirit?
  Val. Neither.
  Pro. What then?
  Val. Nothing.
  Lau. Can nothing fpeake? Mafter, fhall I ftrike?
  Pro. Who wouldft thou ftrike?
  Lau. Nothing.
  Pro. Villaine, forbeare.
  Lau. Why Sir, Ile ftrike nothing : I pray you.
  Pro. Sirha, I fay forbeare : friend *Valentine,* a word.
  Val. My eares are ftopt, & cannot hear good newes,
So much of bad already hath poffeft them.
  Pro. Then in dumbe filence will I bury mine,
For they are harfh, vn-tuneable, and bad..
  Val. Is *Siluia* dead?
  Pro. No, *Valentine.*
  Val. No *Valentine* indeed, for facred *Siluia,*
Hath fhe forfworne me?
  Pro. No, *Valentine.*
  Val. No *Valentine,* if *Siluia* haue forfworne me.
What is your newes?
  Lau. Sir, there is a proclamation, ỹ you are vanifhed.
  Pro. That thou art banifh'd : oh that's the newes,
From hence, from *Siluia,* and from me thy friend.
  Val. Oh, I haue fed vpon this woe already,
And now exceffe of it will make me furfet.
Doth *Siluia* know that I am banifh'd?
  Pro. I, I : and fhé hath offered to the doome

(Which vn-reuerft ftands in effectuall force)
A Sea of melting pearle, which fome call teares;
Thofe at her fathers churlifh feete fhe tenderd,
With them vpon her knees, her humble felfe,
Wringing her haⁱⁿds, whofe whitenes fo became them,
As if but now they waxed pale for woe :
But neither bended knees, pure hands held vp,
Sad fighes, deepe grones, nor filuer-fhedding teares
Could penetrate her vncompaffionate Sire ;
But *Valentine,* if he be tane, muft die.
Befides, her interceffion chaf'd him fo,
When fhe for thy repeale was fuppliant,
That to clofe prifon he commanded her,
With many bitter threats of biding there.
  Val. No more: vnles the next word that thou fpeak'ft
Haue fome malignant power vpon my life :
If fo : I pray thee breath it in mine eare,
As ending Antheme of my endleffe dolor.
  Pro. Ceafe to lament for that thou canft not helpe,
And ftudy helpe for that which thou lament'ft,
Time is the Nurfe, and breeder of all good ;
Here, if thou ftay, thou canft not fee thy loue :
Befides, thy ftaying will abridge thy life :
Hope is a louers ftaffe, walke hence with that
And manage it, againft defpairing thoughts :
Thy letters may be here, though thou art hence,
Which, being writ to me, fhall be deliuer'd
Euen in the milke-white bofome of thy Loue.
The time now ferues not to expoftulate,
Come, Ile conuey thee through the City-gate.
And ere I part with thee, confer at large
Of all that may concerne thy Loue-affaires :
As thou lou'ft *Siluia* (though not for thy felfe)
Regard thy danger, and along with me.
  Val. I pray thee *Launce,* and if thou feeft my Boy
Bid him make hafte, and meet me at the North-gate.
  Pro. Goe firha, finde him out : Come *Valentine.*
  Val. Oh my deere *Siluia* ; haplefle *Valentine.*
  Launce. I am but a foole, looke you, and yet I haue
the wit to thinke my Mafter is a kinde of a knaue : but
that's all one, if he be but one knaue : He liues not now
that knowes me to be in loue, yet I am in loue, but a
Teeme of horfe fhall not plucke that from me : nor who
'tis I loue : and yet 'tis a woman ; but what woman, I
will not tell my felfe : and yet 'tis a Milke-maid : yet 'tis
not a maid : for fhee hath had Goffips : yet 'tis a maid,
for fhe is her Mafters maid, and ferues for wages. Shee
hath more qualities then a Water-Spaniell, which is
much in a bare Chriftian : Heere is the Cate-log of her
Condition. *Inprimis.* Shee can fetch and carry : why
a horfe can doe no more ; nay, a horfe cannot fetch, but
onely carry, therefore is fhee better then a Iade. *Item.*
She can milke, looke you, a fweet vertue in a maid with
cleane hands.
  Speed. How now Signior *Launce?* what newes with
your Mafterfhip?
  La. With my Mafterfhip? why, it is at Sea :
  Sp. Well, your old vice ftill : miftake the word : what
newes then in your paper?
  La. The black'ft newes that euer thou heard'ft.
  Sp. Why man? how blacke?
  La. Why, as blacke as Inke.
  Sp. Let me read them?
  La. Fie on thee Iolt-head, thou canft not read.
  Sp. Thou lyeft : I can.
  La. I will try thee : tell me this? who begot thee?
                                            Sp. Marry,

Sp. Marry, the fon of my Grand-father.

La. Oh illiterate loyterer; it was the fonne of thy Grand-mother: this proues that thou canft not read.

Sp. Come foole, come: try me in thy paper.

La. There: and S. *Nicholas* be thy fpeed.

Sp. Inprimis fhe can milke.

La. I that fhe can.

Sp. Item, fhe brewes good Ale.

La. And thereof comes the prouerbe: (*Bleffing of your heart, you brew good Ale.*)

Sp. Item, fhe can fowe.

La. That's as much as to fay (*Can fhe fo?*)

Sp. Item fhe can knit.

La. What neede a man care for a ftock with a wench, When fhe can knit him a ftocke?

Sp. Item, fhe can wafh and fcoure.

La. A fpeciall vertue: for then fhee neede not be wafh'd, and fcowr'd.

Sp. Item, fhe can fpin.

La. Then may I fet the world on wheeles, when fhe can fpin for her liuing.

Sp. Item, fhe hath many namelefle vertues.

La. That's as much as to fay *Baftard-vertues*: that indeede know not their fathers; and therefore haue no names.

Sp. Here follow her vices.

La. Clofe at the heeles of her vertues.

Sp. Item, fhee is not to be fafting in refpect of her breath.

La. Well: that fault may be mended with a break-faft: read on.

Sp. Item, fhe hath a fweet mouth.

La. That makes amends for her foure breath.

Sp. Item, fhe doth talke in her fleepe.

La. It's no matter for that; fo fhee fleepe not in her talke.

Sp. Item, fhe is flow in words.

La. Oh villaine, that fet this downe among her vices; To be flow in words, is a womans onely vertue: I pray thee out with't, and place it for her chiefe vertue.

Sp. Item, fhe is proud.

La. Out with that too: It was *Eues* legacie, and cannot be t'ane from her.

Sp. Item, fhe hath no teeth.

La. I care not for that neither: becaufe I loue crufts.

Sp. Item, fhe is curft.

La. Well: the beft is, fhe hath no teeth to bite.

Sp. Item, fhe will often praife her liquor.

La. If her liquor be good, fhe fhall: if fhe will not, I will; for good things fhould be praifed.

Sp. Item, fhe is too liberall.

La. Of her tongue fhe cannot; for that's writ downe fhe is flow of: of her purfe, fhee fhall not, for that fhe keepe fhut: Now, of another thing fhee may, and that cannot I helpe. Well, proceede.

Sp. Item, fhee hath more haire then wit, and more faults then haires, and more wealth then faults.

La. Stop there: Ile haue her: fhe was mine, and not mine, twice or thrice in that laft Article: rehearfe that once more.

Sp. Item, fhe hath more haire then wit.

La. More haire then wit: it may be ile proue it: The couer of the falt, hides the falt, and therefore it is more then the falt; the haire that couers the wit, is more then the wit; for the greater hides the lefle: What's next?

Sp. And more faults then haires.

La. That's monftrous: oh that that were out.

Sp. And more wealth then faults.

La. Why that word makes the faults gracious: Well, ile haue her: and if it be a match, as nothing is impoffible.

Sp. What then?

La. Why then, will I tell thee, that thy Mafter ftaies for thee at the North gate.

Sp. For me?

La. For thee? I, who art thou? he hath ftaid for a better man then thee.

Sp. And muft I goe to him?

La. Thou muft run to him; for thou haft ftaid fo long, that going will fcarce ferue the turne.

Sp. Why didft not tell me fooner? 'pox of your loue Letters.

La. Now will he be fwing'd for reading my Letter; An vnmannerly flaue, that will thruft himfelfe into fecrets: Ile after, to reioyce in the boyes correctiõ. *Exeunt.*

Scena Secunda.

Enter Duke, Thurio, Protheus.

Du. Sir *Thurio*, feare not, but that fhe will loue you Now *Valentine* is banifh'd from her fight.

Th. Since his exile fhe hath defpis'd me moft, Forfworne my company, and rail'd at me, That I am defperate of obtaining her.

Du. This weake impreffe of Loue, is as a figure Trenched in ice, which with an houres heate Diffolues to water, and doth loofe his forme. A little time will melt her frozen thoughts, And worthlefle *Valentine* fhall be forgot. How now fir *Protheus*, is your countriman (According to our Proclamation) gon?

Pro. Gon, my good Lord.

Du. My daughter takes his going grieuoufly?

Pro. A little time (my Lord) will kill that griefe.

Du. So I beleeue: but *Thurio* thinkes not fo: *Protheus*, the good conceit I hold of thee, (For thou haft fhowne fome figne of good defert) Makes me the better to confer with thee.

Pro. Longer then I proue loyall to your Grace, Let me not liue, to looke vpon your Grace.

Du. Thou know'ft how willingly, I would effect The match betweene fir *Thurio*, and my daughter?

Pro. I doe my Lord.

Du. And alfo, I thinke, thou art not ignorant How fhe oppofes her againft my will?

Pro. She did my Lord, when *Valentine* was here.

Du. I, and peruerfly, fhe perfeuers fo: What might we doe to make the girle forget The loue of *Valentine*, and loue fir *Thurio*?

Pro. The beft way is, to flander *Valentine*, With falfehood, cowardize, and poore difcent: Three things, that women highly hold in hate.

Du. I, but fhe'll thinke, that it is fpoke in hate.

Pro. I, if his enemy deliuer it. Therefore it muft with circumftance be fpoken By one, whom fhe efteemeth as his friend.

Du. Then you muft vndertake to flander him.

Pro.

Pro. And that (my Lord) I ſhall be loath to doe :
'Tis an ill office for a Gentleman,
Eſpecially againſt his very friend.

Du. Where your good word cannot aduantage him,
Your ſlander neuer can endamage him ;
Therefore the office is indifferent,
Being intreated to it by your friend.

Pro. You haue preuail'd (my Lord) if I can doe it
By ought that I can ſpeake in his diſpraiſe,
She ſhall not long continue loue to him :
But ſay this weede her loue from *Valentine*,
It followes not that ſhe will loue ſir *Thurio.*

Th. Therefore, as you vnwinde her loue from him ;
Leaſt it ſhould rauell, and be good to none,
You muſt prouide to bottome it on me :
Which muſt be done, by praiſing me as much
As you, in worth diſpraiſe, ſir *Ualentine.*

Du. And *Protheus*, we dare truſt you in this kinde,
Becauſe we know (on *Valentines* report)
You are already loues firme votary,
And cannot ſoone reuolt, and change your minde.
Vpon this warrant, ſhall you haue acceſſe,
Where you, with *Siluia*, may conferre at large.
For ſhe is lumpiſh, heauy, mellancholly,
And (for your friends ſake) will be glad of you ;
Where you may temper her, by your perſwaſion,
To hate yong *Ualentine*, and loue my friend.

Pro. As much as I can doe, I will effect :
But you ſir *Thurio*, are not ſharpe enough :
You muſt lay Lime, to tangle her deſires
By walefull Sonnets, whoſe compoſed Rimes
Should be full fraught with ſeruiceable vowes.

Du. I, much is the force of heauen-bred Poeſie.

Pro. Say that vpon the altar of her beauty
You ſacrifice your teares, your ſighes, your heart :
Write till your inke be dry ; and with your teares
Moiſt it againe : and frame ſome feeling line,
That may diſcouer ſuch integrity :
For *Orpheus* Lute, was ſtrung with Poets ſinewes,
Whoſe golden touch could ſoften ſteele and ſtones ;
Make Tygers tame, and huge *Leuiathans*
Forſake vnſounded deepes, to dance on Sands.
After your dire-lamenting Elegies,
Viſit by night your Ladies chamber-window
With ſome ſweet Conſort ; To their Inſtruments
Tune a deploring dumpe : the nights dead ſilence
Will well become ſuch ſweet complaining grieuance :
This, or elſe nothing, will inherit her.

Du. This diſcipline, ſhowes thou haſt bin in loue.

Th. And thy aduice, this night, ile put in practiſe :
Therefore, ſweet *Protheus*, my direction-giuer,
Let vs into the City preſently
To ſort ſome Gentlemen, well skil'd in Muſicke.
I haue a Sonnet, that will ſerue the turne
To giue the on-ſet to thy good aduiſe.

Du. About it Gentlemen.

Pro. We'll wait vpon your Grace, till after Supper,
And afterward determine our proceedings.

Du. Euen now about it, I will pardon you.			*Exeunt.*

Actus Quartus. Scæna Prima.

Enter Valentine, Speed, and certaine Out-lawes.

1.*Out-l.* Fellowes, ſtand faſt : I ſee a paſſenger.

2.*Out.* If there be ten, ſhrinke not, but down with'em.

3.*Out.* Stand ſir, and throw vs that you haue about'ye.
If not : we'll make you ſit, and riſle you.

Sp. Sir we are vndone ; theſe are the Villaines
That all the Trauailers doe feare ſo much.

Val. My friends.

1.*Out.* That's not ſo, ſir : we are your enemies.

2.*Out.* Peace : we'll heare him.

3.*Out.* I by my beard will we : for he is a proper man.

Val. Then know that I haue little wealth to looſe ;
A man I am, croſs'd with aduerſitie :
My riches, are theſe poore habiliments,
Of which, if you ſhould here disfurniſh me,
You take the ſum and ſubſtance that I haue.

2.*Out.* Whether trauell you ?

Val. To *Verona.*

1.*Out.* Whence came you ?

Val. From *Millaine.*

3.*Out.* Haue you long ſoiourn'd there ?		(ſtaid,

Val. Some ſixteene moneths, and longer might haue
If crooked fortune had not thwarted me.

1.*Out.* What, were you baniſh'd thence ?

Val. I was.

2.*Out.* For what offence ?

Val. For that which now torments me to rehearſe ;
I kil'd a man, whoſe death I much repent,
But yet I ſlew him manfully, in fight,
Without falſe vantage, or baſe treachery.

1.*Out.* Why nere repent it, if it were done ſo;
But were you baniſht for ſo ſmall a fault ?

Val. I was, and held me glad of ſuch a doome.

2.*Out.* Haue you the Tongues ?

Val. My youthfull trauaile, therein made me happy,
Or elſe I often had beene often miſerable.

3.*Out.* By the bare ſcalpe of *Robin Hoods* fat Fryer,
This fellow were a King, for our wilde faction.

1.*Out.* We'll haue him : Sirs, a word.

Sp. Maſter, be one of them :
It's an honourable kinde of theeuery.

Val. Peace villaine.

2.*Out.* Tell vs this : haue you any thing to take to ?

Val. Nothing but my fortune.

3.*Out.* Know then, that ſome of vs are Gentlemen,
Such as the fury of vngouern'd youth
Thruſt from the company of awfull men.
My ſelfe was from *Verona* baniſhed,
For practiſing to ſteale away a Lady,
And heire and Neece, aliede vnto the Duke.

2.*Out.* And I from *Mantua*, for a Gentleman,
Who, in my moode, I ſtab'd vnto the heart.

1.*Out.* And I, for ſuch like petty crimes as theſe.
But to the purpoſe : for we cite our faults,
That they may hold excuſ'd our lawleſſe liues ;
And partly ſeeing you are beautifide
With goodly ſhape ; and by your owne report,
A Linguiſt, and a man of ſuch perfection,
As we doe in our quality much want.

2.*Out.* Indeede becauſe you are a baniſh'd man,
Therefore, aboue the reſt, we parley to you :
Are you content to be our Generall ?
To make a vertue of neceſſity,
And liue as we doe in this wilderneſſe ?

3.*Out.* What ſaiſt thou ? wilt thou be of our conſort ?
Say I, and be the captaine of vs all :
We'll doe thee homage, and be rul'd by thee,
Loue thee, as our Commander, and our King.

1.*Out.*

1.*Out.* But if thou ſcorne our curteſie, thou dyeſt.

2.*Out.* Thou ſhalt not liue, to brag what we haue of-

Val. I take your offer, and will liue with you,   (fer'd.

Prouided that you do no outrages

On ſilly women, or poore paſſengers.

3.*Out.* No, we deteſt ſuch vile baſe practiſes.

Come, goe with vs, we'll bring thee to our Crewes,

And ſhow thee all the Treaſure we haue got;

Which, with our ſelues, all reſt at thy diſpoſe.   *Exeunt.*

Scœna Secunda.

Enter Protheus, Thurio, Iulia, Hoſt, Muſitian, Siluia.

Pro. Already haue I bin falſe to *Valentine,*

And now I muſt be as vniuſt to *Thurio,*

Vnder the colour of commending him,

I haue acceſſe my owne loue to prefer.

But *Siluia* is too faire, too true, too holy,

To be corrupted with my worthleſſe guiſts;

When I proteſt true loyalty to her,

She twits me with my falſehood to my friend;

When to her beauty I commend my vowes,

She bids me thinke how I haue bin forſworne

In breaking faith with *Iulia,* whom I lou'd;

And notwithſtanding all her ſodaine quips,

The leaſt whereof would quell a louers hope:

Yet (Spaniel-like) the more ſhe ſpurnes my loue,

The more it growes, and fawneth on her ſtill;

But here comes *Thurio;* now muſt we to her window,

And giue ſome euening Muſique to her eare.

Th. How now, ſir *Protheus,* are you crept before vs?

Pro. I gentle *Thurio,* for you know that loue

Will creepe in ſeruice, where it cannot goe.

Th. I, but I hope, Sir, that you loue not here.

Pro. Sir, but I doe: or elſe I would be hence.

Th. Who, *Siluia?*

Pro. I, *Siluia,* for your ſake.

Th. I thanke you for your owne: Now Gentlemen

Let's tune: and too it luſtily a while.

Ho. Now, my yong gueſt; me thinks your' allycholly;

I pray you why is it?

Iu. Marry (mine *Hoſt*) becauſe I cannot be merry.

Ho. Come, we'll haue you merry: ile bring you where

you ſhall heare Muſique, and ſee the Gentleman that

you ask'd for.

Iu. But ſhall I heare him ſpeake.

Ho. I that you ſhall.

Iu. That will be Muſique.

Ho. Harke, harke.

Iu. Is he among theſe?

Ho. I: but peace, let's heare'm.

Song. Who is Siluia? what is ſhe?

That all our Swaines commend her?

Holy, faire, and wiſe is ſhe,

The heauen ſuch grace did lend her,

that ſhe might admired be.

Is ſhe kinde as ſhe is faire?

For beauty liues with kindneſſe:

Loue doth to her eyes repaire,

To helpe him of his blindneſſe:

And being help'd, inhabits there.

Then to Siluia, let vs ſing,

That Siluia is excelling;

She excels each mortall thing

Vpon the dull earth dwelling.

To her let vs Garlands bring.

Ho. How now? are you ſadder then you were before;

How doe you, man? the Muſicke likes you not.

Iu. You miſtake: the Muſitian likes me not.

Ho. Why, my pretty youth?

Iu. He plaies falſe (father.)

Ho. How, out of tune on the ſtrings.

Iu. Not ſo: but yet

So falſe that he grieues my very heart-ſtrings.

Ho. You haue a quicke eare.   (heart.

Iu. I, I would I were deaſe: it makes me haue a ſlow

Ho. I perceiue you delight not in Muſique.

Iu. Not a whit, when it iars ſo.

Ho. Harke, what fine change is in the Muſique.

Iu. I: that change is the ſpight.

Ho. You would haue them alwaies play but one thing.

Iu. I would alwaies haue one play but one thing.

But Hoſt, doth this Sir *Protheus,* that we talke on,

Often reſort vnto this Gentlewoman?

Ho. I tell you what *Launce* his man told me,

He lou'd her out of all nicke.

Iu. Where is *Launce?*

Ho. Gone to ſeeke his dog, which to morrow, by his

Maſters command, hee muſt carry for a preſent to his

Lady.

Iu. Peace, ſtand aſide, the company parts.

Pro. Sir *Thurio,* feare not you, I will ſo pleade,

That you ſhall ſay, my cunning drift excels.

Th. Where meete we?

Pro. At Saint *Gregories* well.

Th. Farewell.

Pro. Madam: good eu'n to your Ladiſhip.

Sil. I thanke you for your Muſique (Gentlemen)

Who is that that ſpake?

Pro. One (Lady) if you knew his pure hearts truth,

You would quickly learne to know him by his voice.

Sil. Sir *Protheus,* as I take it.

Pro. Sir *Protheus* (gentle Lady) and your Seruant.

Sil. What's your will?

Pro. That I may compaſſe yours.

Sil. You haue your wiſh: my will is euen this;

That preſently you hie you home to bed:

Thou ſubtile, periur'd, falſe, diſloyall man:

Think'ſt thou I am ſo ſhallow, ſo conceitleſſe,

To be ſeduced by thy flattery,

That has't deceiu'd ſo many with thy vowes?

Returne, returne and make thy loue amends:

For me (by this pale queene of night I ſweare)

I am ſo farre from granting thy requeſt,

That I deſpiſe thee, for thy wrongfull ſuite;

And by and by intend to chide my ſelfe,

Euen for this time I ſpend in talking to thee.

Pro. I grant (ſweet loue) that I did loue a Lady,

But ſhe is dead.

Iu. 'Twere falſe, if I ſhould ſpeake it;

For I am ſure ſhe is not buried.

Sil. Say that ſhe be: yet *Valentine* thy friend

Suruiues; to whom (thy ſelfe art witneſſe)

I am betroth'd; and art thou not aſham'd

To wrong him, with thy importunacy?

Pro.

Pro. I likewife heare that *Valentine* is dead.
Sil. And fo fuppofe am I ; for in her graue
Affure thy felfe, my loue is buried.
Pro. Sweet Lady, let me rake it from the earth.
Sil. Goe to thy Ladies graue and call hers thence,
Or at the leaft, in hers, fepulcher thine.
Iul. He heard not that.
Pro. Madam : if your heart be fo obdurate :
Vouchfafe me yet your Picture for my loue,
The Picture that is hanging in your chamber :
To that ile fpeake, to that ile figh and weepe :
For fince the fubftance of your perfect felfe
Is elfe deuoted, I am but a fhadow;
And to your fhadow, will I make true loue.
Iul. If'twere a fubftance you would fure deceiue it,
And make it but a fhadow, as I am.
Sil. I am very loath to be your Idoll Sir ;
But, fince your falfehood fhall become you well
To worfhip fhadowes, and adore falfe fhapes,
Send to me in the morning, and ile fend it :
And fo, good reft.
Pro. As wretches haue ore-night
That wait for execution in the morne.
Iul. Hoft, will you goe ?
Ho. By my hallidome, I was faft afleepe.
Iul. Pray you, where lies Sir *Protheus ?*
Ho. Marry, at my houfe :
Truft me, I thinke 'tis almoft day.
Iul. Not fo : but it hath bin the longeft night
That ere I watch'd, and the moft heauieft.

Scœna Tertia.

Enter Eglamore, Siluia.

Eg. This is the houre that Madam *Siluia*
Entreated me to call, and know her minde :
Ther's fome great matter fhe'ld employ me in.
Madam, Madam.
Sil. Who cals?
Eg. Your feruant, and your friend ;
One that attends your Ladifhips command.
Sil. Sir *Eglamore,* a thoufand times good morrow.
Eg. As many (worthy Lady) to your felfe :
According to your Ladifhips impofe,
I am thus early come, to know what feruice
It is your pleafure to command me in.
Sil. Oh *Eglamoure,* thou art a Gentleman :
Thinke not I flatter (for I fweare I doe not)
Valiant, wife, remorfe-full, well accomplifh'd.
Thou art not ignorant what deere good will
I beare vnto the banifh'd *Valentine :*
Nor how my father would enforce me marry
Vaine *Thurio* (whom my very foule abhor'd.)
Thy felfe haft lou'd, and I haue heard thee fay
No griefe did euer come fo neere thy heart,
As when thy Lady, and thy true-loue dide,
Vpon whofe Graue thou vow'dft pure chaftitie :'
Sir *Eglamore :* I would to *Valentine*
To *Mantua,* where I heare, he makes aboad ;
And for the waies are dangerous to paffe,
I doe defire thy worthy company,

Vpon whofe faith and honor, I repofe.
Vrge not my fathers anger (*Eglamoure*)
But thinke vpon my griefe (a Ladies griefe)
And on the iuftice of my flying hence,
To keepe me from a moft vnholy match,
Which heauen and fortune ftill rewards with plagues.
I doe defire thee, euen from a heart
As full of forrowes, as the Sea of fands,
To beare me company, and goe with me :
If not, to hide what I haue faid to thee,
That I may venture to depart alone.
Egl. Madam, I pitty much your grieuances,
Which, fince I know they vertuoufly are plac'd,
I giue confent to goe along with you,
Wreaking as little what betideth me,
As much, I wifh all good befortune you.
When will you goe ?
Sil. This euening comming.
Eg. Where fhall I meete you ?
Sil. At *Frier Patrickes* Cell,
Where I intend holy Confeffion.
Eg. I will not faile your Ladifhip :
Good morrow (gentle Lady.)
Sil. Good morrow, kinde Sir *Eglamoure.*   *Exeunt.*

Scena Quarta.

Enter Launce, Protheus, Iulia, Siluia.

Lau. When a mans feruant fhall play the Curre with
him (looke you) it goes hard : one that I brought vp of
a puppy : one that I fau'd from drowning, when three or
foure of his blinde brothers and fifters went to it : I haue
taught him (euen as one would fay precifely, thus I
would teach a dog) I was fent to deliuer him, as a prefent to Miftris *Siluia,* from my Mafter ; and I came no
fooner into the dyning-chamber, but he fteps me to her
Trencher, and fteales her Capons-leg : O, 'tis a foule
thing, when a Cur cannot keepe himfelfe in all compa-
nies : I would haue (as one fhould fay) one that takes vpon him to be a dog indeede, to be, as it were, a dog at all
things. If I had not had more wit then he, to take a fault
vpon me that he did, I thinke verily hee had bin hang'd
for't : fure as I liue he had fuffer'd for't ; you fhall iudge :
Hee thrufts me himfelfe into the company of three or
foure gentleman-like-dogs, vnder the Dukes table : hee
had not bin there (bleffe the marke) a piffing while, but
all the chamber fmelt him : out with the dog (faies one)
what cur is that (faies another) whip him out (faies the
third) hang him vp (faies the Duke.) I hauing bin acquainted with the fmell before, knew it was Crab ; and
goes me to the fellow that whips the dogges : friend
(quoth I) you meane to whip the dog : I marry doe I
(quoth he) you doe him the more wrong (quoth I) 'twas
I did the thing you wot of : he makes me no more adoe,
but whips me out of the chamber : how many Mafters
would doe this for his Seruant ? nay, ile be fworne I haue
fat in the ftockes, for puddings he hath ftolne, otherwife
he had bin executed : I haue ftood on the Pillorie for
Geefe he hath kil'd, otherwife he had fufferd for't : thou
think'ft not of this now : nay, I remember the tricke you
feru'd me, when I tooke my leaue of Madam *Siluia* : did
not

not I bid thee ſtill marke me, and doe as I do ; when did'ſt
thou ſee me heaue vp my leg, and make water againſt a
Gentlewomans farthingale ? did'ſt thou euer ſee me doe
ſuch a tricke ?

Pro. *Sebaſtian* is thy name : I like thee well,
And will imploy thee in ſome ſeruice preſently.

Iu. In what you pleaſe, ile doe what I can.

Pro. I hope thou wilt.
How now you whor-ſon pezant,
Where haue you bin theſe two dayes loytering ?

La. Marry Sir, I carried Miſtris *Siluia* the dogge you
bad me.

Pro. And what ſaies ſhe to my little Iewell ?

La. Marry ſhe ſaies your dog was a cur, and tels you
curriſh thanks is good enough for ſuch a preſent.

Pro. But ſhe receiu'd my dog ?

La. No indeede did ſhe not :
Here haue I brought him backe againe.

Pro. What, didſt thou offer her this from me ?

La. I Sir, the other Squirrill was ſtolne from me
By the Hangmans boyes in the market place,
And then I offer'd her mine owne, who is a dog
As big as ten of yours, & therefore the guiſt the greater.

Pro. Goe, get thee hence, and finde my dog againe,
Or nere returne againe into my ſight.
Away, I ſay : ſtayeſt thou to vexe me here ;
A Slaue, that ſtill an end, turnes me to ſhame :
Sebaſtian, I haue entertained thee,
Partly that I haue neede of ſuch a youth,
That can with ſome diſcretion doe my buſineſſe :
For 'tis no truſting to yond fooliſh Lowt ;
But chiefely, for thy face, and thy behauiour,
Which (if my Augury deceiue me not)
Witneſſe good bringing vp, fortune, and truth :
Therefore know thee, for this I entertaine thee.
Go preſently, and take this Ring with thee,
Deliuer it to Madam *Siluia* ;
She lou'd me well, deliuer'd it to me.

Iul. It ſeemes you lou'd not her, not leaue her token :
She is dead belike ?

Pro. Not ſo : I thinke ſhe liues.

Iul. Alas.

Pro. Why do'ſt thou cry alas ?

Iul. I cannot chooſe but pitty her.

Pro. Wherefore ſhould'ſt thou pitty her ?

Iul. Becauſe, me thinkes that ſhe lou'd you as well
As you doe loue your Lady *Siluia* :
She dreames on him, that has forgot her loue,
You doate on her, that cares not for your loue.
'Tis pitty Loue, ſhould be ſo contrary :
And thinking on it, makes me cry alas.

Pro. Well : giue her that Ring, and therewithall
This Letter : that's her chamber : Tell my Lady,
I claime the promiſe for her heauenly Picture :
Your meſſage done, hye home vnto my chamber,
Where thou ſhalt finde me ſad, and ſolitarie.

Iul. How many women would doe ſuch a meſſage ?
Alas poore *Protheus*, thou haſt entertain'd
A Foxe, to be the Shepheard of thy Lambs ;
Alas, poore foole, why doe I pitty him
That with his very heart deſpiſeth me ?
Becauſe he loues her, he deſpiſeth me,
Becauſe I loue him, I muſt pitty him.
This Ring I gaue him, when he parted from me,
To binde him to remember my good will :
And now am I (vnhappy Meſſenger)

To plead for that, which I would not obtaine ;
To carry that, which I would baue refus'd ;
To praiſe his faith, which I would haue diſprais'd.
I am my Maſters true confirmed Loue,
But cannot be true ſeruant to my Maſter,
Vnleſſe I proue falſe traitor to my ſelfe.
Yet will I woe for him, but yet ſo coldly,
As (heauen it knowes) I would not haue him ſpeed.
Gentlewoman, good day : I pray you be my meane
To bring me where to ſpeake with Madam *Siluia*.

Sil. What would you with her, if that I be ſhe ?

Iul. If you be ſhe, I doe intreat your patience
To heare me ſpeake the meſſage I am ſent on.

Sil. From whom ?

Iul. From my Maſter, Sir *Protheus*, Madam.

Sil. Oh : he ſends you for a Picture ?

Iul. I, Madam.

Sil. *Vrſula*, bring my Picture there ,
Goe, giue your Maſter this : tell him from me,
One *Iulia*, that his changing thoughts forget
Would better fit his Chamber, then this Shadow.

Iul. Madam, pleaſe you peruſe this Letter ;
Pardon me (Madam) I haue vnaduis'd
Deliuer'd you a paper that I ſhould not ;
This is the Letter to your Ladiſhip.

Sil. I pray thee let me looke on that againe.

Iul. It may not be : good Madam pardon me.

Sil. There, hold :
I will not looke vpon your Maſters lines :
I know they are ſtuft with proteſtations,
And full of new-found oathes, which he will breake
As eaſily as I doe teare his paper.

Iul. Madam, he ſends your Ladiſhip this Ring.

Sil. The more ſhame for him, that he ſends it me ;
For I haue heard him ſay a thouſand times,
His *Iulia* gaue it him, at his departure :
Though his falſe finger haue prophan'd the Ring,
Mine ſhall not doe his *Iulia* ſo much wrong.

Iul. She thankes you.

Sil. What ſai'ſt thou ?

Iul. I thanke you Madam, that you tender her :
Poore Gentlewoman, my Maſter wrongs her much.

Sil. Do'ſt thou know her ?

Iul. Almoſt as well as I doe know my ſelfe.
To thinke vpon her woes, I doe proteſt
That I haue wept a hundred ſeuerall times.

Sil. Belike ſhe thinks that *Protheus* hath forſook her ?

Iul. I thinke ſhe doth : and that's her cauſe of ſorrow.

Sil. Is ſhe not paſſing faire ?

Iul. She hath bin fairer (Madam) then ſhe is,
When ſhe did thinke my Maſter lou'd her well ;
She, in my iudgement, was as faire as you.
But ſince ſhe did neglect her looking-glaſſe,
And threw her Sun-expelling Maſque away,
The ayre hath ſtaru'd the roſes in her cheekes,
And pinch'd the lilly-tincture of her face,
That now ſhe is become as blacke as I.

Sil. How tall was ſhe ?

Iul. About my ſtature : for at *Pentecoſt*,
When all our Pageants of delight were plaid,
Our youth got me to play the womans part,
And I was trim'd in Madam *Iulias* gowne,
Which ſerued me as fit, by all mens iudgements,
As if the garment had bin made for me :
Therefore I know ſhe is about my height,
And at that time I made her weepe a good,

For I did play a lamentable part.
(Madam) 'twas *Ariadne*, paſſioning
For *Theſus* periury, and vniuſt flight ;
Which I ſo liuely acted with my teares :
That my poore Miſtris moued therewithall,
Wept bitterly : and would I might be dead,
If I in thought felt not her very ſorrow.
   Sil. She is beholding to thee (gentle youth)
Alas (poore Lady) defolate, and left ;
I weepe my ſelfe to thinke vpon thy words :
Here youth : there is my purſe ; I giue thee this   (well.
For thy ſweet Miſtris ſake, becauſe thou lou'ſt her.   Fare-
   Iul. And ſhe ſhall thanke you for't, if ere you know
A vertuous gentlewoman, milde, and beautifull.   (her.
I hope my Maſters ſuit will be but cold,
Since ſhe reſpects my Miſtris loue ſo much.
Alas, how loue can trifle with it ſelfe :
Here is her Picture : let me ſee, I thinke
If I had ſuch a Tyre, this face of mine
Were full as louely, as is this of hers ;
And yet the Painter flatter'd her a little,
Vnleſſe I flatter with my ſelfe too much.
Her haire is *Aburne*, mine is perfect *Yellow*;
If that be all the difference in his loue,
Ile get me ſuch a coulour'd Perrywig :
Her eyes are grey as glaſſe, and ſo are mine :
I, but her fore-head's low, and mine's as high :
What ſhould it be that he reſpects in her,
But I can make reſpectiue in my ſelfe ?
If this fond Loue, were not a blinded god.
Come ſhadow, come, and take this ſhadow vp,
For 'tis thy riuall : O thou ſenceleſſe forme,
Thou ſhalt be worſhip'd, kiſs'd, lou'd, and ador'd ;
And were there ſence in his Idolatry,
My ſubſtance ſhould be ſtatue in thy ſtead.
Ile vſe thee kindly, for thy Miſtris ſake
That vs'd me ſo : or elſe by *Ioue*, I vow,
I ſhould haue ſcratch'd out your vnſeeing eyes,
To make my Maſter out of loue with thee.   *Exeunt.*

Actus Quintus. Scœna Prima.

Enter Eglamoure, Siluia.

   Egl. The Sun begins to guild the weſterne skie,
And now it is about the very houre
That *Siluia*, at Fryer *Patricks* Cell ſhould meet me,
She will not faile ; as Louers breake not houres,
Vnleſſe it be to come before their time,
So much they ſpur their expedition.
See where ſhe comes : Lady a happy euening.
   Sil. Amen, Amen : goe on (good *Eglamoure*)
Out at the Poſterne by the Abbey wall ;
I feare I am attended by ſome Spies.
   Egl. Feare not : the Forreſt is not three leagues off,
If we recouer that, we are ſure enough.   *Exeunt.*

Scœna Secunda.

Enter Thurio, Protheus, Iulia, Duke.
   Th. Sir *Protheus*, what ſaies *Siluia* to my ſuit ?

   Pro. Oh Sir, I finde her milder then ſhe was,
And yet ſhe takes exceptions at your perſon.
   Thu. What ? that my leg is too long ?
   Pro. No, that it is too little.   (der.
   Thu. Ile weare a Boote, to make it ſomewhat roun-
   Pro. But loue will not be ſpurd to what it loathes.
   Thu. What ſaies ſhe to my face ?
   Pro. She ſaies it is a faire one.
   Thu. Nay then the wanton lyes : my face is blacke.
   Pro. But Pearles are faire ; and the old ſaying is,
Blacke men are Pearles, in beauteous Ladies eyes.
   Thu. 'Tis true, ſuch Pearles as put out Ladies eyes,
For I had rather winke, then looke on them.
   Thu. How likes ſhe my diſcourſe ?
   Pro. Ill, when you talke of war.
   Thu. But well, when I diſcourſe of loue and peace.
   Iul. But better indeede, when you hold you peace.
   Thu. What ſayes ſhe to my valour ?
   Pro. Oh Sir, ſhe makes no doubt of that.
   Iul. She needes not, when ſhe knowes it cowardize.
   Thu. What ſaies ſhe to my birth ?
   Pro. That you are well deriu'd.
   Iul. True : from a Gentleman, to a foole.
   Thu. Confiders ſhe my Poſſeſſions ?
   Pro. Oh, I : and pitties them.
   Thu. Wherefore ?
   Iul. That ſuch an Aſſe ſhould owe them.
   Pro. That they are out by Leaſe.
   Iul. Here comes the Duke.
   Du. How now ſir *Protheus* ; how now *Thurio* ?
Which of you ſaw *Eglamoure* of late ?
   Thu. Not I.
   Pro. Nor I.
   Du. Saw you my daughter ?
   Pro. Neither.
   Du. Why then
She's fled vnto that pezant, *Valentine* ;
And *Eglamoure* is in her Company :
'Tis true ; for Frier *Laurence* met them both
As he, in peannce wander'd through the Forreſt :
Him he knew well : and gueſd that it was ſhe,
But being mask'd, he was not ſure of it.
Beſides ſhe did intend Confeſſion
At *Patricks* Cell this euen, and there ſhe was not.
Theſe likelihoods confirme her flight from hence ;
Therefore I pray you ſtand, not to diſcourſe,
But mount you preſently, and meete with me
Vpon the riſing of the Mountaine foote
That leads toward *Mantua*, whether they are fled :
Diſpatch (ſweet Gentlemen) and follow me.
   Thu. Why this it is, to be a peeuiſh Girle,
That flies her fortune when it followes her :
Ile after ; more to be reueng'd on *Eglamoure*,
Then for the loue of reck-leſſe *Siluia*.
   Pro. And I will follow, more for *Siluas* loue
Then hate of *Eglamoure* that goes with her.
   Iul. And I will follow, more to croſſe that loue
Then hate for *Siluia*, that is gone for loue.   *Exeunt.*

Scena Tertia.

Siluia, Out-lawes.
   1.*Out.* Come, come be patient :

We muſt bring you to our Captaine.

Sil. A thouſand more miſchances then this one
Haue learn'd me how to brooke this patiently.

2 Out. Come, bring her away.

1 Out. Where is the Gentleman that was with her?

3 Out. Being nimble footed, he hath out-run vs.

But *Moyſes* and *Valerius* follow him:
Goe thou with her to the Weſt end of the wood,
There is our Captaine: Wee'll follow him that's fled,
The Thicket is beſet, he cannot ſcape.

1 Out. Come, I muſt bring you to our Captains caue.
Feare not: he beares an honourable minde,
And will not vſe a woman lawleſly.

Sil. O *Valentine*: this I endure for thee.

Exeunt.

Scæna Quarta.

*Enter Valentine, Protheus, Siluia, Iulia, Duke, Thurio,
Out-lawes.*

Val. How vſe doth breed a habit in a man?
This ſhadowy deſart, vnfrequented woods
I better brooke then flouriſhing peopled Townes:
Here can I ſit alone, vn-ſeene of any,
And to the Nightingales complaining Notes
Tune my diſtreſtes, and record my woes.
O thou that doſt inhabit in my breſt,
Leaue not the Manſion ſo long Tenant-leſſe,
Leſt growing ruinous, the building fall,
And leaue no memory of what it was,
Repaire me, with thy preſence, *Siluia*:
Thou gentle Nimph, cheriſh thy for-lorne ſwaine.
What hallowing, and what ſtir is this to day?
Theſe are my mates, that make their wills their Law,
Haue ſome vnhappy paſſenger in chace;
They loue me well: yet I haue much to doe
To keepe them from vnciuill outrages.
Withdraw thee *Valentine*: who's this comes heere?

Pro. Madam, this ſeruice I haue done for you
(Though you reſpect not aught your ſeruant doth)
To hazard life, and reskew you from him,
That would haue forc'd your honour, and your loue,
Vouchſafe me for my meed, but one faire looke:
(A ſmaller boone then this I cannot beg,
And leſſe then this, I am ſure you cannot giue.)

Val. How like a dreame is this? I ſee, and heare:
Loue, lend me patience to forbeare a while.

Sil. O miſerable, vnhappy that I am.

Pro. Vnhappy were you (Madam) ere I came:
But by my comming, I haue made you happy.

Sil. By thy approach thou mak'ſt me moſt vnhappy.

Iul. And me, when he approcheth to your preſence.

Sil. Had I beene ceazed by a hungry Lion,
I would haue beene a break-faſt to the Beaſt,
Rather then haue falſe *Protheus* reskue me:
Oh heauen be iudge how I loue *Valentine*,
Whoſe life's as tender to me as my ſoule,
And full as much (for more there cannot be)
I doe deteſt falſe periur'd *Protheus*:
Therefore be gone, ſollicit me no more.

Pro. What dangerous action, ſtood it next to death
Would I not vndergoe, for one calme looke:
Oh 'tis the curſe in Loue, and ſtill approu'd

When women cannot loue, where they're belou'd.

Sil. When *Protheus* cannot loue, where he's belou'd:
Read ouer *Iulia's* heart, (thy firſt beſt Loue)
For whoſe deare ſake, thou didſt then rend thy faith
Into a thouſand oathes; and all thoſe oathes,
Deſcended into periury, to loue me,
Thou haſt no faith left now, vnleſſe thou'dſt two,
And that's farre worſe then none: better haue none
Then plurall faith, which is too much by one:
Thou Counterfeyt, to thy true friend.

Pro. In Loue,
Who reſpects friend?

Sil. All men but *Protheus.*

Pro. Nay, if the gentle ſpirit of mouing words
Can no way change you to a milder forme;
Ile wooe you like a Souldier, at armes end,
And loue you 'gainſt the nature of Loue: force ye.

Sil. Oh heauen.

Pro. Ile force thee yeeld to my deſire.

Val. Ruffian: let goe that rude vnciuill touch,
Thou friend of an ill faſhion.

Pro. *Valentine.*

Val. Thou common friend, that's without faith or loue,
For ſuch is a friend now: treacherous man,
Thou haſt beguil'd my hopes; nought but mine eye
Could haue perſwaded me: now I dare not ſay
I haue one friend aliue; thou wouldſt diſproue me:
Who ſhould be truſted, when ones right hand
Is periured to the boſome? *Protheus*
I am ſorry I muſt neuer truſt thee more,
But count the world a ſtranger for thy ſake:
The priuate wound is deepeſt: oh time, moſt accurſt:
'Mongſt all foes that a friend ſhould be the worſt?

Pro. My ſhame and guilt confounds me:
Forgiue me *Valentine*: if hearty ſorrow
Be a ſufficient Ranſome for offence,
I tender't heere: I doe as truely ſuffer,
As ere I did commit.

Val. Then I am paid:
And once againe, I doe receiue thee honeſt;
Who by Repentance is not ſatisfied,
Is nor of heauen, nor earth; for theſe are pleas'd:
By Penitence th'Eternalls wrath's appeas'd:
And that my loue may appeare plaine and free,
All that was mine, in *Siluia*, I giue thee.

Iul. Oh me vnhappy.

Pro. Looke to the Boy.

Val. Why, Boy?

Iul. O good ſir, my maſter charg'd me to deliuer a ring
to Madam *Siluia*: w (out of my neglect) was neuer done.

Pro. Where is that ring? boy?

Iul. Heere 'tis: this is it.

Pro. How? let me ſee.
Why this is the ring I gaue to *Iulia.*

Iul. Oh, cry you mercy ſir, I haue miſtooke:
This is the ring you ſent to *Siluia.*

Pro. But how cam'ſt thou by this ring? at my depart
I gaue this vnto *Iulia.*

Iul. And *Iulia* her ſelfe did giue it me,
And *Iulia* her ſelfe hath brought it hither.

Pro. How? *Iulia?*

Iul. Behold her, that gaue ayme to all thy oathes,
And entertain'd 'em deeply in her heart.
How oft haſt thou with periury cleft the roote?
Oh *Protheus*, let this habit make thee bluſh.

D   Be

Be thou asham'd that I haue tooke vpon me,
Such an immodest rayment; if shame liue
In a disguise of loue?
It is the lesser blot modesty findes,
Women to change their shapes, then men their minds.

Pro. Then men their minds? tis true: oh heuen, were man
But Constant, he were perfect; that one error
Fils him with faults: makes him run through all th'sins;
Inconstancy falls-off, ere it begins:
What is in *Siluia's* face, but I may spie
More fresh in *Iulia's,* with a constant eye?

Val. Come, come : a hand from either :
Let me be blest to make this happy close :
'Twere pitty two such friends should be long foes.

Pro. Beare witnes (heauen) I haue my wish for euer.

Iul. And I mine.

Out-l. A prize : a prize : a prize.

Val. Forbeare, forbeare I say : It is my Lord the *Duke.*
Your Grace is welcome to a man disgrac'd,
Banished *Valentine.*

Duke. Sir *Valentine?*

Thu. Yonder is *Siluia* : and *Siluia's* mine.

Val. *Thurio* giue backe; or else embrace thy death :
Come not within the measure of my wrath :
Doe not name *Siluia* thine : if once againe,
Verona shall not hold thee : heere she stands,
Take but possession of her, with a Touch :
I dare thee, but to breath vpon my Loue.

Thur. Sir *Valentine,* I care not for her, I :
I hold him but a foole that will endanger
His Body, for a Girle that loues him not :
I claime her not, and therefore she is thine.

Duke. The more degenerate and base art thou
To make such meanes for her, as thou hast done,
And leaue her on such slight conditions.

Now, by the honor of my Ancestry,
I doe applaud thy spirit, *Valentine,*
And thinke thee worthy of an Empresse loue :
Know then, I heere forget all former greefes,
Cancell all grudge, repeale thee home againe,
Plead a new state in thy vn-riual'd merit,
To which I thus subscribe : Sir *Valentine,*
Thou art a Gentleman, and well deriu'd,
Take thou thy *Siluia,* for thou hast deseru'd her.

Val. I thank your Grace, ẙ gift hath made me happy :
I now beseech you (for your daughters sake)
To grant one Boone that I shall aske of you.

Duke. I grant it (for thine owne) what ere it be.

Val. These banish'd men, that I haue kept withall,
Are men endu'd with worthy qualities :
Forgiue them what they haue committed here,
And let them be recall'd from their Exile :
They are reformed, ciuill, full of good,
And fit for great employment (worthy Lord.)

Duke. Thou hast preuaild, I pardon them and thee :
Dispose of them, as thou knowst their deserts.
Come, let vs goe, we will include all Iarres,
With Triumphes, Mirth, and rare solemnity.

Val. And as we walke along, I dare be bold
With our discourse, to make your Grace to smile.
What thinke you of this Page (my Lord ?)

Duke. I think the Boy hath grace in him, he blushes.

Val. I warrant you (my Lord) more grace, then Boy.

Duke. What meane you by that saying?

Val. Please you, Ile tell you, as we passe along,
That you will wonder what hath fortuned :
Come *Protheus,* 'tis your pennance, but to heare
The story of your Loues discouered.
That done, our day of marriage shall be yours,
One Feast, one house, one mutuall happinesse.   *Exeunt.*

The names of all the Actors.

Duke : *Father to Siluia.*
Valentine. } *the two Gentlemen.*
Protheus. }
Anthonio : *father to Protheus.*
Thurio : *a foolish riuall to Valentine.*

Eglamoure : *Agent for Siluia in her escape.*
Host : *where Iulia lodges.*
Out-lawes *with Valentine.*
Speed : *a clownish seruant to Valentine.*
Launce : *the like to Protheus.*
Panthion : *seruant to Antonio.*
Iulia : *beloued of Protheus.*
Siluia : *beloued of Valentine.*
Lucetta : *waighting-woman to Iulia.*

FINIS.

THE

THE
Merry Wiues of Windsor.

Actus primus, Scena prima.

Enter Iustice Shallow, Slender, *Sir* Hugh Euans, *Master* Page, Falstoffe, Bardolph, Nym, Pistoll, Anne Page, *Mistresse* Ford, *Mistresse* Page, Simple.

Shallow.

Ir *Hugh*, persswade me not: I will make a Star-Chamber matter of it, if hee were twenty Sir *Iohn Falstoffs*, he shall not abuse *Robert Shallow* Esquire.   (*Coram*.

Slen. In the County of *Glousler*, Iustice of Peace and *Shal.* I (Cosen *Slender*) and *Cust-alorum*.

Slen. I, and *Rato lorum* too; and a Gentleman borne (Master Parson) who writes himselfe *Armigero*, in any Bill, Warrant, Quittance, or Obligation, *Armigero*.

Shal. I that I doe, and haue done any time these three hundred yeeres.

Slen. All his successors (gone before him) hath don't: and all his Ancestors (that come after him) may: they may giue the dozen white Luces in their Coate.

Shal. It is an olde Coate.

Euans. The dozen white Lowses doe become an old Coat well: it agrees well passant: It is a familiar beast to man, and signifies Loue.

Shal. The Luse is the fresh-fish, the salt-fish, is an old Coate.

Slen. I may quarter (Coz).

Shal. You may, by marrying.

Euans. It is marring indeed, if he quarter it.

Shal. Not a whit.

Euan. Yes per-lady: if he ha's a quarter of your coat, there is but three Skirts for your selfe, in my simple coniectures; but that is all one: if Sir *Iohn Falstaffe* haue committed disparagements vnto you, I am of the Church and will be glad to do my beneuolence, to make attonements and compremises betweene you.

Shal. The Councell shall heare it, it is a Riot.

Euan. It is not meet the Councell heare a Riot: there is no feare of Got in a Riot: The Councell (looke you) shall desire to heare the feare of Got, and not to heare a Riot: take your viza-ments in that.

Shal. Ha; o' my life, if I were yong againe, the sword should end it.

Euans. It is petter that friends is the sword, and end it: and there is also another deuice in my praine, which peraduenture prings goot discretions with it. There is *Anne Page*, which is daughter to Master *Thomas Page*, which is pretty virginity.

Slen. *Mistris Anne Page?* she has browne haire, and speakes small like a woman.

Euans. It is that ferry person for all the orld, as iust as you will desire, and seuen hundred pounds of Moneyes, and Gold, and Siluer, is her Grand-sire vpon his deaths-bed, (Got deliuer to a ioyfull resurrections) giue, when she is able to ouertake seuenteene yeeres old. It were a goot motion, if we leaue our pribbles and prabbles, and desire a marriage betweene Master *Abraham*, and Mistris *Anne Page*.

Slen. Did her Grand-sire leaue her seauen hundred pound?

Euan. I, and her father is make her a petter penny.

Slen. I know the young Gentlewoman, she has good gifts.

Euan. Seuen hundred pounds, and possibilities, is goot gifts.

Shal. Wel, let vs see honest Mr. *Page*: is *Falstaffe* there?

Euan. Shall I tell you a lye? I doe despise a lyer, as I doe despise one that is false, or as I despise one that is not true: the Knight Sir *Iohn* is there, and I beseech you be ruled by your well-willers: I will peat the doore for Mr. *Page*.   What hoa? Got-plesse your house heere.

Mr. Page. Who's there?

Euan. Here is go't's plessing and your friend, and Iustice *Shallow*, and heere yong Master *Slender*: that peraduentures shall tell you another tale, if matters grow to your likings.

Mr. Page. I am glad to see your Worships well: I thanke you for my Venison Master *Shallow*.

Shal. Master *Page*, I am glad to see you: much good doe it your good heart: I wish'd your Venison better, it was ill killd: how doth good Mistresse *Page?* and I thank you alwaies with my heart, la: with my heart.

M. Page. Sir, I thanke you.

Shal. Sir, I thanke you: by yea, and no I doe.

M. Pa. I am glad to see you, good Master *Slender*.

Slen. How do's your fallow Greyhound, Sir, I heard say he was out-run on *Cotsall*.

M. Pa. It could not be iudg'd, Sir.

Slen. You'll not confesse: you'll not confesse.

Shal. That he will not, 'tis your fault, 'tis your fault: 'tis a good dogge.

M. Pa. A Cur, Sir.

Shal. Sir: hee's a good dog, and a faire dog, can there be more said? he is good, and faire. Is Sir *Iohn Falstaffe* heere?

M. Pa. Sir, hee is within: and I would I could doe a good office betweene you.

Euan. It is spoke as a Christians ought to speake.

Shal. He hath wrong'd me (Master *Page*.)

M. Pa. Sir, he doth in some sort confesse it.

D 2   *Sha.)*

Shal. If it be confeſſed, it is not redreſſed; is not that
ſo (M.*Page?*) he hath wrong'd me, indeed he hath, at a
word he hath : beleeue me, *Robert Shallow* Eſquire, ſaith
he is wronged.

Ma.Pa. Here comes Sir *Iohn*.

Fal. Now, Maſter *Shallow*, you'll complaine of me to
the King?

Shal. Knight, you haue beaten my men, kill'd my
deere, and broke open my Lodge.

Fal. But not kiſs'd your Keepers daughter?

Shal. Tut, a pin : this ſhall be anſwer'd.

Fal. I will anſwere it ſtrait, I haue done all this:
That is now anſwer'd.

Shal. The Councell ſhall know this.

Fal. 'Twere better for you if it were known in councell : you'll be laugh'd at.

Eu. *Pauca verba* ; (Sir *Iohn*) good worts.

Fal. Good worts? good Cabidge ; *Slender*, I broke
your head : what matter haue you againſt me?

Slen. Marry ſir, I haue matter in my head againſt you,
and againſt your cony-catching Raſcalls, *Bardolf*, *Nym*,
and *Piſtoll*.

Bar. You Banbery Cheeſe.

Slen. I, it is no matter.

Piſt. How now, *Mephoſtophilus*?

Slen. I, it is no matter.

Nym. Slice, I ſay ; *pauca, pauca* : Slice, that's my humor.

Slen. Where's *Simple* my man? can you tell, Coſen?

Eua. Peace, I pray you : now let vs vnderſtand : there
is three Vmpires in this matter, as I vnderſtand ; that is,
Maſter *Page* (fidelicet Maſter *Page*,) & there is my ſelfe,
(fidelicet my ſelfe) and the three party is (laſtly, and fi-
nally) mine Hoſt of the Gater.

Ma.Pa. We three to heare it, & end it between them.

Euan. Ferry goo't, I will make a prieſe of it in my
note-booke, and we wil afterwards orke vpon the cauſe,
with as great diſcreetly as we can.

Fal. *Piſtoll*.

Piſt. He heares with eares.

Euan. The Teuill and his Tam : what phraſe is this?
he heares with eare? why, it is affeĉtations.

Fal. *Piſtoll*, did you picke M. *Slenders* purſe?

Slen. I, by theſe gloues did hee, or I would I might
neuer come in mine owne great chamber againe elſe, of
ſeauen groates in mill-ſixpences, and two *Edward* Sho-
uelboords, that coſt me two ſhilling and two pence a
peece of *Yead Miller* : by theſe gloues.

Fal. Is this true, *Piſtoll?*

Euan. No, it is falſe, if it is a picke-purſe.

Piſt. Ha, thou mountaine Forreyner : Sir *Iohn*, and
Maſter mine, I combat challenge of this Latine Bilboe :
word of deniall in thy *labras* here ; word of denial ; froth,
and ſcum thou lieſt.

Slen. By theſe gloues, then 'twas he.

Nym. Be auis'd ſir, and paſſe good humours : I will
ſay marry trap with you, if you runne the nut-hooks humor on me, that is the very note of it.

Slen. By this hat, then he in the red face had it : for
though I cannot remember what I did when you made
me drunke, yet I am not altogether an aſſe.

Fal. What ſay you *Scarlet*, and *Iohn?*

Bar. Why ſir, (for my part) I ſay the Gentleman had
drunke himſelfe out of his fiue ſentences.

Eu. It is his fiue ſences : fie, what the ignorance is.

Bar. And being fap, ſir, was (as they ſay) caſheerd :
ſo concluſions paſt the Car-eires.

Slen. I, you ſpake in Latten then to: but 'tis no matter ; Ile nere be drunk whilſt I liue againe, but in honeſt,
ciuill, godly company for this tricke : if I be drunke, Ile
be drunke with thoſe that haue the feare of God, and not
with drunken knaues.

Euan. So got-udge me, that is a vertuons minde.

Fal. You heare all theſe matters deni'd, Gentlemen ;
you heare it.

Mr.Page. Nay daughter, carry the wine in, wee'll
drinke within.

Slen. Oh heauen : This is Miſtreſſe *Anne Page*.

Mr.Page. How now Miſtris *Ford?*

Fal. Miſtris *Ford*, by my troth you are very wel met:
by your leaue good Miſtris.

Mr.Page. Wife, bid theſe gentlemen welcome : come,
we haue a hot Veniſon paſty to dinner ; Come gentlemen, I hope we ſhall drinke downe all vnkindneſſe.

Slen. I had rather then forty ſhillings I had my booke
of Songs and Sonnets heere : How now *Simple*, where
haue you beene ? I muſt wait on my ſelfe, muſt I ? you
haue not the booke of Riddles about you, haue you ?

Sim. Booke of Riddles ? why did you not lend it to
Alice Short-cake vpon Alhallowmas laſt, a fortnight a-
fore Michaelmas.

Shal. Come Coz, come Coz, we ſtay for you : a word
with you Coz : marry this, Coz : there is as 'twere a tender, a kinde of tender, made a farre-off by Sir *Hugh* here :
doe you vnderſtand me?

Slen. I Sir, you ſhall finde me reaſonable ; if it be ſo,
I ſhall doe that that is reaſon.

Shal. Nay, but vnderſtand me.

Slen. So I doe Sir.

Euan. Glue eare to his motions ; (Mr.*Slender*) I will
deſcription the matter to you, if you be capacity of it.

Slen. Nay, I will doe as my Cozen *Shallow* ſaies : I
pray you pardon me, he's a Iuſtice of Peace in his Countrie, ſimple though I ſtand here.

Euan. But that is not the queſtion : the queſtion is
concerning your marriage.

Shal. I, there's the point Sir.

Eu. Marry is it : the very point of it, to Mi. *An Page*.

Slen. Why if it be ſo ; I will marry her vpon any reaſonable demands.

Eu. But can you affeĉtion the 'o-man, let vs command
to know that of your mouth, or of your lips : for diuers
Philoſophers hold, that the lips is parcell of the mouth :
therfore preciſely, c̃a you carry your good wil to y̆ maid ?

Sh. Coſen *Abraham Slender*, can you loue her?

Slen. I hope ſir, I will do as it ſhall become one that
would doe reaſon.

Eu. Nay, got's Lords, and his Ladies, you muſt ſpeake
poſſitable, if you can carry-her your deſires towards her.

Shal. That you muſt :
Will you, (vpon good dowry) marry her ?

Slen. I will doe a greater thing then that, vpon your
requeſt (Coſen) in any reaſon.

Shal. Nay conceiue me, conceiue mee, (ſweet Coz) :
what I doe is to pleaſure you (Coz:) can you loue the
maid ?

Slen. I will marry her (Sir) at your requeſt ; but if
there be no great loue in the beginning, yet Heauen
may decreaſe it vpon better acquaintance , when wee
are married, and haue more occaſion to know one another : I hope vpon familliarity will grow more content :
but if you ſay mary-her, I will mary-her, that I am freely
diſſolued, and diſſolutely.

Eu. It

Eu. It is a fery difcretion-anfwere ; faue the fall is in the'ord, diffolutely : the ort is (according to our meaning) refolutely : his meaning is good.

Sb. I : I thinke my Cofen meant well.

Sl. I, or elfe I would I might be hang'd (la.)

Sb. Here comes faire Miftris *Anne* ; would I were yong for your fake, Miftris *Anne.*

An. The dinner is on the Table, my Father defires your worfhips company.

Sb. I will wait on him, (faire Miftris *Anne.*)

Eu. Od's pleffed-wil : I wil not be ablêce at the grace.

An. Wil't pleafe your worfhip to come in, Sir ?

Sl. No, I thank you forfooth, hartely ; I am very well.

An. The dinner attends you, Sir.

Sl. I am not a-hungry, I thanke you, forfooth : goe, Sirha, for all you are my man, goe wait vpon my Cofen *Shallow* : a Iuftice of peace fometime may be beholding to his friend, for a Man ; I keepe but three Men, and a Boy yet, till my Mother be dead : but what though, yet I liue like a poore Gentleman borne.

An. I may not goe in without your worfhip : they will not fit till you come.

Sl. I'faith, ile eate nothing : I thanke you as much as though I did.

An. I pray you Sir walke in.

Sl. I had rather walke here (I thanke you) I bruiz'd my fhin th'other day, with playing at Sword and Dagger with a Mafter of Fence (three veneys for a difh of ftew'd Prunes) and by my troth, I cannot abide the fmell of hot meate fince. Why doe your dogs barke fo ? be there Beares ich' Towne ?

An. I thinke there are, Sir, I heard them talk'd of.

Sl. I loue the fport well, but I fhall as foone quarrell at it, as any man in *England* : you are afraid if you fee the Beare loofe, are you not ?

An. I indeede Sir.

Sl. That's meate and drinke to me now : I haue feene *Sackerfon* loofe, twenty times, and haue taken him by the Chaine : but (I warrant you) the women haue fo cride and fhrekt at it, that it paft : But women indeede, cannot abide'em , they are very ill-fauour'd rough things.

Ma.Pa. Come, gentle M. *Slender,* come ; we ftay for you.

Sl. Ile eate nothing, I thanke you Sir.

Ma.Pa. By cocke and pie, you fhall not choofe, Sir : come, come.

Sl. Nay, pray you lead the way.

Ma.Pa. Come on, Sir.

Sl. Miftris *Anne* : your felfe fhall goe firft.

An. Not I Sir, pray you keepe on.

Sl. Truely I will not goe firft : truely-la : I will not doe you that wrong.

An. I pray you Sir.

Sl. Ile rather be vnmannerly, then troublefome : you doe your felfe wrong indeede-la. *Exeunt.*

Scena Secunda.

Enter Euans, and Simple.

Eu. Go your waies, and aske of Doctor *Caius* houfe, which is the way ; and there dwels one Miftris *Quickly* ; which is in the manner of his Nurfe ; or his dry-Nurfe ; or his Cooke ; or his Laundry ; his Wafher, and his Ringer.

Si. Well Sir.

Eu. Nay, it is petter yet : giue her this letter ; for it is a'oman that altogeathers acquaintâce with Miftris *Anne Page* ; and the Letter is to defire, and require her to folicite your Mafters defires, to Miftris *Anne Page* : I pray you be gon : I will make an end of my dinner ; ther's Pippins and Cheefe to come. *Exeunt.*

Scena Tertia.

Enter Falftaffe, Hoft, Bardolfe, Nym, Piftoll, Page.

Fal. Mine *Hoft* of the *Garter* ?

Ho. What faies my Bully Rooke ? fpeake fchollerly, and wifely.

Fal. Truely mine *Hoft* ; I muft turne away fome of my followers.

Ho. Difcard, (bully *Hercules*) cafheere ; let them wag ; trot, trot.

Fal. I fit at ten pounds a weeke.

Ho. Thou'rt an Emperor (*Cefar*, *Keifer* and *Pheazar*) I will entertaine *Bardolfe* : he fhall draw ; he fhall tap ; faid I well (bully *Hector* ?)

Fa. Doe fo (good mine *Hoft.*)

Ho. I haue fpoke : let him follow : let me fee thee froth, and liue : I am at a word : follow.

Fal. Bardolfe, follow him : a *Tapfter* is a good trade : an old Cloake, makes a new Ierkin : a wither'd Seruingman, a frefh Tapfter : goe, adew.

Ba. It is a life that I haue defir'd : I will thriue.

Pift. O bafe hungarian wight : wilt ÿ the fpigot wield.

Ni. He was gotten in drink : is not the humor cõceited ?

Fal. I am glad I am fo acquit of this Tinderbox : his Thefts were too open : his filching was like an vnskilfull Singer, he kept not time.

Ni. The good humor is to fteale at a minutes reft.

Pift. Conuay the wife it call : Steale ? foh : a fico for the phrafe.

Fal. Well firs, I am almoft out at heeles.

Pift. Why then let Kibes enfue.

Fal. There is no remedy : I muft conicatch, I muft fhift.

Pift. Yong Rauens muft haue foode.

Fal. Which of you know *Ford* of this Towne ?

Pift. I ken the wight : he is of fubftance good.

Fal. My honeft Lads, I will tell you what I am about.

Pift. Two yards, and more.

Fal. No quips now *Piftoll* : (Indeede I am in the wafte two yards about : but I am now about no wafte : I am about thrift) briefely : I doe meane to make loue to *Fords* wife : I fpie entertainment in her : fhee difcourfes : fhee carues : fhe giues the leere of inuitation : I can conftrue the action of her familier ftile, & the hardeft voice of her behauior (to be englifh'd rightly) is, *I am Sir Iohn Falftafs.*

Pift. He hath ftudied her will ; and tranflated her will : out of honefty, into Englifh.

Ni. The Anchor is deepe : will that humor paffe ?

Fal. Now, the report goes, fhe has all the rule of her husbands Purfe : he hath a legend of Angels.

Pift. As many diuels entertaine : and to her Boy fay I.

Ni. The humor rifes : it is good : humor me the angels.

Fal. I haue writ me here a letter to her : & here another to *Pages* wife, who euen now gaue mee good eyes too ; examind my parts with moft iudicious illiads : fometimes the beame of her view, guilded my foote : fometimes my portly belly.

Pift.

Piſt. Then did the Sun on dung-hill ſhine.

Ni. I thanke thee for that humour.

Fal. O ſhe did ſo courſe o're my exteriors with ſuch a greedy intention, that the appetite of her eye, did ſeeme to ſcorch me vp like a burning-glaſſe: here's another letter to her : She beares the Purſe too : She is a Region in *Guiana* : all gold, and bountie : I will be Cheaters to them both, and they ſhall be Exchequers to mee : they ſhall be my Eaſt and Weſt Indies, and I will trade to them both : Goe, beare thou this Letter to Miſtris *Page*; and thou this to Miſtris *Ford* : we will thriue (Lads) we will thriue.

Piſt. Shall I Sir *Pandarus* of *Troy* become, And by my ſide weare Steele? then Lucifer take all.

Ni. I will run no baſe humor : here take the humor-Letter ; I will keepe the hauior of reputation.

Fal. Hold Sirha, beare you theſe *Letters* tightly, Saile like my Pinnaſſe to theſe golden ſhores. Rogues, hence, auaunt, vaniſh like haile-ſtones ; goe, Trudge ; plod away ith' hoofe : ſeeke ſhelter, packe : *Falſtaffe* will learne the honor of the age, French-thrift, you Rogues, my ſelfe, and skirted *Page*.

Piſt. Let Vultures gripe thy guts : for gourd, and Fullam holds : & high and low beguiles the rich & poore, Teſter ile haue in pouch when thou ſhalt lacke, Baſe *Phrygian* Turke.

Ni. I haue opperations, Which be humors of reuenge.

Piſt. Wilt thou reuenge?

Ni. By Welkin, and her Star.

Piſt. With wit, or Steele?

Ni. WIth both the humors, I : I will diſcuſſe the humour of this Loue to *Ford*.

Piſt. And I to *Page* ſhall eke vnfold How *Falſtaffe* (varlet vile) His Doue will proue ; his gold will hold, And his ſoft couch defile.

Ni. My humour ſhall not coole : I will incenſe *Ford* to deale with poyſon : I will poſſeſſe him with yallow-neſſe, for the reuolt of mine is dangerous : that is my true humour.

Piſt. Thou art the *Mars* of *Malecontents* : I ſecond thee : troope on.   *Exeunt.*

Scœna Quarta.

Enter Miſtris Quickly, Simple, Iohn Rugby, Doctor, Caius, Fenton.

Qu. What, *Iohn Rugby*, I pray thee goe to the Caſement, and ſee if you can ſee my Maſter, Maſter Docter *Caius* comming : if he doe (I'faith) and finde any body in the houſe; here wille be an old abuſing of Gods patience, and the Kings Engliſh.

Ru. Ile goe watch.

Qu. Goe, and we'll haue a poſſet for't ſoone at night, (in faith) at the latter end of a Sea-cole-fire : An honeſt, willing, kinde fellow, as euer ſeruant ſhall come in houſe withall : and I warrant you, no tel-tale, nor no breede-bate : his worſt fault is, that he is giuen to prayer ; hee is ſomething peeuiſh that way : but no body but has his fault : but let that paſſe. *Peter Simple*, you ſay your name is ?

Si. I : for fault of a better.

Qu. And Maſter *Slender's* your Maſter ?

Si. I forſooth.

Qu. Do's he not weare a great round Beard, like a Glouers pairing-knife?

Si. No forſooth : he hath but a little wee-face; with a little yellow Beard : a Caine colourd Beard.

Qu. A ſoftly-ſprighted man, is he not?

Si. I forſooth : but he is as tall a man of his hands, as any is betweene this and his head : he hath fought with a Warrener.

Qu. How ſay you : oh, I ſhould remember him : do's he not hold vp his head (as it were?) and ſtrut in his gate?

Si. Yes indeede do's he.

Qu. Well, heauen ſend *Anne Page*, no worſe fortune : Tell Maſter Parſon *Euans*, I will doe what I can for your Maſter : *Anne* is a good girle, and I wiſh—

Ru. Out alas : here comes my Maſter.

Qu. We ſhall all be ſhent : Run in here, good young man : goe into this Cloſſet : he will not ſtay long : what *Iohn Rugby? Iohn* : what *Iohn* I ſay ? goe *Iohn*, goe enquire for my Maſter, I doubt he be not well, that hee comes not home : (*and downe, downe, adowne'a. &c.*)

Ca. Vat is you ſing? I doe not like des-toyes : pray you goe and vetch me in my Cloſſet, vnboyteene verd ; a Box, a greene-a-Box : do intend vat I ſpeake? a greene-a-Box.

Qu. I forſooth ile fetch it you : I am glad hee went not in himſelfe : if he had found the yong man he would haue bin horne-mad.

Ca. Fe, fe, fe, fe, mai foy, il fait for ehando, Ie man voi a le Court la grand affaires.

Qu. Is it this Sir?

Ca. Ouy mette le au mon pocket, de-peech quickly : Vere is dat knaue *Rugby*?

Qu. What *Iohn Rugby, Iohn* ?

Ru. Here Sir.

Ca. You are *Iohn Rugby*, aad you are *Iacke Rugby* : Come, take-a-your Rapier, and come after my heele to the Court.

Ru. 'Tis ready Sir, here in the Porch.

Ca. By my trot : I tarry too long : od's-me : *que ay ie oublie* : dere is ſome Simples in my Cloſſet, dat I vill not for the varld I ſhall leaue behinde.

Qu. Ay-me, he'll finde the yong man there, & be mad.

Ca. O *Diable, Diable* : vat is in my Cloſſet? Villanie, La-roone : *Rugby*, my Rapier.

Qu. Good Maſter be content.

Ca. Wherefore ſhall I be content-a?

Qu. The yong man is an honeſt man.

Ca. What ſhall de honeſt man do in my Cloſſet : dere is no honeſt man dat ſhall come in my Cloſſet.

Qu. I beſeech you be not ſo flegmaticke : heare the truth of it. He came of an errand to mee, from Parſon *Hugh*.

Ca. Vell.

Si. I forſooth : to deſire her to—

Qu. Peace, I pray you.

Ca. Peace-a-your tongue : ſpeake-a-your Tale.

Si. To deſire this honeſt Gentlewoman (your Maid) to ſpeake a good word to Miſtris *Anne Page*, for my Maſter in the way of Marriage.

Qu. This is all indeede-la : but ile nere put my finger in the fire, and neede not.

Ca. Sir *Hugh* ſend-a you ? *Rugby*, ballow mee ſome paper : tarry you a littell-a-while.   *Qu.* I

Qui. I am glad he is ſo quiet : if he had bin through-ly moued, you ſhould haue heard him ſo loud, and ſo me-lancholly : but notwithſtanding man, Ile doe yoe your Maſter what good I can : and the very yea, & the no is, ỹ French Doctor my Maſter, (I may call him my Maſter, looke you, for I keepe his houſe ; and I waſh, ring, brew, bake, ſcowre, dreſſe meat and drinke, make the beds, and doe all my ſelfe.)

Simp. 'Tis a great charge to come vnder one bodies hand.

Qui. Are you a-uis'd o'that? you ſhall finde it a great charge : and to be vp early, and down late : but notwith-ſtanding, (to tell you in your eare, I wold haue no words of it) my Maſter himſelfe is in loue with Miſtris *Anne Page* : but notwithſtanding that I know *Ans* mind, that's neither heere nor there.

Caius. You, Iack 'Nape : giue-'a this Letter to Sir *Hugh*, by gar it is a ſhallenge : I will cut his troat in de Parke, and I will teach a ſcuruy Iack-a-nape Prieſt to meddle, or make : —————you may be gon : it is not good you tarry here : by gar I will cut all his two ſtones : by gar, he ſhall not haue a ſtone to throw at his dogge.

Qui. Alas : he ſpeakes but for his friend.

Caius. It is no matter'a ver dat : do not you tell-a-me dat I ſhall haue *Anne Page* for my ſelfe ? by gar, I vill kill de Iack-Prieſt : and I haue appointed mine Hoſt of de Iarteer to meaſure our weapon : by gar, I wil my ſelfe haue *Anne Page*.

Qui. Sir, the maid loues you, and all ſhall bee well : We muſt giue folkes leaue to prate : what the good-ier.

Caius. *Rugby*, come to the Court with me : by gar, if I haue not *Anne Page*, I ſhall turne your head out of my dore : follow my heeles, *Rugby*.

Qui. You ſhall haue *An*-fooles head of your owne : No, I know *Ans* mind for that : neuer a woman in *Wind-ſor* knowes more of *Ans* minde then I doe, nor can doe more then I doe with her, I thanke heauen.

Fenton. Who's with in there, hoa ?

Qui. Who's there, I troa ? Come neere the houſe I pray you.

Fen. How now (good woman) how doſt thou ?

Qui. The better that it pleaſes your good Worſhip to aske ?

Fen. What newes ? how do's pretty Miſtris *Anne* ?

Qui. In truth Sir, and ſhee is pretty, and honeſt, and gentle, and one that is your friend, I can tell you that by the way, I praiſe heauen for it.

Fen. Shall I doe any good thinkſt thou ? ſhall I not looſe my ſuit ?

Qui. Troth Sir, all is in his hands aboue : but not-withſtanding (Maſter *Fenton*) Ile be ſworne on a booke ſhee loues you : haue not your Worſhip a wart aboue your eye ?

Fen. Yes marry haue I, what of that ?

Qui. Wel, thereby hangs a tale : good faith, it is ſuch another *Nan* ; (but (I deteſt) an honeſt maid as euer broke bread : wee had an howres talke of that wart ; I ſhall neuer laugh but in that maids company : but (in-deed) ſhee is giuen too much to Allicholy and muſing : but for you ——— well — goe too————

Fen. Well : I ſhall ſee her to day : hold, there's mo-ney for thee : Let mee haue thy voice in my behalfe : if thou ſeeſt her before me, commend me.————

Qui. Will I ? I faith that wee will : And I will tell your Worſhip more of the Wart, the next time we haue confidence, and of other wooers.

Fen. Well, fare-well, I am in great haſte now.

Qui. Fare-well to your Worſhip : truely an honeſt Gentleman : but *Anne* loues hiim not : for I know *Ans* minde as well as another do's : out vpon't : what haue I forgot.   *Exit.*

Actus Secundus. Scœna Prima.

Enter Miſtris Page, Miſtris Ford, Maſter Page, Maſter Ford, Piſtoll, Nim, Quickly, Hoſt, Shallow.

Miſ. Page. What, haue ſcap'd Loue-letters in the holly-day-time of my beauty, and am I now a ſubiect for them ? let me ſee ?

Aske me no reaſon why I loue you, for though Loue vſe Rea-ſon for his preciſian, hee admits him not for his Counſailour : you are not yong, no more am I : goe to then, there's ſimpathie : you are merry, ſo am I : ba, ba, then there's more ſimpathie : you loue ſacke, and ſo do I : would you deſire better ſimpathie ? Let it ſuffice thee (Miſtris Page) at the leaſt if the Loue of Souldier can ſuffice, that I loue thee : I will not ſay pitty mee, 'tis not a Souldier-like phraſe ; but I ſay, loue me :
By me, thine owne true Knight, by day or night :
Or any kinde of light, with all his might ,
For thee to fight,   Iohn Falſtaffe.

What a *Herod* of *Iurie* is this ? O wicked, wicked world : One that is well-nye worne to peeces with age To ſhow himſelfe a yong Gallant ? What an vnwaied Behauiour hath this Flemiſh drunkard pickt (with The Deuills name) out of my conuerſation, that he dares In this manner aſſay me ? why, hee hath not beene thrice In my Company : what ſhould I ſay to him ? I was then Frugall of my mirth : (heauen forgiue mee :) why Ile Exhibit a Bill in the Parliament for the putting downe of men : how ſhall I be reueng'd on him ? for reueng'd I will be ? as ſure as his guts are made of puddings.

Miſ Ford. Miſtris *Page*, truſt me, I was going to your houſe.

Miſ. Page. And truſt me, I was comming to you : you looke very ill.

Miſ.Ford. Nay, Ile nere beleeee that ; I haue to ſhew to the contrary.

Miſ.Page. 'Faith but you doe in my minde.

Miſ.Ford. Well : I doe then : yet I ſay, I could ſhew you to the contrary : O Miſtris *Page*, giue mee ſome counſaile.

Miſ.Page. What's the matter, woman ?

Mi. Ford. O woman : if it were not for one trifling re-ſpect, I could come to ſuch honour.

Miſ.Page. Hang the trifle (woman) take the honour : what is it ? diſpence with trifles : what is it ?

Miſ. Ford. If I would but goe to hell, for an eternall moment, or ſo : I could be knighted.

Miſ.Page. What thou lieſt ? Sir *Alice Ford* ? theſe Knights will hacke, and ſo thou ſhouldſt not alter the ar-ticle of thy Gentry.

Miſ.Ford. Wee burne day-light : heere , read, read : perceiue how I might bee knighted , I ſhall thinke the worſe of fat men , as long as I haue an eye to make diffe-rence of mens liking : and yet hee would not ſweare :
praiſe

praife womens modefty: and gaue fuch orderly and wel-
behaued reproofe to al vncomelineffe, that I would haue
fworne his difpofition would haue gone to the truth of
his words: but they doe no more adhere and keep place
together, then the hundred Pfalms to the tune of Green-
fleeues : What tempeft (I troa) threw this Whale, (with
fo many Tuns of oyle in his belly) a'fhoare at Windfor?
How fhall I bee reuenged on him? I thinke the beft way
were, to entertaine him with hope, till the wicked fire
of luft haue melted him in his owne greace : Did you e-
uer heare the like?

Mif.Page. Letter for letter; but that the name of
Page and *Ford* differs : to thy great comfort in this my-
ftery of ill opinions, heere's the twyn-brother of thy Letter : but let thine inherit firft, for I proteft mine neuer
fhall : I warrant he hath a thoufand of thefe Letters, writ
with blancke-fpace for different names (fure more) : and
thefe are of the fecond edition : hee will print them out
of doubt: for he cares not what hee puts into the preffe,
when he would put vs two : I had rather be a Gianteffe,
and lye vnder Mount *Pelion*: Well; I will find you twentie lafciuious Turtles ere one chafte man.

Mif.Ford. Why this is the very fame : the very hand:
the very words : what doth he thinke of vs?

Mif.Page. Nay I know not: it makes me almoft readie to wrangle with mine owne honefty : Ile entertaine
my felfe like one that I am not acquainted withall : for
fure vnleffe hee know fome ftraine in mee, that I know
not my felfe, hee would neuer haue boorded me in this
furie.

Mi. Ford. Boording, call you it? Ile bee fure to keepe
him aboue decke.

Mi.Page. So will I : if hee come vnder my hatches,
Ile neuer to Sea againe : Let's bee reueng'd on him : let's
appoint him a meeting : giue him a fhow of comfort in
his Suit, and lead him on with a fine baited delay, till hee
hath pawn'd his horfes to mine Hoft of the Garter.

Mi. Ford. Nay, I wil· confent to act any villany againft
him, that may not fully the charineffe of our honefty : oh
that my husband faw this Letter : it would giue eternall
food to his iealoufie.

Mif.Page. Why look where he comes; and my good
man too : hee's as farre from iealoufie, as I am from giuing him caufe, and that (I hope) is an vnmeafurable diftance.

Mif.Ford. You are the happier woman.

Mif.Page. Let's confult together againft this greafie
Knight : Come hither.

Ford. Well : I hope, it be not fo.

Pift. Hope is a curtall-dog in fome affaires :
Sir *Iohn* affects thy wife.

Ford. Why fir, my wife is not young.

Pift. He wooes both high and low, both rich & poor,
both yong and old, one with another (*Ford*) he loues the
Gally-mawfry (*Ford*) perpend.

Ford. Loue my wife?

Pift. With liuer, burning hot : preuent :
Or goe thou like Sir *Acteon* he, with
Ring-wood at thy heeles : O, odious is the name.

Ford. What name Sir?

Pift. The horne I fay : Farewell :
Take heed, haue open eye, for theeues doe foot by night.
Take heed, ere fommer comes, or Cuckoo-birds do fing.
Away fir Corporall *Nim* :
Beleeue it *(Page)* he fpeakes fence.

Ford. I will be patient : I will find out this.

Nim. And this is true : I like not the humor of lying:
hee hath wronged mee in fome humors: I fhould haue
borne the humour'd Letter to her : but I haue a fword :
and it fhall bite vpon my neceffitie : he loues your wife;
There's the fhort and the long : My name is Corporall
Nim: I fpeak, and I auouch; 'tis true : my name is *Nim*:
and *Falftaffe* loues your wife : adieu, I loue not the humour of bread and cheefe : adieu.

Page. The humour of it (quoth'a?) heere's a fellow
frights Englifh out of his wits.

Ford. I will feeke out *Falftaffe*.

Page. I neuer heard fuch a drawling-affecting rogue.

Ford. If I doe finde it : well.

Page. I will not beleeue fuch a *Cataian*, though the
Prieft o' th'Towne commended him for a true man.

Ford. 'Twas a good fenfible fellow : well.

Page. How now *Meg*?

Mift. Page. Whether goe you (*George*?) harke you.

Mif Ford. How now (fweet *Frank*) why art thou melancholy?

Ford. I melancholy? I am not melancholy :
Get you home : goe.

Mif.Ford. Faith, thou haft fome crochets in thy head,
Now: will you goe, *Miftris Page*?

Mif.Page. Haue with you : you'll come to dinner
George? Looke who comes yonder : fhee fhall bee our
Meffenger to this paltrie Knight.

Mif.Ford. Truft me, I thought on her : fhee'll fit it.

Mif. Page. You are come to fee my daughter *Anne*?

Qui. I forfooth : and I pray how do's good Miftreffe
Anne?

Mif.Page. Go in with vs and fee : we haue an houres
talke with you.

Page. How now Mafter Ford?

For. You heard what this knaue told me, did you not?

Page. Yes, and you heard what the other told me?

Ford. Doe you thinke there is truth in them?

Pag. Hang 'em flaues : I doe not thinke the Knight
would offer it : But thefe that accufe him in his intent
towards our wiues, are a yoake of his difcarded men: very rogues, now they be out of feruice.

Ford. Were they his men?

Page. Marry were they.

Ford. I like it neuer the beter for that,
Do's he lye at the Garter?

Page. I marry do's he : if hee fhould intend this voyage toward my wife, I would turne her loofe to him;
and what hee gets more of her, then fharpe words, let it
lye on my head.

Ford. I doe not mifdoubt my wife : but I would bee
loath to turne them together : a man may be too confident : I would haue nothing lye on my head : I cannot
be thus fatisfied.

Page. Looke where my ranting-Hoft of the Garter
comes : there is eyther liquor in his pate, or mony in his
purfe, when hee lookes fo merrily : How now mine
Hoft?

Hoft. How now Bully-Rooke : thou'rt a Gentleman
Caueleiro Iuftice, I fay.

Shal. I follow, (mine Hoft) I follow : Good-euen,
and twenty (good Mafter *Page*.) Mafter *Page*, wil you go
with vs? we haue fport in hand.

Hoft. Tell him Caueleiro-Iuftice : tell him Bully-
Rooke.

Sball. Sir, there is a fray to be fought, betweene Sir
Hugb the Welch Prieft, and *Caius* the French Doctor.

Ford. Good

Ford. Good mine Hoſt o'th'Garter: a word with you.

Hoſt. What ſaiſt thou, my Bully-Rooke?

Shal. Will you goe with vs to behold it? My merry Hoſt hath had the meaſuring of their weapons ; and (I thinke) hath appointed them contrary places : for (beleeue mee) I heare the Parſon is no Ieſter : harke, I will tell you what our ſport ſhall be.

Hoſt. Haſt thou no ſuit againſt my Knight ? my gueſt-Caualeire?

Shal. None, I proteſt : but Ile giue you a pottle of burn'd ſacke, to giue me recourſe to him, and tell him my name is *Broome* : onely for a ieſt.

Hoſt. My hand, (Bully :) thou ſhalt haue egreſſe and regreſſe, (ſaid I well?) and thy name ſhall be *Broome.* It is a merry Knight : will you goe An-heires?

Shal. Haue with you mine Hoſt.

Page. I haue heard the French-man hath good skill in his Rapier.

Shal. Tut ſir : I could haue told you more : In theſe times you ſtand on diſtance: your Paſſes, Stoccado's, and I know not what : 'tis the heart (Maſter *Page*) 'tis heere, 'tis heere : I haue ſeene the time, with my long-ſword, I would haue made you fowre tall fellowes skippe like Rattes.

Hoſt. Heere boyes, heere, heere : ſhall we wag?

Page. Haue with you : I had rather heare them ſcold, then fight.

Ford. Though *Page* be a ſecure foole, and ſtands ſo firmely on his wiues frailty ; yet, I cannot put-off my o-pinion ſo eaſily : ſhe was in his company at *Pages* houſe : and what they made there, I know not. Well, I wil looke further into't, and I haue a diſguiſe, to ſound *Falſtaffe* ; if I finde her honeſt, I looſe not my labor : if ſhe be otherwiſe, 'tis labour well beſtowed. *Exeunt.*

Scœna Secunda.

Enter Falſtaffe, Piſtoll, Robin, Quickly, Bardolfe, Ford.

Fal. I will not lend thee a penny.

Piſt. Why then the world's mine Oyſter, which I, with ſword will open.

Fal. Not a penny : I haue beene content (Sir,) you ſhould lay my countenance to pawne : I haue grated vp-on my good friends for three Repreeues for you, and your Coach-fellow *Nim* ; or elſe you had look'd through the grate, like a Geminy of Baboones : I am damn'd in hell, for ſwearing to Gentlemen my friends , you were good Souldiers, and tall-fellowes. And when Miſtreſſe *Briget* loſt the handle of her Fan, I took't vpon mine ho-nour thou hadſt it not.

Piſt. Didſt not thou ſhare? hadſt thou not fifteene pence?

Fal. Reaſon, you roague, reaſon : thinkſt thou Ile en-danger my ſoule, *gratis* ? at a word, hang no more about mee , I am no gibbet for you : goe, a ſhort knife, and a throng, to your Mannor of *Pickt-hatch* : goe, you'll not beare a Letter for mee you roague ? you ſtand vpon your honor : why, (thou vnconfinable baſeneſſe) it is as much as I can doe to keepe the termes of my hononor preciſe : I, I, I my ſelfe ſometimes, leauing the feare of heauen on

the left hand, and hiding mine honor in my neceſſity, am faine to ſhuffle : to hedge, and to lurch, and yet , you Rogue, will en-ſconce your raggs ; your Cat-a-Moun-taine-lookes, your red-lattice phraſes , and your bold-beating-oathes, vnder the ſhelter of your honor? you will not doe it? you?

Piſt. I doe relent : what would thou more of man ?

Robin. Sir, here's a woman would ſpeake with you.

Fal. Let her approach.

Qui. Giue your worſhip good morrow.

Fal. Good-morrow, good-wife.

Qui. Not ſo, and't pleaſe your worſhip.

Fal. Good maid then.

Qui. Ile be ſworne,
As my mother was the firſt houre I was borne.

Fal. I doe beleeue the ſwearer ; what with me ?

Qui. Shall I vouch-ſafe your worſhip a word, or two ?

Fal. Two thouſand (faire woman) and ile vouchſafe thee the hearing.

Qui. There is one Miſtreſſe *Ford,* (Sir) I pray come a little neerer this waies : I my ſelfe dwell with M.Doctor *Caius* :

Fal. Well, on ; Miſtreſſe *Ford,* you ſay.

Qui. Your worſhip ſaies very true : I pray your wor-ſhip come a little neerer this waies.

Fal. I warrant thee, no-bodie heares : mine owne people, mine owne people.

Qui. Are they ſo ? heauen-bleſſe them , and make them his Seruants.

Fal. Well ; Miſtreſſe *Ford,* what of her ?

Qui. Why, Sir ; ſhee's a good-creature ; Lord, Lord, your Worſhip's a wanton : well : heauen forgiue you, and all of vs, I pray———.

Fal. Miſtreſſe *Ford* : come, Miſtreſſe *Ford.*

Qui. Marry this is the ſhort, and the long of it : you haue brought her into ſuch a Canaries, as 'tis wonder-full : the beſt Courtier of them all (when the Court lay at *Windſor*) could neuer haue brought her to ſuch a Ca-narie : yet there has beene Knights, and Lords, and Gen-tlemen, with their Coaches ; I warrant you Coach after Coach, letter after letter, gift after gift, ſmelling ſo ſweet-ly ; all Muske, and ſo ruſhling, I warrant you, in ſilke and golde, and in ſuch alligant termes, and in ſuch wine and ſuger of the beſt, and the faireſt, that would haue wonne any womans heart : and I warrant you, they could neuer get an eye-winke of her : I had my ſelfe twentie Angels giuen me this morning, but I defie all Angels (in any ſuch ſort, as they ſay) but in the way of honeſty : and I warrant you, they could neuer get her ſo much as ſippe on a cup with the prowdeſt of them all, and yet there has beene Earles : nay, (which is more) Pentioners, but I warrant you all is one with her.

Fal. But what ſaies ſhee to mee ? be briefe my good ſhee-*Mercurie.*

Qui. Marry, ſhe hath receiu'd your Letter : for the which ſhe thankes you a thouſand times ; and ſhe giues you to notifie, that her husband will be abſence from his houſe, betweene ten and eleuen.

Fal. Ten, and eleuen.

Qui. I, forſooth : and then you may come and ſee the picture (ſhe ſayes) that you wot of : Maſter *Ford* her huſ-band will be from home : alas, the ſweet woman leades an ill life with him : hee's a very iealouſie-man ; ſhe leads a very frampold life with him, (good hart.)

Fal. Ten, and eleuen.

Woman

Woman, commend me to her, I will not faile her.

Qui. Why, you fay well : But I haue another meffenger to your worfhip : Miftreffe *Page* hath her heartie
commendations to you to : and let mee tell you in your
eare, fhee's as fartuous a ciuill modeft wife, and one (I
tell you) that will not miffe you morning nor euening
prayer, as any is in *Windfor*, who ere bee the other : and
fhee bade me tell your worfhip, that her husband is feldome from home, but fhe hopes there will come a time.
I neuer knew a woman fo doate vpon a man ; furely I
thinke you haue charmes, la : yes in truth.

Fal. Not I, I affure thee ; fetting the attraction of my
good parts afide, I haue no other charmes.

Qui. Bleffing on your heart for't.

Fal. But I pray thee tell me this : has *Fords* wife, and
Pages wife acquainted each other, how they loue me ?

Qui. That were a ieft indeed : they haue not fo little
grace I hope, that were a tricke indeed : But Miftris *Page*
would defire you to fend her your little Page of al loues:
her husband has a maruellous infectiō to the little Page :
and truely Mafter *Page* is an honeft man : neuer a wife in
Windfor leades a better life then fhe do's : doe what fhee
will, fay what fhe will, take all, pay all, goe to bed when
fhe lift, rife when fhe lift, all is as fhe will : and truly fhe
deferues it ; for if there be a kinde woman in *Windfor*, fhe
is one : you muft fend her your Page, no remedie.

Fal. Why, I will.

Qu. Nay, but doe fo then, and looke you, hee may
come and goe betweene you both : and in any cafe haue
a nay-word, that you may know one anothers minde,
and the Boy neuer neede to vnderftand any thing ; for
'tis not good that children fhould know any wickednes :
olde folkes you know, haue difcretion, as they fay, and
know the world.

Fal. Farethee-well, commend mee to them both :
there's my purfe, I am yet thy debter : Boy, goe along
with this woman, this newes diftracts me.

Pif. This Puncke is one of *Cupids* Carriers,
Clap on more failes, purfue : vp with your fights :
Giue fire : fhe is my prize, or Ocean whelme them all.

Fal. Saift thou fo (old *Iacke*) go thy wales : Ile make
more of thy olde body then I haue done : will they yet
looke after thee? wilt thou after the expence of fo much
money, be now a gainer? good Body, I thanke thee : let
them fay 'tis groffely done, fo it bee fairely done, no
matter.

Bar. Sir *Iohn*, there's one Mafter *Broome* below would
faine fpeake with you, and be acquainted with you ; and
hath fent your worfhip a mornings draught of Sacke.

Fal. *Broome* is his name ?

Bar. I Sir.

Fal. Call him in : fuch *Broomes* are welcome to mee,
that ore'flowes fuch liquor : ah ha, Miftreffe *Ford* and Miftreffe *Page*, haue I encompafs'd you ? goe to, *via.*

Ford. 'Bleffe you fir.

Fal. And you fir : would you fpeake with me?

Ford. I make bold, to preffe, with fo little preparation vpon you.

Fal. You'r welcome, what's your will ? giue vs leaue
Drawer.

Ford. Sir, I am a Gentleman that haue fpent much,
my name is *Broome.*

Fal. Good Mafter *Broome*, I defire more acquaintance
of you.

Ford. Good Sir *Iohn*, I fue for yours : not to charge
you, for I muft let you vnderftand, I thinke my felfe in

better plight for a Lender, then you are : the which hath
fomething emboldned me to this vnfeafon'd intrufion :
for they fay, if money goe before, all waies doe lye
open.

Fal. Money is a good Souldier (Sir) and will on.

Ford. Troth, and I haue a bag of money heere troubles me : if you will helpe to beare it (Sir *Iohn*) take all,
or halfe, for eafing me of the carriage.

Fal. Sir, I know not how I may deferue to bee your
Porter.

Ford. I will tell you fir, if you will giue mee the hearing.

Fal. Speake (good Mafter *Broome*) I fhall be glad to
be your Seruant.

Ford. There is a Gentlewoman in this Towne, her
husbands name is Ford.

Fal. Well Sir.

Ford. I haue long lou'd her, and I proteft to you, beftowed much on her : followed her with a doating obferuance : Ingrofs'd opportunities to meete her : fee'd e-
uery flight occafion that could but nigardly giue mee
fight of her : not only bought many prefents to giue her,
but haue giuen largely to many, to know what fhee
would haue giuen : briefly, I haue purfu'd her, as Loue
hath purfued mee, which hath beene on the wing of all
occafions : but whatfoeuer I haue merited, either in my
minde, or in my meanes, meede I am fure I haue receiued
none, vnleffe Experience be a Iewell, that I haue purchafed at an infinite rate, and that hath taught mee to fay
this,

"*Loue like a fhadow flies, when fubftance Loue purfues,*
"*Purfuing that that flies, and flying what purfues.*

Fal. Haue you receiu'd no promife of fatisfaction at
her hands?

Ford. Neuer.

Fal. Haue you importun'd her to fuch a purpofe ?

Ford. Neuer.

Fal. Of what qualitie was your loue then ?

Ford. Like a faire houfe, built on another mans ground,
fo that I haue loft my edifice, by miftaking the place,
where I erected it.

Fal. To what purpofe haue you vnfolded this to me ?

For. When I haue told you that, I haue told you all :
Some fay, that though fhe appeare honeft to mee, yet in
other places fhee enlargeth her mirth fo farre, that there
is fhrewd conftruction made of her. Now (Sir *Iohn*) here
is the heart of my purpofe : you are a gentleman of excellent breeding, admirable difcourfe, of great admittance, authenticke in your place and perfon, generally
allow'd for your many war-like, court-like, and learned
preparations.

Fal. O Sir.

Ford. Beleeue it, for you know it : there is money,
fpend it, fpend it, fpend more ; fpend all I haue, onely
giue

giue me fo much of your time in enchange of it, as to lay
an amiable fiege to the honefty of this *Fords* wife : vfe
your Art of wooing ; win her to confent to you : if any
man may, you may as foone as any.

Fal. Would it apply well to the vehemency of your
affe&ion that I fhould win what you would enioy? Me-
thinkes you prefcribe to your felfe very prepofteroufly.

Ford. O, vnderftand my drift : fhe dwells fo fecurely
on the excellency of her honor, that the folly of my foule
dares not prefent it felfe : fhee is too bright to be look'd
againft. Now, could I come to her with any dete&ion
in my hand ; my defires had inftance and argument to
commend themfelues, I could driue her then from the
ward of her purity, her reputation, her marriage-vow,
and a thoufand other her defences, which now are too-
too ftrongly embattaild againft me : what fay you too't,
Sir *Iohn*?

Fal. Mafter *Broome*, I will firft make bold with your
money : next, giue mee your hand : and laft, as I am a
gentleman, you fhall, if you will, enioy *Fords* wife.

Ford. O good Sir.

Fal. I fay you fhall.

Ford. Want no money (Sir *Iohn*)you fhall want none.

Fal. Want no *Miftreffe* Ford(Mafter *Broome*)you fhall
want none :'I fhall be with her (I may tell you) by her
owne appointment, euen as you came in to me, her affi-
ftant, or goe-betweene, parted from me : I fay I fhall be
with her betweene ten and eleuen : for at that time the
iealious-rafcally-knaue her husband will be forth : come
you to me at night, you fhall know how I fpeed.

Ford. I am bleft in your acquaintance : do you know
Ford Sir?

Fal. Hang him (poore Cuckoldly knaue) I know
him not : yet I wrong him to call him poore : They fay
the iealous wittolly-knaue hath maffes of money, for
the which his wife feemes to me well-fauourd : I will vfe
her as the key of the Cuckoldly-rogues Coffer, & ther's
my harueft-home.

Ford. I would you knew *Ford*, fir, that you might a-
uoid him, if you faw him.

Fal. Hang him, mechanicall-falt-butter rogue; I wil
ftare him out of his wits : I will awe-him with my cudgell : it fhall hang like a Meteor ore the Cuckolds horns:
Mafter *Broome*, thou fhalt know, I will predominate o-
uer the pezant, and thou fhalt lye with his wife. Come
to me foone at night : *Ford's* a knaue, and I will aggrauate his ftile : thou (Mafter *Broome*) fhalt know him for
knaue, and Cuckold. Come to me foone at night.

Ford. What a damn'd Epicurian-Rafcall is this? my
heart is ready to cracke with impatience : who faies this
is improuident iealoufie? my wife hath fent to him, the
howre is fixt, the match is made : would any man haue
thought this? fee the hell of hauing a falfe woman : my
bed fhall be abus'd, my Coffers ranfack'd, my reputation gnawne at, and I fhall not onely receiue this villanous
wrong, but ftand vnder the adoption of abhominable
termes, and by him that does mee this wrong : Termes,
names : *Amaimon* founds well : *Lucifer*, well : *Barbafon*,
well : yet they are Diuels additions, the names of fiends :
But Cuckold, Wittoll, Cuckold? the Diuell himfelfe
hath not fuch a name. *Page* is an Affe, a fecure Affe ; hee
will truft his wife, hee will not be iealous : I will rather
truft a *Fleming* with my butter, Parfon *Hugh* the *Welfh*-
man with my Cheefe, an *Irifh*-man with my Aqua-vitæ-
bottle, or a Theefe to walke my ambling gelding, then
my wife with her felfe. Then fhe plots, then fhee rumi-

uates, then fhee deuifes : and what they thinke in their
hearts they may effe& ; they will breake their hearts but
they will effe&. Heauen bee prais'd for my iealoufie :
eleuen o' clocke the howre, I will preuent this, dete&
my wife, bee reueng'd on *Falftaffe*, and laugh at *Page*. I
will about it, better three houres too foone, then a my-
nute too late : fie, fie, fie : Cuckold, Cuckold, Cuckold.

Exit.

Scena Tertia.

Enter Caius, Rugby, Page, Shallow, Slender, Hoft.

Caius. Iacke Rugby.

Rug. Sir.

Caius. Vat is the clocke, *Iack*.

Rug. 'Tis paft the howre (Sir) that Sir *Hugh* promis'd
to meet.

Cai. By gar, he has faue his foule, dat he is no-come :
hee has pray his Pible well, dat he is no-come : by gar·
(*Iack Rugby*) he is dead already, if he be come.

Rug. Hee is wife Sir : hee knew your worfhip would
kill him if he came.

Cai. By gar, de herring is no dead, fo as I vill kill
him : take your Rapier, (*Iacke*) I vill tell you how I vill
kill him.

Rug. Alas fir, I cannot fence.

Cai. Villanie, take your Rapier.

Rug. Forbeare : heer's company.

Hoft. 'Bleffe thee, bully-Do&or.

Shal. 'Saue you M^r. Do&or *Caius*.

Page. Now good M^r. Do&or.

Slen. 'Giue you good-morrow, fir.

Caius. Vat be all you one, two, tree, fowre, come for?

Hoft. To fee thee fight, to fee thee foigne, to fee thee
trauerfe, to fee thee heere, to fee thee there, to fee thee
paffe thy pun&o, thy ftock, thy reuerfe, thy diftance, thy
montant : Is he dead, my Ethiopian? Is he dead, my Francifco? ha Bully? what faies my *Efculapius*? my *Galien*? my
heart of Elder? ha? is he dead bully-Stale? is he dead?

Çai. By gar, he is de Coward-Iack-Prieft of dorld:
he is not fhow his face.

Hoft. Thou art a Caftalion-king-Vrinall : He&or of
Greece(my Boy)

Cai. I pray you beare witneffe, that me haue ftay,
fixe or feuen, two tree howres for him, and hee is no-
come.

Shal. He is the wifer man (M.Do&or)rhe is a curer of
foules, and you a curer of bodies : if you fhould fight, you
goe againft the haire of your profeffions : is it not true,
Mafter *Page*?

Page. Mafter *Shallow*; you haue your felfe beene a
great fighter, though now a man of peace.

Shal. Body-kins M. *Page*, though I now be old, and
of the peace ; if I fee a fword out, my finger itches to
make one : though wee are Iuftices, and Do&ors, and
Church-men (M. *Page*) wee haue fome falt of our youth
in vs, we are the fons of women (M.*Page*.)

Page. 'Tis true, M^r. *Shallow*.

Shal. It wil be found fo, (M.*Page*:) M.Do&or *Caius*,
I am come to fetch you home : I am fworn of the peace:
you haue fhow'd your felfe a wife Phyfician, and Sir
Hugh hath fhowne himfelfe a wife and patient Churchman : you muft goe with me, M.Do&or.

Hoft. Par-

Hoſt. Pardon , Gueſt-Iuſtice ; a Mounſeur Mocke-water.

Cai. Mock-vater? vat is dat?

Hoſt. Mock-water, in our Engliſh tongue, is Valour (Bully.)

Cai. By gar, then I haue as much Mock-vater as de Engliſhman : ſcuruy-Iack-dog-Prieſt : by gar, mee vill cut his eares.

Hoſt. He will Clapper-claw thee tightly (Bully.)

Cai. Clapper-de-claw? vat is dat?

Hoſt. That is, he will make thee amends.

Cai. By gar, me doe looke hee ſhall clapper-de-claw me, for by-gar, me vill haue it.

Hoſt. And I will prouoke him to't, or let him wag.

Cai. Me tanck you for dat.

Hoſt. And moreouer, (Bully) but firſt , Mr. Ghueſt, and M. *Page*, & eeke Caualeiro *Slender* goe you through the Towne to *Frogmore*.

Page. Sir *Hugh* is there, is he?

Hoſt. He is there, ſee what humor he is in : and I will bring the Doctor about by the Fields : will it doe well?

Shal. We will doe it.

All. Adieu, good M. Doctor.

Cai. By-gar, me vill kill de Prieſt, for he ſpeake for a Iack-an-Ape to *Anne Page.*

Hoſt. Let him die : ſheath thy impatience : throw cold water on thy Choller : goe about the fields with mee through *Frogmore*, I will bring thee where Miſtris *Anne Page* is, at a Farm-houſe a Feaſting : and thou ſhalt wooe he r : Cride-game, ſaid I well?

Cai. By-gar, mee dancke you vor dat : by gar I loue you : and I ſhall procure 'a you de good Gueſt : de Earle, de Knight, de Lords, de Gentlemen, my patients.

Hoſt. For the which, I will be thy aduerſary toward *Anne Page* : ſaid I well?

Cai. By-gar, 'tis good : vell ſaid.

Hoſt. Let vs wag then.

Cai. Come at my heeles, *Iack Rugby.*

Exeunt.

Actus Tertius. Scœna Prima.

Enter Euans, Simple, Page, Shallow, Slender, Hoſt, Caius, Rugby.

Euans. I pray you now, good Maſter *Slenders* ſeruing-man, and friend *Simple* by your name ; which way haue you look'd for Maſter *Caius*, that calls himſelfe Doctor of Phiſicke.

Sim. Marry Sir, the pittie-ward, the Parke-ward : euery way : olde *Windſor* way, and euery way but the Towne-way.

Euan. I moſt ſehemently deſire you, you will alſo looke that way.

Sim. I will ſir.

Euan. 'Pleſſe my ſoule: how full of Chollors I am, and trempling of minde : I ſhall be glad if he haue deceiued me : how melancholies I am? I will knog his Vrinalls a-bout his knaues coſtard, when I haue good oportunities for the orke : 'Pleſſe my ſoule : *To ſhallow Ruiers to whoſe falls : melodious Birds ſings Madrigalls : There will we make our Peds of Roſes : and a thouſand fragrant poſies. To ſhallow :* 'Mercie on mee, I haue a great diſpoſitions to cry.

Melodious birds ſing Madrigalls : ——*When as I ſat in Pabilon : and a thouſand vagram Poſies. To ſhallow, &c.*

Sim. Yonder he is comming, this way, Sir *Hugh.*

Euan. Hee's welcome : *To ſhallow Riuers, to whoſe fals :* Heauen proſper the right : what weapons is he?

Sim. No weapons, Sir : there comes my Maſter, Mr. *Shallow*, and another Gentleman ; from *Frogmore* , ouer the ſtile, this way.

Euan. Pray you giue mee my gowne, or elſe keepe it in your armes.

Shal. How now Maſter Parſon? good morrow good Sir *Hugh* : keepe a Gameſter from the dice, and a good Studient from his booke, and it is wonderfull.

Slen. Ah ſweet *Anne Page.*

Page. 'Saue you, good Sir *Hugh.*

Euan. 'Pleſſe you from his mercy-ſake, all of you.

Shal. What? the Sword, and the Word? Doe you ſtudy them both, Mr. Parſon?

Page. And youthfull ſtill, in your doublet and hoſe, this raw-rumaticke day?

Euan. There is reaſons, and cauſes for it.

Page. We are come to you, to doe a good office, Mr. Parſon.

Euan. Fery-well : what is it?

Page. Yonder is a moſt reuerend Gentleman ; who ('be-like) hauing receiued wrong by ſome perſon, is at moſt odds with his owne grauity and patience, that euer you ſaw.

Shal. I haue liued foure-ſcore yeeres, and vpward : I neuer heard a man of his place, grauity, and learning, ſo wide of his owne reſpect.

Euan. What is he?

Page. I thinke you know him : Mr. Doctor *Caius* the renowned French Phyſician.

Euan. Got's-will, and his paſſion of my heart : I had as lief you would tell me of a meſſe of porredge.

Page. Why?

Euan. He has no more knowledge in *Hibocrates* and *Galen*, and hee is a knaue beſides : a cowardly knaue , as you would deſires to be acquaiuted withall.

Page. I warrant you, hee's the man ſhould fight with him.

Slen. O ſweet *Anne Page.*

Shal. It appeares ſo by his weapons : keepe them a-ſunder : here comes Doctor *Caius.*

Page. Nay good Mr. Parſon, keepe in your weapon.

Shal. So doe you, good Mr. Doctor.

Hoſt. Diſarme them, and let them queſtion : let them keepe their limbs whole, and hack our Engliſh.

Cai. I pray you let-a-mee ſpeake a word with your eare ; vherefore vill you not meet-a me?

Euan. Pray you vſe your patience in good time.

Cai. By-gar, you are de Coward : de Iack dog : John Ape.

Euan. Pray you let vs not be laughing-ſtocks to other mens humors : I deſire you in friendſhip, and I will one way or other make you amends : I will knog your Vrinal about your knaues Cogs-combe.

Cai. Diable : Iack Rugby : mine Hoſt de Iarteer : haue I not ſtay for him, to kill him? haue I not at de place I did appoint?

Euan. As I am a Chriſtians-ſoule , now looke you : this is the place appointed, Ile bee iudgement by mine Hoſt of the Garter.

Hoſt. Peace, I ſay, *Gallia* and *Gaule*, French & Welch, Soule-Curer, and Body-Curer.

Cai. I,

Cai. I, dat is very good, excallant.

Hoſt. Peace, I ſay : heare mine Hoſt of the Garter,
Am I politicke? Am I ſubtle? Am I a Machiuell?
Shall I looſe my Doctor? No, hee giues me the Potions
and the Motions. Shall I looſe my Parſon? my Prieſt?
my Sir *Hugh*? No, he giues me the Prouerbes, and the
No-verbes. Giue me thy hand (Celeſtiall) ſo : Boyes of
Art, I haue deceiu'd you both : I haue directed you to
wrong places : your hearts are mighty, your ſkinnes are
whole, and let burn'd Sacke be the iſſue : Come, lay their
ſwords to pawne : Follow me, Lad of peace, follow, follow, follow.

Shal. Truſt me, a mad Hoſt : follow Gentlemen, follow.

Slen. O ſweet *Anne Page.*

Cai. Ha' do I perceiue dat? Haue you make-a-de-ſot
of vs, ha, ha?

Eua. This is well, he has made vs his vlowting-ſtog :
I deſire you that we may be friends : and let vs knog our
praines together to be reuenge on this ſame ſcall-ſcur-
uy-cogging-companion the Hoſt of the Garter.

Cai. By gar, with all my heart : he promiſe to bring
me where is *Anne Page* : by gar he deceiue me too.

Euan. Well, I will ſmite his noddles : pray you follow.

Scena Secunda.

Miſt. Page, Robin, Ford, Page, Shallow, Slender, Hoſt,
Euans, Caius.

Miſt. Page. Nay keepe your way (little Gallant) you
were wont to be a follower, but now you are a Leader :
whether had you rather lead mine eyes, or eye your maſters heeles?

Rob. I had rather (forſooth) go before you like a man,
then follow him like a dwarfe. (Courtier.

M. Pa. O you are a flattering boy, now I ſee you'l be a
Ford. Well met miſtris *Page,* whether go you.

M. Pa. Truly Sir, to ſee your wife, is ſhe at home?

Ford. I, and as idle as ſhe may hang together for want
of company : I thinke if your husbands were dead, you
two would marry.

M. Pa. Be ſure of that, two other husbands.

Ford. Where had you this pretty weather-cocke?

M. Pa. I cannot tell what (the dickens) his name is my
husband had him of, what do you cal your Knights name

Rob. Sir *Iohn Falſtaffe.* (ſirrah?

Ford. Sir *Iohn Falſtaffe.*

M. Pa. He, he, I can neuer hit on's name ; there is ſuch a
league betweene my goodman, and he : is your Wife at
Ford. indeed ſhe is. (home indeed?

M. Pa. By your leaue ſir, I am ſicke till I ſee her.

Ford. Has *Page* any braines? Hath he any eies? Hath he
any thinking? Sure they ſleepe, he hath no vſe of them :
why this boy will carrie a letter twentie mile as eaſie, as
a Canon will ſhoot point-blanke twelue ſcore : hee peeces out his wiues inclination : he giues her folly motion
and aduantage : and now ſhe's going to my wife, & *Fal-*
ſtaffes boy with her : A man may heare this ſhowre ſing
in the winde ; and *Falſtaffes* boy with her : good plots,
they are laide, and our reuolted wiues ſhare damnation
together. Well, I will take him, then torture my wife,
plucke the borrowed vaile of modeſtie from the ſo-ſee-
ming *Miſt. Page,* divulge *Page* himſelfe for a ſecure and

wilfull *Actæon,* and to theſe violent proceedings all my
neighbors ſhall cry aime. The clocke giues me my Qu,
and my aſſurance bids me ſearch, there I ſhall finde *Fal-*
ſtaffe : I ſhall be rather praiſd for this, then mock'd, for
it is as poſſitiue, as the earth is firme, that *Falſtaffe* is
there : I will go.

Shal. Page, &c. Well met Mr *Ford.*

Ford. Truſt me, a good knotte ; I haue good cheere at
home, and I pray you all go with me.

Shal. I muſt excuſe my ſelfe Mr *Ford.*

Slen. And ſo muſt I Sir,
We haue appointed to dine with Miſtris *Anne,*
And I would not breake with her for more mony
Then Ile ſpeake of.

Shal. We haue linger'd about a match betweene *An*
Page, and my cozen *Slender,* and this day wee ſhall haue
our anſwer.

Slen. I hope I haue your good will Father *Page.*

Pag. You haue Mr *Slender,* I ſtand wholly for you,
But my wife (Mr Doctor) is for you altogether.

Cai. I be-gar, and de Maid is loue-a-me : my nurſh-
a-Quickly tell me ſo muſh.

Hoſt. What ſay you to yong Mr *Fenton?* He capers,
he dances, he has eies of youth : he writes verſes, hee
ſpeakes holliday, he ſmels April and May, he wil carry't,
he will carry't, 'tis in his buttons, he will carry't.

Page. Not by my conſent I promiſe you. The Gentleman is of no hauing, hee kept companie with the wilde
Prince, and *Pointz* : he is of too high a Region, he knows
too much : no, hee ſhall not knit a knot in his fortunes,
with the finger of my ſubſtance : if he take her, let him
take her ſimply : the wealth I haue waits on my conſent,
and my conſent goes not that way.

Ford. I beſeech you heartily, ſome of you goe home
with me to dinner : beſides your cheere you ſhall haue
ſport, I will ſhew you a monſter : Mr Doctor, you ſhal
go, ſo ſhall you Mr *Page,* and you Sir *Hugh.*

Shal. Well, fare you well :
We ſhall haue the freer woing at Mr *Pages.*

Cai. Go home *Iohn Rugby,* I come anon.

Hoſt. Farewell my hearts, I will to my honeſt Knight
Falſtaffe, and drinke Canarie with him.

Ford. I thinke I ſhall drinke in Pipe-wine firſt with
him, Ile make him dance. Will you go, Gentles?

All. Haue with you, to ſee this Monſter. *Exeunt*

Scena Tertia.

Enter M. Ford, M. Page, Seruants, Robin, Falſtaffe,
Ford, Page, Caius, Euans.

Miſt. Ford. What *Iohn,* what *Robert.*

M. Page. Quickly, quickly : Is the Buck-basket——

Miſ. Ford. I warrant. What *Robin* I ſay.

Miſ. Page. Come, come, come.

Miſt. Ford. Heere, ſet it downe.

M. Pag. Giue your men the charge, we muſt be briefe.

M. Ford. Marrie, as I told you before (*Iohn* & *Robert*)
be ready here hard-by in the Brew-houſe, & when I ſodainly call you, come forth, and (without any pauſe, or
ſtaggering) take this basket on your ſhoulders : ẙ done,
trudge with it in all haſt, and carry it among the Whit-
ſters in *Dotchet* Mead, and there empty it in the muddie
ditch, cloſe by the Thames ſide.

M. Page. You will do it? (direction.

M. Ford. I ha told them ouer and ouer, they lacke no
E Bg

Be gone, and come when you are call'd.

M.Page. Here comes little *Robin.*   (with you?

Miſt.Ford. How now my Eyas-Musket, what newes *Rob.* My M.Sir *Iohn* is come in at your backe doore ('Miſt.Ford*, and requeſts your company.

M.Page. You litle Iack-a-lent, haue you bin true to vs *Rob.* I, Ile be fworne : my Maſter knowes not of your being heere : and hath threatned to put me into euerla- ſting liberty, if I tell you of it : for he fweares he'll turne me away.

Miſt.Pag. Thou'rt a good boy : this fecrecy of thine ſhall be a Tailor to thee, and ſhal make thee a new dou- blet and hofe. Ile go hide me.

Mi.Ford. Do fo : go tell thy Maſter, I am alone : Mi- ſtris *Page*, remember you your *Qu.*

*Miſt.Pag.*I warrant thee, if I do not aſt it, hiſſe me.

Miſt.Ford. Go-too then : we'l vfe this vnwholſome humidity, this groſſe-watry Pumpion ; we'll teach him to know Turtles from Iayes.

Fal. Haue I caught thee, my heauenly Iewell? Why now let me die, for I haue liu'd long enough : This is the period of my ambition : O this bleſſed houre.

Miſt.Ford. O fweet Sir *Iohn.*

Fal. Miſtris *Ford*, I cannot cog, I cannot prate (Miſt. *Ford*) now ſhall I fin in my wiſh ; I would thy Husband were dead, Ile fpeake it before the beſt Lord, I would make thee my Lady.

Miſt.Ford. I your Lady Sir *Iohn*? Alas, I ſhould bee a pittifull Lady.

Fal. Let the Court of France ſhew me fuch another : I fee how thine eye would emulate the Diamond : Thou haſt the right arched-beauty of the brow, that becomes the Ship-tyre, the Tyre-valiant, or any Tire of Venetian admittance.

Miſ.Ford. A plaine Kerchiefe, Sir *Iohn* : My browes become nothing elfe, nor that well neither.

Fal. Thou art a tyrant to fay fo : thou wouldſt make an abſolute Courtier, and the firme fixture of thy foote, would giue an excellent motion to thy gate, in a femi- circled Farthingale. I fee what thou wert if Fortune thy foe, were not Nature thy friend : Come, thou canſt not hide it.

*Miſt.Ford.*Beleeue me, ther's no fuch thing in me.

Fal. What made me loue thee? Let that perfwade thee. Ther's fomething extraordinary in thee : Come, I cannot cog, and fay thou art this and that, like a-manie of thefe lifping-hauthorne buds, that come like women in mens apparrell, and fmell like Bucklers-berry in fim- ple time : I cannot, but I loue thee, none but thee ; and thou deferu'ſt it.

*M.Ford.*Do not betray me fir, I fear you loue M.*Page.*

Fal. Thou mightſt as well fay, I loue to walke by the Counter-gate, which is as hatefull to me, as the reeke of a Lime-kill.

*Miſ.Ford.*Well, heauen knowes how I loue you, And you ſhall one day finde it.

Fal. Keepe in that minde, Ile deferue it.

Miſt.Ford: Nay, I muſt tell you, fo you doe ; Or elfe I could not be in that minde.

*Rob.*Miſtris *Ford*, Miſtris *Ford* : heere's Miſtris *Page* at the doore, fweating, and blowing, and looking wildely, and would needs fpeake with you prefently.

Fal. She ſhall not fee me, I will enfconce mee behinde the Arras.

*M.Ford.*Pray you do fo, ſhe's a very tatling woman. Whats the matter? How now?

Miſt.Page. O miſtris *Ford* what haue you done? You'r ſham'd, y'are ouerthrowne, y'are vndone for euer.

M.Ford. What's the matter, good miſtris *Page?*

M.Page. O weladay, miſt.*Ford*, hauing an honeſt man to your husband, to giue him fuch caufe of fufpition.

M.Ford. What caufe of fufpition?

M.Page. What caufe of fufpition? Out vpon you : How am I miſtooke in you?

M.Ford. Why (alas) what's the matter?

M.Page. Your husband's comming hether (Woman) with all the Officers in Windfor, to fearch for a Gentle- man, that he fayes is heere now in the houfe ; by your confent to take an ill aduantage of his abfence : you are vndone.

M.Ford. 'Tis not fo, I hope.

M.Page. Pray heauen it be not fo, that you haue fuch a man heere : but 'tis moſt certaine your husband's com- ming, with halfe Windfor at his heeles, to ferch for fuch a one, I come before to tell you : If you know your felfe cleere, why I am glad of it : but if you haue a friend here, conuey, conuey him out. Be not amaz'd, call all your fenfes to you, defend your reputation, or bid farwell to your good life for euer.

M.Ford. What ſhall I do? There is a Gentleman my deere friend : and I feare not mine owne ſhame fo much, as his perill. I had rather then a thoufand pound he were out of the houfe.

M.Page. For ſhame, neuer ſtand (you had rather, and you had rather :) your husband's heere at hand, bethinke you of fome conueyance : in the houfe you cannot hide him. Oh, how haue you deceiu'd me? Looke, heere is a basket, if he be of any reafonable ſtature, he may creepe in heere, and throw fowle linnen vpon him, as if it were going to bucking : Or it is whiting time, fend him by your two men to *Datchet*-Meade.

M.Ford. He's too big to go in there : what ſhall I do?

Fal. Let me fee't, let me fee't, O let me fee't : Ile in, Ile in : Follow your friends counfell, Ile in.

M.Page. What Sir *Iohn Faiſtaſſe?* Are thefe your Let- ters, Knight?

Fal. I loue thee, helpe mee away : let me creepe in heere : ile neuer——

M.Page. Helpe to couer your maſter (Boy :) Call your men (Miſt.*Ford.*) You diſſembling Knight.

M.Ford. What *Iohn, Robert, Iohn* ; Go, take vp thefe cloathes heere, quickly : Wher's the Cowle-ſtaffe? Look how you drumble? Carry them to the Landreſſe in Dat- chet mead ; quickly, come.

Ford. 'Pray you come nere : if I fufpeſt without caufe, Why then make fport at me, then let me be your ieſt, I deferue it : How now? Whether beare you this?

Ser. To the Landreſſe forfooth?

M.Ford. Why, what haue you to doe whether they beare it? You were beſt meddle with buck-waſhing.

Ford. Buck? I would I could waſh my felfe of ỹ Buck : Bucke, bucke, bucke, I bucke : I warrant you Bucke, And of the feafon too ; it ſhall appeare. Gentlemen, I haue dream'd to night, Ile tell you my dreame : heere, heere, heere bee my keyes, afcend my Chambers, fearch, feeke, finde out : Ile warrant wee'le vnkennell the Fox. Let me ſtop this way firſt : fo, now vncape.

Page. Good maſter *Ford*, be contented : You wrong your felfe too much.

Ford. True (maſter *Page*) vp Gentlemen, You ſhall fee fport anon :

                                   Follow

Follow me Gentlemen.

Euans. This is fery fantafticall humors and iealoufies.

Caius. By gar, 'tis no-the fafhion of France:
It is not iealous in France.

Page. Nay follow him (Gentlemen) fee the yffue of his fearch.

Mif.Page Is there not a double excellency in this?

Mif.Ford. I know not which pleafes me better,
That my husband is deceiued, or Sir *Iohn.*

Mif.Page. What a taking was hee in, when your husband askt who was in the basket?

Mif.Ford. I am halfe affraid he will haue neede of wafhing: fo throwing him into the water, will doe him a benefit.

Mif.Page. Hang him difhoneft rafcall: I would all of the fame ftraine, were in the fame diftreffe.

Mif.Ford. I thinke my husband hath fome fpeciall fufpition of *Falftaffs* being heere: for I neuer faw him fo groffe in his iealoufie till now.

Mif.Page. I will lay a plot to try that, and wee will yet haue more trickes with *Falftaffe*: his diffolute difeafe will fcarfe obey this medicine.

Mif.Ford. Shall we fend that foolifhion Carion, Mift. *Quickly* to him, and excufe his throwing into the water, and giue him another hope, to betray him to another punifhment?

Mif.Page. We will do it: let him be fent for to-morrow eight a clocke to haue amends.

Ford. I cannot finde him: may be the knaue bragg'd of that he could not compaffe.

Mif.Page. Heard you that?

Mif.Ford. You vfe me well, M.*Ford?* Do you?

Ford. I, I do fo.

M.Ford. Heauen make you better then your thoghts

Ford. Amen.

Mi.Page. You do your felfe mighty wrong (M.*Ford*)

Ford. I, I: I muft beare it.

Eu. If there be any pody in the houfe, & in the chambers, and in the coffers, and in the preffes: heauen forgiue my fins at the day of iudgement.

Caius. Be gar, nor I too: there is no-bodies.

Page. Fy, fy, M.*Ford*, are you not afham'd? What fpirit, what diuell fuggefts this imagination? I wold not ha your diftemper in this kind, for ÿ welth of *Windfor caftle.*

Ford. 'Tis my fault (M.*Page*) I fuffer for it.

Euans. You fuffer for a pad confcience: your wife is as honeft a o'mans, as I will defires among fiue thoufand, and fiue hundred too.

Cai. By gar, I fee 'tis an honeft woman.

Ford. Well, I promifd you a dinner: come, come, walk in the Parke, I pray you pardon me: I wil hereafter make knowne to you why I haue done this. Come wife, come Mi.*Page,* I pray you pardon me. Pray hartly pardon me.

Page. Let's go in Gentlemen, but (truft me) we'l mock him: I doe inuite you to morrow morning to my houfe to breakfaft: after we'll a Birding together, I haue a fine Hawke for the bufh. Shall it be fo:

Ford. Any thing.

Eu. If there is one, I fhall make two in the Companie

Ca. If there be one, or two, I fhall make-a-theturd.

Ford. Pray you go, M.*Page.*

Eua. I pray you now remembrance to morrow on the lowfie knaue, mine Hoft.

Cai. Dat is good by gar, withall my heart.

Eua. A lowfie knaue, to haue his gibes, and his mockeries.   *Exeunt.*

Scœna Quarta.

*Enter Fenton, Anne, Page, Shallow, Slender,
Quickly, Page, Mif. Page.*

Fen: I fee I cannot get thy Fathers loue,
Therefore no more turne me to him (fweet Nan.)

Anne. Alas, how then?

Fen. Why thou muft be thy felfe.
He doth obiect, I am too great of birth,
And that my ftate being gall'd with my expence,
I feeke to heale it onely by his wealth.
Befides thefe, other barres he layes before me,
My Riots paft, my wilde Societies,
And tels me 'tis a thing impoffible
I fhould loue thee, but as a property.

An. May be he tels you true.
No, heauen fo fpeed me in my time to come,
Albeit I will confeffe, thy Fathers wealth
Was the firft motiue that I woo'd thee (*Anne*:)
Yet wooing thee, I found thee of more valew
Then ftampes in Gold, or fummes in fealed bagges:
And 'tis the very riches of thy felfe,
That now I ayme at.

An. Gentle M. *Fenton,*
Yet feeke my Fathers loue, ftill feeke it fir,
If opportunity and humbleft fuite
Cannot attaine it, why then harke you hither.

Shal. Breake their talke Miftris *Quickly,*
My Kinfman fhall fpeake for himfelfe.

Slen. Ile make a fhaft or a bolt on't, flid, tis but ventu-

Shal. Be not difmaid.   (ring.

Slen. No, fhe fhall not difmay me:
I care not for that, but that I am affeard.

Qui. Hark ye, M.*Slender* would fpeake a word with you

An. I come to him. This is my Fathers choice:
O what a world of vilde ill-fauour'd faults
Lookes handfome in three hundred pounds a yeere?

Qui. And how do's good Mafter *Fenton?*
Pray you a word with you,

Shal. Shee's comming; to her Coz:
O boy, thou hadft a father.

Slen. I had a father (M.*An*) my vncle can tel you good iefts of him: pray you Vncle, tel Mift. *Anne* the ieft how my Father ftole two Geefe out of a Pen, good Vnckle.

Shal. Miftris *Anne,* my Cozen loues you.

Slen. I that I do, as well as I loue any woman in Glocefterfhire.

Shal. He will maintaine you like a Gentlewoman.

Slen. I that I will, come cut and long-taile, vnder the degree of a Squire.

Shal. He will make you a hundred and fiftie pounds ioynture.

Anne. Good Maifter *Shallow* let him woo for himfelfe.

Shal. Marrie I thanke you for it: I thanke you for that good comfort: fhe cals you (Coz) Ile leaue you.

Anne. Now Mafter *Slender.*

Slen. Now good Miftris *Anne.*

Anne. What is your will?

Slen. My will? Odd's-hart-lings, that's a prettie ieft indeede: I ne're made my Will yet (I thanke Heauen:) I am not fuch a fickely creature, I giue Heauen praife.

Anne. I meane (M.*Slender*) what wold you with me?

Slen. Truely, for mine owne part, I would little or nothing with you: your father and my vncle hath made motions: if it be my lucke, ſo; if not, happy man bee his dole, they can tell you how things go, better then I can: you may aske your father, heere he comes.

Page. Now Mr *Slender*; Loue him daughter *Anne.* Why how now? What does Mr *Fenter* here? You wrong me Sir, thus ſtill to haunt my houſe. I told you Sir, my daughter is diſpoſd of.

Fen. Nay Mr *Page,* be not impatient.

Miſt.Page. Good M. *Fenton.*come not to my child.

Page. She is no match for you.

Fen. Sir, will you heere me?

Page. No, good M. *Fenton.*

Come M. *Shallow*: Come ſonne *Slender,* in; Knowing my minde, you wrong me (M. *Fenton.*)

Qui. Speake to Miſtris *Page.*

Fen. Good Miſt. *Page,* for that I loue your daughter In ſuch a righteous faſhion as I do, Perforce, againſt all checkes, rebukes, and manners, I muſt aduance the colours of my loue, And not retire. Let me haue your good will.

An. Good mother, do not marry me to yond foole.

Miſt.Page. I meane it not, I ſeeke you a better huſband.

Qui. That's my maſter, M.*Doctor.*

*An.*Alas I had rather be ſet quick i'th earth, And bowl'd to death with Turnips.

Miſt. Page. Come, trouble not your ſelfe good M. *Fenton,* I will not be your friend, nor enemy: My daughter will I queſtion how ſhe loues you, And as I finde her, ſo am I affected: Till then, farewell Sir, ſhe muſt needs go in, Her father will be angry.

Fen. Farewell gentle Miſtris: farewell *Nan.*

Qui. This is my doing now: Nay, ſaide I, will you caſt away your childe on a Foole, and a Phyſitian: Looke on M. *Fenton,* this is my doing.

Fen. I thanke thee: and I pray thee once to night, Giue my ſweet *Nan* this Ring: there's for thy paines.

Qui. Now heauen ſend thee good fortune, a kinde heart he hath: a woman would run through fire & water for ſuch a kinde heart. But yet, I would my Maiſter had Miſtris *Anne,* or I would M.*Slender* had her: or (in ſooth) I would M.*Fenton* had her; I will do what I can for them all three, for ſo I haue promiſd, and Ile bee as good as my word, but ſpeciouſly for M. *Fenton.* Well, I muſt of another errand to Sir *Iohn Falſtaffe* from my two Miſtreſſes: what a beaſt am I to ſlacke it.   *Exeunt*

Scena Quinta.

Enter Falſtaffe, Bardolfe, Quickly, Ford.

Fal. *Bardolfe* I ſay.

Bar. Heere Sir.

Fal. Go, fetch me a quart of Sacke, put a toſt in't. Haue I liu'd to be carried in a Basket like a barrow of butchers Offall? and to be throwne in the Thames? Wel, if I be ſeru'd ſuch another tricke, Ile haue my braines 'tane out and butter'd, and giue them to a dogge for a New-yeares gift. The rogues ſlighted me into the riuer with as little remorſe, as they would haue drown'de a

blinde bitches Puppies, fifteene i'th litter: and you may know by my ſize, that I haue a kinde of alacrity in ſinking: if the bottome were as deepe as hell, I ſhold down. I had beene drown'd, but that the ſhore was ſheluy and ſhallow: a death that I abhorre: for the water ſwelles a man; and what a thing ſhould I haue beene, when I had beene ſwel'd? I ſhould haue beene a Mountaine of Mummie.

Bar. Here's M.*Quickly* Sir to ſpeake with you.

Fal. Come, let me poure in ſome Sack to the Thames water: for my bellies as cold as if I had ſwallow'd ſnow-bals, for pilles to coole the reines. Call her in.

Bar. Come in woman.

Qui. By your leaue: I cry you mercy? Giue your worſhip good morrow.

Fal. Take away theſe Challices: Go, brew me a pottle of Sacke finely.

Bard. With Egges, Sir?

Fal. Simple of it ſelfe: Ile no Pullet-Sperſme in my brewage. How now?

Qui. Marry Sir, I come to your worſhip from M. *Ford.*

Fal.Miſt.Ford? I haue had Ford enough`: I was thrown into the Ford; I haue my belly full of Ford.

Qui. Alas the day, (good-heart) that was not her fault: ſhe do's ſo take on with her men; they miſtooke their erection.   (promiſe.

Fal. So did I mine, to build vpon a fooliſh Womans

Qui. Well, ſhe laments Sir for it, that it would yern your heart to ſee it: her husband goes this morning a birding; ſhe deſires you once more to come to her, betweene eight and nine: I muſt carry her word quickely, ſhe'll make you amends I warrant you.

Fal. Well, I will viſit her, tell her ſo: and bidde her thinke what a-man is: Let her conſider his frailety, and then iudge of my merit.

Qui. I will tell her.

Fal. Do ſo. Betweene nine and ten ſaiſt thou?

Qui. Eight and nine Sir.

Fal. Well, be gone: I will not miſſe her.

Qui. Peace be with you Sir.

Fal. I meruaile I heare not of Mr *Broome*: he ſent me word to ſtay within: I like his money well. Oh, heere he comes.

Ford. Bleſſe you Sir.

Fal. Now M. *Broome,* you come to know What hath paſt betweene me, and *Fords* wife.

Ford. That indeed (Sir *Iohn*) is my buſineſſe.

Fal. M.*Broome* I will not lye to you, I was at her houſe the houre ſhe appointed me.

Ford. And ſped you Sir?

Fal. very ill-fauouredly M. *Broome.*

Ford. How ſo ſir, did ſhe change her determination?

Fal. No (M.*Broome*) but the peaking Curnuto her huſband (M.*Broome*) dwelling in a continual larum of ielouſie, coms me in the inſtant of our encounter, after we had embraſt, kiſt, proteſted, & (as it were) ſpoke the prologue of our Comedy: and at his heeles, a rabble of his companions, thither prouoked and inſtigated by his diſtemper, and (forſooth) to ſerch his houſe for his wiues Loue.

Ford. What? While you were there?

Fal. While I was there.

For. And did he ſearch for you, & could not find you?

Fal. You ſhall heare. As good lucke would haue it, comes in one *Miſt. Page,* giues intelligence of *Fords* approch: and in her inuention, and *Fords* wiues diſtraction, they conuey'd me into a bucke-basket.

Ford

Ford. A Buck-basket?

Fal. Yes : a Buck-basket : ram'd mee in with foule Shirts and Smockes, Socks, foule Stockings, greaſie Napkins, that (Maſter *Broome*) there was the rankeſt compound of villanous ſmell, that euer offended no-ſtrill.

Ford. And how long lay you there?

Fal. Nay, you ſhall heare (Maſter *Broome*) what I haue ſufferd, to bring this woman to euill, for your good : Being thus cram'd in the Basket, a couple of *Fords* knaues, his Hindes, were cald forth by their Mi-ſtris, to carry mee in the name of foule Cloathes to *Datchet-lane* : they tooke me on their ſhoulders : met the iealous knaue their Maſter in the doore; who ask'd them once or twice what they had in their Baſ-ket? I quak'd for feare leaſt the Lunatique Knaue would haue ſearch'd it : but Fate (ordaining he ſhould be a Cuckold) held his hand : well, on went hee, for a ſearch, and away went I for foule Cloathes : But marke the ſequell (Maſter *Broome*) I ſuffered the pangs of three ſeuerall deaths : Firſt, an intollerable fright, to be detected with a iealous rotten Bell-weather : Next to be compaſs'd like a good Bilbo in the circum-ference of a Pecke, hilt to point, heele to head. And then to be ſtopt in like a ſtrong diſtillation with ſtink-ing Cloathes, that fretted in their owne greaſe : thinke of that, a man of my Kidney; thinke of that, that am as ſubiect to heate as butter; a man of conti-nuall diſſolution, and thaw : it was a miracle to ſcape ſuffocation. And in the height of this Bath (when I was more then halfe ſtew'd in greaſe (like a Dutch-diſh) to be throwne into the Thames, and coold, glowing-hot, in that ſerge like a Horſe-ſhoo; thinke of that; hiſſing hot : thinke of that (Maſter *Broome*.)

Ford. In good ſadneſſe Sir, I am ſorry, that for my ſake you haue ſufferd all this. My ſuite then is deſperate : You'll vndertake her no more?

Fal. Maſter *Broome* : I will be throwne into *Etna*, as I haue beene into Thames, ere I will leaue her thus; her Husband is this morning gone a Birding : I haue receiued from her another ambaſſie of mee-ting : 'twixt eight and nine is the houre (Maſter *Broome*.)

Ford. 'Tis paſt eight already Sir.

Fal. Is it? I will then addreſſe mee to my appoint-ment : Come to mee at your conuenient leiſure, and you ſhall know how I ſpeede : and the concluſion ſhall be crowned with your enioying her : adiew : you ſhall haue her (Maſter *Broome*) Maſter *Broome*, you ſhall cuckold *Ford*.

Ford. Hum : ha? Is this a viſion? Is this a dreame? doe I ſleepe? Maſter *Ford* awake, awake Maſter *Ford* : ther's a hole made in your beſt coate (Maſter *Ford* :) this 'tis to be married; this 'tis to haue Lynnen, and Buck-baskets : Well, I will proclaime my ſelfe what I am : I will now take the Leacher : hee is at my houſe : hee cannot ſcape me : 'tis impoſſible hee ſhould : hee can-not creepe into a halfe-penny purſe, nor into a Pepper-Boxe : But leaſt the Diuell that guides him, ſhould aide him, I will ſearch impoſſible places : though what I am, I cannot auoide; yet to be what I would not, ſhall not make me tame : If I haue hornes, to make one mad, let the prouerbe goe with me, Ile be horne-mad.   *Exeunt.*

Actus Quartus. Scœna Prima.

Enter Miſtris Page, Quickly, William, Euans.

Miſt.Pag. Is he at M.*Fords* already think'ſt thou?

Qui. Sure he is by this; or will be preſently; but truely he is very couragious mad, about his throwing into the water. Miſtris *Ford* deſires you to come ſo-dainely.

Miſt.Pag. Ile be with her by and by : Ile but bring my yong-man here to Schoole : looke where his Maſter comes; 'tis a playing day I ſee : how now Sir *Hugh*, no Schoole to day?

Eua. No : Maſter *Slender* is let the Boyes leaue to play.

Qui. 'Bleſſing of his heart.

Miſt.Pag. Sir *Hugh*, my husband ſaies my ſonne pro-fits nothing in the world at his Booke : I pray you aske him ſome queſtions in his Accidence.

Eu. Come hither *William*; hold vp your head; come.

Miſt.Pag. Come-on Sirha; hold vp your head; an-ſwere your Maſter, be not afraid.

Eua. *William*, how many Numbers is in Nownes?

Will. Two.

Qui. Truely, I thought there had bin one Number more, becauſe they ſay od's-Nownes.

Eua. Peace, your tatlings. What is (*Faire*)*William*?

Will. Pulcher.

Qu. Powlcats? there are fairer things then Powlcats, ſure.

Eua. You are a very ſimplicity o'man : I pray you peace. What is (*Lapis*)*William*?

Will. A Stone.

Eua. And what is a Stone (*William*?)

Will. A Peeble.

Eua. No; it is *Lapis* : I pray you remember in your praine.

Will. *Lapis*.

Eua. That is a good *William* : what is he (*William*) that do's lend Articles.

Will. Articles are borrowed of the Pronoune; and be thus declined. *Singulariter nominatiuo hic, hæc, hoc.*

Eua. *Nominatiuo hig, hag, hog* : pray you marke : *geni-tiuo huius* : Well : what is your *Accuſatiue-caſe*?

Will. *Accuſatiuo hinc.*

Eua. I pray you haue your remembrance (childe) *Ac-cuſatiuo hing, hang, hog.*

Qy. Hang-hog, is latten for Bacon, I warrant you.

Eua. Leaue your prables (o'man) What is the *Foca-tiue caſe* (*William*?)

Will. O, *Vocatiuo*, O.

Eua. Remember *William*, *Focatiue*, is *caret*.

Qy. And that's a good roote.

Eua. O' man, forbeare.

Miſt.Pag. Peace.

Eua: What is your *Genitiue caſe plurall* (*William*?)

Will. *Genitiue caſe*?

Eua. I.

Will. *Genitiue horum, harum, horum.*

Qu. 'Vengeance of Ginyes caſe; fie on her; neuer name her(childe) if ſhe be a whore.

Eua. For ſhame o'man.

Qy. You doe ill to teach the childe ſuch words : hee teaches him to hic, and to hac; which they'll doe faſt enough of themſelues, and to call *horum* ; fie vpon you.

E 3   *Eua.* 'Oman

Euans. O'man, art thou Lunaties? Haſt thou no vn-
derſtandings for thy Caſes, & the numbers of the Gen-
ders? Thou art as fooliſh Chriſtian creatures, as I would
deſires.
Mi.Page. Pre'thee hold thy peace.
Eu. Shew me now (*William*) ſome declenſions of your
Pronounes.
Will. Forſooth, I haue forgot.
Eu. It is *Qui, quæ, quod*; if you forget your *Quies*,
your *Ques*, and your *Quods*, you muſt be preeches: Goe
your waies and play, go.
M.Pag. He is a better ſcholler then I thought he was.
Eu. He is a good ſprag-memory: Farewel *Mis.Page.*
Miſ.Page. Adieu good Sir *Hugh*:
Get you home boy, Come we ſtay too long.   *Exeunt.*

Scena Secunda.

Enter Falſtoffe, Miſſ. Ford, Miſſ. Page, Seruants, Ford,
Page, Caius, Euans, Shallow.

Fal. Mi.*Ford*, Your ſorrow hath eaten vp my ſufferance; I ſee you are obſequious in your loue, and I pro-
feſſe requitall to a haires bredth, not onely Miſt. *Ford*,
in the ſimple office of loue, but in all the accuſtrement,
complement, and ceremony of it: But are you ſure of
your busband now?
Miſ.Ford. Hee's a birding (ſweet Sir *Iohn*.)
Mi.Page. What hoa, goſſip Ford: what hoa.
Mi.Ford. Step into th'chamber, Sir *Iohn.*
Mis. Page. How now (ſweete heart) whoſe at home
beſides your ſelfe?
Miſ Ford. Why none but mine owne people.
Miſ.Page. Indeed?
Miſ.Ford. No certainly: Speake louder.
Miſ.Pag. Truly, I am ſo glad you haue no body here.
Mis.Ford. Why?
Miſ.Page. Why woman, your husband is in his olde
lines againe: he ſo railes on yonder with my husband, ſo
railes againſt all married mankinde; ſo curſes all *Eues*
daughters, of what complexion ſoeuer; and ſo buffettes
himſelfe on the for-head: crying peere-out, peere-out,
that any madneſſe I euer yet beheld, ſeem'd but tame-
neſſe, ciuility, and patience to this his diſtemper he is in
now: I am glad the fat Knight is not heere.
Miſt.Ford. Why, do's he talke of him?
Miſt.Page. Of none but him, and ſweares he was ca-
ried out the laſt time hee ſearch'd for him, in a Basket:
Proteſts to my husband he is now heere, & hath drawne
him and the reſt of their company from their ſport, to
make another experiment of his ſuſpition: But I am glad
the Knight is not heere; now he ſhall ſee his owne foolerie.
Miſ.Ford. How neere is he Miſtris *Page*?
Miſ.Pag. Hard by, at ſtreet end; he will be here anon.
Miſt.Ford. I am vndone, the Knight is heere.
Miſt.Page. Why then you are vtterly ſham'd, & hee's
but a dead man. What a woman are you? Away with
him, away with him: Better ſhame, then murther.
Miſſ.Ford. Which way ſhould he go? How ſhould I
beſtow him? Shall I put him into the basket againe?
Fal. No, Ile come no more I'th Basket:
May I not go out ere he come?

Miſt.Page. Alas: three of M*r*. *Fords* brothers watch
the doore with Piſtols, that none ſhall iſſue out: other-
wiſe you might ſlip away ere hee came: But what make
you heere?
Fal. What ſhall I do? Ile creepe vp into the chimney.
Miſt.Ford. There they alwaies vſe to diſcharge their
Birding-peeces: creepe into the Kill-hole.
Fal. Where is it?
Miſt.Ford. He will ſeeke there on my word: Neyther
Preſſe, Coffer, Cheſt, Trunke, Well, Vault, but he hath
an abſtract for the remembrance of ſuch places, and goes
to them by his Note: There is no hiding you in the
houſe.
Fal. Ile go out then.
Miſt.Ford. If you goe out in your owne ſemblance,
you die Sir *Iohn*, vnleſſe you go out diſguis'd.
Miſt. Ford. How might we diſguiſe him?
Miſt.Page. Alas the day I know not, there is no wo-
mans gowne bigge enough for him: otherwiſe he might
put on a hat, a muffler, and a kerchiefe, and ſo eſcape.
Fal. Good hearts, deuiſe ſomething: any extremitie,
rather then a miſchiefe.
Miſt. Ford. My Maids Aunt the fat woman of *Brainford*, has a gowne aboue.
Miſt. Page. On my word it will ſerue him: ſhee's as
big as he is: and there's her thrum'd hat, and her muffler
too: run vp Sir *Iohn.*
Miſt.Ford. Go, go, ſweet Sir *Iohn*: *Miſtriſ Page* and
I will looke ſome linnen for your head.
Miſt.Page. Quicke, quicke, wee'le come dreſſe you
ſtraight: put on the gowne the while.
Miſt.Ford. I would my husband would meete him
in this ſhape: he cannot abide the old woman of Brainford; he ſweares ſhe's a witch, forbad her my houſe, and
hath threatned to beate her.
Miſt.Page. Heauen guide him to thy husbands cudgell: and the diuell guide him a cudgell afterwards.
Miſt.Ford. But is my husband comming?
Miſt.Page. I in good ſadneſſe is he, and talkes of the
basket too, howſoeuer he hath had intelligence.
Miſ.Ford. Wee'l try that: for Ile appoint my men to
carry the basket againe, to meete him at the doore with
it, as they did laſt time.
Miſt.Page. Nay, but hee'l be heere preſently: let's go
dreſſe him like the witch of *Brainford.*
Miſt. Ford. Ile firſt direct direct my men, what they
ſhall do with the basket: Goe vp, Ile bring linnen for
him ſtraight.
Miſt.Page. Hang him diſhoneſt Varlet,
We cannot miſuſe enough:
We'll leaue a proofe by that which we will doo,
Wiues may be merry, and yet honeſt too:
We do not aſte that often, ieſt, and laugh,
'Tis old, but true, Still Swine eats all the draugh.
Miſt.Ford. Go Sirs, take the basket againe on your
ſhoulders: your Maſter is hard at doore: if hee bid you
ſet it downe, obey him: quickly, diſpatch.
1 *Ser.* Come, come, take it vp.
2 *Ser.* Pray heauen it be not full of Knight againe.
1 *Ser.* I hope not, I had liefe as beare ſo much lead.
Ford. I, but if it proue true (M*r*. *Page*) haue you any
way then to vnfoole me againe. Set downe the basket
villaine: ſome body call my wife: Youth in a basket?
Oh you Panderly Raſcals, there's a knot: a gin, a packe,
a conſpiracie againſt me: Now ſhall the diuel be ſham'd.
What wife I ſay: Come, come forth: behold what honeſt

neft cloathes you fend forth to bleaching.

Page. Why, this paffes M. *Ford*: you are not to goe loofe any longer, you muft be pinnion'd.

Euans. Why, this is Lunaticks: this is madde, as a mad dogge.

Sbal. Indeed M. *Ford*, thi is not well indeed.

Ford. So fay I too Sir, come hither Miftris *Ford*, Miftris *Ford*, the honeft woman, the modeft wife, the vertuous creature, that hath the iealious foole to her husband : I fufpect without caufe (Miftris) do I ?

Mift. Ford. Heauen be my witneffe you doe, if you fufpect me in any difhonefty.

Ford. Well faid Brazon-face, hold it out : Come forth firrah.

Page. This paffes.

Mift.Ford. Are you not afham'd, let the cloths alone.

Ford. I fhall finde you anon.

Eua. 'Tis vnreafonable ; will you take vp your wiues cloathes ? Come, away.

Ford. Empty the basket I fay.

M.Ford. Why man, why ?

Ford. Mafter *Page*, as I am a man, there was one conuay'd out of my houfe yefterday in this basket : why may not he be there againe, in my houfe I am fure he is : my Intelligence is true, my iealoufie is reafonable, pluck me out all the linnen.

Mift.Ford. If you find a man there, he fhall dye a Fleas death.

Page. Heer's no man.

Sbal. By my fidelity this is not well Mr. *Ford* : This wrongs you.

Euans. Mr *Ford*, you muft pray, and not follow the imaginations of your owne heart : this is iealoufies.

Ford. Well, hee's not heere I feeke for.

Page. No, nor no where elfe but in your braine.

Ford. Helpe to fearch my houfe this one time : if I find not what I feeke, fhew no colour for my extremity : Let me for euer be your Table-fport : Let them fay of me, as iealous as *Ford*, that fearch'd a hollow Wall-nut for his wiues Lemman. Satisfie me once more, once more ferch with me.

M.Ford. What hoa (Miftris *Page*,) come you and the old woman downe : my husband will come into the Chamber.

Ford. Old woman ? what old womans that ?

M.Ford. Why it is my maids Aunt of *Brainford*.

Ford. A witch, a Queane, an olde couzening queane : Haue I not forbid her my houfe. She comes of errands do's fhe ? We are fimple men, wee doe not know what's brought to paffe vnder the profeffion of Fortune-telling. She workes by Charmes, by Spels, by th'Figure, & fuch dawbry as this is, beyond our Element : wee know nothing. Come downe you Witch, you Hagge you, come downe I fay.

Mift.Ford. Nay, good fweet husband, good Gentlemen, let him ftrike the old woman.

Mift.Page. Come mother *Prat*, Come giue me your hand.

Ford. Ile *Prat*-her : Out of my doore, you Witch, you Ragge, you Baggage, you Poulcat, you Runnion, out, out : Ile coniure you, Ile fortune-tell you.

Mift.Page. Are you not afham'd ?
I thinke you haue kill'd the poore woman.

Mift.Ford. Nay he will do it, 'tis a goodly credite for you.

Ford. Hang her witch.

Eua. By yea, and no, I thinke the o'man is a witch indeede : I like not when a o'man has a great peard ; I fpie a great peard vnder his muffler.

Ford. Will you follow Gentlemen, I befeech you follow : fee but the iffue of my iealoufie : If I cry out thus vpon no traile, neuer truft me when I open againe.

Page. Let's obey his humour a little further :
Come Gentlemen.

Mift.Page. Truft me he beate him moft pittifully.

Mift.Ford. Nay by th'Maffe that he did not : he beate him moft vnpittifully, me thought.

Mift.Page. Ile haue the cudgell hallow'd, and hung ore the Altar, it hath done meritorious feruice.

Mift.Ford. What thinke you ? May we with the warrant of woman-hood, and the witneffe of a good confcience, purfue him with any further reuenge ?

M.Page. The fpirit of wantonneffe is fure fcar'd out of him, if the diuell haue him not in fee-fimple, with fine and recouery, he will neuer (I thinke) in the way of wafte, attempt vs againe.

Mift.Ford. Shall we tell our husbands how wee haue feru'd him.

Mift.Page. Yes, by all meanes : if it be but to fcrape the figures out of your husbands braines : if they can find in their hearts, the poore vnuertuous fat Knight fhall be any further afflicted, wee two will ftill bee the minifters.

Mift.Ford. Ile warrant, they'l haue him publiquely fham'd, and me thinkes there would be no period to the ieft, fhould he not be publikely fham'd.

Mift.Page. Come, to the Forge with it, then fhape it : I would not haue things coole.   *Exeunt.*

Scena Tertia.

Enter Hoft and Bardolfe.

Bar. Sir, the Germane defires to haue three of your horfes : the Duke himfelfe will be to morrow at Court, and they are going to meet him.

Hoft. What Duke fhould that be comes fo fecretly ? I heare not of him in the Court : let mee fpeake with the Gentlemen, they fpeake Englifh ?

Bar. I Sir ? Ile call him to you.

Hoft. They fhall haue my horfes, but Ile make them pay : Ile fauce them, they haue had my houfes a week at commaund : I haue turn'd away my other guefts, they muft come off, Ile fawce them, come.   *Exeunt*

Scena Quarta.

*Enter Page, Ford, Miftris Page, Miftris
Ford, and Euans.*

Eua. 'Tis one of the beft difcretions of a o'man as euer I did looke vpon.

Page. And did he fend you both thefe Letters at an inftant ?

Mift.Page. VVithin a quarter of an houre.

Ford. Pardon me (wife) henceforth do what ȳ wilt :
I rather will fufpect the Sunne with gold,
Then thee with wantonnes : Now doth thy honor ftand
(In

(In him that was of late an Heretike)
As firme as faith.

Page. 'Tis well, 'tis well, no more :
Be not as extreme in fubmiffion, as in offence,
But let our plot go forward : Let our wiues
Yet once againe (to make vs publike fport)
Appoint a meeting with this old fat-fellow,
Where we may take him, and difgrace him for it.

Ford. There is no better way then that they fpoke of.

Page. How ? to fend him word they'll meete him in
the Parke at midnight ? Fie, fie, he'll neuer come.

Eu. You fay he has bin throwne in the Riuers : and
has bin greeuoufly peaten, as an old o'man : me-thinkes
there fhould be terrors in him, that he fhould not come :
Me-thinkes his flefh is punifh'd, hee fhall haue no defires.

Page. So thinke I too.

M.Ford. Deuife but how you'l vfe him whē he comes,
And let vs two deuife to bring him thether.

Mif.Page. There is an old tale goes, that *Herne* the
Hunter (fometime a keeper heere in Windfor Forreft)
Doth all the winter time, at ftill midnight
Walke round about an Oake, with great rag'd-hornes,
And there he blafts the tree, and takes the cattle,
And make milch-kine yeeld blood, and fhakes a chaine
In a moft hideous and dreadfull manner.
You haue heard of fuch a Spirit, and well you know
The fuperftitious idle-headed-Eld
Receiu'd, and did deliuer to our age
This tale of *Herne* the Hunter, for a truth.

Page. Why yet there want not many that do feare
In deepe of night to walke by this Hernes Oake :
But what of this ?

Mift.Ford. Marry this is our deuife,
That *Falftaffe* at that Oake fhall meete with vs.

Page. Well, let it not be doubted but he'll come,
And in this fhape, when you haue brought him thether,
What fhall be done with him ? What is your plot ?

Mift.Pa. That likewife haue we thoght vpon : & thus :
Nan Page (my daughter) and my little fonne,
And three or foure more of their growth, wee'l dreffe
Like Vrchins, Ouphes, and Fairies, greene and white,
With rounds of waxen Tapers on their heads,
And rattles in their hands ; vpon a fodaine,
As *Falftaffe*, fhe, and I, are newly met,
Let them from forth a faw-pit rufh at once
With fome diffufed fong : Vpon their fight
We two, in great amazedneffe will flye :
Then let them all encircle him about,
And Fairy-like to pinch the vncleane Knight ;
And aske him why that houre of Fairy Reuell,
In their fo facred pathes, he dares to tread
In fhape prophane.

Ford. And till he tell the truth,
Let the fuppofed Fairies pinch him, found,
And burne him with their Tapers.

Mift.Page. The truth being knowne,
We'll all prefent our felues ; dif-horne the fpirit,
And mocke him home to Windfor.

Ford. The children muft
Be practis'd well to this, or they'll neu'r doo't.

Eua. I will teach the children their behauiours : and I
will be like a Iacke-an-Apes alfo, to burne the Knight
with my Taber.

Ford. That will be excellent,
Ile go buy them vizards.

Mift.Page. My *Nan* fhall be the Queene of all the
Fairies, finely attired in a robe of white.

Page. That filke will I go buy, and in that time
Shall M. *Slender* fteale my *Nan* away,
And marry her at *Eaton* : go, fend to *Falftaffe* ftraight.

Ford. Nay, Ile to him againe in name of *Broome*,
Hee'l tell me all his purpofe : fure hee'l come.

Mift.Page. Feare not you that : Go get vs properties
And tricking for our Fayries.

Euans. Let vs about it,
It is admirable pleafures, and ferry honeft knaueries.

*Mif.Page.*Go *Mift.Ford*,
Send quickly to Sir *Iohn*, to know his minde :
Ile to the Doctor, he hath my good will,
And none but he to marry with *Nan Page* :
That *Slender* (though well landed) is an Ideot :
And he, my husband beft of all affects :
The Doctor is well monied, and his friends
Potent at Court : he, none but he fhall haue her,
Though twenty thoufand worthier come to craue her.

Scena Quinta.

*Enter Hoft, Simple, Falftaffe, Bardolfe, Euans,
Caius, Quickly.*

*Hoft.*What wouldft thou haue? (Boore) what? (thick
skin) fpeake, breathe, difcuffe : breefe, fhort, quicke,
fnap.

Simp. Marry Sir, I come to fpeake with Sir *Iohn* Falftaffe from M. *Slender.*

Hoft. There's his Chamber, his Houfe, his Caftle,
his ftanding-bed and truckle-bed : 'tis painted about
with the ftory of the Prodigall, frefh and new : go, knock
and call : hee'l fpeake like an Anthropophaginian vnto
thee : Knocke I fay.

Simp. There's an olde woman, a fat woman gone vp
into his chamber : Ile be fo bold as ftay Sir till fhe come
downe : I come to fpeake with her indeed.

Hoft. Ha ? A fat woman ? The Knight may be robb'd :
Ile call. Bully-Knight, Bully Sir *Iohn*: fpeake from thy
Lungs Military : Art thou there ? It is thine Hoft, thine
Ephefian cals.

Fal. How now, mine Hoft ?

Hoft. Here's a Bohemian-Tartar taries the comming
downe of thy fat-woman : Let her defcend (Bully) let
her defcend : my Chambers are honourable : Fie, priua-
cy ? Fie.

Fal. There was (mine Hoft) an old-fat-woman euen
now with me, but fhe's gone.

Simp. Pray you Sir, was't not the Wife-woman of
Brainford ?

Fal. I marry was it (Muffel-fhell) what would you
with her ?

Simp. My Mafter (Sir) my mafter *Slender*, fent to her
feeing me go thorough the ftreets, to know (Sir) whether one *Nim* (Sir) that beguil'd him of a chaine, had the
chaine, or no.

Fal. I fpake with the old woman about it.

Sim. And what fayes fhe, I pray Sir ?

Fal. Marry fhee fayes, that the very fame man that
beguil'd Mafter *Slender* of his Chaine, cozon'd him of it.

Simp. I would I could haue fpoken with the Woman
her

her felfe, I had other things to haue fpoken with her too, from him.

Fal. What are they? let vs know.

Hoſt. I : come : quicke.

Fal. I may not conceale them (Sir.)

Hoſt. Conceale them, or thou di'ſt.

Sim. Why fir, they were nothing but about Miſtris *Anne Page*, to know if it were my Maſters fortune to haue her, or no.

Fal. 'Tis, 'tis his fortune.

Sim. What Sir?

Fal. To haue her, or no : goe ; fay the woman told me fo.

Sim. May I be bold to fay fo Sir?

Fal. I Sir : like who more bold.

Sim. I thanke your worſhip : I ſhall make my Maſter glad with thefe tydings.

Hoſt. Thou are clearkly : thou art clearkly (Sir *Iohn*) was there a wife woman with thee?

Fal. I that there was (mine *Hoſt*) one that hath taught me more wit, then euer I learn'd before in my life : and I paid nothing for it neither, but was paid for my learning.

Bar. Out alas (Sir) cozonage : meere cozonage.

Hoſt. Where be my horfes? fpeake well of them varletto.

Bar. Run away with the cozoners : for fo foone as I came beyond *Eaton*, they threw mee off, from behinde one of them, in a flough of myre ; and fet fpurres, and away ; like three *Germane-diuels* ; three *Doĉtor Fauſtaſſes.*

Hoſt. They are gone but to meete the Duke (villaine) doe not fay they be fled : *Germanes* are honeft men.

Euan. Where is mine *Hoſt*?

Hoſt. What is the matter Sir?

Euan. Haue a care of your entertainments : there is a friend of mine come to Towne, tels mee there is three Cozen-Iermans, that has cozend all the *Hoſts* of *Readins*, of *Maidenhead* ; of *Cole-brooke*, of horfes and money : I tell you for good will (looke you) you are wife, and full of gibes, and vlouting-ſtocks : and 'tis not conuenient you ſhould be cozoned. Fare you well.

Cai. Ver'is mine *Hoſt de Iarteere*?

Hoſt. Here (Maſter *Doĉtor*) in perplexitie, and doubtfull delemma.

Cai. I cannot tell vat is dat : but it is tell-a-me, dat you make grand preparation for a Duke *de Iamanie* : by my trot : der is no Duke that the Court is know, to come : I tell you for good will : adieu.

Hoſt. Huy and cry, (villaine) goe : aſſiſt me Knight, I am vndone : fly, run : huy, and cry (villaine) I am vndone.

Fal. I would all the world might be cozond, for I haue beene cozond and beaten too : if it ſhould come to the eare of the Court, how I haue beene transformed ; and how my transformation hath beene waſhd, and cudgeld, they would melt mee out of my fat drop by drop, and liquor Fiſhermens-boots with me : I warrant they would whip me with their fine wits, till I were as creſt-falne as a dride-peare : I neuer profper'd, fince I forfwore my felfe at *Primero* : well, if my winde were but long enough ; I would repent : Now? Whence come you?

Qui. From the two parties forfooth.

Fal. The Diuell take one partie, and his Dam the other : and fo they ſhall be both beſtowed ; I haue fuf-

fer'd more for their fakes ; more then the villanous inconſtancy of mans difpoſition is able to beare.

Qui. And haue not they fuffer'd? Yes, I warrant ; fpeciouſly one of them ; Miſtris *Ford* (good heart) is beaten blacke and blew, that you cannot fee a white fpot about her.

Fal. What tell'ſt thou mee of blacke, and blew? I was beaten my felfe into all the colours of the Rainebow : and I was like to be apprehended for the Witch of *Braineford*, but that my admirable dexteritie of wit, my counterfeiting the aĉtion of an old woman deliuer'd me, the knaue Conftable had fet me ith' Stocks, ith' common Stocks, for a Witch.

Quy. Sir : let me fpeake with you in your Chamber, you ſhall heare how things goe, and (I warrant) to your content : here is a *Letter* will fay fomewhat : (goodhearts) what a-doe here is to bring you together? Sure, one of you do's not ferue heauen well, that you are fo croſt'd.

Fal. Come vp into my Chamber. *Exeunt.*

Scena Sexta.

Enter Fenton, Hoſt.

Hoſt. Maſter *Fenton*, talke not to mee, my minde is heauy : I will giue ouer all.

Fen. Yet heare me fpeake : affiſt me in my purpofe, And (as I am a gentleman) ile giue thee A hundred pound in gold, more then your loſſe.

Hoſt. I will heare you (Maſter *Fenton*) and I will (at the leaſt) keepe your counfell.

Fen. From time to time, I haue acquainted you With the deare loue I beare to faire *Anne Page*, Who, mutually, hath anfwer'd my affeĉtion, (So farre forth, as her felfe might be her choofer) Euen to my wiſh ; I haue a letter from her Of fuch contents, as you will wonder at ; The mirth whereof, fo larded with my matter, That neither (fingly) can be manifeſted Without the ſhew of both : fat *Falſtaffe* Hath a great Scene ; the image of the ieſt Ile ſhow you here at large (harke good mine *Hoſt* :) To night at *Hernes-Oke*, iuſt 'twixt twelue and one, Muſt my fweet *Nan* prefent the *Faerie-Queene* : The purpofe why, is here : in which difguife VVhile other Ieſts are fomething ranke on foote, Her father hath commanded her to flip Away with *Slender*, and with him, at *Eaton* Immediately to Marry : She hath confented : Now Sir, Her Mother, (euen ſtrong againſt that match And firme for Doĉtor *Caius*) hath appointed That he ſhall likewife ſhuffle her away, While other fports are tasking of their mindes, And at the *Deanry*, where a *Prieſt* attends Strait marry her : to this her Mothers plot She feemingly obedient) likewife hath Made promife to the *Doĉtor* : Now, thus it reſts, And firme for Doĉtor *Caius*) hath appointed And in that habit, when *Slender* fees his time To take her by the hand, and bid her goe, She ſhall goe with him : her Mother hath intended (The better to deuote her to the *Doĉtor* ; For they muſt all be mask'd, and vizarded)

That

That quaint in greene, fhe fhall be loofe en-roab'd,
With Ribonds-pendant, flaring 'bout her head ;
And when the Doctor fpies his vantage ripe,
To pinch her by the hand, and on that token,
The maid hath giuen confent to go with him.

Hoft. Which meanes fhe to deceiue? Father, or Mother.

Fen. Both (my good Hoft) to go along with me :
And heere it refts, that you'l procure the Vicar
To ftay for me at Church, 'twixt twelue, and one,
And in the lawfull name of marrying,
To giue our hearts vnited ceremony.

Hoft. Well, husband your deuice ; Ile to the Vicar,
Bring you the Maid, you fhall not lacke a Prieft.

Fen. So fhall I euermore be bound to thee ;
Befides, Ile make a prefent recompence. _Exeunt._

Actus Quintus. Scæna Prima.

Enter Falftoffe, Quickly, and Ford.

Fal. Pre'thee no more pratling : go, Ile hold, this is the third time : I hope good lucke lies in odde numbers : Away, go, they fay there is Diuinity in odde Numbers, either in natiuity, chance, or death : away.

Qgi. Ile prouide you a chaine, and Ile do what I can to get you a paire of hornes.

Fal. Away I fay, time weares, hold vp your head & mince. How now M. _Broome_? Mafter _Broome_, the matter will be knowne to night, or neuer. Bee you in the Parke about midnight, at Hernes-Oake, and you fhall fee wonders.

Ford. Went you not to her yefterday (Sir) as you told me you had appointed?

Fal. I went to her (Mafter _Broome_) as you fee, like a poore-old-man, but I came from her (Mafter _Broome_) like a poore-old-woman ; that fame knaue (_Ford_ hir husband) hath the fineft mad diuell of iealoufie in him (Mafter _Broome_) that euer gouern'd Frenfie. I will tell you, he beate me greeuoufly, in the fhape of a woman : (for in the fhape of Man (Mafter _Broome_) I feare not Goliah with a Weauers beame, becaufe I know alfo, life is a Shuttle) I am in haft, go along with mee, Ile tell you all (Mafter _Broome_:) fince I pluckt Geefe, plaide Trewant, and whipt Top, I knew not what 'twas to be beaten, till lately. Follow mee, Ile tell you ftrange things of this knaue _Ford_, on whom to night I will be reuenged, and I will deliuer his wife into your hand . Follow, ftraunge things in hand (M. _Broome_) follow. _Exeunt._

Scena Secunda.

Enter Page, Shallow, Slender.

Page. Come, come : wee'll couch i'th Caftle-ditch, till we fee the light of our Fairies. Remember fon _Slender_, my

Slen. I forfooth, I haue fpoke with her, & we haue a nay-word, how to know one another. I come to her in white, and cry Mum ; fhe cries Budget, and by that we know one another.

Shal. That's good too : But what needes either your Mum, or her Budget? The white will decipher her well enough. It hath ftrooke ten a'clocke.

Page. The night is darke, Light and Spirits will become it wel : Heauen profper our fport. No man means euill but the deuill, and we fhal know him by his hornes. Lets away : follow me. _Exeunt._

Scena Tertia.

Enter Mift. Page, Mift. Ford, Caius.

Mift. Page. Mr Doctor, my daughter is in green, when you fee your time, take her by the hand, away with her to the Deanerie, and difpatch it quickly : go before into the Parke : we two muft go together.

Cai. I know vat I haue to do, adieu.

Mift. Page. Fare you well (Sir:) my husband will not reioyce fo much at the abufe of _Falftaffe_, as he will chafe at the Doctors marrying my daughter : But 'tis no matter ; better a little chiding, then a great deale of heart-breake.

Mift. Ford. Where is _Nan_ now? and her troop of Fairies? and the Welch-deuill Herne?

Mift. Page. They are all couch'd in a pit hard by Hernes Oake, with obfcur'd Lights ; which at the very inftant of _Falftaffes_ and our meeting, they will at once difplay to the night.

Mift. Ford. That cannot choofe but amaze him.

Mift. Page. If he be not amaz'd he will be mock'd : If he be amaz'd, he will euery way be mock'd.

Mift. Ford. Wee'll betray him finely.

Mift. Page. Againft fuch Lewdfters, and their lechery, Thofe that betray them, do no treachery.

Mift. Ford. The houre drawes-on : to the Oake, to the Oake. _Exeunt._

Scena Quarta.

Enter Euans and Fairies.

Euans. Trib, trib Fairies : Come, and remember your parts : be pold (I pray you) follow me into the pit, and when I giue the watch-'ords, do as I pid you : Come, come, trib, trib. _Exeunt_

Scena Quinta.

_Enter Falftaffe, Miftris Page, Miftris Ford, Euant,
Anne Page, Fairies, Page, Ford, Quickly,
Slender, Fenton, Caius, Piftoll._

Fal. The Windfor-bell hath ftroke twelue : the Minute drawes-on : Now the hot-blooded-Gods affift me : Remember Ioue, thou was't a Bull for thy _Europa_, Loue fet on thy hornes. O powerfull Loue, that in fome refpects makes a Beaft a Man : In fom other, a Man a beaft. You were alfo (Iupiter) a Swan, for the loue of _Leda_ : O omnipotent

omnipotent Loue, how nere the God drew to the complexion of a Gooſe: a fault done firſt in the forme of a beaſt, (O Ioue, a beaſtly fault:) and then another fault, in the ſemblance of a Fowle, thinke on't (Ioue) a fowle-fault. When Gods haue hot backes, what ſhall poore men do? For me, I am heere a Windſor Stagge, and the fatteſt (I thinke) i'th Forreſt. Send me a coole rut-time (Ioue) or who can blame me to piſſe my Tallow? Who comes heere? my Doe?

M. Ford. Sir *Iohn*? Art thou there (my *Deere*?) My male-Deere?

Fal. My Doe, with the blacke Scut? Let the skie raine Potatoes: let it thunder, to the tune of Greene-ſleeues, haile-kiſſing Comfits, and ſnow Eringoes: Let there come a tempeſt of prouocation, I will ſhelter mee heere.

M. Ford. Miſtris *Page* is come with me (ſweet hart.)

Fal. Diuide me like a brib'd-Bucke, each a Haunch: I will keepe my ſides to my ſelfe, my ſhoulders for the fellow of this walke; and my hornes I bequeath your husbands. Am I a Woodman, ha? Speake I like *Herne* the Hunter? Why, now is Cupid a child of conſcience, he makes reſtitution. As I am a true ſpirit, welcome.

M. Page. Alas, what noiſe?

M. Ford. Heauen forgiue our ſinnes.

Fal. What ſhould this be?

M. Ford. M. Page Away, away.

Fal. I thinke the diuell wil not haue me damn'd, Leaſt the oyle that's in me ſhould ſet hell on fire; He would neuer elſe croſſe me thus.

Enter Fairies.

Qui. Fairies blacke, gray, greene, and white, You Moone-ſhine reuellers, and ſhades of night. You Orphan heires of fixed deſtiny, Attend your office, and your quality. Crier Hob-goblyn, make the Fairy Oyes.

Piſt. Elues, lift your names: Silence you aiery toyes. Cricket, to Windſor-chimnies ſhalt thou leape; Where fires thou find'ſt vnrak'd, and hearths vnſwept, There pinch the Maids as blew as Bill-berry, Our radiant Queene, hates Sluts, and Sluttery.

Fal. They are Fairies, he that ſpeaks to them ſhall die, Ile winke, and couch: No man their workes muſt eie.

Eu. Wher's *Bede*? Go you, and where you find a maid That ere ſhe ſleepe has thrice her prayers ſaid, Raiſe vp the Organs of her fantaſie, Sleepe ſhe as ſound as careleſſe infancie, But thoſe as ſleepe, and thinke not on their ſins, Pinch them armes, legs, backes, ſhoulders, ſides, & ſhins.

Qy. About, about: Search Windſor Caſtle (Elues) within, and out. Strew good lucke (Ouphes) on euery ſacred roome, That it may ſtand till the perpetuall doome, In ſtate as wholſome, as in ſtate 'tis fit, Worthy the Owner, and the Owner it. The ſeuerall Chaires of Order, looke you ſcowre With iuyce of Balme; and euery precious flowre, Each faire Inſtalment, Coate, and ſeu'rall Creſt, With loyall Blazon, euermore bleſt. And Nightly-meadow-Fairies, looke you ſing Like to the *Garters*-Compaſſe, in a ring, Th'expreſſure that it beares: Greene let it be, Mote fertile-freſh then all the Field to ſee: And, *Hony Soit Qui Mal-y-Pence*, write In Emrold-tuffes, Flowres purple, blew, and white, Like Saphire-pearle, and rich embroiderie,

Buckled below faire Knight-hoods bending knee; Fairies vſe Flowres for their charaĉterie. Away, diſperſe: But till 'tis one a clocke, Our Dance of Cuſtome, round about the Oke Of *Herne* the Hunter, let vs not forget. (ſet:

Euan. Pray you lock hand in hand: your ſelues in order And twenty glow-wormes ſhall our Lanthornes bee To guide our Meaſure round about the Tree. But ſtay, I ſmell a man of middle earth.

Fal. Heauens defend me from that Welſh Fairy, Leaſt he transforme me to a peece of Cheeſe.

Piſt. Vilde worme, thou waſt ore-look'd euen in thy birth.

Qu. With Triall-fire touch me his finger end: If he be chaſte, the flame will backe deſcend And turne him to no paine: but if he ſtart, It is the fleſh of a corrupted hart.

Piſt. A triall, come.

Eua. Come: will this wood take fire?

Fal. Oh, oh, oh.

Qui. Corrupt, corrupt, and tainted in deſire. About him (Fairies) ſing a ſcornfull rime, And as you trip, ſtill pinch him to your time.

The Song.

Fie on ſinnefull phantaſie: Fie on Luſt, and Luxurie: Luſt is but a bloudy fire, kindled with vnchaſte deſire, Fed in heart whoſe flames aſpire, As thoughts do blow them higher and higher. Pinch him (Fairies) mutually: Pinch him for his villanie. Pinch him, and burne him, and turne him about, Till Candles, & Star-light, & Moone-ſhine be out.

Page. Nay do not flye, I thinke we haue watcht you now: VVill none but *Herne* the Hunter ſerue your turne?

M. Page. I pray you come, hold vp the ieſt no higher. Now (good Sir *Iohn*) how like you *Windſor* wiues? See you theſe husband? Do not theſe faire yoakes Become the Forreſt better then the Towne?

Ford. Now Sir, whoſe a Cuckold now?

Mr *Broome*, *Falſtaffes* a Knaue, a Cuckoldly knaue, Heere are his hornes Maſter *Broome*: And Maſter *Broome*, he hath enioyed nothing of *Fords*, but his Buck-basket, his cudgell, and twenty pounds of money, which muſt be paid to Mr *Broome*, his horſes are arreſted for it, Mr *Broome*.

M. Ford. Sir *Iohn*, we haue had ill lucke: wee could neuer meete: I will neuer take you for my Loue againe, but I will alwayes count you my Deere.

Fal. I do begin to perceiue that I am made an Aſſe.

Ford. I, and an Oxe too: both the proofes are extant.

Fal. And theſe are not Fairies: I was three or foure times in the thought they were not Fairies, and yet the guiltineſſe of my minde, the ſodaine ſurprize of my powers, droue the groſſeneſſe of the foppery into a receiu'd beleefe, in deſpight of the teeth of all rime and reaſon, that they were Fairies. See now how wit may be made a Iacke-a-Lent, when 'tis vpon ill imployment.

Euant. Sir *Iohn Falſtaffe*, ſerue Got, and leaue your deſires, and Fairies will not pinſe you.

Ford. VVell ſaid Fairy *Hugh*.

Euans. And leaue you your iealouzies too, I pray you.

Ford.

Ford. I will neuer miſtruſt my wife againe, till thou art able to woo her in good Engliſh.

Fal. Haue I laid my braine in the Sun, and dri'de it, that it wants matter to preuent ſo groſſe ore-reaching as this? Am I ridden with a Welch Goate too? Shal I haue a Coxcombe of Frize? Tis time I were choak'd with a peece of toaſted Cheeſe.

Eu. Seeſe is not good to glue putter; your belly is al putter.

Fal. Seeſe, and Putter? Haue I liu'd to ſtand at the taunt of one that makes Fritters of Engliſh? This is e-nough to be the decay of luſt and late-walking through the Realme.

Miſt. Page. Why Sir *Iohn,* do you thinke though wee would haue thruſt vertue out of our hearts by the head and ſhoulders, and haue giuen our ſelues without ſcru-ple to hell, that euer the deuill could haue made you our delight?

Ford. What, a hodge-pudding? A bag of flax?

Miſt. Page. A puſt man?

Page. Old, cold, wither'd, and of intollerable en-trailes?

Ford. And one that is as ſlanderous as Sathan?

Page. And as poore as Iob?

Ford. And as wicked as his wife?

Euan. And giuen to Fornications, and to Tauernes, and Sacke, and Wine, and Metheglins, and to drinkings and ſwearings, and ſtarings? Pribles and prables?

Fal. Well, I am your Theame : you haue the ſtart of me, I am deiected : I am not able to anſwer the Welch Flannell, Ignorance it ſelfe is a plummet ore me, vſe me as you will.

Ford. Marry Sir, wee'l bring you to Windſor to one Mr *Broome,* that you haue cozon'd of money, to whom you ſhould haue bin a Pander : ouer and aboue that you haue ſuffer'd, I thinke, to repay that money will be a bi-ting affliction.

Page. Yet be cheerefull Knight : thou ſhalt eat a poſ-ſet to night at my houſe, wher I will deſire thee to laugh at my wife, that now laughes at thee : Tell her Mr *Slen-der* hath married her daughter.

Miſt. Page. Doctors doubt that; If *Anne Page* be my daughter, ſhe is (by this) Doctour *Caius* wife.

Slen. Whoa hoe, hoe, Father *Page.*

Page. Sonne? How now? How now Sonne, Haue you diſpatch'd?

Slen. Diſpatch'd? Ile make the beſt in Gloſterſhire know on't : would I were hang'd la, elſe.

Page. Of what ſonne?

Slen. I came yonder at *Eaton* to marry Miſtris *Anne Page,* and ſhe's a great lubberly boy. If it had not beene i'th Church, I would haue ſwing'd him, or hee ſhould haue ſwing'd me. If I did not thinke it had beene *Anne Page,* would I might neuer ſtirre, and 'tis a Poſt-maſters Boy.

Page. Vpon my life then, you tooke the wrong.

Slen. What neede you tell me that? I think ſo, when I tooke a Boy for a Girle : If I had bene married to him, (for all he was in womans apparrell) I would not haue had him.

Page. Why this is your owne folly, Did not I tell you how you ſhould know my daughter, By her garments?

Slen. I went to her in greene, and cried Mum, and ſhe cride budget, as *Anne* and I had appointed, and yet it was not *Anne,* but a Poſt-maſters boy.

Miſt. Page. Good *George* be not angry, I knew of your purpoſe : turn'd my daughter into white, and in-deede ſhe is now with the Doctor at the Deanrie, and there married.

Cai. Ver is Miſtris *Page* : by gar I am cozoned, I ha married oon Garſoon, a boy; oon peſant, by gar. A boy, it is not *An Page,* by gar, I am cozened.

M. Page. VVhy? did you take her in white?

Cai. I bee gar, and 'tis a boy : be gar, Ile raiſe all Windſor.

Ford. This is ſtrange : Who hath got the right *Anne?*

Page. My heart miſgiues me, here comes Mr *Fenton.* How now Mr *Fenton?*

Anne. Purdon good father, good my mother pardon

Page. Now Miſtris : How chance you went not with Mr *Slender?*

M. Page. Why went you not with Mr Doctor, maid?

Fen. You do amaze her : heare the truth of it, You would haue married her moſt ſhamefully, Where there was no proportion held in loue : The truth is, ſhe and I (long ſince contracted) Are now ſo ſure that nothing can diſſolue vs : Th'offence is holy, that ſhe hath committed, And this deceit looſes the name of craft, Of diſobedience, or vnduteous title, Since therein ſhe doth euitate and ſhun A thouſand irreligious curſed houres Which forced marriage would haue brought vpon her.

Ford. Stand not amaz'd, here is no remedie : In Loue, the heauens themſelues do guide the ſtate, Money buyes Lands, and wiues are ſold by fate.

Fal. I am glad, though you haue tane a ſpecial ſtand to ſtrike at me, that your Arrow hath glanc'd.

Page. Well, what remedy? *Fenton,* heauen giue thee Ioy, what cannot be eſchew'd, muſt be embrac'd.

Fal. When night-dogges run, all ſorts of Deere are chac'd.

Miſt Page. Well, I will muſe no further : Mr *Fenton,* Heauen giue you many, many merry dayes : Good husband, let vs euery one go home, And laugh this ſport ore by a Countrie fire, Sir *Iohn* and all.

Ford. Let it be ſo (Sir *Iohn:*) To Maſter *Broome,* you yet ſhall hold yourword, For he, to night, ſhall lye with Miſtris *Ford:*   *Exeunt.*

FINIS.

MEASVRE,
For Meafure.

Actus primus, Scena prima.

Enter Duke, Efcalus, Lords.

Duke.

Scalus.

Efc. My Lord. (fold,

Duk. Of Gouernment, the properties to vn-
Would feeme in me t'affect fpeech & difcourfe,
Since I am put to know, that your owne Science
Exceedes (in that) the lifts of all aduice
My ftrength can giue you : Then no more remaines
But that, to your fufficiency, as your worth is able,
And let them worke : The nature of our People,
Our *Cities Inftitutions*, and the Termes
For Common Iuftice, y'are as pregnant in
As Art, and practife, hath inriched any
That we remember : There is our Commiffion,
From which, we would not haue you warpe ; call hither,
I fay, bid come before vs *Angelo* :
What figure of vs thinke you, he will beare.
For you muft know, we haue with fpeciall foule
Elected him our abfence to fupply ;
Lent him our terror, dreft him with our loue,
And giuen his Deputation all the Organs
Of our owne powre : What thinke you of it?

Efc. If any in *Vienna* be of worth
To vndergoe fuch ample grace, and honour,
It is Lord *Angelo*.

Enter Angelo.

Duk. Looke where he comes.

Ang. Always obedient to your Graces will,
I come to know your pleafure.

Duke. *Angelo* :
There is a kinde of Character in thy life,
That to th'obferuer, doth thy hiftory
Fully vnfold : Thy felfe, and thy belongings
Are not thine owne fo proper, as to wafte
Thy felfe vpon thy vertues ; they on thee :
Heauen doth with vs, as we, with Torches doe,
Not light them for themfelues : For if our vertues
Did not goe forth of vs, 'twere all alike
As if we had them not : Spirits are not finely tonch'd,
But to fine iffues : nor nature neuer lends
The fmalleft fcruple of her excellence,
But like a thrifty goddeffe, fhe determines
Her felfe the glory of a creditour,
Both thanks, and vfe ; but I do bend my fpeech

To one that can my part in him aduertife ;
Hold therefore *Angelo* :
In our remoue, be thou at full, our felfe :
Mortallitie and Mercie in *Vienna*
Liue in thy tongue, and heart : Old *Efcalus*
Though firft in queftion, is thy fecondary.
Take thy Commiffion.

Ang. Now good my Lord
Let there be fome more teft, made of my mettle,
Before fo noble, and fo great a figure
Be ftamp'd vpon it.

Duk. No more euafion :
We haue with a leauen'd, and prepared choice
Proceeded to you ; therefore take your honors :
Our hafte from hence is of fo quicke condition,
That it prefers it felfe, and leaues vnqueftion'd
Matters of needfull value : We fhall write to you
As time, and our concernings fhall importune,
How it goes with vs, and doe looke to know
What doth befall you here. So fare you well :
To th' hopefull execution doe I leaue you,
Of your Commiffions.

Ang. Yet giue leaue (my Lord,)
That we may bring you fomething on the way.

Duk. My hafte may not admit it,
Nor neede you (on mine honor) haue to doe
With any fcruple : your fcope is as mine owne,
So to inforce, or qualifie the Lawes
As to your foule feemes good : Giue me your hand,
Ile priuily away : I loue the people,
But doe not like to ftage me to their eyes :
Though it doe well, I doe not rellifh well
Their lowd applaufe, and Aues vehement :
Nor doe I thinke the man of fafe difcretion
That do's affect it. Once more fare you well.

Ang. The heauens giue fafety to your purpofes.

Efc. Lead forth, and bring you backe in happineffe. *Exit.*

Duk. I thanke you, fare you well.

Efc. I fhall defire you, Sir, to giue me leaue
To haue free fpeech with you ; and it concernes me
To looke into the bottome of my place :
A powre I haue, but of what ftrength and nature,
I am not yet inftructed.

Ang. 'Tis fo with me : Let vs with-draw together,
And we may foone our fatisfaction haue
Touching that point.

Efc. Ile wait vpon your honor. *Exeunt.*

F *Scæna*

Scena Secunda.

Enter Lucio, and two other Gentlemen.

Luc. If the *Duke*, with the other Dukes, come not to
compoſition with the King of *Hungary*, why then all the
Dukes fall vpon the King.

1.Gent. Heauen grant vs its peace, but not the King
of *Hungaries*.

2.Gent. Amen.

Luc. Thou eonclud'ſt like the Sanctimonious Pirat,
that went to ſea with the ten Commandements, but
ſcrap'd one out of the Table.

2.Gent. Thou ſhalt not Steale?

Luc. I, that he raz'd.

1.Gent. Why? 'twas a commandement, to command
the Captaine and all the reſt from their functions: they
put forth to ſteale: There's not a Souldier of vs all, that
in the thankſ-giuing before meate, do ralliſh the petition
well, that praies for peace.

2.Gent. I neuer heard any Souldier diſlike it.

Luc. I beleeue thee: for I thinke thou neuer was't
where Grace was ſaid.

2.Gent. No? a dozen times at leaſt.

1.Gent. What? In meeter?

Luc. In any proportion: or in any language.

1.Gent. I thinke, or in any Religion.

Luc. I, why not? Grace, is Grace, deſpight of all controuerſie: as for example; Thou thy ſelfe art a wicked
villaine, deſpight of all Grace.

1.Gent. Well: there went but a paire of ſheeres betweene vs.

Luc. I grant: as there may betweene the Liſts, and
the Veluet. Thou art the Liſt.

1.Gent. And thou the Veluet; thou art good veluet;
thou'rt a three pild-peece I warrant thee: I had as lieſe
be a Lyſt of an Engliſh Kerſey, as be pil'd, as thou art
pil'd, for a French Veluet. Do I ſpeake feelingly now?

Luc. I thinke thou do'ſt: and indeed with moſt painfull feeling of thy ſpeech: I will, out of thine owne confeſſion, learne to begin thy health; but, whilſt I liue forget to drinke after thee.

1.Gen. I think I haue done my ſelfe wrong, haue I not?

2.Gent. Yes, that thou haſt; whether thou art tainted,
or free.   *Enter Bawde.*

Luc. Behold, behold, where Madam *Mitigation* comes.
I haue purchaſ'd as many diſeaſes vnder her Roofe,
As come to

2.Gent. To what, I pray?

Luc. Iudge.

2.Gent. To three thouſand Dollours a yeare.

1.Gent. I, and more.

Luc. A French crowne more.

1.Gent. Thou art alwayes figuring diſeaſes in me; but
thou art full of error, I am ſound.

Luc. Nay, not (as one would ſay) healthy: but ſo
ſound, as things that are hollow; thy bones are hollow;
Impiety has made a feaſt of thee.

1.Gent. How now, which of your hips has the moſt
profound Ciatica?

Bawd. Well, well: there's one yonder arreſted, and
carried to priſon, was worth fiue thouſand of you all.

2.Gent. Who's that I pray'thee?

Bawd. Marry Sir, that's *Claudio*, Signior *Claudio*.

1.Gent. *Claudio* to priſon? 'tis not ſo.

Bawd. Nay, but I know 'tis ſo: I ſaw him arreſted:
ſaw him carried away: and which is more, within theſe
three daies his head to be chop'd off.

Luc. But, after all this fooling, I would not haue it ſo:
Art thou ſure of this?

Bawd. I am too ſure of it: and it is for getting Madam
Iulietta with childe.

Luc. Beleeue me this may be: he promis'd to meete
me two howres ſince, and he was euer preciſe in promiſe
keeping.

2.Gent. Beſides you know, it drawes ſomthing neere
to the ſpeech we had to ſuch a purpoſe.

1.Gent. But moſt of all agreeing with the proclamatiõ.

Luc. Away: let's goe learne the truth of it.   *Exit.*

Bawd. Thus, what with the war; what with the ſweat,
what with the gallowes, and what with pouerty, I am
Cuſtom-ſhrunke. How now? what's the newes with
you.   *Enter Clowne.*

Clo. Yonder man is carried to priſon.

Baw. Well: what has he done?

Clo. A Woman.

Baw. But what's his offence?

Clo. Groping for Trowts, in a peculiar Riuer.

Baw. What? is there a maid with child by him?

Clo. No: but there's a woman with maid by him:
you haue not heard of the proclamation, haue you?

Baw. What proclamation, man?

Clow. All howſes in the Suburbs of *Vienna* muſt bee
pluck'd downe.

Bawd. And what ſhall become of thoſe in the Citie?

Clow. They ſhall ſtand for ſeed: they had gon down
to, but that a wiſe Burger put in for them.

Bawd. But ſhall all our houſes of reſort in the Suburbs be puld downe?

Clow. To the ground, Miſtris.

Bawd. Why heere's a change indeed in the Common-
wealth: what ſhall become of me?

Clow. Come: feare not you: good Counſellors lacke
no Clients: though you change your place, you neede
not change your Trade: Ile bee your Tapſter ſtill; courage, there will bee pitty taken on you; you that haue
worne your eyes almoſt out in the ſeruice, you will bee
conſidered.

Bawd. What's to doe heere, *Thomas* Tapſter? let's
withdraw?

Clo. Here comes Signior *Claudio*, led by the Prouoſt
to priſon: and there's Madam *Iuliet*.   *Exeunt.*

Scena Tertia.

Enter Prouoſt, Claudio, Iuliet, Officers, Lucio, & 2.Gent.

Cla. Fellow, why do'ſt thou ſhow me thus to th'world?
Beare me to priſon, where I am committed.

Pro. I do it not in euill diſpoſition,
But from Lord *Angelo* by ſpeciall charge.

Clau. Thus can the demy-god (Authority)
Make vs pay downe, for our offence, by waight
The words of heauen; on whom it will, it will,
On whom it will not (ſoe) yet ſtill 'tis iuſt.   (ſtraint.

Luc. Why how now *Claudio*? whence comes this re-

Cla. From too much liberty, (my *Lucio*) Liberty
As ſurfet is the father of much faſt,
So euery Scope by the immoderate vſe
Turnes to reſtraint: Our Natures doe purſue

                                 Like

Like Rats that rauyn downe their proper Bane,
A thirſty euill, and when we drinke, we die.

 Luc. If I could ſpeake ſo wiſely vnder an arreſt, I
would ſend for certaine of my Creditors *:* and yet, to ſay
the truth, I had as lief haue the foppery of freedome, as
the mortality of impriſonment : what's thy offence,
Claudio ?

 Cla. What (but to ſpeake of) would offend againe.

 Luc. What, is't murder ?

 Cla. No.

 Luc. Lecherie ?

 Cla. Call it ſo.

 Pro. Away, Sir, you muſt goe.

 Cla. One word, good friend :
Lucio, a word with you.

 Luc. A hundred :
If they'll doe you any good : Is *Lechery* ſo look'd after ?

 Cla. Thus ſtands it with me : vpon a true contract
I got poſſeſſion of *Iuliet* as bed,
You know the Lady, ſhe is faſt my wife,
Saue that we doe the denunciation lacke
Of outward Order.   This we came not to,
Onely for propogation of a Dowre
Remaining in the Coffer of her friends,
From whom we thought it meet to hide our Loue
Till Time had made them for vs. But it chances
The ſtealth of our moſt mutuall entertainment
With Character too groſſe, is writ on *Iuliet.*

 Luc. With childe, perhaps?

 Cla. Vnhappely, euen ſo.
And the new Deputie, now for the Duke,
Whether it be the fault and glimpſe of newnes,
Or whether that the body publique, be
A horſe whereon the Gouernor doth ride,
Who newly in the Seate, that it may know
He can command ; lets it ſtrait feele the ſpur :
Whether the Tirranny be in his place,
Or in his Eminence that fills it vp
I ſtagger in : But this new Gouernor
Awakes me all the inrolled penalties
Which haue (like vn-ſcowr'd Armor) hung by th'wall
So long, that ninteene Zodiacks haue gone round,
And none of them beene worne ; and for a name
Now puts the drowſie and negleƈed Aƈ
Freſhly on me : 'tis ſurely for a name.

 Luc. I warrant it is : And thy head ſtands ſo tickle on
thy ſhoulders, that a milke-maid, if ſhe be in loue, may
ſigh it off : Send after the Duke, and appeale to him.

 Cla. I haue done ſo, but hee's not to be found.
I pre'thee (*Lucio*) doe me this kinde ſeruice *:*
This day, my ſiſter ſhould the Cloyſter enter,
And there receiue her approbation.
Acquaint her with the danger of my ſtate,
Implore her, in my voice, that ſhe make friends
To the ſtriƈ deputie : bid her ſelfe aſſay him,
I haue great hope in that : for in her youth
There is a prone and ſpeechleſſe dialeƈ,
Such as moue men : beſide, ſhe hath proſperous Art
When ſhe will play with reaſon, and diſcourſe,
And well ſhe can perſwade.

 Luc. I pray ſhee may ; aſwell for the encouragement
of the like, which elſe would ſtand vnder greeuous im-
poſition *:* as for the enioying of thy life, who I would be
ſorry ſhould bee thus fooliſhly loſt, at a game of ticke-
tacke *:* Ile to her.

 Cla. I thanke you good friend *Lucio.*

 Luc. Within two houres.

 Cla. Come Officer, away.   *Exeunt.*

Scena Quarta.

Enter Duke and Frier Thomas.

 Duk. No : holy Father, throw away that thought,
Beleeue not that the dribling dart of Loue
Can pierce a compleat boſome : why, I deſire thee
To giue me ſecret harbour, hath a purpoſe
More graue, and wrinkled, then the aimes, and ends
Of burning youth.

 Fri. May your Grace ſpeake of it ?

 Duk. My holy Sir, none better knowes then you
How I haue euer lou'd the life remoued
And held in idle price, to haunt aſſemblies
Where youth, and coſt, witleſſe brauery keepes.
I haue deliuer'd to Lord *Angelo*
(A man of ſtriƈure and firme abſtinence)
My abſolute power, and place here in *Vienna,*
And he ſuppoſes me trauaild to *Poland,*
(For ſo I haue ſtrewd it in the common eare)
And ſo it is receiu'd : Now (pious Sir)
You will demand of me, why I do this.

 Fri. Gladly, my Lord.

 Duk. We haue ſtriƈ Statutes, and moſt biting Laws,
(The needfull bits and curbes to headſtrong weedes,)
Which for this foureteene yeares, we haue let ſlip,
Euen like an ore-growne Lyon in a Caue
That goes not out to prey : Now, as fond Fathers,
Hauing bound vp the threatning twigs of birch,
Onely to ſticke it in their childrens ſight,
For terror, not to vſe : in time the rod
More mock'd, then fear'd : ſo our Decrees,
Dead to infliƈion, to themſelues are dead,
And libertie, plucks Iuſtice by the noſe ;
The Baby beates the Nurſe, and quite athwart
Goes all decorum.

 Fri. It reſted in your Grace
To vnlooſe this tyde-vp Iuſtice, when you pleaſ'd :
And it in you more dreadfull would haue ſeem'd
Then in Lord *Angelo.*

 Duk. I doe feare : too dreadfull :
Sith 'twas my fault, to giue the people ſcope,
'Twould be my tirrany to ſtrike and gall them,
For what I bid them doe : For, we bid this be done
When euill deedes haue their permiſſiue paſſe,
And not the puniſhment : therefore indeede (my father)
I haue on *Angelo* impos'd the office,
Who may in th'ambuſh of my name, ſtrike home,
And yet, my nature neuer in the fight
To do in ſlander : And to behold his ſway
I will, as 'twere a brother of your Order,
Viſit both Prince, and People : Therefore I pre'thee
Supply me with the habit, and inſtruƈ me
How I may formally in perſon beare
Like a true *Frier* : Moe reaſons for this aƈion
At our more leyſure, ſhall I render you ;
Onely, this one : Lord *Angelo* is preciſe,
Stands at a guard with Enuie : ſcarce confeſſes
That his blood flowes : or that his appetite
Is more to bread then ſtone : hence ſhall we ſee
If power change purpoſe : what our Seemers be.   *Exit.*

Scena Quinta.

Enter Iſabell and Franciſca a Nun.

Iſa. And haue you *Nuns* no farther priuiledges?
Nun. Are not theſe large enough?
Iſa. Yes truely; I ſpeake not as deſiring more,
But rather wiſhing a more ſtrict reſtraint
Vpon the Siſterſtood, the Votariſts of Saint *Clare.*
Lucio within.
Luc. Hoa? peace be in this place.
Iſa: Who's that which cals?
Nun. It is a mans voice: gentle *Iſabella*
Turne you the key, and know his buſineſſe of him;
You may; I may not: you are yet vnſworne:
When you haue vowd, you muſt not ſpeake with men,
But in the preſence of the *Prioreſſe*;
Then if you ſpeake, you muſt not ſhow your face;
Or if you ſhow your face, you muſt not ſpeake.
He cals againe: I pray you anſwere him.
Iſa. Peace and proſperitie: who is't rhat cals?
Luc. Haile Virgin, (if you be) as thoſe cheeke-Roſes
Proclaime you are no leſſe: can you ſo ſteed me,
As bring me to the ſight of *Iſabella*,
A Nouice of this place, and the faire Siſter
To her vnhappie brother *Claudio*?
Iſa. Why her vnhappy Brother? Let me aske,
The rather for I now muſt make you know
I am her *Iſabella*, and his Siſter.
Luc. Gentle & faire: your Brother kindly greets you;
Not to be weary with you; he's in priſon.
Iſa. Woe me; for what?
Luc. For that, which if my ſelfe might be his Iudge,
He ſhould receiue his puniſhment, in thankes:
He hath got his friend with childe.
Iſa. Sir, make me not your ſtorie.
Luc. 'Tis true; I would not, though 'tis my familiar ſin,
With Maids to ſeeme the Lapwing, and to ieſt
Tongue, far from heart: play with all Virgins ſo:
I hold you as a thing en-skied, and ſainted,
By your renouncement, an imortall ſpirit
And to be talk'd with in ſincerity,
As with a Saint.
Iſa. You doe blaſpheme the good, in mocking me.
Luc. Doe not beleeue it: ſewnes, and truth; tis thus,
Your brother, and his louer haue embrac'd;
As thoſe that feed, grow full: as bloſſoming Time
That from the ſeednes, the bare fallow brings
To teemiug foyſon: euen ſo her plenteous wombe
Expreſſeth his full Tilth, and husbandry.
Iſa. Some one with childe by him? my coſen *Iuliet*?
Luc. Is ſhe your coſen?
Iſa. Adoptedly, as ſchoole-maids change their names
By vaine, though apt affection.
Luc. She it is.
Iſa. Oh, let him marry her.
Luc. This is the point.
The Duke is very ſtrangely gone from hence;
Bore many gentlemen (my ſelfe being one)
In hand, and hope of action: but we doe learne,
By thoſe that know the very Nerues of State,
His giuing-out, were of an infinite diſtance
From his true meant deſigne: vpon his place,

(And with full line of his authority)
Gouernes Lord *Angelo*; A man, whoſe blood
Is very ſnow-broth: one, who neuer feeles
The wanton ſtings, and motions of the ſence;
But doth rebate, and blunt his naturall edge
With profits of the minde: Studie, and faſt
He (to giue feare to vſe, and libertie,
Which haue, for long, run-by the hideous law,
As Myce, by Lyons) hath pickt out an act,
Vnder whoſe heauy ſence, your brothers life
Fals into forfeit: he arreſts him on it,
And followes cloſe the rigor of the Statute
To make him an example: all hope is gone,
Vnleſſe you haue the grace, by your faire praier
To ſoften *Angelo*: And that's my pith of buſineſſe
'Twixt you, and your poore brother.
Iſa. Doth he ſo,
Seeke his life?
Luc. Has cenſur'd him already,
And as I heare, the Prouoſt hath a warrant
For's execution.
Iſa. Alas: what poore
Abilitie's in me, to doe him good.
Luc. Aſſay the powre you haue.
Iſa. My power? alas, I doubt.
Luc. Our doubts are traitors
And makes vs looſe the good we oft might win,
By fearing to attempt: Goe to Lord *Angelo*
And let him learne to know, when Maidens ſue
Men giue like gods: but when they weepe and kneele,
All their petitions, are as freely theirs
As they themſelues would owe them.
Iſa. Ile ſee what I can doe.
Luc. But ſpeedily.
Iſa. I will about it ſtrait;
No longer ſtaying, but to giue the Mother
Notice of my affaire: I humbly thanke you:
Commend me to my brother: ſoone at night
Ile ſend him certaine word of my ſucceſſe.
Luc. I take my leaue of you.
Iſa. Good ſir, adieu.   *Exeunt.*

Actus Secundus. Scœna Prima.

Enter Angelo, Eſcalus, and ſeruants, Iuſtice.

Ang. We muſt not make a ſcar-crow of the Law,
Setting it vp to feare the Birds of prey,
And let it keepe one ſhape, till cuſtome make it
Their pearch, and not their terror.
Eſc. I, but yet
Let vs be keene, and rather cut a little
Then fall, and bruiſe to death: alas, this gentleman
Whom I would ſaue, had a moſt noble father,
Let but your honour know
(Whom I beleeue to be moſt ſtrait in vertue)
That in the working of your owne affections,
Had time coheard with Place, or place with wiſhing,
Or that the reſolute acting of our blood
Could haue attaind th'effect of your owne purpoſe,
Whether you had not ſometime in your life
Er'd in this point, which now you cenſure him,
And puld the Law vpon you.
Ang. 'Tis one thing to be tempted (*Eſcalus*)
                                      Another

Another thing to fall : I not deny
The Iury paffing on the Prifoners life
May in the fworne-twelue haue a thiefe, or two
Guiltier then him they try; what's open made to Iuftice,
That Iuftice ceizes; What knowes the Lawes
That theeues do paffe on theeues? 'Tis very pregnant,
The Iewell that we finde, we ftoope, and take't,
Becaufe we fee it; but what we doe not fee,
We tread vpon, and neuer thinke of it.
You may not fo extenuate his offence,
For I haue had fuch faults; but rather tell me
When I, that cenfure him, do fo offend,
Let mine owne Iudgement patterne out my death,
And nothing come in partiall. Sir, he muft dye.

Enter Prouoft.

Efc. Be it as your wifedome will.

Ang. Where is the *Prouoft* ?

Pro. Here if it like your honour.

Ang. See that *Claudio*
Be executed by nine to morrow morning,
Bring him his Confeffor, let him be prepar'd,
For that's the vtmoft of his pilgrimage.

Efc. Well : heauen forgiue him ; and forgiue vs all :
Some rife by finne, and fome by vertue fall :
Some run from brakes of Ice, and anfwere none,
And fome condemned for a fault alone.

Enter Elbow, Froth, Clowne, Officers.

Elb. Come, bring them away : if thefe be good people in a Common-weale, that doe nothing but vfe their
abufes in common houfes, I know no law : bring them
away.

Ang. How now Sir, what's your name ? And what's
the matter?

Elb. If it pleafe your honour, I am the poore *Dukes*
Conftable, and my name is *Elbow*; I doe leane vpon Iuftice Sir, and doe bring in here before your good honor,
two notorious Benefactors.

Ang. Benefactors? Well: What Benefactors are they?
Are they not Malefactors?

Elb. If it pleafe your honour, I know not well what
they are : But precife villaines they are, that I am fure of,
and void of all prophanation in the world, that good
Chriftians ought to haue.

Efc. This comes off well : here's a wife Officer.

Ang. Goe to : What quality are they of ? *Elbow* is
your name ?
Why do'ft thou not fpeake *Elbow* ?

Clo. He cannot Sir : he's out at Elbow.

Ang. What are you Sir?

Elb. He Sir : a Tapfter Sir : parcell Baud : one that
ferues a bad woman : whofe houfe Sir was (as they fay)
pluckt downe in the Suburbs : and now fhee profeffes a
hot-houfe ; which, I thinke is a very ill houfe too.

Efc. How know you that?

Elb. My wife Sir? whom I deteft before heauen, and
your honour.

Efc. How? thy wife?

Elb. I Sir: whom I thanke heauen is an honeft woman.

Efc. Do'ft thou deteft her therefore?

Elb. I fay fir, I will deteft my felfe alfo, as well as fhe,
that this houfe, if it be not a Bauds houfe, it is pitty of her
life, for it is a naughty houfe.

Efc. How do'ft thou know that, Conftable ?

Elb. Marry fir, by my wife, who, if fhe had bin a woman Cardinally giuen, might haue bin accus'd in forni-

cation, adultery, and all vncleanlineffe there.

Efc. By the womans meanes ?

Elb. I fir, by Miftris *Ouer-don* meanes: but as fhe fpit
in his face, fo fhe defide him.

Clo. Sir, if it pleafe your honor, this is not fo.

Elb. Proue it before thefe varlets here, thou honorable man, proue it.

Efc. Doe you heare how he mifplaces?

Clo. Sir, fhe came in great with childe : and longing
(fauing your honors reuerence) for ftewd prewyns ; fir,
we had but two in the houfe, which at that very diftant
time ftood, as it were in a fruit difh (a difh of fome three
pence ; your honours haue feene fuch difhes) they are not
China-difhes, but very good difhes.

Efc. Go too : go too : no matter for the difh fir.

Clo. No indeede fir not of a pin ; you are therein in
the right : but, to the point : As I fay, this Miftris *Elbow*,
being (as I fay) with childe, and being great bellied, and
longing (as I faid) for prewyns : and hauing but two in
the difh (as I faid) Mafter *Froth* here, this very man, hauing eaten the reft (as I faid) & (as I fay) paying for them
very honeftly : for, as you know Mafter *Froth*, I could not
giue you three pence againe.

Fro. No indeede.

Clo. Very well : you being then (if you be remembred) cracking the ftones of the forefaid prewyns.

Fro. I, fo I did indeede.

Clo. Why, very well : I telling you then (if you be
remembred) that fuch a one, and fuch a one, were paft
cure of the thing you wot of, vnleffe they kept very good
diet, as I told you.

Fro. All this is true.

Clo. Why very well then.

Efc. Come : you are a tedious foole : to the purpofe :
what was done to *Elbowes* wife, that hee hath caufe to
complaine of? Come me to what was done to her.

Clo. Sir, your honor cannot come to that yet.

Efc. No fir, nor I meane it not.

Clo. Sir, but you fhall come to it, by your honours
leaue : And I befeech you, looke into Mafter *Froth* here
fir, a man of foure-fcore pound a yeare ; whofe father
died at *Hallowmas* : Was't not at *Hallowmas* Mafter
Froth ?

Fro. Allhallond-Eue.

Clo. Why very well : I hope here be truthes : he Sir,
fitting (as I fay) in a lower chaire, Sir, 'twas in the bunch
of Grapes, where indeede you haue a delight to fit, haue
you not ?

Fro. I haue fo, becaufe it is an open roome, and good
for winter.

Clo. Why very well then : I hope here be truthes.

Ang. This will laft out a night in *Rufsia*
When nights are longeft there : Ile take my leaue,
And leaue you to the hearing of the caufe ;
Hoping youle finde good caufe to whip them all. *Exit.*

Efc. I thinke no leffe : good morrow to your Lordfhip. Now Sir, come on : What was done to *Elbowes*
wife, once more?

Clo. Once Sir ? there was nothing done to her once.

Elb. I befeech you Sir, aske him what this man did to
my wife.

Clo. I befeech your honor, aske me.

Efc. Well fir, what did this Gentleman to her ?

Clo. I befeech you fir, looke in this Gentlemans face:
good Mafter *Froth* looke vpon his honor; 'tis for a good
purpofe : doth your honor marke his face ?

F 3 *Efc.* I

Efc. I fir, very well.

Clo. Nay, I befeech you marke it well.

Efc. Well, I doe fo.

Clo. Doth your honor fee any harme in his face ?

Efc. Why no.

Clo. Ile be fuppofd vpon a booke, his face is the worft thing about him : good then : if his face be the worft thing about him, how could Mafter *Froth* doe the Conftables wife any harme ? I would know that of your honour.

Efc. He's in the right (Conftable) what fay you to it ?

Elb. Firft, and it like you, the houfe is a refpected houfe ; next, this is a refpected fellow ; and his Miftris is a refpected woman.

Clo. By this hand Sir, his wife is a more refpected perfon then any of vs all.

Elb. Varlet, thou lyeft; thou lyeft wicked varlet : the time is yet to come that fhee was euer refpected with man, woman, or childe.

Clo. Sir, fhe was refpected with him, before he married with her.

Efc. Which is the wifer here ; *Iuftice* or *Iniquitie* ? Is this true ?

Elb. O thou caytiffe : O thou varlet : O thou wicked *Hanniball* ; I refpected with her, before I was married to her ? If euer I was refpected with her, or fhe with me, let not your worfhip thinke mee the poore *Dukes* Officer : proue this, thou wicked *Hanniball* , or ile haue mine action of battry on thee.

Efc. If he tooke you a box 'oth'eare, you might haue your action of flander too.

Elb. Marry I thanke your good worfhip for it : what is't your Worfhips pleafure I fhall doe with this wicked Caitiffe ?

Efc. Truely Officer, becaufe he hath fome offences in him, that thou wouldft difcouer, if thou couldft, let him continue in his courfes, till thou knowft what they are.

Elb. Marry I thanke your worfhip for it : Thou feeft thou wicked varlet now, what's come vpon thee. Thou art to continue now thou Varlet, thou art to continue.

Efc. Where were you borne, friend ?

Froth. Here in *Vienna*, Sir.

Efc. Are you of fourefcore pounds a yeere ?

Froth. Yes, and 't pleafe you fir.

Efc. So : what trade are you of, fir ?

Clo. A Tapfter, a poore widdowes Tapfter.

Efc. Your Miftris name ?

Clo. Miftris *Ouer-don.*

Efc. Hath fhe had any more then one husband ?

Clo. Nine, fir : *Ouer-don* by the laft.

Efc. Nine ? come hether to me, Mafter *Froth* ; Mafter *Froth*, I would not haue you acquainted with Tapfters ; they will draw you Mafter *Froth*, and you wil hang them : get you gon, and let me heare no more of you.

Fro. I thanke your worfhip : for mine owne part, I neuer come into any roome in a Tap-houfe, but I am drawne in.

Efc. Well : no more of it Mafter *Froth* : farewell : Come you hether to me, M^r. Tapfter : what's your name Mr. Tapfter ?

Clo. *Pompey.*

Efc. What elfe ?

Clo. *Bum*, Sir.

Efc. Troth, and your bum is the greateft thing about you, fo that in the beaftlieft fence, you are *Pompey* the

great; *Pompey*, you are partly a bawd, *Pompey* ; howfoeuer you colour it in being a Tapfter, are you not ? come, tell me true, it fhall be the better for you.

Clo. Truely fir, I am a poore fellow that would liue.

Efc. How would you liue *Pompey* ? by being a bawd ? what doe you thinke of the trade *Pompey* ? is it a lawfull trade ?

Clo. If the Law would allow it, fir.

Efc. But the Law will not allow it *Pompey* ; nor it fhall not be allowed in *Vienna*.

Clo. Do's your Worfhip meane to geld and fplay all the youth of the City ?

Efc. No, *Pompey.*

Clo. Truely Sir, in my poore opinion they will too't then : if your worfhip will take order for the drabs and the knaues, you need not to feare the bawds.

Efc. There is pretty orders beginning I can tell you : It is but heading, and hanging.

Clo. If you head, and hang all that offend that way but for ten yeare together ; you'll be glad to giue out a Commiffion for more heads : if this law hold in *Vienna* ten yeare, ile rent the faireft houfe in it after three pence a Bay : if you liue to fee this come to paffe, fay *Pompey* told you fo.

Efc. Thanke you good *Pompey* ; and in requitall of your prophefie, harke you : I aduife you let me not finde you before me againe vpon any complaint whatfoeuer ; no, not for dwelling where you doe : if I doe *Pompey*, I fhall beat you to your Tent, and proue a fhrewd *Cæfar* to you : in plaine dealing *Pompey*, I fhall haue you whipt ; fo for this time, *Pompey*, fare you well.

Clo. I thanke your Worfhip for your good counfell ; but I fhall follow it as the flefh and fortune fhall better determine. Whip me ? no, no, let Carman whip his Iade, The valiant heart's not whipt out of his trade. *Exit.*

Efc. Come hether to me, Mafter *Elbow* : come hither Mafter Conftable : how long haue you bin in this place of Conftable ?

Elb. Seuen yeere, and a halfe fir.

Efc. I thought by the readineffe in the office, you had continued in it fome time : you fay feauen yeares together.

Elb. And a halfe fir.

Efc. Alas, it hath beene great paines to you : they do you wrong to put you fo oft vpon't. Are there not men in your Ward fufficient to ferue it ?

Elb. 'Faith fir, few of any wit in fuch matters : as they are chofen, they are glad to choofe me for them ; I do it for fome peece of money, and goe through with all.

Efc. Looke you bring mee in the names of fome fixe or feuen, the moft fufficient of your parifh.

Elb. To your Worfhips houfe fir ?

Efc. To my houfe : fare you well : what's a clocke, thinke you ?

Iuft. Eleuen, Sir.

Efc. I pray you home to dinner with me.

Iuft. I humbly thanke you.

Efc. It grieues me for the death of *Claudio*
But there's no remedie :

Iuft. Lord *Angelo* is feuere.

Efc. It is but needfull.
Mercy is not it felfe, that oft lookes fo,
Pardon is ftill the nurfe of fecond woe :
But yet, poore *Claudio* ; there is no remedie.
Come Sir. *Exeunt.*

Scæna

Scena Secunda.

Enter Prouoſt, Seruant.

Ser. Hee's hearing of a Cauſe; he will come ſtraight,
I'le tell him of you.

Pro. 'Pray you doe; Ile know
His pleaſure, may be he will relent; alas
He hath but as offended in a dreame,
All Sects, all Ages ſmack of this vice, and he
To die for't?

Enter Angelo.

Ang. Now, what's the matter *Prouoſt?*

Pro. Is it your will *Claudio* ſhall die to morrow?

Ang. Did not I tell thee yea? hadſt thou not order?
Why do'ſt thou aske againe?

Pro. Leſt I might be too raſh:
Vnder your good correction, I haue ſeene
When after execution, Iudgement hath
Repented ore his doome.

Ang. Goe to; let that be mine,
Doe you your office, or giue vp your Place,
And you ſhall well be ſpar'd.

Pro. I craue your Honours pardon:
What ſhall be done Sir, with the groaning *Iuliet?*
Shee's very neere her howre.

Ang. Diſpoſe of her
To ſome more fitter place; and that with ſpeed.

Ser. Here is the ſiſter of the man condemn'd,
Deſires acceſſe to you.

Ang. Hath he a Siſter?

Pro. I my good Lord, a very vertuous maid,
And to be ſhortlie of a Siſter-hood,
If not alreadie.

Ang. Well: let her be admitted,
See you the Fornicatreſſe be remou'd,
Let her haue needfull, but not lauiſh meanes,
There ſhall be order for't.

Enter Lucio and Iſabella.

Pro. 'Saue your Honour.   (will?

Ang. Stay a little while; y'are welcome: what's your

Iſab. I am a wofull Sutor to your Honour,
'Pleaſe but your Honor heare me.

Ang. Well: what's your ſuite.

Iſab. There is a vice that moſt I doe abhorre,
And moſt deſire ſhould meet the blow of Iuſtice;
For which I would not plead, but that I muſt,
For which I muſt not plead, but that I am
At warre, twixt will, and will not.

Ang. Well: the matter?

Iſab. I haue a brother is condemn'd to die,
I doe beſeech you let it be his fault,
And not my brother.

Pro. Heauen giue thee mouing graces.

Ang. Condemne the fault, and not the actor of it,
Why euery fault's condemnd ere it be done:
Mine were the verie Cipher of a Function
To fine the faults, whoſe fine ſtands in record,
And let goe by the Actor.

Iſab. Oh iuſt, but ſeuere Law:
I had a brother then; heauen keepe your honour.

Luc. Giue 't not ore ſo: to him againe, entreat him,
Kneele downe before him, hang vpon his gowne,
You are too cold: if you ſhould need a pin,

You could not with more tame a tongue deſire it:
To him, I ſay.

Iſab. Muſt he needs die?

Ang. Maiden, no remedie.

Iſab. Yes: I doe thinke that you might pardon him,
And neither heauen, nor man grieue at the mercy.

Ang. I will not doe't.

Iſab. But can you if you would?

Ang. Looke what I will not, that I cannot doe.

Iſab. But might you doe't & do the world no wrong
If ſo your heart were touch'd with that remorſe,
As mine is to him?

Ang. Hee's ſentenc'd, tis too late.

Luc. You are too cold.

Iſab. Too late? why no: I that doe ſpeak a word
May call it againe: well, beleeue this
No ceremony that to great ones longs,
Not the Kings Crowne; nor the deputed ſword,
The Marſhalls Truncheon, nor the Iudges Robe
Become them with one halfe ſo good a grace
As mercie does: If he had bin as you, and you as he,
You would haue ſlipt like him, but he like you
Would not haue beene ſo ſterne.

Ang. Pray you be gone.

Iſab. I would to heauen I had your potencie,
And you were *Iſabell:* ſhould it then be thus?
No: I would tell what 'twere to be a Iudge,
And what a priſoner.

Luc. I, touch him: there's the vaine.

Ang. Your Brother is a forfeit of the Law,
And you but waſte your words.

Iſab. Alas, alas:
Why all the ſoules that were, were forfeit once,
And he that might the vantage beſt haue tooke,
Found out the remedie: how would you be,
If he, which is the top of Iudgement, ſhould
But iudge you, as you are? Oh, thinke on that,
And mercie then will breathe within your lips
Like man new made.

Ang. Be you content, (faire Maid)
It is the Law, not I, condemne your brother,
Were he my kinſman, brother, or my ſonne,
It ſhould be thus with him: he muſt die to morrow.

Iſab. To morrow? oh, that's ſodaine,
Spare him, ſpare him:
Hee's not prepar'd for death; euen for our kitchins
We kill the fowle of ſeaſon: ſhall we ſerue heauen
With leſſe reſpect then we doe miniſter
To our groſſe-ſelues? good, good my Lord, bethink you;
Who is it that hath di'd for this offence?
There's many haue committed it.

Luc. I, well ſaid.

Ang. The Law hath not bin dead, thogh it hath ſlept
Thoſe many had not dar'd to doe that euill
If the firſt, that did th' Edict infringe
Had anſwer'd for his deed: Now 'tis awake,
Takes note of what is done, and like a Prophet
Lookes in a glaſſe that ſhewes what future euils
Either now, or by remiſſeneſſe, new conceiu'd,
And ſo in progreſſe to be hatch'd, and borne,
Are now to haue no ſucceſſiue degrees,
But here they liue to end.

Iſab. Yet ſhew ſome pittie.

Ang. I ſhew it moſt of all, when I ſhow Iuſtice;
For then I pittie thoſe I doe not know,
Which a diſmis'd offence, would after gaule

And

And doe him right, that anfwering one foule wrong
Liues not to act another. Be fatisfied ;
Your Brother dies to morrow ; be content.
Ifab. So you muft be y̆ firft that giues this fentence,
And hee, that fuffers : Oh, it is excellent
To haue a Giants ftrength : but it is tyrannous
To vfe it like a Giant.
  Luc. That's well faid.
  Ifab. Could great men thunder
As *Ioue* himfelfe do's, *Ioue* would neuer be quiet,
For euery pelting petty Officer
Would vfe his heauen for thunder;
Nothing but thunder : Mercifull heauen,
Thou rather with thy fharpe and fulpherous bolt
Splits the vn-wedgable and gnarled Oke,
Then the foft Mertill : But man, proud man,
Dreft in a little briefe authoritie,
Moft ignorant of what he's moft affur'd,
(His glaffie Effence) like an angry Ape
Plaies fuch phantaftique tricks before high heauen,
As makes the Angels weepe: who with our fpleenes,
Would all themfelues laugh mortall.
  Luc. Oh, to him, to him wench : he will relent,
Hee's comming : I perceiue't.
  Pro. Pray heauen fhe win him.
  Ifab. We cannot weigh our brother with our felfe,
Great men may left with Saints: tis wit in them,
But in the leffe fowle prophanation.
  Luc. Thou'rt i'th right (Girle) more o'that.
  Ifab. That in the Captaine's but a chollericke word,
Which in the Souldier is flat blafphemie.
  Luc. Art auis'd o'that? more on't.
  Ang. Why doe you put thefe fayings vpon me ?
  Ifab. Becaufe Authoritie, though it erre like others,
Hath yet a kinde of medicine in it felfe
That skins the vice o'th top ; goe to your bofome,
Knock there, and aske your heart what it doth know
That's like my brothers fault : if it confeffe
A naturall guiltineffe, fuch as is his,
Let it not found a thought vpon your tongue
Againft my brothers life.
  Ang. Shee fpeakes, and 'tis fuch fence
That my Sence breeds with it ; fare you well.
  Ifab. Gentle my Lord, turne backe.
  Ang. I will bethinke me : come againe to morrow.
  Ifa. Hark, how Ile bribe you : good my Lord turn back.
  Ang. How ? bribe me ?
  If. I, with fuch gifts that heauen fhall fhare with you.
  Luc. You had mar'd all elfe.
  Ifab. Not with fond Sickles of the tefted-gold,
Or Stones, whofe rate are either rich, or poore
As fancie values them : but with true prayers,
That fhall be vp at heauen, and enter there
Ere Sunne rife : prayers from preferued foules,
From fafting Maides, whofe mindes are dedicate
To nothing temporall.
  Ang. Well : come to me to morrow.
  Luc. Goe to : 'tis well ; away.
  Ifab. Heauen keepe your honour fafe.
  Ang. Amen.
For I am that way going to temptation,
Where prayers croffe.
  Ifab. At what hower to morrow,
Shall I attend your Lordfhip ?
  Ang. At any time 'fore-noone.
  Ifab. 'Saue your Honour.

  Ang. From thee : euen from thy vertue.
What's this ? what's this ? is this her fault, or mine ?
The Tempter, or the Tempted, who fins moft ? ha ?
Not fhe : nor doth fhe tempt : but it is I,
That, lying by the Violet in the Sunne ,
Doe as the Carrion do's, not as the flowre,
Corrupt with vertuous feafon : Can it be,
That Modefty may more betray our Sence
Then womans lightneffe ? hauing wafte ground enough,
Shall we defire to raze the Sanctuary
And pitch our euils there ? oh fie, fie, fie :
What doft thou ? or what art thou *Angelo* ?
Doft thou defire her fowly, for thofe things
That make her good ? oh, let her brother liue :
Theeues for their robbery haue authority,
When Iudges fteale themfelues : what, doe I loue her,
That I defire to heare her fpeake againe ?
And feaft vpon her eyes ? what is't I dreame on ?
Oh cunning enemy, that to catch a Saint,
With Saints doft bait thy hooke : moft dangerous
Is that temptation, that doth goad vs on
To finne, in louing vertue : neuer could the Strumpet
With all her double vigor, Art, and Nature
Once ftir my temper : but this vertuous Maid
Subdues me quite : Euer till now
When men were fond, I fmild, and wondred how. *Exit.*

Scena Tertia.

Enter Duke and Prouoft.

  Duke. Haile to you, *Prouoft*, fo I thinke you are.
  Pro. I am the Prouoft : whats your will, good Frier ?
  Duke. Bound by my charity, and my bleft order,
I come to vifite the afflicted fpirits
Here in the prifon : doe me the common right
To let me fee them : and to make me know
The nature of their crimes, that I may minifter
To them accordingly.
  Pro. I would do more then that, if more were needfull
Enter Iuliet.
Looke here comes one : a Gentlewoman of mine,
Who falling in the flawes of her owne youth,
Hath blifterd her report : She is with childe,
And he that got it, fentenc'd : a yong man,
More fit to doe another fuch offence,
Then dye for this.
  Duk. When muft he dye ?
  Pro. As I do thinke to morrow.
I haue prouided for you, ftay a while
And you fhall be conducted.
  Duk. Repent you (faire one) of the fin you carry ?
  Iul. I doe ; and beare the fhame moft patiently.
  Du. Ile teach you how you fhal araign your confciêce
And try your penitence, if it be found,
Or hollowly put on.
  Iul. Ile gladly learne.
  Duk. Loue you the man that wrong'd you ?
  Iul. Yes, as I loue the woman that wrong'd him.
  Duk. So then it feemes your moft offence full act
Was mutually committed.
  Iul. Mutually.
  Duk. Then was your fin of heauier kinde then his.
  Iul. I doe confeffe it, and repent it (Father.)

  Du. 'Tis

Duk. 'Tis meet fo (daughter) but leaft you do repent
As that the fin hath brought you to this fhame,
Which forrow is alwaies toward our felues, not heauen,
Showing we would not fpare heauen, as we loue it,
But as we ftand in feare.

Iul. I doe repent me, as it is an euill,
And take the fhame with ioy.

Duke. There reft :
Your partner (as I heare) muft die to morrow,
And I am going with inftruction to him :
Grace goe with you, *Benedicite.*   *Exit.*

Iul. Muft die to morrow ? oh iniurious Loue
That refpits me a life, whofe very comfort
Is ftill a dying horror.

Pro. 'Tis pitty of him.   *Exeunt.*

Scena Quarta.

Enter Angelo.

An. When I would pray, & think, I thinke, and pray
To feuerall fubiects : heauen hath my empty words,
Whilft my Inuention, hearing not my Tongue,
Anchors on *Ifabell* : heauen in my mouth,
As if I did but onely chew his name,
And in my heart the ftrong and fwelling euill
Of my conception : the ftate whereon I ftudied
Is like a good thing, being often read
Growne feard, and tedious : yea, my Grauitie
Wherein (let no man heare me) I take pride,
Could I, with boote, change for an idle plume
Which the ayre beats for vaine : oh forme,
How often doft thou with thy cafe, thy habit
Wrench awe from fooles, and tye the wifer foules
To thy falfe feeming ? Blood, thou art blood ,
Let's write good Angell on the Deuills horne
'Tis not the Deuills Creft : how now ? who's there ?

Enter Seruant.

Ser. One *Ifabell*, a Sifter, defires acceffe to you.

Ang. Teach her the way : oh, heauens
Why doe's my bloud thus mufter to my heart,
Making both it vnable for it felfe ,
And difpoffefsing all my other parts
Of neceffary fitneffe ?
So play the foolifh throngs with one that fwounds,
Come all to help him, and fo ftop the ayre
By which hee fhould reuiue : and euen fo
The generall fubiect to a wel-witht King
Quit their owne part, and in obfequious fondneffe
Crowd to his prefence, where their vn-taught loue
Muft needs appeare offence : how now faire Maid.

Enter Ifabella.

Ifab. I am come to know your pleafure.   (me,
An. That you might know it, wold much better pleafe
Then to demand what 'tis : your Brother cannot liue.

Ifab. Euen fo : heauen keepe your Honor.

Ang. Yet may he liue a while : and it may be
As long as you, or I : yet he muft die.

Ifab. Vnder your Sentence ?

Ang. Yea.

Ifab. When, I befeech you : that in his Reprieue
(Longer, or fhorter) he may be fo fitted
That his foule ficken not.

Ang. Ha ? fie, thefe filthy vices : It were as good

To pardon him, that hath from nature ftolne
A man already made, as to remit
Their fawcie fweetnes, that do coyne heauens Image
In ftamps that are forbid : 'tis all as eafie,
Falfely to take away a life true made,
As to put mettle in reftrained meanes
To make a falfe one.

Ifab. 'Tis fet downe fo in heauen, but not in earth.

Ang. Say you fo : then I fhall poze you quickly.
Which had you rather, that the moft iuft Law
Now tooke your brothers life, and to redeeme him
Giue vp your body to fuch fweet vncleanneffe
As fhe that he hath ftaind ?

Ifab. Sir, beleeue this.
I had rather giue my body, then my foule.

Ang. I talke not of your foule : our compel'd fins
Stand more for number, then for accompt.

Ifab. How fay you ?

Ang. Nay Ile not warrant that : for I can fpeake
Againft the thing I fay : Anfwere to this,
I (now the voyce of the recorded Law)
Pronounce a fentence on your Brothers life,
Might there not be a charitie in finne,
To faue this Brothers life ?

Ifab. Pleafe you to doo't,
Ile take it as a perill to my foule,
It is no finne at all, but charitie.

Ang. Pleaf'd you to doo't, at perill of your foule
Were equall poize of finne, and charitie.

Ifab. That I do beg his life, if it be finne
Heauen let me beare it : you granting of my fuit,
If that be fin, Ile make it my Morne-praier,
To haue it added to the faults of mine,
And nothing of your anfwere.

Ang. Nay, but heare me,
Your fence purfues not mine : either you are ignorant,
Or feeme fo crafty ; and that's not good.

Ifab. Let be ignorant, and in nothing good,
But gracioufly to know I am no better.

Ang. Thus wifdome wifhes to appeare moft bright,
When it doth taxe it felfe : As thefe blacke Mafques
Proclaime an en-fhield beauty ten times louder
Then beauty could difplaied : But marke me,
To be receiued plaine, Ile fpeake more groffe :
Your Brother is to dye.

Ifab. So.

Ang. And his offence is fo, as it appeares,
Accountant to the Law, vpon that paine.

Ifab. True.

Ang. Admit no other way to faue his life
(As I fubfcribe not that, nor any other,
But in the loffe of queftion) that you, his Sifter,
Finding your felfe defir'd of fuch a perfon,
Whofe creadit with the Iudge, or owne great place,
Could fetch your Brother from the Manacles
Of the all-building-Law : and that there were
No earthly meane to faue him, but that either
You muft lay downe the treafures of your body,
To this fuppofed, or elfe to let him fuffer :
What would you doe ?

Ifab. As much for my poore Brother, as my felfe ;
That is : were I vnder the tearmes of death,
Th'impreffion of keene whips, I'ld weare as Rubies,
And ftrip my felfe to death, as to a bed,
That longing haue bin ficke for, ere I'ld yeeld
My body vp to fhame.

Ang. That

Ang. Then muſt your brother die.

Iſa. And 'twer the cheaper way :
Better it were a brother dide at once,
Then that a ſiſter, by redeeming him
Should die for euer.

Ang. Were not you then as cruell as the Sentence,
That you haue ſlander'd ſo ?

Iſa. Ignomie in ranſome, and free pardon
Are of two houſes : lawfull mercie,
Is nothing kin to fowle redemption.

Ang. You ſeem'd of late to make the Law a tirant,
And rather prou'd the ſliding of your brother
A merriment, then a vice.

Iſa. Oh pardon me my Lord, it oft fals out
To haue, what we would haue,
We ſpeake not what vve meane ;
I ſomething do excuſe the thing I hate,
For his aduantage that I dearely loue.

Ang. We are all fraile.

Iſa. Elſe let my brother die,
If not a fedarie but onely he
Owe, and ſucceed thy weakneſſe.

Ang. Nay, women are fraile too.

Iſa. I, as the glaſſes where they view themſelues,
Which are as eaſie broke as they make formes :
Women? Helpe heauen ; men their creation marre
In profiting by them : Nay, call vs ten times fraile,
For we are ſoft, as our complexions are,
And credulous to falſe prints.

Ang. I thinke it well :
And from this teſtimonie of your owne ſex
(Since I ſuppoſe we are made to be no ſtronger
Then faults may ſhake our frames) let me be bold ;
I do arreſt your words. Be that you are,
That is a woman ; if you be more, you'r none.
If you be one (as you are well expreſt
By all externall warrants) ſhew it now,
By putting on the deſtin'd Liuerie.

Iſa. I haue no tongue but one; gentle my Lord,
Let me entreate you ſpeake the former language.

Ang. Plainlie conceiue I loue you.

Iſa. My brother did loue *Iuliet,*
And you tell me that he ſhall die for't.

Ang. He ſhall not *Iſabell* if you giue me loue.

Iſa. I know your vertue hath a licence in't,
Which ſeemes a little fouler then it is,
To plucke on others.

Ang. Beleeue me on mine Honor,
My words expreſſe my purpoſe.

Iſa. Ha? Little honor, to be much beleeu'd,
And moſt pernitious purpoſe : Seeming, ſeeming.
I will proclaime thee *Angelo,* looke for't.
Signe me a preſent pardon for my brother,
Or with an out-ſtretcht throate Ile tell the world aloud
What man thou art.

Ang. Who will beleeue thee *Iſabell* ?
My vnſoild name, th'auſteerneſſe of my life,
My vouch againſt you, and my place i'th State,
Will ſo your accuſation ouer-weigh,
That you ſhall ſtifle in your owne reporr,
And ſmell of calumnie. I haue begun,
And now I glue my ſenſuall race, the reine,
Fit thy conſent to my ſharpe appetite,
Lay by all nicetie, and prolixious bluſhes
That baniſh what they ſue for : Redeeme thy brother,
By yeelding vp thy bodie to my will,

Or elſe he muſt not onelie die the death,
But thy vnkindneſſe ſhall his death draw out
To lingring ſufferance : Anſwer me to morrow,
Or by the affeſtion that now guides me moſt,
Ile proue a Tirant to him. As for you,
Say what you can ; my falſe, ore-weighs your true. *Exit*

Iſa. To whom ſhould I complaine ? Did I tell this,
Who would beleeue me ? O perilous mouthes
That beare in them, one and the ſelfeſame tongue,
Either of condemnation, or approofe,
Bidding the Law make curtſie to their will,
Hooking both right and wrong to th'appetite,
To follow as it drawes. Ile to my brother,
Though he hath falne by prompture of the blood,
Yet hath he in him ſuch a minde of Honor,
That had he twentie heads to tender downe
On twentie bloodie blockes, hee'ld yeeld them vp,
Before his ſiſter ſhould her bodie ſtoope
To ſuch abhord pollution.
Then *Iſabell* liue chaſte, and brother die ;
"More then our Brother, is our Chaſtitie.
Ile tell him yet of *Angelo's* requeſt,
And fit his minde to death, for his ſoules reſt.   *Exit.*

Actus Tertius. Scena Prima.

Enter Duke, Claudio, and Prouoſt.

Du. So then you hope of pardon from Lord *Angelo* ?

Cla. The miſerable haue no other medicine
But onely hope : I'haue hope to liue, and am prepar'd to
die.

Duke. Be abſolute for death : either death or life
Shall thereby be the ſweeter. Reaſon thus with life :
If I do looſe thee, I do looſe a thing
That none but fooles would keepe : a breath thou art,
Seruile to all the skyle-influences,
That doſt this habitation where thou keepſt
Hourely afflict : Meerely, thou art deaths foole,
For him thou labourſt by thy flight to ſhun,
And yet runſt toward him ſtill. Thou art not noble,
For all th'accommodations that thou bearſt,
Are nurſt by baſeneſſe : Thou'rt by no meanes valiant,
For thou doſt feare the ſoft and tender forke
Of a poore worme : thy beſt of reſt is ſleepe,
And that thou oft prouoakſt, yet groſſelie fearſt
Thy death, which is no more. Thou art not thy ſelfe,
For thou exiſts on manie a thouſand graines
That iſſue out of duſt. Happie thou art not,
For what thou haſt not, ſtill thou ſtriu'ſt to get,
And what thou haſt forgetſt. Thou art not certaine,
For thy complexion ſhifts to ſtrange effects,
After the Moone : If thou art rich, thou'rt poore,
For like an Aſſe, whoſe backe with Ingots bowes;
Thou bearſt thy heauie riches but a iournie,
And death vnloads thee ; Friend haſt thou none.
For thine owne bowels which do call thee, ſire
The meere effuſion of thy proper loines
Do curſe the Gowt, Sapego, and the Rheume
For ending thee no ſooner. Thou haſt nor youth, nor age
But as it were an after-dinners ſleepe
Dreaming on both, for all thy bleſſed youth
Becomes as aged, and doth begge the almes
Of palſied-Eld : and when thou art old, and rich

Thou

Thou haft neither heate, affeﬆion, limbe, nor beautie
To make thy riches pleaſant : what's yet in this
That beares the name of life ? Yet in this life
Lie hid moe thouſand deaths; yet death we feare
That makes theſe oddes, all euen.
 Cla. I humblie thanke you.
To ſue to liue, I ﬁnde I ſeeke to die,
And ſeeking death, ﬁnde life : Let it come on.
   Enter Iſabella.
*Iſab.*What hoa? Peace heere; Grace, and good companie.
 Pro. Who's there ? Come in, the wiſh deſerues a welcome.
 Duke. Deere ſir, ere long Ile viſit you againe.
 Cla. Moﬆ holie Sir, I thanke you.
 Iſa. My buſineſſe is a word or two with *Claudio.*
 Pro. And verie welcom : looke Signior, here's your ſiﬆer.
 Duke. Prouoﬆ, a word with you.
 Pro. As manie as you pleaſe.
 *Duke.*Bring them to heare me ſpeak, where I may be conceal'd.
 Cla. Now ſiﬆer, what's the comfort?
 Iſa. Why,
As all comforts are : moﬆ good, moﬆ good indeede,
Lord *Angelo* hauing affaires to heauen
Intends you for his ſwift Ambaſſador,
Where you ſhall be an euerlaﬆing Leiger ;
Therefore your beﬆ appointment make with ſpeed,
To Morrow you ſet on.
 Clau. Is there no remedie ?
 Iſa. None, but ſuch remedie, as to ſaue a head
To cleaue a heart in twaine:
 Clau. But is there anie?
 Iſa. Yes brother, you may liue;
There is a diuelliſh mercie in the Iudge,
If you'l implore it, that will free your life,
But fetter you till death.
 Cla. Perpetuall durance?
 Iſa. I juﬆ, perpetuall durance, a reﬆraint
Through all the worlds vaﬆiditie you had
To a determin'd ſcope.
 Clau. But in what nature ?
 Iſa. In ſuch a one, as you conſenting too't,
Would barke your honor from that trunke you beare,
And leaue you naked.
 Clau. Let me know the point.
 Iſa. Oh, I do feare thee *Claudio,* and I quake,
Leaﬆ thou a feauorous life ſhouldﬆ entertaine,
And ſix or ſeuen winters more reſpeﬆ
Then a perpetuall Honor. Dar'ſt thou die ?
The ſence of death is moﬆ in apprehenſion,
And the poore Beetle that we treade vpon
In corporall ſufferance, ﬁnds a pang as great,
As when a Giant dies.
 Cla. Why giue you me this ſhame ?
Thinke you I can a reſolution fetch
From ﬂowrie tenderneſſe ? If I muſt die,
I will encounter darkneſſe as a bride,
And hugge it in mine armes.
 *Iſa.*There ſpake my brother : there my fathers graue
Did vtter forth a voice. Yes, thou muﬆ die :
Thou art too noble, to conſerue a life
In baſe appliances. This outward ſainted Deputie,
Whoſe ſetled viſage, and deliberate word
Nips youth i'th head, and follies doth emmew

As Falcon doth the Fowle, is yet a diuell :
His ﬁlth within being caﬆ, he would appeare
A pond, as deepe as hell.
 Cla. The prenzie, *Angelo* ?
 Iſa. Oh 'tis the cunning Liuerie of hell,
The damneﬆ bodie to inueﬆ, and couer
In prenzie gardes ; doﬆ thou thinke *Claudio,*
If I would yeeld him my virginitie
Thou might'ﬆ be freed ?
 Cla. Oh heauens, it cannot be.
 Iſa. Yes, he would giu't thee; from this rank offence
So to offend him ﬆill. This night's the time
That I ſhould do what I abhorre to name,
Or elſe thou dieſt to morrow.
 Clau. Thou ſhalt not do't.
 Iſa. O, were it but my life,
I'de throw it downe for your deliuerance
As frankely as a pin.
 Clau. Thankes deere *Iſabell.*
 Iſa. Be readie *Claudio,* for your death to morrow.
 Clau. Yes. Has he affeﬆions in him,
That thus can make him bite the Law by th'noſe,
When he would force it? Sure it is no ſinne,
Or of the deadly ſeuen it is the leaﬆ.
 Iſa. Which is the leaﬆ ?
 Cla. If it were damnable, he being ſo wiſe,
Why would he for the momentarie tricke
Be perdurable ﬁn'de ? Oh *Iſabell.*
 Iſa. What ſaies my brother ?
 Cla. Death is a fearefull thing.
 Iſa. And ſhamed life, a hatefull.
 Cla. I, but to die, and go we know not where,
To lie in cold obﬆruﬆion, and to rot,
This ſenſible warme motion, to become
A kneaded clod ; And the delighted ſpirit
To bath in ﬁerie ﬂoods, or to reſide
In thrilling Region of thicke-ribbed Ice,
To be impriſon'd in the viewleſſe windes
And blowne with reﬆleſſe violence round about
The pendant world : or to be worſe then worﬆ
Of thoſe, that lawleſſe and incertaine thought,
Imagine howling, 'tis too horrible.
The wearieﬆ, and moﬆ loathed worldly life
That Age, Ache, periury, and impriſonment
Can lay on nature, is a Paradiſe
To what we feare of death.
 Iſa. Alas, alas.
 Cla. Sweet Siﬆer, let me liue.
What ſinne you do, to ſaue a brothers life,
Nature diſpenſes with the deede ſo farre,
That it becomes a vertue.
 Iſa. Oh you beaﬆ,
Oh faithleſſe Coward, oh diſhoneﬆ wretch,
Wilt thou be made a man, out of my vice ?
Is't not a kinde of Inceﬆ, to take life
From mine owne ſiﬆers ſhame ? What ſhould I thinke,
Heauen ſhield my Mother plaid my Father faire :
For ſuch a warped ſlip of wilderneſſe
Nere iſſu'd from his blood. Take my deﬁance,
Die, periſh : Might but my bending downe
Repreeue thee from thy fate, it ſhould proceede.
Ile pray a thouſand praiers for thy death,
No word to ſaue thee.
 Cla. Nay heare me *Iſabell.*
 Iſa. Oh ﬁe, ﬁe, ﬁe:
Thy ſinn's not accidentall, but a Trade ;

         Mercie

Mercy to thee would proue it ſelfe a Bawd,
'Tis beſt that thou dieſt quickly.

Cla. Oh heare me *Iſabella.*

Duk. Vouchſafe a word, yong ſiſter, but one word.

Iſa. What is your Will.

Duk. Might you diſpenſe with your leyſure, I would
by and by haue ſome ſpeech with you : the ſatiſfaction I
would require, is likewiſe your owne benefit.

Iſa. I haue no ſuperfluous leyſure, my ſtay muſt be
ſtolen out of other affaires : but I will attend you a while.

Duke. Son, I haue ouer-heard what hath paſt between
you & your ſiſter. *Angelo* had neuer the purpoſe to corrupt her ; onely he hath made an aſſay of her vertue, to
practiſe his iudgement with the diſpoſition of natures.
She (hauing the truth of honour in her) hath made him
that gracious deniall, which he is moſt glad to receiue : I
am Confeſſor to *Angelo*, and I know this to be true, therfore prepare your ſelfe to death : do not ſatisfie your reſolution with hopes that are fallible, to morrow you
muſt die, goe to your knees, and make ready.

Cla. Let me aſk my ſiſter pardon, I am ſo out of loue
with life, that I will ſue to be rid of it.

Duke. Hold you there : farewell : *Prouoſt*, a word
with you.

Pro. What's your will (father ?)

Duk. That now you are come, you wil be gone : leaue
me a while with the Maid, my minde promiſes with my
habit, no loſſe ſhall touch her by my company.

Pro. In good time.　　　　　　　　　　　　*Exit.*

Duk. The hand that hath made you faire, hath made
you good : the goodnes that is cheape in beauty, makes
beauty briefe in goodnes ; but grace being the ſoule of
your complexion, ſhall keepe the body of it euer faire :
the aſſault that *Angelo* hath made to you, Fortune hath
conuaid to my vnderſtanding ; and but that frailty hath
examples for his falling, I ſhould wonder at *Angelo*: how
will you doe to content this Subſtitute, and to ſaue your
Brother?

Iſab. I am now going to reſolue him : I had rather
my brother die by the Law, then my ſonne ſhould be vn-
lawfullie borne. But (oh) how much is the good Duke
deceiu'd in *Angelo* : if euer he returne, and I can ſpeake
to him, I will open my lips in vaine, or diſcouer his gouernment.

Duke. That ſhall not be much amiſſe : yet, as the matter now ſtands, he will auoid your accuſation : he made
triall of you onelie. Therefore faſten your eare on my
aduiſings, to the loue I haue in doing good ; a remedie
preſents it ſelfe. I doe make my ſelfe beleeue that you
may moſt vprighteouſly do a poor wronged Lady a merited benefit; redeem your brother from theangry Law;
doe no ſtaine to your owne gracious perſon, and much
pleaſe the abſent Duke, if peraduenture he ſhall euer returne to haue hearing of this buſineſſe.

Iſab. Let me heare you ſpeake farther; I haue ſpirit to
do any thing that appeares not fowle in the truth of my
ſpirit.

Duke. Vertue is bold, and goodnes neuer fearefull :
Haue you not heard ſpeake of *Mariana* the ſiſter of *Fredericke* the great Souldier, who miſcarried at Sea?

Iſa. I haue heard of the Lady, and good words went
with her name.

Duke. Shee ſhould this *Angelo* haue married : was affianced to her oath, and the nuptiall appointed: between
which time of the contract, and limit of the ſolemnitie,
her brother *Fredericke* was wrackt at Sea, hauing in that

periſhed veſſell, the dowry of his ſiſter : but marke how
heauily this befell to the poore Gentlewoman, there ſhe
loſt a noble and renowned brother, in his loue toward
her, euer moſt kinde and naturall : with him the portion
and ſinew of her fortune, her marriage dowry : with
both, her combynate-husband, this well-ſeeming
Angelo.

Iſab. Can this be ſo ? did *Angelo* ſo leaue her?

Duke. Left her in her teares, & dried not one of them
with his comfort : ſwallowed his vowes whole, preten-
ding in her, diſcoueries of diſhonor : in few, beſtow'd
her on her owne lamentation, which ſhe yet weares for
his ſake : and he, a marble to her teares, is waſhed with
them, but relents not.

Iſab. What a merit were it in death to take this poore
maid from the world? what corruption in this life, that
it will let this man liue ? But how out of this can ſhee a-
uaile ?

Duke. It is a rupture that you may eaſily heale: and the
cure of it not onely ſaues your brother, but keepes you
from diſhonor in doing it.

Iſab. Shew me how (good Father.)

Duk. This fore-named Maid hath yet in her the continuance of her firſt affection : his vniuſt vnkindeneſſe
(that in all reaſon ſhould haue quenched her loue) hath
(like an impediment in the Current) made it more violent and vnruly : Goe you to *Angelo*, anſwere his requi-
ring with a plauſible obedience, agree with his demands
to the point : onely referre your ſelfe to this aduantage ;
firſt, that your ſtay with him may not be long : that the
time may haue all ſhadow, and ſilence in it : and the place
anſwere to conuenience : this being granted in courſe,
and now followes all : wee ſhall aduiſe this wronged
maid to ſteed vp your appointment, goe in your place:
if the encounter acknowledge it ſelfe heereafter, it may
compell him to her recompence ; and heere, by this is
your brother ſaued, your honor vntainted, the poore
Mariana aduantaged, and the corrupt Deputy ſcaled.
The Maid will I frame, and make fit for his attempt : if
you thinke well to carry this as you may, the doubleneſ
of the benefit defends the deceit from reproofe. What
thinke you of it ?

Iſab. The image of it giues me content already, and I
truſt it will grow to a moſt proſperous perfection.

Duk. It lies much in your holding vp : haſte you ſpeedily to *Angelo*, if for this night he intreat you to his bed,
giue him promiſe of ſatisfaction : I will preſently to S.
Lukes, there at the moated-Grange recides this deiected *Mariana*; at that place call vpon me, and diſpatch
with *Angelo*, that it may be quickly.

Iſab. I thank you for this comfort : fare youwell good
father.　　　　　　　　　　　　　　　　　　　　*Exit.*

Enter Elbow, Clowne, Officers.

Elb. Nay, if there be no remedy for it, but that you
will needes buy and ſell men and women like beaſts, we
ſhall haue all the world drinke browne & white baſtard.

Duk. Oh heauens, what ſtuffe is heere.

Clow. Twas neuer merry world ſince of two vſuries
the merrieſt was put downe, and the worſer allow'd by
order of Law ; a fur'd gowne to keepe him warme ; and
furd with Foxe and Lamb-skins too, to ſignifie, that craft
being richer then Innocency, ſtands for the facing.

Elb. Come your way ſir : 'bleſſe you good Father
Frier.

Duk. And you good Brother Father ; what offence
hath this man made you, Sir ?

　　　　　　　　　　　　　　　　　　　　　　Elb. Marry

Elb. Marry Sir, he hath offended the Law; and Sir, we take him to be a Theefe too Sir : for wee haue found vpon him Sir, a ſtrange Pick-lock, which we haue ſent to the Deputie.

Duke. Fie, ſirrah, a Bawd, a wicked bawd, The euill that thou cauſeſt to be done, That is thy meanes to liue. Do thou but thinke What 'tis to cram a maw, or cloath a backe From ſuch a filthie vice : ſay to thy ſelfe, From their abhominable and beaſtly touches I drinke, I eate away my ſelfe, and liue : Canſt thou beleeue thy liuing is a life, So ſtinkingly depending ? Go mend, go mend.

Clo. Indeed, it do's ſtinke in ſome ſort, Sir : But yet Sir I would proue.

Duke. Nay, if the diuell haue giuen thee proofs for ſin Thou wilt proue his. Take him to priſon Officer : Correction, and Inſtruction muſt both worke Ere this rude beaſt will profit.

Elb. He muſt before the Deputy Sir, he ha's giuen him warning : the Deputy cannot abide a Whore-maſter : if he be a Whore-monger, and comes before him, he were as good go a mile on his errand.

Duke. That we were all, as ſome would ſeeme to bee From our faults, as faults from ſeeming free.

Enter Lucio.

Elb. His necke will come to your waſt, a Cord ſir.

Clo. I ſpy comfort, I cry baile: Here's a Gentleman, and a friend of mine.

Luc. How now noble *Pompey?* What, at the wheels of *Cæſar* ? Art thou led in triumph ? What is there none of *Pigmalions* Images newly made woman to bee had now, for putting the hand in the pocket, and extracting clutch'd ? What reply ? Ha ? What ſaiſt thou to this Tune, Matter, and Method ? Is't not drown'd i'th laſt raine ? Ha ? What ſaiſt thou Trot ? Is the world as it was Man ? Which is the vvay ? Is it ſad, and few words ? Or how ? The tricke of it ?

Duke. Still thus, and thus : ſtill vvorſe ?

Luc. How doth my deere Morſell, thy Miſtris ? Procures ſhe ſtill ? Ha ?

Clo. Troth ſir, ſhee hath eaten vp all her beefe, and ſhe is her ſelfe in the tub.

Luc. Why 'tis good : It is the right of it : it muſt be ſo. Euer your freſh Whore, and your pouder'd Baud, an vnſhun'd conſequence, it muſt be ſo. Art going to priſon *Pompey* ?

Clo. Yes faith ſir.

Luc. Why 'tis not amiſſe *Pompey* : farewell : goe ſay I ſent thee thether : for debt *Pompey?* Or how ?

Elb. For being a baud, for being a baud.

Luc. Well, then impriſon him : If impriſonment be the due of a baud, why 'tis his right. Baud is he doubtleſſe, and of antiquity too : Baud borne. Farewell good *Pompey* : Commend me to the priſon *Pompey*, you will turne good husband now *Pompey*, you vvill keepe the houſe.

Clo. I hope Sir, your good Worſhip wil be my baile ?

Luc. No indeed vvil I not *Pompey*, it is not the wear : I will pray (*Pompey*) to encreaſe your bondage if you take it not patiently : Why, your mettle is the more : Adieu truſtie *Pompey.* Bleſſe you Friar.

Duke. And you.

Luc. Do's *Bridget* paint ſtill, *Pompey* ? Ha ?

Elb. Come your waies ſir, come.

Clo. You will not baile me then Sir ?

Luc. Then *Pompey*, nor now : what newes abroad Frier ? What newes ?

Elb. Come your waies ſir, come.

Luc. Goe to kennell (*Pompey*) goe : What newes *Frier of the Duke ?*

Duke. I know none : can you tell me of any ?

Luc. Some ſay he is with the Emperor of *Ruſſia* : other ſome, he is in *Rome* : but where is he thinke you ?

Duke. I know not where : but whereſoeuer, I wiſh him well.

Luc. It was a mad fantaſticall tricke of him to ſteale from the State, and vſurpe the beggerie hee was neuer borne to : Lord *Angelo* Dukes it well in his abſence : he puts tranſgreſſion too't.

Duke. He do's well in't.

Luc. A little more lenitie to Lecherie would doe no harme in him : Something too crabbed that way, *Frier.*

Duk. It is too general a vice, and ſeueritie muſt cure it.

Luc. Yes in good ſooth, the vice is of a great kindred; it is vvell allied, but it is impoſſible to extirpe it quite, Frier, till eating and drinking be put downe. They ſay this *Angelo* vvas not made by Man and Woman, after this downe-right vvay of Creation : is it true, thinke you ?

Duke. How ſhould he be made then ?

Luc. Some report, a Sea-mald ſpawn'd him. Some, that he vvas begot betweene two Stock-fiſhes . But it is certaine, that when he makes water, his Vrine is congeal'd ice, that I know to bee true : and he is a motion generatiue, that's infallible.

Duke. You are pleaſant ſir, and ſpeake apace.

Luc. Why, what a ruthleſſe thing is this in him, for the rebellion of a Cod-peece, to take away the life of a man ? Would the Duke that is abſent haue done this ? Ere he vvould haue hang'd a man for the getting a hundred Baſtards, he vvould haue paide for the Nurſing a thouſand. He had ſome feeling of the ſport, hee knew the ſeruice, and that inſtructed him to mercie.

Duke. I neuer heard the abſent Duke much detected for Women, he was not enclin'd that vvay.

Luc. Oh Sir, you are deceiu'd.

Duke. 'Tis not poſſible.

Luc. Who, not the Duke ? Yes, your beggar of fifty : and his vſe was, to put a ducket in her Clack-diſh ; the Duke had Crochets in him. Hee would be drunke too, that let me informe you.

Duke. You do him wrong, ſurely.

Luc. Sir, I vvas an inward of his : a ſhie fellow vvas the Duke, and I beleeue I know the cauſe of his vvithdrawing.

Duke. What (I prethee) might be the cauſe ?

Luc. No, pardon : 'Tis a ſecret muſt bee lockt within the teeth and the lippes : but this I can let you vnderſtand, the greater file of the ſubiect held the Duke to be vviſe.

Duke. Wiſe ? Why no queſtion but he was.

Luc. A very ſuperficiall, ignorant, vnweighing fellow

Duke. Either this is Enuie in you, Folly, or miſtaking : The very ſtreame of his life, and the buſineſſe he hath helmed, muſt vppon a warranted neede, giue him a better proclamation. Let him be but teſtimonied in his owne bringings forth, and hee ſhall appeare to the enuious, a Scholler, a Stateſman, and a Soldier : therefore you ſpeake vnſkilfully : or, if your knowledge bee more, it is much darkned in your malice.

G   *Luc.*

Luc. Sir, I know him, and I loue him.

Duke. Loue talkes with better knowledge, & knowledge with deare loue.

Luc. Come Sir, I know what I know.

Duke. I can hardly beleeue that, fince you know not what you fpeake. But if euer the Duke returne (as our praiers are he may) let mee defire you to make your anfwer before him : if it bee honeft you haue fpoke, you haue courage to maintaine it ; I am bound to call vppon you, and I pray you your name ?

Luc. Sir my name is *Lucio,* wel known to the Duke.

Duke. He fhall know you better Sir, if I may liue to report you.

Luc. I feare you not.

Duke. O, you hope the Duke will returne no more: or you imagine me to vnhurtfull an oppofite : but indeed I can doe you little harme : You'll for-fweare this a-gaine ?

Luc. Ile be hang'd firft : Thou art deceiu'd in mee Friar. But no more of this : Canft thou tell if *Claudio* die to morrow, or no ?

Duke. Why fhould he die Sir ?

Luc. Why ? For filling a bottle with a Tunne-difh : I would the Duke we talke of were return'd againe: this vngenitur'd Agent will vn-people the Prouince with Continencie. Sparrowes muft not build in his houfe-ceues, becaufe they are lecherous: The Duke yet would haue darke deeds darkelie anfwered, hee would neuer bring them to light : would hee were return'd. Marrie this *Claudio* is condemned for vntruffing.Farwell good Friar, I prethee pray for me : The Duke (I fay to thee againe) would eate Mutton on Fridaies. He's now paft it, yet (and I fay to thee) hee would mouth with a beggar, though fhe fmelt browne-bread and Oarlicke : fay that I faid fo : Farewell.   *Exit.*

Duke. No might, nor greatneffe in mortality Can cenfure fcape : Back-wounding calumnie The whiteft vertue ftrikes. What King fo ftrong, Can tie the gall vp in the flanderous tong ? But who comes heere ?

Enter Efcalus, Prouoft, and Bawd.

Efc. Go, away with her to prifon.

Bawd. Good my Lord be good to mee, your Honor is accounted a mercifull man : good my Lord.

Efc. Double, and trebble admonition, and ftill forfeite in the fame kinde ? This would make mercy fweare and play the Tirant.

Pro. A Bawd of eleuen yeares continuance, may it pleafe your Honor.

Bawd. My Lord, this is one *Lucio's* information againft me, Miftris *Kate Keepe-downe* was with childe by him in the Dukes time, he promis'd her marriage : his Childe is a yeere and a quarter olde come *Philip* and *Iacob* : I haue kept it my felfe; and fee how hee goes about to abufe me.

Efc. That fellow is a fellow of much Licenfe : Let him be call'd before vs. Away with her to prifon : Goe too, no more words. Prouoft, my Brother *Angelo* will not be alter'd, *Claudio* muft die to morrow : Let him be furnifh'd with Diuines, and haue all charitable preparation. If my brother wrought by my pitie, it fhould not be fo with him.

Pro. So pleafe you, this Friar hath beene with him, and aduis'd him for th'entertainment of death.

Efc. Good'euen, good Father.

Duke. Bliffe, and goodneffe on you.

Efc. Of whence are you ?

*Duke.*Not of this Countrie, though my chance is now To vfe it for my time : I am a brother Of gracious Order, late come from the Sea, In fpeciall bufineffe from his Holineffe.

Efc. What newes abroad i'th World ?

Duke. None, but that there is fo great a Feauor on goodneffe, that the diffolution of it muft cure it. Noueltie is onely in requeft, and as it is as dangerous to be aged in any kinde of courfe, as it is vertuous to be conftant in any vndertaking. There is fcarfe truth enough aliue to make Societies fecure, but Securitie enough to make Fellowfhips accurft: Much vpon this riddle runs the wifedome of the world : This newes is old enough, yet it is euerie daies newes. I pray you Sir, of what difpofition was the Duke ?

Efc. One, that aboue all other ftrifes, Contended efpecially to know himfelfe.

Duke. What pleafure was he giuen to ?

Efc. Rather reioycing to fee another merry, then merrrie at anie thing which profeft to make him reioice. A Gentleman of all temperance. But leaue wee him to his euents, with a praier they may proue profperous, & let me defire to know, how you finde *Claudio* prepar'd ? I am made to vnderftand, that you haue lent him vifitation.

Duke. He profeffes to haue receiued no finifter meafure from his Iudge, but moft willingly humbles himfelfe to the determination of Iuftice : yet had he framed to himfelfe (by the inftruction of his frailty) manie deceyuing promifes of life, which I (by my good leifure) haue difcredited to him, and now is he refolu'd to die.

Efc. You haue paid the heauens your Function, and the prifoner the verie debt of your Calling. I haue labour'd for the poore Gentleman, to the extremeft fhore of my modeftie, but my brother-Iuftice haue I found fo feuere, that he hath forc'd me to tell him, hee is indeede Iuftice.

Duke. If his owne life, Anfwere the ftraitneffe of his proceeding, It fhall become him well : wherein if he chance to faile he hath fentenc'd himfelfe.

Efc. I am going to vifit the prifoner, Fare you well.

Duke. Peace be with you.

He who the fword of Heauen will beare, Should be as holy, as feueare : Patterne in himfelfe to know, Grace to ftand, and Vertue go : More, nor leffe to others paying, Then by felfe-offences weighing. Shame to him, whofe cruell ftriking, Kils for faults of his owne liking : Twice trebble fhame on *Angelo,* To vveede my vice, and let his grow. Oh, what may Man within him hide, Though Angel on the outward fide ? How may likeneffe made in crimes, Making practife on the Times, To draw with ydle Spiders ftrings Moft ponderous and fubftantiall things? Craft againft vice, I muft applie. With *Angelo* to night fhall lye His old betroathed (but defpifed:) So difguife fhall by th'difguifed Pay with falfhood, falfe exacting, And performe an olde contracting.

Exit Actus

Actus Quartus. Scæna Prima.

Enter Mariana, and Boy finging.

Song.   *Take, oh take thofe lips away,*
that fo fweetly were forfworne,
And thofe eyes : the breake of day
lights that doe miflead the Morne ;
But my kiffes bring againe, bring againe,
Seales of loue, but feal'd in vaine, feal'd in vaine.

Enter Duke.

Mar. Breake off thy fong, and hafte thee quick away,
Here comes a man of comfort, whofe aduice
Hath often ftill'd my brawling difcontent.
I cry you mercie, Sir, and well could wifh
You had not found me here fo muficall.
Let me excufe me, and beleeue me fo,
My mirth it much difpleaf'd, but pleaf'd my woe.

Duk. 'Tis good ; though Mufick oft hath fuch a charme
To make bad, good ; and good prouoake to harme.
I pray you tell me, hath any body enquir'd for mee here
to day ; much vpon this time haue I promif'd here to
meete.

Mar. You haue not bin enquir'd after : I haue fat
here all day.

Enter Ifabell.

Duk. I doe conftantly beleeue you : the time is come
euen now. I fhall craue your forbearance alittle, may be
I will call vpon you anone for fome aduantage to your
felfe.

Mar. I am alwayes bound to you.   *Exit.*

Duk. Very well met, and well come :
What is the newes from this good Deputie?

Ifab. He hath a Garden circummur'd with Bricke,
Whofe wefterne fide is with a Vineyard back't ;
And to that Vineyard is a planched gate,
That makes his opening with this bigger Key :
This other doth command a little doore,
Which from the Vineyard to the Garden leades,
There haue I made my promife, vpon the
Heauy midle of the night, to call vpon him.

Duk. But fhall you on your knowledge find this way?

Ifab. I haue t'ane a due, and wary note vpon't,
With whifpering, and moft guiltie diligence,
In action all of precept, he did fhow me
The way twice ore.

Duk. Are there no other tokens
Betweene you 'greed, concerning her obferuance?

Ifab. No : none but onely a repaire ith' darke,
And that I haue poffeft him, my moft ftay
Can be but briefe : for I haue made him know,
I haue a Seruant comes with me along
That ftaies vpon me ; whofe perfwafion is,
I come about my Brother.

Duk. 'Tis well borne vp.
I haue not yet made knowne to *Mariana*

Enter Mariana.

A word of this : what hoa, within; come forth,
I pray you be acquainted with this Maid,
She comes to doe you good.

Ifab. I doe defire the like.

Duk. Do you perfwade your felfe that I refpect you?

Mar. Good Frier, I know you do, and haue found it.

Duke. Take then this your companion by the hand
Who hath a ftorie readie for your eare :
I fhall attend your leifure, but make hafte
The vaporous night approaches.

Mar. Wilt pleafe you walke afide.   *Exit.*

Duke. Oh Place, and greatnes : millions of falfe eies
Are ftucke vpon thee : volumes of report
Run with thefe ftorie, and moft contrarius Queft
Vpon thy doings : thoufand efcapes of wit
Make thee the father of their idle dreame,
And racke thee in their fancies. Welcome, how agreed ?

Enter Mariana and Ifabella.

Ifab. Shee'll take the enterprize vpon her father,
If you aduife it.

Duke. It is not my confent,
But my entreaty too.

Ifa. Little haue you to fay
When you depart from him, but foft and low,
Remember now my brother.

Mar. Feare me not.

Duk. Nor gentle daughter, feare you not at all :
He is your husband on a pre-contract :
To bring you thus together 'tis no finne,
Sith that the Iuftice of your title to him
Doth flourifh the deceit. Come, let vs goe,
Our Corne's to reape, for yet our Tithes to fow.   *Exeunt.*

Scena Secunda.

Enter Prouoft and Clowne.

Pro. Come hither firha ; can you cut off a mans head?

Clo. If the man be a Bachelor Sir, I can :
But if he be a married man, he's his wiues head,
And I can neuer cut off a womans head.

Pro. Come fir, leaue me your fnatches, and yeeld mee
a direct anfwere. To morrow morning are to die *Claudio* and *Barnardine* : heere is in our prifon a common executioner, who in his office lacks a helper, if you will take
it on you to affift him , it fhall redeeme you from your
Gyues : if not, you fhall haue your full time of imprifon-
ment, and your deliuerance with an vnpittied whipping;
for you haue beene a notorious bawd.

Clo. Sir, I haue beene an vnlawfull bawd, time out of
minde , but yet I will bee content to be a lawfull hang-
man : I would bee glad to receiue fome inftruction from
my fellow partner.

Pro. What hoa, *Abhorfon* : where's *Abhorfon* there ?

Enter Abhorfon.

Abh. Doe you call fir ?

Pro. Sirha, here's a fellow will helpe you to morrow
in your execution : if you thinke it meet, compound with
him by the yeere, and let him abide here with you, if not,
vfe him for the prefent, and difmiffe him , hee cannot
plead his eftimation with you : he hath beene a Bawd.

Abh. A Bawd Sir? fie vpon him, he will difcredit our
myfterie.

Pro. Goe too Sir, you waigh equallie : a feather will
turne the Scale.   *Exit.*

Clo. Pray fir, by your good fauor : for furely fir, a
good fauor you haue, but that you haue a hanging look :
Doe you call fir, your occupation a Myfterie ?

                 G 2   *Abh.* I,

Abb. I Sir, a Miſterie.

Clo. Painting Sir, I haue heard ſay, is a Miſterie; and your Whores ſir, being members of my occupation, v-ſing painting, do proue my Occupation, a Miſterie: but what Miſterie there ſhould be in hanging, if I ſhould be hang'd, I cannot imagine.

Abb. Sir, it is a Miſterie.

Clo. Proofe.

Abb. Euerie true mans apparrell fits your Theefe.

Clo. If it be too little for your theefe, your true man thinkes it bigge enough. If it bee too bigge for your Theefe, your Theefe thinkes it little enough : So euerie true mans apparrell fits your Theefe.

Enter Prouoſt.

Pro. Are you agreed ?

Clo. Sir, I will ſerue him : For I do finde your Hang-man is a more penitent Trade then your Bawd: he doth oftner aske forgiueneſſe.

Pro. You ſirrah, prouide your blocke and your Axe to morrow, foure a clocke.

Abb. Come on (Bawd) I will inſtruct thee in my Trade : follow.

Clo. I do deſire to learne ſir : and I hope, if you haue occaſion to vſe me for your owne turne, you ſhall finde me y'are. For truly ſir, for your kindneſſe, I owe you a good turne.   *Exit*

Pro. Call hether *Barnardine* and *Claudio* : Th'one has my pitie ; not a iot the other, Being a Murtherer, though he were my brother.

Enter Claudio.

Looke, here's the Warrant *Claudio*, for thy death, 'Tis now dead midnight, and by eight to morrow Thou muſt be made immortall. Where's *Barnardine?*

Cla. As faſt lock'd vp in ſleepe, as guiltleſſe labour, When it lies ſtarkely in the Trauellers bones, He will not wake.

Pro. Who can do good on him ? Well, go, prepare your ſelfe. But harke, what noiſe ? Heauen giue your ſpirits comfort : by, and by, I hope it is ſome pardon, or repreeue For the moſt gentle *Claudio.* Welcome Father.

Enter Duke.

Duke. The beſt, and wholſomſt ſpirits of the night, Inuellop you, good Prouoſt: who call'd heere of late?

Pro. None ſince the Curphew rung.

Duke. Not *Iſabell* ?

Pro. No.

Duke. They will then er't be long.

Pro. What comfort is for *Claudio* ?

Duke. There's ſome in hope.

Pro. It is a bitter Deputie.

Duke. Not ſo, not ſo : his life is paralel'd Euen with the ſtroke and line of his great Iuſtice : He doth with holie abſtinence ſubdue That in himſelfe, which he ſpurres on his powre To qualifie in others: were he meal'd with that Which he corrects, then were he tirrannous, But this being ſo, he's iuſt. Now are they come. This is a gentle Prouoſt, ſildome when The ſteeled Gaoler is the friend of men : How now? what noiſe ? That ſpirit's poſſeſt with haſt, That wounds th'vnſiſting Poſterne with theſe ſtrokes.

Pro. There he muſt ſtay vntill the Officer Ariſe to let him in : he is call'd vp.

Duke. Haue you no countermand for *Claudio* yet ?

But he muſt die to morrow ?

Pro. None Sir, none.

Duke. As neere the dawning Prouoſt, as it is, You ſhall heare more ere Morning.

Pro. Happely You ſomething know : yet I beleeue there comes No countermand : no ſuch example haue we: Beſides, vpon the verie ſiege of Iuſtice, Lord *Angelo* hath to the publike eare Profeſt the contrarie.

Enter a Meſſenger.

Duke. This is his Lords man.

Pro. And heere comes *Claudio's* pardon.

Meſſ. My Lord hath ſent you this note, And by mee this further charge ; That you ſwerue not from the ſmalleſt Article of it, Neither in time, matter, or other circumſtance. Good morrow: for as I take it, it is almoſt day.

Pro. I ſhall obey him.

Duke. This is his Pardon purchas'd by ſuch ſin, For which the Pardoner himſelfe is in : Hence hath offence his quicke celeritie, When it is borne in high Authority. When Vice makes Mercie ; Mercie's ſo extended, That for the faults loue, is th'offender friended. Now Sir, what newes?

Pro. I told you :
Lord *Angelo* (be-like) thinking me remiſſe In mine Office, awakens mee With this vnwonted putting on, methinks ſtrangely : For he hath not vs'd it before.

Duk. Pray you let's heare.

The Letter.

Whatſoeuer you may heare to the contrary, let Claudio be ex-ecuted by foure of the clocks, and in the afternoone Barnar-dine : For my better ſatiſfaction , let mee haue Claudios head ſent me by fiue. Let this be duely performed with a thought that more depends on it, then we muſt yet deliuer. Thus faile not to doe your Office, as you will anſwere it at your perill.

What ſay you to this Sir ?

Duke. What is that *Barnardine*, who is to be execu-ted in th'afternoone ?

Pro. A Bohemian borne : But here nurſt vp & bred, One that is a priſoner nine yeeres old.

Duke. How came it, that the abſent Duke had not either deliuer'd him to his libertie, or executed him ? I haue heard it was euer his manner to do ſo.

Pro. His friends ſtill wrought Repreeues for him : And indeed his fact till now in the gouernment of Lord *Angelo*, came not to an vndoubtfull proofe.

Duke. It is now apparant ?

Pro. Moſt manifeſt, and not denied by himſelfe.

Duke. Hath he borne himſelfe penitently in priſon ? How ſeemes he to be touch'd ?

Pro. A man that apprehends death no more dread-fully, but as a drunken ſleepe, careleſſe, wreakleſſe, and feareleſſe of what's paſt, preſent, or to come : inſenſible of mortality, and deſperately mortall.

Duke. He wants aduice.

Pro. He wil heare none: he hath euermore had the li-berty of the priſon: giue him leaue to eſcape hence, hee would not. Drunke many times a day, if not many daies entirely drunke. We haue verie oft awak'd him, as if to carrie him to execution, and ſhew'd him a ſeeming war-rant for it, it hath not moued him at all.

                              Duke.

Duke. More of him anon : There is written in your brow *Prouoft*, honefty and conftancie ; if I reade it not truly, my ancient skill beguiles me : but in the boldnes of my cunning, I will lay my felfe in hazard : *Claudio*, whom heere you haue warrant to execute, is no greater forfeit to the Law, then *Angelo* who hath fentenc'd him. To make you vnderftand this in a manifefted effect, I craue but foure daies refpit : for the which, you are to do me both a prefent, and a dangerous courtefie.

Pro. Pray Sir, in what ?

Duke. In the delaying death.

Pro. Alacke, how may I do it ? Hauing the houre li-mited, and an expreffe command, vnder penaltie, to de-liuer his head in the view of *Angelo* ? I may make my cafe as *Claudio*'s, to croffe this in the fmalleft.

Duke. By the vow of mine Order, I warrant you, If my inftructions may be your guide, Let this *Barnardine* be this morning executed, And his head borne to *Angelo*.

Pro. *Angelo* hath feene them both, And will difcouer the fauour.

Duke. Oh, death's a great difguifer, and you may adde to it ; Shaue the head, and tie the beard, and fay it was the defire of the penitent to be fo bar'de before his death : you know the courfe is common. If any thing fall to you vpon this, more then thankes and good for-tune, by the Saint whom I profeffe, I will plead againft it with my life.

Pro. Pardon me, good Father, it is againft my oath.

Duke. Were you fworne to the Duke, or to the De-putie ?

Pro. To him, and to his Subftitutes.

Duke. You will thinke you haue made no offence, if the Duke auouch the iuftice of your dealing ?

Pro. But what likelihood is in that ?

Duke. Not a refemblance, but a certainty ; yet fince I fee you fearfull, that neither my coate, integrity, nor perfwafion, can with eafe attempt you, I wil go further then I meant, to plucke all feares out of you. Looke you Sir, heere is the hand and Seale of the Duke : you know the Charracter I doubt not, and the Signet is not ftrange to you ?

Pro. I know them both.

Duke. The Contents of this, is the returne of the Duke ; you fhall anon ouer-reade it at your pleafure : where you fhall finde within thefe two daies, he wil be heere. This is a thing that *Angelo* knowes not, for hee this very day receiues letters of ftrange tenor, perchance of the Dukes death, perchance entering into fome Mo-nafterie, but by chance nothing of what is writ.Looke, th'vnfolding Starre calles vp the Shepheard ; put not your felfe into amazement, how thefe things fhould be; all difficulties are but eafie vvhen they are knowne. Call your executioner, and off with *Barnardines* head : I will giue him a prefent fhrift, and aduife him for a better place. Yet you are amaz'd, but this fhall abfolutely re-folue you : Come away, it is almoft cleere dawne. *Exit.*

Scena Tertia.

Enter Clowne.

Clo. I am as well acquainted heere, as I was in our houfe of profeffion : one would thinke it vvere Miftris

Ouer-*dons* owne houfe, for heere be manie of her olde Cuftomers. Firft, here's yong Mr *Rafh*, hee's in for a commoditie of browne paper, and olde Ginger, nine fcore and feuenteene pounds, of which hee made fiue Markes readie money : marrie then, Ginger was not much in requeft, for the olde Women vvere all dead. Then is there heere one Mr *Caper*, at the fuite of Mafter *Three-Pile* the Mercer, for fome foure fuites of Peach-colour'd Satten, which now peaches him a beggar. Then haue vve heere, yong *Dizie*, and yong Mr *Deepe-vow*, and Mr *Copperfpurre*, and Mr *Starue-Lackey* the Ra-pier and dagger man, and yong *Drop-heire* that kild lu-ftie *Pudding*, and Mr *Forthlight* the Tilter, and braue Mr *Shootie* the great Traueller, and wilde *Halfe-Canne* that ftabb'd Pots, and I thinke fortie more, all great doers in our Trade, and are now for the Lords fake.

Enter Abhorfon.

Abh. Sirrah, bring *Barnardine* hether.

Clo. Mr *Barnardine*, you muft rife and be hang'd, Mr *Barnardine*.

Abh. What hoa *Barnardine*.

Barnardine within.

Bar. A pox o'your throats : who makes that noyfe there ? What are you ?

Clo. Your friends Sir, the Hangman : You muft be fo good Sir to rife,and be put to death.

Bar. Away you Rogue, away, I am fleepie.

Abh. Tell him he muft awake, And that quickly too.

Clo: Pray Mafter *Barnardine*, awake till you areex-ecuted, and fleepe afterwards.

Ab. Go in to him, and fetch him out.

Clo. He is comming Sir, he is comming : I heare his Straw ruffle.

Enter Barnardine.

Abh. Is the Axe vpon the blocke, firrah?

Clo. Verie readie Sir.

Bar. How now *Abhorfon* ? What's the newes vvith you ?

Abh. Truly Sir, I would defire you to clap into your prayers : for looke you, the Warrants come.

Bar. You Rogue, I haue bin drinking all night, I am not fitted for't.

Clo. Oh, the better Sir: for he that drinkes all night, and is hanged betimes in the morning , may fleepe the founder all the next day.

Enter Duke.

Abh. Looke you Sir, heere comes your ghoftly Fa-'ther : do we ieft now thinke you ?

Duke. Sir, induced by my charitie, and hearing how haftily you are to depart, I am come to aduife you, Comfort you, and pray with you.

Bar. Friar, not I : I haue bin drinking hard all night, and I will haue more time to prepare mee, or they fhall beat out my braines with billets : I will not confent to die this day, that's certaine.

Duke. Oh fir, you muft : and therefore I befeech you Looke forward on the iournie you fhall go.

Bar. I fweare I will not die to day for anie mans per-fwafion.

Duke. But heare you:

Bar. Not a word : if you haue anie thing to fay to me, come to my Ward : for thence will not I to day. *Exit*

Enter Prouoft.

Duke. Vnfit to liue, or die : oh grauell heart.

G 3   After

After him (Fellowes) bring him to the blocke.

Pro. Now Sir, how do you finde the priſoner?

Duke. A creature vnpre-par'd, vnmeet for death,
And to tranſport him in the minde he is,
Were damnable.

Pro. Heere in the priſon, Father,
There died this morning of a cruell Feauor,
One *Ragozine*, a moſt notorious Pirate,
A man of *Claudio's* yeares : his beard, and head
Iuſt of his colour.   What if we do omit
This Reprobate, til he were wel enclin'd,
And ſatisfie the Deputie with the viſage
Of *Ragozine*, more like to *Claudio?*

Duke. Oh, 'tis an accident that heauen prouides :
Diſpatch it preſently, the houre drawes on
Prefixt by *Angelo* : See this be done,
And ſent according to command, whiles I
Perſwade this rude wretch willingly to die.

Pro. This ſhall be done (good Father) preſently :
But *Barnardine* muſt die this afternoone,
And how ſhall we continue *Claudio,*
To ſaue me from the danger that might come,
If he were knowne aliue?

Duke. Let this be done,
Put them in ſecret holds, both *Barnardine* and *Claudio,*
Ere twice the Sun hath made his iournall greeting
To yond generation, you ſhal finde
Your ſafetie manifeſted.

Pro. I am your free dependant.   *Exit.*

Duke. Quicke, diſpatch, and ſend the head to *Angelo*
Now wil I write Letters to *Angelo,*
(The Prouoſt he ſhal beare them) whoſe contents
Shal witneſſe to him I am neere at home :
And that by great Iniunctions I am bound
To enter publikely : him Ile deſire
To meet me at the conſecrated Fount,
A League below the Citie : and from thence,
By cold gradation, and weale-ballanc'd forme.
We ſhal proceed with *Angelo.*

Enter Prouoſt.

Pro. Heere is the head, Ile carrie it my ſelfe.

Duke. Conuenient is it : Make a ſwift returne,
For I would commune with you of ſuch things,
That want no eare but yours.

Pro. Ile make all ſpeede.   *Exit*

Iſabell within.

Iſa. Peace hoa, be heere.

Duke. The tongue of *Iſabell.* She's come to know,
If yet her brothers pardon be come hither :
But I will keepe her ignorant of her good,
To make her heauenly comforts of diſpaire,
When it is leaſt expected.

Enter Iſabella.

Iſa. Hoa, by your leaue.

Duke. Good morning to you, faire, and gracious
daughter.

Iſa. The better giuen me by ſo holy a man,
Hath yet the Deputie ſent my brothers pardon?

Duke. He hath releaſd him, *Iſabell,* from the world,
His head is off, and ſent to *Angelo.*

Iſa. Nay, but it is not ſo.

Duke. It is no other,
Shew your wiſedome daughter in your cloſe patience.

Iſa. Oh, I wil to him, and plucke out his eies.

Duk. You ſhal not be admitted to his ſight.

Iſa. Vnhappie *Claudio,* wretched *Iſabell,*

Iniurious world, moſt damned *Angelo.*

Duke. This nor hurts him, nor profits you a iot,
Forbeare it therefore, giue your cauſe to heauen,
Marke what I ſay, which you ſhal finde
By euery ſitlable a faithfull veritie.
The Duke comes home to morrow : nay drie your eyes,
One of our Couent, and his Confeſſor
Giues me this inſtance : Already he hath carried
Notice to *Eſcalus* and *Angelo,*
Who do prepare to meete him at the gates,   (dome,
There to giue vp their powre : If you can pace your wiſ-
In that good path that I would wiſh it go,
And you ſhal haue your boſome on this wretch,
Grace of the Duke, reuenges to your heart,
And generall Honor.

Iſa. I am directed by you.

Duk. This Letter then to Friar *Peter* giue,
'Tis that he ſent me of the Dukes returne :
Say, by this token, I deſire his companie
At *Mariana's* houſe to night. Her cauſe, and yours
Ile perfect him withall, and he ſhal bring you
Before the Duke ; and to the head of *Angelo*
Accuſe him home and home. For my poore ſelfe,
I am combined by a ſacred Vow,
And ſhall be abſent. Wend you with this Letter :
Command theſe fretting waters from your eies
With a light heart ; truſt not my holie Order
If I peruert your courſe : whoſe heere?

Enter Lucio.

Luc. Good 'euen ;
Frier, where's the Prouoſt?

Duke. Not within Sir.

Luc. Oh prettie *Iſabella,* I am pale at mine heart, to
ſee thine eyes ſo red : thou muſt be patient; I am faine
to dine and ſup with water and bran : I dare not for my
head fill my belly. One fruitfull Meale would ſet mee
too't : but they ſay the Duke will be heere to Morrow.
By my troth *Iſabell* I lou'd thy brother, if the olde fantaſtical Duke of darke corners had bene at home, he had
liued.

Duke. Sir, the Duke is maruellous little beholding
to your reports, but the beſt is, he liues not in them.

Luc. Friar, thou knoweſt not the Duke ſo wel as I
do : he's a better woodman then thou tak'ſt him for.

Duke. Well : you'l anſwer this one day. Fare ye well.

Luc. Nay tarrie, Ile go along with thee,
I can tel thee pretty tales of the Duke.

Duke. You haue told me too many of him already ſir
if they be true : if not true, none were enough.

Lucio. I was once before him for getting a Wench
with childe.

Duke. Did you ſuch a thing?

Luc. Yes marrie did I; but I was faine to forſwear it,
They would elſe haue married me to the rotten Medler.

Duke. Sir your company is fairer then honeſt, reſt you
well.

Lucio. By my troth Ile go with thee to the lanes end:
if baudy talke offend you, we'el haue very litle of it : nay
Friar, I am a kind of Burre, I ſhal ſticke.   *Exeunt*

Scena Quarta.

Enter Angelo & Eſcalus.

Eſc. Euery Letter he hath writ, hath diſuouch'd other.

Ang.

An. In moſt vneuen and diſtracted manner, his actions ſhow much like to madneſſe, pray heauen his wiſedome bee not tainted : and why meet him at the gates and re-luer ou rauthorities there?

Eſc. I gheſſe not.

Ang. And why ſhould wee proclaime it in an howre before his entring, that if any craue redreſſe of iniuſtice, they ſhould exhibit their petitions in the ſtreet?

Eſc. He ſhowes his reaſon for that: to haue a diſpatch of Complaints, and to deliuer vs from deuices heere-after, which ſhall then haue no power to ſtand againſt vs.

Ang. Well : I beſeech you let it bee proclaim'd be-times i'th'morne, Ile call you at your houſe : giue notice to ſuch men of ſort and ſuite as are to meete him.

Eſc. I ſhall fir : fareyouwell. *Exit.*

Ang. Good night.
This deede vnſhapes me quite, makes me vnpregnant
And dull to all proceedings. A deflowred maid,
And by an eminent body, that enforc'd
The Law againſt it? But that her tender ſhame
Will not proclaime againſt her maiden loſſe,
How might ſhe tongue me? yet reaſon dares her no,
For my Authority beares of a credent bulke,
That no particular ſcandall once can touch
But it confounds the breather. He ſhould haue liu'd,
Saue that his riotous youth with dangerous ſence
Might in the times to come haue ta'ne reuenge
By ſo receiuing a diſhonor'd life
With ranſome of ſuch ſhame : would yet he had liued.
Alack, when once our grace we haue forgot,
Nothing goes right, we would, and we would not. *Exit.*

Scena Quinta.

Enter Duke and Frier Peter.

Duke. Theſe Letters at fit time deliuer me,
The Prouoſt knowes our purpoſe and our plot,
The matter being a foote, keepe your inſtruction
And hold you euer to our ſpeciall drift,
Though ſometimes you doe blench from this to that
As cauſe doth miniſter : Goe call at *Flauia's* houſe,
And tell him where I ſtay : giue the like notice
To *Valencius, Rowland,* and to *Craſſus,*
And bid them bring the Trumpets to the gate :
But ſend me *Flauius* firſt.

Peter. It ſhall be ſpeeded well.

Enter Varrius.

Duke. I thank thee *Varrius,* thou haſt made good haſt,
Come, we will walke : There's other of our friends
Will greet vs heere anon : my gentle *Varrius.* *Exeunt.*

Scena Sexta.

Enter Iſabella and Mariana.

Iſab. To ſpeak ſo indirectly I am loath,
I would ſay the truth, but to accuſe him ſo
That is your part, yet I am aduis'd to doe it,
He ſaies, to vaile full purpoſe.

Mar. Be rul'd by him.

Iſab. Beſides he tells me, that if peraduenture
He ſpeake againſt me on the aduerſe ſide,
I ſhould not thinke it ſtrange, for 'tis a phyſicke
That's bitter, to ſweet end.

Enter Peter.

Mar. I would *Frier Peter*

Iſab. Oh peace, the *Frier* is come.

Peter. Come I haue found you out a ſtand moſt fit,
Where you may haue ſuch vantage on the *Duke*
He ſhall not paſſe you :
Twice haue the Trumpets ſounded.
The generous, and graueſt Citizens
Haue hent the gates, and very neere vpon
The *Duke* is entring :
Therefore hence away. *Exeunt.*

Actus Quintus. Scæna Prima.

Enter Duke, Varrius, Lords, Angelo, Eſculus, Lucio, Citizens at ſeuerall doores.

Duk. My very worthy Coſen, fairely met,
Our old, and faithfull friend, we are glad to ſee you.

Ang.Eſc. Happy returne be to yonr royall grace.

Duk. Many and harty thankings to you both :
We haue made enquiry of you, and we heare
Such goodneſſe of your Iuſtice, that our ſoule
Cannot but yeeld you forth to publique thankes
Forerunning more requitall.

Ang. You make my bonds ſtill greater.

Duk. Oh your deſert ſpeaks loud, & I ſhould wrong it
To locke it in the wards of couert boſome
When it deſerues with characters of braſſe
A forted reſidence 'gainſt the tooth of time,
And razure of obliuion : Giue we your hand
And let the Subiect ſee, to make them know
That outward curteſies would faine proclaime
Fauours that keepe within : Come *Eſcalus,*
You muſt walke by vs, on our other hand :
And good ſupporters are you.

Enter Peter and Iſabella.

Peter. Now is your time
Speake loud, and kneele before him.

Iſab. Iuſtice, O royall *Duke,* vaile your regard
Vpon a wrong'd (I would faine haue ſaid a Maid)
Oh worthy Prince, diſhonor not your eye
By throwing it on any other obiect,
Till you haue heard me, in my true complaint,
And giuen me Iuſtice, Iuſtice, Iuſtice, Iuſtice.

Duk. Relate your wrongs ;
In what, by whom? be briefe :
Here is Lord *Angelo* ſhall giue you Iuſtice,
Reueale your ſelfe to him.

Iſab. Oh worthy *Duke,*
You bid me ſeeke redemption of the diuell,
Heare me your ſelfe : for that which I muſt ſpeake
Muſt either puniſh me, not being beleeu'd,
Or wring redreſſe from you : heare me : oh heare me, heere.

Ang. My Lord, her wits I feare me are not firme :
She hath bin a ſuitor to me, for her Brother
Cut off by courſe of Iuſtice.

Iſab. By courſe of Iuſtice.

Ang. And ſhe will ſpeake moſt bitterly, and ſtrange.

Iſab. Moſt

Iſab. Moſt ſtrange : but yet moſt truely wil I ſpeake,
That *Angelo's* forſworne, is it not ſtrange?
That *Angelo's* a murtherer, is't not ſtrange?
That *Angelo* is an adulterous thiefe,
An hypocrite, a virgin violator,
Is it not ſtrange? and ſtrange?
　Duke. Nay it is ten times ſtrange?
　Iſa. It is not truer he is *Angelo,*
Then this is all as true, as it is ſtrange;
Nay, it is ten times true, for truth is truth
To th'end of reckning.
　Duke. Away with her : poore ſoule
She ſpeakes this, in th'infirmity of ſence.
　Iſa. Oh Prince, I coniure thee, as thou beleeu'ſt
There is another comfort, then this world,
That thou negleſt me not, with that opinion
That I am touch'd with madneſſe : make not impoſſible
That which but ſeemes vnlike, 'tis not impoſſible
But one, the wickedſt caitiffe on the ground
May ſeeme as ſhie, as graue, as iuſt, as abſolute :
As *Angelo,* euen ſo may *Angelo*
In all his dreſſings, caraſts, titles, formes,
Be an arch-villaine : Beleeue it, royall Prince
If he be leſſe, he's nothing, but he's more,
Had I more name for badneſſe.
　Duke. By mine honeſty
If ſhe be mad, as I beleeue no other,
Her madneſſe hath the oddeſt frame of ſenſe,
Such a dependancy of thing, on thing,
As ere I heard in madneſſe.
　Iſab. Oh gracious *Duke*
Harpe not on that ; nor do not baniſh reaſon
For inequality, but let your reaſon ſerue
To make the truth appeare, where it ſeemes hid,
And hide the falſe ſeemes true.
　Duk. Many that are not mad
Haue ſure more lacke of reaſon :
What would you ſay?
　Iſab. I am the Siſter of one *Claudio,*
Condemn'd vpon the Aſt of Fornication
To looſe his head, condemn'd by *Angelo,*
I, (in probation of a Siſterhood)
Was ſent to by my Brother ; one *Lucio*
As then the Meſſenger.
　Luc. That's I, and't like your Grace :
I came to her from *Claudio,* and deſir'd her,
To try her gracious fortune with Lord *Angelo,*
For her poore Brothers pardon.
　Iſab. That's he indeede.
　Duk. You were not bid to ſpeake.
　Luc. No, my good Lord,
Nor wiſh'd to hold my peace.
　Duk. I wiſh you now then,
Pray you take note of it : and when you haue
A buſineſſe for your ſelfe : pray heauen you then
Be perfeſt.
　Luc. I warrant your honor.
　Duk. The warrant's for your ſelfe : take heede to't.
　Iſab. This Gentleman told ſomewhat of my Tale.
　Luc. Right.
　Duk. It may be right, but you are i'the wrong
To ſpeake before your time : proceed,
　Iſab. I went
To this pernicious Caitiffe Deputie.
　Duk. That's ſomewhat madly ſpoken.
　Iſab: Pardon it,

The phraſe is to the matter.
　Duke. Mended againe : the matter : proceed.
　Iſab. In briefe, to ſet the needleſſe proceſſe by :
How I perſwaded, how I praid, and kneel'd,
How he refeld me, and how I replide
(For this was of much length) the vild concluſion
I now begin with griefe, and ſhame to vtter.
He would not, but by gift of my chaſte body
To his concupiſcible intemperate luſt
Releaſe my brother ; and after much debatement,
My ſiſterly remorſe, confutes mine honour,
And I did yeeld to him : But the next morne betimes,
His purpoſe ſurfetting, he ſends a warrant
For my poore brothers head.
　Duke. This is moſt likely.
　Iſab. Oh that it were as like as it is true.　(ſpeak'ſt,
　Duk. By heauen (fond wretch) ẙ knowſt not what thou
Or elſe thou art ſuborn'd againſt his honor
In hatefull praſtiſe : firſt his Integritie
Stands without blemiſh : next it imports no reaſon,
That with ſuch vehemency he ſhould purſue
Faults proper to himſelfe : if he had ſo offended
He would haue waigh'd thy brother by himſelfe,
And not haue cut him off : ſome one hath ſet you on :
Confeſſe the truth, and ſay by whoſe aduice
Thou cam'ſt heere to complaine.
　Iſa. And is this all?
Then oh you bleſſed Miniſters aboue
Keepe me in patience, and with ripened time
Vnfold the euill, which is heere wrapt vp
In countenance : heauen ſhield your Grace from woe,
As I was wrong'd, hence vnbeleeued goe.
　Duke. I know you'ld faine be gone: An Officer :
To priſon with her : Shall we thus permit
A blaſting and a ſcandalous breath to fall,
On him ſo neere vs? This needs muſt be a praſtiſe;
Who knew of your intent and comming hither?
　Iſa. One that I would were heere, *Frier Lodowick.*
　Duk. A ghoſtly Father, belike :
Who knowes that *Lodowicke* ?
　Luc. My Lord, I know him, 'tis a medling Fryer,
I doe not like the man : had he been Lay my Lord,
For certaine words hee ſpake againſt your Grace
In your retirment, I had ſwing'd him ſoundly.
　Duke. Words againſt mee? this 'a good Fryer belike
And to ſet on this wretched woman here
Againſt our Subſtitute : Let this Fryer be found.
　Luc. But yeſternight my Lord, ſhe and that Fryer
I ſaw them at the priſon : a ſawcy Fryar,
A very ſcuruy fellow.
　Peter. Bleſſed be your Royall Grace :
I haue ſtood by my Lord, and I haue heard
Your royall eare abus'd : firſt hath this woman
Moſt wrongfully accus'd your Subſtitute,
Who is as free from touch, or ſoyle with her
As ſhe from one vngot.
　Duke. We did beleeue no leſſe.
Know you that Frier *Lodowick* that ſhe ſpeakes of?
　Peter. I know him for a man diuine and holy,
Not ſcuruy, nor a temporary medler
As he's reported by this Gentleman :
And on my truſt, a man that neuer yet
Did (as he vouches) miſ-report your Grace.
　Luc. My Lord, moſt villanouſly, beleeue it.
　Peter. Well : he in time may come to cleere himſelfe;
But at this inſtant he is ſicke, my Lord :

Of a ſtrange Feauor : vpon his meere requeſt
Being come to knowledge, that there was complaint
Intended 'gainſt Lord *Angelo*, came I hether
To ſpeake as from his mouth, what he doth know
Is true, and falſe : And what he with his oath
And all probation will make vp full cleare
Whenſoeuer he's conuented : Firſt for this woman,
To iuſtifie this worthy Noble man
So vulgarly and perſonally accus'd,
Her ſhall you heare diſproued to her eyes,
Till ſhe her ſelfe confeſſe it.

Duk. Good Frier, let's heare it :
Doe you not ſmile at this, Lord *Angelo* ?
Oh heauen, the vanity of wretched fooles.
Giue va ſome ſeates, Come coſen *Angelo*,
In this I'll be impartiall : be you Iudge
Of your owne Cauſe : Is this the Witnes Frier ?

    Enter Mariana.

Firſt, let her ſhew your face, and after, ſpeake.
Mar. Pardon my Lord, I will not ſhew my face
Vntill my husband bid me.
Duke. What, are you married ?
Mar. No my Lord.
Duke. Are you a Maid ?
Mar. No my Lord.
Duk. A Widow then ?
Mar. Neither, my Lord.
Duk. Why you are nothing then: neither Maid, Widow, nor Wife ?
Luc. My Lord, ſhe may be a Puncke : for many of them, are neither Maid, Widow, nor Wife.
Duk. Silence that fellow : I would he had ſome cauſe to prattle for himſelfe.
Luc. Well my Lord.
Mar. My Lord, I doe confeſſe I nere was married,
And I confeſſe beſides, I am no Maid,
I haue known my husband, yet my husband
Knowes not, that euer he knew me.
Luc. He was drunk then, my Lord, it can be no better.
Duk. For the benefit of ſilence, would thou wert ſo to.
Luc. Well, my Lord.
Duk. This is no witneſſe for Lord *Angelo*.
Mar. Now I come to't, my Lord.
Shee that accuſes him of Fornication,
In ſelfe-ſame manner, doth accuſe my husband,
And charges him, my Lord, with ſuch a time,
When I'le depoſe I had him in mine Armes
With all th'effect of Loue.
Ang. Charges ſhe moe then me ?
Mar. Not that I know.
Duk. No ? you ſay your husband.
Mar. Why iuſt, my Lord, and that is *Angelo*,
Who thinkes he knowes, that he nere knew my body,
But knows, he thinkes, that he knowes *Iſabels*.
Ang. This is a ſtrange abuſe : Let's ſee thy face.
Mar. My husband bids me, now I will vnmaske.
This is that face, thou cruell *Angelo*
Which once thou ſworſt, was worth the looking on :
This is the hand, which with a vowd contract
Was faſt belockt in thine : This is the body
That tooke away the match from *Iſabell*,
And did ſupply thee at thy garden-houſe
In her Imagin'd perſon.
Duke. Know you this woman ?
Luc. Carnallie ſhe ſaies.

Duk Sirha, no more.
Luc. Enoug my Lord.
Ang. My Lord, I muſt confeſſe, I know this woman,
And ſiue yeres ſince there was ſome ſpeech of marriage
Betwixt my ſelfe, and her : which was broke off,
Partly for that her promis'd proportions
Came ſhort of Compoſition : But in chiefe
For that her reputation was diſ-valued
In leuitie : Since which time of ſiue yeres
I neuer ſpake with her, ſaw her, nor heard from her
Vpon my faith, and honor.
Mar. Noble Prince,
As there comes light from heauen, and words frō breath,
As there is ſence in truth, and truth in vertue,
I am affianced this mans wife, as ſtrongly
As words could make vp vowes : And my good Lord,
But Tueſday night laſt gon, in's garden houſe,
He knew me as a wife. As this is true,
Let me in ſafety raiſe me from my knees,
Or elſe for euer be confixed here
A Marble Monument.
Ang. I did but ſmile till now,
Now, good my Lord, giue me the ſcope of Iuſtice,
My patience here is touch'd : I doe perceiue
Theſe poore informall women, are no more
But inſtruments of ſome more mightier member
That ſets them on. Let me haue way, my Lord
To finde this practiſe out.
Duke. I, with my heart,
And puniſh them to your height of pleaſure.
Thou fooliſh Frier, and thou pernicious woman
Compact with her that's gone : thinkſt thou, thy oathes,
Though they would ſwear downe each particular Saint,
Were teſtimonies againſt his worth, and credit
That's ſeald in approbation ? you, Lord *Eſcalus*
Sit with my Cozen, lend him your kinde paines
To finde out this abuſe, whence 'tis deriu'd.
There is another Frier that ſet them on,
Let him be ſent for.
Peter. Would he were here, my Lord, for he indeed
Hath ſet the women on to this Complaint ;
Your Prouoſt knowes the place where he abides ,
And he may fetch him.
Duke. Goe, doe it inſtantly :
And you, my noble and well-warranted Coſen
Whom it concernes to heare this matter forth,
Doe with your iniuries as ſeemes you beſt
In any chaſtiſement ; I for a while
Will leaue you ; but ſtir not you till you haue
Well determin'd vpon theſe Slanderers.   *Exit.*
Eſc. My Lord, wee'll doe it throughly : Signior *Lucio*, did not you ſay you knew that Frier *Lodowick* to be a diſhoneſt perſon ?
Luc. *Cucullus non facit Monachum*, honeſt in nothing but in his Clothes , and one that hath ſpoke moſt villanous ſpeeches of the Duke.
Eſc. We ſhall intreat you to abide heere till he come, and inforce them againſt him : we ſhall finde this Frier a notable fellow.
Luc. As any in *Vienna*, on my word.
Eſc. Call that ſame *Iſabell* here once againe, I would ſpeake with her : pray you, my Lord, giue mee leaue to queſtion, you ſhall ſee how Ile handle her.
Luc. Not better then he, by her owne report.
Eſc. Say you ?
Luc. Marry ſir, I thinke, if you handled her priuately
            ſhee

She would ſooner confeſſe, perchance publikely ſhe'll be
aſham'd.

Enter Duke, Prouoſt, Iſabella.

Eſc. I will goe darkely to worke with her.
Luc. That's the way : for women are light at mid-
night.
Eſc. Come on Miſtris, here's a Gentlewoman,
Denies all that you haue ſaid.
Luc. My Lord, here comes the raſcall I ſpoke of,
Here, with the *Prouoſt.*
Eſc. In very good time : ſpeake not you to him, till
we call vpon you.
Luc. Mum.
Eſc. Come Sir, did you ſet theſe women on to ſlan-
der Lord *Angelo ?* they haue confeſ'd you did.
Duk. 'Tis falſe.
Eſc. How ? Know you where you are ?
Duk. Reſpect to your great place ; and let the diuell
Be ſometime honour'd, for his burning throne.
Where is the *Duke ?* 'tis he ſhould heare me ſpeake.
Eſc. The *Duke's* in vs : and we will heare you ſpeake,
Looke you ſpeake iuſtly.
Duk. Boldly, at leaſt. But oh poore ſoules,
Come you to ſeeke the Lamb here of the Fox ;
Good night to your redreſſe : Is the *Duke* gone ?
Then is your cauſe gone too : The *Duke's* vniuſt,
Thus to retort your manifeſt Appeale,
And put your triall in the villaines mouth,
Which here you come to accuſe.
Luc. This is the raſcall : this is he I ſpoke of.
Eſc. Why thou vnreuerend, and vnhallowed Fryer :
Is't not enough thou haſt ſuborn'd theſe women,
To accuſe this worthy man ? but in foule mouth,
And in the witneſſe of his proper eare,
To call him villaine; and then to glance from him,
To th'*Duke* himſelfe, to taxe him with Iniuſtice ?
Take him hence; to th'racke with him : we'll towze you
Ioynt by ioynt, but we will know his purpoſe :
What ? vniuſt ?
Duk. Be not ſo hot : the *Duke* dare
No more ſtretch this finger of mine, then he
Dare racke his owne : his Subiect am I not,
Nor here Prouinciall : My buſineſſe in this State
Made me a looker on here in *Vienna,*
Where I haue ſeene corruption boyle and bubble,
Till it ore-run the Stew : Lawes, for all faults,
But faults ſo countenanc'd, that the ſtrong Statutes
Stand like the forfeites in a Barbers ſhop,
As much in mocke, as marke.
Eſc. Slander to th' State :
Away with him to priſon.
Ang. What can you vouch againſt him Signior *Lucio ?*
Is this the man that you did tell vs of ?
Luc. 'Tis he, my Lord : come hither goodman bald-
pate, doe you know me ?
Duk. I remember you Sir, by the ſound of your voice,
I met you at the Priſon, in the abſence of the *Duke.*
Luc. Oh, did you ſo? and do you remember what you
ſaid of the *Duke.*
Duk. Moſt notedly Sir.
Luc. Do you ſo Sir : And was the *Duke* a fleſh-mon-
ger, a foole, and a coward, as you then reported him
to be ?
Duk. You muſt (Sir) change perſons with me, ere you
make that my report : you indeede ſpoke ſo of him, and

much more, much worſe.
Luc. Oh thou damnable fellow : did not I plucke thee
by the noſe, for thy ſpeeches ?
Duk. I proteſt, I loue the *Duke,* as I loue my ſelfe.
Ang. Harke how the villaine would cloſe now, after
his treaſonable abuſes.
Eſc. Such a fellow is not to be talk'd withall : Away
with him to priſon : Where is the *Prouoſt ?* away with
him to priſon : lay bolts enough vpon him: let him ſpeak
no more : away with thoſe Giglets too, and with the o-
ther confederate companion.
Duk. Stay Sir, ſtay a while.
Ang. What, reſiſts he ? helpe him *Lucio.*
Luc. Come ſir, come ſir, come ſir : foh ſir, why you
bald-pated lying raſcall; you muſt be hooded muſt you ?
ſhow your knaues viſage with a poxe to you: ſhow your
ſheepe-biting face, and be hang'd an houre : will't
not off ?
Duk. Thou art the firſt knaue, that ere mad'ſt a *Duke.*
Firſt *Prouoſt,* let me bayle theſe gentle three :
Sneake not away Sir, for the Fryer, and you,
Muſt haue a word anon: lay hold on him.
Luc. This may proue worſe then hanging.
Duk. What you haue ſpoke, I pardon: ſit you downe,
We'll borrow place of him ; Sir, by your leaue :
Ha'ſt thou or word, or wit, or impudence,
That yet can doe thee office ? If thou ha'ſt
Rely vpon it, till my tale be heard,
And hold no longer out.
Ang. Oh, my dread Lord,
I ſhould be guiltier then my guiltineſſe,
To thinke I can be vndiſcerneable,
When I perceiue your grace, like powre diuine,
Hath look'd vpon my paſſes. Then good Prince,
No longer Seſſion hold vpon my ſhame,
But let my Triall, be mine owne Confeſſion :
Immediate ſentence then, and ſequent death,
Is all the grace I beg.
Duk. Come hither *Mariana,*
Say : was't thou ere contracted to this woman ?
Ang. I was my Lord.
Duk. Goe take her hence, and marry her inſtantly.
Doe you the office (*Fryer*) which conſummate,
Returne him here againe : goe with him *Prouoſt.*   *Exit.*
Eſc. My Lord, I am more amaz'd at his diſhonor,
Then at the ſtrangeneſſe of it.
Duk. Come hither *Iſabell,*
Your *Frier* is now your Prince : As I was then
Aduertyſing, and holy to your buſineſſe,
(Not changing heart with habit) I am ſtill,
Atturnied at your ſeruice.
Iſab. Oh giue me pardon
That I, your vaſſaile, haue imploid, and pain'd
Your vnknowne Soueraigntie.
Duk. You are pardon'd *Iſabell* :
And now, deere Maide, be you as free to vs.
Your Brothers death I know ſits at your heart :
And you may maruaile, why I obſcur'd my ſelfe,
Labouring to ſaue his life : and would not rather
Make raſh remonſtrance of my hidden powre,
Then let him ſo be loſt : oh moſt kinde Maid,
It was the ſwift celeritie of his death,
Which I did thinke, with ſlower foot came on,
That brain'd my purpoſe : but peace be with him,
That life is better life paſt fearing death,
Then that which liues to feare : make it your comfort,
So

So happy is your Brother.

Enter Angelo, Maria, Peter, Prouoſt.

Iſab. I doe my Lord.

Duk. For this new-maried man, approaching here,
Whoſe ſalt imagination yet hath wrong'd
Your well defended honor : you muſt pardon
For *Mariana's* ſake : But as he adiudg'd your Brother,
Being criminall, in double violation
Of ſacred Chaſtitie, and of promiſe-breach,
Thereon dependant for your Brothers life,
The very mercy of the Law cries out
Moſt audible, euen from his proper tongue.
An *Angelo* for *Claudio*, death for death :
Haſte ſtill paies haſte, and leaſure, anſwers leaſure ;
Like doth quit like, and *Meaſure* ſtill for *Meaſure* :
Then *Angelo*, thy fault's thus manifeſted ;
Which though thou would'ſt deny, denies thee vantage.
We doe condemne thee to the very Blocke
Where *Claudio* ſtoop'd to death, and with like haſte.
Away with him.

Mar. Oh my moſt gracious Lord,
I hope you will not mocke me with a husband ?

Duk. It is your husband mock't you with a husband,
Conſenting to the ſafe-guard of your honor,
I thought your marriage fit : elſe Imputation,
For that he knew you, might reproach your life,
And choake your good to come : For his Poſſeſſions,
Although by confutation they are ours ;
We doe en-ſtate, and widow you with all,
To buy you a better husband.

Mar. Oh my deere Lord,
I craue no other, nor no better man.

Duke. Neuer craue him, we are definitiue.

Mar: Gentle my Liege.

Duke. You doe but looſe your labour.
Away with him to death : Now Sir, to you.

Mar. Oh my good Lord, ſweet *Iſabell*, take my part,
Lend me your knees, and all my life to come,
I'll lend you all my life to doe you ſeruice.

Duke. Againſt all ſence you doe importune her,
Should ſhe kneele downe, in mercie of this fact,
Her Brothers ghoſt, his paued bed would breake,
And take her hence in horror.

Mar. *Iſabell* ;
Sweet *Iſabel*, doe yet but kneele by me,
Hold vp your hands, ſay nothing : I'll ſpeake all.
They ſay beſt men are moulded out of faults,
And for the moſt, become much more the better
For being a little bad : So may my husband.
Oh *Iſabel* : will you not lend a knee ?

Duke. He dies for *Claudio's* death.

Iſab. Moſt bounteous Sir.
Looke if it pleaſe you, on this man condemn'd,
As if my Brother liu'd : I partly thinke,
A due ſinceritie gouerned his deedes,
Till he did looke on me : Since it is ſo,
Let him not die : my Brother had but Iuſtice,
In that he did the thing for which he dide.
For *Angelo*, his Act did not ore-take his bad intent,
And muſt be buried but as an intent
That periſh'd by the way : thoughts are no ſubiects
Intents, but meerely thoughts.

Mar. Meerely my Lord.

Duk. Your ſuite's vnprofitable : ſtand vp I ſay :
I haue bethought me of another fault.
Prouoſt, how came it *Claudio* was beheaded

At an vnuſuall howre ?

Pro. It was commanded ſo.

Duke. Had you a ſpeciall warrant for the deed ?

Pro. No my good Lord : it was by priuate meſſage.

Duke. For which I doe diſcharge you of your office,
Giue vp your keyes.

Pro. Pardon me, noble Lord,
I thought it was a fault, but knew it not,
Yet did repent me after more aduice,
For teſtimony whereof, one in the priſon
That ſhould by priuate order elſe haue dide,
I haue reſeru'd aliue.

Duk. What's he ?

Pro. His name is *Barnardine*.

Duke. I would thou hadſt done ſo by *Claudio* :
Goe fetch him hither, let me looke vpon him.

Eſc. I am ſorry, one ſo learned, and ſo wiſe
As you, Lord *Angelo*, haue ſtil appear'd,
Should ſlip ſo groſſelie, both in the heat of bloud
And lacke of temper'd iudgement afterward.

Ang. I am ſorrie, that ſuch ſorrow I procure,
And ſo deepe ſticks it in my penitent heart,
That I craue death more willingly then mercy,
'Tis my deſeruing, and I doe entreat it.

Enter Barnardine and Prouoſt, Claudio, Iulietta.

Duke. Which is that *Barnardine* ?

Pro. This my Lord.

Duke. There was a Friar told me of this man.
Sirha, thou art ſaid to haue a ſtubborne ſoule
That apprehends no further then this world,
And ſquar'ſt thy life according : Thou'rt condemn'd,
But for thoſe earthly faults, I quit them all,
And pray thee take this mercie to prouide
For better times to come : Frier aduiſe him,
I leaue him to your hand . What muffeld fellow's that ?

Pro. This is another priſoner, for his ſake
Who ſhould haue di'd when *Claudio* loſt his head,
As like almoſt to *Claudio*, as himſelfe.

Duke. If he be like your brother, for his ſake
Is he pardon'd, and for your louelie ſake
Giue me your hand, and ſay you will be mine,
He is my brother too : But fitter time for that :
By this Lord *Angelo* perceiues he's ſafe,
Methinkes I ſee a quickning in his eye :
Well *Angelo*, your euill quits you well.
Looke that you loue your wife : her worth, worth yours
I finde an apt remiſſion in my ſelfe :
And yet heere's one in place I cannot pardon,
You ſirha, that knew me for a foole, a Coward,
One all of Luxurie, an aſſe, a mad man :
Wherein haue I ſo deſeru'd of you
That you extoll me thus ?

Luc. 'Faith my Lord, I ſpoke it but according to the
trick : if you will hang me for it you may : but I had rather it would pleaſe you, I might be whipt.

Duke. Whipt firſt, ſir, and hang'd after.
Proclaime it Prouoſt round about the Citie,
If any woman wrong'd by this lewd fellow
(As I haue heard him ſweare himſelfe there's one
whom he begot with childe) let her appeare,
And he ſhall marry her : the nuptiall finiſh'd,
Let him be whipt and hang'd.

Luc. I beſeech your Highneſſe doe not marry me to
a Whore : your Highneſſe ſaid euen now I made you a
Duke, good my Lord do not recompence me, in making
me a Cuckold.

Duk. Vpon

Duke. Vpon mine honor thou fhalt marrie her.
Thy flanders I forgiue, and therewithall
Remit thy other forfeits : take him to prifon,
And fee our pleafure herein executed.
  Luc. Marrying a punke my Lord, is preffing to death,
Whipping and hanging.
  Duke. Slandering a Prince deferues it.
She *Claudio* that you wrong'd, looke you reftore.
I oy to you *Mariana*, loue her *Angelo* :
I haue confes'd her, and I know her vertue.
Thanks good friend, *Efcalus*, for thy much goodneffe,

There's more behinde that is more gratulate.
Thanks *Prouoft* for thy care, and fecrecie,
We fhall imploy thee in a worthier place.
Forgiue him *Angelo*, that brought you home
The head of *Ragozine* for *Claudio's*,
Th'offence pardons it felfe. Deere *Ifabell*,
I haue a motion much imports your good,
Whereto if you'll a willing eare incline ;
What's mine is yours, and what is yours is mine.
So bring vs to our Pallace, where wee'll fhow
What's yet behinde, that meete you all fhould know.

The Scene Vienna.

The names of all the Actors.

Vincentio : the Duke.
Angelo, the Deputie.
Efcalus, an ancient Lord.
Claudio, a yong Gentleman.
Lucio, a fantaftique.
2. *Other like Gentlemen.*
Prouoft.

Thomas.
Peter. } 2. *Friers.*
Elbow, a fimple Conftable.
Froth, a foolifh Gentleman.
Clowne.
Abborfon, an Executioner.
Barnardine, a diffolute prifoner.
Ifabella, fifter to Claudio.
Mariana, betrothed to Angelo.
Iuliet, beloued of Claudio.
Francifca, a Nun.
Miftris Ouer-don, a Bawd.

FINIS.

The Comedie of Errors.

Actus primus, Scena prima.

Enter the Duke of Ephesus, with the Merchant of Siracusa, Iaylor, and other attendants.

 Marchant.

Proceed *Solinus* to procure my fall,
And by the doome of death end woes and all.
 Duke. Merchant of *Siracusa*, plead no more.
I am not partiall to infringe our Lawes;
The enmity and difcord which of late
Sprung from the rancorous outrage of your Duke,
To Merchants our well-dealing Countrimen,
Who wanting gilders to redeeme their liues,
Haue feal'd his rigorous ftatutes with their blouds,
Excludes all pitty from our threatning lookes:
For fince the mortall and inteftine iarres
Twixt thy feditious Countrimen and vs,
It hath in folemne Synodes beene decreed,
Both by the *Siracufians* and our felues,
To admit no trafficke to our aduerfe townes:
Nay more, if any borne at *Ephefus*
Be feene at any *Siracufian* Marts and Fayres:
Againe, if any *Siracufian* borne
Come to the Bay of *Ephefus*, he dies:
His goods confifcate to the Dukes difpofe,
Vnleffe a thoufand markes be leuied
To quit the penalty, and to ranfome him:
Thy fubftance, valued at the higheft rate,
Cannot amount vnto a hundred Markes,
Therefore by Law thou art condemn'd to die.
 Mer. Yet this my comfort, when your words are done,
My woes end likewife with the euening Sonne.
 Duk. Well *Siracufian*; fay in briefe the caufe
Why thou departedft from thy natiue home?
And for what caufe thou cam'ft to *Ephefus*.
 Mer. A heauier taske could not haue beene impos'd,
Then I to fpeake my griefes vnfpeakeable:
Yet that the world may witneffe that my end
Was wrought by nature, not by vile offence,
Ile vtter what my forrow giues me leaue.
In *Syracufa* was I borne, and wedde
Vnto a woman, happy but for me,
And by me ; had not our hap beene bad :
With her I liu'd in ioy, our wealth increaft
By profperous voyages I often made
To *Epidamium*, till my factors death,
And he great care of goods at randone left,
Drew me from kinde embracements of my fpoufe;
From whom my abfence was not fixe moneths olde,
Before her felfe (almoft at fainting vnder

The pleafing punifhment that women beare)
Had made prouifion for her following me,
And foone, and fafe, arriued where I was :
There had fhe not beene long, but fhe became
A ioyfull mother of two goodly fonnes :
And, which was ftrange, the one fo like the other,
As could not be diftinguifh'd but by names.
That very howre, and in the felfe-fame Inne,
A meane woman was deliuered
Of fuch a burthen Male, twins both alike :
Thofe, for their parents were exceeding poore,
I bought, and brought vp to attend my fonnes.
My wife, not meanely proud of two fuch boyes,
Made daily motions for our home returne:
Vnwilling I agreed, alas, too foone wee came aboord.
A league from *Epidamium* had we faild
Before the alwaies winde-obeying deepe
Gaue any Tragicke Inftance of our harme :
But longer did we not retaine much hope ;
For what obfcured light the heauens did grant,
Did but conuay vnto our fearefull mindes
A doubtfull warrant of immediate death,
Which though my felfe would gladly haue imbrac'd,
Yet the inceffant weepings of my wife,
Weeping before for what fhe faw muft come,
And pitteous playnings of the prettie babes
That mourn'd for fafhion, ignorant what to feare,
Forft me to feeke delayes for them and me,
And this it was: (for other meanes was none)
The Sailors fought for fafety by our boate,
And left the fhip then finking ripe to vs.
My wife, more carefull for the latter borne,
Had faftned him vnto a fmall fpare Maft,
Such as fea-faring men prouide for ftormes :
To him one of the other twins was bound,
Whil'ft I had beene like heedfull of the other.
The children thus difpos'd, my wife and I,
Fixing our eyes on whom our care was fixt,
Faftned our felues at eyther end the maft,
And floating ftraight, obedient to the ftreame,
Was carried towards *Corinth*, as we thought.
At length the fonne gazing vpon the earth,
Difperft thofe vapours that offended vs,
And by the benefit of his wifhed light
The feas waxt calme, and we difcouered
Two fhippes from farre, making amaine to vs :
Of *Corinth* that, of *Epidarus* this ,
But ere they came, oh let me fay no more,
Gather the fequell by that went before.
 Duk. Nay forward old man, doe not breake off fo,
           H   For

For we may pitty, though not pardon thee.

Merch. Oh had the gods done fo,I had not now
Worthily tearm'd them mercileſſe to vs :
For ere the ſhips could meet by twice fiue leagues,
We were encountred by a mighty rocke,
Which being violently borne vp,
Our helpefull ſhip was ſplitted in the midſt ;
So that in this vniuſt diuorce of vs,
Fortune had left to both of vs alike,
What to delight in, what to forrow for,
Her part, poore foule, feeming as burdened
With leſſer waight, but not with leſſer woe,
Was carried with more ſpeed before the winde,
And in our ſight they three were taken vp
By Fiſhermen of *Corinth*, as we thought.
At length another ſhip had ſeiz'd on vs,
And knowing whom it was their hap to faue,
Gaue healthfull welcome to their ſhip-wrackt gueſts,
And would haue reſt the Fiſhers of their prey,
Had not their backe beene very ſlow of faile ;
And therefore homeward did they bend their courſe.
Thus haue you heard me ſeuer'd from my bliſſe,
That by misfortunes was my life prolong'd,
To tell ſad ſtories of my owne miſhaps.

Duke. And for the fake of them thou forroweſt for,
Doe me the fauour to dilate at full,
What haue befalne of them and they till now.

Merch. My yongeſt boy,and yet my eldeſt care,
At eighteene yeeres became inquiſitiue
After his brother ; and importun'd me
That his attendant, fo his caſe was like,
Might beare him company in the queſt of him:
Whom whil'ſt I laboured of a loue to fee,
I hazarded the loſſe of whom I lou'd.
Fiue Sommers haue I ſpent in fartheſt *Greece*,
Roming cleane through the bounds of *Aſia*,
And coaſting homeward, came to *Epheſus* :
Hopeleſſe to finde, yet loth to leaue vnſought
Or that, or any place that harbours men :
But heere muſt end the ſtory of my life,
And happy were I in my timelie death,
Could all my trauells warrant me they liue.

Duke. Hapleſſe *Egeon* whom the fates haue markt
To beare the extremitie of dire miſhap:
Now truſt me, were it not againſt our Lawes,
Againſt my Crowne, my oath, my dignity,
Which Princes would they may not difanull,
My foule ſhould fue as aduocate for thee :
But though thou art adiudged to the death,
And paſſed ſentence may not be recal'd
But to our honours great difparagement :
Yet will I fauour thee in what I can ;
Therefore Marchant, Ile limit thee this day
To feeke thy helpe by beneficiall helpe,
Try all the friends thou haſt in *Epheſus* ,
Beg thou, or borrow, to make vp the fumme,
And liue: if no, then thou art doom'd to die:
Iaylor, take him to thy cuſtodie.

Iaylor. I will my Lord.

Merch. Hopeleſſe and helpeleſſe doth *Egean* wend,
But to procraſtinate his liueleſſe end. *Exeunt.*

Enter Antipholis Erotes, a Marchant ,and Dromio.

Mer. Therefore giue out you are of *Epidamium*,
Left that your goods too foone be confiſcate :

This very day a *Syracuſian* Marchant
Is apprehended for a riuall here,
And not being able to buy out his life,
According to the ſtatute of the towne,
Dies ere the wearie funne fet in the Weſt :
There is your monie that I had to keepe.

Ant. Goe beare it to the Centaure, where we hoſt,
And ſtay there *Dromio*, till I come to thee ;
Within this houre it will be dinner time,
Till that Ile view the manners of the towne,
Peruſe the traders, gaze vpon the buildings,
And then returne and ſleepe within mine Inne,
For with long trauaile I am ſtiffe and wearie.
Get thee away.

Dro. Many a man would take you at your word,
And goe indeede, hauing fo good a meane.
Exit Dromio.

Ant. A truſtie villaine ſir, that very oft,
When I am dull with care and melancholly,
Lightens my humour with his merry ieſts :
What will you walke with me about the towne,
And then goe to my Inne and dine with me?

E.Mar. I am inuited ſir to certaine Marchants,
Of whom I hope to make much benefit :
I craue your pardon, foone at fiue a clocke,
Pleaſe you, Ile meete with you vpon the Mart,
And afterward confort you till bed time :
My preſent buſineſſe cals me from you now.

Ant. Farewell till then : I will goe loofe my ſelfe,
And wander vp and downe to view the Citie.

E.Mar. Sir, I commend you to your owne content.
Exeunt.

Ant. He that commends me to mine owne content,
Commends me to the thing I cannot get :
I to the world am like a drop of water,
That in the Ocean ſeekes another drop,
Who falling there to finde his fellow forth,
(Vnſeene, inquiſitiue) confounds himſelfe.
So I, to finde a Mother and a Brother,
In queſt of them (vnhappiea)loofe my ſelfe.

Enter Dromio of Epheſus.

Here comes the almanacke of my true date :
What now ? How chance thou art return'd fo foone.

E.Dro. Return'd fo foone, rather approacht too late:
The Capon burnes, the Pig fals from the ſpit;
The clocke hath ſtrucken twelue vpon the bell :
My Miſtris made it one vpon my cheeke :
She is fo hot becauſe the meate is colde :
The meate is colde, becauſe you come not home :
You come not home, becauſe you haue no ſtomacke :
You haue no ſtomacke, hauing broke your faſt :
But we that know what 'tis to faſt and pray,
Are penitent for your default to day.

Ant. Stop in your winde ſir, tell me this I pray ?
Where haue you left the mony that I gaue you.

E.Dro. Oh fixe pence that I had a wenſday laſt,
To pay the Sadler for my Miſtris crupper:
The Sadler had it Sir, I kept it not.

Ant. I am not in a ſportiue humor now :
Tell me, and dally not, where is the monie ?
We being ſtrangers here, how dar'ſt thou truſt
So great a charge from thine owne cuſtodie.

E.Dro. I pray you ieſt ſir as you ſit at dinner :
I from my Miſtris come to you in poſt :
If I returne I ſhall be poſt indeede.

For

For she will scoure your fault vpon my pate :
Me thinkes your maw, like mine, should be your cooke,
And strike you home without a messenger.
Ant. Come *Dromio*, come, these iests are out of season,
Reserue them till a merrier houre then this:
Where is the gold I gaue in charge to thee?
E.Dro. To me sir? why you gaue no gold to me?
Ant. Come on sir knaue, haue done your foolishnes,
And tell me how thou hast dispos'd thy charge.
E.Dro. My charge was but to fetch you frō the Mart
Home to your house, the *Phœnix* sir, to dinner;
My Mistris and her sister staies for you.
Ant. Now as I am a Christian answer me,
In what safe place you haue bestow'd my monie ;
Or I shall breake that merrie sconce of yours
That stands on tricks, when I am vndispos'd :
Where is the thousand Markes thou hadst of me?
E.Dro. I haue some markes of yours vpon my pate :
Some of my Mistris markes vpon my shoulders :
But not a thousand markes betweene you both.
If I should pay your worship those againe,
Perchance you will not beare them patiently.
Ant. Thy Mistris markes? what Mistris slaue hast thou?
E.Dro. Your worships wife, my Mistris at the *Phœnix*;
She that doth fast till you come home to dinner :
And praies that you will hie you home to dinner.
Ant. What wilt thou flout me thus vnto my face
Being forbid? There take you that sir knaue.
E.Dro. What meane you sir, for God sake hold your
Nay, and you will not sir, Ile take my heeles. (hands :
          Exeunt Dromio Ep.
Ant. Vpon my life by some deuise or other,
The villaine is ore-wrought of all my monie.
They say this towne is full of cosenage :
As nimble Iuglers that deceiue the eie :
Darke working Sorcerers that change the minde :
Soule-killing Witches, that deforme the bodie :
Disguised Cheaters, prating Mountebankes ;
And manie such like liberties of sinne :
If it proue so, I will be gone the sooner :
Ile to the Centaur to goe seeke this slaue,
I greatly feare my monie is not safe.   *Exit.*

Actus Secundus.

*Enter Adriana, wife to Antipholis Sereptus, with
Luciana her Sister.*

Adr. Neither my husband nor the slaue return'd,
That in such haste I sent to seeke his Master ?
Sure *Luciana* it is two a clocke.
Luc. Perhaps some Merchant hath inuited him,
And from the Mart he's somewhere gone to dinner :
Good Sister let vs dine, and neuer fret ;
A man is Master of his libertie :
Time is their Master, and when they see time,
They'll goe or come ; if so, be patient Sister.
Adr. Why should their libertie then ours be more?
Luc. Because their businesse still lies out adore.
Adr. Looke when I serue him so, he takes it thus.
Luc. Oh, know he is the bridle of your will.
Adr. There's none but asses will be bridled so.

Luc. Why, headstrong liberty is lasht with woe :
There's nothing situate vnder heauens eye,
But hath his bound in earth, in sea, in skie.
The beasts, the fishes, and the winged fowles
Are their males subiects, and at their controules :
Man more diuine, the Master of all these,
Lord of the wide world, and wilde watry seas,
Indued with intellectuall sence and soules,
Of more preheminence then fish and fowles,
Are masters to their females, and their Lords :
Then let your will attend on their accords.
Adri. This seruitude makes you to keepe vnwed.
Luci. Not this, but troubles of the marriage bed.
Adr. But were you wedded, you wold bear some sway
Luc. Ere I learne loue, Ile practise to obey.
Adr. How if your husband start some other where ?
Luc. Till he come home againe, I would forbeare.
Adr. Patience vnmou'd, no maruel though she pause,
They can be meeke, that haue no other cause :
A wretched soule bruis'd with aduersitie,
We bid be quiet when we heare it crie.
But were we burdned with like waight of paine,
As much, or more, we should our selues complaine :
So thou that hast no vnkinde mate to greeue thee,
With vrging helpelesse patience would releeue me ;
But if thou liue to see like right bereft,
This foole-beg'd patience in thee will be left.
Luci. Well, I will marry one day but to trie:
Heere comes your man, now is your husband nie.

          Enter Dromio Eph.

Adr. Say, is your tardie master now at hand ?
E.Dro. Nay, hee's at too hands with mee, and that my
two eares can witnesse.
Adr. Say, didst thou speake with him ? knowst thou
his minde ?
E. Dro. I, I, he told his minde vpon mine eare,
Beshrew his hand, I scarce could vnderstand it.
Luc. Spake hee so doubtfully, thou couldst not feele
his meaning.
E. Dro. Nay, hee strooke so plainly, I could too well
feele his blowes ; and withall so doubtfully, that I could
scarce vnderstand them.
Adri. But say, I prethee, is he comming home ?
It seemes he hath great care to pleafe his wife.
E.Dro. Why Mistresse, sure my Master is horne mad.
Adri. Horne mad, thou villaine ?
E.Dro. I meane not Cuckold mad,
But sure he is starke mad :
When I desir'd him to come home to dinner,
He ask'd me for a hundred markes in gold :
'Tis dinner time quoth I : my gold, quoth he :
Your meat doth burne, quoth I : my gold quoth he :
Will you come, quoth I : my gold, quoth he ;
Where is the thousand markes I gaue thee villaine ?
The Pigge quoth I, is burn'd : my gold, quoth he :
My mistresse, sir, quoth I : hang vp thy Mistresse :
I know not thy mistresse, out on thy mistresse.
Luci. Quoth who ?
E.Dr. Quoth my Master, I know quoth he, no house,
no wife , no mistresse : so that my arrant due vnto my
tongue, I thanke him, I bare home vpon my shoulders :
for in conclusion, he did beat me there.
Adri. Go back againe, thou slaue, & fetch him home.
Dro. Goe backe againe, and be new beaten home ?
For Gods sake send some other messenger.

Adri. Backe flaue, or I will breake thy pate a-croffe.
Dro. And he will bleffe ẙ croffe with other beating :
Betweene you, I fhall haue a holy head.
Adri. Hence prating pefant, fetch thy Mafter home.
Dro. Am I fo round with you, as you with me,
That like a foot-ball you doe fpurne me thus :
You fpurne me hence, and he will fpurne me hither,
If I laft in this feruice, you muft cafe me in leather.
Luci. Fie how impatience lowreth in your face.
Adri. His company muft do his minions grace,
Whil'ft I at home ftarue for a merrie looke :
Hath homelie age th'alluring beauty tooke
From my poore cheeke ? then he hath wafted it.
Are my difcourfes dull ? Barren my wit,
If voluble and fharpe difcourfe be mar'd,
Vnkindneffe blunts it more then marble hard.
Doe their gay veftments his affeɗions baite ?
That's not my fault , hee's mafter of my ftate.
What ruines are in me that can be found ,
By him not ruin'd ? Then is he the ground
Of my defeatures. My decayed faire,
A funnie looke of his, would foone repaire.
But, too vnruly Deere, he breakes the pale,
And feedes from home ; poore I am but his ftale.
Luci. Selfe-harming Iealoufie ; fie beat it hence.
Ad. Vnfeeling fools can with fuch wrongs difpence :
I know his eye doth homage other-where,
Or elfe, what lets it but he would be here ?
Sifter, you know he promis'd me a chaine ,
Would that alone, a loue he would detaine,
So he would keepe faire quarter with his bed :
I fee the Iewell beft enamfled
Will loofe his beautie : yet the gold bides ftill
That others touch, and often touching will,
Where gold and no man that hath a name,
By falfhood and corruption doth it fhame :
Since that my beautie cannot pleafe his eie,
Ile weepe (what's left away) and weeping die.
Luci. How manie fond fooles ferue mad Ieloufie?
                         Exit.

        Enter Antipholis Errotis.

Ant. The gold I gaue to *Dromio* is laid vp
Safe at the *Centaur*, and the heedfull flaue
Is wandred forth in care to feeke me out
By computation and mine hofts report.
I could not fpeake with *Dromio*, fince at firft
I fent him from the Mart ? fee here he comes.

        Enter Dromio Siracufia.

How now fir, is your merrie humor alter'd ?
As you loue ftroakes, fo ieft with me againe :
You know no *Centaur* ? you receiu'd no gold ?
Your Miftreffe fent to haue me home to dinner ?
My houfe was at the *Phœnix* ? Waft thou mad,
That thus fo madlie thou did didft anfwere me?
   S.Dro. What anfwer fir ? when fpake I fuch a word ?
E.Ant. Euen now, euen here, not halfe an howre fince.
   S.Dro. I did not fee you fince you fent me hence
Home to the *Centaur* with the gold you gaue me.
   Ant. Villaine, thou didft denie the golds receit,
And toldft me of a Miftreffe, and a dinner,
For which I hope thou feltft I was difpleas'd.
   S.Dro. I am glad to fee you in this merrie vaine,
What meanes this ieft, I pray you Mafter tell me ?
   Ant. Yes, doft thou ieere & flowt me in the teeth ?
Thinkft ẙ I ieft? hold, take thou that, & that. *Beats Dro.*
   S.Dr. Hold fir, for Gods fake, now your ieft is earneft,

Vpon what bargaine do you giue it me ?
   Antiph. Becaufe that I familiarlie fometimes
Doe vfe you for my foole, and chat with you,
Your fawcineffe will ieft vpon my loue,
And make a Common of my ferious howres,
When the funne fhines, let foolifh gnats make fport ,
But creepe in crannies, when he hides his beames :
If you will ieft with me, know my afpeɗ ,
And fafhion your demeanor to my lookes,
Or I will beat this method in your fconce.
   S.Dro. Sconce call you it? fo you would leaue batte-
ring, I had rather haue it a head, and you vfe thefe blows
long , I muft get a fconce for my head, and Infconce it
to, or elfe I fhall feek my wit in my fhoulders, but I pray
fir, why am I beaten ?
   Ant. Doft thou not know ?
   S.Dro, Nothing fit, but that I am beaten.
   Ant. Shall I tell you why ?
   S.Dro. I fir, and wherefore ; for they fay , euery why
hath a wherefore.
   Ant. Why firft for flowting me, and then wherefore,
for vrging it the fecond time to me.
   S.Dro. Was there euer anie man thus beaten out of
feafon, when in the why and the wherefore , is neither
rime nor reafon. Well fir, I thanke you,
   Ant. Thanke me fir, for what ?
   S.Dro. Marry fir, for this fomething that you gaue me
for nothing.
   Ant. Ile make you amends next, to giue you nothing
for fomething. But fay fir, is it dinner time ?
   S.Dro. No fir, I thinke the meat wants that I haue.
   Ant. In good time fir : what's that ?
   S.Dro. Bafting.
   Ant. Well fir, then 'twill be drie.
   S.Dro. If it be fir, I pray you eat none of it.
   Ant. Your reafon?
   S.Dro. Left it make you chollericke, and purchafe me
another drie bafting.
   Ant. Well fir, learne to ieft in good time , there's a
time for all things.
   S.Dro. I durft haue denied that before it vvere fo
chollericke.
   Anti. By what rule fir?
   S.Dro. Marry fir, by a rule as plaine as the plaine bald
pate of Father time himfelfe.
   Ant. Let's heare it.
   S.Dro. There's no time for a man to recouer his haire
that growes bald by nature.
   Ant. May he not doe it by fine and recouerie ?
   S.Dro. Yes, to pay a fine for a perewig, and recouer
the loft haire of another man.
   Ant. Why, is Time fuch a niggard of haire , being (as
it is) fo plentifull an excrement?
   S.Dro. Becaufe it is a bleffing that hee beftowes on
beafts, and what he hath fcanted them in haire, hee hath
giuen them in wit.
   Ant. Why, but theres manie a man hath more haire
then wit.
   S.Dro. Not a man of thofe but he hath the wit to lofe
his haire.
   Ant. Why thou didft conclude hairy men plain dea-
lers without wit.
   S.Dro. The plainer dealer, the fooner loft ; yet he loo-
feth it in a kinde of iollitie.
   An. For what reafon.
   S.Dro. For two, and found ones to.

                                  An. Nay

An. Nay not found I pray you.

S.Dro. Sure ones then.

An. Nay, not fure in a thing falsing.

S.Dro. Certaine ones then.

An. Name them.

S.Dro. The one to faue the money that he fpends in trying : the other, that at dinner they fhould not drop in his porrage.

An. You would all this time haue prou'd, there is no time for all things.

S.Dro. Marry and did fir : namely, in no time to recouer haire loft by Nature.

An. But your reafon was not fubftantiall, why there is no time to recouer.

S.Dro. Thus I mend it : Time himfelfe is bald, and therefore to the worlds end, will haue bald followers.

An. I knew 'twould be a bald conclufion : but foft, who wafts vs yonder.

Enter Adriana and Luciana.

Adri. I, I, *Antipholus*, looke ftrange and frowne, Some other Miftreffe hath thy fweet afpects : I am not *Adriana*, nor thy wife.

The time was once, when thou vn-vrg'd wouldft vow, That neuer words were muficke to thine eare, That neuer obiect pleafing in thine eye, That neuer touch well welcome to thy hand, That neuer meat fweet–fauour'd in thy tafte, Vnleffe I fpake, or look'd, or touch'd, or caru'd to thee. How comes it now, my Husband, oh how comes it, That thou art then eftranged from thy felfe ? Thy felfe I call it, being ftrange to me: That vndiuidable Incorporate Am better then thy deere felfes better part. Ah doe not teare away thy felfe from me ; For know my loue : as eafie maift thou fall A drop of water in the breaking gulfe , And take vnmingled thence that drop againe Without addition or diminifhing, As take from me thy felfe, and not me too. How deerely would it touch thee to the quicke, Shouldft thou but heare I were licencious ? And that this body confecrate to thee, By Ruffian Luft fhould be contaminate ? Wouldft thou not fpit at me, and fpurne at me, And hurle the name of husband in my face, And teare the ftain'd skin of my Harlot brow, And from my falfe hand cut the wedding ring, And breake it with a deepe-diuorcing vow ? I know thou canft, and therefore fee thou doe it. I am poffeft with an adulterate blot : My bloud is mingled with the crime of luft : For if we two be one, and thou play falfe, I doe digeft the poifon of thy flefh, Being ftrumpeted by thy contagion : Keepe then faire league and truce with thy true bed , I liue diftain'd, thou vndifhonoured.

Antip. Plead you to me faire dame ? I know you not : In *Ephefus* I am but two houres old , As ftrange vnto your towne, as to your talke, Who euery word by all my wit being fcan'd, Wants wit in all, one word to vnderftand.

Luci. Fie brother, how the world is chang'd with you: When were you wont to vfe my fifter thus ? She fent for you by *Dromio* home to dinner.

Ant. By *Dromio*?   *Drom.* By me.

Adr. By thee, and this thou didft returne from him. That he did buffet thee, and in his blowes, Denied my houfe for his, me for his wife.

Ant. Did you conuerfe fir with this gentlewoman: What is the courfe and drift of your compact?

S.Dro. I fir? I neuer faw her till this time.

Ant. Villaine thou lieft, for euen her verie words, Didft thou deliuer to me on the Mart.

S.Dro. I neuer fpake with her in all my life.

Ant. How can fhe thus then call vs by our names ? Vnleffe it be by infpiration.

Adri. How ill agrees it with your grauitie, To counterfeit thus grofely with your flaue, Abetting him to thwart me in my moode ; Be it my wrong, you are from me exempt, But wrong not that wrong with a more contempt. Come I will faften on this fleeue of thine : Thou art an Elme my husband, I a Vine : Whofe weakneffe married to thy ftranger ftate, Makes me with thy ftrength to communicate : If ought poffeffe thee from me, it is droffe, Vsurping Iuie, Brier, or idle Moffe, Who all for want of pruning, with intrufion, Infect thy fap, and liue on thy confufion.

Ant. To mee fhee fpeakes, fhee moues mee for her theame ; What, was I married to her in my dreame ? Or fleepe I now, and thinke I heare all this ? What error driues our eies and eares amiffe ? Vntill I know this fure vncertaintie, Ile entertaine the free'd fallacie.

Luc. Dromio, goe bid the feruants fpred for dinner.

S.Dro. Oh for my beads, I croffe me for a finner. This is the Fairie land, oh fpight of fpights, We talke with Goblins, Owles and Sprights ; If we obay them not, this will infue : They'll fucke our breath, or pinch vs blacke and blew.

Luc. Why prat'ft thou to thy felfe, and anfwer'ft not? *Dromio*, thou *Dromio*, thou fnaile, thou flug, thou fot.

S.Dro. I am transformed Mafter, am I not ?

Ant. I thinke thou art in minde, and fo am I.

S.Dro. Nay Mafter, both in minde, and in my fhape.

Ant. Thou haft thine owne forme.

S.Dro. No, I am mine Ape.

Luc. If thou art chang'd to ought, 'tis to an Affe.

S.Dro. 'Tis true fhe rides me, and I long for graffe. 'Tis fo, I am an Affe, elfe it could neuer be, But I fhould know her as well as fhe knowes me.

Adr. Come, come, no longer will I be a foole, To put the finger in the eie and weepe ; Whil'ft man and Mafter laughes my woes to fcorne : Come fir to dinner, *Dromio* keepe the gate : Husband Ile dine aboue with you to day, And fhriue you of a thoufand idle prankes : Sirra, if any aske you for your Mafter, Say he dines forth, and let no creature enter : Come fifter, *Dromio* play the Porter well.

Ant. Am I in earth, in heauen, or in hell ? Sleeping or waking, mad or well aduifde : Knowne vnto thefe, and to my felfe difguifde : Ile fay as they fay, and perfeuer fo : And in this mift at all aduentures go.

S.Dro. Mafter, fhall I be Porter at the gate ?

Adr. I, and let none enter, leaft I breake your pate.

Luc. Come, come, *Antipholus*, we dine to late.

Actus Tertius. Scena Prima.

*Enter Antipholus of Ephesus, his man Dromio, Angelo the
Goldsmith, and Balthasar the Merchant.*

E.Anti. Good fignior *Angelo* you muft excufe vs all,
My wife is fhrewifh when I keepe not howres ;
Say that I lingerd with you at your fhop
To fee the making of her Carkanet,
And that to morrow you will bring it home.
But here's a villaine that would face me downe
He met me on the Mart, and that I beat him,
And charg'd him with a thoufand markes in gold,
And that I did denie my wife and houfe ;
Thou drunkard thou, what didft thou meane by this ?
  E.Dro. Say what you wil fir, but I know what I know,
That you beat me at the Mart I haue your hand to fhow;
If ỹ skin were parchment, & ỹ blows you gaue were ink,
Your owne hand-writing would tell you what I thinke.
  E.Ant. I thinke thou art an affe.
  E.Dro. Marry fo it doth appeare
By the wrongs I fuffer, and the blowes I beare,
I fhould kicke being kickt, and being at that paffe,
You would keepe from my heeles, and beware of an affe.
  E.An. Y'are fad fignior *Balthazar*, pray God our cheer
May anfwer my good will, and your good welcom here.
  Bal. I hold your dainties cheap fir, & your welcom deer.
  E.An. Oh fignior *Balthazar*, either at flefh or fifh,
A table full of welcome, makes fcarce one dainty difh.
  Bal. Good meat fir is cõmon that euery churle affords.
  Anti. And welcome more common, for thats nothing
but words.
  Bal. Small cheere and great welcome, makes a mer-
rie feaft.
  Anti. I, to a niggardly Hoft, and more fparing gueft:
But though my cates be meane, take them in good part,
Better cheere may you haue, but not with better hart.
But foft, my doore is lockt ; goe bid them let vs in.
  E.Dro. Maud, Briget, Marian, Cifley, Gillian, Ginn.
  S.Dro. Mome, Malthorfe, Capon,   Coxcombe , Idi-
ot, Patch,
Either get thee from the dore, or fit downe at the hatch :
Doft thou coniure for wenches, that ỹ calft for fuch ftore,
When one is one too many, goe get thee from the dore.
  E.Dro. What patch is made our Porter ? my Mafter
ftayes in the ftreet.
  S.Dro. Let him walke from whence he came, left hee
catch cold on's feet.
  E.Ant. Who talks within there ? hoa, open the dore.
  S.Dro. Right fir, Ile tell you when , and you'll tell
me wherefore.
  Ant. Wherefore ? for my dinner : I haue not din'd to
day.
  S.Dro. Nor to day here you muft not come againe
when you may.
  Anti. What art thou that keep'ft mee out from the
howfe I owe?
  S.Dro. The Porter for this time Sir, and my name is
Dromio.
  E.Dro. O villaine, thou haft ftolne both mine office
and my name,
The one nere got me credit, the other mickle blame :
If thou hadft beene *Dromio* to day in my place,

Thou wouldft haue chang'd thy face for a name , or thy
name for an affe.
                    Enter Luce.
  Luce. What a coile is there *Dromio* ? who are thofe
at the gate?
  E.Dro. Let my Mafter in *Luce.*
  Luce. Faith no , hee comes too late, and fo tell your
Mafter.
  E.Dro. O Lord I muft laugh, haue at you with a Pro-
uerbe,
Shall I fet in my ftaffe.
  Luce. Haue at you with another , that's when ? can
you tell?
  S.Dro. If thy name be called *Luce*, *Luce* thou haft an-
fwer'd him well.
  Anti. Doe you heare you minion, you'll let vs in I
hope?
  Luce. I thought to haue askt you.
  S.Dro. And you faid no.
  E.Dro. So come helpe, well ftrooke, there was blow
for blow.
  Anti. Thou baggage let me in.
  Luce. Can you tell for whofe fake?
  E.Drom. Mafter, knocke the doore hard.
  Luce. Let him knocke till it ake.
  Anti. You'll crie for this minion , if I beat the doore
downe.
  Luce. What needs all that, and a paire of ftocks in the
towne?
                    Enter Adriana.
  Adr. Who is that at the doore ỹ keeps all this noife?
  S.Dro. By my troth your towne is troubled with vn-
ruly boies.
  Anti. Are you there Wife ? you might haue come
before.
  Adri. Your wife fir knaue ? go get you from the dore.
  E.Dro. If you went in paine Mafter, this knaue wold
goe fore.
  Angelo. Heere is neither cheere fir, nor welcome, we
would faine haue either.
  Balt. In debating which was beft , wee fhall part
with neither.
  E.Dro. They ftand at the doore , Mafter , bid them
welcome hither.
  Anti. There is fomething in the winde, that we can-
not get in.
  S.Dro. You would fay fo Mafter, if your garments
were thin.
Your cake here is warme within : you ftand here in the
cold.
It would make a man mad as a Bucke to be fo bought
and fold.
  Ant. Go fetch me fomething, Ile break ope the gate.
  S.Dro. Breake any breaking here, and Ile breake your
knaues pate.
  E.Dro. A man may breake a word with your fir, and
words are but winde :
I and breake it in your face, fo be break it not behinde.
  S.Dro. It feemes thou want'ft breaking, out vpon thee
hinde.
  E.Dro. Here's too much out vpon thee, I pray thee let
me in.
  S.Dro. I, when fowles haue no feathers, and fifh haue
no fin.
  Ant. Well, Ile breake in: go borrow me a crow.
  E.Dro. A crow without feather, Mafter meane you fo;
                                              For

For a fish without a finne, ther's a fowle without afether,
If a crow help vs in firra, wee'll plucke a crow together.
Ant. Go,get thee gon, fetch me an iron Crow.
Balth. Haue patience fir, oh let it not be fo,
Heerein you warre againft your reputation,
And draw within the compaffe of fufpect
Th'vnuiolated honor of your wife.
Once this your long experience of your wifedome,
Her fober vertue, yeares, and modeftie,
Plead on your part fome caufe to you vnknowne ;
And doubt not fir, but fhe will well excufe
Why at this time the dores are made againft you.
Be rul'd by me, depart in patience,
And let vs to the Tyger all to dinner,
And about euening come your felfe alone,
To know the reafon of this ftrange reftraint :
If by ftrong hand you offer to breake in
Now in the ftirring paffage of the day,
A vulgar comment will be made of it ;
And that fuppofed by the common rowt
Againft your yet vngalled eftimation,
That may with foule intrufion enter in,
And dwell vpon your graue when you are dead ;
For flander liues vpon fucceffion;
For euer hows'd, where it gets poffeffion.
Anti. You haue preuail'd, I will depart in quiet,
And in defpight af mirth meane to be merrie :
I know a wench of excellent difcourfe ,
Prettie and wittie; wilde, and yet too gentle ;
There will we dine : this woman that I meane
My wife (but I proteft without defert)
Hath oftentimes vpbraided me withall :
To her will we to dinner, get you home
And fetch the chaine, by this I know 'tis made,
Bring it I pray you to the *Porpentine* ,
For there's the houfe: That chaine will I beftow
(Be it for nothing but to fpight my wife)
Vpon mine hofteffe there, good fir make hafte :
Since mine owne doores refufe to entertaine me ,
Ile knocke elfe-where, to fee if they'll difdaine me.
Ang. Ile meet you at that place fome houre hence.
Anti. Do fo, this left fhall coft me fome expence.
Exeunt.

Enter Iuliana, with Antipholus of Siracufia.
Iulia. And may it be that you haue quite forgot
A husbands office ? fhall *Antipholus*
Euen in the fpring of Loue, thy Loue-fprings rot?
Shall loue in buildings grow fo ruinate?
If you did wed my fifter for her wealth,
Then for her wealths-fake vfe her with more kindneffe :
Or if you like elfe-where doe it by ftealth,
Muffle your falfe loue with fome fhew of blindneffe :
Let not my fifter read it in your eye :
Be not thy tongue thy owne fhames Orator :
Looke fweet, fpeake faire, become difloyaltie :
Apparell vice like vertues harbenger :
Beare a faire prefence, though your heart be tainted,
Teach finne the carriage of a holy Saint ,
Be fecret falfe : what need fhe be acquainted ?
What fimple thiefe brags of his owne attaine ?
'Tis double wrong to truant with your bed ,
And let her read it in thy lookes at boord :
Shame hath a baftard fame, well managed,
Ill deeds is doubled with an euill word :
Alas poore women, make vs not beleeue
(Being compact of credit) that you loue vs,

Though others haue the arme, fhew vs the fleeue :
We in your motion turne, and you may moue vs.
Then gentle brother get you in againe ;
Comfort my fifter, cheere her, call her wife ;
'Tis holy fport to be a little vaine,
When the fweet breath of flatterie conquers ftrife.
S. Anti. Sweete Miftris, what your name is elfe I
   know not ;
Nor by what wonder you do hit of mine:
Leffe in your knowledge, and your grace you fhow not,
Then our earths wonder, more then earth diuine.
Teach me deere creature how to thinke and fpeake :
Lay open to my earthie groffe conceit :
Smothred in errors, feeble, fhallow, weake,
The foulded meaning of your words deceit :
Againft my foules pure truth, why labour you,
To make it wander in an vnknowne field ?
Are you a god ? would you create me new ?
Transforme me then, and to your powre Ile yeeld.
But if that I am I, then well I know,
Your weeping fifter is no wife of mine,
Nor to her bed no homage doe I owe :
Farre more, farre more, to you doe I decline:
Oh traine me not fweet Mermaide with thy note,
To drowne me in thy fifter floud of teares :
Sing Siren for thy felfe, and I will dote :
Spread ore the filuer waues thy golden haires ;
And as a bud Ile take thee, and there lie :
And in that glorious fuppofition thinke,
He gaines by death, that hath fuch meanes to die :
Let Loue, being light, be drowned if fhe finke.
Luc. What are you mad, that you doe reafon fo ?
Ant. Not mad, but mated, how I doe not know.
Luc. It is a fault that fpringeth from your eie.
Ant. For gazing on your beames faire fun being by.
Luc. Gaze when you fhould, and that will cleere
   your fight.
Ant. As good to winke fweet loue, as looke on night.
Luc. Why call you me loue? Call my fifter fo.
Ant. Thy fifters fifter.
Luc. That's my fifter.
Ant. No : it is thy felfe, mine owne felfes better part:
Mine eies cleere eie, my deere hearts deerer heart ;
My foode, my fortune, and my fweet hopes aime ;
My fole earths heauen, and my heauens claime.
Luc. All this my fifter is, or elfe fhould be.
Ant. Call thy felfe fifter fweet, for I am thee :
Thee will I loue, and with thee lead my life ;
Thou haft no husband yet, nor I no wife :
Giue me thy hand.
Luc. Oh foft fir, hold you ftill :
Ile fetch my fifter to get her good will.   *Exit.*
Enter Dromio, Siracufia.
Ant. Why how now *Dromio*, where run'ft thou fo
   faft ?
S. Dro. Doe you know me fir? Am I *Dromio* ? Am I
   your man ? Am I my felfe ?
Ant. Thou art *Dromio*, thou art my man, thou art
   thy felfe.
Dro. I am an affe, I am a womans man, and befides
   my felfe.
Ant. What womans man ? and how befides thy
   felfe ?
Dro. Marrie fir, befides my felfe, I am due to a woman:
One that claimes me, one that haunts me, one that will
haue me.
                                          Ant. What

Anti. What claime laies fhe to thee?

Dro. Marry fir, fuch claime as you would lay to your horfe, and fhe would haue me as a beaft, not that I beeing a beaft fhe would haue me, but that fhe being a verie beaftly creature layes claime to me.

Anti. What is fhe?

Dro. A very reuerent body: I fuch a one, as a man may not fpeake of, without he fay fir reuerence, I haue but leane lucke in the match, and yet is fhe a wondrous fat marriage.

Anti. How doft thou meane a fat marriage?

Dro. Marry fir, fhe's the Kitchin wench, & al greafe, and I know not what vfe to put her too, but to make a Lampe of her, and run from her by her owne light. I warrant, her ragges and the Tallow in them, will burne a *Poland* Winter: If fhe liues till doomefday, fhe'l burne a weeke longer then the whole World.

Anti. What complexion is fhe of?

Dro. Swart like my fhoo, but her face nothing like fo cleane kept: for why? fhe fweats a man may goe ouer-fhooes in the grime of it.

Anti. That's a fault that water will mend.

Dro. No fir, 'tis in graine, *Noahs* flood could not do it.

Anti. What's her name?

Dro. Nell Sir: but her name is three quarters, that's an Ell and three quarters, will not meafure her from hip to hip.

Anti. Then fhe beares fome bredth?

Dro. No longer from head to foot, then from hippe to hippe: fhe is fphericall, like a globe: I could find out Countries in her.

Anti. In what part of her body ftands *Ireland*?

Dro. Marry fir in her buttockes, I found it out by the bogges.

Ant, Where *Scotland*?

Dro. I found it by the barrenneffe, hard in the palme of the hand.

Ant. Where *France*?

Dro. In her forhead, arm'd and reuerted, making warre againft her heire.

Ant. Where *England*?

Dro. I look'd for the chalkle Cliffes, but I could find no whiteneffe in them. But I gueffe, it ftood in her chin by the falt rheume that ranne betweene *France*, and it.

Ant. Where *Spaine*?

Dro. Faith I faw it not: but I felt it hot in her breth.

Ant. Where *America*, the *Indies*?

Dro. Oh fir, vpon her nofe, all ore embellifhed with Rubies, Carbuncles, Saphires, declining their rich Afpeft to the hot breath of Spaine, who fent whole Armadoes of Carrects to be ballaft at her nofe.

Anti. Where ftood *Belgia*, the *Netherlands*?

Dro. Oh fir, I did not looke fo low. To conclude, this drudge or Diuiner layd claime to mee, call'd mee *Dromio*, fwore I was affur'd to her, told me what priuie markes I had about mee, as the marke of my fhoulder, the Mole in my necke, the great Wart on my left arme, that I amaz'd ranne from her as a witch. And I thinke, if my breft had not beene made of faith, and my heart of fteele, fhe had transform'd me to a Curtull dog, & made me turne i'th wheele.

Anti. Go hie thee prefently, poft to the rode, And if the winde blow any way from fhore, I will not harbour in this Towne to night. If any Barke put forth, come to the Mart,

Where I will walke till thou returne to me: If euerie one knowes vs, and we know none, 'Tis time I thinke to trudge, packe, and be gone.

Dro. As from a Beare a man would run for life, So flie I from her that would be my wife.   *Exit*

Anti. There's none but Witches do inhabite heere, And therefore 'tis hie time that I were hence: She that doth call me husband, euen my foule Doth for a wife abhorre. But her faire fifter Poffeft with fuch a gentle foueraigne grace, Of fuch inchanting prefence and difcourfe, Hath almoft made me Traitor to my felfe: But leaft my felfe be guilty to felfe wrong, Ile ftop mine eares againft the Mermaids fong.

Enter Angelo with the Chaine.

Ang. M.r *Antipholus.*

Anti. I that's my name.

Ang. I know it well fir, loe here's the chaine, I thought to haue tane you at the *Porpentine,* The chaine vnfinifh'd made me ftay thus long.

Anti. What is your will that I fhal do with this?

Ang. What pleafe your felfe fir: I haue made it for you.

Anti. Made it for me fir, I befpoke it not.

Ang. Not once, nor twice, but twentie times you haue:

Go home with it, and pleafe your Wife withall, And foone at fupper time Ile vifit you, And then receiue my money for the chaine.

Anti. I pray you fir receiue the money now, For feare you ne're fee chaine, nor mony more.

Ang. You are a merry man fir, fare you well.   *Exit.*

Ant. What I fhould thinke of this, I cannot tell: But this I thinke, there's no man is fo vaine, That would refufe fo faire an offer'd Chaine. I fee a man heere needs not liue by fhifts, When in the ftreets he meetes fuch Golden gifts: Ile to the Mart, and there for *Dromio* ftay, If any fhip put out, then ftraight away.   *Exit.*

Actus Quartus. Scœna Prima.

Enter a Merchant, Goldfmith, and an Officer.

Mar. You know fince Pentecoft the fum is due, And fince I haue not much importun'd you, Nor now I had not, but that I am bound To *Perfia*, and want Gilders for my voyage: Therefore make prefent fatisfaction, Or Ile attach you by this Officer.

Gold. Euen iuft the fum that I do owe to you, Is growing to me by *Antipholus,* And in the inftant that I met with you, He had of me a Chaine, at fiue a clocke I fhall receiue the money for the fame: Pleafeth you walke with me downe to his houfe, I will difcharge my bond, and thanke you too.

Enter Antipholus Ephef. Dromio from the Courtizans.

Offi. That labour may you faue: See where he comes.

Ant. While I go to the Goldfmiths houfe, go thou

And

And buy a ropes end, that will I beftow
Among my wife, and their confederates,
For locking me out of my doores by day :
But foft I fee the Goldfmith ; get thee gone,
Buy thou a rope, and bring it home to me.

Dro. I buy a thoufand pound a yeare, I buy a rope.

Exit Dromio

Eph. Ant. A man is well holpe vp that trufts to you,
I promifed your prefence, and the Chaine,
But neither Chaine nor Goldfmith came to me :
Belike you thought our loue would laft too long
If it were chain'd together : and therefore came not.

Gold. Sauing your merrie humor : here's the note
How much your Chaine weighs to the vtmoft chareƈt,
The finenefſe of the Gold, and conuei'd fafhion,
Which doth amount to three odde Duckets more
Then I ftand debted to this Gentleman,
I pray you fee him prefently difcharg'd,
For he is bound to Sea, and ftayes but for it.

Anti. I am not furnifh'd with the prefent monie :
Befides I haue fome bufineffe in the towne,
Good Signior take the ftranger to my houfe,
And with you take the Chaine,and bid my wife
Disburfe the fumme, on the receit thereof,
Perchance I will be there as foone as you.

Gold. Then you will bring the Chaine to her your
felfe.

Anti. No beare it with you, leaft I come not time e-
nough.

Gold. Well fir, I will ? Haue you the Chaine about
you?

Ant. And if I haue not fir, I hope you haue:
Or elfe you may returne without your money.

Gold. Nay come I pray you fir, giue me the Chaine :
Both winde and tide ftayes for this Gentleman,
And I too blame haue held him heere too long.

Anti. Good Lord, you vfe this dalliance to excufe
Your breach of promife to the *Porpentine*,
I fhould haue chid you for not bringing it,
But like a fhrew you firft begin to brawle.

Mar. The houre fteales on, I pray you fir difpatch.

Gold. You heare how he importunes me, the Chaine.

Ant. Wh y giue it to my wife, and fetch your mony.

Gold. Come,come,you know I gaue it you euen now.
Either fend the Chaine, or fend me by fome token.

Ant. Fie, now you run this humor out of breath,
Come where's the Chaine, I pray you let me fee it.

Mar. My bufineffe cannot brooke this dalliance,
Good fir fay, whe'r you'l anfwer me, or no :
If not, Ile leaue him to the Officer.

Ant. I anfwer you ? What fhould I anfwer you.

Gold. The monie that you owe me for the Chaine.

Ant. I owe you none, till I receiue the Chaine.

Gold. You know I gaue it you halfe an houre fince.

Ant. You gaue me none, you wrong mee much to
fay fo.

Gold. You wrong me more fir in denying it.
Confider how it ftands vpon my credit.

Mar. Well Officer, arreft him at my fuite.

Offi. I do, and charge you in the Dukes name to o-
bey me.

Gold. This touches me in reputation.
Either confent to pay this fum for me,
Or I attach you by this Officer.

Ant. Confent to pay thee that I neuer had :
Arreft me foolifh fellow if thou dar'ft.

Gold. Heere is thy fee, arreft him Officer.
I would not fpare my brother in this cafe,
If he fhould fcorne me fo apparantly.

Offic. I do arreft you fir, you heare the fuite.

Ant. I do obey thee, till I giue thee baile.
But firrah, you fhall buy this fport as deere,
As all the mettall in your fhop will anfwer.

Gold. Sir, fir, I fhall haue Law in *Ephefus*,
To your notorious fhame, I doubt it not.

Enter Dromio Sira. from the Bay.

Dro. Mafter, there's a Barke of *Epidamium*,
That ftaies but till her Owner comes aboord,
And then fir fhe beares away. Our fraughtage fir,
I haue conuei'd aboord, and I haue bought
The Oyle, the *Balfamum*, and Aqua-vitæ.
The fhip is in her trim, the merrie winde
Blowes faire from land : they ftay for nought at all,
But for their Owner, Mafter, and your felfe.

An. How now? a Madman? Why thou peeuifh fheep
What fhip of *Epidamium* ftaies for me.

S.Dro. A fhip you fent me too, to hier waftage.

Ant. Thou drunken flaue, I fent thee for a rope,
And told thee to what purpofe,and what end.

S.Dro. You fent me for a ropes end as foone,
You fent me to the Bay fir, for a Barke.

Ant. I will debate this matter at more leifure
And teach your eares to lift me with more heede :
To *Adriana* Villaine hie thee ftraight:
Giue her this key,and tell her in the Deske
That's couer'd o're with Turkifh Tapiftrie,
There is a purfe of Duckets, let her fend it:
Tell her, I am arrefted in the ftreete,
And that fhall baile me : hie thee flaue, be gone,
On Officer to prifon, till it come.

Exeunt

S. Dromio. To *Adriana*,that is where we din'd,
Where Dowfabell did claime me for her husband,
She is too bigge I hope for me to compaffe,
Thither I muft, although againft my will :
For feruants muft their Mafters mindes fulfill.

Exit

Enter Adriana and Luciana.

Adr. Ah *Luciana*, did he tempt thee fo ?
Might'ft thou perceiue aufteerely in his eie,
That he did plead in earneft, yea or no :
Look'd he or red or pale, or fad or merrily ?
What obferuation mad'ft thou in this cafe ?
Oh, his hearts Meteors tilting in his face.

Luc. Firft he deni'de you had in him no right.

Adr. He meant he did me none : the more my fpight

Luc. Then fwore he that he was a ftranger heere.

Adr. And true he fwore, though yet forfworne hee
were.

Luc. Then pleaded I for you.

Adr. And what faid he ?

Luc. That loue I begg'd for you, he begg'd of me.

Adr. With what perfwafion did he tempt thy loue ?

Luc. With words, that in an honeft fuit might moue.
Firft, he did praife my beautie, then my fpeech.

Adr. Did'ft fpeake him faire ?

Luc. Haue patience I befeech.

Adr. I cannot, nor I will not hold me ftill,
My tongue, though not my heart, fhall haue his will.
He is deformed, crooked, old, and fere,
Ill-fac'd, worfe bodied, fhapeleffe euery where :
Vicious, vngentle, foolifh, blunt, vnkinde,

Stigma-

Stigmaticall in making worſe in minde.

Luc. Who would be iealous then of ſuch a one?
No euill loſt is wail'd, when it is gone.

Adr. Ah but I thinke him better then I ſay :
And yet would herein others eies were worſe :
Farre from her neſt the Lapwing cries away ;
My heart praies for him, though my tongue doe curſe.

Enter S. Dromio.

Dro. Here goe : the deske, the purſe, ſweet now make
haſte.

Luc. How haſt thou loſt thy breath?

S. Dro. By running faſt.

Adr. Where is thy Maſter Dromio? Is he well?

S. Dro. No, he's in Tartar limbo, worſe then hell :
A diuell in an euerlaſting garment hath him ;
On whoſe hard heart is button'd vp with ſteele :
A Feind, a Fairie, pittileſſe and ruffe :
A Wolfe, nay worſe, a fellow all in buffe :
A back friend, a ſhoulder-clapper, one that countermãds
The paſſages of allies, creekes, and narrow lands :
A hound that runs Counter, and yet draws drifoot well,
One that before the Iudgmẽt carries poore ſoules to hel.

Adr. Why man, what is the matter?

S. Dro. I doe not know the matter, hee is reſted on
the caſe.

Adr. What is he arreſted? tell me at whoſe ſuite?

S. Dro. I know not at whoſe ſuite he is areſted well;
but is in a ſuite of buffe which reſted him, that can I tell,
will you ſend him Miſtris redemption, the monie in
his deske.

Adr. Go fetch it Siſter ; this I wonder at.
           Exit Luciana.

Thus he vnknowne to me ſhould be in debt :
Tell me, was he areſted on a band?

S. Dro. Not on a band, but on a ſtronger thing :
A chaine, a chaine, doe you not here it ring.

Adria. What, the chaine?

S. Dro. No, no, the bell, 'tis time that I were gone :
It was two ere I left him, and now the clocke ſtrikes one.

Adr. The houres come backe, that did I neuer heare.

S. Dro. Oh yes, if any houre meete a Serieant, a turnes
backe for verie feare.

Adri. As if time were in debt : how fondly do'ſt thou
reaſon?

S. Dro. Time is a verie bankerout, and owes more then
he's worth to ſeaſon.
Nay, he's a theefe too : haue you not heard men ſay,
That time comes ſtealing on by night and day?
If I be in debt and theft, and a Serieant in the way,
Hath he not reaſon to turne backe an houre in a day?

Enter Luciana.

Adr. Go Dromio, there's the monie, beare it ſtraight,
And bring thy Maſter home imediately.
Come ſifter, I am preſt downe with conceit :
Conceit, my comfort and my iniurie.   *Exit.*

Enter Antipholus Siracuſia.

There's not a man I meete but doth ſalute me
As if I were their well acquainted friend,
And euerie one doth call me by my name :
Some tender monie to me, ſome inuite me ;
Some other giue me thankes for kindneſſes ;
Some offer me Commodities to buy.
Euen now a tailor cal'd me in his ſhop,

And ſhow'd me Silkes that he had bought for me,
And therewithall tooke meaſure of my body.
Sure theſe are but imaginarie wiles,
And lapland Sorcerers inhabite here.

Enter Dromio. Sir.

S. Dro. Maſter, here's the gold you ſent me for : what
haue you got the picture of old *Adam* new apparel'd?

Ant. What gold is this? What *Adam* do'ſt thou
meane?

S. Dro. Not that *Adam* that kept the Paradiſe : but
that *Adam* that keepes the priſon ; hee that goes in the
calues-skin, that was kil'd for the Prodigall : hee that
came behinde you ſir, like an euill angel, and bid you forſake your libertie.

Ant. I vnderſtand thee not.

S. Dro. No? why 'tis a plaine caſe : he that went like
a Baſe-Viole in a caſe of leather ; the man ſir, that when
gentlemen are tired giues them a ſob, and reſts them :
he ſir, that takes pittie on decaied men, and giues them
ſuites of durance : he that ſets vp his reſt to doe more ex-
ploits with his Mace, then a Moris Pike.

Ant. What thou mean'ſt an officer?

S. Dro. I ſir, the Serieant of the Band : he that brings
any man to anſwer it that breakes his Band : one that
thinkes a man alwaies going to bed, and ſaies, God giue
you good reſt.

Ant. Well ſir, there reſt in your foolerie :
Is there any ſhips puts forth to night? may we be gone?

S. Dro. Why ſir, I brought you word an houre ſince,
that the Barke *Expedition* put forth to night, and then
were you hindred by the Serieant to tarry for the *Hoy
Delay* : Here are the angels that you ſent for to deliuer
you.

Ant. The fellow is diſtract, and ſo am I,
And here we wander in illuſions :
Some bleſſed power deliuer vs from hence.

Enter a Curtizan.

Cur. Well met, well met, Maſter *Antipholus* :
I ſee ſir you haue found the Gold-ſmith now :
Is that the chaine you promis'd me to day.

Ant. Sathan auoide, I charge thee tempt me not.

S. Dro. Maſter, is this Miſtris *Satban?*

Ant. It is the diuell.

S. Dro. Nay, ſhe is worſe, ſhe is the diuels dam :
And here ſhe comes in the habit of a light wench, and
thereof comes, that the wenches ſay God dam me, That's
as much to ſay, God make me a light wench : It is written, they appeare to men like angels of light, light is an
effect of fire, and fire will burne : *ergo,* light wenches will
burne, come not neere her.

Cur. Your man and you are maruailous merrie ſir.
Will you goe with me, wee'll mend our dinner here?

S. Dro. Maſter, if do expect ſpoon-meate, or beſpeake
a long ſpoone.

Ant. Why *Dromio?*

S. Dro. Marrie he muſt haue a long ſpoone that muſt
eate with the diuell.

Ant. Auoid then fiend, what tel'ſt thou me of ſup-
Thou art, as you are all a ſorcereſſe :   (ping?
I coniure thee to leaue me, and be gon.

Cur. Giue me the ring of mine you had at dinner,
Or for my Diamond the Chaine you promis'd,
And Ile be gone ſir, and not trouble you.

S. Dro. Some diuels aske but the parings of ones naile,

                                            a

a ruſh, a haire, a drop of blood, a pin, a nut, a cherrie-
ſtone : but ſhe more couetous, wold haue a chaine: Maſter be wiſe, and if you giue it her, the diuell will ſhake
her Chaine, and fright vs with it.

  Cur. I pray you ſir my Ring, or elſe the Chaine,
I hope you do not meane to cheate me ſo ?
  Ant. Auant thou witch : Come *Dromio* let vs go.
  S.Dro. Flie pride ſaies the Pea-cocke, Miſtris that
you know.   *Exit.*
  Cur. Now out of doubt *Antipholus* is mad,
Elſe would he neuer ſo demeane himſelfe,
A Ring he hath of mine worth fortie Duckets,
And for the ſame he promis'd me a Chaine,
Both one and other he denies me now :
The reaſon that I gather he is mad,
Beſides this preſent inſtance of his rage,
Is a mad tale he told to day at dinner,
Of his owne doores being ſhut againſt his entrance.
Belike his wife acquainted with his fits,
On purpoſe ſhut the doores againſt his way :
My way is now to hie home to his houſe,
And tell his wife, that being Lunaticke,
He ruſh'd into my houſe, and tooke perforce
My Ring away. This courſe I fitteſt chooſe,
For fortie Duckets is too much to looſe.

       Enter Antipholus Ephes. with a Iailor.

  An. Feare me not man, I will not breake away,
Ile giue thee ere I leaue thee ſo much money
To warrant thee as I am reſted for.
My wife is in a wayward moode to day,
And will not lightly truſt the Meſſenger,
That I ſhould be attach'd in *Epheſus*,
I tell you 'twill ſound harſhly in her eares.

       Enter Dromio Eph. with a ropes end.
Heere comes my Man, I thinke he brings the monie.
How now ſir? Haue you that I ſent you for?
  E.Dro. Here's that I warrant you will pay them all.
  Anti. But where's the Money ?
  E. Dro. Why ſir, I gaue the Monie for the Rope.
  Ant. Fiue hundred Duckets villaine for a rope ?
  E. Dro. Ile ſerue you ſir fiue hundred at the rate.
  Ant. To what end did I bid thee hie thee home?
  E.Dro. To a ropes end ſir, and to that end am I re-
turn'd.
  Offi. Good ſir be patient.
  E. Dro. Nay 'tis for me to be patient, I am in aduer-
ſitie.
  Offi. Good now hold thy tongue.
  E.Dro. Nay, rather perſwade him to hold his hands.
  Anti. Thou whoreſon ſenſeleſſe Villaine.
  E.Dro. I would I were ſenſeleſſe ſir, that I might
not feele your blowes.
  Anti. Thou art ſenſible in nothing but blowes, and
ſo is an Aſſe.
  E. Dro. I am an Aſſe indeede, you may prooue it by
my long eares. I haue ſerued him from the houre of my
Natiuitie to this inſtant, and haue nothing at his hands
for my ſeruice but blowes. When I am cold, he heates
me with beating : when I am warme, he cooles me with
beating : I am wak'd with it when I ſleepe, rais'd with
it when I ſit, driuen out of doores with it when I goe
from home, welcom'd home with it when I returne, nay

I beare it on my ſhoulders, as a begger woont her brat :
and I thinke when he hath lam'd me, I ſhall begge with
it from doore to doore.

   Enter Adriana, Luciana, Courtizan, and a Schoole-
          maſter, call'd Pinch.

  Ant. Come goe along, my wife is comming yon-
der.
  E.Dro. Miſtris *reſpice finem*, reſpect your end, or ra-
ther the propheſie like the Parrat, beware the ropes end.
  Anti. Wilt thou ſtill talke?   *Beats Dro.*
  Curt. How ſay you now? Is not your husband mad?
  Adri. His inciuility confirmes no leſſe :
Good Doctor *Pinch*, you are a Coniurer,
Eſtabliſh him in his true ſence againe,
And I will pleaſe you what you will demand.
  Luc. Alas how fiery, and how ſharpe he lookes.
  Cur. Marke, how he trembles in his extaſie.
  Pinch. Giue me your hand, and let mee feele your
pulſe.
  Ant. There is my hand, and let it feele your eare.
  Pinch. I charge thee Sathan, hous'd within this man,
To yeeld poſſeſſion to my holie praiers,
And to thy ſtate of darkneſſe hie thee ſtraight,
I coniure thee by all the Saints in heauen.
  Anti. Peace doting wizard, peace ; I am not mad.
  Adr. Oh that thou wer't not, poore diſtreſſed ſoule.
  Anti. You Minion you, are theſe your Cuſtomers?
Did this Companion with the ſaffron face
Reuell and feaſt it at my houſe to day,
Whil'ſt vpon me the guiltie doores were ſhut,
And I denied to enter in my houſe.
  Adr. O husband, God doth know you din'd at home
Where would you had remain'd vntill this time,
Free from theſe ſlanders, and this open ſhame.
  Anti. Din'd at home ? Thou Villaine, what ſayeſt
thou ?
  Dro. Sir ſooth to ſay, you did not dine at home.
  Ant. Were not my doores lockt vp, and I ſhut out ?
  Dro. Perdie, your doores were lockt, and you ſhut
out.
  Anti. And did not ſhe her ſelfe reuile me there?
  Dro. Sans Fable, ſhe her ſelfe reuil'd you there.
  Anti. Did not her Kitchen maide raile, taunt, and
ſcorne me ?
  Dro. Certis ſhe did, the kitchin veſtall ſcorn'd you.
  Ant. And did not I in rage depart from thence ?
  Dro. In veritie you did, my bones beares witneſſe,
That ſince haue felt the vigor of his rage.
  Adr. Is't good to ſooth him in theſe crontraries?
  Pinch. It is no ſhame, the fellow finds his vaine,
And yeelding to him, humors well his frenſie.
  Ant. Thou haſt ſubborn'd the Goldſmith to arreſt
mee.
  Adr. Alas, I ſent you Monie to redeeme you,
By *Dromio* heere, who came in haſt for it.
  Dro. Monie by me? Heart and good will you might,
But ſurely Maſter not a ragge of Monie.
  Ant. Wentſt not thou to her for a purſe of Duckets.
  Adri. He came to me, and I deliuer'd it.
  Luci. And I am witneſſe with her that ſhe did:
  Dro. God and the Rope-maker beare me witneſſe,
That I was ſent for nothing but a rope.
  Pinch. Miſtris, both Man and Maſter is poſſeſt,
I know it by their pale and deadly lookes,

                         They

They muſt be bound and laide in ſome darke roome.
*Ant.*Say wherefore didſt thou locke me forth to day,
And why doſt thou denie the bagge of gold?
Adr. I did not gentle husband locke thee forth.
Dro. And gentle Mr I receiu'd no gold :
But I confeſſe ſir, that we were lock'd out.
Adr. Diſſembling Villain, thou ſpeak'ſt falſe in both
Ant. Diſſembling harlot, thou art falſe in all,
And art confederate with a damned packe,
To make a loathſome abiect ſcorne of me :
But with theſe nailes, Ile plucke out theſe falſe eyes,
That would behold in me this ſhamefull ſport.

   Enter three or foure, and offer to binde him:
       Hee ſtriues.
Adr. Oh binde him, binde him, let him not come
neere me.
*Pinch.*More company, the fiend is ſtrong within him
Luc. Aye me poore man, how pale and wan he looks.
Ant. What will you murther me, thou Iailor thou ?
I am thy priſoner, wilt thou ſuffer them to make a reſ-
cue ?
Offi. Maſters let him go : he is my priſoner, and you
ſhall not haue him.
Pinch. Go binde this man, for he is franticke too.
Adr. What wilt thou do, thou peeuiſh Officer ?
Haſt thou delight to ſee a wretched man
Do outrage and diſpleaſure to himſelfe?
Offi. He is my priſoner, if I let him go,
The debt he owes will be requir'd of me.
Adr. I will diſcharge thee ere I go from thee,
Beare me forthwith vnto his Creditor,
And knowing how the debt growes I will pay it.
Good Maſter Doctor ſee him ſafe conuey'd
Home to my houſe, oh moſt vnhappy day.
Ant. Oh moſt vnhappie ſtrumpet.
Dro. Maſter, I am heere entred in bond for you.
Ant. Out on thee Villaine, wherefore doſt thou mad
mee ?
Dro. Will you be bound for nothing, be mad good
Maſter, cry the diuell.
Luc. God helpe poore ſoules, how idlely doe they
talke.
Adr. Go beare him hence, ſiſter go you with me:
Say now, whoſe ſuite is he arreſted at ?
    Exeunt. Manet Offic. Adri. Luci. Courtizan
Off. One *Angelo* a Goldſmith, do you know him?
Adr. I know the man : what is the ſumme he owes ?
Off. Two hundred Duckets.
Adr. Say, how growes it due.
Off. Due for a Chaine your husband had of him.
Adr. He did beſpeake a Chain for me, but had it not.
Cur. When as your husband all in rage to day
Came to my houſe, and tooke away my Ring,
The Ring I ſaw vpon his finger now,
Straight after did I meete him with a Chaine.
Adr. It may be ſo, but I did neuer ſee it.
Come Iailor, bring me where the Goldſmith is,
I long to know the truth heereof at large.

  Enter Antipholus Siracuſia with his Rapier drawne,
    and Dromio Sirac.

Luc. God for thy mercy, they are looſe againe.
Adr. And come with naked ſwords,
Let's call more helpe to haue them bound againe.
        Runne all out.

Off. Away, they'l kill vs.
   Exeunt omnes, as faſt as may be, frighted.
S. Ant. I ſee theſe Witches are affraid of ſwords.
S. Dro. She that would be your wife, now ran from
you.
Ant. Come to the Centaur, fetch our ſtuffe from
thence :
I long that we were ſafe and ſound aboord.
Dro. Faith ſtay heere this night, they will ſurely do
vs no harme : you ſaw they ſpeake vs faire, giue vs gold:
me thinkes they are ſuch a gentle Nation, that but for
the Mountaine of mad fleſh that claimes mariage of me,
I could finde in my heart to ſtay heere ſtill, and turne
Witch.
Ant. I will not ſtay to night for all the Towne,
Therefore away, to get our ſtuffe aboord .   *Exeunt*

Actus Quintus. Scœna Prima.

   Enter the Merchant and the Goldſmith.

Gold. I am ſorry Sir that I haue hindred you,
But I proteſt he had the Chaine of me,
Though moſt diſhoneſtly he doth denie it.
Mar. How is the man eſteem'd heere in the Citie?
Gold. Of very reuerent reputation ſir,
Of credit infinite, highly belou'd,
Second to none that liues heere in the Citie :
His word might beare my wealth at any time.
Mar. Speake ſoftly, yonder as I thinke he walkes.

   Enter Antipholus and Dromio againe.

Gold. 'Tis ſo : and that ſelfe chaine about his necke,
Which he forſwore moſt monſtrouſly to haue.
Good ſir draw neere to me, Ile ſpeake to him :
Signior *Antipholus*, I wonder much
That you would put me to this ſhame and trouble,
And not without ſome ſcandall to your ſelfe,
With circumſtance and oaths, ſo to denie
This Chaine, which now you weare ſo openly.
Beſide the charge, the ſhame, impriſonment,
You haue done wrong to this my honeſt friend,
Who but for ſtaying on our Controuerſie,
Had hoiſted ſaile, and put to ſea to day:
This Chaine you had of me, can you deny it?
Ant. I thinke I had, I neuer did deny it.
Mar. Yes that you did ſir, and forſwore it too.
Ant. Who heard me to denie it or forſweare it ?
Mar. Theſe eares of mine thou knowſt did hear thee :
Fie on thee wretch, 'tis pitty that thou liu'ſt
To walke where any honeſt men reſort.
Ant. Thou art a Villaine to impeach me thus,
Ile proue mine honor, and mine honeſtie
Againſt thee preſently, if thou dar'ſt ſtand:
Mar. I dare and do defie thee for a villaine.

They draw. Enter Adriana, Luciana, Courtezan, & others.
Adr. Hold, hurt him not for God ſake, he is mad,
Some get within him, take his ſword away :
Binde *Dromio* too, and beare them to my houſe.
S. Dro. Runne maſter run, for Gods ſake take a houſe,
This is ſome Priorie, in, or we are ſpoyl'd.
      Exeunt to the Priorie.
            Enter

Enter Ladie Abbeſſe.

Ab. Be quiet people, wherefore throng you hither?
Adr. To fetch my poore diſtracted husband hence,
Let vs come in, that we may binde him faſt,
And beare him home for his recouerie.
Gold. I knew he vvas not in his perfect wits.
Mar. I am ſorry now that I did draw on him.
Ab. How long hath this poſſeſſion held the man.
Adr. This weeke he hath beene heauie, ſower ſad,
And much different from the man he was:
But till this afternoone his paſſion
Ne're brake into extremity of rage.
Ab. Hath he not loſt much wealth by wrack of ſea,
Buried ſome deere friend, hath not elſe his eye
Stray'd his affection in vnlawfull loue,
A ſinne preuailing much in youthfull men,
Who giue their eies the liberty of gazing.
Which of theſe ſorrowes is he ſubiect too?
Adr. To none of theſe, except it be the laſt,
Namely, ſome loue that drew him oft from home.
Ab. You ſhould for that haue reprehended him.
Adr. Why ſo I did.
Ab. I but not rough enough.
Adr. As roughly as my modeſtie would let me.
Ab. Haply in priuate.
Adr. And in aſſemblies too.
Ab. I, but not enough.
Adr. It was the copie of our Conference.
In bed he ſlept not for my vrging it,
At boord he fed not for my vrging it:
Alone, it was the ſubiect of my Theame:
In company I often glanced it:
Still did I tell him, it was vilde and bad.
Ab. And thereof came it, that the man was mad.
The venome clamors of a iealous woman,
Poiſons more deadly then a mad dogges tooth.
It ſeemes his ſleepes were hindred by thy railing,
And thereof comes it that his head is light.
Thou ſaiſt his meate was ſawc'd with thy vpbraidings,
Vnquiet meales make ill digeſtions,
Thereof the raging fire of feauer bred,
And what's a Feauer, but a fit of madneſſe?
Thou ſayeſt his ſports were hindred by thy bralles.
Sweet recreation barr'd, what doth enſue
But moodie and dull melancholly,
Kinſman to grim and comfortleſſe diſpaire,
And at her heeles a huge infectious troope
Of pale diſtemperatures, and foes to life?
In food, in ſport, and life-preſeruing reſt
To be diſturb'd, would mad or man, or beaſt:
The conſequence is then, thy iealous fits
Hath ſcar'd thy husband from the vſe of wits.
Luc. She neuer reprehended him but mildely,
When he demean'd himſelfe, rough, rude, and wildly,
Why beare you theſe rebukes, and anſwer not?
Adri. She did betray me to my owne reproofe,
Good people enter, and lay hold on him.
Ab. No, not a creature enters in my houſe.
Ad. Then let your ſeruants bring my husband forth
Ab. Neither: he tooke this place for ſanctuary,
And it ſhall priuiledge him from your hands,
Till I haue brought him to his wits againe,
Or looſe my labour in aſſaying it.
Adr. I will attend my husband, be his nurſe,

Diet his ſickneſſe, for it is my Office,
And will haue no atturney but my ſelfe,
And therefore let me haue him home with me.
Ab. Be patient, for I will not let him ſtirre,
Till I haue vs'd the approoued meanes I haue,
With wholſome ſirrups, drugges, and holy prayers
To make of him a formall man againe:
It is a branch and parcell of mine oath,
A charitable dutie of my order,
Therefore depart, and leaue him heere with me.
Adr. I will not hence, and leaue my husband heere:
And ill it doth beſeeme your holineſſe
To ſeparate the husband and the wife.
Ab. Be quiet and depart, thou ſhalt not haue him.
Luc. Complaine vnto the Duke of this indignity.
Adr. Come go, I will fall proſtrate at his feete,
And neuer riſe vntill my teares and prayers
Haue won his grace to come in perſon hither,
And take perforce my husband from the Abbeſſe.
Mar. By this I thinke the Diall points at fiue:
Anon I'me ſure the Duke himſelfe in perſon
Comes this way to the melancholly vale;
The place of depth, and ſorrie execution,
Behinde the ditches of the Abbey heere.
Gold. Vpon what cauſe?
Mar. To ſee a reuerent *Siracuſian* Merchant,
Who put vnluckily into this Bay
Againſt the Lawes and Statutes of this Towne,
Beheaded publikely for his offence.
Gold. See where they come, we wil behold his death
Luc. Kneele to the Duke before he paſſe the Abbey.

Enter the Duke of Epheſus, and the Merchant of Siracuſe bare head, with the Headſman, & other Officers.

Duke. Yet once againe proclaime it publikely,
If any friend will pay the ſumme for him,
He ſhall not die, ſo much we tender him.
Adr. Iuſtice moſt ſacred Duke againſt the Abbeſſe.
Duke. She is a vertuous and a reuerend Lady,
It cannot be that ſhe hath done thee wrong.
Adr. May it pleaſe your Grace, *Antipholus* my husbād,
Who I made Lord of me, and all I had,
At your important Letters this ill day,
A moſt outragious fit of madneſſe tooke him:
That deſp'rately he hurried through the ſtreete,
With him his bondman, all as mad as he,
Doing diſpleaſure to the Citizens,
By ruſhing in their houſes: bearing thence
Rings, Iewels, any thing his rage did like.
Once did I get him bound, and ſent him home,
Whil'ſt to take order for the wrongs I went,
That heere and there his furie had committed,
Anon I wot not, by what ſtrong eſcape
He broke from thoſe that had the guard of him,
And with his mad attendant and himſelfe,
Each one with irefull paſſion, with drawne ſwords
Met vs againe, and madly bent on vs
Chac'd vs away: till raiſing of more aide
We came againe to binde them: then they fled
Into this Abbey, whether we purſu'd them,
And heere the Abbeſſe ſhuts the gates on vs,
And will not ſuffer vs to fetch him out,
Nor ſend him forth, that we may beare him hence.

I   Therefore

Therefore moſt gracious Duke with thy command,
Let him be brought forth,and borne hence for helpe.
 Duke. Long ſince thy husband ſeru'd me in my wars
And I to thee ingag'd a Princes word,
When thou didſt make him Maſter of thy bed,
To do him all the grace and good I could.
Go ſome of you, knocke at the Abbey gate,
And bid the Lady Abbeſſe come to me :
I will determine this before I ſtirre.
 Enter a Meſſenger.
Oh Miſtris,Miſtris, ſhift and ſaue your ſelfe,
My Maſter and his man are both broke looſe,
Beaten the Maids a-row, and bound the Doctor,
Whoſe beard they haue ſindg'd off with brands of fire,
And euer as it blaz'd, they threw on him
Great pailes of puddled myre to quench the haire ;
My Mr preaches patience to him, and the while
His man with Cizers nickes him like a foole :
And ſure (vnleſſe you ſend ſome preſent helpe)
Betweene them they will kill the Coniurer.
 Adr. Peace foole, thy Maſter and his man are here,
And that is falſe thou doſt report to vs.
 Meſſ. Miſtris, vpon my life I tel you true,
I haue not breath'd almoſt ſince I did ſee it.
He cries for you, and vowes if he can take you,
To ſcorch your face, and to disfigure you :
 Cry within.
Harke, harke, I heare him Miſtris : flie, be gone.
 Duke. Come ſtand by me,feare nothing: guard with
Halberds.
 Adr. Ay me, it is my husband : witneſſe you,
That he is borne about inuiſible,
Euen now we hous'd him in the Abbey heere.
And now he's there, paſt thought of humane reaſon.

 Enter Antipholus, and E . Dromio of Epheſus.
 (ſtice,
 E.Ant. Iuſtice moſt gracious Duke,oh grant me iu-
Euen for the ſeruice that long ſince I did thee,
When I beſtrid thee in the warres, and tooke
Deepe ſcarres to ſaue thy life ; euen for the blood
That then I loſt for thee, now grant me iuſtice.
 Mar.Fat. Vnleſſe the feare of death doth make me
dote, I ſee my ſonne *Antipholus* and *Dromio.*
 E.Ant. Iuſtice (ſweet Prince) againſt ỹ Woman there:
She whom thou gau'ſt to me to be my wife ;
That hath abuſed and diſhonored me,
Euen in the ſtrength and height of iniurie :
Beyond imagination is the wrong
That ſhe this day hath ſhameleſſe throwne on me.
 Duke. Diſcouer how,and thou ſhalt finde me iuſt.
 E.Ant. This day (great Duke) ſhe ſhut the doores
vpon me,
While ſhe with Harlots feaſted in my houſe.
 Duke. A greeuous fault : ſay woman,didſt thou ſo ?
 Adr. No my good Lord. My ſelfe, he,and my ſiſter,
To day did dine together : ſo befall my ſoule,
As this is falſe he burthens me withall.
 Luc. Nere may I looke on day, nor ſleepe on night,
But ſhe tels to your Highneſſe ſimple truth.
 Gold. O periur'd woman! They are both forſworne,
In this the Madman iuſtly chargeth them.
 E. Ant. My Liege, I am aduiſed what I ſay,
Neither diſturbed with the effect of Wine,
Nor headie-raſh prouoak'd with raging ire,
Albeit my wrongs might make one wiſer mad.

This woman lock'd me out this day from dinner ;
That Goldſmith there, were he not pack'd with her,
Could witneſſe it : for he was with me then,
Who parted with me to go fetch a Chaine,
Promiſing to bring it to the Porpentine,
Where *Balthaſar* and I did dine together.
Our dinner done, and he not comming thither,
I went to ſeeke him. In the ſtreet I met him,
And in his companie that Gentleman.
There did this periur'd Goldſmith ſweare me downe,
That I this day of him receiu'd the Chaine,
Which God he knowes, I ſaw not. For the which,
He did arreſt me with an Officer.
I did obey, and ſent my Peſant home
For certaine Duckets : he with none return'd.
Then fairely I beſpoke the Officer
To go in perſon with me to my houſe.
By th'way, we met my wife,her ſiſter,and a rabble more
Of vilde Confederates : Along with them
They brought one *Pinch*,a hungry leane-fac'd Villaine ;
A meere Anatomie, a Mountebanke,
A thred-bare Iugler, and a Fortune-teller,
A needy-hollow-ey'd-ſharpe-looking-wretch ;
A liuing dead man. This pernicious ſlaue,
Forſooth tooke on him as a Coniurer :
And gazing in mine eyes, feeling my pulſe,
And with no-face (as 'twere) out-facing me,
Cries out, I was poſſeſt. Then altogether
They fell vpon me, bound me, bore me thence,
And in a darke and dankiſh vault at home
There left me and my man, both bound together,
Till gnawing with my teeth my bonds in ſunder,
I gain'd my freedome ; and immediately
Ran hether to your Grace, whom I beſeech
To giue me ample ſatisfaction
For theſe deepe ſhames, and great indignities.
 Gold. My Lord, in truth, thus farre I witnes with him :
That he din'd not at home, but was lock'd out.
 Duke. But had he ſuch a Chaine of thee,or no ?
 Gold. He had my Lord, and when he ran in heere,
Theſe people ſaw the Chaine about his necke.
 Mar. Beſides, I will be ſworne theſe eares of mine,
Heard you confeſſe you had the Chaine of him,
After you firſt forſwore it on the Mart,
And thereupon I drew my ſword on you:
And then you fled into this Abbey heere,
From whence I thinke you are come by Miracle.
 E.Ant. I neuer came within theſe Abbey wals,
Nor euer didſt thou draw thy ſword on me :
I neuer ſaw the Chaine, ſo helpe me heauen :
And this is falſe you burthen me withall.
 Duke. Why what an intricate impeach is this ?
I thinke you all haue drunke of *Circes* cup :
If heere you hous'd him, heere he would haue bin.
If he were mad, he would not pleade ſo coldly :
You ſay he din'd at home, the Goldſmith heere
Denies that ſaying. Sirra, what ſay you?
 E.Dro. Sir he din'de with her there,at the Porpen-
tine.
 Cur. He did, and from my finger ſnacht that Ring.
 E.Anti. Tis true (my Liege) this Ring I had of her.
 Duke. Saw'ſt thou him enter at the Abbey heere ?
 Curt. As ſure (my Liege) as I do ſee your Grace.
 Duke. Why this is ſtraunge : Go call the Abbeſſe hi-
ther.
I thinke you are all mated, or ſtarke mad.

 Exit

Exit one to the Abbeſſe.

Fa. Moſt mighty Duke, vouchſafe me ſpeak a word:
Haply I ſee a friend will ſaue my life,
And pay the ſum that may deliuer me.
Duke. Speake freely *Siracuſian* what thou wilt.
Fath. Is not your name ſir call'd *Antipholus?*
And is not that your bondman *Dromio?*
E. Dro. Within this houre I was his bondman ſir,
But he I thanke him gnaw'd in two my cords,
Now am I *Dromio,* and his man, vnbound.
Fath. I am ſure you both of you remember me.
Dro. Our ſelues we do remember ſir by you:
For lately we were bound as you are now.
You are not *Pinches* patient, are you ſir?
Father. Why looke you ſtrange on me? you know
me well.
E. Ant. I neuer ſaw you in my life till now.
Fa. Oh! griefe hath chang'd me ſince you ſaw me laſt,
And carefull houres with times deformed hand,
Haue written ſtrange defeatures in my face:
But tell me yet, doſt thou not know my voice?
Ant. Neither.
Fat. Dromio, nor thou?
Dro. No truſt me ſir, nor I.
Fa. I am ſure thou doſt?
E. Dromio. I ſir, but I am ſure I do not, and whatſo-
euer a man denies, you are now bound to beleeue him.
Fath. Not know my voice, oh times e tremity
Haſt thou ſo crack'd and ſplitted my poore tongue
In ſeuen ſhort yeares, that heere my onely ſonne
Knowes not my feeble key of vntun'd cares?
Though now this grained face of mine be hid
In ſap-conſuming Winters drizled ſnow,
And all the Conduits of my blood froze vp:
Yet hath my night of life ſome memorie:
My waſting lampes ſome fading glimmer left;
My dull deafe eares a little vſe to heare:
All theſe old witneſſes, I cannot erre.
Tell me, thou art my ſonne *Antipholus.*
Ant. I neuer ſaw my Father in my life.
Fa. But ſeuen yeares ſince, in *Siracuſa* boy
Thou know'ſt we parted, but perhaps my ſonne,
Thou ſham'ſt to acknowledge me in miſerie.
Ant. The Duke, and all that know me in the City,
Can witneſſe with me that it is not ſo.
I ne're ſaw *Siracuſa* in my life.
Duke. I tell thee *Siracuſian,* twentie yeares
Haue I bin Patron to *Antipholus,*
During which time, he ne're ſaw *Siracuſa:*
I ſee thy age and dangers make thee dote.

*Enter the Abbeſſe with Antipholus Siracuſa,
and Dromio Sir.*

Abbeſſe. Moſt mightie Duke, behold a man much
wrong'd.
All gather to ſee them.
Adr. I ſee two husbands, or mine eyes deceiue me.
Duke. One of theſe men is *genius* to the other:
And ſo of theſe, which is the naturall man,
And which the ſpirit? Who deciphers them?
S. Dromio. I Sir am *Dromio,* command him away.
E. Dro. I Sir am *Dromio,* pray let me ſtay.
S. Ant. Egeon art thou not? or elſe his ghoſt.

S. Drom. Oh my olde Maſter, who hath bound him
heere?
Abb. Who euer bound him, I will loſe his bonds,
And gaine a husband by his libertie:
Speake olde *Egeon,* if thou bee'ſt the man
That hadſt a wife once call'd *Æmilia,*
That bore thee at a burthen two faire ſonnes?
Oh if thou bee'ſt the ſame *Egeon,* ſpeake:
And ſpeake vnto the ſame *Æmilia.*
Duke. Why heere begins his Morning ſtorie right:
Theſe two *Antipholus,* theſe two ſo like,
And theſe two *Dromio's,* one in ſemblance:
Beſides her vrging of her wracke at ſea,
Theſe are the parents to theſe children,
Which accidentally are met together.
Fa. If I dreame not, thou art *Æmilia,*
If thou art ſhe, tell me, where is that ſonne
That floated with thee on the fatall raſte.
Abb. By men of *Epidamium,* he, and I,
And the twin *Dromio,* all were taken vp;
But by and by, rude Fiſhermen of *Corinth*
By force tooke *Dromio,* and my ſonne from them,
And me they left with thoſe of *Epidamium.*
What then became of them, I cannot tell:
I, to this fortune that you ſee mee in.
Duke. Antipholus thou cam'ſt from *Corinth* firſt.
S. Ant. No ſir, not I, I came from *Siracuſe.*
Duke. Stay, ſtand apart, I know not which is which.
E. Ant. I came from *Corinth* my moſt gracious Lord
E. Dro. And I with him.
E. Ant. Brought to this Town by that moſt famous
Warriour,
Duke *Menaphon,* your moſt renowned Vnckle.
Adr. Which of you two did dine with me to day?
S. Ant. I, gentle Miſtris.
Adr. And are not you my husband?
E. Ant. No, I ſay nay to that.
S. Ant. And ſo do I, yet did ſhe call me ſo:
And this faire Gentlewoman her ſiſter heere
Did call me brother. What I told you then,
I hope I ſhall haue leiſure to make good,
If this be not a dreame I ſee and heare.
Goldſmith. That is the Chaine ſir, which you had of
mee.
S. Ant. I thinke it be ſir, I denie it not.
E. Ant. And you ſir for this Chaine arreſted me.
Gold. I thinke I did ſir, I deny it not.
Adr. I ſent you monie ſir to be your baile
By *Dromio,* but I thinke he brought it not.
E. Dro. No, none by me.
S. Ant. This purſe of Duckets I receiu'd from you,
And *Dromio* my man did bring them me:
I ſee we ſtill did meete each others man,
And I was tane for him, and he for me,
And thereupon theſe errors are aroſe.
E. Ant. Theſe Duckets pawne I for my father heere.
Duke. It ſhall not neede, thy father hath his life.
Cur. Sir I muſt haue that Diamond from you.
E. Ant. There take it, and much thanks for my good
cheere.
Abb. Renowned Duke, vouchſafe to take the paines
To go with vs into the Abbey heere,
And heare at large diſcourſed all our fortunes,
And all that are aſſembled in this place:
That by this ſimpathized one daies error
Haue ſuffer'd wrong. Goe, keepe vs companie,

I 2   And

And we fhall make full fatisfaction.
Thirtie three yeares haue I but gone in trauaile
Of you my fonnes, and till this prefent houre
My heauie burthen are deliuered :
The Duke my husband, and my children both,
And you the Kalenders of their Natiuity,
Go to a Goffips feaft, and go with mee,
After fo long greefe fuch Natiuitie.
   Duke. With all my heart, Ile Goffip at this feaft.

    Exeunt omnes.   *Manet the two Dromio's and*
           two Brothers.
S.Dro. Maft.fhall I fetch your ftuffe from fhipbord?
E.An.Dromio, what ftuffe of mine haft thou imbarkt
*S.Dro.*Your goods that lay at hoft fir in the Centaur.
S.Ant. He fpeakes to me, I am your mafter *Dromio*.

Come go with vs, wee'l looke to that anon,
Embrace thy brother there, reioyce with him.   *Exit*
   S.Dro. There is a fat friend at your mafters houfe,
That kitchin'd me for you to day at dinner :
She now fhall be my fifter, not my wife,
   *E.D.*Me thinks you are my glaffe, & not my brother:
I fee by you, I am a fweet-fac'd youth,
Will you walke in to fee their goffipping?
   S.Dro. Not I fir, you are my elder.
   E.Dro. That's a queftion, how fhall we trie it.
   S.Dro. Wee'l draw Cuts for the Signior, till then,
lead thou firft.
   E.Dro. Nay then thus :
We came into the world like brother and brother :
And now let's go hand in hand, not one before another.
                     Exeunt.

FINIS.

Much adoe about Nothing.

Actus primus, Scena prima.

Enter Leonato Gouernour of Meſſina, Innogen his wife, Hero his daughter, and Beatrice his Neece, with a meſſenger.

Leonato.

Learne in this Letter, that *Don Peter of Arragon*, comes this night to *Meſſina*.

Meſſ. He is very neere by this : he was not three Leagues off when I left him.

Leon. How many Gentlemen haue you loſt in this action?

Meſſ. But few of any ſort, and none of name.

Leon. A victorie is twice it ſelfe, when the atchieuer brings home full numbers : I finde heere, that Don *Peter* hath beſtowed much honor on a yong *Florentine*, called *Claudio*.

Meſſ. Much deſeru'd on his part, and equally remembred by Don *Pedro*, he hath borne himſelfe beyond the promiſe of his age, doing in the figure of a Lambe, the feats of a Lion, he hath indeede better bettred expectation, then you muſt expect of me to tell you how.

Leo. He hath an Vnckle heere in *Meſſina*, wil be very much glad of it.

Meſſ. I haue alreadie deliuered him letters, and there appeares much ioy in him, euen ſo much, that ioy could not ſhew it ſelfe modeſt enough, without a badg of bitterneſſe.

Leo. Did he breake out into teares?

Meſſ. In great meaſure.

Leo. A kinde ouerflow of kindneſſe, there are no faces truer, then thoſe that are ſo waſh'd, how much better is it to weepe at ioy, then to ioy at weeping?

Bea. I pray you, is Signior *Mountanto* return'd from the warres, or no?

Meſſ. I know none of that name, Lady, there was none ſuch in the armie of any ſort.

Leon. What is he that you aske for Neece?

Hero. My couſin meanes Signior Benedick of *Padua*

Meſſ. O he's return'd, and as pleaſant as euer he was.

Beat. He ſet vp his bils here in *Meſſina*, & challeng'd Cupid at the Flight: and my Vnckles foole reading the Challenge, ſubſcrib'd for Cupid, and challeng'd him at the Burbolt. I pray you, how many hath hee kil'd and eaten in theſe warres? But how many hath he kil'd? for indeed, I promis'd to eate all of his killing.

Leon. 'Faith Neece, you taxe Signior Benedicke too much, but hee'l be meet with you, I doubt it not.

Meſſ. He hath done good ſeruice Lady in theſe wars.

Beat. You had muſty victuall, and he hath holpe to eaſe it : he's a very valiant Trencher-man, hee hath an excellent ſtomacke.

Meſſ. And a good ſouldier too Lady.

Beat. And a good ſouldier to a Lady. But what is he to a Lord?

Meſſ. A Lord to a Lord, a man to a man, ſtuft with all honourable vertues.

Beat, It is ſo indeed, he is no leſſe then a ſtuft man : but for the ſtuffing well, we are all mortall.

Leon. You muſt not (ſir) miſtake my Neece, there is a kind of merry war betwixt Signior Benedick, & her : they neuer meet, but there's a skirmiſh of wit between them.

Bea. Alas, he gets nothing by that. In our laſt conflict, foure of his ſiue wits went halting off, and now is the whole man gouern'd with one : ſo that if hee haue wit enough to keepe himſelfe warme, let him beare it for a difference betweene himſelfe and his horſe : For it is all the wealth that he hath left, to be knowne a reaſonable creature. Who is his companion now? He hath euery month a new ſworne brother.

Meſſ. I'ſt poſſible?

Beat. Very eaſily poſſible : he weares his faith but as the faſhion of his hat, it euer changes with $\tilde{y}$ next block.

Meſſ. I ſee (Lady) the Gentleman is not in your bookes.

Bea. No, and he were, I would burne my ſtudy. But I pray you, who is his companion? Is there no young ſquarer now, that will make a voyage with him to the diuell?

Meſſ. He is moſt in the company of the right noble *Claudio.*

Beat. O Lord, he will hang vpon him like a diſeaſe : he is ſooner caught then the peſtilence, and the taker runs preſently mad. God helpe the noble *Claudio*, if hee haue caught the Benedict, it will coſt him a thouſand pound ere he be cur'd.

Meſſ. I will hold friends with you Lady.

Bea. Do good friend.

Leo. You'l ne're run mad Neece.

Bea. No, not till a hot Ianuary.

Meſſ. Don Pedro is approach'd.

Enter don Pedro, Claudio, Benedicke, Balthaſar, and Iohn the baſtard.

Pedro. Good Signior *Leonato*, you are come to meet your trouble : the faſhion of the world is to auoid coſt, and you encounter it.

Leon. Neuer came trouble to my houſe in the likenes of your Grace : for trouble being gone, comfort ſhould remaine : but when you depart from me, ſorrow abides, and happineſſe takes his leaue.

I 3   *Pedro.*

Pedro. You embrace your charge too willingly: I thinke this is your daughter.

Leonato. Her mother hath many times told me fo.

Bened. Were you in doubt that you askt her?

Leonato. Signior Benedicke, no, for then were you a childe.

Pedro. You haue it full Benedicke, we may gheſſe by this, what you are, being a man, truely the Lady fathers her felfe: be happie Lady, for you are like an honorable father.

Ben. If Signior *Leonato* be her father, ſhe would not haue his head on her ſhoulders for al Meſſina, as like him as ſhe is.

Beat. I wonder that you will ſtill be talking, ſignior Benedicke, no body markes you.

Ben. What my deere Ladie Diſdaine ʼ are you yet liuing?

Beat. Is it poſſible Diſdaine ſhould die, while ſhee hath fuch meete foode to feede it, as Signior Benedicke? Curteſie it felfe muſt conuert to Diſdaine, if you come in her prefence.

Bene. Then is curteſie a turne-coate, but it is certaine I am loued of all Ladies, onely you excepted: and I would I could finde in my heart that I had not a hard heart, for truely I loue none.

Beat. A deere happineſſe to women, they would elfe haue beene troubled with a pernitious Suter, I thanke God and my cold blood, I am of your humour for that, I had rather heare my Dog barke at a Crow, than a man fweare he loues me.

Bene. God keepe your Ladiſhip ſtill in that minde, fo fome Gentleman or other ſhall ſcape a predeſtinate ſcratcht face.

Beat. Scratching could not make it worſe, and ʼtwere fuch a face as yours were.

Bene. Well, you are a rare Parrat teacher.

Beat. A bird of my tongue, is better than a beaſt of your.

Ben. I would my horſe had the fpeed of your tongue, and fo good a continuer, but keepe your way a Gods name, I haue done.

Beat. You alwaies end with a Iades tricke, I know you of old.

Pedro. This is the fumme of all: *Leonato*, ſignior *Claudio*, and ſignior *Benedicke*; my deere friend *Leonato*, hath inuited you all, I tell him we ſhall ſtay here, at the leaſt a moneth, and he heartily praies fome occaſion may detaine vs longer: I dare fweare hee is no hypocrite, but praies from his heart.

Leon. If you fweare, my Lord, you ſhall not be for-fworne, let mee bid you welcome, my Lord, being reconciled to the Prince your brother: I owe you all duetie.

Iohn. I thanke you, I am not of many words, but I thanke you.

Leon. Pleaſe it your grace leade on?

Pedro. Your hand *Leonato*, we will goe together.

Exeunt. Manet Benedicke and Claudio.

Clau. Benedicke, didſt thou note the daughter of ſignior *Leonato*?

Bene. I noted her not, but I lookt on her.

Clau. Is ſhe not a modeſt yong Ladie?

Bene. Doe you queſtion me as an honeſt man ſhould doe, for my ſimple true iudgement? or would you haue me fpeake after my cuſtome, as being a profeſſed tyrant to their ſexe?

Clau. No, I pray thee fpeake in fober iudgement.

Bene. Why yfaith me thinks ſhee's too low for a hie praiſe, too browne for a faire praiſe, and too little for a great praiſe, onely this commendation I can afford her, that were ſhee other then ſhe is, ſhe were vnhandſome, and being no other, but as ſhe is, I doe not like her.

Clau. Thou think'ſt I am in fport, I pray thee tell me truely how thou lik'ſt her.

Bene. Would you buie her, that you enquier after her?

Clau. Can the world buie fuch a iewell?

Ben. Yea, and a caſe to put it into, but fpeake you this with a fad brow? Or doe you play the flowting iacke, to tell vs Cupid is a good Hare-finder, and Vulcan a rare Carpenter: Come, in what key ſhall aman take you to goe in the fong?

Clau. In mine eie, ſhe is the fweeteſt Ladie that euer I lookt on.

Bene. I can fee yet without fpeĉtacles, and I fee no fuch matter: there's her cofin, and ſhe were not poſſeſt with a furie, exceedes her as much in beautie, as the firſt of Maie doth the laſt of December: but I hope you haue no intent to turne husband, haue you?

Clau. I would fcarce truſt my felfe, though I had fworne the contrarie, if *Hero* would be my wife.

Bene. Iſt come to this? in faith hath not the world one man but he will weare his cap with fuſpition? ſhall I neuer fee a batcheller of three ſcore againe? goe to yfaith, and thou wilt needes thruſt thy necke into a yoke, weare the print of it, and figh away fundaies: looke, *don Pedro* is returned to feeke you.

Enter don Pedro, Iohn the baſtard.

Pedr. What fecret hath held you here, that you followed not to *Leonatoes*?

Bened. I would your Grace would conſtraine mee to tell.

Pedro. I charge thee on thy allegeance.

Ben. You heare, Count *Claudio*, I can be fecret as a dumbe man, I would haue you thinke fo (but on my allegiance, marke you this, on my allegiance) hee is in loue, With who? now that is your Graces part: marke how ſhort his anſwere is, with *Hero*, *Leonatoes* ſhort daughter.

Clau. If this were fo, fo were it vttred.

Bened. Like the old tale, my Lord, it is not fo, nor ʼtwas not fo: but indeede, God forbid it ſhould be fo.

Clau. If my paſſion change not ſhortly, God forbid it ſhould be otherwiſe.

Pedro. Amen, if you loue her, for the Ladie is verie well worthie.

Clau. You fpeake this to fetch me in, my Lord.

Pedr. By my troth I fpeake my thought.

Clau. And in faith, my Lord, I fpoke mine.

Bened. And by my two faiths and troths, my Lord, I fpeake mine.

Clau. That I loue her, I feele.

Pedr. That ſhe is worthie, I know.

Bened. That I neither feele how ſhee ſhould be loued, nor know how ſhee ſhould be worthie, is the opinion that fire cannot melt out of me, I will die in it at the ſtake.

Pedr. Thou waſt euer an obſtinate heretique in the defpight of Beautie.

Clau. And neuer could maintaine his part, but in the force of his will.

Bene. That

Ben. That a woman conceiued me, I thanke her : that
she brought mee vp, I likewife giue her moft humble
thankes : but that I will haue a rechate winded in my
forehead, or hang my bugle in an inuifible baldricke, all
women fhall pardon me: becaufe I will not do them the
wrong to miftruft any, I will doe my felfe the right to
truft none : and the fine is, (for the which I may goe the
finer) I will liue a Batchellor.

Pedro. I fhall fee thee ere I die, looke pale with loue.

Bene. With anger, with ficknefle, or with hunger,
my Lord, not with loue : proue that euer I loofe more
blood with loue, then I will get againe with drinking,
picke out mine eyes with a Ballet-makers penne, and
hang me vp at the doore of a brothel-houfe for the figne
of blinde Cupid.

Pedro. Well, if euer thou dooft fall from this faith,
thou wilt proue a notable argument.

Bene. If I do, hang me in a bottle like a Cat, & fhoot
at me, and he that hit's me, let him be clapt on the fhoulder, and cal'd *Adam.*

Pedro. Well, as time fhall trie : In time the fauage
Bull doth beare tne yoake.

Bene. The fauage bull may, but if euer the fenfible
Beneaicke beare it, plucke off the bulles hornes, and fet
them in my forehead, and let me be vildely painted, and
in fuch great Letters as they write, heere is good horfe
to hire : let them fignifie vnder my figne, here you may
fee *Benedicke* the married man.

Clau. If this fhould euer happen, thou wouldft bee
horne mad.

Pedro. Nay, if Cupid haue not fpent all his Quiuer in
Venice, thou wilt quake for this fhortly.

Bene. I looke for an earthquake too then.

Pedro. Well, you will temporize with the houres, in
the meane time, good Signior *Benedicke,* repaire to *Leonatoes,* commend me to him, and tell him I will not faile
him at fupper, for indeede he hath made great preparation.

Bene. I haue almoft matter enough in me for fuch an
Embaffage, and fo I commit you.

Clau. To the tuition of God. From my houfe, if I
had it.

Pedro. The fixt of Iuly. Your louing friend, *Benedick.*

Bene. Nay mocke not, mocke not ; the body of your
difcourfe is fometime guarded with fragments, and the
guardes are but flightly bafted on neither, ere you flout
old ends any further, examine your confcience, and fo I
leaue you.   *Exit.*

Clau. My Liege, your Highneffe now may doe mee
good.

Pedro. My loue is thine to teach, teach it but how,
And thou fhalt fee how apt it is to learne
Any hard Leffon that may do thee good.

Clau. Hath *Leonato* any fonne my Lord ?

Pedro. No childe but *Hero,* fhe's his onely heire.
Doft thou affeﬆ her *Claudio* ?

Clau. O my Lord,
When you went onward on this ended aﬆion,
I look'd vpon her with a fouldiers eie,
That lik'd, but had a rougher taske in hand,
Than to driue liking to the name of loue:
But now I am return'd, and that warre-thoughts
Haue left their places vacant : in their roomes,
Come thronging foft and delicate defires,
All prompting mee how faire yong *Hero* is,
Saying I lik'd her ere I went to warres.

Pedro. Thou wilt be like a louer prefently,
And tire the bearer with a booke of words:
If thou doft loue faire *Hero,* cherifh it,
And I will breake with her : waft not to this end,
That thou beganft to twift fo fine a ftory ?

Clau. How fweetly doe you minifter to loue,
That know loues griefe by his complexion !
But left my liking might too fodaine feeme,
I would haue falu'd it with a longer treatife.

Ped. What need ẙ bridge much broder then the flood?
The faireft graunt is the neceffitie :
Looke what will ferue, is fit : 'tis once, thou loueft,
And I will fit thee with the remedie,
I know we fhall haue reuelling to night,
I will affume thy part in fome difguife,
And tell faire *Hero* I am *Claudio,*
And in her bofome Ile vnclafpe my heart,
And take her hearing prifoner with the force
And ftrong incounter of my amorous tale :
Then after, to her father will I breake,
And the conclufion is, fhee fhall be thine,
In praﬆife let vs put it prefently.   *Exeunt.*

Enter Leonato and an old man, brother to Leonato.

Leo. How now brother, where is my cofen your fon :
hath he prouided this muficke?

Old. He is very bufie about it, but brother, I can tell
you newes that you yet dreamt not of.

Leo. Are they good ?

Old. As the euents ftamps them, but they haue a good
couer : they fhew well outward, the Prince and Count
Claudio walking in a thick pleached alley in my orchard,
were thus ouer-heard by a man of mine : the Prince difcouered to *Claudio* that hee loued my niece your daughter, and meant to acknowledge it this night in a dance,
and if hee found her accordant, hee meant to take the
prefent time by the top, and inftantly breake with you
of it.

Leo. Hath the fellow any wit that told you this?

Old. A good fharpe fellow, I will fend for him, and
queftion him your felfe.

Leo. No, no ; wee will hold it as a dreame, till it appeare it felfe : but I will acquaint my daughter withall,
that fhe may be the better prepared for an anfwer, if peraduenture this bee true : goe you and tell her of it : coo-
fins, you know what you haue to doe, O I crie you mercie friend, goe you with mee and I will vfe your skill,
good cofin haue a care this bufie time.   *Exeunt.*

Enter Sir Iohn the Baftard, and Conrade his companion.

Con. What the good yeere my Lord, why are you
thus out of meafure fad ?

Ioh. There is no meafure in the occafion that breeds,
therefore the fadneffe is without limit.

Con. You fhould heare reafon.

Iohn. And when I haue heard it, what bleffing bringeth it?

Con. If not a prefent remedy, yet a patient fufferance.

Ioh. I wonder that thou (being as thou faift thou art,
borne vnder *Saturne*) goeft about to apply a morall medicine, to a mortifying mifchiefe : I cannot hide what I
am : I muft be fad when I haue caufe, and fmile at no
mans iefts, eat when I haue ftomacke, and wait for no
mans leifure : fleepe when I am drowfie, and tend on no
mans bufineffe, laugh when I am merry, and claw no man
in his humor.

Con. Yea, but you muft not make the ful fhow of this,
till you may doe it without controllment, you haue of
late

late ftood out againft your brother, and hee hath tane you newly into his grace, where it is impoffible you fhould take root, but by the faire weather that you make your felfe, it is needful that you frame the feafon for your owne harueft.

Iohn. I had rather be a canker in a hedge, then a rofe in his grace, and it better fits my bloud to be difdain'd of all, then to fafhion a carriage to rob loue from any: in this (though I cannot be faid to be a flattering honeft man) it muft not be denied but I am a plaine dealing villaine, I am trufted with a muffell, and enfranchifde with a clog, therefore I haue decreed, not to fing in my cage : if I had my mouth, I would bite : if I had my liberty, I would do my liking : in the meane time, let me be that I am, and feeke not to alter me.

Con. Can you make no vfe of your difcontent?

Iohn. I will make all vfe of it, for I vfe it onely. Who comes here? what newes *Borachio?*

Enter *Borachio.*

Bor. I came yonder from a great fupper, the Prince your brother is royally entertained by *Leonato*, and I can giue you intelligence of an intended marriage.

Iohn. Will it ferue for any Modell to build mifchiefe on? What is hee for a foole that betrothes himfelfe to vnquietneffe?

Bor. Mary it is your brothers right hand.

Iohn. Who, the moft exquifite *Claudio* ?

Bor. Euen he.

Iohn. A proper fquier, and who, and who, which way lookes he ?

Bor. Mary on *Hero*, the daughter and Heire of *Leonato.*

Iohn. A very forward March-chicke, how came you to this ?

Bor. Being entertain'd for a perfumer, as I was fmoaking a mufty roome, comes me the Prince and *Claudio*, hand in hand in fad conference : I whipt behind the Arras, and there heard it agreed vpon, that the Prince fhould wooe *Hero* for himfelfe, and hauing obtain'd her, giue her to Count *Claudio.*

Iohn. Come, come, let vs thither, this may proue food to my difpleafure, that young ftart-vp hath all the glorie of my ouerthrow : if I can croffe him any way, I bleffe my felfe euery way, you are both fure, and will affift mee ?

Conr. To the death my Lord.

Iohn. Let vs to the great fupper, their cheere is the greater that I am fubdued, would the Cooke were of my minde: fhall we goe proue whats to be done ?

Bor. Wee'll wait vpon your Lordfhip.

Exeunt.

Actus Secundus.

Enter Leonato, his brother, his wife, Hero his daughter, and Beatrice his neece, and a kinfman.

Leonato. Was not Count *Iohn* here at fupper?

Brother. I faw him not.

Beatrice. How tartly that Gentleman lookes, I neuer can fee him, but I am heart-burn'd an howre after.

Hero. He is of a very melancholy difpofition.

Beatrice. Hee were an excellent man that were made iuft in the mid-way betweene him and *Benedicke*, the one is too like an image and faies nothing, and the other too like my Ladies eldeft fonne, euermore tatling.

Leon. Then halfe fignior *Benedicks* tongue in Count *Iohns* mouth, and halfe Count *Iohns* melancholy in Signior *Benedicks* face.

Beat. With a good legge, and a good foot vnckle, and money enough in his purfe, fuch a man would winne any woman in the world, if he could get her good will.

Leon. By my troth Neece, thou wilt neuer get thee a husband, if thou be fo fhrewd of thy tongue.

Brother. Infaith fhee's too curft.

Beat. Too curft is more then curft, I fhall leffen Gods fending that way: for it is faid, God fends a curft Cow fhort hornes, but to a Cow too curft he fends none.

Leon. So, by being too curft, God will fend you no hornes.

Beat. Iuft, if he fend me no husband, for the which bleffing, I am at him vpon my knees euery morning and euening : Lord, I could not endure a husband with a beard on his face, I had rather lie in the woollen.

Leonato. You may light vpon a husband that hath no beard.

Batrice. What fhould I doe with him ? dreffe him in my apparell, and make him my waiting gentlewoman? he that hath a beard, is more then a youth : and he that hath no beard, is leffe then a man : and hee that is more then a youth, is not for mee : and he that is leffe then a man, I am not for him : therefore I will euen take fixpence in earneft of the Berrord, and leade his Apes into hell.

Leon. Well then, goe you into hell.

Beat. No, but to the gate, and there will the Deuill meete mee like an old Cuckold with hornes on his head, and fay, get you to heauen *Beatrice*, get you to heauen, heere's no place for you maids, fo deliuer I vp my Apes, and away to S. *Peter* : for the heauens, hee fhewes mee where the Batchellers fit, and there liue wee as merry as the day is long.

Brother. Well neece, I truft you will be rul'd by your father.

Beatrice. Yes faith, it is my cofens dutie to make curtfie, and fay, as it pleafe you : but yet for all that cofin, let him be a handfome fellow, or elfe make an other curfie, and fay, father, as it pleafe me.

Leonato. Well neece, I hope to fee you one day fitted with a husband.

Beatrice. Not till God make men of fome other mettall then earth, would it not grieue a woman to be ouermaftred with a peece of valiant duft ? to make account of her life to a clod of waiward marle ? no vnckle, ile none : *Adams* fonnes are my brethren, and truly I hold it a finne to match in my kinred.

Leon. Daughter, remember what I told you, if the Prince doe folicit you in that kinde, you know your anfwere.

Beatrice. The fault will be in the muficke cofin, if you be not woed in good time : if the Prince bee too important, tell him there is meafure in euery thing, & fo dance out the anfwere, for heare me *Hero*, wooing, wedding, & repenting, is as a Scotch ijgge, a meafure, and a cinquepace : the firft fuite is hot and hafty like a Scotch ijgge (and full as fantafticall) the wedding manerly modeft, (as a meafure) full of ftate & aunchentry, and then comes repentance, and with his bad legs falls into the cinquepace fafter and fafter, till he finkes into his graue.

Leonato.

Leonata. Cofin you apprehend paffing fhrewdly.

Beatrice. I haue a good eye vnckle,I can fee a Church by daylight.

Leon. The reuellers are entring brother , make good roome.

Enter Prince, Pedro, Claudio, and Benedicke, and Balthaſar, or dumbe Iohn, Maskers with a drum.

Pedro. Lady,will you walke about with your friend?

Hero. So you walke foftly,and looke fweetly, and fay nothing,I am yours for the walke, and efpecially when I walke away.

Pedro. With me in your company.

Hero. I may fay fo when I pleafe.

Pedro. And when pleaſe you to fay fo?

Hero. When I like your fauour , for God defend the Lute fhould be like the cafe.

Pedro. My vifor is *Philemons* roofe , within the houfe is Loue.

Hero. Why then your vifor fhould be thatcht.

Pedro. Speake low if you fpeake Loue.

Bene. Well, I would you did like me.

Mar. So would not I for your owne fake,for I haue manie ill qualities.

Bene. Which is one?

Mar. I fay my prayers alowd.

Ben. I loue you the better , the hearers may cry Amen.

Mar. God match me with a good dauncer.

Balt. Amen.

Mar. And God keepe him out of my fight when the daunce is done : anfwer Clarke.

Balt. No more words, the Clarke is anfwered.

Vrſula. I know you well enough,you are Signior *Anthonio.*

Anth. At a word , I am not.

Vrſula. I know you by the wagling of your head.

Anth. To tell you true, I counterfet him.

Vrſu. You could neuer doe him fo ill well , vnleffe you were the very man : here's his dry hand vp & down, you are he, you are he.

Anth. At a word I am not.

Urſula. Come, come,doe you thinke I doe not know you by your excellent wit? can vertue hide it felfe? goe to, mumme, you are he, graces will appeare , and there's an end.

Beat. Will you not tell me who told you fo?

Bene. No, you fhall pardon me.

Beat. Nor will you not tell me who you are?

Bened. Not now.

Beat. That I was difdainfull, and that I had my good wit out of the hundred merry tales : well,this was Signior *Benedicke* that faid fo.

Bene. What's he?

Beat. I am fure you know him well enough.

Bene. Not I, beleeue me.

Beat. Did he neuer make you laugh?

Bene. I pray you what is he?

Beat. Why he is the Princes ieafter,a very dull foole, onely his gift is , in deuifing impoſible flanders , none but Libertines delight in him, and the commendation is not in his witte, but in his villanie, for hee both pleafeth men and angers them, and then they laugh at him, and beat him: I am fure he is in the Fleet , I would he had boorded me.

Bene. When I know the Gentleman,Ile tell him what you fay.

Beat. Do, do, hee'l but breake a comparifon or two on me, which peraduenture (not markt, or not laugh'd at) ftrikes him into melancholly, and then there's a Partridge wing faued, for the foole will eate no fupper that night. We muft follow the Leaders.

Ben. In every good thing.

Bea. Nay, if they leade to any ill, I will leaue them at the next turning.   *Exeunt.*

Muſicke for the dance.

Iohn. Sure my brother is amorous on *Hero,* and hath withdrawne her father to breake with him about it: the Ladies follow her,and but one viſor remaines.

Borachio. And that is *Claudio,*I know him by his bearing.

Iohn. Are not you ſignior *Benedicke*?

Clau. You know me well, I am hee.

Iohn. Signior,you are verie neere my Brother in his loue, he is enamor'd on *Hero,* I pray you diſſwade him from her, fhe is no equall for his birth : you may do the part of an honeſt man in it.

Claudio. How know you he loues her?

Iohn. I heard him fweare his affection,

Bor. So did I too, and he fwore he would marrie her to night.

Iohn. Come, let vs to the banquet.   *Ex.manet Clau.*

Clau. Thus anfwere I in name of Benedicke,
But heare thefe Ill newes with the eares of *Claudio*:
'Tis certaine fo, the Prince woes for himſelfe :
Friendſhip is conftant in all other things,
Saue in the Office and affaires of loue :
Therefore all hearts in loue vfe their owne tongues.
Let euerie eye negotiate for it felfe,
And truft no Agent : for beautie is a witch,
Againft whofe charmes, faith melteth into blood :
This is an accident of hourely proofe,
Which I miftrufted not. Farewell therefore *Hero.*

Enter Benedicke.

Ben. Count *Claudio.*

Clau. Yea, the fame.

Ben. Come, will you go with me?

Clau. Whither?

Ben. Euen to the next Willow, about your own bufineffe, Count. What fafhion will you weare the Garland off? About your necke, like an Vfurers chaine? Or vnder your arme, like a Lieutenants fcarfe? You muſt weare it one way, for the Prince hath got your *Hero.*

Clau. I wifh him ioy of her.

Ben. Why that's fpoken like an honeft Drouier, fo they fel Bullockes : but did you thinke the Prince wold haue ferued you thus?

Clau. I pray you leaue me.

Ben. Ho now you ftrike like the blindman,'twas the boy that ftole your meate, and you'l beat the poft.

Clau. If it will not be, Ile leaue you.   *Exit.*

Ben. Alas poore hurt fowle, now will he creepe into fedges: But that my Ladie *Beatrice* fhould know me, & not know me : the Princes foole! Hah? It may be I goe vnder that title, becaufe I am merrie : yea but fo I am apt to do my felfe wrong : I am not fo reputed, it is the bafe (though bitter) difpofition of *Beatrice,* that putt's the world into her perfon, and fo giues me out: well,Ile be reuenged as I may.

Enter the Prince.

Pedro. Now Signior, where's the Count, did you fee him?

Ben·

Bene. Troth my Lord, I haue played the part of Lady Fame, I found him heere as melancholy as a Lodge in a Warren, I told him, and I thinke, told him true, that your grace had got the will of this young Lady, and I offered him my company to a willow tree, either to make him a garland, as being forfaken, or to binde him a rod, as being worthy to be whipt.

Pedro. To be whipt, what's his fault?

Bene. The flat tranfgreffion of a Schoole-boy, who being ouer-ioyed with finding a birds neft, fhewes it his companion, and he fteales it.

Pedro. Wilt thou make a truft, a tranfgreffion ? the tranfgreffion is in the ftealer.

Ben. Yet it had not beene amiffe the rod had beene made, and the garland too, for the garland he might haue worne himfelfe, and the rod hee might haue beftowed on you, who (as I take it) haue ftolne his birds neft.

Pedro. I will but teach them to fing, and reftore them to the owner.

Bene. If their finging anfwer your faying, by my faith you fay honeftly.

Pedro. The Lady *Beatrice* hath a quarrell to you, the Gentleman that daunft with her, told her fhee is much wrong'd by you.

Bene. O fhe mifufde me paft the indurance of a block: an oake but with one greene leafe on it, would haue anfwered her: my very vifor began to affume life, and fcold with her : fhee told mee, not thinking I had beene my felfe, that I was the Princes Iefter, and that I was duller then a great thaw, hudling ieft vpon ieft, with fuch impoffible conueiance vpon me, that I ftood like a man at a marke, with a whole army fhooting at me : fhee fpeakes poynyards, and euery word ftabbes : if her breath were as terrible as terminations, there were no liuing neere her, fhe would infect to the north ftarre : I would not marry her, though fhe were indowed with all that *Adam* had left him before he tranfgreft, fhe would haue made *Hercules* haue turnd fpit, yea, and haue cleft his club to make the fire too : come, talke not of her, you fhall finde her the infernall Ate in good apparell. I would to God fome fcholler would coniure her, for certainely while fhe is heere, a man may liue as quiet in hell, as in a fanctuary, and people finne vpon purpofe, becaufe they would goe thither, fo indeed all difquiet, horror, and perturbation followes her.

Enter Claudio and Beatrice, Leonato, Hero.

Pedro. Looke heere fhe comes.

Bene. Will your Grace command mee any feruice to the worlds end ? I will goe on the flighteft arrand now to the Antypodes that you can deuife to fend me on : I will fetch you a tooth-picker now from the furtheft inch of Afia : bring you the length of *Prefter Iohns* foot: fetch you a hayre off the great *Chams* beard : doe you any embaffage to the Pigmies, rather then hould three words conference, with this Harpy : you haue no employment for me ?

Pedro. None, but to defire your good company.

Bene. O God fir, heeres a difh I loue not, I cannot indure this Lady tongue. *Exit.*

Pedr. Come Lady, come, you haue loft the heart of Signior *Benedicke.*

Beatr. Indeed my Lord, hee lent it me a while, and I gaue him vfe for it, a double heart for a fingle one, marry once before he wonne it of mee, with falfe dice, therefore your Grace may well fay I haue loft it.

Pedro. You haue put him downe Lady, you haue put him downe.

Beat. So I would not he fhould do me, my Lord, left I fhould prooue the mother of fooles : I haue brought Count *Claudio,* whom you fent me to feeke.

Pedro. Why how now Count, wherfore are you fad ?

Claud. Not fad my Lord.

Pedro. How then ? ficke ?

Claud. Neither, my Lord.

Beat. The Count is neither fad, nor ficke, nor merry, nor well : but ciuill Count, ciuill as an Orange, and fomething of a iealous complexion.

Pedro. Ifaith Lady, I thinke your blazon to be true, though Ile be fworne, if hee be fo, his conceit is falfe : heere *Claudio,* I haue wooed in thy name, and faire *Hero* is won, I haue broke with her father, and his good will obtained, name the day of marriage, and God giue thee ioy.

Leona. Count, take of me my daughter, and with her my fortunes : his grace hath made the match, & all grace fay, Amen to it.

Beatr. Speake Count, tis your Qu.

Claud. Silence is the perfecteft Herault of ioy, I were but little happy if I could fay, how much ? Lady, as you are mine, I am yours, I giue away my felfe for you, and doat vpon the exchange.

Beat. Speake cofin, or (if you cannot) ftop his mouth with a kiffe, and let not him fpeake neither.

Pedro. Infaith Lady you haue a merry heart.

Beatr. Yea my Lord I thanke it, poore foole it keepes on the windy fide of Care, my coofin tells him in his eare that he is in my heart.

Clau. And fo fhe doth coofin.

Beat. Good Lord for alliance : thus goes euery one to the world but I, and I am fun-burn'd, I may fit in a corner and cry, heigh ho for a husband.

Pedro. Lady *Beatrice,* I will get you one.

Beat. I would rather haue one of your fathers getting : hath your Grace ne're a brother like you ? your father got excellent husbands, if a maid could come by them.

Prince. Will you haue me ? Lady.

Beat. No, my Lord, vnleffe I might haue another for working-daies, your Grace is too coftly to weare euerie day : but I befeech your Grace pardon mee, I was borne to fpeake all mirth, and no matter.

Prince. Your filence moft offends me, and to be merry, beft becomes you, for out of queftion, you were born in a merry howre.

Beatr. No fure my Lord, my Mother cried, but then there was a ftarre daunft, and vnder that was I borne : cofins God giue you ioy.

Leonato. Neece, will you looke to thofe rhings I told you of ?

Beat. I cry you mercy Vncle, by your Graces pardon. *Exit Beatrice.*

Prince. By my troth a pleafant fpirited Lady.

Leon. There's little of the melancholy element in her my Lord, fhe is neuer fad, but when fhe fleepes, and not euer fad then: for I haue heard my daughter fay, fhe hath often dreamt of vnhappineffe, and wakt her felfe with laughing.

Pedro. Shee cannot indure to heare tell of a husband.

Leonato. O, by no meanes, fhe mocks all her wooers out of fuite.

Prince. She were an excellent wife for *Benedick.*

Leonato. O Lord, my Lord, if they were but a weeke married,

married, they would talke themselues madde.

Prince. Counte *Claudio*, when meane you to goe to Church?

Clau. To morrow my Lord, Time goes on crutches, till Loue haue all his rites.

Leonata. Not till monday, my deare sonne, which is hence a iust seuen night, and a time too briefe too, to haue all things answer minde.

Prince. Come, you shake the head at so long a breathing, but I warrant thee *Claudio*, the time shall not goe dully by vs, I will in the *interim*, vndertake one of *Hercules* labors, which is, to bring Signior *Benedicke* and the Lady *Beatrice* into a mountaine of affection, th'one with th'other, I would faine haue it a match, and I doubt not but to fashion it, if you three will but minister such assistance as I shall giue you direction.

Leonata. My Lord, I am for you, though it cost mee ten nights watchings.

Claud. And I my Lord.

Prin. And you to gentle *Hero?*

Hero. I will doe any modest office, my Lord, to helpe my cosin to a good husband.

Prin. And *Benedick* is not the vnhopefullest husband that I know : thus farre can I praise him, hee is of a noble straine, of approued valour, and confirm'd honesty, I will teach you how to humour your cosin, that shee shall fall in loue with *Benedicke*, and I, with your two helpes, will so practise on *Benedicke*, that in despight of his quicke wit, and his queasie stomacke, hee shall fall in loue with *Beatrice* : if wee can doe this, *Cupid* is no longer an Archer, his glory shall be ours, for wee are the onely louegods, goe in with me, and I will tell you my drift. *Exit.*

Enter Iohn and Borachio.

Ioh. It is so, the Count *Claudio* shal marry the daughter of *Leonato.*

Bora. Yea my Lord, but I can crosse it.

Iohn. Any barre, any crosse, any impediment, will be medicinable to me, I am sicke in displeasure to him, and whatsoeuer comes athwart his affection, ranges euenly with mine, how canst thou crosse this marriage?

Bor. Not honestly my Lord, but so couertly, that no dishonesty shall appeare in me.

Iohn. Shew me breefely how.

Bor. I thinke I told your Lordship a yeere since, how much I am in the fauour of *Margaret*, the waiting gentlewoman to *Hero.*

Iohn. I remember.

Bor. I can at any vnseasonable instant of the night, appoint her to look out at her Ladies chamber window.

Iohn. What life is in that, to be the death of this marriage?

Bor. The poyson of that lies in you to temper, goe you to the Prince your brother, spare not to tell him, that hee hath wronged his Honor in marrying the renowned *Claudio*, whose estimation do you mightily hold vp, to a contaminated stale, such a one as *Hero.*

Iohn. What proofe shall I make of that?

Bor. Proofe enough, to misuse the Prince, to vexe *Claudio*, to vndoe *Hero*, and kill *Leonato*, looke you for any other issue?

Iohn. Onely to despight them, I will endeauour any thing.

Bor. Goe then, finde me a meete howre, to draw on *Pedro* and the Count *Claudio* alone, tell them that you know that *Hero* loues me, intend a kinde of zeale both to the Prince and *Claudio* (as in a loue of your brothers

honor who hath made this match) and his friends reputation, who is thus like to be cosen'd with the semblance of a maid, that you haue discouer'd thus: they will scarcely beleeue this without triall: offer them instances which shall beare no lesse likelihood, than to see mee at her chamber window, heare me call *Margaret*, *Hero*; heare *Margaret* terme me *Claudio*, and bring them to see this the very night before the intended wedding, for in the meane time, I will so fashion the matter, that *Hero* shall be absent, and there shall appeare such seeming truths of *Heroes* disloyaltie, that iealousie shall be cal'd assurance, and all the preparation ouerthrowne.

Iohn. Grow this to what aduerse issue it can, I will put it in practise : be cunning in the working this, and thy fee is a thousand ducates.

Bor. Be thou constant in the accusation, and my cunning shall not shame me.

Iohn. I will presentlie goe learne their day of marriage. *Exit.*

Enter Benedicke alone.

Bene. Boy.

Boy. Signior.

Bene. In my chamber window lies a booke, bring it hither to me in the orchard.

Boy. I am heere already sir. *Exit.*

Bene. I know that, but I would haue thee hence, and heere againe. I doe much wonder, that one man seeing how much another man is a foole, when he dedicates his behauiours to loue, will after hee hath laught at such shallow follies in others, become the argument of his owne scorne, by falling in loue, & such a man is *Claudio*, I haue known when there was no musicke with him but the drum and the fife, and now had hee rather heare the taber and the pipe : I haue knowne when he would haue walkt ten mile afoot, to see a good armor, and now will he lie ten nights awake caruing the fashion of a new dublet: he was wont to speake plaine, & to the purpose (like an honest man & a souldier) and now is he turn'd orthography, his words are a very fantasticall banquet, iust so many strange dishes : may I be so conuerted, & see with these eyes? I cannot tell, I thinke not : I will not bee sworne, but loue may transforme me to an oyster, but Ile take my oath on it, till he haue made an oyster of me, he shall neuer make me such a foole : one woman is faire, yet I am well : another is wise, yet I am well: another vertuous, yet I am well : but till all graces be in one woman, one woman shall not come in my grace : rich shee shall be, that's certaine : wise, or Ile none : vertuous, or Ile neuer cheapen her : faire, or Ile neuer looke on her : milde, or come not neere me : Noble, or not for an Angell : of good discourse : an excellent Musitian, and her haire shal be of what colour it please God, hah! the Prince and Monsieur Loue, I will hide me in the Arbor.

Enter Prince, Leonato, Claudio, and Iacke Wilson.

Prin. Come, shall we heare this musicke?

Claud. Yea my good Lord : how still the euening is, As husht on purpose to grace harmonic.

Prin. See you where *Benedicke* hath hid himselfe?

Clau. O very well my Lord: the musicke ended, Wee'l fit the kid-foxe with a penny worth.

Prince. Come *Balthasar*, wee'l heare that song again.

Balth. O good my Lord, taxe not so bad a voyce, To slander musicke any more then once.

Prin. It is the witnesse still of excellency,

To

To flander Muficke any more then once.

Prince. It is the witneffe ftill of excellencie,
To put a ftrange face on his owne perfe&ion,
I pray thee fing, and let me woe no more.

Balth. Becaufe you talke of wooing, I will fing,
Since many a wooer doth commence his fuit,
To her he thinkes not worthy, yet he wooes,
Yet will he fweare he loues.

Prince. Nay pray thee come,
Or if thou wilt hold longer argument,
Doe it in notes.

Balth. Note this before my notes,
Theres not a note of mine that's worth the noting.

Prince. Why thefe are very crotchets that he fpeaks,
Note notes forfooth, and nothing.

Bene. Now diuine aire, now is his foule raulfht, is it
not ftrange that fheepes guts fhould hale foules out of
mens bodies? well, a horne for my money when all's
done.

The Song.

Sigh no more Ladies, figh no more,
Men were deceiuers euer,
One foote in Sea, and one on fhore,
To one thing conftant neuer,
Then figh not fo, but let them goe,
And be you blithe and bonnie,
Conuerting all your founds of woe,
Into hey nony nony.

Sing no more ditties, fing no moe,
Of dumps fo dull and heauy,
The fraud of men were euer fo,
Since fummer firft was leauy,
Then figh not fo, &c.

Prince. By my troth a good song.

Balth. And an ill finger, my Lord.

Prince. Ha, no, no faith, thou fingft well enough for a
fhift.

Ben. And he had been a dog that fhould haue howld
thus, they would haue hang'd him, and I pray God his
bad voyce bode no mifchiefe, I had as liefe haue heard
the night-rauen, come what plague could haue come after it.

Prince. Yea marry, doft thou heare *Balthafar*? I pray
thee get vs fome excellent muficke: for to morrow night
we would haue it at the Lady *Heroes* chamber window.

Balth. The beft I can, my Lord.   *Exit Balthafar.*

Prince. Do fo, farewell. Come hither *Leonato*, what
was it you told me of to day, that your Niece *Beatrice*
was in loue with figniur *Benedicke*?

Cla. O I, ftalke on, ftalke on, the foule fits. I did neuer thinke that Lady would haue loued any man.

Leon. No, nor I neither, but moft wonderful, that fhe
fhould fo dote on Signior *Benedicke*, whom fhee hath in
all outward behauiours feemed euer to abhorre.

Bene. Is't poffible? fits the winde in that corner?

Leo. By my troth my Lord, I cannot tell what to
thinke of it, but that fhe loues him with an inraged affe-
&ion, it is paft the infinite of thought.

Prince. May be fhe doth but counterfeit.

Claud. Faith like enough.

Leon. O God! counterfeit? there was neuer counterfeit of paffion, came fo neere the life of paffion as fhe dif-
couers it.

Prince. Why what effe&s of paffion fhewes fhe?

Claud. Baite the hooke well, this fifh will bite.

Leon. What effe&s my Lord? fhee will fit you, you
heard my daughter tell you how.

Clau. She did indeed.

Prin. How, how I pray you? you amaze me, I would
haue thought her fpirit had beene inuincible againft all
affaults of affe&ion.

Leo. I would haue fworne it had, my Lord, efpecially
againft *Benedicke*.

Bene. I fhould thinke this a gull, but that the white-
bearded fellow fpeakes it: knauery cannot fure hide
himfelfe in fuch reuerence.

Claud. He hath tane th'infe&ion, hold it vp.

Prince. Hath fhee made her affe&ion knowne to *Benedicke*?

Leonato. No, and fweares fhe neuer will, that's her
torment.

Claud. 'Tis true indeed, fo your daughter faies: fhall
I, faies fhe, that haue fo oft encountred him with fcorne,
write to him that I loue him?

Leo. This faies fhee now when fhee is beginning to
write to him, for fhee'll be vp twenty times a night, and
there will fhe fit in her fmocke, till fhe haue writ a fheet
of paper: my daughter tells vs all.

Clau. Now you talke of a fheet of paper, I remember
a pretty ieft your daughter told vs of.

Leon. O when fhe had writ it, & was reading it ouer,
fhe found *Benedicke* and *Beatrice* betweene the fheete.

Clau. That.

Leon. O fhe tore the letter into a thoufand halfpence,
raild at her felf, that fhe fhould be fo immodeft to write,
to one that fhee knew would flout her: I meafure him,
faies fhe, by my owne fpirit, for I fhould flout him if hee
writ to mee, yea though I loue him, I fhould.

Clau. Then downe vpon her knees fhe falls, weepes,
fobs, beates her heart, teares her hayre, praies, curfes, O
fweet *Benedicke*, God giue me patience.

Leon. She doth indeed, my daughter faies fo, and the
extafie hath fo much ouerborne her, that my daughter is
fomtime afeard fhe will doe a defperate out-rage to her
felfe, it is very true.

Prin. It were good that *Benedicke* knew of it by fome
other, if fhe will not difcouer it.

Clau. To what end? he would but make a fport of it,
and torment the poore Lady worfe.

Prin. And he fhould, it were an almes to hang him,
fhee's an excellent fweet Lady, and (out of all fufpition,)
fhe is vertuous.

Claudio. And fhe is exceeding wife.

Prince. In euery thing, but in louing *Benedicke*.

Leon. O my Lord, wifedome and bloud combating in
fo tender a body, we haue ten proofes to one, that bloud
hath the vi&ory, I am forry for her, as I haue iuft caufe,
being her Vncle, and her Guardian.

Prince. I would fhee had beftowed this dotage on
mee, I would haue daft all other refpe&s, and made her
halfe my felfe: I pray you tell *Benedicke* of it, and heare
what he will fay.

Leon. Were it good thinke you?

Clau. *Hero* thinkes furely fhe wil die, for fhe faies fhe
will die, if hee loue her not, and fhee will die ere fhee
make her loue knowne, and fhe will die if hee wooe her,
rather than fhee will bate one breath of her accuftomed
croffeneffe.

Prin. She doth well, if fhe fhould make tender of her
loue,

loue, 'tis very poffible hee'l fcorne it, for the man (as you know all) hath a contemptible fpirit.

Clau. He is a very proper man.

Prin. He hath indeed a good outward happines.

Clau. 'Fore God, and in my minde very wife.

Prin. He doth indeed fhew fome fparkes that are like wit.

Leon. And I take him to be valiant.

Prin. As *Hector*, I affure you, and in the managing of quarrels you may fee hee is wife, for either hee auoydes them with great difcretion, or vndertakes them with a Chriftian-like feare.

Leon. If hee doe feare God, a muft neceffarilie keepe peace, if hee breake the peace, hee ought to enter into a quarrell with feare and trembling.

Prin. And fo will he doe, for the man doth feare God, howfoeuer it feemes not in him, by fome large leafts hee will make: well, I am forry for your niece, fhall we goe fee *Benedicke*, and tell him of her loue.

Claud. Neuer tell him, my Lord, let her weare it out with good counfell.

Leon. Nay that's impoffible, fhe may weare her heart out firft.

Prin. Well, we will heare further of it by your daughter, let it coole the while, I loue *Benedicke* well, and I could wifh he would modeftly examine himfelfe, to fee how much he is vnworthy to haue fo good a Lady.

Leon. My Lord, will you walke? dinner is ready.

Clau. If he do not doat on her vpon this, I will neuer truft my expectation.

Prin. Let there be the fame Net fpread for her, and that muft your daughter and her gentlewoman carry: the fport will be, when they hold one an opinion of anothers dotage, and no fuch matter, that's the Scene that I would fee, which will be meerely a dumbe fhew: let vs fend her to call him into dinner.		*Exeunt.*

Bene. This can be no tricke, the conference was fadly borne, they haue the truth of this from *Hero*, they feeme to pittie the Lady: it feemes her affections haue the full bent: loue me? why it muft be requited: I heare how I am cenfur'd, they fay I will beare my felfe proudly, if I perceiue the loue come from her: they fay too, that fhe will rather die than giue any figne of affection: I did neuer thinke to marry, I muft not feeme proud, happy are they that heare their detractions, and can put them to mending: they fay the Lady is faire, 'tis a truth, I can beare them witneffe: and vertuous, tis fo, I cannot reprooue it, and wife, but for louing me, by my troth it is no addition to her witte, nor no great argument of her folly; for I will be horribly in loue with her, I may chance haue fome odde quirkes and remnants of witte broken on mee, becaufe I haue rail'd fo long againft marriage: but doth not the appetite alter? a man loues the meat in his youth, that he cannot indure in his age. Shall quips and fentences, and thefe paper bullets of the braine awe a man from the careere of his humour? No, the world muft be peopled. When I faid I would die a batcheler, I did not thinke I fhould liue till I were maried, here comes *Beatrice*: by this day, fhee's a faire Lady, I doe fpie fome markes of loue in her.

Enter Beatrice.

Beat. Againft my wil I am fent to bid you come in to dinner.

Bene. Faire *Beatrice*, I thanke you for your paines.

Beat. I tooke no more paines for thofe thankes, then you take paines to thanke me, if it had been painefull, I would not haue come.

Bene. You take pleafure then in the meffage.

Beat. Yea iuft fo much as you may take vpon a kniues point, and choake a daw withall: you haue no ftomacke fignior, fare you well.		*Exit.*

Bene. Ha, againft my will I am fent to bid you come into dinner: there's a double meaning in that: I tooke no more paines for thofe thankes then you tooke paines to thanke me, that's as much as to fay, any paines that I take for you is as eafie as thankes: if I doe not take pitty of her I am a villaine, if I doe not loue her I am a Iew, I will goe get her picture.		*Exit.*

Actus Tertius.

Enter Hero and two Gentlemen, Margaret, and Vrfula.

Hero. Good *Margaret* runne thee to the parlour,
There fhalt thou finde my Cofin *Beatrice*,
Propofing with the Prince and *Claudio*,
Whifper her eare, and tell her I and *Vrfula*,
Walke in the Orchard, and our whole difcourfe
Is all of her, fay that thou ouer-heardft vs,
And bid her fteale into the pleached bower,
Where hony-fuckles ripened by the funne,
Forbid the funne to enter: like fauourites,
Made proud by Princes, that aduance their pride,
Againft that power that bred it, there will fhe hide her,
To liften our purpofe, this is thy office,
Beare thee well in it, and leaue vs alone.

Marg. Ile make her come I warrant you prefently.

Hero. Now *Vrfula*, when *Beatrice* doth come,
As we do trace this alley vp and downe,
Our talke muft onely be of *Benedicke*,
When I doe name him, let it be thy part,
To praife him more then euer man did merit,
My talke to thee muft be how *Benedicke*
Is ficke in loue with *Beatrice*: of this matter,
Is little *Cupids* crafty arrow made,
That onely wounds by heare-fay: now begin,
			Enter Beatrice.
For looke where *Beatrice* like a Lapwing runs
Clofe by the ground, to heare our conference.

Vrf. The pleafant'ft angling is to fee the fifh
Cut with her golden ores the filuer ftreame,
And greedily deuoure the treacherous baite:
So angle we for *Beatrice*, who euen now,
Is couched in the wood-bine couerture,
Feare you not my part of the Dialogue.

Her. Then go we neare her that her eare loofe nothing,
Of the falfe fweete baite that we lay for it:
No truely *Vrfula*, fhe is too difdainfull,
I know her fpirits are as coy and wilde,
As Haggerds of the rocke.

Vrfula. But are you fure,
That *Benedicke* loues *Beatrice* fo intirely?

Her. So faies the Prince, and my new trothed Lord.

Vrf. And did they bid you tell her of it, Madam?

Her. They did intreate me to acquaint her of it,
But I perfwaded them, if they lou'd *Benedicke*,

K					To

To wiſh him wraſtle with affeċtion,
And neuer to let *Beatrice* know of it.
  Vrſula. Why did you ſo, doth not the Gentleman
Deſerue as full as fortunate a bed,
As euer *Beatrice* ſhall couch vpon ?
  Hero. O God of loue! I know he doth deſerue,
As much as may be yeelded to a man :
But Nature neuer fram'd a womans heart,
Of prowder ſtuffe then that of *Beatrice* :
Diſdaine and Scorne ride ſparkling in her eyes,
Miſ-prizing what they looke on, and her wit
Values it ſelfe ſo highly, that to her
All matter elſe ſeemes weake : ſhe cannot loue,
Nor take no ſhape nor proieċt of affeċtion,
Shee is ſo ſelfe indeared.
  Vrſula. Sure I thinke ſo,
And therefore certainely it were not good
She knew his loue, leſt ſhe make ſport at it.
  Hero. Why you ſpeake truth, I neuer yet ſaw man,
How wiſe, how noble, yong, how rarely featur'd.
But ſhe would ſpell him backward : if faire fac'd,
She would ſweare the gentleman ſhould be her ſiſter :
If blacke, why Nature drawing of an anticke,
Made a foule blot : if tall, a launce ill headed :
If low, an agot very vildlie cut :
If ſpeaking, why a vane blowne with all windes :
If ſilent, why a blocke moued with none.
So turnes ſhe euery man the wrong ſide out,
And neuer giues to Truth and Vertue, that
Which ſimpleneſſe and merit purchaſeth.
  Vrſu. Sure, ſure, ſuch carping is not commendable.
  Hero. No, not to be ſo odde, and from all faſhions,
As *Beatrice* is, cannot be commendable,
But who dare tell her ſo ? if I ſhould ſpeake,
She would mocke me into ayre, O ſhe would laugh me
Out of my ſelfe, preſſe me to death with wit,
Therefore let *Benedicke* like couered fire,
Conſume away in ſighes, waſte inwardly :
It were a better death, to die with mockes,
Which is as bad as die with tickling.
  Vrſu. Yet tell her of it, heare what ſhee will ſay.
  Hero. No, rather I will goe to *Benedicke*,
And counſaile him to fight againſt his paſſion,
And truly Ile deuiſe ſome honeſt ſlanders,
To ſtaine my coſin with, one doth not know,
How much an ill word may impoiſon liking.
  Vrſu. O doe not doe your coſin ſuch a wrong,
She cannot be ſo much without true iudgement,
Hauing ſo ſwift and excellent a wit
As ſhe is priſde to haue, as to refuſe
So rare a Gentleman as ſignior *Benedicke*.
  Hero. He is the onely man of Italy,
Alwaies excepted, my deare *Claudio*.
  Vrſu. I pray you be not angry with me, Madame,
Speaking my fancy : Signior *Benedicke*,
For ſhape, for bearing argument and valour,
Goes formoſt in report through Italy.
  Hero. Indeed he hath an excellent good name.
  Vrſu. His excellence did earne it ere he had it :
When are you married Madame ?
  Hero. Why euerie day to morrow, come goe in,
Ile ſhew thee ſome attires, and haue thy counſell,
Which is the beſt to furniſh me to morrow.
  Vrſu. Shee's tane I warrant you,
We haue caught her Madame ?
  Hero. If it proue ſo, then louing goes by haps,

Some *Cupid* kills with arrowes, ſome with traps.   *Exit.*
  Beat. What fire is in mine eares? can this be true?
Stand I condemn'd for pride and ſcorne ſo much?
Contempt, farewell, and maiden pride, adew,
No glory liues behinde the backe of ſuch.
And *Benedicke*, loue on, I will requite thee,
Taming my wilde heart to thy louing hand :
If thou doſt loue, my kindeneſſe ſhall incite thee
To binde our loues vp in a holy band.
For others ſay thou doſt deſerue, and I
Beleeue it better then reportingly.   *Exit.*

  Enter Prince, Claudio, Benedicke, and Leonato.
  Prince. I doe but ſtay till your marriage be conſummate, and then go I toward Arragon.
  Clau. Ile bring you thither my Lord, if you'l vouchſafe me.
  Prin. Nay, that would be as great a ſoyle in the new
gloſſe of your marriage, as to ſhew a childe his new coat
and forbid him to weare it, I will onely bee bold with
Benedicke for his companie, for from the crowne of his
head, to the ſole of his foot, he is all mirth, he hath twice
or thrice cut *Cupids* bow-ſtring, and the little hang-man
dare not ſhoot at him, he hath a heart as ſound as a bell,
and his tongue is the clapper, for what his heart thinkes,
his tongue ſpeakes.
  Bene. Gallants, I am not as I haue bin.
  Leo. So ſay I, methinkes you are ſadder.
  Claud. I hope he be in loue.
  Prin. Hang him truant, there's no true drop of bloud
in him to be truly toucht with loue, if he be ſad, he wants
money.
  Bene. I haue the tooth-ach.
  Prin. Draw it.
  Bene. Hang it.
  Claud. You muſt hang it firſt, and draw it afterwards.
  Prin. What ? ſigh for the tooth-ach.
  Leon. Where is but a humour or a worme.
  Bene. Well, euery one cannot maſter a griefe, but hee
that has it.
  Clau. Yet ſay I, he is in loue.
  Prin. There is no appearance of fancie in him, vnleſſe
it be a fancy that he hath to ſtrange diſguiſes, as to bee a
Dutchman to day, a Frenchman to morrow : vnleſſe hee
haue a fancy to this foolery, as it appeares hee hath, hee
is no foole for fancy, as you would haue it to appeare
he is.
  Clau. If he be not in loue vvith ſome vvoman, there
is no beleeuing old ſignes, a bruſhes his hat a mornings,
What ſhould that bode?
  Prin. Hath any man ſeene him at the Barbers?
  Clau. No, but the Barbers man hath beene ſeen with
him, and the olde ornament of his cheeke hath alreadie
ſtuft tennis balls.
  Leon. Indeed he lookes yonger then hee did, by the
loſſe of a beard.
  Prin. Nay a rubs himſelfe vvith Ciuit, can you ſmell
him out by that ?
  Clau. That's as much as to ſay, the ſweet youth's in
loue.
  Prin. The greateſt note of it is his melancholy.
  Clau. And vvhen vvas he vvont to vvaſh his face ?
  Prin. Yea, or to paint himſelfe ? for the which I heare
vvhat they ſay of him.
  Clau. Nay, but his ieſting ſpirit, vvhich is now crept
into a lute-ſtring, and now gouern'd by ſtops.

                          Prince.

Prin. Indeed that tels a heauy tale for him: conclude, he is in loue.

Clau. Nay, but I know who loues him.

Prince. That would I know too, I warrant one that knowes him not.

Cla. Yes, and his ill conditions, and in defpight of all, dies for him.

Prin. Shee fhall be buried with her face vpwards.

Bene. Yet is this no charme for the tooth-ake, old fignior, walke afide with mee, I haue ftudied eight or nine wife words to fpeake to you, which thefe hobby-horfes muft not heare.

Prin. For my life to breake with him about *Beatrice.*

Clau. 'Tis euen fo, *Hero* and *Margaret* haue by this played their parts with *Beatrice*, and then the two Beares will not bite one another when they meete.

Enter Iohn the Baftard.

Baft. My Lord and brother, God faue you.

Prin. Good den brother.

Baft. If your leifure feru'd, I would fpeake with you.

Prince. In priuate?

Baft. If it pleafe you, yet Count *Claudio* may heare, for what I would fpeake of, concernes him.

Prin. What's the matter?

Bafta. Meanes your Lordfhip to be married to morrow?

Prin. You know he does.

Baft. I know not that when he knowes what I know.

Clau. If there be any impediment, I pray you difcouer it.

Baft. You may thinke I loue you not, let that appeare hereafter, and ayme better at me by that I now will manifeft, for my brother (I thinke, he holds you well, and in dearenefle of heart) hath holpe to effect your enfuing marriage: furely fute ill fpent, and labour ill beftowed.

Prin. Why, what's the matter?

Baftard. I came hither to tell you, and circumftances fhortned, (for fhe hath beene too long a talking of) the Lady is difloyall.

Clau. Who *Hero?*

Baft. Euen fhee, *Leonatoes Hero*, your *Hero*, euery mans *Hero.*

Clau. Difloyall?

Baft. The word is too good to paint out her wickednefle, I could fay fhe were worfe, thinke you of a worfe title, and I will fit her to it: wonder not till further warrant: goe but with mee to night, you fhal fee her chamber window entred, euen the night before her wedding day, if you loue her, then to morrow wed her: But it would better fit your honour to change your minde.

Claud. May this be fo?

Princ. I will not thinke it.

Baft. If you dare not truft that you fee, confefle not that you know: if you will follow mee, I will fhew you enough, and when you haue feene more, & heard more, proceed accordingly.

Clau. If I fee any thing to night, why I fhould not marry her to morrow in the congregation, where I fhold wedde, there will I fhame her.

Prin. And as I wooed for thee to obtaine her, I will ioyne with thee to difgrace her.

Baft. I will difparage her no farther, till you are my witnefles, beare it coldly but till night, and let the iffue fhew it felfe.

Prin. O day vntowardly turned!

Claud. O mifchiefe ftrangelie thwarting!

Buftard. O plague right well preuented! fo will you fay, when you haue feene the fequele.   *Exit.*

Enter Dogbery and his compartner with the watch.

Dog. Are you good men and true?

Verg. Yea, or elfe it were pitty but they fhould fuffer faluation body and foule.

Dogb. Nay, that were a punifhment too good for them, if they fhould haue any allegiance in them, being chofen for the Princes watch.

Verges. Well, giue them their charge, neighbour Dogbery.

Dog. Firft, who thinke you the moft defartlefle man to be Conftable?

Watch. 1. *Hugh Ote-cake* fir, or *George Sea-coale*, for they can write and reade.

Dogb. Come hither neighbour Sea-coale, God hath bleft you with a good name: to be a wel-fauoured man, is the gift of Fortune, but to write and reade, comes by Nature.

Watch 2. Both which Mafter Conftable

Dogb. You haue: I knew it would be your anfwere: well, for your fauour fir, why giue God thankes, & make no boaft of it, and for your writing and reading, let that appeare when there is no need of fuch vanity, you are thought heere to be the moft fenfible and fit man for the Conftable of the watch: therefore beare you the lanthorne: this is your charge: You fhall comprehend all vagrom men, you are to bid any man ftand in the Princes name.

Watch 2. How if a will not ftand?

Dogb. Why then take no note of him, but let him go, and prefently call the reft of the Watch together, and thanke God you are ridde of a knaue.

Verges. If he will not ftand when he is bidden, hee is none of the Princes fubiects.

Dogb. True, and they are to meddle with none but the Princes fubiects: you fhall alfo make no noife in the ftreetes: for, for the Watch to babble and talke, is moft tollerable, and not to be indured.

Watch. We will rather fleepe than talke, wee know what belongs to a Watch.

Dog. Why you fpeake like an ancient and moft quiet watchman, for I cannot fee how fleeping fhould offend: only haue a care that your bills be not ftolne: well, you are to call at all the Alehoufes, and bid them that are drunke get them to bed.

Watch. How if they will not?

Dogb. Why then let them alone till they are fober, if they make you not then the better anfwere, you may fay, they are not the men you tooke them for.

Watch. Well fir.

Dogb. If you meet a theefe, you may fufpect him, by vertue of your office, to be no true man: and for fuch kinde of men, the lefle you meddle or make with them, why the more is for your honefty.

Watch. If wee know him to be a thiefe, fhall wee not lay hands on him.

Dogb. Truly by your office you may, but I thinke they that touch pitch will be defil'd: the moft peaceable way for you, if you doe take a theefe, is, to let him fhew himfelfe what he is, and fteale out of your company.

Ver. You haue bin alwaies cal'd a merciful mã partner.

Dog. Truely I would not hang a dog by my will, much more a man who hath anie honeftie in him.

K 2   *Verges.*

Verges. If you heare a child crie in the night you muſt call to the nurſe, and bid her ſtill it.

Watch. How if the nurſe be aſleepe and will not heare vs?

Dog. Why then depart in peace, and let the childe wake her with crying, for the ewe that will not heare her Lambe when it baes, will neuer anſwere a calfe when he bleates.

Verges. 'Tis verie true.

Dog. This is the end of the charge : you conſtable are to preſent the Princes owne perſon, if you meete the Prince in the night, you may ſtaie him.

Verges. Nay birladie that I thinke a cannot.

Dog. Fiue ſhillings to one on't with anie man that knowes the Statues, he may ſtaie him, marrie not without the prince be willing, for indeed the watch ought to offend no man, and it is an offence to ſtay a man againſt his will.

Verges. Birladie I thinke it be ſo.

Dog. Ha, ah ha, well maſters good night, and there be anie matter of weight chances, call vp me, keepe your fellowes counſailes, and your owne, and good night, come neighbour.

Watch. Well maſters, we heare our charge, let vs go ſit here vpon the Church bench till two, and then all to bed.

Dog. One word more, honeſt neighbors. I pray you watch about ſignior *Leonatoes* doore, for the wedding being there to morrow, there is a great coyle to night, adiew, be vigitant I beſeech you.   *Exeunt.*

Enter Borachio and Conrade.

Bor. What, *Conrade?*

Watch. Peace, ſtir not.

Bor. *Conrade* I ſay.

Con. Here man, I am at thy elbow.

Bor. Mas and my elbow itcht, I thought there would a ſcabbe follow.

Con. I will owe thee an anſwere for that, and now forward with thy tale.

Bor. Stand thee cloſe then vnder this penthouſe, for it driſſels raine, and I will, like a true drunkard, vtter all to thee.

Watch. Some treaſon maſters, yet ſtand cloſe.

Bor. Therefore know, I haue earned of *Don Iohn* a thouſand Ducates.

Con. Is it poſſible that anie villanie ſhould be ſo deare?

Bor. Thou ſhould'ſt rather aske if it were poſſible anie villanie ſhould be ſo rich? for when rich villains haue neede of poore ones, poore ones may make what price they will.

Con. I wonder at it.

Bor. That ſhewes thou art vnconfirm'd, thou knoweſt that the faſhion of a doublet, or a hat, or a cloake, is nothing to a man.

Con. Yes, it is apparell.

Bor. I meane the faſhion.

Con. Yes the faſhion is the faſhion.

Bor. Tuſh, I may as well ſay the foole's the foole, but ſeeſt thou not what a deformed theefe this faſhion is?

Watch. I know that deformed, a has bin a vile theefe, this vii. yeares, a goes vp and downe like a gentle man : I remember his name.

Bor. Did'ſt thou not heare ſome bodie?

Con. No, 'twas the vaine on the houſe.

Bor. Seeſt thou not (I ſay) what a deformed thiefe this faſhion is, how giddily a turnes about all the Hot-

blouds, betweene foureteene & fiue & thirtie, ſometimes faſhioning them like *Pharaoes* fouldiours in the rechie painting, ſometime like god Bels prieſts in the old Church window, ſometime like the ſhauen *Hercules* in the ſmircht worm eaten tapeſtrie, where his cod-peece ſeemes as maſſie as his club.

Con. All this I ſee, and ſee that the faſhion weares out more apparrell then the man; but art not thou thy ſelfe giddie with the faſhion too that thou haſt ſhifted out of thy tale into telling me of the faſhion ?

Bor. Not ſo neither, but know that I haue to night wooed *Margaret* the Lady *Heroes* gentle-woman, by the name of *Hero,* ſhe leanes me out at her miſtris chamber-vvindow, bids me a thouſand times good night : I tell this tale vildly. I ſhould firſt tell thee how the Prince *Claudio* and my Maſter planted, and placed, and poſſeſſed by my Maſter *Don Iohn,* ſaw a far off in the Orchard this amiable incounter.

Con. And thought thy *Margaret* was *Hero?*

Bor. Two of them did, the Prince and *Claudio,* but the diuell my Maſter knew ſhe was *Margaret* and partly by his oathes, which firſt poſſeſt them, partly by the darke night which did deceiue them, but cheifely, by my villanie, which did confirme any ſlander that *Don Iohn* had made, away vvent *Claudio* enraged, ſwore hee vvould meete her as he was apointed next morning at the Temple, and there, before the whole congregation ſhame her with vvhat he ſaw o're night, and ſend her home againe vvithout a husbaud.

Watch. 1. We charge you in the Princes name ſtand.

Watch. 2. Call vp the right maſter Conſtable, vve haue here recouered the moſt dangerous peece of lechery, that euer vvas knowne in the Common-wealth.

Watch. 1. And one Deformed is one of them, I know him, a vveares a locke.

Conr. Maſters, maſters.

Watch. 2. Youle be made bring deformed forth I warrant you,

Conr. Maſters, neuer ſpeake, vve charge you, let vs obey you to goe vvith vs.

Bor. We are like to proue a goodly commoditie, being taken vp of theſe mens bils.

Conr. A commoditie in queſtion I warrant you, come vveele obey you.   *Exeunt.*

Enter Hero, and Margaret, and Vrſula.

Hero. Good *Vrſula* wake my coſin *Beatrice,* and deſire her to riſe..

Vrſu. I will Lady.

Her. And bid her come hither.

Vrſ. Well.

Mar. Troth I thinke your other rebato were better.

Bero. No pray thee good *Meg,* Ile vveare this.

Marg. By my troth's not ſo good, and I vvarrant your coſin vvill ſay ſo.

Bero. My coſin's a foole, and thou art another, ile vveare none but this.

Mar. I like the new tire vvithin excellently, if the haire vvere a thought browner : and your gown's a moſt rare faſhion yfaith, I ſaw the Dutcheſſe of *Millaines* gowne that they praiſe ſo.

Bero. O that exceedes they ſay.

Mar. By my troth's but a night-gowne in reſpeĉt of yours, cloth a gold and cuts, and lac'd with ſiluer, ſet with pearles, downe ſleeues, ſide ſleeues, and ſkirts, round vnderborn with a blewiſh tinſel, but for a fine queint gracefull and excellent faſhion, yours is worth ten on't.

Bero. God

Hero. God giue mee ioy to weare it, for my heart is exceeding heauy.

Marga. 'Twill be heauier foone, by the waight of a man.

Hero. Fie vpon thee, art not afham'd?

Marg. Of what Lady? of fpeaking honourably? is not marriage honourable in a beggar? is not your Lord honourable without marriage? I thinke you would haue me fay, fauing your reuerence a husband : and bad thinking doe not wreft true fpeaking, Ile offend no body, is there any harme in the heauier for a husband? none I thinke, and it be the right husband, and the right wife, otherwife 'tis light and not heauy, aske my Lady *Beatrice* elfe, here fhe comes.

Enter Beatrice.

Hero. Good morrow Coze.

Beat. Good morrow fweet *Hero.*

Hero. Why how now? do you fpeake in the fick tune?

Beat. I am out of all other tune, me thinkes.

Mar. Claps into Light a loue , (that goes without a burden,) do you fing it and Ile dance it.

Beat. Ye Light aloue with your heeles, then if your husband haue ftables enough, you'll looke he fhall lacke no barnes.

Mar. O illegitimate conftruction! I faorne that with my heeles.

Beat. 'Tis almoft fiue a clocke cofin, 'tis time you were ready, by my troth I am exceeding ill, hey ho.

Mar. For a hauke, a horfe, or a husband?

Beat. For the letter that begins them all, H.

Mar. Well, and you be not turn'd Turke, there's no more fayling by the ftarre.

Beat. What meanes the foole trow?

Mar. Nothing I, but God fend euery one their harts defire.

Hero. Thefe gloues the Count fent mee , they are an excellent perfume.

Beat. I am ftuft cofin, I cannot fmell.

Mar. A maid and ftuft! there's goodly catching of colde.

Beat. O God helpe me, God help me, how long haue you profeft apprehenfion?

Mar. Euer fince you left it, doth not my wit become me rarely?

Beat. It is not feene enough, you fhould weare it in your cap, by my troth I am ficke.

Mar. Get you fome of this diftill'd *carduus beuedictus* and lay it to your heart, it is the onely thing for a qualm.

Hero. There thou prickft her with a thiffell.

Beat. Benedictus, why *benedictus?* you haue fome morall in this *benedictus.*

Mar. Morall? no by my troth, I haue no morall meaning, I meant plaine holy thiffell , you may thinke perchance that I thinke you are in loue, nay birlady I am not fuch a foole to thinke what I lift, nor I lift not to thinke what I can, nor indeed I cannot thinke, if I would thinke my hart out of thinking, that you are in loue, or that you will be in loue, or that you can be in loue : yet *Benedicke* was fuch another, and now is he become a man, he fwore hee would neuer marry, and yet now in defpight of his heart he eates his meat without grudging, and how you may be conuerted I know not, but me thinkes you looke with your eies as other women doe.

Beat. What pace is this that thy tongue keepes.

Mar. Not a falfe gallop.

Enter Vrfula.

Vrfula. Madam, withdraw, the Prince, the Count, fignior *Benedicke*, Don *Iohn*, and all the gallants of the towne are come to fetch you to Church.

Hero. Helpe to dreffe mee good coze, good *Meg*, good *Vrfula.*

Enter Leonato, and the Conftable, and the Headborough.

Leonato. What would you with mee , honeft neighbour?

Conft.Dog. Mary fir I would haue fome confidence with you, that decernes you nearely.

Leon. Briefe I pray you , for you fee it is a bufie time with me.

Conft.Dog. Mary this it is fir.

Headb. Yes in truth it is fir.

Leon. What is it my good friends?

Con.Do. Goodman *Verges* fir fpeakes a little of the matter, an old man fir, and his wits are not fo blunt, as God helpe I would defire they were, but infaith honeft as the skin betweene his browes.

Head. Yes I thank God, I am as honeft as any man liuing, that is an old man, and no honefter then I.

Con.Dog. Comparifons are odorous, palabras, neighbour Verges.

Leon. Neighbours, you are tedious.

Con.Dog. It pleafes your worfhip to fay fo, but we are the poore Dukes officers, but truely for mine owne part, if I were as tedious as a King I could finde in my heart to beftow it all of your worfhip.

Leon. All thy tedioufneffe on me, ah?

Conft.Dog. Yea , and 'twere a thoufand times more than 'tis, for I heare as good exclamation on your Worfhip as of any man in the Citie , and though I bee but a poore man, I am glad to heare it.

Head. And fo am I.

Leon. I would faine know what you haue to fay.

Head. Marry fir our watch to night , excepting your worfhips prefence, haue tane a couple of as arrant knaues as any in Meffina.

Con.Dog. A good old man fir, hee will be talking as they fay, when the age is in, the wit is out, God helpe vs, it is a world to fee : well faid yfaith neighbour *Verges*, well, God's a good man , and two men ride of a horfe, one muft ride behinde, an honeft foule yfaith fir, by my troth he is, as euer broke bread, but God is to bee worfhipt, all men are not alike, alas good neighbour.

Leon. Indeed neighbour he comes too fhort of you.

Con.Do. Gifts that God giues.

Leon. I muft leaue you.

Con.Dog. One word fir, our watch fir haue indeede comprehended two afpitious perfons, & we would haue them this morning examined before your worfhip.

Leon. Take their examination your felfe, and bring it me, I am now in great hafte, as may appeare vnto you.

Conft. It fhall be fuffigance.   (*Exit.*

Leon. Drinke fome wine ere you goe : fare you well.

Meffenger. My Lord, they ftay for you to giue your daughter to her husband.

Leon. Ile wait vpon them, I am ready.

Dogb. Goe good partner, goe get you to *Francis Seacoale*, bid him bring his pen and inkehorne to the Gaole : we are now to examine thofe men.

Verges. And we muft doe it wifely.

Dogb. Wee will fpare for no witte I warrant you : heeres

heere's that fhall driue fome of them to a non-come, only get the learned writer to fet downe our excommuni-
cation, and meet me at the Iaile.   *Exeunt.*

Actus Quartus.

Enter Prince, Baftard, Leonato, Frier, Claudio, Benedicke,
Hero, and Beatrice.

Leonato. Come Frier *Francis,* be briefe, onely to the
plaine forme of marriage, and you fhal recount their particular duties afterwards.

Fran. You come hither, my Lord, to marry this Lady.

Clau. No.

Leo. To be married to her : Frier, you come to marrie her.

Frier. Lady, you come hither to be married to this
Count.

Hero. I doe.

Frier. If either of you know any inward impediment
why you fhould not be conioyned, I charge you on your
foules to vtter it.

Claud. Know you anie, *Hero?*

Hero. None my Lord.

Frier. Know you anie, Count?

Leon. I dare make his anfwer, None.

Clau. O what men dare do! what men may do! what
men daily do!

Bene. How now! interiections? why then, fome be
of laughing, as ha, ha, he.

Clau. Stand thee by Frier, father, by your leaue,
Will you with free and vnconftrained foule
Giue me this maid your daughter?

Leon. As freely fonne as God did giue her me.

Cla. And what haue I to giue you back, whofe worth
May counterpoife this rich and precious gift?

Prin. Nothing, vnleffe you render her againe.

Clau. Sweet Prince, you learn me noble thankfulnes:
There *Leonato,* take her backe againe,
Giue not this rotten Orenge to your friend,
Shee's but the figne and femblance of her honour:
Behold how like a maid fhe blufhes heere!
O what authoritie and fhew of truth
Can cunning finne couer it felfe withall!
Comes not that bloud, as modeft euidence,
To witneffe fimple Vertue? would you not fweare
All you that fee her, that fhe were a maide,
By thefe exterior fhewes? But fhe is none:
She knowes the heat of a luxurious bed:
Her blufh is guiltineffe, not modeftie.

Leonato. What doe you meane, my Lord?

Clau. Not to be married,
Not to knit my foule to an approued wanton.

Leon. Deere my Lord, if you in your owne proofe,
Haue vanquifht the refiftance of her youth,
And made defeat of her virginitie.   (her,

Clau. I know what you would fay: if I haue knowne
You will fay, fhe did imbrace me as a husband,
And fo extenuate the forehand finne : No *Leonato,*
I neuer tempted her with word too large,
But as a brother to his fifter, fhewed
Bafhfull finceritie and comely loue.

Hero. And feem'd I euer otherwife to you?

Clau. Out on thee feeming, I will write againft it,
You feeme to me as *Diane* in her Orbe,
As chafte as is the budde ere it be blowne:
But you are more intemperate in your blood,
Than *Venus,* or thofe pampred animalls,
That rage in fauage fenfualitie.

Hero. Is my Lord well, that he doth fpeake fo wide?

Leon. Sweete Prince, why fpeake not you?

Prin. What fhould I fpeake?
I ftand difhonour'd that haue gone about,
To linke my deare friend to a common ftale.

Leon. Are thefe things fpoken, or doe I but dreame?

Baft. Sir, they are fpoken, and thefe things are true.

Bene. This lookes not like a nuptiall.

Hero. True, O God!

Clau. Leonato, ftand I here?
Is this the Prince? is this the Princes brother?
Is this face *Heroes?* are our eies our owne?

Leon. All this is fo, but what of this my Lord?

Clau. Let me but moue one queftion to your daugh-
And by that fatherly and kindly power,   (ter,
That you haue in her, bid her anfwer truly.

Leo. I charge thee doe, as thou art my childe.

Hero. O God defend me how am I befet,
What kinde of catechizing call you this?

Clau. To make you anfwer truly to your name.

Hero. Is it not *Hero?* who can blot that name
With any iuft reproach?

Claud. Marry that can *Hero,*
Hero it felfe can blot out *Heroes* vertue.
What man was he, talkt with you yefternight,
Out at your window betwixt twelue and one?
Now if you are a maid, anfwer to this.

Hero. I talkt with no man at that howre my Lord.

Prince. Why then you are no maiden. *Leonato,*
I am forry you muft heare : vpon mine honor,
My felfe, my brother, and this grieued Count
Did fee her, heare her, at that howre laft night,
Talke with a ruffian at her chamber window,
Who hath indeed moft like a liberall villaine,
Confeft the vile encounters they haue had
A thoufand times in fecret.

Iohn. Fie, fie, they are not to be named my Lord,
Not to be fpoken of,
There is not chaftitie enough in language,
Without offence to vtter them: thus pretty Lady
I am forry for thy much mifgouernment.

Claud. O *Hero!* what a *Hero* hadft thou beene
If halfe thy outward graces had beene placed
About thy thoughts and counfailes of thy heart?
But fare thee well, moft foule, moft faire, farewell
Thou pure impiery, and impious puritie,
For thee Ile locke vp all the gates of Loue,
And on my eie-lids fhall Coniecture hang,
To turne all beauty into thoughts of harme,
And neuer fhall it more be gracious.

Leon. Hath no mans dagger here a point for me?

Beat. Why how now cofin, wherfore fink you down?

Baft. Come, let vs go: thefe things come thus to light,
Smother her fpirits vp.

Bene. How doth the Lady?

Beat. Dead I thinke, helpe vncle,
Hero, why *Hero,* Vncle, Signor *Benedicke,* Frier.

Leonato. O Fate! take not away thy heauy hand,
Death is the faireft couer for her fhame
That may be wifht for.

                       Beat. How

Beatr. How now cofin *Hero?*

Fri. Haue comfort Ladie.

Leon. Doſt thou looke vp?

Frier. Yea, wherefore ſhould ſhe not?

Leon. Wherfore? Why doth not euery earthly thing
Cry ſhame vpon her? Could ſhe heere denie
The ſtorie that is printed in her blood?
Do not liue *Hero,* do not ope thine eyes:
For did I thinke thou wouldſt not quickly die,
Thought I thy ſpirits were ſtronger then thy ſhames,
My ſelfe would on the reward of reproaches
Strike at thy life. Grieu'd I, I had but one?
Chid I, for that at frugal Natures frame?
O one too much by thee: why had I one?
Why euer was't thou louelie in my eies?
Why had I not with charitable hand
Tooke vp a beggars iſſue at my gates,
Who ſmeered thus, and mir'd with infamie,
I might haue ſaid, no part of it is mine:
This ſhame deriues it ſelfe from vnknowne loines,
But mine, and mine I lou'd, and mine I prais'd,
And mine that I was proud on mine ſo much,
That I my ſelfe, was to my ſelfe not mine:
Valewing of her, why ſhe, O ſhe is falne
Into a pit of Inke, that the wide ſea
Hath drops too few to waſh her cleane againe,
And ſalt too little, which may ſeaſon giue
To her foule tainted fleſh.

Ben. Sir, ſir, be patient: for my part, I am ſo attired
in wonder, I know not what to ſay.

Bea. O on my ſoule my coſin is belied.

Ben. Ladie, were you her bedfellow laſt night?

Bea. No truly: not although vntill laſt night,
I haue this tweluemonth bin her bedfellow.

Leon. Confirm'd, confirm'd, O that is ſtronger made
Which was before barr'd vp with ribs of iron.
Would the Princes lie, and *Claudio* lie,
Who lou'd her ſo, that ſpeaking of her foulneſſe,
Waſh'd it with teares? Hence from her, let her die.

Fri. Heare me a little, for I haue onely bene ſilent ſo
long, and giuen way vnto this courſe of fortune, by no-
ting of the Ladie, I haue markt,
A thouſand bluſhing apparitions,
To ſtart into her face, a thouſand innocent ſhames,
In Angel whiteneſſe beare away thoſe bluſhes,
And in her eie there hath appear'd a fire
To burne the errors that theſe Princes hold
Againſt her maiden truth. Call me a foole,
Truſt not my reading, nor my obſeruations,
Which with experimentall ſeale doth warrant
The tenure of my booke: truſt not my age,
My reuerence, calling, nor diuinitie,
If this ſweet Ladie lye not guiltleſſe heere,
Vnder ſome biting error.

Leo. Friar, it cannot be:
Thou ſeeſt that all the Grace that ſhe hath left,
Is, that ſhe wil not adde to her damnation,
A ſinne of periury, ſhe not denies it:
Why ſeek'ſt thou then to couer with excuſe,
That which appeares in proper nakedneſſe?

Fri. Ladie, what man is he you are accus'd of?

Hero. They know that do accuſe me, I know none:
If I know more of any man aliue
Then that which maiden modeſtie doth warrant,
Let all my ſinnes lacke mercy. O my Father,
Proue you that any man with me conuerſt,

At houres vnmeete, or that I yeſternight
Maintain'd the change of words with any creature,
Refuſe me, hate me, torture me to death.

Fri. There is ſome ſtrange miſpriſion in the Princes.

Ben. Two of them haue the verie bent of honor,
And if their wiſedomes be miſled in this:
The practiſe of it liues in *Iohn* the baſtard,
Whoſe ſpirits toile in frame of villanies.

Leo. I know not: if they ſpeake but truth of her,
Theſe hands ſhall teare her: If they wrong her honour,
The proudeſt of them ſhall wel heare of it.
Time hath not yet ſo dried this bloud of mine,
Nor age ſo eate vp my inuention,
Nor Fortune made ſuch hauocke of my meanes,
Nor my bad life reſt me ſo much of friends,
But they ſhall finde, awak'd in ſuch a kinde,
Both ſtrength of limbe, and policie of minde,
Ability in meanes, and choiſe of friends,
To quit me of them throughly.

Fri. Pauſe awhile:
And let my counſell ſway you in this caſe,
Your daughter heere the Princeſſe (left for dead)
Let her awhile be ſecretly kept in,
And publiſh it, that ſhe is dead indeed:
Maintaine a mourning oſtentation,
And on your Families old monument,
Hang mournfull Epitaphes, and do all rites,
That appertaine vnto a buriall.

Leon. What ſhall become of this? What wil this do?

Fri. Marry this wel carried, ſhall on her behalfe,
Change ſlander to remorſe, that is ſome good,
But not for that dreame I on this ſtrange courſe,
But on this trauaile looke for greater birth:
She dying, as it muſt be ſo maintain'd,
Vpon the inſtant that ſhe was accus'd,
Shal be lamented, pitied, and excuſ'd
Of euery hearer: for it ſo fals out,
That what we haue, we prize not to the worth,
Whiles we enioy it; but being lack'd and loſt,
Why then we racke the value, then we finde
The vertue that poſſeſſion would not ſhew vs
Whiles it was ours, ſo will it fare with *Claudio*:
When he ſhal heare ſhe dyed vpon his words,
Th'Idea of her life ſhal ſweetly creepe
Into his ſtudy of imagination.
And euery louely Organ of her life,
Shall come apparel'd in more precious habite:
More mouing delicate, and ful of life,
Into the eye and proſpect of his ſoule
Then when ſhe liu'd indeed: then ſhal he mourne,
If euer Loue had intereſt in his Liuer,
And wiſh he had not ſo accuſed her:
No, though he thought his accuſation true:
Let this be ſo, and doubt not but ſucceſſe
Wil faſhion the euent in better ſhape,
Then I can lay it downe in likelihood.
But if all ayme but this be leuelld falſe,
The ſuppoſition of the Ladies death,
Will quench the wonder of her infamie.
And if it ſort not well, you may conceale her,
As beſt befits her wounded reputation,
In ſome recluſiue and religious life,
Out of all eyes, tongues, mindes and iniuries.

Bene. Signior *Leonato,* let the Frier aduiſe you,
And though you know my inwardneſſe and loue
Is very much vnto the Prince and *Claudio.*

Yet

Yet, by mine honor, I will deale in this,
As secretly and iustlie, as your soule
Should with your bodie.
Leon. Being that I flow in greefe,
The smallest twine may lead me.
Frier. 'Tis well consented, presently away,
For to strange sores, strangely they straine the cure,
Come Lady, die to liue, this wedding day
Perhaps is but prolong'd, haue patience & endure.   *Exit.*
Bene. Lady *Beatrice*, haue you wept all this while?
Beat. Yea, and I will weepe a while longer.
Bene. I will not desire that.
Beat. You haue no reason, I doe it freely.
Bene. Surelie I do beleeue your faire cosin is wrong'd.
Beat. Ah, how much might the man deserue of mee
that would right her!
Bene. Is there any way to shew such friendship?
Beat. A verie euen way, but no such friend.
Bene. May a man doe it?
Beat. It is a mans office, but not yours.
Bene. I doe loue nothing in the world so well as you,
is not that strange?
Beat. As strange as the thing I know not, it were as
possible for me to say, I loued nothing so well as you, but
beleeue me not, and yet I lie not, I confesse nothing, nor
I deny nothing, I am sorry for my cousin.
Bene. By my sword *Beatrice* thou lou'st me.
Beat. Doe not sweare by it and eat it.
Bene. I will sweare by it that you loue mee, and I will
make him eat it that sayes I loue not you.
Beat. Will you not eat your word?
Bene. With no sawce that can be deuised to it, I pro-
test I loue thee.
Beat. Why then God forgiue me.
Bene. What offence sweet Beatrice?
Beat. You haue stayed me in a happy howre, I was a-
bout to protest I loued you.
Bene. And doe it with all thy heart.
Beat. I loue you with so much of my heart, that none
is left to protest.
Bened. Come, bid me doe any thing for thee.
Beat. Kill *Claudio.*
Bene. Ha, not for the wide world.
Beat. You kill me to denie, farewell.
Bene. Tarrie sweet *Beatrice.*
Beat. I am gone, though I am heere, there is no loue
in you, nay I pray you let me goe.
Bene. Beatrice.
Beat. Infaith I will goe.
Bene. Wee'll be friends first.
Beat. You dare easier be friends with mee, than fight
with mine enemy.
Bene. Is *Claudio* thine enemie?
Beat. Is a not approued in the height a villaine, that
hath slandered, scorned, dishonoured my kinswoman? O
that I were a man! what, beare her in hand vntill they
come to take hands, and then with publike accusation
vncouered slander, vnmittigated rancour? O God that I
were a man! I would eat his heart in the market-place.
Bene. Heare me Beatrice.
Beat. Talke with a man out at a window, a proper
saying.
Bene. Nay but Beatrice.
Beat. Sweet *Hero*, she is wrong'd, shee is slandered,
she is vndone.
Bene. Beat?

Beat. Princes and Counties! surelie a Princely testi-
monie, a goodly Count, Comfect, a sweet Gallant surelie, O that I were a man for his sake! or that I had any
friend would be a man for my sake! But manhood is melted into cursies, valour into complement, and men are
onelie turned into tongue, and trim ones too: he is now
as valiant as *Hercules*, that only tells a lie, and sweares it:
I cannot be a man with wishing, therfore I will die a woman with grieuing.
Bene. Tarry good *Beatrice*, by this hand I loue thee.
Beat. Vse it for my loue some other way then swea-
ring by it.
Bened. Thinke you in your soule the Count *Claudio*
hath wrong'd *Hero*?
Beat. Yea, as sure as I haue a thought, or a soule.
Bene. Enough, I am engagde, I will challenge him, I
will kisse your hand, and so leaue you: by this hand *Claudio* shall render me a deere account: as you heare of me,
so thinke of me: goe comfort your coosin, I must say she
is dead, and so farewell.

*Enter the Constables, Borachio, and the Towne Clerke
in gownes.*

Keeper. Is our whole dissembly appeard?
Cowley. O a stoole and a cushion for the Sexton.
Sexton. Which be the malefactors?
Andrew. Marry that am I, and my partner.
Cowley. Nay that's certaine, wee haue the exhibition
to examine.
Sexton. But which are the offenders that are to be ex-
amined, let them come before master Constable.
Kemp. Yea marry, let them come before mee, what is
your name, friend?
Bor. Borachio.
Kem. Pray write downe *Borachio.* Yours sirra.
Con. I am a Gentleman sir, and my name is Conrade.
Kee. Write downe Master gentleman Conrade: mai-
sters, doe you serue God? maisters, it is proued alreadie
that you are little better than false knaues, and it will goe
neere to be thought so shortly, how answer you for your
selues?
Con. Marry sir, we say we are none.
Kemp. A maruellous witty fellow I assure you, but I
will goe about with him: come you hither sirra, a word
in your eare sir, I say to you, it is thought you are false
knaues.
Bor. Sir, I say to you, we are none.
Kemp. Well, stand aside, 'fore God they are both in
a tale: haue you writ downe that they are none?
Sext. Master Constable, you goe not the way to examine, you must call forth the watch that are their ac-
cusers.
Kemp. Yea marry, that's the eftest way, let the watch
come forth: maisters, I charge you in the Princes name,
accuse these men.
Watch 1. This man said sir, that *Don Iohn* the Princes
brother was a villaine.
Kemp. Write down, Prince *Iohn* a villaine: why this
is flat periurie, to call a Princes brother villaine.
Bora. Master Constable.
Kemp. Pray thee fellow peace, I do not like thy looke
I promise thee.
Sexton. What heard you him say else?
Watch 2. Mary that he had receiued a thousand Du-
kates of *Don Iohn*, for accusing the Lady Hero wrong-
fully.   *Kem.*

Kemp. Flat Burglarie as euer was committed.
Conſt. Yea by th'maſſe that it is.
Sexton. What elſe fellow?
Watch 1. And that Count *Claudio* did meane vpon his words, to diſgrace *Hero* before the whole aſſembly, and not marry her.
Kemp. O villaine!thou wilt be condemn'd into euerlaſting redemption for this.
Sexton. What elſe?
Watch. This is all.
Sexton. And this is more maſters then you can deny, Prince *Iohn* is this morning ſecretly ſtolne away : *Hero* was in this manner accus'd, in this very manner refus'd, and vpon the griefe of this ſodainely died : Maſter Conſtable, let theſe men be bound, and brought to *Leonato*, I will goe before,and ſhew him their examination.
Conſt. Come, let them be opinion'd.
Sex. Let them be in the hands of *Coxcombe.*
Kem. Gods my life, where's the Sexton?let him write downe the Princes Officer *Coxcombe* : come, binde them thou naughty varlet.
Couley. Away, you are an aſſe, you are an aſſe.
Kemp. Doſt thou not ſuſpect my place? doſt thou not ſuſpect my yeeres ? O that hee were heere to write mee downe an aſſe ! but maſters, remember that I am an aſſe : though it be not written down, yet forget not ÿ I am an aſſe:No thou villaine,ÿ art full of piety as ſhall be prou'd vpon thee by good witneſſe, I am a wiſe fellow, and which is more, an officer,and which is more, a houſhoulder,and which is more,as pretty a peece of fleſh as any in Meſſina, and one that knowes the Law,goe to, & a rich fellow enough,goe to, and a fellow that hath had loſſes, and one that hath two gownes, and euery thing handſome about him: bring him away:O that I had been writ downe an aſſe! *Exit.*

Actus Quintus.

Enter Leonato and his brother.

Brother. If you goe on thus,you will kill your ſelfe, And 'tis not wiſedome thus to ſecond griefe, Againſt your ſelfe.
Leon. I pray thee ceaſe thy counſaile, Which falls into mine eares as profitleſſe, As water in a ſiue : giue not me counſaile, Nor let no comfort delight mine eare, But ſuch a one whoſe wrongs doth ſute with mine. Bring me a father that ſo lou'd his childe, Whoſe ioy of her is ouer-whelmed like mine, And bid him ſpeake of patience, Meaſure his woe the length and bredth of mine, And let it anſwere euery ſtraine for ſtraine, As thus for thus, and ſuch a griefe for ſuch, In euery lineament, branch,ſhape,and forme : If ſuch a one will ſmile and ſtroke his beard, And ſorrow,wagge, crie hem,when he ſhould grone, Patch griefe with prouerbs, make misfortune drunke, With candle-waſters : bring him yet to me, And I of him will gather patience : But there is no ſuch man,for brother, men Can counſaile, and ſpeake comfort to that griefe, Which they themſelues not feele, but taſting it, Their counſaile turnes to paſſion, which before,

Would giue preceptiall medicine to rage, Fetter ſtrong madneſſe in a ſilken thred, Charme ache with ayre, and agony with words, No,no, 'tis all mens office, to ſpeake patience To thoſe that wring vnder the load of ſorrow: But no mans vertue nor ſufficiencie To be ſo morall, when he ſhall endure The like himſelfe : therefore giue me no counſaile, My griefs cry lowder then aduertiſement.
Broth. Therein do men from children nothing differ.
Leonato. I pray thee peace,I will be fleſh and bloud, For there was neuer yet Philoſopher, That could endure the tooth-ake patiently, How euer they haue writ the ſtile of gods, And made a puſh at chance and ſufferance.
Brother. Yet bend not all the harme vpon your ſelfe, Make thoſe that doe offend you, ſuffer too.
Leon. There thou ſpeak'ſt reaſon,nay I will doe ſo, My ſoule doth tell me, *Hero* is belied, And that ſhall *Claudio* know,ſo ſhall the Prince, And all of them that thus diſhonour her.

Enter Prince and Claudio.

Brot. Here comes the *Prince* and *Claudio* haſtily.
Prin. Good den,good den.
Clau. Good day to both of you.
Leon. Heare you my Lords?
Prin. We haue ſome haſte *Leonato.*
Leo. Some haſte my Lord! wel, fareyouwel my Lord, Are you ſo haſty now? well, all is one.
Prin. Nay,do not quarrell with vs,good old man.
Brot. If he could rite himſelfe with quarrelling, Some of vs would lie low.
Claud. Who wrongs him?
Leon. Marry ÿ doſt wrong me, thou diſſembler,thou: Nay, neuer lay thy hand vpon thy ſword, I feare thee not.
Claud. Marry beſhrew my hand, If it ſhould giue your age ſuch cauſe of feare, Infaith my hand meant nothing to my ſword.
Leonato. Tuſh, tuſh,man, neuer fleere and ieſt at me, I ſpeake not like a dotard, nor a foole, As vnder priuiledge of age to bragge, What I haue done being yong, or what would doe, Were I not old, know *Claudio* to thy head, Thou haſt ſo wrong'd my innocent childe and me, That I am forc'd to lay my reuerence by, And with grey haires and bruiſe of many daies, Doe challenge thee to triall of a man, I ſay thou haſt belied mine innocent childe. Thy ſlander hath gone through and through her heart, And ſhe lies buried with her anceſtors : O in a tombe where neuer ſcandall ſlept, Saue this of hers, fram'd by thy villanie.
Claud. My villany?
Leonato. Thine *Claudio*, thine I ſay.
Prin. You ſay not right old man.
Leon. My Lord, my Lord, Ile proue it on his body if he dare, Deſpight his nice fence, and his active practiſe, His Maie of youth, and bloome of luſtihood.
Claud. Away, I will not haue to do with you.
Leo. Canſt thou ſo daffe me?thou haſt kild my child, If thou kilſt me,boy,thou ſhalt kill a man.
Bro. He ſhall kill two of vs, and men indeed, But that's no matter, let him kill one firſt :

Win

Win me and weare me, let him anfwere me,
Come follow me boy, come fir boy, come follow me
Sir boy, ile whip you from your foyning fence,
Nay, as I am a gentleman, I will.
Leon. Brother.
Brot. Content your felf, God knows I lou'd my neece,
And fhe is dead, flander'd to death by villaines,
That dare as well anfwer a man indeede,
As I d are take a ferpent by the tongue.
Boyes, apes, braggarts, I ackes, milke-fops.
Leon. Brother *Anthony.*
Brot. Hold you content, what man? I know them, yea
And what they weigh, euen to the vtmoft fcruple,
Scambling, out-facing, fafhion-monging boyes,
That lye, and cog, and flout, depraue, and flander,
Goe antiquely, and fhow outward hidioufneffe,
And fpeake of halfe a dozen dang'rous words,
How they might hurt their enemies, if they durft.
And this is all.
Leon. But brother *Anthonie.*
Ant. Come, 'tis no matter,
Do not you meddle, let me deale in this.
Pri. Gentlemen both, we will not wake your patience
My heart is forry for your daughters death:
But on my honour fhe was charg'd with nothing
But what was true, and very full of proofe.
Leon. My Lord, my Lord.
Prin. I will not heare you.
              Enter Benedicke.
Leo. No come brother, away, I will be heard.
              Exeunt ambo.
Bro. And fhall, or fome of vs will fmart for it.
Prin. See, fee, here comes the man we went to feeke.
Clau. Now fignior, what newes?
Ben. Good day my Lord.
Prin. Welcome fignior, you are almoft come to part
almoft a fray.
Clau. Wee had likt to haue had our two nofes fnapt
off with two old men without teeth.
Prin. *Leonato* and his brother, what think'ft thou? had
wee fought, I doubt we fhould haue beene too yong for
them.
Ben. In a falfe quarrell there is no true valour, I came
to feeke you both.
Clau. We haue beene vp and downe to feeke thee, for
we are high proofe melancholly, and would faine haue it
beaten away, wilt thou vfe thy wit?
Ben. It is in my fcabberd, fhall I draw it?
Prin. Dooft thou weare thy wit by thy fide?
Clau. Neuer any did fo, though verie many haue been
befide their wit, I will bid thee drawe, as we do the min-
ftrels, draw to pleafure vs.
Prin. As I am an honeft man he lookes pale, art thou
ficke, or angrie?
Clau. What, courage man: what though care kil'd a
cat, thou haft mettle enough in thee to kill care.
Ben. Sir, I fhall meete your wit in the careere, and
you charge it againft me, I pray you chufe another fub-
ieƈt.
Clau. Nay then giue him another ftaffe, this laft was
broke croffe.
Prin. By this light, he changes more and more, I thinke
he be angrie indeede.
Clau. If he be, he knowes how to turne his girdle.
Ben. Shall I fpeake a word in your eare?
Clau. God bleffe me from a challenge.

Ben. You are a villaine, I left not, I will make it good
how you dare, with what you dare, and when you dare:
do me right, or I will proteƈt your cowardife: you haue
kill'd a fweete Ladie, and her death fhall fall heauie on
you, let me heare from you.
Clau. Well, I will meete you, fo I may haue good
cheare.
Prin. What, a feaft, a feaft?
Clau. I faith I thanke him, he hath bid me to a calues
head and a Capon, the which if I doe not carue moft curioufly, fay my knife's naught, fhall I not finde a woodcocke too?
Ben. Sir, your wit ambles well, it goes eafily.
Prin. Ile tell thee how *Beatrice* prais'd thy wit the o-
ther day: I faid thou hadft a fine wit: true faies fhe, a fine
little one: no faid I, a great wit: right faies fhee, a great
groffe one: nay faid I, a good wit: iuft faid fhe, it hurts
no body: nay faid I, the gentleman is wife: certain faid
fhe, a wife gentleman: nay faid I, he hath the tongues:
that I beleeue faid fhee, for hee fwore a thing to me on
munday night, which he forfwore on tuefday morning:
there's a double tongue, there's two tongues: thus did
fhee an howre togither praife thy particular vertues, yet at laft fhe concluded with a figh, thou waft the
propreft man in Italie.
Claud. For the which fhe wept heartily, and faid fhee
car'd not.
Prin. Yea that fhe did, but yet for all that, and if fhee
did not hate him deadlie, fhee would loue him dearely,
the old mans daughter told vs all.
Clau. All, all, and moreouer, God faw him vvhen he
was hid in the garden.
Prin. But when fhall we fet the fauage Bulls hornes
on the fenfible *Benedicks* head?
Clau. Yea and text vnder-neath, heere dwells *Benedicke* the married man.
Ben. Fare you well, Boy, you know my minde, I will
leaue you now to your goffep-like humor, you breake
iefts as braggards do their blades, which God be thanked hurt not: my Lord, for your manie courtefies I thank
you, I muft difcontinue your companie, your brother
the Baftard is fled from *Meffina*: you haue among you,
kill'd a fweet and innocent Ladie: for my Lord Lacke-
beard there, he and I fhall meete, and till then peace be
with him.
Prin. He is in earneft.
Clau. In moft profound earneft, and Ile warrant you,
for the loue of Beatrice.
Prin. And hath challeng'd thee.
Clau. Moft fincerely.
Prin. What a prettie thing man is, when he goes in his
doublet and hofe, and leaues off his wit.

Enter Conftable, Conrade, and Borachio.

Clau. He is then a Giant to an Ape, but then is an Ape
a Doƈtor to fuch a man.
Prin. But foft you, let me be, plucke vp my heart, and
be fad, did he not fay my brother was fled?
Conf. Come you fir, if iuftice cannot tame you, fhee
fhall nere weigh more reafons in her ballance, nay, and
you be a curfing hypocrite once, you muft be lookt to.
Prin. How now, two of my brothers men bound? *Bo-
rachio* one.
Clau. Harken after their offence my Lord.
Prin. Officers, what offence haue thefe men done?
Con. Marrie

Conſt. Marrie ſir, they haue committed falſe report, moreouer they haue ſpoken vntruths, ſecondarily they are ſlanders, ſixt and laſtly, they haue belyed a Ladie, thirdly, they haue verified vniuſt things, and to conclude they are lying knaues.

Prin. Firſt I aske thee what they haue done, thirdlie I aske thee vvhat's their offence, ſixt and laſtlie why they are committed, and to conclude, what you lay to their charge.

Clau. Rightlie reaſoned, and in his owne diuiſion, and by my troth there's one meaning vvell ſuted.

Prin. Who haue you offended maſters, that you are thus bound to your anſwer? this learned Conſtable is too cunning to be vnderſtood, vvhat's your offence?

Bor. Sweete Prince, let me go no farther to mine anſwere: do you heare me, and let this Count kill mee: I haue deceiued euen your verie eies: vvhat your wiſe-domes could not diſcouer, theſe ſhallow fooles haue brought to light, vvho in the night ouerheard me confeſſing to this man, how *Don Iohn* your brother incenſed me to ſlander the Ladie *Hero,* how you were brought into the Orchard, and ſaw me court *Margaret* in *Heroes* garments, how you diſgrac'd her vvhen you ſhould marrie her: my villanie they haue vpon record, vvhich I had rather ſeale vvith my death, then repeate ouer to my ſhame: the Ladie is dead vpon mine and my maſters falſe accuſation: and brieſelie, I deſire nothing but the reward of a villaine.

Prin. Runs not this ſpeech like yron through your bloud?

Clau. I haue drunke poiſon whiles he vtter'd it.

Prin. But did my Brother ſet thee on to this?

Bor. Yea, and paid me richly for the practiſe of it.

Prin. He is compos'd and fram'd of treacherie, And fled he is vpon this villanie.

Clau. Sweet *Hero,* now thy image doth appeare In the rare ſemblance that I lou'd it firſt.

Conſt. Come, bring away the plaintiffes, by this time our *Sexton* hath reformed *Signior Leonato* of the matter: and maſters, do not forget to ſpecifie when time & place ſhall ſerue, that I am an Aſſe.

Con. 2. Here, here comes maſter *Signior Leonato,* and the *Sexton* too.

Enter Leonato.

Leon. Which is the villaine? let me ſee his eies, That when I note another man like him, I may auoide him: vvhich of theſe is he?

Bor. If you vvould know your wronger, looke on me.

Leon. Art thou thou the ſlaue that with thy breath haſt kild mine innocent childe?

Bor. Yea, euen I alone.

Leo. No, not ſo villaine, thou belieſt thy ſelfe, Here ſtand a paire of honourable men, A third is fled that had a hand in it: I thanke you Princes for my daughters death, Record it with your high and worthie deedes, 'Twas brauely done, if you bethinke you of it.

Clau. I know not how to pray your patience, Yet I muſt ſpeake, chooſe your reuenge your ſelfe, Impoſe me to what penance your inuention Can lay vpon my ſinne, yet ſinn'd I not, But in miſtaking.

Prin. By my ſoule nor I, And yet to ſatisfie this good old man,

I vvould bend vnder anie heauie vvaight, That heele enioyne me to.

Leon. I cannot bid you bid my daughter liue, That vvere impoſſible, but I praie you both, Poſſeſſe the people in *Meſſina* here, How innocent ſhe died, and if your loue Can labour aught in ſad inuention, Hang her an epitaph vpon her toomb, And ſing it to her bones, ſing it to night: To morrow morning come you to my houſe, And ſince you could not be my ſonne in law, Be yet my Nephew: my brother hath a daughter, Almoſt the copie of my childe that's dead, And ſhe alone is heire to both of vs, Giue her the right you ſhould haue giu'n her coſin, And ſo dies my reuenge.

Clau. O noble ſir! Your ouerkindneſſe doth wring teares from me, I do embrace your offer, and diſpoſe For henceforth of poore *Claudio.*

Leon. To morrow then I will expeſt your comming, To night I take my leaue, this naughtie man Shall face to face be brought to *Margaret,* Who I beleeue was packt in all this wrong, Hired to it by your brother.

Bor. No by my ſoule ſhe was not, Nor knew not what ſhe did when ſhe ſpoke to me, But alwaies hath bin iuſt and vertuous, In anie thing that I do know by her.

Conſt. Moreouer ſir, which indeede is not vnder white and black, this plaintiffe here, the offendour did call mee aſſe, I beſeech you let it be remembred in his puniſh-ment, and alſo the vvatch heard them talke of one Deformed, they ſay he weares a keyin his eare and a lock hang-ing by it, and borrowes monie in Gods name, the which he hath vs'd ſo long, and neuer paied, that now men grow hard-harted and will lend nothing for Gods ſake: praie you examine him vpon that point.

Leon. I thanke thee for thy care and honeſt paines.

Conſt. Your vvorſhip ſpeakes like a moſt thankefull and reuerend youth, and I praiſe God for you.

Leon. There's for thy paines.

Conſt. God ſaue the foundation.

Leon. Goe, I diſcharge thee of thy priſoner, and I thanke thee.

Conſt. I leaue an arrant knaue vvith your vvorſhip, which I beſeech your worſhip to correſt your ſelfe, for the example of others: God keepe your vvorſhip, I wiſh your worſhip vvell, God reſtore you to health, I humblie giue you leaue to depart, and if a mer-rie meeting may be wiſht, God prohibite it: come neighbour.

Leon. Vntill to morrow morning, Lords, farewell.
Exeunt.

Brot. Farewell my Lords, vve looke for you to mor-row.

Prin. We will not faile.

Clau. To night Ile mourne with *Hero.*

Leon. Bring you theſe fellowes on, weel talke vvith *Margaret,* how her acquaintance grew vvith this lewd fellow.
Exeunt.

Enter Benedicke and Margaret.

Ben. Praie thee ſweete Miſtris *Margaret,* deſerue vvell at my hands, by helping mee to the ſpeech of *Bea-trice.*

Mar. Will

Mar. Will you then write me a Sonnet in praise of my beautie?

Bene. In fo high a ftile *Margaret*, that no man liuing fhall come ouer it, for in moft comely truth thou deferueft it.

Mar. To haue no man come ouer me, why, fhall I alwaies keepe below ftaires?

Bene. Thy wit is as quicke as the grey-hounds mouth, it catches.

Mar. And yours, as blunt as the Fencers foiles, which hit, but hurt not.

Bene. A moft manly wit *Margaret*, it will not hurt a woman : and fo I pray thee call *Beatrice*, I giue thee the bucklers.

Mar. Giue vs the fwords, wee haue bucklers of our owne.

Bene. If you vfe them *Margaret*, you muft put in the pikes with a vice, and they are dangerous weapons for Maides.

Mar. Well, I will call *Beatrice* to you, who I thinke hath legges.   *Exit Margarite.*

Ben. And therefore will come. The God of loue that fits aboue, and knowes me, and knowes me, how pittifull I deferue. I meane in finging, but in louing, Leander the good fwimmer, Troilous the firft imploier of pandars, and a whole booke full of thefe quondam carpet-mongers, whofe name yet runne fmoothly in the euen rode of a blanke verfe, why they were neuer fo truely turned ouer and ouer as my poore felfe in loue : marrie I cannot fhew it rime, I haue tried, I can finde out no rime to Ladie but babie, an innocent rime : for fcorne, horne, a hard time : for fchoole foole, a babling time : verie ominous endings, no, I was not borne vnder a riming Plannet, for I cannot wooe in feftiuall tearmes :

Enter Beatrice.

fweete *Beatrice* would'ft thou come when I cal'd thee?

Beat. Yea Signior, and depart when you bid me.

Bene. O ftay but till then.

Beat. Then, is fpoken : fare you well now, and yet ere I goe, let me goe with that I came, which is, with knowing what hath paft betweene you and *Claudio.*

Bene. Onely foule words, and thereupon I will kiffe thee.

Beat. Foule words is but foule wind, and foule wind is but foule breath, and foule breath is noifome, therefore I will depart vnkift.

Bene. Thou haft frighted the word out of his right fence, fo forcible is thy wit, but I muft tell thee plainely, *Claudio* vndergoes my challenge, and either I muft fhortly heare from him, or I will fubfcribe him a coward, and I pray thee now tell me, for which of my bad parts didft thou firft fall in loue with me?

Beat. For them all together, which maintain'd fo politique a ftate of euill, that they will not admit any good part to intermingle with them : but for which of my good parts did you firft fuffer loue for me?

Bene. Suffer loue! a good epithite, I do fuffer loue indeede, for I loue thee againft my will.

Beat. In fpight of your heart I think, alas poore heart, if you fpight it for my fake, I will fpight it for yours, for I will neuer loue that which my friend hates.

Bened. Thou and I are too wife to wooe peaceablie.

Bea. It appeares not in this confeffion, there's not one wife man among twentie that will praife himfelfe.

Bene. An old, an old inftance *Beatrice*, that liu'd in the time of good neighbours, if a man doe not erect in this age his owne tombe ere he dies, hee fhall liue no longer in monuments, then the Bels ring, & the Widdow weepes.

Beat. And how long is that thinke you?

Bene. Queftion, why an hower in clamour and a quarter in rhewme, therfore is it moft expedient for the wife, if Don worme (his confcience) finde no impediment to the contrarie, to be the trumpet of his owne vertues, as I am to my felfe fo much for praifing my felfe, who I my felfe will beare witneffe is praife worthie, and now tell me, how doth your cofin?

Beat. Verie ill.

Bene. And how doe you?

Beat. Verie ill too.

Enter Urfula.

Bene. Serue God, loue me, and mend, there will I leaue you too, for here comes one in hafte.

Vrf. Madam, you muft come to your Vncle, yonders old coile at home, it is prooued my Ladie *Hero* hath bin falfelie accufde, the *Prince* and *Claudio* mightilie abufde, and *Don Iohn* is the author of all, who is fled and gone : will you come prefentlie?

Beat. Will you go heare this newes Signior?

Bene. I will liue in thy heart, die in thy lap, and be buried in thy eies : and moreouer, I will goe with thee to thy Vncles.   *Exeunt.*

Enter Claudio, Prince, and three or foure with Tapers.

Clau. Is this the monument of *Leonato?*

Lord. It is my Lord.   *Epitaph.*

Done to death by flanderous tongues,
Was the Hero that here lies :
Death in guerdon of her wrongs,
Giues her fame which neuer dies :
So the life that dyed with fhame,
Liues in death with glorious fame.

Hang thou there vpon the tombe,
Praifing her when I am dombe.

Clau. Now mufick found & fing your folemn hymne.

Song.

Pardon goddeffe of the night,
Thofe that flew thy virgin knight,
For the which with fongs of woe,
Round about her tombe they goe :
Midnight affift our mone, helpe vs to figh and grone,
Heauily, heauily.

Graues yawne and yeelde your dead,
Till death be vttered,
Heauenly, heauenly.

     (this right.

Lo. Now vnto thy bones good night, yeerely will I do

Prin. Good morrow mafters, put your Torches out, The wolues haue preied, and looke, the gentle day Before the wheeles of Phœbus, round about Dapples the drowfie Eaft with fpots of grey : Thanks to you all, and leaue vs, fare you well.

Clau. Good morrow mafters, each his feuerall way.

Prin. Come let vs hence, and put on other weedes, And then to *Leonatoes* we will goe.

Clau. And Hymen now with luckier iffue fpeeds,

             Then

Then this for whom we rendred vp this woe. *Exeunt.*
Enter Leonato, Bene. Marg. Vrsula, old man, Frier, Hero.
Frier. Did I not tell you she was innocent?
Leo. So are the *Prince* and *Claudio* who accus'd her,
Vpon the errour that you heard debated :
But *Margaret* was in some fault for this,
Although against her will as it appeares,
In the true course of all the question.
Old. Well, I am glad that all things sort so well.
Bene. And so am I, being elfe by faith enforc'd
To call young *Claudio* to a reckoning for it.
Leo. Well daughter, and you gentlewomen all,
Withdraw into a chamber by your selues,
And when I send for you, come hither mask'd :
The *Prince* and *Claudio* promis'd by this howre
To visit me, you know your office Brother,
You must be father to your brothers daughter,
And giue her to young *Claudio.* *Exeunt Ladies.*
Old. Which I will doe with confirm'd countenance.
Bene. Frier, I must intreat your paines, I thinke.
Frier. To doe what Signior?
Bene. To binde me, or vndoe me, one of them:
Signior *Leonato,* truth it is good Signior,
Your neece regards me with an eye of fauour.
Leo. That eye my daughter lent her, 'tis most true.
Bene. And I doe with an eye of loue requite her.
Leo. The sight whereof I thinke you had from me,
From *Claudio,* and the *Prince,* but what's your will?
Bened. Your answer sir is Enigmaticall,
But for my will, my will is, your good will
May stand with ours, this day to be conioyn'd,
In the state of honourable marriage,
In which (good Frier) I shall desire your helpe.
Leon. My heart is with your liking.
Frier. And my helpe.
Enter Prince and Claudio, with attendants.
Prin. Good morrow to this faire assembly.
Leo. Good morrow *Prince,* good morrow *Claudio:*
We heere attend you, are you yet determin'd,
To day to marry with my brothers daughter?
Claud. Ile hold my minde were she an Ethiope.
Leo. Call her forth brother, heres the Frier ready.
Prin. Good morrow *Benedike,* why what's the matter?
That you haue such a Februarie face,
So full of frost, of storme, and clowdinesse.
Claud. I thinke he thinkes vpon the sauage bull:
Tush, feare not man, wee'll tip thy hornes with gold,
And all *Europa* shall reioyce at thee,
As once *Europa* did at lusty *Ioue,*
When he would play the noble beast in loue.
Ben. Bull *Ioue* sir, had an amiable low,
And some such strange bull leapt your fathers Cow,
A got a Calfe in that same noble feat,
Much like to you, for you haue iust his bleat.
Enter brother, Hero, Beatrice, Margaret, Vrsula.
Cla. For this I owe you: here comes other recknings.
Which is the Lady I must seize vpon?
Leo. This same is she, and I doe giue you her.
Cla. Why then she's mine, sweet let me see your face.
Leon. No that you shal not, till you take her hand,
Before this Frier, and sweare to marry her.
Claud. Giue me your hand before this holy Frier,
I am your husband if you like of me.
Hero. And when I liu'd I was your other wife,
And when you lou'd, you were my other husband.
Clau. Another *Hero*?

Hero. Nothing certainer.
One *Hero* died, but I doe liue,
And surely as I liue, I am a maid.
Prin. The former *Hero, Hero* that is dead.
Leon. Shee died my Lord, but whiles her slander liu'd.
Frier. All this amazement can I qualifie,
When after that the holy rites are ended,
Ile tell you largely of faire *Heroes* death :
Meane time let wonder seeme familiar,
And to the chappell let vs presently.
Ben. Soft and faire Frier, which is *Beatrice*?
Beat. I answer to that name, what is your will?
Bene. Doe not you loue me?
Beat. Why no, no more then reason.
Bene. Why then your Vncle, and the Prince, & *Clau-*
dio, haue beene deceiued, for they sweare you did.
Beat. Doe not you loue mee?
Bene. Troth no, no more then reason.
Beat. Why then my Cosin *Margaret* and *Vrsula*
Are much deceiu'd, for they did sweare you did.
Bene. They sweare you were almost sicke for me.
Beat. They sweare you were wel-nye dead for me.
Bene. 'Tis no matter, then you doe not loue me?
Beat. No truly, but in friendly recompence.
Leon. Come Cosin, I am sure you loue the gentleman.
Clau. And Ile be sworne vpon't, that he loues her,
For heere a paper written in his hand,
A halting sonnet of his owne pure braine,
Fashioned to *Beatrice.*
Hero. And heeres another,
Writ in my cosins hand, stolne from her pocket,
Containing her affection vnto *Benedicke.*
Bene. A miracle, here's our owne hands against our
hearts : come I will haue thee, but by this light I take
thee for pittie.
Beat. I would not denie you, but by this good day, I
yeeld vpon great perswasion, & partly to saue your life,
for I was told, you were in a consumption.
Leon. Peace I will stop your mouth.
Prin. How dost thou *Benedicke* the married man?
Bene. Ile tell thee what Prince : a Colledge of witte-
crackers cannot flout mee out of my humour, dost thou
think I care for a Satyre or an Epigram? no, if a man will
be beaten with braines, a shall weare nothing handsome
about him : in briefe, since I do purpose to marry, I will
thinke nothing to any purpose that the world can say a-
gainst it, and therefore neuer flout at me, for I haue said
against it : for man is a giddy thing, and this is my conclusion: for thy part *Claudio,* I did thinke to haue beaten
thee, but in that thou art like to be my kinsman, liue vn-
bruis'd, and loue my cousin.
Cla. I had well hop'd ÿ wouldst haue denied *Beatrice,* ÿ
I might haue cudgel'd thee out of thy single life, to make
thee a double dealer, which out of question thou wilt be,
if my Cousin do not looke exceeding narrowly to thee.
Bene. Come, come, we are friends, let's haue a dance
ere we are married, that we may lighten our own hearts,
and our wiues heeles.
Leon. Wee'll haue dancing afterward.
Bene. First, of my vvord, therfore play musick. *Prince,*
thou art sad, get thee a vvife, get thee a vvife, there is no
staff more reuerend then one tipt with horn. *Enter. Mes.*
Messen. My Lord, your brother *Iohn* is tane in flight,
And brought with armed men backe to *Messina.*
Bene. Thinke not on him till to morrow, ile deuise
thee braue punishments for him: strike vp Pipers. *Dance.*

L   *FINIS.*

Loues Labour's loft.

Actus primus.

Enter Ferdinand King of Nauarre, Berowne, Longauill, and Dumane.

Ferdinand.

Et *Fame*, that all hunt after in their liues,
Liue regiftred vpon our brazen Tombes,
And then grace vs in the difgrace of death:
when fpight of cormorant deuouring Time,
Th'endeuour of this prefent breath may buy:
That honour which fhall bate his fythes keene edge,
And make vs heyres of all eternitie.
Therefore braue Conquerours, for fo you are,
That warre againft your owne affections,
And the huge Armie of the worlds defires.
Our late edict fhall ftrongly ftand in force,
Nauar fhall be the wonder of the world.
Our Court fhall be a little Achademe,
Still and contemplatiue in liuing Art.
You three, *Berowne, Dumaine,* and *Longauill,*
Haue fworne for three yeeres terme, to liue with me:
My fellow Schollers, and to keepe thofe ftatutes
That are recorded in this fcedule heere.
Your oathes are paft, and now fubfcribe your names:
That his owne hand may ftrike his honour downe,
That violates the fmalleft branch heerein:
If you are arm'd to doe, as fworne to do,
Subfcribe to your deepe oathes, and keepe it to.

Longauill. I am refolu'd, 'tis but a three yeeres faft:
The minde fhall banquet, though the body pine,
Fat paunches haue leane pates: and dainty bits,
Make rich the ribs, but bankerout the wits.

Dumane. My louing Lord, *Dumane* is mortified,
The groffer manner of thefe worlds delights,
He throwes vpon the groffe worlds bafer flaues:
To loue, to wealth, to pompe, I pine and die,
With all thefe liuing in Philofophie.

Berowne. I can but fay their proteftation ouer,
So much, deare Liege, I haue already fworne,
That is, to liue and ftudy heere three yeeres.
But there are other ftrict obferuances:
As not to fee a woman in that terme,
Which I hope well is not enrolled there.
And one day in a weeke to touch no foode:
And but one meale on euery day befide:
The which I hope is not enrolled there.
And then to fleepe but three houres in the night,
And not be feene to winke of all the day.
When I was wont to thinke no harme all night,
And make a darke night too of halfe the day:

Which I hope well is not enrolled there.
O, thefe are barren taskes, too hard to keepe,
Not to fee Ladies, ftudy, faft, not fleepe.

Ferd. Your oath is paft, to paffe away from thefe.

Berow. Let me fay no my Liedge, and if you pleafe,
I onely fwore to ftudy with your grace,
And ftay heere in your Court for three yeeres fpace.

Longa. You fwore to that *Berowne*, and to the reft.

Berow. By yea and nay fir, than I fwore in ieft.
What is the end of ftudy, let me know?

Fer. Why that to know which elfe wee fhould not know.

Ber. Things hid & bard (you meane) fr cmon fenfe.

Ferd. I, that is ftudies god-like recompence.

Bero. Come on then, I will fweare to ftudie fo,
To know the thing I am forbid to know:
As thus, to ftudy where I well may dine,
When I to faft expreffely am forbid.
Or ftudie where to meet fome Miftreffe fine,
When Miftreffes from common fenfe are hid.
Or hauing fworne too hard a keeping oath,
Studie to breake it, and not breake my troth.
If ftudies gaine be thus, and this be fo,
Studie knowes that which yet it doth not know,
Sweare me to this, and I will nere fay no.

Ferd. Thefe be the ftops that hinder ftudie quite,
And traine our intellects to vaine delight.

Ber. Why? all delights are vaine, and that moft vaine
Which with paine purchas'd, doth inherit paine,
As painefully to poare vpon a Booke,
To feeke the light of truth, while truth the while
Doth falfely blinde the eye-fight of his looke:
Light feeeking light, doth light of light beguile:
So ere you finde where light in darkeneffe lies,
Your light growes darke by lofing of your eyes.
Studie me how to pleafe the eye indeede,
By fixing it vpon a fairer eye,
Who dazling fo, that eye fhall be his heed,
And giue him light that it was blinded by.
Studie is like the heauens glorious Sunne,
That will not be deepe fearch'd with fawcy lookes:
Small haue continuall plodders euer wonne,
Saue bafe authoritie from others Bookes.
Thefe earthly Godfathers of heauens lights,
That giue a name to euery fixed Starre,
Haue no more profit of their fhining nights,
Then thofe that walke and wot not what they are.
Too much to know, is to know nought but fame:
And euery Godfather can giue a name.

Fer. How well hee's read, to reafon againft reading.

Dum.

Dum. Proceeded well, to ftop all good proceeding.

Lon. Hee weedes the corne, and ftill lets grow the weeding.

Ber. The Spring is neare when greene geeffe are a breeding.

Dum. How followes that?

Ber. Fit in his place and time.

Dum. In reafon nothing.

Ber. Something then in rime.

Ferd. *Berowne* is like an enuious fneaping Froft,
That bites the firft borne infants of the Spring.

Ber. Wel, fay I am, why fhould proud Summer boaft,
Before the Birds haue any caufe to fing?
Why fhould I ioy in any abortiue birth?
At Chriftmas I no more defire a Rofe,
Then wifh a Snow in Mayes new fangled fhowes:
But like of each thing that in feafon growes.
So you to ftudie now it is too late,
That were to clymbe ore the houfe to vnlocke the gate.

Fer. Well, fit you out: go home *Berowne*: adue.

Ber. No my good Lord, I haue fworn to ftay with you.
And though I haue for barbarifme fpoke more,
Then for that Angell knowledge you can fay,
Yet confident Ile keepe what I haue fworne,
And bide the pennance of each three yeares day.
Giue me the paper, let me reade the fame,
And to the ftricteft decrees Ile write my name.

Fer. How well this yeelding refcues thee from fhame.

Ber. Item. That no woman fhall come within a mile of my Court.
Hath this bin proclaimed?

Lon. Foure dayes agoe.

Ber. Let's fee the penaltie.
On paine of loofing her tongue.
Who deuis'd this penaltie?

Lon. Marry that did I.

Ber. Sweete Lord, and why?

Lon. To fright them hence with that dread penaltie,
A dangerous law againft gentilitie.

Item, If any man be feene to talke with a woman within the tearme of three yeares, hee fhall indure fuch publiqe fhame as the reft of the Court fhall poffibly deuife.

Ber. This Article my Liedge your felfe muft breake,
For well you know here comes in Embaffie
The *French* Kings daughter, with your felfe to fpeake:
A Maide of grace and compleate maieftie,
About furrender vp of *Aquitaine*:
To her decrepit, ficke, and bed-rid Father.
Therefore this Article is made in vaine,
Or vainly comes th'admired Princeffe hither.

Fer. What fay you Lords?
Why, this was quite forgot.

Ber. So Studie euermore is ouerfhot,
While it doth ftudy to haue what it would,
It doth forget to doe the thing it fhould:
And when it hath the thing it hunteth moft,
'Tis won as townes with fire, fo won, fo loft.

Fer. We muft of force difpence with this Decree,
She muft lye here on meere neceffitie.

Ber. Neceffity will make vs all forfworne
Three thoufand times within this three yeeres fpace:
For euery man with his affects is borne,
Not by might maftred, but by fpeciall grace.
If I breake faith, this word fhall breake for me,
I am forfworne on meere neceffitie.

So to the Lawes at large I write my name,
And he that breakes them in the leaft degree,
Stands in attainder of eternall fhame.
Suggeftions are to others as to me:
But I beleeue although I feeme fo loth,
I am the laft that will laft keepe his oth.
But is there no quicke recreation granted?

Fer. I that there is, our Court you know is hanted
With a refined trauailer of *Spaine*,
A man in all the worlds new fafhion planted,
That hath a mint of phrafes in his braine:
One, who the muficke of his owne vaine tongue,
Doth rauifh like inchanting harmonie:
A man of complements whom right and wrong
Haue chofe as vmpire of their mutinie.
This childe of fancie that *Armado* hight,
For interim to our ftudies fhall relate,
In high-borne words the worth of many a Knight:
From tawnie *Spaine* loft in the worlds debate.
How you delight my Lords, I know not I,
But I proteft I loue to heare him lie,
And I will vfe him for my Minftrelfie.

Bero. *Armado* is a moft illuftrious wight,
A man of fire, new words, fafhions owne Knight.

Lon. *Coftard* the fwaine and he, fhall be our fport,
And fo to ftudie, three yeeres is but fhort.

Enter a Conftable with Coftard with a Letter.

Conft. Which is the Dukes owne perfon.

Ber. This fellow, What would'ft?

Con. I my felfe reprehend his owne perfon, for I am his graces Tharborough: But I would fee his own perfon in flefh and blood.

Ber. This is he.

Con. Signeor *Arme, Arme* commends you:
Ther's villanie abroad, this letter will tell you more.

Clow. Sir the Contempts thereof are as touching mee.

Fer. A letter from the magnificent *Armado*.

Ber. How low foeuer the matter, I hope in God for high words.

Lon. A high hope for a low heauen, God grant vs patience.

Ber. To heare, or forbeare hearing.

Lon. To heare meekely fir, and to laugh moderately, or to forbeare both.

Ber. Well fir, be it as the ftile fhall giue vs caufe to clime in the merrineffe.

Clo. The matter is to me fir, as concerning *Iaquenetta*.
The manner of it is, I was taken with the manner.

Ber. In what manner?

Clo. In manner and forme following fir all thofe three.
I was feene with her in the Mannor houfe, fitting with her vpon the Forme, and taken following her into the Parke: which put to gether, is in manner and forme following. Now fir for the manner; It is the manner of a man to fpeake to a woman, for the forme in fome forme.

Ber. For the following fir.

Clo. As it fhall follow in my correction, and God defend the right.

Fer. Will you heare this Letter with attention?

Ber. As we would heare an Oracle.

Clo. Such is the fimplicitie of man to harken after the flefh.

Fer. Great

Ferdinand.

GReat Deputie, the Welkins Vicegerent, and ſole domi-
nator of Nauar, my ſoules earths God, and bodies fo-
ſtring patrone :

Coſt. Not a vvord of *Coſtard* yet.

Ferd. So it is.

Coſt. It may be ſo: but if he ſay it is ſo, he is in telling
true : but ſo.

Ferd. Peace,

Clow. Be to me, and euery man that dares not fight.

Ferd. No words,

Clow. Of other mens ſecrets I beſeech you.

Ferd. So it is beſieged with ſable coloured melancholie, I
did commend the blacke oppreſſing humour to the moſt whole-
ſome Phyſicke of thy health-giuing ayre : And as I am a Gentleman, betooke my ſelfe to walke : the time When ? about the
ſixt houre, When beaſts moſt graſe, birds beſt pecke, and men
ſit downe to that nouriſhment which is called ſupper : So much
for the time When. Now for the ground Which ? which I
meane I walkt vpon, it is ycliped, Thy Parke. Then for the
place Where ? where I meane I did encounter that obſcene and
moſt prepoſterous euent that draweth from my ſnow-white pen
the ebon coloured Inke, which heere thou vieweſt, beholdeſt,
ſuruayeſt, or ſeeſt. But to the place Where ? It ſtandeth
North North-eaſt and by Eaſt from the Weſt corner of thy
curious knotted garden ; There did I ſee that low ſpiri-
ted Swaine , that baſe Minow of thy myrth, (Clown. Mee?)
that vnletered ſmall knowing ſoule, (Clow Me?) that ſhallow
vaſſall (Clow. Still mee?) which as I remember, hight Coſtard, (Clow. O me) ſorted and conſorted contrary to thy e-
ſtabliſhed proclaymed Edict and Continet, Cannon : Which
with, ô with, but with this I paſſion to ſay wherewith:

Clo. With a Wench.

Ferd. With a childe of our Grandmother Eue, a female ;
or for thy more ſweet vnderſtanding a woman : him, I (as my
euer eſteemed dutie prickes me on) haue ſent to thee, to receiue
the meed of puniſhment by thy ſweet Graces Officer Anthony
Dull, a man of good repute, carriage, bearing, & eſtimation.

Anth. Me, an't ſhall pleaſe you? I am *Anthony Dull.*

Ferd. For Iaquenetta (ſo is the weaker veſſell called)
which I apprehended with the aforeſaid Swaine, I keeper her
as a veſſell of thy Lawes furie, and ſhall at the leaſt of thy
ſweet notice, bring her to triall. Thine in all complements of
deuoted and heart-burning heat of dutie.

Don Adriana de Armado.

Ber. This is not ſo well as I looked for, but the beſt
that euer I heard.

Fer. I the beſt, for the worſt. But ſirra, What ſay you
to this?

Clo. Sir I confeſſe the Wench.

Fer. Did you heare the Proclamation?

Clo. I doe confeſſe much of the hearing it, but little
of the marking of it.

Fer. It was proclaimed a yeeres impriſonment to bee
taken with a Wench.

Clow. I was taken with none ſir, I was taken vvith a
Damoſell.

Fer. Well, it was proclaimed Damoſell.

Clo. This was no Damoſell neyther ſir, ſhee was a
Virgin.

Fer. It is ſo varried to, for it was proclaimed Virgin.

Clo. If it were, I denie her Virginitie : I was taken
with a Maide.

Fer. This Maid will not ſerue your turne ſir.

Clo. This Maide will ſerue my turne ſir.

Kin. Sir I will pronounce your ſentence : You ſhall
faſt a Weeke with Branne and water.

Clo. I had rather pray a Moneth with Mutton and
Porridge.

Kin. And *Don Armado* ſhall be your keeper.
My Lord *Berowne*, ſee him deliuer'd ore,
And goe we Lords to put in practice that,
Which each to other hath ſo ſtrongly ſworne.

Bero. Ile lay my head to any good mans hat,
Theſe oathes and lawes will proue an idle ſcorne.
Sirra, come on.

Clo. I ſuffer for the truth ſir : for true it is, I was taken with *Iaquenetta*, and *Iaquenetta* is a true girle, and
therefore welcome the ſowre cup of proſperitie, affliction
on may one day ſmile againe, and vntill then ſit downe
ſorrow. *Exit.*

Enter Armado and Moth his Page.

Arma. Boy, What ſigne is it when a man of great
ſpirit growes melancholy ?

Boy. A great ſigne ſir, that he will looke ſad.

Brag. Why? ſadneſſe is one and the ſelfe-ſame thing
deare impe.

Boy. No no, O Lord ſir no.

Brag. How canſt thou part ſadneſſe and melancholy
my tender *Iuuenall* ?

Boy. By a familiar demonſtration of the working, my
tough ſigneur.

Brag. Why tough ſigneur ? Why tough ſigneur ?

Boy. Why tender *Iuuenall* ? Why tender *Iuuenall?*

Brag. I ſpoke it tender *Iuuenall*, as a congruent apa-
thaton, appertaining to thy young daies, which we may
nominate tender.

Boy. And I tough ſigneur, as an appertinent title to
your olde time, which we may name tough.

Brag. Pretty and apt.

Boy. How meane you ſir, I pretty, and my ſaying apt?
or I apt, and my ſaying prettie?

Brag. Thou pretty becauſe little.

Boy. Little pretty, becauſe little : wherefore apt?

Brag. And therefore apt, becauſe quicke.

Boy. Speake you this in my praiſe Maſter ?

Brag. In thy condigne praiſe.

Boy. I will praiſe an Eele with the ſame praiſe.

Brag. What? that an Eele is ingenuous.

Boy. That an Eeele is quicke.

Brag. I doe ſay thou art quicke in anſweres. Thou
heat'ſt my bloud.

Boy. I am anſwer'd ſir.

Brag. I loue not to be croſt.   (him.

Boy. He ſpeakes the meere contrary, croſſes loue not

Br. I haue promis'd to ſtudy iij. yeres with the Duke.

Boy. You may doe it in an houre ſir.

Brag. Impoſſible.

Boy. How many is one thrice told ?

Bra. I am ill at reckning, it fits the ſpirit of a Tapſter.

Boy. You are a gentleman and a gameſter ſir.

Brag. I confeſſe both, they are both the varniſh of a
compleat man.

Boy. Then I am ſure you know how much the groſſe
ſumme of deuſ-ace amounts to.

Brag. It doth amount to one more then two.

Boy. Which the baſe vulgar call three.

Br. True. *Boy.* Why ſir is this ſuch a peece of ſtudy?
Now here's three ſtudied, ere you'll thrice wink, & how
eaſie it is to put yeres to the word three, and ſtudy three
yeeres in two words, the dancing horſe will tell you.

                                   Brag. A

Brag. A moſt fine Figure.

Boy. To proue you a Cypher.

Brag. I will heereupon confeſſe I am in loue : and as it is baſe for a Souldier to loue ; ſo am I in loue with a baſe wench. If drawing my ſword againſt the humour of affeƈtion, would deliuer mee from the reprobate thought of it, I would take Deſire priſoner, and ranſome him to any French Courtier for a new deuis'd curtſie. I thinke ſcorne to ſigh, me thinkes I ſhould out-ſweare *Cupid.* Comfort me Boy, What great men haue beene in loue?

Boy. Hercules Maſter.

Brag. Moſt ſweete *Hercules* : more authority deare Boy, name more; and ſweet my childe let them be men of good repute and carriage.

Boy. Sampſon Maſter, he was a man of good carriage, great carriage : for hee carried the Towne-gates on his backe like a Porter: and he was in loue.

Brag. O well-knit *Sampſon,* ſtrong ioynted *Sampſon;* I doe excell thee in my rapier, as much as thou didſt mee in carrying gates. I am in loue too. Who was *Sampſons* loue my deare *Moth* ?

Boy. A Woman, Maſter.

Brag. Of what complexion *?*

Boy. Of all the foure, or the three, or the two, or one of the foure.

Brag. Tell me preciſely of what complexion *?*

Boy. Of the ſea-water Greene ſir.

Brag. Is that one of the foure complexions ?

Boy. As I haue read ſir, and the beſt of them too.

Brag. Greene indeed is the colour of Louers : but to haue a Loue of that colour, methinkes *Sampſon* had ſmall reaſon for it. He ſurely affeƈted her for her wit.

Boy. It was ſo ſir, for ſhe had a greene wit.

Brag. My Loue is moſt immaculate white and red.

Boy. Moſt immaculate thoughts Maſter, are mask'd vnder ſuch colours.

Brag. Define, define, well educated infant.

Boy. My fathers witte, and my mothers tongue aſſiſt mee.

Brag. Sweet inuocation of a childe, moſt pretty and patheticall.

Boy. If ſhee be made of white and red,
Her faults will nere be knowne :
For bluſh-in cheekes by faults are bred,
And feares by pale white ſhowne :
Then if ſhe feare, or be to blame,
By this you ſhall not know,
For ſtill her cheekes poſſeſſe the ſame,
Which natiue ſhe doth owe :
A dangerous rime maſter againſt the reaſon of white and redde.

Brag. Is there not a ballet Boy, of the King and the Begger ?

Boy. The world was very guilty of ſuch a Ballet ſome three ages ſince, but I thinke now 'tis not to be found: or if it were, it would neither ſerue for the writing, nor the tune.

Brag. I will haue that ſubieƈt newly writ ore, that I may example my digreſſion by ſome mighty preſident. Boy, I doe loue that Countrey girle that I tooke in the Parke with the rationall hinde *Coſtard*: ſhe deſerues well.

Boy. To bee whip'd : and yet a better loue then my Maſter.

Brag. Sing Boy, my ſpirit growes heauy in loue.

Boy. And that's great maruell, louing a light wench.

Brag. I ſay ſing.

Boy. Forbeare till this company be paſt.

Enter Clowne, Conſtable, and Wench.

Conſt. Sir, the Dukes pleaſure, is that you keepe *Co-ſtard* ſafe, and you muſt let him take no delight, nor no penance, but hee muſt faſt three daies a weeke : for this Damſell, I muſt keepe her at the Parke, ſhee is alowd for the Day-woman. Fare you well.   *Exit.*

Brag. I doe betray my ſelfe with bluſhing : Maide.

Maid. Man.

Brag. I wil viſit thee at the Lodge.

Maid. That's here by.

Brag. I know where it is ſituate.

Mai. Lord how wiſe you are !

Brag. I will tell thee wonders.

Ma. With what face?

Brag. I loue thee.

Mai. So I heard you ſay.

Brag. And ſo farewell.

Mai. Faire weather after you.

Clo. Come *Iaquenetta,* away.   *Exeunt.*

Brag. Villaine, thou ſhalt faſt for thy offences ere thou be pardoned.

Clo. Well ſir, I hope when I doe it, I ſhall doe it on a full ſtomacke.

Brag. Thou ſhalt be heauily puniſhed.

Clo. I am more bound to you then your fellowes, for they are but lightly rewarded.

Clo. Take away this villaine, ſhut him vp.

Boy. Come you tranſgreſſing ſlaue, away.

Clow. Let mee not bee pent vp ſir , I will faſt being looſe.

Boy. No ſir, that were faſt and looſe : thou ſhalt to priſon.

Clow. Well, if euer I do ſee the merry dayes of deſolation that I haue ſeene, ſome ſhall ſee.

Boy. What ſhall ſome ſee?

Clow. Nay nothing, Maſter *Moth,* but what they looke vpon. It is not for priſoners to be ſilent in their words, and therefore I will ſay nothing : I thanke God, I haue as little patience as another man, and therefore I can be quiet.   *Exit.*

Brag. I doe affeƈt the very ground (which is baſe) where her ſhooe (which is baſer) guided by her foote (which is baſeſt) doth tread. I ſhall be forſworn (which is a great argument of falſhood) if I loue. And how can that be true loue, which is falſly attempted? Loue is a fa-miliar, Loue is a Diuell. There is no euill Angell but Loue, yet *Sampſon* was ſo tempted, and he had an excel-lent ſtrength : Yet was *Salomon* ſo ſeduced, and hee had a very good witte. *Cupids* Butſhaft is too hard for *Her-cules* Clubbe, and therefore too much ods for a Spa-niards Rapier : The firſt and ſecond cauſe will not ſerue my turne : the *Paſſado* hee reſpeƈts not, the *Duello* he regards not ; his diſgrace is to be called Boy , but his glorie is to ſubdue men. Adue Valour, ruſt Rapier, bee ſtill Drum, for your manager is in loue ; yea hee loueth. Aſſiſt me ſome extemporall god of Rime, for I am ſure I ſhall turne Sonnet. Deuiſe Wit, write Pen, for I am for whole volumes in folio.   *Exit.*

Finis Aƈtus Primus.

Actus Secunda.

Enter the Princeffe of France, with three attending Ladies, and three Lords.

Boyet. Now Madam fummon vp your deareft fpirits,
Confider who the King your father fends :
To whom he fends, and what's his Embaffie.
Your felfe, held precious in the worlds efteeme,
To parlee with the fole inheritour
Of all perfections that a man may owe,
Matchleffe *Nauarre,* the plea of no leffe weight
Then *Aquitaine,* a Dowrie for a Queene.
Be now as prodigall of all deare grace,
As Nature was in making Graces deare,
When fhe did ftarue the generall world befide,
And prodigally gaue them all to you.

Queen. Good L. *Boyet,* my beauty though but mean,
Needs not the painted flourifh of your praife :
Beauty is bought by iudgement of the eye,
Not vttred by bafe fale of chapmens tongues :
I am leffe proud to heare you tell my worth,
Then you much wiling to be counted wife,
In fpending your wit in the praife of mine.
But now to taske the tasker, good *Boyet,*

Prin. You are not ignorant all-telling fame
Doth noyfe abroad *Nauar* hath made a vow,
Till painefull ftudie fhall out-weare three yeares,
No woman may approach his filent Court :
Therefore to's feemeth it a needfull courfe,
Before we enter his forbidden gates,
To know his pleafure, and in that behalfe
Bold of your worthineffe, we fingle you,
As our beft mouing faire foliciter :
Tell him, the daughter of the King of France,
On ferious bufineffe crauing quicke difpatch,
Importunes perfonall conference with his grace.
Hafte, fignifie fo much while we attend,
Like humble vifag'd futers his high will.

Boy. Proud of imployment, willingly I goe.   *Exit.*

Prin. All pride is willing pride, and yours is fo :
Who are the Votaries my louing Lords, that are vow-
fellowes with this vertuous Duke ?

Lor. *Longauill* is one.

Princ. Know you the man ?

1 *Lady.* I know him Madame at a marriage feaft,
Betweene L. *Perigort* and the beautious heire
Of *Iaques Fauconbridge* folemnized.
In *Normandie* faw I this *Longauill* ,
A man of foueraigne parts he is efteem'd :
Well fitted in Arts, glorious in Armes :
Nothing becomes him ill that he would well.
The onely foyle of his faire vertues gloffe,
If vertues gloffe will ftaine with any foile,
Is a fharp wit match'd with too blunt a Will :
Whofe edge hath power to cut whofe will ftill wills,
It fhould none fpare that come within his power.

Prin. Some merry mocking Lord belike, ift fo ?

Lad. 1. They fay fo moft, that moft his humors know.

Prin. Such fhort liu'd wits do wither as they grow.
Who are the reft ?

2. *Lad.* The yong *Dumaine,* a well accomplifht youth,

Of all that Vertue loue, for Vertue loued.
Moft power to doe moft harme, leaft knowing ill :
For he hath wit to make an ill fhape good,
And fhape to win grace though fhe had no wit.
I faw him at the Duke *Alanfoes* once,
And much too little of that good I faw,
Is my report to his great worthineffe.

Roffa. Another of thefe Students at that time,
Was there with him, as I haue heard a truth.
Berowne they call him, but a merrier man,
Within the limit of becomming mirth,
I neuer fpent an houres talke withall.
His eye begets occafion for his wit,
For euery obiect that the one doth catch,
The other turnes to a mirth-mouing ieft.
Which his faire tongue (conceits expofitor)
Deliuers in fuch apt and gracious words,
That aged eares play treuant at his tales,
And yonger hearings are quite rauifhed.
So fweet and voluble is his difcourfe.

Prin. God bleffe my Ladies, are they all in loue ?
That euery one her owne hath garnifhed,
With fuch bedecking ornaments of praife.

Ma. Heere comes *Boyet.*

Enter Boyet.

Prin. Now, what admittance Lord ?

Boyet. *Nauar* had notice of your faire approach ;
And he and his competitors in oath,
Were all addreft to meete you gentle Lady
Before I came : Marrie thus much I haue learnt,
He rather meanes to lodge you in the field,
Like one that comes heere to befiege his Court,
Then feeke a difpenfation for his oath :
To let you enter his vnpeopled houfe.

Enter Nauar, Longauill, Dumaine, and Berowne.

Heere comes *Nauar.*

Nau. Faire Princeffe, welcom to the Court of *Nauar.*

Prin. Faire I giue you backe againe, and welcome I
haue not yet : the roofe of this Court is too high to bee
yours, and welcome to the wide fields, too bafe to be
mine.

Nau. You fhall be welcome Madam to my Court.

Prin. I will be welcome then, Conduct me thither.

Nau. Heare me deare Lady, I haue fworne an oath.

Prin. Our Lady helpe my Lord, he'll be forfworne.

Nau. Not for the world faire Madam, by my will.

Prin. Why, will fhall breake it will, and nothing els.

Nau. Your Ladifhip is ignorant what it is.

Prin. Were my Lord fo, his ignorance were wife,
Where now his knowledge muft proue ignorance.
I heare your grace hath fworne out Houfekeeping :
'Tis deadly finne to keepe that oath my Lord,
And finne to breake it :
But pardon me, I am too fodaine bold,
To teach a Teacher ill befeemeth me.
Vouchfafe to read the purpofe of my comming,
And fodainly refolue me in my fuite.

Nau. Madam, I will, if fodainly I may.

Prin. You will the fooner that I were away,
For you'll proue periur'd if you make me ftay.

Berow. Did not I dance with you in *Brabant* once ?

Rofa. Did not I dance with you in *Brabant* once ?

                        Ber. I

Ber. I know you did.
Rofa. How needleffe was it then to ask the queftion?
Ber. You muft not be fo quicke.
Rofa. 'Tis long of you ý fpur me with fuch queftions.
Ber. Your wit's too hot, it fpeeds too faft, 'twill tire.
Rofa. Not till it leaue the Rider in the mire.
Ber. What time a day?
Rofa. The howre that fooles fhould aske.
Ber. Now faire befall your maske.
Rofa. Faire fall the face it couers.
Ber. And fend you many louers.
Rofa. Amen, fo you be none.
Ber. Nay then will I be gone.
Kin. Madame, your father heere doth intimate,
The paiment of a hundred thoufand Crownes,
Being but th'one halfe, of an intire fumme,
Disburfed by my father in his warres.
But fay that he, or we, as neither haue
Receiu'd that fumme ; yet there remaines vnpaid
A hundred thoufand more : in furety of the which,
One part of *Aquitaine* is bound to vs,
Although not valued to the moneys worth.
If then the King your father will reftore
But that one halfe which is vnfatisfied,
We will giue vp our right in *Aquitaine*,
And hold faire friendfhip with his Maieftie :
But that it feemes he little purpofeth,
For here he doth demand to haue repaie,
An hundred thoufand Crownes, and not demands
One paiment of a hundred thoufand Crownes,
To haue his title liue in *Aquitaine*.
Which we much rather had depart withall,
And haue the money by our father lent,
Then *Aquitane*, fo guelded as it is.
Deare Princeffe, were not his requefts fo farre
From reafons yeelding, your faire felfe fhould make
A yeelding'gainft fome reafon in my breft,
And goe well fatisfied to *France* againe.
Prin. You doe the King my Father too much wrong,
And wrong the reputation of your name,
In fo vnfeeming to confeffe receyt
Of that which hath fo faithfully beene paid.
Kin. I doe proteft I neuer heard of it,
And if you proue it, Ile repay it backe,
Or yeeld vp *Aquitaine*.
Prin. We arreft your word :
Boyet, you can produce acquittances
For fuch a fumme, from fpeciall Officers,
Of *Charles* his Father.
Kin. Satisfie me fo.
Boyet. So pleafe your Grace, the packet is not come
Where that and other fpecialties are bound,
To morrow you fhall haue a fight of them.
Kin. It fhall fuffice me ; at which enteruiew,
All liberall reafon would I yeeld vnto :
Meane time, receiue fuch welcome at my hand,
As Honour, without breach of Honour may
Make tender of, to thy true worthineffe.
You may not come faire Princeffe in my gates,
But heere without you fhall be fo receiu'd,
As you fhall deeme your felfe lodg'd in my heart,
Though fo deni'd farther harbour in my houfe :
Your owne good thoughts excufe me, and farewell,
To morrow we fhall vifit you againe.
Prin. Sweet health & faire defires confort your grace.
Kin. Thy own wifh wifh I thee, in euery place. *Exit.*

Boy. Lady, I will commend you to my owne heart.
La. Ro. Pray you doe my commendations,
I would be glad to fee it.
Boy. I would you heard it grone.
La. Ro. Is the foule ficke?.
Boy. Sicke at the heart.
La. Ro. Alacke, let it bloud.
Boy. Would that doe it good?
La. Ro. My Phificke faies I.
Boy. Will you prick't with your eye.
La. Ro. No poynt, with my knife.
Boy. Now God faue thy life.
La. Ro. And yours from long liuing.
Ber. I cannot ftay thankf-giuing.   *Exit.*

Enter Dumane.

Dum. Sir, I pray you a word : What Lady is that fame?
Boy. The heire of *Alanfon*, *Rofalin* her name.
Dum. A gallant Lady, Mounfier fare you well.
Long. I befeech you a word : what is fhe in the white?
Long. A woman fomtimes, if you faw her in the light.
Long. Perchance light in the light : I defire her name.
Boy. Shee hath but one for her felfe,
To defire that were a fhame.
Long. Pray you fir, whofe daughter ?
Boy. Her Mothers, I haue heard.
Long. Gods bleffing a your beard.
Boy. Good fir be not offended,
Shee is an heyre of *Faulconbridge.*
Long. Nay, my choller is ended :
Shee is a moft fweet Lady.   *Exit. Long.*
Boy. Not vnlike fir, that may be.

Enter Beroune.

Ber. What's her name in the cap.
Boy. *Katherine* by good hap.
Ber. Is fhe wedded, or no.
Boy. To her will fir, or fo.
Ber. You are welcome fir, adiew.
Boy. Fare well to me fir, and welcome to you. *Exit.*
La. Ma. That laft is *Beroune*, the mery mad-cap Lord.
Not a word with him, but a ieft.
Boy. And euery ieft but a word.
Pri. It was well done of you to take him at his word.
Boy. I was as willing to grapple, as he was to boord.
La. Ma. Two hot Sheepes marie :
And wherefore not Ships?   (lips.
Boy. No Sheepe (fweet Lamb) vnleffe we feed on your
La. You Sheep and I pafture : fhall that finifh the ieft ?
Boy. So you grant pafture for me.
La. Not fo gentle beaft.
My lips are no Common, though feuerall they be.
Bo. Belonging to whom ?
La. To my fortunes and me.
Prin. Good wits wil be iangling, but gentles agree.
This ciuill warre of wits were much better vfed
On *Nauar* and his bookemen, for heere 'tis abus'd.
Bo. If my obferuation (which very feldome lies
By the hearts ftill rhetoricke, difclofed with eyes)
Deceiue me not now, *Nauar* is infected.
Prin. With what?
Bo. With that which we Louers intitle affected.
Prin. Your reafon.
Bo. Why all his behauiours doe make their retire,
To the court of his eye, peeping thorough defire.
His hart like an Agot with your print impreffed,

Proud

Proud with his forme,in his eie pride expreffed,
His tongue all impatient to fpeake and not fee,
Did ftumble with hafte in his eie-fight to be,
All fences to that fence did make their repaire,
To feele onely looking on faireft of faire :
Me thought all his fences were lockt in his eye,
As Iewels in Chriftall for fome Prince to buy.   (glaft,
Who tendring their own worth from whence they were
Did point out to buy them along as you paft.
His faces owne margent did coate fuch amazes,
That all eyes faw his eies inchanted with gazes.
Ile giue you *Aquitaine*,and all that is his,
And you giue him for my fake,but one louing Kiffe.
  Prin. Come to our Pauillion, *Boyet* is difpofde.
  *Bro.*But to fpeak that in words, which his eie hath dif-
I onelie haue made a mouth of his eie,   (clos'd,
By adding a tongue, which I know will not lie.
  Lad.Ro. Thou art an old Loue-monger,and fpeakeft
skilfully.
  Lad.Ma. He is *Cupids* Grandfather,and learnes news
of him.
  *Lad.*2. Then was *Venus* like her mother, for her fa-
ther is but grim.
  Boy. Do you heare my mad wenches?
  *La.*1. No.
  Boy. What then,do you fee ?
  *Lad.*2. I, our way to be gone.
  Boy. You are too hard for me.   *Exeunt omnes.*

Actus Tertius.

Enter Broggart and Boy.
Song.
  Bra. Warble childe,make paffionate my fenfe of hea-
ring.
  Boy. Concolinel.
  Brag. Sweete Ayer, go tenderneffe of yeares : take
this Key, giue enlargement to the fwaine, bring him fe-
ftinatly hither : I muft imploy him in a letter to my
Loue.
  .Boy. Will you win your loue with a French braule?
  Bra. How meaneft thou,brauling in French ?
  Boy. No my compleat mafter, but to Iigge off a tune
at the tongues end, canarie to it with the feete, humour
it with turning vp your eie : figh a note and fing a note,
fometime through the throate : if you fwallowed loue
with finging, loue fometime through : nofe as if you
fnuft vp loue by fmelling loue with your hat penthoufe-
like ore the fhop of your eies, with your armes croft on
your thinbellie doublet , like a Rabbet on a fpit, or your
hands in your pocket, like a man after the old painting,
and keepe not too long in one tune, but a fnip and away :
thefe are complements, thefe are humours, thefe betraie
nice wenches that would be betraied without thefe, and
make them men of note : do you note men that moft are
affected to thefe?
  Brag. How haft thou purchafed this experience ?
  Boy. By my penne of obferuation.
  Brag. But O, but O.
  Boy. The Hobbie-horfe is forgot.
  Bra. Cal'ft thou my loue Hobbi-horfe.
  Boy. No Mafter,the Hobbie-horfe is but a Colt, and
and your Loue perhaps, a Hacknie :

But haue you forgot your Loue ?
  Brag. Almoft I had.
  Boy. Negligent ftudent,learne her by heart.
  Brag. By heart, and in heart Boy.
  Boy. And out of heart Mafter : all thofe three I will
proue.
  Brag. What wilt thou proue?
  Boy. A man,if I liue(and this)by,in,and without,vp-
on the inftant : by heart you loue .her,becaufe your heart
cannot come by her : in heart you loue her,becaufe your
heart is in loue with her : and out of heart you loue her,
being out of heart that you cannot enioy her.
  Brag. I am all thefe three.
  Boy. And three times as much more,and yet nothing
at all.
  Brag. Fetch hither the Swaine, he muft carrie mee a
letter.
  Boy. A meffage well fimpathis'd, a Horfe to be em-
baffadour for an Affe.
  Brag. Ha,ha,What faieft thou ?
  *Boy.*Marrie fir,you muft fend the Affe vpon the Horfe
for he is verie flow gated : but I goe.
  Brag. The way is but fhort,away.
  Boy. As fwift as Lead fir.
  Brag. Thy meaning prettie ingenious, is not Lead a
mettall heauie, dull,and flow ?
  Boy. Minnime honeft Mafter,or rather Mafter no.
  Brad. I fay Lead is flow.
  Boy. You are too fwift fir to fay fo.
Is that Lead flow which is fir'd from a Gunne ?
  Brag. Sweete fmoke of Rhetorike,
He reputes me a Cannon,and the Bullet that's he :
I fhoote thee at the Swaine.
  Boy. Thump then,and I flee.
  Bra. A moft acute Iuuenall, voluble and free of grace,
By thy fauour fweet Welkin, I muft figh in thy face.
Moft rude melancholie, Valour glues thee place.
My Herald is return'd.

Enter Page and Clowne.

  Pag. A wonder Mafter,here's a *Coftard* broken in a
fhin.
  Ar. Some enigma, fome riddle, come, thy *Lenuoy*
begin.
  Clo. No egma,no riddle,no *lenuoy*, no falue, in thee
male fir. Or fir, Plantan, a plaine Plantan : no *lenuoy*,no
lenuoy,no Salue fir,but a Plantan.
  Ar. By vertue thou inforceft laughter, thy fillie
thought, my fpleene, the heauing of my lunges prouokes
me to rediculous fmyling : O pardon me my ftars, doth
the inconfiderate take *falue* for *lenuoy*, and the word *len-
uoy* for a *falue?*
  Pag. Doe the wife thinke them other, is not *lenuoy* a
falue?   (plaine,
  Ar. No *Page*, it is an epilogue or difcourfe to make
Some obfcure precedence that hath tofore bin faine.
Now will I begin your morrall, and do you follow with
my *lenuoy*.
The Foxe, the Ape,and the Humble-Bee,
  Were at oddes,being but three.
  Arm. Vntill the Goofe came out of doore,
  Staying the oddes by adding foure.
  *Pag.*A good *Lenuoy*, ending in the Goofe: would you
defire more ?
  Clo. The Boy hath fold him a bargaine,a Goofe, that's
flat

Sir, your penny-worth is good, and your Goofe be fat.
To fell a bargaine well is as cunning as faft and loofe:
Let me fee a fat *Lenuoy*, I that's a fat Goofe.

Ar. Come hither, come hither:
How did this argument begin?

Boy. By faying that a *Coftard* was broken in a fhin.
Then cal'd you for the *Lenuoy*.

Clow. True, and I for a Plantan:
Thus came your argument in:
Then the Boyes fat *Lenuoy*, the Goofe that you bought,
And he ended the market.

Ar. But tell me: How was there a *Coftard* broken in
a fhin?

Pag. I will tell you fencibly.

Clow. Thou haft no feeling of it *Moth*,
I will fpeake that *Lenuoy*.
I *Coftard* running out, that was fafely within,
Fell ouer the threfhold, and broke my fhin.

Arm. We will talke no more of this matter.

Clow. Till there be more matter in the fhin.

Arm. Sirra *Coftard*, I will infranchife thee.

Clow. O, marrie me to one *Francis*, I fmell fome *Lenuoy*, fome Goofe in this.

Arm. By my fweete foule, I meane, fetting thee at libertie. Enfreedoming thy perfon: thou wert emured,
reftrained, captiuated, bound.

Clow. True, true, and now you will be my purgation,
and let me loofe.

Arm. I giue thee thy libertie, fet thee from durance,
and in lieu thereof, impofe on thee nothing but this:
Beare this fignificant to the countrey Maide *Iaquenetta*:
there is remuneration, for the beft ward of mine honours
is rewarding my dependants. *Moth*, follow.

Pag. Like the fequell I.

Signeur *Coftard* adew.   *Exit.*

Clow. My fweete ounce of mans flefh, my in-conie
Iew: Now will I looke to his remuneration.
Remuneration, O, that's the Latine word for three-farthings: Three-farthings remuneration, What's the price
of this yncle? i.d.no, Ile giue you a remuneration: Why?
It carries it remuneration: Why? It is a fairer name then
a French-Crowne. I will neuer buy and fell out of this
word.

Enter Berowne.

Ber. O my good knaue *Coftard*, exceedingly well met.

Clow. Pray you fir, How much Carnation Ribbon
may a man buy for a remuneration?

Ber. What is a remuneration?

Coft. Marrie fir, halfe pennie farthing.

Ber. O, Why then threefarthings worth of Silke.

Coft. I thanke your worfhip, God be wy you.

Ber. O ftay flaue, I muft employ thee:
As thou wilt win my fauour, good my knaue,
Doe one thing for me that I fhall intreate.

Clow. When would you haue it done fir?

Ber. O this after-noone.

Clo. Well, I will doe it fir: Fare you weil.

Ber. O thou knoweft not what it is.

Clo. I fhall know fir, when I haue done it.

Ber. Why villaine thou muft know firft.

Clo. I wil come to your worfhip to morrow morning.

Ber. It muft be done this after-noone,
Harke flaue, it is but this:
The Princeffe comes to hunt here in the Parke,

And in her traine there is a gentle Ladie:
When tongues fpeak fweetly, then they name her name,
And *Rofaline* they call her, aske for her:
And to her white hand fee thou do commend
This feal'd-vp counfaile. Ther's thy guerdon: goe.

Clo. Gardon, O fweete gardon, better then remuneration, a leuenpence-farthing better: moft fweete gardon. I will doe it fir in print: gardon, remuneration.
     Exit.

Ber. O, and I forfooth in loue,
I that haue beene loues whip?
A verie Beadle to a humerous figh: A Criticke,
Nay, a night-watch Conftable.
A domineering pedant ore the Boy,
Then whom no mortall fo magnificent.
This wimpled, whyning, purblinde waiward Boy,
This fignior *Iunios* gyant drawfe, don *Cupid*,
Regent of Loue-rimes, Lord of folded armes,
Th'annointed foueraigne of fighes and groanes:
Liedge of all loyterers and malecontents:
Dread Prince of Placcats, King of Codpeeces.
Sole Emperator and great generall
Of trotting Parrators (O my little heart.)
And I to be a Corporall of his field,
And weare his colours like a Tumblers hoope.
What? I loue, I fue, I feeke a wife,
A woman that is like a Germane Cloake,
Still a repairing: euer out of frame,
And neuer going a right, being a Watch:
But being watcht, that it may ftill goe right.
Nay, to be periurde, which is worft of all:
And among three, to loue the worft of all,
A whitly wanton, with a veluet brow.
With two pitch bals ftucke in her face for eyes.
I, and by heauen, one that will doe the deede,
Though *Argus* were her Eunuch and her garde.
And I to figh for her, to watch for her,
To pray for her, go to: it is a plague
That *Cupid* will impofe for my neglect,
Of his almighty dreadfull little might.
Well, I will loue, write, figh, pray, fhue, grone,
Some men muft loue my Lady, and fome Ione.

Actus Quartus.

*Enter the Princeffe, a Forrefter, her Ladies, and
her Lords.*

Qu. Was that the King that fpurd his horfe fo hard,
Againft rhe fteepe vprifing of the hill?

Boy. I know not, but I thinke it was not he.

Qu. Who ere a was, a fhew'd a mounting minde:
Well Lords, to day we fhall haue our difpatch,
On Saterday we will returne to *France*.
Then *Forrefter* my friend, Where is the Bufh
That we muft ftand and play the murtherer in?

For. Hereby vpon the edge of yonder Coppice,
A Stand where you may make the faireft fhoote.

Qu. I thanke my beautie, I am faire that fhoote,
And thereupon thou fpeak'ft the faireft fhoote.

For. Pardon me Madam, for I meant not fo.

Qu. What, what? Firft praife me, & then again fay no.
O fhort liu'd pride. Not faire? alacke for woe.

     For. Yes

For. Yes Madam faire.

Qu. Nay, neuer paint me now,
Where faire is not, praife cannot mend the brow.
Here (good my glaffe) take this for telling true:
Faire paiment for foule words, is more then due.

For. Nothing but faire is that which you inherit.

Qu. See, fee, my beautie will be fau'd by merit.
O herefie in faire, fit for thefe dayes,
A giuing hand, though foule, fhall haue faire praife.
But come, the Bow: Now Mercie goes to kill,
And fhooting well, is then accounted ill:
Thus will I faue my credit in the fhoote,
Not wounding, pittie would not let me do't:
If wounding, then it was to fhew my skill,
That more for praife, then purpofe meant to kill.
And out of queftion, fo it is fometimes:
Glory growes guiltie of detefted crimes,
When for Fames fake, for praife an outward part,
We bend to that, the working of the hart.
As I for praife alone now feeke to fpill
The poore Deeres blood, that my heart meanes no ill.

Boy. Do not curft wiues hold that felfe-foueraigntie
Onely for praife fake, when they ftriue to be
Lords ore their Lords?

Qu. Onely for praife, and praife we may afford,
To any Lady that fubdewes a Lord.

Enter Clowne.

Boy. Here comes a member of the common-wealth.

Clo. God dig-you-den all, pray you which is the head
Lady?

Qu. Thou fhalt know her fellow, by the reft that haue
no heads.

Clo. Which is the greateft Lady, the higheft?

Qu. The thickeft, and the talleft.

Clo. The thickeft, & the talleft: it is fo, truth is truth.
And your wafte Miftris, were as flender as my wit,
One a thefe Maides girdles for your wafte fhould be fit.
Are not you the chiefe woma? You are the thickeft here?

Qu. What's your will fir? What's your will?

Clo. I haue a Letter from Monfier *Berowne*,
To one Lady *Rofaline*.

Qu. O thy letter, thy letter: He's a good friend of mine.
Stand a fide good bearer.
Boyet, you can carue,
Breake vp this Capon.

Boyet. I am bound to ferue.
This Letter is miftooke: it importeth none here:
It is writ to *Iaquenetta*.

Qu. We will reade it, I fweare.
Breake the necke of the Waxe, and euery one giue eare.

Boyet reades.

BY heauen, that thou art faire, is moft infallible: true
that thou art beauteous, truth it felfe that thou art
louely: more fairer then faire, beautifull then beautious,
truer then truth it felfe: haue comiferation on thy heroi-
call Vaffall. The magnanimous and moft illuftrate King
Cophetua fet eie vpon the pernicious and indubitate Begger *Zenelophon*: and he it was that might rightly fay, *Ve-
ni, vidi, vici:* Which to annothanize in the vulgar, O
bafe and obfcure vulgar; *videlifet*, He came, See, and o-
uercame: hee came one; fee, two; couercame three:
Who came? the King. Why did he come? to fee. Why

did he fee? to ouercome. To whom came he? to the
Begger. What faw he? the Begger. Who ouercame
he? the Begger. The conclufion is victorie: On whofe
fide? the King: the captiue is inricht: On whofe fide?
the Beggers. The cataftrophe is a Nuptiall: on whofe
fide? the Kings: no, on both in one, or one in both. I am
the King (for fo ftands the comparifon) thou the Begger, for fo witneffeth thy lowlineffe. Shall I command
thy loue? I may. Shall I enforce thy loue? I could.
Shall I entreate thy loue? I will. What, fhalt thou exchange for ragges, roabes: for tittles titles, for thy felfe
mee. Thus expecting thy reply, I prophane my lips on
thy foote, my eyes on thy picture, and my heart on thy
euerie part.

Thine in the deareft defigne of induftrie,

Don Adriana de Armatho.

Thus doft thou heare the Nemean Lion roare,
Gainft thee thou Lambe, that ftandeft as his pray:
Submiffiue fall his princely feete before,
And he from forrage will incline to play.
But if thou ftriue (poore foule) what art thou then?
Foode for his rage, repafture for his den.

Qu. What plume of feathers is hee that indited this
Letter? What veine? What Wethercocke? Did you
euer heare better?

Boy. I am much deceiued, but I remember the ftile.

Qu. Elfe your memorie is bad, going ore it erewhile.

Boy. This *Armado* is a *Spaniard* that keeps here in court
A Phantafime, a Monarcho, and one that makes fport
To the Prince and his Booke-mates.

Qu. Thou fellow, a word.
Who gaue thee this Letter?

Clow. I told you, my Lord.

Qu. To whom fhould'ft thou giue it?

Clo. From my Lord to my Lady.

Qu. From which Lord, to which Lady?

Clo. From my Lord *Berowne*, a good mafter of mine,
To a Lady of *France*, that he call'd *Rofaline*.

Qu. Thou haft miftaken his letter. Come Lords away.
Here fweete, put vp this, 'twill be thine another day.

Exeunt.

Boy. Who is the fhooter? Who is the fhooter?

Rofa. Shall I teach you to know.

Boy. I my continent of beautie.

Rofa. Why fhe that beares the Bow. Finely put off.

Boy. My Lady goes to kill hornes, but if thou marrie,
Hang me by the necke, if hornes that yeare mifcarrie.
Finely put on.

Rofa. Well then, I am the fhooter.

Boy. And who is your Deare?

Rofa. If we choofe by the hornes, your felfe come not
neare. Finely put on indeede.

Maria. You ftill wrangle with her *Boyet*, and fhee
ftrikes at the brow.

Boyet. But fhe her felfe is hit lower:
Haue I hit her now.

Rofa. Shall I come vpon thee with an old faying, that
was a man when King *Pippin* of *France* was a little boy, as
touching the hit it.

Boyet. So I may anfwere thee with one as old that
was a woman when Queene *Guinouer* of *Brittaine* was a
little wench, as touching the hit it.

                            Rofa. Thou

Roſa. Thou canſt not hit it, hit it, hit it,
Thou canſt not hit it my good man.
Boy. I cannot, cannot, cannot :
And I cannot, another can.   *Exit.*
Clo. By my troth moſt pleaſant, how both did fit it.
Mar. A marke marueilous well ſhot, for they both
did hit.
Boy. A mark, O marke but that marke : a marke ſaies
my Lady.
Let the mark haue a pricke in't, to meat at, if it may be.
Mar. Wide a'th bow hand, yſaith your hand is out.
Clo. Indeede a'muſt ſhoote nearer, or heele ne're hit
the clout.
Boy. And if my hand be out, then belike your hand
is in.
Clo. Then will ſhee get the vpſhoot by cleauing the
is in.
Ma. Come, come, you talke greaſely, your lips grow
foule.
Clo. She's too hard for you at pricks, ſir challenge her
to boule.
Boy. I feare too much rubbing : good night my good
Oule.
Clo. By my ſoule a Swaine, a moſt ſimple Clowne.
Lord, Lord, how the Ladies and I haue put him downe.
O my troth moſt ſweete ieſts, moſt inconie vulgar wit,
When it comes ſo ſmoothly off, ſo obſcenely, as it were,
ſo fit.
Armathor ath to the ſide, O a moſt dainty man.
To ſee him walke before a Lady, and to beare her Fan.
To ſee him kiſſe his hand, and how moſt ſweetly a will
ſweare :
And his Page atother ſide, that handfull of wit,
Ah heauens, it is moſt patheticall nit.
Sowla, ſowla.   *Exeunt.*

Shoote within.

Enter Dull, Holofernes, the Pedant and Nathaniel.

Nat. Very reuerent ſport truely, and done in the teſtimony of a good conſcience.
Ped. The Deare was (as you know) ſanguis in blood,
ripe as a Pomwater, who now hangeth like a Iewell in
the eare of *Cœlo* the ſkie ; the welken the heauen, and a-
non falleth like a Crab on the face of *Terra,* the ſoyle, the
land, the earth.
Curat. Nath. Truely M. *Holofernes,* the epythithes are
ſweetly varied like a ſcholler at the leaſt : but ſir I aſſure
ye, it was a Bucke of the firſt head.
Hol. Sir *Nathaniel, haud credo.*
Dul. 'Twas not a *haud credo,* 'twas a Pricket.
Hol. Moſt barbarous intimation : yet a kinde of inſi-
nuation, as it were in *via,* in way of explication *facere* : as
it were replication, or rather *oſtentare,* to ſhow as it were
his inclination after his vndreſſed, vnpoliſhed, vneduca-
ted, vnpruned, vntrained, or rather vnlettered, or rathe-
reſt vnconfirmed faſhion, to inſert againe my *haud credo*
for a Deare.
Dul. I ſaid the Deare was not a *haud credo,* 'twas a
Pricket.
Hol. Twice ſod ſimplicitie, *bis coctus,* O thou monſter Ignorance, how deformed dooſt thou looke.
Nath. Sir hee hath neuer fed of the dainties that are
bred in a booke.
He hath not eate paper as it were :
He hath not drunke inke.

His intellect is not repleniſhed, hee is onely an animall,
onely ſenſible in the duller parts: and ſuch barren plants
are ſet before vs, that we thankfull ſhould be : which we
taſte and feeling, are for thoſe parts that doe fructifie in
vs more then he.
For as it would ill become me to be vaine, indiſcreet, or
a foole ;
So were there a patch ſet on Learning, to ſee him in a
Schoole.
But *omne bene* ſay I, being of an old Fathers minde,
Many can brooke the weather, that loue not the winde.
Dul. You two are book-men: Can you tell by your
wit, What was a month old at *Cains* birth, that's not fiue
weekes old as yet ?
Hol. *Dictiſima* goodman *Dull, dictiſima* goodman
Dull.
Dul. What is *dictina* ?
Nath. A title to *Phebe,* to *Luna,* to the *Moone.*
Hol. The Moone was a month old when *Adam* was
no more.   (ſcore.
And wrought not to fiue-weekes when he came to fiue-
Th'alluſion holds in the Exchange.
Dul. 'Tis true indeede, the Colluſion holds in the
Exchange.
Hol. God comfort thy capacity, I ſay th'alluſion holds
in the Exchange.
Dul. And I ſay the poluſion holds in the Exchange :
for the Moone is neuer but a month old : and I ſay be-
ſide that, 'twas a Pricket that the Princeſſe kill'd.
Hol. Sir *Nathaniel,* will you heare an extemporall
Epytaph on the death of the Deare, and to humour
the ignorant call'd the Deare, the Princeſſe kill'd a
Pricket.
Nath. Perge, good M. *Holofernes, perge,* ſo it ſhall
pleaſe you to abrogate ſcurilitie.
Hol. I will ſomething affect the letter, for it argues
facilitie.

The prayfull Princeſſe pearſt and prickt
   a prettie pleaſing Pricket,
Some ſay a Sore, but not a ſore,
   till now made ſore with ſhooting.
The Dogges did yell, put ell to Sore,
   then Sorell iumps from thicket :
Or Pricket-ſore, or elſe Sorell,
   the people fall a hooting.
If Sore be ſore, then ell to Sore,
   makes fiftie ſores O ſorell :
Of one ſore I an hundred make
   by adding but one more L.

Nath. A rare talent.
Dul. If a talent be a claw, looke how he clawes him
with a talent.
Nath. This is a gift that I haue ſimple: ſimple, a fooliſh extrauagant ſpirit, full of formes, figures, ſhapes, obiects, Ideas, apprehenſions, motions, reuolutions. Theſe
are begot in the ventricle of memorie, nouriſht in the
wombe of primater, and deliuered vpon the mellowing
of occaſion : but the gift is good in thoſe in whom it is
acute, and I am thankfull for it.
Hol. Sir, I praiſe the Lord for you, and ſo may my
pariſhioners, for their Sonnes are well tutor'd by you,
and their Daughters profit very greatly vnder you : you
are a good member of the common-wealth.
Nath. Me hercle, If their Sonnes be ingenuous, they
                  ſhall

ſhall want no inſtruction: If their Daughters be capable,
I will put it to them. But *Vir ſapis qui pauca loquitur,* a
ſoule Feminine ſaluteth vs.

Enter Iaquenetta and the Clowne.

Iaqu. God giue you good morrow M.*Perſon.*
Nath. Maſter Perſon,*quaſi* Perſon? And if one ſhould
be perſt, Which is the one?
Clo. Marry M. Schoolemaſter, hee that is likeſt to a
hogſhead.
Nath. Of perſing a Hogshead, a good luſter of conceit in a turph of Earth, Fire enough for a Flint, Pearle
enough for a Swine : 'tis prettie, it is well.
Iaqu. Good Maſter Parſon be ſo good as reade mee
this Letter, it was giuen mee by *Coſtard,* and ſent mee
from *Don Armatho* : I beſeech you reade it.
Nath. *Facile precor gellida, quando pecas omnia ſub vm-
bra ruminat,* and ſo forth. Ah good old *Mantuan,* I
may ſpeake of thee as the traueiler doth of *Venice, vem-
chie, vencha, que non te vnde, que non te perreche.* Old *Man-
tuam,* old *Mantuan.* Who vnderſtandeth thee not, *vt re
ſol la mi fa* : Vnder pardon ſir, What are the contents? or
rather as *Horrace* ſayes in his, What my ſoule verſes.
Hol. I ſir, and very learned.
Nath. Let me heare a ſtaffe, a ſtanze, a verſe, *Lege do-
mine.*
If Loue make me forſworne, how ſhall I ſweare to loue?
Ah neuer faith could hold, if not to beautie vowed.
Though to my ſelfe forſworn, to thee Ile faithfull proue.
Thoſe thoughts to mee were Okes, to thee like Oſiers
    bowed.
Studie his byas leaues, and makes his booke thine eyes.
Where all thoſe pleaſures liue, that Art would compre-
    hend.
If knowledge be the marke, to know thee ſhall ſuffice.
Well learned is that tongue, that well can thee cōmend.
All ignorant that ſoule, that ſees thee without wonder.
Which is to me ſome praiſe, that I thy parts admire ;
Thy eye *Ioues* lightning beares, thy voyce his dreadfull
    thunder.
Which not to anger bent, is muſique, and ſweet fire.
Celeſtiall as thou art, Oh pardon loue this wrong,
That ſings heauens praiſe, with ſuch an earthly tongue.
Ped. You finde not the apoſtraphas, and ſo miſſe the
accent. Let me ſuperuiſe the cangenet.
Nath. Here are onely numbers ratified, but for the
elegancy, facility, & golden cadence of poeſie *caret* : *O-
uiddius Naſo* was the man. And why in deed *Naſo,* but
for ſmelling out the odoriferous flowers of fancy? the
ierkes of inuention imitarie is nothing : So doth the
Hound his maſter, the Ape his keeper, the tyred Horſe
his rider : But *Damoſella virgin,* Was this directed to
you?
Iaq. I ſir from one mounſier *Berowne,* one of the
ſtrange Queenes Lords.
Nath. I will ouerglance the ſuperſcript.
To the ſnow-white hand of the moſt beautious Lady Roſaline.
I will looke againe on the intellect of the Letter, for
the nomination of the partie written to the perſon written vnto.
Your Ladiſhips in all deſired imployment , Berowne.
Per. Sir Holofernes, this *Berowne* is one of the Votaries
with the King, and here he hath framed a Letter to a ſequent of the ſtranger Queenes : which accidentally, or
by the way of progreſſion, hath miſcarried. Trip and

goe my ſweete, deliuer this Paper into the hand of the
King, it may concerne much : ſtay not thy complement, I
forgiue thy duetie, adue.
Maid. Good *Cuſtard* go with me :
Sir God ſaue your life.
  Coſt. Haue with thee my girle.   *Exit.*
Hol. Sir you haue done this in the feare of God very
religiouſly : and as a certaine Father ſaith
Ped. Sir tell not me of the Father, I do feare coloura-
ble colours. But to returne to the Verſes, Did they pleaſe
you ſir *Nathaniel?*
Nath. Marueilous well for the pen.
 Peda. I do dine to day at the fathers of a certaine Pu-
pill of mine, where if (being repaſt) it ſhall pleaſe you to
gratifie the table with a Grace, I will on my priuiledge I
haue with the parents of the foreſaid Childe or Pupill,
vndertake your *bien vonuto,* where I will proue thoſe
Verſes to be very vnlearned , neither ſauouring of
Poetrie, Wit, nor Inuention. I beſeech your Societie.
Nat. And thanke you to: for ſocietie (ſaith the text)
is the happineſſe of life.
Pida. And certes the text moſt infallibly concludes it.
Sir I do inuite you too, you ſhall not ſay me nay : *pauca
verba.*
Away, the gentles are at their game, and we will to our
recreation.   *Exeunt.*

Enter Berowne with a Paper in his hand, alone.

Bero. The King he is hunting the Deare,
I am courſing my ſelfe.
  They haue pitcht a Toyle, I am toyling in a pytch,
pitch that defiles ; defile, a foule word : Well, ſet thee
downe ſorrow ; for ſo they ſay the foole ſaid, and ſo ſay
I, and I the foole : Well proued wit. By the Lord this
Loue is as mad as *Aiax,* it kils ſheepe, it kils mee, I a
ſheepe: Well proued againe a my ſide. I will not loue;
if I do hang me : yſaith I will not. O but her eye : by
this light, but for her eye, I would not loue her; yes, for
her two eyes. Well, I doe nothing in the world but lye,
and lye in my throate. By heauen I doe loue, and it hath
taught mee to Rime, and to be mallicholie : and here is
part of my Rime, and heere my mallicholie. Well, ſhe
hath one a'my Sonnets already, the Clowne bore it, the
Foole ſent it, and the Lady hath it : ſweet Clowne, ſweeter Foole, ſweeteſt Lady. By the world, I would not care
a pin, if the other three were in. Here comes one with a
paper, God giue him grace to grone.
  He ſtands aſide.   *The King entreth.*
Kin. Ay mee !
Ber. Shot by heauen: proceede ſweet *Cupid,* thou haſt
thumpt him with thy Birdbolt vnder the left pap: in faith
ſecrets.
King. So ſweete a kiſſe the golden Sunne giues not,
To thoſe freſh morning drops vpon the Roſe,
As thy eye beames, when their freſh rayſe haue ſmot.
The night of dew that on my cheekes downe flowes.
Nor ſhines the ſiluer Moone one halfe ſo bright,
Through the tranſparent boſome of the deepe,
As doth thy face through teares of mine giue light :
Thou ſhin'ſt in euery teare that I doe weepe,
No drop, but as a Coach doth carry thee :
So rideſt thou triumphing in my woe.
Do but behold the teares that ſwell in me,
And they thy glory through my griefe will ſhow :

                                      But

But doe not loue thy ſelfe, then thou wilt keepe
My teares for glaſſes, and ſtill make me weepe.
O Queene of Queenes, how farre doſt thou excell,
No thought can thinke, nor tongue of mortall tell.
How ſhall ſhe know my griefes? Ile drop the paper.
Sweet leaues ſhade folly. Who is he comes heere?

     Enter Longauile.   *The King ſteps aſide.*
What *Longauill*, and reading : liſten eare.
  Ber. Now in thy likeneſſe, one more foole appeare.
  Long. Ay me, I am forſworne.
  Ber. Why he comes in like a periure, wearing papers.
  Long. In loue I hope, ſweet fellowſhip in ſhame.
  Ber. One drunkard loues another of the name.
  Lon. Am I the firſt ẙ haue been periur'd ſo? (know,
  Ber. I could put thee in comfort, not by two that I
Thou makeſt the triumphery, the corner cap of ſocietie,
The ſhape of Loues Tiburne, that hangs vp ſimplicitie.
  Lon. I feare theſe ſtubborn lines lack power to moue.
O ſweet *Maria*, Empreſſe of my Loue,
Theſe numbers will I teare, and write in proſe.
  Ber. O Rimes are gards on wanton *Cupids* hoſe,
Disfigure not his Shop.
  Lon. This ſame ſhall goe.   *He reades the Sonnet.*
Did not the heauenly Rhetoricke of thine eye,
'Gainſt whom the world cannot hold argument,
Perſwade my heart to this falſe periurie?
Vowes for thee broke deſerue not puniſhment.
A Woman I forſwore, but I will proue,
Thou being a Goddeſſe, I forſwore not thee.
My Vow was earthly, thou a heauenly Loue.
Thy grace being gain'd, cures all diſgrace in me.
Vowes are but breath, and breath a vapour is.
Then thou faire Sun, which on my earth doeſt ſhine,
Exhaleſt this vapor-vow, in thee it is :
If broken then, it is no fault of mine :
If by me broke, What foole is not ſo wiſe,
To looſe an oath, to win a Paradiſe?
  Ber. This is the liuer veine, which makes fleſh a deity.
A greene Gooſe, a Coddeſſe, pure pure Idolatry.
God amend vs, God amend, we are much out o'th'way.

     Enter Dumaine.
  Lon. By whom ſhall I ſend this (company?) Stay.
  Bero. All hid, all hid, an old infant play,
Like a demie God, here ſit I in the skie,
And wretched fooles ſecrets heedfully ore-eye.
More Sacks to the myll. O heauens I haue my wiſh,
Dumaine transform'd, foure Woodcocks in a diſh.
  Dum. O moſt diuine *Kate.*
  Bero. O moſt prophane coxcombe.
  Dum. By heauen the wonder of a mortall eye.
  Bero. By earth ſhe is not, corporall, there you lye.
  Dum. Her Amber haires for foule hath amber coted.
  Ber. An Amber eoloured Rauen was well noted.
  Dum. As vpright as the Cedar.
  Ber. Stoope I ſay, her ſhoulder is with-child.
  Dum. As faire as day.
  Ber. I as ſome daies, but then no ſunne muſt ſhine.
  Dum. O that I had my wiſh?
  Lon. And I had mine.
  Kin. And mine too good Lord.
  Ber. Amen, ſo I had mine : Is not that a good word?
  Dum. I would forget her, but a Feuer ſhe
Raignes in my bloud, and will remembred be.
  Ber. A Feuer in your bloud, why then inciſion

Would let her out in Sawcers, ſweet miſpriſion.
  Dum. Once more Ile read the Ode that I haue writ.
  Ber. Once more Ile marke how Loue can varry Wit.

    Dumane reades his Sonnet.

On a day, alack the day :
Loue, whoſe Month is euery May,
Spied a bloſſome paſſing faire,
Playing in the wanton ayre :
Through the Veluet, leaues the winde,
All vnſeene, can paſſage finde.
That the Louer ſicke to death,
Wiſh himſelfe the heauens breath.
Ayre (quoth he) thy cheekes may blowe,
Ayre, would I might triumph ſo.
But alacke my hand is ſworne,
Nere to plucke thee from thy throne :
Vow alacke for youth vnmeete,
Youth ſo apt to plucke a ſweet.
Doe not call it ſinne in me,
That I am forſworne for thee.
Thou for whom loue would ſweare,
Iuno but an Æthiop were,
And denie himſelfe for Ioue.
Turning mortall for thy Loue.

This will I ſend, and ſomething elſe more plaine.
That ſhall expreſſe my true-loues faſting paine.
O would the *King, Berowne* and *Longauill,*
Were Louers too, ill to example ill,
Would from my forehead wipe a periur'd note :
For none offend, where all alike doe dote.
  Lon. *Dumaine*, thy Loue is farre from charitie,
That in Loues griefe deſir'ſt ſocietie :
You may looke pale, but I ſhould bluſh I know,
To be ore-heard, and taken napping ſo.
  Kin. Come ſir, you bluſh : as his, your caſe is ſuch,
You chide at him, offending twice as much.
You doe not loue *Maria*? *Longauile,*
Did neuer Sonnet for her ſake compile ;
Nor neuer lay his wreathed armes athwart
His louing boſome, to keepe downe his heart.
I haue beene cloſely ſhrowded in this buſh,
And markt you both, and for you both did bluſh.
I heard your guilty Rimes, obſeru'd your faſhion :
Saw ſighes reeke from you, noted well your paſſion.
Aye me, ſayes one! O *Ioue*, the other cries!
On her haires were Gold, Chriſtall the others eyes.
You would for Paradiſe breake Faith and troth,
And *Ioue* for your Loue would infringe an oath.
What will *Berowne* ſay when that he ſhall heare
Faith infringed, which ſuch zeale did ſweare.
How will he ſcorne? how will he ſpend his wit?
How will he triumph, leape, and laugh at it?
For all the wealth that euer I did ſee,
I would not haue him know ſo much by me.
  Bero. Now ſtep I forth to whip hypocriſie.
Ah good my Liedge, I pray thee pardon me.
Good heart, What grace haſt thou thus to reproue
Theſe wormes for louing, that art moſt in loue?
Your eyes doe make no couches in your teares.
There is no certaine Princeſſe that appeares.
You'll not be periur'd, 'tis a hatefull thing :
Tuſh, none but Minſtrels like of Sonnetting.
But are you not aſham'd? nay, are you not

           M   All

All three of you, to be thus much ore'ſhot?
You found his Moth, the King your Moth did ſee:
But I a Beame doe finde in each of three.
O what a Scene of fool'ry haue I ſeene.
Of ſighes, of grones, of ſorrow, and of teene:
O me, with what ſtrict patience haue I ſat,
To ſee a King transformed to a Gnat?
To ſee great *Hercules* whipping a Gigge,
And profound *Salomon* tuning a Iygge?
And *Neſtor* play at puſh-pin with the boyes,
And *Critticke Tymon* laugh at idle toyes.
Where lies thy griefe? O tell me good *Dumaine*;
And gentle *Longauill*, where lies thy paine?
And where my Liedges? all about the breſt:
  A Candle hoa!
  Kin. Too bitter is thy ieſt.
Are wee betrayed thus to thy ouer-view?
  Ber. Not you by me, but I betrayed to you.
I that am honeſt, I that hold it ſinne
To breake the vow I am ingaged in.
I am betrayed by keeping company
With men, like men of inconſtancie.
When ſhall you ſee me write a thing in time?
Or grone for *Ioone*? or ſpend a minutes time,
In pruning mee, when ſhall you heare that I will praiſe a
hand, a foot, a face, an eye : a gate, a ſtate, a brow, a breſt,
a waſte, a legge, a limme.
  Kin. Soft, Whither a-way ſo faſt?
A true man, or a theefe, that gallops ſo.
  Ber. I poſt from Loue, good Louer let me go.

Enter Iaquenetta and Clowne.
  Iaqu. God bleſſe the King.
  Kin. What Preſent haſt thou there?
  Clo. Some certaine treaſon.
  Kin. What makes treaſon heere?
  Clo. Nay it makes nothing ſir.
  Kin. If it marre nothing neither,
The treaſon and you goe in peace away together.
  Iaqu. I beſeech your Grace let this Letter be read,
Our perſon miſ-doubts it : it was treaſon he ſaid.
  Kin. Berowne, read it ouer.   *He reades the Letter.*
  Kin. Where hadſt thou it?
  Iaqu. Of *Coſtard.*
  King. Where hadſt thou it?
  Coſt. Of *Dun Adramadio, Dun Adramadio.*
  Kin. How now, what is in you? why doſt thou tear it?
  Ber. A toy my Liedge, a toy : your grace needes not
feare it.
  Long. It did moue him to paſſion, and therefore let's
heare it.
  Dum. It is *Berowns* writing, and heere is his name.
  Ber. Ah you whoreſon loggerhead, you were borne
to doe me ſhame.
Guilty my Lord, guilty : I confeſſe, I confeſſe.
  Kin. What?
  Ber. That you three fooles, lackt mee foole, to make
vp the meſſe.
He, he, and you : and you my Liedge, and I,
Are picke-purſes in Loue, and we deſerue to die.
O diſmiſſe this audience, and I ſhall tell you more.
  Dum. Now the number is euen.
  Berow. True true, we are fowre : will theſe Turtles
be gone?
  Kin. Hence ſirs, away.
  Clo. Walk aſide the true folke, & let the traytors ſtay.

  Ber. Sweet Lords, ſweet Louers, O let vs imbrace,
As true we are as fleſh and bloud can be,
The Sea will ebbe and flow, heauen will ſhew his face:
Young bloud doth not obey an old decree.
We cannot croſſe the cauſe why we are borne:
Therefore of all hands muſt we be forſworne.
  King. What, did theſe rent lines ſhew ſome loue of
thine?   (*Roſaline,*
  Ber. Did they, quoth you ? Who ſees the heauenly
That (like a rude and ſauage man of *Inde.*)
At the firſt opening of the gorgeous Eaſt,
Bowes not his vaſſall head, and ſtrooken blinde,
Kiſſes the baſe ground with obedient breaſt?
What peremptory Eagle-ſighted eye
Dares looke vpon the heauen of her brow,
That is not blinded by her maieſtie?
  Kin. What zeale, what furie, hath inſpir'd thee now?
My Loue (her Miſtres) is a gracious Moone,
Shee (an attending Starre) ſcarce ſeene a light.
  Ber. My eyes are then no eyes, nor I *Berowne.*
O, but for my Loue, day would turne to night,
Of all complexions the cul'd ſoueraignty,
Doe meet as at a faire in her faire cheeke,
Where ſeuerall Worthies make one dignity,
Where nothing wants, that want it ſelfe doth ſeeke.
Lend me the flouriſh of all gentle tongues,
Fie painted Rethoricke, O ſhe needs it not,
To things of ſale, a ſellers praiſe belongs:
She paſſes prayſe, then prayſe too ſhort doth blot.
A withered Hermite, fiueſcore winters worne,
Might ſhake off fiftie, looking in her eye:
Beauty doth varniſh Age, as if new borne,
And giues the Crutch the Cradles infancie.
O 'tis the Sunne that maketh all things ſhine.
  King. By heauen, thy Loue is blacke as Ebonie.
  Berow. Is Ebonie like her? O word diuine?
A wife of ſuch wood were felicitie.
O who can giue an oth? Where is a booke?
That I may ſweare Beauty doth beauty lacke,
If that ſhe learne not of her eye to looke:
No face is faire that is not full ſo blacke.
  Kin. O paradoxe, Blacke is the badge of hell,
The hue of dungeons, and the Schoole of night:
And beauties creſt becomes the heauens well.
  Ber. Diuels ſooneſt tempt reſembling ſpirits of light.
O if in blacke my Ladies browes be deckt,
It mournes, that painting vſurping haire
Should rauiſh doters with a falſe aſpect:
And therfore is ſhe borne to make blacke, faire.
Her fauour turnes the faſhion of the dayes,
For natiue bloud is counted painting now:
And therefore red that would auoyd diſpraiſe,
Paints it ſelfe blacke, to imitate her brow.
  Dum. To look like her are Chimny-ſweepers blacke.
  Lon. And ſince her time, are Colliers counted bright.
  King. And Æthiops of their ſweet complexion crake.
  Dum. Dark needs no Candles now, for dark is light.
  Ber. Your miſtreſſes dare neuer come in raine,
For feare their colours ſhould be waſht away.
  Kin. 'Twere good yours did: for ſir to tell you plaine,
Ile finde a fairer face not waſht to day.
  Ber. Ile proue her faire, or talke till dooms-day here.
  Kin. No Diuell will fright thee then ſo much as ſhee.
  Duma. I neuer knew man hold vile ſtuffe ſo deere.
  Lon. Looke, heer's thy loue, my foot and her face ſee.
  Ber. O if the ſtreets were paued with thine eyes,
                                                    Her

Her feet were much too dainty for fuch tread.
Duma. O vile, then as fhe goes what vpward lyes?
The ftreet fhould fee as fhe walk'd ouer head.
Kin. But what of this, are we not all in loue?
Ber. O nothing fo fure, and thereby all forfworne.
Kin. Then leaue this chat, & good *Berown* now proue
Our louing lawfull, and our fayth not torne.
Dum. I marie there, fome flattery for this euill.
Long. O fome authority how to proceed,
Some tricks, fome quillets, how to cheat the diuell.
Dum. Some falue for periurie.
Ber. O 'tis more then neede.
Haue at you then affections men at armes,
Confider what you firft did fweare vnto :
To faft, to ftudy, and to fee no woman :
Flat treafon againft the Kingly ftate of youth.
Say, Can you faft? your ftomacks are too young:
And abftinence ingenders maladies.
And where that you haue vow'd to ftudie (Lords)
In that each of you haue forfworne his Booke.
Can you ftill dreame and pore, and thereon looke.
For when would you my Lord, or you, or you,
Haue found the ground of ftudies excellence,
Without the beauty of a womans face;
From womens eyes this doctrine I deriue,
They are the Ground, the Bookes, the Achadems,
From whence doth fpring the true *Promethean* fire.
Why, vniuerfall plodding poyfons vp
The nimble fpirits in the arteries,
As motion and long during action tyres
The finnowy vigour of the trauailer.
Now for not looking on a womans face,
You haue in that forfworne the vfe of eyes :
And ftudie too, the caufer of your vow.
For where is any Author in the world,
Teaches fuch beauty as a womans eye :
Learning is but an adiunct to our felfe,
And where we are, our Learning likewife is.
Then when our felues we fee in Ladies eyes,
With our felues.
Doe we not likewife fee our learning there?
O we haue made a Vow to ftudie, Lords,
And in that vow we haue forfworne our Bookes :
For when would you (my Leege) or you, or you?
In leaden contemplation haue found out
Such fiery Numbers as the prompting eyes,
Of beauties tutors haue inrich'd you with :
Other flow Arts intirely keepe the braine :
And therefore finding barraine practizers,
Scarce fhew a harueft of their heauy toyle.
But Loue firft learned in a Ladies eyes,
Liues not alone emured in tbe braine :
But with the motion of all elements,
Courfes as fwift as thought in euery power,
And giues to euery power a double power,
Aboue their functions and their offices.
It addes a precious feeing to the eye:
A Louers eyes will gaze an Eagle blinde.
A Louers eare will heare the loweft found.
When the fufpicious head of theft is ftopt.
Loues feeling is more foft and fenfible,
Then are the tender hornes of Cockled Snayles.
Loues tongue proues dainty, *Bachus* groffe in tafte,
For Valour, is not Loue a *Hercules*?
Still climing trees in the *Hefperides*.
Subtill as *Sphinx*, as fweet and muficall,

As bright *Apollo's* Lute, ftrung with his haire.
And when Loue fpeakes, the voyce of all the Gods,
Make heauen drowfie with the harmonie.
Neuer durft Poet touch a pen to write,
Vntill his Inke were tempred with Loues fighes:
O then his lines would rauifh fauage eares,
And plant in Tyrants milde humilitie.
From womens eyes this doctrine I deriue.
They fparcle ftill the right promethean fire,
They are the Bookes, the Arts, the Achademes,
That fhew, containe, and nourifh all the world.
Elfe none at all in ought proues excellent.
Then fooles you were thefe women to forfweare :
Or keeping what is fworne, you will proue fooles,
For Wifedomes fake, a word that all men loue :
Or for Loues fake, a word that loues all men.
Or for Mens fake, the author of thefe Women :
Or Womens fake, by whom we men are Men.
Let's once loofe our oathes to finde our felues,
Or elfe we loofe our felues, to keepe our oathes :
It is religion to be thus forfworne.
For Charity it felfe fulfills the Law :
And who can feuer loue from Charity.
Kin. Saint *Cupid* then, and Souldiers to the field.
Ber. Aduance your ftandards, & vpon them Lords.
Pell, mell, downe with them : but be firft aduis'd,
In conflict that you get the Sunne of them.
Long. Now to plaine dealing, Lay thefe glozes by,
Shall we refolue to woe thefe girles of France?
Kin. And winne them too, therefore let vs deuife,
Some entertainment for them in their Tents.
Ber. Firft from the Park let vs conduct them thither,
Then homeward euery man attach the hand
Of his faire Miftreffe, in the afternoone
We will with fome ftrange paftime folace them :
Such as the fhortneffe of the time can fhape,
For Reuels, Dances, Maskes, and merry houres,
Fore-runne faire Loue, ftrewing her way with flowres.
Kin. Away, away, no time fhall be omitted,
That will be time, and may by vs be fitted.
Ber. Alone, alone fowed Cockell, reap'd no Corne,
And Iuftice alwaies whirles in equall meafure :
Light Wenches may proue plagues to men forfworne,
If fo, our Copper buyes no better treafure. *Exeunt.*

Actus Quartus.

Enter the Pedant, Curate and Dull.

Pedant. Satis quid fufficit.
Curat. I praife God for you fir, your reafons at dinner
haue beene fharpe & fententious:pleafant without fcur-
rillity, witty without affection, audacious without im-
pudency, learned without opinion, and ftrange without
herefie : I did conuerfe this *quondam* day with a companion of the Kings, who is intituled, nominated, or called,
Don Adriano de Armatho.
Ped. Noui hominum tanquam te, His humour is lofty,
his difcourfe peremptorie : his tongue filed, his eye
ambitious, his gate maiefticall, and his generall behauiour vaine, ridiculous, and thrafonicall. He is too picked,
too fpruce, too affected, too odde, as it were, too pere-
grinat, as I may call it.

Curat. A moft fingular and choife Epithat,
    Draw out his Table-booke.
Peda. He draweth out the thred of his verbofitie, finer then the ftaple of his argument. I abhor fuch pha-
naticall phantafims, fuch infociable and poynt deuife
companions, fuch rackers of ortagriphie, as to fpeake
dout fine, when he fhould fay doubt; det, when he fhold
pronounce debt; d e b t, not det: he clepeth a Calf, Caufe:
halfe, haufe : neighbour *vocatur* nebour; neigh abreuiated
ne : this is abhominable, which he would call abhomi-
nableit infinuateth me of infamie : *ne inteligis domine,* to
make franticke, lunaticke ?
Cura. *Laus deo, bene intelligo.*
Peda. *Bome boon for boon prefcian,* a little fcratcht, 'twil
ferue.

    Enter Bragart, Boy.

Curat. *Video ne quis venit ?*
Peda. *Video, & gaudio.*
Brag. Chirra.
Peda. *Quari* Chirra, not Sirra ?
Brag. Men of peace well incountred.
Ped. Moft millitarie fir falutation.
Boy. They haue beene at a great feaft of Languages,
and ftolne the fcraps.
Clow. O they haue liu'd long on the almes-basket of
words. I maruell thy M. hath not eaten thee for a word,
for thou art not fo long by the head as honorificabilitu-
dinitatibus : Thou art eafier fwallowed then a flapdra-
gon.
Page. Peace, the peale begins.
Brag. Mounfier, are you not lettred ?
Page. Yes, yes, he teaches boyes the Horne-booke :
What is Ab fpeld backward with the horn on his head ?
Peda. Ba, *puericia* with a horne added.
Pag. Ba moft feely Sheepe, with a horne : you heare
his learning.
Peda. *Quis quis,* thou Confonant?
Pag. The laft of the fiue Vowels if You repeat them,
or the fift if I.
Peda. I will repeat them : a e I.
Pag. The Sheepe, the other two concludes it o u.
Brag. Now by the falt waue of the mediteranium, a
fweet tutch, a quicke vene we of wit, fnip fnap, quick &
home, it reioyceth my intellect, true wit.
Page. Offered by a childe to an olde man : which is
wit-old.
Peda. What is the figure ? What is the figure ?
Page. Hornes.
Peda. Thou difputes like an Infant : goe whip thy
Gigge.
Pag. Lend me your Horne to make one, and I will
whip about your Infamie *vnum cita* a gigge of a Cuck-
olds horne.
Clow. And I had but one penny in the world, thou
fhouldft haue it to buy Ginger bread: Hold, there is the
very Remuneration I had of thy Maifter, thou halfpenny
purfe of wit, thou Pidgeon-egge of difcretion. O & the
heauens were fo pleafed, that thou wert but my Baftard;
What a ioyfull father wouldft thou make mee ? Goe to,
thou haft it *ad dungil,* at the fingers ends, as they fay.
Peda. Oh I fmell falfe Latine, *dungbel* for *vnguem.*
Brag. *Artf-man preambulat,* we will bee fingled from
the barbarous. Do you not educate youth at the Charg-
houfe on the top of the Mountaine?
Peda. Or *Mons* the hill.

Brag. At your fweet pleafure, for the Mountaine.
Peda. I doe *fans queftion.*
Bra. Sir, it is the Kings moft fweet pleafure and affection, to congratulate the Princeffe at her Paullion, in
the *pofteriors* of this day, which the rude multitude call
the after-noone.
Ped. The *pofterior* of the day, moft generous fir, is lia-
ble, congruent, and meafurable for the after-noone : the
word is well culd, chofe, fweet, and apt I doe affure you
fir, I doe affure.
Brag. Sir, the King is a noble Gentleman, and my familiar, I doe affure ye very good friend : for what is inward betweene vs, let it paffe. I doe befeech thee remember thy curtefie. I befeech thee apparell thy head :
and among other importunate & moft ferious defignes,
and of great import indeed too : but let that paffe, for I
muft tell thee it will pleafe his Grace (by the world)
fometime to leane vpon my poore fhoulder, and with
his royall finger thus dallie with my excrement, with my
muftachio : but fweet heart let that paffe. By the world
I recount no fable, fome certaine fpeciall honours it
pleafeth his greatneffe to impart to *Armado* a Souldier,
a man of trauell, that hath feene the world : but let that
paffe ; the very all of all is: but fweet heart, I do implore
fecrecie, that the King would haue mee prefent the
Princeffe (fweet chucke) with fome delightfull oftenta-
tion, or fhow, or pageant, or anticke, or fire-worke :
Now, vnderftanding that the Curate and your fweet felf
are good at fuch eruptions, and fodaine breaking out of
myrth (as it were) I haue acquainted you withall, to
the end to craue your affiftance.
Peda. Sir, you fhall prefent before her the Nine Worthies. Sir *Holofernes,* as concerning fome entertainment
of time, fome fhow in the pofterior of this day, to bee
rendred by our affiftants the Kings command : and this
moft gallant, illuftrate and learned Gentleman, before
the Princeffe : I fay none fo fit as to prefent the Nine
Worthies.
Curat. Where will you finde men worthy enough to
prefent them ?
Peda. *Iofua,* your felfe: my felfe, and this gallant gentleman *Iudas Machabeus* ; this Swaine (becaufe of his
great limme or ioynt) fhall paffe *Pompey* the great, the
Page *Hercules.*
Brag. Pardon fir, error : He is not quantitie enough
for that Worthies thumb, hee is not fo big as the end of
his Club.
Peda. Shall I haue audience ? he fhall prefent *Hercu-
les* in minoritie : his *enter* and *exit* fhall bee ftrangling a
Snake ; and I will haue an Apologie for that purpofe.
Pag. An excellent deuice : fo if any of the audience
hiffe, you may cry, Well done *Hercules,* now thou cru-
fheft the Snake ; that is the way to make an offence gra-
cious, though few haue the grace to doe it.
Brag. For the reft of the Worthies ?
Peda. I will play three my felfe.
Pag. Thrice worthy Gentleman.
Brag. Shall I tell you a thing ?
Peda. We attend.
Brag. We will haue, if this fadge not, an Antique. I
befeech you follow.
Ped. *Via* good-man *Dull,* thou haft fpoken no word
all this while.
Dull. Nor vnderftood none neither fir.
Ped. Alone, we will employ thee.
Dull. Ile make one in a dance, or fo : or I will play
               on

on the taber to the Worthies, & let them dance the hey.
Ped. Moſt *Dull*, honeſt *Dull*, to our ſport away. *Exit.*

Enter Ladies.

Qu. Sweet hearts we ſhall be rich ere we depart,
If fairings come thus plentifully in.
A Lady wal'd about with Diamonds : Look you, what I
haue from the louing King.

Roſa. Madam, came nothing elſe along with that?

Qu. Nothing but this : yes as much loue in Rime,
As would be cram'd vp in a ſheet of paper
Writ on both ſides the leafe, margent and all,
That he was faine to ſeale on *Cupids* name.

Roſa. That was the way to make his god-head wax:
For he hath beene fiue thouſand yeeres a Boy.

Kath. I, and a ſhrewd vnhappy gallowes too.

Roſ. You'll nere be friends with him, a kild your ſiſter.

Kath. He made her melancholy, ſad, and heauy, and
ſo ſhe died : had ſhe beene Light like you, of ſuch a merrie nimble ſtirring ſpirit, ſhe might a bin a Grandam ere
ſhe died. And ſo may you : For a light heart liues long.

Roſ. What's your darke meaning mouſe, of this light
word?

Kat. A light condition in a beauty darke.

Roſ. We need more light to finde your meaning out.

Kat. You'll marre the light by taking it in ſnuffe :
Therefore Ile darkely end the argument.

Roſ. Look what you doe, you doe it ſtill i'th darke.

Kat. So do not you, for you are a light Wench.

Roſ. Indeed I waigh not you, and therefore light.

Ka. You waigh me not, O that's you care not for me.

Roſ. Great reaſon : for paſt care, is ſtill paſt cure.

Qu. Well bandied both, a ſet of Wit well played.
But *Roſaline*, you haue a Fauour too?
Who ſent it? and what is it?

Roſ. I would you knew.
And if my face were but as faire as yours,
My Fauour were as great, be witneſſe this.
Nay, I haue Verſes too, I thanke *Berowne*,
The numbers true, and were the numbring too,
I were the faireſt goddeſſe on the ground.
I am compar'd to twenty thouſand fairs.

Qu. Any thing like?

Roſ. Much in the letters, nothing in the praiſe.

Qu. Beauteous as Incke : a good concluſion.

Kat. Faire as a text B. in a Coppie booke.

Roſ. Ware penſals. How? Let me not die your debtor,
My red Dominicall, my golden letter.
O that your face were full of Oes.

Qu. A Pox of that ieſt, and I beſhrew all Shrowes:
But *Katherine*, what was ſent to you
From faire *Dumaine*?

Kat. Madame, this Gloue.

Qu. Did he not ſend you twaine?

Kat. Yes Madame : and moreouer,
Some thouſand Verſes of a faithfull Louer.
A huge tranſlation of hypocriſie,
Vildly compiled, profound ſimplicitie.

Mar. This, and theſe Pearls, to me ſent *Longauile*.
The Letter is too long by halfe a mile.

Qu. I thinke no leſſe : Doſt thou wiſh in heart
The Chaine were longer, and the Letter ſhort.

Mar. I, or I would theſe hands might neuer part.

Quee. We are wiſe girles to mocke our Louers ſo.

Roſ. They are worſe fooles to purchaſe mocking ſo.

That ſame *Berowne* ile torture ere I goe.
O that I knew he were but in by th'weeke,
How I would make him fawne, and begge, and ſeeke,
And wait the ſeaſon, and obſerue the times,
And ſpend his prodigall wits in booteles rimes.
And ſhape his ſeruice wholly to my deuice,
And make him proud to make me proud that ieſts.
So pertaunt like would I o'reſway his ſtate,
That he ſhold be my foole, and I his fate.

Qu. None are ſo ſurely caught, when they are catcht,
As Wit turn'd foole, follie in Wiſedome hatch'd :
Hath wiſedoms warrant, and the helpe of Schoole,
And Wits owne grace to grace a learned Foole ?

Roſ. The bloud of youth burns not with ſuch exceſſe,
As grauities reuolt to wantons be.

Mar. Follie in Fooles beares not ſo ſtrong a note,
As fool'ry in the Wife, when Wit doth dote :
Since all the power thereof it doth apply,
To proue by Wit, worth in ſimplicitie.

Enter Boyet.

Qu. Heere comes *Boyet*, and mirth in his face.

Boy. O I am ſtab'd with laughter, Wher's her Grace?

Qu. Thy newes *Boyet*?

Boy. Prepare Madame, prepare.
Arme Wenches arme, incounters mounted are,
Againſt your Peace, Loue doth approach, diſguis'd :
Armed in arguments, you'll be ſurpriz'd.
Muſter your Wits, ſtand in your owne defence,
Or hide your heads like Cowards, and flie hence.

Qu. Saint *Dennis* to S. *Cupid* : What are they,
That charge their breath ag ·ſt vs ? Say ſcout ſay.

Boy. Vnder the coole ſh de of a Siccamore,
I thought to cloſe mine eye ſome halfe an houre :
When lo to interrupt my purpos'd reſt,
Toward that ſhade I might behold addreſt,
The King and his companions : warely
I ſtole into a neighbour thicket by,
And ouer-heard, what you ſhall ouer-heare :
That by and by diſguis'd they will be heere.
Their Herald is a pretty knauiſh Page :
That well by heart hath con'd his embaſſage,
Action and accent did they teach him there.
Thus muſt thou ſpeake, and thus thy body beare.
And euer and anon they made a doubt,
Preſence maieſticall would put him out :
For quoth the King, an Angell ſhalt thou ſee :
Yet feare not thou, but ſpeake audaciouſly.
The Boy reply'd, An Angell is not euill :
I ſhould haue fear'd her, had ſhe beene a deuill.
With that all laugh'd, and clap'd him on the ſhoulder,
Making the bold wagg by their praiſes bolder.
One rub'd his elboe thus, and fleer'd, and ſwore,
A better ſpeech was neuer ſpoke before.
Another with his finger and his thumb,
Cry'd *via*, we will doo't, come what will come.
The third he caper'd and cried, All goes well.
The fourth turn'd on the toe, and downe he fell :
With that they all did tumble on the ground,
With ſuch a zelous laughter ſo profound,
That in this ſpleene ridiculous appeares,
To checke their folly paſſions ſolemne teares.

Quee. But what, but what, come they to viſit vs ?

Boy. They do, they do ; and are apparel'd thus,
Like *Muſcouites*, or *Ruſſians*, as I geſſe.
Their purpoſe is to parlee, to court, and dance,

And euery one his Loue-feat will aduance,
Vnto his ſeuerall Miſtreſſe: which they'll know
By fauours ſeuerall, which they did beſtow.
  Queen. And will they ſo? the Gallants ſhall be taskt:
For Ladies; we will euery one be maskt,
And not a man of them ſhall haue the grace
Deſpight of ſute, to ſee a Ladies face.
Hold *Roſaline,* this Fauour thou ſhalt weare,
And then the King will court thee for his Deare:
Hold, take thou this my ſweet, and giue me thine,
So ſhall *Berowne* take me for *Roſaline.*
And change your Fauours too, ſo ſhall your Loues
Woo contrary, deceiu'd by theſe remoues.
  Roſa. Come on then, weare the fauours moſt in ſight.
  Kath. But in this changing, What is your intent?
  Queen. The effect of my intent is to croſſe theirs:
They doe it but in mocking merriment,
And mocke for mocke is onely my intent.
Their ſeuerall counſels they vnboſome ſhall,
To Loues miſtooke, and ſo be mockt withall.
Vpon the next occaſion that we meete,
With Viſages diſplayd to talke and greete.
  Roſ. But ſhall we dance, if they deſire vs too't?
  Quee. No, to the death we will not moue a foot,
Nor to their pen'd ſpeech render we no grace:
But while 'tis ſpoke, each turne away his face.
  Boy. Why that contempt will kill the keepers heart,
And quite diuorce his memory from his part.
  Quee. Therefore I doe it, and I make no doubt,
The reſt will ere come in, if he be out.
Theres no ſuch ſport, as ſport by ſport orethrowne:
To make theirs ours, and ours none but our owne.
So ſhall we ſtay mocking entended game,
And they well mockt, depart away with ſhame.   *Sound.*
  Boy. The Trompet ſounds, be maskt, the maskers
come.

*Enter Black moores with muſicke, the Boy with a ſpeech,
and the reſt of the Lords diſguiſed.*

  Page. All haile, the richeſt Beauties on the earth.
  Ber. Beauties no richer then rich Taffata.
  *Pag. A holy parcell of the faireſt dames that euer turn'd
their backes to mortall viewes.*
      The Ladies turne their backes to him.
  Ber. Their eyes villaine, their eyes.
  Pag. That euer turn'd their eyes to mortall viewes.
Out
  Boy. True, out indeed.
  *Pag. Out of your fauours heauenly ſpirits vouchſafe
Not to beholde.*
  Ber. Once to behold, rogue.
  *Pag. Once to behold with your Sunne beamed eyes,
With your Sunne beamed eyes.*
  Boy. They will not anſwer to that Epythite,
You were beſt call it Daughter beamed eyes.
  Pag. They do not marke me, and that brings me out.
  Bero. Is this your perfeĉtneſſe? be gon you rogue.
  Roſa. What would theſe ſtrangers?
Know their mindes *Boyet.*
If they doe ſpeake our language, 'tis our will
That ſome plaine man recount their purpoſes.
Know what they would?
  Boyet. What would you with the Princes?
  Ber. Nothing but peace, and gentle viſitation.
  Roſ. What would they, ſay they?

  Boy. Nothing but peace, and gentle viſitation.
  Roſa. Why that they haue, and bid them ſo be gon.
  Boy. She ſaies you haue it, and you may be gon.
  Kin. Say to her we haue meaſur'd many miles,
To tread a Meaſure with you on the graſſe.
  Boy. They ſay that they haue meaſur'd many a mile,
To tread a Meaſure with you on this graſſe.
  Roſa. It is not ſo. Aske them how many inches
Is in one mile? If they haue meaſur'd manie,
The meaſure then of one is eaſlie told.
  Boy. If to come hither, you haue meaſur'd miles,
And many miles: the Princeſſe bids you tell,
How many inches doth fill vp one mile?
  Ber. Tell her we meaſure them by weary ſteps.
  Boy. She heares her ſelfe.
  Roſa. How manie wearie ſteps,
Of many wearie miles you haue ore-gone,
Are numbred in the trauell of one mile?
  Bero. We number nothing that we ſpend for you,
Our dutie is ſo rich, ſo infinite,
That we may doe it ſtill without accompt.
Vouchſafe to ſhew the ſunſhine of your face,
That we (like ſauages) may worſhip it.
  Roſa. My face is but a Moone, and clouded too.
  Kin. Bleſſed are clouds, to doe as ſuch clouds do.
Vouchſafe bright Moone, and theſe thy ſtars to ſhine,
(Thoſe clouds remooued) vpon our waterie eyne.
  Roſa. O vaine peticioner, beg a greater matter,
Thou now requeſts but Mooneſhine in the water.
  Kin. Then in our meaſure, vouchſafe but one change.
Thou bidſt me begge, this begging is not ſtrange.
  Roſa. Play muſicke then: nay you muſt doe it ſoone.
Not yet nor dance: thus change I like the Moone.
  Kin. Will you not dance? How come you thus e-
ſtranged?
  Roſa. You tooke the Moone at full, but now ſhee's
changed?
  Kin. Yet ſtill ſhe is the Moone, and I the Man.
  Roſa. The muſick playes, vouchſafe ſome motion to
it: Our eares vouchſafe it.
  Kin. But your legges ſhould doe it.
  Roſ. Since you are ſtrangers, & come here by chance,
Wee'll not be nice, take hands, we will not dance.
  Kin. Why take you hands then?
  Roſa. Onelie to part friends.
Curtſie ſweet hearts, and ſo the Meaſure ends.
  Kin. More meaſure of this meaſure, be not nice.
  Roſa. We can afford no more at ſuch a price.
  Kin. Priſe your ſelues: What buyes your companie?
  Roſa. Your abſence onelie.
  Kin. That can neuer be.
  Roſa. Then cannot we be bought: and ſo adue,
Twice to your Viſore, and halfe once to you.
  Kin. If you denie to dance, let's hold more chat.
  Roſ. In priuate then.
  Kin. I am beſt pleas'd with that.
  Be. White handed Miſtris, one ſweet word with thee.
  Qu. Hony, and Milke, and Suger: there is three.
  Ber. Nay then two treyes, an if you grow ſo nice
Methegline, Wort, and Malmſey; well runne dice:
There's halfe a dozen ſweets.
  Qu. Seuenth ſweet adue, ſince you can cogg,
Ile play no more with you.
  Ber. One word in ſecret.
  Qu. Let it not be ſweet.
  Ber. Thou greeu'ſt my gall.
                                          Queen,

Qu. Gall, bitter.
Ber. Therefore meete.
Du. Will you vouchfafe with me to change a word?
Mar. Name it.
Dum. Faire Ladie.
Mar. Say you fo? Faire Lord:
Take you that for your faire Lady.
Du. Pleafe it you,
As much in priuate, and Ile bid adieu.
Mar. What, was your vizard made without a tong?
Long. I know the reafon Ladie why you aske.
Mar. O for your reafon, quickly fir, I long.
Long. You haue a double tongue within your mask.
And would affoord my fpeechleffe vizard halfe.
Mar. Veale quoth the Dutch-man: is not Veale a
Calfe?
Long. A Calfe faire Ladie?
Mar. No, a faire Lord Calfe.
Long. Let's part the word.
Mar. No, Ile not be your halfe:
Take all and weane it, it may proue an Oxe.
Long. Looke how you but your felfe in thefe fharpe
mockes.
Will you giue hornes chaft Ladie? Do not fo.
Mar. Then die a Calfe before your horns do grow.
Lon. One word in priuate with you ere I die.
Mar. Bleat foftly then, the Butcher heares you cry.
Boyet. The tongues of mocking wenches are as keen
As is the Razors edge, inuifible:
Cutting a fmaller haire then may be feene,
Aboue the fenfe of fence fo fenfible:
Seemeth their conference, their conceits haue wings,
Fleeter then arrows, bullets wind, thoght, fwifter things
Rofa. Not one word more my maides, breake off,
breake off.
Ber. By heauen, all drie beaten with pure fcoffe.
King. Farewell madde Wenches, you haue fimple
wits. *Exeunt.*
Qu. Twentie adieus my frozen Mufcouits.
Are thefe the breed of wits fo wondred at?
Boyet. Tapers they are, with your fweete breathes
puft out.
Rofa. Wel-liking wits they haue, groffe, groffe, fat, fat.
Qu. O pouertie in wit, Kingly poore flout.
Will they not (thinke you) hang themfelues to night?
Or euer but in vizards fhew their faces:
This pert *Berowne* was out of count'nance quite.
Rofa. They were all in lamentable cafes.
The King was vveeping ripe for a good word.
Qu. *Berowne* did fweare himfelfe out of all fuite.
Mar. Dumaine was at my feruice, and his fword:
No point (quoth I:) my feruant ftraight vvas mute.
Ka. Lord *Longauill* faid I came ore his hart:
And trow you vvhat he call'd me?
Qu. Qualme perhaps.
Kat. Yes in good faith.
Qu. Go fickneffe as thou art.
Rof. Well, better wits haue worne plain ftatute caps,
But vvil you heare; the King is my loue fworne.
Qu. And quicke *Berowne* hath plighted faith to me.
Kat. And *Longauill* was for my feruice borne.
Mar. *Dumaine* is mine as fure as barke on tree.
Boyet. Madam, and prettie miftreffes glue eare,
Immediately they will againe be heere
In their owne fhapes: for it can neuer be,
They will digeft this harfh indignitie.

Qu. Will they returne?
Boy. They will they will, God knowes,
And leape for ioy, though they are lame with blowes:
Therefore change Fauours, and when they repaire,
Blow like fweet Rofes, in this fummer aire.
Qu. How blovv? how blovv? Speake to bee vnder-
ftood.
Boy. Faire Ladies maskt, are Rofes in their bud:
Difmaskt, their damaske fweet commixture fhowne,
Are Angels vailing clouds, or Rofes blowne.
Qu. Auant perplexitie: What fhall vve do,
If they returne in their owne fhapes to wo?
Rofa. Good Madam, if by me you'l be aduis'd,
Let's mocke them ftill as well knowne as difguis'd:
Let vs complaine to them vvhat fooles were heare,
Difguis'd like Mufcouites in fhapeleffe geare:
And wonder what they were, and to what end
Their fhallow fhowes, and Prologue vildely pen'd:
And their rough carriage fo ridiculous,
Should be prefented at our Tent to vs.
Boyet. Ladies, withdraw: the gallants are at hand.
Quee. Whip to our Tents, as Roes runnes ore Land.
Exeunt.

Enter the King and the reft.

King. Faire fir, God faue you. Wher's the Princeffe?
Boy. Gone to her Tent.
Pleafe it your Maieftie command me any feruice to her?
King. That fhe vouchfafe me audience for one word.
Boy. I will, and fo will fhe, I know my Lord. *Exit.*
Ber. This fellow pickes vp wit as Pigeons peafe,
And vtters it againe, when *Ioue* doth pleafe.
He is Wits Pedler, and retailes his Wares,
At Wakes, and Waffels, Meetings, Markets, Faires.
And we that fell by groffe, the Lord doth know,
Haue not the grace to grace it with fuch fhow.
This Gallant pins the Wenches on his fleeue.
Had he bin *Adam*, he had tempted *Eua*.
He can carue too, and lifpe: Why this is he,
That kift away his hand in courtefie.
This is the Ape of Forme, Monfieur the nice,
That when he plaies at Tables, chides the Dice
In honorable tearmes: Nay he can fing
A meane moft meanly, and in Vfhering
Mend him who can: the Ladies call him fweete.
The ftaires as he treads on them kiffe his feete.
This is the flower that fmiles on euerie one,
To fhew his teeth as white as Whales bone.
And confciences that wil not die in debt,
Pay him the dutie of honie-tongued *Boyet.*
King. A blifter on his fweet tongue with my hart,
That put *Armatbees* Page out of his part.

Enter the Ladies.

Ber. See where it comes. Behauiour what wer't thou,
Till this madman fhew'd thee? And what art thou now?
King. All haile fweet Madame, and faire time of day.
Qu. Faire in all Haile is foule, as I conceiue.
King. Conftrue my fpeeches better, if you may.
Qu. Then wifh me better, I wil giue you leaue.
King. We came to vifit you, and purpofe now
To leade you to our Court, vouchfafe it then.
Qu. This field fhal hold me, and fo hold your vow:
Nor God, nor I, delights in periur'd men.
King. Rebuke me not for that which you prouoke:
The

The vertue of your eie muſt breake my oth.

Qu. You nickname vertue: vice you ſhould haue ſpoke:
For vertues office neuer breakes men troth,
Now by my maiden honor, yet as pure
As the vnſallied Lilly, I proteſt,
A world of torments though I ſhould endure,
I would not yeeld to be your houſes gueſt :
So much I hate a breaking cauſe to be
Of heauenly oaths, vow'd with integritie.

Kin. O you haue liu'd in deſolation heere,
Vnſeene, vnuiſited, much to our ſhame.

Qu. Not ſo my Lord, it is not ſo I ſweare,
We haue had paſtimes heere, and pleaſant game,
A meſſe of Ruſſians left vs but of late.

Kin. How Madam? Ruſſians?

Qu. I in truth, my Lord.
Trim gallants, full of Courtſhip and of ſtate.

Roſa. Madam ſpeake true. It is not ſo my Lord :
My Ladie (to the manner of the daies)
In curteſie giues vndeſeruing praiſe.
We foure indeed confronted were with foure
In Ruſſia habit : Heere the⁀ yed an houre,
And talk'd apace : and in that houre (my Lord)
They did not bleſſe vs with one happy word.
I dare not call them fooles ; but this I thinke,
When they are thirſtie, fooles would faine haue drinke.

Ber. This ieſt is drie to me. Gentle ſweete,
Your wits makes wiſe things fooliſh when we greete
With eies beſt ſeeing, heauens fierie eie :
By light we looſe light ; your capacitie
Is of that nature, that to your huge ſtoore,
Wiſe things ſeeme fooliſh, and rich things but poore.

Roſ. This proues you wiſe and rich : for in my eie

Ber. I am a foole, and full of pouertie.

Roſ. But that you take what doth to you belong,
It were a fault to ſnatch words from my tongue.

Ber. O, I am yours, and all that I poſſeſſe.

Roſ. All the foole mine.

Ber. I cannot giue you leſſe.

Roſ. Which of the Vizards what it that you wore?

Ber. Where? when? What Vizard?
Why demand you this?

Roſ. There, then, that vizard, that ſuperfluous caſe,
That hid the worſe, and ſhew'd the better face.

Kin. We are diſcried,
They'l mocke vs now downeright.

Du. Let vs confeſſe, and turne it to a ieſt.

Que. Amaz'd my Lord? Why lookes your Highnes
ſadde?

Roſa. Helpe hold his browes, hee'l ſound: why looke
you pale?
Sea-ſicke I thinke comming from Muſcouie.

Ber. Thus poure the ſtars down plagues for periury.
Can any face of braſſe hold longer out?
Heere ſtand I, Ladie dart thy skill at me,
Bruiſe me with ſcorne, confound me with a flout.
Thruſt thy ſharpe wit quite through my ignorance.
Cut me to peeces with thy keene conceit :
And I will wiſh thee neuer more to dance,
Nor neuer more in Ruſſian habit waite.
O! neuer will I truſt to ſpeeches pen'd,
Nor to the motion of a Schoole-boies tongue.
Nor neuer come in vizard to my friend,
Nor woo in rime like a blind-harpers ſongue.
Taffata phraſes, ſilken tearmes preciſe,
Three-pil'd Hyperboles, ſpruce affection ;

Figures pedanticall, theſe ſummer flies,
Haue blowne me full of maggot oſtentation.
I do forſweare them, and I heere proteſt,
By this white Gloue (how white the hand God knows)
Henceforth my woing minde ſhall be expreſt
In ruſſet yeas, and honeſt kerſie noes.
And to begin Wench, ſo God helpe me law,
My loue to thee is ſound, ſans cracke or flaw.

Roſa. Sans, ſans, I pray you.

Ber. Yet I haue a tricke
Of the old rage : beare with me, I am ſicke.
Ile leaue it by degrees : ſoft, let vs ſee,
Write *Lord haue mercie on vs,* on thoſe three,
They are infected, in their hearts it lies :
They haue the plague, and caught it of your eyes :
Theſe Lords are viſited, you are not free :
For the Lords tokens on you do I ſee.

Qu. No, they are free that gaue theſe tokens to vs.

Ber. Our ſtates are forfeit, ſeeke not to vndo vs.

Roſ. It is not ſo ; for how can this be true,
That you ſtand forfeit, being thoſe that ſue.

Ber. Peace, for I will not haue to do with you.

Roſ. Nor ſhall not, if I do as I intend.

Ber. Speake for your ſelues, my wit is at an end.

King. Teach vs ſweete Madame, for our rude tranſgreſſion, ſome faire excuſe.

Qu. The faireſt is confeſſion.
Were you not heere but euen now, diſguis'd?

Kin. Madam, I was.

Qu. And were you well aduis'd?

Kin. I was faire Madam.

Qu. When you then were heere,
What did you whiſper in your Ladies eare?

King. That more then all the world I did reſpect her

Qu. When ſhee ſhall challenge this, you will reiect
her.

King. Vpon mine Honor no.

Qu. Peace, peace, forbeare :
your oath once broke, you force not to forſweare.

King. Deſpiſe me when I breake this oath of mine.

Qu. I will, and therefore keepe it. *Roſaline,*
What did the Ruſſian whiſper in your eare?

Roſ. Madam, he ſwore that he did hold me deare
As precious eye-ſight, and did value me
Aboue this World : adding thereto moreouer,
That he vvould Wed me, or elſe die my Louer.

Qu. God giue thee ioy of him : the Noble Lord
Moſt honorably doth vphold his word.

King. What meane you Madame?
By my life, my troth,
I neuer ſwore this Ladie ſuch an oth.

Roſ. By heauen you did ; and to confirme it plaine,
you gaue me this : But take it ſir againe.

King. My faith and this, the Princeſſe I did giue,
I knew her by this Iewell on her ſleeue.

Qu. Pardon me ſir, this Iewell did ſhe weare,
And Lord *Berowne* (I thanke him) is my deare.
What? Will you haue me, or your Pearle againe?

Ber. Neither of either, I remit both twaine.
I ſee the tricke on't : Heere was a conſent,
Knowing aforehand of our merriment,
To daſh it like a Chriſtmas Comedie.
Some carry-tale, ſome pleaſe-man, ſome ſlight Zanie,
Some mumble-newes, ſome trencher-knight, ſom Dick
That ſmiles his cheeke in yeares, and knowes the trick
To make my Lady laugh, when ſhe's diſpos'd ;

Told

Told our intents before : which once diſclos'd,
The Ladies did change Fauours; and then we
Following the ſignes, woo'd but the ſigne of ſhe.
Now to our periurie, to adde more terror,
We are againe forſworne in will and error.
Much vpon this 'tis : and might not you
Foreſtall our ſport, to make vs thus vntrue ?
Do not you know my Ladies foot by'th ſquier ?
And laugh vpon the apple of her eie ?
And ſtand betweene her backe ſir, and the fire,
Holding a trencher, ieſting merrilie ?
You put our Page out : go, you are alowd.
Die when you will, a ſmocke ſhall be your ſhrowd.
You leere vpon me, do you ? There's an eie
Wounds like a Leaden ſword.

Boy. Full merrily hath this braue manager, this car-
reere bene run.

Ber. Loe, he is tilting ſtraight. Peace, I haue don.

Enter Clowne.

Welcome pure wit, thou part'ſt a faire fray.

Clo. O Lord ſir, they would kno,
Whether the three worthies ſhall come in, or no.

Ber. What, are there but three ?

Clo. No ſir, but it is vara fine,
For euerie one purſents three.

Ber. And three times thrice is nine.

Clo. Not ſo ſir, vnder correction ſir, I hope it is not ſo.
You cannot beg vs ſir, I can aſſure you ſir, we know what
we know : I hope ſir three times thrice ſir.

Ber. Is not nine.

Clo. Vnder correction ſir, wee know where-vntill it
doth amount.

Ber. By Ioue, I alwaies tooke three threes for nine.

Clow. O Lord ſir, it were pittie you ſhould get your
liuing by reckning ſir.

Ber. How much is it ?

Clo. O Lord ſir, the parties themſelues, the actors ſir
will ſhew where-vntill it doth amount : for mine owne
part, I am (as they ſay, but to perfect one man in one
poore man) *Pompion* the great ſir.

Ber. Art thou one of the Worthies ?

Clo. It pleaſed them to thinke me worthie of *Pompey*
the great : for mine owne part, I know not the degree of
the Worthie, but I am to ſtand for him.

Ber. Go, bid them prepare.   *Exit.*

Clo. We will turne it finely off ſir, we wil take ſome
care.

King. *Berowne*, they will ſhame vs :
Let them not approach.

Ber. We are ſhame-proofe my Lord : and 'tis ſome
policie, to haue one ſhew worſe then the Kings and his
companie.

Kin. I ſay they ſhall not come.

Qu. Nay my good Lord, let me ore-rule you now;
That ſport beſt pleaſes, that doth leaſt know how.
Where Zeale ſtriues to content, and the contents
Dies in the Zeale of that which it preſents :
Their forme confounded, makes moſt forme in mirth,
When great things labouring periſh in their birth.

Ber. A right deſcription of our ſport my Lord.

Enter Braggart.

Brag. Annointed, I implore ſo much expence of thy

royall ſweet breath, as will vtter a brace of words.

Qu. Doth this man ſerue God ?

Ber. Why aske you ?

Qu. He ſpeak's not like a man of God's making.

Brag. That's all one my faire ſweet honie Monarch:
For I proteſt, the Schoolmaſter is exceeding fantaſticall:
Too too vaine, too too vaine. But we wil put it (as they
ſay) to *Fortuna delaguar*, I wiſh you the peace of minde
moſt royall cupplement.

King. Here is like to be a good preſence of Worthies;
He preſents *Hector* of Troy, the Swaine *Pompey* ẙ great,
the Pariſh Curate *Alexander*, *Armadoes* Page *Hercules*,
the Pedant *Iudas Machabeus* : And if theſe foure Worthies in their firſt ſhew thriue, theſe foure will change
habites, and preſent the other fiue.

Ber. There is fiue in the firſt ſhew.

Kin. You are deceiued, tis not ſo.

Ber. The Pedant, the Braggart, the Hedge-Prieſt, the
Foole, and the Boy,
Abate throw at Novum, and the whole world againe,
Cannot pricke out fiue ſuch, take each one in's vaine.

Kin. The ſhip is vnder ſaile, and here ſhe coms amain.

Enter Pompey.

Clo. I *Pompey* am.

Ber. You lie, you are not he.

Clo. I *Pompey* am.

Boy. With Libbards head on knee.

Ber. Well ſaid old mocker,
I muſt needs be friends with thee.

Clo. I *Pompey* am, *Pompey ſurnam'd the big.*

Du. The great.

Clo. It is great ſir : *Pompey ſurnam'd the great :*
That oft in field, with Targe and Shield,
did make my foe to ſweat :
And trauailing along this coaſt, I heere am come by chance,
And lay my Armes before the legs of this ſweet Laſſe of
France.
If your Ladiſhip would ſay thankes *Pompey*, I had done.

La. Great thankes great *Pompey*.

Clo. Tis not ſo much worth : but I hope I was perfect. I made a little fault in great.

Ber. My hat to a halfe-penie, *Pompey* prooues the
beſt Worthie.

Enter Curate for Alexander.

Curat. *When in the world I liu'd, I was the worldes Com-*
mander :
By Eaſt, Weſt, North, & South, I ſpred my conquering might
My Scutcheon plaine declares that I am Aliſander.

Boiet. Your noſe ſaies no, you are not :
For it ſtands too right.

Ber. Your noſe ſmels no, in this moſt tender ſmelling Knight.

Qu. The Conqueror is diſmaid :
Proceede good *Alexander.*

Cur. *When in the world I liued, I was the worldes Com-*
mander.

Boiet. Moſt true, 'tis right : you were ſo *Aliſander.*

Ber. *Pompey* the great.

Clo. your ſeruant and *Coſtard.*

Ber. Take away the Conqueror, take away *Aliſander.*

Clo. O ſir, you haue ouerthrowne *Aliſander* the conqueror : you will be ſcrap'd out of the painted cloth for
this.

this : your Lion that holds his Pollax fitting on a clofe
ftoole, will be giuen to Aiax. He will be the ninth worthie. A Conqueror, and affraid to fpeake? Runne away
for fhame *Alifander.* There an't fhall pleafe you : a foolifh milde man, an honeft man, looke you, & foon dafht.
He is a maruellous good neighbour infooth, and a verie
good Bowler : but for *Alifander,* alas you fee, how 'tis a
little ore-parted. But there are Worthies a comming,
will fpeake their minde in fome other fort.   *Exit Cu.*
Qu. Stand afide good Pompey.

Enter Pedant for Iudas, and the Boy for Hercules.

Ped. Great *Hercules* is prefented by this Impe,
Whofe Club kil'd *Cerberus* that three-headed *Canus,*
And when he was a babe, a childe, a fhrimpe,
Thus did he ftrangle Serpents in his *Manus* :
Quoniam, he feemeth in minoritie,
Ergo, I come with this Apologie.
Keepe fome ftate in thy *exit,* and vanifh.   *Exit Boy*
Ped. Iudas *I am.*
Dum. A Iudas?
Ped. Not *Ifcariot fir.*
Iudas I am, ycliped Machabeus.
Dum. Iudas Machabeus clipt, is plaine Iudas.
Ber. A kiffing traitor. How art thou prou'd *Iudas?*
Ped. Iudas I am.
Dum. The more fhame for you *Iudas.*
Ped. What meane you fir?
Boi. To make *Iudas* hang himfelfe.
Ped. Begin fir, you are my elder.
Ber. Well follow'd, *Iudas* was hang'd on an Elder.
Ped. I will not be put out of countenance.
Ber. Becaufe thou haft no face.
Ped. What is this?
Boi. A Citterne head.
Dum. The head of a bodkin.
Ber. A deaths face in a ring.
Lon. The face of an old Roman coine, fcarce feene.
Boi. The pummell of *Cæfars* Faulchion.
Dum. The caru'd-bone face on a Flaske.
Ber. S.Georges halfe cheeke in a brooch.
Dum. I, and in a brooch of Lead.
Ber. I, and worne in the cap of a Tooth-drawer.
And now forward, for we haue put thee in countenance
Ped. You haue put me out of countenance.
Ber. Falfe, we haue giuen thee faces.
Ped. But you haue out-fac'd them all.
Ber. And thou wer't a Lion, we would do fo.
Boy. Therefore as he is, an Affe, let him go :
And fo adieu fweet *Iude.* Nay, why doft thou ftay?
Dum. For the latter end of his name.
Ber. For the *Affe* to the *Iude :* giue it him.   *Iud-as* a-
way.
Ped. This is not generous, not gentle, not humble.
Boy. A light for monfieur *Iudas,* it growes darke, he
may ftumble.
Que. Alas poore *Machabeus,* how hath hee beene
baited.

Enter Braggart.

Ber. Hide thy head *Achilles,* heere comes *Hector* in
Armes.
Dum. Though my mockes come home by me, I will
now be merrie.
King. Hector was but a Troyan in refpect of this.

Boi. But is this *Hector?*
Kin. I thinke *Hector* was not fo cleane timber'd.
Lon. His legge is too big for *Hector.*
Dum. More Calfe certaine.
Boi. No, he is beft indued in the fmall.
Ber. This cannot be *Hector.*
Dum. He's a God or a Painter, for he makes faces.
Brag. The Armipotent Mars, of Launces the almighty,
gaue Hector *a gift.*
Dum. A gilt Nutmegge.
Ber. A Lemmon.
Lon. Stucke with Cloues.
Dum. No clouen.
Brag. The Armipotent Mars of Launces the almighty,
Gaue Hector a gift, the heire of Illion ;
A man fo breathed, that certaine he would fight : yea
From morne till night, out of his Pauillion.
I am that Flower.
Dum. That Mint.
Long. That Cullambine.
Brag. Sweet Lord *Longauill* reine thy tongue.
Lon. I muft rather giue it the reine : for it runnes a-
gainft *Hector.*
Dum. I, and *Hector's* a Grey-hound.
Brag. The fweet War-man is dead and rotten,
Sweet chuckes, beat not the bones of the buried :
But I will forward with my deuice ;
Sweet Royaltie beftow on me the fence of hearing.

Berowne fteppes forth.

Qu. Speake braue *Hector,* we are much delighted.
Brag. I do adore thy fweet Graces flipper.
Boy. Loues her by the foot.
Dum. He may not by the yard.
Brag. This Hector farre furmounted Hanniball.
The partie is gone.
Clo. Fellow *Hector,* fhe is gone ; fhe is two moneths
on her way.
Brag. What meaneft thou?
Clo. Faith vnleffe you play the honeft Troyan, the
poore Wench is caft away: fhe's quick, the child brags
in her belly alreadie : tis yours.
Brag. Doft thou infamonize me among Potentates?
Thou fhalt die.
Clo. Then fhall Hector be whipt for *Iaquenetta* that
is quicke by him, and hang'd for *Pompey,* that is dead by
him.
Dum. Moft rare *Pompey.*
Boi. Renowned *Pompey.*
Ber. Greater then great, great, great, great *Pompey :*
Pompey the huge.
Dum. Hector trembles.
Ber. Pompey is moued, more Atees more Atees ftirre
them, or ftirre them on.
Dum. Hector will challenge him.
Ber. I, if a'haue no more mans blood in's belly, then
will fup a Flea.
Brag. By the North-pole I do challenge thee.
Clo. I wil not fight with a pole like a Northern man;
Ile flafh, Ile do it by the fword : I pray you let mee bor-
row my Armes againe.
Dum. Roome for the incenfed Worthies.
Clo. Ile do it in my fhirt.
Dum. Moft refolute *Pompey.*
Page. Mafter, let me take you a button hole lower :
Do you not fee Pompey is vncafing for the combat: what
meane

meane you? you will lofe your reputation.

Brag. Gentlemen and Souldiers pardon me, I will not combat in my fhirt.

Du. You may not denie it, *Pompey* hath made the challenge.

Brag. Sweet bloods, I both may, and will .

Ber. What reafon haue you for't?

Brag. The naked truth of it is, I haue no fhirt, I go woolward for penance.

Boy. True, and it was inioyned him in *Rome* for want of Linnen : fince when, Ile be fworne he wore none, but a difhclout of *Iaquenetta*, and that hee weares next his heart for a fauour.

Enter a Meffenger, Monfieur Marcade.

Mar. God faue you Madame.

Qu. Welcome *Marcade*, but that thou interrupteft our merriment.

Marc. I am forrie Madam, for the newes I bring is heauie in my tongue. The King your father

Qu. Dead for my life.

Mar. Euen fo : My tale is told.

Ber. Worthies away, the Scene begins to cloud.

Brag. For mine owne part, I breath free breath : I haue feene the day of wrong, through the little hole of difcretion, and I will right my felfe like a Souldier.

Exeunt Worthies

Kin. How fare's your Maieftie?

Qu. *Boyet* prepare, I will away to night.

Kin. Madame not fo, I do befeech you ftay.

Qu. Prepare I fay. I thanke you gracious Lords For all your faire endeuours and entreats : Out of a new fad-foule, that you vouchfafe, In your rich wifedome to excufe, or hide, The liberall oppofition of our fpirits, If ouer-boldly we haue borne our felues, In the conuerfe of breath (your gentlenefse Was guiltie of it.) Farewell worthie Lord : A heauie heart beares not a humble tongue. Excufe me fo, comming fo fhort of thankes, For my great fuite, fo eafily obtain'd.

Kin. The extreme parts of time, extremelie formes All caufes to the purpofe of his fpeed : And often at his verie loofe decides That, which long procefse could not arbitrate. And though the mourning brow of progenie Forbid the fmiling curtefie of Loue : The holy fuite which faine it would conuince, Yet fince loues argument was firft on foote, Let not the cloud of forrow iuftle it From what it purpos'd : fince to waile friends loft, Is not by much fo wholfome profitable, As to reioyce at friends but newly found.

Qu. I vnderftand you not, my greefes are double.

Ber. Honeft plain words, beft pierce the ears of griefe And by thefe badges vnderftand the King, For your faire fakes haue we negleated time, Plaid foule play with our oaths: your beautie Ladies Hath much deformed vs, fafhioning our humors Euen to the oppofed end of our intents : And what in vs hath feem'd ridiculous : As Loue is full of vnbefitting ftraines, All wanton as a childe, skipping and vaine. Form'd by the eie, and therefore like the eie. Full of ftraying fhapes, of habits, and of formes

Varying in fubieets as the eie doth roule, To euerie varied obieet in his glance : Which partie-coated prefence of loofe loue Put on by vs, if in your heauenly eies, Haue misbecom'd our oathes and grauities. Thofe heauenlie eies that looke into thefe faults, Suggefted vs to make : therefore Ladies Our loue being yours, the error that Loue makes Is likewife yonrs. We to our felues proue falfe, By being once falfe, for euer to be true To thofe that make vs both, faire Ladies you. And euen that falfhood in it felfe a finne, Thus purifies it felfe, and turnes to grace.

Qu. We haue receiu'd your Letters, full of Loue: Your Fauours, the Ambaffadors of Loue. And in our maiden counfaile rated them, At courtfhip, pleafant ieft, and curtefie, As bumbaft and as lining to the time: But more deuout then thefe are our refpeets Haue we not bene, and therefore met your loues In their owne fafhion, like a merriment.

Du. Our letters Madam, fhew'd much more then ieft.

Lon. So did our lookes.

Rofa. We did not coat them fo.

Kin. Now at the lateft minute of the houre, Grant vs your loues.

Qu. A time me thinkes too fhort, To make a world-without-end bargaine in ; No, no my Lord, your Grace is periur'd much, Full of deare guiltineffe, and therefore this : If for my Loue (as there is no fuch caufe) You will do ought, this fhall you do for me. Your oth I will not truft: but go with fpeed To fome forlorne and naked Hermitage, Remote from all the pleafures of the world : There ftay, vntill the twelue Celeftiall Signes Haue brought about their annuall reckoning. If this aufteere infociable life, Change not your offer made in heate of blood : If frofts, and fafts, hard lodging, and thin weeds Nip not the gaudie bloffomes of your Loue, But that it beare this triall, and laft loue : Then at the expiration of the yeare, Come challenge me, challenge me by thefe deferts, And by this Virgin palme, now kiffing thine, I will be thine : and till that inftant fhut My wofull felfe vp in a mourning houfe, Raining the teares of lamentation, For the remembrance of my Fathers death. If this thou do denie, let our hands part, Neither intitled in the others hart.

Kin. If this, or more then this, I would denie, To flatter vp thefe powers of mine with reft, The fodaine hand of death clofe vp mine eie. Hence euer then, my heart is in thy breft.

Ber. And what to me my Loue? and what to me ?

Rof. You muft be purged too, your fins are rack'd. You are attaint with faults and periurie : Therefore if you my fauor meane to get, A tweluemonth fhall you fpend, and neuer reft, But feeke the wearie beds of people ficke.

Du. But what to me my loue? but what to me ?

Kat. A wife? a beard, faire health, and honeftie, With three-fold loue, I wifh you all thefe three.

Du. O fhall I fay, I thanke you gentle wife?

Kat. Not fo my Lord, a tweluemonth and a day,

Ile

Ile marke no words that ſmoothfac'd wooers ſay.
Come when the King doth to my Ladie come :
Then if I haue much loue, Ile giue you ſome.
Dum. Ile ſerue thee true and faithfully till then.
Kath. Yet ſweare not, leaſt ye be forſworne agen.
Lon. What ſaies *Maria?*
Mari. At the tweluemonths end,
Ile change my blacke Gowne, for a faithfull friend.
Lon. Ile ſtay with patience : but the time is long.
Mari. The liker you, few taller are ſo yong.
Ber. Studies my Ladie? Miſtreſſe, looke on me,
Behold the window of my heart, mine eie :
What humble ſuite attends thy anſwer there,
Impoſe ſome ſeruice on me for my loue.
Roſ. Oft haue I heard of you my Lord *Berowne,*
Before I ſaw you : and the worlds large tongue
Proclaimes you for a man replete with mockes,
Full of compariſons, and wounding floutes :
Which you on all eſtates will execute,
That lie within the mercie of your wit.
To weed this Wormewood from your fruitfull braine,
And therewithall to win me, if you pleaſe,
Without the which I am not to be won :
You ſhall this tweluemonth terme from day to day,
Viſite the ſpeechleſſe ſicke, and ſtill conuerſe
With groaning wretches : and your taske ſhall be,
With all the fierce endeuour of your wit,
To enforce the pained impotent to ſmile.
Ber. To moue wilde laughter in the throate of death ?
It cannot be, it is impoſſible.
Mirth cannot moue a ſoule in agonie.
Roſ. Why that's the way to choke a gibing ſpirit,
Whoſe influence is begot of that looſe grace,
Which ſhallow laughing hearers giue to fooles :
A ieſts proſperitie, lies in the eare
Of him that heares it, neuer in the tongue
Of him that makes it : then, if ſickly eares,
Deaft with the clamors of their owne deare grones,
Will heare your idle ſcornes; continue then,
And I will haue you, and that fault withall.
But if they will not, throw away that ſpirit,
And I ſhal finde you emptie of that fault,
Right ioyfull of your reformation.
Ber. A tweluemonth? Well : befall what will befall,
Ile ieſt a tweluemonth in an Hoſpitall.
Qu. I ſweet my Lord, and ſo I take my leaue.
King. No Madam, we will bring you on your way.
Ber. Our woing doth not end like an old Play:
Iacke hath not Gill : theſe Ladies courteſie
Might wel haue made our ſport a Comedie.
Kin. Come ſir, it wants a tweluemonth and a day,
And then 'twil end.
Ber. That's too long for a play.

Enter Braggart.
Brag. Sweet Maieſty vouchſafe me.
Qu. Was not that Hector ?
Dum. The worthie Knight of Troy.
Brag. I wil kiſſe thy royal finger, and take leaue.
I am a Votarie, I haue vow'd to *Iaquenetta* to holde the

Plough for her ſweet loue three yeares. But moſt eſteemed greatneſſe, wil you heare the Dialogue that the two
Learned men haue compiled, in praiſe of the Owle and
the Cuckow? It ſhould haue followed in the end of our
ſhew.
Kin. Call them forth quickely, we will do ſo.
Brag. Holla, Approach.

Enter all.
This ſide is *Hiems,* Winter.
This *Ver,* the Spring : the one maintained by the Owle,
Th'other by the Cuckow.
Ver, begin.

The Song.

When Daſies pied, and Violets blew,
And Cuckow-buds of yellow hew :
And Ladie-ſmockes all ſiluer white,
Do paint the Medowes with delight.
The Cuckow then on euerie tree,
Mockes married men, for thus ſings he,
Cuckow.
Cuckow, Cuckow : O word of feare,
Vnpleaſing to a married eare.

When Shepheards pipe on Oaten ſtrawes,
And merrie Larkes are Ploughmens clockes :
When Turtles tread, and Rookes and Dawes,
And Maidens bleach their ſummer ſmockes :
The Cuckow then on euerie tree
Mockes married men ; for thus ſings he,
Cuckow.
Cuckow, Cuckow : O word of feare,
Vnpleaſing to a married eare.

Winter.
When Iſicles hang by the wall,
And Dicke the Sphepheard blowes his naile ;
And Tom beares Logges into the hall,
And Milke comes frozen home in paile :
When blood is nipt, and waies be fowle,
Then nightly ſings the ſtaring Owle
Tu-whit to-who.
    A merrie note,
While greaſie Ione doth keele the pot.

When all aloud the winde doth blow,
And coffing drownes the Parſons ſaw :
And birds ſit brooding in the ſnow,
And Marrians noſe lookes red and raw :
When roaſted Crabs hiſſe in the bowle,
Then nightly ſings the ſtaring Owle,
Tu-whit to who :
    A merrie note,
While greaſie Ione doth keele the pot.

Brag. The Words of Mercurie,
Are harſh after the ſongs of Apollo :
You that way ; we this way.
                Exeunt omnes.

FINIS.

A MIDSOMMER Nights Dreame.

Actus primus.

Enter Theseus, Hippolita, with others.

Theseus.

Ow faire Hippolita, our nuptiall houre
Drawes on apace: foure happy daies bring in
Another Moon: but oh, me thinkes, how flow
This old Moon wanes; She lingers my defires
Like to a Step-dame, or a Dowager,
Long withering out a yong mans reuennew.

*Hip.*Foure daies wil quickly fteep thēfelues in nights
Foure nights wil quickly dreame away the time:
And then the Moone, like to a filuer bow,
Now bent in heauen, fhal behold the night
Of our folemnities.

The. Go *Philoftrate,*
Stirre vp the Athenian youth to merriments,
Awake the pert and nimble fpirit of mirth,
Turne melancholy forth to Funerals:
The pale companion is not for our pompe,
Hippolita, I woo'd thee with my fword,
And wonne thy loue, doing thee iniuries:
But I will wed thee in another key,
With pompe, with triumph, and with reuelling.

*Enter Egeus and his daughter Hermia, Lyfander,
and Demetrius.*

Ege. Happy be *Thefeus,* our renowned Duke.

*The.*Thanks good *Egeus*:what's the news with thee?

Ege. Full of vexation, come I, with complaint
Againft my childe, my daughter Hermia.

Stand forth Demetrius.

My Noble Lord,
This man hath my confent to marrie her.

Stand forth Lyfander.

And my gracious Duke,
This man hath bewitch'd the bofome of my childe:
Thou, thou *Lyfander,* thou haft giuen her rimes,
And interchang'd loue-tokens with my childe:
Thou haft by Moone-light at her window fung,
With faining voice, verfes of faining loue,
And ftolne the impreffion of her fantafie,
With bracelets of thy haire, rings, gawdes, conceits,
Knackes, trifles, Nofe-gaies, fweet meats(meffengers
Of ftrong preuailment in vnhardned youth)

With cunning haft thou filch'd my daughters heart,
Turn'd her obedience (which is due to me)
To ftubborne harfhneffe. And my gracious Duke,
Be it fo fhe will not heere before your Grace,
Confent to marrie with *Demetrius,*
I beg the ancient priuiledge of Athens;
As fhe is mine, I may difpofe of her;
Which fhall be either to this Gentleman,
Or to her death, according to our Law,
Immediately prouided in that cafe.

The. What fay you Hermia? be aduis'd faire Maide,
To you your Father fhould be as a God;
One that compos'd your beauties; yea and one
To whom you are but as a forme in waxe
By him imprinted: and within his power,
To leaue the figure, or disfigure it:
Demetrius is a worthy Gentleman.

Her. So is *Lyfander.*

The. In himfelfe he is.
But in this kinde, wanting your fathers voyce.
The other muft be held the worthier.

Her. I would my father look'd but with my eyes.

*The.*Rather your eies muft with his iudgment looke.

Her. I do entreat your Grace to pardon me.
I know not by what power I am made bold,
Nor how it may concerne my modeftie
In fuch a prefence heere to pleade my thoughts:
But I befeech your Grace, that I may know
The worft that may befall me in this cafe,
If I refufe to wed *Demetrius.*

The. Either to dye the death, or to abiure
For euer the fociety of men.
Therefore faire Hermia queftion your defires,
Know of your youth, examine well your blood,
Whether (if you yeeld not to your fathers choice)
You can endure the liuerie of a Nunne,
For aye to be in fhady Cloifter mew'd,
To liue a barren fifter all your life,
Chanting faint hymnes to the cold fruitleffe Moone,
Thrice bleffed they that mafter fo their blood,
To vndergo fuch maiden pilgrimage,
But earthlier happie is the Rofe diftil'd,
Then that which withering on the virgin thorne,
Growes, liues, and dies, in fingle bleffedneffe.

N

Her.

Her. So will I grow, ſo liue, ſo die my Lord,
Ere I will yeeld my virgin Patent vp
Vnto his Lordſhip, whoſe vnwiſhed yoake,
My ſoule conſents not to giue ſoueraignty.

The. Take time to pauſe, and by the next new Moon
The ſealing day betwixt my loue and me,
For euerlaſting bond of fellowſhip :
Vpon that day either prepare to dye,
For diſobedience to your fathers will,
Or elſe to wed *Demetrius* as hee would,
Or on *Dianaes* Altar to proteſt
For aie, auſterity, and ſingle life.

Dem. Relent ſweet *Hermia*, and *Lyſander*, yeelde
Thy crazed title to my certaine right.

Lyſ. You haue her fathers loue, *Demetrius* :
Let me haue *Hermiaes* : do you marry him.

Egeus. Scornfull *Lyſander*, true, he hath my Loue;
Aud what is mine, my loue ſhall render him.
And ſhe is mine, and all my right of her,
I'do eſtate vnto *Demetrius*.

Lyſ. I am my Lord, as well deriu'd as he,
As well poſſeſt : my loue is more then his :
My fortunes euery way as fairely ranck'd
(If not with vantage) as *Demetrius* :
And (which is more then all theſe boaſts can be)
I am belou'd of beauteous *Hermia*.
Why ſhould not I then proſecute my right?
Demetrius, Ile auouch it to his head,
Made loue to *Nedars* daughter, *Helena*,
And won her ſoule : and ſhe (ſweet Ladie)dotes,
Deuoutly dotes, dotes in Idolatry,
Vpon this ſpotted and inconſtant man.

The. I muſt confeſſe, that I haue heard ſo much,
And with *Demetrius* thought to haue ſpoke thereof :
But being ouer-full of ſelfe-affaires,
My minde did loſe it. But *Demetrius* come,
And come *Egeus*, you ſhall go with me,
I haue ſome priuate ſchooling for you both.
For you faire *Hermia*, looke you arme your ſelfe,
To fit your fancies to your Fathers will ;
Or elſe the Law of Athens yeelds you vp
(Which by no meanes we may extenuate)
To death, or to a vow of ſingle life.
Come my *Hippolita*, what cheare my loue ?
Demetrius and *Egeus* go along :
I muſt imploy you in ſome buſineſſe
Againſt our nuptiall, and conferre with you
Of ſomething, neerely that concernes your ſelues.

Ege. With dutie and deſire we follow you.   *Exeunt*

      Manet Lyſander and Hermia.

Lyſ. How now my loue? Why is your cheek ſo pale?
How chance the Roſes there do fade ſo faſt?

Her. Belike for want of raine, which I could well
Beteeme them, from the tempeſt of mine eyes.

Lyſ. For ought that euer I could reade,
Could euer heare by tale or hiſtorie,
The courſe of true loue neuer did run ſmooth,
But either it was different in blood.

Her. O croſſe! too high to be enthral'd to loue.

Lyſ. Or elſe miſgraffed, in reſpect of yeares.

Her. O ſpight! too old to be ingag'd to yong.

Lyſ. Or elſe it ſtood vpon the choiſe of merit.

Her. O hell ! to chooſe loue by anothers eie.

Lyſ. Or if there were a ſimpathie in choiſe,
Warre, death, or ſickneſſe, did lay ſiege to it ;
Making it momentarie, as a ſound:

Swift as a ſhadow, ſhort as any dreame,
Briefe as the lightning in the collied night,
That (in a ſpleene) vnfolds both heauen and earth ;
And ere a man hath power to ſay, behold,
The iawes of darkneſſe do deuoure it vp :
So quicke bright things come to confuſion.

Her. If then true Louers haue beene euer croſt,
It ſtands as an edict in deſtinie :
Then let vs teach our triall patience,
Becauſe it is a cuſtomarie croſſe,
As due to loue, as thoughts, and dreames, and ſighs,
Wiſhes and teares ; poore Fancies followers.

Lyſ. A good perſwaſion ; therefore heare me *Hermia*,
I haue a Widdow Aunt, a dowager,
Of great reuennew, and ſhe hath no childe,
From Athens is her houſe remou'd ſeuen leagues,
And ſhe reſpects me, as her onely ſonne :
There gentle *Hermia*, may I marrie thee,
And to that place, the ſharpe Athenian Law
Cannot purſue vs. If thou lou'ſt me, then
Steale forth thy fathers houſe to morrow night :
And in the wood, a league without the towne,
(Where I did meete thee once with *Helena*,
To do obſeruance for a morne of May)
There will I ſtay for thee.

Her. My good *Lyſander*,
I ſweare to thee, by Cupids ſtrongeſt bow,
By his beſt arrow with the golden head,
By the ſimplicitie of Venus Doues,
By that which knitteth ſoules, and proſpers loue,
And by that fire which burn'd the Carthage Queene,
When the falſe Troyan vnder ſaile was ſeene,
By all the vowes that euer men haue broke,
(In number more then euer women ſpoke)
In that ſame place thou haſt appointed me,
To morrow truly will I meete with thee.

Lyſ. Keepe promiſe loue : looke here comes *Helena*.

      Enter Helena.

Her. God ſpeede faire *Helena*, whither away ?

Hel. Cal you me faire? that faire againe vnſay,
Demetrius loues you faire : O happie faire !
Your eyes are loadſtarres, and your tongues ſweet ayre
More tuneable then Larke to ſhepheards eare,
When wheate is greene, when hauthorne buds appeare,
Sickneſſe is catching : O were fauor ſo,
Your words I catch, faire *Hermia* ere I go,
My eare ſhould catch your voice, my eye, your eye,
My tongue ſhould catch your tongues ſweet melodie,
Were the world mine, *Demetrius* being bated,
The reſt Ile giue to be to you tranſlated.
O teach me how you looke, and with what art
you ſway the motion of *Demetrius* hart.

Her. I frowne vpon him, yet he loues me ſtill.

Hel. O that your frownes would teach my ſmiles
ſuch skill.

Her. I giue him curſes, yet he giues me loue.

Hel. O that my prayers could ſuch affection mpoue.

Her. The more I hate, the more he followes me.

Hel. The more I loue, the more he hateth me.

Her. His folly Helena is none of mine.

Hel. None but your beauty, wold that fault wer mine

Her. Take comfort : he no more ſhall ſee my face,
Lyſander and my ſelfe will flie this place.
Before the time I did *Lyſander* ſee,
Seem'd Athens like a Paradiſe to mee.

                                O

O then, what graces in my Loue do dwell,
That he hath turn'd a heauen into hell.

Lyf. *Helen,* to you our mindes we will vnfold,
To morrow night, when *Phœbe* doth behold
Her siluer visage, in the watry glasse,
Decking with liquid pearle, the bladed grasse
(A time that Louers flights doth still conceale)
Through *Athens* gates, haue we deuis'd to steale.

Her. And in the wood, where often you and I,
Vpon faint Primrose beds, were wont to lye,
Emptying our bosomes, of their counsell sweld :
There my *Lysander,* and my selfe shall meete,
And thence from *Athens* turne away our eyes
To seeke new friends and strange companions,
Farwell sweet play-fellow, pray thou for vs,
And good lucke grant thee thy *Demetrius.*
Keepe word *Lysander* we must starue our sight,
From louers foode, till morrow deepe midnight.

Exit Hermia.

Lyf. I will my *Hermia. Helena* adieu,
As you on him, *Demetrius* dotes on you. *Exit Lysander.*

Hele. How happy some, ore othersome can be ?
Through *Athens* I am thought as faire as she.
But what of that ? *Demetrius* thinkes not so :
He will not know, what all, but he doth know,
And as hee erres, doting on *Hermias* eyes ;
So I, admiring of his qualities :
Things base and vilde, holding no quantity,
Loue can transpose to forme and dignity,
Loue lookes not with the eyes, but with the minde,
And therefore is wing'd *Cupid* painted blinde.
Nor hath loues minde of any iudgement taste :
Wings and no eyes, figure, vnheedy haste.
And therefore is Loue said to be a childe,
Because in choise he is often beguil'd,
As waggish boyes in game themselues forsweare ;
So the boy Loue is periur'd euery where.
For ere *Demetrius* lookt on *Hermias* eyne,
He hail'd downe oathes that he was onely mine.
And when this Haile some heat from *Hermia* felt,
So he dissolu'd, and showres of oathes did melt,
I will goe tell him of faire *Hermias* flight :
Then to the wood will he, to morrow night
Pursue her ; and for his intelligence,
If I haue thankes, it is a deere expence :
But heerein meane I to enrich my paine,
To haue his sight thither, and backe againe. *Exit.*

Enter Quince the Carpenter, Snug the Ioyner, Bottome the Weauer, Flute the bellowes-mender, Snout the Tinker, and Starueling the Taylor.

Qyin. Is all our company heere ?

Bot. You were best to call them generally, man by man, accoding to the scrip.

Qui. Here is the scrowle of euery mans name, which is thought fit through all *Athens,* to play in our Enterlude before the Duke and the Dutches, on his wedding day at night.

Bot. First, good *Peter Quince,* say what the play treats on : then read the names of the Actors : and so grow on to a point.

Quin. Marry our play is the most lamentable Comedy, and most cruell death of *Pyramus* and *Thisbie.*

Bot. A very good peece of worke I assure you, and a

merry. Now good *Peter Quince,* call forth your Actors by the scrowle. Masters spread your selues.

Quince. Answere as I call you. Nick Bottome the Weauer.

Bottome. Ready ; name what part I am for, and proceed.

Quince. You *Nicke Bottome* are set downe for *Pyramus.*

Bot. What is *Pyramus,* a louer, or a tyrant ?

Quin. A Louer that kills himselfe most gallantly for loue.

Bot. That will aske some teares in the true performing of it : if I do it, let the audience looke to their eies : I will mooue stormes ; I will condole in some measure. To the rest yet, my chiefe humour is for a tyrant. I could play *Ercles* rarely, or a part to teare a Cat in, to make all split the raging Rocks; and shiuering shocks shall break the locks of prison gates, and *Phibbus* carre shall shine from farre, and make and marre the foolish Fates. This was lofty. Now name the rest of the Players. This is *Ercles* vaine, a tyrants vaine : a louer is more condoling.

Quin. Francis Flute the Bellowes-mender.

Flu. Heere *Peter Quince.*

Quin. You must take *Thisbie* on you.

Flut. What is *Thisbie,* a wandring Knight ?

Qui. It is the Lady that *Pyramus* must loue.

Flut. Nay faith, let not mee play a woman, I haue a beard comming.

Qui. That's all one, you shall play it in a Maske, and you may speake as small as you will.

Bot. And I may hide my face, let me play *Thisbie* too : Ile speake in a monstrous little voyce ; *Thisne, Thisne,* ah *Pyramus* my louer deare, thy *Thisbie* deare, and Lady deare.

Quin. No no, you must play *Pyramus,* and *Flute,* you *Thisby.*

Bot. Well, proceed.

Qu. Robin Starueling the Taylor.

Star. Heere *Peter Quince.*

Quince. Robin Starueling, you must play *Thisbies* mother ?

Tom Snowt, the Tinker.

Snowt. Heere *Peter Quince.*

Quin. You, *Pyramus* father ; my self, *Thisbies* father ; *Snugge* the Ioyner, you the Lyons part : and I hope there is a play fitted.

Snug. Haue you the Lions part written ? pray you if be, giue it me, for I am slow of studie.

Quin. You may doe it *extemporie,* for it is nothing but roaring.

Bot. Let mee play the Lyon too, I will roare that I will doe any mans heart good to heare me. I will roare, that I will make the Duke say, Let him roare againe, let him roare againe.

Quin. If you should doe it too terribly, you would fright the Dutchesse and the Ladies, that they would shrike, and that were enough to hang vs all.

All. That would hang vs euery mothers sonne.

Bottome. I graunt you friends, if that you should fright the Ladies out of their Wittes, they would haue no more discretion but to hang vs : but I will aggrauate my voyce so, that I will roare you as gently as any sucking Doue ; I will roare and 'twere any Nightingale.

Quin. You can play no part but *Piramus,* for *Pira—*

N 2   *mus*

mus is a fweet-fac'd man, a proper man as one fhall fee in a fummers day ; a moft louely Gentleman-like man, therfore you muft needs play *Piramus.*

Bot. Well, I will vndertake it. What beard were I beft to play it in ?

Quin. Why, what you will.

Bot. I will difcharge it, in either your ftraw-colour beard, your orange tawnie beard, your purple in graine beard, or your French-crowne colour'd beard, your perfect yellow.

Quin. Some of your French Crownes haue no haire at all, and then you will play bare-fac'd. But mafters here are your parts, and I am to Intreat you, requeft you, and defire you, to con them by too morrow night : and meet me in the palace wood, a mile without the Towne, by Moone-light, there we will rehearfe : for if we meete in the Citie, we fhalbe dog'd with company, and our deuifes knowne. In the meane time, I wil draw a bil of properties, fuch as our play wants. I pray you faile me not.

Bottom. We will meete, and there we may rehearfe more obfcenely and couragioufly. Take paines, be perfect, adieu.

Quin. At the Dukes oake we meete.

Bot. Enough, hold or cut bow-ftrings.   *Exeunt*

Actus Secundus.

Enter a Fairie at one doore, and Robin good-fellow at another.

Rob. How now fpirit, whether wander you ?

Fai. Ouer hil, ouer dale, through bufh, through briar, Ouer parke, ouer pale, through flood, through fire, I do wander euerie where, fwifter then ŷ Moons fphere ; And I ferue the Fairy Queene, to dew her orbs vpon the The Cowflips tall, her penfioners bee,   (green. In their gold coats, fpots you fee, Thofe be Rubies, Fairie fauors, In thofe freckles, llue their fauors, I muft go feeke fome dew drops heere, And hang a pearle in euery cowflips eare. Farewell thou Lobe of fpirits, Ile be gon, Our Queene and all her Elues come heere anon.

Rob. The King doth keepe his Reuels here to night, Take heed the Queene come not within his fight, For *Oberon* is paffing fell and wrath, Becaufe that fhe, as her attendant, hath A louely boy ftolne from an Indian King, She neuer had fo fweet a changeling, And iealous *Oberon* would haue the childe Knight of his traine, to trace the Forrefts wilde. But fhe (perforce) with-holds the loued boy, Crownes him with flowers, and makes him all her ioy. And now they neuer meete in groue, or greene, By fountaine cleere, or fpangled ftar-light fheene, But they do fquare, that all their Elues for feare Creepe into Acorne cups and hide them there.

Fai. Either I miftake your fhape and making quite, Or elfe you are that fhrew'd and knauifh fpirit Cal'd Robin Good-fellow. Are you not hee, That frights the maidens of the Villagree, Skim milke, and fometimes labour in the querne, And bootleffe make the breathleffe hufwife cherne, And fometime make the drinke to beare no barme,

Mifleade night-wanderers, laughing at their harme, Thofe that Hobgoblin call you, and fweet Pucke, You do their worke, and they fhall haue good lucke. Are not you he ?

Rob. Thou fpeak'ft aright ; I am that merrie wanderer of the night : I left to *Oberon*, and make him fmile, When I a fat and beane fed horfe beguile, Neighing in likeneffe of a filly foale, And fometime lurke I in a Goffips bole, In very likeneffe of a roafted crab : And when fhe drinkes, againft her lips I bob, And on her withered dewlop poure the Ale. The wifeft Aunt telling the faddeft tale, Sometime for three-foot ftoole, miftaketh me, Then flip I from her bum, downe topples fhe, And tailour cries, and fals into a coffe. And then the whole quire hold their hips, and loffe, And waxen in their mirth, and neeze, and fweare, A merrier houre vvas neuer wafted there. But roome Fairy, heere comes Oberon.

Fair. And heere my Miftris : Would that he vvere gone.

Enter the King of Fairies at one doore with his traine, and the Queene at another with hers.

Ob. Ill met by Moone-light, Proud *Tytania.*

Qu. What, iealous Oberon? Fairy skip hence. I haue forfworne his bed and companie.

Ob. Tarrie rafh Wanton ; am not I thy Lord ?

Qu. Then I muft be thy Lady : but I know When thou vvaft ftolne away from Fairy Land, And in the fhape of *Corin*, fate all day, Playing on pipes of Corne, and verfing loue To amorous *Phillida.* Why art thou heere Come from the fartheft fteepe of *India* ? But that forfooth the bouncing *Amazon* Your buskin'd Miftreffe, and your Warrior loue, To *Thefeus* muft be Wedded ; and you come, To giue their bed ioy and profperitie.

Ob. How canft thou thus for fhame *Tytania*, Glance at my credite, vvith *Hippolita* ? Knowing I knovv thy loue to *Thefeus* ? Didft thou not leade him through the glimmering night From *Peregenia*, whom he rauifhed ? And make him vvith faire Eagles breake his faith With *Ariadne*, and *Atiopa* ?

Que. Thefe are the forgeries of iealoufie, And neuer fince the middle Summers fpring Met vve on hil, in dale, forreft, or mead, By paued fountaine, or by rufhie brooke, Or in the beached margent of the fea, To dance our ringlets to the whiftling Winde, But vvith thy braules thou haft difturb'd our fport. Therefore the Windes, piping to vs in vaine, As in reuenge, haue fuck'd vp from the fea Contagious fogges : Which falling in the Land, Hath euerie petty Riuer made fo proud, That they haue ouer-borne their Continents. The Oxe hath therefore ftretch'd his yoake in vaine, The Ploughman loft his fweat, and the greene Corne Hath rotted, ere his youth attain'd a beard : The fold ftands empty in the drowned field, And Crowes are fatted vvith the murrion flocke,

    The

The nine mens Morris is fild vp with mud,
And the queint Mazes in the wanton greene,
For lacke of tread are vndiftinguiſhable.
The humane mortals want their winter heere,
No night is now with hymne or caroll bleſt ;
Therefore the Moone (the gouerneſſe of floods)
Pale in her anger, waſhes all the aire ;
That Rheumaticke diſeaſes doe abound.
And through this diſtemperature, we ſee
The ſeaſons alter ; hoared headed froſts
Fall in the freſh lap of the crimſon Roſe,
And on old *Hyems* chinne and Icie crowne,
An odorous Chaplet of ſweet Sommer buds
Is as in mockry ſet. The Spring, the Sommer,
The childing Autumne, angry Winter change
Their wonted Liueries, and the mazed world ,
By their increaſe, now knowes not which is which ;
And this ſame progeny of euills,
Comes from our debate, from our diſſention,
We are their parents and originall.
Ober. Do you amend it then, it lies in you,
Why ſhould *Titania* croſſe her *Oberon* ?
I do but beg a little changeling boy,
To be my Henchman.
Qu. Set your heart at reſt,
The Fairy land buyes not the childe of me,
His mother was a Votreſſe of my Order,
And in the ſpiced *Indian* aire, by night
Full often hath ſhe goſſipt by my ſide,
And ſat with me on *Neptunes* yellow ſands,
Marking th'embarked traders on the flood,
When we haue laught to ſee the ſailes conceiue,
And grow big bellied with the wanton winde :
Which ſhe with pretty and with ſwimming gate,
Following (her wombe then rich with my yong ſquire)
Would imitate, and ſaile vpon the Land,
To fetch me trifles, and returne againe,
As from a voyage, rich with merchandize.
But ſhe being mortall, of that boy did die,
And for her ſake I doe reare vp her boy,
And for her ſake I will not part with him.
Ob. How long within this wood intend you ſtay ?
Qu. Perchance till after *Theſeus* wedding day.
If you will patiently dance in our Round,
And ſee our Moone-light reuels, goe with vs ;
If not, ſhun me and I will ſpare your haunts.
Ob. Giue me that boy, and I will goe with thee.
Qu. Not for thy Fairy Kingdome. Fairies away :
We ſhall chide downe right, if I longer ſtay. *Exeunt.*
Ob. Wel, go thy way : thou ſhalt not from this groue,
Till I torment thee for this iniury.
My gentle *Pucke* come hither ; thou remembreſt
Since once I ſat vpon a promontory,
And heard a Meare-maide on a Dolphins backe,
Vttering ſuch dulcet and harmonious breath,
That the rude ſea grew ciuill at her ſong,
And certaine ſtarres ſhot madly from their Spheares,
To heare the Sea-maids muſicke.
Puc. I remember.
Ob. That very time I ſay (but thou couldſt not)
Flying betweene the cold Moone and the earth,
Cupid all arm'd ; a certaine aime he tooke
At a faire Veſtall, throned by the Weſt,
And loos'd his loue-ſhaft ſmartly from his bow,
As it ſhould pierce a hundred thouſand hearts,
But I might ſee young *Cupids* fiery ſhaft

Quencht in the chaſte beames of the watry Moone ;
And the imperiall Votreſſe paſſed on,
In maiden meditation, fancy free.
Yet markt I where the bolt of *Cupid* fell.
It fell vpon a little weſterne flower ;
Before, milke-white ; now purple with loues wound,
And maidens call it, Loue in idleneſſe.
Fetch me that flower ; the hearb I ſhew'd thee once,
The iuyce of it, on ſleeping eye-lids laid,
Will make or man or woman madly dote
Vpon the next liue creature that it ſees.
Fetch me this hearbe, and be thou heere againe,
Ere the *Leuiathan* can ſwim a league.
Pucke. Ile put a girdle about the earth, in forty mi-
nutes.
Ober. Hauing once this iuyce,
Ile watch *Titania*, when ſhe is aſleepe,
And drop the liquor of it in her eyes :
The next thing when ſhe waking lookes vpon,
(Be it on Lyon, Beare, or Wolfe, or Bull,
On medling Monkey, or on buſie Ape)
Shee ſhall purſue it, with the ſoule of loue.
And ere I take this charme off from her ſight,
(As I can take it with another hearbe)
Ile make her render vp her Page to me.
But who comes heere? I am inuiſible,
And I will ouer-heare their conference.

Enter Demetrius, Helena following him.

Deme. I loue thee not, therefore purſue me not,
Where is *Lyſander*, and faire *Hermia* ?
The one Ile ſtay, the other ſtayeth me.
Thou toldſt me they were ſtolne into this wood ;
And heere am I, and wood within this wood,
Becauſe I cannot meet my *Hermia.*
Hence, get thee gone, and follow me no more.
Hel. You draw me, you hard-hearted Adamant,
But yet you draw not Iron, for my heart
Is true as ſteele. Leaue you your power to draw,
And I ſhall haue no power to follow you.
Deme. Do I entice you ? do I ſpeake you faire ?
Or rather doe I not in plaineſt truth,
Tell you I doe not, nor I cannot loue you ?
Hel. And euen for that doe I loue thee the more ;
I am your ſpaniell, and *Demetrius* ,
The more you beat me, I will fawne on you.
Vſe me but as your ſpaniell ; ſpurne me, ſtrike me,
Neglect me, loſe me ; onely giue me leaue
(Vnworthy as I am) to follow you.
What worſer place can I beg in your loue,
(And yet a place of high reſpect with me)
Then to be vſed as you doe your dogge.
Dem. Tempt not too much the hatred of my ſpirit,
For I am ſicke when I do looke on thee.
Hel. And I am ſicke when I looke not on you.
Dem. You doe impeach your modeſty too much,
To leaue the Citty, and commit your ſelfe
Into the hands of one that loues you not,
To truſt the opportunity of night,
And the ill counſell of a deſert place,
With the rich worth of your virginity.
Hel. Your vertue is my priuiledge : for that
It is not night when I doe ſee your face.
Therefore I thinke I am not in the night,
Nor doth this wood lacke worlds of company ,

N 3   For

For you in my respect are nll the world.
Then how can it be said I am alone,
When all the world is heere to looke on me?
Dem. Ile run from thee, and hide me in the brakes,
And leaue thee to the mercy of wilde beasts.
Hel. The wildest hath not such a heart as you;
Runne when you will, the story shall be chang'd:
Apollo flies, and *Daphne* holds the chase;
The Doue pursues the Griffin, the milde Hinde
Makes speed to catch the Tyger. Bootlesse speede,
When cowardise pursues, and valour flies.
Demet. I will not stay thy questions, let me go;
Or if thou follow me, doe not beleeue,
But I shall doe thee mischiefe in the wood.
Hel. I, in the Temple, in the Towne, and Field
You doe me mischiefe. Fye *Demetrius*,
Your wrongs doe set a scandall on my sexe:
We cannot fight for loue, as men may doe;
We should be woo'd, and were not made to wooe.
I follow thee, and make a heauen of hell,
To die vpon the hand I loue so well.   *Exit.*
Ob. Fare thee well Nymph, ere he do leaue this groue,
Thou shalt flie him, and he shall seeke thy loue.
Hast thou the flower there? Welcome wanderer.

       Enter Pucke.
Puck. I, there it is.
Ob. I pray thee giue it me.
I know a banke where the wilde time blowes,
Where Oxslips and the nodding Violet growes,
Quite ouer-cannopied with luscious woodbine,
With sweet muske roses, and with Eglantine;
There sleepes *Tytania*, sometime of the night,
Lul'd in these flowers, with dances and delight:
And there the snake throwes her enammel'd skinne,
Weed wide enough to rap a Fairy in.
And with the iuyce of this Ile streake her eyes,
And make her full of hatefull fantasies.
Take thou some of it, and seek through this groue;
A sweet *Athenian* Lady is in loue
With a disdainefull youth: anoint his eyes,
But doe it when the next thing he espies,
May be the Lady. Thou shalt know the man,
By the *Athenian* garments he hath on.
Effect it with some care, that he may proue
More fond on her, then she vpon her loue;
And looke thou meet me ere the first Cocke crow.
Pu. Feare not my Lord, your seruant shall do so. *Exit.*

    Enter Queene of Fairies, with her traine.
Queen. Come, now a Roundell, and a Fairy song;
Then for the third part of a minute hence,
Some to kill Cankers in the muske rose buds,
Some warre with Reremise, for their leathern wings,
To make my small Elues coates, and some keepe backe
The clamorous Owle that nightly hoots and wonders
At our queint spirits : Sing me now asleepe,
Then to your offices, and let me rest.

       Fairies Sing.

You spotted Snakes with double tongue,
Thorny Hedgehogges be not seene,
Newts and blinde wormes do no wrong,
Come not neere our Fairy Queene.
Philomele with melodie,

Sing in your sweet Lullaby,
Lulla, lulla, lullaby, lulla, lulla, lullaby,
Neuer harme, nor spell, nor charme,
Come our louely Lady nye,
So good night with Lullaby.
    2. *Fairy. Weauing Spiders come not heere,*
Hence you long leg'd Spinners, hence:
Beetles blacke approach not neere;
Worme nor Snayle doe no offence.
Philomele with melody, &c.
    1. *Fairy. Hence away, now all is well;*
One aloofe, stand Centinell.   *Shee sleepes.*

       Enter Oberon.
Ober. What thou seest when thou dost wake,
Doe it for thy true Loue take :
Loue and languish for his sake.
Be it Ounce, or Catte, or Beare,
Pard, or Boare with bristled haire,
In thy eye that shall appeare,
When thou wak'st, it is thy deare,
Wake when some vile thing is neere.

    Enter Lisander and Hermia.

Lis. Faire loue, you faint with wandring in ŷ woods,
And to speake troth I haue forgot our way :
Wee'll rest vs *Hermia*, if you thinke it good,
And tarry for the comfort of the day.
Her. Be it so *Lysander*; finde you out a bed,
For I vpon this banke will rest my head.
Lys. One turfe shall serue as pillow for vs both,
One heart, one bed, two bosomes, and one troth.
Her. Nay good *Lysander*, for my sake my deere
Lie further off yet, doe not lie so neere.
Lys. O take the sence sweet, of my innocence,
Loue takes the meaning, in loues conference,
I meane that my heart vnto yours is knit,
So that but one heart can you make of it.
Two bosomes interchanged with an oath,
So then two bosomes, and a single troth.
Then by your side, no bed-roome me deny,
For lying so, *Hermia*, I doe not lye.
Her. *Lysander* riddles very prettily;
Now much beshrew my manners and my pride,
If *Hermia* meant to say, *Lysander* lied.
But gentle friend, for loue and courtesie
Lie further off, in humane modesty,
Such separation, as may well be said,
Becomes a vertuous batchelour, and a maide,
So farre be distant, and good night sweet friend;
Thy loue nere alter, till thy sweet life end.
Lys. Amen, amen, to that faire prayer, say I,
And then end life, when I end loyalty :
Heere is my bed, sleepe giue thee all his rest.
Her. With halfe that wish, the wishers eyes be prest.
       Enter Pucke.   *They sleepe.*
Puck. Through the Forrest haue I gone,
But *Athenian* finde I none,
One whose eyes I might approue
This flowers force in stirring loue.
Night and silence : who is heere?
Weedes of *Athens* he doth weare :
This is he (my master said)
Despised the *Athenian* maide :
And heere the maiden sleeping found,

           On

On the danke and durty ground.
Pretty ſoule, ſhe durſt not lye
Neere this Iacke-loue, this kill-curteſie.
Churle, vpon thy eyes I throw
All the power this charme doth owe :
When thou wak'ſt, let loue forbid
Sleepe his ſeate on thy eye-lid.
So awake when I am gone :
For I muſt now to Oberon.   *Exit.*

Enter Demetrius and Helena running.

Hel. Stay, though thou kill me, ſweete *Demetrius.*
De. I charge thee hence, and do not haunt me thus.
Hel. O wilt thou darkling leaue me? do not ſo.
De. Stay on thy perill, I alone will goe.
                                        Exit Demetrius.
Hel. O I am out of breath, in this fond chace,
The more my prayer, the leſſer is my grace,
Happy is *Hermia,* whereſoere ſhe lies ;
For ſhe hath bleſſed and attractiue eyes.
How came her eyes ſo bright? Not with ſalt teares.
If ſo, my eyes are oftner waſht then hers.
No, no, I am as vgly as a Beare ;
For beaſts that meete me, runne away for feare,
Therefore no maruaile, though *Demetrius*
Doe as a monſter, flie my preſence thus.
What wicked and diſſembling glaſſe of mine,
Made me compare with *Hermias* ſphery eyne?
But who is here? *Lyſander* on the ground ;
Deade or aſleepe? I ſee no bloud, no wound,
Lyſander, if you liue, good ſir awake.
Lyſ. And run through fire I will for thy ſweet ſake.
Tranſparent *Helena,* nature her ſhewes art,
That through thy boſome makes me ſee thy heart.
Where is *Demetrius?* oh how fit a word
Is that vile name, to periſh on my ſword !
Hel. Do not ſay ſo *Lyſander,* ſay not ſo :
What though he loue your *Hermia?* Lord, what though?
Yet *Hermia* ſtill loues you ; then be content.
Lyſ. Content with *Hermia?* No, I do repent
The tedious minutes I with her haue ſpent.
Not *Hermia,* but *Helena* now I loue ;
Who will not change a Rauen for a Doue?
The will of man is by his reaſon ſway'd :
And reaſon ſaies you are the worthier Maide.
Things growing are not ripe vntill their ſeaſon ;
So I being yong, till now ripe not to reaſon,
And touching now the point of humane skill,
Reaſon becomes the Marſhall to my will,
And leades me to your eyes, where I orelooke
Loues ſtories, written in Loues richeſt booke.
Hel. Wherefore was I to this keene mockery borne?
When at your hands did I deſerue this ſcorne ?
Iſt not enough, iſt not enough, yong man,
That I did neuer, no nor neuer can,
Deſerue a ſweete looke from *Demetrius* eye,
But you muſt flout my inſufficiency ?
Good troth you do me wrong(good-ſooth you do)
In ſuch diſdainfull manner, me to wooe.
But fare you well ; perforce I muſt confeſſe,
I thought you Lord of more true gentleneſſe.
Oh, that a Lady of one man refus'd,
Should of another therefore be abus'd.   *Exit.*
Lyſ. She ſees not *Hermia* : *Hermia* ſleepe thou there,
And neuer maiſt thou come *Lyſander* neere ;

For as a ſurfeit of the ſweeteſt things
The deepeſt loathing to the ſtomacke brings :
Or as the hereſies that men do leaue,
Are hated moſt of thoſe that did deceiue :
So thou, my ſurfeit, and my hereſie,
Of all be hated ; but the moſt of me ;
And all my powers addreſſe your loue and might,
To honour *Helen,* and to be her Knight.   *Exit.*
Her. Helpe me *Lyſander,* helpe me ; do thy beſt
To plucke this crawling ſerpent from my breſt.
Aye me, for pitty; what a dreame was here ?
Lyſander, looke, how I do quake with feare :
Me-thought a ſerpent eate my heart away,
And yet ſat ſmiling at his cruell prey.
Lyſander, what remoou'd ? *Lyſander,* Lord,
What, out of hearing, gone? No ſound, no word ?
Alacke where are you ? ſpeake and if you heare :
Speake of all loues ; I found almoſt with feare.
No, then I well perceiue you are not nye,
Either death or you Ile finde immediately.   *Exit.*

Actus Tertius.

Enter the Clownes.

Bot. Are we all met ?
Quin. Pat, pat, and here's a maruailous conuenient
place for our rehearſall. This greene plot ſhall be our
ſtage, this hauthorne brake our tyring houſe, and we will
do it in action, as we will do it before the Duke.
Bot. Peter quince ?
Peter. What ſaiſt thou, bully *Bottome* ?
Bot. There are things in this Comedy of *Piramus* and
Thisby, that will neuer pleaſe. Firſt, *Piramus* muſt draw a
ſword to kill himſelfe ; which the Ladies cannot abide.
How anſwere you that ?
Snout. Berlaken, a parlous feare.
Star. I beleeue we muſt leaue the killing out, when
all is done.
Bot. Not a whit, I haue a deuice to make all well.
Write me a Prologue, and let the Prologue ſeeme to ſay,
we will do no harme with our ſwords, and that *Pyramus*
is not kill'd indeede : and for the more better aſſurance,
tell them, that I *Piramus* am not *Piramus,* but *Bottome* the
Weauer; this will put them out of feare.
Quin. Well, we will haue ſuch a Prologue, and it ſhall
be written in eight and ſixe.
Bot. No, make it two more, let it be written in eight
and eight.
Snout. Will not the Ladies be afear'd of the Lyon ?
Star. I feare it, I promiſe you.
Bot. Maſters, you ought to conſider with your ſelues, to
bring in(God ſhield vs)a Lyon among Ladies, is a moſt
dreadfull thing. For there is not a more fearefull wilde
foule then your Lyon liuing : and wee ought to looke
to it.
Snout. Therefore another Prologue muſt tell he is not
a Lyon.
Bot. Nay, you muſt name his name, and halfe his face
muſt be ſeene through the Lyons necke, and he himſelfe
muſt ſpeake through, ſaying thus, or to the ſame defect ;
Ladies, or faire Ladies, I would wiſh you, or I would
                                                    requeſt

requeſt you,or I would entreate you, not to feare, not to tremble: my life for yours. If you thinke I come hither as a Lyon, it were pitty of my life. No, I am no ſuch thing,I am a man as other men are ; and there indeed let him name his name, and tell him plainly hee is *Snug* the ioyner.

Quin. Well, it ſhall be ſo; but there is two hard things, that is, to bring the Moone-light into a chamber: for you know, *Piramus* and *Thiſby* meete by Moonelight.

Sn. Doth the Moone ſhine that night wee play our play ?

Bot. A Calender, a Calender, looke in the Almanack, finde out Moone-ſhine, finde out Moone-ſhine.

Enter Pucke.

Quin. Yes, it doth ſhine that night.

Bot. Why then may you leaue a caſement of the great chamber window (where we play) open, and the Moone may ſhine in at the caſement.

Quin. I, or elſe one muſt come in with a buſh of thorns and a lanthorne, and ſay he comes to disfigure, or to preſent the perſon of Moone-ſhine. Then there is another thing, we muſt haue a wall in the great Chamber; for *Piramus* and *Thiſby* (ſaies the ſtory) did talke through the chinke of a wall.

Sn. You can neuer bring in a wall. What ſay you *Bottome* ?

Bot. Some man or other muſt preſent wall, and let him haue ſome Plaſter, or ſome *Lome*, or ſome rough caſt about him, to ſignifie wall; or let him hold his fingers thus; and through that cranny, ſhall *Piramus* and *Thiſby* whiſper.

Quin. If that may be, then all is well. Come, ſit downe euery mothers ſonne, and rehearſe your parts. *Piramus,* you begin ; when you haue ſpoken your ſpeech, enter into that Brake, and ſo euery one according to his cue.

Enter Robin.

Rob. What hempen home-ſpuns haue we ſwaggering here,
So neere the Cradle of the Faierie Queene ?
What, a Play toward ? Ile be an auditor,
An Actor too perhaps, if I ſee cauſe.

Quin. Speake *Piramus* : *Thiſby* ſtand forth.

Pir. *Thiſby,* the flowers of odious ſauors ſweete,

Quin. Odours, odours.

Pir. Odours ſauors ſweete,
So hath thy breath, my deareſt *Thiſby* deare.
But harke, a voyce : ſtay thou but here a while,
And by and by I will to thee appeare.   *Exit. Pir.*

Puck. A ſtranger *Piramus,* then ere plaid here.

Thiſ. Muſt I ſpeake now ?

Pet. I marry muſt you. For you muſt vnderſtand, he goes but to ſee a noyſe that he heard, and is to come againe.

Thyſ. Moſt radiant *Piramus,* moſt Lilly white of hue,
Of colour like the red roſe on triumphant bryer,
Moſt brisky Iuuenall, and eke moſt louely Iew,
As true as trueſt horſe, that yet would neuer tyre,
Ile meete thee *Piramus,* at Ninnies toombe.

Pet. *Ninus* toombe man: why, you muſt not ſpeake that yet ; that you anſwere to *Piramus* : you ſpeake all your part at once, cues and all. *Piramus* enter, your cue is paſt ; it is neuer tyre.

Thyſ. O, as true as trueſt horſe, that yet would neuer tyre:

Pir. If I were faire, *Thiſby* I were onely thine.

Pet. O monſtrous. O ſtrange. We are hanted; pray maſters, flye maſters, helpe.

The Clownes all Exit.

Puk. Ile follow you, Ile leade you about a Round,
Through bogge, through buſh, through brake, through bryer,
Sometime a horſe Ile be, ſometime a hound :
A hogge, a headleſſe beare, ſometime a fire,
And neigh, and barke, and grunt, and rore, and burne,
Like horſe, hound, hog, beare, fire, at euery turne.   *Exit.*

Enter Piramus with the Aſſe head.

Bot. Why do they run away ? This is a knauery of them to make me afeard.   *Enter Snowt.*

Sn. O *Bottom,* thou art chang'd; What doe I ſee on thee ?

Bot. What do you ſee ? You ſee an Aſſe-head of your owne, do you ?

Enter Peter Quince.

Pet. Bleſſe thee *Bottome,* bleſſe thee; thou art tranſlated.   *Exit.*

Bot. I ſee their knauery; this is to make an aſſe of me, to fright me if they could ; but I will not ſtirre from this place, do what they can. I will walke vp and downe here, and I will ſing that they ſhall heare I am not afraid.

The Wooſell cocke, ſo blacke of hew,
With Orenge-tawny bill.
The Throſtle, with his note ſo true,
The Wren and little quill.

Tyta. What Angell wakes me from my flowry bed ?

Bot. The Finch, the Sparrow, and the Larke,
The plainſong Cuckow gray ;
Whoſe note full many a man doth marke,
And dares not anſwere, nay.
For indeede, who would ſet his wit to ſo fooliſh a bird ?
Who would giue a bird the lye, though he cry Cuckow,
neuer ſo ?

Tyta. I pray thee gentle mortall, ſing againe,
Mine eare is much enamored of thy note ;
On the firſt view to ſay, to ſweare I loue thee.
So is mine eye enthralled to thy ſhape,
And thy faire vertues force (perforce) doth moue me.

Bot. Me-thinkes miſtreſſe, you ſhould haue little reaſon for that : and yet to ſay the truth, reaſon and loue keepe little company together , now-adayes. The more the pittie, that ſome honeſt neighbours will not make them friends. Nay, I can gleeke vpon occaſion.

Tyta. Thou art as wiſe, as thou art beautifull.

Bot. Not ſo neither : but if I had wit enough to get out of this wood, I haue enough to ſerue mine owne turne.

Tyta. Out of this wood, do not deſire to goe,
Thou ſhalt remaine here, whether thou wilt or no.
I am a ſpirit no common rate :
The Summer ſtill doth tend vpon my ſtate,
And I doe loue thee ; therefore goe with me,
Ile giue thee Fairies to attend on thee ;
And they ſhall fetch thee Iewels from the deepe,
And ſing, while thou on preſſed flowers doſt ſleepe :
And I will purge thy mortall groſſeneſſe ſo,
That thou ſhalt like an airie ſpirit go.

Enter Peaſe-bloſſome, Cobweb, Moth, Muſtard-
ſeede, and foure Fairies.

Fai. Ready ; and I, and I, and I, Where ſhall we go ?

Tita. Be

Tita. Be kinde and curteous to this Gentleman,
Hop in his walkes, and gambole in his eies,
Feede him with Apricocks, and Dewberries,
With purple Grapes, greene Figs, and Mulberries,
The honie-bags fteale from the humble Bees,
And for night-tapers crop their waxen thighes,
And light them at the fierie-Glow-wormes eyes,
To haue my loue to bed, and to arife :
And plucke the wings from painted Butterflies,
To fan the Moone-beames from his fleeping eies.
Nod to him Elues, and doe him curtefies.
  1.Fai. Haile mortall, haile.
  2.Fai. Haile.
  3.Fai. Haile.
  Bot. I cry your worfhips mercy hartily ; I befeech
your worfhips name.
  Cob. Cobweb.
  Bot. I fhall defire you of more acquaintance, good
Mafter *Cobweb* : if I cut my finger, I fhall make bold
with you.
Your name honeft Gentleman ?
  Peaf. Peafe bloffome.
  Bot. I pray you commend mee to miftreffe *Squafh* ,
your mother, and to mafter *Peafcod* your father. Good
mafter *Peafe-bloffome,* I fhal defire of you more acquain-
tance to. Your name I befeech you fir ?
  Muf. a *Muftard feeds.*
  Peaf. Peafe-bloffome.
  Bot. Good mafter *Muftard feede,* I know your pati-
ence well : that fame cowardly gyant-like Oxe-beefe
hath deuoured many a gentleman of your houfe. I pro-
mife you, your kindred hath made my eyes water ere
now. I defire you more acquaintance, good Mafter
Muftard-feede.
  Tita. Come waite vpon him, lead him to my bower.
The Moone me-thinks, lookes with a watrie eie,
And when fhe weepes, weepe euerie little flower,
Lamenting fome enforced chaftitie.
Tye vp my louers tongue, bring him filently.   *Exit.*

Enter King of Pharies, folus.

  Ob. I wonder if *Titania* be awak't ;
Then what it was that next came in her eye,
Which fhe muft dote on, in extremitie.
  Enter Pucke.
Here comes my meffenger : how now mad fpirit,
What night-rule now about this gaunted groue?
  Puck. My Miftris with a monfter is in loue,
Neere to her clofe and confecrated bower,
While fhe was in her dull and fleeping hower,
A crew of patches, rude Mcehanicals,
That worke for bread vpon *Athenian* ftals,
Were met together to rehearfe a Play,
Intended for great *Thefeus* nuptiall day :
The fhalloweft thick-skin of that barren fort,
Who *Piramus* prefented, in their fport,
Forfooke his Scene, and entred in a brake,
When I did him at this aduantage take,
An Affes nole I fixed on his head.
Anon his *Thisbie* muft be anfwered,
And forth my Mimmick comes : when they him fpie,
As Wilde-geefe, that the creeping Fowler eye,
Or ruffed-pated choughes, many in fort
(Rifing and cawing at the guns report)
Seuer themfelues, and madly fweepe the skye :

So at his fight, away his fellowes flye,
And at our ftampe, here ore and ore one fals ;
He murther cries, and helpe from *Athens* cals.
Their fenfe thus weake, loft with their fears thus ftrong,
Made fenfeleffe things begin to do them wrong.
For briars and thornes at their apparell fnatch,
Some fleeues, fome hats, from yeelders all things catch,
I led them on in this diftracted feare,
And left fweete *Piramus* tranflated there :
When in that moment (fo it came to paffe)
Tytania waked, and ftraightway lou'd an Affe.
  Ob. This fals out better then I could deuife :
But haft thou yet lacht the *Athenians* eyes,
With the loue iuyce, as I did bid thee doe ?
  Rob. I tooke him fleeping (that is finifht to)
And the *Athenian* woman by his fide,
That when he wak't, of force fhe muft be eyde.

Enter Demetrius and Hermia.

  Ob. Stand clofe, this is the fame *Athenian.*
  Rob. This is the woman, but not this the man.
  Dem. O why rebuke you him that loues you fo ?
Lay breath fo bitter on your bitter foe.
  Her. Now I but chide, but I fhould vfe thee worfe.
For thou (I feare) haft giuen mee caufe to curfe,
If thou haft flaine *Lyfander* In his fleepe,
Being ore fhooes in bloud, plunge in the deepe, and kill
                    me too :
The Sunne was not fo true vnto the day,
As he to me. Would he haue ftollen away,
From fleeping *Hermia* ? Ile beleeue as foone
This whole earth may be bord, and that the Moone
May through the Center creepe, and fo difpleafe
Her brothers noonetide, with th'*Antipodes.*
It cannot be but thou haft murdred him,
So fhould a mutrherer looke, fo dead, fo grim.
  Dem. So fhould the murderer looke, and fo fhould I,
Pierft through the heart with your ftearne cruelty :
Yet you the murderer looks as bright as cleare,
As yonder *Venus* in her glimmering fpheare.
  Her. What's this to my *Lyfander* ? where is he ?
Ah good *Demetrius,* wilt thou giue him me ?
  Dem. I'de rather giue his carkaffe to my hounds.
  Her. Out dog, out cur, thou driu'ft me paft the bounds
Of maidens patience. Haft thou flaine him then?
Henceforth be neuer numbred among men.
Oh, once tell true, euen for my fake,
Durft thou a lookt vpon him, being awake?
And haft thou kill'd him fleeping? O braue tutch :
Could not a worme, an Adder do fo much ?
An Adder did it : for with doubler tongue
Then thine (thou ferpent) neuer Adder ftung.
  Dem. You fpend your paffion on a mifpri'sd mood,
I am not guiltie of *Lyfanders* blood :
Nor is he dead for ought that I can tell.
  Her. I pray thee tell me then that he is well.
  Dem. And if I could, what fhould I get therefore ?
  Her. A priuiledge, neuer to fee me more ;
And from thy hated prefence part I : fee me no more
Whether he be dead or no.   *Exit.*
  Dem. There is no following her in this fierce vaine,
Here therefore for a while I will remaine.
So forrowes heauineffe doth heauier grow :
For debt that bankrout flip doth forrow owe,
Which now in fome flight meafure it will pay,

                                                             If

If for his tender here I make ſome ſtay.   *Lie downe.*
Ob. What haſt thou done?Thou haſt miſtaken quite
And laid the loue iuyce on ſome true loues ſight:
Of thy miſpriſion, muſt perforce enſue
Some true loue turn'd, and not a falſe turn'd true.
   Rob. Then fate ore-rules, that one man hoiding troth,
A million faile, confounding oath on oath.
   Ob. About the wood, goe ſwifter then the winde,
And *Helena* of *Athens* looke thou finde.
All fancy ſicke ſhe is, and pale of cheere,
With ſighes of loue, that coſts the freſh bloud deare.
By ſome illuſion ſee thou bring her heere,
Ile charme his eyes againſt ſhe doth appeare.
   Robin. I go, I go, looke how I goe,
Swifter then arrow from the *Tartars* bowe.   *Exit.*
   Ob. Flower of this purple die,
Hit with *Cupids* archery,
Sinke in apple of his eye,
When his loue he doth eſpie,
Let her ſhine as gloriouſly
As the *Venus* of the sky.
When thou wak'ſt if ſhe be by,
Beg of her for remedy.

Enter Pucke.

   Puck. Captaine of our Fairy band,
Helena is heere at hand,
And the youth, miſtooke by me,
Pleading for a Louers fee.
Shall we their fond Pageant ſee?
Lord, what fooles theſe mortals be!
   Ob. Stand aſide: the noyſe they make,
Will cauſe *Demetrius* to awake.
   Puck. Then will two at once wooe one,
That muſt needs be ſport alone:
And thoſe things doe beſt pleaſe me,
That befall prepoſterouſly.

Enter Lyſander and Helena.

   Lyſ. Why ſhould you think y̌ I ſhould wooe in ſcorn?
Scorne and deriſion neuer comes in teares:
Looke when I vow I weepe; and vowes ſo borne,
In their natiuity all truth appeares.
How can theſe things in me, ſeeme ſcorne to you?
Bearing the badge of faith to proue them true.
   Hel. You doe aduance your cunning more & more,
When truth kils truth, O diueliſh holy fray!
Theſe vowes are *Hermias*. Will you giue her ore?
Weigh oath with oath, and you will nothing weigh.
Your vowes to her, and me, (put in two ſcales)
Will euen weigh, and both as light as tales.
   Lyſ. I had no iudgement, when to her I ſwore.
   Hel. Nor none in my minde, now you giue her ore.
   Lyſ. Demetrius loues her, and he loues not you. *Awa.*
   Dem. O *Helen,* goddeſſe, nimph, perfect, diuine,
To what my, loue, ſhall I compare thine eyne!
Chriſtall is muddy, O how ripe in ſhow,
Thy lips, thoſe kiſſing cherries, tempting grow!
That pure congealed white, high *Taurus* ſnow,
Fan'd with the Eaſterne winde, turnes to a crow,
When thou holdſt vp thy hand. O let me kiſſe
This Princeſſe of pure white, this ſeale of bliſſe.
   Hell. O ſpight! O hell! I ſee you are all bent
To ſet againſt me, for your merriment:
If you were ciuill, and knew curteſie,
You would not doe me thus much iniury.

Can you not hate me, as I know you doe,
But you muſt ioyne in ſoules to mocke me to?
If you are men, as men you are in ſhow,
You would not vſe a gentle Lady ſo;
To vow, and ſweare, and ſuperpraiſe my parts,
When I am ſure you hate me with your hearts.
You both are Riuals, and loue *Hermia*;
And now both Riuals to mocke *Helena*.
A trim exploit, a manly enterprize,
To coniure teares vp in a poore maids eyes,
With your deriſion; none of noble ſort,
Would ſo offend a Virgin, and extort
A poore ſoules patience, all to make you ſport.
   Lyſa. You are vnkind *Demetrius*; be not ſo,
For you loue *Hermia*; this you know I know;
And here with all good will, with all my heart,
In *Hermias* loue I yeeld you vp my part;
And yours of *Helena,* to me bequeath,
Whom I do loue, and will do to my death.
   Hel. Neuer did mockers waſt more idle breth.
   Dem. Lyſander, keep thy *Hermia,* I will none:
If ere I lou'd her, all that loue is gone.
My heart to her, but as gueſt-wiſe ſoiourn'd,
And now to *Helen* it is home return'd,
There to remaine.
   Lyſ. It is not ſo.
   De. Diſparage not the faith thou doſt not know,
Leſt to thy perill thou abide it deare.
Looke where thy Loue comes, yonder is thy deare.

Enter Hermia.

   Her. Dark night, that from the eye his function takes,
The eare more quicke of apprehenſion makes,
Wherein it doth impaire the ſeeing ſenſe,
It paies the hearing double recompence.
Thou art not by mine eye, *Lyſander* found,
Mine eare (I thanke it) brought me to that ſound.
But why vnkindly didſt thou leaue me ſo?   (to go?
   Lyſan. Why ſhould hee ſtay whom Loue doth preſſe
   Her. What loue could preſſe *Lyſander* from my ſide?
   Lyſ. Lyſanders loue (that would not let him bide)
Faire *Helena;* who more engilds the night,
Then all yon fierie oes, and eies of light.
Why ſeek'ſt thou me? Could not this make thee know,
The hate I bare thee, made me leaue thee ſo?
   Her. You ſpeake not as you thinke; it cannot be.
   Hel. Loe, ſhe is one of this confederacy,
Now I perceiue they haue conioyn'd all three,
To faſhion this falſe ſport in ſpight of me.
Iniurious *Hermia,* moſt vngratefull maid,
Haue you conſpir'd, haue you with theſe contriu'd
To baite me, with this foule deriſion?
Is all the counſell that we two haue ſhar'd,
The ſiſters vowes, the houres that we haue ſpent,
When wee haue chid the haſty footed time,
For parting vs; O, is all forgot?
All ſchooledaies friendſhip, child-hood innocence?
We *Hermia,* like two Artificiall gods,
Haue with our needles, created both one flower,
Both on one ſampler, ſitting on one cuſhion,
Both warbling of one ſong, both in one key;
As if our hands, our ſides, voices, and mindes
Had beene incorporate. So we grew together,
Like to a double cherry, ſeeming parted,
But yet a vnion in partition,

                                     Two

Two louely berries molded on one ſtem,
So with two ſeeming bodies, but one heart,
Two of the firſt life coats in Heraldry,
Due but to one and crowned with one creſt.
And will you rent our ancient loue aſunder,
To ioyne with men in ſcorning your poore friend?
It is not friendly, 'tis not maidenly.
Our ſexe as well as I, may chide you for it,
Though I alone doe feele the iniurie.
  Her. I am amazed at your paſſionate words,
I ſcorne you not; It ſeemes that you ſcorne me.
  Hel. Haue you not ſet *Lyſander*, as in ſcorne
To follow me, and praiſe my eies and face?
And made your other loue, *Demetrius*
(Who euen but now did ſpurne me with his foote)
To call me goddeſſe, nimph, diuine, and rare,
Precious, celeſtiall? Wherefore ſpeakes he this
To her he hates? And wherefore doth *Lyſander*
Denie your loue (ſo rich within his ſoule)
And tender me (forſooth) affection,
But by your ſetting on, by your conſent?
What though I be not ſo in grace as you,
So hung vpon with loue, ſo fortunate?
(But miſerable moſt, to loue vnlou'd)
This you ſhould pittie, rather then deſpiſe.
  Her. I vnderſtand not what you meane by this.
  Hel. I, doe, perſeuer, counterfeit ſad lookes,
Make mouthes vpon me when I turne my backe,
Winke each at other, hold the ſweete ieſt vp:
This ſport well carried, ſhall be chronicled.
If you haue any pittie, grace, or manners,
You would not make me ſuch an argument:
But fare ye well, 'tis partly mine owne fault,
Which death or abſence ſoone ſhall remedie.
  Lyſ. Stay gentle *Helena*, heare my excuſe,
My loue, my life, my ſoule, faire *Helena*.
  Hel. O excellent!
  Her. Sweete, do not ſcorne her ſo.
  Dem. If ſhe cannot entreate, I can compell.
  Lyſ. Thou canſt compell, no more then ſhe entreate.
Thy threats haue no more ſtrength then her weak praiſe.
Helen, I loue thee, by my life I doe;
I ſweare by that which I will loſe for thee,
To proue him falſe, that ſaies I loue thee not.
  Dem. I ſay, I loue thee more then he can doe.
  Lyſ. If thou ſay ſo, with-draw and proue it too.
  Dem. Quick, come.
  Her. *Lyſander*, whereto tends all this?
  Lyſ. Away, you *Ethiope*.
  Dem. No, no, Sir, ſeeme to breake looſe;
Take on as you would follow,
But yet come not: you are a tame man, go.
  Lyſ. Hang off thou cat, thou bur; vile thing let looſe,
Or I will ſhake thee from me like a ſerpent.
  Her. Why are you growne ſo rude?
What change is this ſweete Loue?
  Lyſ. Thy loue? out tawny *Tartar*, out;
Out loathed medicine; O hated poiſon hence.
  Her. Do you ieſt?
  Hel. Yes ſooth, and ſo do you.
  Lyſ. *Demetrius*: I will keepe my word with thee.
  Dem. I would I had your bond: for I perceiue
A weake bond holds you; Ile not truſt your word.
  Lyſ. What, ſhould I hurt her, ſtrike her, kill her dead?
Although I hate her, Ile not harme her ſo.
  Her. What, can you do me greater harme then hate?

Hate me, wherefore? O me, what newes my Loue?
Am not I *Hermia*? Are not you *Lyſander*?
I am as faire now, as I was ere while.
Since night you lou'd me; yet ſince night you left me.
Why then you left me (O the gods forbid
In earneſt, ſhall I ſay?
  Lyſ. I, by my life;
And neuer did deſire to ſee thee more.
Therefore be out of hope, of queſtion, of doubt;
Be certaine, nothing truer: 'tis no ieſt,
That I doe hate thee, and loue *Helena*.
  Her. O me, you iugler, you canker bloſſome,
You theefe of loue; What, haue you come by night,
And ſtolne my loues heart from him?
  Hel. Fine yfaith:
Haue you no modeſty, no maiden ſhame,
No touch of baſhfulneſſe? What, will you teare
Impatient anſwers from my gentle tongue?
Fie, fie, you counterfeit, you puppet, you.
  Her. Puppet? why ſo? I, that way goes the game.
Now I perceiue that ſhe hath made compare
Betweene our ſtatures, ſhe hath vrg'd her height,
And with her perſonage, her tall perſonage,
Her height (forſooth) ſhe hath preuail'd with him.
And are you growne ſo high in his eſteeme,
Becauſe I am ſo dwarfiſh, and ſo low?
How low am I, thou painted May-pole? Speake,
How low am I? I am not yet ſo low,
But that my nailes can reach vnto thine eyes.
  Hel. I pray you though you mocke me, gentlemen,
Let her not hurt me; I was neuer curſt:
I haue no gift at all in ſhrewiſhneſſe;
I am a right maide for my cowardize;
Let her not ſtrike me: you perhaps may thinke,
Becauſe ſhe is ſomething lower then my ſelfe,
That I can match her.
  Her. Lower? harke againe.
  Hel. Good *Hermia*, do not be ſo bitter with me,
I euermore did loue you *Hermia*,
Did euer keepe your counſels, neuer wronged you,
Saue that in loue vnto *Demetriu*,
I told him of your ſtealth vnto this wood.
He followed you, for loue I followed him,
But he hath chid me hence, and threatned me
To ſtrike me, ſpurne me, nay to kill me too;
And now, ſo you will let me quiet go,
To *Athens* will I beare my folly backe,
And follow you no further. Let me go.
You ſee how ſimple, and how fond I am.
  Her. Why get you gone: who iſt that hinders you?
  Hel. A fooliſh heart, that I leaue here behinde.
  Her. What, with *Lyſander*?
  Hel. With *Demetrius*.
  Lyſ. Be not afraid, ſhe ſhall not harme thee *Helena*.
  Dem. No ſir, ſhe ſhall not, though you take her part.
  Hel. O me, ſhe's angry, ſhe is keene and ſhrewd,
She was a vixen when ſhe went to ſchoole,
And though ſhe be but little, ſhe is fierce.
  Her. Little againe? Nothing but low and little?
Why will you ſuffer her to flout me thus?
Let me come to her.
  Lyſ. Get you gone you dwarfe,
You *minimus*, of hindring knot-graſſe made,
You bead, you acorne.
  Dem. You are too officious,
In her behalfe that ſcornes your ſeruices.

Let

Let her alone, speake not of *Helena*,
Take not her part. For if thou dost intend
Neuer so little shew of loue to her,
Thou shalt abide it.

Lyf. Now she holds me not,
Now follow if thou dar'st, to try whose right,
Of thine or mine is most in *Helena*.

Dem. Follow? Nay, Ile goe with thee cheeke by
iowle. *Exit Lysander and Demetrius.*

Her. You Mistris, all this coyle is long of you.
Nay, goe not backe.

Hel. I will not trust you I,
Nor longer stay in your curst companie.
Your hands then mine, are quicker for a fray,
My legs are longer though to runne away.

Enter Oberon and Pucke.

Ob. This is thy negligence, still thou mistak'st,
Or else committ'st thy knaueries willingly.

Puck. Beleeue me, King of shadowes, I mistooke,
Did not you tell me, I should know the man,
By the *Athenian* garments he hath on?
And so farre blamelesse proues my enterprize,
That I haue nointed an Athenians eies,
And so farre am I glad, it so did sort,
As this their iangling I esteeme a sport.

Ob. Thou seest these Louers seeke a place to fight,
Hie therefore *Robin*, ouercast the night,
The starrie Welkin couer thou anon,
With drooping fogge as blacke as *Acheron*,
And lead these testie Riuals so astray,
As one come not within anothers way.
Like to *Lysander*, sometime frame thy tongue,
Then stirre *Demetrius* vp with bitter wrong;
And sometime raile thou like *Demetrius*;
And from each other looke thou leade them thus,
Till ore their browes, death-counterfeiting, sleepe
With leaden legs, and Battie-wings doth creepe;
Then crush this hearbe into *Lysanders* eie,
Whose liquor hath this vertuous propertie,
To take from thence all error, with his might,
And make his eie-bals role with wonted sight.
When they next wake, all this derision
Shall seeme a dreame, and fruitlesse vision,
And backe to *Athens* shall the Louers wend
With league, whose date till death shall neuer end.
Whiles I in this affaire do thee imply,
Ile to my Queene, and beg her *Indian* Boy;
And then I will her charmed eie release
From monsters view, and all things shall be peace.

Puck. My Fairie Lord, this must be done with haste,
For night-swift Dragons cut the Clouds full fast,
And yonder shines *Auroras* harbinger;
At whose approach Ghosts wandring here and there,
Troope home to Church-yards; damned spirits all,
That in crosse-waies and floods haue buriall,
Alreadie to their wormie beds are gone;
For feare least day should looke their shames vpon,
They wilfully themselues dxile from light,
And must for aye consort with blacke browd night.

Ob. But we are spirits of another sort:
I, with the mornings loue haue oft made sport,
And like a Forrester, the groues may tread,
Euen till the Easterne gate all fierie red,
Opening on *Neptune*, with faire blessed beames,
Turnes into yellow gold, his salt greene streames.

But notwithstanding haste, make no delay:
We may effect this businesse, yet ere day.

Puck. Vp and downe, vp and downe, I will leade
them vp and downe: I am fear'd in field and towne.
Goblin, lead them vp and downe: here comes one.

Enter Lysander.

Lys. Where art thou, proud *Demetrius*?
Speake thou now.

Rob. Here villaine, drawne & readie. Where art thou?

Lys. I will be with thee straight.

Rob. Follow me then to plainer ground.

Enter Demetrius.

Dem. *Lysander*, speake againe;
Thou runaway, thou coward, art thou fled?
Speake in some bush: Where dost thou hide thy head?

Rob. Thou coward, art thou bragging to the stars,
Telling the bushes that thou look'st for wars,
And wilt not come? Come recreant, come thou childe,
Ile whip thee with a rod. He is defil'd
That drawes a sword on thee.

Dem. Yea, art thou there?

Ro. Follow my voice, we'l try no manhood here. *Exit.*

Lys. He goes before me, and still dares me on,
When I come where he cals, then he's gone.
The villaine is much lighter heel'd then I:
I followed fast, but faster he did flye; *shifting places.*
That fallen am I in darke vneuen way,
And here will rest me. Come thou gentle day: *lye down.*
For if but once thou shew me thy gray light,
Ile finde *Demetrius*, and reuenge this spight.

Enter Robin and Demetrius.

Rob. Ho, ho, ho; coward, why com'st thou not?

Dem. Abide me, if thou dar'st. For well I wot,
Thou runst before me, shifting euery place,
And dar'st not stand, nor looke me in the face.
Where art thou?

Rob. Come hither, I am here.

Dem. Nay then thou mock'st me; thou shalt buy this
deere,
If euer I thy face by day-light see.
Now goe thy way: faintnesse constraineth me,
To measure out my length on this cold bed,
By daies approach looke to be visited.

Enter Helena.

Hel. O weary night, O long and tedious night,
Abate thy houres, shine comforts from the East,
That I may backe to *Athens* by day-light,
From these that my poore companie detest;
And sleepe that sometime shuts vp sorrowes eie,
Steale me a while from mine owne companie. *Sleepe.*

Rob. Yet but three? Come one more,
Two of both kindes makes vp foure.
Here she comes, curst and sad,
Cupid is a knauish lad,

Enter Hermia.

Thus to make poore females mad.

Her. Neuer so wearie, neuer so in woe,
Bedabbled with the dew, and torne with briars,
I can no further crawle, no further goe;
My legs can keepe no pace with my desires.
Here will I rest me till the breake of day,
Heauens shield *Lysander*, if they meane a fray.

Rob. On the ground sleepe found,
Ile apply your eie gentle louer, remedy.
When thou wak'st, thou tak'st
True delight in the sight of thy former Ladies eye,

And

And the Country Prouerb knowne,
That euery man should take his owne,
In your waking shall be showne.
Iacke shall haue *Iill*, nought shall goe ill,
The man shall haue his Mare againe, and all shall bee
well.

They sleepe all the Act.

Actus Quartus.

*Enter Queene of Fairies, and Clowne, and Fairies, and the
King behinde them.*

Tita. Come, sit thee downe vpon this flowry bed,
While I thy amiable cheekes doe coy,
And sticke muske roses in thy sleeke smoothe head,
And kisse thy faire large eares, my gentle ioy.
 Clow. Where's *Pease blossome?*
 Peas. Ready.
 Clow. scratch my head, *Pease-blossome.* Wher's Moun-
sieur *Cobweb.*
 Cob. Ready.
 Clowne. Mounsieur *Cobweb,* good Mounsier get your
weapons in your hand, & kill me a red hipt humble-Bee,
on the top of a thistle ; and good Mounsieur bring mee
the hony bag. Doe not fret your selfe too much in the
action, Mounsieur; and good Mounsieur haue a care the
hony bag breake not, I would be loth to haue yon ouer-
flowne with a hony-bag signiour. Where's Mounsieur
Mustardseed?
 Must. Ready.
 Clo. Giue me your neafe, Mounsieur *Mustardseed.*
Pray you leaue your courtesie good Mounsieur.
 Mus. What's your will ?
 Clo. Nothing good Mounsieur, but to help Caualery
Cobweb to scratch. I must to the Barbers Mounsieur, for
me-thinkes I am maruellous hairy about the face. And I
am such a tender asse, if my haire do but tickle me, I must
scratch.
 Tita. What, wilt thou heare some musicke, my sweet
loue.
 Clow. I haue a reasonable good eare in musicke. Let
vs haue the tongs and the bones.
 　　　　Musicke Tongs, Rurall Musicke.
 Tita. Or say sweete Loue, what thou desirest to eat.
 Clowne. Truly a pecke of Prouender ; I could munch
your good dry Oates. Me-thinkes I haue a great desire
to a bottle of hay : good hay, sweete hay hath no fel-
low.
 Tita. I haue a venturous Fairy,
That shall seeke the Squirrels hoard,
And fetch thee new Nuts.
 Clown. I had rather haue a handfull or two of dried
pease. But I pray you let none of your people stirre me, I
haue an exposition of sleepe come vpon me.
 Tyta. Sleepe thou, and I will winde thee in my armes,
Fairies be gone, and be alwaies away.
So doth the woodbine, the sweet Honisuckle,
Gently entwist ; the female Iuy so
Enrings the barky fingers of the Elme.

O how I loue thee ! how I dote on thee !

Enter Robin goodfellow and Oberon.
 Ob. Welcome good *Robin :*
Seest thou this sweet sight ?
Her dotage now I doe begin to pitty.
For meeting her of late behinde the wood,
Seeking sweet sauors for this hatefull foole,
I did vpbraid her, and fall out with her.
For she his hairy temples then had rounded,
With coronet of fresh and fragrant flowers.
And that same dew which somtime on the buds,
Was wont to swell like round and orient pearles ;
Stood now within the pretty flouriets eyes,
Like teares that did their owne disgrace bewaile.
When I had at my pleasure taunted her,
And she in milde termes beg'd my patience,
I then did aske of her, her changeling childe,
Which straight she gaue me, and her Fairy sent
To beare him to my Bower in Fairy Land.
And now I haue the Boy, I will vndoe
This hatefull imperfection of her eyes.
And gentle *Pucke,* take this transformed scalpe,
From off the head of this *Athenian* swaine ;
That he awaking when the other doe,
May all to *Athens* backe againe repaire,
And thinke no more of this nights accidents,
But as the fierce vexation of a dreame.
But first I will release the Fairy Queene.

 Be thou as thou wast wont to be ;
 See as thou wast wont to see.
 Dians bud, or Cupids flower,
 Hath such force and blessed power.

Now my *Titania* wake you my sweet Queene.
 Tita. My *Oberon,* what visions haue I seene !
Me-thought I was enamoured of an Asse.
 Ob. There lies your loue.
 Tita. How came these things to passe ?
Oh, how mine eyes doth loath this visage now !
 Ob. Silence a while. *Robin* take off his head :
Titania, musicke call, and strike more dead
Then common sleepe ; of all these, fine the sense.
 Tita. Musicke, ho musicke, such as charmeth sleepe.
 　　　　　　　　　　　　　　　Musick still.
 Rob. When thou wak'st, with thine owne fooles eies
peepe.　　　　　　　　　　　　　　　　　　　(me
 Ob. Sound musick; come my Queen, take hands with
And rocke the ground whereon these sleepers be.
Now thou and I are new in amity,
And will to morrow midnight, solemnly
Dance in Duke *Theseus* house triumphantly,
And blesse it to all faire posterity.
There shall the paires of faithfull Louers be
Wedded, with *Theseus,* all in iollity.
 Rob. Faire King attend, and marke,
I doe heare the morning Larke.
 Ob. Then my Queene in silence sad,
Trip we after the nights shade ;
We the Globe can compasse soone,
Swifter then the wandring Moone.
 Tita. Come my Lord, and in our flight,
Tell me how it came this night,
That I sleeping heere was found,
 　　　　　　　　　　　　　Sleepers Lye still.
　　　　O　　　　　　　　　　　　　With

With theſe mortals on the ground.   *Exeunt.*
                        Winde Hornes.

Enter Theſeus, Egeus, Hippolita and all his trainc.

Theſ. Goe one of you, finde out the Forreſter,
For now our obſeruation is perform'd;
And ſince we haue the vaward of the day,
My Loue ſhall heare the muſicke of my hounds.
Vncouple in the Weſterne valley, let them goe;
Diſpatch I ſay, and finde the Forreſter.
We will faire Queene, vp to the Mountaines top.
And marke the muſicall confuſion
Of hounds and eccho in coniunction.
   Hip. I was with *Hercules* and *Cadmus* once,
When in a wood of *Creete* they bayed the Beare
With hounds of *Sparta*; neuer did I heare
Such gallant chiding. For beſides the groues,
The skies, the fountaines, euery region neere,
Seeme all one mutuall cry. I neuer heard
So muſicall a diſcord, ſuch ſweet thunder.
   Theſ. My hounds are bred out of the *Spartan* kinde,
So flew'd, ſo ſanded, and their heads are hung
With eares that ſweepe away the morning dew,
Crooke kneed, and dew-lapt, like *Theſſalian* Buls,
Slow in purſuit, but match'd in mouth like bels,
Each vnder each. A cry more tuneable
Was neuer hallowed to, nor cheer'd with horne,
In *Creete*, in *Sparta*, nor in *Theſſaly*;
Iudge when you heare. Bnt ſoft, what nimphs are theſe?
   Egeus. My Lord, this is my daughter heere aſleepe,
And this *Lyſander*, this *Demetrius* is,
This *Helena*, olde *Nedars* *Helena*,
I wonder of this being heere together.
   The. No doubt they roſe vp early, to obſerue
The right of May; and hearing our intent,
Came heere in grace of our ſolemnity.
But ſpeake *Egeus*, is not this the day
That *Hermia* ſhould giue anſwer of her choice?
   Egeus. It is, my Lord.
   Theſ. Goe bid the huntſ-men wake them with their
hornes.

Hornes and they wake.
Shout within, they all ſtart vp.

   Theſ. Good morrow friends: Saint *Valentine* iʃ paſt,
Begin theſe wood birds but to couple now?
   Lyſ. Pardon my Lord.
   Theſ. I pray you all ſtand vp.
I know you two are Riuall enemies.
How comes this gentle concord in the world,
That hatred is is ſo farre from iealouſie,
To ſleepe by hate, and feare no enmity.
   Lyſ. My Lord, I ſhall reply amazedly,
Halfe ſleepe, halfe waking. But as yet, I ſweare,
I cannot truly ſay how I came heere.
But as I thinke (for truly would I ſpeake)
And now I doe bethinke me, ſo it is;
I came with *Hermia* hither. Our intent
Was to be gone from *Athens*, where we might be
Without the perill of the *Athenian* Law.
   Ege. Enough, enough, my Lord: you haue enough;
I beg the Law, the Law, vpon his head:
They would haue ſtolne away, they would *Demetrius*,
Thereby to haue defeated you and me:
You of your wife, and me ôf my conſent;
Of my conſent, that ſhe ſhould be your wife.
   Dem. My Lord, faire *Helen* told me of their ſtealth,
Of this their purpoſe hither, to this wood,

And I in furie hither followed them;
Faire *Helena*, in fancy followed me.
But my good Lord, I wot not by what power,
(But by ſome power it is) my loue
To *Hermia* (melted as the ſnow)
Seems to me now as the remembrance of an idle gaude,
Which in my childehood I did doat vpon:
And all the faith, the vertue of my heart,
The obiect and the pleaſure of mine eye,
Is onely *Helena*. To her, my Lord,
Was I betroth'd, ere I ſee *Hermia*,
But like a ſickeneſſe did I loath this food,
But as in health, come to my naturall taſte,
Now doe I wiſh it, loue it, long for it,
And will for euermore be true to it.
   Theſ. Faire Louers, you are fortunately met;
Of this diſcourſe we ſhall heare more anon.
Egeus, I will ouer-beare your will;
For in the Temple, by and by with vs,
Theſe couples ſhall eternally be knit.
And for the morning now is ſomething worne,
Our purpoſ'd hunting ſhall be ſet aſide.
Away, with vs to *Athens*; three and three,
Wee'll hold a feaſt in great ſolemnitie.
Come *Hippolita*.   *Exit Duke and Lords.*
   Dem. Theſe things ſeeme ſmall & vndiſtinguiſhable,
Like farre off mountaines turned into Clouds.
   Her. Me-thinks I ſee theſe things with parted eye,
When euery things ſeemes double.
   Hel. So me-thinkes:
And I haue found *Demetrius*, like a iewell,
Mine owne, and not mine owne.
   Dem. It ſeemes to mee,
That yet we ſleepe, we dreame. Do not you thinke,
The Duke was heere, and bid vs follow him?
   Her. Yea, and my Father.
   Hel. And *Hippolita*.
   Lyſ. And he bid vs follow to the Temple.
   Dem. Why then we are awake; lets follow him, and
by the way let vs recount our dreames.

Bottome wakes.   *Exit Louers.*

   Clo. When my cue comes, call me, and I will anſwer.
My next is, moſt faire *Piramus*. Hey ho. *Peter Quince?*
Flute the bellowes-mender? *Snout* the tinker? *Starue-*
ling? Gods my life! Stolne hence, and left me aſleepe: I
haue had a moſt rare viſion. I had a dreame, paſt the wit
of man, to ſay, what dreame it was. Man is but an Aſſe,
if he goe about to expound this dreame. Me-thought I
was, there is no man can tell what. Me-thought I was,
and me-thought I had. But man is but a patch'd foole,
if he will offer to ſay, what me-thought I had. The eye of
man hath not heard, the eare of man hath not ſeen, mans
hand is not able to taſte, his tongue to conceiue, nor his
heart to report, what my dreame was. I will get *Peter*
Quince to write a ballet of this dreame, it ſhall be called
Bottomes Dreame, becauſe it hath no bottome; and I will
ſing it in the latter end of a play, before the Duke. Peraduenture, to make it the more gracious, I ſhall ſing it
at her death.   *Exit.*

Enter Quince, Flute, Thisbie, Snout, and Starueling.

   Quin. Haue you ſent to *Bottomes* houſe? Is he come
home yet?
   Staru. He cannot be heard of. Out of doubt hee is
tranſported.

                                       Thiſ. If

Thiſ. If he come not, then the play is mar'd. It goes not forward, doth it?

Quin. It is not poſſible : you haue not a man in all *Athens*, able to diſcharge *Piramus* but he.

Thiſ. No, hee hath ſimply the beſt wit of any handy-craft man in *Athens.*

Quin. Yea, and the beſt perſon too, and hee is a very Paramour, for a ſweet voyce.

Thiſ. You muſt ſay, Paragón. A Paramour is (God bleſſe vs) a thing of nought.

Enter Snug the Ioyner.

Snug. Maſters, the Duke is comming from the Temple, and there is two or three Lords & Ladies more married : If our ſport had gone forward, we had all bin made men.

Thiſ. O ſweet bully *Bottome* : thus hath he loſt ſixepence a day, during his life; he could not haue ſcaped ſixpence a day. And the Duke had not giuen him ſixpence a day for playing *Piramus*, Ile be hang'd. He would haue deſerued it. Sixpence a day in *Piramus*, or nothing.

Enter Bottome.

Bot. Where are theſe Lads? Where are theſe hearts?

Quin. *Bottome*, ô moſt couragious day! O moſt happie houre!

Bot. Maſters, I am to diſcourſe wonders; but ask me not what. For if I tell you , I am no true *Athenian.* I will tell you euery thing as it fell out.

Qu. Let vs heare, ſweet *Bottome.*

Bot. Not a word of me : all that I will tell you, is, that the Duke hath dined. Get your apparell together, good ſtrings to your beards, new ribbands to your pumps, meete preſently at the Palace , euery man looke ore his part : for the ſhort and the long is, our play is preferred : In any caſe let *Thiſby* haue cleane linnen : and let not him that playes the Lion, paire his nailes, for they ſhall hang out for the Lions clawes. And moſt deare Actors, eate no Onions, nor Garlicke ; for wee are to vtter ſweete breath, and I doe not doubt but to heare them ſay, it is a ſweet Comedy. No more words : away, go away.

Exeunt.

Actus Quintus.

Enter Theſeus, Hippolita, Egeus and his Lords.

Hip. 'Tis ſtrange my *Theſeus*, ỹ theſe louers ſpeake of.

The. More ſtrange then true. I neuer may beleeue Theſe anticke fables, nor theſe Fairy toyes, Louers and mad men haue ſuch ſeething braines, Such ſhaping phantaſies, that apprehend more Then coole reaſon euer comprehends. The Lunaticke, the Louer, and the Poet, Are of imagination all compact. One ſees more diuels then vaſte hell can hold ; That is the mad man. The Louer, all as franticke, Sees *Helens* beauty in a brow of *Egipt.* The Poets eye in a fine frenzy rolling, doth glance From heauen to earth, from earth to heauen. And as imagination bodies forth the forms of things Vnknowne ; the Poets pen turnes them to ſhapes, And giues to aire nothing, a locall habitation, And a name. Such tricks hath ſtrong imagination,

That if it would but apprehend ſome ioy, It comprehends ſome bringer of that ioy. Or in the night, imagining ſome feare, How eaſie is a buſh ſuppos'd a Beare? *Hip.* But all the ſtorie of the night told ouer, And all their minds transfigur'd ſo together, More witneſſeth than fancies images, And growes to ſomething of great conſtancie; But howſoeuer, ſtrange, and admirable.

Enter louers, Lyſander, Demetrius, Hermia, and Helena.

The. Heere come the louers, full of ioy and mirth : Ioy, gentle friends, ioy and freſh dayes Of loue accompany your hearts.

Lyſ. More then to vs, waite in your royall walkes, your boord, your bed.

The. Come now, what maskes, what dances ſhall we haue, To weare away this long age of three houres, Between our after ſupper, and bed-time ? Where is our vſuall manager of mirth ? What Reuels are in hand ? Is there no play, To eaſe the anguiſh of a torturing houre? Call *Egeus.*

Ege. Heere mighty *Theſeus.*

The. Say, what abridgement haue you for this euening? What maske? What muſicke? How ſhall we beguile The lazie time, if not with ſome delight?

Ege. There is a breefe how many ſports are rife : Make choiſe of which your Highneſſe will ſee firſt.

Liſ. The battell with the Centaurs to be ſung By an Athenian Eunuch, to the Harpe.

The. Wee'l none of that. That haue I told my Loue In glory of my kinſman Hercules.

Liſ. The riot of the tipſie Bachanals, Tearing the Thracian ſinger, in their rage?

The. That is an old deuice, and it was plaid When I from *Thebes* came laſt a Conqueror.

Liſ. The thrice three Muſes, mourning for the death of learning, late deceaſt in beggerie.

The. That is ſome Satire keene and criticall, Not ſorting with a nuptiall ceremonie.

Liſ. A tedious breefe Scene of yong *Piramus*, And his loue *Thiſby* ; very tragicall mirth.

The. Merry and tragicall? Tedious, and briefe? That is, hot ice, and wondrous ſtrange ſnow. How ſhall wee finde the concord of this diſcord ?

Ege. A play there is, my Lord, ſome ten words long, Which is as breefe, as I haue knowne a play ; But by ten words, my Lord, it is too long ; Which makes it tedious. For in all the play, There is not one word apt, one Player fitted. And tragicall my noble Lord it is : for *Piramus* Therein doth kill himſelfe. Which when I ſaw Rehearſt, I muſt confeſſe, made mine eyes water : But more merrie teares, the paſſion of loud laughter Neuer ſhed.

Theſ. What are they that do play it?

Ege. Hard handed men, that worke in Athens heere, Which neuer labour'd in their mindes till now ; And now haue toyled their vnbreathed memories With this ſame play, againſt your nuptiall.

The. And we will heare it.

O 2 *Phil.*

Phi. No, my noble Lord, it is not for you. I haue heard
It ouer, and it is nothing, nothing in the world ;
Vnleſſe you can finde ſport in their intents,
Extreamely ſtretcht, and cond with cruell paine,
To doe you ſeruice.

Theſ. I will heare that play. For neuer any thing
Can be amiſſe, when ſimpleneſſe and duty tender it.
Goe bring them in, and take your places, Ladies.

Hip. I loue not to ſee wretchedneſſe orecharged ;
And duty in his ſeruice periſhing.

Theſ. Why gentle ſweet, you ſhall ſee no ſuch thing.

Hip. He ſaies, they can doe nothing in this kinde.

Theſ. The kinder we, to giue them thanks for nothing
Our ſport ſhall be, to take what they miſtake ;
And what poore duty cannot doe, noble reſpect
Takes it in might, not merit.
Where I haue come, great Clearkes haue purpoſed
To greete me with premeditated welcomes ;
Where I haue ſeene them ſhiuer and looke pale,
Make periods in the midſt of ſentences,
Throttle their practiz'd accent in their feares,
And in concluſion, dumbly haue broke off,
Not paying me a welcome. Truſt me ſweete,
Out of this ſilence yet, I pickt a welcome :
And in the modeſty of fearefull duty,
I read as much, as from the ratling tongue
Of ſaucy and audacious eloquence.
Loue therefore, and tongue-tide ſimplicity,
In leaſt, ſpeake moſt, to my capacity.

Egeus. So pleaſe your Grace, the Prologue is addreſt.

Duke. Let him approach.   *Flor. Trum.*

Enter the Prologue.   *Quince.*

Pro. If we offend, it is with our good will.
That you ſhould thinke, we come not to offend,
But with good will. To ſhew our ſimple skill,
That is the true beginning of our end.
Conſider then, we come but in deſpight.
We do not come, as minding to content you,
Our true intent is. All for your delight,
We are not heere. That you ſhould here repent you,
The Actors are at hand ; and by their ſhow,
You ſhall know all, that you are like to know.

Theſ. This fellow doth not ſtand vpon points.

Lyſ. He hath rid his Prologue, like a rough Colt : he
knowes not the ſtop. A good morall my Lord. It is not
enough to ſpeake, but to ſpeake true.

Hip. Indeed hee hath plaid on his Prologue, like a
childe on a Recorder, a ſound, but not in gouernment.

Theſ. His ſpeech was like a tangled chaine: nothing
impaired, but all diſordered. Who is next ?

Tawyer with a Trumpet before them.

Enter Pyramus and Thiſby, Wall, Moone-ſhine, and Lyon.

Prol. Gentles, perchance you wonder at this ſhow,
But wonder on, till truth make all things plaine.
This man is *Piramus*, if you would know ;
This beauteous Lady, *Thiſby* is certaine.
This man, with lyme and rough-caſt, doth preſent
Wall, that vile wall, which did theſe louers ſunder :
And through walls chink (poor ſoules) they are content
To whiſper. At the which, let no man wonder.
This man, with Lanthorne, dog, and buſh of thorne,
Preſenteth moone-ſhine. For if you will know,
By moone-ſhine did theſe Louers thinke no ſcorne
To meet at *Ninus* toombe, there, there to wooe :

This grizy beaſt (which Lyon hight by name)
The truſty *Thiſby*, comming firſt by night,
Did ſcarre away, or rather did affright :
And as ſhe fled, her mantle ſhe did fall ;
Which Lyon vile with bloody mouth did ſtaine.
Anon comes *Piramus*, ſweet youth and tall,
And findes his *Thiſbies* Mantle ſlaine ;
Whereat, with blade, with bloody blamefull blade,
He brauely broacht his boiling bloudy breaſt,
And *Thiſby*, tarrying in Mulberry ſhade,
His dagger drew, and died. For all the reſt,
Let *Lyon, Moone-ſhine, Wall*, and Louers twaine,
At large diſcourſe, while here they doe remaine.

Exit all but Wall.

Theſ. I wonder if the Lion be to ſpeake.

Deme. No wonder, my Lord : one Lion may, when
many Aſſes doe.

Exit Lyon, Thiſbie, and Mooneſhine.

Wall. In this ſame Interlude, it doth befall,
That I, one *Snowt* (by name) preſent a wall :
And ſuch a wall, as I vvould haue you thinke,
That had in it a crannied hole or chinke :
Through which the Louers, *Piramus* and *Thiſbie*
Did whiſper often, very ſecretly.
This loame, this rough-caſt, and this ſtone doth ſhew,
That I am that ſame Wall ; the truth is ſo.
And this the cranny is, right and ſiniſter,
Through which the fearefull Louers are to whiſper.

Theſ. Would you deſire Lime and Haire to ſpeake
better ?

Deme. It is the vvittieſt partition, that euer I heard
diſcourſe, my Lord.

Theſ. Pyramus drawes neere the Wall, ſilence.

Enter Pyramus.

Pir. O grim lookt night, ô night with hue ſo blacke,
O night, which euer art, when day is not :
O night, ô night, alacke, alacke, alacke,
I feare my *Thiſbies* promiſe is forgot.
And thou ô vvall, thou ſweet and louely vvall,
That ſtands betweene her fathers ground and mine,
Thou vvall, ô vvall, ô ſweet and louely vvall,
Shew me thy chinke, to blinke through vvith mine eine.
Thankes courteous vvall. *Ioue* ſhield thee vvell for this.
But vvhat ſee I ? No *Thiſbie* doe I ſee.
O vvicked vvall, through vvhom I ſee no bliſſe,
Curſt be thy ſtones for thus deceiuing mee.

Theſ. The vvall me-thinkes being ſenſible, ſhould
curſe againe.

Pir. No in truth ſir, he ſhould not. *Deceiuing me*,
Is *Thiſbies* cue ; ſhe is to enter, and I am to ſpy
Her through the vvall. You ſhall ſee it vvill fall.

Enter Thiſbie.

Pat as I told you ; yonder ſhe comes.

Thiſ. O vvall, full often haſt thou heard my mones,
For parting my faire *Piramus*, and me.
My cherry lips haue often kiſt thy ſtones ;
Thy ſtones vvith Lime and Haire knit vp in thee.

Pyra. I ſee a voyce ; now vvill I to the chinke,
To ſpy and I can heare my *Thiſbies* face. *Thiſbie* ?

Thiſ. My Loue thou art, my Loue I thinke.

Pir. Thinke vvhat thou vvilt, I am thy Louers grace,
And like *Limander* am I truſty ſtill.

Thiſ. And like *Helen* till the Fates me kill.

Pir. Not *Shafalus* to *Procrus*, was ſo true.

Thiſ. As *Shafalus* to *Procrus*, I to you.

Pir. O

Pir. O kiffe me through the hole of this vile wall.

Thif. I kiffe the wals hole, not your lips at all.

Pir. Wilt thou at *Ninnies* tombe meete me ftraight way?

Thif. Tide life, tide death, I come without delay.

Wall. Thus haue I *Wall*, my part difcharged fo; And being done, thus *Wall* away doth go.   *Exit Clow.*

Du. Now is the morall downe betweene the two Neighbors.

Dem. No remedie my Lord, when Wals are fo wil-full, to heare without vvarning.

Dut. This is the fillieft ftuffe that ere I heard.

Du. The beft in this kind are but fhadowes, and the worft are no worfe, if imagination amend them.

Dut. It muft be your imagination then, & not theirs.

Duk. If wee imagine no worfe of them then they of themfelues, they may paffe for excellent men. Here com two noble beafts, in a man and a Lion.

Enter Lyon and Moone-fhine.

Lyon. You Ladies, you (whofe gentle harts do feare The fmalleft monftrous moufe that creepes on floore) May now perchance, both quake and tremble heere, When Lion rough in wildeft rage doth roare. Then know that I, one *Snug* the Ioyner am A Lion fell, nor elfe no Lions dam : For if I fhould as Lion come in ftrife Into this place, 'twere pittie of my life.

Du. A verie gentle beaft, and of a good confcience.

Dem. The verie beft at a beaft, my Lord, ỹ ere I faw.

Lif. This Lion is a verie Fox for his valor.

Du. True, and a Goofe for his difcretion.

Dem. Not fo my Lord : for his valor cannot carrie his difcretion, and the Fox carries the Goofe.

Du. His difcretion I am fure cannot carrie his valor : for the Goofe carries not the Fox. It is well ; leaue it to his difcretion, and let vs hearken to the Moone.

Moon. This Lanthorne doth the horned Moone pre-fent.

De. He fhould haue worne the hornes on his head.

Du. Hee is no crefcent, and his hornes are inuifible, within the circumference.

Moon. This lanthorne doth the horned Moone pre-fent : My felfe, the man i'th Moone doth feeme to be.

Du. This is the greateft error of all the reft; the man fhould be put into the Lanthorne. How is it els the man i'th Moone?

Dem. He dares not come there for the candle. For you fee, it is already in fnuffe.

Dut. I am vvearie of this Moone ; vvould he would change.

Du. It appeares by his fmal light of difcretion, that he is in the wane : but yet in courtefie, in all reafon, vve muft ftay the time.

Lyf. Proceed Moone.

Moon. All that I haue to fay, is to tell you, that the Lanthorne is the Moone; I, the man in the Moone; this thorne bufh, my thorne bufh; and this dog, my dog.

Dem. Why all thefe fhould be in the Lanthorne: for they are in the Moone. But filence, heere comes *Thifby.*

Enter Thifby.

Thif. This is old *Ninnies* tombe : where is my loue?

Lyon. Oh.

The Lion roares, Thifby runs off.

Dem. Well roar'd Lion.

Du. Well run *Thifby.*

Dut. Well fhone Moone. Truly the Moone fhines with a good grace.

Du. Wel mouz'd Lion.

Dem. And then came *Piramus.*

Lyf. And fo the Lion vanifht.

Enter Piramus.

Pyr. Sweet Moone, I thank thee for thy funny beames, I thanke thee Moone, for fhining now fo bright: For by thy gracious, golden, glittering beames, I truft to tafte of trueft *Thifbies* fight. But ftay : O fpight! but marke, poore Knight, What dreadful dole is heere? Eyes do you fee! How can it be! O dainty Ducke : O Deere! Thy mantle good ; what ftaind with blood! Approch you Furies fell : O Fates! come, come : Cut thred and thrum, Quaile, crufh, conclude, and quell.

Du. This paffion, and the death of a deare friend, Would go neere to make a man looke fad.

Dut. Befhrew my heart, but I pittie the man.

Pir. O wherefore Nature, did'ft thou Lions frame? Since Lion vilde hath heere deflour'd my deere : Which is : no, no, which was the faireft Dame That liu'd, that lou'd, that lik'd, that look'd with cheere. Come teares, confound : Out fword, and wound The pap of *Piramus* : I, that left pap, where heart doth hop ; Thus dye I, thus, thus, thus. Now am I dead, now am I fled, my foule is in the sky, Tongue lofe thy light, Moone take thy flight, Now dye, dye, dye, dye, dye.

Dem. No Die, but an ace for him ; for he is but one.

Lif. Leffe then an ace man. For he is dead, he is no-thing.

Du. With the helpe of a Surgeon, he might yet reco-uer, and proue an Affe.

Dut. How chance Moone-fhine is gone before? *Thifby* comes backe, and findes her Louer.

Enter Thifby.

Duke. She wil finde him by ftarre-light. Heere fhe comes, and her paffion ends the play.

Dut. Me thinkes fhee fhould not vfe a long one for fuch a *Piramus* : I hope fhe will be breefe.

Dem. A Moth wil turne the ballance, which *Piramus* which *Thifby* is the better.   (eyes.

Lyf. She hath fpyed him already, with thofe fweete

Dem. And thus fhe meanes, *videlicit.*

This. Afleepe my Loue? What, dead my Doue? O *Piramus* arife : Speake, Speake. Quite dumbe? Dead, dead? A tombe Muft couer thy fweet eyes. Thefe Lilly Lips, this cherry nofe, Thefe yellow Cowflip cheekes Are gone, are gone : Louers make mone : His eyes were greene as Leekes. O fifters three, come, come to mee, With hands as pale as Milke, Lay them in gore, fince you haue fhore With fheeres, his thred of filke. Tongue not a word : Come trufty fword : Come blade, my breft imbrue :

O 3   And

And farwell friends, thus *Thiſbie* ends ;
Adieu, adieu, adieu.

   Duk. Moon-ſhine & Lion are left to burie the dead.

   Deme. I, and Wall too.

   Bot. No, I aſſure you, the wall is downe, that parted their Fathers. Will it pleaſe you to ſee the Epilogue, or to heare a Bergomask dance, betweene two of our company ?

   Duk. No Epilogue, I pray you ; for your play needs no excuſe. Neuer excuſe ; for when the plaiers are all dead, there need none to be blamed. Marry, if hee that writ it had plaid *Piramus*, and hung himſelfe in *Thiſbies* garter, it would haue beene a fine Tragedy : and ſo it is truely, and very notably diſcharg'd. But come, your Burgomaske ; let your Epilogue alone.
The iron tongue of midnight hath told twelue.
Louers to bed, 'tis almoſt Fairy time.
I feare we ſhall out-ſleepe the comming morne,
As much as we this night haue ouer-watcht.
This palpable groſſe play hath well beguil'd
The heauy gate of night. Sweet friends to bed.
A fortnight hold we this ſolemnity.
In nightly Reuels; and new iollitie.   *Exeunt.*

Enter Pucke.

Puck Now the hungry Lyons rores,
And the Wolfe beholds the Moone :
Whileſt the heauy ploughman ſnores,
All with weary taske fore-done.
Now the waſted brands doe glow,
Whil'ſt the ſcritch-owle, ſcritching loud,
Puts the wretch that lies in woe,
In remembrance of a ſhrowd.
Now it is the time of night,
That the graues, all gaping wide,
Euery one lets forth his ſpright,
In the Church-way paths to glide.
And we Fairies, that do runne,
By the triple *Hecates* teame,
From the preſence of the Sunne,
Following darkeneſſe like a dreame,
Now are frollicke ; not a Mouſe
Shall diſturbe this hallowed houſe.
I am ſent with broome before,
To ſweep the duſt behinde the doore.

   Enter King and Queene of Fairies, with their traine.
   Ob. Through the houſe giue glimmering light,

By the dead and drowſie fier,
Euerie Elfe and Fairie ſpright,
Hop as light as bird from brier,
And this Ditty after me, ſing and dance it trippinglie.

   Tita. Firſt rehearſe this ſong by roate,
To each word a warbling note.
Hand in hand, with Fairie grace,
Will we ſing and bleſſe this place.

     The Song.
Now vntill the breake of day,
Through this houſe each Fairy ſtray.
To the beſt Bride-bed will we,
Which by vs ſhall bleſſed be :
And the iſſue there create,
Euer ſhall be fortunate :
So ſhall all the couples three,
Euer true in louing be :
And the blots of Natures hand,
Shall not in their iſſue ſtand.
Neuer mole, harelip, nor ſcarre,
Nor marke prodigious, ſuch as are
Deſpiſed in Natiuitie,
Shall vpon their children be.
With this field dew conſecrate,
Euery Fairy take his gate,
And each ſeuerall chamber bleſſe,
Through this Pallace with ſweet peace,
Euer ſhall in ſafety reſt,
And the owner of it bleſt.
Trip away, make no ſtay ;
Meet me all by breake of day.

   Robin. If we ſhadowes haue offended,
Thinke but this (and all is mended)
That you haue but ſlumbred heere,
While theſe viſions did appeare.
And this weake and idle theame,
No more yeelding but a dreame,
Centles, doe not reprehend.
If you pardon, we will mend.
And as I am an honeſt *Pucke*,
If we haue vnearned lucke,
Now to ſcape the Serpents tongue,
We will make amends ere long :
Elſe the *Pucke* a lyar call.
So good night vnto you all.
Giue me your hands, if we be friends,
And *Robin* ſhall reſtore amends.

FINIS.

The Merchant of Venice.

Actus primus.

Enter Anthonio, Salarino, and Salanio.

Anthonio.

IN footh I know not why I am fo fad,
It wearies me : you fay it wearies you ;
But how I caught it, found it, or came by it,
What ftuffe 'tis made of, whereof it is borne,
I am to learne : and fuch a Want-wit fadneffe makes of
mee,
That I haue much ado to know my felfe.

Sal. Your minde is toffing on the Ocean,
There where your Argofies with portly faile
Like Signiors and rich Burgers on the flood,
Or as it were the Pageants of the fea,
Do ouer-peere the pettie Traffiquers
That curtfie to them, do them reuerence
As they flye by them with their wouen wings.

Salar. Beleeue me fir, had I fuch venture forth,
The better part of my affections, would
Be with my hopes abroad. I fhould be ftill
Plucking the graffe to know where fits the winde,
Peering in Maps for ports, and peers, and rodes:
And euery obiect that might make me feare
Misfortune to my ventures, out of doubt
Would make me fad.

Sal. My winde cooling my broth,
Would blow me to an Ague, when I thought
What harme a winde too great might doe at fea.
I fhould not fee the fandie houre-glaffe runne,
But I fhould thinke of fhallows,and of flats,
And fee my wealthy *Andrew* docks in fand,
Vailing her high top lower then her ribs
To kiffe her buriall ; fhould I goe to Church
And fee the holy edifice of ftone,
And not bethinke me ftraight of dangerous rocks,
Which touching but my gentle Veffels fide
Would fcatter all her fpices on the ftreame,
Enrobe the roring waters with my filkes,
And in a word, but euen now worth this,
And now worth nothing. Shall I haue the thought
To thinke on this, and fhall I lacke the thought
That fuch a thing bechaunc'd would make me fad?
But tell not me, I know *Anthonio*
Is fad to thinke vpon his merchandize.

Anth. Beleeue me no, I thanke my fortune for it,
My ventures are not in one bottome trufted,
Nor to one place ; nor is my whole eftate

Vpon the fortune of this prefent yeere :
Therefore my merchandize makes me not fad.

Sola. Why then you are in loue.

Anth. Fie, fie.

Sola. Not in loue neither : then let vs fay you are fad
Becaufe you are not merry ; and 'twere as eafie
For you to laugh and leape,and fay you are merry
Becaufe you are not fad. Now by two-headed *Ianus*,
Nature hath fram'd ftrange fellowes in her time :
Some that will euermore peepe through their eyes,
And laugh like Parrats at a bag-piper.
And other of fuch vineger afpect,
That they'll not fhew their teeth in way of fmile,
Though *Neftor* fweare the left be laughable.

Enter Baffanio, Lorenfo, and Gratiano.

Sola. Heere comes *Baffanio*,
Your moft noble Kinfman,
Gratiano, and *Lorenfo*. Faryewell,
We leaue you now with better company.

Sala. I would haue ftaid till I had made you merry,
If worthier friends had not preuented me.

Ant. Your worth is very deere in my regard.
I take it your owne bufines calls on you,
And you embrace th'occafion to depart.

Sal. Good morrow my good Lords. (when?

Baff. Good figniors both, when fhall we laugh? fay,
You grow exceeding ftrange : muft it be fo?

Sal. Wee'll make our leyfures to attend on yours.
Exeunt Salarino, and Solanio.

Lor. My Lord *Baffanio*,fince you haue found *Anthonio*
We two will leaue you, but at dinner time
I pray you haue in minde where we muft meete.

Baff. I will not faile you.

Grat. You looke not well fignior *Anthonio*,
You haue too much refpect vpon the world :
They loofe it that doe buy it with much care,
Beleeue me you are maruelloufly chang'd.

Ant. I hold the world but as the world *Gratiano*,
A ftage, where euery man muft play a part,
And mine a fad one.

Grati. Let me play the foole,
With mirth and laughter let old wrinckles come,
And let my Liuer rather heate with wine,
Then my heart coole with mortifying grones.
Why fhould a man whofe bloud is warme within,
Sit like his Grandfire, cut in Alablafter?
Sleepe when he wakes? and creep into the Iaundies

By

By being peeuiſh? I tell thee what *Anthonio*,
I loue thee, and it is my loue that ſpeakes:
There are a fort of men, whoſe viſages
Do creame and mantle like a ſtanding pond,
And do a wilfull ſtilneſſe entertaine,
With purpoſe to be dreſt in an opinion
Of wiſedome, grauity, profound conceit,
As who ſhould ſay, I am ſir an Oracle,
And when I ope my lips, let no dogge barke.
O my *Anthonio*, I do know of theſe
That therefore onely are reputed wiſe,
For ſaying nothing; when I am verie ſure
If they ſhould ſpeake, would almoſt dam thoſe eares
Which hearing them would call their brothers fooles:
Ile tell thee more of this another time.
But fiſh not with this melancholly baite
For this foole Gudgin, this opinion:
Come good *Lorenzo*, faryewell a while,
Ile end my exhortation after dinner.
 Lor. Well, we will leaue you then till dinner time.
I muſt be one of theſe ſame dumbe wiſe men,
For *Gratiano* neuer let's me ſpeake.
 Gra. Well, keepe me company but two yeares mo,
Thou ſhalt not know the ſound of thine owne tongue.
 Ant. Far you well, Ile grow a talker for this geare.
 Gra. Thankes ifaith, for ſilence is onely commendable
In a neats tongue dri'd, and a maid not vendible. *Exit.*
 Ant. It is that any thing now.
 Baſ. *Gratiano* ſpeakes an infinite deale of nothing,
more then any man in all Venice, his reaſons are two
graines of wheate hid in two buſhels of chaffe: you ſhall
ſeeke all day ere you finde them, & when you haue them
they are not worth the ſearch.
 An. Well: tel me now, what Lady is the ſame
To whom you ſwore a ſecret Pilgrimage
That you to day promis'd to tel me of?
 Baſ. Tis not vnknowne to you *Anthonio*
How much I haue diſabled mine eſtate,
By ſomething ſhewing a more ſwelling port
Then my faint meanes would grant continuance:
Nor do I now make mone to be abridg'd
From ſuch a noble rate, but my cheefe care
Is to come fairely off from the great debts
Wherein my time ſomething too prodigall
Hath left me gag'd: to you *Anthonio*
I owe the moſt in money, and in loue,
And from your loue I haue a warrantie
To vnburthen all my plots and purpoſes,
How to get cleere of all the debts I owe.
 An. I pray you good *Baſſanio* let me know it,
And if it ſtand as you your ſelfe ſtill do,
Within the eye of honour, be aſſur'd
My purſe, my perſon, my extreameſt meanes
Lye all vnlock'd to your occaſions.
 Baſſ. In my ſchoole dayes, when I had loſt one ſhaft
I ſhot his fellow of the ſelfeſame flight
The ſelfeſame way, with more aduiſed watch
To finde the other forth, and by aduenturing both,
I oft found both. I vrge this child-hoode proofe,
Becauſe what followes is pure innocence.
I owe you much, and like a wilfull youth, ·
That which I owe is loſt: but if you pleaſe
To ſhoote another arrow that ſelfe way
Which you did ſhoot the firſt, I do not doubt,
As I will watch the ayme: Or to finde both,
Or bring your latter hazard backe againe,

And thankfully reſt debter for the firſt.
 An. You know me well, and herein ſpend but time
To winde about my loue with circumſtance,
And out of doubt you doe more wrong
In making queſtion of my vttermoſt
Then if you had made waſte of all I haue:
Then doe but ſay to me what I ſhould doe
That in your knowledge may by me be done,
And I am preſt vnto it: therefore ſpeake.
 Baſſ. In *Belmont* is a Lady richly left,
And ſhe is faire, and fairer then that word,
Of wondrous vertues, ſometimes from her eyes
I did receiue faire ſpeechleſſe meſſages:
Her name is *Portia*, nothing vndervallewd
To *Cato's* daughter, *Brutus Portia*,
Nor is the wide world ignorant of her worth,
For the foure windes blow in from euery coaſt
Renowned ſutors, and her ſunny locks
Hang on her temples like a golden fleece,
Which makes her ſeat of *Belmont Cholcbos* ſtrond,
And many *Iaſons* come in queſt of her.
O my *Anthonio*, had I but the meanes
To hold a riuall place with one of them,
I haue a minde preſages me ſuch thrift,
That I ſhould queſtionleſſe be fortunate.
 Anth. Thou knowſt that all my fortunes are at ſea,
Neither haue I money, nor commodity
To raiſe a preſent ſumme, therefore goe forth
Try what my credit can in *Venice* doe,
That ſhall be rackt euen to the vttermoſt,
To furniſh thee to *Belmont* to faire *Portia*.
Goe preſently enquire, and ſo will I
Where money is, and I no queſtion make
To haue it of my truſt, or for my ſake. *Exeunt.*

Enter Portia with her waiting woman Neriſſa.

 Portia. By my troth *Nerriſſa*, my little body is a wearie of this great world.
 Ner. You would be ſweet Madam, if your miſeries
were in the ſame abundance as your good fortunes are:
and yet for ought I ſee, they are as ſicke that ſurfet with
too much, as they that ſtarue with nothing; it is no ſmal
happineſſe therefore to be ſeated in the meane, ſuper-
fluitie comes ſooner by white haires, but competencie
liues longer.
 Portia. Good ſentences, and well pronounc'd.
 Ner. They would be better if well followed.
 Portia. If to doe were as eaſie as to know what were
good to doe, Chappels had beene Churches, and poore
mens cottages Princes Pallaces: it is a good Diuine that
followes his owne inſtructions; I can eaſier teach twentie what were good to be done, then be one of the twentie to follow mine owne teaching: the braine may deuiſe lawes for the blood, but a hot temper leapes ore a
colde decree, ſuch a hare is madneſſe the youth, to skip
ore the meſhes of good counſaile the cripple; but this
reaſon is not in faſhion to chooſe me a husband: O mee,
the word chooſe, I may neither chooſe whom I would,
nor refuſe whom I diſlike, ſo is the wil of a liuing daughter curb'd by the will of a dead father: it is not hard *Nerriſſa*, that I cannot chooſe one, nor refuſe none.
 Ner. Your father was euer vertuous, and holy men
at their death haue good inſpirations, therefore the lot-
terie that hee hath deuiſed in theſe three cheſts of gold,
ſiluer, and leade, whereof who chooſes his meaning,
chooſes

chooſes you, wil no doubt neuer be choſen by any rightly, but one who you ſhall rightly loue : but what warmth
is there in your affection towards any of theſe Princely
ſuters that are already come?

Por. I pray thee ouer-name them, and as thou nameſt
them, I will deſcribe them, and according to my deſcription leuell at my affection.

Ner. Firſt there is the Neopolitane Prince.

Por. I that's a colt indeede, for he doth nothing but
talke of his horſe, and hee makes it a great appropria-
tion to his owne good parts that he can ſhoo him himſelfe : I am much afraid my Ladie his mother plaid falſe
with a Smyth.

Ner. Than is there the Countie Palentine.

Por. He doth nothing but frowne (as who ſhould
ſay, and you will not haue me, chooſe : he heares merrie
tales and ſmiles not, I feare hee will proue the weeping
Phyloſopher when he growes old, being ſo full of vnmannerly ſadneſſe in his youth.) I had rather to be married to a deaths head with a bone in his mouth, then to either of theſe : God defend me from theſe two.

Ner. How ſay you by the French Lord, Mounſier
Le Boune?

Pro. God made him, and therefore let him paſſe for a
man, in truth I know it is a ſinne to be a mocker, but he,
why he hath a horſe better then the Neopolitans, a better had habite of frowning then the Count Palentine, he
is euery man in no man, if a Traſſell ſing, he fals ſtraight
a capring, he will fence with his own ſhadow. If I ſhould
marry him, I ſhould marry twentie husbands : if hee
would deſpiſe me, I would forgiue him, for if he loue me
to madneſſe, I ſhould neuer requite him.

Ner. What ſay you then to *Fauconbridge*, the yong
Baron of *England?*

Por. You know I ſay nothing to him, for hee vnderſtands not me, nor I him : he hath neither *Latine, French,*
nor *Italian,* and you will come into the Court & ſweare
that I haue a poore pennie-worth in the *Engliſh* : hee is a
proper mans picture, but alas who can conuerſe with a
dumbe ſhow? how odly he is ſuited, I thinke he bought
his doublet in *Italie,* his round hoſe in *France,* his bonnet
in *Germanie,* and his behauiour euery where.

Ner. What thinke you of the other Lord his neighbour?

Por. That he hath a neighbourly charitie in him, for
he borrowed a boxe of the eare of the *Engliſhman,* and
ſwore he would pay him againe when hee was able : I
thinke the *Frenchman* became his ſuretie, and ſeald vnder
for another.

Ner. How like you the yong *Germaine,* the Duke of
Saxonies Nephew?

Por. Very vildely in the morning when hee is ſober,
and moſt vildely in the afternoone when hee is drunke :
when he is beſt, he is a little worſe then a man, and when
he is worſt, he is little better then a beaſt : and the worſt
fall that euer fell, I hope I ſhall make ſhift to goe without him.

Ner. If he ſhould offer to chooſe, and chooſe the right
Casket, you ſhould refuſe to performe your Fathers will,
if you ſhould refuſe to accept him.

Por. Therefore for feare of the worſt, I pray thee ſet
a deepe glaſſe of Reiniſh-wine on the contrary Casket,
for if the diuell be within, and that temptation without,
I know he will chooſe it. I will doe any thing *Nerriſſa*
ere I will be married to a ſpunge.

Ner. You neede not feare Lady the hauing any of

theſe Lords, they haue acquainted me with their deter-
minations, which is indeede to returne to their home,
and to trouble you with no more ſuite, vnleſſe you may
be won by ſome other ſort then your Fathers impoſiti-
on, depending on the Caskets.

Por. If I liue to be as olde as *Sibilla,* I will dye as
chaſte as *Diana*: vnleſſe I be obtained by the manner
of my Fathers will : I am glad this parcell of wooers
are ſo reaſonable, for there is not one among them but
I doate on his verie abſence : and I wiſh them a faire departure.

Ner. Doe you not remember Ladie in your Fathers time, a *Venecian,* a Scholler and a Souldior that
came hither in companie of the Marqueſſe of *Mount-
ferrat?*

Por. Yes, yes, it was *Baſſanio,* as I thinke, ſo was hee
call'd.

Ner. True Madam, hee of all the men that euer my
fooliſh eyes look'd vpon, was the beſt deſeruing a faire
Lady.

Por. I remember him well, and I remember him worthy of thy praiſe.

Enter a Seruingman.

Ser. The foure Strangers ſeeke you Madam to take
their leaue : and there is a fore-runner come from a fift,
the Prince of *Moroco,* who brings word the Prince his
Maiſter will be here to night.

Por. If I could bid the fift welcome with ſo good
heart as I can bid the other foure farewell, I ſhould be
glad of his approach : if he haue the condition of a Saint,
and the complexion of a diuell, I had rather hee ſhould
ſhriue me then wiue me. Come *Nerriſſa,* ſirra go before;
whiles wee ſhut the gate vpon one wooer, another
knocks at the doore.   *Exeunt.*

Enter Baſſanio with Shylocke the Iew.

Shy. Three thouſand ducates, well.

Baſſ. I ſir, for three months.

Shy. For three months, well.

Baſſ. For the which, as I told you,
Anthonio ſhall be bound.

Shy. *Anthonio* ſhall become bound, well.

Baſſ. May you ſted me? Will you pleaſure me?
Shall I know your anſwere?

Shy. Three thouſand ducats for three months,
and *Anthonio* bound.

Baſſ. Your anſwere to that.

Shy. *Anthonio* is a good man.

Baſſ. Haue you heard any imputation to the contrary.

Shy. Ho no, no, no, no, no : my meaning in ſaying he is a
good man, is to haue you vnderſtand me that he is ſuffi-
ent, yet his meanes are in ſuppoſition : he hath an Argoſie bound to Tripolis, another to the Indies, I vnderſtand moreouer vpon the Ryalta, he hath a third at Mexico, a fourth for England, and other ventures hee hath
ſquandred abroad, but ſhips are but boords, Saylers but
men, there be land rats, and water rats, water theeues,
and land theeues, I meane Pyrats, and then there is the
perrill of waters, windes, and rocks : the man is no twith-
ſtanding ſufficient, three thouſand ducats, I thinke I may
take his bond.

Baſ. Be aſſured you may.

Iew. I

Iew. I will be assured I may : and that I may be assured, I will bethinke mee, may I speake with *Anthonio ?*
Baſſ. If it pleaſe you to dine with vs,
Iew. Yes, to ſmell porke, to eate of the habitation
which your Prophet the Nazarite coniured the diuell
into : I will buy with you, ſell with you, talke with
you, walke with you, and ſo following : but I will
not eate with you, drinke with you, nor pray with you.
What newes on the Ryalta, who is he comes here ?

Enter Anthonio.

Baſſ. This is ſignior *Anthonio.*
Iew. How like a fawning publican he lookes.
I hate him for he is a Chriſtian :
But more, for that in low ſimplicitie
He lends out money gratis, and brings downe
The rate of vſance here with vs in *Venice.*
If I can catch him once vpon the hip,
I will feede fat the ancient grudge I beare him.
He hates our ſacred Nation, and he railes
Euen there where Merchants moſt doe congregate
On me, my bargaines, and my well-worne thrift,
Which he cals Interreſt : Curſed be my Trybe
If I forgiue him.
Baſſ. Shylock, doe you heare.
Shy. I am debating of my preſent ſtore,
And by the neere geſſe of my memorie
I cannot inſtantly raiſe vp the groſſe
Of full three thouſand ducats : what of that?
Tuball a wealthy Hebrew of my Tribe
Will furniſh me; but ſoft, how many months
Doe you deſire ? Reſt you faire good ſignior,
Your worſhip was the laſt man in our mouthes.
Ant. Shylocke, albeit I neither lend nor borrow
By taking, nor by giuing of exceſſe,
Yet to ſupply the ripe wants of my friend,
Ile breake a cuſtome : is he yet poſſeſt
How much he would ?
Shy. I, I, three thouſand ducats.
Ant. And for three months.
Shy. I had forgot, three months, you told me ſo.
Well then, your bond : and let me ſee, but heare you,
Me thoughts you ſaid, you neither lend nor borrow
Vpon aduantage.
Ant. I doe neuer vſe it.
Shy. When *Iacob* graz'd his Vncle *Labans* ſheepe,
This *Iacob* from our holy *Abram* was
(As his wife mother wrought in his behalfe)
The third poſſeſſer ; I, he was the third.
Ant. And what of him, did he take interreſt ?
Shy. No, not take intereſt, not as you would ſay
Directly intereſt, marke what *Iacob* did,
When *Laban* and himſelfe were compremyz'd
That all the eanelings which were ſtreakt and pied
Should fall as *Iacobs* hier, the Ewes being rancke,
In end of Autumne turned to the Rammes,
And when the worke of generation was
Betweene theſe woolly breeders in the act,
The skilfull ſhepheard pil'd me certaine wands,
And in the dooing of the deede of kinde,
He ſtucke them vp before the fulſome Ewes,
Who then conceauing, did in eaning time
Fall party-colour'd lambs, and thoſe were *Iacobs.*
This was a way to thriue, and he was bleſt :

And thrift is bleſſing if men ſteale it not.
Ant. This was a venture ſir that *Iacob* ſeru'd for,
A thing not in his power to bring to paſſe,
But ſway'd and faſhion'd by the hand of heauen.
Was this inſerted to make interreſt good ?
Or is your gold and ſiluer Ewes and Rams ?
Shy. I cannot tell, I make it breede as faſt,
But note me ſignior.
Ant. Marke you this *Baſſanio,*
The diuell can cite Scripture for his purpoſe,
An euill ſoule producing holy witneſſe,
Is like a villaine with a ſmiling cheeke,
A goodly apple rotten at the heart.
O what a goodly outſide falſehood hath.
Shy. Three thouſand ducats, 'tis a good round ſum.
Three months from twelue, then let me ſee the rate.
Ant. Well Shylocke, ſhall we be beholding to you ?
Shy. Signior *Anthonio,* many a time and oft
In the Ryalto you haue rated me
About my monies and my vſances :
Still haue I borne it with a patient ſhrug,
(For ſuffrance is the badge of all our Tribe.)
You call me miſbeleeuer, cut-throate dog,
And ſpet vpon my Iewiſh gaberdine,
And all for vſe of that which is mine owne.
Well then, it now appeares you neede my helpe :
Goe to then, you come to me, and you ſay,
Shylocke, we would haue moneyes, you ſay ſo :
You that did voide your rume vpon my beard,
And foote me as you ſpurne a ſtranger curre
Ouer your threſhold, moneyes is your ſuite.
What ſhould I ſay to you ? Should I not ſay,
Hath a dog money ? Is it poſſible
A curre ſhould lend three thouſand ducats ? or
Shall I bend low, and in a bond-mans key
With bated breath, and whiſpring humbleneſſe,
Say this : Faire ſir, you ſpet on me on Wedneſday laſt ;
You ſpurn'd me ſuch a day; another time
You cald me dog : and for theſe curteſies
Ile lend you thus much moneyes.
Ant. I am as like to call thee ſo againe,
To ſpet on thee againe, to ſpurne thee too.
If thou wilt lend this money, lend it not
As to thy friends, for when did friendſhip take
A breede of barraine mettall of his friend?
But lend it rather to thine enemie,
Who if he breake, thou maiſt with better face
Exact the penalties.
Shy. Why looke you how you ſtorme,
I would be friends with you, and haue your loue,
Forget the ſhames that you haue ſtaind me with,
Supplie your preſent wants, and take no doite
Of vſance for my moneyes, and youle not heare me,
This is kinde I offer.
Baſſ. This were kindneſſe.
Shy. This kindneſſe will I ſhowe,
Goe with me to a Notarie, ſeale me there
Your ſingle bond, and in a merrie ſport
If you repaie me not on ſuch a day,
In ſuch a place, ſuch ſum or ſums as are
Expreſt in the condition, let the forfeite
Be nominated for an equall pound
Of your faire fleſh, to be cut off and taken
In what part of your bodie it pleaſeth me.
Ant. Content infaith, Ile ſeale to ſuch a bond,
And ſay there is much kindneſſe in the Iew.
Baſſ. You

Baſſ. You ſhall not ſeale to ſuch a bond for me,
Ile rather dwell in my neceſſitie.

Ant. Why feare not man, I will not forfaite it,
Within theſe two months, that's a month before
This bond expires, I doe expect returne
Of thrice three times the valew of this bond.

Shy. O father *Abram*, what theſe Chriſtians are,
Whoſe owne hard dealings teaches them ſuſpect
The thoughts of others: Praie you tell me this,
If he ſhould breake his daie, what ſhould I gaine
By the exaction of the forfeiture?
A pound of mans fleſh taken from a man,
Is not ſo eſtimable, profitable neither
As fleſh of Muttons, Beefes, or Goates, I ſay
To buy his fauour, I extend this friendſhip,
If he will take it, ſo: if not adiew,
And for my loue I praie you wrong me not.

Ant. Yes *Shylocke*, I will ſeale vnto this bond.

Shy. Then meete me forthwith at the Notaries,
Giue him direction for this merrie bond,
And I will goe and purſe the ducats ſtraite.
See to my houſe left in the fearefull gard
Of an vnthriftie knaue: and preſentlie
Ile be with you.   *Exit.*

Ant. Hie thee gentle *Iew.* This Hebrew will turne
Chriſtian, he growes kinde.

Baſſ. I like not faire teames, and a villaines minde.

Ant. Come on, in this there can be no diſmaie,
My Shippes come home a month before the daie.
                                          Exennt.

Actus Secundus.

*Enter Morochus a tawnie Moore all in white, and three or
foure followers accordingly, with Portia,
Nerriſſa, and their traine.
Flo. Cornets.*

Mor. Miſlike me not for my complexion,
The ſhadowed liuerie of the burniſht ſunne,
To whom I am a neighbour, and neere bred.
Bring me the faireſt creature North-ward borne,
Where *Phœbus* fire ſcarce thawes the yſicles,
And let vs make inciſion for your loue,
To proue whoſe blood is reddeſt, his or mine.
I tell thee Ladie this aſpect of mine
Hath feard the valiant, (by my loue I ſweare)
The beſt regarded Virgins of our Clyme
Haue lou'd it too: I would not change this hue,
Except to ſteale your thoughts my gentle Queene.

Por. In tearmes of choiſe I am not ſolie led
By nice direction of a maidens eies:
Beſides, the lottrie of my deſtenie
Bars me the right of voluntarie chooſing:
But if my Father had not ſcanted me,
And hedg'd me by his wit to yeelde my ſelfe
His wife, who wins me by that meanes I told you,
Your ſelfe (renowned Prince) than ſtood as faire
As any commer I haue look'd on yet
For my affection.

Mor. Euen for that I thanke you,
Therefore I pray you leade me to the Caskets
To trie my fortune: By this Symitare

That ſlew the Sophie, and a Perſian Prince
That won three fields of Sultan Solyman,
I would ore-ſtare the ſterneſt eies that looke:
Out-braue the heart moſt daring on the earth:
Plucke the yong ſucking Cubs from the ſhe Beare,
Yea, mocke the Lion when he rores for pray
To win the Ladie. But alas, the while
If *Hercules* and *Lychas* plaie at dice
Which is the better man, the greater throw
May turne by fortune from the weaker hand:
So is *Alcides* beaten by his rage,
And ſo may I, blinde fortune leading me
Miſſe that which one vnworthier may attaine,
And die with grieuing.

Port. You muſt take your chance,
And either not attempt to chooſe at all,
Or ſweare before you chooſe, if you chooſe wrong
Neuer to ſpeake to Ladie afterward
In way of marriage, therefore be aduis'd.

Mor. Nor will not, come bring me vnto my chance.

Por. Firſt forward to the temple, after dinner
Your hazard ſhall be made.

Mor. Good fortune then,   *Cornets.*
To make me bleſt or curſed'ſt among men.   *Exeunt.*

Enter the Clowne alone.

Clo. Certainely, my conſcience will ſerue me to run
from this Iew my Maiſter: the fiend is at mine elbow,
and tempts me, ſaying to me, *Iobbe*, *Launcelet Iobbe*, good
Launcelet, or good *Iobbe*, or good *Launcelet Iobbe*, vſe
your legs, take the ſtart, run awaie: my conſcience ſaies
no; take heede honeſt *Launcelet*, take heed honeſt *Iobbe*,
or as afore-ſaid honeſt *Launcelet Iobbe*, doe not runne,
ſcorne running with thy heeles; well, the moſt coragious fiend bids me packe, ſia ſaies the fiend, away ſaies
the fiend, for the heauens rouſe vp a braue minde ſaies
the fiend, and run; well, my conſcience hanging about
the necke of my heart, ſaies verie wiſely to me: my honeſt friend *Launcelet*, being an honeſt mans ſonne, or rather an honeſt womans ſonne, for indeede my Father did
ſomething ſmack, ſomething grow too; he had a kinde of
taſte; wel, my conſcience ſaies *Lancelet* bouge not, bouge
ſaies the fiend, bouge not ſaies my conſcience, conſcience
ſay I you counſaile well, fiend ſay I you counſaile well,
to be rul'd by my conſcience I ſhould ſtay with the *Iew*
my Maiſter, (who God bleſſe the marke) is a kinde of diuell; and to run away from the *Iew* I ſhould be ruled by
the fiend, who ſauing your reuerence is the diuell himſelfe: certainely the *Iew* is the verie diuell incarnation,
and in my conſcience, my conſcience is a kinde of hard
conſcience, to offer to counſaile me to ſtay with the *Iew*;
the fiend giues the more friendly counſaile: I will runne
fiend, my heeles are at your commandement, I will
runne.

Enter old Gobbo with a Baſket.

Gob. Maiſter yong-man, you I praie you, which is the
waie to Maiſter *Iewes*?

Lan. O heauens, this is my true begotten Father, who
being more then ſand-blinde, high grauel blinde, knows
me not, I will trie confuſions with him.

Gob. Maiſter yong Gentleman, I praie you which is
the waie to Maiſter *Iewes*.

Laun. Turne vpon your right hand at the next turn-
ning

ning, but at the next turning of all on your left; marrie at the verie next turning, turne of no hand, but turn down indirectlie to the *Iewes* houſe.

Gob. Be Gods ſonties 'twill be a hard waie to hit, can you tell me whether one *Launcelet* that dwels with him, dwell with him or no.

Laun. Talke you of yong Maſter *Launcelet*, marke me now, now will I raiſe the waters; talke you of yong Maiſter *Launcelet*?

Gob. No Maiſter ſir, but a poore mans ſonne, his Father though I ſay't is an honeſt exceeding poore man, and God be thanked well to liue.

Lan. Well, let his Father be what a will, wee talke of yong Maiſter *Launcelet*.

Gob. Your worſhips friend and *Launcelet*.

Laun. But I praie you *ergo* old man, *ergo* I beſeech you, talke you of yong Maiſter *Launcelet*.

Gob. Of *Launcelet*, ant pleaſe your maiſterſhip.

Lan. Ergo Maiſter *Lancelet*, talke not of maiſter *Lancelet* Father, for the yong gentleman according to fates and deſtinies, and ſuch odde ſayings, the ſiſters three, & ſuch branches of learning, is indeede deceaſed, or as you would ſay in plaine tearmes, gone to heauen.

Gob. Marrie God forbid, the boy was the verie ſtaffe of my age, my verie prop.

Lau. Do I look like a cudgell or a howell-poſt, a ſtaffe or a prop: doe you know me Father.

Gob. Alacke the day, I know you not yong Gentleman, but I praie you tell me, is my boy God reſt his ſoule aliue or dead.

Lan. Doe you not know me Father.

Gob. Alacke ſir I am ſand blinde, I know you not.

Lan. Nay, indeede if you had your eies you might faile of the knowing me: it is a wiſe Father that knowes his owne childe. Well, old man, I will tell you newes of your ſon, giue me your bleſſing, truth will come to light, murder cannot be hid long, a mans ſonne may, but in the end truth will out.

Gob. Praie you ſir ſtand vp, I am ſure you are not *Lancelet* my boy.

Lan. Praie you let's haue no more fooling about it, but giue mee your bleſſing: I am *Lancelet* your boy that was, your ſonne that is, your childe that ſhall be.

Gob. I cannot thinke you are my ſonne.

Lan. I know not what I ſhall thinke of that: but I am *Lancelet* the *Iewes* man, and I am ſure *Margerie* your wife is my mother.

Gob. Her name is *Margerie* indeede, Ile be ſworne if thou be *Lancelet*, thou art mine owne fleſh and blood: Lord worſhipt might he be, what a beard haſt thou got; thou haſt got more haire on thy chin, then Dobbin my philhorſe h as on his taile.

Lan. It ſhould ſeeme then that Dobbins taile growes backeward: I am ſure he had more haire of his taile then I haue of my face when I loſt ſaw him.

Gob. Lord how art thou chang'd: how dooſt thou and thy Maſter agree, I haue brought him a preſent; how gree you now?

Lan. Well, well, but for mine owne part, as I haue ſet vp my reſt to run awaie, ſo I will not reſt till I haue run ſome ground; my Maiſter's a verie *Iew*, giue him a preſent, giue him a halter, I am famiſht in his ſeruice. You may tell euerie finger I haue with my ribs: Father I am glad you are come, giue me your preſent to one Maiſter *Baſſanio*, who indeede giues rare new Liuories, if I ſerue

not him, I will run as far as God has anie ground. O rare fortune, here comes the man, to him Father, for I am a *Iew* if I ſerue the *Iew* anie longer.

Enter Baſſanio with a follower or two.

Baſſ. You may doe ſo, but let it be ſo haſted that ſupper be readie at the fartheſt by fiue of the clocke: ſee theſe Letters deliuered, put the Liueries to making, and deſire *Gratiano* to come anone to my lodging.

Lan. To him Father.

Gob. God bleſſe your worſhip.

Baſſ. Gramercie, would'ſt thou ought with me.

Gob. Here's my ſonne ſir, a poore boy.

Lan. Not a poore boy ſir, but the rich *Iewes* man that would ſir as my Father ſhall ſpecifie.

Gob. He hath a great infection ſir, as one would ſay to ſerue.

Lan. Indeede the ſhort and the long is, I ſerue the *Iew*, and haue a deſire as my Father ſhall ſpecifie.

Gob. His Maiſter and he (ſauing your worſhips reuerence) are ſcarce catercoſins.

Lan. To be briefe, the verie truth is, that the *Iew* hauing done me wrong, doth cauſe me as my Father being I hope an old man ſhall frutifie vnto you.

Gob. I haue here a diſh of Doues that I would beſtow vpon your worſhip, and my ſuite is.

Lan. In verie briefe, the ſuite is impertinent to my ſelfe, as your worſhip ſhall know by this honeſt old man, and though I ſay it, though old man, yet poore man my Father.

Baſſ. One ſpeake for both, what would you?

Lan. Serue you ſir.

Gob. That is the verie defect of the matter ſir.

Baſſ. I know thee well, thou haſt obtain'd thy ſuite, *Shylocke* thy Maiſter ſpoke with me this daie, And hath prefer'd thee, if it be preferment To leaue a rich *Iewes* ſeruice, to become The follower of ſo poore a Gentleman.

Clo. The old prouerbe is verie well parted betweene my Maiſter *Shylocke* and you ſir, you haue the grace of God ſir, and he hath enough.

Baſſ. Thou ſpeak'ſt it well; go Father with thy Son, Take leaue of thy old Maiſter, and enquire My lodging out, giue him a Liuerie More garded then his fellowes: ſee it done.

Clo. Father in, I cannot get a ſeruice, no, I haue nere a tongue in my head, well: if anie man in *Italie* haue a fairer table which doth offer to ſweare vpon a booke, I ſhall haue good fortune; goe too, here's a ſimple line of life, here's a ſmall trifle of wiues, alas, fifteene wiues is nothing, a leuen widdowes and nine maides is a ſimple comming in for one man, and then to ſcape drowning thrice, and to be in perill of my life with the edge of a featherbed, here are ſimple ſcapes: well, if Fortune be a woman, ſhe's a good wench for this gere: Father come, Ile take my leaue of the *Iew* in the twinkling.

Exit Clowne.

Baſſ. I praie thee good *Leonardo* thinke on this, Theſe things being bought and orderly beſtowed Returne in haſte, for I doe feaſt to night My beſt eſteemd acquaintance, hie thee goe.

Leon. My beſt endeuors ſhall be done herein. *Exit. Le.*

Enter Gratiano.

Gra. Where's your Maiſter.

Leon. Yonder

Leon. Yonder fir he walkes.

Gra. Signior *Baffanio.*

Baf. Gratiano.

Gra. I haue a fute to you.

Baff. You haue obtain'd it.

Gra. You muft not denie me, I muft goe with you to Belmont.

Baff. Why then you muft : but heare thee *Gratiano,*
Thou art to wilde, to rude, and bold of voyce,
Parts that become thee happily enough,
And in fuch eyes as ours appeare not faults;
But where they are not knowne, why there they fhow
Something too liberall, pray thee take paine
To allay with fome cold drops of modeftie
Thy skipping fpirit, leaft through thy wilde behauiour
I be mifconfterd in the place I goe to,
And loofe my hopes.

Gra. Signor *Baffanio,* heare me,
If I doe not put on a fober habite,
Talke with refpect, and fweare but now and than,
Weare prayer bookes in my pocket, looke demurely,
Nay more, while grace is faying hood mine eyes
Thus with my hat, and figh and fay Amen :
Vfe all the obferuance of ciuillitie
Like one well ftudied in a fad oftent
To pleafe his Grandam, neuer truft me more.

Baf. Well, we fhall fee your bearing.

Gra. Nay but I barre to night, you fhall not gage me
By what we doe to night.

Baf. No that were pittie,
I would intreate you rather to put on
Your boldeft fuite of mirth, for we haue friends
That purpofe merriment : but far you well,
I haue fome bufineffe.

Gra. And I muft to *Lorenfo* and the reft,
But we will vifite you at fupper time.   *Exeunt.*

Enter Ieffica and the Clowne.

Ief. I am forry thou wilt leaue my Father fo,
Our houfe is hell, and thou a merrie diuell
Did'ft rob it of fome tafte of tedioufneffe ;
But far thee well, there is a ducat for thee,
And *Lancelet,* foone at fupper fhalt thou fee
Lorenzo, who is thy new Maifters gueft,
Giue him this Letter, doe it fecretly,
And fo farwell : I would not haue my Father
See me talke with thee.

Clo. Adue, teares exhibit my tongue, moft beautifull
Pagan, moft fweete Iew, if a Chriftian doe not play the
knaue and get thee, I am much deceiued; but adue, thefe
foolifh drops doe fomewhat drowne my manly fpirit :
adue.   *Exit.*

Ief. Farewell good *Lancelet.*
Alacke, what hainous finne is jt in me
To be afhamed to be my Fathers childe,
But though I am a daughter to his blood,
I am not to his manners : O *Lorenzo,*
If thou keepe promife I fhall end this ftrife,
Become a Chriftian, and thy louing wife.   *Exit.*

Enter Gratiano, Lorenzo, Slarino, and Salanio.

Lor. Nay, we will flinke away in fupper time,
Difguife vs at my lodging, and returne all in an houre.

Gra. We haue not made good preparation.

Sal. We haue not fpoke vs yet of Torch-bearers.

Sol. 'Tis vile vnleffe it may be quaintly ordered,
And better in my minde not vndertooke.

Lor. 'Tis now but foure of clock, we haue two houres
To furnifh vs ; friend *Lancelet* what's the newes.

Enter Laucelet with a Lettor.

Lan. And it fhall pleafe you to breakᵉ vp this, fhall it feeme to fignifie.

Lor. I know the hand, in faith 'tis a faire hand
And whiter then the paper it writ on,
I the faire hand that writ.

Gra. Loue newes in faith.

Lan. By your leaue fir.

Lor. Whither goeft thou?

Lan. Marry fir to bid my old Mafter the *Iew* to fup
to night with my new Mafter the Chriftian.

Lor. Hold here, take this, tell gentle *Ieffica*
I will not faile her, fpeake it priuately :
Go Gentlemen, will you prepare you for this Maske to
night,
I am prouided of a Torch-bearer.   *Exit. Clowne.*

Sal. I marry, ile be gone about it ftrait.

Sol. And fo will I.

Lor. Meete me and *Gratiano* at *Gratianos* lodging
Some houre hence.

Sal. 'Tis good we do fo.   *Exit.*

Gra. Was not that Letter from faire *Ieffica?*

Lor. I muft needes tell thee all, fhe hath directed
How I fhall take her from her Fathers houfe,
What gold and iewels fhe is furnifht with,
What Pages fuite fhe hath in readineffe:
If ere the *Iew* her Father come to heauen,
It will be for his gentle daughters fake ;
And neuer dare misfortune croffe her foote,
Vnleffe fhe doe it vnder this excufe,
That fhe is iffue to a faithleffe *Iew* :
Come goe with me, p ervfe this as thou goeft,
Faire *Ieffica* fhall be my Torch-bearer.   *Exit.*

Enter Iew, and his man that was the Clowne.

Iew. Well, thou fhall fee, thy eyes fhall be thy iudge,
The difference of old *Shylocke* and *Baffanio* ;
What *Ieffica,* thou fhalt not gurmandize
As thou haft done with me : what *Ieffica?*
And fleepe, and fnore, and rend apparrell out.
Why *Ieffica* I fay.

Clo. Why *Ieffica.*

Shy. Who bids thee call ? I do not bid thee call.

Clo. Your worfhip was wont to tell me
I could doe nothing without bidding.

Enter Ieffica.

Ief. Call you ? what is your will ?

Shy. I am bid forth to fupper *Ieffica,*
There are my Keyes : but wherefore fhould I go?
I am not bid for loue, they flattr me,
But yet Ile goe in hate, to feede vpon
The prodigall Chriftian. *Ieffica* my girle,
Looke to my houfe, I am right loath to goe,
There is fome ill a bruing towards my reft,
For I did dreame of money bags to night.

Clo. I befeech you fir goe, my yong Mafter
Doth expect your reproach.

Shy. So doe I his.

Clo. And they haue confpired together, I will not fay
you fhall fee a Maske, but if you doe, then jt was not for
nothing that my nofe fell a bleeding on blacke monday
laft,

P

laſt, at ſix a clocke ith morning, falling out that yeere on
aſhwenſday was foure yeere in th'afternoone.
  Shy. What are their maskes? heare you me *Ieſſica,*
Lock vp my doores, and when you heare the drum
And the vile ſquealing of the wry-neckt Fife,
Clamber not you vp to the caſements then,
Nor thruſt your head into the publique ſtreete
To gaze on Chriſtian fooles with varniſht faces:
But ſtop my houſes eares, I meane my caſements,
Let not the ſound of ſhallow fopperie enter
My ſober houſe. By *Iacobs* ſtaffe I ſweare,
I haue no minde of feaſting forth to night:
But I will goe : goe you before me ſirra,
Say I will come.
  Clo. I will goe before ſir.
Miſtris looke out at window for all this;
There will come a Chriſtian by,
Will be worth a Iewes eye.
  Shy. What ſaies that foole of *Hagars* off-ſpring?
ha.
  Ieſ. His words were farewell miſtris, nothing elſe.
  Shy. The patch is kinde enough, but a huge feeder:
Snaile-ſlow in profit, but he ſleepes by day
More then the wilde-cat : drones hiue not with me,
Therefore I part with him, and part with him
To one that I would haue him helpe to waſte
His borrowed purſe. Well *Ieſſica* goe in,
Perhaps I will returne immediately;
Doe as I bid you, ſhut dores after you, faſt binde, faſt
finde,
A prouerbe neuer ſtale in thriftie minde.   *Exit.*
  Ieſ. Farewell, and if my fortune be not croſt,
I haue a Father, you a daughter loſt.   *Exit.*

    Enter the Maskers, Gratiano and Salino.

  Gra. This is the penthouſe vnder which *Lorenzo*
Deſired vs to make a ſtand.
  Sal. His houre is almoſt paſt.
  Gra. And it is meruaile he out-dwels his houre,
For louers euer run before the clocke.
  Sal. O ten times faſter *Venus* Pidgions flye
To ſteale loues bonds new made, then they are wont
To keepe obliged faith vnforfaited.
  Gra. That euer holds, who riſeth from a feaſt
With that keene appetite that he ſits downe?
Where is the horſe that doth vntread againe
His tedious meaſures with the vnbated fire,
That he did pace them firſt : all things that are,
Are with more ſpirit chaſed then enioy'd.
How like a yonger or a prodigall
The skarfed barke puts from her natiue bay,
Hudg'd and embraced by the ſtrumpet winde:
How like a prodigall doth ſhe returne
With ouer-wither'd ribs and ragged ſailes,
Leane, rent, and begger'd by the ſtrumpet winde?

    Enter Lorenzo.

  Salino. Heere comes *Lorenzo,* more of this here-
after.
  Lor. Sweete friends, your patience for my long a-
bode,
Not I, but my affaires haue made you wait:
When you ſhall pleaſe to play the theeues for wiues
Ile watch as long for you then: approach

Here dwels my father Iew.   Hoa, who's within?

    Ieſſica aboue.

  Ieſſ. Who are you? tell me for more certainty,
Albeit Ile ſweare that I do know your tongue.
  Lor. Lorenzo, and thy Loue.
  Ieſ. Lorenzo certaine, and my loue indeed,
For who loue I ſo much? and now who knowes
But you *Lorenzo,* whether I am yours?
  Lor. Heauen and thy thoughts are witneſs that thou
art.
  Ieſ. Heere, catch this casket, it is worth the paines,
I am glad 'tis night, you do not looke on me,
For I am much aſham'd of my exchange:
But loue is blinde, and louers cannot ſee
The pretty follies that themſelues commit,
For if they could, *Cupid* himſelfe would bluſh
To ſee me thus transformed to a boy.
  Lor. Deſcend, for you muſt be my torch-bearer.
  Ieſ. What, muſt I hold a Candle to my ſhames?
They in themſelues goodſooth are too too light.
Why, 'tis an office of diſcouery Loue,
And I ſhould be obſcur'd.
  Lor. So you are ſweet,
Euen in the louely garniſh of a boy: but come at once,
For the cloſe night doth play the run-away,
And we are ſtaid for at *Baſſanio's* feaſt.
  Ieſ. I will make faſt the doores and guild my ſelfe
With ſome more ducats, and be with you ſtraight.
  Gra. Now by my hood, a gentle, and no Iew.
  Lor. Beſhrew me but I loue her heartily.
For ſhe is wiſe, if I can iudge of her,
And faire ſhe is, if that mine eyes be true,
And true ſhe is, as ſhe hath prou'd her ſelfe:
And therefore like her ſelfe, wiſe, faire, and true,
Shall ſhe be placed in my conſtant ſoule.

    Enter Ieſſica.

What, art thou come? on gentlemen, away,
Our masking mates by this time for vs ſtay.   *Exit.*

    Enter Anthonio.

  Ant. Who's there?
  Gra. Signior *Anthonio?*
  Ant. Fie, fie, *Gratiano,* where are all the reſt?
'Tis nine a clocke, our friends all ſtay for you,
No maske to night, the winde is come about,
Baſſanio preſently will goe aboard,
I haue ſent twenty out to ſeeke for you.
  Gra. I am glad on't, I deſire no more delight
Then to be vnder ſaile, and gone to night.   *Exeunt.*

    Enter Portia with Morrocho, and both their traines.

  Por. Goe, draw aſide the curtaines, and diſcouer
The ſeuerall Caskets to this noble Prince :
Now make your choyſe.
  Mor. The firſt of gold, who this inſcription beares,
Who chooſeth me, ſhall gaine what men deſire.
The ſecond ſiluer, which this promiſe carries,
Who chooſeth me, ſhall get as much as he deſerues.
This third, dull lead, with warning all as blunt,
Who chooſeth me, muſt giue and hazard all he hath.
How ſhall I know if I doe chooſe the right?
  Por. The

How shall I know if I doe choose the right.

Por. The one of them containes my picture Prince,
If you choose that, then I am yours withall.

Mor. Some God direct my iudgement, let me see,
I will suruay the inscriptions, backe againe :
What saies this leaden casket?
Who chooseth me, must giue and hazard all he hath.
Must giue, for what? for lead, hazard for lead?
This casket threatens men that hazard all
Doe it in hope of faire aduantages :
A golden minde stoopes not to showes of drosse,
Ile then nor giue nor hazard ought for lead.
What saies the Siluer with her virgin hue?
Who chooseth me, shall get as much as he deserues.
As much as he deserues ; pause there *Morocho*,
And weigh thy value with an euen hand,
If thou beest rated by thy estimation
Thou doost deserue enough, and yet enough
May not extend so farre as to the Ladie :
And yet to be afeard of my deseruing,
Were but a weake disabling of my selfe.
As much as I deserue, why that's the Lady.
I doe in birth deserue her, and in fortunes,
In graces, and in qualities of breeding :
But more then these, in loue I doe deserue.
What if I strai'd no farther, but chose here?
Let's see once more this saying grau'd in gold.
Who chooseth me shall gaine what many men desire:
Why that's the Lady, all the world desires her :
From the foure corners of the earth they come
To kisse this shrine, this mortall breathing Saint.
The Hircanion deserts, and the vaste wildes
Of wide Arabia are as throughfares now
For Princes to come view faire *Portia*.
The waterie Kingdome, whose ambitious head
Spets in the face of heauen, is no barre
To stop the forraine spirits, but they come
As ore a brooke to see faire *Portia*.
One of these three containes her heauenly picture.
Is't like that Lead containes her? 'twere damnation
To thinke so base a thought, it were too grose
To rib her searecloath in the obscure graue :
Or shall I thinke in Siluer she's immur'd
Being ten times vndervalued to tride gold ;
O sinfull thought, neuer so rich a Iem
Was set in worse then gold ! They haue in England
A coyne that beares the figure of an Angell
Stampt in gold, but that's insculpt vpon :
But here an Angell in a golden bed
Lies all within. Deliuer me the key :
Here doe I choose, and thriue I as I may.

Por. There take it Prince, and if my forme lye there
Then I am yours.

Mor. O hell ! what haue we here, a carrion death,
Within whose emptie eye there is a written scroule ;
Ile reade the writing.

   All that glisters is not gold,
   Often haue you heard that told ;
   Many a man his life hath sold
   But my out side to behold ;
   Guilded timber doe wormes infold :
   Had you beene as wise as bold,
   Yong in limbs, in iudgement old,
   Your answere had not beene inscrold,
   Fareyouwell, your suite is cold,

Mor. Cold indeede, and labour lost,
Then farewell heate, and welcome frost :
Portia adew, I haue too grieu'd a heart
To take a tedious leaue : thus loosers part.   *Exit.*

Por. A gentle riddance : draw the curtaines, go :
Let all of his complexion choose me so.   *Exeunt.*

Enter Salarino and Solanio.
Flo. Cornets.

Sal. Why man I saw *Bassanio* vnder sayle,
With him is *Gratiano* gone along ;
And in their ship I am sure *Lorenzo* is not.

Sol. The villaine *Iew* with outcries rais'd the Duke.
Who went with him to search *Bassanios* ship.

Sal. He comes too late, the ship was vndersaile ;
But there the Duke was giuen to vnderstand
That in a Gondilo were seene together
Lorenzo and his amorous *Iessica.*
Besides, *Anthonio* certified the Duke
They were not with *Bassanio* in his ship.

Sol. I neuer heard a passion so confus'd,
So strange, outragious, and so variable,
As the dogge *Iew* did vtter in the streets ;
My daughter, O my ducats, O my daughter,
Fled with a Christian, O my Christian ducats !
Iustice, the law, my ducats, and my daughter ;
A sealed bagge, two sealed bags of ducats,
Of double ducats, stolne from me by my daughter,
And iewels, two stones, two rich and precious stones,
Stolne by my daughter : iustice, finde the girle,
She hath the stones vpon her, and the ducats.

Sal. Why all the boyes in Venice follow him,
Crying his stones, his daughter, and his ducats.

Sol. Let good *Anthonio* looke he keepe his day
Or he shall pay for this.

Sal. Marry well remembred,
I reason'd with a Frenchman yesterday,
Who told me, in the narrow seas that part
The French and English, there miscaried
A vessell of our countrey richly fraught :
I thought vpon *Anthonio* when he told me,
And wisht in silence that it were not his.

Sol. Yo were best to tell *Anthonio* what you heare.
Yet doe not suddainely, for it may grieue him.

Sal. A kinder Gentleman treads not the earth,
I saw *Bassanio* and *Anthonio* part,
Bassanio told him he would make some speede
Of his returne : he answered, doe not so,
Slubber not businesse for my sake *Bassanio*,
But stay the very riping of the time,
And for the *Iewes* bond which he hath of me,
Let it not enter in your minde of loue :
Be merry, and imploy your chiefest thoughts
To courtship, and such faire ostents of loue
As shall conueniently become you there ;
And euen there his eye being big with teares,
Turning his face, he put his hand behinde him,
And with affection wondrous sencible
He wrung *Bassanios* hand, and so they parted.

Sol. I thinke he onely loues the world for him,
I pray thee let vs goe and finde him out
And quicken his embraced heauinesse
With some delight or other.

Sal. Doe we so.   *Exeunt.*

Enter Nerrissa and a Seruiture.
Ner. Quick, quick I pray thee, draw the curtain strait,
        P 2   The

The Prince of Arragon hath tane his oath,
And comes to his election prefently.

Enter Arragon, his traine, and Portia.
Flor. Cornets.

Por. Behold, there ftand the caskets noble Prince,
If you choofe that wherein I am contain'd,
Straight fhall our nuptiall rights be folemniz'd :
But if thou faile, without more fpeech my Lord,
You muft be gone from hence immediately.

Ar. I am enioynd by oath to obferue three things;
Firft, neuer to vnfold to any one
Which casket 'twas I chofe ; next, if I faile
Of the right casket, neuer in my life
To wooe a maide in way of marriage :
Laftly, if I doe faile in fortune of my choyfe,
Immediately to leaue you, and be gone.

Por. To thefe iniunctions euery one doth fweare
That comes to hazard for my worthleffe felfe.

Ar. And fo haue I addreft the, fortune now
To my hearts hope : gold, filuer, and bafe lead.
Who choofeth me muft giue and hazard all he hath.
You fhall looke fairer ere I giue or hazard.
What faies the golden cheft, ha, let me fee :
Who choofeth me, fhall gaine what many men defire:
What many men defire, that many may be meant
By the foole multitude that choofe by fhow,
Not learning more then the fond eye doth teach,
Which pries not to th'interior, but like the Martlet
Builds in the weather on the outward wall,
Euen in the force and rode of cafualtie.
I will not choofe what many men defire,
Becaufe I will not iumpe with common fpirits,
And ranke me with the barbarous multitudes.
Why then to thee thou Siluer treafure houfe,
Tell me once more, what title thou dooft beare ;
Who choofeth me fhall get as much as he deferues :
And well faid too ; for who fhall goe about
To cofen Fortune, and be honourable
Without the ftampe of merrit, let none prefume
To weare an vnderferued dignitie :
O that eftates, degrees, and offices,
Were not deriu'd corruptly, and that cleare honour
Were purchaft by the merrit of the wearer ;
How many then fhould couer that ftand bare ?
How many be commanded that command ?
How much low pleafantry would then be gleaned
From the true feede of honor ? And how much honor
Pickt from the chaffe and ruine of the times,
To be new varnifht : Well, but to my choife.
Who choofeth me fhall get as much as he deferues.
I will affume defert ; giue me a key for this,
And inftantly vnlocke my fortunes here.

Por. Too long a paufe for that which you finde there.

Ar. What's here, the portrait of a blinking idiot
Prefenting me a fcedule, I will reade it :
How much vnlike art thou to *Portia* ?
How much vnlike my hopes and my deferuings ?
Who choofeth me, fhall haue as much as he deferues.
Did I deferue no more then a fooles head,
Is that my prize, and are my deferts no better ?

Por. To offend and iudge are diftinct offices,
And of oppofed natures.

Ar. What is here ?

The fier feauen times tried this,

Seauen times tried that iudement is,
That did neuer choofe amis,
Some there be that fhadowes kiffe,
Such haue but a fhadowes bliffe :
There be fooles aliue I wis
Siluer'd o're, and fo was this :
Take what wife you will to bed,
I will euer be your head :
So be gone, you are fped.

Ar. Still more foole I fhall appeare
By the time I linger here,
With one fooles head I came to woo,
But I goe away with two.
Sweet adue, Ile keepe mine oath,
Patiently to beare my wroath.

Por. Thus hath the candle fing'd the moath :
O thefe deliberate fooles when they doe choofe,
They haue the wifdome by their wit to loofe.

Ner. The ancient faying is no herefie,
Hanging and wiuing goes by deftinie.

Por. Come draw the curtaine *Nerriffa.*

Enter Meffenger.

Mef. Where is my Lady ?

Por. Here, what would my Lord ?

Mef. Madam, there is a-lighted at your gate
A yong Venetian, one that comes before
To fignifie th'approaching of his Lord,
From whom he bringeth fenfible regreets ;
To wit (befides commends and curteous breath)
Gifts of rich value ; yet I haue not feene
So likely an Embaffador of loue.
A day in Aprill neuer came fo fweete
To fhow how coftly Sommer was at hand,
As this fore-fpurrer comes before his Lord.

Por. No more I pray thee, I am halfe a-feard
Thou wilt fay anone he is fome kin to thee,
Thou fpend'ft fuch high-day wit in praifing him :
Come, come *Nerriffa*, for I long to fee
Quicke *Cupids* Poft, that comes fo mannerly.

Ner. *Baffanio* Lord, loue if thy will it be.   *Exeunt.*

Actus Tertius.

Enter Solanio and Salarino.

Sol. Now, what newes on the Ryalto ?

Sal. Why yet it liues there vncheckt, that *Anthonio*
hath a fhip of rich lading wrackt on the narrow feas; the
Goodwins I thinke they call the place, a very dangerous
flat, and fatall, where the carcaffes of many a tall fhip, lye
buried, as they fay, if my goffips report be an honeft woman of her word.

Sol. I would fhe were as lying a goffip in that, as euer
knapt Ginger, or made her neighbours beleeue fhe wept
for the death of a third husband : but it is true, without
any flips of prolixity, or croffing the plaine high-way of
talke, that the good *Anthonio*, the honeft *Anthonio*; ô that
I had a title good enough to keepe his name company !

Sal. Come, the full ftop.

Sol. Ha, what fayeft thou, why the end is, he hath loft
a fhip.

Sal. I

Sal. I would it might proue the end of his loſſes.

Sol. Let me ſay Amen betimes, leaſt the diuell croſſe my praier, for here he comes in the iikenes of a *Iew.* How now *Shylocke*, what newes among the Merchants?

Enter Shylocke.

Sby. You knew none ſo well, none ſo well as you, of my daughters flight.

Sal. That's certaine, I for my part knew the Tailor that made the wings ſhe flew withall.

Sol. And *Shylocke* for his own part knew the bird was fledg'd, and then it is the complexion of them al to leaue the dam.

Sby. She is damn'd for it.

Sal. That's certaine, if the diuell may be her Iudge.

Sby. My owne fleſh and blood to rebell.

Sol. Out vpon it old carrion, rebels it at theſe yeeres.

Sby. I ſay my daughter is my fleſh and bloud.

Sal. There is more difference betweene thy fleſh and hers, then betweene Iet and Iuorie, more betweene your bloods, then there is betweene red wine and renniſh : but tell vs, doe you heare whether *Anthonio* haue had anie loſſe at ſea or no?

Sby. There I haue another bad match, a bankrout, a prodigall, who dare ſcarce ſhew his head on the Ryalto, a begger that was vſd to come ſo ſmug vpon the Mart : let him look to his bond, he was wont to call me Vſurer, let him looke to his bond, he was wont to lend money for a Chriſtian curtſie, let him looke to his bond.

Sal. Why I am ſure if he forſaite, thou wilt not take his fleſh, what's that good for?

Sby. To baite fiſh withall, if it will feede nothing elſe, it will feede my reuenge ; he hath diſgrac'd me, and hindred me halfe a million, laught at my loſſes, mockt at my gaines, ſcorned my Nation, thwarted my bargaines, cooled my friends, heated mine enemies, and what's the reaſon? I am a *Iewe* : Hath not a *Iew* eyes? hath not a *Iew* hands, organs, dementions, ſences, affeƈtions, paſſions, fed with the ſame foode, hurt with the ſame weapons, ſubieƈt to the ſame diſeaſes, healed by the ſame meanes, warmed and cooled by the ſame Winter and Sommmer as a Chriſtian is : if you pricke vs doe we not bleede? if you tickle vs, doe we not laugh? if you poiſon vs doe we not die? and if you wrong vs ſhall we not reuenge? If we are like you in the reſt, we will reſemble you in that. If a *Iew* wrong a *Chriſtian*, what is his humility, reuenge? If a *Chriſtian* wrong a *Iew*, what ſhould his ſufferance be by Chriſtian example, why reuenge? The villanie you teach me I will execute, and it ſhall goe hard but I will better the inſtruƈtion.

Enter a man from Anthonio.

Gentlemen, my maiſter *Anthonio* is at his houſe, and deſires to ſpeake with you both.

Sal. We haue beene vp and downe to ſeeke him.

Enter Tuball.

Sol. Here comes another of the Tribe, a third cannot be matcht, vnleſſe the diuell himſelfe turne *Iew*.

Exeunt Gentlemen.

Sby. How now *Tuball*, what newes from *Genowa?* haſt thou found my daughter?

Tub. I often came where I did heare of ſter, but cannot finde her.

Sby. Why there, there, there, there, a diamond gone coſt me two thouſand ducats in Franckford, the curſe neuer fell vpon our Nation till now, I neuer felt it till now, two thouſand ducats in that, and other precious, precious iewels : I would my daughter were dead at my foot, and the iewels in her eare : would ſhe were hearſt at my foote, and the duckets in her coffin : no newes of them, why ſo? and I know not how much is ſpent in the ſearch: why thou loſſe vpon loſſe, the theefe gone with ſo much, and ſo much to finde the theefe, and no ſatisfaƈtion, no reuenge, nor no ill luck ſtirring but what lights a my ſhoulders, no ſighes but a my breathing, no teares but a my ſhedding.

Tub. Yes, other men haue ill lucke too, *Anthonio* as I heard in Genowa?

Sby. What, what, what, ill lucke, ill lucke.

Tub. Hath an Argoſie caſt away comming from Tripolis.

Sby. I thanke God, I thanke God, is it true, is it true?

Tub. I ſpoke with ſome of the Saylers that eſcaped the wracke.

Sby. I thanke thee good *Tuball*, good newes, good newes : ha, ha, here in Genowa.

Tub. Your daughter ſpent in Genowa, as I heard, one night foureſcore ducats.

Sby. Thou ſtick'ſt a dagger in me, I ſhall neuer ſee my gold againe, foureſcore ducats at a fitting, foureſcore ducats.

Tub. There came diuers of *Anthonios* creditors in my company to Venice, that ſweare hee cannot chooſe but breake.

Sby, I am very glad of it, ile plague him, ile torture him, I am glad of it,

Tub. One of them ſhewed me a ring that bee had of your daughter for a Monkie.

Sby. Out vpon her, thou tortureſt me *Tuball*, it was my Turkies, I had it of *Leah* when I was a Batcheler : I would not haue giuen it for a wilderneſſe of Monkies.

Tub. But *Anthonio* is certainely vndone.

Sby. Nay, that's true, that's very true, goe *Tuball*, fee me an Officer, beſpeake him a fortnight before, I will haue the heart of him if he forſeit, for were he out of Venice, I can make what merchandize I will : goe *Tuball*, and meete me at our Sinagogue, goe good *Tuball*, at our Sinagogue *Tuball*.   *Exeunt.*

Enter Baſſanio, Portia, Gratiano, *and all their traine.*

Por. I pray you tarrie, pauſe a day or two
Before you hazard, for in chooſing wrong
I looſe your companie ; therefore forbeare a while,
There's ſomething tels me (but it is not loue)
I would not looſe you, and you know your ſelfe,
Hate counſailes not in ſuch a quallicie;
But leaſt you ſhould not vnderſtand me well,
And yet a maiden hath no tongue, but thought,
I would detaine you here ſome month or two
Before you venture for me. I could teach you
How to chooſe right, but then I am forſworne,
So will I neuer be, ſo may you miſſe me,
But if you doe, youle make me wiſh a ſinne,
That I had beene forſworne : Beſhrow your eyes,
They haue ore-lookt me and deuided me,
One halfe of me is yours, the other halfe yours,
Mine owne I would ſay : but of mine then yours,
And ſo all yours ; O theſe naughtie times
Puts bars betweene the owners and their rights.
And ſo though yours, not yours (proue it ſo)
Let Fortune goe to hell for it, not I.
I ſpeake too long, but 'tis to peize the time,
To ich it, and to draw it out in length,
To ſtay you from election.

P 3   *Baſſ.* Let

Baſſ. Let me chooſe,
For as I am, I liue vpon the racke.
Por. Vpon the racke *Baſſanio,* then confeſſe
What treaſon there is mingled with your loue.
Baſſ. None but that vglie treaſon of miſtruſt.
Which makes me feare the enioying of my loue :
There may as well be amitie and life,
'Tweene ſnow and fire, as treaſon and my loue:
Por. I, but I feare you ſpeake vpon the racke,
Where men enforced doth ſpeake any thing.
Baſſ. Promiſe me life, and ile confeſſe the truth.
Por. Well then, confeſſe and liue.
Baſſ. Confeſſe and loue
Had beene the verie ſum of my confeſſion :
O happie torment, when my torturer
Doth teach me anſwers for deliuerance :
But let me to my fortune and the caskets.
Por. Away then, I am lockt in one of them,
If you doe loue me, you will finde me out.
Nerryſſa and the reſt, ſtand all alooſe,
Let muſicke ſound while he doth make his choiſe,
Then if he looſe he makes a Swan-like end,
Fading in muſique. That the compariſon
May ſtand more proper, my eye ſhall be the ſtreame
And watrie death-bed for him : he may win,
And what is muſique than ? Than muſique is
Euen as the flouriſh, when true ſubiects bowe
To a new crowned Monarch : Such it is,
As are thoſe dulcet ſounds in breake of day,
That creepe into the dreaming bride-groomes eare,
And ſummon him to marriage. Now he goes
With no leſſe preſence, but with much more loue
Then yong *Alcides,* when he did redeeme
The virgine tribute, paled by howling *Troy*
To the Sea-monſter : I ſtand for ſacrifice,
The reſt alooſe are the Dardanian wiues :
With bleared viſages come forth to view
The iſſue of th'exploit : Goe Hercules,
Liue thou, I liue with much more diſmay
I view the fight, then thou that mak'ſt the fray.
Here Muſicke.

A Song the whilſt Baſſanio *comments on the Caskets to himſelfe.*

Tell me where is fancie bred,
Or in the heart, or in the head :
How begot, how nouriſhed.   *Replie, replie.*
It is engendred in the eyes,
With gazing fed, and Fancie dies,
In the cradle where it lies :
Let vs all ring Fancies knell.
Ile begin it.
Ding, dong, bell.
    All. Ding, dong, bell.

Baſſ. So may the outward ſhowes be leaſt themſelues
The world is ſtill deceiu'd with ornament.
In Law, what Plea ſo tanted and corrupt,
But being ſeaſon'd with a gracious voice,
Obſcures the ſhow of euill ? In Religion,
What damned error, but ſome ſober brow
Will bleſſe it, and approue it with a text,
Hiding the groſeneſſe with faire ornament :
There is no voice ſo ſimple, but aſſumes
Some marke of vertue on his outward parts ;

How manie cowards, whoſe hearts are all as falſe
As ſtayers of ſand, weare yet vpon their chins
The beards of *Hercules* and frowning *Mars,*
Who inward ſearcht, haue lyuers white as milke,
And theſe aſſume but valors excrement,
To render them redoubted. Looke on beautie,
And you ſhall ſee 'tis purchaſt by the weight,
Which therein workes a miracle in nature,
Making them lighteſt that weare moſt of it :
So are thoſe criſped ſnakie golden locks
Which makes ſuch wanton gambols with the winde
Vpon ſuppoſed faireneſſe, often knowne
To be the dowrie of a ſecond head,
The ſcull that bred them in the Sepulcher.
Thus ornament is but the guiled ſhore
To a moſt dangerous ſea : the beautious ſcarfe
Vailing an Indian beautie ; In a word,
The ſeeming truth which cunning times put on
To intrap the wiſeſt. Therefore then thou gaudie gold,
Hard food for *Midas,* I will none of thee,
Nor none of thee thou pale and common drudge
'Tweene man and man : but thou, thou meager lead
Which rather threatneſt then doſt promiſe ought,
Thy paleneſſe moues me more then eloquence,
And here chooſe I, ioy be the conſequence.
Por. How all the other paſſions fleet to ayre,
As doubtfull thoughts, and raſh imbrac'd deſpaire :
And ſhuddring feare, and greene-eyed iealouſie.
O loue be moderate, allay thy extaſie,
In meaſure raine thy ioy, ſcant this exceſſe,
I feele too much thy bleſſing, make it leſſe,
For feare I ſurfeit.
Baſ. What finde I here ?
Faire *Portias* counterfeit. What demie God
Hath come ſo neere creation ? moue theſe eies ?
Or whether riding on the bals of mine
Seeme they in motion ? Here are ſeuer'd lips
Parted with ſuger breath, ſo ſweet a barre
Should ſunder ſuch ſweet friends : here in her haires
The Painter plaies the Spider, and hath wouen
A golden meſh t'intrap the hearts of men
Faſter then gnats in cobwebs : but her eies,
How could he ſee to doe them ? hauing made one,
Me thinkes it ſhould haue power to ſteale both his
And leaue it ſelfe vnfurniſht : Yet looke how farre
The ſubſtance of my praiſe doth wrong this ſhadow
In vnderpriſing it, ſo farre this ſhadow
Doth limpe behinde the ſubſtance. Here's the ſcroule,
The continent, and ſummarie of my fortune.

You that chooſe not by the view
Chance as faire, and chooſe as true :
Since this fortune fals to you,
Be content, and ſeeke no new.
If you be well pleaſd with this,
And hold your fortune for your bliſſe,
Turne you where your Lady is,
And claime her with a louing kiſſe.

Baſſ. A gentle ſcroule : Faire Lady, by your leaue,
I come by note to giue, and to receiue,
Like one of two contending in a prize
That thinks he hath done well in peoples eies :
Hearing applauſe and vniuerſall ſhout,
Giddie in ſpirit, ſtill gazing in a doubt
Whether thoſe peales of praiſe be his or no.

           So

So thrice faire Lady ſtand I euen ſo,
As doubtfull whether what I ſee be true,
Vntill confirm'd, ſign'd, ratified by you.
  Por. You ſee my Lord *Baſſiano* where I ſtand,
Such as I am ; though for my ſelfe alone
I would not be ambitious in my wiſh,
To wiſh my ſelfe much better, yet for you,
I would be trebled twenty times my ſelfe,
A thouſand times more faire, ten thouſand times
More rich, that onely to ſtand high in your account,
I might in vertues, beauties, liuings, friends,
Exceed account : but the full ſumme of me
Is ſum of nothing : which to terme in groſſe,
Is an vnleſſoned girle, vnſchool'd, vnpractiz'd,
Happy in this, ſhe is not yet ſo old
But ſhe may learne : happier then this,
Shee is not bred ſo dull but ſhe can learne ;
Happieſt of all, is that her gentle ſpirit
Commits it ſelfe to yours to be directed,
As from her Lord, her Gouernour, her King.
My ſelfe, and what is mine, to you and yours
Is now conuerted. But now I was the Lord
Of this faire manſion, maſter of my ſeruants,
Queene ore my ſelfe : and euen now, but now,
This houſe, theſe ſeruants, and this ſame my ſelfe
Are yours, my Lord, I giue them with this ring,
Which when you part from, looſe, or giue away,
Let it preſage the ruine of your loue,
And be my vantage to exclaime on you.
  Baſſ. Maddam, you haue bereft me of all words,
Onely my bloud ſpeakes to you in my vaines,
And there is ſuch confuſion in my powers,
As after ſome oration fairely ſpoke
By a beloued Prince, there doth appeare
Among the buzzing pleaſed multitude,
Where euery ſomething being blent together,
Turnes to a wilde of nothing, ſaue of ioy
Expreſt, and not expreſt : but when this ring
Parts from this finger, then parts life from hence,
O then be bold to ſay *Baſſanio's* dead.
  Ner. My Lord and Lady, it is now our time
That haue ſtood by and ſeene our wiſhes proſper,
To cry good Ioy, good Ioy my Lord and Lady.
  Gra. My Lord *Baſſanio,* and my gentle Lady,
I wiſh you all the ioy that you can wiſh :
For I am ſure you can wiſh none from me :
And when your Honours meane to ſolemnize
The bargaine of your faith : I doe beſeech you
Euen at that time I may be married too.
  Baſſ. With all my heart, ſo thou canſt get a wife.
  Gra. I thanke your Lordſhip, you gaue got me one.
My eyes my Lord can looke as ſwift as yours :
You ſaw the miſtres, I beheld the maid :
You lou'd, I lou'd for intermiſſion,
No more pertaines to me my Lord then you ;
Your fortune ſtood vpon the caskets there,
And ſo did mine too, as the matter falls :
For wooing heere vntill I ſwet againe,
And ſwearing till my very rough was dry
With oathes of loue, at laſt, if promiſe laſt,
I got a promiſe of this faire one heere
To haue her loue : prouided that your fortune
Atchieu'd her miſtreſſe.
  Por. Is this true *Nerriſſa* ?
  Ner. Madam it is ſo, ſo you ſtand pleas'd withall.
  Baſſ. And doe you *Gratiano* meane good faith ?

  Gra. Yes faith my Lord.
  Baſſ. Our feaſt ſhall be much honored in your mar-
riage.
  Gra. Weele play with them the firſt boy for a thou-
ſand ducats.
  Ner. What and ſtake downe ?
  Gra. No, we ſhal nere win at that ſport, and ſtake
downe.
But who comes heere ? *Lorenzo* and his Infidell ?
What and my old Venetian friend *Salerio* ?

Enter Lorenzo, Ieſſica, and Salerio.

  Baſ. *Lorenzo* and *Salerio,* welcome hether,
If that the youth of my new intereſt heere
Haue power to bid you welcome : by your leaue
I bid my verie friends and Countrimen
Sweet *Portia* welcome.
  Por. So do I my Lord, they are intirely welcome.
  Lor. I thanke your honor ; for my part my Lord,
My purpoſe was not to haue ſeene you heere,
But meeting with *Salerio* by the way,
He did intreate mee paſt all ſaying nay
To come with him along.
  Sal. I did my Lord,
And I haue reaſon for it, Signior *Anthonio*
Commends him to you.
  Baſſ. Ere I ope his Letter
I pray you tell me how my good friend doth.
  Sal. Not ſicke my Lord, vnleſſe it be in minde,
Nor wel, vnleſſe in minde : his Letter there
Wil ſhew you his eſtate.
          Opens the Letter.
  Gra. *Nerriſſa,* cheere yond ſtranger, bid her welcom.
Your hand *Salerio,* what's the newes from Venice ?
How doth that royal Merchant good *Anthonio*;
I know he vvil be glad of our ſucceſſe,
We are the *Iaſons,* we haue won the fleece.
  Sal. I would you had vvon the fleece that hee hath
loſt.
  Por. There are ſome ſhrewd contents in yond ſame
Paper,
That ſteales the colour from *Baſſanos* cheeke,
Some deere friend dead, elſe nothing in the world
Could turne ſo much the conſtitution
Of any conſtant man. What, worſe and worſe?
With leaue *Baſſanio* I am halfe your ſelfe,
And I muſt freely haue the halfe of any thing
That this ſame paper brings you.
  Baſſ. O ſweet *Portia,*
Heere are a few of the vnpleaſant'ſt words
That euer blotted paper. Gentle Ladie
When I did firſt impart my loue to you,
I freely told you all the wealth I had
Ran in my vaines: I was a Gentleman,
And then I told you true : and yet deere Ladie,
Rating my ſelfe at nothing, you ſhall ſee
How much I was a Braggart, when I told you
My ſtate was nothing, I ſhould then haue told you
That I vvas worſe then nothing : for indeede
I haue ingag'd my ſelfe to a deere friend,
Ingag'd my friend to his meere enemie
To feede my meanes. Heere is a Letter Ladie,
The paper as the bodie of my friend,
And euerie word in it a gaping wound
Iſſuing life blood. But is it true *Salerio,*

                                             Hath

Hath all his ventures faild, what not one hit,
From Tripolis, from Mexico and England,
From Lisbon, Barbary, and India,
And not one veſſell ſcape the dreadfull touch
Of Merchant-marring rocks?

Sal. Not one my Lord.

Beſides, it ſhould appeare, that if he had
The preſent money to diſcharge the Iew,
He would not take it : neuer did I know
A creature that did beare the ſhape of man
So keene and greedy to confound a man.
He plyes the Duke at morning and at night,
And doth impeach the freedome of the ſtate
If they deny him iuſtice. Twenty Merchants,
The Duke himſelfe, and the Magnificoes
Of greateſt port haue all perſwaded with him,
But none can driue him from the enuious plea
Of forfeiture, of iuſtice, and his bond.

Ieſſi. When I was with him, I haue heard him ſweare
To *Tuball* and to *Chus*, his Countri-men,
That he would rather haue *Anthonio's* fleſh,
Then twenty times the value of the ſumme
That he did owe him : and I know my Lord,
If law, authoritie, and power denie not,
It will goe hard with poore *Anthonio.*

Por. Is it your deere friend that is thus in trouble?

Baſſ. The deereſt friend to me, the kindeſt man,
The beſt condition'd, and vnwearied ſpirit
In doing curteſies : and one in whom
The ancient Romane honour more appeares
Then any that drawes breath in Italie.

Por. What ſumme owes he the Iew?

Baſſ. For me three thouſand ducats.

Por. What, no more?

Pay him ſixe thouſand, and deface the bond :
Double ſixe thouſand, and then treble that,
Before a friend of this deſcription
Shall loſe a haire through *Baſſano's* fault.
Firſt goe with me to Church, and call me wife,
And then away to Venice to your friend :
For neuer ſhall you lie by *Portias* ſide
With an vnquiet foule. You ſhall haue gold
To pay the petty debt twenty times ouer.
When it is payd, bring your true friend along,
My maid *Nerriſſa*, and my ſelfe meane time
Will liue as maids and widdowes ; come away,
For you ſhall hence vpon your wedding day :
Bid your friends welcome, ſhow a merry cheere,
Since you are deere bought, I will loue you deere.
But let me heare the letter of your friend.

*Sweet Baſſanio, my ſhips haue all miſcarried, my Credi-
tors grow cruell, my eſtate is very low, my bond to the Iew is
forfeit, and ſince in paying it, it is impoſſible I ſhould liue, all
debts are cleerd betweene you and I, if I might ſee you at my
death : notwithſtanding, vſe your pleaſure, if your loue doe not
perſwade you to come, let not my letter.*

Por. O loue! diſpach all buſines and be gone.

Baſſ. Since I haue your good leaue to goe away,
I will make haſt ; but till I come againe,
No bed ſhall ere be guilty of my ſtay,
Nor reſt be interpoſer twixt vs twaine.   *Exeunt.*

*Enter the Iew, and Solanio, and Anthonio,
and the Iaylor.*

Iew. Iaylor, looke to him, tell not me of mercy,

This is the foole that lends out money *gratis.*
Iaylor, looke to him.

Ant. Heare me yet good *Shylok.*

Iew. Ile haue my bond, ſpeake not againſt my bond,
I haue ſworne an oath that I will haue my bond :
Thou call'dſt me dog before thou hadſt a cauſe,
But ſince I am a dog, beware my phangs,
The Duke ſhall grant me iuſtice, I do wonder
Thou naughty Iaylor, that thou art ſo fond
To come abroad with him at his requeſt.

Ant. I pray thee heare me ſpeake.

Iew. Ile haue my bond, I will not heare thee ſpeake,
Ile haue my bond, and therefore ſpeake no more.
Ile not be made a ſoft and dull ey'd foole,
To ſhake the head, relent, and ſigh, and yeeld
To Chriſtian interceſſors : follow not,
Ile haue no ſpeaking, I will haue my bond.   *Exit Iew.*

Sol. It is the moſt impenetrable curre
That euer kept with men.

Ant. Let him alone,
Ile follow him no more with bootleſſe prayers :
He ſeekes my life, his reaſon well I know ;
I oft deliuer'd from his forfeitures
Many that haue at times made mone to me,
Therefore he hates me.

Sol. I am ſure the Duke will neuer grant
this forfeiture to hold.

An. The Duke cannot deny the courſe of law :
For the commoditie that ſtrangers haue
With vs in Venice, if it be denied,
Will much impeach the iuſtice of the State,
Since that the trade and profit of the citty
Conſiſteth of all Nations. Therefore goe,
Theſe greefes and loſſes haue ſo bated mee,
That I ſhall hardly ſpare a pound of fleſh
To morrow, to my bloudy Creditor.
Well Iaylor, on, pray God *Baſſanio* come
To ſee me pay his debt, and then I care not.   *Exeunt.*

*Enter Portia, Nerriſſa, Lorenzo, Ieſſica, and a man of
Portias.*

Lor. Madam, although I ſpeake it in your preſence,
You haue a noble and a true conceit
Of god-like amity, which appeares moſt ſtrongly
In bearing thus the abſence of your Lord.
But if you knew to whom you ſhew this honour,
How true a Gentleman you ſend releeſe,
How deere a louer of my Lord your husband,
I know you would be prouder of the worke
Then cuſtomary bounty can enforce you.

Por. I neuer did repent for doing good,
Nor ſhall not now : for in companions
That do conuerſe and waſte the timetogether,
Whoſe ſoules doe beare an egal yoke of loue,
There muſt be needs a like proportion
Of lyniaments, of manners, and of ſpirit ;
Which makes me thinke that this *Anthonio*
Being the boſome louer of my Lord,
Muſt needs be like my Lord. If it be ſo,
How little is the coſt I haue beſtowed
In purchaſing the ſemblance of my ſoule ;
From out the ſtate of helliſh cruelty,
This comes too neere the praiſing of my ſelfe,
Therefore no more of it : heere other things
Lorenſo I commit into your hands,

The

The husbandry and mannage of my houfe,
Vntill my Lords returne; for mine owne part
I haue toward heauen breath'd a fecret vow,
To liue in prayer and contemplation,
Onely attended by *Nerriffa* heere,
Vntill her husband and my Lords returne:
There is a monaftery too miles off,
And there we will abide. I doe defire you
Not to denie this impofition,
The which my loue and fome neceffity
Now layes vpon you.
Lorenf. Madame, with all my heart,
I fhall obey you in all faire commands.
  Por. My people doe already know my minde,
And will acknowledge you and *Ieffica*
In place of Lord *Baffanio* and my felfe.
So far you well till we fhall meete againe.
  Lor. Faire thoughts & happy houres attend on you.
  Ieffi. I wifh your Ladifhip all hearts content.
  Por. I thanke you for your wifh, and am well pleas'd
To wifh it backe on you: faryouwell *Ieffica.*   *Exeunt.*
Now *Balthafer,* as I haue euer found thee honeft true,
So let me finde thee ftill : take this fame letter,
And vfe thou all the indeauor of a man,
In fpeed to Mantua, fee thou render this
Into my cofins hand, Doctor *Belario,*
And looke what notes and garments he doth giue thee,
Bring them I pray thee with imagin'd fpeed
Vnto the Tranect, to the common Ferrie
Which trades to Venice; wafte no time in words,
But get thee gone, I fhall be there before thee.
  Balth. Madam, I goe with all conuenient fpeed.
  Por. Come on *Neriffa,* I haue worke in hand
That you yet know not of; wee'll fee our husbands
Before they thinke of vs?
  Nerriffa. Shall they fee vs?
  Portia. They fhall *Nerriffa* : but in fuch a habit,
That they fhall thinke we are accomplifhed
With that we lacke; Ile hold thee any wager
When we are both accoutred like yong men,
Ile proue the prettier fellow of the two,
And weare my dagger with the brauer grace,
And fpeake betweene the change of man and boy,
With a reede voyce, and turne two minfing fteps
Into a manly ftride; and fpeake of frayes
Like a fine bragging youth : and tell quaint lyes
How honourable Ladies fought my loue,
Which I denying, they fell ficke and died.
I could not doe withall : then Ile repent,
And wifh for all that, that I had not kil'd them;
And twentie of thefe punie lies Ile tell,
That men fhall fweare I haue difcontinued fchoole
Aboue a twelue moneth : I haue within my minde
A thoufand raw tricks of thefe bragging Iacks,
Which I will practife.
  Nerrif. Why, fhall wee turne to men?
  Portia. Fie, what a queftions that?
If thou wert nere a lewd interpreter :
But come, Ile tell thee all my whole deuice
When I am in my coach, which ftayes for vs
At the Parke gate; and therefore hafte away,
For we muft meafure twentie miles to day.   *Exeunt.*

Enter Clowne and Ieffica.

Clown. Yes truly; for looke you, the finnes of the Fa-

ther are to be laid vpon the children, therefore I promife
you, I feare you, I was alwaies plaine with you, and fo
now I fpeake my agitation of the matter : therfore be of
good cheere, for truly I thinke you are damn'd, there is
but one hope in it that can doe you anie good, and that is
but a kinde of baftard hope neither.
  Ieffica. And what hope is that I pray thee?
  Clow. Marrie you may partlie hope that your father
got you not, that you are not the Iewes daughter.
  Ief. That were a kinde of baftard hope indeed, fo the
fins of my mother fhould be vifited vpon me.
  Clow. Truly then I feare you are damned both by father and mother : thus when I fhun *Scilla* your father, I
fall into *Charibdis* your mother; well, you are gone both
waies.
  Ief. I fhall be fau'd by my husband, he hath made me
a Chriftian.
  Clow. Truly the more to blame he, we were Chriftians enow before, e'ne as many as could wel liue one by a-
nother : this making of Chriftians will raife the price of
Hogs, if wee grow all to be porke-eaters, wee fhall not
fhortlie haue a rafher on the coales for money.

Enter Lorenzo.

  Ief. Ile tell my husband *Lancelet* what you fay, heere
he comes.
  Loren. I fhall grow iealous of you fhortly *Lancelet*,
if you thus get my wife into corners?
  Ief. Nay, you need not feare vs *Lorenzo,* Launcelet
and I are out, he tells me flatly there is no mercy for mee
in heauen, becaufe I am a Iewes daughter : and hee faies
you are no good member of the common wealth, for
in conuerting Iewes to Chriftians, you raife the price
of Porke.
  Loren. I fhall anfwere that better to the Common-
wealth, than you can the getting vp of the Negroes bel-
lie : the Moore is with childe by you *Launcelet?*
  Clow. It is much that the Moore fhould be more then
reafon : but if fhe be leffe then an honeft woman, fhee is
indeed more then I tooke her for.
  Loren. How euerie foole can play vpon the word, I
thinke the beft grace of witte will fhortly turne into filence, and difcourfe grow commendable in none onely
but Parrats : goe in firra, bid them prepare for dinner?
  Clow. That is done fir, they haue all ftomacks?
  Loren. Goodly Lord, what a witte-fnapper are you,
then bid them prepare dinner.
  Clow. That is done to fir, onely couer is the word.
  Loren. Will you couer than fir?
  Clow. Not fo fir neither, I know my dutie.
  Loren. Yet more quarrelling with occafion, wilt thou
fhew the whole wealth of thy wit in an inftant; I pray
thee vnderftand a plaine man in his plaine meaning: goe
to thy fellowes, bid them couer the table, ferue in the
meat, and we will come in to dinner.
  Clow. For the table fir, it fhall be feru'd in, for the
meat fir, it fhall bee couered, for your comming in to
dinner fir, why let it be as humors and conceits fhall go-
uerne.   *Exit Clowne.*
  Lor. O deare difcretion, how his words are futed,
The foole hath planted in his memory
An Armie of good words, and I doe know
A many fooles that ftand in better place,
Garnifht like him, that for a trickfie word
Defie the matter: how cheer'ft thou *Ieffica,*
And now good fweet fay thy opinion,
                                                      How

How doſt thou like the Lord *Baſſiano*'s wife ?

Ieſſi. Paſt all expreſſing, it is very meete
The Lord *Baſſanio* liue an vpright life
For hauing ſuch a bleſſing in his Lady,
He findes the ioyes of heauen heere on earth,
And if on earth he doe not meane it, it
Is reaſon he ſhonld neuer come to heauen ?
Why, if two gods ſhould play ſome heauenly match,
And on the wager lay two earthly women,
And *Portia* one : there muſt be ſomething elſe
Paund with the other, for the poore rude world
Hath not her fellow.

Loren. Euen ſuch a husband
Haſt thou of me, as ſhe is for a wife.

Ieſ. Nay, but aske my opinion to of that ?

Lor. I will anone, firſt let vs goe to dinner ?

Ieſ. Nay, let me praiſe you while I haue a ſtomacke ?

Lor. No pray thee, let it ſerue for table talke,
Then how ſom ere thou ſpeakſt 'mong other things,
I ſhall digeſt it ?

Ieſſi. Well, Ile ſet you forth.　　　　　　*Exeunt.*

Actus Quartus.

Enter the Duke, the Magnificoes, Anthonio, Baſſanio, and Gratiano.

Duke. What, is *Anthonio* heere ?

Ant. Ready, ſo pleaſe your grace ?

Duke. I am ſorry for thee, thou art come to anſwere
A ſtonie aduerſary, an inhumane wretch,
Vncapable of pitty, voyd, and empty
From any dram of mercie.

Ant. I haue heard
Your Grace hath tane great paines to qualifie
His rigorous courſe : but ſince he ſtands obdurate,
And that no lawful meanes can carrie me
Out of his enuies reach, I do oppoſe
My patience to his fury, and am arm'd
To ſuffer with a quietneſſe of ſpirit,
The very tiranny and rage of his.

Du. Go one and cal the Iew into the Court.

Sal. He is ready at the doore, he comes my Lord.

Enter Shylocke.

Du. Make roome, and let him ſtand before our face.
Shylocke the world thinkes, and I thinke ſo to
That thou but leadeſt this faſhion of thy mallice
To the laſt houre of act, and then 'tis thought
Thou'lt ſhew thy mercy and remorſe more ſtrange,
Than is thy ſtrange apparant cruelty :
And where thou now exact'ſt the penalty,
Which is a pound of this poore Merchants fleſh,
Thou wilt not onely looſe the forfeiture,
But touch'd with humane gentleneſſe and loue :
Forgiue a moytie of the principall ,
Glancing an eye of pitty on his loſſes
That haue of late ſo hudled on his backe,
Enow to preſſe a royall Merchant downe ;
And plucke commiſeration of his ſtate
From braſſie boſomes, and rough hearts of flints ,
From ſtubborne Turkes and Tarters neuer traind

To offices of tender curteſie,
We all expect a gentle anſwer Iew ?

Iew. I haue poſſeſt your grace of what I purpoſe,
And by our holy Sabbath haue I ſworne
To haue the due and forfeit of my bond.
If you denie it, let the danger light
Vpon your Charter, and your Cities freedome.
You'l aske me why I rather chooſe to haue
A weight of carrion fleſh, then to receiue
Three thouſand Ducats ? Ile not anſwer that :
But ſay it is my humor ; Is it anſwered ?
What if my houſe be troubled with a Rat,
And I be pleas'd to giue ten thouſand Ducates
To haue it bain'd ? What, are you anſwer'd yet ?
Some men there are loue not a gaping Pigge :
Some that are mad, if they behold a Cat :
And others, when the bag-pipe ſings i'th noſe,
Cannot containe their Vrine for affection.
Maſters of paſſion ſwayes it to the moode
Of what it likes or loaths, now for your anſwer :
As there is no firme reaſon to be rendred
Why he cannot abide a gaping Pigge ?
Why he a harmleſſe neceſſarie Cat ?
Why he a woollen bag-pipe : but of force
Muſt yeeld to ſuch ineuitable ſhame,
As to offend himſelfe being offended :
So can I giue no reaſon, nor I will not,
More then a lodg'd hate, and a certaine loathing
I beare *Anthonio*, that I follow thus
A looſing ſuite againſt him ? Are you anſwered ?

Baſſ. This is no anſwer thou vnfeeling man,
To excuſe the currant of thy cruelty.

Iew. I am not bound to pleaſe thee with my anſwer.

Baſſ. Do all men kil the things they do not loue?

Iew. Hates any man the thing he would not kill?

Baſſ. Euerie offence is not a hate at firſt.

Iew. What wouldſt thou haue a Serpent ſting thee twice ?

Ant. I pray you thinke you queſtion with the Iew :
You may as well go ſtand vpon the beach,
And bid the maine flood baite his vſuall height,
Or euen as well vſe queſtion with the Wolfe,
The Ewe bleate for the Lambe :
You may as well forbid the Mountaine Pines
To wagge their high tops, and to make no noiſe
When they are fretted with the guſts of heauen :
You may as well do any thing moſt hard,
As ſeeke to ſoften that, then which what harder ?
His Iewiſh heart.　Therefore I do beſeech you
Make no more offers, vſe no farther meanes,
But with all briefe and plaine conueniencie
Let me haue iudgement, and the Iew his will.

Baſ. For thy three thouſand Ducates heereis fix.

Iew. If euerie Ducat in fixe thouſand Ducates
Were in fixe parts, and euery part a Ducate,
I would not draw them, I would haue my bond ?

Du. How ſhalt thou hope for mercie, rendring none ?

Iew. What iudgement ſhall I dread doing no wrong?
You haue among you many a purchaſt ſlaue,
Which like your Aſſes, and your Dogs and Mules,
You vſe in abiect and in ſlauiſh parts,
Becauſe you bought them.　Shall I ſay to you,
Let them be free, marrie them to your heires ?
Why ſweate they vnder burthens? Let their beds
Be made as ſoft as yours : and let their pallats
Be ſeaſon'd with ſuch Viands : you will anſwer

The

The flaues are ours. So do I anfwer you.
The pound of flefh which I demand of him
Is deerely bought, 'tis mine, and I will haue it.
If you deny me ; fie vpon your Law,
There is no force in the decrees of Venice;
I ftand for iudgement, anfwer, Shall I haue it?
  Du. Vpon my power I may difmiffe this Court,
Vnleffe *Bellario* a learned Doctor,
Whom I haue fent for to determine this,
Come heere to day.
  Sal. My Lord, heere ftayes without
A Meffenger with Letters from the Doctor,
New come from Padua.
  Du. Bring vs the Letters, Call the Meffengers.
  Baff. Good cheere *Anthonio.* What man, corage yet:
The Iew fhall haue my flefh, blood, bones, and all,
Ere thou fhalt loofe for me one drop of blood.
  Ant. I am a tainted Weather of the flocke,
Meeteft for death, the weakeft kinde of fruite
Drops earlieft to the ground, and fo let me;
You cannot better be employ'd *Baffanio,*
Then to liue ftill, and write mine Epitaph.

Enter Nerriffa.
  Du. Came you from Padua from *Bellario?*
  Ner. From both.
My Lord *Bellario* greets your Grace.
  Baf. Why doft thou whet thy knife fo earneftly?
  Iew. To cut the forfeiture from that bankrout there.
  Gra. Not on thy foale : but on thy foule harfh Iew
Thou mak'ft thy knife keene: but no mettall can,
No, not the hangmans Axe beare halfe the keenneffe
Of thy fharpe enuy. Can no prayers pierce thee?
  Iew. No, none that thou haft wit enough to make.
  Gra. O be thou damn'd, inexecrable dogge,
And for thy life let iuftice be accus'd:
Thou almoft mak'ft me wauer in my faith;
To hold opinion with *Pythagoras,*
That foules of Animals infufe themfelues
Into the trunkes of men. Thy currifh fpirit
Gouern'd a Wolfe, who hang'd for humane flaughter,
Euen from the gallowes did his fell foule fleet;
And whil'ft thou layeft in thy vnhallowed dam,
Infus'd it felfe in thee : For thy defires
Are Woluifh, bloody, fteru'd, and rauenous.
  Iew. Till thou canft raile the feale from off my bond
Thou but offend'ft thy Lungs to fpeake fo loud :
Repaire thy wit good youth, or it will fall
To endleffe ruine. I ftand heere for Law.
  Dn. This Letter from *Bellario* doth commend
A yong and Learned Doctor in our Court;
Where is he?
  Ner. He attendeth heere hard by
To know your anfwer, whether you'l admit him.
  Du. With all my heart. Some three or four of you
Go giue him curteous conduct to this place,
Meane time the Court fhall heare *Bellarioes* Letter.

Your Grace fhall vnderftand, that at the receite of your
Letter I am very ficke : but in the inftant that your meffenger came, in louing vifitation, was with me a young Doctor of Rome, his name is Balthafar : I acquained him with
the caufe in Controuerfie, betweene the Iew and Anthonio
the Merchant : We turn'd ore many Bookes together : bee is
furnifhed with my opinion, which bettred with his owne learning, the greatneffe whereof I cannot enough commend, comes

with him at my importunity, to fill vp your Graces requeft in
my fted. I befeech you, let his lacke of years be no impediment
to let him lacke a reuerend eftimation : for I neuer knewe fo
yong a body, with fo old a head. I leaue him to your gracious
acceptance, whofe trial fhall better publifh his commendation.

Enter Portia for Balthazar.

  Duke. You heare the learn'd *Bellario* what he writes,
And heere (I take it) is the Doctor come.
Giue me your hand : Came you from old *Bellario?*
  Por. I did my Lord.
  Du. You are welcome : take your place;
Are you acquainted with the difference
That holds this prefent queftion in the Court.
  Por. I am enformed throughly of the caufe.
Which is the Merchant heere? and which the Iew?
  Du. Anthonio and old *Shylocke,* both ftand forth.
  Por. Is your name *Shylocke?*
  Iew. Shylocke is my name.
  Por. Of a ftrange nature is the fute you follow,
Yet in fuch rule, that the Venetian Law
Cannot impugne you as you do proceed.
You ftand within his danger, do you not?
  Ant. I, fo he fayes.
  Por. Do you confeffe the bond?
  Ant. I do.
  Por. Then muft the Iew be mercifull.
  Iew. On what compulfion muft I? Tell me that.
  Por. The quality of mercy is not ftrain'd,
It droppeth as the gentle raine from heauen
Vpon the place beneath. It is twice bleft,
It bleffeth him that giues, and him that takes,
'Tis mightieft in the mightieft, it becomes
The throned Monarch better then his Crowne.
His Scepter fhewes the force of temporall power,
The attribute to awe and Maieftie,
Wherein doth fit the dread and feare of Kings:
But mercy is aboue this fceptred fway,
It is enthroned in the hearts of Kings,
It is an attribute to God himfelfe;
And earthly power doth then fhew likeft Gods
When mercie feafons Iuftice. Therefore Iew,
Though Iuftice be thy plea, confider this,
That in the courfe of Iuftice, none of vs
Should fee faluation : we do pray for mercie,
And that fame prayer, doth teach vs all to render
The deeds of mercie. I haue fpoke thus much
To mitigate the iuftice of thy plea :
Which if thou follow, this ftrict courfe of Venice
Muft needes giue fentence 'gainft the Merchant there.
  Shy. My deeds vpon my head, I craue the Law,
The penaltie and forfeite of my bond.
  Por. Is he not able to difcharge the money?
  Baf. Yes, heere I tender it for him in the Court,
Yea, twice the fumme, if that will not fuffice,
I will be bound to pay it ten times ore,
On forfeit of my hands, my head, my heart :
If this will not follow, it muft appeare
That malice beares downe truth. And I befeech you
Wreft once the Law to your authority.
To do a great right, do a little wrong,
And curbe this cruell diuell of his will.
  Por. It muft not be, there is no power in Venice
Can alter a decree eftablifhed :
'Twill be recorded for a Prefident,

And

And many an error by the same example,
Will rush into the state : It cannot be.
Iew. A *Daniel* come to iudgement, yea a *Daniel.*
O wise young Iudge, how do I honour thee.
Por. I pray you let me looke vpon the bond.
Iew. Heere 'tis most reuerend Doctor, heere it is.
Por. Shylocke, there's thrice thy monie offered thee.
Shy. An oath, an oath, I haue an oath in heauen :
Shall I lay periurie vpon my soule?
No not for Venice.
Por. Why this bond is forfeit,
And lawfully by this the Iew may claime
A pound of flesh, to be by him cut off
Neerest the Merchants heart ; be mercifull,
Take thrice thy money, bid me teare the bond.
Iew. When it is paid according to the tenure.
It doth appeare you are a worthy Iudge :
you know the Law, your exposition
Hath beene most found. I charge you by the Law,
Whereof you are a well-deseruing pillar,
Proceede to iudgement : By my soule I sweare,
There is no power in the tongue of man
To alter me : I stay heere on my bond.
An. Most heartily I do beseech the Court
To giue the iudgement.
Por. Why then thus it is :
you must prepare your bosome for his knife.
Iew. O noble Iudge, O excellent yong man.
Por. For the intent and purpose of the Law
Hath full relation to the penaltie,
Which heere appeareth due vpon the bond.
Iew. 'Tis verie true : O wise and vpright Iudge,
How much more elder art thou then thy lookes?
Por. Therefore lay bare your bosome.
Iew. I, his brest,
So sayes the bond, doth it not noble Iudge?
Neerest his heart, those are the very words.
Por. It is so : Are there ballance heere to weigh the
flesh?
Iew. I haue them ready.
Por. Haue by some Surgeon *Shylock* on your charge
To stop his wounds, least he should bleede to death.
Iew. It is not nominated in the bond?
Por. It is not so exprest: but what of that?
'Twere good you do so much for charitie.
Iew. I cannot finde it, 'tis not in the bond.
Por. Come Merchant, haue you any thing to say?
Ant. But little : I am arm'd and well prepar'd.
Giue me your hand *Bassanio,* fare you well.
Greeue not that I am falne to this for you :
For heerein fortune shewes her selfe more kinde
Then is her custome. It is still her vse
To let the wretched man out-liue his wealth,
To view with hollow eye, and wrinkled brow
An age of pouerty. From which lingring penance
Of such miserie, doth she cut me off:
Commend me to your honourable Wife,
Tell her the processe of *Anthonio's* end :
Say how I lou'd you ; speake me faire in death :
And when the tale is told, bid her be iudge,
Whether *Bassanio* had not once a Loue :
Repent not you that you shall loose your friend,
And he repents not that he payes your debt.
For if the Iew do cut but deepe enough,
Ile pay it instantly, with all my heart.
Bas. Anthonio, I am married to a wife,

Which is as deere to me as life it selfe,
But life it selfe, my wife, and all the world,
Are not with me esteem'd aboue thy life.
I would loose all, I sacrifice them all
Heere to this deuill, to deliuer you.
Por. Your wife would giue you little thanks for that
If she were by to heare you make the offer.
Gra. I haue a wife whom I protest I loue,
I would she were in heauen, so she could
Intreat some power to change this currish Iew.
Ner. 'Tis well you offer it behinde her backe,
The wish would make else an vnquiet house. (ter
Iew. These be the Christian husbands: I haue a daugh-
Would any of the stocke of *Barrabas*
Had beene her husband, rather then a Christian.
We trifle time, I pray thee pursue sentence.
Por. A pound of that same marchants flesh is thine,
The Court awards it, and the law doth giue it.
Iew. Most rightfull Iudge.
Por. And you must cut this flesh from off his brest,
The Law allowes it, and the Court awards it.
Iew. Most learned Iudge, a sentence, come prepare.
Por. Tarry a little, there is something else,
This bond doth giue thee heere no iot of bloud,
The words expresly are a pound of flesh :
Then take thy bond, take thou thy pound of flesh,
But in the cutting it, if thou dost shed
One drop of Christian bloud, thy lands and goods
Are by the Lawes of Venice confiscate
Vnto the state of Venice.
Gra. O vpright Iudge,
Marke Iew, ô learned Iudge.
Shy. Is that the law?
Por. Thy selfe shalt see the Act :
For as thou vrgest iustice, be assur'd
Thou shalt haue iustice more then thou desirest.
Gra. O learned Iudge, mark Iew, a learned Iudge.
Iew. I take this offer then, pay the bond thrice,
And let the Christian goe.
Bass. Heere is the money.
Por. Soft, the Iew shall haue all iustice, soft, no haste,
He shall haue nothing but the penalty.
Gra. O Iew, an vpright Iudge, a learned Iudge.
Por. Therefore prepare thee to cut off the flesh,
Shed thou no bloud, nor cut thou lesse nor more
But iust a pound of flesh : if thou tak'st more
Or lesse then a iust pound, be it so much
As makes it light or heauy in the substance,
Or the deuision of the twentieth part
Of one poore scruple, nay if the scale doe turne
But in the estimation of a hayre,
Thou diest, and all thy goods are confiscate.
Gra. A second *Daniel,* a *Daniel* Iew,
Now infidell I haue thee on the hip.
Por. Why doth the Iew pause, take thy forfeiture.
Shy. Giue me my principall, and let me goe.
Bass. I haue it ready for thee, heere it is.
Por. He hath refus'd it in the open Court,
He shall haue meerly iustice and his bond.
Gra. A Daniel still say I, a second *Daniel,*
I thanke thee Iew for teaching me that word.
Shy. Shall I not haue barely my principall?
Por. Thou shalt haue nothing but the forfeiture,
To be taken so at thy perill Iew.
Shy. Why then the Deuill giue him good of it:
Ile stay no longer question.

Por. Tarry

Por. Tarry Iew,
The Law hath yet another hold on you.
It is enacted in the Lawes of Venice,
If it be proued againſt an Alien,
That by direct, or indirect attempts
He ſeeke the life of any Citizen,
The party gainſt the which he doth contriue,
Shall ſeaze one halfe his goods, the other halfe
Comes to the priuie coffer of the State,
And the offenders life lies in the mercy
Of the Duke onely, gainſt all other voice.
In which predicament I ſay thou ſtandſt :
For it appeares by manifeſt proceeding,
That indirectly, and directly to,
Thou haſt contriu'd againſt the very life
Of the defendant : and thou haſt incur'd
The danger formerly by me rehearſt.
Downe therefore, and beg mercy of the Duke.

Gra. Beg that thou maiſt haue leaue to hang thy ſelfe,
And yet thy wealth being forfeit to the ſtate,
Thou haſt not left the value of a cord,
Therefore thou muſt be hang'd at the ſtates charge.

Duk. That thou ſhalt ſee the difference of our ſpirit,
I pardon thee thy life before thou aske it :
For halfe thy wealth, it is *Anthonio's*,
The other halfe comes to the generall ſtate,
Which humbleneſſe may driue vnto a fine.

Por. I for the ſtate, not for *Anthonio*.

Shy. Nay, take my life and all, pardon not that,
You take my houſe, when you do take the prop
That doth ſuſtaine my houſe : you take my life
When you doe take the meanes whereby I liue.

Por. What mercy can you render him *Anthonio?*

Gra. A halter *gratis*, nothing elſe for Gods ſake.

Ant. So pleaſe my Lord the Duke, and all the Court
To quit the fine for one halfe of his goods,
I am content : ſo he will let me haue
The other halfe in vſe, to render it
Vpon his death, vnto the Gentleman
That lately ſtole his daughter.
Two things prouided more, that for this fauour
He preſently become a Chriſtian :
The other, that he doe record a gift
Heere in the Court of all he dies poſſeſt
Vnto his ſonne *Lorenzo*, and his daughter.

Duk. He ſhall doe this, or elſe I doe recant
The pardon that I late pronounced heere.

Por. Art thou contented Iew? what doſt thou ſay?

Shy. I am content.

Por. Clarke, draw a deed of gift.

Shy. I pray you giue me leaue to goe from hence,
I am not well, ſend the deed after me,
And I will ſigne it.

Duke. Get thee gone, but doe it.

Gra. In chriſtning thou ſhalt haue two godfathers,
Had I been iudge, thou ſhouldſt haue had ten more,
To bring thee to the gallowes, not to the font.   *Exit.*

Du. Sir I intreat you with me home to dinner.

Por. I humbly doe deſire your Grace of pardon,
I muſt away this night toward Padua,
And it is meete I preſently ſet forth.

Duk. I am ſorry that your leyſure ſerues you not :
Anthonio, gratifie this gentleman,
For in my minde, you are much bound to him.
          Exit Duke and his traine.

Baſſ. Moſt worthy gentleman, I and my friend

Haue by your wiſedome beene this day acquitted
Of greeuous penalties, in lieu whereof,
Three thouſand Ducats due vnto the Iew
We freely cope your curteous paines withall.

An. And ſtand indebted ouer and aboue
In loue and ſeruice to you euermore.

Por. He is well paid that is well ſatisfied,
And I deliuering you, am ſatisfied,
And therein doe account my ſelfe well paid,
My minde was neuer yet more mercinarie.
I pray you know me when we meete againe,
I wiſh you well, and ſo I take my leaue.

Baſſ. Deare ſir, of force I muſt attempt you further,
Take ſome remembrance of vs as a tribute,
Not as fee : grant me two things, I pray you
Not to denie me, and to pardon me.

Por. You preſſe mee farre, and therefore I will yeeld,
Giue me your gloues, Ile weare them for your ſake,
And for your loue Ile take this ring from you,
Doe not draw backe your hand, ile take no more,
And you in loue ſhall not deny me this ?

Baſſ. This ring good ſir, alas it is a trifle,
I will not ſhame my ſelfe to giue you this.

Por. I wil haue nothing elſe but onely this,
And now methinkes I haue a minde to it.

Baſ. There's more depends on this then on the value,
The deareſt ring in Venice will I giue you,
And finde it out by proclamation,
Onely for this I pray you pardon me.

Por. I ſee ſir you are liberall in offers,
You taught me firſt to beg, and now me thinkes
You teach me how a beggar ſhould be anſwer'd.

Baſ. Good ſir, this ring was giuen me by my wife,
And when ſhe put it on, ſhe made me vow
That I ſhould neither ſell, nor giue, nor loſe it.

Por. That ſcuſe ſerues many men to ſaue their gifts,
And if your wife be not a mad woman,
And know how well I haue deſeru'd this ring,
Shee would not hold out enemy for euer
For giuing it to me : well, peace be with you.   *Exeunt.*

Ant. My L. *Baſſanio*, let him haue the ring,
Let his deſeruings and my loue withall
Be valued againſt your wiues commandement.

Baſſ. Goe *Gratiano*, run and ouer-take him,
Giue him the ring, and bring him if thou canſt
Vnto *Anthonios* houſe, away, make haſte.   *Exit Grati.*
Come, you and I will thither preſently,
And in the morning early will we both
Flie toward *Belmont*, come *Anthonio*.   *Exeunt.*

Enter Portia and Nerriſſa.

Por. Enquire the Iewes houſe out, giue him this deed,
And let him ſigne it, wee'll away to night,
And be a day before our husbands home :
This deed will be well welcome to *Lorenzo*.

Enter Gratiano.

Gra. Faire ſir, you are well ore-tane :
My L. *Baſſanio* vpon more aduice,
Hath ſent you heere this ring, and doth intreat
Your company at dinner.

Por. That cannot be ;
His ring I doe accept moſt thankfully,
And ſo I pray you tell him : furthermore,
I pray you ſhew my youth old *Shylockes* houſe.

Gra. That will I doe.

Ner. Sir, I would ſpeake with you :

Q   Ile

Ile fee if I can get my husbands ring
Which I did make him fweare to keepe for euer.
Por. Thou maift I warrant, we fhal haue old fwearing
That they did giue the rings away to men ;
But weele out-face them, and out-fweare them to :
Away, make hafte, thou know'ft where I will tarry.
Ner. Come good fir, will you fhew me to this houfe.
Exeunt.

eActus Quintus.

Enter Lorenzo and Ieffica.

Lor. The moone fhines bright. In fuch a night as this,
When the fweet winde did gently kiffe the trees,
And they did make no nnyfe, in fuch a night
Troylus me thinkes mounted the Troian walls,
And figh'd his foule toward the Grecian tents
Where *Creffed* lay that night.
Ief. In fuch a night
Did *Thisbie* fearefully ore-trip the dewe,
And faw the Lyons fhadow ere himfelfe,
And ranne difmayed away.
Loren. In fuch a night
Stood *Dido* with a Willow in her hand
Vpon the wilde fea bankes, and waft her Loue
To come againe to Carthage.
Ief. In fuch a night
Medea gathered the inchanted hearbs
That did renew old *Eſon.*
Loren. In fuch a night
Did *Ieffica* fteale from the wealthy Iewe,
And with an Vnthrift Loue did runne from Venice,
As farre as Belmont.
Ief. In fuch a night
Did young *Lorenzo* fweare he lou'd her well,
Stealing her foule with many vowes of faith,
And nere a true one.
Loren. In fuch a night
Did pretty *Ieffica* (like a little fhrow)
Slander her Loue, and he forgaue it her.
Ieffi. I would out-night you did no body come :
But harke, I heare the footing of a man.

Enter Meffenger.

Lor. Who comes fo faft in filence of the night?
Mef. A friend. (friend?
Loren. A friend, what friend ? your name I pray you
Mef. Stephano is my name, and I bring word
My Miftreffe will before the breake of day
Be heere at Belmont, fhe doth ftray about
By holy croffes where fhe kneeles and prayes
For happy wedlocke houres.
Loren. .Who comes with her ?
Mef. None but a holy Hermit and her maid :
I pray you it my Mafter yet rnturn'd ?
Loren. He is not, nor we haue not heard from him,
But goe we in I pray thee *Ieffica*,
And ceremonioufly let vs vs prepare
Some welcome for the Miftreffe of the houfe,

Enter Clowne.

Clo. Sola, fola : wo ha ho, fola, fola.

Loren. Who calls ?
Clo. Sola, did you fee M. *Lorenzo*, & M. *Lorenzo*, fola,
Lor. Leaue hollowing man, heere. (fola.
Clo. Sola, where, where ?
Lor. Heere ?
Clo. Tel him ther's a Poft come from my Mafter, with
his horne full of good newes, my Mafter will be here ere
morning fweet foule.
Loren. Let's in, and there expect his comming.
And yet no matter : why fhould we goe in?
My friend *Stephen*, fignifie pray you
Within the houfe, your Miftreffe is at hand ,
And bring your mufique foorth into the ayre.
How fweet the moone-light fleepes vpon this banke,
Heere will we fit, and let the founds of muficke
Creepe in our eares foft ftilnes, and the night
Become the tutches of fweet harmonie :
Sit *Ieffica*, looke how the floore of heauen
Is thicke inlayed with pattens of bright gold ,
There's not the fmalleft orbe which thou beholdft
But in his motion like an Angell fings,
Still quiring to the young eyed Cherubins ;
Such harmonie is in immortall foules,
But whilft this muddy vefture of decay
Doth grofly clofe in it, we cannot heare it :
Come hoe, and wake *Diana* with a hymne,
With fweeteft tutches pearce your Miftreffe eare,
And draw her home with muficke.
Ieffi. I am neuer merry when I heare fweet mufique.
Play mufieke.
Lor. The reafon is, your fpirits are attentiue :
For doe but note a wilde and wanton heard
Or race of youthful and vnhandied colts,
Fetching mad bounds, bellowing and neighing loud,
Which is the hot condition of their bloud,
If they but heare perchance a trumpet found,
Or any ayre of muficke touch their eares,
You fhall perceiue them make a mutuall ftand,
Their fauage eyes turn'd to a modeft gaze,
By the fweet power of muficke : therefore the Poet
Did faine that *Orpheus* drew trees, ftones, and floods.
Since naught fo ftockifh, hard, and full of rage,
But muficke for time doth change his nature,
The man that hath no muficke in himfelfe,
Nor is not moued with concord of fweet founds,
Is fit for treafons, ftratagems, and fpoyles,
The motions of his fpirit are dull as night,
And his affections darke as *Erobus*,
Let no fuch man be trufted : marke the muficke.

Enter Portia and Nerriffa.

Por. That light we fee is burning in my hall :
How farre that little candell throwes his beames,
So fhines a good deed in a naughty world. (dle?
Ner. When the moone fhone we did not fee the can
Por. So doth the greater glory dim the leffe,
A fubftitute fhines brightly as a King
Vntill a King be by, and then his ftate
Empties it felfe, as doth an inland brooke
Into the maine of waters : mufique, harke. *Muficke.*
Ner. It is your mufieke Madame of the houfe.
Por. Nothing is good I fee without refpect,
Methinkes it founds much fweeter then by day ?
Ner: Silence beftowes that vertue on it Madam.
Por. The Crow doth fing as fweetly as the Larke
When

When neither is attended : and I thinke
The Nightingale if fhe fhould fing by day
When euery Goofe is cackling, would be thought
No better a Mufitian then the Wren ?
How many things by feafon, feafon'd are
To their right praife, and true perfe&ion :
Peace, how the Moone fleepes with Endimion,
And would not be awak'd.
                                Muficke ceafes.
  Lor. That is the voice,
Or I am much deceiu'd of *Portia.*
  Por. He knowes me as the blinde man knowes the
Cuckow by the bad voice?
  Lor. Deere Lady welcome home?
  Por. We haue bene praying for our husbands welfare
Which fpeed we hope the better for our words,
Are they return'd ?
  Lor. Madam, they are not yet :
But there is come a Meffenger before
To fignifie their comming.
  Por. Go in *Nerriffa,*
Giue order to my feruants, that they take
No note at all of our being abfent hence,
Nor you *Lorenzo, Ieffica* nor you.
                                A Tucket founds.
  Lor. Your husband is at hand, I heare his Trumpet,
We are no tell-tales Madam, feare you not.
  Por. This night methinkes is but the daylight ficke,
It lookes a little paler, 'tis a day,
Such as the day is, when the Sun is hid.

        *Enter Baffanio, Anthonio, Gratiano, and their
                        Followers.*

  Baf. We fhould hold day with the Antipodes,
If you would walke in abfence of the funne.
  Por. Let me giue light, but let me not be light,
For a light wife doth make a heauie husband,
And neuer be *Baffanio* fo for me,
But God fort all: you are welcome home my Lord.
  Baff. I thanke you Madam, giue welcom to my friend
This is the man, this is *Anthonio,*
To whom I am fo infinitely bound.
  Por. You fhould in all fence be much bound to him,
For as I heare he was much bound for you.
  Anth. No more then I am wel acquitted of.
  Por. Sir, you are verie welcome to our houfe :
It muft appeare in other waies then words,
Therefore I fcant this breathing curtefie.
  Gra. By yonder Moone I fweare you do me wrong,
Infaith I gaue it to the Iudges Clearke,
Would he were gelt that had it for my part,
Since you do take it Loue fo much at hart.
  Por. A quarrel hoe alreadie, what's the matter ?
  Gra. About a hoope of Gold, a paltry Ring
That fhe did giue me, whofe Poefie was
For all the world like Cutlers Poetry
Vpon a knife ; *Loue mee, and leaue mee not.*
  Ner. What talke you of the Poefie or the valew:
You fwore to me when I did giue it you,
That you would weare it til the houre of death,
And that it fhould lye with you in your graue,
Though not for me, yet for your vehement oaths,
You fhould haue beene refpe&iue and haue kept it.
Gaue it a Iudges Clearke: but wel I know
The Clearke wil nere weare haire on's face that had it.

  Gra. He wil, and if he liue to be a man.
  Nerriffa. I, if a Woman liue to be a man.
  Gra. Now by this hand I gaue it to a youth,
A kinde of boy, a little fcrubbed boy,
No higher then thy felfe, the Iudges Clearke,
A prating boy that begg'd it as a Fee,
I could not for my heart deny it him.
  Por. You were too blame, I muft be plaine with you,
To part fo flightly with your wiues firft gift,
A thing ftucke on with oathes vpon your finger,
And fo riueted with faith vnto your flefh.
I gaue my Loue a Ring, and made him fweare
Neuer to part with it, and heere he ftands :
I dare be fworne for him, he would not leaue it,
Nor plucke it from his finger, for the wealth
That the world mafters. Now in faith *Gratiano,*
You giue your wife too vnkinde a caufe of greefe,
And 'twere to me I fhould be mad at it.
  Baff. Why I were beft to cut my left hand off,
And fweare I loft the Ring defending it.
  Gra. My Lord *Baffanio* gaue his Ring away
Vnto the Iudge that beg'd it, and indeede
Deferu'd it too : and then the Boy his Clearke
That tooke fome paines in writing, he begg'd mine,
And neyther man nor mafter would take ought
But the two Rings.
  Por. What Ring gaue you my Lord ?
Not that I gaue you, nor that which you receiu'd of me.
  Baff. If I could adde a lie vnto a fault,
I would deny it : but you fee my finger
Hath not the Ring vpon it, it is gone.
  Por. Euen fo voide is your falfe heart of truth.
By heauen I wil nere come in your bed
Vntil I fee the Ring.
  Ner. Nor I in yours, til I againe fee mine.
  Baff. Sweet *Portia,*
If you did know to whom I gaue the Ring,
If you did know for whom I gaue the Ring,
And would conceiue for what I gaue the Ring,
And how vnwillingly I left the Ring,
When nought would be accepted but the Ring,
You would abate the ftrength of your difpleafure?
  Por. If you had knowne the vertue of the Ring,
Or halfe her worthineffe that gaue the Ring,
Or your owne honour to containe the Ring,
You would not then haue parted with the Ring :
What man is there fo much vnreafonable,
If you had pleas'd to haue defended it
With any termes of Zeale : wanted the modeftie
To vrge the thing held as a ceremonie :
Nerriffa teaches me what to beleeue,
Ile die for't, but fome Woman had the Ring?
  Baff. No by mine honor Madam, by my foule
No Woman had it, but a ciuill Do&or,
Which did refufe three thoufand Ducates of me,
And beg'd the Ring; the which I did denie him,
And fuffer'd him to go difpleas'd away :
Euen he that had held vp the verie life
Of my deere friend. What fhould I fay fweete Lady ?
I was inforc'd to fend it after him,
I was befet with fhame and curtefie,
My honor would not let ingratitude
So much befmeare it. Pardon me good Lady,
And by thefe bleffed Candles of the night,
Had you bene there, I thinke you would haue beg'd
The Ring of me, to giue the worthie Do&or?

                                    Q 2   *Por.*

Por. Let not that Doctor ere come neere my houfe,
Since he hath got the iewell that I loued,
And that which you did fweare to keepe for me,
I will become as liberall as you,
Ile not deny him any thing I haue,
No, not my body, nor my husbands bed :
Know him I fhall, I am well fure of it.
Lie not a night from home. Watch me like Argos,
If you doe not, if I be left alone,
Now by mine honour which is yet mine owne,
Ile haue the Doctor for my bedfellow.
Nerriffa. And I his Clarke: therefore be well aduis'd
How you doe leaue me to mine owne protection.
Gra. Well, doe you fo : let not me take him then,
For if I doe, ile mar the yong Clarks pen.
Ant. I am th'vnhappy fubiect of thefe quarrels.
Por. Sir, grieue not you,
You are welcome notwithftanding.
Baf. Portia, forgiue me this enforced wrong,
And in the hearing of thefe manie friends
I fweare to thee, euen by thine owne faire eyes
Wherein I fee my felfe.
Por. Marke you but that?
In both my eyes he doubly fees himfelfe :
In each eye one, fweare by your double felfe,
And there's an oath of credit.
Baf. Nay, but heare me.
Pardon this fault, and by my foule I fweare
I neuer more will breake an oath with thee.
Anth. I once did lend my bodie for thy wealth,
Which but for him that had your husbands ring
Had quite mifcarried. I dare be bound againe,
My foule vpon the forfeit, that your Lord
Will neuer more breake faith aduifedlie.
Por. Then you fhall be his furetie : giue him this,
And bid him keepe it better then the other.
Ant. Heere Lord *Baffanio,* fwear to keep this ring.
Baff. By heauen it is the fame I gaue the Doctor.
Por. I had it of him : pardon *Baffanio,*
For by this ring the Doctor lay with me.
Ner. And pardon me my gentle *Gratiano,*
For that fame fcrubbed boy the Doctors Clarke
In liew of this, laft night did lye with me.
Gra. Why this is like the mending of high waies
In Sommer, where the waies are faire enough :
What, are we Cuckolds ere we haue deferu'd it.

Por. Speake not fo groffely, you are all amaz'd ;
Heere is a letter, reade it at your leyfure,
It comes from Padua from *Bellario,*
There you fhall finde that *Portia* was the Doctor,
Nerriffa there her Clarke. *Lorenzo* heere
Shall witneffe I fet forth as foone as you,
And but eu'n now return'd: I haue not yet
Entred my houfe. *Anthonio* you are welcome,
And I haue better newes in ftore for you
Then you expect : vnfeale this letter foone,
There you fhall finde three of your Argofies
Are richly come to harbour fodainlie.
You fhall not know by what ftrange accident
I chanced on this letter.
Antho. I am dumbe.
Baff. Were you the Doctor, and I knew you not?
Gra. Were you the Clark that is to make me cuckold.
Ner. I, but the Clark that neuer meanes to doe it,
Vnleffe he liue vntill he be a man.
Baff. (Sweet Doctor) you fhall be my bedfellow,
When I am abfent, then lie with my wife.
An. (Sweet Ladie) you haue giuen me life & liuing ;
For heere I reade for certaine that my fhips
Are fafelie come to Rode.
Por. How now *Lorenzo* ?
My Clarke hath fome good comforts to for you.
Ner. I, and Ile giue them him without a fee.
There doe I giue to you and *Ieffica*
From the rich Iewe, a fpeciall deed of gift
After his death, of all he dies poffeff'd of.
Loren. Faire Ladies you drop Manna in the way
Of ftarued people.
Por. It is almoft morning,
And yet I am fure you are not fatisfied
Of thefe euents at full. Let vs goe in,
And charge vs there vpon intergatories,
And we will anfwer all things faithfully.
Gra. Let it be fo, the firft intergatory
That my *Nerriffa* fhall be fworne on, is,
Whether till the next night fhe had rather ftay,
Or goe to bed, now being two houres to day,
But were the day come, I fhould wifh it darke,
Till I were couching with the Doctors Clarke.
Well, while I liue, Ile feare no other thing
So fore, as keeping fafe *Nerriffas* ring.

Exeunt.

FINIS.

As you Like it.

Actus primus. Scæna Prima.

Enter Orlando and Adam.

Orlando.

AS I remember *Adam*, it was vpon this fashion bequeathed me by will, but poore a thousand Crownes, and as thou faist, charged my brother on his blessing to breed mee well : and there begins my sadnesse : My brother *Iaques* he keepes at schoole, and report speakes goldenly of his profit : for my part, he keepes me rustically at home, or (to speak more properly) staies heere at home vnkept : for call you that keeping for a gentleman of my birth, that differs not from the stalling of an Oxe? his horses are bred better, for besides that they are faire with their feeding, they are taught their mannage, and to that end Riders deerely hir'd : but I (his brother) gaine nothing vnder him but growth, for the which his Animals on his dunghils are as much bound to him as I : besides this nothing that he so plentifully giues me, the something that nature gaue mee, his countenance seemes to take from me : hee lets mee feede with his Hindes, barres mee the place of a brother, and as much as in him lies, mines my gentility with my education. This is it *Adam* that grieues me, and the spirit of my Father, which I thinke is within mee, begins to mutinie against this seruitude. I will no longer endure it, though yet I know no wise remedy how to auoid it.

Enter Oliuer.

Adam. Yonder comes my Master, your brother.

Orlan. Goe a-part *Adam*, and thou shalt heare how he will shake me vp.

Oli. Now Sir, what make you heere?

Orl. Nothing : I am not taught to make any thing.

Oli. What mar you then sir?

Orl. Marry sir, I am helping you to mar that which God made, a poore vnworthy brother of yours with idlenesse.

Oliuer. Marry sir be better employed, and be naught a while.

Orlan. Shall I keepe your hogs, and eat huskes with them? what prodigall portion haue I spent, that I should come to such penury?

Oli. Know you where you are sir?

Orl. O sir, very well : heere in your Orchard.

Oli. Know you before whom sir?

Orl. I, better then him I am before knowes mee : I know you are my eldest brother, and in the gentle condition of bloud you should so know me : the courtesie of nations allowes you my better, in that you are the first borne, but the same tradition takes not away my bloud, were there twenty brothers betwixt vs : I haue as much

of my father in mee, as you, albeit I confesse your comming before me is neerer to his reuerence.

Oli. What Boy? (this.

Orl. Come, come elder brother, you are too yong in this.

Oli. Wilt thou lay hands on me villaine?

Orl. I am no villaine : I am the yongest sonne of Sir *Rowland de Boys*, he was my father, and he is thrice a villaine that saies such a father begot villaines : wert thou not my brother, I would not take this hand from thy throat, till this other had puld out thy tongue for saying so, thou hast raild on thy selfe.

Adam. Sweet Masters bee patient, for your Fathers remembrance, be at accord.

Oli. Let me goe I say.

Orl. I will not till I please : you shall heare mee : my father charg'd you in his will to giue me good education : you haue train'd me like a pezant, obscuring and hiding from me all gentleman-like qualities : the spirit of my father growes strong in mee, and I will no longer endure it : therefore allow me such exercises as may become a gentleman, or giue mee the poore allottery my father left me by testament, with that I will goe buy my fortunes.

Oli. And what wilt thou do? beg when that is spent? Well sir, get you in . I will not long be troubled with you : you shall haue some part of your will, I pray you leaue me.

Orl. I will no further offend you, then becomes mee for my good.

Oli. Get you with him, you olde dogge.

Adam. Is old dogge my reward : most true, I haue lost my teeth in your seruice : God be with my olde master, he would not haue spoke such a word. *Ex. Orl. Ad.*

Oli. Is it euen so, begin you to grow vpon me? I will physicke your ranckenesse, and yet giue no thousand crownes neyther : holla *Dennis.*

Enter Dennis.

Den. Calls your worship?

Oli. Was not *Charles* the Dukes Wrastler heere to speake with me?

Den. So please you, he is heere at the doore, and importunes accesse to you.

Oli. Call him in : 'twill be a good way : and to morrow the wrastling is.

Enter Charles,

Cha. Good morrow to your worship.

Oli. Good Mounsier *Charles* : what's the new newes at the new Court?

Charles. There's no newes at the Court Sir, but the olde newes : that is, the old Duke is banished by his yonger brother the new Duke, and three or foure louing

Q 3 Lords

Lords haue put themſelues into voluntary exile with him, whoſe lands and reuenues enrich the new *Duke*, therefore he giues them good leaue to wander.

Oli. Can you tell if *Roſalind* the *Dukes* daughter bee baniſhed with her Father?

Cha. O no ; for the *Dukes* daughter her *Coſen* ſo loues her, being euer from their Cradles bred together, that hee would haue followed her exile, or haue died to ſtay behind her ; ſhe is at the Court, and no leſſe beloued of her *Vncle*, then his owne daughter, and neuer two Ladies loued as they doe.

Oli. Where will the old *Duke* liue ?

Cha. They ſay hee is already in the Forreſt of *Arden*, and a many merry men with him ; and there they liue like the old *Robin Hood* of *England*: they ſay many yong Gentlemen flocke to him euery day, and fleet the time careleſly as they did in the golden world.

Oli. What, you wraſtle to morrow before the new *Duke*.

Cha. Marry doe I ſir : and I came to acquaint you with a matter : I am giuen ſir ſecretly to vnderſtand, that your yonger brother *Orlando* hath a diſpoſition to come in diſguis'd againſt mee to try a fall : to morrow ſir I wraſtle for my credit, and hee that eſcapes me without ſome broken limbe, ſhall acquit him well : your brother is but young and tender, and for your loue I would bee loth to foyle him, as I muſt for my owne honour if hee come in : therefore out of my loue to you, I came hither to acquaint you withall, that either you might ſtay him from his intendment, or brooke ſuch diſgrace well as he ſhall runne into, in that it is a thing of his owne ſearch, and altogether againſt my will.

Oli. *Charles*, I thanke thee for thy loue to me, which thou ſhalt finde I will moſt kindly requite : I had my ſelfe notice of my Brothers purpoſe heerein, and haue by vnder-hand meanes laboured to diſſwade him from it ; but he is reſolute. Ile tell thee *Charles*, it is the ſtubborneſt yong fellow of France, full of ambition, an enuious emulator of euery mans good parts, a ſecret & villanous contriuer againſt mee his naturall brother : therefore vſe thy diſcretion, I had as liefe thou didſt breake his necke as his finger. And thou wert beſt looke to't ; for if thou doſt him any ſlight diſgrace, or if hee doe not mightilie grace himſelfe on thee, hee will practiſe againſt thee by poyſon, entrap thee by ſome treacherous deuiſe, and neuer leaue thee till he hath tane thy life by ſome indirect meanes or other : for I aſſure thee, (and almoſt with teares I ſpeake it) there is not one ſo young, and ſo villanous this day liuing. I ſpeake but brotherly of him, but ſhould I anathomize him to thee, as hee is, I muſt bluſh, and weepe, and thou muſt looke pale and wonder.

Cha. I am heartily glad I came hither to you : if hee come to morrow, Ile giue him his payment : if euer hee goe alone againe, Ile neuer wraſtle for prize more : and ſo God keepe your worſhip. *Exit.*

Farewell good *Charles*. Now will I ſtirre this Gameſter : I hope I ſhall ſee an end of him ; for my ſoule (yet I know not why) hates nothing more then he : yet hee's gentle, neuer ſchool'd, and yet learned, full of noble deuiſe, of all ſorts enchantingly beloued, and indeed ſo much in the heart of the world, and eſpecially of my owne people, who beſt know him, that I am altogether miſpriſed : but it ſhall not be ſo long, this wraſtler ſhall cleare all : nothing remaines, but that I kindle the boy thither, which now Ile goe about. *Exit.*

Scœna Secunda.

Enter Roſalind, and Cellia.

Cel. I pray thee *Roſalind*, ſweet my Coz, be merry.

Roſ. Deere *Cellia*; I ſhow more mirth then I am miſtreſſe of, and would you yet were merrier : vnleſſe you could teach me to forget a baniſhed father, you muſt not learne me how to remember any extraordinary pleaſure.

Cel. Heerein I ſee thou lou'ſt mee not with the full waight that I loue thee ; if my Vncle thy baniſhed father had baniſhed thy Vncle the Duke my Father, ſo thou hadſt beene ſtill with mee, I could haue taught my loue to take thy father for mine ; ſo wouldſt thou, if the truth of thy loue to me were ſo righteouſly temper'd, as mine is to thee.

Roſ. Well, I will forget the condition of my eſtate, to reioyce in yours.

Cel. You know my Father hath no childe, but I, nor none is like to haue ; and truely when he dies, thou ſhalt be his heire ; for what hee hath taken away from thy father perforce, I will render thee againe in affection : by mine honor I will, and when I breake that oath, let mee turne monſter:therefore my ſweet *Roſe*, my deare *Roſe*, be merry.

Roſ. From henceforth I will Coz, and deuiſe ſports: let me ſee, what thinke you of falling in Loue ?

Cel. Marry I prethee doe, to make ſport withall: but loue no man in good earneſt, nor no further in ſport neyther, then with ſafety of a pure bluſh, thou maiſt in honor come off againe.

Roſ. What ſhall be our ſport then ?

Cel. Let vs ſit and mocke the good houſwife *Fortune* from her wheele, that her gifts may henceforth bee beſtowed equally.

Roſ. I would wee could doe ſo : for her benefits are mightily miſplaced, and the bountifull blinde woman doth moſt miſtake in her gifts to women.

Cel. 'Tis true, for thoſe that ſhe makes faire, ſhe ſcarce makes honeſt, & thoſe that ſhe makes honeſt, ſhe makes very illfauouredly.

Roſ. Nay now thou goeſt from Fortunes office to Natures : Fortune reignes in gifts of the world, not in the lineaments of Nature.

Enter Clowne.

Cel. No ; when Nature hath made a faire creature, may ſhe not by Fortune fall into the fire ? though nature hath giuen vs wit to flout at Fortune, hath not Fortune ſent in this foole to cut off the argument ?

Roſ. Indeed there is fortune too hard for nature, when fortune makes natures naturall, the cutter off of natures witte.

Cel. Peraduenture this is not Fortunes work neither, but Natures, who perceiueth our naturall wits too dull to reaſon of ſuch goddeſſes, hath ſent this Naturall for our whetſtone. for alwaies the dulneſſe of the foole, is the whetſtone of the wits. How now Witte, whether wander you ?

Clow. Miſtreſſe, you muſt come away to your farher.

Cel. Were you made the meſſenger ?

Clo. No by mine honor, but I was bid to come for you *Roſ.*

Rof. Where learned you that oath foole?

Clo. Of a certaine Knight, that fwore by his Honour they were good Pan-cakes, and fwore by his Honor the Muftard was naught : Now Ile ftand to it, the Pancakes were naught, and the Muftard was good, and yet was not the Knight forfworne.

Cel. How proue you that in the great heape of your knowledge ?

Rof. I marry, now vnmuzzle your wifedome.

Clo. Stand you both forth now : ftroke your chinnes, and fweare by your beards that I am a knaue.

Cel. By our beards(if we had them)thou art.

Clo. By my knauerie (if I had it) then I were : but if you fweare by that that is not, you are not forfworn : no more was this knight fwearing by his Honor, for he neuer had anie ; or if he had, he had fworne it away, before euer he faw thofe Pancakes, or that Muftard.

Cel. Prethee, who is't that thou means't?

Clo. One that old *Fredericke* your Father loues.

Rof. My Fathers loue is enough to honor him enough; fpeake no more of him, you'l be whipt for taxation one of thefe daies.

Clo. The more pittie that fooles may not fpeak wifely, what Wifemen do foolifhly.

Cel. By my troth thou faieft true : For, fince the little wit that fooles haue was filenced, the little foolerie that wife men haue makes a great fhew ; Heere comes Monfieur the *Beu.*

Enter le Beau.

Rof. With his mouth full of newes.

Cel. Which he vvill put on vs, as Pigeons feed their young.

Rof. Then fhal we be newes-cram'd.

Cel. All the better : we fhalbe the more Marketable. Boon-iour *Monfieur le Beu,* what's the newes?

Le Beu. Faire Princeffe,
you haue loft much good fport.

Cel. Sport : of what colour ?

Le Beu. What colour Madame? How fhall I aunfwer you ?

Rof. As wit and fortune will.

Clo. Or as the deftinies decrees.

Cel. Well faid, that was laid on with a trowell.

Clo. Nay, if I keepe not my ranke.

Rof. Thou loofeft thy old fmell.

Le Beu. You amaze me Ladies : I would haue told you of good wraftling, which you haue loft the fight of.

Rof. Yet tell vs the manner of the Wraftling.

Le Beu. I will tell you the beginning : and if it pleafe your Ladifhips, you may fee the end, for the beft is yet to doe, and heere where you are, they are comming to performe it.

Cel. Well, the beginning that is dead and buried.

Le Beu. There comes an old man, and his three fons.

Cel. I could match this beginning with an old tale.

Le Beu. Three proper yong men, of excellent growth and prefence.

Rof. With bils on their neckes : Be it knowne vnto all men by thefe prefents.

Le Beu. The eldeft of the three, wraftled with *Charles* the Dukes Wraftler, which *Charles* in a moment threw him, and broke three of his ribbes, that there is little hope of life in him : So he feru'd the fecond, and fo the third : yonder they lie, the poore old man their Father, making fuch pittiful dole ouer them, that all the beholders take his part with weeping.

Rof. Alas.

Clo. But what is the fport Monfieur, that the Ladies haue loft?

Le Beu. Why this that I fpeake of.

Clo. Thus men may grow wifer euery day. It is the firft time that euer I heard breaking of ribbes was fport for Ladies.

Cel. Or I, I promife thee.

Rof. But is there any elfe longs to fee this broken Muficke in his fides ? Is there yet another doates vpon rib-breaking? Shall we fee this wraftling Cofin?

Le Beu. You muft if you ftay heere, for heere is the place appointed for the wraftling, and they are ready to performe it.

Cel. Yonder fure they are comming. Let vs now ftay and fee it.

Flourifh. Enter Duke, Lords, Orlando, Charles, and Attendants.

Duke. Come on, fince the youth will not be intreated His owne perill on his forwardneffe.

Rof. Is yonder the man ?

Le Beu. Euen he, Madam.

Cel. Alas, he is too yong : yet he looks fucceffefully

Du. How now daughter, and Coufin:
Are you crept hither to fee the wraftling?

Rof. I my Liege, fo pleafe you giue vs leaue.

Du. You wil take little delight in it, I can tell you there is fuch oddes in the man : In pitie of the challengers youth, I would faine diffwade him, but he will not bee entreated. Speake to him Ladies, fee if you can mooue him.

Cel. Call him hether good Monfieuer *Le Beu.*

Duke. Do fo : Ile not be by.

Le Beu. Monfieur the Challenger, the Princeffe cals for you.

Orl. I attend them with all refpect and dutie.

Rof. Young man, haue you challeng'd *Charles* the Wraftler?

Orl. No faire Princeffe : he is the generall challenger, I come but in as others do, to try with him the ftrength of my youth.

Cel. Yong Gentleman, your fpirits are too bold for your yeares : you haue feene cruell proofe of this mans ftrength, if you faw your felfe with your eies, or knew your felfe with your iudgment, the feare of your aduenture would counfel you to a more equall enterprife. We pray you for your owne fake to embrace your own fafetie, and giue ouer this attempt.

Rof. Do yong Sir, your reputation fhall not therefore be mifprifed : we wil make it our fuite to the Duke, that the wraftling might not go forward.

Orl. I befeech you, punifh mee not with your harde thoughts, wherein I confeffe me much guiltie to denie fo faire and excellent Ladies anie thing. But let your faire eies, and gentle wifhes go with mee to my triall ; wherein if I bee foil'd, there is but one fham'd that vvas neuer gracious : if kil'd, but one dead that is willing to be fo : I fhall do my friends no wrong, for I haue none to lament me:the world no iniurie, for in it I haue nothing: onely in the world I fil vp a place, which may bee better fupplied, when I haue made it emptie.

Rof. The little ftrength that I haue, I would it vvere with you.

Cel.

Cel. And mine to eeke out hers.

Rof. Fare you well:praie heauen I be deceiu'd in you.

Cel. Your hearts defires be with you.

Char. Come, where is this yong gallant, that is fo defirous to lie with his mother earth ?

Orl. Readie Sir,but his will hath in it a more modeft working.

Duk. You fhall trie but one fall.

Cha. No, I warrant your Grace you fhall not entreat him to a fecond, that haue fo mightilie perfwaded him from a firft.

Orl. You meane to mocke me after : you fhould not haue mockt me before : but come your waies.

Rof. Now Hercules, be thy fpeede yong man.

Cel. I would I were inuifible,to catch the ftrong fel-low by the legge.   *Wraftle.*

Rof. Oh excellent yong man.

Cel. If I had a thunderbolt in mine eie,I can tell who fhould downe.   *Shout.*

Duk. No more, no more.

Orl. Yes I befeech your Grace, I am not yet well breath'd.

Duk. How do'ft thou *Charles?*

Le Beu. He cannot fpeake my Lord.

Duk. Beare him awaie :

What is thy name yong man ?

Orl. Orlando my Liege, the yongeft fonne of Sir Ro-land *de Boys.*

Duk. I would thou hadft beene fon to fome man elfe,

The world efteem'd thy father honourable,

But I did finde him ftill mine enemie :

Thou fhould'ft haue better pleas'd me with this deede,

Hadft thou defcended from another houfe :

But fare thee well, thou art a gallant youth,

I would thou had'ft told me of another Father.

                                    Exit Duke.

Cel. Were I my Father (Coze) would I do this?

Orl. I am more proud to be Sir *Rolands* fonne,

His yongeft fonne, and would not change that calling

To be adopted heire to *Fredricke.*

Rof. My Father lou'd Sir *Roland* as his foule,

And all the world was of my Fathers minde,

Had I before knowne this yong man his fonne,

I fhould haue giuen him teares vnto entreaties,

Ere he fhould thus haue ventur'd.

Cel. Gentle Cofen,

Let vs goe thanke him,and encourage him :

My Fathers rough and enuious difpofition

Sticks me at heart : Sir,you haue well deferu'd,

If you doe keepe your promifes in loue;

But iuftly as you haue exceeded all promife,

Your Miftris fhall be happie.

Rof. Gentleman,

Weare this for me : one out of fuites with fortune

That could giue more,but that her hand lacks meanes.

Shall we goe Coze?

Cel. I : fare you well faire Gentleman.

Orl. Can I not fay,I thanke you? My better parts

Are all throwne downe, and that which here ftands vp

Is but a quintine, a meere liueleffe blocke.

Rof. He cals vs back : my pride fell with my fortunes,

Ile aske him what he would : Did you call Sir ?

Sir, you haue wraftled well, and ouerthrowne

More then your enemies.

Cel. Will you goe Coze ?

Rof. Haue with you : fare you well.   *Exit.*

*Orl.*What paffion hangs thefe waights vpõ my toong?

I cannot fpeake to her, yet fhe vrg'd conference.

Enter Le Beu.

O poore *Orlando!* thou art ouerthrowne

Or Charles,or fomething weaker mafters thee.

*Le Beu.*Good Sir, I do in friendfhip counfaile you

Te leaue this place ; Albeit you haue deferu'd

High commendation, true applaufe,and loue ;

Yet fuch is now the Dukes condition,

That he mifconfters all that you haue done :

The Duke is humorous, what he is indeede

More fuites you to conceiue,then I to fpeake of.

Orl. I thanke you Sir, and pray you tell me this,

Which of the two was daughter of the Duke,

That here was at the Wraftling ?

*Le Beu.*Neither his daughter,if we iudge by manners,

But yet indeede the taller is his daughter,

The other is daughter to the banifh'd Duke,

And here detain'd by her vfurping Vncle

To keepe his daughter companie, whofe loues

Are deerer then the naturall bond of Sifters :

But I can tell you, that of late this Duke

Hath tane difpleafure'gainft his gentle Neece,

Grounded vpon no other argument,

But that the people praife her for her vertues,

And pittie her, for her good Fathers fake ;

And on my life his malice 'gainft the Lady

Will fodainly breake forth : Sir,fare you well,

Hereafter in a better world then this,

I fhall defire more loue and knowledge of you.

Orl. I reft much bounden to you : fare you well.

Thus muft I from the fmoake into the fmother,

From tyrant Duke,vnto a tyrant Brother.

But heauenly *Rofaline.*   *Exit*

Scena Tertius.

Enter Celia and Rofaline.

Cel. Why Cofen, why *Rofaline* : *Cupid* haue mercie, Not a word ?

Rof. Not one to throw at a dog.

Cel. No, thy words are too precious to be caft away vpon curs,throw fome of them at me; come lame mee with reafons.

Rof. Then there were two Cofens laid vp, when the one fhould be lam'd with reafons, and the other mad without any.

Cel. But is all this for your Father ?

Rof. No, fome of it is for my childes Father : Oh how full of briers is this working day world.

Cel. They are but burs, Cofen, throwne vpon thee in holiday foolerie, if we walke not in the trodden paths our very petty-coates will catch them.

Rof. I could fhake them off my coate, thefe burs are in my heart.

Cel. Hem them away.

Rof. I would try if I could cry hem,and haue him.

Cel. Come, come,wraftle with thy affe&ions.

Rof. O they take the part of a better wraftler then my felfe.

Cel. O, a good wifh vpon you : you will trie in time

                                    in

in difpight of a fall: but turning thefe iefts out of feruice,
let vs talke in good earneft : Is it poffible on fuch a fodaine, you fhould fall into fo ftrong a liking with old Sir
Roulands yongeft fonne?

Rof. The Duke my Father lou'd his Father deerelie.

Cel. Doth it therefore enfue that you fhould loue his
Sonne deerelie ? By this kinde of chafe, I fhould hate
him, for my father hated his father deerely ; yet I hate
not *Orlando.*

Rof. No faith, hate him not for my fake.

Cel. Why fhould I not ? doth he not deferue well?

Enter Duke with Lords.

Rof. Let me loue him for that, and do you loue him
Becaufe I doe. Looke, here comes the Duke.

Cel. With his eies full of anger.

Duk. Miftris, difpatch you with your fafeft hafte,
And get you from our Court.

Rof. Me Vncle.

Duk. You Cofen,
Within thefe ten daies if that thou beeft found
So neere our publike Court as twentie miles,
Thou dieft for it.

Rof. I doe befeech your Grace
Let me the knowledge of my fault beare with me :
If with my felfe I hold intelligence,
Or haue acquaintance with mine owne defires,
If that I doe not dreame, or be not franticke,
(As I doe truft I am not) then deere Vncle,
Neuer fo much as in a thought vnborne,
Did I offend your highneffe.

Duk. Thus doe all Traitors,
If their purgation did confift in words,
They are as innocent as grace it felfe ;
Let it fuffice thee that I truft thee not.

Rof. Yet your miftruft cannot make me a Traitor ;
Tell me whereon the likelihoods depends?

Duk. Thou art thy Fathers daughter, there's enough.

Rof. So was I when your highnes took his Dukdome,
So was I when your highneffe banifht him ;
Treafon is not inherited my Lord,
Or if we did deriue it from our friends,
What's that to me, my Father was no Traitor,
Then good my Leige, miftake me not fo much,
To thinke my pouertie is treacherous.

Cel. Deere Soueraigne heare me fpeake.

Duk. I *Celia*, we ftaid her for your fake,
Elfe had fhe with her Father rang'd along.

Cel. I did not then intreat to haue her ftay,
It was your pleafure. and your owne remorfe,
I was too yong that time to value her,
But now I know her : if fhe be a Traitor,
Why fo am I : we ftill haue flept together,
Rofe at an inftant, learn'd, plaid, eate together,
And wherefoere we went, like *Iunos* Swans,
Still we went coupled and infeperable.

Duk. She is too fubtile for thee, and her fmoothnes;
Her verie filence, and per patience,
Speake to the people, and they pittie her :
Thou art a foole, fhe robs thee of thy name,
And thou wilt fhow more bright, & feem more vertuous
When fhe is gone : then open not thy lips
Firme, and irreuocable is my doombe,
Which I haue paft vpon her, fhe is banifh'd.

Cel. Pronounce that fentence then on me my Leige,
I cannot liue out of her companie.

Duk. You are a foole : you Neice prouide your felfe,
If you out-ftay the time, vpon mine honor,
And in the greatneffe of my word you die.

Exit Duke, &c.

Cel. O my poore *Rofaline,* whether wilt thou goe?
Wilt thou change Fathers ? I will giue thee mine :
I charge thee be not thou more grieu'd then I am.

Rof. I haue more caufe.

Cel. Thou haft not Cofen,
Prethee be cheerefull ; know'ft thou not the Duke
Hath banifh'd me his daughter?

Rof. That he hath not.

Cel. No, hath not ? *Rofaline* lacks then the loue
Which teacheth thee that thou and I am one,
Shall we be fundred ? fhall we part fweete girle ?
No, let my Father feeke another heire :
Therefore deuife with me how we may flie
Whether to goe, and what to beare with vs,
And doe not feeke to take your change vpon you,
To beare your griefes your felfe, and leaue me out :
For by this heauen, now at our forrowes pale ;
Say what thou canft, Ile goe along with thee.

Rof. Why, whether fhall we goe ?

Cel. To feeke my Vncle in the Forreft of *Arden.*

Rof. Alas, what danger will it be to vs,
(Maides as we are) to trauell forth fo farre ?
Beautie prouoketh theeues fooner then gold.

Cel. Ile put my felfe in poore and meane attire,
And with a kinde of vmber fmirch my face,
The like doe you, fo fhall we paffe along,
And neuer ftir affailants.

Rof. Were it not better,
Becaufe that I am more then common tall,
That I did fuite me all points like a man,
A gallant curtelax vpon my thigh,
A bore-fpeare in my hand, and in my heart
Lye there what hidden womans feare there will,
Weele haue a fwafhing and a marfhall outfide,
As manie other mannifh cowards haue,
That doe outface it with their femblances.

Cel. What fhall I call thee when thou art a man ?

Rof. Ile haue no worfe a name then *Ioues* owne Page,
And therefore looke you call me *Ganimed.*
But what will you by call'd?

Cel. Something that hath a reference to my ftate :
No longer *Celia*, but *Aliena.*

Rof. But Cofen, what if we affaid to fteale
The clownifh Foole out of your Fathers Court :
Would he not be a comfort to our trauaile ?

Cel. Heele goe along ore the wide world with me,
Leaue me alone to woe him ; Let's away
And get our Iewels and our wealth together,
Deuife the fitteft time, and fafeft way
To hide vs from purfuite that will be made
After my flight : now goe in we content
To libertie, and not to banifhment.

Exeunt.

Actus Secundus. Scoena Prima.

*Enter Duke Senior : Amyens, and two or three Lords
like Forreſters.*

Duk. Sen. Now my Coe-mates, and brothers in exile :
Hath not old cuftome made this life more fweete

Then

Then that of painted pompe? Are not thefe woods
More free from perill then the enuious Court?
Heere feele we not the penaltie of *Adam*,
The feafons difference, as the Icie phange
And churlifh chiding of the winters winde,
Which when it bites and blowes vpon my body
Euen till I fhrinke with cold, I fmile, and fay
This is no flattery : thefe are counfellors
That feelingly perfwade me what I am :
Sweet are the vfes of aduerfitie
Which like the toad, ougly and venemous,
Weares yet a precious Iewell in his head :
And this our life exempt from publike haunt,
Findes tongues in trees, bookes in the running brookes,
Sermons in ftones, and good in euery thing.
  Amien. I would not change it, happy is your Grace
That can tranflate the ftubbornneffe of fortune
Into fo quiet and fo fweet a ftile.
  Du. Sen. Come, fhall we goe and kill vs venifon?
And yet it irkes me the poore dapled fooles
Being natiue Burgers of this defert City,
Should intheir owne confines with forked heads
Haue their round hanches goard.
  1.*Lord.* Indeed my Lord
The melancholy *Iaques* grieues at that,
And in that kinde fweares you doe more vfurpe
Then doth your brother that hath banifh'd you :
To day my Lord of *Amiens*, and my felfe,
Did fteale behinde him as he lay along
Vnder an oake, whofe anticke roote peepes out
Vpon the brooke that brawles along this wood,
To the which place a poore fequeftred Stag
That from the Hunters aime had tane a hurt,
Did come to languifh ; and indeed my Lord
The wretched annimall heau'd forth fuch groanes
That their difcharge did ftretch his leatherne coat
Almoft to burfting, and the big round teares
Cours'd one another downe his innocent nofe
In pitteous chafe : and thus the hairie foole,
Much marked of the melancholie *Iaques*,
Stood on th'extremeft verge of the fwift brooke,
Augmenting it with teares.
  Du. Sen. But what faid *Iaques*?
Did he not moralize this fpectacle?
  1.*Lord.* O yes, into a thoufand fimilies.
Firft, for his weeping into the needleffe ftreame ;
Poore Deere quoth he, thou mak'ft a teftament
As worldlings doe, giuing thy fum of more
To that which had too muft : then being there alone,
Left and abandoned of his veluet friend ;
'Tis right quoth he, thus miferie doth part
The Fluxe of companie : anon a careleffe Heard
Full of the pafture, iumps along by him
And neuer ftaies to greet him : I quoth *Iaques*,
Sweepe on you fat and greazie Citizens,
'Tis iuft the fafhion ; wherefore doe you looke
Vpon that poore and broken bankrupt there?
Thus moft inuectiuely he pierceth through
The body of Countrie, Citie, Court,
Yea, and of this our life, fwearing that we
Are meere vfurpers, tyrants, and whats worfe
To fright the Annimals, and to kill them vp
In their affign'd and natiue dwelling place.
  D. Sen. And did you leaue him in this contemplation?
  2.*Lord.* We did my Lord, weeping and commenting
Vpon the fobbing Deere.

  Du. Sen. Show me the place,
I loue to cope him in thefe fullen fits,
For then he's full of matter.
  1.*Lor.* Ile bring you to him ftrait.   *Exeunt.*

Scena Secunda.

Enter Duke, with Lords.

  Duk. Can it be poffible that no man faw them?
It cannot be, fome villaines of my Court
Are of confent and fufferance in this.
  1.*Lo.* I cannot heare of any that did fee her,
The Ladies her attendants of her chamber
Saw her a bed, and in the morning early,
They found the bed vntreafur'd of their Miftris.
  2.*Lor.* My Lord, the roynifh Clown, at whom fo oft,
Your Grace was wont to laugh is alfo miffing,
Hifperia the Princeffe Gentlewoman
Confeffes that fhe fecretly ore-heard
Your daughter and her Cofen much commend
The parts and graces of the Wraftler
That did but lately foile the finowie *Charles*,
And fhe beleeues where euer they are gone
That youth is furely in their companie.
  Duk. Send to his brother, fetch that gallant hither,
If he be abfent, bring his Brother to me,
Ile make him finde him : do this fodainly ;
And let not fearch and inquifition quaile,
To bring againe thefe foolifh runawaies.   *Exunt.*

Scena Tertia.

Enter Orlando and Adam.

  Orl. Who's there?
  Ad. What my yong Mafter, oh my gentle mafter,
Oh my fweet mafter, O you memorie
Of old Sir *Rowland*; why, what make you here?
Why are you vertuous? Why do people loue you?
And wherefore are you gentle, ftrong, and valiant?
Why would you be fo fond to ouercome
The bonnie prifer of the humorous Duke?
Your praife is come too fwiftly home before you.
Know you not Mafter, to feeme kinde of men,
Their graces ferue them but as enemies,
No more doe yours : your vertues gentle Mafter
Are fanctified and holy traitors to you :
Oh what a world is this, when what is comely
Enuenoms him that beares it?
Why, what's the matter?
  Ad. O vnhappie youth,
Come not within thefe doores : within this roofe
The enemie of all your graces liues
Your brother, no, no brother, yet the fonne
(Yet not the fon, I will not call him fon)
Of him I was about to call his Father,
Hath heard your praifes, and this night he meanes,
To burne the lodging where you vfe to lye,
And you within it : if he faile of that

                                                      He

He will haue other meanes to cut you off;
I ouerheard him: and his praƈtiſes:
This is no place, this houſe is but a butcherie;
Abhorre it,feare it, doe not enter it.
 Ad. Why whether *Adam* would'ſt thou haue me go?
 Ad. No matter whether,ſo you come not here.
 Orl. What, would'ſt thou haue me go& beg my food,
Or with a baſe and boiſtrous Sword enforce
A theeuiſh liuing on the common rode?
This I muſt do,or know not what to do :
Yet this I will not do, do how I can.
I rather will ſubieƈt me to the malice
Of a diuerted blood,and bloudie brother.
 Ad. But do not ſo : I haue fiue hundred Crownes,
The thriftie hire I ſaued vnder your Father,
Which I did ſtore to be my foſter Nurſe,
When ſeruice ſhould in my old limbs lie lame,
And vnregarded age in corners throwne,
Take that, and he that doth the Rauens feede,
Yea prouidently caters for the Sparrow,
Be comfort to my age : here is the gold,
All this I giue you, let me be your ſeruant,
Though I looke old, yet I am ſtrong and luſtie;
For in my youth I neuer did apply
Hot,and rebellious liquors in my bloud,
Nor did not with vnbaſhfull forehead woe,
The meanes of weakneſſe and debilitie,
Therefore my age is as a luſtie winter,
Froſtie, but kindely ; let me goe with you,
Ile doe the ſeruice of a yonger man
In all your buſineſſe and neceſſities.
 Orl. Oh good old man, how well in thee appeares
The conſtant ſeruice of the antique world,
When ſeruice ſweate for dutie,not for meede:
Thou art not for the faſhion of theſe times,
Where none will ſweate, but for promotion,
And hauing that do choake their ſeruice vp,
Euen with the hauing, it is not ſo with thee :
But poore old man, thou prun'ſt a rotten tree,
That cannot ſo much as a bloſſome yeelde,
In lieu of all thy paines and husbandrie,
But come thy waies, weele goe along together,
And ere we haue thy youthfull wages ſpent,
Weele light vpon ſome ſetied low content.
 Ad. Maſter goe on,and I will follow thee
To the laſt gaſpe with truth and loyaltie,
From ſeauentie yeeres, till now almoſt foureſcore
Here liued I, but now liue here no more
At ſeauenteene yeeres, many their fortunes ſeeke
But at foureſcore, it is too late a weeke,
Yet fortune cannot recompence me better
Then to die well, and not my Maſters debter. *Exeunt.*

Scena Quarta.

*Enter Roſaline for Ganimed, Celia for Aliena,and
  Clowne, alias Touchſtone.*

 Roſ. O *Iupiter,* how merry are my ſpirits?
 Clo. I care not for my ſpirits, if my legges were not
wearie.
 Roſ. I could finde in my heart to diſgrace my mans
apparell, and to cry like a woman : but I muſt comfort

the weaker veſſell, as doublet and hoſe ought to ſhow it
ſelfe coragious to petty-coate; therefore courage, good
Aliena.
 Cel. I pray you beare with me, I cannot goe no further.
 Clo. For my part, I had rather beare with you, then
beare you : yet I ſhould beare no croſſe if I did beare
you, for I thinke you haue no money in your purſe.
 Roſ. Well, this is the Forreſt of *Arden.*
 Clo. I, now am I in *Arden,* the more foole I, when I
was at home I was in a better place, but Trauellers muſt
be content.

Enter Corin and Siluius.

 Roſ. I, be ſo good *Touchſtone:* Look you, who comes
here, a yong man and an old in ſolemne talke.
 Cor. That is the way to make her ſcorne you ſtill.
 Sil. Oh *Corin,* that thou knew'ſt how I do loue her.
 Cor. I partly gueſſe: for I haue lou'd ere now.
 Sil. No *Corin,* being old, thou canſt not gueſſe,
Though in thy youth thou waſt as true a louer
As euer ſigh'd vpon a midnight pillow :
But if thy loue were euer like to mine,
As ſure I thinke did neuer man loue ſo :
How many aƈtions moſt ridiculous,
Haſt thou beene drawne to by thy fantaſie?
 Cor. Into a thouſand that I haue forgotten.
 Sil. Oh thou didſt then neuer loue ſo hartily,
If thou remembreſt not the ſlighteſt folly,
That euer loue did make thee run into,
Thou haſt not lou'd.
Or if thou haſt not ſat as I doe now,
Wearing thy hearer in thy Miſtris praiſe,
Thou haſt not lou'd.
Or if thou haſt not broke from companie,
Abruptly as my paſſion now makes me,
Thou haſt not lou'd.
O *Phebe, Phebe, Phebe.*   *Exit.*
 Roſ. Alas poore Shepheard ſearching of they would,
I haue by hard aduenture found mine owne.
 Clo. And I mine : I remember when I was in loue, I
broke my ſword vpon a ſtone, and bid him take that for
comming a night to *Iane Smile,* and I remember the kiſ-
ſing of her batler, and the Cowes dugs that her prettie
chopt hands had milk'd ; and I remember the wooing
of a peaſcod inſtead of her, from whom I tooke two
cods, and giuing her them againe, ſaid with weeping
teares, weare theſe for my ſake: wee that are true Lo-
uers, runne into ſtrange capers; but as all is mortall in
nature, ſo is all nature in loue, mortall in folly.
 Roſ. Thou ſpeak'ſt wiſer then thou art ware of.
 Clo. Nay,I ſhall nere be ware of mine owne wit, till
I breake my ſhins againſt it.
 Roſ. Ioue,Ioue, this Shepherds paſſion,
Is much vpon my faſhion.
 Clo. And mine, but it growes ſomething ſtale with
mee.
 Cel. I pray you, one of you queſtion yon'd man,
If he for gold will giue vs any foode,
I faint almoſt to death.
 Clo. Holla ; you Clowne.
 Roſ. Peace foole, he's not thy kinſman.
 Cor. Who cals?
 Clo. Your betters Sir.
 Cor. Elſe are they very wretched.
               Roſ. Peace

Rof. Peace I fay; good euen to your friend.
Cor. And to you gentle Sir, and to you all.
Rof. I prethee Shepheard, if that loue or gold
Can in this defert place buy entertainment,
Bring vs where we may reft our felues, and feed :
Here's a yong maid with trauaile much oppreffed,
And faints for fuccour.
Cor. Faire Sir, I pittie her,
And wifh for her fake more then for mine owne,
My fortunes were more able to releeue her :
But I am fhepheard to another man,
And do not fheere the Fleeces that I graze :
My mafter is of churlifh difpofition,
And little wreakes to finde the way to heauen
By doing deeds of hofpitalitie.
Befides his Coate, his Flockes, and bounds of feede
Are now on fale, and at our fheep-coat now
By reafon of his abfence there is nothing
That you will feed on : but what is, come fee,
And in my voice moft welcome fhall you be.
Rof. What is he that fhall buy his flocke and pafture?
Cor. That yong Swaine that you faw heere but ere-
while,
That little cares for buying any thing.
Rof. I pray thee, if it ftand with honeftie,
Buy thou the Cottage, pafture, and the flocke,
And thou fhalt haue to pay for it of vs.
Cel. And we will mend thy wages :
I like this place, and willingly could
Wafte my time in it.
Cor. Affuredly the thing is to be fold :
Go with me, if you like vpon report,
The foile, the profit, and this kinde of life,
I will your very faithfull Feeder be,
And buy it with your Gold right fodainly.   *Exeunt.*

Scena Quinta.

Enter, Amyens, Iaques, & others.
Song.
Vnder the greene wood tree,
who loues to lye with mee,
And turne his merrie Note,
vnto the fweet Birds throte :
Come hither, come hither, come hither :
Heere fhall he fee no enemie,
But Winter and rough Weather.

Iaq. More, more, I pre'thee more.
Amy. It will make you melancholly Monfieur *Iaques*
Iaq. I thanke it : More, I prethee more,
I can fucke melancholly out of a fong,
As a Weazel fuckes egges : More, I pre'thee more.
Amy. My voice is ragged, I know I cannot pleafe
you.
Iaq. I do not defire you to pleafe me,
I do defire you to fing :
Come, more, another ftanzo : Cal you'em ftanzo's ?
Amy. What you wil Monfieur *Iaques.*
Iaq. Nay, I care not for their names, they owe mee
nothing. Wil you fing ?
Amy. More at your requeft, then to pleafe my felfe.
Iaq. Well then, if euer I thanke any man, Ile thanke

you : but that they cal complement is like th'encounter
of two dog-Apes. And when a man thankes me hartily,
me thinkes I haue giuen him a penie, and he renders me
the beggerly thankes. Come fing ; and you that wil not
hold your tongues.
Amy. Wel, Ile end the fong. Sirs, couer the while,
the Duke wil drinke vnder this tree; he hath bin all this
day to looke you.
Iaq. And I haue bin all this day to auoid him :
He is too difputeable for my companie :
I thinke of as many matters as he, but I giue
Heauen thankes, and make no boaft of them.
Come, warble, come.

Song.   *Altogether heere.*
Who doth ambition fhunne,
and loues to liue i'th Sunne:
Seeking the food he eates,
and pleas'd with what he gets :
Come hither, come hither, come hither,
Heere fhall he fee.&c.

Iaq. Ile giue you a verfe to this note,
That I made yefterday in defpight of my Inuention.
Amy. And Ile fing it.
Amy. Thus it goes.
If it do come to paffe, that any man turne Affe :
Leauing his wealth and eafe,
A ftubborne will to pleafe,
Ducdame, ducdame, ducdame:
Heere fhall he fee, groffe fooles as he,
And if he will come to me.
Amy. What's that Ducdame ?
Iaq. 'Tis a Greeke inuocation, to call fools into a cir-
cle. Ile go fleepe if I can : if I cannot, Ile raile againft all
the firft borne of Egypt.
Amy. And Ile go feeke the Duke,
His banket is prepar'd.   *Exeunt*

Scena Sexta.

Enter Orlando, & Adam.

Adam. Deere Mafter, I can go no further :
O I die for food. Heere lie I downe,
And meafure out my graue. Farwel kinde mafter.
Orl. Why how now *Adam?* No greater heart in thee:
Liue a little, comfort a little, cheere thy felfe a little.
If this vncouth Forreft yeeld any thing fauage,
I wil either be food for it, or bring it for foode to thee :
Thy conceite is neerer death, then thy powers.
For my fake be comfortable, hold death a while
At the armes end : I wil heere be with thee prefently,
And if I bring thee not fomething to eate,
I will giue thee leaue to die : but if thou dieft
Before I come, thou art a mocker of my labor.
Wel faid, thou look'ft cheerely,
And Ile be with thee quickly : yet thou lieft
In the bleake aire. Come, I wil beare thee
To fome fhelter, and thou fhalt not die
For lacke of a dinner,
If there liue any thing in this Defert.
Cheerely good *Adam.*   *Exeunt*
Scena

Scena Septima.

Enter Duke Sen. & Lord, like Out-lawes.
Du.Sen. I thinke he be transform'd into a beaft,
For I can no where finde him, like a man.
1.Lord. My Lord, he is but euen now gone hence,
Heere was he merry, hearing of a Song.
Du.Sen. If he compact of iarres, grow Muficall,
We fhall haue fhortly difcord in the Spheares :
Go feeke him, tell him I would fpeake with him.

Enter Iaques.

1.Lord. He faues my labor by his owne approach.
Du.Sen. Why how now Monfieur, what a life is this
That your poore friends muft woe your companie,
What, you looke merrily.
Iaq. A Foole, a foole : I met a foole i'th Forreft,
A motley Foole (a miferable world:)
As I do liue by foode, I met a foole,
Who laid him downe, and bask'd him in the Sun,
And rail'd on Lady Fortune in good termes,
In good fet termes, and yet a motley foole.
Good morrow foole (quoth I:) no Sir, quoth he,
Call me not foole, till heauen hath fent me fortune,
And then he drew a diall from his poake,
And looking on it, with lacke-luftre eye,
Sayes, very wifely, it is ten a clocke :
Thus we may fee (quoth he) how the world wagges :
'Tis but an houre agoe, fince it was nine,
And after one houre more, 'twill be eleuen,
And fo from houre to houre, we ripe,and ripe,
And then from houre to houre, we rot,and rot,
And thereby hangs a tale. When I did heare
The motley Foole, thus morall on the time,
My Lungs began to crow like Chanticleere,
That Fooles fhould be fo deepe contemplatiue :
And I did laugh, fans intermiffion
An houre by his diall. Oh noble foole,
A worthy foole : Motley's the onely weare.
Du.Sen. What foole is this?
Iaq. O worthie Foole : One that hath bin a Courtier
And fayes, if Ladies be but yong, and faire,
They haue the gift to know it : and in his braine,
Which is as drie as the remainder bisket
After a voyage : He hath ftrange places cram'd
With obferuation, the which he vents
In mangled formes. O that I were a foole,
I am ambitious for a motley coat.
Du.Sen. Thou fhalt haue one.
Iaq. It is my onely fuite,
Prouided that you weed your better iudgements
Of all opinion that growes ranke in them,
That I am wife. I muft haue liberty
Wiithall, as large a Charter as the winde,
To blow on whom I pleafe, for fo fooles haue :
And they that are moft gauled with my folly,
They moft muft laugh : And why fir muft they fo ?
The why is plaine, as way to Parifh Church :
Hee, that a Foole doth very wifely hit,
Doth very foolifhly, although he fmart
Seeme fenfeleffe of the bob. If not,
The Wife-mans folly is anathomiz'd
Euen by the fquandring glances of the foole.
Inueft me in my motley : Giue me leaue
To fpeake my minde, and I will through and through
Cleanfe the foule bodie of th'infected world,
If they will patiently receiue my medicine.
Du.Sen. Fie on thee. I can tell what thou wouldft do.
Iaq. What, for a Counter, would I do, but good ?
Du.Sen. Moft mifcheeuous foule fin,in chiding fin :
For thou thy felfe haft bene a Libertine,
As fenfuall as the brutifh fting it felfe,
And all th'imboffed fores, and headed euils,
That thou with licenfe of free foot haft caught,
Would'ft thou difgorge into the generall world.
Iaq. Why who cries out on pride,
That can therein taxe any priuate party :
Doth it not flow as hugely as the Sea,
Till that the wearie verie meanes do ebbe.
What woman in the Citie do I name,
When that I fay the City woman beares
The coft of Princes on vnworthy fhoulders ?
Who can come in, and fay that I meane her,
When fuch a one as fhee, fuch is her neighbor ?
Or what is he of bafeft function,
That fayes his brauerie is not on my coft,
Thinking that I meane him, but therein fuites
His folly to the mettle of my fpeech,
There then, how then, what then, let me fee wherein
My tongue hath wrong'd him : If it do him right,
Then he hath wrong'd himfelfe : if he be free,
why then my taxing like a wild-goofe flies
Vnclaim'd of any man.But who come here?

Enter Orlando.

Orl. Forbeare, and eate no more.
Iaq. Why I haue eate none yet.
Orl. Nor fhalt not, till neceffity be feru'd.
Iaq. Of what kinde fhould this Cocke come of ?
Du.Sen. Art thou thus bolden'd man by thy diftres?
Or elfe a rude defpifer of good manners,
That in ciuility thou feem'ft fo emptie?
Orl. You touch'd my veine at firft, the thorny point
Of bare diftreffe, hath tane from me the fhew
Of fmooth ciuility : yet am I in-land bred,
And know fome nourture : But forbeare, I fay,
He dies that touches any of this fruite,
Till I, and my affaires are anfwered.
Iaq. And you will not be anfwer'd with reafon,
I muft dye.
Du.Sen. What would you haue?
Your gentleneffe fhall force, more then your force
Moue vs to gentleneffe.
Orl. I almoft die for food,and let me haue it.
Du.Sen. Sit downe and feed,& welcom to our table
Orl. Speake you fo gently? Pardon me I pray you,
I thought that all things had bin fauage heere,
And therefore put I on the countenance
Of fterne command'ment. But what ere you are
That in this defert inacceffible,
Vnder the fhade of melancholly boughes,
Loofe, and neglect the creeping houres of time :
If euer you haue look'd on better dayes :
If euer beene where bels haue knoll'd to Church :
If euer fate at any good mans feaft :
If euer from your eye-lids wip'd a teare,
And know what 'tis to pittie, and be pittied :
Let gentleneffe my ftrong enforcement be,
In the which hope, I blufh, and hide my Sword.

R   *Duke*

Du. Sen. True is it, that we haue feene better dayes,
And haue with holy bell bin knowld to Church,
And fat at good mens feafts, and wip'd our eies
Of drops, that facred pity hath engendred :
And therefore fit you downe in gentleneffe,
And take vpon command, what helpe we haue
That to your wanting may be miniftred.

Orl. Then but forbeare your food a little while :
Whiles (like a Doe) I go to finde my Fawne,
And giue it food.   There is an old poore man,
Who after me, hath many a weary fteppe
Limpt in pure loue : till he be firft fuffic'd,
Oppreft with two weake euils, age, and hunger,
I will not touch a bit.

Duke Sen. Go finde him out.
And we will nothing wafte till you returne.

Orl. I thanke ye, and be bleft for your good comfort.

Du. Sen. Thou feeft, we are not all alone vnhappie:
This wide and vniuerfall Theater
Prefents more wofull Pageants then the Sceane
Wherein we play in.

Ia. All the world's a ftage,
And all the men and women, meerely Players;
They haue their *Exits* and their Entrances,
And one man in his time playes many parts,
His Acts being feuen ages.   At firft the Infant,
Mewling, and puking in the Nurfes armes :
Then, the whining Schoole-boy with his Satchell
And fhining morning face, creeping like fnaile
Vnwillingly to fchoole.   And then the Louer,
Sighing like Furnace, with a wofull ballad
Made to his Miftreffe eye-brow.   Then, a Soldier,
Full of ftrange oaths, and bearded like the Pard,
Ielous in honor, fodaine, and quicke in quarrell,
Seeking the bubble Reputation
Euen in the Canons mouth : And then, the Iuftice
In faire round belly, with good Capon lin'd,
With eyes feuere, and beard of formall cut,
Full of wife fawes, and moderne inftances,
And fo he playes his part.   The fixt age fhifts
Into the leane and flipper'd Pantaloone,
With fpectacles on nofe, and pouch on fide,
His youthfull hofe well fau'd, a world too wide,
For his fhrunke fhanke, and his bigge manly voice,
Turning againe toward childifh trebble pipes,
And whiftles in his found.   Laft Scene of all,
That ends this ftrange euentfull hiftorie,
Is fecond childifhneffe, and meere obliuion,
Sans teeth, fans eyes, fans tafte, fans euery thing.

Enter Orlando with Adam.

Du Sen. Welcome : fet downe your venerable burthen, and let him feede.

Orl. I thanke you moft for him.

Ad. So had you neede,
I fcarce can fpeake to thanke you for my felfe.

Du. Sen. Welcome, fall too : I wil not trouble you,
As yet to queftion you about your fortunes :
Giue vs fome Muficke, and good Cozen, fing.

Song.

Blow, blow, thou winter winde,
Thou art not fo vnkinde, as mans ingratitude
Thy tooth is not fo keene, becaufe thou art not feene,
although thy breath be rude.

Heigh ho, fing heigh ho, vnto the greene holly,
Moft frendfhip, is fayning; moft Louing, meere folly:
    The heigh ho, the holly,
    This Life is moft iolly.

Freize, freize, thou bitter skie that doft not bight fo nigh
    as benefitts forgot :
Though thou the waters warpe, thy fting is not fo fharpe,
    as freind remembred not.
    Heigh ho, fing, &c.

Duke Sen. If that you were the good Sir *Rowlands* fon,
As you haue whifper'd faithfully you were,
And as mine eye doth his effigies witneffe,
Moft truly limn'd, and liuing in your face,
Be truly welcome hither : I am the Duke
That lou'd your Father, the refidue of your fortune,
Go to my Caue, and tell mee.   Good old man,
Thou art right welcome, as thy mafters is :
Support him by the arme : giue me your hand,
And let me all your fortunes vnderftand.   *Exeunt.*

Actus Tertius. Scena Prima.

Enter Duke, Lords, & Oliuer.

Du. Not fee him fince ? Sir, fir, that cannot be :
But were I not the better part made mercie,
I fhould not feeke an abfent argument
Of my reuenge, thou prefent : but looke to it,
Finde out thy brother wherefoere he is,
Seeke him with Candle : bring him dead, or liuing
Within this tweluemonth, or turne thou no more
To feeke a liuing in our Territorie.
Thy Lands and all things that thou doft call thine,
Worth feizure, do we feize into our hands,
Till thou canft quit thee by thy brothers mouth,
Of what we thinke againft thee.

Ol. Oh that your Highneffe knew my heart in this:
I neuer lou'd my brother in my life.

Duke. More villaine thou.   Well pufh him out of dores
And let my officers of fuch a nature
Make an extent vpon his houfe and Lands:
Do this expediently, and turne him going.   *Exeunt*

Scena Secunda.

Enter Orlando.

Orl. Hang there my verfe, in witneffe of my loue,
And thou thrice crowned Queene of night furuey
With thy chafte eye, from thy pale fpheare aboue
Thy Huntreffe name, that my full life doth fway.
O *Rofalind*, thefe Trees fhall be my Bookes,
And in their barkes my thoughts Ile charracter,
That euerie eye, which in this Forreft lookes,
Shall fee thy vertue witneft euery where.
Run, run *Orlando*, carue on euery Tree,
The faire, the chafte, and vnexpreffiue fhee.   *Exit*

Enter Corin & Clowne.

Co. And how like you this fhepherds life M꜀ *Touchftone?*
                                    Clo.

Clow. Truely Shepheard, in respect of it selfe, it is a good life ; but in respect that it is a shepheards life, it is naught. In respect that it is solitary, I like it verie well : but in respect that it is priuate, it is a very vild life. Now in respect it is in the fields, it pleaseth mee well : but in respect it is not in the Court, it is tedious. As it is a spare life (looke you) it fits my humor well : but as there is no more plentie in it, it goes much against my stomacke. Has't any Philosophie in thee shepheard?

Cor. No more, but that I know the more one sickens, the worse at ease he is : and that hee that wants money, meanes, and content, is without three good frends. That the propertie of raine is to wet, and fire to burne : That pood pasture makes fat sheepe : and that a great cause of the night, is lacke of the Sunne : That hee that hath learned no wit by Nature, nor Art, may complaine of good breeding, or comes of a very dull kindred.

Clo. Such a one is a naturall Philosopher :
Was't euer in Court, Shepheard?

Cor. No truly.

Clo. Then thou art damn'd.

Cor. Nay, I hope.

Clo. Truly thou art damn'd, like an ill roasted Egge, all on one side.

Cor. For not being at Court? your reason.

Clo. Why, if thou neuer was't at Court, thou neuer saw'st good manners : If thou neuer saw'st good maners, then thy manners must be wicked, and wickednes is sin, and sinne is damnation: Thou art in a parlous state shepheard.

Cor. Not a whit *Touchstone*, those that are good maners at the Court, are as ridiculous in the Countrey, as the behauiour of the Countrie is most mockeable at the Court. You told me, you salute not at the Court, but you kisse your hands; that courtesie would be vncleanlie if Courtiers were shepheards.

Clo. Instance, briefly : come, instance.

Cor. Why we are still handling our Ewes, and their Fels you know are greasie.

Clo. Why do not your Courtiers hands sweate? and is not the grease of a Mutton, as wholesome as the sweat of a man? Shallow, shallow : A better instance I say : Come.

Cor. Besides, our hands are hard.

Clo. Your lips wil feele them the sooner. Shallow agen : a more sounder instance, come.

Cor. And they are often tarr'd ouer, with the surgery of our sheepe : and would you haue vs kisse Tarre? The Courtiers hands are perfum'd with Ciuet.

Clo. Most shallow man : Thou wormes meate in respect of a good peece of flesh indeed : learne of the wise and perpend : Ciuet is of a baser birth then Tarre, the verie vncleanly fluxe of a Cat. Mend the instance Shepheard.

Cor. You haue too Courtly a wit, for me, Ile rest.

Clo. Wilt thou rest damn'd? God helpe thee shallow man : God make incision in thee, thou art raw.

Cor. Sir, I am a true Labourer, I earne that I eate: get that I weare; owe no man hate, enuie no mans happinesse : glad of other mens good content with my harme: and the greatest of my pride, is to see my Ewes graze, & my Lambes sucke.

Clo. That is another simple sinne in you, to bring the Ewes and the Rammes together, and to offer to get your liuing, by the copulation of Cattle, to be bawd to a Belweather, and to betray a shee-Lambe of a tweluemonth to a crooked-pated olde Cuckoldly Ramme, out of all reasonable match. If thou bee'st not damn'd for this, the diuell himselfe will haue no shepherds, I cannot see else how thou shouldst scape.

Cor. Heere comes yong Mr *Ganimed*, my new Mistrisses Brother.

Enter Rosalind.

Ros. *From the east to westerne Inde,*
no iewel is like Rosalinde,
Hir worth being mounted on the winde,
through all the world beares Rosalinde.
All the pictures fairest Linde,
are but blacke to Rosalinde :
Let no face bee kept in mind,
but the faire of Rosalinde.

Clo. Ile rime you so, eight yeares together ; dinners, and suppers, and sleeping hours excepted : it is the right Butter-womens ranke to Market.

Ros. Out Foole.

Clo. For a taste.
If a Hart doe lacke a Hinde,
Let him seeke out Rosalinde :
If the Cat will after kinde,
so be sure will Rosalinde :
Wintred garments must be linde,
so must slender Rosalinde :
They that reap must sheafe and binde,
then to cart with Rosalinde.
Sweetest nut, hath sowrest rinde,
such a nut is Rosalinde.
He that sweetest rose will finde,
must finde Loues pricke, & Rosalinde.

This is the verie false gallop of Verses, why doe you infect your selfe with them?

Ros. Peace you dull foole, I found them on a tree.

Clo. Truely the tree yeelds bad fruite.

Ros. Ile graffe it with you, and then I shall graffe it with a Medler : then it will be the earliest fruit i'th country : for you'l be rotten ere you bee halfe ripe, and that's the right vertue of the Medler.

Clo. You haue said : but whether wisely or no, let the Forrest iudge.

Enter Celia with a writing.

Ros. Peace, here comes my sister reading, stand aside.

Cel. *Why should this Desert bee,*
for it is vnpeopled? Noe :
Tonges Ile hang on euerie tree,
that shall ciuill sayings shoe.
Some, how briefe the Life of man
runs his erring pilgrimage,
That the stretching of a span,
buckles in his summe of age.
Some of violated vowes,
twixt the soules of friend, and friend:
But vpon the fairest bowes,
or at euerie sentence end;
Will I Rosalinda write,
teaching all that reade, to know
The quintessence of euerie sprite,
heauen would in little show.
Therefore heauen Nature charg'd,
that one bodie should be fill'd
With all Graces wide enlarg'd,
nature presently distill'd

R 2 *Helens*

Helens cheeke, but not his heart,
Cleopatra's *Maieſtie* :
Attalanta's *better part,*
ſad Lucrecia's *Modeſtie.*
Thus Roſalinde *of manie parts,*
by Heauenly Synode was deuis'd,
Of manie faces, eyes, and hearts,
to haue the touches deereſt pris'd.
Heauen would that ſhee theſe gifts ſhould haue,
and I to liue and die her ſlaue.

Roſ. O moſt gentle Iupiter, what tedious homilie of Loue haue you wearied your pariſhioners withall, and neuer cri'de, haue patience good people.

Cel. How now backe friends : Shepheard, go off a little : go with him ſirrah.

Clo. Come Shepheard, let vs make an honorable retreit, though not with bagge and baggage, yet with ſcrip and ſcrippage. *Exit.*

Cel. Didſt thou heare theſe verſes?

Roſ. O yes, I heard them all, and more too, for ſome of them had in them more feete then the Verſes would beare.

Cel. That's no matter : the feet might beare ẙ verſes.

Roſ. I, but the feet were lame, and could not beare themſelues without the verſe, and therefore ſtood lamely in the verſe.

Cel. But didſt thou heare without wondering, how thy name ſhould be hang'd and carued vpon theſe trees?

Roſ. I was ſeuen of the nine daies out of the wonder, before you came : for looke heere what I found on a Palme tree; I was neuer ſo berim'd ſince *Pythagoras* time that I was an Iriſh Rat, which I can hardly remember.

Cel. Tro you, who hath done this ?

Roſ. Is it a man ?

Cel. And a chaine that you once wore about his neck: change you colour ?

Roſ. I pre'thee who ?

Cel. O Lord, Lord, it is a hard matter for friends to meete ; but Mountaines may bee remoou'd with Earthquakes, and ſo encounter.

Roſ. Nay, but who is it ?

Cel. Is it poſſible?

Roſ. Nay, I pre'thee now, with moſt petitionary vehemence, tell me who it is.

Cel. O wonderfull, wonderfull, and moſt wonderfull wonderfull, and yet againe wonderful, and after that out of all hooping.

Roſ. Good my complection, doſt thou think though I am capariſon'd like a man, I haue a doublet and hoſe in my diſpoſition ? One inch of delay more, is a South-ſea of diſcouerie. I pre'thee tell me, who is it quickely, and ſpeake apace : I would thou couldſt ſtammer, that thou might'ſt powre this conceal'd man out of thy mouth, as Wine comes out of a narrow-mouth'd bottle:either too much at once, or none at all. I pre'thee take the Corke out of thy mouth, that I may drinke thy tydings.

Cel. So you may put a man in your belly.

Roſ. Is he of Gods making ? What manner of man ? Is his head worth a hat? Or his chin worth a beard ?

Cel. Nay, he hath but a little beard.

Roſ. Why God will ſend more, if the man will bee thankful : let me ſtay the growth of his beard, if thou delay me not the knowledge of his chin.

Cel. It is yong *Orlando,* that tript vp the Wraſtlers heeles, and your heart, both in an inſtant.

Roſ. Nay, but the diuell take mocking : ſpeake ſadde brow, and true maid.

Cel. I'faith(Coz) tis he.

Roſ. *Orlando* ?

Cel. *Orlando.*

Roſ. Alas the day, what ſhall I do with my doublet & hoſe ? What did he when thou ſaw'ſt him ? What ſayde he? How look'd he?̈ Wherein went he? What makes hee heere? Did he aske for me ? Where remaines he ? How parted he with thee ? And when ſhalt thou ſee him againe? Anſwer me in one vvord.

Cel. You muſt borrow me Gargantuas mouth firſt : 'tis a Word too great for any mouth of this Ages ſize, to ſay I and no, to theſe particulars, is more then to anſwer in a Catechiſme.

Roſ. But doth he know that I am in this Forreſt, and in mans apparrell ? Looks he as freſhly, as he did the day he Wraſtled ?

Cel. It is as eaſie to count Atomies as to reſolue the propoſitions of a Louer : but take a taſte of my finding him, and relliſh it with good obſeruance. I found him vnder a tree like a drop'd Acorne.

Roſ. It may vvel be cal'd Ioues tree, when it droppes forth fruite.

Cel. Giue me audience, good Madam.

Roſ. Proceed.

Cel. There lay hee ſtretch'd along like a Wounded knight.

Roſ. Though it be pittie to ſee ſuch a ſight, it vvell becomes the ground.

Cel. Cry holla, to the tongue, I prethee : it curuettes vnſeaſonably. He was furniſh'd like a Hunter.

Roſ. O ominous, he comes to kill my Hart.

Cel. I would ſing my ſong without a burthen, thou bring'ſt me out of tune.

Roſ. Do you not know I am a woman, when I thinke, I muſt ſpeake : ſweet, ſay on.

Enter Orlando & Iaques.

Cel. You bring me out. *Soft,* comes he not heere ?

Roſ. 'Tis he, ſlinke by, and note him.

Iaq I thanke you for your company, but good faith I had as liefe haue beene my ſelfe alone.

Orl. And ſo had I : but yet for faſhion ſake I thanke you too, for your ſocietie.

Iaq. God buy you, let's meet as little as we can.

Orl. I do deſire we may be better ſtrangers.

Iaq. I pray you marre no more trees vvith Writing Loue-ſongs in their barkes.

Orl. I pray you marre no moe of my verſes with reading them ill-fauouredly.

Iaq. Roſalinde is your loues name? *Orl.* Yes, Iuſt.

Iaq. I do not like her name.

Orl. There was no thought of pleaſing you when ſhe was chriſten'd.

Iaq. What ſtature is ſhe of?

Orl. Iuſt as high as my heart.

Iaq. You are full of prety anſwers: haue you not bin acquainted with goldſmiths wiues, & cond thē out of rings

Orl. Not ſo : but I anſwer you right painted cloath, from whence you haue ſtudied your queſtions.

Iaq. You haue a nimble wit ; I thinke 'twas made of *Attalanta's* heeles. Will you ſitte downe with me, and wee two, will raile againſt our Miſtris the world, and all our miſerie.

Orl, I wil chide no breather in the world but my ſelfe againſt

againſt whom I know moſt faults.

Iaq. The worſt fault you haue, is to be in loue.

Orl. 'Tis a fault I will not change, for your beſt vertue : I am wearie of you.

Iaq. By my troth, I was ſeeking for a Foole, when I found you.

Orl. He is drown'd in the brooke, looke but in, and you ſhall ſee him.

Iaq. There I ſhal ſee mine owne figure.

Orl. Which I take to be either a foole, or a Cipher.

Iaq. Ile tarrie no longer with you, farewell good ſignior Loue.

Orl. I am glad of your departure : Adieu good Monſieur Melancholly.

Roſ. I wil ſpeake to him like a ſawcie Lacky. and vnder that habit play the knaue with him, do you hear For-

Orl. Verie wel, what would you ?   (reſter.

Roſ. I pray you, what i'ſt a clocke ?

Orl. You ſhould aske me what time o'day: there's no clocke in the Forreſt.

Roſ. Then there is no true Louer in the Forreſt, elſe ſighing euerie minute. and groaning euerie houre wold deteɛ̃ the lazie foot of time, as wel as a clocke.

Orl. And why not the ſwift foote of time ? Had not that bin as proper ?

Roſ. By no meanes ſir ; Time trauels in diuers paces, with diuers perſons : Ile tel you who Time ambles withall, who Time trots withal, who Time gallops withal, and who he ſtands ſtil withall.

Orl. I prethee, who doth he trot withal ?

Roſ. Marry he trots hard with a yong maid, between the contract of her marriage, and the day it is ſolemnizd: if the interim be but a ſennight, Times pace is ſo hard, that it ſeemes the length of ſeuen yeare.

Orl. Who ambles Time withal ?

Roſ. With a Prieſt that lacks Latine, and a rich man that hath not the Gowt : for the one ſleepes eaſily becauſe he cannot ſtudy, and the other liues merrily, becauſe he feeles no paine : the one lacking the burthen of leane and waſteful Learning; the other knowing no burthen of heauie tedious penurie. Theſe Time ambles withal.

Orl. Who doth he gallop withal ?

Roſ. With a theefe to the gallowes : for though hee go as ſoftly as foot can fall, he thinkes himſelfe too ſoon there.

Orl. Who ſtaies it ſtil withal ?

Roſ. With Lawiers in the vacation : for they ſleepe betweene Terme and Terme, and then they perceiue not how time moues.

Orl. Where dwel you prettie youth ?

Roſ. With this Shepheardeſſe my ſiſter : heere in the skirts of the Forreſt, like fringe vpon a petticoat.

Orl. Are you natiue of this place ?

Roſ. As the Conie that you ſee dwell where ſhee is kindled.

Orl. Your accent is ſomething finer, then you could purchaſe in ſo remoued a dwelling.

Roſ. I haue bin told ſo of many : but indeed, an olde religious Vnckle of mine taught me to ſpeake, who was in his youth an inland man, one that knew Courtſhip too well : for there he fel in loue. I haue heard him read many Lectors againſt it, and I thanke God, I am not a Woman to be touch'd with ſo many giddie offences as hee hath generally tax'd their whole ſex withal.

Orl. Can you remember any of the principall euils,

that he laid to the charge of women?

Roſ. There were none principal, they were all like one another, as halfe pence are, euerie one fault ſeeming monſtrous, til his fellow-fault came to match it.

Orl. I prethee recount ſome of them.

Roſ. No: I wil not caſt away my phyſick, but on thoſe that are ſicke. There is a man haunts the Forreſt, that abuſes our yong plants with caruing *Roſalinde* on their barkes; hangs Oades vpon Hauthornes, and Elegies on brambles; all (forſooth) defying the name of *Roſalinde.* If I could meet that Fancie-monger, I would giue him ſome good counſel, for he ſeemes to haue the Quotidian of Loue vpon him.

Orl. I am he that is ſo Loue-ſhak'd, I pray you tel me your remedie.

Roſ. There is none of my Vnckles markes vpon you: he taught me to know a man in loue : in which cage of ruſhes, I am ſure you art not priſoner.

Orl. What were his markes?

Roſ. A leane cheeke, which you haue not : a blew eie and ſunken, which you haue not : an vnqueſtionable ſpirit, which you haue not : a beard neglected, which you haue not; (but I pardon you for that, for ſimply your hauing in beard, is a yonger brothers reuennew) then your hoſe ſhould be vngarter'd, your bonnet vnbanded, your ſleeue vnbutton'd, your ſhoo vnti'de, and euerie thing about you, demonſtrating a careleſſe deſolation : but you are no ſuch man; you are rather point deuice in your accouſtrements, as louing your ſelfe, then ſeeming the Louer of any other.   (I Loue.

Orl. Faire youth, I would I could make thee beleeue

Roſ. Me beleeue it ? You may aſſoone make her that you Loue beleeue it, which I warrant ſhe is apter to do, then to confeſſe ſhe do's: that is one of the points, in the which women ſtil giue the lie to their conſciences. But in good ſooth, are you he that hangs the verſes on the Trees, wherein *Roſalind* is ſo admired ?

Orl. I ſweare to thee youth, by the white band of *Roſalind,* I am he that, that vnfortunate he.

Roſ. But are you ſo much in loue, as your rimes ſpeak ?

Orl. Neither rime nor reaſon can expreſſe how much.

Roſ: Loue is meerely a madneſſe, and I tel you, deſerues as wel a darke houſe, and a whip, as madmen do : and the reaſon why they are not ſo puniſh'd and cured, is that the Lunacie is ſo ordinarie, that the whippers are in loue too : yet I profeſſe curing it by counſel.

Orl. Did you euer cure any ſo ?

Roſ. Yes one, and in this manner. Hee was to imagine me his Loue, his Miſtris : and I ſet him euerie day to woe me. At which time would I, being but a mooniſh youth, greeue, be effeminate, changeable, longing, and liking, proud, fantaſtical, apiſh, ſhallow, inconſtant, ful of teares, ful of ſmiles ; for euerie paſſion ſomething, and for no paſſion truly any thing, as boyes and women are for the moſt part, cattle of this colour : would now like him, now loath him : then entertaine him, then forſwear him : now weepe for him, then ſpit at him ; that I draue my Sutor from his mad humor of loue, to a liuing humor of madnes, ẃ was to forſweare the ful ſtream of ẏ world, and to liue in a nooke meerly Monaſtick : and thus I cur'd him, and this way wil I take vpon mee to waſh your Liuer as cleane as a ſound ſheepes heart, that there ſhal not be one ſpot of Loue in't.

Orl. I would not be cured, youth.

Roſ. I would cure you, if you would but call me *Roſalind,* and come euerie day to my Coat, and woe me.

R 3   *Orl.*

Orlan. Now by the faith of my loue, I will ; Tel me where it is.

Rof. Go with me to it, and Ile ſhew it you : and by the way, you ſhal tell me, where in the Forreſt you liue : Wil you go ?

Orl. With all my heart, good youth.

Rof. Nay, you muſt call mee *Roſalind* : Come ſiſter, will you go ?   *Exeunt.*

Scœna Tertia.

Enter Clowne, Audrey, & Iaques :

Clo. Come apace good *Audrey*, I wil fetch vp your Goates, *Audrey* : and how *Audrey* am I the man yet ? Doth my ſimple feature content you ?

Aud. Your features, Lord warrant vs : what features ?

Clo. I am heere with thee, and thy Goats, as the moſt capricious Poet honeſt *Ouid* was among the Gothes.

Iaq. O knowledge ill inhabited, worſe then Ioue in a thatch'd houſe.

Clo. When a mans verſes cannot be vnderſtood, nor a mans good wit ſeconded with the forward childe, vnderſtanding : it ſtrikes a man more dead then a great reckoning in a little roome : truly, I would the Gods hadde made thee poeticall.

Aud. I do not know what Poeticall is : is it honeſt in deed and word : is it a true thing ?

Clo. No trulie : for the trueſt poetrie is the moſt faining, and Louers are giuen to Poetrie : and what they ſweare in Poetrie, may be ſaid as Louers, they do feigne.

Aud. Do you wiſh then that the Gods had made me Poeticall ?

Clow. I do truly : for thou ſwear'ſt to me thou art honeſt : Now if thou wert a Poet, I might haue ſome hope thou didſt feigne.

Aud. Would you not haue me honeſt ?

Clo. No truly, vnleſſe thou wert hard fauour'd : for honeſtie coupled to beautie, is to haue Honie a ſawce to Sugar.

Iaq. A materiall foole.

Aud. Well, I am not faire, and therefore I pray the Gods make me honeſt.

Clo. Truly, and to caſt away honeſtie vppon a foule ſlut, were to put good meate into an vncleane diſh.

Aud. I am not a ſlut, though I thanke the Goddes I am foule.

Clo. Well, praiſed be the Gods, for thy foulneſſe; ſluttiſhneſſe may come heereafter. But be it, as it may bee, I wil marrie thee : and to that end, I haue bin with Sir *Oliuer Mar-text*, the Vicar of the next village, who hath promis'd to meete me in this place of the Forreſt, and to couple vs.

Iaq. I would faine ſee this meeting.

Aud. Wel, the Gods giue vs ioy.

Clo. Amen. A man may if he were of a fearful heart, ſtagger in this attempt : for heere wee haue no Temple but the wood, no aſſembly but horne-beaſts. But what though? Courage. As hornes are odious, they are neceſſarie. It is ſaid, many a man knowes no end of his goods; right : Many a man has good Hornes, and knows no end of them. Well, that is the dowrie of his wife, 'tis none of his owne getting ; hornes, euen ſo poore men alone :

No, no, the nobleſt Deere hath them as huge as the Raſcall : Is the ſingle man therefore bleſſed ? No, as a wall'd Towne is more worthier then a village, ſo is the forehead of a married man, more honourable then the bare brow of a Batcheller : and by how much defence is better then no skill, by ſo much is a horne more precious then to want.

Enter Sir Oliuer Mar-text.

Heere comes Sir *Oliuer* : Sir *Oliuer Mar-text* you are wel met. Will you diſpatch vs heere vnder this tree, or ſhal we go with you to your Chappell ?

Ol. Is there none heere to giue the woman ?

Clo. I wil not take her on guiſt of any man.

Ol. Truly ſhe muſt be giuen, or the marriage is not lawfull.

Iaq. Proceed, proceede : Ile giue her.

Clo. Good euen good M*r* what ye cal't : how do you Sir, you are verie well met : goddild you for your laſt companie, I am verie glad to ſee you, euen a toy in hand heere Sir : Nay, pray be couer'd.

Iaq. Wil you be married, Motley ?

Clo. As the Oxe hath his bow ſir, the horſe his curb, and the Falcon her bels, ſo man hath his deſires, and as Pigeons bill, ſo wedlocke would be nibling.

Iaq. And wil you (being a man of your breeding) be married vnder a buſh like a begger ? Get you to church, and haue a good Prieſt that can tel you what marriage is, this fellow wil but ioyne you together, as they ioyne Wainſcot, then one of you wil proue a ſhrunke pannell, and like greene timber, warpe, warpe.

Clo. I am not in the minde, but I were better to bee married of him then of another, for he is not like to marrie me wel : and not being wel married, it wil be a good excuſe for me heereafter, to leaue my wife.

Iaq. Goe thou with mee,
And let me counſel thee.

Ol. Come ſweete *Audrey*,
We muſt be married, or we muſt liue in baudrey :
Farewel good M*r Oliuer* : Not O ſweet *Oliuer*, O braue *Oliuer* leaue me not behind thee : But winde away, bee gone I ſay, I wil not to wedding with thee.

Ol. 'Tis no matter; Ne're a fantaſticall knaue of them all ſhal flout me out of my calling.   *Exeunt*

Scœna Quarta.

Enter Roſalind & Celia.

Rof. Neuer talke to me, I wil weepe.

Cel. Do I prethee, but yet haue the grace to conſider, that teares do not become a man.

Rof. But haue I not cauſe to weepe ?

Cel. As good cauſe as one would deſire,
Therefore weepe.

Rof. His very haire
Is of the diſſembling colour.

Cel. Something browner then Iudaſſes :
Marrie his kiſſes are Iudaſſes owne children.

Rof. I'faith his haire is of a good colour.

Cel. An excellent colour :
Your Cheſſenut was euer the onely colour :

Rof. And his kiſſing is as ful of ſanctitie,
As the touch of holy bread.

                         Cel.

Cel. Hee hath bought a paire of caſt lips of *Diana*: a Nun of winters ſiſterhood kiſſes not more religiouſlie, the very yce of chaſtity is in them.

Roſa. But why did hee ſweare hee would come this morning, and comes not?

Cel. Nay certainly there is no truth in him.

Roſ. Doe you thinke ſo?

Cel. Yes, I thinke he is not a picke purſe, nor a horſe-ſtealer, but for his verity in loue, I doe thinke him as concaue as a couered goblet, or a Worme-eaten nut.

Roſ. Not true in loue?

Cel. Yes, when he is in, but I thinke he is not in.

Roſ. You haue heard him ſweare downright he was.

Cel. Was, is not is: beſides, the oath of Louer is no ſtronger then the word of a Tapſter, they are both the confirmer of falſe reckonings, he attends here in the forreſt on the Duke your father.

Roſ. I met the Duke yeſterday, and had much queſtion with him: he askt me of what parentage I was; I told him of as good as he, ſo he laugh'd and let mee goe. But what talke wee of Fathers, when there is ſuch a man as *Orlando*?

Cel. O that's a braue man, hee writes braue verſes, ſpeakes braue words, ſweares braue oathes, and breakes them brauely, quite trauers athwart the heart of his louer, as a puiſny Tilter, ỹ ſpurs his horſe but on one ſide, breakes his ſtaffe like a noble gooſe; but all's braue that youth mounts, and folly guides: who comes heere?

Enter Corin.

Corin. Miſtreſſe and Maſter, you haue oft enquired After the Shepherd that complain'd of loue, Who you ſaw ſitting by me on the Turph, Praiſing the proud diſdainfull Shepherdeſſe That was his Miſtreſſe.

Cel. Well: and what of him?

Cor. If you will ſee a pageant truely plaid Betweene the pale complexion of true Loue, And the red glowe of ſcorne and prowd diſdaine, Goe hence a little, and I ſhall conduct you If you will marke it.

Roſ. O come, let vs remoue, The ſight of Louers feedeth thoſe in loue: Bring vs to this ſight, and you ſhall ſay Ile proue a buſie actor in their play. *Exeunt*.

Scena Quinta.

Enter Siluius and Phebe.

Sil. Sweet *Phebe* doe not ſcorne me, do not *Phebe* Say that you loue me not, but ſay not ſo In bitterneſſe; the common executioner Whoſe heart th'accuſtom'd ſight of death makes hard Falls not the axe vpon the humbled neck, But firſt begs pardon: will you ſterner be Then he that dies and liues by bloody drops?

Enter Roſalind, Celia, and Corin.

Phe. I would not be thy executioner, I flye thee, for I would not iniure thee: Thou tellſt me there is murder in mine eye, 'Tis pretty ſure, and very probable,

That eyes that are the frailſt, and ſofteſt things, Who ſhut their coward gates on atomyes, Should be called tyrants, butchers, murtherers. Now I doe frowne on thee with all my heart, And if mine eyes can wound, now let them kill thee: Now counterfeit to ſwound, why now fall downe, Or if thou canſt not, oh for ſhame, for ſhame, Lye not, to ſay mine eyes are murtherers: Now ſhew the wound mine eye hath made in thee, Scratch thee but with a pin, and there remaines Some ſcarre of it: Leaue vpon a ruſh The Cicatrice and capable impreſſure Thy palme ſome moment keepes: but now mine eyes Which I haue darted at thee, hurt thee not, Nor I am ſure there is no force in eyes That can doe hurt.

Sil. O deere *Phebe*, If euer (as that euer may be neere) You meet in ſome freſh cheeke the power of fancie, Then ſhall you know the wouuds inuiſible That Loues keene arrows make.

Phe. But till that time Come not thou neere me: and when that time comes, Afflict me with thy mockes, pitty me not, As till that time I ſhall not pitty thee.

Roſ. And why I pray you? who might be your mother That you inſult, exult, and all at once Ouer the wretched? what though you hau no beauty As by my faith, I ſee no more in you Then without Candle may goe darke to bed: Muſt you be therefore prowd and pittileſſe? Why what meanes this? why do you looke on me? I ſee no more in you then in the ordinary Of Natures ſale-worke? 'ods my little life, I thinke ſhe meanes to tangle my eies too: No faith proud Miſtreſſe, hope not after it, 'Tis not your inkie browes, your blacke ſilke haire, Your bugle eye-balls, nor your cheeke of creame That can entame my ſpirits to your worſhip: You fooliſh Shepheard, wherefore do you follow her Like foggy South, puffing with winde and raine, You are a thouſand times a properer man Then ſhe a woman. 'Tis ſuch fooles as you That makes the world full of ill-fauourd children: 'Tis not her glaſſe, but you that flatters her, And out of you ſhe ſees her ſelfe more proper Then any of her lineaments can ſhow her: But Miſtris, know your ſelfe, downe on your knees And thanke heauen, faſting, for a good mans loue; For I muſt tell you friendly in your eare, Sell when you can, you are not for all markets: Cry the man mercy, loue him, take his offer, Foule is moſt foule, being foule to be a ſcoffer. So take her to thee Shepheard, fareyouwell.

Phe. Sweet youth, I pray you chide a yere together, I had rather here you chide, then this man wooe.

Ros. Hees falne in loue with your foulneſſe, & ſhee'll Fall in loue with my anger. If it be ſo, as faſt As ſhe anſweres thee with frowning lookes, ile ſauce Her with bitter words: why looke you ſo vpon me?

Phe. For no ill will I beare you.

Roſ. I pray you do not fall in loue with mee, For I am falſer then vowes made in wine: Beſides, I like you not: if you will know my houſe, 'Tis at the tufft of Oliues, here hard by: Will you goe Siſter? Shepheard ply her hard:

Come

Come Sifter : Shepheardeffe, looke on him better
And be not proud, though all the world could fee,
None could be fo abus'd in fight as hee.
Come, to our flocke, *Exit.*
Phe. Dead Shepheard, now I find thy faw of might,
Who euer lov'd, that lou'd not at firft fight?
Sil. Sweet *Phebe.*
Phe. Hah: what faift thou *Siluius* ?
Sil. Sweet *Phebe* pitty me.
Phe. Why I am forry for thee gentle *Siluius.*
Sil. Where euer forrow is, reliefe would be :
If you doe forrow at my griefe in loue,
By giuing loue your forrow, and my griefe
Were both extermin'd'
Phe. Thou haft my loue, is not that neighbourly ?
Sil. I would haue you.
Phe. Why that were couetoufneffe :
Siluius; the time was, that I hated thee ;
And yet it is not, that I beare thee loue,
But fince that thou canft talke of loue fo well,
Thy company, which erft was irkefome to me
I will endure ; and Ile employ thee too :
But doe not looke for further recompence
Then thine owne gladneffe, that thou art employd.
Sil. So holy, and fo perfect is my loue,
And I in fuch a pouerty of grace,
That I fhall thinke it a moft plenteous crop
To gleane the broken eares after the man
That the maine harueft reapes: loofe now and then
A fcattred fmile, and that Ile liue vpon. ʃwhile ?
Phe. Knowft thou the youth that fpoke to mee yere-
Sil. Not very well, but I haue met him oft,
And he hath bought the Cottage and the bounds
That the old *Carlot* once was Mafter of.
Phe. Thinke not I loue him, though I ask for him,
'Tis but a peeuifh boy, yet he talkes well ;
But what care I for words ? yet words doe well
When he that fpeakes them pleafes thofe that heare:
It is a pretty youth, not very prettie ,
But fure hee's proud, and yet his pride becomes him ;
Hee'll make a proper man: the beft thing in him
Is his complexion : and fafter then his tongue
Did make offence, his eye did heale it vp :
He is not very tall, yet for his yeeres hee's tall :
His leg is but fo fo, and yet 'tis well :
There was a pretty redneffe in his lip,
A little riper, and more luftie red
Then that mixt in his cheeke: 'twas iuft the difference
Betwixt the conftant red, and mingled Damaske.
There be fome women *Siluius*, had they markt him
In parcells as I did, would haue gone neere
To fall in loue with him : but for my part
I loue him not, nor hate him not : and yet
Haue more caufe to hate him then to loue him,
For what had he to doe to chide at me ?
He faid mine eyes were black, and my haire blacke ,
And now I am remembred, fcorn'd at me :
I marueil why I anfwer'd not againe,
But that's all one : omittance is no quittance :
Ile write to him a very tanting Letter,
And thou fhalt beare it, wilt thou *Siluius* ?
Sil. Phebe, with all my heart.
Phe. Ile write it ftrait :
The matter's in my head, and in my heart,
I will be bitter with him, and paffing fhort ;
Goe with me *Siluius*. *Exeunt.*

Actus Quartus. Scena Prima.

Enter Rofalind, and Celia, and Iaques.

Iaq. I prethee, pretty youth, let me better acquainted
with thee.
Rof They fay you are a melancholly fellow.
Iaq. I am fo : I doe loue it better then laughing.
Rof. Thofe that are in extremity of either, are abhominable fellowes, and betray themfelues to euery moderne cenfure, worfe then drunkards.
Iaq. Why, 'tis good to be fad and fay nothing.
Rof. Why then 'tis good to be a pofte.
Iaq. I haue neither the Schollers melancholy, which
is emulation : nor the Mufitians, which is fantafticall ;
nor the Courtiers, which is proud : nor the Souldiers,
which is ambitious : nor the Lawiers, which is politick :
nor the Ladies, which is nice : nor the Louers, which
is all thefe : but it is a melancholy of mine owne, com-
pounded of many fimples, extracted from many obiects,
and indeed the fundrie contemplation of my trauells, in
which by often rumination, wraps me in a moft humorous fadneffe.
Rof. A Traueller : by my faith you haue great reafon to be fad : I feare you haue fold your owne Lands,
to fee other mens ; then to haue feene much, and to haue
nothing, is to haue rich eyes and poore hands.
Iaq. Yes, I haue gain'd my experience.
Enter Orlando.
Rof. And your experience makes you fad : I had rather haue a foole to make me merrie, then experience to
make me fad, and to trauaile for it too.
Orl. Good day, and happineffe, deere *Rofalind.*
Iaq. Nay then God buy you, and you talke in blanke
verfe.
Rof. Farewell Mounfieur Trauellor : looke you
lifpe, and weare ftrange fuites ; difable all the benefits
of your owne Countrie : be out of loue with your
natiuitie , and almoft chide God for making you that
countenance you are ; or I will fcarce thinke you haue
fwam in a Gundello. Why how now *Orlando,* where
haue you bin all this while ? you a louer ? and you
ferue me fuch another tricke, neuer come in my fight
more.
Orl. My faire *Rofalind,* I come within an houre of my
promife.
Rof. Breake an houres promife in loue ? hee that
will diuide a minute into a thoufand parts, and breake
but a part of the thoufand part of a minute in the affairs
of loue, it may be faid of him that *Cupid* hath clapt
him oth' fhoulder, but Ile warrant him heart hole.
Orl. Pardon me deere *Rofalind.*
Rof. Nay, and you be fo tardie, come no more in my
fight, I had as liefe be woo'd of a Snaile.
Orl. Of a Snaile ?
Rof. I, of a Snaile : for though he comes flowly, hee
carries his houfe on his head ; a better ioyncture I thinke
then you make a woman : befides, he brings his deftinie
with him.
Orl. What's that ?
Rof. Why hornes : w̄ fuch as youare faine to be beholding to your wiues for : but he comes armed in his
fortune, and preuents the flander of his wife.

Orl. Vertue

Orl. Vertue is no horne-maker : and my *Rofalind* is vertuous.

Rof. And I am your *Rofalind*.

Cel. It pleafes him to call you fo : but he hath a *Rofalind* of a better leere then you.

Rof. Come, wooe me, wooe mee : for now I am in a holy-day humor, and like enough to confent : What would you fay to me now, and I were your verie, verie *Rofalind* ?

Orl. I would kiffe before I fpoke.

Rof. Nay, you were better fpeake firft, and when you were grauel'd, for lacke of matter, you might take occafion to kiffe : verie good Orators when they are out, they will fpit, and for louers, lacking (God warne vs) matter, the cleanlieft fhift is to kiffe.

Orl. How if the kiffe be denide ?

Rof. Then fhe puts you to entreatie, and there begins new matter.

Orl. Who could be out, being before his beloued Miftris ?

Rof. Marrie that fhould you if I were your Miftris, or I fhould thinke my honeftie ranker then my wit.

Orl. What, of my fuite ?

Rof. Not out of your apparrell, and yet out of your fuite :
Am not I your *Rofalind* ?

Orl. I take fome ioy to fay you are, becaufe I would be talking of her.

Rof. Well, in her perfon, I fay I will not haue you.

Orl. Then in mine owne perfon, I die.

Rof. No faith, die by Attorney : the poore world is almoft fix thoufand yeeres old, and in all this time there was not anie man died in his owne perfon (*videlicet*) in a loue caufe : *Troilous* had his braines dafh'd out with a Grecian club, yet he did what hee could to die before, and he is one of the patternes of loue. *Leander*, he would haue liu'd manie a faire yeere though *Hero* had turn'd Nun ; If it had not bin for a hot Midfomer-night, for (good youth) he went but forth to wafh him in the Hellefpont, and being taken with the crampe, was droun'd, and the foolifh Chronoclers of that age, found it was *Hero* of Ceftos. But thefe are all lies, men haue died from time to time, and wormes haue eaten them, but not for loue.

Orl. I would not haue my right *Rofalind* of this mind, for I proteft her frowne might kill me.

Ref. By this hand, it will not kill a flie : but come, now I will be your *Rofalind* in a more comming-on difpofition : and aske me what you will, I will grant it.

Orl. Then loue me *Rofalind*.

Rof. Yes faith will I, fridaies and faterdaies, and all.

Orl. And wilt thou haue me ?

Rof. I, and twentie fuch.

Orl. What faieft thou ?

Ref. Are you not good ?

Orl. I hope fo.

Rofalind. Why then, can one defire too much of a good thing : Come fifter, you fhall be the Prieft, and marrie vs : giue me your hand *Orlando* : What doe you fay fifter ?

Orl. Pray thee marrie vs.

Cel. I cannot fay the words.

Rof. You muft begin, will you *Orlando*.

Cel. Goe too : wil you *Orlando*, haue to wife this *Rofalind* ?

Orl. I will.

Rof. I, but when ?

Orl. Why now, as faft as fhe can marrie vs.

Rof. Then you muft fay, I take thee *Rofalind* for wife.

Orl. I take thee *Rofalind* for wife.

Rof. I might aske you for your Commiffion, But I doe take thee *Orlando* for my husband : there's a girle goes before the Prieft, and certainely a Womans thought runs before her actions.

Orl. So do all thoughts, they are wing'd.

Rof. Now tell me how long you would haue her, after you haue poffeft her ?

Orl. For euer, and a day.

Rof. Say a day, without the euer : no, no *Orlando*, men are Aprill when they woe, December when they wed : Maides are May when they are maides, but the sky changes when they are wiues : I will bee more iealous of thee, then a Barbary cocke-pidgeon ouer his hen, more clamorous then a Parrat againft raine, more new-fangled then an ape, more giddy in my defires, then a monkey : I will weepe for nothing, like *Diana* in the Fountaine, & I wil do that when you are difpos'd to be merry : I will laugh like a Hyen, and that when thou art inclin'd to fleepe.

Orl. But will my *Rofalind* doe fo ?

Rof. By my life, fhe will doe as I doe.

Orl. O but fhe is wife.

Ros. Or elfe fhee could not haue the wit to doe this : the wifer, the waywarder : make the doores vpon a womans wit, and it will out at the cafement : fhut that, and 'twill out at the key-hole : ftop that, 'twill flie with the fmoake out at the chimney.

Orl. A man that had a wife with fuch a wit, he might fay, wit whether wil't ?

Rof. Nay, you might keepe that checke for it, till you met your wiues wit going to your neighbours bed.

Orl. And what wit could wit haue, to excufe that ?

Rofa. Marry to fay, fhe came to feeke you there : you fhall neuer take her without her anfwer, vnleffe you take her without her tongue : ô that woman that cannot make her fault her hufbands occafion, let her neuer nurfe her childe her felfe, for fhe will breed it like a foole.

Orl. For thefe two houres *Rofalinde*, I wil leaue thee.

Rof. Alas, deere loue, I cannot lacke thee two houres.

Orl. I muft attend the Duke at dinner, by two a clock I will be with thee againe.

Rof. I, goe your waies, goe your waies : I knew what you would proue, my friends told mee as much, and I thought no leffe : that flattering tongue of yours wonne me : 'tis but one caft away, and fo come death : two o' clocke is your howre.

Orl. I, fweet *Rofalind*.

Rof. By my troth, and in good earneft, and fo God mend mee, and by all pretty oathes that are not dangerous, if you breake one iot of your promife, or come one minute behinde your houre, I will thinke you the moft patheticall breake-promife, and the moft hollow louer, and the moft vnworthy of her you call *Rofalinde*, that may bee chofen out of the groffe band of the vnfaithfull : therefore beware my cenfure, and keep your promife.

Orl. With no leffe religion, then if thou wert indeed my *Rofalind* : fo adieu.

Rof. Well, Time is the olde Iuftice that examines all fuch offenders, and let time try : adieu. *Exit.*

Cel. You haue fimply mifus'd our fexe in your loueprate :

prate : we muſt haue your doublet and hoſe pluckt ouer your head, and ſhew the world what the bird hath done to her owne neaſt.

Roſ. O coz, coz, coz : my pretty little coz, that thou didſt know how many fathome deepe I am in loue : but it cannot bee ſounded : my affeꝗion hath an vnknowne bottome, like the Bay of Portugall.

Cel. Or rather bottomleſſe, that as faſt as you poure affeꝗion in, in runs out.

Roſ. No, that ſame wicked Baſtard of *Venus*, that was begot of thought, conceiu'd of ſpleene, and borne of madneſſe, that blinde raſcally boy, that abuſes euery ones eyes, becauſe his owne are out, let him bee iudge, how deepe I am in loue : ile tell thee *Aliena*, I cannot be out of the ſight of *Orlando* : Ile goe finde a ſhadow, and ſigh till he come.

Cel. And Ile ſleepe.   *Exeunt.*

Scena Secunda.

Enter Iaques and Lords, Forreſters.

Iaq. Which is he that killed the Deare?

Lord. Sir, it was I.

Iaq. Let's preſent him to the Duke like a Romane Conquerour, and it would doe well to ſet the Deares horns vpon his head, for a branch of viꝗory ; haue you no ſong Forreſter for this purpoſe?

Lord. Yes Sir.

Iaq. Sing it : 'tis no matter how it bee in tune, ſo it make noyſe enough.

Muſicke, Song.

What ſhall he haue that kild the Deare?
His Leather skin, and hornes to weare :
Then ſing him home, the reſt ſhall beare this burthen ;
Take thou no ſcorne to weare the horne,
It was a creſt ere thou waſt borne,
Thy fathers father wore it,
And thy father bore it,
The horne, the horne, the luſty horne,
Is not a thing to laugh to ſcorne.   *Exeunt.*

Scæna Tertia.

Enter Roſalind and Celia.

Roſ. How ſay you now, is it not paſt two a clock? And heere much *Orlando.*

Cel. I warrant you, with pure loue, & troubled brain,
Enter Siluius.
He hath t'ane his bow and arrowes, and is gone forth To ſleepe : looke who comes heere.

Sil. My errand is to you, faire youth,
My gentle *Phebe*, did bid me giue you this :
I know not the contents, but as I gueſſe
By the ſterne brow, and waſpiſh aꝗion
Which ſhe did vſe, as ſhe was writing of it,
It beares an angry tenure ; pardon me,
I am but as a guiltleſſe meſſenger.

Roſ. Patience her ſelfe would ſtartle at this letter,

And play the ſwaggerer, beare this, beare all :
Shee ſaies I am not faire, that I lacke manners,
She calls me proud, and that ſhe could not loue me
Were man as rare as Phenix : 'od's my will,
Her loue is not the Hare that I doe hunt,
Why writes ſhe ſo to me? well Shepheard, well,
This is a Letter of your owne deuice.

Sil. No, I proteſt, I know not the contents,
Phebe did write it.

Roſ. Come, come, you are a foole,
And turn'd into the extremity of loue.
I ſaw her hand, ſhe has a leatherne hand,
A freeſtone coloured hand : I verily did thinke
That her old gloues were on, but twas her hands:
She has a huſwiues hand, but that's no matter :
I ſay ſhe neuer did inuent this letter,
This is a mans inuention, and his hand.

Sil. Sure it is hers.

Roſ. Why, tis a boyſterous and a cruell ſtile,
A ſtile for challengers : why, ſhe defies me,
Like Turke to Chriſtian : vvomens gentle braine
Could not drop forth ſuch giant rude inuention,
Such Ethiop vvords, blacker in their effeꝗ
Then in their countenance : vvill you heare the letter?

Sil. So pleaſe you, for I neuer heard it yet :
Yet heard too much of *Phebes* crueltie.

Roſ. She *Phebes* me : marke how the tyrant vvrites.
Read. *Art thou god, to Shepherd turn'd?*
That a maidens heart hath burn'd?
Can a vvoman raile thus?

Sil. Call you this railing?

Roſ. Read. *Why, thy godhead laid a part,*
War'ſt thou with a womans heart?
Did you euer heare ſuch railing?
Whiles the eye of man did wooe me,
That could do no vengeance to me.
Meaning me a beaſt.
If the ſcorne of your bright eine
Haue power to raiſe ſuch loue in mine,
Alacke, in me, what ſtrange effeꝗ
Would they worke in milde aſpeꝗ?
Whiles you chid me, I did loue,
How then might your praiers moue?
He that brings this loue to thee,
Little knowes this Loue in me :
And by him ſeale vp thy minde,
Whether that thy youth and kinde
Will the faithfull offer take
Of me, and all that I can make,
Or elſe by him my loue denie,
And then Ile ſtudie how to die.

Sil. Call you this chiding?

Cel. Alas poore Shepheard.

Roſ. Doe you pitty him? No, he deſerues no pitty:
wilt thou loue ſuch a woman? what to make thee an inſtrument, and play falſe ſtraines vpon thee? not to be endur'd. Well, goe your way to her; (for I ſee Loue hath
made thee a tame ſnake) and ſay this to her; That if ſhe
loue me, I charge her to loue thee : if ſhe will not, I will
neuer haue her, vnleſſe thou intreat for her : if you bee a
true louer hence, and not a word ; for here comes more
company.   *Exit. Sil.*

Enter Oliuer.   know)

Oliu. Good morrow, faire ones : pray you, (if you
Where in the Purlews of this Forreſt, ſtands

A

A fheep-coat, fenc'd about with Oliue-trees.

Cel. Weft of this place, down in the neighbor bottom
The ranke of Oziers, by the murmuring ftreame
Left on your right hand, brings you to the place:
But at this howre, the houfe doth keepe it felfe,
There's none within.

Oli. If that an eye may profit by a tongue,
Then fhould I know you by defcription,
Such garments, and fuch yeeres : the boy is faire,
Of femall fauour, and beftowes himfelfe
Like a ripe fifter : the woman low
And browner then her brother : are not you
The owner of the houfe I did enquire for ?

Cel. It is no boaft, being ask'd, to fay we are.

Oli. *Orlando* doth commend him to you both,
And to that youth hee calls his *Rofalind*,
He fends this bloudy napkin ; are yuu he ?

Rof. I am : what muft we vnderftand by this ?

Oli. Some of my fhame, if you will know of me
What man I am, and how, and why, and where
This handkercher was ftain'd.

Cel. I pray you tell it.

Oli. When laft the yong *Orlando* parted from you,
He left a promife to returne againe
Within an houre, and pacing through the Forreft,
Chewing the food of fweet and bitter fancie,
Loe vvhat befull : he threw his eye afide,
And marke vvhat obiect did prefent it felfe
Vnder an old Oake, whofe bows were mofs'd with age
And high top, bald with drie antiquitie :
A wretched ragged man, ore-grovvne with haire
Lay fleeping on his back ; about his necke
A greene and guilded fnake had wreath'd it felfe,
Who with her head, nimble in threats approach'd
The opening of his mouth : but fodainly
Seeing *Orlando*, it vnlink'd it felfe,
And with indented glides, did flip away
Into a bufh, vnder which bufhes fhade
A Lyonneffe, with vdders all drawne drie,
Lay cowching head on ground, with catlike watch
When that the fleeping man fhould ftirre ; for 'tis
The royall difpofition of that beaft
To prey on nothing, that doth feeme as dead :
This feene, *Orlando* did approach the man,
And found it was his brother, his elder brother.

Cel. O I haue heard him fpeake of that fame brother,
And he did render him the moft vnnaturall
That liu'd amongft men.

Oli. And well he might fo doe,
For well I know he was vnnaturall.

Rof. But to *Orlando* : did he leaue him there
Food to the fuck'd and hungry Lyonneffe ?

Oli. Twice did he turne his backe, and purpos'd fo :
But kindneffe, nobler euer then reuenge,
And Nature ftronger then his iuft occafion,
Made him giue battell to the Lyonneffe :
Who quickly fell before him, in which hurtling
From miferable flumber I awaked.

Cel. Are you his brother ?

Rof. Was't you he refcu'd ?

Cel. Was't you that did fo oft contriue to kill him ?

Oli. 'Twas I : but 'tis not I : I doe not fhame
To tell you what I was, fince my conuerfion
So fweeetly taftes, being the thing I am.

Rof. But for the bloody napkin ?

Oli. By and by :

When from the firft to laft betwixt vs two,
Teares our recountments had moft kindely bath'd,
As how I came into that Defert place.
I briefe, he led me to the gentle Duke,
Who gaue me frefh aray, and entertainment,
Committing me vnto my brothers loue,
Who led me inftantly vnto his Caue,
There ftript himfelfe, and heere vpon his arme
The Lyonneffe had torne fome flefh away,
Which all this while had bled ; and now he fainted,
And cride in fainting vpon *R:falinde*.
Briefe, I recouer'd him, bound vp his wound,
And after fome fmall fpace, being ftrong at heart,
He fent me hither, ftranger as I am
To tell this ftory, that you might excufe
His broken promife, and to giue this napkin
Died in this bloud, vnto the Shepheard youth,
That he in fport doth call his *Rofalind*.

Cel. Why how now *Ganimed*, fweet *Ganimed*.

Oli. Many will fwoon when they do look on bloud.

Cel. There is more in it ; Cofen *Ganimed*.

Oli. Looke, he recouers.

Rof. I would I were at home.

Cel. Wee'll lead you thither :
I pray you will you take him by the arme.

Oli. Be of good cheere youth : you a man?
You lacke a mans heart.

Rof. I doe fo, I confeffe it :
Ah, firra, a body would thinke this was well counterfei-
ted, I pray you tell your brother how well I counterfei-
ted : heigh-ho.

Oli. This was not counterfeit, there is too great teftimony in your complexion, that it was a paffion of earneft.

Rof. Counterfeit, I affure you.

Oli. Well then, take a good heart, and counterfeit to
be a man.

Rof. So I doe : but yfaith, I fhould haue beene a woman by right.

Cel. Come, you looke paler and paler : pray you draw
homewards : good fir, goe with vs.

Oli. That will I : for I muft beare anfwere backe
How you excufe my brother, *Rofalind*.

Rof. I fhall deuife fomething : but I pray you commend my counterfeiting to him : will you goe ?

Exeunt.

Actus Quintus. Scena Prima.

Enter Clowne and Awdrie.

Clow. We fhall finde a time *Awdrie*, patience gentle *Awdrie*.

Awd. Faith the Prieft was good enough, for all the
olde gentlemans faying.

Clow. A moft wicked Sir *Oliuer*, *Awdrie*, a moft vile
Mar-text. But *Awdrie*, there is a youth heere in the
Forreft layes claime to you.

Awd. I, I know who 'tis : he hath no intereft in mee
in the world : here comes the man you meane.

Enter William.

Clo. It is meat and drinke to me to fee a Clowne, by
my

my troth, we that haue good wits, haue much to anſwer for : we ſhall be flouting : we cannot hold.

Will. Good eu'n *Audrey.*

Aud. God ye good eu'n *William.*

Will. And good eu'n to you Sir.

Clo. Good eu'n gentle friend. Couer thy head, couer thy head : Nay prethee bee eouer'd. How olde are you Friend?

Will. Fiue and twentie Sir.

Clo. A ripe age : Is thy name *William*?

Will. William, ſir.

Clo. A faire name. Was't borne i'th Forreſt heere?

Will. I ſir, I thanke God.

Clo. Thanke God : A good anſwer : Art rich?

Will. 'Faith ſir, ſo, ſo.

Clo. So, ſo, is good, very good, very excellent good: and yet it is not, it is but ſo, ſo : Art thou wiſe?

Will. I ſir, I haue a prettie wit.

Clo. Why, thou ſaiſt well. I do now remember a ſaying : The Foole doth thinke he is wiſe, but the wiſeman knowes himſelfe to be a Foole. The Heathen Philoſopher, when he had a deſire to eate a Grape, would open his lips when he put it into his mouth, meaning thereby, that Grapes were made to eate, and lippes to open. You do loue this maid?

Will. I do ſir.

Clo. Giue me your hand : Art thou Learned?

Will. No ſir.

Clo. Then learne this of me, To haue, is to haue. For it is a figure in Rhetoricke, that drink being powr'd out of a cup into a glaſſe, by filling the one, doth empty the other. For all your Writers do conſent, that *ipſe* is hee : now you are not *ipſe,* for I am he.

Will. Which he ſir?

Clo. He ſir, that muſt marrie this woman: Therefore you Clowne, abandon : which is in the vulgar, leaue the ſocietie : which in the booriſh, is companie, of this female : which in the common, is woman : which together, is, abandon the ſociety of this Female, or Clowne thou periſheſt: or to thy better vnderſtanding, dyeſt ; or (to wit) I kill thee, make thee away, tranſlate thy life into death, thy libertie into bondage : I will deale in poyſon with thee, or in baſtinado, or in ſteele : I will bandy with thee in faction, I will ore-run thee with police : I will kill thee a hundred and fifty wayes, therefore tremble and depart.

Aud. Do good *William.*

Will. God reſt you merry ſir.   *Exit*

Enter Corin.

Cor. Our Maſter and Miſtreſſe ſeekes you : come away, away.

Clo. Trip *Audry,* trip *Audry,* I attend, I attend.   *Exeunt*

Scæna Secunda.

Enter Orlando & Oliuer.

Orl. Is't poſſible, that on ſo little acquaintance you ſhould like her? that, but ſeeing, you ſhould loue her?

And louing woo? and wooing, ſhe ſhould graunt? And will you perſeuer to enioy her?

Ol. Neither call the giddineſſe of it in queſtion ; the pouertie of her, the ſmall acquaintance, my ſodaine wooing, nor ſudaine conſenting : but ſay with mee, I loue *Aliena* : ſay with her, that ſhe loues mee ; conſent with both, that we may enioy each other : it ſhall be to your good : for my fathers houſe, and all the reuennew, that was old Sir *Rowlands* will I eſtate vpon you, and heere liue and die a Shepherd.

Enter Roſalind.

Orl. You haue my conſent.
Let your Wedding be to morrow : thither will I Inuite the Duke, and all's contented followers: Go you, and prepare *Aliena*; for looke you, Heere comes my *Roſalinde.*

Roſ. God ſaue you brother.

Ol. And you faire ſiſter.

Roſ. Oh my deere *Orlando,* how it greeues me to ſee thee weare thy heart in a ſcarfe.

Orl. It is my arme.

Roſ. I thought thy heart had beene wounded with the clawes of a Lion.

Orl. Wounded it is, but with the eyes of a Lady.

Roſ. Did your brother tell you how I counterfeyted to ſound, when he ſhew'd me your handkercher?

Orl. I, and greater wonders then that.

Roſ. O, I know where you are : nay, tis true : there was neuer any thing ſo ſodaine, but the fight of two Rammes, and *Ceſars* Thraſonicall bragge of I came, ſaw, and ouercome. For your brother, and my ſiſter, no ſooner met, but they look'd : no ſooner look'd, but they lou'd ; no ſooner lou'd, but they ſigh'd : no ſooner ſigh'd but they ask'd one another the reaſon : no ſooner knew the reaſon, but they ſought the remedie : and in theſe degrees, haue they made a paire of ſtaires to marriage, which they will climbe incontinent, or elſe bee incontinent before marriage ; they are in the verie wrath of loue, and they will together . Clubbes cannot part them.

Orl. They ſhall be married to morrow : and I will bid the Duke to the Nuptiall. But O, how bitter a thing it is, to looke into happines through another mans eies : by ſo much the more ſhall I to morrow be at the height of heart heauineſſe. by how much I ſhal thinke my brother happie, in hauing what he wiſhes for.

Roſ. Why then to morrow, I cannot ſerue your turne for *Roſalind?*

Orl. I can liue no longer by thinking.

Roſ. I will wearie you then no longer with idle talking. Know of me then (for now I ſpeake to ſome purpoſe) that I know you are a Gentleman of good conceit: I ſpeake not this, that you ſhould beare a good opinion of my knowledge: inſomuch (I ſay) I know you are:neither do I labor for a greater eſteeme then may in ſome little meaſure draw a beleeſe from you, to do your ſelfe good, and not to grace me. Beleeue then, if you pleaſe, that I can do ſtrange things : I haue ſince I was three yeare olde conuerſt with a Magitian, moſt profound in his Art, and yet not damnable. If you do loue *Roſalinde* ſo neere the hart, as your geſture cries it out : when your brother marries *Aliena,* ſhall you marrie her. I know into what ſtraights of Fortune ſhe is driuen, and it is not impoſſible to me, if it appeare not inconuenient to you, to to fet her before your eyes to morrow, humane as fhe is, and without any danger.

Orl. Speak'ft thou in fober meanings?

Rof. By my life I do, which I tender deerly, though I fay I am a Magitian : Therefore put you in your beft a-ray, bid your friends : for if you will be married to morrow, you fhall : and to *Rofalind* if you will.

Enter Siluius & Phebe.

Looke, here comes a Louer of mine, and a louer of hers.

Phe. Youth, you haue done me much vngentleneffe, To fhew the letter that I writ to you.

Rof. I care not if I haue : it is my ftudie To feeme defpightfull and vngentle to you : you are there followed by a faithful fhepheard, Looke vpon him, loue him : he worfhips you.

Phe. Good fhepheard, tell this youth what 'tis to loue

Sil. It is to be all made of fighes and teares, And fo am I for *Phebe.*

Phe. And I for *Ganimed.*

Orl. And I for *Rofalind.*

Rof And I for no woman.

Sil. It is to be all made of faith and feruice, And fo am I for *Phebe.*

Phe. And I for *Ganimed.*

Orl. And I for *Rofalind.*

Rof. And I for no woman.

Sil. It is to be all made of fantafie, All made of paffion, and all made of wifhes, All adoration, dutie, and obferuance, All humbleneffe, all patience, and impatience, All puritie, all triall, all obferuance : And fo am I for *Phebe.*

Phe. And fo am I for *Ganimed.*

Orl. And fo am I for *Rofalind.*

Rof. And fo am I for no woman.

Phe. If this be fo, why blame you me to loue you?

Sil. If this be fo, why blame you me to loue you?

Orl. If this be fo, why blame you me to loue you?

Rof. Why do you fpeake too, Why blame you mee to loue you.

Orl. To her, that is not heere, nor doth not heare.

Rof. Pray you no more of this, 'tis like the howling of Irifh Wolues againft the Moone : I will helpe you if I can : I would loue you if I could : To morrow meet me altogether : I wil marrie you, if euer I marrie Woman, and Ile be married to morrow : I will fatisfie you, if euer I fatisfi'd man, and you fhall bee married to morrow. I wil content you, if what pleafes you contents you, and you fhal be married to morrow : As you loue *Rofalind* meet, as you loue *Phebe* meet, and as I loue no woman, Ile meet : fo fare you wel : I haue left you commands.

Sil. Ile not faile, if I liue.

Phe. Nor I.

Orl. Nor I.   *Exeunt.*

Scæna Tertia.

Enter Clowne and Audrey.

Clo. To morrow is the ioyfull day *Audrey*, to morrow will we be married.

Aud. I do defire it with all my heart : and I hope it is no difhoneft defire, to defire to be a woman of ỹ world?

Heere come two of the banifh'd Dukes Pages.

Enter two Pages.

1.Pa. Wel met honeft Gentleman.

Clo. By my troth well met : come, fit, fit, and a fong.

2.Pa. We are for you, fit i'th middle.

1.Pa. Shal we clap into't roundly, without hauking, or fpitting, or faying we are hoarfe, which are the onely prologues to a bad voice.

2.Pa. I faith, y'faith, and both in a tune like two gipfies on a horfe.

Song.

It was a Louer, and his laffe,
  With a hey, and a ho, and a hey nonino,
That o're the greene corne feild did paffe,
  In the fpring time, the onely pretty rang time.
When Birds do fing, hey ding a ding, ding.
Sweet Louers loue the fpring,
And therefore take the prefent time,
  With a hey, & a ho, and a hey nonino,
For loue is crowned with the prime.
  In fpring time, &c.

Betweene the acres of the Rie,
  With a hey, and a ho, & a hey nonino :
Thefe prettie Country folks would lie.
  In fpring time, &c.

This Carroll they began that houre,
  With a hey and a ho, & a hey nonino :
How that a life was but a Flower,
  In fpring time, &c.

Clo. Truly yong Gentlemen, though there vvas no great matter in the dittie, yet ỹ note was very vntunable

1.Pa. you are deceiu'd Sir, we kept time, we loft not our time.

Clo. By my troth yes : I count it but time loft to heare fuch a foolifh fong. God buy you, and God mend your voices. Come *Audrie.*   *Exeunt.*

Scena Quarta.

Enter Duke Senior, Amyens, Iaques, Orlando, Oliuer, Celia.

Du. Sen. Doft thou beleeue *Orlando*, that the boy Can do all this that he hath promifed?

Orl. I fometimes do beleeue, and fomtimes do not, As thofe that feare they hope, and know they feare.

Enter Rofalinde, Siluius, & Phebe.

Rof. Patience once more, whiles our cõpact is vrg'd : You fay, if I bring in your *Rofalinde,* You will beftow her on *Orlando* heere?

Du. Se. That would I, had I kingdoms to giue with hir.

Rof. And you fay you wil haue her, when I bring hir?

Orl. That would I, were I of all kingdomes King.

Rof. You fay, you'l marrie me, if I be willing.

Phe. That will I, fhould I die the houre after.

Rof. But if you do refufe to marrie me, You'l giue your felfe to this moft faithfull Shepheard.

Phe. So is the bargaine.

Rof. You fay that you'l haue *Phebe* if fhe will.

Sil. Though to haue her and death, were both one thing.

S   *Rof.*

Rof. I haue promis'd to make all this matter euen :
Keepe you your word, O Duke, to giue your daughter,
You yours *Orlando*, to receiue his daughter:
Keepe you your word *Phebe*, that you'l marrie me,
Or elfe refuſing me to wed this ſhepheard :
Keepe your word *Siluius*, that you'l marrie her
If ſhe refuſe me, and from hence I go
To make theſe doubts all euen. *Exit Rof. and Celia.*

Du.Sen. I do remember in this ſhepheard boy,
Some liuely touches of my daughters fauour.

Orl. My Lord, the firſt time that I euer ſaw him,
Me thought he was a brother to your daughrer:
But my good Lord, this Boy is Forreſt borne,
And hath bin tutor'd in the rudiments
Of many deſperate ſtudies, by his vnckle,
Whom he reports to be a great Magitian.

Enter Clowne and Audrey.
Obſcured in the circle of this Forreſt.

Iaq. There is ſure another flood toward, and theſe
couples are comming to the Arke. Here comes a payre
of verie ſtrange beaſts, which in all tongues, are call'd
Fooles.

Clo. Salutation and greeting to you all.

Iaq. Good my Lord, bid him welcome : This is the
Motley-minded Gentleman, that I haue ſo often met in
the Forreſt: he hath bin a Courtier he ſweares.

Clo. If any man doubt that, let him put mee to my
purgation, I haue trod a meaſure : I haue flattred a Lady,
I haue bin politicke with my friend, ſmooth with mine
enemie, I haue vndone three Tailors, I haue had foure
quarrels, and like to haue fought one.

Iaq. And how was that tane vp ?

Clo. 'Faith we met, and found the quarrel was vpon
the ſeuenth cauſe.

Iaq. How ſeuenth cauſe? Good my Lord, like this
fellow.

Du.Se. I like him very well.

Clo. God'ild you ſir, I defire you of the like : I preſſe
in heere ſir, amongſt the reſt of the Country copulatiues
to ſweare, and to forſweare, according as mariage binds
and blood breakes : a poore virgin ſir, an il-fauor'd thing
ſir, but mine owne, a poore humour of mine ſir, to take
that that no man elſe will : rich honeſtie dwels like a mi-
ſer ſir, in a poore houſe, as your Pearle in your foule oyſter.

Du.Se. By my faith, he is very ſwift, and ſententious

Clo. According to the fooles bolt ſir, and ſuch dulcet
diſeaſes.

Iaq. But for the ſeuenth cauſe. How did you finde
the quarrell on the ſeuenth cauſe?

Clo. Vpon a lye, ſeuen times remoued : (beare your
bodie more ſeeming *Audry*) as thus ſir : I did diſlike the
cut of a certaine Courtiers beard : he ſent me word, if I
ſaid his beard was not cut well, hee was in the minde it
was : this is call'd the retort courteous. If I ſent him
word againe, it was not well cut, he wold ſend me word
he cut it to pleaſe himſelfe:this is call'd the quip modeſt.
If againe, it was not well cut, he diſabled my iudgment :
this is called, the reply churliſh.If againe it was not well
cut, he would anſwer I ſpake not true : this is call'd the
reproofe valiant. If againe, it was not well cut, he wold
ſay, I lie : this is call'd the counter-checke quarrelſome :
and ſo ro lye circumſtantiall, and the lye direct.

Iaq. And how oft did you ſay his beard was not well
cut ?

Clo. I durſt go no further then the lye circumſtantial:

nor he durſt not giue me the lye direct : and ſo wee meafur'd ſwords, and parted.

Iaq. Can you nominate in order now, the degrees of
the lye.

Clo. O ſir, we quarrel in print, by the booke : as you
haue bookes for good manners : I will name you the degrees. The firſt, the Retort courteous : the ſecond, the
Quip-modeſt : the third, the reply Churliſh:the fourth,
the Reproofe valiant : the fift, the Counterchecke quarrelſome : the ſixt, the Lye with circumſtance : the ſea-
uenth, the Lye direct : all theſe you may auoyd, but the
Lye direct : and you may auoide that too, with an If. I
knew when ſeuen Iuſtices could not take vp a Quarrell,
but when the parties were met themſelues, one of them
thought but of an If; as if you ſaide ſo, then I ſaide ſo :
and they ſhooke hands, and ſwore brothers. Your If, is
the onely peace-maker: much vertue in if.

Iaq. Is not this a rare fellow my Lord ? He's as good
at any thing, and yet a foole.

Du.Se. He vſes his folly like a ſtalking-horſe, and vnder the preſentation of that he ſhoots his wit.

Enter Hymen, Rofalind, and Celia.
Still Muſicke.

Hymen. *Then is there mirth in heauen,*
When earthly things made eauen
attone together.
Good Duke receiue thy daughter,
Hymen from Heauen brought her,
Yea brought her hether.
That thou mightſt ioyne his hand with his,
Whoſe heart within his boſome is.

Rof. To you I giue my ſelfe, for I am yours.
To you I giue my ſelfe, for I am yours.

Du.Se. If there be truth in ſight, you are my daughter.

Orl. If there be truth in ſight, you are my *Rofalind.*

Phe. If ſight & ſhape be true, why then my loue adieu

Rof. Ile haue no Father, if you be not he :
Ile haue no Husband, if you be not he :
Nor ne're wed woman, if you be not ſhee.

Hy. Peace hoa : I barre confuſion,
'Tis I muſt make concluſion
Of theſe moſt ſtrange euents :
Here's eight that muſt take hands,
To ioyne in *Hymens* bands,
If truth holds true contents.
You and you, no croſſe ſhall part;
You and you, are hart in hart :
You, to his loue muſt accord,
Or haue a Woman to your Lord.
You and you, are ſure together,
As the Winter to fowle Weather :
Whiles a Wedlocke Hymne we ſing,
Feede your ſelues with queſtioning :
That reaſon, wonder may diminiſh
How thus we met, and theſe things finiſh.

Song.
Wedding is great Iunos crowne,
O bleſſed bond of boord and bed :
'Tis Hymen peoples euerie towne,
High wedlock then be honored :
Honor, high honor and renowne
To Hymen, God of euerie Towne.

Du.Se. O my deere Neece, welcome thou art to me,
Euen daughter welcome, in no leſſe degree.

Phe.

Phe. I will not eate my word, now thou art mine,
Thy faith, my fancie to thee doth combine.

Enter Second Brother.

2.Bro. Let me haue audience for a word or two:
I am the second sonne of old *Sir Rowland,*
That bring thefe tidings to this faire affembly.
Duke Frederick hearing how that euerie day
Men of great worth reforted to this forreft,
Addreft a mightie power, which were on foote
In his owne conduct, purpofely to take
His brother heere, and put him to the fword :
And to the skirts of this wilde Wood he came ;
Where, meeting with an old Religious man,
After fome queftion with him, was conuerted
Both from his enterprize, and from the world :
His crowne bequeathing to his banifh'd Brother,
And all their Lands reftor'd to him againe
That were with him exil'd.   This to be true,
I do engage my life.

Du.Se. Welcome yong man :
Thou offer'ft fairely to thy brothers wedding :
To one his lands with-held, and to the other
A land it felfe at large, a potent Dukedome.
Firft, in this Forreft, let vs do thofe ends
That heere vvere well begun, and wel begot :
And after, euery of this happie number
That haue endur'd fhrew'd daies, and nights with vs,
Shal fhare the good of our returned fortune,
According to the meafure of their ftates.
Meane time, forget this new-falne dignitie,
And fall into our Rufticke Reuelrie :
Play Muficke, and you Brides and Bride-groomes all,
With meafure heap'd in ioy, to'th Meafures fall.

Iaq. Sir, by your patience : if I heard you rightly,
The Duke hath put on a Religious life,
And throwne into neglect the pompous Court.

2.Bro. He hath.

Iaq. To him will I : out of thefe conuertites,
There is much matter to be heard, and learn'd :
you to your former Honor, I bequeath
your patience, and your vertue, well deferues it.
you to a loue, that your true faith doth merit :
you to your land, and loue, and great allies :
you to a long, and well-deferued bed :
And you to wrangling, for thy louing voyage
Is but for two moneths victuall'd : So to your pleafures,
I am for other, then for dancing meazures.

Du.Se. Stay, *Iaques,* ftay.

Iaq. To fee no paftime, I : what you would haue,
Ile ftay to know, at your abandon'd caue.   *Exit.*

Du.Se. Proceed, proceed : wee'l begin thefe rights,
As we do truft, they'l end in true delights.   *Exit*

Rof. It is not the fafhion to fee the Ladie the Epilogue : but it is no more vnhandfome, then to fee the
Lord the Prologue.   If it be true, that good wine needs
no bufh, 'tis true, that a good play needes no Epilogue.
Yet to good wine they do vfe good bufhes : and good
playes proue the better by the helpe of good Epilogues:
What a cafe am I in then, that am neither a good Epilogue, nor cannot infinuate with you in the behalfe of a
good play?   I am not furnifh'd like a Begger, therefore
to begge will not become mee.   My way is to coniure
you, and Ile begin with the Women.   I charge you (O
women) for the loue you beare to men, to like as much
of this Play, as pleafe you : And I charge you (O men)
for the loue you beare to women (as I perceiue by your
fimpring,none of you hates them) that betweene you,
and the women, the play may pleafe.   If I were a Woman, I would kiffe as many of you as had beards that
pleas'd me, complexions that lik'd me, and breaths that
I defi'de not : And I am fure, as many as haue good
beards, or good faces, or fweet breaths,will for my kind
offer,when I make curt'fie,bid me farewell.   *Exit.*

FINIS.

S 2

THE
Taming of the Shrew.

Actus primus. Scæna Prima.

Enter Begger and Hostes, Christophero Sly.

Begger.
Le pheeze you infaith.
Host. A paire of stockes you rogue.
Beg. Y'are a baggage, the *Slies* are no
Rogues. Looke in the Chronicles, we come
in with *Richard Conqueror* : therefore *Pau-*
cas pallabris, let the world slide : Sessa.
Host. You will not pay for the glasses you haue burst ?
Beg. No, not a deniere : go by S. *Ieronimie*, goe to thy
cold bed, and warme thee.
Host. I know my remedie, I must go fetch the Head-
borough.
Beg. Third, or fourth, or fift Borough, Ile answere
him by Law. Ile not budge an inch boy : Let him come,
and kindly. *Falles asleepe.*

Winde hornes. Enter a Lord from hunting, with his traine.
Lo. Huntsman I charge thee, tender wel my hounds,
Brach *Merriman*, the poore Curre is imbost,
And couple *Clowder* with the deepe-mouth'd brach,
Saw'st thou not boy how *Silver* made it good
At the hedge corner, in the couldest fault,
I would not loose the dogge for twentie pound.
Hunts. Why *Belman* is as good as he my Lord,
He cried vpon it at the meerest losse,
And twice to day pick'd out the dullest sent,
Trust me, I take him for the better dogge.
Lord. Thou art a Foole, if *Eccho* were as fleete,
I would esteeme him worth a dozen such :
But sup them well, and looke vnto them all,
To morrow I intend to hunt againe.
Hunts. I will my Lord.
Lord. What's heere? One dead, or drunke? See doth
he breath ?
2.Hun. He breath's my Lord. Were he not warm'd
with Ale, this were a bed but cold to sleepe so soundly.
Lord. Oh monstrous beast, how like a swine he lyes.
Grim death, how foule and loathsome is thine image :
Sirs, I will practise on this drunken man.
What thinke you, if he were conuey'd to bed,
Wrap'd in sweet cloathes : Rings put vpon his fingers :
A most delicious banquet by his bed,
And braue attendants neere him when he wakes,
Would not the begger then forget himselfe?
1.Hun. Beleeue me Lord, I thinke he cannot choose.
2.H. It would seeme strange vnto him when he wak'd
Lord. Euen as a flatt'ring dreame, or worthles fancie.

Then take him vp, and manage well the iest :
Carrie him gently to my fairest Chamber,
And hang it round with all my vvanton pictures:
Balme his foule head in warme distilled waters,
And burne sweet Wood to make the Lodging sweete:
Procure me Musicke readie when he vvakes,
To make a dulcet and a heauenly sound :
And if he chance to speake, be readie straight
(And with a lowe submissiue reuerence)
Say, what is it your Honor vvil command :
Let one attend him vvith a siluer Bason
Full of Rose-water, and bestrew'd with Flowers,
Another beare the Ewer : the third a Diaper,
And say wilt please your Lordship coole your hands.
Some one be readie with a costly suite,
And aske him what apparrel he will weare :
Another tell him of his Hounds and Horse,
And that his Ladie mournes at his disease,
Perswade him that he hath bin Lunaticke,
And when he sayes he is, say that he dreames,
For he is nothing but a mightie Lord :
This do, and do it kindly, gentle sirs,
It wil be pastime passing excellent,
If it be husbanded with modestie.
1.Hunts. My Lord I warrant you we wil play our part
As he shall thinke by our true diligence
He is no lesse then what we say he is.
Lord. Take him vp gently, and to bed with him,
And each one to his office when he wakes. *Sound trumpets.*
Sirrah, go see what Trumpet 'tis that sounds,
Belike some Noble Gentleman that meanes
(Trauelling some iourney) to repose him heere.
Enter Seruingman.
How now? who is it ?
Ser. An't please your Honor, Players
That offer seruice to your Lordship.

Enter Players.
Lord. Bid them come neere:
Now fellowes, you are welcome.
Players. We thanke your Honor.
Lord. Do you intend to stay with me to night ?
2.Player. So please your Lordshippe to accept our
dutie.
Lord. With all my heart. This fellow I remember,
Since once he plaide a Farmers eldest sonne,
'Twas where you woo'd the Gentlewoman so well :
I haue forgot your name : but sure that part

Was

Was aptly fitted, and naturally perform'd.

Sinclo. I thinke 'twas *Soto* that your honor meanes.

Lord. 'Tis verie true, thou didſt it excellent :
Well you are come to me in happie time,
The rather for I haue ſome ſport in hand,
Wherein your cunning can aſſiſt me much.

There is a Lord will heare you play to night;
But I am doubtfull of your modeſties,
Leaſt (ouer-eying of his odde behauiour,
For yet his honor neuer heard a play)
You breake into ſome merrie paſſion,
And ſo offend him : for I tell you ſirs,
If you ſhould ſmile, he growes impatient.

Plai. Feare not my Lord, we can contain our ſelues,
Were he the verieſt anticke in the world.

Lord. Go ſirra, take them to the Butterie,
And giue them friendly welcome euerie one,
Let them want nothing that my houſe affoords.

Exit one with the Players.

Sirra go you to Bartholmew my Page,
And ſee him dreſt in all ſuites like a Ladie :
That done, conduct him to the drunkards chamber,
And call him Madam, do him obeiſance :
Tell him from me (as he will win my loue)
He beare himſelfe with honourable action,
Such as he hath obſeru'd in noble Ladies
Vnto their Lords, by them accompliſhed,
Such dutie to the drunkard let him do :
With ſoft lowe tongue, and lowly curteſie,
And ſay : What iſ't your Honor will command,
Wherein your Ladie, and your humble wife,
May ſhew her dutie, and make knowne her loue.
And then with kinde embracements, tempting kiſſes,
And with declining head into his boſome
Bid him ſhed teares, as being ouer-ioyed
To ſee her noble Lord reſtor'd to health,
Who for this ſeuen yeares hath eſteemed him
No better then a poore and loathſome begger :
And if the boy haue not a womans guilt
To raine a ſhower of commanded teares,
An Onion wil do well for ſuch a ſhift,
Which in a Napkin (being cloſe conuei'd)
Shall in deſpight enforce a waterie eie :
See this diſpatch'd with all the haſt thou canſt,
Anon Ile giue thee more inſtructions.

Exit a ſeruingman.

I know the boy will wel vſurpe the grace,
Voice, gate, and action of a Gentlewoman :
I long to heare him call the drunkard husband,
And how my men will ſtay themſelues from laughter,
When they do homage to this ſimple peaſant,
Ile in to counſell them : haply my preſence
May well abate the ouer-merrie ſpleene,
Which otherwiſe would grow into extreames.

*Enter aloft the drunkard with attendants, ſome with apparel,
Baſon and Ewer, & other appurtenances, & Lord.*

Beg. For Gods ſake a pot of ſmall Ale.

1. Ser. Wilt pleaſe your Lord drink a cup of ſacke ?

2. Ser. Wilt pleaſe your Honor taſte of theſe Conſerues ?

3. Ser. What raiment wil your honor weare to day.

Beg. I am *Chriſtophero Sly*, call not mee Honour nor
Lordſhip : I ne're drank ſacke in my life : and if you giue
me any Conſerues, giue me conſerues of Beefe : nere ask
me what raiment Ile weare, for I haue no more doub-

lets then backes : no more ſtockings then legges : nor
no more ſhooes then feet, nay ſometime more feete then
ſhooes, or ſuch ſhooes as my toes looke through the o-
uer-leather.

Lord. Heauen ceaſe this idle humor in your Honor.
Oh that a mightie man of ſuch diſcent,
Of ſuch poſſeſſions, and ſo high eſteeme
Should be infuſed with ſo foule a ſpirit.

Beg. What would you make me mad ? Am not I *Chriſtopher Slie*, old *Sies* ſonne of Burton-heath, by byrth a
Pedler, by education a Cardmaker, by tranſmutation a
Beare-heard, and now by preſent profeſſion a Tinker.
Aske *Marrian Hacket* the fat Alewife of Wincot, if ſhee
know me not : if ſhe ſay I am not xiiii.d. on the ſcore for
ſheere Ale, ſcore me vp for the lyingſt knaue in Chriſten
dome. What I am not beſtraught : here's————

1. Man. Oh this it is that makes your Ladie mourne.

2. Man. Oh this is it that makes your ſeruants droop.

Lord. Hence comes it, that your kindred ſhuns your
As beaten hence by your ſtrange Lunacie.   (houſe
Oh Noble Lord, bethinke thee of thy birth,
Call home thy ancient thoughts from baniſhment,
And baniſh hence theſe abiect lowlie dreames :
Looke how thy ſeruants do attend on thee,
Each in his office ready at thy becke.
Wilt thou haue Muſicke ? Harke Apollo plaies,   *Muſick*
And twentie caged Nightingales do ſing.
Or wilt thou ſleepe ? Wee'l haue thee to a Couch,
Softer and ſweeter then the luſtfull bed
On purpoſe trim'd vp for Semiramis.
Say thou wilt walke : we wil beſtrow the ground.
Or wilt thou ride ? Thy horſes ſhal be trap'd,
Their harneſſe ſtudded all with Gold and Pearle.
Doſt thou loue hawking ? Thou haſt hawkes will ſoare
Aboue the morning Larke. Or wilt thou hunt,
Thy hounds ſhall make the Welkin anſwer them
And fetch ſhrill ecchoes from the hollow earth.

1. Man. Say thou wilt courſe, thy gray-hounds are as
As breathed Stags : ſ fleeter then the Roe.   (ſwift

2. M. Doſt thou loue pictures ? we wil fetch thee ſtrait
Adonis painted by a running brooke,
And Cithera all in ſedges hid,
Which ſeeme to moue and wanton with her breath,
Euen as the wauing ſedges play with winde.

Lord. Wee'l ſhew thee *Io*, as ſhe was a Maid,
And how ſhe was beguiled and ſurpriz'd,
As liuelie painted, 'as the deede was done.

3. Man. Or *Daphne* roming through a thornie wood,
Scratching her legs, that one ſhal ſweare ſhe bleeds,
And at that ſight ſhal ſad Apollo weepe,
So workmanlie the blood and teares are drawne.

Lord. Thou art a Lord, and nothing but a Lord :
Thou haſt a Ladie farre more Beautifull,
Then any woman in this waining age.

1. Man. And til the teares that ſhe hath ſhed for thee,
Like enuious flouds ore-run her louely face,
She was the faireſt creature in the world,
And yet ſhee is inferiour to none.

Beg. Am I a Lord, and haue I ſuch a Ladie ?
Or do I dreame ? Or haue I dream'd till now ?
I do not ſleepe : I ſee, I heare, I ſpeake :
I ſmel ſweet ſauours, and I feele ſoft things :
Vpon my life I am a Lord indeede,
And not a Tinker, nor Chriſtopher Slie.
Well, bring our Ladie hither to our ſight,
And once againe a pot o'th ſmalleſt Ale.

2.*Man.* Wilt pleafe your mightineffe to wafh your
hands :
Oh how we ioy to fee your wit reftor'd,
Oh that once more you knew but what you are :
Thefe fifteene yeeres you haue bin in a dreame,
Or when you wak'd, fo wak'd as if you flept.
  Beg. Thefe fifteene yeeres, by my fay, a goodly nap,
But did I neuer fpeake of all that time.
  1.*Man.* Oh yes my Lord, but verie idle words,
For though you lay heere in this goodlie chamber,
Yet would you fay, ye were beaten out of doore,
And raile vpon the Hofteffe of the houfe,
And fay you would prefent her at the Leete,
Becaufe fhe brought ftone-Iugs, and no feal'd quarts :
Sometimes you would call out for Cicely Hacket.
  Beg. I, the womans maide of the houfe.
  3.*man.* Why fir you know no houfe, nor no fuch maid
Nor no fuch men as you haue reckon'd vp,
As *Stephen Slie*, and old *Iohn Naps* of Greece,
And *Peter Turph*, and *Henry Pimpernell*,
And twentie more fuch names and men as thefe,
Which neuer were, nor no man euer faw.
  Beg. Now Lord be thanked for my good amends.
  All. Amen.

     Enter Lady with Attendants.
  Beg. I thanke thee, thou fhalt not loofe by it.
  Lady. How fares my noble Lord ?
  Beg. Marrie I fare well, for heere is cheere enough.
Where is my wife ?
  La. Heere noble Lord, what is thy will with her ?
  Beg. Are you my wife, and will not cal me husband ?
My men fhould call me Lord, I am your good-man.
  La. My husband and my Lord, my Lord and husband
I am your wife in all obedience.
  Beg. I know it well, what muft I call her ?
  Lord. Madam.
  Beg. *Alce* Madam, or *Ione* Madam ?
  Lord. Madam, and nothing elfe, fo Lords cal Ladies
  Beg. Madame wife, they fay that I haue dream'd,
And flept aboue fome fifteene yeare or more.
  Lady. I, and the time feeme's thirty vnto me,
Being all this time abandon'd from your bed.
  Beg. 'Tis much, feruants leaue me and her alone :
Madam vndreffe you, and come now to bed.
  La. Thrice noble Lord, let me intreat of you
To pardon me yet for a night or two :
Or if not fo, vntill the Sun be fet.
For your Phyfitians haue expreffely charg'd,
In perill to incurre your former malady,
That I fhould yet abfent me from your bed :
I hope this reafon ftands for my excufe.
  Beg. I, it ftands fo that I may hardly tarry fo long :
But I would be loth to fall into my dreames againe : I
wil therefore tarrie in defpight of the flefh & the blood

     Enter a Meffenger.
  Mef. Your Honors Players hearing your amendment,
Are come to play a pleafant Comedie,
For fo your doctors hold it very meete,
Seeing too much fadneffe hath congeal'd your blood,
And melancholly is the Nurfe of frenzie,
Therefore they thought it good you heare a play,
And frame your minde to mirth and merriment,
Which barres a thoufand harmes, and lengthens life.
  Beg. Marrie I will let them play, it is not a Comon-

tie, a Chriftmas gambold, or a tumbling tricke?
  Lady. No my good Lord, it is more pleafing ftuffe.
  Beg. What, houfhold ftuffe.
  Lady. It is a a kinde of hiftory.
  Beg. Well, we'l fee't :
Come Madam wife fit by my fide,
And let the world flip, we fhall nere be yonger.

    Flourifh. Enter Lucentio, and his man Triano.
  Luc. *Tranio*, fince for the great defire I had
To fee faire *Padua*, nurferie of Arts,
I am arriu'd for fruitfull *Lumbardie*,
The pleafant garden of great *Italy*,
And by my fathers loue and leaue am arm'd
With his good will, and thy good companie.
My truftie feruant well approu'd in all,
Heere let vs breath, and haply inftitute
A courfe of Learning, and ingenious ftudies.
Pifa renowned for graue Citizens
Gaue me my being, and my father firft
A Merchant of great Trafficke through the world :
Vincentio's come of the *Bentiuolii*,
Vincentio's fonne, brough vp in *Florence*,
It fhall become to ferue all hopes conceiu'd
To decke his fortune with his vertuous deedes :
And therefore *Tranio*, for the time I ftudie,
Vertue and that part of Philofophie
Will I applie, that treats of happineffe,
By vertue fpecially to be atchieu'd.
Tell me thy minde, for I haue *Pifa* left,
And am to *Padua* come, as he that leaues
A fhallow plafh, to plunge him in the deepe,
And with facietie feekes to quench his thirft.
  Tra. *Me Pardonato*, gentle mafter mine :
I am in all affected as your felfe,
Glad that you thus continue your refolue,
To fucke the fweets of fweete Philofophie.
Onely (good mafter) while we do admire
This vertue, and this morall difcipline,
Let's be no Stoickes, nor no ftockes I pray,
Or fo deuote to *Arift*otles checkes
As *Ouid*; be an out-caft quite abiur'd :
Balke Lodgicke with acquaintaince that you haue,
And practife Rhetoricke in your common talke,
Muficke and Poefie vfe, to quicken you ,
The Mathematickes, and the Metaphyfickes
Fall to them as you finde your ftomacke ferues you :
No profit growes, where is no pleafure tane :
In briefe fir, ftudie what you moft affect.
  Luc. Gramercies *Tranio*, well doft thou aduife,
If *Biondello* thou wert come afhore,
We could at once put vs in readineffe,
And take a Lodging fit to entertaine
Such friends (as time) in *Padua* fhall beget.
But ftay a while, what companie is this ?
  Tra. Mafter fome fhew to welcome vs to Towne.

Enter Baptifta with his two daughters, Katerina & Bianca,
  Gremio a Pantelowne, Hortentio fifter to Bianca.
     Lucen. Tranio, ftand by.

  Bap. Gentlemen, importune me no farther,
For how I firmly am refolu'd you know :
That is, not to beftow my yongeft daughter,
Before I haue a husband for the elder :
If either of you both loue *Katherina*,

Becaufe

Becaufe I know you well, and loue you well,
Leaue fhall you haue to court her at your pleafure.

Gre. To cart her rather. She's to rough for mee,
There, there *Hortenfio*, will you any Wife?

Kate. I pray you fir, is it your will
To make a ftale of me amongft thefe mates?

Hor. Mates maid, how meane you that?
No mates for you,
Vnleffe you were of gentler milder mould.

Kate. I'faith fir, you fhall neuer neede to feare,
I-wis it is not halfe way to her heart:
But if it were, doubt not, her care fhould be,
To combe your noddle with a three-legg'd ftoole,
And paint your face, and vfe you like a foole.

Hor. From all fuch diuels, good Lord deliuer vs.

Gre. And me too, good Lord.

Tra. Hufht mafter, heres fome good paftime toward;
That wench is ftarke mad, or wonderfull froward.

Lucen. But in the others filence do I fee,
Maids milde behauiour and fobrietie.
Peace *Tranio.*

Tra. Well faid M*r*, mum, and gaze your fill.

Bap. Gentlemen, that I may foone make good
What I haue faid, *Bianca* get you in,
And let it not difpleafe thee good *Bianca*,
For I will loue thee nere the leffe my girle.

Kate. A pretty peate, it is beft put finger in the eye,
and fhe knew why.

Bian. Sifter content you, in my difcontent.
Sir, to your pleafure humbly I fubfcribe:
My bookes and inftruments fhall be my companie,
On them to looke, and praƈtife by my felfe.

Luc. Harke *Tranio*, thou maift heare *Minerua* fpeak.

Hor. Signior *Baptifta*, will you be fo ftrange,
Sorrie am I that our good will effeƈts
Bianca's greefe.

Gre. Why will you mew her vp
(Signior *Baptifta*) for this fiend of hell,
And make her beare the pennance of her tongue.

Bap. Gentlemen content ye: I am refould:
Go in *Bianca*.
And for I know fhe taketh moft delight
In Muficke, Inftruments, and Poetry,
Schoolemafters will I keepe within my houfe,
Fit to inftruƈt her youth. If you *Hortenfio*,
Or fignior *Gremio* you know any fuch,
Preferre them hither: for to cunning men,
I will be very kinde and liberall,
To mine owne children, in good bringing vp,
And fo farewell: *Katherina* you may ftay,
For I haue more to commune with *Bianca*.   *Exit.*

Kate. Why, and I truft I may go too, may I not?
What fhall I be appointed houres, as though
(Belike) I knew not what to take,
And what to leaue? Ha.   *Exit*

Gre. You may go to the diuels dam: your guifts are
fo good heere's none will holde you: Their loue is not
fo great *Hortenfio*, but we may blow our nails together,
and faft it fairely out. Our cakes dough on both fides.
Farewell: yet for the loue I beare my fweet *Bianca*, if
I can by any meanes light on a fit man to teach her that
wherein fhe delights, I will wifh him to her father.

Hor. So will I figniour *Gremio*: but a word I pray:
Though the nature of our quarrell yet neuer brook'd
parle, know now vpon aduice, it toucheth vs both: that
we may yet againe haue acceffe to our faire Miftris, and

be happie riuals in *Bianca's* loue, to labour and effeƈt
one thing fpecially.

Gre. What's that I pray?

Hor. Marrie fir to get a husband for her Sifter.

Gre. A husband: a diuell.

Hor. I fay a husband.

Gre. I fay, a diuell: Think'ft thou *Hortenfio*, though
her father be verie rich, any man is fo verie a foole to be
married to hell?

Hor. Tufh *Gremio*: though it paffe your patience &
mine to endure her lowd alarums, why man there bee
good fellowes in the world, and a man could light on
them, would take her with all faults, and mony enough.

Gre. I cannot tell: but I had as lief take her dowrie
with this condition; To be whipt at the hie croffe euerie
morning.

Hor. Faith (as you fay) there's fmall choife in rotten
apples: but come, fince this bar in law makes vs friends,
it fhall be fo farre forth friendly maintain'd, till by helping *Baptiftas* eldeft daughter to a husband, wee fet his
yongeft free for a husband, and then haue too t afrefh:
Sweet *Bianca*, happy man be his dole: hee that runnes
fafteft, gets the Ring: How fay you fignior *Gremio*?

Grem. I am agreed, and would I had giuen him the
beft horfe in *Padua* to begin his woing that would thoroughly woe her, wed her, and bed her, and ridde the
houfe of her. Come on.

Exeunt ambo. Manet Tranio and Lucentio

Tra. I pray fir tel me, is it poffible
That loue fhould of a fodaine take fuch hold.

Luc. Oh *Tranio*, till I found it to be true,
I neuer thought it poffible or likely.
But fee, while idely I ftood looking on,
I found the effeƈt of Loue in idleneffe,
And now in plainneffe do confeffe to thee
That art to me as fecret and as deere
As *Anna* to the Queene of Carthage was:
Tranio I burne, I pine, I perifh *Tranio*,
If I atchieue not this yong modeft gyrle:
Counfaile me *Tranio*, for I know thou canft:
Affift me *Tranio*, for I know thou wilt.

Tra. Mafter, it is no time to chide you now,
Affeƈtion is not rated from the heart:
If loue haue touch'd you, naught remaines but fo,
Redime te captam quam queas minimo.

Luc. Gramercies Lad: Go forward, this contents,
The reft will comfort, for thy counfels found.

Tra. Mafter, you look'd fo longly on the maide,
Perhaps you mark'd not what's the pith of all.

Luc. Oh yes, I faw fweet beautie in her face,
Such as the daughter of *Agenor* had,
That made great *Ioue* to humble him to her hand,
When with his knees he kift the Cretan ftrond.

Tra. Saw you no more? Mark'd you not how hir fifter
Began to fcold, and raife vp fuch a ftorme,
That mortal eares might hardly indure the din.

Luc. *Tranio*, I faw her corrall lips to moue,
And with her breath fhe did perfume the ayre,
Sacred and fweet was all I faw in her.

Tra. Nay, then 'tis time to ftirre him frõ his trance:
I pray awake fir: if you loue the Maide,
Bend thoughts and wits to atcheeue her. Thus it ftands:
Her elder fifter is fo curft and fhrew'd,
That til the Father rid his hands of her,
Mafter, your Loue muft liue a maide at home,
And therefore has he clofely meu'd her vp,

Becaufe

Becaufe fhe will not be annoy'd with futers.

Luc. Ah *Tranio,* what a cruell Fathers he :
But art thou not aduis'd, he tooke fome care
To get her cunning Schoolemafters to inftruct her.

Tra. I marry am I fir, and now 'tis plotted.

Luc. I haue it *Tranio.*

Tra. Mafter, for my hand,
Both our inuentions meet and iumpe in one.

Luc. Tell me thine firft.

Tra. You will be fchoole-mafter,
And vndertake the teaching of the maid :
That's your deuice.

Luc. It is : May it be done ?

Tra. Not poffible : for who fhall beare your part,
And be in *Padua* heere *Vincentio's* fonne,
Keepe houfe, and ply his booke, welcome his friends,
Vifit his Countrimen, and banquet them ?

Luc. *Bafta,* content thee : for I haue it full.
We haue not yet bin feene in any houfe,
Nor can we be diftinguifh'd by our faces,
For man or mafter : then it followes thus ;
Thou fhalt be mafter, *Tranio* in my fted :
Keepe houfe, and port, and feruants, as I fhould,
I will fome other be, fome *Florentine,*
Some *Neapolitan,* or meaner man of *Pifa.*
'Tis hatch'd, and fhall be fo : *Tranio* at once
Vncafe thee : take my Conlord hat and cloake,
When *Biondello* comes, he waites on thee,
But I will charme him firft to keepe his tongue.

Tra. So had you neede :
In breefe Sir, fith it your pleafure is,
And I am tyed to be obedient,
For fo your father charg'd me at our parting ?
Be feruiceable to my fonne (quoth he)
Although I thinke 'twas in another fence,
I am content to bee *Lucentio,*
Becaufe fo well I loue *Lucentio.*

Luc. *Tranio* be fo, becaufe *Lucentio* loues,
And let me be a flaue, t'atchieue that maide,
Whofe fodaine fight hath thral'd my wounded eye.

Enter *Biondello.*

Heere comes the rogue. Sirra, where haue you bin ?

Bion. Where haue I beene ? Nay how now, where
are you ? Maifter, ha's my fellow *Tranio* ftolne your
cloathes, or you ftolne his, or both ? Pray what's the
newes?

Luc. Sirra come hither, 'tis no time to ieft,
And therefore frame your manners to the time
Your fellow *Tranio* heere to faue my life,
Puts my apparrell, and my count'nance on,
And I for my efcape haue put on his :
For in a quarrell fince I came a fhore,
I kil'd a man, and feare I was defcried :
Waite you on him, I charge you, as becomes :
While I make way from hence to faue my life :
You vnderftand me ?

Bion. I fir, ne're a whit.

Luc. And not a iot of *Tranio* in your mouth,
Tranio is chang'd into *Lucentio.*

Bion. The better for him, would I were fo too.

Tra. So could I 'faith boy, to haue the next wifh after, that *Lucentio* indeede had *Baptiftas* yongeft daughter. But firra, not for my fake, but your mafters, I aduife you vfe your manners difcreetly in all kind of com-
panies : When I am alone, why then I am *Tranio* : but in

all places elfe, you mafter *Lucentio.*

Luc. *Tranio* let's go :
One thing more refts, that thy felfe execute,
To make one among thefe wooers : if thou ask me why,
Sufficeth my reafons are both good and waighty.

Exeunt. *The Prefenters aboue fpeakes.*

1. *Man.* My Lord you nod, you do not minde the
play.

Beg. Yes by Saint Anne do I, a good matter furely :
Comes there any more of it ?

Lady. My Lord, 'tis but begun.

Beg. 'Tis a verie excellent peece of worke, Madame
Ladie : would 'twere done.   *They fit and marke.*

Enter *Petruchio, and his man Grumio.*

Petr. *Verona,* for a while I take my leaue,
To fee my friends in *Padua* ; but of all
My beft beloued and approued friend
Hortenfio : & I trow this is his houfe :
Heere firra *Grumio,* knocke I fay.

Gru. Knocke fir ? whom fhould I knocke ? Is there
any man ha's rebus'd your worfhip ?

Petr. Villaine I fay, knocke me heere foundly.

Gru. Knocke you heere fir ? Why fir, what am I fir,
that I fhould knocke you heere fir.

Petr. Villaine I fay, knocke me at this gate,
And rap me well, or Ile knocke your knaues pate.

Gru. My Mr is growne quarrelfome :
I fhould knocke you firft,
And then I know after who comes by the worft.

Petr. Will it not be ?
'Faith firrah, and you'l not knocke, Ile ring it,
Ile trie how you can *Sol, Fa,* and fing it.

He rings him by the eares

Gru. Helpe miftris helpe, my mafter is mad.

Petr. Now knocke when I bid you : firrah villaine.

Enter *Hortenfio.*

Hor. How now, what's the matter? My olde friend
Grumio, and my good friend *Petruchio* ? How do you all
at *Verona* ?

Petr. Signior *Hortenfio,* come you to part the fray ?
Contutti le core bene trobatto, may I fay.

Hor. *Alla noftra cafa bene venuto multo honorata figni-
or mio Petruchio.*

Rife *Grumio* rife, we will compound this quarrell.

Gru. Nay 'tis no matter fir, what he leges in Latine.
If this be not a lawfull caufe for me to leaue his feruice,
looke you fir : He bid me knocke him, & rap him foundly fir. Well, was it fit for a feruant to vfe his mafter fo,
being perhaps (for ought I fee) two and thirty, a peepe
out ? Whom would to God I had well knockt at firft,
then had not *Grumio* come by the worft.

Petr. A fenceleffe villaine : good *Hortenfio,*
I bad the rafcall knocke vpon your gate,
And could not get him for my heart to do it.

Gru. Knocke at the gate? O heauens ! fpake you not
thefe words plaine ? Sirra, Knocke me heere : rappe me
heere : knocke me well, and knocke me foundly ? And
come you now with knocking at the gate ?

Petr. Sirra be gone, or talke not I aduife you.

Hor. *Petruchio* patience, I am *Grumio's* pledge :
Why this a heauie chance twixr him and you,
Your ancient truftie pleafant feruant *Grumio* :
And tell me now (fweet friend) what happie gale
Blowes you to *Padua* heere, from old *Verona* ?

Petr. Such wind as fcatters yongmen throgh ÿ world,

To

To feeke their fortunes farther then at home,
Where fmall experience growes but in a few.
Signior *Hortenfio*, thus it ftands with me,
Antonio my father is deceaft,
And I haue thruſt my ſelfe into this maze,
Happily to wiue and thriue, as beſt I may:
Crownes in my purſe I haue, and goods at home,
And ſo am come abroad to ſee the world.

Hor. *Petrucbio*, ſhall I then come roundly to thee,
And wiſh thee to a ſhrew'd ill-fauour'd wife?
Thou'dſt thanke me but a little for my counſell:
And yet Ile promiſe thee ſhe ſhall be rich,
And verie rich: but th'art too much my friend,
And Ile not wiſh thee to her.

Petr. Signior *Hortenfio*, 'twixt ſuch friends as wee,
Few words ſuffice: and therefore, if thou know
One rich enough to be *Petruchio's* wife:
(As wealth is burthen of my woing dance)
Be ſhe as foule as was *Florentius* Loue,
As old as *Sibell*, and as curſt and ſhrow'd
As *Socrates Zentippe*, or a worſe:
She moues me not, or not remoues at leaſt
Affections edge in me. Were ſhe is as rough
As are the ſwelling *Adriaticke* ſeas.
I come to wiue it wealthily in *Padua*:
If wealthily, then happily in *Padua*.

Gru. Nay looke you ſir, hee tels you flatly what his
minde is: why giue him Gold enough, and marrie him
to a Puppet or an Aglet babie, or an old trot with ne're a
tooth in her head, though ſhe haue as manie diſeaſes as
two and fiftie horſes. Why nothing comes amiſſe, ſo
monie comes withall.

Hor. *Petrucbio*, ſince we are ſtept thus farre in,
I will continue that I broach'd in ieſt,
I can *Petruchio* helpe thee to a wife
With wealth enough, and yong and beautious,
Brought vp as beſt becomes a Gentlewoman.
Her onely fault, and that is faults enough,
Is, that ſhe is intollerable curſt,
And ſhrow'd, and froward, ſo beyond all meaſure,
That were my ſtate farre worſer then it is,
I would not wed her for a mine of Gold.

Petr. *Hortenfio* peace: thou knowſt not golds effect,
Tell me her fathers name, and 'tis enough:
For I will boord her, though ſhe chide as loud
As thunder, when the clouds in Autumne cracke.

Hor. Her father is *Baptiſta* *Minola*,
An affable and courteous Gentleman,
Her name is *Katherina Minola*,
Renown'd in *Padua* for her ſcolding tongue.

Petr. I know her father, though I know not her,
And he knew my deceaſed father well:
I will not ſleepe *Hortenfio* til I ſee her,
And therefore let me be thus bold with you,
To giue you ouer at this firſt encounter,
Vnleſſe you wil accompanie me thither.

Gru. I pray you Sir let him go while the humor laſts.
A my word, and ſhe knew him as wel as I do, ſhe would
thinke ſcolding would doe little good vpon him. Shee
may perhaps call him halfe a ſcore Knaues, or ſo: Why
that's nothing; and he begin once, hee'l raile in his rope
trickes. Ile tell you what ſir, and ſhe ſtand him but a litle, he wil throw a figure in her face, and ſo disfigure hir
with it, that ſhee ſhal haue no more eies to ſee withall
then a Cat: you know him not ſir.

Hor. Tarrie *Petruchio*, I muſt go with thee,

For in *Baptiſtas* keepe my treaſure is:
He hath the Iewel of my life in hold,
His yongeſt daughter, beautiful *Bianca*,
And her with-holds from me. Other more
Suters to her, and riuals in my Loue:
Suppofing it a thing impoſſible,
For thoſe defects I haue before rehearſt,
That euer *Katherina* wil be woo'd:
Therefore this order hath *Baptiſta* tane,
That none ſhal haue acceſſe vnto *Bianca*,
Til *Katherine* the Curſt, haue got a husband.

Gru. *Katherine* the curſt,
A title for a maide, of all titles the worſt.

Hor. Now ſhal my friend *Petruchio* do me grace,
And offer me disguis'd in ſober robes,
To old *Baptiſta* as a ſchoole-maſter
Well ſeene in Muficke, to inſtruct *Bianca*,
That ſo I may by this deuice at leaſt
Haue leaue and leiſure to make loue to her,
And vnſuſpected court her by her ſelfe.

Enter Gremio and Lucentio disguis'd.

Gru. Heere's no knauerie. See, to beguile the olde-
folkes, how the young folkes lay their heads together.
Maſter, maſter, looke about you: Who goes there? ha.

Hor. Peace *Grumio*, it is the riuall of my Loue.

Petruchio ſtand by a while.

Grumio. A proper ſtripling, and an amorous.

Gremio. O very well, I haue perus'd the note:
Hearke you ſir, Ile haue them verie fairely bound,
All bookes of Loue, ſee that at any hand,
And ſee you reade no other Lectures to her:
You vnderſtand me. Ouer and beſide
Signior *Baptiſtas* liberalitie,
Ile mend it with a Largeſſe. Take your paper too,
And let me haue them verie wel perfum'd;
For ſhe is ſweeter then perfume it ſelfe
To whom they go to: what wil you reade to her.

Luc. What ere I reade to her, Ile pleade for you,
As for my patron, ſtand you ſo aſſur'd,
As firmely as your ſelfe were ſtill in place,
Yea and perhaps with more ſucceſſefull words
Then you; vnleſſe you were a ſcholler ſir.

Gre. Oh this learning, what a thing it is.

Gru. Oh this Woodcocke, what an Aſſe it is.

Petru. Peace ſirra.

Hor. *Grumio* mum: God ſaue you ſignior *Gremio*.

Gre. And you are wel met, Signior *Hortenfio*.
Trow you whither I am going? To *Baptiſta Minola*,
I promiſt to enquire carefully
About a ſchoolemaſter for the faire *Bianca*,
And by good fortune I haue lighted well
On this yong man: For learning and behauiour
Fit for her turne, well read in Poetrie
And other bookes, good ones, I warrant ye.

Hor. 'Tis well: and I haue met a Gentleman
Hath promiſt me to helpe one to another,
A fine Muſitian to inſtruct our Miſtris,
So ſhal I no whit be behinde in dutie
To faire *Bianca*, ſo beloued of me.

Gre. Beloued of me, and that my deeds ſhal proue.

Gru. And that his bags ſhal proue.

Hor. *Gremio*, 'tis now no time to vent our loue,
Liſten to me, and if you ſpeake me faire,
Ile tel you newes indifferent good for either.
Heere is a Gentleman whom by chance I met

Vpon

Vpon agreement from vs to his liking,
Will vndertake to woo curſt *Katherine*,
Yea, and to marrie her, if her dowrie pleaſe.
  Gre. So ſaid, ſo done, is well :
Hortenſio, haue you told him all her faults ?
  Petr. I know ſhe is an irkeſome brawling ſcold :
If that be all Maſters, I heare no harme.
  Gre. No, ſayſt me ſo, friend ? What Countreyman ?
  Petr. Borne in *Verona*, old *Butonios* ſonne :
My father dead, my fortune liues for me,
And I do hope, good dayes and long, to ſee.
  Gre. Oh ſir, ſuch a life with ſuch a wife, were ſtrange:
But if you haue a ſtomacke, too't a Gods name,
You ſhal haue me aſſiſting you in all.
But will you woo this Wilde-cat ?
  Petr. Will I liue ?
  Gru. Wil he woo her ? I : or Ile hang her.
  Petr. Why came I hither, but to that intent ?
Thinke you, a little dinne can daunt mine eares ?
Haue I not in my time heard Lions rore ?
Haue I not heard the ſea, puſt vp with windes,
Rage like an angry Boare, chafed with ſweat ?
Haue I not heard great Ordnance in the field?
And heauens Artillerie thunder in the skies ?
Haue I not in a pitched battell heard
Loud larums, neighing ſteeds, & trumpets clangue ?
And do you tell me of a womans tongue ?
That giues not halfe ſo great a blow to heare,
As wil a Cheſſe-nut in a Farmers fire.
Tuſh, tuſh, feare boyes with bugs.
  Gru. For he feares none.
  Grem. *Hortenſio* hearke :
This Gentleman is happily arriu'd,
My minde preſumes for his owne good, and yours.
  Hor. I promiſt we would be Contributors,
And beare his charge of wooing whatſoere.
  Gremio. And ſo we wil, prouided that he win her.
  Gru. I would I were as ſure of a good dinner.

Enter *Tranio* braue, and *Biondello*.

  Tra. Gentlemen God ſaue you. If I may be bold
Tell me I beſeech you, which is the readieſt way
To the houſe of Signior *Baptiſta Minola* ?
  Bion. He that ha's the two faire daughters: iſt he you
meane ?
  Tra. Euen he *Biondello*.
  Gre. Hearke you ſir, you meane not her to———
  Tra. Perhaps him and her ſir, what haue you to do ?
  Petr. Not her that chides ſir, at any hand I pray.
  Tranio. I loue no chiders ſir : *Biondello*, let's away.
  Luc Well begun *Tranio*.
  Hor. Sir, a word ere you goe:
Are you a ſutor to the Maid you talke of, yea or no ?
  Tra. And if I be ſir, is it any offence ?
  Gremio. No : if without more words you will get you
hence.
  Tra. Why ſir, I pray are not the ſtreers as free
For me, as for you ?
  Gre. But ſo is not ſhe.
  Tra. For what reaſon I beſeech you.
  Gre. For this reaſon if you'l kno,
That ſhe's the choiſe loue of Signior *Gremio*.
  Hor. That ſhe's the choſen of ſignior *Hortenſio*.
  Tra. Softly my Maſters : If you be Gentlemen
Do me this right : heare me with patience.
Baptiſta is a noble Gentleman,

To whom my Father is not all vnknowne,
And were his daughter fairer then ſhe is,
She may more ſutors haue, and me for one.
Faire *Lædaes* daughter had a thouſand wooers,
Then well one more may faire *Bianca* haue ;
And ſo ſhe ſhall : *Lucentio* ſhal make one,
Though *Paris* came, in hope to ſpeed alone.
  Gre. What, this Gentleman will out-talke vs all.
  Luc. Sir giue him head, I know hee'l proue a Iade.
  Petr. *Hortenſio*, to what end are all theſe words ?
  Hor. Sir, let me be ſo bold as aske you,
Did you yet euer ſee *Baptiſtas* daughter ?
  Tra. No ſir, but heare I do that he hath two :
The one, as famous for a ſcolding tongue,
As is the other, for beauteous modeſtie.
  Petr. Sir, ſir, the firſt's for me, let her go by.
  Gre. Yea, leaue that labour to great *Hercules*,
And let it be more then *Alcides* twelue.
  Petr. Sir vnderſtand you this of me (inſooth)
The yongeſt daughter whom you hearken for,
Her father keepes from all acceſſe of ſutors,
And will not promiſe her to any man,
Vntill the elder ſiſter firſt be wed.
The yonger then is free, and not before.
  Tranio. If it be ſo ſir, that you are the man
Muſt ſteed vs all, and me amongſt the reſt :
And if you breake the ice, and do this ſeeke,
Atchieue the elder : ſet the yonger free,
For our acceſſe, whoſe hap ſhall be to haue her,
Wil not ſo graceleſſe be, to be ingrate.
  Hor. Sir you ſay wel, and wel you do conceiue,
And ſince you do profeſſe to be a ſutor,
You muſt as we do, gratifie this Gentleman,
To whom we all reſt generally beholding.
  Tranio. Sir, I ſhal not be ſlacke, in ſigne whereof,
Pleaſe ye we may contriue this afternoone,
And quaffe carowſes to our Miſtreſſe health,
And do as aduerſaries do in law,
Striue mightily, but eate and drinke as friends.
  Gru. Bion. Oh excellent motion: fellowes let's be gon.
  Hor. The motions good indeed, and be it ſo,
Petruchio, I ſhal be your *Been venuto*.   *Exeunt.*

Enter *Katherina* and *Bianca*.

  Bian. Good ſiſter wrong me not, nor wrong your ſelf,
To make a bondmaide and a ſlaue of mee,
That I diſdaine : but for theſe other goods,
Vnbinde my hands, Ile pull them off my ſelfe,
Yea all my raiment, to my petticoate,
Or what you will command me, wil I do,
So well I know my dutie to my elders.
  Kate. Of all thy ſutors heere I charge tel
Whom thou lou'ſt beſt : ſee thou diſſemble not.
  Bianca. Beleeue me ſiſter, of all the men aliue,
I neuer yet beheld that ſpeciall face,
Which I could fancie, more then any other.
  Kate. Minion thou lyeſt : Is't not *Hortenſio* ?
  Bian. If you affect him ſiſter, heere I ſweare
Ile pleade for you my ſelfe, but you ſhal haue him.
  Kate. Oh then belike you fancie riches more,
You wil haue *Gremio* to keepe you faire.
  Bian. Is it for him you do enuie me ſo ?
Nay then you ieſt, and now I wel perceiue
You haue but ieſted with me all this while :
I prethee ſiſter Kate, vntie my hands.
  Ka. If that be ieſt, then all the reſt was ſo.   *Strikes her*
                                                                    Enter

Enter Baptista.

Bap. Why how now Dame, whence growes this infolence?
Bianca ftand afide, poore gyrle fhe weepes:
Go ply thy Needle, meddle not with her.
For fhame thou Hilding of a diuellifh fpirit,
Why doft thou wrong her, that did nere wrong thee?
When did fhe croffe thee with a bitter word?
Kate. Her filence flouts me, and Ile be reueng'd.

Flies after Bianca

Bap. What in my fight? *Bianca* get thee in.   *Exit.*
Kate. What will you not fuffer me: Nay now I fee
She is your treafure, fhe muft haue a husband,
I muft dance bare-foot on her wedding day,
And for your loue to her, leade Apes in hell.
Talke not to me, I will go fit and weepe,
Till I can finde occafion of reuenge.

Bap. Was euer Gentleman thus greeu'd as I?
But who comes heere.

*Enter Gremio, Lucentio, in the habit of a meane man,
Petruchio with Tranio, with his boy
bearing a Lute and Bookes.*

Gre. Good morrow neighbour *Baptifta.*
Bap. Good morrow neighbour *Gremio:* God faue you Gentlemen.
Pet. And you good fir: pray haue you not a daughter, cal'd *Katerina,* faire and vertuous.
Bap. I haue a daughter fir, cal'd *Katerina.*
Gre. You are too blunt, go to it orderly.
Pet. You wrong me fignior *Gremio,* giue me leaue.
I am a Gentleman of *Verona* fir,
That hearing of her beautie, and her wit,
Her affability and bafhfull modeftie:
Her wondrous qualities, and milde behauiour,
Am bold to fhew my felfe a forward gueft
Within your houfe, to make mine eye the witneffe
Of that report, which I fo oft haue heard,
And for an entrance to my entertainment,
I do prefent you with a man of mine
Cunning in Muficke, and the Mathematickes,
To inftruct her fully in thofe fciences,
Whereof I know fhe is not ignorant,
Accept of him, or elfe you do me wrong,
His name is *Litio,* borne in *Mantua.*
Bap. Y'are welcome fir, and he for your good fake.
But for my daughter *Katerine,* this I know,
She is not for your turne, the more my greefe.
Pet. I fee you do not meane to part with her,
Or elfe you like not of my companie.
Bap. Miftake me not, I fpeake but as I finde,
Whence are you fir? What may I call your name.
Pet. *Petruchio* is my name, *Antonio's* fonne,
A man well knowne throughout all Italy.
Bap. I know him well: you are welcome for his fake.
Gre. Sauing your tale *Petruchio,* I pray let vs that are poore petitioners fpeake too? *Bacare,* you are meruaylous forward.
Pet. Oh, Pardon me fignior *Gremio,* I would faine be doing.
Gre. I doubt it not fir. But you will curfe Your wooing neighbors: this is a guift Very gratefull, I am fure of it, to expreffe The like kindneffe my felfe, that haue beene More kindely beholding to you then any:

Freely giue vnto this yong Scholler, that hath
Beene long ftudying at *Rbemes,* as cunning
In Greeke, Latine, and other Languages,
As the other in Muficke and Mathematickes:
His name is *Cambio:* pray accept his feruice.
Bap. A thoufand thankes fignior *Gremio:*
Welcome good *Cambio.* But gentle fir,
Me thinkes you walke like a ftranger,
May I be fo bold, to know the caufe of your comming?
Tra. Pardon me fir, the boldneffe is mine owne,
That being a ftranger in this Cittie heere,
Do make my felfe af utor to your daughter,
Vnto *Bianca,* faire and vertuous:
Nor is your firme refolue vnknowne to me,
In the preferment of the eldeft fifter.
This liberty is all that I requeft,
That vpon knowledge of my Parentage,
I may haue welcome 'mongft the reft that woo,
And free acceffe and fauour as the reft.
And toward the education of your daughters:
I heere beftow a fimple inftrument,
And this fmall packet of Greeke and Latine bookes:
If you accept them, then their worth is great:
Bap. *Lucentio* is your name, of whence I pray.
Tra. Of *Pifa* fir, fonne to *Vincentio.*
Bap. A mightie man of *Pifa* by report,
I know him well: you are verie welcome fir:
Take you the Lute, and you the fet of bookes,
You fhall go fee your Pupils prefently.
Holla, within.

Enter a Seruant.

Sirrah, leade thefe Gentlemen
To my daughters, and tell them both
Thefe are their Tutors, bid them vfe them well,
We will go walke a little in the Orchard,
And then to dinner: you are paffing welcome,
And fo I pray you all to thinke your felues.
Pet. Signior *Baptifta,* my bufineffe asketh hafte,
And euerie day I cannot come to woo,
You knew my father well, and in him me,
Left folie heire to all his Lands and goods,
Which I haue bettered rather then decreaft,
Then tell me, if I get your daughters loue,
What dowrie fhall I haue with her to wife.
Bap. After my death, the one halfe of my Lands,
And in poffeffion twentie thoufand Crownes.
Pet And for that dowrie, Ile affure her of
Her widdow-hood, be it that fhe furuiue me
In all my Lands and Leafes whatfoeuer,
Let fpecialties be therefore drawne betweene vs,
That couenants may be kept on either hand.
Bap. I, when the fpeciall thing is well obtain'd,
That is her loue: for that is all in all.
Pet. Why that is nothing: for I tell you father,
I am as peremptorie as fhe proud minded:
And where two raging fires meete together,
They do confume the thing that feedes their furie.
Though little fire growes great with little winde,
yet extreme gufts will blow out fire and all:
So I to her, and fo fhe yeelds to me,
For I am rough, and woo not like a babe.
Bap. Well maift thou woo, and happy be thy fpeed:
But be thou arm'd for fome vnhappie words.
Pet. I to the proofe, as Mountaines are for windes,
That fhakes not, though they blow perpetually.

Enter Hortenfio with his head broke.

B pa.

Bap. How now my friend, why doſt thou looke ſo
pale ?

Hor. For feare I promiſe you, if I looke pale.

Bap. What, will my daughter proue a good Muſitian ?

Hor. I thinke ſhe'l ſooner proue a ſouldier,
Iron may hold with her, but neuer Lutes.

Bap. Why then thou canſt not break her to the Lute?

Hor. Why no, for ſhe hath broke the Lute to me :
I did but tell her ſhe miſtooke her frets,
And bow'd her hand to teach her fingering,
When (with a moſt impatient diuelliſh ſpirit)
Frets call you theſe? (quoth ſhe) Ile fume with them :
And with that word ſhe ſtroke me on the head,
And through the inſtrument my pate made way,
And there I ſtood amazed for a while,
As on a Pillorie, looking through the Lute,
While ſhe did call me Raſcall, Fidler,
And twangling Iacke, with twentie ſuch vilde tearmes,
As had ſhe ſtudied to miſvſe me ſo.

Pet. Now by the world, it is a luſtie Wench,
I loue her ten times more then ere I did,
Oh how I long to haue ſome chat with her.

Bap. Wel go with me, and be not ſo diſcomfited.
Proceed in practiſe with my yonger daughter,
She's apt to learne, and thankefull for good turnes :
Signior *Petruchio*, will you go with vs,
Or ſhall I ſend my daughter *Kate* to you.

       Exit. Manet Petruchio.

Pet. I pray you do. Ile attend her heere,
And woo her with ſome ſpirit when ſhe comes,
Say that ſhe raile, why then Ile tell her plaine,
She ſings as ſweetly as a Nightinghale :
Say that ſhe frowne, Ile ſay ſhe lookes as cleere
As morning Roſes newly waſht with dew :
Say ſhe be mute, and will not ſpeake a word,
Then Ile commend her volubility,
And ſay ſhe vttereth piercing eloquence :
If ſhe do bid me packe, Ile giue her thankes,
As though ſhe bid me ſtay by her a weeke :
If ſhe denie to wed, Ile craue the day
When I ſhall aske the banes, and when be married.
But heere ſhe comes, and now *Petruchio* ſpeake.

       Enter Katerina.

Good morrow *Kate*, for thats your name I heare.

Kate. Well haue you heard, but ſomething hard of
hearing :
They call me *Katerine*, that do talke of me.

Pet. You lye infaith, for you are call'd plaine *Kate*,
And bony *Kate*, and ſometimes *Kate* the curſt :
But *Kate*, the prettieſt *Kate* in Chriſtendome,
Kate of *Kate*-hall, my ſuper-daintie *Kate*,
For dainties are all *Kates*, and therefore *Kate*
Take this of me, *Kate* of my conſolation,
Hearing thy mildneſſe prais'd in euery Towne,
Thy vertues ſpoke of, and thy beautie ſounded,
Yet not ſo deepely as to thee belongs,
My ſelfe am moou'd to woo thee for my wife.

Kate. Mou'd, in good time, let him that mou'd you
hether
Remoue you hence : I knew you at the firſt
You were a mouable.

Pet. Why, what's a mouable ?

Kat. A ioyn'd ſtoole.

Pet. Thou haſt hit it : come ſit on me.

Kate. Aſſes are made to beare, and ſo are you.

Pet. Women are made to beare, and ſo are you.

Kate. No ſuch Iade as you, if me you meane.

Pet. Alas good *Kate*, I will not burthen thee,
For knowing thee to be but yong and light.

Kate. Too light for ſuch a ſwaine as you to catch,
And yet as heauie as my waight ſhould be.

Pet. Shold be, ſhould : buzze.

Kate. Well tane, and like a buzzard.

Pet. Oh ſlow-wing'd Turtle, ſhal a buzard take thee?

Kat. I for a Turtle, as he takes a buzard.

Pet. Come, come you Waſpe, y'faith you are too
angrie.

Kate. If I be waſpiſh, beſt beware my ſting.

Pet. My remedy is then to plucke it out.

Kate. I, if the foole could finde it where it lies.

Pet. Who knowes not where a Waſpe does weare
his ſting ? In his taile.

Kate. In his tongue ?

Pet. Whoſe tongue.

Kate. Yours if you talke of tales, and ſo farewell.

Pet. What with my tongue in your taile.
Nay, come againe, good *Kate*, I am a Gentleman,

Kate. That Ile trie.   *ſhe ſtrikes him*

Pet. I ſweare Ile cuffe you, if you ſtrike againe.

Kate. So may you looſe your armes,
If you ſtrike me, you are no Gentleman,
And if no Gentleman, why then no armes.

Pet. A Herald *Kate*? Oh put me in thy bookes.

Kate. What is your Creſt, a Coxcombe?

Pet. A combleſſe Cocke, ſo *Kate* will be my Hen.

Kate. No Cocke of mine, you crow too like a crauen

Pet. Nay come *Kate*, come : you muſt not looke ſo
ſowre.

Kate. It is my faſhion when I ſee a Crab.

Pet. Why heere's no crab, and therefore looke not
ſowre.

Kate. There is, there is.

Pet. Then ſhew it me.

Kate. Had I a glaſſe, I would.

Pet. What, you meane my face.

Kate. Well aym'd of ſuch a yong one.

Pet. Now by S. George I am too yong for you.

Kate. Yet you are wither'd.

Pet. 'Tis with cares.

Kate. I care not.

Pet. Nay heare you *Kate*. Inſooth you ſcape not ſo.

Kate. I chafe you if I tarrie. Let me go.

Pet. No, not a whit, I finde you paſſing gentle :
'Twas told me you were rough, and coy, and ſullen,
And now I finde report a very liar :
For thou art pleaſant, gameſome, paſſing courteous,
But ſlow in ſpeech : yet ſweet as ſpring-time flowers.
Thou canſt not frowne, thou canſt not looke a ſconce,
Nor bite the lip, as angry wenches will,
Nor haſt thou pleaſure to be croſſe in talke :
But thou with mildneſſe entertain'ſt thy wooers,
With gentle conference, ſoft, and affable.
Why does the world report that *Kate* doth limpe ?
Oh ſland'rous world : *Kate* like the hazle twig
Is ſtraight, and ſlender, and as browne in hue
As hazle nuts, and ſweeter then the kernels :
Oh let me ſee thee walke : thou doſt not halt.

Kate. Go foole, and whom thou keep'ſt commaud.

Pet. Did euer *Dian* ſo become a Groue
As *Kate* this chamber with her princely gate :
O be thou *Dian*, and let her be *Kate*,

                      And

And then let *Kate* be chafte, and *Dian* fportfull.
Kate. Where did you ftudy all this goodly fpeech?
Petr. It is *extempore*, from my mother wit.
Kate. A witty mother, witleffe elfe her fonne.
Pet. Am I not wife?
Kat. Yes, keepe you warme.
Pet. Marry fo I meane fweet *Katherine* in thy bed :
And therefore fetting all this chat afide,
Thus in plaine termes : your father hath confented
That you fhall be my wife ; your dowry 'greed on,
And will you, nill you, I will marry you.
Now *Kate*, I am a husband for your turne,
For by this light, whereby I fee thy beauty,
Thy beauty that doth make me like thee well,
Thou muft be married to no man but me,

Enter Baptifta, Gremio, Trayno.

For I am he am borne to tame you *Kate*,
And bring you from a wilde *Kate* to a *Kate*
Conformable as other houfhold *Kates*:
Heere comes your father, neuer make deniall ,
I muft, and will haue *Katherine* to my wife. (daughter?
Bap. Now Signior *Petruchio*, how fpeed you with my
Pet. How but well fit?how but well?
It were impoffible I fhould fpeede amiffe. (dumps?
Bap. Why how now daughter *Katherine* , in your
Kat. Call you me daughter? now I promife you
You haue fhewd a tender fatherly regard,
To wifh me wed to one halfe Lunaticke,
A mad-cap ruffian, and a fwearing Iacke,
That thinkes with oathes to face the matter out.
Pet. Father, 'tis thus, your felfe and all the world
That talk'd of her, haue talk'd amiffe of her :
If fhe be curft, it is for pollicie ,
For fhee's not froward, but modeft as the Doue,
Shee is not hot, but temperate as the morne ,
For patience fhee will proue a fecond *Griffell*,
And Romane *Lucrece* for her chaftitie :
And to conclude, we haue 'greed fo well together ,
That vpon fonday is the wedding day.
Kate. Ile fee thee hang'd on fonday firft. (firft.
Gre. Hark *Petruchio*, fhe faies fhee'll fee thee hang'd
Tra. Is this your fpeeding? nay the godnight our part.
Pet. Be patient gentlemen, I choofe her for my felfe,
If fhe and I be pleas'd, what's that to you?
'Tis bargain'd 'twixt vs twaine being alone ,
That fhe fhall ftill be curft in company.
I tell you 'tis incredible to beleeue
How much fhe loues me : oh the kindeft *Kate*,
Shee hung about my necke, and kiffe on kiffe
Shee vi'd fo faft, protefting oath on oath ,
That in a twinke fhe won me to her loue.
Oh you are nouices, 'tis a world to fee
How tame when men and women are alone,
A meacocke wretch can make the curfteft fhrew :
Giue me thy hand *Kate*, I will vnto *Venice*
To buy apparell 'gainft the wedding day ;
Prouide the feaft father, and bid the guefts,
I will be fure my *Katherine* fhall be fine.
Bap. I know not what to fay, but giue me your hads,
God fend you ioy, *Petruchio*, 'tis a match.
Gre.Tra. Amen fay we, we will be witneffes.
Pet. Father, and wife, and gentlemen adieu,
I will to *Venice*, fonday comes apace,
We will haue rings, and things, and fine array,

And kiffe me *Kate*, we will be married a fonday.
      Exit Petrucbio and Katherine.
Gre. Was euer match clapt vp fo fodainly?
Bap. Faith Gentlemen now I play a marchants part,
And venture madly on a defperate Mart.
Tra. Twas a commodity lay fretting by you,
'Twill bring you gaine, or perifh on the feas.
Bap. The gaine I feeke, is quiet me the match.
Gre. No doubt but he hath got a quiet catch:
But now *Baptifta*, to your yonger daughter,
Now is the day we long haue looked for,
I am your neighbour, and was futer firft.
Tra. And I am one that loue *Bianca* more
Then words can witneffe, or your thoughts can gueffe.
Gre. Yongling thou canft not loue fo deare as I.
Tra. Gray-beard thy loue doth freeze.
Gre. But thine doth frie,
Skipper ftand backe, 'tis age that nourifheth.
Tra. But youth in Ladies eyes that florifheth.
Bap. Content you gentlemen, I wil copound this ftrife
'Tis deeds muft win the prize, and he of both
That can affure my daughter greateft dower,
Shall haue my *Biancas* loue.
Say fignior *Gremio*, what can you affure her?
Gre. Firft, as you know, my houfe within the City
Is richly furnifhed with plate and gold,
Bafons and ewers to laue her dainty hands,
My hangings all of *tirian* tapeftry :
In Iuory cofers I haue ftuft my crownes :
In Cypres chefts my arras counterpoints,
Coftly apparell, tents, and Canopies,
Fine Linnen, Turky cufhions boft with pearle,
Vallens of *Venice* gold, in needle worke :
Pewter and braffe, and all things that belongs
To houfe or houfe-keeping : then at my farme
I haue a hundred milch-kine to the pale,
Sixe-fcore fat Oxen ftanding in my ftalls,
And all things anfwerable to this portion.
My felfe am ftrooke in yeeres I muft confeffe ,
And if I die to morrow this is hers,
If whil'ft I liue fhe will be onely mine.
Tra. That onely came well in : fir, lift to me,
I am my fathers heyre and onely fonne,
If I may haue your daughter to my wife,
Ile leaue her houfes three or foure as good
Within rich *Pifa* walls, as any one
Old Signior *Gremio* has in *Padua*,
Befides, two thoufand Duckets by the yeere
Of fruitfull land, all which fhall be her ioynter.
What, haue I pincht you Signior *Gremio*?
Gre. Two thoufand Duckets by the yeere of land,
My Land amounts not to fo much in all :
That fhe fhall haue, befides an Argofie
That now is lying in Marcellus roade :
What, haue I choakt you with an Argofie?
Tra. *Gremio*, 'tis knowne my father hath no leffe
Then three great Argofies, befides two Galliaffes
And twelue tite Gallies, thefe I will affure her,
And twice as much what are thou offreft next.
Gre. Nay, I haue offred all, I haue no more,
And fhe can haue no more then all I haue ,
If you like me, fhe fhall haue me and mine.
Tra. Why then the maid is mine from all the world
By your firme promife, *Gremio* is out-vied.
Bap. I muft confeffe your offer is the beft,
And let your father make her the affurance,

                      T   Shee

Shee is your owne, elfe you muſt pardon me:
If you ſhould die before him, where's her dower?
  Tra. That's but a cauill: he is olde, I young.
  Gre. And may not yong men die as well as old?
  Bap. Well gentlemen, I am thus refolu'd,
On ſonday next, you know
My daughter *Katherine* is to be married:
Now on the ſonday following, ſhall *Bianca*
Be Bride to you, if you make this aſſurance:
If not, to Signior *Gremio*:
And ſo I take my leaue, and thanke you both.   *Exit.*
  Gre. Adieu good neighbour: now I feare thee not:
Sirra, yong gameſter, your father were a foole
To giue thee all, and in his wayning age
Set foot vnder thy table: tut, a toy,
An olde Italian foxe is not ſo kinde my boy.   *Exit.*
  Tra. A vengeance on your crafty withered hide,
Yet I haue fac'd it with a card of ten:
'Tis in my head to doe my maſter good:
I ſee no reaſon but ſuppos'd *Lucentio*
Muſt get a father, call'd ſuppos'd *Vincentio*,
And that's a wonder: fathers commonly
Doe get their children: but in this caſe of woing,
A childe ſhall get a ſire, if I faile not of my cunning. *Exit.*

Actus Tertia.

Enter Lucentio, Hortentio, and Bianca.

  Luc. Fidler forbeare, you grow too forward Sir,
Haue you ſo ſoone forgot the entertainment
Her ſiſter *Katherine* welcom'd you withall.
  Hort. But wrangling pedant, this is
The patroneſſe of heauenly harmony:
Then giue me leaue to haue prerogatiue,
And when in Muſicke we haue ſpent an houre,
Your Lecture ſhall haue leifure for as much.
  Luc. Prepoſterous Aſſe that neuer read ſo farre,
To know the cauſe why muſicke was ordain'd:
Was it not to refreſh the minde of man
After his ſtudies, or his vſuall paine?
Then giue me leaue to read Philoſophy,
And while I pauſe, ſerue in your harmony.
  Hort. Sirra, I will not beare theſe braues of thine.
  Bianc. Why gentlemen, you doe me double wrong,
To ſtriue for that which reſteth in my choice:
I am no breeching ſcholler in the ſchooles,
Ile not be tied to howres, nor pointed times,
But learne my Leſſons as I pleaſe my ſelfe,
And to cut off all ſtrife: heere ſit we downe,
Take you your inſtrument, play you the whiles,
His Lecture will be done ere you haue tun'd.
  Hort. You'll leaue his Lecture when I am in tune?
  Luc. That will be neuer, tune your inſtrument.
  Bian. Where left I laſt?
  Luc. Heere Madam: *Hic Ibat Simois, bit eſt ſigeria tellus, bic ſteterat Priami regia Celſa ſenis.*
  Bian. Conſter them.
  Luc. Hic Ibat, as I told you before, *Simois,* I am Lucentio, *bic eſt,* ſonne vnto Vincentio of Piſa, *Sigeria tellus,* diſguiſed thus to get your loue, *bic ſteterat,* and that Lucentio that comes a wooing, *priami,* is my man Tranio, *regia,* bearing my port, *celſa ſenis* that we might beguile the old Pantalowne.

  Hort. Madam, my Inſtrument's in tune.
  Bian. Let's heare, oh fie, the treble iarres.
  Luc. Spit in the hole man, and tune againe.
  Bian. Now let mee ſee if I can conſter it.   *Hic ibat ſimois,* I know you not, *bic eſt ſigeria tellus,* I truſt you not, *bic ſtaterat priami,* take heede he heare vs not, *regia* preſume not, *Celſa ſenis,* deſpaire not.
  Hort. Madam, tis now in tune.
  Luc. All but the baſe.
  Hort. The baſe is right, 'tis the baſe knaue that iars.
  Luc. How fiery and forward our Pedant is,
Now for my life the knaue doth court my loue,
Pedaſcule, Ile watch you better yet:
In time I may beleeue, yet I miſtruſt.
  Bian. Miſtruſt it not, for ſure eÆacides
Was *Aiax* cald ſo from his grandfather.
  Hort. I muſt beleeue my maſter, elſe I promiſe you,
I ſhould be arguing ſtill vpon that doubt:,
But let it reſt, now *Litio* to you:
Good maſter take it not vnkindly pray
That I haue beene thus pleaſant with you both.
  Hort. You may go walk, and giue me leaue a while,
My Leſſons make no muſicke in three parts.
  Luc. Are you ſo formall ſir, well I muſt waite
And watch withall, for but I be deceiu'd,
Our fine Muſitian groweth amorous.
  Hor. Madam, before you touch the inſtrument,
To learne the order of my fingering,
I muſt begin with rudiments of Art,
To teach you gamoth in a briefer ſort,
More pleaſant, pithy, and effectuall,
Then hath beene taught by any of my trade,
And there it is in writing fairely drawne.
  Bian. Why, I am paſt my gamouth long agoe.
  Hor. Yet read the gamouth of *Hortensio.*
  Bian. Gamouth I am, the ground of all accord:
Are, to plead *Hortenſio's* paſſion:
Beeme, Bianca take him for thy Lord
Cfavt, that loues with all affection:
D ſol re, one Cliffe, two notes haue I,
Elami, ſhow pitty or I die.
Call you this gamouth? tut I like it not,
Old faſhions pleaſe me beſt, I am not ſo nice
To charge true rules for old inuentions.

Enter a Meſſenger.

  Nicke. Miſtreſſe, your father prayes you leaue your
And helpe to dreſſe your ſiſters chamber vp,   (books,
You know to morrow is the wedding day.
  Bian. Farewell ſweet maſters both, I muſt be gone.
  Luc. Faith Miſtreſſe then I haue no cauſe to ſtay.
  Hor. But I haue cauſe to pry into this pedant,
Methinkes he lookes as though he were in loue:
Yet if thy thoughts *Bianca* be ſo humble
To caſt thy wandring eyes on euery ſtale:
Seize thee that Liſt, if once I finde thee ranging,
Hortenſio will be quit with thee by changing.   *Exit.*

Enter Baptiſta, Gremio, Tranio, Katherine, Bianca, and others, attendants.

  Bap. Signior *Lucentio,* this is the pointed day
That *Katherine* and *Petruchio* ſhould be married,
And yet we heare not of our ſonne in Law:
What will be ſaid, what mockery will it be?
To want the Bride-groome when the Prieſt attends
To ſpeake the ceremoniall rites of marriage?
What ſaies *Lucentio* to this ſhame of ours?

                                      No

Kate. No fhame but mine, I muft forfooth be forft
To giue my hand oppos'd againft my heart
Vnto a mad-braine rudesby, full of fpleene,
Who woo'd in hafte, and meanes to wed at leyfure :
I told you I, he was a franticke foole,
Hiding his bitter iefts in blunt behauiour ,
And to be noted for a merry man ;
Hee'll wooe a thoufand, point the day of marriage,
Make friends, inuite, and proclaime the banes ,
Yet neuer meanes to wed where he hath woo'd :
Now muft the world point at poore *Katherine,*
And fay, loe, there is mad *Petruchio's* wife
If it would pleafe him come and marry her.

Tra. Patience good *Katherine* and *Baptifta* too,
Vpon my life *Petruchio* meanes but well,
What euer fortune ftayes him from his word,
Though he be blunt, I know him paffing wife ,
Though he be merry, yet withall he 's honeft.

Kate. Would *Katherine* had neuer feen him though.

Exit weeping.

Bap. Goe girle, I cannot blame thee now to weepe,
For fuch an iniurie would vexe a very faint,
Much more a fhrew of impatient humour.

Enter Biondello.

Bion. Mafter, mafter, newes, and fuch newes as you
neuer heard of,

Bap. Is it new and olde too ? how may that be ?

Bion. Why, is it not newes to heard of *Petruchio's*

Bap. Is he come ?   (comming?

Bion. Why no fir.

Bap. What then ?

Bion. He is comming.

Bap. When will he be heere ?

Bion. When he ftands where I am, and fees you there.

Tra. But fay, what to thine olde newes ?

Bion. Why *Petruchio* is comming, in a new hat and
an old ierkin, a paire of olde breeches thrice turn'd ; a
paire of bootes that haue beene candle-cafes, one buckled, another lac'd : an olde rufty fword tane out of the
Towne Armory, with a broken hilt, and chapeleffe : with
two broken points : his horfe hip'd with an olde mo-
thy faddle, and ftirrops of no kindred : befides poffeft
with the glanders, and like to mofe in the chine , troubled with the Lampaffe, infected with the fafhions, full
of Windegalls, fped with Spauins, raied with the Yel-
lowes , paft cure of the Fiues, ftarke fpoyl'd with the
Staggers, begnawne with the Bots, Waid in the backe,
and fhoulder-fhotten , neere leg'd before, and with a
halfe-chekt Bitte, & a headftall of fheepes leather, which
being reftrain'd to keepe him from ftumbling, hath been
often burft, and now repaired with knots : one girth fixe
times peec'd, and a womans Crupper of velure , which
hath two letters for her name, fairely fet down in ftuds,
and beere and there peec'd with packthred.

Bap. Who comes with him ?

Bion. Oh fir, his Lackey, for all the world Capari-
fon'd like the horfe : with a linnen ftock on one leg, and
a kerfey boot-hofe on the other, gartred with a red and
blew lift;an old hat, & the humor of forty fancies prickt
in't for a feather : a monfter, a very monfter in apparell ,
& not like a Chriftian foot-boy, or a gentlemans Lacky.

Tra. 'Tis fome od humor pricks him to this fafhion,
Yet oftentimes he goes but meane apparel'd.

Bap. I am glad he's come, howfoere he comes.

Bion. Why fir, he comes not.

Bap. Didft thou not fay hee comes?

Bion. Who, that *Petruchio* came?

Bap. I, that *Petruchio* came.   (backe.

Bion. No fir, I fay his horfe comes with him on his

Bap. Why that's all one.

Bion. Nay by S.*Iamy,* I hold you a penny, a horfe and
a man is more then one, and yet not many.

Enter Petruchio and Grumio.

Pet. Come, where be thefe gallants? who's at home ?

Bap. You are welcome fir.

Petr. And yet I come not well.

Bap. And yet you halt not.

Tra. Not fo well apparell'd as I wifh you were.

Petr. Were it better I fhould rufh in thus :
But where is *Kate* ? where is my louely Bride ?
How does my father? gentles methinkes you frowne ,
And wherefore gaze this goodly company ,
As if they faw fome wondrous monument,
Some Commet, or vnufuall prodigie ?

Bap. Why fir, you know this is your wedding day :
Firft were we fad, fearing you would not come,
Now fadder that you come fo vnprouided :
Fie, doff this habit, fhame to your eftate,
An eye-fore to our folemne feftiuall.

Tra. And tell vs what occafion of import
Hath all fo long detain'd you from your wife,
And fent you hither fo vnlike your felfe ?

Petr. Tedious it were to tell, and harfh to heare,
Sufficeth I am come to keepe my word ,
Though in fome part inforced to digreffe ,
Which at more leyfure I will fo excufe,
As you fhall well be fatisfied with all.
But where is *Kate* ? I ftay too long from her,
The morning weares, 'tis time we were at Church.

Tra. See not your Bride in thefe vnreuerent robes,
Goe to my chamber, put on clothes of mine.

Pet. Not I, beleeue me, thus Ile vifit her.

Bap. But thus I truft you will not marry her.   (words,

Pet. Good footh man thus : therefore ha done with
To me fhe's married, not vnto my cloathes :
Could I repaire what fhe will weare in me,
As I can change thefe poore accoutrements,
'Twere well for *Kate,* and better for my felfe.
But what a foole am I to chat with you,
When I fhould bid good morrow to my Bride?
And feale the title with a louely kiffe.   *Exit.*

Tra. He hath fome meaning in his mad attire,
We will perfwade him be it poffible,
To put on better ere he goe to Church.

Bap. Ile after him, and fee the euent of this.   *Exit.*

Tra. But fir, Loue concerneth vs to adde
Her fathers liking, which to bring to paffe
As before imparted to your worfhip,
I am to get a man what ere he be,
It skills not much, weele fit him to our turne,
And he fhall be *Vincentio* of *Pifa,*
And make affurance heere in *Padua*
Of greater fummes then I haue promifed,
So fhall you quietly enioy your hope,
And marry fweet *Bianca* with confent.

Luc. Were it not that my fellow fchoolemafter
Doth watch *Bianca's* fteps fo narrowly :
'Twere good me-thinkes to fteale our marriage,
Which once perform'd, let all the world fay no,
Ile keepe mine owne defpite of all the world.

Tra. That by degrees we meane to looke into,

And

T 2

And watch our vantage in this bufineſſe,
Wee'll ouer-reach the grey-beard *Gremio*,
The narrow prying father *Minola*,
The quaint Muſician, amorous *Litio*,
All for my Maſters ſake *Lucentio*.

Enter Gremio.

Signior *Gremio*, came you from the Church?
Gre. As willingly as ere I came from ſchoole.
Tra. And is the Bride & Bridegroom coming home?
Gre. A bridegroome ſay you? 'tis a groome indeed,
A grumlling groome, and that the girle ſhall finde.
Tra. Curſter then ſhe, why 'tis impoſſible.
Gre. Why hee's a deuill, a deuill, a very fiend.
Tra. Why ſhe's a deuill, a deuill, the deuils damme.
Gre. Tut, ſhe's a Lambe, a Doue, a foole to him:
Ile tell you ſir *Lucentio*; when the Prieſt
Should aske if *Katherine* ſhould be his wife,
I, by gogge woones quoth he, and ſwore ſo loud,
That all amaz'd the Prieſt let fall the booke,
And as he ſtoop'd againe to take it vp,
This mad-brain'd bridegroome tooke him ſuch a cuffe,
That downe fell Prieſt and booke, and booke and Prieſt,
Now take them vp quoth he, if any lift.
Tra. What ſaid the wench when he roſe againe?
Gre. Trembled and ſhooke : for why, he ſtamp'd and
ſwore, as if the Vicar meant to cozen him : but after ma-
ny ceremonies done, hee calls for wine, a health quoth
he, as if he had beene aboord carowſing to his Mates after a ſtorme, quaft off the Muſcadell, and threw the ſops
all in the Sextons face : hauing no other reaſon, but that
his beard grew thinne and hungerly, and ſeem'd to aske
him ſops as hee was drinking : This done, hee tooke the
Bride about the necke, and kiſt her lips with ſuch a clamorous ſmacke, that at the parting all the Church did
eccho: and I ſeeing this, came thence for very ſhame, and
after mee I know the rout is comming, ſuch a mad mar-
ryage neuer was before : harke, harke, I heare the minſtrels play.   *Muſicke playes.*

Enter Petruchio, Kate, Bianca, Hortenſio, Baptiſta.

Petr. Gentlemen & friends, I thank you for your pains,
I know you thinke to dine with me to day,
And haue prepar'd great ſtore of wedding cheere,
But ſo it is, my haſte doth call me hence,
And therefore heere I meane to take my leaue.
Bap. Is't poſſible you will away to night?
Pet. I muſt away to day before night come,
Make it no wonder : if you knew my buſineſſe,
You would intreat me rather goe then ſtay :
And honeſt company, I thanke you all,
That haue beheld me giue away my ſelfe
To this moſt patient, ſweet, and vertuous wife,
Dine with my father, drinke a health to me,
For I muſt hence, and farewell to you all.
Tra. Let vs intreat you ſtay till after dinner.
Pet. It may not be.
Gra. Let me intreat you.
Pet. It cannot be.
Kat. Let me intreat you.
Pet. I am content.
Kat. Are you content to ſtay?
Pet. I am content you ſhall entreat me ſtay,
But yet not ſtay, entreat me how you can.

Kat. Now if you loue me ſtay.
Pet. *Grumio*, my horſe.
Gru. I ſir, they be ready, the Oates haue eaten the
horſes.
Kate. Nay then,
Doe what thou canſt, I will not goe to day,
No, nor to morrow, not till I pleaſe my ſelfe,
The dore is open ſir, there lies your way,
You may be iogging whiles your bootes are greene :
For me, Ile not be gone till I pleaſe my ſelfe,
'Tis like you'll proue a iolly ſurly groome,
That take it on you at the firſt ſo roundly.
Pet. O *Kate* content thee, prethee be not angry.
Kat. I will be angry, what haſt thou to doe?
Father, be quiet, he ſhall ſtay my leiſure.
Gre. I marry ſir, now it begins to worke.
Kat. Gentlemen, forward to the bridall dinner,
I ſee a woman may be made a foole
If ſhe had not a ſpirit to reſiſt.
Pet. They ſhall goe forward *Kate* at thy command,
Obey the Bride you that attend on her.
Goe to the feaſt, reuell and domineere,
Carowſe full meaſure to her maiden-head,
Be madde and merry, or goe hang your ſelues :
But for my bonny *Kate*, ſhe muſt with me :
Nay, looke not big, nor ſtampe, nor ſtare, nor fret,
I will be maſter of what is mine owne,
Shee is my goods, my chattels, ſhe is my houſe,
My houſhold-ſtuffe, my field, my barne,
My horſe, my oxe, my aſſe, my any thing,
And heere ſhe ſtands, touch her who euer dare,
Ile bring mine action on the proudeſt he
That ſtops my way in *Padua* : *Grumio*
Draw forth thy weapon, we are beſet with theeues,
Reſcue thy Miſtreſſe if thou be a man :
Feare not ſweet wench, they ſhall not touch thee *Kate*,
Ile buckler thee againſt a Million.   *Exeunt. P. Ka.*
Bap. Nay, let them goe, a couple of quiet ones.   (ing.
Gre. Went they not quickly, I ſhould die with laugh-
Tra. Of all mad matches neuer was the like.
Luc. Miſtreſſe, what's your opinion of your ſiſter?
Bian. That being mad her ſelfe, ſhe's madly mated.
Gre. I warrant him *Petruchio* is Kated.
Bap. Neighbours and friends, though Bride & Bride-
For to ſupply the places at the table,   (groom wants
You know there wants no iunkets at the feaſt :
Lucentio, you ſhall ſupply the Bridegroomes place,
And let *Bianca* take her ſiſters roome.
Tra. Shall ſweet *Bianca* practiſe how to bride it?
Bap. She ſhall *Lucentio*: come gentlemen lets goe.
     Enter Grumio.   *Exeunt.*
Gru. Fie, fie on all tired Iades, on all mad Maſters, &
all foule waies : was euer man ſo beaten ? was euer man
ſo raide ? was euer man ſo weary ? I am ſent before to
make a fire, and they are comming after to warme them:
now were not I a little pot, & ſoone hot ; my very lippes
might freeze to my teeth, my tongue to the roofe of my
mouth, my heart in my belly, ere I ſhould come by a fire
to thaw me, but I with blowing the fire ſhall warme my
ſelfe : for conſidering the weather, a taller man then I
will take cold : Holla, hoa *Curtis.*

     Enter Curtis.
Curt. Who is that calls ſo coldly?
Gru. A piece of Ice : if thou doubt it, thou maiſt
ſlide from my ſhoulder to my heele, with no
                                 greater

greater a run but my head and my necke. A fire good
Curtis.

Cur. Is my mafter and his wife comming *Grumio?*

Gru. Oh I *Curtis* I, and therefore fire, fire, caft on no
water.

Cur. Is fhe fo hot a fhrew as fhe's reported.

Gru. She was good *Curtis* before this froft: but thou
know'ft winter tames man, woman, and beaft : for it
hath tam'd my old mafter, and my new miftris, and my
felfe fellow *Curtis.*

Gru. Away you three inch foole, I am no beaft.

Gru. Am I but three inches? Why thy horne is a foot
and fo long am I at the leaft. But wilt thou make a fire,
or fhall I complaine on thee to our miftris, whofe hand
(fhe being now at hand) thou fhalt foone feele, to thy
cold comfort, for being flow in thy hot office.

Cur. I prethee good *Grumio*, tell me, how goes the
world ?

Gru. A cold world *Curtis* in euery office but thine, &
therefore fire : do thy duty, and haue thy dutie, for my
Mafter and miftris are almoft frozen to death.

Cur. There's fire readie, and therefore good *Grumio*
the newes.

Gru. Why Iacke boy, ho boy, and as much newes as
wilt thou.

Cur. Come, you are fo full of conicatching.

Gru. Why therefore fire, for I haue caught extreme
cold. Where's the Cooke, is fupper ready, the houfe
trim'd, rufhes ftrew'd, cobwebs fwept, the feruingmen
in their new fuftian, the white ftockings, and euery officer his wedding garment on ? Be the Iackes faire within, the Gils faire without, the Carpets laide, and euerie
thing in order ?

Cur. All readie : and therefore I pray thee newes.

Gru. Firft know my horfe is tired, my mafter & miftris falne out. *Cur.* How ?

Gru. Out of their faddles into the durt, and thereby
hangs a tale.

Cur. Let's ha't good *Grumio.*

Gru. Lend thine eare.

Cur. Heere.

Gru. There.

Cur. This 'tis to feele a tale, not to heare a tale.

Gru. And therefore 'tis cal'd a fenfible tale : and this
Cuffe was but to knocke at your eare, and befeech lift-
ning : now I begin, Inprimis wee came downe a fowle
hill, my Mafter riding behinde my Miftris.

Cur. Both of one horfe ?

Gru. What's that to thee ?

Cur. Why a horfe.

Gru. Tell thou the tale : but hadft thou not croft me,
thou fhouldft haue heard how her horfe fel, and fhe vnder her horfe : thou fhouldft haue heard in how miery a
place, how fhe was bemoil'd, how hee left her with the
horfe vpon her, how he beat me becaufe her horfe ftum-
bled, how fhe waded through the durt to plucke him off
me : how he fwore, how fhe prai'd, that neuer prai'd before : how I cried, how the horfes ranne away, how her
bridle was burft ; how I loft my crupper, with manie
things of worthy memorie, which now fhall die in obliuion, and thou returne vnexperienc'd to thy graue.

Cur. By this reckning he is more fhrew than fhe.

Gru. I, and that thou and the proudeft of you all fhall
finde when he comes home. But what talke I of this ?
Call forth *Nathaniel, Iofeph, Nicholas, Phillip, Walter, Su-
gerfop* and the reft : let their heads bee flickely comb'd,

their blew coats brufh'd, and their garters of an indifferent knit, let them curtfie with their left legges, and not
prefume to touch a haire of my Mafters horfe-taile, till
they kiffe their hands. Are they all readie ?

Cur. They are.

Gru. Call them forth.

Cur. Do you heare ho? you muft meete my maifter
to countenance my miftris.

Gru. Why fhe hath a face of her owne.

Cur. Who knowes not that ?

Gru. Thou it feemes, that cals for company to countenance her.

Cur. I call them forth to credit her.

Enter foure or fiue feruingmen.

Gru. Why fhe comes to borrow nothing of them.

Nat. Welcome home *Grumio.*

Phil. How now *Grumio.*

Iof. What *Grumio.*

Nick. Fellow *Grumio.*

Nat. How now old lad.

Gru. Welcome you : how now you : what you: fellow you : and thus much for greeting. Now my fpruce
companions, is all readie, and all things neate?

Nat. All things is readie, how neere is our mafter ?

Gre. E'ne at hand, alighted by this: and therefore be
not———Cockes paffion, filence, I heare my mafter.

Enter Petruchio and Kate.

Pet. Where be thefe knaues? What no man at doore
To hold my ftirrop, nor to take my horfe ?
Where is *Nathaniel, Gregory, Phillip.*

All fer. Heere, heere fir, heere fir.

Pet. Heere fir, heere fir, heere fir, heere fir.
You logger-headed and vnpollifht groomes :
What? no attendance? no regard? no dutie?
Where is the foolifh knaue I fent before ?

Gru. Heere fir, as foolifh as I was before.

Pet. You pezant, fwain, you horfon malt-horfe drudg
Did I not bid thee meete me in the Parke,
And bring along thefe rafcal knaues with thee?

Grumio. *Nathaniels* coate fir was not fully made,
And *Gabrels* pumpes were all vnpinkt i'th heele :
There was no Linke to colour *Peters* hat,
And *Walters* dagger was not come from fheathing :
There were none fine, but *Adam, Rafe,* and *Gregory,*
The reft were ragged, old, and beggerly,
Yet as they are, here are they come to meete you.

Pet. Go rafcals, go, and fetch my fupper in. *Ex.Ser.*
Where is the life that late I led?
Where are thofe ? Sit downe *Kate,*
And welcome. Soud, foud, foud, foud.

Enter feruants with fupper.

Why when I fay? Nay good fweete *Kate* be merrie.
Off with my boots, you rogues : you villaines, when ?
It was the Friar of Orders gray,
As he forth walked on his way.
Out you rogue, you plucke my foote awrie,
Take that, and mend the plucking of the other.
Be merrie *Kate* : Some water heere : what hoa.

Enter one with water.

Where's my Spaniel *Troilus?* Sirra, get you hence,
And bid my cozen *Ferdinand* come hither :
One *Kate* that you muft kiffe, and be acquaint_ed with.
Where are my Slippers? Shall I haue fome w_ater ?
Come *Kate* and wafh, & welcome heartily :
you horfon villaine, will you let it fall ?

T 3　　　　　　　　　　　*Kate*

Kate. Patience I pray you, 'twas a fault vnwilling.

Pet. A horſon beetle-headed flap-ear'd knaue :
Come *Kate* ſit downe, I know you haue a ſtomacke,
Will you giue thankes, ſweete *Kate*, or elſe ſhall I ?
What's this, Mutton ?

1. Ser. I.

Pet. Who brought it ?

Peter. I.

Pet. 'Tis burnt, and ſo is all the meate :
What dogges are theſe ? Where is the raſcall Cooke ?
How durſt you villaines bring it from the dreſſer
And ſerue it thus to me that loue it not ?
There, take it to you, trenchers, cups, and all :
You heedleſſe iolt-heads, and vnmanner'd ſlaues.
What, do you grumble? Ile be with you ſtraight.

Kate. I pray you husband be not ſo diſquiet,
The meate was well, if you were ſo contented.

Pet. I tell thee *Kate*, 'twas burnt and dried away,
And I expreſſely am forbid to touch it :
For it engenders choller, planteth anger,
And better 'twere that both of vs did faſt,
Since of our ſelues, our ſelues are chollericke,
Then feede it with ſuch ouer-roſted fleſh:
Be patient, to morrow't ſhalbe mended,
And for this night we'l faſt for companie.
Come I wil bring thee to thy Bridall chamber.   *Exeunt.*

Enter Seruants ſeuerally.

Nath. Peter didſt euer ſee the like.

Peter. He kils her in her owne humor.

Grumio. Where is he?

Enter Curtis a Seruant.

Cur. In her chamber, making a ſermon of continencie to her, and railes, and ſweares, and rates, that ſhee
(poore ſoule) knowes not which way to ſtand, to looke,
to ſpeake, and ſits as one new riſen from a dreame. A-
way, away, for he is comming hither.

Enter Petruchio.

Pet. Thus haue I politickely begun my reigne,
And 'tis my hope to end ſucceſſefully :
My Faulcon now is ſharpe, and paſſing emptie,
And til ſhe ſtoope, ſhe muſt not be full gorg'd,
For then ſhe neuer lookes vpon her lure.
Another way I haue to man my Haggard,
To make her come, and know her Keepers call :
That is, to watch her, as we watch theſe Kites,
That baite, and beate, and will not be obedient :
She eate no meate to day, nor none ſhall eate.
Laſt night ſhe ſlept not, nor to night ſhe ſhall not :
As with the meate, ſome vndeſerued fault
Ile finde about the making of the bed,
And heere Ile fling the pillow, there the boulſter,
This way the Couerlet, another way the ſheets :
I, and amid this hurlie I intend,
That all is done in reuerend care of her,
And in concluſion, ſhe ſhal watch all night,
And if ſhe chance to nod, Ile raile and brawle,
And with the clamor keepe her ſtil awake :
This is a way to kil a Wife with kindneſſe,
And thus Ile curbe her mad and headſtrong humor :
He that knowes better how to tame a ſhrew,
Now let him ſpeake, 'tis charity to ſhew.   *Exit*

Enter Tranio and Hortenſio:

Tra. Is't poſſible friend *Liſio*, that miſtris *Bianca*
Doth fancie any other but *Lucentio*,
I tel you ſir, ſhe beares me faire in hand.

Luc. Sir, to ſatisfie you in what I haue ſaid,

Stand by, and marke the manner of his teaching.

Enter Bianca.

Hor. Now Miſtris, profit you in what you reade?

Bian. What Maſter reade you firſt, reſolue me that ?

Hor. I reade, that I profeſſe the Art to loue.

Bian And may you proue ſir Maſter of your Art.

Luc. While you ſweet deere ptoue Miſtreſſe of my
heart.

Hor. Quicke proceeders marry, now tel me I pray,
you that durſt ſweare that your miſtris *Bianca*
Lou'd me in the World ſo wel as *Lucentio.*

Tra. Oh deſpightful Loue, vnconſtant womankind,
I tel thee *Liſio* this is wonderfull.

Hor. Miſtake no more, I am not *Liſio*,
Nor a Muſitian as I ſeeme to bee,
But one that ſcorne to liue in this diſguiſe,
For ſuch a one as leaues a Gentleman,
And makes a God of ſuch a Cullion ;
Know ſir, that I am cal'd *Hortenſio.*

Tra. Signior *Hortenſio*, I haue often heard
Of your entire affection to *Bianca*,
And ſince mine eyes are witneſſe of her lightneſſe,
I will with you, if you be ſo contented,
Forſweare *Bianca*, and her loue for euer.

Hor. See how they kiſſe and court: Signior *Lucentio,*
Heere is my hand, and heere I firmly vow
Neuer ro woo her more, but do forſweare her
As one vnworthle all the former fauours
That I haue fondly flatter'd of them withall.

Tra. And heere I take the like vnſained oath,
Neuer to marrie with her, though ſhe would intreate,
Fie on her, ſee how beaſtly ſhe doth court him.

Hor. Would all the world but he had quite forſworn
For me, that I may ſurely keepe mine oath.
I wil be married to a wealthy Widdow,
Ere three dayes paſſe, which hath as long lou'd me,
As I haue lou'd this proud diſdainful Haggard,
And ſo farewel ſignior *Lucentio,*
Kindneſſe in women, not their beauteous lookes
Shal win my loue, and ſo I take my leaue,
In reſolution, as I ſwore before.

Tra. Miſtris *Bianca*, bleſſe you with ſuch grace,
As longeth to a Louers bleſſed caſe :
Nay, I haue tane you napping gentle Loue,
And haue forſworne you with *Hortenſio.*

Bian. *Tranio* you ieſt, but haue you both forſworne
mee ?

Tra. Miſtris we haue.

Luc. Then we are rid of *Liſio.*

Tra. I'faith hee'l haue a luſtie Widdow now,
That ſhalbe woo'd, and wedded in a day.

Bian. God giue him ioy.

Tra. I, and hee'l tame her.

Bianca. He ſayes ſo *Tranio.*

Tra. Faith he is gone vnto the taming ſchoole.

Bian. The taming ſchoole: what is there ſuch a place?

Tra. I miſtris, and *Petruchio* is the maſter,
That teacheth trickes eleuen and twentie long,
To tame a ſhrew, and charme her chattering tongue.

Enter Biondello.

Bion. Oh Maſter, maſter I haue watcht ſo long,
That I am dogge-wearie, but at laſt I ſpied
An ancient Angel comming downe the hill,
Wil ſerue the turne.

Tra. What is he *Biondello* ?

Bio. Maſter, a Marcantant, or a pedant,

I know not what, but formall in apparrell,
In gate and eountenance surely like a Father.
Luc. And what of him *Tranio*?
Tra. If he be credulous, and trust my tale,
Ile make him glad to seeme *Vincentio*,
And giue assurance to *Baptista Minola*.
As if he were the right *Vincentio*.
Par. Take me your loue, and then let me alone.

Enter a Pedant.

Ped. God saue you sir,
Tra. And you sir, you are welcome,
Trauaile you farre on, or are you at the farthest?
Ped. Sir at the farthest for a weeke or two,
But then vp farther, and as farre as Rome,
And so to Tripolie, if God lend me life.
Tra. What Countreyman I pray?
Ped. Of *Mantua.*
Tra. Of *Mantua* Sir, marrie God forbid,
And come to Padua carelesse of your life.
Ped. My life sir? how I pray? for that goes hard.
Tra. 'Tis death for any one in Mantua
To come to Padua, know you not the cause?
Your ships are staid at Venice, and the Duke
For priuate quarrel 'twixt your Duke and him,
Hath publish'd and proclaim'd it openly:
'Tis meruaile, but that you are but newly come,
you might haue heard it else proclaim'd about.
Ped. Alas sir, it is worse for me then so,
For I haue bils for monie by exchange
From Florence, and must heere deliuer them.
Tra. Wel sir, to do you courtesie,
This wil I do, and this I wil aduise you,
First tell me, haue you euer beene at Pisa?
Ped. I sir, in Pisa haue I often bin,
Pisa renowned for graue Citizens.
Tra. Among them know you one *Vincentio*?
Ped. I know him not, but I haue heard of him:
A Merchant of incomparable wealth.
Tra. He is my father sir, and sooth to say,
In count'nance somewhat doth resemble you.
Bion. As much as an apple doth an oyster, & all one.
Tra. To saue your life in this extremitie,
This fauor wil I do you for his sake,
And thinke it not the worst of all your fortunes,
That you are like to Sir *Vincentio.*
His name and credite shal you vndertake,
And in my house you shal be friendly lodg'd,
Looke that you take vpon you as you should,
you vnderstand me sir: so shal you stay
Til you haue done your businesse in the Citie:
If this be court'sie sir, accept of it.
Ped. Oh sir I do, and wil repute you euer
The patron of my life and libertie.
Tra. Then go with me, to make the matter good,
This by the way I let you vnderstand,
My father is heere look'd for euerie day,
To passe assurance of a dowre in marriage
'Twixt me, and one *Baptistas* daughter heere:
In all these circumstances Ile instruct you,
Go with me to cloath you as becomes you.   *Exeunt.*

Actus Quartus. Scena Prima.

Enter Katherina and Grumio.

Gru. No, no forsooth I dare not for my life.
Ka. The more my wrong, the more his spite appears.
What, did he marrie me to famish me?
Beggers that come vnto my fathers doore,
Vpon intreatie haue a present almes,
If not, elsewhere they meete with charitie:
But I, who neuer knew how to intreat,
Nor neuer needed that I should intreate,
Am staru'd for meate, giddie for lacke of sleepe:
With oathes kept waking, and with brawling fed,
And that which spights me more then all these wants,
He does it vnder name of perfect loue:
As who should say, if I should sleepe or eate
'Twere deadly sicknesse, or else present death.
I prethee go, aud get me some repast,
I care not what, so it be holsome foode.
Gru. What say you to a Neats foote?
Kate. 'Tis passing good, I prethee let me haue it.
Gru. I feare it is too chollericke a meate.
How say you to a fat Tripe finely broyl'd?
Kate. I like it well, good Grumio fetch it me.
Gru. I cannot tell, I feare 'tis chollericke.
What say you to a peece of Beefe and Mustard?
Kate. A dish that I do loue to feede vpon.
Gru. I, but the Mustard is too hot a little.
Kate. Why then the Beefe, and let the Mustard rest.
Gru. Nay then I wil not, you shal haue the Mustard
Or else you get no beefe of Grumio.
Kate. Then both or one, or any thing thou wilt.
Gru. Why then the Mustard without the beefe.
Kate. Go get thee gone, thou false deluding slaue,

Beats him.

That feed'st me with the verie name of meate.
Sorrow on thee, and all the packe of you
That triumph thus vpon my misery:
Go get thee gone, I say.

Enter Petruchio, and Hortensio with meate.

Petr. How fares my Kate, what sweeting all a-mort?
Hor. Mistris, what cheere?
Kate. Faith as cold as can be.
Pet. Plucke vp thy spirits, looke cheerfully vpon me.
Heere Loue, thou seest how diligent I am,
To dresse thy meate my selfe, and bring it thee.
I am sure sweet Kate, this kindnesse merites thankes.
What, not a word? Nay then, thou lou'st it not:
And all my paines is sorted to no proofe.
Heere take away this dish.
Kate. I pray you let it stand.
Pet. The poorest seruice is repaide with thankes,
And so shall mine before you touch the meate.
Kate. I thanke you sir.
Hor. Signior Petruchio, fie you are too blame:
Come Mistris Kate, Ile beare you companie.
Petr. Eate it vp all *Hortensio*, if thou louest mee:
Much good do it vnto thy gentle heart:
Kate eate apace; and now my honie Loue,
Will we returne vnto thy Fathers house,
And reuell it as brauely as the best,
With silken coats and caps, and golden Rings,
With Ruffes and Cuffes, and Fardingales, and things:
With Scarfes, and Fannes, & double change of brau'ry,
With Amber Bracelets, Beades, and all this knau'ry.
What hast thou din'd? The Tailor staies thy leasure,
To decke thy bodie with his ruffling treasure.

Enter Tailor.

Come

Come Tailor, let vs fee thefe ornaments.

Enter Haberdafber.

Lay forth the gowne. What newes with you fir?

Fel. Heere is the cap your Worfhip did befpeake.

Pet. Why this was moulded on a porrenger,
A Veluet difh : Fie,fie, 'tis lewd and filthy,
Why 'tis a cockle or a walnut-fhell,
A knacke, a toy, a tricke, a babies cap :
Away with it, come let me haue a bigger.

Kate. Ile haue no bigger, this doth fit the time,
And Gentlewomen weare fuch caps as thefe.

Pet. When you are gentle, you fhall haue one too,
And not till then.

Hor. That will not be in haft.

Kate. Why fir I truft I may haue leaue to fpeake,
And fpeake I will. I am no childe, no babe,
Your betters haue indur'd me fay my minde,
And If you cannot, beft you ftop your eares,
My tongue will tell the anger of my heart,
Or els my heart concealing it wil breake,
And rather then it fhall, I will be free,
Euen to the vttermoft as I pleafe in words.

Pet. Why thou faift true, it is paltrie cap,
A cuftard coffen, a bauble, a filken pie,
I loue thee well in that thou lik'ft it not.

Kate. Loue me, or loue me not, I like the cap,
And it I will haue, or I will haue none.

Pet. Thy gowne, why I : come Tailor let vs fee't.
Oh mercie God, what masking ftuffe is heere ?
Whats this? a fleeue ? 'tis like demi cannon,
What, vp and downe caru'd like an apple Tart?
Heers fnip, and nip, and cut, and flifh and flafh,
Like to a Cenfor in a barbers fhoppe :
Why what a deuils name Tailor cal'ft thou this ?

Hor. I fee fhees like to haue neither cap nor gowne.

Tai. You bid me make it orderlie and well,
According to the fafhion, and the time.

Pet. Marrie and did : but if you be remembred,
I did not bid you marre it to the time,
Go hop me ouer euery kennell home,
For you fhall hop without my cuftome fir;
Ile none of it ; hence, make your beft of it.

Kate. I neuer faw a better fafhion'd gowne,
More queint, more pleafing, nor more commendable :
Belike you meane to make a puppet of me.

Pet. Why true, he meanes to make a puppet of thee.

Tail. She faies your Worfhip meanes to make a
puppet of her.

Pet. Oh monftrous arrogance :
Thou lyeft, thou thred, thou thimble,
Thou yard three quarters, halfe yard, quarter, naile,
Thou Flea, thou Nit, thou winter cricket thou :
Brau'd in mine owne houfe with a skeine of thred :
Away thou Ragge, thou quantitie, thou remnant,
Or I fhall fo be-mete thee with thy yard,
As thou fhalt thinke on prating whil'ft thou liu'ft :
I tell thee I, that thou haft marr'd her gowne.

Tail. Your worfhip is deceiu'd, the gowne is made
Iuft as my mafter had direction :
Grumio gaue order how it fhould be done.

Gru. I gaue him no order, I gaue him the ftuffe.

Tail. But how did you defire it fhould be made ?

Gru. Marrie fir with needle and thred.

Tail. But did you not requeft to haue it cut ?

Gru. Thou haft fac'd many things.

Tail. I haue.

Gru. Face not mee : thou haft brau'd manie men,
braue not me ; I will neither bee fac'd nor brau'd. I fay
vnto thee, I bid thy Mafter cut out the gowne, but I did
not bid him cut it to peeces.Ergo thou lieft.

Tail. Why heere is the note of the fafhion to teftify.

Pet. Reade it.

Gru. The note lies in's throate if he fay I faid fo.

Tail. Inprimis,a loofe bodied gowne.

Gru. Mafter, if euer I faid loofe-bodied gowne, fow
me in the skirts of it, and beate me to death with a bottome of browne thred : I faid a gowne.

Pet. Proceede.

Tai. With a fmall compaft cape.

Gru. I confeffe the cape.

Tai. With a trunke fleeue.

Gru. I confeffe two fleeues.

Tai. The fleeues curioufly cut.

Pet. I there's the villanie.

Gru. Error i'th bill fir, error i'th bill? I commanded
the fleeues fhould be cut out, and fow'd vp againe, and
that Ile proue vpon thee, though thy little finger be armed in a thimble.

Tail. This is true that I fay, and I had thee in place
where thou fhouldft know it.

Gru. I am for thee ftraight : take thou the bill, giue
me thy meat-yard, and fpare not me.

Hor. God-a-mercie *Grumio*, then hee fhall haue no
oddes.

Pet. Well fir in breefe the gowne is not for me.

Gru. You are i'th right fir, 'tis for my miftris.

Pet. Go take it vp vnto thy mafters vfe.

Gru. Villaine, not for thy life : Take vp my Miftreffe
gowne for thy mafters vfe.

Pet. Why fir, what's your conceit in that?

Gru. Oh fir, the conceit is deeper then you think for:
Take vp my Miftris gowne to his mafters vfe.
Oh fie, fie, fie.

Pet. Hortenfio, fay thou wilt fee the Tailor paide:
Go take it hence, be gone, and fay no more.

Hor. Tailor, Ile pay thee for thy gowne to morrow,
Take no vnkindneffe of his haftie words :
Away I fay,commend me to thy mafter. *Exit Tail.*

Pet. Well, come my *Kate*, we will vnto your fathers,
Euen in thefe honeft meane habiliments :
Our purfes fhall be proud, our garments poore :
For 'tis the minde that makes the bodie rich.
And as the Sunne breakes through the darkeft clouds,
So honor peereth in the meaneft habit.
What is the Iay more precious then the Larke?
Becaufe his feathers are more beautifull.
Or is the Adder better then the Eele,
Becaufe his painted skin contents the eye.
Oh no good *Kate* : neither art thou the worfe
For this poore furniture, and meane array.
If thou accountedft it fhame, lay it on me,
And therefore frolicke, we will hence forthwith,
To feaft and fport vs at thy fathers houfe,
Go call my men, and let vs ftraight to him,
And bring our horfes vnto Long-lane end,
There wil we mount, and thither walke on foote,
Let's fee, I thinke 'tis now fome feuen a clocke,
Aud well we may come there by dinner time.

Kate. I dare affure you fir,'tis almoft two,
And 'twill be fupper time ere you come there.

Pet. It fhall be feuen ere I go to horfe :
Looke what I fpeake, or do, or thinke to doe,

You

You are still croffing it, firs let't alone,
I will not goe to day, and ere I doe,
It fhall be what a clock I fay it is.
Hor. Why fo this gallant will command the funne.

Enter Tranio, and the Pedant dreft like Vincentio.
Tra. Sirs, this is the houfe, pleafe it you that I call.
Ped. I what elfe, and but I be deceiued,
Signior *Baptifta* may remember me
Neere twentie yeares a goe in *Genoa*.
Tra. Where we were lodgers, at the *Pegafus*,
Tis well, and hold your owne in any cafe
With fuch aufteritie as longeth to a father.

Enter Biondello.
Ped. I warrant you : but fir here comes your boy,
, Twere good he were fchool'd.
Tra. Feare you not him : firra *Biondello*,
Now doe your dutie throughlie I aduife you :
Imagine 'twere the right *Vincentio*.
Bion. Tut, feare not me.
Tra. But haft thou done thy errand to *Baptifta*.
Bion. I told him that your father was at *Venice*,
And that you look't for him this day in *Padua*.
Tra. Th'art a tall fellow, hold thee that to drinke,
Here comes *Baptifta* : fet your countenance fir.

Enter Baptifta and Lucentio : Pedant booted
and bare headed.
Tra. Signior *Baptifta* you are happilie met :
Sir, this is the gentleman I told you of,
I pray you ftand good father to me now,
Giue me *Bianca* for my patrimony.
Ped. Soft fon : fir by your leaue, hauing com to *Padua*
To gather in fome debts, my fon *Lucentio*
Made me acquainted with a waighty caufe
Of loue betweene your daughter and himfelfe :
And for the good report I heare of you,
And for the loue he beareth to your daughter,
And fhe to him : to ftay him not too long,
I am content in a good fathers care
To haue him matcht, and if you pleafe to like
No worfe then I, vpon fome agreement
Me fhall you finde readie and willing
With one confent to haue her fo beftowed :
For curious I cannot be with you
Signior *Baptifta*, of whom I heare fo well.
Bap. Sir, pardon me in what I haue to fay,
Your plainneffe and your fhortneffe pleafe me well :
Right true it is your fonne *Lucentio* here
Doth loue my daughter, and fhe loueth him,
Or both diffemble deeply their affections :
And therefore if you fay no more then this,
That like a Father you will deale with him,
And paffe my daughter a fufficient dower,
The match is made, and all is done,
Your fonne fhall haue my daughter with confent.
Tra. I thanke you fir, where then doe you know beft
We be affied and fuch affurance tane,
As fhall with either parts agreement ftand.
Bap. Not in my houfe *Lucentio*, for you know
Pitchers haue eares, and I haue manie feruants,
Befides old *Gremio* is harkning ftill,
And happilie we might be interrupted.
Tra. Then at my lodging, and it like you,
There doth my father lie : and there this night

Weele paffe the bufineffe priuately and well :
Send for your daughter by your feruant here,
My Boy fhall fetch the Scriuener prefentlie,
The worft is this that at fo flender warning,
You are like to haue a thin and flender pittance.
Bap. It likes me well :
Cambio hie you home, and bid *Bianca* make her readie
ftraight :
And if you will tell what hath hapned,
Lucentios Father is arriued in *Padua*,
And how fhe's like to be *Lucentios* wife.
Biond. I praie the gods fhe may withall my heart.
Exit.
Tran. Dallie not with the gods, but get thee gone.
Enter Peter.
Signior *Baptifta*, fhall I leade the way,
Welcome, one meffe is like to be your cheere,
Come fir, we will better it in *Pifa*.
Bap. I follow you.
Exeunt.

Enter Lucentio and Biondello.
Bion. Cambio.
Luc. What faift thou *Biondello*.
Biond. You faw my Mafter winke and laugh vpon
you?
Luc. *Biondello*, what of that?
Biond. Faith nothing : but has left mee here behinde
to expound the meaning or morrall of his fignes and to-
kens.
Luc. I pray thee moralize them.
Biond. Then thus : *Baptifta* is fafe talking with the
deceiuing Father of a deceitfull fonne.
Luc. And what of him?
Biond. His daughter is to be brought by you to the
fupper.
Luc. And then.
Bio. The old Prieft at Saint *Lukes* Church is at your
command at all houres.
Luc. And what of all this.
Bion. I cannot tell, expect they are bufied about a
counterfeit affurance : take you affurance of her, *Cum
preuilegio ad Impremendum folem*, to th' Church take the
Prieft, Clarke, and fome fufficient honeft witneffes :
If this be not that you looke fot, I haue no more to fay,
But bid *Bianca* farewell for euer and a day.
Luc. Hear'ft thou *Biondello*.
Biond. I cannot tarry : I knew a wench maried in an
afternoone as fhee went to the Garden for Parfeley to
ftuffe a Rabit, and fo may you fir : and fo adew fir, my
Mafter hath appointed me to goe to Saint *Lukes* to bid
the Prieft be readie to come againft you come with your
appendix.
Exit.
Luc. I may and will, if fhe be fo contented :
She will be pleas'd, then wherefore fhould I doubt :
Hap what hap may, Ile roundly goe about her :
It fhall goe hard if *Cambio* goe without her.
Exit.

Enter Petruchio, Kate, Hortentio
Petr. Come on a Gods name, once more toward our
fathers :
Good Lord how bright and goodly fhines the Moone.
Kate. The Moone, the Sunne : it is not Moonelight
now.
Pet. I fay it is the Moone that fhines fo bright.
Kate. I know it is the Sunne that fhines fo bright.
Pet. Now by my mothers fonne, and that's my felfe,
It

It fhall be moone, or ftarre, or what I lift,
Or ere I iourney to your Fathers houfe :
Goe on, and fetch our horfes backe againe,
Euermore croft and croft, nothing but croft.

Hort. Say as he faies, or we fhall neuer goe.

Kate. Forward I pray, fince we haue come fo farre,
And be it moone, or funne, or what you pleafe :
And if you pleafe to call it a rufh Candle,
Henceforth I vowe it fhall be fo for me.

Petr. I fay it is the Moone.

Kate. I know it is the Moone.

Petr. Nay then you lye : it is the bleffed Sunne.

Kate. Then God be bleft, it in the bleffed fun,
But funne it is not, when you fay it is not,
And the Moone changes euen as your minde :
What you will haue it nam'd, euen that it is,
And fo it fhall be fo for *Katherine*.

Hort. Petruchio, goe thy waies, the field is won.

Petr. Well, forward, forward, thus the bowle fhould
And not vnluckily againft the Bias :   (run,
But foft, Company is comming here·

Enter Vincentio.

Good morrow gentle Miftris, where away :
Tell me fweete *Kate*, and tell me truely too,
Haft thou beheld a frefher Gentlewoman :
Such warre of white and red within her cheekes :
What ftars do fpangle heauen with fuch beautie,
As thofe two eyes become that heauenly face ?
Faire louely Maide, once more good day to thee :
Sweete *Kate* embrace her for her beauties fake.

Hort. A will make the man mad to make the woman
of him.

Kate. Yong budding Virgin, faire, and frefh, & fweet,
Whether away, or whether is thy aboade?
Happy the Parents of fo faire a childe ;
Happier the man whom fauourable ftars
A lots thee for his louely bedfellow.

Petr. Why how now *Kate*, I hope thou art not mad,
This is a man old, wrinckled, faded, withered,
And not a Maiden, as thou faift he is.

Kate. Pardon old father my miftaking eies,
That haue bin fo bedazled with the funne,
That euery thing I looke on feemeth greene :
Now I perceiue thou art a reuerent Father :
Pardon I pray thee for my mad miftaking.

Petr. Do good old grandfire, & withall make known
Which way thou trauelleft, if along with vs,
We fhall be ioyfull of thy companie.

Vin. Faire Sir, and you my merry Miftris,
That with your ftrange encounter much amafde me :
My name is call'd *Vincentio*, my dwelling *Pifa*,
And bound I am to *Padua*, there to vifite
A fonne of mine, which long I haue not feene.

Petr. What is his name?

Vinc. Lucentio gentle fir.

Petr. Happily met, the happier for thy fonne:
And now by Law, as well as reuerent age,
I may intitle thee my louing Father,
The fifter to my wife, this Gentlewoman,
Thy Sonne by this hath married : wonder not,
Nor be not grieued, fhe is of good efteeme,
Her dowrie wealthie, and of worthie birth ;
Befide, fo qualified, as may befeeme
The Spoufe of any noble Gentleman :
Let me imbrace with old *Vincentio*,

And wander we to fee thy honeft fonne,
Who will of thy arriuall be full ioyous.

Vinc. But is this true, or is it elfe your pleafure,
Like pleafant trauailors to breake a Ieft
Vpon the companie you ouertake?

Hort. I doe affure thee father fo it is.

Petr. Come goe along and fee the truth hereof,
For our firft merriment hath made thee iealous.   *Exeunt.*

Hor. Well *Petruchio*, this has put me in heart;
Haue to my Widdow, and if fhe froward,
Then haft thou taught *Hortentio* to be vntoward.   *Exit.*

Enter Biondello, Lucentio and Bianca, Gremio is out before.

Biond. Softly and fwiftly fir, for the Prieft is ready.

Luc. I flie *Biondello* ; but they may chance to neede
thee at home, therefore leaue vs.

Biond. Nay faith, Ile fee the Church a your backe,
and then come backe to my miftris as foone as I can.

Gre. I maruaile *Cambio* comes not all this while.

Enter Petruchio, Kate, Vincentio, Grumio with Attendants.

Petr. Sir heres the doore, this is *Lucentios* houfe,
My Fathers beares more toward the Market-place,
Thither muft I, and here I leaue you fir.

Vin. You fhall not choofe but drinke before you go,
I thinke I fhall command your welcome here ;
And by all likelihood fome cheere is toward.   *Knock.*

Grem. They're bufie within, you were beft knocke
lowder.

Pedant lookes out of the window.

Ped. What's he that knockes as he would beat downe
the gate?

Vin. Is Signior *Lucentio* within fir?

Ped. He's within fir, but not to be fpoken withall.

Vinc. What if a man bring him a hundred pound or
two to make merrie withall.

Ped. Keepe your hundred pounds to your felfe, hee
fhall neede none fo long as I liue.

Petr. Nay, I told you your fonne was well beloued in
Padua : doe you heare fir, to leaue friuolous circumftances, I pray you tell fignior *Lucentio* that his Father is
come from *Pifa*, and is here at the doore to fpeake with
him.

Ped. Thou lieft his Father is come from *Padua*, and
here looking out at the window.

Vin. Art thou his father?

Ped. I fir, fo his mother faies, if I may beleeue her.

Petr. Why how now gentleman : why this is flat knauerie to take vpon you another mans name.

Peda. Lay hands on the villaine, I beleeue a meanes
to cofen fome bodie in this Citie vnder my countenance.

Enter Biondello.

Bio. I haue feene them in the Church together, God
fend'em good fhipping : but who is here? mine old Mafter *Vincentio* : now wee are vndone and brough to nothing.

Vin. Come hither crackhempe.

Bion. I hope I may choofe Sir.

Vin. Come hither you rogue, what haue you forgot
mee ?

Biond. Forgot you, no fir : I could not forget you, for
I neuer faw you before in all my life.

Vinc. What, you notorious villaine, didft thou neuer
fee thy Miftris father, *Vincentio* ?

                                      Bion. What

Bion. What my old worſhipfull old maſter? yes marie ſir ſee where he lookes out of the window.

Uin. Iſt ſo indeede.   *He beates Biondello.*

Bion. Helpe, helpe, helpe, here's a mad man will murder me.

Pedan. Helpe, ſonne, helpe ſignior *Baptiſta.*

Petr. Pree the *Kate* let's ſtand aſide and ſee the end of this controuerſie.

Enter Pedant with ſeruants, Baptiſta, Tranio.

Tra. Sir, what are you that offer to beate my ſeruant?

Vinc. What am I ſir: nay what are you ſir : oh immortall Goddes : oh fine villaine, a ſilken doubtlet, a veluet hoſe, a ſcarlet cloake, and a copataine hat : oh I am vndone, I am vndone : while I plaie the good husband at home, my ſonne and my ſeruant ſpend all at the vniuerſitie.

Tra. How now, what's the matter?

Bapt. What is the man lunaticke?

Tra. Sir, you ſeeme a ſober ancient Gentleman by your habit : but your words ſhew you a mad man : why ſir, what cernes it you, if I weare Pearle and gold: I thank my good Father, I am able to maintaine it.

Vin. Thy father : oh villaine, he is a Saile-maker in *Bergamo.*

Bap. You miſtake ſir, you miſtake ſir, praie what do you thinke is his name?

Vin. His name, as if I knew not his name : I haue brought him vp euer ſince he was three yeeres old, and his name is *Tronio.*

Ped. Awaie, awaie mad aſſe, his name is *Lucentio*, and he is mine onelie ſonne and heire to the Lands of me ſignior *Vincentio.*

Ven. Lucentio : oh he hath murdred his Maſter ; laie hold on him I charge you in the Dukes name : oh my ſonne, my ſonne : tell me thou villaine, where is my ſon *Lucentio?*

Tra. Call forth an officer : Carrie this mad knaue to the Iaile : father *Baptiſta*, I charge you ſee that hee be forth comming.

Vinc. Carrie me to the Iaile?

Gre. Staie officer, he ſhall not go to priſon.

Bap. Talke not ſignior *Gremio*: I ſaie he ſhall goe to priſon.

Gre. Take heede ſignior *Baptiſta*, leaſt you be coniкатcht in this buſineſſe : I dare ſweare this is the right *Vincentio.*

Ped. Sweare if thou dar'ſt.

Gre. Naie, I dare not ſweare it.

Tran. Then thou wert beſt ſaie that I am not *Lucentio.*

Gre. Yes, I know thee to be ſignior *Lucentio.*

Bap. Awaie with the dotard, to the Iaile with him.

Enter Biondello, Lucentio and Biancu.

Vin. Thus ſtrangers may be haild and abuſd : oh monſtrous villaine.

Bion. Oh we are ſpoil'd, and yonder he is, denie him, forſweare him, or elſe we are all vndone.

Exit Biondello, Tranio and Pedant as faſt as may be.

Luc. Pardon ſweete father.   *Kneele.*

Vin. Liues my ſweete ſonne?

Bian. Pardon deere father.

Bap. How haſt thou offended, where is *Lucentio?*

Luc. Here's *Lucentio*, right ſonne to the right *Vincentio,*

That haue by marriage made thy daughter mine, While counterfeit ſuppoſes bleer'd thine eine.

Gre. Here's packing with a witneſſe to deceiue vs all.

Vin. Where is that damned villaine *Tranio*, That fac'd and braued me in this matter ſo?

Bup. Why, tell me is not this my *Cambio?*

Bian. Cambio is chang'd into *Lucentio.*

Luc. Loue wrought theſe miracles. *Biancas* loue Made me exchange my ſtate with *Tranio*, While he did beare my countenance in the towne, And happilie I haue arriued at the laſt Vnto the wiſhed hauen of my bliſſe : What *Tranio* did, my ſelfe enforſt him to ; Then pardon him ſweete Father for my ſake.

Uin. Ile ſlit the villaines noſe that would haue ſent me to the Iaile.

Bap. But doe you heare ſir, haue you married my daughter without asking my good will?

Vin. Feare not *Baptiſta*, we will content you, goe to : but I will in to be reueng'd for this villanie.   *Exit.*

Bap. And I to ſound the depth of this knauerie.   *Exit.*

Luc. Looke not pale *Bianca*, thy father will not frown.   *Exeunt.*

Gre. My cake is doug, hbut Ile in among the reſt, Out of hope of all, but my ſhare of the feaſt.

Kate. Husband let's follow, to ſee the end of this adoe.

Petr. Firſt kiſſe me *Kate*, and we will.

Kate. What in the midſt of the ſtreete?

Petr. What art thou aſham'd of me?

Kate. Mo ſir, God forbid, but aſham'd to kiſſe.

Petr. Why then let's home againe : Come Sirra let's awaie.

Kate. Nay, I will giue thee a kiſſe, now praie thee Loue ſtaie.

Petr. Is not this well? come my ſweete *Kate.* Better once then neuer, for neuer to late.   *Exeunt.*

Actus Quintus.

Enter Baptiſta, Vincentio, Gremio, the Pedant, Lucentio, and Bianca. Tranio, Biondello Grumio, and Widdow : The Seruingmen with Tranio bringing in a Banquet.

Luc. At laſt, though long, our iarring notes agree, And time it is when raging warre is come, To ſmile at ſcapes and perils ouerblowne : My faire *Bianca* bid my father welcome, While I with ſelfeſame kindneſſe welcome thine: Brother *Petruchio*, ſiſter *Katerina*, And thou *Hortentio* with thy louing *Widdow*: Feaſt with the beſt, and welcome to my houſe, My Banket is to cloſe our ſtomakes vp After our great good cheere : praie you ſit downe, For now we ſit to chat as well as eate.

Petr. Nothing but ſit and ſit, and eate and eate.

Bap. Padua affords this kindneſſe, ſonne *Petruchio.*

Peir. Padua affords nothing but what is kinde.

Hor. For both our ſakes I would that word were true.

Pet. Now for my life *Hortentio* feares his Widow.

Wid. Then neuer truſt me if I be affeard.

Petr. You are verie ſencible, and yet you miſſe my ſenſe : I meane *Hortentio* is afeard of you.

Wid. H**ᵉ**

Wid. He that is giddie thinks the world turns round.

Petr. Roundlie replied.

Kat. Miftris, how meane you that?

Wid. Thus I conceiue by him.

Petr. Conceiues by me, how likes *Hortentio* that?

Hor. My Widdow faies, thus fhe conceiues her tale.

Petr. Verie well mended : kiffe him for that good
Widdow.

Kat. He that is giddie thinkes the world turnes round,
I praie you tell me what you meant by that.

Wid. Your housband being troubled with a fhrew,
Meafures my husbands forrow by his woe :
And now you know my meaning.

Kate. A verie meane meaning.

Wid. Right, I meane you.

Kat. And I am meane indeede, refpecting you.

Petr. To her *Kate.*

Hor. To her *Widdow.*

Petr. A hundred marks, my *Kate* does put her down.

Hor. That's my office.

Petr. Spoke like an Officer : ha to the lad .
Drinkes to Hortentio.

Bap. How likes *Gremio* thefe quicke witted folkes?

Gre. Beleeue me fir, they But together well.

Bian. Head, and but an haftie witted bodie,
Would fay your Head and But were head and horne.

Vin. I Miftris Bride, hath that awakened you?

Bian. I, but not frighted me, therefore Ile fleepe a-
gaine.

Petr. Nay that you fhall not fince you haue begun :
Haue at you for a better ieft or too.

Bian. Am I your Bird, I meane to fhift my bufh,
And then purfue me as you draw your Bow.
You are welcome all.   *Exit Bianca.*

Petr. She hath preuented me, here fignior *Tranio,*
This bird you aim'd at, though you hit her not,
Therefore a health to all that fhot and mift.

Tri. Oh fir, *Lucentio* flipt me like his Gray-hound,
Which runs himfelfe, and catches for his Mafter.

Petr. A good fwift fimile, but fomething currifh.

Tra. 'Tis well fir that you hunted for your felfe :
'Tis thought your Deere does hold you at a baie.

Bap. Oh, oh *Petruchio, Tranio* hits you now.

Luc. I thanke thee for that gird good *Tranio.*

Hor. Confeffe, confeffe, hath he not hit you here?

Petr. A has a little gald me I confeffe :
And as the Ieft did glaunce awaie from me,
'Tis ten to one it maim'd you too out right.

Bap. Now in good fadneffe fonne *Petruchio,*
I thinke thou haft the verieft fhrew of all.

Petr. Well, I fay no : and therefore fir affurance,
Let's each one fend vnto his wife,
And he whofe wife is moft obedient,
To come at firft when he doth fend for her,
Shall win the wager which we will propofe.

Hort. Content, what's the wager ?

Luc. Twentie crownes.

Petr. Twentie crownes,
Ile venture fo much of my Hawke or Hound,
But twentie times fo much vpon my Wife.

Luc. A hundred then.

Hor. Content.

Petr. A match, 'tis done.

Hor. Who fhall begin?

Luc. That will I.

Goe *Biondello,* bid your Miftris come to me.

Bio. Igoe.   *Exit.*

Bap. Sonne, Ile be your halfe, *Bianca* comes.

Luc. Ile haue no halues : Ile beare it all my felfe.
Enter Biondello.
How now, what newes?

Bio. Sir, my Miftris fends you word
That fhe is bufie, and fhe cannot come.

Petr. How? fhe's bufie, and fhe cannot come : is that
an anfwere?

Gre. I, and a kinde one too :
Praie God fir your wife fend you not a worfe.

Petr. I hope better.

Hor. Sirra *Biondello,* goe and intreate my wife to
come to me forthwith.   *Exit. Bion.*

Pet. Oh ho, intreate her, nay then fhee muft needes
come.

Hor. I am affraid fir, doe what you can
Enter Biondello.
Yours will not be entreated : Now, where's my wife ?

Bion. She faies you haue fome goodly Ieft in hand,
She will not come : fhe bids you come to her.

Petr. Worfe and worfe, fhe will not come :
Oh vilde, intollerable, not to be indur'd :
Sirra *Grumio,* goe to your Miftris,
Say I command her come to me.   *Exit.*

Hor. I know her anfwere,

Pet. What?

Hor. She will not.

Petr. The fouler fortune mine, and there an end.

Enter Katerina.

Bap. Now by my hollidam here comes *Katerina.*

Kat. What is your will fir, that you fend for me?

Petr. Where is your fifter, and *Hortenfios* wife?

Kate. They fit conferring by the Parler fire.

Petr. Goe fetch them hither, if they denie to come,
Swinge me them foundly forth vnto their husbands :
Away I fay, and bring them hither ftraight.

Luc. Here is a wonder, if you talke of a wonder.

Hor. And fo it is : I wonder what it boads.

Petr. Marrie peace it boads, and loue, and quiet life,
An awfull rule, and right fupremicie :
And to be fhort, what not, that's fweete and happie.

Bap. Now faire befall thee good *Petruchio ;*
The wager thou haft won, and I will adde
Vnto their loffes twentie thoufand crownes,
Another dowrie to another daughter,
For fhe is chang'd as fhe had neuer bin.

Petr. Nay, I will win my wager better yet,
And fhow more figne of her obedience,
Her new built vertue and obedience.

Enter Kate, Bianca, and Widdow.

See where fhe comes, and brings your froward Wiues
As prifoners to her womanlie perfwafion :
Katerine, that Cap of yours becomes you not,
Off with that bable, throw it vnderfoote.

Wid. Lord let me neuer haue a caufe to figh,
Till I be brought to fuch a fillie paffe.

Bian. Fie what a foolifh dutie call you this?

Luc. I would your dutie were as foolifh too :
The wifdome of your dutie faire *Bianca,*
Hath coft me fiue hundred crownes fince fupper time.

Bian. The more foole you for laying on my dutie.

Pet. *Katherine* I charge thee tell thefe head-ftrong
women, what dutie they doe owe their Lords and hufbands.

Wid. Come,

Wid. Come, come, your mocking: we will haue no telling.

Pet. Come on I fay, and firſt begin with her.

Wid. She ſhall not.

Pet. I fay ſhe ſhall, and firſt begin with her.

Kate. Fie, fie, vnknit that thretaning vnkinde brow,
And dart not ſcornefull glances from thoſe eies,
To wound thy Lord, thy King, thy Gouernour.
It blots thy beautie, as froſts doe bite the Meads,
Confounds thy fame, as whirlewinds ſhake faire budds,
And in no ſence is meete or amiable .
A woman mou'd, is like a fountaine troubled,
Muddie, ill ſeeming, thicke, bereft of beautie,
And while it is ſo, none ſo dry or thirſtie
Will daigne to ſip, or touch one drop of it.
Thy husband is thy Lord, thy life, thy keeper,
Thy head, thy ſoueraigne : One that cares for thee,
And for thy maintenance. Commits his body
To painfull labour, both by ſea and land :
To watch the night in ſtormes, the day in cold,
Whil'ſt thou ly'ſt warme at home, ſecure and ſafe,
And craues no other tribute at thy hands,
But loue, faire lookes, and true obedience ;
Too little payment for ſo great a debt.
Such dutie as the ſubiect owes the Prince,
Euen ſuch a woman oweth to her husband :
And when ſhe is froward, peeuiſh, ſullen, ſowre,
And not obedient to his honeſt will,
What is ſhe but a foule contending Rebell,
And graceleſſe Traitor to her louing Lord?
I am aſham'd that women are ſo ſimple,

To offer warre, where they ſhould kneele for peace :
Or ſeeke for rule, ſupremacie, and ſway,
When they are bound to ſerue, loue, and obay.
Why are our bodies ſoft, and weake, and ſmooth,
Vnapt to toyle and trouble in the world,
But that our ſoft conditions, and our harts,
Should well agree with our externall parts ?
Come, come, you froward and vnable wormes,
My minde hath bin as bigge as one of yours,
My heart as great, my reaſon haplie more,
To bandie word for word, and frowne for frowne ;
But now I ſee our Launces are but ſtrawes :
Our ſtrength as weake, our weakeneſſe paſt compare,
That ſeeming to be moſt, which we indeed leaſt are.
Then vale your ſtomackes, for it is no boote,
And place your hands below your husbands foote :
In token of which dutie, if he pleaſe,
My hand is readie, may it do him eaſe.

Pet. Why there's a wench : Come on, and kiſſe mee
Kate.

Luc. Well go thy waies olde Lad for thou ſhalt ha't.

Vin. Tis a good hearing, when children are toward.

Luc. But a harſh hearing, when women are froward,

Pet. Come *Kate*, weee'le to bed,
We three are married, but you two are ſped.
'Twas I wonne the wager, though you hit the white,
And being a winner, God giue you good night.

Exit Petruchio

Horten. Now goe thy wayes, thou haſt tam'd a curſt
Shrow.

Luc. Tis a wonder, by your leaue, ſhe wil be tam'd ſo.

FINIS.

V v

ALL'S
Well, that Ends Well.

Actus primus. Scæna Prima.

Enter yong Bertram Count of Rossillion, his Mother, and Helena, Lord Lafew, all in blacke.

Mother.

N deliuering my sonne from me, I burie a second husband.

Rof. And I in going Madam, weep ore my fathers death anew; but I must attend his maiesties command, to whom I am now in Ward, euermore in subiection.

Laf. You shall find of the King a husband Madame, you sir a father. He that so generally is at all times good, must of necessitie hold his vertue to you, whose worthinesse would stirre it vp where it wanted rather then lack it where there is such abundance.

Mo. What hope is there of his Maiesties amendment?

Laf. He hath abandon'd his Phisitions Madam, vnder whose practises he hath persecuted time with hope, and finds no other aduantage in the processe, but onely the loosing of hope by time.

Mo. This yong Gentlewoman had a father, O that had, how sad a passage tis, whose skill was almost as great as his honestie, had it stretch'd so far, would haue made nature immortall, and death should haue play for lacke of worke. Would for the Kings sake hee were liuing, I thinke it would be the death of the Kings disease.

Laf. How call'd you the man you speake of Madam?

Mo. He was famous sir in his profession, and it was his great right to be so : *Gerard de Narbon.*

Laf. He was excellent indeed Madam, the King very latelie spoke of him admiringly, and mourningly : hee was skilfull enough to haue liu'd stil, if knowledge could be set vp against mortallitie.

Rof. What is it (my good Lord) the King languishes of?

Laf. A Fistula my Lord.

Rof. I heard not of it before.

Laf. I would it were not notorious. Was this Gentlewoman the Daughter of *Gerard de Narbon?*

Mo. His sole childe my Lord, and bequeathed to my ouer looking. I haue those hopes of her good, that her education promises her dispositions shee inherits, which makes faire gifts fairer : for where an vncleane mind carries vertuous qualities, there commendations go with pitty, they are vertues and traitors too : in her they are the better for their simplenesse; she deriues her honestie,

and atcheeues her goodnesse.

Lafew. Your commendations Madam get from her teares.

Mo. 'Tis the best brine a Maiden can season her praise in. The remembrance of her father neuer approches her heart, but the tirrany of her sorrowes takes all luelihood from her cheeke. No more of this *Helena*, go too, no more least it be rather thought you affect a sorrow, then to haue——

Hell. I doe affect a sorrow indeed, but I haue it too.

Laf. Moderate lamentation is the right of the dead, excessiue greefe the enemie to the liuing.

Mo. If the liuing be enemie to the greefe, the excesse makes it soone mortall.

Rof. Maddam I desire your holie wishes.

Laf. How vnderstand we that?

Mo. Be thou blest *Bertrame*, and succeed thy father
In manners as in shape : thy blood and vertue
Contend for Empire in thee, and thy goodnesse
Share with thy birth-right. Loue all, trust a few,
Doe wrong to none : be able for thine enemie
Rather in power then vse : and keepe thy friend
Vnder thy owne lifes key. Be checkt for silence,
But neuer tax'd for speech. What heauen more wil,
That thee may furnish, and my prayers plucke downe,
Fall on thy head. Farwell my Lord,
'Tis an vnseason'd Courtier, good my Lord
Aduise him.

Laf. He cannot want the best
That shall attend his loue.

Mo. Heauen blesse him : Farwell *Bertram.*

Ro. The best wishes that can be forg'd in your thoghts be seruants to you : be comfortable to my mother, your Mistris, and make much of her.

Laf. Farewell prettie Lady, you must hold the credit of your father.

Hell. O were that all, I thinke not on my father,
And these great teares grace his remembrance more
Then those I shed for him. What was he like?
I haue forgott him. My imagination
Carries no fauour in't but *Bertrams.*
I am vndone, there is no liuing, none,
If *Bertram* be away. 'Twere all one,
That I should loue a bright particuler starre,
And think to wed it, he is so aboue me
In his bright radience and colaterall light,

Must

Muſt I be comforted, not in his ſphere;
Th'ambition in my loue thus plagues it ſelfe:
The hind that would be mated by the Lion
Muſt die for loue. 'Twas prettie, though a plague
To ſee him euerie houre to fit and draw
His arched browes, his hawking eie, his curles
In our hearts table : heart too capeable
Of euerie line and tricke of his ſweet fauour.
But now he's gone, and my idolatrous fancie
Muſt ſanctifie his Reliques. Who comes heere?

Enter Parrolles.

One that goes with him : I loue him for his ſake,
And yet I know him a notorious Liar,
Thinke him a great way foole, ſolie a coward,
Yet theſe fixt euils ſit ſo fit in him,
That they take place, when Vertues ſteely bones
Lookes bleake i'th cold wind : withall, full ofte we ſee
Cold wiſedome waighting on ſuperfluous follie.
  Par. Saue you faire Queene.
  Hel. And you Monarch.
  Par. No.
  Hel. And no.
  Par. Are you meditating on virginitie?
  Hel. It you haue ſome ſtaine of ſouldier in you : Let
mee aske you a queſtion. Man is enemie to virginitie,
how may we barracado it againſt him?
  Par. Keepe him out.
  Hel. But he aſſailes, and our virginitie though vail-
ant, in the defence yet is weak : vnfold to vs ſome war-
like reſiſtance.
  Par. There is none : Man ſetting downe before you,
will vndermine you, and blow you vp.
  Hel. Bleſſe our poore Virginity from vnderminers
and blowers vp. Is there no Military policy how Virgins might blow vp men ?
  Par. Virginity beeing blowne downe , Man will
quicklier be blowne vp : marry in blowing him downe
againe, with the breach your ſelues made, you loſe your
Citty. It is not politicke, in the Common-wealth of
Nature, to preſerue virginity. Loſſe of Virginitie, is
rationall encreaſe, and there was neuer Virgin goe, till
virginitie was firſt loſt. That you were made of, is mettall to make Virgins. Virginitie, by beeing once loſt,
may be ten times found : by being euer kept, it is euer
loſt: 'tis too cold a companion: Away with't.
  Hel. I will ſtand for't a little, though therefore I die
a Virgin.
  Par. There's little can bee ſaide in't, 'tis againſt the
rule of Nature. To ſpeake on the part of virginitie, is
to accuſe your Mothers; which is moſt infallible diſobedience. He that hangs himſelfe is a Virgin : Virginitie murthers it ſelfe, and ſhould be buried in highwayes
out of all ſanctified limit, as a deſperate Offendreſſe a-
gainſt Nature. Virginitie breedes mites, much like a
Cheeſe, conſumes it ſelfe to the very payring, and ſo
dies with feeding his owne ſtomacke. Beſides, Virginitie is peeuiſh, proud, ydle, made of ſelfe-loue, which
is the moſt inhibited ſinne in the Cannon. Keepe it not,
you cannot chooſe but looſe by't. Out with't : within
ten yeare it will make it ſelfe two, which is a goodly increaſe, and the principall it ſelfe not much the worſe .
Away with't.
  Hel. How might one do ſir, to looſe it to her owne
liking?

  Par. Let mee ſee . Marry ill, to like him that ne're
it likes. 'Tis a commoditie wil loſe the gloſſe with lying:
The longer kept, the leſſe worth : Off with't while 'tis
vendible. Anſwer the time of requeſt, Virginitie like
an olde Courtier, weares her cap out of faſhion, richly
ſuted, but vnſuteable, iuſt like the brooch & the tooth-
pick, which were not now : your Date is better in your
Pye and your Porredge, then in your cheeke : and your
virginity, your old virginity, is like one of our French
wither'd peares, it lookes ill, it eates drily, marry 'tis a
wither'd peare : it was formerly better, marry yet 'tis a
wither'd peare : Will you any thing with it?
  Hel. Not my virginity yet :
There ſhall your Maſter haue a thouſand loues,
A Mother, and a Miſtreſſe, and a friend,
A Phenix, Captaine, and an enemy,
A guide, a Goddeſſe, and a Soueraigne,
A Counſellor, a Traitoreſſe, and a Deare :
His humble ambition, proud humility :
His iarring, concord : and his diſcord, dulcet:
His faith, his ſweet diſaſter : with a world
Of pretty fond adoptious chriſtendomes
That blinking Cupid goſſips. Now ſhall he:
I know not what he ſhall, God ſend him well,
The Courts a learning place, and he is one.
  Par. What one iſaith?
  Hel. That I wiſh well, 'tis pitty.
  Par. What's pitty?
  Hel. That wiſhing well had not a body in't,
Which might be felt, that we the poorer borne,
Whoſe baſer ſtarres do ſhut vs vp in wiſhes,
Might vvith effects of them follow our friends,
And ſhew what vve alone muſt thinke, which neuer
Returnes vs thankes.

Enter Page.

  Pag. Monſieur Parrolles,
My Lord cals for you.
  Par. Little *Hellen* farewell, if I can remember thee, I
will thinke of thee at Court.
  Hel. Monſieur Parolles, you were borne vnder a
charitable ſtarre.
  Par. Vnder Mars I.
  Hel. I eſpecially thinke, vnder Mars.
  Par. Why vnder Mars?
  Hel. The warres hath ſo kept you vnder, that you
muſt needes be borne vnder Mars.
  Par. When he was predominant.
  Hel. When he was retrograde I thinke rather.
  Par. Why thinke you ſo?
  Hel. You go ſo much backward when you fight.
  Par. That's for aduantage.
  Hel. So is running away,
When feare propoſes the ſafetie :
But the compoſition that your valour and feare makes
in you , is a vertue of a good wing, and I like the
weare well.
  Paroll. I am ſo full of buſineſſes, I cannot anſwere
thee acutely : I will returne perfect Courtier, in the
which my inſtruction ſhall ſerue to naturalize thee, ſo
thou wilt be capeable of a Courtiers councell, and vnderſtand what aduice ſhall thruſt vppon thee, elſe thou
dieſt in thine vnthankfulnes, and thine ignorance makes
thee away, farewell : When thou haſt leyſure, ſay thy
praiers : when thou haſt none, remember thy Friends:
Get

Get thee a good husband , and vſe him as he vſes thee :
So farewell.

Hel. Our remedies oft in our ſelues do lye,
Which we aſcribe to heauen : the fated skye
Giues vs free ſcope, onely doth backward pull
Our ſlow deſignes, when we our ſelues are dull.
What power is it, which mounts my loue ſo hye,
That makes me ſee, and cannot feede mine eye ?
The mightieſt ſpace in fortune, Nature brings
To ioyne like, likes ; and· kiſſe like natiue things.
Impoſſible be ſtrange attempts to thoſe
That weigh their paines in ſence, and do ſuppoſe
What hath beene, cannot be. Who euer ſtroue
To ſhew her merit, that did miſſe her loue ?
(The Kings diſeaſe) my proiect may deceiue me,
But my intents are fixt, and will not leaue me.   *Exit*

Flouriſh Cornets.
Enter the King of France with Letters, and
diuers Attendants.

King. The *Florentines* and *Senoys* are by th'eares,
Haue ſought with equall fortune, and continue
A brauing warre.

1.*Lo.G.* So tis reported ſir.

King. Nay tis moſt credible, we heere receiue it,
A certaintie vouch'd from our Coſin *Auſtria,*
With caution, that the *Florentine* will moue vs
For ſpeedie ayde: wherein our decreſt friend
Preiudicates the buſineſſe, and would ſeeme
To haue vs make deniall.

1.*Lo.G.* His loue and wiſedome
Approu'd ſo to your Maieſty, may pleade
For ampleſt credence.

King. He hath arm'd our anſwer,
And *Florence* is deni'de before he comes :
Yet for our Gentlemen that meane to ſee
The *Tuſcan* ſeruice, freely haue they leaue
To ſtand on either part.

2.*Lo.E.* It well may ſerue
A nurſſerie to our Gentrie, who are ſicke
For breathing, and exploit.

King. What's he comes heere.

Enter Bertram, Lafew, and Parolles.

1.*Lor.G.* It is the Count *Roſignoll* my good Lord,
Yong *Bertram.*

King. Youth, thou bear'ſt thy Fathers face,
Franke Nature rather curious then in haſt
Hath well compos'd thee : Thy Fathers morall parts
Maiſt thou inherit too : Welcome to *Paris.*

Ber. My thankes and dutie are your Maieſties.

Kin. I would I had that corporall ſoundneſſe now,
As when thy father, and my ſelfe, in friendſhip
Firſt tride our ſouldierſhip : he did looke farre
Into the ſeruice of the time, and was
Diſcipled of the braueſt. He laſted long,
But on vs both did haggiſh Age ſteale on,
And wore vs out of act : It much repaires me
To talke of your good father ; in his youth
He had the wit, which I can well obſerue
To day in our yong Lords : but they may ieſt
Till their owne ſcorne returne to them vnnoted
Ere they can hide their leuitie in honour :
So like a Courtier, contempt nor bitterneſſe

Were in his pride, or ſharpneſſe ; if they were,
His equall had awak'd them, and his honour
Clocke to it ſelfe, knew the true minute when
Exception bid him ſpeake : and at this time
His tongue obey'd his hand. Who were below him,
He vs'd as creatures of another place,
Aud bow'd his eminent top to their low rankes,
Making them proud of his humilitie,
In their poore praiſe he humbled : Such a man
Might be a copie to theſe yonger times ;
Which followed well, would demonſtrate them now
But goers backward.

Ber. His good remembrance ſir
Lies richer in your thoughts, then on his tombe:
So in approofe liues not his Epitaph, ·
As in your royall ſpeech.

King. Would I were with him he would alwaies ſay,
(Me thinkes I heare him now) his plauſiue words
He ſcatter'd not in eares, but grafted them
To grow there and to beare : Let me not liue,
This his good melancholly oft began
On the Cataſtrophe and heele of paſtime
When it was out : Let me not liue (quoth hee)
After my flame lackes oyle, to be the ſnuffe
Of yonger ſpirits, whoſe apprehenſiue ſenſes
All but new things diſdaine ; whoſe iudgements are
Meere fathers of their garments : whoſe conſtancies
Expire before their faſhions : this he wiſh'd.
I after him, do after him wiſh too :
Since I nor wax nor honie can bring home,
I quickly were diſſolued from my hiue
To giue ſome Labourers roome.

L.2.E. You'r loued Sir,
They that leaſt lend it you, ſhall lacke you firſt.

Kin. I fill a place I know't : how long iſt Count
Since the Phyſitian at your fathers died?
He was much fam'd.

Ber. Some ſix moneths ſince my Lord.

Kin. If he were liuing, I would try him yet.
Lend me an arme : the reſt haue worne me out
With ſeuerall applications : Nature and ſickneſſe
Debate it at their leiſure. Welcome Count,
My ſonne's no deerer.

Ber. Thanke your Maieſty.   *Exit*

Flouriſh.

Enter Counteſſe, Steward, and Clowne.

Coun. I will now heare, what ſay you of this gentlewoman.

Ste. Maddam the care I haue had to euen your content, I wiſh might be found in the Kalender of my paſt
endeuours, for then we wound our Modeſtie, and make
foule the clearneſſe of our deſeruings, whenof our ſelues
we publiſh them.

Coun. What doe's this knaue heere? Get you gone
ſirra: the complaints I haue heard of you I do not all beleeue, 'tis my ſlowneſſe that I doe not : For I know you
lacke not folly to commit them, & haue abilitie enough
to make ſuch knaueries yours.

Clo. 'Tis not vnknown to you Madam, I am a poore
fellow.

Coun. Well ſir.

Clo. No maddam,
'Tis not ſo well that I am poore, though manie
of

of the rich are damn'd, but if I may haue your Ladiſhips
good will to goe to the world, *Isbell* the woman and w
will doe as we may.

Coun. Wilt thou needes be a begger?

Clo. I doe beg your good will in this caſe.

Cou. In what caſe?

Clo. In *Isbels* caſe and mine owne : ſeruice is no heri-
tage, and I thinke I ſhall neuer haue the bleſſing of God,
till I haue iſſue a my bodie : for they ſay barnes are bleſſings.

Cou. Tell me thy reaſon why thou wilt marrie?

Clo. My poore bodie Madam requires it, I am driuen
onby the fleſh, and hee muſt needes goe that the diuell
driues.

Cou. Is this all your worſhips reaſon?

Clo. Faith Madam I haue other holie reaſons, ſuch as
they are.

Con. May the world know them?

Clo. I haue beene Madam a wicked creature, as you
and all fleſh and blood are, and indeede I doe marrie that
I may repent.

Cou. Thy marriage ſooner then thy wickedneſſe.

Clo. I am out a friends Madam, and I hope to haue
friends for my wiues ſake.

Cou. Such friends are thine enemies knaue.

Clo. Y'are ſhallow Madam in great friends, for the
knaues come to doe that for me which I am a wearie of:
he that eres my Land, ſpares my teame, and giues mee
leaue to Inne the crop : if I be his cuckold hee's my
drudge; he that comforts my wife, is the cheriſher of
my fleſh and blood; hee that cheriſhes my fleſh and
blood, loues my fleſh and blood; he that loues my fleſh
and blood is my friend:*ergo*, he that kiſſes my wife is my
friend : if men could be contented to be what they are,
there were no feare in marriage, for yong *Charbon* the
Puritan, and old *Poyſam* the Papiſt, how ſomere their
hearts are ſeuer'd in Religion, their heads are both one,
they may ioule horns together like any Deare i'th Herd.

Cou. Wilt thou euer be a foule mouth'd and calum-
nious knaue?

Clo. A Prophet I Madam, and I ſpeake the truth the
next waie, for I the Ballad will repeate, which men full
true ſhall finde, your marriage comes by deſtinie, your
Cuckow ſings by kinde.

Cou. Get you gone ſir, Ile talke with you more anon.

Stew. May it pleaſe you Madam, that hee bid *Hellen*
come to you, of her I am to ſpeake.

Cou. Sirra tell my gentlewoman I would ſpeake with
her, *Hellen* I meane.

Clo. Was this faire face the cauſe, quoth ſhe,
Why the Grecians ſacked *Troy*,
Fond done, done, fond was this King *Priams* ioy,
With that ſhe ſighed as ſhe ſtood, *bis*
And gaue this ſentence then, among nine bad if one be
good, among nine bad if one be good, there's yet one
good in ten.

Cou. What, one good in tenne? you corrupt the ſong
ſirra.

Clo. One good woman in ten Madam, which is a pu-
rifying ath'ſong : would God would ſerue the world ſo
all the yeere, weed finde no fault with the tithe woman
if I were the Parſon, one in ten quoth a? and wee might
haue a good woman borne but ore euerie blazing ſtarre,
or at an earthquake, 'twould mend the Lotteriewell, a
man may draw his heart out ere a plucke one.

Cou. Youle begone ſir knaue, and doe as I command
you?

Clo. That man ſhould be at womans command, and
yet no hurt done, though honeſtie be no Puritan, yet
it will doe no hurt, it will weare the Surplis of humilitie
ouer the blacke-Gowne of a bigge heart : I am going forſooth, the buſineſſe is for *Helen* to come hither.
Exit.

Cou. Well now.

Stew. I know Madam you loue your Gentlewoman
intirely.

Cou. Faith I doe : her Father bequeath'd her to mee,
and ſhe her ſelfe without other aduantage, may lawfullie make title to as much loue as ſhee findes, there is
more owing her then is paid, and more ſhall be paid
her then ſheele demand.

Stew. Madam, I was verie late more neere her then
I thinke ſhee wiſht mee, alone ſhee was, and did
communicate to her ſelfe her owne words to her
owne eares, ſhee thought, I dare vowe for her, they
toucht not anie ſtranger ſence, her matter was, ſhee
loued your Sonne; Fortune ſhee ſaid was no goddeſſe, that had put ſuch difference betwixt their two
eſtates : Loue no god, that would not extend his might
onelie, where qualities were leuell, Queene of Virgins, that would ſuffer her poore Knight ſurpris'd
without reſcue in the firſt aſſault or ranſome afterward : This ſhee deliuer'd in the moſt bitter touch of
ſorrow that ere I heard Virgin exclaime in, which I held
my dutie ſpeedily to acquaint you withall, ſithence in
the loſſe that may happen, it concernes you ſomething
to know it.

Cou. You haue diſcharg'd this honeſtlie, keepe it
to your ſelfe, manie likelihoods inform'd mee of this
before, which hung ſo tottring in the ballance, that
I could neither beleeue nor miſdoubt : praie you
leaue mee, ſtall this in your boſome, and I thanke
you for your honeſt care : I will ſpeake with you further anon. *Exit Steward.*

Enter Hellen.

Old.Cou. Euen ſo it vvas vvith me when I was yong:
If euer vve are natures, theſe are ours, this thorne
Doth to our Roſe of youth righlie belong
Our bloud to vs, this to our blood is borne,
It is the ſhow, and ſeale of natures truth,
Where loues ſtrong paſſion is impreſt in youth,
By our remembrances of daies forgon,
Such were our faults, or then we thought them none,
Her eie is ſicke on't, I obſerue her now.

Hell. What is your pleaſure Madam?

Ol.Cou. You know *Hellen* I am a mother to you.

Hell. Mine honorable Miſtris.

Ol.Cou. Nay a mother, why not a mother? when I
ſed a mother
Me thought you ſaw a ſerpent, what's in mother,
That you ſtart at it? I ſay I am your mother,
And put you in the Catalogue of thoſe
That were enwombed mine, 'tis often ſeene
Adoption ſtriues vvith nature, and choiſe breedes
A natiue ſlip to vs from forraine ſeedes :
You nere oppreſt me with a mothers groane,
Yet I expreſſe to you a mothers care,
(Gods mercie maiden) dos it curd thy blood
To ſay I am thy mother? vvhat's the matter,
That this diſtempered meſſenger of wet?

The

The manie colour'd Iris rounds thine eye?
————Why, that you are my daughter?
Hell. That I am not.
Old.Cou. I fay I am your Mother.
Hell. Pardon Madam.
The Count *Rofilion* cannot be my brother:
I am from humble, he from honored name:
No note vpon my Parents, his all noble,
My Mafter, my deere Lord he is, and I
His feruant liue, and will his vaffall die:
He muft not be my brother.
Ol.Cou. Nor I your Mother.
Hell. You are my mother Madam, would you were
So that my Lord your fonne were not my brother,
Indeede my mother, or were you both our mothers,
I care no more for, then I doe for heauen,
So I were not his fifter, cant no other,
But I your daughter, he muft be my brother.
Old.Cou. Yes *Hellen*, you might be my daughter in law,
God fhield you meane it not, daughter and mother
So ftriue vpon your pulfe; vvhat pale agen?
My feare hath catcht your fondneffe! now I fee
The miftrie of your louelineffe, and finde
Your falt teares head, now to all fence 'tis groffe:
You loue my fonne, inuention is afham'd
Againft the proclamation of thy paffion
To fay thou dooft not: therefore tell me true,
But tell me then 'tis fo, for looke, thy cheekes
Confeffe it 'ton tooth to th'other, and thine eies
See it fo grofely fhowne in thy behauiours,
That in their kinde they fpeake it, onely finne
And hellifh obftinacie tye thy tongue
That truth fhould be fufpected, fpeake, ift fo?
If it be fo, you haue wound a goodly clewe:
If it be not, forfweare't how ere I charge thee,
As heauen fhall worke in me for thine auaile
To tell me truelie.
Hell. Good Madam pardon me.
Cou. Do you loue my Sonne?
Hell. Your pardon noble Miftris.
Cou. Loue you my Sonne?
Hell. Doe not you loue him Madam?
Cou. Goe not about; my loue hath in't a bond
Whereof the world takes note: Come, come, difclofe:
The ftate of your affection, for your paffions
Haue to the full appeach'd.
Hell. Then I confeffe
Here on my knee, before high heauen and you,
That before you, and next vnto high heauen, I loue your
Sonne:
My friends were poore but honeft, fo's my loue:
Be not offended, for it hurts not him
That he is lou'd of me; I follow him not
By any token of prefumptuous fuite,
Nor would I haue him, till I doe deferue him,
Yet neuer know how that defert fhould be:
I know I loue in vaine, ftriue againft hope:
Yet in this captious, and intemible Slue.
I ftill poure in the waters of my loue
And lacke not to loofe ftill; thus *Indian* like
Religious in mine error, I adore
The Sunne that lookes vpon his worfhipper,
But knowes of him no more. My deereft Madam,
Let not your hate incounter with my loue,
For louing where you doe; but if your felfe,
Whofe aged honor cites a vertuous youth,

Did euer, in fo true a flame of liking,
Wifh chaftly, and loue dearely, that your *Dian*
Was both her felfe and loue, O then giue pittie
To her whofe ftate is fuch, that cannot choofe
But lend and giue where fhe is fure to loofe;
That feekes not to finde that, her fearch implies,
But riddle like, liues fweetely where fhe dies.
Cou. Had you not lately an intent, fpeake truely,
To goe to *Paris?*
Hell. Madam I had.
Cou. Wherefore? tell true.
Hell. I will tell truth, by grace it felfe I fweare:
You know my Father left me fome prefcriptions
Of rare and prou'd effects, fuch as his reading
And manifeft experience, had collected
For generall foueraigntie: and that he wil'd me
In heedefull'ft referuation to beftow them,
As notes, whofe faculties inclufiue were,
More then they were in note: Amongft the reft,
There is a remedie, approu'd, fet downe,
To cure the defperate languifhings whereof
The King is render'd loft.
Cou. This was your motiue for *Paris*, was it, fpeake?
Hell. My Lord, your fonne, made me to think of this;
Elfe *Paris*, and the medicine, and the King,
Had from the conuerfation of my thoughts,
Happily beene abfent then.
Cou. But thinke you *Hellen*,
If you fhould tender your fuppofed aide,
He would receiue it? He and his Phifitions
Are of a minde, he, that they cannot helpe him:
They, that they cannot helpe, how fhall they credit
A poore vnlearned Virgin, when the Schooles
Embowel'd of their doctrine, haue left off
The danger to it felfe.
Hell. There's fomething in't
More then my Fathers skill, which was the great'ft
Of his profeffion, that his good receipt,
Shall for my legacie be fanctified
Byth'luckieft ftars in heauen, and would your honor
But giue me leaue to trie fucceffe, I'de venture
The well loft life of mine, on his Graces cure,
By fuch a day, an houre.
Cou. Doo'ft thou beleeue't?
Hell. I Madam knowingly.
Cou. Why *Hellen* thou fhalt haue my leaue and loue,
Meanes and attendants, and my louing greetings
To thofe of mine in Court, Ile ftaie at home
And praie Gods bleffing into thy attempt:
Begon to morrow, and be fure of this,
What I can helpe thee to, thou fhalt not miffe. *Exeunt.*

Actus Secundus.

*Enter the King with diuers yong Lords, taking leaue for
the Florentine warre: Count, Roffe, and
Parrolles. Florifh Cornets.*

King. Farewell yong Lords, thefe warlike principles
Doe not throw from you, and you my Lords farewell:
Share the aduice betwixt you, if both gaine, all
The guift doth ftretch it felfe as 'tis receiu'd,
And is enough for both.
Lord.G. 'Tis our hope fir,

After

After well entred fouldiers, to returne
And finde your grace in health.

King. No, no, it cannot be ; and yet my heart
Will not confeffe he owes the mallady
That doth my life befiege : farwell yong Lords,
Whether I liue or die, be you the fonnes
Of worthy French men : let higher Italy
(Thofe bated that inherit but the fall
Of the laft Monarchy) fee that you come
Not to wooe honour, but to wed it, when
The braueft queftant fhrinkes : finde what you feeke,
That fame may cry you loud : I fay farewell.

L.G. Health at your bidding ferue your Maiefty.

King. Thofe girles of Italy, take heed of them,
They fay our French, lacke language to deny
If they demand : beware of being Captiues
Before you ferue.

Bo. Our hearts receiue your warnings.

King. Farewell, come hether to me.

1.Lo.G. Oh my fweet Lord ỹ you wil ftay behind vs.

Parr. 'Tis not his fault the fpark.

2.Lo.E. Oh 'tis braue warres.

Parr. Moft admirable, I haue feene thofe warres.

Roffill. I am commanded here, and kept a coyle with,
Too young, and the next yeere, and 'tis too early.

Parr. And thy minde ftand too't boy,
Steale away brauely.

Roffill. I fhal ftay here the for-horfe to a fmocke,
Creeking my fhooes on the plaine Mafonry,
Till honour be bought vp, and no fword worne
But one to dance with : by heauen, Ile fteale away.

1.Lo.G. There's honour in the theft.

Parr. Commit it Count.

2.Lo.E. I am your acceffary, and fo farewell.

Rof. I grow to you, & our parting is a tortur'd body.

1.Lo.G. Farewll Captaine.

2.Lo.E. Sweet Mounfier *Parolles.*

Parr. Noble *Heroes* ; my fword and yours are kinne,
good fparkes and luftrous, a word good mettals. You
fhall finde in the Regiment of the Spinij, one Captaine
Spurio his ficatrice, with an Embleme of warre heere on
his finifter cheeke ; it was this very fword entrench'd it :
fay to him I liue, and obferue his reports for me.

Lo.G. We fhall noble Captaine.

Parr. Mars doate on you for his nouices, what will
ye doe ?

Roff. Stay the King.

Parr. Vfe a more fpacious ceremonie to the Noble
Lords, you haue reftrain'd your felfe within the Lift of
too cold an adieu : be more expreffiue to them ; for they
weare themfelues in the cap of the time, there do mufter
true gate; eat, fpeake, and moue vnder the influence of
the moft receiu'd ftarre, and though the deuill leade the
meafure, fuch are to be followed: after them, and take a
more dilated farewell.

Roff. And I will doe fo.

Parr. Worthy fellowes, and like to prooue moft fi-
newie fword-men. *Exeunt.*

Enter Lafew.

L.Laf. Pardon my Lord for mee and for my tidings.

King. Ile fee thee to ftand vp. (pardon,

L.Laf. Then heres a man ftands that has brought his
I would you had kneel'd my Lord to aske me mercy,
And that at my bidding you could fo ftand vp.

King. I would I had, fo I had broke thy pate

And askt thee mercy for't.

Laf. Goodfaith a-croffe, but my good Lord 'tis thus,
Will you be cur'd of your infirmitie ?

King. No.

Laf. O will you eat no grapes my royall foxe ?
Yes but you will, my noble grapes, and if
My royall foxe could reach them: I haue feen a medicine
That's able to breath life into a ftone,
Quicken a rocke, and make you dance Canari
With fprightly fire and motion, whofe fimple touch
Is powerfull to arayfe King *Pippen*, nay
To giue great *Charlemaine* a pen in's hand
And write to her a loue-line.

King. What her is this ?

Laf. Why doctor fhe is : my Lord, there's one arriu'd,
If you will fee her : now by my faith and honour,
If ferioufly I may conuay my thoughts
In this my light deliuerance, I haue fpoke
With one, that in her fexe, her yeeres, profeffion,
Wifedome and conftancy, hath amaz'd mee more
Then I dare blame my weakeneffe : will you fee her ?
For that is her demand, and know her bufineffe ?
That done, laugh well at me.

King. Now good *Lafew*,
Bring in the admiration, that we with thee
May fpend our wonder too, or take off thine
By wondring how thou tookft it.

Laf. Nay, Ile fit you,
And not be all day neither.

King. Thus he bis fpeciall nothing euer prologues.

Laf. Nay, come your waies.

Enter Hellen.

King. This hafte hath wings indeed.

Laf. Nay, come your waies,
This is his Maieftie, fay your minde to him,
A Traitor you doe looke like, but fuch traitors
His Maiefty feldome feares, I am *Creffeds* Vncle,
That dare leaue two together, far you well. *Exit.*

King. Now faire one, do's your bufines follow vs ?

Hel. I my good Lord,
Gerard de Narbon was my father,
In what he did profeffe, well found.

King. I knew him.

Hel. The rather will I fpare my praifes towards him,
Knowing him is enough : on's bed of death,
Many receits he gaue me, chieflie one,
Which as the deareft iffue of his practice
And of his olde experience, th'onlie darling,
He bad me ftore vp, as a triple eye,
Safer then mine owne two : more deare I haue fo,
And hearing your high Maieftie is toucht
With that malignant caufe, wherein the honour
Of my deare fathers gift, ftands cheefe in power,
I come to tender it, and my appliance,
With all bound humbleneffe.

King. We thanke you maiden,
But may not be fo credulous of cure,
When our moft learned Doctors leaue vs, and
The congregated Colledge haue concluded,
That labouring Art can neuer ranfome nature
From her inaydible eftate : I fay we muft not
So ftaine our iudgement, or corrupt our hope,
To proftitute our paft-cure malladie
To emericks, or to diffeuer fo
Our great felfe and our credit, to efteeme
A fenceleffe helpe, when helpe paft fence we deeme.
Hel. My

Hell. My dutie then fhall pay me for my paines :
I will no more enforce mine office on you ,
Humbly intreating from your royall thoughts,
A modeſt one to beare me backe againe.

King. I cannot giue thee leſſe to be cal'd gratefull :
Thou thoughteſt to helpe me, and ſuch thankes I giue,
As one neere death to thoſe that wiſh him liue:
But what at full I know, thou knowſt no part,
I knowing all my perill, thou no Art.

Hell. What I can doe, can doe no hurt to try,
Since you ſet vp your reſt 'gainſt remedie :
He that of greateſt workes is finiſher,
Oft does them by the weakeſt miniſter :
So holy Writ, in babes hath iudgement ſhowne,
When Iudges haue bin babes; great flouds haue flowne
From ſimple ſources : and great Seas haue dried
When Miracles haue by the great'ſt beene denied.
Oft expectation failes, and moſt oft there
Where moſt it promiſes : and oft it hits,
Where hope is coldeſt, and deſpaire moſt ſhifts.

King. I muſt not heare thee, fare thee wel kind maide,
Thy paines not vs'd, muſt by thy ſelfe be paid,
Proffers not tooke, reape thanks for their reward.

Hel. Inſpired Merit ſo by breath is bard,
It is not ſo with him that all things knowes
As 'tis with vs, that ſquare our gueſſe by ſhowes:
But moſt it is preſumption in vs, when
The help of heauen we count the act of men.
Deare ſir, to my endeauors giue conſent,
Of heauen, not me, make an experiment.
I am not an Impoſtrue, that proclaime
My ſelfe againſt the leuill of mine aime ,
But know I thinke, and thinke I know moſt ſure,
My Art is not paſt power, nor you paſt cure.

King. Art thou ſo confident? Within what ſpace
Hop'ſt thou my cure?

Hel. The greateſt grace lending grace,
Ere twice the horſes of the ſunne ſhall bring
Their fiery torcher his diurnall ring,
Ere twice in murke and occidentall dampe
Moiſt *Heſperus* hath quench'd her ſleepy Lampe:
Or foure and twenty times the Pylots glaſſe
Hath told the theeuiſh minutes, how they paſſe :
What is infirme, from your ſound parts ſhall flie,
Health ſhall liue free, and ſickeneſſe freely dye.

King. Vpon thy certainty and confidence,
What dar'ſt thou venter ?

Hell. Taxe of impudence,
A ſtrumpets boldneſſe, a divulged ſhame
Traduc'd by odious ballads : my maidens name
Seard otherwiſe, ne worſe of worſt extended
With vildeſt torture, let my life be ended.

Kin. Methinkes in thee ſome bleſſed ſpirit doth ſpeak
His powerfull ſound, within an organ weake :
And what impoſſibility would ſlay
In common ſence, ſence ſaues another way :
Thy life is deere, for all that life can rate
Worth name of life, in thee hath eſtimate :
Youth, beauty, wiſedome, courage, all
That happines and prime, can happy call :
Thou this to hazard, needs muſt intimate
Skill infinite, or monſtrous deſperate,
Sweet practiſer, thy Phyſicke I will try,
That miniſters thine owne death if I die.

Hel. If I breake time, or flinch in property
Of what I ſpoke, vnpittied let me die,

And well deſeru'd: not helping, death's my fee,
But if I helpe, what doe you promiſe me.

Kin. Make thy demand.

Hel. But will you make it euen ?

Kin. I by my Scepter, and my hopes of helpe.

Hel. Then ſhalt thou giue me with thy kingly hand
What husband in thy power I will command :
Exempted be from me the arrogance
To chooſe from forth the royall bloud of France,
My low and humble name to propagate
With any branch or image of thy ſtate :
But ſuch a one thy vaſſall, whom I know
Is free for me to aske, thee to beſtow.

Kin. Heere is my hand, the premiſes obſeru'd,
Thy will by my performance ſhall be ſeru'd:
So make the choice of thy owne time, for I
Thy reſolv'd Patient, on thee ſtill relye :
More ſhould I queſtion thee, and more I muſt,
Though more to know, could not be more to truſt:
From whence thou cam'ſt, how tended on, but reſt
Vnqueſtion'd welcome, and vndoubted bleſt.
Giue me ſome helpe heere hoa, if thou proceed,
As high as word, my deed ſhall match thy deed.

                  Floriſh.   *Exit.*

Enter Counteſſe and Clowne.

Lady. Come on ſir, I ſhall now put you to the height
of your breeding.

Clown. I will ſhew my ſelfe highly fed , and lowly
taught, I know my buſineſſe is but to the Court.

Lady. To the Court, why what place make you ſpeciall, when you put off that with ſuch contempt, but to
the Court?

Clo. Truly Madam, if God haue lent a man any manners, hee may eaſilie put it off at Court : hee that cannot
make a legge, put off's cap, kiſſe his hand, and ſay nothing, has neither legge, hands, lippe, nor cap ; and indeed ſuch a fellow, to ſay preciſely, were not for the
Court, but for me, I haue an anſwere will ſerue all men.

Lady. Marry that's a bountifull anſwere that fits all
queſtions.

Clo. It is like a Barbers chaire that fits all buttockes,
the pin buttocke, the quatch-buttocke, the brawn buttocke, or any buttocke.

Lady. Will your anſwere ſerue fit to all queſtions ?

Clo. It muſt be an anſwere for the hand of an Atturney, as your French Crowne for your taffety punke, as
Tibs ruſh for *Toms* fore-finger, as a pancake for Shroue-
tueſday, a Morris for May-day, as the naile to his hole,
the Cuckold to his horne, as a ſcolding queane to a
wrangling knaue, as the Nuns lip to the Friers mouth,
nay as the pudding to his skin.

Lady. Haue you, I ſay, an anſwere of ſuch fitneſſe for
all queſtions?

Clo. From below your Duke, to beneath your Conſtable, it will fit any queſtion.

Lady. It muſt be an anſwere of moſt monſtrous fize,
that muſt fit all demands.

Clo. But a trifle neither in good faith, if the learned
ſhould ſpeake truth of it : heere it is, and all that belongs
to't. Aske mee if I am a Courtier, it ſhall doe you no
harme to learne.

Lady. To be young againe if we could : I will bee a
foole in queſtion, hoping to bee the wiſer by your anſwer.

                           Lady.

La. I pray you fir, are you a Courtier?

Clo. O Lord fir theres a fimple putting off : more, more, a hundred of them.

La. Sir I am a poore freind of yours, that loues you.

Clo. O Lord fir, thicke, thicke, fpare not me.

La. I thinke fir, you can eate none of this homely meate.

Clo. O Lord fir; nay put me too't, I warrant you.

La. You were lately whipt fir as I thinke.

Clo. O Lord fir, fpare not me.

La. Doe you crie O Lord fir at your whipping, and fpare not me? Indeed your O Lord fir, is very fequent to your whipping : you would anfwere very well to a whipping if you were but bound too't.

Clo. I nere had worfe lucke in my life in my O Lord fir : I fee things may ferue long, but not ferue euer.

La. I play the noble hufwife with the time, to entertaine it fo merrily with a foole.

Clo. O Lord fir, why there't ferues well agen.

La. And end fir to your bufineffe: giue *Hellen* this, And vrge her to a prefent anfwer backe, Commend me to my kinfmen, and my fonne, This is not much .

Clo. Not much commendation to them.

La. Not much imployement for you, you vnderftand me.

Clo. Moft fruitfully, I am there, before my legges.

La. Haft you agen. *Exeunt*

Enter Count, Lafew, and Parolles.

Ol.Laf. They fay miracles are paft, and we haue our Philofophicall perfons, to make moderne and familiar things fupernaturall and caufeleffe. Hence is it, that we make trifles of terrours, enfconcing our felues into feeming knowledge, when we fhould fubmit our felues to an vnknowne feare.

Par. Why 'tis the rareft argument of wonder, that hath fhot out in our latter times.

Rof. And fo 'tis.

Ol.Laf. To be relinquifht of the Artifts.

Par. So I fay both of *Galen* and *Paracelfus.*

Ol.Laf. Of all the learned and authenticke fellowes.

Par. Right fo I fay.

Ol.Laf. That gaue him out incureable.

Par. Why there 'tis, fo fay I too.

Ol.Laf. Not to be help'd.

Par. Right, as 'twere a man affur'd of a——

Ol.Laf. Vncertaine life, and fure death.

Par. Iuft, you fay well : fo would I haue faid.

Ol.Laf. I may truly fay, it is a noueltie to the world.

Par. It is indeede if you will haue it in fhewing, you fhall reade it in what do ye call there.

Ol.Laf. A fhewing of a heauenly effect in an earthly Actor.

Par. That's it, I would haue faid, the verie fame.

Ol.Laf. Why your Dolphin is not luftier : fore mee I fpeake in refpect——

Par. Nay 'tis ftrange, 'tis very ftraunge, that is the breefe and the tedious of it, and he's of a moft facinerious fpirit, that will not acknowledge it to be the——

Ol.Laf. Very hand of heauen.

Par. I, fo I fay.

Ol.Laf. In a moft weake——

Par. And debile minifter great power, great trancendence, which fhould indeede giue vs a further vfe to

be made, then alone the recou'ry of the king, as to bee

Old Laf. Generally thankfull.

Enter King, Hellen, and attendants.

Par. I would haue faid it, you fay well : heere comes the King.

Ol.Laf. Luftique, as the Dutchman faies : Ile like a maide the Better whil'ft I haue a tooth in my head: why he's able to leade her a Carranto.

Par. Mor du vinager, is not this *Helen?*

Ol.Laf. Fore God I thinke fo.

King. Goe call before mee all the Lords in Court, Sit my preferuer by thy patients fide, And with this healthfull hand whofe banifht fence Thou haft repeal'd, a fecond time receyue The confirmation of my promis'd guift, Which but attends thy naming.

Enter 3 or 4 Lords.

Faire Maide fend forth thine eye, this youthfull parcell Of Noble Batchellors, ftand at my beftowing, Ore whom both Soueraigne power, and fathers voice I haue to vfe; thy franke election make, Thou haft power to choofe, and they none to forfake.

Hel. To each of you, one faire and vertuous Miftris; Fall when loue pleafe, marry to each but one.

Old Laf. I'de giue bay curtall, and his furniture My mouth no more were broken then thefe boyes, And writ as little beard.

King. Perufe them well :
Not one of thofe, but had a Noble father.

She addreffes her to a Lord.

Hel. Gentlemen, heauen hath through me , reftor'd the king to health.

All. We vnderftand it, and thanke heauen for you.

Hel. I am a fimple Maide, and therein wealthieft That I proteft, I fimply am a Maide : Pleafe it your Maieftie, I haue done already : The blufhes in my cheekes thus whifper mee, We blufh that thou fhouldft choofe, but be refufed ; Let the white death fit on thy cheeke for euer, Wee'l nere come there againe.

King. Make choife and fee, Who fhuns thy loue, fhuns all his loue in mee.

Hel. Now *'Dian* from thy Altar do I fly, And to imperiall loue, that God moft high Do my fighes ftreame : Sir, wil you heare my fuite?

1.Lo. And grant it.

Hel. Thankes fir, all the reft is mute.

Ol.Laf. I had rather be in this choife, then throw Ames-ace for my life.

Hel. The honor fir that flames in your faire eyes, Before I fpeake too threatningly replies: Loue make your fortunes twentie times aboue Her that fo vvifhes, and her humble loue.

2.Lo. No better if you pleafe.

Hel. My wifh receiue, Which great loue grant, and fo I take my leaue.

Ol.Laf. Do all they denie her? And they were fons of mine, I'de haue them whip'd, or I would fend them to'th Turke to make Eunuches of.

Hel. Be not afraid that I your hand fhould take, Ile neuer do you wrong for your owne fake : Bleffing vpon your vowes, and in your bed Finde fairer fortune, if you euer wed.

Old Laf. Thefe boyes are boyes of Ice, they'le none
haue

haue heere : fure they are baftards to the Englifh, the French nere got em.

La. You are too young, too happie, and too good To make your felfe a fonne out of my blood.

4.Lord. Faire one, I thinke not fo.

Ol.Lord There's one grape yet, I am fure thy father drunke wine. But if thou be'ft not an affe, I am a youth of fourteene : I haue knowne thee already.

Hel. I dare not fay I take you, but I giue Me and my feruice, euer whilſt I liue Into your guiding power : This is the man.

King. Why then young *Bertram* take her fhee's thy wife.

Ber. My wife my Leige? I fhal befeech your highnes In fuch a bufines, giue me leaue to vfe The helpe of mine owne eies.

King. Know'ft thou not *Bertram* what fhee ha's done for mee?

Ber. Yes my good Lord, but neuer hope to know why I fhould marrie her.

King. Thou know'ft fhee ha's rais'd me from my fick-ly bed.

Ber. But followes it my Lord, to bring me downe Muft anfwer for your raifing? I knowe her well : Shee had her breeding at my fathers charge: A poore Phyfitians daughter my wife? Difdaine Rather corrupt me euer.

King. Tis onely title thou difdainft in her, the which I can build vp : ftrange is it that our bloods Of colour, waight, and heat, pour'd all together, Would quite confound diftinction: yet ftands off In differences fo mightie. If fhe bee All that is vertuous (faue what thou difik'ſt) A poore Phifitians daughter, thou difik'ſt Of vertue for the name : but doe not fo : From loweſt place, whence vertuous things proceed, The place is dignified by th' doers deede. Where great additions fwell's, and vertue none, It is a dropfied honour. Good a lone, Is good without a name? Vileneffe is fo : The propertie by what is is, fhould go, Not by the title. Shee is young, wife, faire, In thefe, to Nature fhee's immediate heire : And thefe breed honour : that is honours fcorne, Which challenges it felfe as honours borne, And is not like the fire : Honours thriue, When rather from our acts we them deriue Then our fore-goers : the meere words, a flaue Debofh'd on euerie tombe, on euerie graue : A lying Trophee, and as oft is dumbe, Where duft, and damn'd obliuion is the Tombe. Of honour'd bones indeed, what fhould be faide? If thou canft like this creature, as a maide, I can create the reft : Vertue, and fhee Is her owne dower : Honour and wealth, from mee.

Ber. I cannot loue her, nor will ftriue to doo't.

King. Thou wrong'ft thy felfe, if thou fhold'ft ftriue to choofe.

Hel. That you are well reftor'd my Lord, I'me glad: Let the reft go.

King. My Honor's at the ftake, which to defeate I muft produce my power. Heere, take her hand, Proud fcornfull boy, vnworthie this good gift, That duft in vile mifprifion fhackle vp My loue, and her defert : that canft not dreame, We poizing vs in her defective fcale,

Shall weigh thee to the beame : That wilt not know, It is in Vs to plant thine Honour, where We pleafe to haue it grow. Checke thy contempt: Obey Our will, which trauailes in thy good : Beleeue not thy difdaine, but prefentlie Do thine owne fortunes that obedient right Which both thy dutie owes, and Our power claimes, Or I will throw thee from my care for euer Into the ftaggers, and the careleffe lapfe Of youth and ignorance : both my reuenge and hate Loofing vpon thee, in the name of iuftice, Without all termes of pittie. Speake, thine anfwer.

Ber. Pardon my gracious Lord : for I fubmit My fancie to your eies, when I confider What great creation, and what dole of honour Flies where you bid it : I finde that fhe which late Was in my Nobler thoughts, moft bafe : is now The praifed of the King, who fo ennobled, Is as 'twere borne fo.

King. Take her by the hand, And tell her fhe is thine: to whom I promife A counterpoize : If not to thy eftate, A ballance more repleat.

Ber. I take her hand.

Kin. Good fortune, and the fauour of the King Smile vpon this Contract : whofe Ceremonie Shall feeme expedient on the now borne briefe, And be perform'd to night : the folemne Feaſt Shall more attend vpon the coming fpace, Expecting abfent friends. As thou lou'ſt her, Thy loue's to me Religious : elfe, do's erre.   *Exeunt*

Parolles and Lafew ſtay behind, commen-ting of this wedding.

Laf. Do you heare Monfieur? A word with you.

Par. Your pleafure fir.

Laf. Your Lord and Mafter did well to make his re-cantation.

Par. Recantation? My Lord? my Mafter?

Laf. I : Is it not a Language I fpeake?

Par. A moft harfh one, and not to bee vnderftoode without bloudie fucceeding My Mafter?

Laf. Are you Companion to the Count *Rofillion?*

Par. To any Count, to all Counts : to what is man.

Laf. To what is Counts man : Counts maifter is of another ftile.

Par. You are too old fir : Let it fatisfie you, you are too old.

Laf. I muft tell thee firrah, I write Man : to which title age cannot bring thee.

Par. What I dare too well do, I dare not do.

Laf. I did thinke thee for two ordinaries : to bee a prettie wife fellow, thou didſt make tollerable vent of thy trauell, it might paffe : yet the fcarffes and the ban-nerets about thee, did manifoldlie diffwade me from be-leeuing thee a veffell of too great a burthen. I haue now found thee, when I loofe thee againe, I care not: yet art thou good for nothing but taking vp, and that th' ourt fcarce worth.

Par. Hadſt thou not the priuiledge of Antiquity vp-on thee.

Laf. Do not plundge thy felfe to farre in anger, leaſt thou haften thy triall : which if, Lord haue mercie on thee for a hen, fo my good window of Lettice fare thee well, tby cafement I neede not open, for I look through thee. Giue me thy hand.

Par. My Lord, you giue me moft egregious indignity.

Laf.

Laf. I with all my heart, and thou art worthy of it.

Par. I haue not my Lord deferu'd it.

Laf. Yes good faith, eu'ry dramme of it, and I will not bate thee a fcruple.

Par. Well, I fhall be wifer.

*Laf.*Eu'n as foone as thou can'ft, for thou haft to pull at a fmacke a'th contrarie. If euer thou bee'ft bound in thy skarfe and beaten, thou fhall finde what it is to be proud of thy bondage, I haue a defire to holde my acquaintance with thee, or rather my knowledge, that I may fay in the default, he is a man I know.

Par. My Lord you do me moft infupportable vexation.

Laf. I would it were hell paines for thy fake, and my poore doing eternall : for doing I am paft, as I will by thee, in what motion age will giue me leaue.   *Exit.*

Par. Well, thou haft a fonne fhall take this difgrace off me; fcuruy, old, filthy, fcuruy Lord: Well, I muft be patient, there is no fettering of authority. Ile beate him (by my life) if I can meete him with any conuenience, and he were double and double a Lord. Ile haue no more pittie of his age then I would haue of——Ile beate him, and if I could but meet him agen.

Enter Lafew.

Laf. Sirra, your Lord and mafters married, there's newes for you : you haue a new Miftris.

Par. I moft vnfainedly befeech your Lordfhippe to make fome referuation of your wrongs. He is my good Lord, whom I ferue aboue is my mafter.

Laf. Who? God.

Par. I fir.

Laf. The deuill it is, that's thy mafter. Why dooeft thou garter vp thy armes a this fafhion? Doft make hofe of thy fleeues? Do other feruants fo ? Thou wert beft fet thy lower part where thy nofe ftands. By mine Honor, if I were but two houres yonger, I'de beate thee : meethink'ft thou art a generall offence, and euery man fhold beate thee : I thinke thou waft created for men to breath themfelues vpon thee.

Par. This is hard and vndeferued meafure my Lord.

Laf. Go too fir, you were beaten in *Italy* for picking a kernell out of a Pomgranat, you are a vagabond, and no true traueller : you are more fawcie with Lordes and honourable perfonages, then the Commifsion of your birth and vertue giues you Heraldry. You are not worth another word, elfe I'de call you knaue. I leaue you.   *Exit*

Enter Count Rofsillion.

Par. Good, very good, it is fo then: good, very good, let it be conceal'd awhile.

Rof. Vndone, and forfeited to cares for euer.

Par. What's the matter fweet-heart ?

Rofsill. Although before the folemne Prieft I haue fworne, I will not bed her.

Par. What? what fweet heart?

Rof. O my *Parrolles*, they haue married me: Ile to the *Tufcan* warres, and neuer bed her.

Par. *France* is a dog-hole, and it no more merits, The tread of a mans foot : too'th warres.

Rof. There's letters from my mother : What th'import is, I know not yet.

Par. I that would be knowne : too'th warrs my boy, too'th warres :

He weares his honor in a boxe vnfeene, That hugges his kickie wickie heare at home, Spending his manlie marrow in her armes Which fhould fuftaine the bound and high curuet Of *Marfes* fierie fteed : to other Regions, *France* is a ftable, wee that dwell in't Iades, Therefore too'th warre.

Rof. It fhall be fo, Ile fend her to my houfe, Acquaint my mother with my hate to her, And wherefore I am fled : Write to the King That which I durft not fpeake. His prefent gift Shall furnifh me to thofe Italian fields Where noble fellowes ftrike : Warres is no ftrife To the darke houfe, and the detected wife.

Par. Will this Caprichio hold in thee, art fure?

Rof. Go with me to my chamber, and aduice me. Ile fend her ftraight away : To morrow, Ile to the warres, fhe to her fingle forrow.

Par. Why thefe bals bound, ther's noife in it. Tis hard A yong man maried, is a man that's mard : Therefore away, and leaue her brauely : go, The King ha's done you wrong : but hufh 'tis fo.   *Exit*

Enter Helena and Clowne.

Hel. My mother greets me kindly, is fhe well ?

Clo. She is not well, but yet fhe has her health, fhe's very merrie, but yet fhe is not well : but thankes be giuen fhe's very well, and wants nothing i'th world : but yet fhe is not well.

Hel. If fhe be verie wel, what do's fhe ayle, that fhe's not verie well?

Clo. Truly fhe's very well indeed, but for two things

Hel. What two things ?

Clo. One, that fhe's not in heauen, whether God fend her quickly : the other, that fhe's in earth, from whence God fend her quickly.

Enter Parolles.

Par. Bleffe you my fortunate Ladie.

Hel. I hope fir I haue your good will to haue mine owne good fortune.

Par. You had my prayers to leade them on, and to keepe them on, haue them ftill. O my knaue, how do's my old Ladie ?

Clo. So that you had her wrinkles, and I her money, I would fhe did as you fay.

Par. Why I fay nothing.

Clo. Marry you are the wifer man : for many a mans tongue fhakes out his mafters vndoing : to fay nothing, to do nothing, to know nothing, and to haue nothing, is to be a great part of your title, which is within a verie little of nothing.

Par. Away, th'art a knaue.

Clo. You fhould haue faid fir before a knaue, th'art a knaue, that's before me th'art a knaue : this had beene truth fir.

Par. Go too, thou art a wittie foole, I haue found thee.

Clo. Did you finde me in your felfe fir, or were you taught to finde me?

Clo. The fearch fir was profitable, and much Foole may you find in you, euen to the worlds pleafure, and the encreafe of laughter.

Par. A good knaue ifaith, and well fed.

Madam, my Lord will go awaie to night,

A

A verie ferrious bufineffe call's on him :
The great prerogatiue and rite of loue,
Which as your due time claimes, he do's acknowledge,
But puts it off to a compell'd reftraint :
Whofe want, and whofe delay, is ftrew'd with fweets
Which they diftill now in the curbed time,
To make the comming houre oreflow with ioy,
And pleafure drowne the brim.

Hel. What's his will elfe?

Par. That you will take your inftant leaue a'th king,
And make this haft as your owne good proceeding,
Strengthned with what Apologie you thinke
May make it probable neede.

Hel. What more commands hee?

Par. That hauing this obtain'd, you prefentlie
Attend his further pleafure.

Hel. In euery thing I waite vpon his will.

Par. I fhall report it fo.   *Exit Par.*

Hell. I pray you come firrah.   *Exit*

Enter Lafew and Bertram.

Laf. But I hope your Lordfhippe thinkes not him a
fouldier.

Ber. Yes my Lord and of verie valiant approofe.

Laf. You haue it from his owne deliuerance.

Ber. And by other warranted teftimonie.

Laf. Then my Diall goes not true, I tooke this Larke
for a bunting.

Ber. I do affure you my Lord he is very great in knowledge, and accordinglie valiant.

Laf. I haue then finn'd againft his experience, and
tranfgreft againft his valour, and my ftate that way is
dangerous, fince I cannot yet find in my heart to repent:
Heere he comes, I pray you make vs freinds, I will purfue the amitie.

Enter Parolles.

Par. Thefe things fhall be done fir.

Laf. Pray you fir whofe his Tailor?

Par. Sir?

Laf. O I know him well, I fir, hee firs a good worke-
man, a verie good Tailor.

Ber. Is fhee gone to the king?

Par. Shee is.

Ber. Will fhee away to night?

Par. As you'le haue her.

Ber. I haue writ my letters, casketted my treafure,
Giuen order for our horfes, and to night,
When I fhould take poffeffion of the Bride,
And ere I doe begin.

Laf. A good Trauailer is fomething at the latter end
of a dinner, but on that lies three thirds, and vfes a
known truth to paffe a thoufand nothings with, fhould
bee once hard, and thrice beaten. God faue you Captaine.

Ber. Is there any vnkindnes betweene my Lord and
you Monfieur?

Par. I know not how I haue deferued to run into my
Lords difpleafure.

Laf. You haue made fhift to run into't, bootes and
fpurres and all : like him that leapt into the Cuftard, and
out of it you'le runne againe, rather then fuffer queftion
for your refidence.

Ber. It may bee you haue miftaken him my Lord.

Laf. And fhall doe fo euer, though I tooke him at's
prayers. Fare you well my Lord, and beleeue this of

me, there can be no kernell in this light Nut : the foule
of this man is his cloathes : Truft him not in matter of
heauie confequence : I haue kept of them tame, & know
their natures. Farewell Monfieur, I haue fpoken better
of you, then you haue or will to deferue at my hand, but
we muft do good againft euill.

Par. An idle Lord, I fweare.

Ber. I thinke fo.

Par. Why do you not know him?

Ber. Yes, I do know him well, and common fpeech
Giues him a worthy paffe. Heere comes my clog.

Enter Helena.

Hel. I haue fir as I was commanded from you
Spoke with the King, and haue procur'd his leaue
For prefent parting, onely he defires
Some priuate fpeech with you.

Ber. I fhall obey his will.
You muft not meruaile *Helen* at my courfe,
Which holds not colour with the time, nor does
The miniftration, and required office
On my particular. Prepar'd I was not
For fuch a bufineffe, therefore am I found
So much vnfetled : This driues me to intreate you,
That prefently you take your way for home,
And rather mufe then aske why I intreate you,
For my refpects are better then they feeme,
And my appointments make in them a neede
Greater then fhewes it felfe at the firft view,
To you that know them not. This to my mother,
'Twill be two daies ere I fhall fee you, fo
I leaue you to your wifedome.

Hel. Sir, I can nothing fay,
But that I am your moft obedient feruant.

Ber. Come, come, no more of that.

Hel. And euer fhall
With true obferuance feeke to eeke out that
Wherein toward me my homely ftarres haue faild
To equall my great fortune.

Ber. Let that goe : my haft is verie great. Farewell :
Hie home.

Hel. Pray fir your pardon.

Ber. Well, what would you fay?

Hel. I am not worthie of the wealth I owe,
Nor dare I fay 'tis mine : and yet it is,
But like a timorous theefe, moft faine would fteale
What law does vouch mine owne.

Ber. What would you haue?

Hel. Something, and fcarfe fo much : nothing indeed,
I would not tell you what I would my Lord : Faith yes,
Strangers and foes do funder, and not kiffe.

Ber. I pray you ftay not, but in haft to horfe.

Hel. I fhall not breake your bidding, good my Lord:
Where are my other men? Monfieur, farwell.   *Exit*

Ber. Go thou toward home, where I wil neuer come,
Whilft I can fhake my fword, or heare the drumme :
Away, and for our flight.

Par. Brauely, Coragio.

Actus Tertius.

*Flourifh. Enter the Duke of Florence, the two Frenchmen,
with a troope of Souldiers.*

Duke. So that from point to point, now haue you heard
The

The fundamentall reafons of this warre,
Whofe great decifion hath much blood let forth
And more thirfts after.

1.Lord. Holy feemes the quarrell
Vpon your Graces part : blacke and fearefull
On the oppofer.

Duke. Therefore we meruaile much our Cofin France
Would in fo luft a bufineffe, fhut his bofome
Againft our borrowing prayers.

French E. Good my Lord,
The reafons of our ftate I cannot yeelde,
But like a common and an outward man,
That the great figure of a Counfaile frames,
By felfe vnable motion, therefore dare not
Say what I thinke of it, fince I haue found
My felfe in my incertaine grounds to faile
As often as I gueft.

Duke. Be it his pleafure.

Fren.G. But I am fure the yonger of our nature,
That furfet on their eafe, will day by day
Come heere for Phyficke.

Duke. Welcome fhall they bee :
And all the honors that can flye from vs,
Shall on them fettle : you know your places well,
When better fall, for your auailes they fell,
To morrow to'th the field.   *Flourifh.*

Enter Counteffe and Clowne.

Count. It hath happen'd all, as I would haue had it, faue
that he comes not along with her.

Clo. By my troth I take my young Lord to be a verie melancholly man.

Count. By what obferuance I pray you.

Clo. Why he will looke vppon his boote, and fing :
mend the Ruffe and fing, aske queftions and fing, picke
his teeth, and fing : I know a man that had this tricke of
melancholy hold a goodly Mannor for a fong.

Lad. Let me fee what he writes, and when he meanes
to come.

Clow. I haue no minde to *Isbell* fince I was at Court.
Our old Lings, and our *Isbels* a'th Country, are nothing
like your old Ling and your *Isbels* a'th Court:the brains
of my Cupid's knock'd out, and I beginne to loue, as an
old man loues money, with no ftomacke.

Lad. What haue we heere?

Clo. In that you haue there.   *exit*

A Letter.

*I haue fent you a daughter-in-Law, fhee hath recouered the
King, and vndone me : I haue wedded her, not bedded her,
and fworne to make the not eternall. You fhall heare I am
runne away, know it before the report come. If there bee
bredth enough in the world, I will hold a long diftance. My
duty to you.   Your vnfortunate fonne,
                                                    Bertram.*

This is not well rafh and vnbridled boy,
To flye the fauours of fo good a King,
To plucke his indignation on thy head,
By the mifprifing of a Maide too vertuous
For the contempt of Empire.

Enter Clowne.

Clow. O Madam, yonder is heauie newes within betweene two fouldiers, and my yong Ladie.

La. What is the matter.

Clo. Nay there is fome comfort in the newes, fome
comfort, your fonne will not be kild fo foone as I thoght
he would.

La. Why fhould he be kill'd?

Clo. So fay I Madame, if he runne away, as I beare he
does, the danger is in ftanding too't, that's the loffe of
men, though it be the getting of children. Heere they
come will tell you more. For my part I onely heare your
fonne was run away.

Enter Hellen and two Gentlemen.

French E. Saue you good Madam.

Hel. Madam, my Lord is gone, for euer gone.

French G. Do not fay fo.

La. Thinke vpon patience, pray you Gentlemen,
I haue felt fo many quirkes of ioy and greefe,
That the firft face of neither on the ftart
Can woman me vntoo't. Where is my fonne I pray you?

Fren.G. Madam he's gone to ferue the Duke of Flo-
rence,
We met him thitherward, for thence we came :
And after fome difpatch in hand at Court,
Thither we bend againe.

Hel. Looke on his Letter Madam, here's my Pafport.

*When thou canft get the Ring vpon my finger, which neuer
fhall come off, and fhew mee a childe begotten of thy bodie,
that I am father too, then call me husband: but in fuch a(then)
I write a Neuer.*

This is a dreadfull fentence.

La. Brought you this Letter Gentlemen?

1.G. I Madam, and for the Contents fake are forrie
for our paines.

Old La. I prethee Ladie haue a better cheere,
If thou engroffeft, all the greefes are thine,
Thou robft me of a moity: He was my fonne,
But I do wafh his name out of my blood,
And thou art all my childe. Towards Florence is he?

Fren.G. I Madam.

La. And to be a fouldier.

Fren.G. Such is his noble purpofe, and beleeu't
The Duke will lay vpon him all the honor
That good conuenience claimes.

La. Returne you thither.

Fren.E. I Madam, with the fwifteft wing of fpeed.

Hel. Till I haue no wife, I haue nothing in France,
'Tis bitter.

La. Finde you that there?

Hel. I Madame.

Fren.E. 'Tis but the boldneffe of his hand haply, which
his heart was not confenting too.

Lad. Nothing in France, vntill he haue no wife :
There's nothing heere that is too good for him
But onely fhe, and fhe deferues a Lord
That twenty fuch rude boyes might tend vpon,
And call her hourely Miftris. Who was with him?

Fren.E. A feruant onely, and a Gentleman : which I
haue fometime knowne.

La. Parolles was it not?

Fren.E. I my good Ladie, hee.

La. A verie tainted fellow, and full of wickedneffe,
My fonne corrupts a well deriued nature
With his inducement.

Fren.E. Indeed good Ladie the fellow has a deale of
that, too much, which holds him much to haue.

La. Y'are welcome Gentlemen, I will intreate you
when you fee my fonne, to tell him that his fword can
neuer winne the honor that he loofes : more Ile intreate
                                    X   you

you written to bearealong.

Fren.G. We ferue you Madam in that and all your
worthieft affaires.

La. Not fo, but as we change our courtefies,
Will you draw neere?   *Exit.*

Hel. Till I haue no wife I haue nothing in France.

Nothing in France vntill he has no wife :
Thou fhalt haue none *Roffillion*, none in France,
Then haft thou all againe : poore Lord, is't I
That chafe thee from thy Countrie, and expofe
Thofe tender limbes of thine, to the euent
Of the none-fparing warre? And is it I,
That driue thee from the fportiue Court, where thou
Was't fhot at with faire eyes, to be the marke
Of fmoakie Muskets ? O you leaden meffengers,
That ride vpon the violent fpeede of fire,
Fly with falfe ayme, moue the ftill-peering aire
That fings with piercing, do not touch my Lord :
Who euer fhoots at him, I fet him there.
Who euer charges on his forward breft
I am the Caitiffe that do hold him too't,
And though I kill him not, I am the caufe
His death was fo effe&ted : Better 'twere
I met the rauine Lyon when he roar'd
With fharpe conftraint of hunger : better 'twere,
That all the miferies which nature owes
Were mine at once. No come thou home *Roff.llion*,
Whence honor but of danger winnes a fcarre,
As oft it loofes all. I will be gone :
My being heere it is, that holds thee hence,
Shall I ftay heere to doo't? No, no, although
The ayre of Paradife did fan the houfe,
And Angles offic'd all : I will be gone,
That pittifull rumour may report my flight
To confolate thine eare. Come night, end day,
For with the darke (poore theefe) Ile fteale away.   *Exit.*

Flourifh.   Enter the Duke of Florence, Roffillion,
drum and trumpets, foldiers, Parrolles.

Duke. The Generall of our horfe thou art, and we
Great in our hope, lay our beft loue and credence
Vpon thy promifing fortune.

Ber. Sir it is
A charge too heauy for my ftrength, but yet
Wee'l ftriue to beare it for your worthy fake,
To th'extreme edge of hazard.

Duke. Then go thou forth,
And fortune play vpon thy profperous helme
As thy aufpicious miftris.

Ber. This very day
Great Mars I put my felfe into thy file,
Make me but like my thoughts, and I fhall proue
A louer of thy drumme, hater of loue.   *Exeunt omnes*

Enter Counteffe & Steward.

La. Alas! and would you take the letter of her :
Might you not know fhe would do, as fhe has done,
By fending me a Letter. Reade it a gen.

Letter.

I am S. Iaques Pilgrim, thither gone :
Ambitious loue hath fo in me offended,
That bare-foot plod I the cold ground vpon
With fainted vow my faults to bane amended.

Write, write, that from the bloodie courfe of warre,
My deereft Mafter your deare fonne, may hie,
Bleffe him at home in peace. Whilft I from farre,
His name with zealous feruour fanctifie :
His taken labours bid him me forgiue :
I his defpightfull Iuno fent him forth,
From Courtly friends, with Camping foes to liue,
Where death and danger dogges the heeles of worth.
He is too good and faire for death, and mee,
Whom I my felfe embrace, to fet him free.

Ah what fharpe ftings are in her mildeft words ?
Rynaldo, you did neuer lacke aduice fo much,
As letting her paffe fo : had I fpoke with her,
I could haue well diuerted her intents,
Which thus fhe hath preuented.

Ste. Pardon me Madam,
If I had giuen you this at ouer-night,
She might haue beene ore-tane : and yet fhe writes
Purfuite would be but vaine.

La. What Angell fhall
Bleffe this vnworthy husband, he cannot thriue,
Vnleffe her prayers, whom heauen delights to heare
And loues to grant, repreeue him from the wrath
Of greateft Iuftice. Write, write *Rynaldo*,
To this vnworthy husband of his wife,
Let euerie word waigh heauie of her worth,
That he does waigh too light : my greateft greefe,
Though little he do feele it, fet downe fharpely.
Difpatch the moft conuenient meffenger,
When haply he fhall heare that fhe is gone,
He will returne, and hope I may that fhee
Hearing fo much, will fpeede her foote againe,
Led hither by pure loue : which of them both
Is deereft to me, I haue no skill in fence
To make diftin&tion : prouide this Meffenger :
My heart is heauie, and mine age is weake,
Greefe would haue teares, and forrow bids me fpeake.

                                          Exeunt

A Tucket afarre off.

Enter old Widdow of Florence, her daughter, Violenta
and Mariana, with other
Citizens.

Widdow. Nay come,
For if they do approach the Citty,
We fhall loofe all the fight.

Diana. They fay, the French Count has done
Moft honourable feruice.

Wid. It is reported,
That he has taken their great'ft Commander,
And that with his owne hand he flew
The Dukes brother : we haue loft our labour,
They are gone a contrarie way: harke,
you may know by their Trumpets.

Maria. Come lets returne againe,
And fuffice our felues with the report of it.
Well *Diana*, take heed of this French Earle,
The honor of a Maide is her name,
And no Legacie is fo rich
As honeftie.

Widdow. I haue told my neighbour
How you haue beene folicited by a Gentleman
His Companion.

                                          Maria

Maria. I know that knaue, hang him, one *Parolles,* a filthy Officer he is in thofe fuggeftions for the young Earle, beware of them *Diana;* their promifes, entifements, oathes, tokens, and all thefe engines of luſt, are not the things they go vnder : many a maide hath beene feduced by them, and the miferie is example, that fo terrible ſhewes in the wracke of maiden-hood, cannot for all that diſſwade fucceſſion, but that they are limed with the twigges that threatens them. I hope I neede not to aduife you further, but I hope your owne grace will keepe you where you are, though there were no further danger knowne, but the modeſtie which is fo loft.

Dia. You ſhall not neede to feare me.

Enter Hellen.

Wid. I hope fo : looke here comes a pilgrim, I know ſhe will lye at my houfe, thither they fend one another, Ile queſtion her. God faue you pilgrim, whether are bound?

Hel. To S. *Iaques la grand.*

Where do the Palmers lodge, I do befeech you?

Wid. At the S. *Francis* heere befide the Port.

Hel. Is this the way?   *A march afarre.*

Wid. I marrie ift. Harke you, they come this way : If you will tarrie holy Pilgrime
But till the troopes come by,
I will conduct you where you ſhall be lodg'd,
The rather for I thinke I know your hofteſſe
As ample as my felfe.

Hel. Is it your felfe ?

Wid. If you ſhall pleafe fo Pilgrime.

Hel. I thanke you, and will ſtay vpon your leifure.

Wid. you came I thinke from *France* ?

Hel. I did fo.

Wid. Heere you ſhall fee a Countriman of yours
That has done worthy feruice.

Hel. His name I pray you ?

Dia. The Count *Roſſillion* : know you fuch a one?

Hel. But by the eare that heares moſt nobly of him : His face I know not.

Dia. What fomere he is
He's brauely taken heere. He ſtole from *France*
As 'tis reported : for the King had married him
Againſt his liking. Thinke you it is fo ?

Hel. I furely meere the truth, I know his Lady.

Dia. There is a Gentleman that ferues the Count, Reports but courfely of her.

Hel. What's his name ?

Dia. Monfieur *Parrolles.*

Hel. Oh I beleeue with him,
In argument of praife, or to the worth
Of the great Count himfelfe, ſhe is too meane
To haue her name repeated, all her deferuing
Is a referued honeftie, and that
I haue not heard examin'd.

Dian. Alas poore Ladie,
'Tis a hard bondage to become the wife
Of a deteſting Lord.

Wid. I write good creature, wherefoere ſhe is,
Her hart waighes fadly : this yong maid might do her
A ſhrewd turne if ſhe pleas'd.

Hel. How do you meane?

May be the amorous Count folicites her
In the vnlawfull purpofe.

Wid. He does indeede,
And brokes with all that can in fuch a fuite

Corrupt the tender honour of a Maide :
But ſhe is arm'd for him, and keepes her guard
In honefteſt defence.

Drumme and Colours.
Enter Count Roſſillion, Parrolles, and the whole Armie.

Mar. The goddes forbid elfe.

Wid. So, now they come :
That is *Anthonio* the Dukes eldeſt fonne,
That *Efcalus.*

Hel. Which is the Frenchman ?

Dia. Hee,
That with the plume, 'tis a moſt gallant fellow,
I would he lou'd his wife : if he were honefter
He were much goodlier. Is't not a handfom Gentleman

Hel. I like him well.

Di. 'Tis pitty he is not honeft:yonds that fame knaue
That leades him to thefe places : were I his Ladie,
I would poifon that vile Rafcall.

Hel. Which is he ?

Dia. That Iacke an-apes with fcarfes. Why is hee melancholly?

Hel. Perchance he s hurt i'th battaile.

Par. Loofe our drum ? Well.

Mar. He's ſhrewdly vext at fomething. Looke he has fpyed vs.

Wid. Marrie hang you.

Mar. And your curtefie, for a ring-carrier.   *Exit.*

Wid. The troope is paſt : Come pilgrim, I wil bring you, Where you ſhall hoſt : Of inioyn'd penitents
There's foure or fiue, to great S. *Iaques* bound,
Alreadie at my houfe.

Hel. I humbly thanke you :
Pleafe it this Matron, and this gentle Maide
To eate with vs to night, the charge and thanking
Shall be for me. and to requite you further,
I will beſtow fome precepts of this Virgin,
Worthy the note.

Both. Wee'l take your offer kindly.   *Exeunt.*

Enter Count Roſſillion and the Frenchmen,
as at firſt.

Cap.E. Nay good my Lord put him too't : let him haue his way.

Cap.G. If your Lordſhippe finde him not a Hilding, hold me no more in your refpect.

Cap.E. On my life my Lord, a bubble.

Ber. Do you thinke I am fo farre Deceiued in him.

Cap.E. Beleeue it my Lord, in mine owne direct knowledge, without any malice, but to fpeake of him as my kinfman, hee's a moſt notable Coward, an infinite and endleffe Lyar, an hourely promife-breaker, the owner of no one good qualitie, worthy your Lordſhips entertainment.

Cap.G. It were fit you knew him, leaſt repofing too farre in his vertue which he hath not, he might at fome great and truſtie bufineſſe, in a maine daunger, fayle you.

Ber. I would I knew in what particular action to try him.

Cap. G. None better then to let him fetch off his drumme, which you heare him fo confidently vndertake to do.

C.E. I with a troop of Florentines wil fodainly furprize

X 2   prize

prize him; fuch I will haue whom I am fure he knowes
not from the enemie : wee will binde and hoodwinke
him fo, that he fhall fuppofe no other but that he is carried into the Leager of the aduerfaries, when we bring
him to our owne tents : be but your Lordfhip prefent
at his examination, if he do not for the promife of his
life, and in the higheft compulfion of bafe feare, offer to
betray you, and deliuer all the intelligence in his power
againft you, and that with the diuine forfeite of his
foule vpon oath, neuer truft my iudgement in anie
thing.

Cap.G. O for the loue of laughter, let him fetch his
drumme, he fayes he has a ftratagem for't : when your
Lordfhip fees the bottome of this fucceffe in't, and to
what mettle this counterfeyt lump of ours will be melted if you glue him not Iohn drummes entertainement,
your Inelining cannot be remoued. Heere he comes.

Enter Parrolles.

Cap.E. O for the loue of laughter hinder not the honor of his defigne, let him fetch off his drumme in any
hand.

Ber. How now Monfieur?This drumme fticks fore-
ly in your difpofition.

Cap.G. A pox on't, let it go, 'tis but a drumme.

Par. But a drumme : Ift but a drumme ? A drum fo
loft. There was excellent command, to charge in with
our horfe vpon our owne wings, and to rend our owne
fouldiers.

Cap.G. That was not to be blam'd in the command
of the feruice : it was a difafter of warre that *Cæfar* him
felfe could not haue preuented, if he had beene there to
command.

Ber. Well, wee cannot greatly condemne our fucceffe : fome difhonor wee had in the loffe of that drum,
but it is not to be recouered.

Par. It might haue beene recouered.

Ber. It might, but it is not now.

Par. It is to be recouered, but that the merit of feruice is fildome attributed to the true and exact perfor-
mer, I would haue that drumme or another, or *hic ia-
cet.*

Ber. Why if you haue a ftomacke, too't Monfieur : if
you thinke your myfterie in ftratagem, can bring this
inftrument of honour againe into his natiue quarter, be
magnanimious in the enterprize and go on, I wil graue
the attempt for a worthy exploit : if you fpeede well in
it, the Duke fhall both fpeake of it, and extend to you
what further becomes his greatneffe, euen to the vtmoft
fyllable of your worthineffe.

Par. By the hand of a fouldier I will vndertake it.

Ber. But you muft not now flumber in it.

Par. Ile about it this euening, and I will prefently
pen downe my dilemma's, encourage my felfe in my
certaintie, put my felfe into my mortall preparation :
and by midnight looke to heare further from me.

Ber. May I bee bold to acquaint his grace you are
gone about it.

Par. I know not what the fucceffe wil be my Lord,
but the attempt I vow.

Ber. I know th'art valiant,
And to the poffibility of thy fouldierfhip,
Will fubfcribe for thee : Farewell.

Par. I loue not many words.   *Exit*

Cap.E. No more then a fifh loues water. Is not this

a ftrange fellow my Lord, that fo confidently feemes to
vndertake this bufineffe, which he knowes is not to be
done, damnes himfelfe to do, & dares better be damnd
then to doo't.

Cap.G. You do not know him my Lord as we doe,
certaine it is that he will fteale himfelfe into a mans fauour, and for a weeke efcape a great deale of difcoue-
ries, but when you finde him out, you haue him euer after.

Ber. Why do you thinke he will make no deede at
all of this that fo feriouflie hee dooes addreffe himfelfe
vnto?

Cap.E. None in the world, but returne with an inuention, and clap vpon you two or three probable lies :
but we haue almoft imboft him, you fhall fee his fall to
night; for indeede he is not for your Lordfhippes refpect.

Cap.G. Weele make you fome fport with the Foxe
ere we cafe him. He was firft fmoak'd by the old Lord
Lafew, when his difguife and he is parted, tell me what
a fprat you fhall finde him, which you fhall fee this verie night.

Cap.E. I muft go looke my twigges,
He fhall be caught.

Ber. Your brother he fhall go along with me.

Cap.G. As't pleafe your Lordfhip, Ile leaue you.

Ber. Now wil I lead you to the houfe,and fhew you
The Laffe I fpoke of.

Cap.E. But you fay fhe's honeft.

Ber. That's all the fault : I fpoke with hir but once,
And found her wondrous cold, but I fent to her
By this fame Coxcombe that we haue i'th winde
Tokens and Letters, which fhe did refend,
And this is all I haue done : She's a faire creature,
Will you go fee her?

Cap.E. With all my heart my Lord.   *Exeunt*

Enter Hellen , and Widdow.

Hel. If you mifdoubt me that I am not fhee,
I know not how I fhall affure you further,
But I fhall loofe the grounds I worke vpon.

Wid. Though my eftate be falne,I was well borne,
Nothing acquainted with thefe bufineffes,
And would not put my reputation now
In any ftaining act.

Hel. Nor would I wifh you.
Firft giue me truft, the Count he is my husband,
And what to your fworne counfaile I haue fpoken,
Is fo from word to word : and then you cannot
By the good ayde that I of you fhall borrow,
Erre in beftowing it.

Wid. I fhould beleeue you,
For you haue fhew'd me that which well approues
Y'are great in fortune.

Hel. Take this purfe of Gold,
And let me buy your friendly helpe thus farre,
Which I will ouer-pay, and pay againe
When I haue found it. The Count he woes your
                        daughter,
Layes downe his wanton fiedge before her beautie,
Refolue to carrie her : let her in fine confent
As wee'l direct her how 'tis beft to beare it :
Now his important blood will naught denie,
That fhee'l demand : a ring the Countie weares,
That downward hath fucceeded in his houfe

From

From ſonne to ſonne, ſome foure or fiue diſcents,
Since the firſt father wore it.   This Ring he holds
In moſt rich choice : yet in his idle fire,
To buy his will, it would not ſeeme too deere,
How ere repented after.

Wid. Now I ſee the bottome of your purpoſe.

Hel. You ſee it lawfull then, it is no more,
But that your daughter ere ſhe ſeemes as wonne,
Deſires this Ring ; appoints him an encounter ;
In fine, deliuers me to fill the time,
Her ſelfe moſt chaſtly abſent : after
To marry her, Ile adde three thouſand Crownes
To what is paſt already.

Wid. I haue yeelded :
Inſtruct my daughter how ſhe ſhall perſeuer,
That time and place with this deceite ſo lawfull
May proue coherent. Euery night he comes
With Muſickes of all ſorts, and ſongs compos'd
To her vnworthineſſe : It nothing ſteeds vs
To chide him from our eeues, for he perſiſts
As if his life lay on't.

Hel. Why then to night
Let vs aſſay our plot, which if it ſpeed,
Is wicked meaning in a lawfull deede ;
And lawfull meaning in a lawfull act,
Where both not ſinne, and yet a ſinfull fact.
But let's about it.

Actus Quartus.

Enter one of the Frenchmen, with fiue or ſixe other
ſouldiers in ambuſh.

1.*Lord E.* He can come no other way but by this hedge
corner : when you ſallie vpon him, ſpeake what terrible
Language you will : though you vnderſtand it not your
ſelues, no matter : for we muſt not ſeeme to vnderſtand
him, vnleſſe ſome one among vs, whom wee muſt produce for an Interpreter.

1.*Sol.* Good Captaiue, let me be th'Interpreter.

Lor.E. Art not acquainted with him ? knowes he not
thy voice ?

1.*Sol.* No ſir I warrant you.

Lo.E. But what linſie wolſy haſt thou to ſpeake to vs
againe.

1.*Sol.* E'n ſuch as you ſpeake to me.

Lo.E. He muſt thinke vs ſome band of ſtrangers, i'th
aduerſaries entertainment. Now he hath a ſmacke of all
neighbouring Languages : therefore we muſt euery one
be a man of his owne fancie, not to know what we ſpeak
one to another : ſo we ſeeme to know, is to know ſtraight
our purpoſe : Choughs language, gabble enough, and
good enough. As for you interpreter, you muſt ſeeme
very politicke. But couch hoa, heere hee comes, to beguile two houres in a ſleepe, and then to returne & ſwear
the lies he forges .

Enter Parrolles.

Par. Ten a clocke : Within theſe three houres 'twill
be time enough to goe home. What ſhall I ſay I haue
done ? It muſt bee a very plauſiue inuention that carries
it. They beginne to ſmoake mee, and diſgraces haue of
late, knock'd too often at my doore : I finde my tongue
is too foole-hardie, but my heart hath the feare of Mars

before it, and of his creatures, not daring the reports of
my tongue.

Lo.E. This is the firſt truth that ere thine own tongue
was guiltie of.

Par. What the diuell ſhould moue mee to vndertake
the recouerie of this drumme, being not ignorant of the
impoſſibility, and knowing I had no ſuch purpoſe ? I
muſt giue my ſelfe ſome hurts, and ſay I got them in exploit : yet ſlight ones will not carrie it.   They will ſay,
came you off with ſo little ? And great ones I dare not
giue, wherefore what's the inſtance. Tongue, I muſt put
you into a Butter-womans mouth, and buy my ſelfe another of *Baiazeths* Mule, if you prattle mee into theſe
perilles.

Lo.E. Is it poſſible he ſhould know what hee is, and
be that he is.

Par. I would the cutting of my garments wold ſerue
the turne, or the breaking of my Spaniſh ſword.

Lo.E. We cannot affoord you ſo.

Par. Or the baring of my beard, and to ſay it was in
ſtratagem.

Lo.E. 'Twould not do.

Par. Or to drowne my cloathes, and ſay I was ſtript.

Lo.E. Hardly ſerue.

Par. Though I ſwore I leapt from the window of the
Citadell.

Lo.E. How deepe ?

Par. Thirty fadome.

Lo.E. Three great oathes would ſcarſe make that be
beleeued.

Par. I would I had any drumme of the enemies, I
would ſweare I recouer'd it.

Lo.E. You ſhall heare one anon.

Par. A drumme now of the enemies.

Alarum within.

Lo E. Throca movouſus, cargo, cargo, cargo.

All. Cargo, cargo, cargo, villianda par corbo, cargo.

Par. O ranſome, ranſome,
Do not hide mine eyes.

Inter. Boskos thromuldo boskos.

Par. I know you are the *Muskos* Regiment,
And I ſhall looſe my life for want of language.
If there be heere German or Dane, Low Dutch,
Italian, or French, let him ſpeake to me,
Ile diſcouer that, which ſhal vndo the Florentine.

Int. Boskos vauvado, I vnderſtand thee, & can ſpeake
thy tongue : Kerelybonto ſir, betake thee to thy faith, for
ſeuenteene ponyards are at thy boſome.

Par. Oh.

Inter. Oh pray, pray, pray,
Manka reuania dulche.

Lo.E. Oſcorbidulchos voliuorco.

Int. The Generall is content to ſpare thee yet,
And hoodwinkt as thou art, will leade thee on
To gather from thee. Haply thou mayſt informe
Something to ſaue thy life.

Par. O let me liue,
And all the ſecrets of our campe Ile ſhew,
Their force, their purpoſes : Nay, Ile ſpeake that,
Which you will wonder at.

Inter. But wilt thou faithfully ?

Par. If I do not, damne me.

Inter. Acordo linta.
Come on, thou are granted ſpace.   *Exit*
A ſhort Alarum within.

X 3   *Lo. E.*

L.E. Go tell the Count *Roſſillion* and my brother,
We haue caught the woodcocke, and will keepe him
Till we do heare from them.   (muffed
Sol. Captaine I will.
L.E. A will betray vs all vnto our ſelues,
Informe on that.
Sol. So I will ſir.
L.E. Till then Ile keepe him darke and ſafely lockt.
                                  Exit

       Enter Bertram, and the Maide called
               Diana.

Ber. They told me that your name was *Fontybell.*
Dia. No my good Lord, *Diana.*
Ber. Titled Goddeſſe,
And worth it with addition : but faire ſoule,
In your fine frame hath loue no qualitie?
If the quicke fire of youth light not your minde,
You are no Maiden but a monument
When you are dead you ſhould be ſuch a one
As you are now : for you are cold and ſterne,
And now you ſhould be as your mother was
When your ſweet ſelfe was got.
Dia. She then was honeſt.
Ber. So ſhould you be.
Dia. No :
My mother did but dutie, ſuch(my Lord)
As you owe to your wife.
Ber. No more a'that :
I prethee do not ſtriue againſt my vowes :
I was compell'd to her, but I loue thee
By loues owne ſweet conſtraint, and will for euer
Do thee all rights of ſeruice.
Dia. I ſo you ſerue vs
Till we ſerue you : But when you haue our Roſes,
You barely leaue our thornes to pricke our ſelues,
And mocke vs with our bareneſſe.
Ber. How haue I ſworne.
Dia. Tis not the many oathes that makes the truth,
But the plaine ſingle vow, that is vow'd true :
What is not holie, that we ſweare not by,
But take the high'ſt to witneſſe : then pray you tell me,
If I ſhould ſweare by Ioues great attributes,
I lou'd you deerely, would you beleeue my oathes,
When I did loue you ill ? This ha's no holding
To ſweare by him whom I proteſt to loue
That I will worke againſt him. Therefore your oathes
Are words and poore conditions, but vnſeal'd
At left in my opinion.
Ber. Change it, change it :
Be not ſo holy cruell : Loue is holie,
And my integritie ne're knew the crafts
That you do charge men with : Stand no more off,
But giue thy ſelfe vnto my ſicke deſires,
Who then recouers. Say thou art mine, and euer
My loue as it beginnes, ſhall ſo perſeuer.
Dia. I ſee that men make rope's in ſuch a ſcarre,
That wee'l forſake our ſelues. Giue me that Ring.
Ber. Ile lend it thee my deere; but haue no power
To giue it from me.
Dia. Will you not my Lord ?
Ber. It is an honour longing to our houſe,
Bequeathed downe from manie Anceſtors,
Which were the greateſt obloquie i'th world,
In me to looſe.
Dian. Mine Honors ſuch a Ring,
My chaſtities the Iewell of our houſe,

Bequeathed downe from many Anceſtors,
Which were the greateſt obloquie i'th world,
In mee to looſe. Thus your owne proper wiſedome
Brings in the Champion honor on my part,
Againſt your vaine aſſault.
Ber. Heere, take my Ring,
My houſe, mine honor, yea my life be thine,
And Ile be bid by thee.
Dia. When midnight comes, knocke at my cham-
             ber window :
Ile order take, my mother ſhall not heare.
Now will I charge you in the band of truth,
When you haue conquer'd my yet maiden-bed,
Remaine there but an houre, nor ſpeake to mee :
My reaſons are moſt ſtrong, and you ſhall know them,
When backe againe this Ring ſhall be deliuer'd :
And on your finger in the night, Ile put
Another Ring, that what in time proceeds,
May token to the future, our paſt deeds.
Adieu till then, then faile not : you haue wonne
A wife of me, though there my hope be done.
    Ber. A heauen on earth I haue won by wooing thee.
    Di. For which, liue long to thanke both heauen & me,
You may ſo in the end.
My mother told me iuſt how he would woo,
As if ſhe fate in's heart. She ſayes, all men
Haue the like oathes : He had ſworne to marrie me
When his wife's dead ; therfore Ile lye with him
When I am buried. Since Frenchmen are ſo braide,
Marry that will, I liue and die a Maid :
Onely in this diſguiſe, I think't no ſinne,
To coſen him that would vniuſtly winne.   *Exit*

   Enter the two French Captaines, and ſome two or three
                   Souldiours.

Cap.G. You haue not giuen him his mothers letter.
Cap.E. I haue deliu'red it an houre ſince, there is ſom
thing in't that ſtings his nature : for on the reading it,
he chang'd almoſt into another man.
Cap.G. He hath much worthy blame laid vpon him,
for ſhaking off ſo good a wife, and ſo ſweet a Lady.
Cap.E. Eſpecially, hee hath incurred the euerlaſting
diſpleaſure of the King, who had euen tun'd his bounty
to ſing happineſſe to him. I will tell you a thing, but
you ſhall let it dwell darkly with you.
Cap.G. When you haue ſpoken it 'tis dead, and I am
the graue of it.
Cap.E. Hee hath peruerted a young Gentlewoman
heere in *Florence,* of a moſt chaſte renown, & this night
he fleſhes his will in the ſpoyle of her honour: hee hath
giuen her his monumentall Ring, and thinkes himſelfe
made in the vnchaſte compoſition.
Cap.G. Now God delay our rebellion as we are our
ſelues, what things are we.
Cap.E. Meerely our owne traitours . And as in the
common courſe of all treaſons, we ſtill ſee them reueale
themſelues, till they attaine to their abhorr'd ends : ſo
he that in this action contriues againſt his owne Nobi-
lity in his proper ſtreame, ore-flowes himſelfe.
Cap.G. Is it not meant damnable in vs, to be Trum-
peters of our vnlawfull intents? We ſhall not then haue
his company to night?
Cap.E. Not till after midnight : for hee is dieted to
his houre.
Cap.G. That approaches apace : I would gladly haue
him ſee his company anathomiz'd, that hee might take

                                           a

a meafure of his owne iudgements, wherein fo curioufly he had fet this counterfeit.

Cap.E. We will not meddle with him till he come; for his prefence muft be the whip of the other.

Cap.G. In the meane time, what heare you of thefe Warres ?

Cap.E. I heare there is an ouerture of peace.

Cap.G. Nay, I affure you a peace concluded.

Cap.E. What will Count *Roffillion* do then? Will he trauaile higher, or returne againe into France ?

Cap.G. I perceiue by this demand, you are not altogether of his councell.

Cap.E. Let it be forbid fir, fo fhould I bee a great deale of his act.

Cap.G. Sir, his wife fome two months fince fledde from his houfe, her pretence is a pilgrimage to Saint *Iaques le grand*; which holy vndertaking, with moft auftere fanctimonie fhe accomplifht : and there refiding, the tendernefte of her Nature, became as a prey to her greefe : in fine, made a groane of her laft breath, & now fhe fings in heauen.

Cap.E. How is this iuftified ?

Cap.G. The ftronger part of it by her owne Letters, which makes her ftorie true, euen to the poynt of her death : her death it felfe, which could not be her office to fay, is come : was faithfully confirm'd by the Rector of the place.

Cap.E. Hath the Count all this intelligence ?

Cap.G. I, and the particular confirmations, point from point, to the full arming of the veritie.

Cap.E. I am heartily forrie that hee'l bee gladde of this.

Cap.G. How mightily fometimes, we make vs comforts of our loffes.

Cap.E. And how mightily fome other times, wee drowne our gaine in teares, the great dignitie that his valour hath here acquir'd for him, fhall at home be encountred with a fhame as ample.

Cap.G. The webbe of our life, is of a mingled yarne, good and ill together : our vertues would bee proud, if our faults whipt them not, and our crimes would difpaire if they were not cherifh'd by our vertues.

Enter a Meffenger.

How now? Where's your mafter ?

Ser. He met the Duke in the ftreet fir, of whom hee hath taken a folemne leaue : his Lordfhippe will next morning for France . The Duke hath offered him Letters of commendations to the King.

Cap.E. They fhall bee no more then needfull there, if they were more then they can commend.

Enter Count Roffillion.

Ber. They cannot be too fweete for the Kings tartnefte, heere's his Lordfhip now. How now my Lord, i'ft not after midnight?

Ber. I haue to night difpatch'd fixteene bufineffes, a moneths length a peece, by an abftract of fucceffe : I haue congied with the Duke, done my adieu with his neereft; buried a wife, mourn'd for her, writ to my Ladie mother, I am returning, entertain'd my Conuoy, & betweene thefe maine parcels of difpatch, affected many nicer needs : the laft was the greateft, but that I haue not ended yet.

Cap.E. If the bufineffe bee of any difficulty, and this morning your departure hence, it requires haft of your Lordfhip.

Ber. I meane the bufineffe is not ended, as fearing to heare of it hereafter: but fhall we haue this dialogue betweene the Foole and the Soldiour. Come, bring forth this counterfet module, has deceiu'd mee, like a double-meaning Prophefier.

Cap.E. Bring him forth, ha's fate i'th ftockes all night poore gallant knaue.

Ber. No matter, his heeles haue deferu'd it, in vfurping his fpurres fo long. How does he carry himfelfe ?

Cap.E. I haue told your Lordfhip alreadie : The ftockes carrie him. But to anfwer you as you would be vnderftood, hee weepes like a wench that had fhed her milke, he hath confeft himfelfe to *Morgan*, whom hee fuppofes to be a Friar, frō the time of his remembrance to this very inftant difafter of his fetting i'th ftockes : and what thinke you he hath confeft ?

Ber. Nothing of me, ha's a ?

Cap.E. His confeffion is taken, and it fhall bee read to his face, if your Lordfhippe be in't, as I beleeue you are, you muft haue the patience to heare it.

Enter Parolles with his Interpreter.

Ber. A plague vpon him, muffeld; he can fay nothing of me : hufh, hufh.

Cap.G. Hoodman comes : *Portotartaroffa.*

Inter. He calles for the tortures, what will you fay without em.

Par. I will confeffe what I know without conftraint, If ye pinch me like a Pafty, I can fay no more.

Int. *Bosko Chimurcho.*

Cap. *Boblibindo chicurmurco.*

Int. You are a mercifull Generall : Our Generall bids you anfwer to what I fhall aske you out of a Note.

Par. And truly, as I hope to liue.

Int. Firft demand of him, how many horfe the Duke is ftrong. What fay you to that ?

Par. Fiue or fixe thoufand, but very weake and vnferuiceable : the troopes are all fcattered, and the Commanders verie poore rogues, vpon my reputation and credit, and as I hope to liue.

Int. Shall I fet downe your anfwer fo ?

Par. Do, Ile take the Sacrament on't, how & which way you will : all's one to him.

Ber. What a paft-fauing flaue is this ?

Cap.G. Y'are deceiu'd my Lord, this is Mounfieur *Parrolles* the gallant militarift, that was his owne phrafe that had the whole theoricke of warre in the knot of his fcarfe, and the practife in the chape of his dagger.

Cap.E. I will neuer truft a man againe, for keeping his fword cleane, nor beleeue he can haue euerie thing in him, by wearing his apparrell neatly.

Int. Well, that's fet downe.

Par. Fiue or fix thoufand horfe I fed, I will fay true, or thereabouts fet downe, for Ile fpeake truth.

Cap.G. He's very neere the truth in this.

Ber. But I con him no thankes for't in the nature he deliuers it.

Par. Poore rogues, I pray you fay.

Int. Well, that's fet downe.

Par. I humbly thanke you fir, a truth's a truth, the Rogues are maruailous poore.

Interp. Demaund of him of what ftrength they are a foot. What fay you to that ?

Par. By my troth fir, if I were to liue this prefent houre, I will tell true. Let me fee, *Spurio* a hundred & fiftie,

fiftie, *Sebaſtian* ſo many, *Corambus* ſo many, *Iaques* ſo many : *Guiltian*, *Coſmo*, *Lodowicke*, and *Gratij*, two hundred fiftie each : Mine owne Company, *Chitopher*, *Vaumond*, *Bentij*, two hundred fiftie each : ſo that the muſter file, rotten and ſound, vppon my life amounts not to fifteene thouſand pole, halfe of the which, dare not ſhake the ſnow from off their Caſſockes, leaſt they ſhake themſelues to peeces.

Ber. What ſhall be done to him ?

Cap.G. Nothing, but let him haue thankes. Demand of him my condition : and what credite I haue with the Duke.

Int. Well that's ſet downe : you ſhall demaund of him, whether one Captaine *Dumaine* bee i'th Campe, a Frenchman : what his reputation is with the Duke, what his valour, honeſtie, and expertneſſe in warres : or whether he thinkes it were not poſſible with well-waighing ſummes of gold to corrupt him to a reuolt.What ſay you to this? What do you know of it ?

Par. I beſeech you let me anſwer to the particular of the intergatories. Demand them ſingly.

Int. Do you know this Captaine *Dumaine* ?

Par. I know him, a was a Botchers Prentize in *Paris*, from whence he was whipt for getting the Shrieues fool with childe, a dumbe innocent that could not ſay him nay.

Ber. Nay, by your leaue hold your hands, though I know his braines are forfeite to the next tile that fals.

Int. Well, is this Captaine in the Duke of Florences campe ?

Par. Vpon my knowledge he is, and lowſie.

Cay.G. Nay looke not ſo vpon me : we ſhall heare of your Lord anon.

Int. What is his reputation with the Duke ?

Par. The Duke knowes him for no other, but a poore Officer of mine, and writ to mee this other day, to turne him out a'th band. I thinke I haue his Letter in my pocket.

Int. Marry we'll ſearch.

Par. In good ſadneſſe I do not know, either it is there, or it is vpon a file with the Dukes other Letters, in my Tent.

Int. Heere 'tis, heere's a paper, ſhall I reade it to you?

Par. I do not know if it be it or no.

Ber. Our Interpreter do's it well.

Cap.G. Excellently.

Int. Dian, *the Counts a foole, and full of gold.*

Par. That is not the Dukes letter ſir : that is an aduertiſement to a proper maide in Florence, one *Diana*, to take heede of the allurement of one Count *Roſſillion*, a fooliſh idle boy : but for all that very ruttiſh. I pray you ſir put it vp againe.

Int. Nay, Ile reade it firſt by your fauour.

Par. My meaning in't I proteſt was very honeſt in the behalfe of the maid : for I knew the young Count to be a dangerous and laſciuious boy, who is a whale to Virginity, and deuours vp all the fry it finds.

Ber. Damnable both-ſides rogue.

Int.Let. *When he ſweares oathes, bid him drop gold, and*
　　　　take it :
After he ſcores, he neuer payes the ſcore :
Halfe won is match well made, match and well make it,
He nere payes after-debts, take it before,
And ſay a ſouldier (Dian) told thee this :
Men are to mell with, boyes are not to kis.

For count of this, the Counts a Foole I know it,
Who payes before, but not when he does owe it.
　　　　Thine as he vow'd to thee in thine eare,
　　　　　　　　　　Parolles.

Ber. He ſhall be whipt through the Armie with this rime in's forehead.

Cap.E. This is your deuoted friend ſir, the manifold Linguiſt, and the army-potent ſouldier.

Ber. I could endure any thing before but a Cat, and now he's a Cat to me.

Int. I perceiue ſir by your Generals lookes, wee ſhall be faine to hang you.

Par. My life ſir in any caſe : Not that I am afraide to dye, but that my offences beeing many, I would repent out the remainder of Nature. Let me liue ſir in a dungeon, i'th ſtockes, or any where, ſo I may liue.

Int. Wee'le ſee what may bee done , ſo you confeſſe freely : therefore once more to this Captaine *Dumaine* : you haue anſwer'd to his reputation with the Duke, and to his valour. What is his honeſtie ?

Par. He will ſteale ſir an Egge out of a Cloiſter : for rapes and rauiſhments he paralels *Neſſus.* Hee profeſſes not keeping of oaths, in breaking em he is ſtronger then *Hercules.* He will lye ſir, with ſuch volubilitie, that you would thinke truth were a foole : drunkenneſſe is his beſt vertue, for he will be ſwine-drunke, and in his ſleepe he does little harme, ſaue to his bed-cloathes about him : but they know his conditions, and lay him in ſtraw. I haue but little more to ſay ſir of his honeſty, he ha's euerie thing that an honeſt man ſhould not haue ; what an honeſt man ſhould haue, he has nothing.

Cap.G. I begin to loue him for this.

Ber. For this deſcription of thine honeſtie ? A pox vpon him for me, he's more and more a Cat.

Int. What ſay you to his expertneſſe in warre ?

Par. Faith ſir, ha's led the drumme before the Engliſh Tragedians : to belye him I will not, and more of his ſouldierſhip I know not, except in that Country, he had the honour to be the Officer at a place there called *Mileend*, to inſtruct for the doubling of files. I would doe the man what honour I can, but of this I am not certaine.

Cap.G. He hath out-villain'd villanie ſo farre, that the raritie redeemes him.

Ber. A pox on him, he's a Cat ſtill.

Int. His qualities being at this poore price, I neede not to aske you, if Gold will corrupt him to reuolt.

Par. Sir, for a Cardceue he will ſell the fee-ſimple of his ſaluation, the inheritance of it, and cut th'intaile from all remainders, and a perpetuall ſucceſsion for it perpetually.

Int. What's his Brother, the other Captain *Dumain* ?

Cap.E. Why do's he aske him of me ?

Int. What's he ?

Par. E'ne a Crow a'th ſame neſt : not altogether ſo great as the firſt in goodneſſe, but greater a great deale in euill. He excels his Brother for a coward, yet his Brother is reputed one of the beſt that is. In a retreate hee out-runnes any Lackey; marrie in comming on, hee ha's the Crampe.

Int. If your life be ſaued, will you vndertake to betray the Florentine.

Par. I, and the Captaine of his horſe, Count *Roſſillion.*

Int. Ile whiſper with the Generall, and knowe his pleaſure.

Par. Ile no more drumming, a plague of all drummes, onely to ſeeme to deſerue well, and to beguile the ſuppoſition

fition of that lafciuious yong boy the Count, haue I run
into this danger: yet who would haue fufpected an am-
bufh where I was taken?

Int. There is no remedy fir, but you muft dye : the
Generall fayes, you that haue fo traitoroufly difcouerd
the fecrets of your army, and made fuch peftifferous reports of men very nobly held, can ferue the world for
no honeft vfe : therefore you muft dye. Come headef-
man, off with his head.

Par. O Lord fir let me liue, or let me fee my death.

Int. That fhall you, and take your leaue of all your
friends:
So, looke about you, know you any heere?

Count. Good morrow noble Captaine.

Lo.E. God bleffe you Captaine *Parolles.*

Cap.G. God faue you noble Captaine.

Lo.E. Captain, what greeting will you to my Lord
Lafew? I am for *France*.

Cap.G. Good Captaine will you giue me a Copy of
the fonnet you writ to *Diana* in behalfe of the Count
Roffillion, and I were not a verie Coward, I'de compell
it of you, but far you well. *Exeunt.*

Int. You are vndone Captaine all but your fcarfe,
that has a knot on't yet.

Par. Who cannot be crufh'd with a plot?

Inter. If you could finde out a Countrie where but
women were that had receiued fo much fhame, you
might begin an impudent Nation. Fare yee well fir, I
am for *France* too, we fhall fpeake of you there. *Exit*

Par. Yet am I thankfull : if my heart were great
'Twould burft at this : Captaine Ile be no more,
But I will eate, and drinke, and fleepe as foft
As Captaine fhall. Simply the thing I am
Shall make me liue : who knowes himfelfe a braggart
Let him feare this ; for it will come to paffe,
That euery braggart fhall be found an Affe.
Ruft fword, coole blufhes, and *Parrolles* liue
Safeft in fhame : being fool'd, by fool'rie thriue;
There's place and meanes for euery man aliue.
Ile after them. *Exit.*

Enter Hellen, Widdow, and Diana.

Hel. That you may well perceiue I haue not
wrong'd you,
One of the greateft in the Chriftian world
Shall be my furetie : for whofe throne 'tis needfull
Ere I can perfeƈt mine intents, to kneele.
Time was, I did him a defired office
Deere almoft as his life, which gratitude
Through flintie Tartars bofome would peepe forth,
And anfwer thankes. I duly am inform'd,
His grace is at *Marcellæ*, to which place
We haue conuenient conuoy : you muft know
I am fuppofed dead, the Army breaking,
My husband hies him home, where heauen ayding,
And by the leaue of my good Lord the King,
Wee'l be before our welcome.

Wid. Gentle Madam,
You neuer had a feruant to whofe truft
Your bufines was more welcome.

Hel. Nor your Miftris
Euer a friend, whofe thoughts more truly labour
To recompence your loue : Doubt not but heauen
Hath brought me vp to be your daughters dower,
As it hath fated her to be my motiue

And helper to a husband. But O ftrange men,
That can fuch fweet vfe make of what they hate,
When fawcie trufting of the cofin'd thoughts
Defiles the pitchy night, fo luft doth play
With what it loathes, for that which is away,
But more of this heereafter : you *Diana,*
Vnder my poore inftruƈtions yet muft fuffer
Something in my behalfe.

Dia. Let death and honeftie
Go with your impofitions, I am yours
Vpon your will to fuffer.

Hel. Yet I pray you :
But with the word the time will bring on fummer,
When Briars fhall haue leaues as well as thornes,
And be as fweet as fharpe : we muft away,
Our Wagon is prepar'd, and time reuiues vs,
All's well that ends well, ftill the fines the Crowne ;
What ere the courfe, the end is the renowne. *Exeunt*

Enter Clowne, old Lady, and Lafew.

Laf. No, no, no, your fonne was milled with a fnipt
taffata fellow there, whofe villanous faffron wold haue
made all the vnbak'd and dowy youth of a nation in his
colour : your daughter-in-law had beene aliue at this
houre, and your fonne heere at home, more aduanced
by the King, then by that red-tail'd humble Bee I fpeak
of.

La. I would I had not knowne him, it was the death
of the moft vertuous gentlewoman, that euer Nature
had praife for creating. If fhe had pertaken of my flefh
and coft mee the deereft groanes of a mother, I could
not haue owed her a more rooted loue.

Laf. Twas a good Lady, 'twas a good Lady. Wee
may picke a thoufand fallets ere wee light on fuch another hearbe.

Clo. Indeed fir fhe was the fweete Margerom of the
fallet, or rather the hearbe of grace.

Laf. They are not hearbes you knaue, they are nofe-
hearbes.

Clowne. I am no great *Nabuchadnezar* fir, I haue not
much skill in grace.

Laf. Whether doeft thou profeffe thy felfe, a knaue
or a foole?

Clo. A foole fir at a womans feruice, and a knaue at a
mans.

Laf. Your diftinƈtion.

Clo. I would coufen the man of his wife, and do his
feruice.

Laf. So you were a knaue at his feruice indeed.

Clo. And I would giue his wife my bauble fir to doe
her feruice.

Laf. I will fubfcribe for thee, thou art both knaue
and foole.

Clo. At your feruice.

Laf. No, no, no.

Clo. Why fir, if I cannot ferue you, I can ferue as
great a prince as you are.

Laf. Whofe that, a Frenchman?

Clo. Faith fir a has an Englifh maine, but his fifno-
mie is more hotter in France then there.

Laf. What prince is that?

Clo. The blacke prince fir, alias the prince of darkeneffe, alias the diuell.

Laf. Hold there's my purfe, I giue thee not this
to fuggeft thee from thy mafter thou talk'ft off, ferue
him ftill.

Clow

Clo. I am a woodland fellow fir, that alwaies loued
a great fire, and the mafter I fpeak of euer keeps a good
fire, but fure he is the Prince of the world, let his No-
bilitie remaine in's Court. I am for the houfe with the
narrow gate, which I take to be too little for pompe to
enter : fome that humble themfelues may, but the manie will be too chill and tender, and theyle bee for the
flowrie way that leads to the broad gate, and the great
fire.

Laf. Go thy waies, I begin to bee a wearie of thee,
and I tell thee fo before, becaufe I would not fall out
with thee. Go thy wayes, let my horfes be wel look'd
too, without any trickes.

Clo. If I put any trickes vpon em fir, they fhall bee
Iades trickes, which are their owne right by the law of
Nature.   *exit*

Laf. A fhrewd knaue and an vnhappie.

Lady. So a is. My Lord that's gone made himfelfe
much fport out of him, by his authoritie hee remaines
heere, which he thinkes is a pattent for his fawcineffe,
and indeede he has no pace, but runnes where he will.

Laf. I like him well, 'tis not amiffe:and I was about
to tell you, fince I heard of the good Ladies death, and
that my Lord your fonne was vpon his returne home. I
moued the King my mafter to fpeake in the behalfe of
my daughter, which in the minoritie of them both, his
Maieftie out of a felfe-gracious remembrance did firft
propofe, his Highneffe hath promis'd me to doe it, and
to ftoppe vp the difpleafure he hath conceiued againft
your fonne, there is no fitter matter. How do's your
Ladyfhip like it?

La. With verie much content my Lord, and I wifh
it happily effected.

Laf. His Highneffe comes poft from *Marcellus,* of as
able bodie as when he number'd thirty, a will be heere
to morrow, or I am deceiu'd, by him that in fuch intelligence hath feldome fall'd.

La. It reioyces me, that I hope I fhall fee him ere I
die. I haue letters that my fonne will be heere to night:
I fhall befeech your Lordfhip to remaine with mee, till
they meete together.

Laf. Madam, I was thinking with what manners I
might fafely be admitted.

Lad. You neede but pleade your honourable priuiledge.

Laf. Ladie, of that I haue made a bold charter, but
I thanke my God, it holds yet.

Enter Clowne.

Clo. O Madam, yonders my Lord your fonne with
a patch of veluet on's face, whether there bee a fcar vnder't or no, the Veluet knowes, but 'tis a goodly patch
of Veluet, his left cheeke is a cheeke of two pile and a
halfe, but his right cheeke is worne bare.

Laf. A fcarre nobly got,
Or a noble fcarre, is a good liu'rie of honor,
So belike is that.

Clo. But it is your carbinado'd face.

Laf. Let vs go fee
your fonne I pray you, I long to talke
With the yong noble fouldier.

Clowne. 'Faith there's a dozen of em, with delicate
fine hats, and moft courteous feathers, which bow the
head, and nod at euerie man.   *Exeunt*

Actus Quintus.

*Enter Hellen, Widdow, and Diana, with
two Attendants.*

Hel. But this exceeding pofting day and night,
Muft wear your fpirits low, we cannot helpe it :
But fince you haue made the daies and nights as one,
To weare your gentle limbes in my affayres,
Be bold you do fo grow in my requitall,
As nothing can vnroote you. In happie time,

Enter a gentle Aftringer.

This man may helpe me to his Maiefties eare,
If he would fpend his power. God faue you fir.

Gent. And you.

Hel. Sir, I haue feene you in the Court of France.

Gent. I haue beene fometimes there.

Hel. I do prefume fir, that you are not falne
From the report that goes vpon your goodneffe,
And therefore goaded with moft fharpe occafions,
Which lay nice manners by, I put you to
The vfe of your owne vertues, for the which
I fhall continue thankefull.

Gent. What's your will?

Hel. That it will pleafe you
To giue this poore petition to the King,
And ayde me with that ftore of power you haue
To come into his prefence.

Gen. The Kings not heere.

Hel. Not heere fir?

Gen. Not indeed,
He hence remou'd laft night, and with more haft
Then is his vfe.

Wid. Lord how we loofe our paines.

Hel. All's well that ends well yet,
Though time feeme fo aduerfe, and meanes vnfit:
I do befeech you, whither is he gone?

Gent. Marrie as I take it to *Roffillion,*
Whither I am going.

Hel. I do befeech you fir,
Since you are like to fee the King before me,
Commend the paper to his gracious hand,
Which I prefume fhall render you no blame,
But rather make you thanke your paines for it,
I will come after you with what good fpeede
Our meanes will make vs meanes.

Gent. This Ile do for you.

Hel. And you fhall finde your felfe to be well thankt
what e're falles more. We muft to horfe againe, Go, go,
prouide.

Enter Clowne and Parrolles.

Par. Good Mr *Lauatch* giue my Lord *Lafew* this letter, I haue ere now fir beene better knowne to you, when
I haue held familiaritie with frefher cloathes : but I am
now fir muddied in fortunes mood, and fmell fomewhat
ftrong of her ftrong difpleafure.

Clo, Truely, Fortunes difpleafure is but fluttifh if it
fmell fo ftrongly as.thou fpeak'ft of : I will henceforth
eate no Fifh of Fortunes butt'ring. Pre thee alow the
winde.

Par. Nay you neede not to ftop your nofe fir : I fpake
but by a Metaphor.

Clo. Indeed fir, if your Metaphor ftinke, I will ftop
my nofe, or againft any mans Metaphor.Prethe get thee
further.   *Par.*

Par. Pray you fir deliuer me this paper.

Clo. Foh, prethee ftand away : a paper from fortunes clofe-ftoole, to giue to a Nobleman . Looke heere he comes himfelfe.

Enter Lafew.

Clo. Heere is a purre of Fortunes fir, or of Fortunes Cat, but not a Mufcat, that ha's falne *into the vncleane* fifh-pond of her difpleafure, and as he fayes is muddied withall. Pray you fir, vfe the Carpe as you may , for he lookes like a poore decayed, ingenious, foolifh, rafcally knaue. I doe pittie his diftreffe in my fmiles of comfort, and leaue him to your Lordfhip.

Par. My Lord I am a man whom fortune hath cruelly fcratch'd.

Laf. And what would you haue me to doe ? 'Tis too late to paire her nailes now. Wherein haue you played the knaue with fortune that fhe fhould fcratch you, who of her felfe is a good Lady, and would not haue knaues thriue long vnder ? There's a Cardegue for you : Let the Iuftices make you and fortune friends ; I am for other bufineffe.

Par. I befeech your honour to heare mee one fingle word,

Laf. you begge a fingle peny more : Come you fhall ha't, faue your word.

Par. My name my good Lord is *Parrolles.*

Laf. You begge more then word then. Cox my paffion, giue me your hand : How does your drumme?

Par. O my good Lord, you were the firft that found mee.

Laf. Was I infooth?And I was the firft that loft thee.

Par. It lies in you my Lord to bring me in fome grace for you did bring me out.

Laf. Out vpon thee knaue, doeft thou put vpon mee at once both the office of God and the diuel: one brings thee in grace, and the other brings thee out. The Kings comming I know by his Trumpets. Sirrah, inquire further after me, I had talke of you laft night, though you are a foole and a knaue, you fhall eate, go too, follow.

Par. I praife God for you.

Flourifh. Enter King, old Lady, Lafew, the two French Lords, with attendants.

Kin. We loft a Iewell of her, and our efteeme Was made much poorer by it : but your fonne, As mad in folly, lack'd the fence to know Her eftimation home.

Old La. 'Tis paft my Liege, And I befeech your Maieftie to make it Naturall rebellion, done i'th blade of youth, When oyle and fire, too ftrong for reafons force, Ore-beares it, and burnes on.

Kin. My honour'd Lady, I haue forgiuen and forgotten all, Though my reuenges were high bent vpon him, And watch'd the time to fhoote.

Laf. This I muft fay, But firft I begge my pardon : the yong Lord Did to his Maiefty, his Mother, and his Ladie, Offence of mighty note; but to himfelfe The greateft wrong of all. He loft a wife, Whofe beauty did aftonifh the furuey Of richeft eies : whofe words all eares tooke captiue, Whofe deere perfection, hearts that fcorn'd to ferue,

Humbly call'd Miftris.

Kin. Praifing what is loft, Makes the remembrance deere. Well, call him hither, We are reconcil'd, and the firft view fhall kill All repetition : Let him not aske our pardon, The nature of his great offence is dead, And deeper then obliuion, we do burie Th'incenfing reliques of it. Let him approach A ftranger, no offender ; and informe him So 'tis our will he fhould.

Gent. I fhall my Liege.

Kin. What fayes he to your daughter, Haue you fpoke ?

Laf. All that he is, hath reference to your Highnes.

Kin. Then fhall we haue a match. I haue letters fent me, that fets him high in fame.

Enter Count Bertram.

Laf. He lookes well on't.

Kin. I am not a day of feafon, For thou maift fee a fun-fhine, and a haile In me at once : But to the brighteft beames Diftracted clouds giue way, fo ftand thou forth, The time is faire againe.

Ber. My high repented blames Deere Soueraigne pardon to me.

Kin. All is whole, Not one word more of the confumed time, Let's take the inftant by the forward top : For we are old, and on our quick'ft decrees Th'inaudible, and noifeleffe foot of time Steales, ere we can effect them. You remember The daughter of this Lord ?

Ber. Admiringly my Liege, at firft I ftucke my choice vpon her, ere my heart Durft make too bold a herauld of my tongue : Where the impreffion of mine eye enfixing, Contempt his fcornfull Perfpectiue did lend me, Which warpt the line of euerie other fauour, Scorn'd a faire colour, or expreft it ftolne, Extended or contracted all proportions To a moft hideous obiect. Thence it came, That fhe whom all men prais'd, and whom my felfe, Since I haue loft, haue lou'd; was in mine eye The duft that did offend it.

Kin. Well excus'd : That thou didft loue her, ftrikes fome fcores away From the great compt : but loue that comes too late, Like a remorfefull pardon flowly carried To the great fender, turnes a fowre offence, Crying, that's good that's gone : Our rafh faults, Make triuiall price of ferious things we haue, Not knowing them, vntill we know their graue. Oft our difpleafures to our felues vniuft, Deftroy our friends, and after weepe their duft: Our owne loue waking, cries to fee what's don,e While fhamefull hate fleepes out the afternoone. Be this fweet *Helens* knell, and now forget her. Send forth your amorous token for faire *Maudlin,* The maine confents are had, and heere wee'l ftay To fee our widdowers fecond marriage day : Which better then the firft, O deere heauen bleffe, Or, ere they meete in me, O Nature ceffe.

Laf. Come on my fonne, in whom my houfes name Muft be digefted : giue a fauour from you To fparkle in the fpirits of my daughter,

That

That fhe may quickly come. By my old beard,
And eu'rie haire that's on't, *Helen* that's dead
Was a fweet creature : fuch a ring as this,
The laft that ere I tooke her leaue at Court,
I faw vpon her finger.

Ber. Hers it was not.

King. Now pray you let me fee it. For mine eye,
While I was fpeaking, oft was faften'd too't :
This Ring was mine, and when I gaue it *Hellen*,
I bad her if her fortunes euer ftoode
Neceffitied to helpe, that by this token
I would releeue her. Had you that craft to reaue her
Of what fhould ftead her moft ?

Ber. My gracious Soueraigne,
How ere it pleafes you to take it fo,
The ring was neuer hers.

Old La. Sonne, on my life
I haue feene her weare it, and fhe reckon'd it
At her liues rate.

Laf. I am fure I faw her weare it.

Ber. You are deceiu'd my Lord, fhe neuer faw it :
In Florence was it from a cafement throwne mee,
Wrap'd in a paper, which contain'd the name
Of her that threw it : Noble fhe was, and thought
I ftood ingag'd . but when I had fubfcrib'd
To mine owne fortune, and inform'd her fully,
I could not anfwer in that courfe of Honour
As fhe had made the ouerture, fhe ceaft
In heauie fatisfaction, and would neuer
Receiue the Ring againe.

Kin. *Platus* himfelfe,
That knowes the tinct and multiplying med'cine,
Hath not in natures myfterie more fcience,
Then I haue in this Ring. 'Twas mine, 'twas *Helens*,
Who euer gaue it you : then if you know
That you are well acquainted with your felfe,
Confeffe 'twas hers, and by what rough enforcement
You got it from her. She call'd the Saints to furetie,
That fhe would neuer put it from her finger,
Vnleffe fhe gaue it to your felfe in bed,
Where you haue neuer come : or fent it vs
Vpon her great difafter.

Ber. She neuer faw it.

Kin. Thou fpeak'ft it falfely : as I loue mine Honor,
And mak'ft connecturall feares to come into me,
Which I would faine fhut out, if it fhould proue
That rhou art fo inhumane, 'twill not proue fo :
And yet I know not, thou didft hate her deadly,
And fhe is dead, which nothing but to clofe
Her eyes my felfe, could win me to beleeue,
More then to fee this Ring. Take him away,
My fore-paft proofes, how ere the matter fall
Shall taze my feares of little vanitie,
Hauing vainly fear'd too little. Away with him,
Wee'l fift this matter further.

Ber. If you fhall proue
This Ring was euer hers, you fhall as eafie
Proue that I husbanded her bed in Florence,
Where yet fhe neuer was.

Enter a Gentleman.

King. I am wrap d in difmall thinkings.

Gen. Gracious Soueraigne,
Whether I haue beene too blame or no, I know not,
Here's a petition from a Florentine,
Who hath for foure or fiue remoues come fhort,
To tender it her felfe. I vndertooke it,

Vanquifh'd thereto by the faire grace and fpeech
Of the poore fuppliant, who by this I know
Is heere attending : her bufineffe lookes in her
With an importing vifage, and fhe told me
In a fweet verball breefe, it did concerne
Your Highneffe with her felfe.

A Letter.

*Vpon his many proteftations to marrie mee when his wife was
dead, I blufh to fay it, he wonne me. Now is the Count Roffillion a Widdower, his vowes are forfeited to mee, and my
honors payed to him. Hee ftole from Florence, taking no
leaue, and I follow him to his Countrey for Iuftice : Grant
it me, O King, in you it beft lies, otherwife a feducer flou-
rifhes, and a poore Maid is vndone.*

               Diana Capilet.

Laf. I will buy me a fonne in Law in a faire, and toule
for this. Ile none of him.

Kin. The heauens haue thought well on thee *Lafew*,
To bring forth this difcou'rie, feeke thefe futors :
Go fpeedily, and bring againe the Count.

Enter Bertram.

I am a-feard the life of *Hellen* (Ladie)
Was fowly fnatcht.

Old La. Now iuftice on the doers.

King. I wonder fir, fir, wiues are monfters to you,
And that you flye them as you fweare them Lordfhip,
Yet you defire to marry. What woman's that ?

Enter Widdow, Diana, and Parrolles.

Dia. I am my Lord a wretched Florentine,
Deriued from the ancient Capilet,
My fuite as I do vnderftand you know,
And therefore know how farre I may be pittied.

Wid. I am her Mother fir, whofe age and honour
Both fuffer vnder this complaint we bring,
And both fhall ceafe, without your remedie.

King. Come hether Count, do you know thefe Women ?

Ber. My Lord, I neither can nor will denie,
But that I know them, do they charge me further ?

Dia. Why do you looke fo ftrange vpon your wife ?

Ber. She's none of mine my Lord.

Dia. If you fhall marrie
You giue away this hand, and that is mine,
You giue away heauens vowes, and thofe are mine :
You giue away my felfe, which is knowne mine :
For I by vow am fo embodied yours,
That fhe which marries you, muft marrie me,
Either both or none.

Laf. your reputation comes too fhort for my daughter, you are no husband for her.

Ber. My Lord, this is a fond and defp'rate creature,
Whom fometime I haue laugh'd with : Let your highnes
Lay a more noble thought vpon mine honour,
Then for to thinke that I would thinke it heere.

Kin. Sir for my thoughts, you haue them in to friend,
Till your deeds gaine them fairer : proue your honor,
Then in my thought it lies.

Dian. Good my Lord,
Aske him vpon his oath, if hee do's thinke
He had not my virginity.

Kin. What faift thou to her ?

Ber. She's impudent my Lord,
And was a common gamefter to the Campe.

Dia. He do's me wrong my Lord : If I were fo,
He might haue bought me at a common price.

Do

Do not beleeue him. O behold this Ring,
Whose high respe&t and rich validitie
Did lacke a Paralell : yet for all that
He gaue it to a Commoner a'th Campe
If I be one.

Coun. He blushes, and 'tis hit :
Of sixe preceding Ancestors, that Iemme
Confer'd by testament to'th sequent issue
Hath it beene owed and worne. This is his wife,
That Ring's a thousand proofes.

King. Me thought you saide
You saw one heere in Court could witnesse it.

Dia. I did my Lord, but loath am to produce
So bad an instrument, his names *Parrolles.*

Laf. I saw the man to day, if man he bee.

Kin. Finde him, and bring him hether.

Rof. What of him :
He's quoted for a most pe fidious slaue
With all the spots a'th world, taxt and debosh'd,
Whose nature sickens : but to speake a truth,
Am I, or that or this for what he'l vtter,
That will speake any thing.

Kin. She hath that Ring of yours.

Rof. I thinke she has; certaine it is I lyk'd her,
And boorded her i'th wanton way of youth :
She knew her distance, and did angle for mee,
Madding my eagernesse with her restraint,
As all impediments in fancies course
Are motiues of more fancie, and in fine,
Her insuite comming with her moderne grace,
Subdu'd me to her rate, she got the Ring,
And I had that which any inferiour might
At Market price haue bought.

Dia. I must be patient :
You that haue turn'd off a first so noble wife,
May iustly dyet me. I pray you yet,
(Since you lacke vertue, I will loose a husband)
Send for your Ring, I will returne it home,
And giue me mine againe.

Rof. I haue it not.

Kin. What Ring was yours I pray you?

Dian. Sir much like the same vpon your finger.

Kin. Know you this Ring, this Ring was his of late.

Dia. And this was it I gaue him being a bed.

Kin. The story then goes false, you threw it him
Out of a Casement.

Dia. I haue spoke the truth. *Enter Parolles.*

Rof. My Lord, I do confesse the ring was hers.

Kin. You boggle shrewdly, euery feather starts you :
Is this the man you speake of?

Dia. I, my Lord.

Kin. Tell me sirrah, but tell me true I charge you,
Not fearing the displeasure of your master :
Which on your lust proceeding, Ile keepe off,
By him and by this woman heere, what know you?

Par. So please your Maiesty, my master hath bin an
honourable Gentleman. Trickes hee hath.had in him,
which Gentlemen haue.

Kin. Come, come, to'th'purpose : Did hee loue this
woman?

Par. Faith sir he did loue her, but how.

Kin. How I pray you?

Par. He did loue her sir, as a Gent. loues a Woman.

Kin. How is that?

Par. He lou'd her sir, and lou'd her not.

Kin. As thou art a knaue and no knaue, what an equi-

uocall Companion is this?

Par. I am a poore man, and at your Maiesties command.

Laf. Hee's a good drumme my Lord, but a naughtie
Orator.

Dian. Do you know he promist me marriage?

Par. Faith I know more then Ile speake.

Kin. But wilt thou not speake all thou know'st?

Par. Yes so please your Maiesty : I did goe betweene
them as I said, but more then that he loued her, for indeede he was madde for her, and talkt of Sathan, and of
Limbo, and of Furies, and I know not what : yet I was in
that credit with them at that time, that I knewe of their
going to bed, and of other motions, as promising her
marriage, and things which would deriue mee ill will to
speake of, therefore I will not speake what I know.

Kin. Thou hast spoken all alreadie, vnlesse thou canst
say they are maried, but thou art too fine in thy euidence,
therefore stand aside. This Ring you say was yours.

Dia. I my good Lord.

Kin. Where did you buy it? Or who gaue it you?

Dia. It was not giuen me, nor I did not buy it.

Kin. Who lent it you?

Dia. It was not lent me neither.

Kin. Where did you finde it then?

Dia. I found it not.

Kin. If it were yours by none of all these wayes,
How could you giue it him?

Dia. I neuer gaue it him.

Laf. This womans an easie gloue my Lord, she goes
off and on at pleasure.

Kin. This Ring was mine, I gaue it his first wife.

Dia. It might be yours or hers for ought I know.

Kin. Take her away, I do not like her now,
To prison with her : and away with him,
Vnlesse thou telst me where thou hadst this Ring,
Thou diest within this houre.

Dia. Ile neuer tell you.

Kin. Take her away.

Dia. Ile put in baile my liedge.

Kin. I thinke thee now some common Customer.

Dia. By Ioue if euer I knew man 'twas you.

King. Wherefore hast thou accuse him al this while.

Dia. Becaufe he's guiltie, and he is not guilty :
He knowes I am no Maid, and hee'l sweare too't :
Ile sweare I am a Maid, and he knowes not.
Great King I am no strumpet, by my life,
I am either Maid, or else this old mans wife.

Kin. She does abufe our eares, to prison with her.

Dia. Good mother fetch my bayle. Stay Royall sir,
The Ieweller that owes the Ring is sent for,
And he shall surety me. But for this Lord,
Who hath abus'd me as he knowes himselfe,
Though yet he neuer harm'd me, heere I quit him.
He knowes himselfe my bed he hath defil'd,
And at that time he got his wife with childe :
Dead though she be, she feeles her yong one kicke :
So there's my riddle, one that's dead is quicke,
And now behold the meaning.

Enter Hellen and Widdow.

Kin. Is there no exorcist
Beguiles the truer Office of mine eyes?
Is't reall that I see?

Hel. No my good Lord,

Y   'Tis

'Tis but the shadow of a wife you see,
The name, and not the thing.

Rof. Both, both, O pardon.

Hel. Oh my good Lord, when I was like this Maid,
I found you wondrous kinde, there is your Ring,
And looke you, heeres your letter : this it sayes,
When from my finger you can get this Ring,
And is by me with childe, &c. This is done,
Will you be mine now you are doubly wonne?

Rof. If she my Liege can make me know this clearly,
Ile loue her dearely, euer, euer dearly.

Hel. If it appeare not plaine, and proue vntrue,
Deadly diuorce step betweene me and you.
O my deere mother do I see you liuing ?

Laf. Mine eyes smell Onions, I shall weepe anon :
Good Tom Drumme lend me a handkercher.
So I thanke thee, waite on me home, Ile make sport with
thee : Let thy curtsies alone, they are scuruy ones.

King Let vs from point to point this storie know,
To make the euen truth in pleasure flow :
If thou beest yet a fresh vncropped flower,
Choose thou thy husband, and Ile pay thy dower.
For I can guesse, that by thy honest ayde,
Thou keptst a wife her selfe, thy selfe a Maide.
Of that and all the progresse more and lesse,
Resolduedly more leasure shall expresse :
All yet seemes well, and if it end so meete,
The bitter past, more welcome is the sweet.
Flourish.

THe Kings a Begger, now the Play is done,
All is well ended, if this suite be wonne,
That you expresse Content : which we will pay,
With strift to please you, day exceeding day :
Ours be your patience then, and yours our parts,
Your gentle hands lend vs, and take our hearts. Exeunt omn.

FINIS.

TwelfeNight, Orvvhatyouwill.

Actus Primus, Scæna Prima.

Enter Orsino Duke of Illyria, Curio, and other Lords.

Duke.

IF Musicke be the food of Loue, play on,
Giue me excesse of it : that surfetting,
The appetite may sicken, and so dye.
That straine agen, it had a dying fall :
O, it came ore my eare, like the sweet sound
That breathes vpon a banke of Violets;
Stealing, and giuing Odour. Enough, no more,
'Tis not so sweet now, as it was before.
O spirit of Loue, how quicke and fresh art thou,
That notwithstanding thy capacitie,
Receiueth as the Sea. Nought enters there,
Of what validity, and pitch so ere,
But falles into abatement, and low price
Euen in a minute; so full of shapes is fancie,
That it alone, is high fantasticall.
Cu. Will you go hunt my Lord?
Du. What Curio?
Cu. The Hart.
Du. Why so I do, the Noblest that I haue :
O when mine eyes did see Oliuia first,
Me thought she purg'd the ayre of pestilence;
That instant was I turn'd into a Hart,
And my desires like fell and cruell hounds,
Ere since pursue me. How now what newes from her?

Enter Valentine.

Val. So please my Lord, I might not be admitted,
But from her handmaid do returne this answer:
The Element it selfe, till seuen yeares heate,
Shall not behold her face at ample view :
But like a Cloystresse she will vailed walke,
And water once a day her Chamber round
With eye-offending brine : all this to season
A brothers dead loue, which she would keepe fresh
And lasting, in her sad remembrance.
Du. O she that hath a heart of that fine frame
To pay this debt of loue but to a brother,
How will she loue, when the rich golden shaft
Hath kill'd the flocke of all affections else
That liue in her. When Liuer, Braine, and Heart,
These soueraigne thrones, are all supply'd and fill'd
Her sweete perfections with one selfe king :
Away before me, to sweet beds of Flowres,
Loue-thoughts lye rich, when canopy'd with bowres.

Exeunt

Scena Secunda.

Enter Viola, a Captaine, and Saylors.

Vio. What Country (Friends) is this?
Cap. This is Illyria Ladie.
Vio. And what should I do in Illyria?
My brother he is in Elizium,
Perchance he is not drown'd : What thinke you saylors?
Cap. It is perchance that you your selfe were saued.
Vio. O my poore brother, and so perchance may he be.
Cap. True Madam, and to comfort you with chance,
Assure your selfe, after our ship did split,
When you, and those poore number saued with you,
Hung on our driuing boate : I saw your brother
Most prouident in perill, binde himselfe,
(Courage and hope both teaching him the practise)
To a sttong Maste, that liu'd vpon the sea :
Where like Orion on the Dolphines backe,
I saw him hold acquaintance with the waues,
So long as I could see.
Vio. For saying so, there's Gold :
Mine owne escape vnfoldeth to my hope,
Whereto thy speech serues for authoritie
The like of him. Know'st thou this Countrey?
Cap. I Madam well, for I was bred and borne
Not three houres trauaile from this very place:
Vio. Who gouernes heere?
Cap. A noble Duke in nature, as in name.
Vio. What is his name?
Cap. Orsino.
Vio, Orsino : I haue heard my father name him.
He was a Batchellor then.
Cap. And so is now, or was so very late :
For but a month ago I went from hence,
And then 'twas fresh in murmure (as you know
What great ones do, the lesse will prattle of,)
That he did seeke the loue of faire Oliuia.
Vio. What's shee?
Cap. A vertuous maid, the daughter of a Count
That dide some tweluemonth since, then leauing her
In the protection of his sonne, her brother,
Who shortly also dide : for whose deere loue
(They say) she hath abiur'd the sight
And company of men.
Vio. O that I seru'd that Lady,
And might not be deliuered to the world

Till

Till I had made mine owne occasion mellow
What my estate is.
  Cap. That were hard to compasse,
Becauſe ſhe will admit no kinde of ſuite,
No, not the Dukes.
  Vio. There is a faire behauiour in thee Captaine,
And though that nature, with a beauteous wall
Doth oft cloſe in pollution : yet of thee
I will beleeue thou haſt a minde that ſuites
With this thy faire and outward charraĉter,
I prethee (and Ile pay thee bounteouſly)
Conceale me what I am, and be my ayde,
For ſuch diſguiſe as haply ſhall become
The forme of my intent. Ile ſerue this Duke,
Thou ſhalt preſent me as an Eunuch to him,
It may be worth thy paines : for I can ſing,
And ſpeake to him in many ſorts of Muſicke,
That will allow me very worth his ſeruice.
What elſe may hap, to time I will commit,
Onely ſhape thou thy ſilence to my wit.
  Cap. Be you his Eunuch, and your Mute Ile bee,
When my tongue blabs, then let mine eyes not ſee.
  Vio. I thanke thee : Lead me on.   *Exeunt*

Scæna Tertia.

Enter Sir Toby, and Maria.

  Sir To. What a plague meanes my Neece to take the
death of her brother thus ? I am ſure care's an enemie to
life.
  Mar. By my troth ſir *Toby*, you muſt come in earlyer
a nights : your Coſin, my Lady, takes great exceptions
to your ill houres.
  To. Why let her except, before excepted.
  Ma. I, but you muſt confine your ſelfe within the
modeſt limits of order.
  To. Confine? Ile confine my ſelfe no finer then I am :
theſe cloathes are good enough to drinke in, and ſo bee
theſe boots too : and they be not, let them hang them-
ſelues in their owne ſtraps.
  Ma. That quaffing and drinking will vndoe you : I
heard my Lady talke of it yeſterday : and of a fooliſh
knight that you brought in one night here, to be hir woer
  To. Who, Sir *Andrew Ague-cheeke?*
  Ma. I he.
  To. He's as tall a man as any's in Illyria.
  Ma. What's that to th'purpoſe?
  To. Why he ha's three thouſand ducates a yeare.
  Ma. I, but hee'l haue but a yeare in all theſe ducates :
He's a very foole, and a prodigall.
  To. Fie, that you'l ſay ſo : he playes o'th Viol-de-gam-
boys, and ſpeakes three or four languages word for word
without booke, & hath all the good gifts of nature.
  Ma. He hath indeed, almoſt naturall : for beſides that
he's a foole, he's a great quarreller : and but that hee hath
the gift of a Coward, to allay the guſt he hath in quarrelling, 'tis thought among the prudent, he would quickely
haue the gift of a graue.
  Tob. By this hand they are ſcoundrels and ſubſtra-
ĉtors that ſay ſo of him. Who are they?
  Ma. They that adde moreour, hee's drunke nightly
in your company.
  To. With drinking healths to my Neece : Ile drinke

to her as long as there is a paſſage in my throat, & drinke
in Illyria : he's a Coward and a Coyſtrill that will not
drinke to my Neece. till his braines turne o'th toe, like a
pariſh top. What wench? *Caſtiliano vulgo:* for here coms
Sir *Andrew Agueface.*

Enter Sir Andrew.

  And. Sir *Toby Belch.* How now ſir *Toby Belch?*
  To. Sweet ſir *Andrew.*
  And. Bleſſe you faire Shrew.
  Mar. And you too ſir.
  Tob. Accoſt Sir *Andrew,* accoſt.
  And. What's that?
  To. My Neeces Chamber-maid.
  Ma. Good Miſtris accoſt, I deſire better acquaintance
  Ma. My name is *Mary* ſir.
  And. Good miſtris *Mary,* accoſt.
  To, You miſtake knight : Accoſt, is front her, boord
her, woe her, aſſayle her.
  And. By my troth I would not vndertake her in this
company. Is that the meaning of Accoſt?
  Ma. Far you well Gentlemen.
  To. And thou let part ſo Sir *Andrew,* would thou
mightſt neuer draw ſword agen.
  And. And you part ſo miſtris, I would I might neuer
draw ſword agen : Faire Lady, doe you thinke you haue
fooles in hand ?
  Ma. Sir, I haue not you by'th hand.
  An. Marry but you ſhall haue, and heeres my hand.
  Ma. Now ſir, thought is free : I pray you bring your
hand to'th Buttry barre, and let it drinke.
  An. Wherefore (ſweet-heart?) What's your Meta-
phor?
  Ma. It's dry ſir.
  And. Why I thinke ſo : I am not ſuch an aſſe, but I
can keepe my hand dry. But what's your ieſt ?
  Ma. A dry ieſt Sir.
  And. Are you full of them ?
  Ma. I Sir, I haue them at my fingers ends: marry now
I let go your hand, I am barren.   *Exit Maria*
  To. O knight, thou lack'ſt a cup of Canarie: when did
I ſee thee ſo put downe?
  An. Neuer in your life I thinke, vnleſſe you ſee Ca-
narie put me downe : mee thinkes ſometimes I haue no
more wit then a Chriſtian, or an ordinary man ha's : but I
am a great eater of beefe, and I beleeue that does harme
to my wit.
  To. No queſtion.
  An. And I thought that, I'de forſweare it. Ile ride
home to morrow ſir *Toby.*
  To. *Pur-quoy* my deere knight?
  An. What is *purquoy?* Do, or not do ? I would I had
beſtowed that time in the tongues, that I haue in fencing
dancing, and beare-bayting : O had I but followed the
Arts.
  To. Then hadſt thou had an excellent head of haire.
  An. Why, would that haue mended my haire ?
  To. Paſt queſtion, for thou ſeeſt it will not coole my
  An. But it becomes wel enough, doſt not?   (nature
  To. Excellent, it hangs like flax on a diſtaffe: & I hope
to ſee a huſwife take thee between her legs, & ſpin it off.
  An. Faith Ile home to morrow ſir *Toby,* your niece wil
not be ſeene, or if ſhe be it's four to one, ſhe'l none of me :
the Connt himſelfe here hard by, wooes her.
  To. Shee'l none o'th Count, ſhe'l not match aboue hir
degree, neither in eſtate, yeares, nor wit : I haue heard her
ſwear t. Tut there's life in't man.

And.

And. Ile ftay a moneth longer. I am a fellow o'th ftrangeft minde i'th world : I delight in Maskes and Reuels fometimes altogether.

To. Art thou good at thefe kicke-chawfes Knight?

And. As any man in Illyria, whatfoeuer he be, vnder the degree of my betters, & yet I will not compare with an old man.

To. What is thy excellence in a galliard, knight?

And. Faith, I can cut a caper.

To. And I can cut the Mutton too't.

And. And I thinke I haue the backe-tricke, fimply as ftrong as any man in Illyria.

To. Wherefore are thefe things hid? Wherefore haue thefe gifts a Curtaine before 'em? Are they like to take duft, like miftris *Mals* picture? Why doft thou not goe to Church in a Galliard, and come home in a Carranto? My verie walke fhould be a Iigge : I would not fo much as make water but in a Sinke-a-pace : What dooeft thou meane? Is it a world to hide vertues in? I did thinke by the excellent conftitution of thy legge, it was form'd vnder the ftarre of a Galliard.

And, I, 'tis ftrong, and it does indifferent well in a dam'd colour'd ftocke. Shall we fit about fome Reuels?

To. What fhall we do elfe : were we not borne vnder Taurus?

And. Taurus? That fides and heart.

To. No fir, it is leggs and thighes : let me fee thee caper. Ha, higher : ha, ha, excellent. *Exeunt*

Scena Quarta.

Enter Valentine, and Viola in mans attire.

Val. If the Duke continue thefe fauours towards you *Cefario*, you are like to be much adu anc'd, he hath known you but three dayes, and already you are no ftranger.

Vio. You either feare his humour, or my negligence, that you call in queftion the continuance of his loue. Is he inconftant fir, in his fauours. *Val.* No beleeue me.

Enter Duke, Curio, and Attendants.

Vio. I thanke you : heere comes the Count.

Duke. Who faw *Cefario* hoa?

Vio. On your attendance my Lord heere.

Du. Stand you a-while aloofe.
Thou knowft no leffe, but all : I haue vnclafp'd
To thee rhe booke euen of my fecret foule.
Therefore good youth, addreffe thy gate vnto her,
Be not deni'de acceffe, ftand at her doores,
And tell them, there thy fixed foot fhall grow
Till thou haue audience.

Vio. Sure my Noble Lord,
If fhe be fo abandon'd to her forrow
As it is fpoke, fhe neuer will admit me.

Du, Be clamorous, and leape all ciuill bounds,
Rather then make vnprofited returne,

Vio. Say I do fpeake with her (my Lord) what then?

Du. O then, vnfold the paffion of my loue,
Surprize her with difcourfe of my deere faith ;
It fhall become thee well to act my woes :
She will attend it better in thy youth,
Then in a Nuntio's of more graue afpect.

Vio. I thinke not fo, my Lord.

Du. Deere Lad, beleeue it ;

For they fhall yet belye thy happy yeeres,
That fay thou art a man : *Dianas* lip
Is not more fmooth, and rubious : thy fmall pipe
Is as the maidens organ, fhrill, and found,
And all is femblatiue a womans part.
I know thy conftellation is right apt
For this affayre : fome foure or fiue attend him,
All if you will : for I my felfe am beft
When leaft in companie : profper well in this,
And thou fhalt liue as freely as thy Lord,
To call his fortunes thine.

Vio. Ile do my beft
To woe your Lady : yet a barrefull ftrife,
Who ere I woe, my felfe would be his wife. *Exeunt.*

Scena Quinta.

Enter Maria, and Clowne.

Ma. Nay, either tell me where thou haft bin, or I will not open my lippes fo wide as a brifle may enter, in way of thy excufe : my Lady will hang thee for thy abfence.

Clo. Let her hang me : hee that is well hang'de in this world, needs to feare no colours.

Ma. Make that good.

Clo. He fhall fee none to feare.

Ma. A good lenton anfwer : I can tell thee where y̓ faying was borne, of I feare no colours.

Clo. Where good miftris *Mary?*

Ma. In the warrs, & that may you be bolde to fay in your foolerie.

Clo. Well, God giue them wifedome that haue it : & thofe that are fooles, let them vfe their talents.

Ma. Yet you will be hang'd for being fo long abfent, or to be turn'd away : is not that as good as a hanging to you?

Clo. Many a good hanging, preuents a bad marriage : and for turning away, let fummer beare it out.

Ma. You are refolute then?

Clo. Not fo neyther, but I am refolu'd on two points

Ma. That if one breake, the other will hold: or if both breake, your gaskins fall.

Clo. Apt in good faith, very apt: well go thy way, if fir *Toby* would leaue drinking, thou wert as witty a piece of *Eues* flefh, as any in Illyria.

Ma. Peace you rogue, no more o' that: here comes my Lady : make your excufe wifely, you were beft.

Enter Lady Oliuia, with Maluolio.

Clo. Wit, and't be thy will, put me into good fooling : thofe wits that thinke they haue thee, doe very oft proue fooles : and I that am fure I lacke thee, may paffe for a wife man. For what fayes *Quinapalus*, Better a witty foole, then a foolifh wit. God bleffe thee Lady.

Ol. Take the foole away.

Clo. Do you not heare fellowes, take away the Ladie.

Ol. Go too, y'are a dry foole : Ile no more of you: befides you grow dif-honeft.

Clo. Two faults Madona, that drinke & good counfell wil amend : for giue the dry foole drink, then is the foole not dry : bid the difhoneft man mend himfelf, if he mend, he is no longer difhoneft; if hee cannot, let the Botcher mend him : any thing that's mended, is but patch'd : vertu that tranfgreffes, is but patcht with finne, and fin that a-mends, is but patcht with vertue. If that this fimple Sillogifme will ferue, fo : if it will not, vvhat remedy?

As there is no true Cuckold but calamity, ſo beauties a
flower ; The Lady bad take away the foole, therefore I
ſay againe, take her away.

_Ol._ Sir, I bad them take away you.

Clo. Miſpriſion in the higheſt degree. Lady, _Cucullus
non facit monachum_: that's as much to ſay, as I weare not
motley in my braine : good _Madona_, giue mee leaue to
proue you a foole.

_Ol._ Can you do it?

Clo. Dexteriouſly, good Madona.

_Ol._ Make your proofe.

Clo. I muſt catechize you for it Madona, Good my
Mouſe of vertue anſwer mee.

_Ol._ Well ſir, for want of other idleneſſe, Ile bide your
proofe.

Clo. Good Madona, why mournſt thou?

_Ol._ Good foole, for my brothers death.

Clo. I thinke his ſoule is in hell, Madona.

_Ol._ I know his ſoule is in heauen, foole.

Clo. The more foole (Madona) to mourne for your
Brothers ſoule, being in heauen. Take away the Foole,
Gentlemen.

_Ol._ What thinke you of this foole _Maluolio_, doth he
not mend?

Mal. Yes, and ſhall do, till the pangs of death ſhake
him : Infirmity that decaies the wiſe, doth euer make the
better foole.

Clow. God ſend you ſir, a ſpeedie Infirmity, for the
better increaſing your folly : Sir _Toby_ will be ſworn that
I am no Fox, but he wil not paſſe his word for two pence
that you are no Foole.

_Ol._ How ſay you to that _Maluolio_?

Mal. I maruell your Ladyſhip takes delight in ſuch
a barren raſcall : I ſaw him put down the other day, with
an ordinary foole, that has no more braine then a ſtone.
Looke you now, he's out of his gard already : vnles you
laugh and miniſter occaſion to him, he is gag'd. I proteſt
I take theſe Wiſemen, that crow ſo at theſe ſet kinde of
fooles, no better then the fooles Zanies.

_Ol._ O you are ſicke of ſelfe-loue _Maluolio_, and taſte
with a diſtemper'd appetite. To be generous, guitleſſe,
and of free diſpoſition, is to take thoſe things for Bird-
bolts, that you deeme Cannon bullets : There is no ſlander in an allow'd foole, though he do nothing but rayle ;
nor no rayling, in a knowne diſcreet man, though hee do
nothing but reproue.

Clo. Now Mercury indue thee with leaſing, for thou
ſpeak'ſt well of fooles.

Enter Maria.

Mar. Madam, there is at the gate, a young Gentleman, much deſires to ſpeake with you.

_Ol._ From the Count Orſino, is it?

_Ma_ I know not (Madam) 'tis a faire young man, and
well attended.

_Ol._ Who of my people hold him in delay?

_Ma._ Sir _Toby_ Madam, your kinſman.

_Ol._ Fetch him off I pray you, he ſpeakes nothing but
madman : Fie on him. Go you _Maluolio_ ; If it be a ſuit
from the Count, I am ſicke, or not at home. What you
will, to diſmiſſe it.   _Exit Maluo._

Now you ſee ſir, how your fooling growes old, & people diſlike it.

Clo. Thou haſt ſpoke for vs (Madona) as if thy eldeſt
ſonne ſhould be a foole : whoſe ſcull, Ioue cramme with
braines, for heere he comes.   _Enter Sir Toby._

One of thy kin has a moſt weake _Pia-mater._

_Ol._ By mine honor halfe drunke. What is he at the
gate Coſin?

_To._ A Gentleman.

_Ol._ A Gentleman? What Gentleman?

_To._ 'Tis a Gentleman heere. A plague o'theſe pickle
herring : How now Sot.

Clo. Good Sir _Toby._

_Ol._ Coſin, Coſin, how haue you come ſo earely by
this Lethargie?

_To._ Letcherie, I defie Letchery : there's one at the
gate.

_Ol._ I marry, what is he?

_To._ Let him be the diuell and he will, I care not: giue
me faith ſay I. Well, it's all one.   _Exit_

_Ol._ What's a drunken man like, foole?

Clo. Like a drown'd man, a foole, and a madde man :
One draught aboue heate, makes him a foole, the ſecond
maddes him, and a third drownes him.

_Ol._ Go thou and ſeeke the Crowner, and let him ſitte
o'my Coz : for he's in the third degree of drinke : hee's
drown'd : go looke after him.

Clo. He is but mad yet Madona, and the foole ſhall
looke to the madman.

Enter Maluolio.

Mal. Madam, yond young fellow ſweares hee will
ſpeake with you. I told you you were ſicke, he takes on
him to vnderſtand ſo much, and therefore comes to ſpeak
with you. I told him you were aſleepe, he ſeems to haue
a fore knowledge of that too, and therefore comes to
ſpeake with you. What is to be ſaid to him Ladie, hee's
fortified againſt any deniall.

_Ol._ Tell him, he ſhall not ſpeake with me.

Mal. Ha's beene told ſo : and hee ſayes hee'l ſtand at
your doore like a Sheriffes poſt, and be the ſupporter to
a bench, but hee'l ſpeake with you.

_Ol._ What kinde o'man is he?

Mal. Why of mankinde.

_Ol._ What manner of man?

Mal. Of verie ill manner : hee'l ſpeake with you, will
you, or no.

_Ol._ Of what perſonage, and yeeres is he?

Mal. Not yet old enough for a man, nor yong enough
for a boy : as a ſquaſh is before tis a peſcod, or a Codling
when tis almoſt an Apple : Tis with him in ſtanding water, betweene boy and man. He is verie well-fauour'd,
and he ſpeakes verie ſhrewiſhly : One would thinke his
mothers milke were ſcarſe out of him.

_Ol._ Let him approach : Call in my Gentlewoman.

Mal. Gentlewoman, my Lady calles.   _Exit._

Enter Maria.

_Ol._ Giue me my vaile : come throw it ore my face,
Wee'l once more heare Orſinos Embaſſie.

Enter Violenta.

Vio. The honorable Ladie of the houſe, which is ſhe?

_Ol._ Speake to mee, I ſhall anſwer for her : your will.

Vio. Moſt radiant, exquiſite, and vnmatchable beautie. I pray you tell me if this bee the Lady of the houſe,
for I neuer ſaw her. I would bee loath to caſt away my
ſpeech : for beſides that it is excellently well pend, I haue
taken great paines to con it. Good Beauties, let mee ſuſtaine no ſcorne ; I am very comptible, euen to the leaſt
ſiniſter vſage.

_Ol._ Whence came you ſir?

Vio. I can ſay little more then I haue ſtudied, & that
queſtion's out of my part. Good gentle one, giue mee
modeſt aſſurance, if you be the Ladie of the houſe, that

                                                             I

may proceede in my fpeech.

Ol. Are you a Comedian?

Vio. No my profound heart : and yet (by the verie phangs of malice, I fweare) I am not that I play. Are you the Ladie of the houfe?

Ol. If I do not vfurpe my felfe, I am.

Vio. Moft certaine, if you are fhe, you do vfurp your felfe : for what is yours to beftowe, is, not yours to referue. But this is from my Commiffion : I will on with my fpeech in your praife, and then fhew you the heart of my meffage.

Ol. Come to what is important in't : I forgiue you the praife.

Vio. Alas, I tooke great paines to ftudie it, and 'tis Poeticall.

Ol. It is the more like to be feigned, I pray you keep it in. I heard you were fawcy at my gates, & allow'd your approach rather to wonder at you, then to heare you. If you be not mad, be gone : if you haue reafon, be breefe : 'tis not that time of Moone with me, to make one in fo skipping a dialogue.

Ma. Will you hoyft fayle fir, here lies your way.

Vio. No good fwabber, I am to hull here a little longer. Some mollification for your Giant, fweete Ladie; tell me your minde, I am a meffenger.

Ol. Sure you haue fome hiddeous matter to deliuer, when the curtefie of it is fo fearefull. Speake your office.

Vio. It alone concernes your eare : I bring no ouerture of warre, no taxation of homage; I hold the Olyffe in my hand : my words are as full of peace, as matter.

Ol. Yet you began rudely. What are you?
What would you?

Vio. The rudeneffe that hath appear'd in mee, haue I learn'd from my entertainment. What I am, and what I would, are as fecret as maiden-head : to your eares, Diuinity; to any others, prophanation.

Ol. Giue vs the place alone,
We will heare this diuinitie. Now fir, what is your text?

Vio. Moft fweet Ladie.

Ol. A comfortable doctrine, and much may bee faide of it. Where lies your Text?

Vio. In Orfinoes bofome.

Ol. In his bofome? In what chapter of his bofome?

Vio. To anfwer by the method. in the firft of his hart.

Ol. O, I haue read it : it is herefie. Haue you no more to fay?

Vio. Good Madam, let me fee your face.

Ol. Haue you any Commiffion from your Lord, to negotiate with my face : you are now out of your Text : but we will draw the Curtain, and fhew you the picture. Looke you fir, fuch a one I was this prefent : Ift not well done?

Vio. Excellently done, if God did all.

Ol. 'Tis in graine fir, 'twill endure winde and weather.

Vio. 'Tis beauty truly blent, whofe red and white, Natures owne fweet, and cunning hand laid on : Lady, you are the cruell'ft fhee aliue, If you will leade thefe graces to the graue, And leaue the world no copie.

Ol. O fir, I will not be fo hard-hearted : I will giue out diuers fcedules of my beautie. It fhalbe Inuentoried and euery particle and vtenfile labell'd to my will : As, Item two lippes indifferent redde, Item two grey eyes, with lids to them : Item, one necke, one chin, & fo forth. Were you fent hither to praife me?

Vio. I fee you what you are, you are too proud : But if you were the diuell, you are faire : My Lord, and mafter loues you : O fuch loue Could be but recompenc'd, though you were crown'd The non-parell of beautie.

Ol. How does he loue me?

Vio. With adorations, fertill teares, With groanes that thunder loue, with fighes of fire.

Ol. Your Lord does know my mind, I cannot loue him Yet I fuppofe him vertuous, know him noble, Of great eftate, of frefh and ftainleffe youth ; In voyces well divulg'd, free, learn'd, and valiant, And in dimenfion, and the fhape of nature, A gracious perfon ; But yet I cannot loue him : He might haue tooke his anfwer long ago.

Vio. If I did loue you in my mafters flame, With fuch a fuffring, fuch a deadly life : In your deniall, I would finde no fence, I would not vnderftand it.

Ol. Why, what would you?

Vio. Make me a willow Cabine at your gate, And call vpon my foule within the houfe, Write loyall Cantons of contemned loue, And fing them lowd euen in the dead of night : Hallow your name to the reuerberate hilles, And make the babling Goffip of the aire, Cry out Oliuia : O you fhould not reft Betweene the elements of ayre, and earth, But you fhould pittie me.

Ol. You might do much :
What is your Parentage?

Vio. Aboue my fortunes, yet my ftate is well : I am a Gentleman.

Ol. Get you to your Lord :
I cannot loue him : let him fend no more, Vnleffe (perchance) you come to me againe, To tell me how he takes it : Fare you well : I thanke you for your paines : fpend this for mee.

Vio. I am no feede poaft, Lady ; keepe your purfe, My Mafter, not my felfe, lackes recompence. Loue make his heart of flint, that you fhal loue, And let your feruour like my mafters be, Plac'd in contempt : Farwell fayre crueltie.   *Exit*

Ol. What is your Parentage?
Aboue my fortunes, yet my ftate is well ; I am a Gentleman. Ile be fworne thou art, Thy tongue, thy face, thy limbes, actions, and fpirit, Do giue thee fiue-fold blazon : not too faft : foft, foft, Vnleffe the Mafter were the man. How now? Euen fo quickly may one catch the plague? Me thinkes I feele this youths perfections With an inuifible, and fubtle ftealth To creepe in at mine eyes. Well, let it be. What hoa, *Maluolio.*

Enter Maluolio.

Mal. Heere Madam, at your feruice.

Ol. Run after that fame peeuifh Meffenger The Countes man : he left this Ring behinde him Would I, or not : tell him, Ile none of it. Defire him not to flatter with his Lord, Nor hold him vp with hopes, I am not for him : If that the youth will come this way to morrow, Ile giue him reafons for't : hie thee *Maluolio.*

Mal. Madam, I will.   *Exit.*

Ol. I do I know not what, and feare to finde Mine eye too great a flatterer for my minde :

Fate

Pate, fhew thy force, our felues we do not owe,
What is decreed, muft be : and be this fo.
Finis, Actus primus.

Actus Secundus, Scæna prima.

Enter Antonio & Sebaftian.

Ant. Will you ftay no longer : nor will you not that
I go with you.

Seb. By your patience, no : my ftarres fhine darkely
ouer me ; the malignancie of my fate, might perhaps diftemper yours ; therefore I fhall craue of you your leaue,
that I may beare my euils alone. It were a bad recompence for your loue, to lay any of them on you.

_An._ Let me yet know of you, whither you are bound.

Seb. No footh fir : my determinate voyage is meere
extrauagancie.But I perceiue in you fo excellent a touch
of modeftie, that you will not extort from me, what I am
willing to keepe in : therefore it charges me in manners,
the rather to expreffe my felfe : you muft know of mee
then _Antonio_, my name is _Sebaftian_ (which I call'd _Rodo-
rigo_) my father was that _Sebaftian_ of _Meffaline_, whom I
know you haue heard of. He left behinde him, my felfe,
and a fifter, both borne in an houre : if the Heauens had
beene pleas'd, would we had fo ended. But you fir, alter'd that, for fome houre before you tooke me from the
breach of the fea, was my fifter drown'd.

Ant. Alas the day.

Seb. A Lady fir, though it was faid fhee much refem-
bled me, was yet of many accounted beautiful:but thogh
I could not with fuch eftimable wonder ouer-farre beleeue that, yet thus farre I will boldly publifh her, fhee
bore a minde that enuy could not but call faire : Shee is
drown'd already fir with falt water, though I feeme to
drowne her remembrance againe with more.

Ant. Pardon me fir, your bad entertainment.

Seb. O good _Antonio_, forgiue me your trouble.

Ant. If you will not murther me for my loue, let mee
be your feruant.

Seb. If you will not vndo what you haue done, that is
kill him, whom you haue recouer'd, defire it not. Fare
ye well at once, my bofome is full of kindneffe, and I
am yet fo neere the manners of my mother, that vpon the
leaft occafion more, mine eyes will tell tales of me : I am
bound to the Count Orfino's Court, farewell.   _Exit_

Ant. The gentleneffe of all the gods go with thee :
I haue many enemies in Orfino's Court,
Elfe would I very fhortly fee thee there :
But come what may, I do adore thee fo,
That danger fhall feeme fport, and I will go.   _Exit._

Scæna Secunda.

Enter Viola and Maluolio, at feuerall doores.

Mal. Were not you eu'n now, with the Counteffe O-
liuia ?

Vio. Euen now fir, on a moderate pace, I haue fince a-
riu'd but hither.

Mal She returnes this Ring to you (fir) you might
haue faued mee my paines, to haue taken it away your
felfe. She adds moreouer, that you fhould put your Lord

into a defperate affurance, fhe will none of him.And one
thing more, that you be neuer fo hardie to come againe
in his affaires, vnleffe it bee to report your Lords taking
of this : receiue it fo.

Vio. She tooke the Ring of me, Ile none of it.

Mal. Come fir, you peeuifhly threw it to her : and
her will is, it fhould be fo rcturn'd : If it bee worth ftoo-
ping for, there it lies, in your eye : if not, bee it his that
findes it.   _Exit._

Vio. I left no Ring with her : what meanes this Lady?
Fortune forbid my out-fide haue not charm'd her :
She made good view of me, indeed fo much,
That me thought her eyes had loft her tongue,
For fhe did fpeake in ftarts diftractedly.
She loues me fure, the cunning of her paffion
Inuites me in this churlifh meffenger :
None of my Lords Ring ? Why he fent her none ;
I am the man, if it be fo, as tis,
Poore Lady, fhe were better loue a dreame:
Difguife, I fee thou art a wickedneffe,
Wherein the pregnant enemie does much.
How eafie is it, for the proper falfe
In womens waxen hearts to fet their formes :
Alas, O frailtie is the caufe, not wee,
For fuch as we are made, if fuch we bee :
How will this fadge? My mafter loues her deerely,
And I (poore monfter) fond afmuch on him :
And fhe (miftaken) feemes to dote on me :
What will become of this ? As I am man,
My ftate is defperate for my maifters loue:
As I am woman (now alas the day)
What thriftleffe fighes fhall poore _Oliuia_ breath?
O time, thou muft vntangle this, not I,
It is too hard a knot for me t'vnty.

Scæna Tertia.

Enter Sir Toby, and Sir Andrew.

_To._ Approach Sir _Andrew_ : not to bee a bedde after
midnight, is to be vp betimes, and _Deliculo furgere_, thou
know'ft.

And. Nay by my troth I know not : but I know, to
be vp late, is to be vp late.

_To._ A falfe conclufion : I hate it as an vnfill'd Canne.
To be vp after midnight, and to go to bed then is early:
fo that to go to bed after midnight, is to goe to bed betimes. Does not our liues confift of the foure Elements ?

And. Faith fo they fay, but I thinke it rather confifts
of eating and drinking.

_To._ Th'art a fcholler ; let vs therefore eate and drinke,
Marian I fay, a ftoope of wine.

Enter Clowne.

And. Heere comes the foole yfaith.

Clo. How now my harts : Did you neuer fee the Picture of we three?

_To._ Welcome affe, now let's haue a catch.

And. By my troth the foole has an excellent breaft. I
had rather then forty fhillings I had fuch a legge, and fo
fweet a breath to fing, as the foole has. Infooth thou waft
in very gracious fooling laft night, when thou fpok'ft of
Pigrogromitus, of the _Vapians_ paffing the Equinoctial of
Queubus: 'twas very good yfaith : I fent thee fixe pence
for

for thy Lemon, hadſt it?

Clo. I did impeticos thy gratillity : for *Maluolios* noſe is no Whip-ſtocke My Lady has a white hand, and the Mermidons are no bottle-ale houſes.

An. Excellent : Why this is the beſt fooling, when all is done. Now a ſong.

To. Come on, there is ſixe pence for you. Let's haue a ſong.

An. There's a teſtrill of me too : if one knight giue a *Clo.* Would you haue a loue-ſong, or a ſong of good life?

To. A loue ſong, a loue ſong.

An. I, I. I care not for good life.

Clowne ſings.

O Miſtris mine where are you roming?
O ſtay and heare, your true loues coming,
That can ſing both high and low.
Trip no further prettie ſweeting :
Iourneys end in louers meeting,
Euery wiſe mans ſonne doth know.

An. Excellent good, iſaith.

To. Good, good.

Clo. *What is loue, tis not heereafter,*
Preſent mirth, hath preſent laughter :
What's to come, is ſtill vnſure.
In delay there lies no plentie,
Then come kiſſe me ſweet and twentie :
Youths a ſtuffe will not endure.

An. A melliſluous voyce, as I am true knight.

To. A contagious breath.

An. Very ſweet, and contagious iſaith.

To. To heare by the noſe, it is dulcet in contagion. But ſhall we make the Welkin dance indeed? Shall wee rowze the night-Owle in a Catch, that will drawe three ſoules out of one Weauer? Shall we do that?

And. And you loue me, let's doo't : I am dogge at a Catch.

Clo. Byrlady ſir, and ſome dogs will catch well.

An. Moſt certaine : Let our Catch be, *Thou Knaue.*

Clo. Hold thy peace, *thou Knaue* knight. I ſhall be conſtrain'd in't, to call thee knaue, Knight.

An. 'Tis not the firſt time I haue conſtrained one to call me knaue. Begin foole : it begins, *Hold thy peace.*

Clo. I ſhall neuer begin if I hold my peace.

An. Good iſaith : Come begin. *Catch ſung*

Enter Maria.

Mar. What a catterwalling doe you keepe heere? If my Ladie haue not call'd vp her Steward *Maluolio*, and bid him turne you out of doores, neuer truſt me.

To. My Lady's a *Catayan*, we are politicians, *Maluolios* a Peg-a-ramſie, and *Three merry men be wee.* Am not I conſanguinious? Am I not of her blood : tilly vally. Ladie, *There dwelt a man in Babylon, Lady, Lady.*

Clo. Beſhrew me, the knights in admirable fooling.

An. I, he do's well enough if he be diſpos'd, and ſo do I too : he does it with a better grace, but I do it more naturall.

To. *O the twelfe day of December.*

Mar. For the loue o'God peace.

Enter Maluolio.

Mal. My maſters are you mad? Or what are you? Haue you no wit, manners, nor honeſtie, but to gabble like Tinkers at this time of night? Do yee make an Alehouſe of my Ladies houſe, that ye ſqueak out your Coziers Catches without any mitigation or remorſe of voice? Is there no reſpeĉt of place, perſons, nor time in you?

To. We did keepe time ſir in our Catches. Snecke vp.

Mal. Sir *Toby*, I muſt be round with you. My Lady bad me tell you, that though ſhe harbors you as her kinſman, ſhe's nothing ally'd to your diſorders. If you can ſeparate your ſelfe and your miſdemeanors, you are welcome to the houſe : if not, and it would pleaſe you to take leaue of her, ſhe is very willing to bid you farewell.

To. Farewell deere heart, ſince I muſt needs be gone.

Mar. Nay good Sir *Toby.*

Clo. His eyes do ſhew his dayes are almoſt done.

Mal. Is't euen ſo?

To. But I will neuer dye.

Clo. Sir *Toby* there you lye.

Mal. This is much credit to you.

To. Shall I bid him go?

Clo. What and if you do?

To. Shall I bid him go, and ſpare not?

Clo. O no, no, no, no, you dare not.

To. Out o'tune ſir, ye lye : Art any more then a Steward? Doſt thou thinke becauſe thou art vertuous, there ſhall be no more Cakes and Ale?

Clo. Yes by *S. Anne*, and Ginger ſhall bee hotte y'th mouth too.

To. Th'art i'th right. Goe ſir, rub your Chaine with crums. A ſtope of Wine *Maria.*

Mal. Miſtris Mary, if you priz'd my Ladies fauour at any thing more then contempt, you would not giue meanes for this vnciuill rule ; ſhe ſhall know of it by this hand. *Exit*

Mar. Go ſhake your eares.

An. 'Twere as good a deede as to drink when a mans a hungrie, to challenge him the field, and then to breake promiſe with him, and make a foole of him.

To. Doo't knight, Ile write thee a Challenge : or Ile deliuer thy indignation to him by word of mouth.

Mar. Sweet Sir Toby be patient for to night : Since the youth of the Counts was to day with my Lady, ſhe is much out of quiet. For Monſieur *Maluolio*, let me alone with him : If I do not gull him into an aueury, and make him a common recreation, do not thinke I haue witte enough to lye ſtraight in my bed : I know I can do it.

To. Poſſeſſe vs, poſſeſſe vs, tell vs ſomething of him.

Mar. Marrie ſir, ſometimes he is a kinde of Puritane.

To. O, if I thought that, Ide beate him like a dogge.

To. What for being a Puritan, thy exquiſite reaſon, deere knight.

An. I haue no exquiſite reaſon for't, but I haue reaſon good enough.

Mar. The diu'll a Puritane that hee is, or any thing conſtantly but a time-pleaſer, an affeĉtion'd Aſſe, that cons State without booke, and vtters it by great ſwarths. The beſt perſwaded of himſelfe : ſo cram'd (as he thinkes) with excellencies, that it is his grounds of faith, that all that looke on him, loue him : and on that vice in him, will my reuenge ſinde notable cauſe to worke.

To. What wilt thou do?

Mar. I will drop in his way ſome obſcure Epiſtles of loue, wherein by the colour of his beard, the ſhape of his legge, the manner of his gate, the expreſſure of his eye, forehead, and compleĉtion, he ſhall ſinde himſelfe moſt feelingly perſonated. I can write very like my Ladie your Neece, on a forgotten matter wee can hardly make diſtinĉtion of our hands.

To. Excellent, I ſmell a deuice.

An. I hau't in my noſe too.

To. He ſhall thinke by the Letters that thou wilt drop that

that they come from my Neece, and that fhee's in loue
with him.

Mar. My purpofe is indeed a horfe of that colour.

An. And your horfe now would make him an Affe.

Mar. Affe, I doubt not.

An. O twill be admirable.

Mar. Sport royall I warrant you : I know my Phyficke will worke with him, I will plant you two, and let
the Foole make a third, where he fhall finde the Letter :
obferue his conftruction of it : For this night to bed, and
dreame on the euent : Farewell.   *Exit*

To. Good night *Penthifilea.*

An. Before me fhe's a good wench.

To. She's a beagle true bred, and one that adores me :
what o'that?

An. I was ador'd once too.

To. Let's to bed knight : Thou hadft neede fend for
more money.

An. If I cannot recouer your Neece, I am a foule way
out.

To. Send for money knight, if thou haft her not i'th
end, call me Cut.

An. If I do not, neuer truft me, take it how you will.

To. Come, come, Ile go burne fome Sacke, tis too late
to go to bed now : Come knight, come knight.   *Exeunt*

Scena Quarta.

Enter Duke, Viola, Curio, and others.

Du. Giue me fome Muficke; Now good morow frends.
Now good *Cefario,* but that peece of fong,
That old and Anticke fong we heard laft night;
Me thought it did releeue my paffion much,
More then light ayres, and recollected termes
Of thefe moft brifke and giddy-paced times.
Come, but one verfe.

Cur. He is not heere (fo pleafe your Lordfhippe) that
fhould fing it ?

Du. Who was it ?

Cur. Fefte the Iefter my Lord, a foole that the Ladie
Oliuiaes Father tooke much delight in . He is about the
houfe.

Du. Seeke him out, and play the tune the while.
                                             Muficke playes.

Come hither Boy, if euer thou fhalt loue
In the fweet pangs of it, remember me :
For fuch as I am, all true Louers are,
Vnftaid and skittifh in all motions elfe,
Saue in the conftant image of the creature
That is belou'd. How doft thou like this tune ?

Vio. It giues a verie eccho to the feate
Where loue is thron'd.

Du. Thou doft fpeake mafterly,
My life vpon't, yong though thou art, thine eye
Hath ftald vpon fome fauour that it loues :
Hath it not boy ?

Vio. A little, by your fauour.

Du. What kinde of woman ift ?

Vio. Of your complection.

Du. She is not worth thee then. What yeares ifaith?

Vio. About your yeeres my Lord.

Du. Too old by heauen : Let ftill the woman take

An elder then her felfe, fo weares fhe to him;
So fwayes fhe leuell in her husbands heart :
For boy, howeuer we do praife our felues,
Our fancies are more giddie and vnfirme,
More longing, wauering, fooner loft and worne,
Then womens are.

Vio. I thinke it well my Lord.

Du. Then let thy Loue be yonger then thy felfe,
Or thy affection cannot hold the bent :
For women are as Rofes, whofe faire flowre
Being once difplaid, doth fall that verie howre.

Vio. And fo they are : alas, that they are fo :
To die, euen when they to perfection grow.

Enter Curio & Clowne.

Du. O fellow come, the fong we had laft night :
Marke it *Cefario,* it is old and plaine ;
The Spinfters and the Knitters in the Sun,
And the free maides that weaue their thred with bones,
Do vfe to chaunt it : it is filly footh,
And dallies with the innocence of loue,
Like the old age.

Clo. Are you ready Sir ?

Duke. I prethee fing.   *Muficke.*

The Song.

Come away, come away death,
And in fad cypreffe let me be laide .
Fye away, fie away breath,
I am flaine by a faire cruell maide :
    My fhrowd of white, ftuck all with Ew, O prepare it.
    My part of death no one fo true did fhare it.

Not a flower, not a flower fweete
On my blacke coffin, let there be ftrewne :
Not a friend, not a friend greet
My poore corpes, where my bones fhall be throwne :
    A thoufand thoufand fighes to faue, lay me ô where
    Sad true louer neuer find my graue, to weepe there.

Du. There's for thy paines.

Clo. No paines fir, I take pleafure in finging fir.

Du. Ile pay thy pleafure then.

Clo. Truely fir, and pleafure will be paide one time, or
another.

Du. Giue me now leaue, to leaue thee.

Clo. Now the melancholly God protect thee, and the
Tailor make thy doublet of changeable Taffata, for thy
minde is a very Opall . I would haue men of fuch conftancie put to Sea, that their bufineffe might be euery thing,
and their intent euerie where, for that's it, that alwayes
makes a good voyage of nothing. Farewell.   *Exit*

Du. Let all the reft giue place : Once more *Cefario,*
Get thee to yond fame foueraigne crueltie :
Tell her my loue, more noble then the world
Prizes not quantitie of dirtie lands,
The parts that fortune hath beftow'd vpon her :
Tell her I hold as giddily as Fortune :
But 'tis that miracle, and Queene of Iems
That nature prankes her in, attracts my foule.

Vio. But if fhe cannot loue you fir.

Du. It cannot be fo anfwer'd.

Vio. Sooth but you muft.
Say that fome Lady, as perhappes there is,
Hath for your loue as great a pang of heart
As you haue for *Oliuia* : you cannot loue her:
You tel her fo : Muft fhe not then be anfwer'd ?

Du. There is no womans fides

Can

Can bide the beating of fo ftrong a paffion,
As loue doth giue my heart : no womans heart
So bigge, to hold fo much, they lacke retention.
Alas, their loue may be call'd appetite,
No motion of the Liuer, but the Pallat,
That fuffer furfet, cloyment, and reuolt,
But mine is all as hungry as the Sea,
And can digeft as much, make no compare
Betweene that loue a woman can beare me,
And that I owe *Oliuia*.

Vio. I but I know.

Du. What doft thou knowe?

Vio. Too well what loue women to men may owe :
In faith they are as true of heart, as we.
My Father had a daughter lou'd a man
As it might be perhaps, were I a woman
I fhould your Lordfhip.

Du. And what's her hiftory?

Vio. A blanke my Lord : fhe neuer told her loue,
But let concealment like a worme i'th budde
Feede on her damaske cheeke : fhe pin'd in thought,
And with a greene and yellow melancholly,
She fate like Patience on a Monument,
Smiling at greefe. Was not this loue indeede?
We men may fay more, fweare more, but indeed
Our fhewes are more then will : for ftill we proue
Much in our vowes, but little in our loue.

Du. But di'de thy fifter of her loue my Boy?

Vio. I am all the daughters of my Fathers houfe,
And all the brothers too: and yet I know not.
Sir, fhall I to this Lady?

Du. I that's the Theame,
To her in hafte : giue her this Iewell : fay,
My loue can giue no place, bide no denay.   *exeunt*

Scena Quinta.

Enter Sir Toby, Sir Andrew, and Fabian.

To. Come thy wayes Signior *Fabian.*

Fab. Nay Ile come : if I loofe a fcruple of this fport,
let me be boyl'd to death with Melancholly.

To. Wouldft thou not be glad to haue the niggardly Rafcally fheepe-biter, come by fome notable fhame?

Fa. I would exult man : you know he brought me out
o'fauour with my Lady, about a Beare-baiting heere.

To. To anger him wee'l haue the Beare againe, and
we will foole him blacke and blew, fhall we not fir *Andrew?*

An. And we do not, it is pittie of our liues.

Enter Maria.

To. Heere comes the little villaine : How now my
Mettle of India?

Mar. Get ye all three into the box tree : *Maluolio's*
comming downe this walke, he has beene yonder i'the
Sunne practifing behauiour to his own fhadow this halfe
houre : obferue him for the loue of Mockerie : for I know
this Letter wil make a contemplatiue Ideot of him. Clofe
in the name of ieafting, lye thou there : for heere comes
the Trowt, that muft be caught with tickling.   *Exit*

Enter Maluolio.

Mal. 'Tis but Fortune, all is fortune. *Maria* once
told me fhe did affect me, and I haue heard her felf come
thus neere, that fhould fhee fancie, it fhould bee one of
my complection. Befides fhe vfes me with a more ex-
alted refpect, then any one elfe that followes her. What
fhould I thinke on't?

To. Heere's an ouer-weening rogue.

Fa. Oh peace : Contemplation makes a rare Turkey
Cocke of him, how he iets vnder his aduanc'd plumes.

And. Slight I could fo beate the Rogue.

To. Peace I fay.

Mal. To be Count *Maluolio.*

To. Ah Rogue.

An. Piftoll him, piftoll him.

To. Peace, peace.

Mal. There is example for't : The Lady of the *Stra-
chy,* married the yeoman of the wardrobe.

An. Fie on him Iezabel.

Fa. O peace, now he's deeply in : looke how imagination blowes him.

Mal. Hauing beene three moneths married to her,
fitting in my ftate.

To. O for a ftone-bow to hit him in the eye.

Mal. Calling my Officers about me, in my branch'd
Veluet gowne : hauing come from a day bedde, where I
haue left *Oliuia* fleeping.

To. Fire and Brimftone.

Fa. O peace, peace.

Mal. And then to haue the humor of ftate : and after
a demure trauaile regard : telling them I knowe my
place, as I would they fhould doe theirs : to aske for my
kinfman *Toby.*

To. Boltes and fhackles.

Fa. Oh peace, peace, peace, now, now.

Mal. Seauen of my people with an obedient ftart,
make out for him : I frowne the while, and perchance
winde vp my watch, or play with my fome rich Iewell :
Toby approaches; curtfies there to me.

To. Shall this fellow liue?

Fa. Though our filence be drawne from vs with cars,
yet peace.

Mal. I extend my hand to him thus : quenching my
familiar fmile with an auftere regard of controll.

To. And do's not *Toby* take you a blow o'the lippes,
then?

Mal. Saying, Cofine *Toby,* my Fortunes hauing caft
me on your Neece, giue me this prerogatiue of fpeech.

To. What, what?

Mal. You muft amend your drunkenneffe.

To. Out fcab.

Fab. Nay patience, or we breake the finewes of our
plot?

Mal. Befides you wafte the treafure of your time,
with a foolifh knight.

And. That's mee I warrant you.

Mal. One fir *Andrew.*

And. I knew 'twas I, for many do call mee foole.

Mal. What employment haue we heere?

Fa. Now is the Woodcocke neere the gin.

To. Oh peace, and the fpirit of humors intimate reading aloud to him.

Mal. By my life this is my Ladies hand: thefe bee her
very *C's,* her *V's,* and her *T's,* and thus makes fhee her
great *P's.* It is in contempt of queftion her hand.

An. Her *C's,* her *V's,* and her *T's:* why that?

Mal. *To the vnknowne belou'd, this, and my good Wifhes :*
Her very Phrafes : By your leaue wax. Soft, and the im-
preffure her *Lucrece,* with which fhe vfes to feale : tis my
Lady : To whom fhould this be?

Fab. This winnes him, Liuer and all.

Mal.

Mal. Ioue knowes I loue, but who, Lips do not mooue, no man muſt know. No man muſt know. What followes? The numbers alter d : No man muſt know, If this ſhould be thee *Maluolio*?

To. Marrie hang thee brocke.

Mal. I may command where I adore, but ſilence like a Lu- creſſe knife : With bloodleſſe ſtroke my heart doth gore, M. O. A. I. doth ſway my life.

Fa. A fuſtian riddle.

To. Excellent Wench, ſay I.

Mal. M. O. A. I. doth ſway my life. Nay but firſt let me ſee, let me ſee, let me ſee.

Fab. What diſh a poyſon has ſhe dreſt him ?

To. And with what wing the ſtallion checkes at it ?

Mal. I may command, where I adore : Why ſhee may command me : I ſerue her, ſhe is my Ladie. Why this is euident to any formall capacitie. There is no obſtruction in this, and the end : What ſhould that Alphabeticall po- ſition portend, if I could make that reſemble ſomething in me ? Softly, *M. O. A. I.*

To. O I, make vp that, he is now at a cold ſent.

Fab. Sowter will cry vpon't for all this, though it bee as ranke as a Fox.

Mal. M. Maluolio, M. why that begins my name.

Fab. Did not I ſay he would worke it out, the Curre is excellent at faults.

Mal. M. But then there is no conſonancy in the ſequell that ſuffers vnder probation : *A.* ſhould follow, but *O.* does.

Fa. And *O* ſhall end, I hope.

To. I, or Ile cudgell him, and make him cry *O.*

Mal. And then *I.* comes behind.

Fa. I, and you had any eye behinde you, you might ſee more detraction at your heeles, then Fortunes before you.

Mal. M, O, A, I. This ſimulation is not as the former: and yet to cruſh this a little, it would bow to mee, for e- uery one of theſe Letters are in my name. Soft, here fol- lowes proſe : *If this fall into thy hand, reuolue.* In my ſtars I am aboue thee, but be not affraid of greatneſſe : Some are become great, ſome atcheeues greatneſſe, and ſome haue greatneſſe thruſt vppon em. Thy fates open theyr hands, let thy blood and ſpirit embrace them, and to in- vre thy ſelfe to what thou art like to be : caſt thy humble ſlough, and appeare freſh. Be oppoſite with a kinſman, ſurly with ſeruants : Let thy tongue tang arguments of ſtate ; put thy ſelfe into the tricke of ſingularitie. Shee thus aduiſes thee, that ſighes for thee. Remember who commended thy yellow ſtockings, and wiſh'd to ſee thee euer croſſe garter'd : I ſay remember, goe too, thou art made if thou deſir'ſt to be ſo : If not, let me ſee thee a ſte- ward ſtill, the fellow of ſeruants, and not woorthie to touch Fortunes fingers Farewell, Shee that would alter ſeruices with thee, tht fortunate vnhappy daylight and champian diſcouers not more : This is open, I will bee proud, I will reade politicke Authours, I will baffle Sir *Toby,* I will waſh oft groſſe acquaintance, I will be point deuiſe, the very man. I do not now foole my ſelfe, to let imagination iade mee ; for euery reaſon excites to this, that my Lady loues me. She did commend my yellow ſtockings of late, ſhee did praiſe my legge being croſſe- garter'd, and in this ſhe manifeſts her ſelfe to my loue, & with a kinde of iniunction driues mee to theſe habites of her liking. I thanke my ſtarres, I am happy : I will bee ſtrange, ſtout, in yellow ſtockings, and croſſe Garter'd,

euen with the ſwiftneſſe of putting on. Ioue, and my ſtarres be praiſed. Heere is yet a poſtſcript. Thou canſt not chooſe but know who I am. If thou entertainſt my loue, let it appeare in thy ſmiling, thy ſmiles become thee well. There- fore in my preſence ſtill ſmile, deero my ſweete, I prethee. Ioue I thanke thee, I will ſmile, I wil do euery thing that thou wilt haue me. *Exit*

Fab. I will not giue my part of this ſport for a penſi- on of thouſands to be paid from the Sophy.

To. I could marry this wench for this deuice.

An. So could I too.

To. And aske no other dowry with her, but ſuch ano- ther ieſt.

Enter Maria.

An. Nor I neither.

Fab. Heere comes my noble gull catcher.

To. Wilt thou ſet thy foote o'my necke.

An. Or o'mine either ?

To. Shall I play my freedome at tray-trip, and becom thy bondſlaue ?

An. Iſaith, or I either ?

Tob. Why, thou haſt put him in ſuch a dreame, that when the image of it leaues him, he muſt run mad.

Ma. Nay but ſay true, do's it worke vpon him ?

To. Like Aqua vite with a Midwife.

Mar. If you will then ſee the fruites of the ſport, mark his firſt approach before my Lady : hee will come to her in yellow ſtockings, and 'tis a colour ſhe abhorres, and croſſe garter'd, a faſhion ſhee deteſts : and hee will ſmile vpon her, which will now be ſo vnſuteable to her diſpo- ſition, being addicted to a melancholly, as ſhee is, that it cannot but turn him into a notable contempt: if you wil ſee it follow me.

To. To the gates of Tartar, thou moſt excellent diuell of wit.

And. Ile make one too. *Exeunt.*

Finis Actus ſecundus

Actus Tertius, Scæna prima.

Enter Viola and Clowne.

Vio. Saue thee Friend and thy Muſick : doſt thou liue by thy Tabor?

Clo. No ſir, I liue by the Church.

Vio. Art thou a Churchman ?

Clo. No ſuch matter ſir, I do liue by the Church : For, I do liue at my houſe, and my houſe dooth ſtand by the Church.

Vio. So thou maiſt ſay the Kings lyes by a begger, if a begger dwell neer him : or the Church ſtands by thy Ta- bor, if thy Tabor ſtand by the Church.

Clo. You haue ſaid ſir : To ſee this age : A ſentence is but a cheu'rill gloue to a good witte, how quickely the wrong ſide may be turn'd outward.

Vio. Nay that's certaine : they that dally nicely with words, may quickely make them wanton.

Clo. I would therefore my ſiſter had had no name Sir.

Vio. Why man ?

Clo. Why ſir, her names a word, and to dallie with that word, might make my ſiſter wanton : But indeede, words are very Raſcals, ſince bonds diſgrac'd them.

Vio. Thy reaſon man ?

Clo.

Clo. Troth fir, I can yeeld you none without wordes, and wordes are growne fo falfe, I am loath to proue reafon with them.

Vio. I warrant thou art a merry fellow, and car'ft for nothing.

Clo. Not fo fir, I do care for fomething: but in my confcience fir, I do not care for you : if that be to care for nothing fir, I would it would make you inuifible.

Vio. Art not thou the Lady *Oliuia's* foole?

Clo. No indeed fir, the Lady *Oliuia* has no folly, fhee will keepe no foole fir, till fhe be married, and fooles are as like husbands, as Pilchers are to Herrings, the Hufbands the bigger, I am indeede not her foole, but hir corrupter of words.

Vio. I faw thee late at the Count *Orfino's.*

Clo. Foolery fir, does walke about the Orbe like the Sun, it fhines euery where. I would be forry fir, but the Foole fhould be as oft with your Mafter, as with my Miftris : I thinke I faw your wifedome there.

Vio. Nay, and thou paffe vpon me, Ile no more with thee: Hold there's expences for thee.

Clo. Now Ioue in his next commodity of hayre, fend thee a beard.

Vio. By my troth Ile tell thee, I am almoft ficke for one, though I would not haue it grow on my chinne. Is thy Lady within?

Clo Would not a paire of thefe haue bred fir?

Vio. Yes being kept together, and put to vfe.

Clo. I would play Lord *Pandarus* of *Phrygia* fir, to bring a *Creffida* to this *Troylus.*

Vio. I vnderftand you fir, tis well begg'd.

Clo. The matter I hope is not great fir; begging, but a begger : *Creffida* was a begger. My Lady is within fir. I will confter to them whence you come, who you are, and what you would are out of my welkin, I might fay Element, but the word is ouer-worne.   *exit*

Vio. This fellow is wife enough to play the foole, And to do that well, craues a kinde of wit : He muft obferue their mood on whom he iefts, The quality of perfons, and the time : And like the Haggard, checke at euery Feather That comes before his eye. This is a practice, As full of labour as a Wife-mans Art: For folly that he wifely fhewes, is fit; But wifemens folly falne, quite taint their wit.

Enter Sir Toby and Andrew.

To. Saue you Gentleman.

Vio. And you fir.

And. Dieu vou guard *Monfieur.*

Vio. Et vous ouffie voftre feruiture.

An. I hope fir, you are, and I am yours.

To. Will you incounter the houfe, my Neece is defirous you fhould enter, if your trade be to her.

Vio. I am bound to your Neece fir, I meane fhe is the lift of my voyage.

To. Tafte your legges fir, put them to motion.

Vio. My legges do better vnderftand me fir, then I vnderftand what you meane by bidding me tafte my legs.

To. I meane to go fir, to enter.

Vio. I will anfwer you with gate and entrance, but we are preuented.

Enter Oliuia, and Gentlewoman.

Moft excellent accomplifh'd Lady, the heauens raine Odours on you.

And. That youth's a rare Courtier, raine odours, wel.

Vio. My matter hath no voice Lady, but to your owne

moft pregnant and vouchfafed eare.

And. Odours, pregnant, and vouchfafed : Ile get 'em all three already.

Ol. Let the Garden doore be fhut, and leaue mee to my hearing. Giue me your hand fir.

Vio. My dutie Madam, and moft humble feruice

Ol. What is your name?

Vio. *Cefario* is your feruants name, faire Princeffe.

Ol. My feruant fir? 'Twas neuer merry world, Since lowly feigning was call'd complement : y'are feruant to the Count *Orfino* youth.

Vio. And he is yours, and his muft needs be yours : your feruants feruant, is your feruant Madam.

Ol. For him, I thinke not on him : for his thoughts, Would they were blankes, rather then fill'd with me.

Vio. Madam, I come to whet your gentle thoughts On his behalfe.

Ol. O by your leaue I pray you. I bad you neuer fpeake againe of him ; But would you vndertake another fuite I had rather heare you, to folicit that, Then Muficke from the fpheares.

Vio. Deere Lady.

Ol. Giue me leaue, befeech you : I did fend, After the laft enchantment you did heare, A Ring in chace of you. So did I abufe My felfe, my feruant, and I feare me you : Vnder your hard conftruction muft I fit, To force that on you in a fhamefull cunning Which you knew none of yours. What might you think? Haue you not fet mine Honor at the ftake, And baited it with all th'vnmuzled thoughts That tyrannous heart can think? To one of your receiuing Enough is fhewne, a Cipreffe, not a bofome, Hides my heart : fo let me heare you fpeake.

Vio. I pittie you.

Ol. That's a degree to loue.

Vio. No not a grize : for tis a vulgar proofe That verie oft we pitty enemies.

Ol. Why then me thinkes 'tis time to fmile agen: O world, how apt the poore are to be proud? If one fhould be a prey, how much the better To fall before the Lion, then the Wolfe?

Clocke ftrikes.

The clocke vpbraides me with the wafte of time: Be not affraid good youth, I will not haue you, And yet when wit and youth is come to harueft, your wife is like to reape a proper man : There lies your way, due Weft.

Vio. Then Weftward hoe :

Grace and good difpofition attend your Ladyfhip : you'l nothing Madam to my Lord, by me :

Ol. Stay : I prethee tell me what thou thinkft of me?

Vio. That you do thinke you are not what you are.

Ol. If I thinke fo, I thinke the fame of you.

Vio. Then thinke you right : I am not what I am.

Ol. I would you were, as I would haue you be,

Vio. Would it be better Madam, then I am? I wifh it might, for now I am your foole.

Ol. O what a deale of fcorne, lookes beautifull? In the contempt and anger of his lip, A murdrous guilt fhewes not it felfe more foone, Then loue that would feeme hid : Loues night, is noone. *Cefario,* by the Rofes of the Spring, By maid-hood, honor, truth, and euery thing, I loue thee fo, that maugre all thy pride,

Z   Nor

Nor wit, nor reaſon, can my paſſion hide :
Do not extort thy reaſons from this clauſe,
For that I woo, thou therefore haſt no cauſe :
But rather reaſon thus, with reaſon fetter ;
Loue ſought, is good : but giuen vnſought, is better.

Vio. By innocence I ſweare, and by my youth,
I haue one heart, one boſome, and one truth,
And that no woman has, nor neuer none
Shall miſtris be of it, ſaue I alone.
And ſo adieu good Madam, neuer more,
Will I my Maſters teares to you deplore.

Ol. Yet come againe : for thou perhaps mayſt moue
That heart which now abhorres, to like his loue. *Exeunt*

Scæna Secunda.

Enter Sir Toby, Sir Andrew, and Fabian.

And. No faith, Ile not ſtay a iot longer :
To. Thy reaſon deere venom, giue thy reaſon.
Fab. You muſt needes yeelde your reaſon, Sir *An-
drew?*
And. Marry I ſaw your Neece do more fauours to the
Counts Seruing-man, then euer ſhe beſtow'd vpon mee :
I ſaw't i'th Orchard.
To. Did ſhe ſee the while, old boy, tell me that.
And. As plaine as I ſee you now.
Fab. This was a great argument of loue in her toward
you.
And. S'light ; will you make an Aſſe o'me.
Fab. I will proue it legitimate ſir, vpon the Oathes of
iudgement, and reaſon.
To. And they haue beene grand Iurie men, ſince before
Noah was a Saylor.
Fab. Shee did ſhew fauour to the youth in your ſight,
onely to exaſperate you, to awake your dormouſe valour,
to put fire in your Heart, and brimſtone in your Liuer :
you ſhould then haue accoſted her, and with ſome excellent ieſts, fire-new from the mint, you ſhould haue bangd
the youth into dumbeneſſe : this was look'd for at your
hand, and this was baulkt : the double gilt of this oppor-
tunitie you let time waſh off, and you are now ſayld into
the North of my Ladies opinion, where you will hang
like an yſickle on a Dutchmans beard, vnleſſe you do redeeme it, by ſome laudable attempt, either of valour or
policie.
And. And't be any way, it muſt be with Valour, for
policie I hate : I had as liefe be a Browniſt, as a Politi-
cian.
To. Why then build me thy fortunes vpon the baſis of
valour. Challenge me the Counts youth to ſight with him
hurt him in eleuen places, my Neece ſhall take note of it,
and aſſure thy ſelfe, there is no loue-Broker in the world,
can more preuaile in mans commendation with woman,
then report of valour.
Fab. There is no way but this ſir *Andrew.*
An. Will either of you beare me a challenge to him?
To. Go, write it in a martial hand, be curſt and briefe:
it is no matter how wittie, ſo it bee eloquent, and full of
inuention : taunt him with the licenſe of Inke : if thou
thou'ſt him ſome thrice, it ſhall not be amiſſe, and as many Lyes, as will lye in thy ſheete of paper, although the
ſheete were bigge enough for the bedde of *Ware* in Eng-

land, ſet 'em downe, go about it. Let there bee gaulle e-
nough in thy inke, though thou write with a Gooſe-pen,
no matter : about it.
And. Where ſhall I finde you?
To. Wee'l call thee at the Cubiculo : Go.
Exit Sir Andrew.
Fa. This is a deere Manakin to you Sir *Toby.*
To. I haue beene deere to him lad, ſome two thouſand
ſtrong, or ſo.
Fa. We ſhall haue a rare Letter from him; but you'le
not deliuer't.
To. Neuer truſt me then : and by all meanes ſtirre on
the youth to an anſwer. I thinke Oxen and waine-ropes
cannot hale them together. For *Andrew,* if he were open'd
and you finde ſo much blood in his Liuer, as will clog the
foote of a flea, Ile eate the reſt of th'anatomy.
Fab. And his oppoſit the youth beares in his viſage no
great preſage of cruelty.

Enter Maria.

To. Looke where the youngeſt Wren of mine comes.
Mar. If you deſire the ſpleene, and will laughe your
ſelues into ſtitches, follow me ; yond gull *Maluolio* is turned Heathen, a verie Renegatho ; for there is no chriſtian
that meanes to be ſaued by beleeuing rightly, can euer
beleeue ſuch impoſſible paſſages of groſſeneſſe. Hee's in
yellow ſtockings.
To. And croſſe garter'd ?
Mar. Moſt villanouſly : like a Pedant that keepes a
Schoole i'th Church : I haue dogg'd him like his murtherer. He does obey euery point of the Letter that I dropt,
to betray him : He does ſmile his face into more lynes,
then is in the new Mappe, with the augmentation of the
Indies : you haue not ſeene ſuch a thing as tis: I can hardly forbeare hurling things at him, I know my Ladie will
ſtrike him : if ſhee doe, hee'l ſmile, and take't for a great
fauour.
To. Come bring vs, bring vs where he is.
Exeunt Omnes.

Scæna Tertia.

Enter Sebaſtian and Anthonio.

Seb. I would not by my will have troubled yo u,
But ſince you make your pleaſure of your paines,
I will no further chide you.
Ant. I could not ſtay behinde you : my deſire
(More ſharpe then filed ſteele) did ſpurre me forth,
And not all loue to ſee you (though ſo much
As might haue drawne one to a longer voyage)
But iealouſie, what might befall your rrauell,
Being skilleſſe in theſe parts : which to a ſtranger,
Vnguided, and vnfriended, often proue
Rough, and vnhoſpitable. My willing loue,
The rather by theſe arguments of feare
Set forth in your purſuite.
Seb. My kinde *Anthonio,*
I can no other anſwer make, but thankes,
And thankes : and euer oft good turnes,
Are ſhuffel'd off with ſuch vncurrant pay :
But were my worth, as is my conſcience firme,

You

You fhould finde better dealing : what's to do ?
Shall we go fee the reliques of this Towne ?

Ant. To morrow fir, beft firft go fee your Lodging ?

Seb. I am not weary, and 'tis long to night
I pray you let vs fatisfie our eyes
With the memorials, and the things of fame
That do renowne this City.

Ant. Would you'd pardon me :
I do not without danger walke thefe ftreetes.
Once in a fea-fight 'gainft the Count his gallies,
I did fome feruice, of fuch note indeede,
That were I tane heere, it would fcarfe be anfwer'd.

Seb. Belike you flew great number of his people.

Ant. Th offence is not of fuch a bloody nature,
Albeit the quality of the time, and quarrell
Might well haue giuen vs bloody argument :
It might haue fince bene anfwer'd in repaying
What we tooke from them, which for Traffiques fake
Moft of our City did. Onely my felfe ftood out,
For which if I be lapfed in this place
I fhall pay deere.

Seb. Do not then walke too open.

Ant. It doth not fit me : hold fir, here's my purfe,
In the South Suburbes at the Elephant
Is beft to lodge : I will befpeake our dyet,
Whiles you beguile the time, and feed your knowledge
With viewing of the Towne, there fhall you haue me.

Seb. Why I your purfe ?

Ant. Haply your eye fhall light vpon fome toy
You haue defire to purchafe : and your ftore
I thinke is not for idle Markets, fir.

Seb. Ile be your purfe-bearer, and leaue you
For an houre.

Ant. To th'Elephant.

Seb. I do remember.   *Exeunt.*

Scæna Quarta.

Enter Oliuia and Maria.

Ol. I haue fent after him, he fayes hee'l come :
How fhall I feaft him ? What beftow of him ?
For youth is bought more oft, then begg'd, or borrow'd.
I fpeake too loud : Where's *Maluolio*, he is fad, and ciuill,
And fuites well for a feruant with my fortunes,
Where is *Maluolio* ?

Mar. He's comming Madame :
But in very ftrange manner, he is fure poffeft Madam.

Ol. Why what's the matter, does he raue ?

Mar. No Madam, he does nothing but fmile:your Ladyfhip were beft to haue fome guard about you, if hee
come, for fure the man is tainted in's wits.

Ol. Go call him hither.

Enter Maluolio.

I am as madde as hee,
If fad and metry madneffe equall bee.
How now *Maluolio* ?

Mal. Sweet Lady, ho, ho.

Ol. Smil'ft thou ? I fent for thee vpon a fad occafion.

Mal. Sad Lady, I could be fad :
This does make fome obftruction in the blood :
This croffe-gartering, but what of that ?

If it pleafe the eye of one, it is wich me as the very true
Sonnet is : Pleafe one, and pleafe all.

Mal. Why how doeft thou man ?
What is the matter with thee ?

Mal. Not blacke in my minde, though yellow in my
legges : It did come to his hands, and Commaunds fhall
be executed. I thinke we doe know the fweet Romane
hand.

Ol. Wilt thou go to bed *Maluolio* ?

Mal. To bed ? I fweet heart, and Ile come to thee.

Ol. God comfort thee : Why doft thou fmile fo, and
kiffe thy hand fo oft ?

Mar. How do you *Maluolio* ?

Maluo. At your requeft :
Yes Nightingales anfwere Dawes.

Mar. Why appeare you with this ridiculous boldneffe before my Lady.

Mal. Be not afraid of greatneffe : 'twas well writ.

Ol. What meanft thou by that *Maluolio* ?

Mal. Some are borne great.

Ol. Ha ?

Mal. Some atcheeue greatneffe.

Ol. What fayft thou ?

Mal. And fome haue greatneffe thruft vpon them.

Ol. Heauen reftore thee.

Mal. Remember who commended thy yellow ftockings.

Ol. Thy yellow ftockings ?

Mal. And wifh'd to fee thee croffe garter'd.

Ol. Croffe garter'd ?

Mal. Go too, thou art made, if thou defir'ft to be fo.

Ol. Am I made ?

Mal. If not, let me fee thee a feruant ftill.

Ol. Why this is verie Midfommer madneffe.

Enter Seruant.

Ser. Madame, the young Gentleman of the Count
Orfino's is return'd, I could hardly entreate him backe : he
attends your Ladyfhips pleafure.

Ol. Ile come to him.
Good *Maria*, let this fellow be look d too. Where's my
Cofine *Toby*, let fome of my people haue a fpeciall care
of him, I would not haue him mifcarrie for the halfe of
my Dowry.   *exit*

Mal. Oh ho, do you come neere me now : no worfe
man then fir *Toby* to looke to me. This concurres directly with the Letter, fhe fends him on purpofe, that I may
appeare ftubborne to him : for fhe incites me to that in
the Letter. Caft thy humble flough fayes fhe : be oppofite with a Kinfman, furly with feruants, let thy tongue
langer with arguments of ftate, put thy felfe into the
tricke of fingularity : and confequently fetts downe the
manner how : as a fad face, a reuerend carriage, a flow
tongue, in the habite of fome Sir of note, and fo foorth.
I haue lymde her, but it is Ioues doing, and Ioue make me
thankefull. And when fhe went away now, let this Fellow be look'd too : Fellow ? not *Maluolio*, nor after my
degree, but Fellow. Why euery thing adheres togither,
that no dramme of a fcruple, no fcruple of a fcruple, no
obftacle, no incredulous or vnfafe circumftance : What
can be falde ? Nothing that can be, can come betweene
me, and the full profpect of my hopes. Well Ioue, not I,
is the doer of this, and he is to be thanked.

Enter Toby, Fabian, and Maria.

Z 2   *To.*

To. Which way is hee in the name of fanctity. If all the dluels of hell be drawne in little, and Legion himfelfe poffeft him, yet Ile fpeake to him.

Fab. Heere he is, heere he is : how ift with you fir? How ift with you man?

Mal. Go off, I difcard you : let me enioy my priuate: go off.

Mar. Lo, how hollow the fiend fpeakes within him; did not I tell you? Sir *Toby*, my Lady prayes you to haue a care of him.

Mal. Ah ha, does fhe fo?

To. Go too, go too: peace, peace, wee muft deale gently with him : Let me alone. How do you *Maluolio*? How ift with you? What man, defie the diuell : confider, he's an enemy to mankinde.

Mal. Do you know what you fay?

Mar. La you, and you fpeake ill of the diuell, how he takes it at heart. Pray God he be not bewitch'd.

Fab. Carry his water to th'wife woman.

Mar. Marry and it fhall be done to morrow morning if I liue. My Lady would not loofe him for more then ile fay,

Mal. How now miftris?

Mar. Oh Lord.

To. Prethee hold thy peace, this is not the way : Doe you not fee you moue him? Let me alone with him.

Fa. No way but gentleneffe, gently, gently : the Fiend is rough, and will not be roughly vs'd.

To. Why how now my bawcock? how doft ÿ chuck?

Mal. Sir.

To. I biddy, come with me. What man, tis not for grauity to play at cherrie-pit with fathan. Hang him foul Colliar.

Mar. Get him to fay his prayers, good fir *Toby* gette him to pray.

Mal. My prayers Minx.

Mar. No I warrant you, he will not heare of godly-neffe.

Mal. Go hang your felues all : you are ydle fhallowe things, I am not of your element, you fhall knowe more heereafter.   *Exit*

To. Ift poffible?

Fa. If this were plaid vpon a ftage now, I could con-demne it as an improbable fiction.

To. His very genius hath taken the infection of the deuice man.

Mar. Nay purfue him now, leaft the deuice take ayre, and taint.

Fa. Why we fhall make him mad indeede.

Mar. The houfe will be the quieter.

To. Come, wee'l haue him in a darke room & bound. My Neece is already in the beleefe that he's mad: we may carry it thus for our pleafure, and his pennance, til our ve-ry paftime tyred out of breath, prompt vs to haue mercy on him : at which time, we wil bring the deuice to the bar and crowne thee for a finder of madmen : but fee, but fee.

Enter Sir Andrew.

Fa. More matter for a May morning.

An. Heere's the Challenge, reade it: I warrant there's vinegar and pepper in't.

Fab. Ift fo fawcy?

And. I, ift? I warrant him : do but read.

To. Giue me.

Youth, whatfoeuer thou art, thou art but a fcuruy fellow.

Fa. Good, and valiant.

To. Wonder not, nor admire not in thy minde why I doe call

thee fo, for I will fhew thee no reafon for't.   (Law

Fa. A good note, that keepes you from the blow of ÿ

To. Thou comft to the Lady Oliuia, and in my fight fhe vfes thee kindly : but thou lyeft in thy throat, that is not the matter I challenge thee for.

Fa. Very breefe, and to exceeding good fence-leffe.

To. I will way-lay thee going home, where if it be thy chance to kill me.

Fa. Good.

To. Thou kilft me like a rogue and a villaine.

Fa. Still you keepe o'th windie fide of the Law:good.

To. If this Letter moue him not, his legges cannot : Ile giu't him.

Mar. Yon may haue verie fit occafion fot't : he is now in fome commerce with my Ladie, and will by and by depart.

To. Go fir *Andrew* : fcout mee for him at the corner of the Orchard like a bum-Baylie : fo foone as euer thou feeft him, draw, and as thou draw'ft, fweare horrible : for t comes to paffe oft, that a terrible oath, with a fwagge-ring accent fharpely twang'd off, giues manhoode more approbation, then euer proofe it felfe would haue earn'd him. Away.

And. Nay let me alone for fwearing.   *Exit*

To. Now will not I deliuer his Letter : for the behaui-our of the yong Gentleman, giues him out to be of good capacity, and breeding : his employment betweene his Lord and my Neece, confirmes no leffe. Therefore, this Letter being fo excellently ignorant, will breed no terror in the youth : he will finde it comes from a Clodde-pole. But fir, I will deliuer his Challenge by word of mouth ; fet vpon *Ague-cheeke* a notable report of valor, and driue the Gentleman (as I know his youth will aptly receiue it) into a moft hideous opinion of his rage, skill, furie, and impetuofitie. This will fo fright them both, that they wil kill one another by the looke, like Cockatrices.

Enter Oliuia and Viola.

Fab. Heere he comes with your Neece, giue them way till he take leaue, and prefently after him.

To. I wil meditate the while vpon fome horrid meffage for a Challenge.

Ol. I haue faid too much vnto a hart of ftone,
And laid mine honour too vnchary on't :
There's fomething in me that reproues my fault :
But fuch a head-ftrong potent fault it is,
That it but mockes reproofe.

Vio. With the fame hauiour that your paffion beares,
Goes on my Mafters greefes.

Ol. Heere, weare this Iewell for me, tis my picture :
Refufe it not, it hath no tongue, to vex you :
And I befeech you come againe to morrow.
What fhall you afke of me that Ile deny,
That honour (fau'd) may vpon asking giue.

Vio. Nothing but this, your true loue for my mafter.

Ol. How with mine honor may I giue him that,
Which I haue giuen to you.

Vio. I will acquit you.

Ol. Well, come againe to morrow : far-thee-well,
A Fiend like thee might beare my foule to hell.

Enter Toby and Fabian.

To. Gentleman, God faue thee.

                                          Vio.

Vio. And you fir.

To. That defence thou haft, betake the too't : of what nature the wrongs are thou haft done him, I knowe not : but thy intercepter full of defpight, bloody as the Hunter, attends thee at the Orchard end : difmount thy tucke, be yare in thy preparation, for thy affaylant is quick, skilfull, and deadly.

Vio. You miftake fir I am fure, no man hath any quarrell to me : my remembrance is very free and cleere from any image of offence done to any man.

To. You'l finde it otherwife I affure you : therefore, if you hold your life at any price, betake you to your gard : for your oppofite hath in him what youth, ftrength, skill, and wrath, can furnifh man withall.

Vio. I pray you fir what is he?

To. He is knight dubb'd with vnhatch'd Rapier, and on carpet confideration, but he is a diuell in priuate brall, foules and bodies hath he diuorc'd three, and his incenfement at this moment is fo implacable, that fatisfaction can be none, but by pangs of death and fepulcher : Hob, nob, is his word : giu't or take't.

Vio. I will returne againe into the houfe, and defire fome conduct of the Lady. I am no fighter, I haue heard of fome kinde of men, that put quarrells purpofely on o-thers, to tafte their valour : belike this is a man of that quirke.

To. Sir, no : his indignation deriues it felfe out of a very computent iniurie, therefore get you on, and giue him his defire. Backe you fhall not to the houfe, vnleffe you vndertake that with me, which with as much fafetie you might anfwer him : therefore on, or ftrippe your fword ftarke naked : for meddle you muft that's certain, or forfweare to weare iron about you.

Vio. This is as vnciuill as ftrange. I befeech you doe me this courteous office, as to know of the Knight what my offence to him is : it is fomething of my negligence, nothing of my purpofe.

To. I will doe fo. Signiour Fabian, ftay you by this Gentleman, till my returne. *Exit Toby.*

Vio. Pray fir, do you know of this matter?

Fab. I know the knight is incenft againft you, euen to a mortall arbitrement, but nothing of the circumftance more.

Vio. I befeech you what manner of man is he?

Fab. Nothing of that wonderfull promife to read him by his forme, as you are like to finde him in the proofe of his valour. He is indeede fir, the moft skilfull, bloudy,& fatall oppofite that you could pofsibly haue found in anie part of Illyria : will you walke towards him, I will make your peace with him, if I can.

Vio. I fhall bee much bound to you for't : I am one, that had rather go with fir Prieft, then fir knight : I care not who knowes fo much of my mettle. *Exeunt.*

Enter Toby and Andrew.

To. Why man hee's a verie diuell, I haue not feen fuch a firago : I had a paffe with him, rapier, fcabberd, and all : and he giues me the ftucke in with fuch a mortall motion that it is ineuitable : and on the anfwer, he payes you as furely, as your feete hits the ground they ftep on. They fay, he has bin Fencer to the Sophy.

And. Pox on't, Ile not meddle with him.

To. I but he will not now be pacified, Fabian can fcarfe hold him yonder.

An. Plague on't, and I thought he had beene valiant, and fo cunning in Fence, I'de haue feene him damn'd ere I'de haue challeng'd him. Let him let the matter flip, and

Ile giue him my horfe, gray Capilet.

To. Ile make the motion : ftand heere, make a good fhew on't, this fhall end without the perdition of foules, marry Ile ride your horfe as well as I ride you.

Enter Fabian and Viola.

I haue his horfe to take vp the quarrell, I haue perfwaded him the youths a diuell.

Fa. He is as horribly conceited of him : and pants, & lookes pale,as if a Beare were at his heeles.

To. There's no remedie fir, he will fight with you for's oath fake : marrie hee hath better bethought him of his quarrell, and hee findes that now fcarfe to bee worth talking of : therefore draw for the fupportance of his vowe, he protefts he will not hurt you.

Vio. Pray God defend me : a little thing would make me tell them how much I lacke of a man,

Fab. Giue ground if you fee him furious.

To. Come fir *Andrew*, there's no remedie, the Gentleman will for his honors fake haue one bowt with you: he cannot by the Duello auoide it : but hee has promifed me, as he is a Gentleman and a Soldiour, he will not hurt you. Come on, too't.

And. Pray God he keepe his oath.

Enter Antonio.

Vio. I do affure you tis againft my will.

Ant. Put vp your fword : if this yong Gentleman Haue done offence, I take the fault on me : If you offend him, I for him defie you.

To. You fir? Why, what are you?

Ant. One fir, that for his loue dares yet do more Then you haue heard him brag to you he will.

To. Nay,if you be an vndertaker, I am for you.

Enter Officers.

Fab. O good fir Toby hold: heere come the Officers.

To. Ile be with you anon.

Vio. Pray fir, put your fword vp if you pleafe.

And. Marry will I fir : and for that I promis'd you Ile be as good as my word. Hee will beare you eafily, and raines well.

1.*Off.* This is the man, do thy Office.

2 *Off.* Anthonio, I arreft thee at the fuit of Count *Orfino*

An. You do miftake me fir.

1.*Off.* No fir, no iot : I know your fauour well : Though now you haue no fea-cap on your head : Take him away, he knowes I know him well.

Ant. I muft obey. This comes with feeking you : But there's no remedie, I fhall anfwer it : What will you do : now my neceffitie Makes me to aske you for my purfe. It greeues mee Much more, for what I cannot do for you, Then what befals my felfe : you ftand amaz'd, But be of comfort.

2 *Off.* Come fir away.

Ant. I muft entreat of you fome of that money.

Vio. What money fir?

For the fayre kindneffe you haue fhew'd me heere, And part being prompted by your prefent trouble, Out of my leane and low ability Ile lend you fomething : my hauing is not much, Ile make diuifion of my prefent with you : Hold, there's halfe my Coffer.

Ant. Will you deny me now, Ift pofsible that my deferts to you Can lacke perfwafion. Do not tempt my mifery, Leaft that it make me fo vnfound a man As to vpbraid you with thofe kindneffes

Z 3 That

That I haue done for you.

Vio. I know of none,
Nor know I you by voyce, or any feature :
I hate ingratitude more in a man,
Then lying, vainneſſe, babling drunkenneſſe,
Or any taint of vice, whoſe ſtrong corruption
Inhabites our fraile blood.

Ant. Oh heauens themſelues.

2. *Off.* Come ſir, I pray you go.

Ant. Let me ſpeake a little. This youth that you ſee
I ſnatch'd one halfe out of the iawes of death,   (heere,
Releeu'd him with ſuch ſanƈtitie of loue ;
And to his image, which me thought did promiſe
Moſt venerable worth, did I deuotion.

1. *Off.* What's that to vs, the time goes by : Away.

Ant. But oh, how vilde an idoll proues this God :
Thou haſt *Sebaſtian* done good feature, ſhame.
In Nature, there's no blemiſh but the minde :
None can be call'd deform'd, but the vnkinde.
Vertue is beauty, but the beauteous euill
Are empty trunkes, ore-flouriſh'd by the deuill.

1. *Off.* The man growes mad, away with him :
Come, come ſir.

Ant. Leade me on.   *Exit*

Vio. Me thinkes his words do from ſuch paſſion flye
That he beleeues himſelfe, ſo do not I :
Proue true imagination, oh proue ttue,
That I deere brother, be now tane for you.

To. Come hither Knight, come hither *Fabian :* Weel
whiſper ore a couplet or two of moſt ſage ſawes.

Vio. He nam'd *Sebaſtian :* I my brother know
Yet liuing in my glaſſe : euen ſuch, and ſo
In fauour was my Brother, and he went
Still in this faſhion, colour, ornament,
For him I imitate : Oh if it proue,
Tempeſts are kinde, and ſalt waues freſh in loue.

To. A very diſhoneſt paltry boy, and more a coward
then a Hare, his diſhoneſty appeares, in leauing his frend
heere in neceſſity, and denying him : and for his coward-
ſhip aske *Fabian.*

Fab. A Coward, a moſt deuout Coward, religious in
it.

And, Slid Ile after him againe, and beate him.

To. Do, cuffe him ſoundly, but neuer draw thy ſword

And. And I do not.

Fab. Come, let's ſee the euent.

To. I dare lay any money, twill be nothing yet.   *Exit*

Actus Quartus, Scæna prima.

Enter Sebaſtian and Clowne.

Clo. Will you make me beleeue, that I am not ſent for
you ?

Seb. Go too, go too, thou art a fooliſh fellow,
Let me be cleere of thee.

Clo. Well held out yfaith : No, I do not know you,
nor I am not ſent to you by my Lady, to bid you come
ſpeake with her : nor your name is not Maſter *Ceſario,*
nor this is not my noſe neyther : Nothing that is ſo, is ſo.

Seb. I prethee vent thy folly ſome-where elſe, thou
know'ſt not me.

Clo. Vent my folly : He has heard that word of ſome
great man, and now applyes it to a foole. Vent my fol-

ly : I am affraid this great lubber the World will proue a
Cockney : I prethee now vngird thy ſtrangenes, and tell
me what I ſhall vent to my Lady ? Shall I vent to hir that
thou art comming ?

Seb. I prethee fooliſh greeke depart from me, there's
money for thee, if you tarry longer, I ſhall giue worſe
paiment.

Clo. By my troth thou haſt an open hand : theſe Wiſemen that giue fooles money, get themſelues a good report, after foureteene yeares purchaſe.

Enter Andrew, Toby, and Fabian.

And. Now ſir, haue I met you again : ther's for you.

Seb. Why there's for thee, and there, and there,
Are all the people mad ?

To. Hold ſir, or Ile throw your dagger ore the houſe.

Clo. This will I tell my Lady ſtraight, I would not be
in ſome of your coats for two pence.

To. Come on ſir, hold.

An. Nay let him alone, Ile go another way to worke
with him : Ile haue an aƈtion of Battery againſt him, if
there be any law in Illyria : though I ſtroke him firſt, yet
it's no matter for that.

Seb. Let go thy hand.

To. Come ſir, I will not let you go. Come my yong
ſouldier put vp your yron : you are well fleſh'd : Come
on.

Seb. I will be free from thee. What wouldſt ÿ now ?
If thou dar'ſt tempt me further, draw thy ſword.

To. What, what ? Nay then I muſt haue an Ounce or
two of this malapert blood from you.

Enter Oliuia.

Ol. Hold *Toby,* on thy life I charge thee hold.

To. Madam.

Ol. Will it be euer thus ? Vngracious wretch,
Fit for the Mountaines, and the barbarous Caues,
Where manners were preach'd : out of my ſight.
Be not offended, deere *Ceſario :*
Rudesbey be gone. I prethee gentle friend,
Let thy fayre wiſedome, not thy paſſion ſway
In this vnciuill, and vniuſt extent
Againſt thy peace. Go with me to my houſe,
And heare thou there how many fruitleſſe prankes
This Ruffian hath botch'd vp, that thou thereby
Mayſt ſmile at this : Thou ſhalt not chooſe but goe :
Do not denie, beſhrew his ſoule for mee,
He ſtarted one poore heart of mine, in thee.

Seb. What relliſh is in this? How runs the ſtreame ?
Or I am mad, or elſe this is a dreame :
Let fancie ſtill my ſenſe in Lethe ſteepe,
If it be thus to dreame, ſtill let me ſleepe.

Ol. Nay come I prethee, would thoud'ſt be rul'd by me

Seb. Madam, I will.

Ol. O ſay ſo, and ſo be.   *Exeunt*

Scæna Secunda.

Enter Maria and Clowne.

Mar. Nay, I prethee put on this gown, & this beard,
make him beleeue thou art ſir *Topas* the Curate, doe it
quickly. Ile call ſir *Toby* the whilſt.

Clo. Well, Ile put it on, and I will diſſemble my ſelfe
in't, and I would I were the firſt that euer diſſembled in
ſuch

in such a gowne. I am not tall enough to become the function well, nor leane enough to bee thought a good Student : but to be said an honest man and a good housekeeper goes as fairely, as to say, a carefull man, & a great scholler. The Competitors enter.

Enter Toby.

To. Ioue blesse thee M. Parson.

Clo. *Bonos dies* sir *Toby* : for as the old hermit of *Prage* that neuer saw pen and inke, very wittily sayd to a Neece of King *Gorbodacke*, that that is, is : so I being M.Parson, am M. Parson ; for what is that, but that? and is, but is?

To. To him sir *Topas.*

Clow. What hoa, I say, Peace in this prison.

To. The knaue counterfets well : a good knaue.

Maluolio within.

Mal. Who cals there ?

Clo. Sir *Topas* the Curate, who comes to visit *Maluolio* the Lunaticke.

Mal. Sir *Topas*, sir *Topas*, good sir *Topas* goe to my Ladie.

Clo. Out hyperbolicall fiend, how vexest thou this man ? Talkest thou nothing but of Ladies ?

Tob. Well said M. Parson.

Mal. Sir *Topas*, neuer was man thus wronged, good sir *Topas* do not thinke I am mad : they haue layde mee heere in hideous darknesse.

Clo. Fye, thou dishonest sathan : I call thee by the most modest termes, for I am one of those gentle ones, that will vse the diuell himselfe with curtesie : sayst thou that house is darke ?

Mal. As hell sir *Topas.*

Clo. Why it hath bay Windowes transparant as baricadoes, and the cleere stores toward the South north, are as lustrous as Ebony : and yet complainest thou of obstruction ?

Mal. I am not mad sir *Topas*, I say to you this house is darke.

Clo. Madman thou errest : I say there is no darknesse but ignorance, in which thou art more puzel'd then the Ægyptians in their fogge.

Mal. I say this house is as darke as Ignorance, thogh Ignorance were as darke as hell ; and I say there was neuer man thus abus'd, I am no more madde then you are, make the triall of it in any constant question.

Clo. What is the opinion of *Pythagoras* concerning Wilde-fowle ?

Mal. That the soule of our grandam, might happily inhabite a bird.

Clo. What thinkst thou of his opinion ?

Mal. I thinke nobly of the soule, and no way aprooue his opinion.

Clo. Fare thee well : remaine thou still in darknesse, thou shalt hold th'opinion of *Pythagoras*, ere I will allow of thy wits, and feare to kill a Woodcocke, lest thou dispossesse the soule of thy grandam. Fare thee well.

Mal. Sir *Topas*, sir *Topas.*

Tob. My most exquisite sir *Topas.*

Clo. Nay I am for all waters.

Mar. Thou mightst haue done this without thy berd and gowne, he sees thee not.

To. To him in thine owne voyce, and bring me word how thou findst him : I would we were well ridde of this knauery. If he may bee conueniently deliuer'd, I would he were, for I am now so farre in offence with my Niece, that I cannot pursue with any safety this sport the vppeshot. Come by and by to my Chamber. *Exit*

Clo. Hey Robin, iolly Robin, tell me how thy Lady does.

Mal. Foole.

Clo. My Lady is vnkind, *perdie.*

Mal. Foole.

Clo. Alas why is she so ?

Mal. Foole, I say.

Clo. She loues another. Who calles, ha ?

Mal. Good foole, as euer thou wilt deserue well at my hand, helpe me to a Candle, and pen, inke, and paper : as I am a Gentleman, I will liue to bee thankefull to thee for't.

Clo. M. *Maluolio* ?

Mal. I good Foole.

Clo. Alas sir, how fell you besides your fiue witts ?

Mall. Foole, there was neuer man so notorioustie abus'd : I am as well in my wits (foole) as thou art.

Clo. But as well : then you are mad indeede, if you be no better in your wits then a foole.

Mal. They haue heere propertied me : keepe mee in darkenesse, send Ministers to me, Asses, and doe all they can to face me out of my wits.

Clo. Aduise you what you say : the Minister is heere. *Maluolio, Maluolio,* thy wittes the heauens restore : endeauour thy selfe to sleepe, and leaue thy vaine bibble babble.

Mal. Sir *Topas.*

Clo. Maintaine no words with him good fellow. Who I sir, not I sir. God buy you good sir *Topas* : Marry Amen, I will sir, I will.

Mal. Foole, foole, foole I say.

Clo. Alas sir be patient. What say you sir, I am shent for speaking to you.

Mal. Good foole, helpe me to some light, and some paper, I tell thee I am as well in my wittes, as any man in Illyria.

Clo. Well-a-day, that you were sir.

Mal. By this hand I am : good foole, some inke, paper, and light : and conuey what I will set downe to my Lady : it shall aduantage thee more, then euer the bearing of Letter did.

Clo. I will help you too't. But tel me true, are you not mad indeed, or do you but counterfeit.

Mal. Beleeue me I am not, I tell thee true.

Clo. Nay, Ile nere beleeue a madman till I see his brains I will fetch you light, and paper, and inke.

Mal. Foole, Ile requite it in the highest degree : I prethee be goue.

Clo. I am gone sir, and anon sir,
Ile be with you againe :
In a trice, like to the old vice,
your neede to sustaine.
Who with dagger of lath, in his rage and his wrath,
cries ah ha, to the diuell :
Like a mad lad, paire thy nayles dad,
Adieu good man diuell. *Exit*

Scæna Tertia.

Enter Sebastian.

This is the ayre, that is the glorious Sunne,
This pearle she gaue me, I do feel't, and see't,
And though tis wonder that enwraps me thus,

Yet

Yet 'tis not madneſſe. Where's *Anthonio* then,
I could not finde him at the Elephant,
Yet there he was, and there I found this credite,
That he did range the towne to ſeeke me out,
His councell now might do me golden ſeruice,
For though my ſoule diſputes well with my ſence,
That this may be ſome error, but no madneſſe,
Yet doth this accident and flood of Fortune,
So farre exceed all inſtance, all diſcourſe,
That I am readie to diſtruſt mine eyes,
And wrangle with my reaſon that perſwades me
To any other truſt, but that I am mad,
Or elſe the Ladies mad; yet if 'twere ſo,
She could not ſway her houſe, command her followers,
Take, and giue backe affayres, and their diſpatch,
With ſuch a ſmooth, diſcreet, and ſtable bearing
As I perceiue ſhe do's : there's ſomething in't
That is deceiueable. But heere the Lady comes.

Enter Oliuia, and Prieſt.

Ol. Blame not this haſte of mine : if you meane well
Now go with me, and with this holy man
Into the Chantry by : there before him,
And vnderneath that conſecrated roofe,
Plight me the full aſſurance of your faith,
That my moſt iealious, and too doubtfull ſoule
May liue at peace. He ſhall conceale it,
Whiles you are willing it ſhall come to note,
What time we will our celebration keepe
According to my birth, what do you ſay ?

Seb. Ile follow this good man, and go with you,
And hauing ſworne truth, euer will be true.

Ol. Then lead the way good father,& heauens ſo ſhine,
That they may fairely note this acte of mine.　*Exeunt.*

Finis Actus Quartus.

Actus Quintus. Scena Prima.

Enter Clowne and Fabian.

Fab. Now as thou lou'ſt me, let me ſee his Letter.
Clo. Good M. *Fabian*, grant me another requeſt.
Fab. Any thing.
Clo. Do not deſire to ſee this Letter.
Fab. This is to giue a dogge, and in recompence deſire
my dogge againe.

Enter Duke, Viola, Curio, and Lords.

Duke. Belong you to the Lady *Oliuia*, friends?
Clo. I ſir, we are ſome of her trappings.
Duke. I know thee well : how doeſt thou my good
Fellow ?
Clo. Truely ſir, the better for my foes, and the worſe
for my friends.
Du. Iuſt the contrary : the better for thy friends.
Clo. No ſir, the worſe.
Du. How can that be ?
Clo. Marry ſir, they praiſe me, and make an aſſe of me,
now my foes tell me plainly, I am an Aſſe : ſo that by my
foes ſir, I profit in the knowledge of my ſelfe, and by my
friends I am abuſed : ſo that concluſions to be as kiſſes, if
your foure negatiues make your two affirmatiues , why
then the worſe for my friends, and the better for my foes.

Du. Why this is excellent.
Clo. By my troth ſir, no : though it pleaſe you to be
one of my friends.
Du. Thou ſhalt not be the worſe for me, there's gold.
Clo. But that it would be double dealing ſir, I would
you could make it another.
Du. O you giue me ill counſell.
Clo. Put your grace in your pocket ſir, for this once,
and let your fleſh and blood obey it.
Du. Well, I will be ſo much a ſinner to be a double
dealer : there's another.
Clo. Primo, ſecundo, tertio, is a good play, and the olde
ſaying is, the third payes for all : the triplex ſir, is a good
tripping meaſure, or the belles of S. *Bennet* ſir, may put
you in minde, one, two, three.
Du. You can foole no more money out of mee at this
throw: if you will let your Lady know I am here to ſpeak
with her, and bring her along with you, it may awake my
bounty further.
Clo. Marry ſir, lullaby to your bountie till I come a-
gen. I go ſir, but I would not haue you to thinke, that
my deſire of hauing is the ſinne of couetouſneſſe : but as
you ſay ſir, let your bounty take a nappe, I will awake it
anon.　　　　　*Exit*

Enter Anthonio and Officers.

Vio. Here comes the man ſir, that did reſcue mee.
Du. That face of his I do remember well,
yet when I ſaw it laſt, it was beſmear'd
As blacke as Vulcan, in the ſmoake of warre :
A bawbling Veſſell was he Captaine of,
For ſhallow draught and bulke vnprizable,
With which ſuch ſcathfull grapple did he make,
With the moſt noble bottome of our Fleete,
That very enuy, and the tongue of loſſe
Cride fame and honor on him: What's the matter?
1 Offi. *Orſino*, this is that *Anthonio*
That tooke the *Phœnix*, and her fraught from *Candy*,
And this is he that did the *Tiger* boord,
When your yong Nephew *Titus* loſt his legge ;
Heere in the ſtreets, deſperate of ſhame and ſtate,
In priuate brabble did we apprehend him.
Vio. He did me kindneſſe ſir, drew on my ſide,
But in concluſion put ſtrange ſpeech vpon me,
I know not what 'twas, but diſtraction.
Du. Notable Pyrate, thou ſalt-water Theefe,
What fooliſh boldneſſe brought thee to their mercies,
Whom thou in termes ſo bloudie, and ſo deere
Haſt made thine enemies?
Ant. *Orſino* : Noble ſir,
Be pleas'd that I ſhake off theſe names you giue mee :
Anthonio neuer yet was Theefe, or Pyrate,
Though I confeſſe, on baſe and ground enough
Orſino's enemie. A witchcraft drew me hither :
That moſt ingratefull boy there by your ſide,
From the rude ſeas enrag'd and foamy mouth
Did I redeeme : a wracke paſt hope he was :
His life I gaue him, and did thereto adde
My loue without retention, or reſtraint,
All his in dedication. For his ſake,
Did I expoſe my ſelfe (pure for his loue)
Into the danger of this aduerſe Towne,
Drew to defend him, when he was beſet :
Where being apprehended, his falſe cunning
(Not meaning to partake with me in danger)
Taught him to face me out of his acquaintance,

And

And grew a twentie yeeres remoued thing
While one would winke : denide me mine owne purfe,
Which I had recommended to his vfe,
Not halfe an houre before.
Vio. How can this be?
Du. When came he to this Towne?
Ant. To day my Lord : and for three months before,
No *intrim*, not a minutes vacancie,
Both day and night did we keepe companie.
Enter Oliuia and attendants.
Du. Heere comes the Counteffe, now heauen walkes
on earth :
But for thee fellow, fellow thy words are madneffe,
Three monthes this youth hath tended vpon mee,
But more of that anon. Take him afide.
Ol. What would my Lord, but that he may not haue,
Wherein *Oliuia* may feeme feruiceable?
Cefario, you do not keepe promife with me.
Vio. Madam:
Du. Gracious *Oliuia*.
Ol. What do you fay *Cefario?* Good my Lord.
Vio. My Lord would fpeake,my dutie hufhes me.
Ol. If it be ought to the old tune my Lord,
It is as fat and fulfome to mine eare
As howling after Muficke.
Du. Still fo cruell?
Ol. Still fo conftant Lord.
Du. What to peruerfeneffe? you vnciuill Ladie
To whofe ingrate, and vnaufpicious Altars
My foule the faithfull'ft offrings haue breath'd out
That ere deuotion tender'd. What fhall I do?
Ol. Euen what it pleafe my Lord,that fhal becom him
Du. Why fhould I not, (had I the heart to do it)
Like to th'Egyptian theefe, at point of death
Kill what I loue : (a fauage Iealoufie,
That fometime fauours nobly) but heare me this :
Since you to non-regardance caft my faith,
And that I partly know the inftrument
That fcrewes me from my true place in your fauour :
Liue you the Marble-brefted Tirant ftill.
But this your Minion, whom I know you loue,
And whom, by heauen I fweare, I tender deerely,
Him will I teare out of that cruell eye,
Where he fits crowned in his mafters fpight.
Come boy with me, my thoughts are ripe in mifchiefe :
Ile facrifice the Lambe that I do loue,
To fpight a Rauens heart within a Doue.
Vio. And I moft iocund, apt, and willinglie,
To do you reft, a thoufand deaths would dye.
Ol. Where goes *Cefario?*
Vio. After him I loue,
More then I loue thefe eyes, more then my life,
More by all mores, then ere I fhall loue wife.
If I do feigne, you witneffes aboue
Punifh my life, for tainting of my loue.
Ol. Aye me detefted, how am I beguil'd?
*Vio.*Who does beguile you? who does do you wrong?
Ol. Haft thou forgot thy felfe? Is it fo long?
Call forth the holy Father.
Du. Come, away.
Ol. Whether my Lord? *Cefario*, Husband, ftay.
Du. Husband?
Ol. I Husband. Can he that deny?
Du. Her husband, firrah?
Vio. No my Lord, not I.
Ol. Alas, it is the bafeneffe of thy feare,

That makes thee ftrangle thy propriety :
Feare not *Cefario*, take thy fortunes vp,
Be that thou know'ft thou art, and then thou art
As great as that thou fear'ft.
Enter Prieft.
O welcome Father :
Father, I charge thee by thy reuerence
Heere to vnfold, though lately we intended
To keepe in darkeneffe, what occafion now
Reueales before 'tis ripe : what thou doft know
Hath newly paft, betweene this youth, and me.
Prieft. A Contract of eternall bond of loue,
Confirm'd by mutuall ioynder of your hands,
Attefted by the holy clofe of lippes,
Strengthned by enterchangement of your rings,
And all the Ceremonie of this compact
Seal'd in my function, by my teftimony :
Since when, my watch hath told me, toward my graue
I haue trauail'd but two houres.
Du. O thou diffembling Cub : what wilt thou be
When time hath fow'd a grizzle on thy cafe?
Or will not elfe thy craft fo quickely grow,
That thine owne trip fhall be thine ouerthrow :
Farewell, and take her, but direct thy feete,
Where thou, and I (henceforth) may neuer meet.
Vio. My Lord, I do proteft.
Ol. O do not fweare,
Hold little faith, though thou haft too much feare.

Enter Sir Andrew.
And. For the loue of God a Surgeon, fend one pre-
fently to fir *Toby*.
Ol. What's the matter?
And. H'as broke my head a-croffe, and has giuen Sir
Toby a bloody Coxcombe too : for the loue of God your
helpe, I had rather then forty pound I were at home.
Ol. Who has done this fir *Andrew?*
And. The Counts Gentleman, one *Cefario*: we tooke
him for a Coward, but hee's the verie diuell incardinate.
Du. My Gentleman *Cefario?*
And. Odd's lifelings heere he is : you broke my head
for nothing, and that that I did, I was fet on to do't by fir
Toby.
Vio. Why do you fpeake to me, I neuer hurt you :
you drew your fword vpon me without caufe,
But I befpake you faire, and hurt you not.

Enter Toby and Clowne.
And. If a bloody coxcombe be a hurt, you haue hurt
me : I thinke you fet nothing by a bloody Coxcombe.
Heere comes fir *Toby* halting, you fhall heare more: but if
he had not beene in drinke, hee would haue tickel'd you
other gates then he did.
Du. How now Gentleman? how ift with you?
To. That's all one, has hurt me,and there's th'end on't:
Sot, didft fee Dicke Surgeon, fot?
Clo. O he's drunke fir *Toby* an houre agone : his eyes
were fet at eight i'th morning.
To. Then he's a Rogue, and a paffy meafures panyn : I
hate a drunken rogue.
Ol. Away with him? Who hath made this hauocke
with them?
And. Ile helpe you fir *Toby*, becaufe we'll be dreft to-
gether.
To. Will you helpe an Affe-head, and a coxcombe, &
a knaue : a thin fac'd knaue, a gull?
Ol.

Ol. Get him to bed, and let his hurt be look'd too.
    Enter Sebaſtian.
  Seb. I am ſorry Madam I haue hurt your kinſman:
But had it beene the brother of my blood,
I muſt haue done no leſſe with wit and ſafety.
You throw a ſtrange regard vpon me, and by that
I do perceiue it hath offended you :
Pardon me (ſweet one) euen for the vowes
We made each other, but ſo late ago.
  Du. One face, one voice, one habit, and two perſons,
A naturall Perſpectiue, that is, and is not.
  Seb. Anthonio : O my deere *Anthonio,*
How haue the houres rack'd, and tortur'd me,
Since I haue loſt thee ?
  Ant. Sebaſtian are you ?
  Seb. Fear'ſt thou that *Anthonio* ?
  Ant. How haue you made diuiſion of your ſelfe,
An apple cleft in two, is not more twin
Then theſe two creatures. Which is *Sebaſtian* ?
  Ol. Moſt wonderfull.
  Seb. Do I ſtand there ? I neuer had a brother :
Nor can there be that Deity in my nature
Of heere, and euery where. I had a ſiſter,
Whom the blinde waues and ſurges haue deuour'd :
Of charity, what kinne are you to me ?
What Countreyman? What name? What Parentage ?
  Vio. Of *Meſſaline :* *Sebaſtian* was my Father,
Such a *Sebaſtian* was my brother too :
So went he ſuited to his watery tombe :
If ſpirits can aſſume both forme and ſuite,
You come to fright vs.
  Seb. A ſpirit I am indeed,
But am in that dimenſion groſſely clad,
Which from the wombe I did participate.
Were you a woman, as the reſt goes euen,
I ſhould my teares let fall vpon your cheeke,
And ſay, thrice welcome drowned *Viola.*
  Vio. My father had a moale vpon his brow.
  Seb. And ſo had mine.
  Vio. And dide that day when *Viola* from her birth
Had numbred thirteene yeares.
  Seb. O that record is liuely in my ſoule,
He finiſhed indeed his mortall acte
That day that made my ſiſter thirteene yeares.
  Vio. If nothing lets to make vs happie both,
But this my maſculine vſurp'd attyre :
Do not embrace me, till each circumſtance,
Of place, time, fortune, do co-here and iumpe
That I am *Viola,* which to confirme,
Ile bring you to a Captaine in this Towne,
Where lye my maiden weeds : by whoſe gentle helpe,
I was preſeru'd to ſerue this Noble Count :
All the occurrence of my fortune ſince
Hath beene betweene this Lady, and this Lord.
  Seb. So comes it Lady, you haue beene miſtooke :
But Nature to her bias drew in that.
·You would haue bin contracted to a Maid,
Nor are you therein (by my life) deceiu'd,
You are betroth'd both to a maid and man.
  Du. Be not amaz'd, right noble is his blood :
If this be ſo, as yet the glaſſe ſeemes true,
I ſhall haue ſhare in this moſt happy wracke,
Boy, thou haſt ſaide to me a thouſand times,
Thou neuer ſhould'ſt loue woman like to me.
  Vio. And all thoſe ſayings, will I ouer ſweare,
And all thoſe ſwearings keepe as true in ſoule,

As doth that Orbed Continent, the fire,
That ſeuers day ftom night.
  Du. Giue me thy hand,
And let me ſee thee in thy womans weedes.
  Vio. The Captaine that did bring me firſt on ſhore
Hath my Maides garments : he vpon ſome Action
Is now in durance, at *Maluolio's* ſuite,
A Gentleman, and follower of my Ladies.
  Ol. He ſhall inlarge him : fetch *Maluolio* hither,
And yet alas, now I remember me,
They ſay poore Gentleman, he's much diſtract.
    Enter Clowne with a Letter, and Fabian.
A moſt extracting frenſie of mine owne
From my remembrance, clearly baniſht his.
How does he ſi·rah ?
  Cl. Truely Madam, he holds *Belzebub* at the ſtaues end as
well as a man in his caſe may do : has heere writ a letter to
you, I ſhould haue giuen't you to day morning. But as a
madmans Epiſtles are no Goſpels, ſo it skilles not much
when they are deliuer'd.
  Ol. Open't, and read it.
  Clo. Looke then to be well edified, when the Foole
deliuers the Madman. *By the Lord Madam.*
  Ol. How now, art thou mad ?
  Clo. No Madam, I do but reade madneſſe : and your
Ladyſhip will haue it as it ought to bee, you muſt allow
Vox.
  Ol. Prethee reade i'thy right wits.
  Clo. So I do Madona : but to reade his right wits, is to
reade thus : therefore, perpend my Princeſſe, and giue
eare.
  Ol. Read it you, ſirrah.
  Fab. Reads. By the Lord Madam, you wrong me, and
the world ſhall know it : Though you haue put mee into
darkeneſſe, and giuen your drunken Coſine rule ouer me,
yet haue I the benefit of my ſenſes as well as your Ladie-
ſhip. I haue your owne letter, that induced mee to the
ſemblance I put on ; with the which I doubt not, but to
do my ſelfe much right, or you much ſhame : thinke of
me as you pleaſe. I leaue my duty a little vnthought of,
and ſpeake out of my iniury. *The madly vs'd Maluolio.*
  Ol. Did he write this ?
  Clo. I Madame.
  Du. This ſauours not much of diſtraction.
  Ol. See him deliuer'd *Fabian,* bring him hither :
My Lord, ſo pleaſe you, theſe things further thought on,
To thinke me as well a ſiſter, as a wife,
One day ſhall crowne th'alliance on't, ſo pleaſe you,
Heere at my houſe, and at my proper coſt.
  Du. Madam, I am moſt apt t'embrace your offer :
Your Maſter quits you : and for your ſeruice done him,
So much againſt the mettle of your ſex,
So farre beneath your ſoft and tender breeding,
And ſince you call'd me Maſter, for ſo long :
Heere is my hand, you ſhall from this time bee
your Maſters Miſtris.
  Ol. A ſiſter, you are ſhe.
    Enter Maluolio.
  Du. Is this the Madman ?
  Ol. I my Lord, this ſame : How now *Maluolio* ?
  Mal. Madam, you haue done me wrong,
Notorious wrong.
  Ol. Haue I *Maluolio* ? No,
  Mal. Lady you haue, pray you peruſe that Letter.
You muſt not now denie it is your hand,
Write from it if you can, in hand, or phraſe,

Or

Or fay, tis not your feale, not your inuention :
You can fay none of this. Well, grant it then,
And tell me in the modeftie of honor,
Why you haue giuen me fuch cleare lights of fauour,
Bad me come fmiling, and croffe-garter'd to you,
To put on yellow ftockings, and to frowne
Vpon fir *Toby*, and the lighter people :
And acting this in an obedient hope,
Why haue you fuffer'd me to be imprifon'd,
Kept in a darke houfe, vifited by the Prieft,
And made the moft notorious gecke and gull,
That ere inuention plaid on ? Tell me why ?

Ol. Alas *Maluolio*, this is not my writing,
Though I confeffe much like the Charracter :
But out of queftion, tis *Marias* hand.
And now I do bethinke me, it was fhee
Firft told me thou waft mad ; then cam'ft in fmiling,
And in fuch formes, which heere were prefuppos'd
Vpon thee in the Letter : prethee be content,
This practice hath moft fhrewdly paft vpon thee :
But when we know the grounds, and authors of it,
Thou fhalt be both the Plaintiffe and the Iudge
Of thine owne caufe.

Fab. Good Madam heare me fpeake,
And let no quarrell, nor no braule to come,
Taint the condition of this prefent houre,
Which I haue wondred at. In hope it fhall not,
Moft freely I confeffe my felfe, and *Toby*
Set this deuice againft *Maluolio* heere,
Vpon fome ftubborne and vncourteous parts
We had conceiu'd againft him. *Maria* writ
The Letter, at fir *Tobyes* great importance,
In recompence whereof, he hath married her :
How with a fportfull malice it was follow'd,
May rather plucke on laughter then reuenge,
If that the iniuries be iuftly weigh'd,
That haue on both fides paft.

Ol. Alas poore Foole, how haue they baffel'd thee ?

Clo. Why fome are borne great, fome atchieue greatneffe, and fome haue greatneffe throwne vpon them. I
was one fir, in this Enterlude, one fir *Topas* fir, but that's
all one : By the Lord Foole, I am not mad : but do you remember, Madam, why laugh you at fuch a barren rafcall,
and you fmile not he's gag'd : and thus the whirlegigge
of time, brings in his reuenges.

Mal. Ile be reueng'd on the whole packe of you ?

Ol. He hath bene moft notoriouſly abus'd.

Du. Purſue him, and entreate him to a peace :
He hath not told vs of the Captaine yet,
When that is knowne, and golden time conuents
A folemne Combination fhall be made
Of our deere foules. Meane time fweet fifter,
We will not part from hence. *Cefario* come
(For fo you fhall be while you are a man :)
But when in other habites you are feene,
Orfino's Miftris, and his fancies Queene.   *Exeunt*

Clowne fings.

> When that I was and a little tine boy,
>   with hey, ho, the winde and the raine :
> A foolifh thing was but a toy,
>   for the raine it raineth euery day.
>
> But when I came to mans eftate,
>   with hey ho, &c.
> Gainſt Knaues and Theeues men fhut their gate,
>   for the raine, &c.
>
> But when I came alas to wiue,
>   with hey ho, &c.
> By fwaggering could I neuer thriue,
>   for the raine, &c.
>
> But when I came vnto my beds,
>   with hey ho, &c.
> With toffpottes ftill had drunken heades,
>   for the raine, &c.
>
> A great while ago the world begon,
>   hey ho, &c.
> But that's all one, our Play is done,
>   and wee'l ftriue to pleafe you euery day.

FINIS.

The Winters Tale.

Actus Primus. Scæna Prima.

Enter Camillo and Archidamus.

Arch. IF you fhall chance(*Camillo*) to vifit *Bohemia*, on the like occafion whereon my feruices are now on-foot, you fhall fee(as I haue faid)great difference betwixt our *Bohemia*, and your *Sicilia*.

Cam. I thinke, this comming Summer, the King of *Sicilia* meanes to pay *Bohemia* the Vifitation, which bee iuftly owes him.

Arch. Wherein our Entertainment fhall fhame vs: we will be iuftified in our Loues : for indeed---

Cam. 'Befeech you---

Arch. Verely I fpeake it in the freedome of my knowledge : we cannot with fuch magnificence--- in fo rare--- I know not what to fay---Wee will giue you fleepie Drinkes, that your Sences (vn-intelligent of our infufficience) may, though they cannot prayfe vs, as little accufe vs.

Cam. You pay a great deale to deare, for what's giuen freely.

Arch. 'Beleeue me, I fpeake as my vnderftanding inftructs me, and as mine honeftie puts it to vtterance.

Cam. *Sicilia* cannot fhew himfelfe ouer-kind to *Bohemia* : They were trayn'd together in their Child-hoods; and there rooted betwixt them then fuch an affection, which cannot chufe but braunch now. Since their more mature Dignities, and Royall Neceffities, made feperation of their Societie, their Encounters(though not Perfonall) hath beene Royally attornyed with enter-change of Gifts, Letters, louing Embaffies, that they haue feem'd to be together, though abfent: fhooke hands, as ouer a Vaft; and embrac'd as it were from the ends of oppofed Winds. The Heauens continue their Loues.

Arch. I thinke there is not in the World, either Malice or Matter, to alter it. You haue an vnfpeakable comfort of your young Prince *Mamillius*: it is a Gentleman of the greateft Promife, that euer came into my Note.

Cam. I very well agree with you, in the hopes of him : it is a gallant Child ; one, that (indeed)Phyficks the Subiect, makes old hearts frefh : they that went on Crutches ere he was borne, defire yet their life, to fee him a Man.

Arch. Would they elfe be content to die?

Cam. Yes, if there were no other excufe, why they fhould defire to liue.

Arch. If the King had no Sonne, they would defire to liue on Crutches till he had one.   *Exeunt.*

Scæna Secunda.

Enter Leontes, Hermione, Mamillius, Polixenes, Camillo.

Pol. Nine Changes of the Watry-Starre hath been The Shepheards Note, fince we haue left our Throne Without a Burthen : Time as long againe Would be fill'd vp(my Brother)with our Thanks, And yet we fhould, for perpetuitie, Goe hence in debt : And therefore, like a Cypher (Yet ftanding in rich place) I multiply With one we thanke you, many thoufands moe, That goe before it.

Leo. Stay your Thanks a while, And pay them when you part.

Pol. Sir, that's to morrow : I am queftion'd by my feares, of what may chance, Or breed vpon our abfence, that may blow No fneaping Winds at home, to make vs fay, This is put forth too truly : befides, I haue ftay'd To tyre your Royaltie.

Leo. We are tougher (Brother) Then you can put vs to't.

Pol. No longer ftay.

Leo. One Seue'night longer.

Pol. Very footh, to morrow.

Leo. Wee'le part the time betweene's then: and in that Ile no gaine-faying.

Pol. Preffe me not ('befeech you) fo : There is no Tongue that moues; none, none i'th'World So foone as yours, could win me: fo it fhould now, Were there neceffitie in your requeft, although 'Twere needfull I deny'd it. My Affaires Doe euen drag me home-ward : which to hinder, Were (in your Loue) a Whip to me ; my ftay, To you a Charge, and Trouble : to faue both, Farewell (our Brother.)

Leo. Tongue-ty'd our Queene ? fpeake you.

Her. I had thought (Sir)to haue held my peace, vntill You had drawne Oathes from him, not to ftay: you(Sir) Charge him too coldly. Tell him, you are fure All in *Bohemia*'s well : this fatisfaction, The by-gone-day proclaym'd, fay this to him, He's beat from his beft ward.

Leo. Well faid, *Hermione*.

Her. To tell, he longs to fee his Sonne, were ftrong: But let him fay fo then, and let him goe ; But let him fweare fo, and he fhall not ftay, Wee'l thwack him hence with Diftaffes. Yet of your Royall prefence, Ile aduenture The borrow of a Weeke. When at *Bohemia* You take my Lord, Ile giue him my Commiffion, To let him there a Moneth, behind the Geft Prefix'd for's parting : yet(good-deed) *Leontes*, I loue thee not a Iarre o'th'Clock, behind

A a   What

What Lady fhe her Lord. You'le ftay ?
Pol. No, Madame.
Her. Nay, but you will ?
Pol. I may not verely.
Her. Verely ?
You put me off with limber Vowes: but I,
Though you would feek t'vnfphere the Stars with Oaths,
Should yet fay, Sir, no going : Verely
You fhall not goe ; a Ladyes Verely ' is
As potent as a Lords. Will you goe yet ?
Force me to keepe you as a Prifoner,
Not like a Gueft : fo you fhall pay your Fees
When you depart, and faue your Thanks. How fay you?
My Prifoner ? or my Gueft ? by your dread Verely,
One of them you fhall be.
　　Pol. Your Gueft then, Madame :
To be your Prifoner, fhould import offending ;
Which is for me, leffe eafie to commit,
Then you to punifh.
　　Her. Not your Gaoler then,
But your kind Hofteffe. Come, Ile queftion you
Of my Lords Tricks, and yours, when you were Boyes:
You were pretty Lordings then ?
　　Pol. We were (faire Queene)
Two Lads, that thought there was no more behind,
But fuch a day to morrow, as to day,
And to be Boy eternall.
　　Her. Was not my Lord
The veryer Wag o'th' two ?
　　Pol. We were as twyn'd Lambs, that did frisk i'th' Sun,
And bleat the one at th'other: what we chang'd,
Was Innocence, for Innocence : we knew not
The Doctrine of ill-doing, nor dream'd
That any did : Had we purfu'd that life,
And our weake Spirits ne're been higher rear'd
With ftronger blood, we fhould haue anfwer'd Heauen
Boldly, not guilty ; the Impofition clear'd,
Hereditarie ours.
　　Her. By this we gather
You haue tript fince.
　　Pol. O my moft facred Lady,
Temptations haue fince then been borne to's: for
In thofe vnfledg'd dayes, was my Wife a Girle ;
Your precious felfe had then not crofs'd the eyes
Of my young Play-fellow.
　　Her. Grace to boot :
Of this make no conclufion, leaft you fay
Your Queene and I are Deuils : yet goe on,
Th'offences we haue made you doe, wee'le anfwere,
If you firft finn'd with vs : and that with vs
You did continue fault; and that you flipt not
With any, but with vs.
　　Leo. Is he woon yet ?
　　Her. Hee'le ftay (my Lord.)
　　Leo. At my requeft, he would not :
Hermione (my deareft) thou neuer fpoak'ft
To better purpofe.
　　Her. Neuer ?
　　Leo. Neuer, but once.
　　Her. What? haue I twice faid well? when was't before?
I prethee tell me : cram's with prayfe, and make's
As fat as tame things: One good deed, dying tongueleffe,
Slaughters a thoufand, wayting vpon that.
Our prayfes are our Wages. You may ride's
With one foft Kiffe a thoufand Furlongs, ere
With Spur we heat an Acre. But to th' Goale :

My laft good deed, was to entreat his ftay.
What was my firft? it ha's an elder Sifter,
Or I miftake you: O, would her Name were *Grace.*
But once before I fpoke to th' purpofe ? when ?
Nay, let me haue't : I long.
　　Leo. Why, that was when
Three crabbed Moneths had fowr'd themfelues to death,
Ere I could make thee open thy white Hand:
A clap thy felfe my Loue ; then didft thou vtter,
I am yours for euer.
　　Her. 'Tis Grace indeed.
Why lo-you now; I haue fpoke to th' purpofe twice :
The one, for euer earn'd a Royall Husband ;
Th'other, for fome while a Friend.
　　Leo. Too hot, too hot :
To mingle friendfhip farre, is mingling bloods.
I haue *Tremor Cordis* on me : my heart daunces,
But not for ioy ; not ioy. This Entertainment
May a free face put on : deriue a Libertie
From Heartineffe, from Bountie, fertile Bofome,
And well become the Agent: 't may; I graunt :
But to be padling Palmes, and pinching Fingers,
As now they are, and making practis'd Smiles
As in a Looking-Glaffe ; and then to figh, as 'twere
The Mort o'th'Deere : oh, that is entertainment
My Bofome likes not, nor my Browes. *Mamillius,*
Art thou my Boy ?
　　Mam. I, my good Lord.
　　Leo. I'fecks?
Why that's my Bawcock: what? has't fmutch'd thy Nofe?
They fay it is a Coppy out of mine. Come Captaine,
We muft be neat ; not neat, but cleanly, Captaine :
And yet the Steere, the Heycfer, and the Calfe,
Are all call'd Neat. Still Virginalling
Vpon his Palme? How now (you wanton Calfe)
Art thou my Calfe ?
　　Mam. Yes, if you will (my Lord.)
　　Leo. Thou want'ft a rough path, & the fhoots that I haue
To be full, like me : yet they fay we are
Almoft as like as Egges ; Women fay fo,
(That will fay any thing.) But were they falfe
As o're-dy'd Blacks, as Wind, as Waters; falfe
As Dice are to be wifh'd, by one that fixes
No borne 'twixt his and mine ; yet were it true,
To fay this Boy were like me. Come(Sir Page)
Looke on me with your Welkin eye : fweet Villaine,
Moft dear'ft; my Collop: Can thy Dam, may't be
Affection? thy Intention ftabs the Center.
Thou do'ft make poffible things not fo held,
Communicat'ft with Dreames(how can this be?)
With what's vnreall: thou coactiue art,
And fellow'ft nothing. Then 'tis very credent,
Thou may'ft co-ioyne with fomething, and thou do'ft,
(And that beyond Commiffion) and I find it,
(And that to the infection of my Braines,
And hardning of my Browes.
　　Pol. What meanes *Sicilia* ?
　　Her. He fomething feemes vnfetled.
　　Pol. How? my Lord ?
　　Leo. What cheere? how is't with you, beft Brother?
　　Her. You looke as if you held a Brow of much diftraction:
Are you mou'd (my Lord?)
　　Leo. No, in good earneft.
How fometimes Nature will betray it's folly ?
It's tenderneffe? and make it felfe a Paftime
To harder bofomes ? Looking on the Lynes

　　　　　　　　　　　　　　　　　　　　　　　　Of

Of my Boyes face,me thoughts I did requoyle
Twentie three yeeres, and faw my felfe vn-breech'd,
In my greene Veluet Coat ; my Dagger muzzel'd,
Leaft it fhould bite it's Mafter, and fo proue
(As Ornaments oft do's) too dangerous :
How like(me thought) I then was to this Kernell,
This Squafh, this Gentleman. Mine honeft Friend,
Will you take Egges for Money ?

Mam. No (my Lord) Ile fight.

Leo. You will: why happy man be's dole. My Brother
Are you fo fond of your young Prince, as we
Doe feeme to be of ours?

Pol. If at home (Sir)
He's all my Exercife, my Mirth, my Matter ;
Now my fworne Friend,and then mine Enemy ;
My Parafite, my Souldier: Statef-man; all :
He makes a Iulyes day,fhort as December,
And with his varying child-neffe, cures in me
Thoughts, that would thick my blood.

Leo. So ftands this Squire
Offic'd with me : We two will walke(my Lord)
And leaue you to your grauer fteps. *Hermione,*
How thou lou'ft vs,fhew in our Brothers welcome ;
Let what is deare in Sicily, be cheape :
Next to thy felfe,and my young Rouer, he's
Apparant to my heart.

Her. If you would feeke vs,
We are yours i'th'Garden : fhall's attend you there ?

Leo. To your owne bents difpofe you : you'le be found,
Be you beneath the Sky : I am angling now,
(Though you perceiue me not how I giue Lyne)
Goe too, goe too.
How fhe holds vp the Neb? the Byll to him ?
And armes her with the boldneffe of a Wife
To her allowing Husband. Gone already,
Ynch-thick, knee-deepe; ore head and eares a fork'd one.
Goe play (Boy) play : thy Mother playes, and I
Play too; but fo difgrac'd a part, whofe iffue
Will hiffe me to my Graue : Contempt and Clamor
Will be my Knell. Goe play (Boy) play, there haue been
(Or I am much deceiu'd) Cuckolds ere now,
And many a man there is (euen at this prefent,
Now, while I fpeake this) holds his Wife by th'Arme,
That little thinkes fhe ha's been fluyc'd in's abfence,
And his Pond fifh'd by his next Neighbor (by
Sir *Smile,* his Neighbor:) nay, there's comfort in't,
Whiles other men haue Gates, and thofe Gates open'd
(As mine) againft their will. Should all defpaire
That haue reuolted Wiues, the tenth of Mankind
Would hang themfelues. Phyfick for't, there's none :
It is a bawdy Planet, that will ftrike
Where 'tis predominant; and 'tis powrefull: thinke it :
From Eaft, Weft, North, and South, be it concluded,
No Barricado for a Belly. Know't,
It will let in and out the Enemy,
With bag and baggage : many thoufand on's
Haue the Difeafe, and feele't not. How now Boy ?

Mam. I am like you fay.

Leo. Why, that's fome comfort.
What ? *Camillo* there ?

Cam. I, my good Lord.

Leo. Goe play (*Mamillius*) thou'rt an honeft man :
Camillo, this great Sir will yet ftay longer.

Cam. You had much adoe to make his Anchor hold,
When you caft out, it ftill came home.

Leo. Didft note it ?

Cam. He would not ftay at your Petitions, made
His Bufineffe more materiall.

Leo. Didft perceiue it ?
They're here with me already; whifp'ring, rounding :
Sicilia is a fo-forth : 'tis farre gone,
When I fhall guft it laft. How cam't (*Camillo*)
That he did ftay ?

Cam. At the good Queenes entreatie.

Leo. At the Queenes be't : Good fhould be pertinent,
But fo it is, it is not. Was this taken
By any vnderftanding Pate but thine ?
For thy Conceit is foaking, will draw in
More then the common Blocks. Not noted, is't,
But of the finer Natures? by fome Seueralls
Of Head-peece extraordinarie? Lower Meffes
Perchance are to this Bufineffe purblind ? fay.

Cam. Bufineffe, my Lord ? I thinke moft vnderftand
Bohemia ftayes here longer.

Leo. Ha ?

Cam. Stayes here longer.

Leo. I, but why ?

Cam. To fatisfie your Highneffe,and the Entreaties
Of our moft gracious Miftreffe.

Leo. Satisfie ?
Th'entreaties of your Miftreffe? Satisfie?
Let that fuffice. I haue trufted thee (*Camillo*)
With all the neereft things to my heart, as well
My Chamber-Councels, wherein(Prieft-like)thou
Haft cleans'd my Bofome: I, from thee departed
Thy Penitent reform'd : but we haue been
Deceiu'd in thy Integritie, deceiu'd
In that which feemes fo.

Cam. Be it forbid (my Lord.)

Leo. To bide vpon't : thou art not honeft: or
If thou inclin'ft that way, thou art a Coward,
Which hoxes honeftie behind, reftrayning
From Courfe requir'd : or elfe thou muft be counted
A Seruant,grafted in my ferious Truft,
And therein negligent : or elfe a Foole,
That feef't a Game play'd home, the rich Stake drawne,
And tak'ft it all for ieaft.

Cam. My gracious Lord,
I may be negligent, foolifh, and fearefull,
In euery one of thefe, no man is free,
But that his negligence, his folly, feare,
Among the infinite doings of the World,
Sometime puts forth in your affaires (my Lord.)
If euer I were wilfull-negligent,
It was my folly : if induftrioufly
I play'd the Foole, it was my negligence,
Not weighing well the end : if euer fearefull
To doe a thing, where I the iffue doubted,
Whereof the execution did cry out
Againft the non-performance, 'twas a feare
Which oft infects the wifeft : thefe(my Lord)
Are fuch allow'd Infirmities, that honeftie
Is neuer free of. But befeech your Grace
Be plainer with me, let me know my Trefpas
By it's owne vifage ; if I then deny it,
'Tis none of mine.

Leo. Ha' not you feene *Camillo* ?
(But that's paft doubt : you haue, or your eye-glaffe
Is thicker then a Cuckolds Horne) or heard ?
(For to a Vifion fo apparant, Rumor
Cannot be mute? or thought? (for Cogitation
Refides not in that man, that do's not thinke)

My

My Wife is flipperie? If thou wilt confeffe,
Or elfe be impudently negatiue,
To haue nor Eyes, nor Eares, nor Thought, then fay
My Wife's a Holy-Horfe, deferues a Name
As ranke as any Flax-Wench, that puts to
Before her troth-plight : fay't, and luftify't.

Cam. I would not be a ftander-by, to heare
My Soueraigne Miftreffe clouded fo, without
My prefent vengeance taken : 'fhrew my heart,
You neuer fpoke what did become you leffe
Then this; which to reiterate, were fin
As deepe as that, though true.

Leo. Is whifpering nothing?
Is leaning Cheeke to Cheeke? is meating Nofes?
Kiffing with in-fide Lip? ftopping the Cariere
Of Laughter, with a figh? (a Note infallible
Of breaking Honeftie) horfing foot on foot?
Skulking in corners? wifhing Clocks more fwift?
Houres, Minutes? Noone, Mid-night? and all Eyes
Blind with the Pin and Web, but theirs; theirs onely,
That would vnfeene be wicked? Is this nothing?
Why then the World, and all that's in't, is nothing,
The couering Skie is nothing, *Bohemia* nothing,
My Wife is nothing, nor Nothing haue thefe Nothings,
If this be nothing.

Cam. Good my Lord, be cur'd
Of this difeas'd Opinion, and betimes,
For 'tis moft dangerous.

Leo. Say it be, 'tis true.

Cam. No, no, my Lord.

Leo. It is: you lye, you lye :
I fay thou lyeft *Camillo*, and I hate thee,
Pronounce thee a groffe Lowt, a mindleffe Slaue,
Or elfe a houering Temporizer, that
Canft with thine eyes at once fee good and euill,
Inclining to them both: were my Wiues Liuer
Infected (as her life) fhe would not liue
The running of one Glaffe.

Cam. Who do's infect her?

Leo. Why he that weares her like her Medull, hanging
About his neck ('Bohemia') who, if I
Had Seruants true about me, that bare eyes
To fee alike mine Honor, as their Profits,
(Their owne particular Thrifts) they would doe that
Which fhould vndoe more doing : I, and thou
His Cup-bearer, whom I from meaner forme
Haue Bench'd, and rear'd to Worfhip, who may'ft fee
Plainely, as Heauen fees Earth, and Earth fees Heauen,
How I am gall'd, might'ft be-fpice a Cup,
To giue mine Enemy a lafting Winke :
Which Draught to me, were cordiall.

Cam. Sir (my Lord)
I could doe this, and that with no rafh Potion,
But with a lingring Dram, that fhould not worke
Malicioufly, like Poyfon : But I cannot
Beleeue this Crack to be in my dread Miftreffe
(So foueraignely being Honorable.)
I haue lou'd thee,

Leo. Make that thy queftion, and goe rot :
Do'ft thinke I am fo muddy, fo vnfetled,
To appoint my felfe in this vexation?
Sully the puritie and whiteneffe of my Sheetes
(Which to preferue, is Sleepe; which being fpotted,
Is Goades, Thornes. Nettles, Tayles of Wafpes)
Giue fcandall to the blood o'th' Prince, my Sonne,
(Who I doe thinke is mine, and loue as mine)

Without ripe mouing to't? Would I doe this?
Could man fo blench?

Cam. I muft beleeue you(Sir)
I doe, and will fetch off *Bohemia* for't :
Prouided, that when hee's remou'd, your Highneffe
Will take againe your Queene, as yours at firft,
Euen for your Sonnes fake, and thereby for fealing
The Iniurie of Tongues, in Courts and Kingdomes
Knowne, and ally'd to yours.

Leo. Thou do'ft aduife me,
Euen fo as I mine owne courfe haue fet downe :
Ile giue no blemifh to her Honor, none.

Cam. My Lord,
Goe then; and with a countenance as cleare
As Friendfhip weares at Feafts, keepe with *Bohemia*,
And with your Queene : I am his Cup-bearer,
If from me he haue wholefome Beueridge,
Account me not your Seruant.

Leo. This is all :
Do't, and thou haft the one halfe of my heart;
Do't not, thou fplit'ft thine owne.

Cam. Ile do't, my Lord.

Leo. I wil feeme friendly, as thou haft aduis'd me. *Exit*

Cam. O miferable Lady. But for me,
What cafe ftand I in? I muft be the poyfoner
Of good *Polixenes*, and my ground to do't,
Is the obedience to a Mafter ; one,
Who in Rebellion with himfelfe, will haue
All that are his, fo too. To doe this deed,
Promotion followes : If I could find example
Of thoufand's that had ftruck anoynted Kings,
And flourifh'd after, Il'd not do't : But fince
Nor Braffe, nor Stone, nor Parchment beares not one,
Let Villanie it felfe forfwear't. I muft
Forfake the Court : to do't, or no, is certaine
To me a breake-neck. Happy Starre raigne now,
Here comes *Bohemia*.   *Enter Polixenes.*

Pol. This is ftrange : Me thinkes
My fauor here begins to warpe. Not fpeake?
Good day *Camillo*.

Cam. Hayle moft Royall Sir.

Pol. What is the Newes i'th' Court?

Cam. None rare (my Lord.)

Pol. The King hath on him fuch a countenance,
As he had loft fome Prouince, and a Region
Lou'd, as he loues himfelfe : euen now I met him
With cuftomarie complement, when hee
Wafting his eyes to th' contrary, and falling
A Lippe of much contempt, fpeedes from me, and
So leaues me, to confider what is breeding,
That changes thus his Manners.

Cam. I dare not know (my Lord.)

Pol. How, dare not? doe not? doe you know, and dare not?
Be intelligent to me, 'tis thereabouts :
For to your felfe, what you doe know, you muft,
And cannot fay, you dare not. Good *Camillo*,
Your chang'd complexions are to me a Mirror,
Which fhewes me mine chang'd too: for I muft be
A partie in this alteration, finding
My felfe thus alter'd with't.

Cam. There is a fickneffe
Which puts fome of vs in diftemper, but
I cannot name the Difeafe, and it is caught
Of you, that yet are well.

Pol. How caught of me?
Make me not fighted like the Bafilifque.

                    I haue

I haue look'd on thousands, who haue ſped the better
By my regard, but kill'd none ſo : *Camillo*,
As you are certainely a Gentleman, thereto
Clerke-like experienc'd, which no leſſe adornes
Our Gentry, then our Parents Noble Names,
In whoſe ſucceſſe we are gentle : I beſeech you,
If you know ought which do's behoue my knowledge,
Thereof to be inform'd, impriſon't not
In ignorant concealement.
 Cam. I may not anſwere.
 Pol. A Sickneſſe caught of me, and yet I well?
I muſt be anſwer'd. Do'ſt thou heare *Camillo*,
I coniure thee, by all the parts of man,
Which Honor do's acknowledge, whereof the leaſt
Is not this Suit of mine, that thou declare
What incidencie thou do'ſt gheſſe of harme
Is creeping toward me ; how farre off, how neere,
Which way to be preuented, if to be :
If not, how beſt to beare it.
 Cam. Sir, I will tell you,
Since I am charg'd in Honor, and by him
That I thinke Honorable: therefore marke my counſaile,
Which muſt be eu'n as ſwiftly followed, as
I meane to vtter it ; or both your ſelfe, and me,
Cry loſt, and ſo good night.
 Pol. On, good *Camillo*.
 Cam. I am appointed him to murther you.
 Pol. By whom, *Camillo* ?
 Cam. By the King.
 Pol. For what ?
 Cam. He thinkes, nay with all confidence he ſweares,
As he had ſeen't, or beene an Inſtrument
To vice you to't, that you haue toucht his Queene
Forbiddenly.
 Pol. Oh then, my beſt blood turne
To an infected Gelly, and my Name
Be yoak'd with his, that did betray the Beſt :
Turne then my freſheſt Reputation to
A ſauour, that may ſtrike the dulleſt Noſthrill
Where I arriue, and my approch be ſhun'd,
Nay hated too, worſe then the great'ſt Infection
That ere was heard, or read.
 Cam. Sweare his thought ouer
By each particular Starre in Heauen, and
By all their Influences ; you may as well
Forbid the Sea for to obey the Moone,
As (or by Oath) remoue, or (Counſaile) ſhake
The Fabrick of his Folly, whoſe foundation
Is pyl'd vpon his Faith, and will continue
The ſtanding of his Body.
 Pol. How ſhould this grow?
 Cam. I know not : but I am ſure 'tis ſafer to
Auoid what's growne, then queſtion how 'tis borne.
If therefore you dare truſt my honeſtie,
That lyes encloſed in this Trunke, which you
Shall beare along impawnd, away to Night,
Your Followers I will whiſper to the Buſineſſe,
And will by twoes, and threes, at ſeuerall Poſternes,
Cleare them o'th' Citie : For my ſelfe, Ile put
My fortunes to your ſeruice (which are here
By this diſcouerie loſt.) Be not vncertaine,
For by the honor of my Parents, I
Haue vttred Truth : which if you ſeeke to proue,
I dare not ſtand by ; nor ſhall you be ſafer,
Then one condemnd by the Kings owne mouth :
Thereon his Execution ſworne.

 Pol. I doe beleeue thee :
I ſaw his heart in's face. Giue me thy hand,
Be Pilot to me, and thy places ſhall
Still neighbour mine. My Ships are ready, and
My people did expect my hence departure
Two dayes agoe. This Iealouſie
Is for a precious Creature : as ſhee's rare,
Muſt it be great ; and, as his Perſon's mightie,
Muſt it be violent : and, as he do's conceiue,
He is diſhonor'd by a man, which euer
Profeſs'd to him : why his Reuenges muſt
In that be made more bitter. Feare ore-ſhades me :
Good Expedition be my friend, and comfort
The gracious Queene, part of his Theame; but nothing
Of his ill-ta'ne ſuſpition. Come *Camillo*,
I will reſpect thee as a Father, if
Thou bear'ſt my life off, hence : Let vs auoid.
 Cam. It is in mine authoritie to command
The Keyes of all the Poſternes : Pleaſe your Highneſſe
To take the vrgent houre. Come Sir, away. *Exeunt.*

Actus Secundus. Scena Prima.

*Enter Hermione, Mamillius, Ladies : Leontes,
Antigonus, Lords.*

 Her. Take the Boy to you : he ſo troubles me,
'Tis paſt enduring.
 Lady. Come (my gracious Lord)
Shall I be your play-fellow ?
 Mam. No, Ile none of you.
 Lady. Why (my ſweet Lord?)
 Mam. You'le kiſſe me hard, and ſpeake to me, as if
I were a Baby ſtill. I loue you better.
 2. Lady. And why ſo (my Lord ?)
 Mam. Not for becauſe
Your Browes are blacker (yet black-browes they ſay
Become ſome Women beſt, ſo that there be not
Too much haire there, but in a Cemicircle,
Or a halfe-Moone, made with a Pen.)
 2. Lady. Who taught 'this ?
 Mam. I learn'd it out of Womens faces : pray now,
What colour are your eye-browes ?
 Lady. Blew (my Lord.)
 Mam. Nay, that's a mock : I haue ſeene a Ladies Noſe
That ha's beene blew, but not her eye-browes.
 Lady. Harke ye,
The Queene (your Mother) rounds apace : we ſhall
Preſent our ſeruices to a fine new Prince
One of theſe dayes, and then you'd wanton with vs,
If we would haue you.
 2. Lady. She is ſpread of late
Into a goodly Bulke (good time encounter her.)
 Her. What wiſdome ſtirs amongſt you? Come Sir, now
I am for you againe : 'Pray you ſit by vs,
And tell's a Tale.
 Mam. Merry, or ſad, ſhal't be ?
 Her. As merry as you will.
 Mam. A ſad Tale's beſt for Winter :
I haue one of Sprights, and Goblins.
 Her. Let's haue that (good Sir.)
Come-on, ſit downe, come-on, and doe your beſt,
To fright me with your Sprights : you're powrefull at it.
A a 3   *Mam.* There

Mam. There was a man.

Her. Nay, come fit downe : then on.

Mam. Dwelt by a Church-yard: I will tell it foftly,
Yond Crickets fhall not heare it.

Her. Come on then, and giu't me in mine eare.

Leon. Was hee met there? his Traine? *Camillo* with him?

Lord. Behind the tuft of Pines I met them, neuer
Saw I men fcowre fo on their way : I eyed them
Euen to their Ships.

Leo. How bleft am I
In my iuft Cenfure? in my true Opinion?
Alack, for leffer knowledge, how accurs'd,
In being fo bleft? There may be in the Cup
A Spider fteep'd, and one may drinke; depart,
And yet partake no venome: (for his knowledge
Is not infected) but if one prefent
Th'abhor'd Ingredient to his eye, make knowne
How he hath drunke, he cracks his gorge, his fides
With violent Hefts: I haue drunke, and feene the Spider.
Camillo was his helpe in this, his Pandar:
There is a Plot againft my Life, my Crowne;
All's true that is miftrufted: that falfe Villaine,
Whom I employ'd, was pre-employ'd by him:
He ha's difcouer'd my Defigns, and I
Remaine a pinch'd Thing; yea, a very Trick
For them to play at will: how came the Pofternes
So eafily open?

Lord. By his great authority,
Which often hath no leffe preuail'd, then fo,
On your command.

Leo. I know't too well.
Giue me the Boy, I am glad you did not nurfe him:
Though he do's beare fome fignes of me, yet you
Haue too much blood in him.

Her. What is this? Sport?

Leo. Beare the Boy hence, he fhall not come about her,
Away with him, and let her fport her felfe
With that fhee's big-with, for 'tis *Polixenes*
Ha's made thee fwell thus.

Her. But Il'd fay he had not;
And Ile be fworne you would beleeue my faying,
How e're you leane to th'Nay-ward.

Leo. You (my Lords)
Looke on her, marke her well: be but about
To fay fhe is a goodly Lady, and
The iuftice of your hearts will thereto adde
'Tis pitty fhee's not honeft: Honorable;
Prayfe her but for this her without-dore-Forme,
(Which on my faith deferues high fpeech) and ftraight
The Shrug, the Hum, or Ha, (thefe Petty-brands
That Calumnie doth vfe; Oh, I am out,
That Mercy do's, for Calumnie will feare
Vertue it felfe) thefe Shrugs, thefe Hum's, and Ha's,
When you haue faid fhee's goodly, come betweene,
Ere you can fay fhee's honeft: But be't knowne
(From him that ha's moft caufe to grieue it fhould be)
Shee's an Adultreffe.

Her. Should a Villaine fay fo,
(The moft replenifh'd Villaine in the World)
He were as much more Villaine : you (my Lord)
Doe but miftake.

Leo. You haue miftooke (my Lady)
Polixenes for *Leontes* : O thou Thing,
(Which Ile not call a Creature of thy place,
Leaft Barbarifme (making me the precedent)

Should a like Language vfe to all degrees,
And mannerly diftinguifhment leaue out,
Betwixt the Prince and Begger:) I haue faid
Shee's an Adultreffe, I haue faid with whom:
More; fhee's a Traytor, and *Camillo* is
A Federarie with her, and one that knowes
What fhe fhould fhame to know her felfe,
But with her moft vild Principall : that fhee's
A Bed-fwaruer, euen as bad as thofe
That Vulgars giue bold'ft Titles; I, and priuy
To this their late efcape.

Her. No (by my life)
Priuy to none of this: how will this grieue you,
When you fhall come to clearer knowledge, that
You thus haue publifh'd me? Gentle my Lord,
You fcarce can right me throughly, then, to fay
You did miftake.

Leo. No : if I miftake
In thofe Foundations which I build vpon,
The Centre is not bigge enough to beare
A Schoole-Boyes Top. Away with her, to Prifon:
He who fhall fpeake for her, is a farre-off guiltie,
But that he fpeakes.

Her. There's fome ill Planet raignes:
I muft be patient, till the Heauens looke
With an afpect more fauorable. Good my Lords,
I am not prone to weeping (as our Sex
Commonly are) the want of which vaine dew
Perchance fhall dry your pitties : but I haue
That honorable Griefe lodg'd here, which burnes
Worfe then Teares drowne: befeech you all (my Lords)
With thoughts fo qualified, as your Charities
Shall beft inftruct you, meafure me; and fo
The Kings will be perform'd.

Leo. Shall I be heard?

Her. Who is't that goes with me? befeech your Highnes
My Women may be with me, for you fee
My plight requires it. Doe not weepe (good Fooles)
There is no caufe: When you fhall know your Miftris
Ha's deferu'd Prifon, then abound in Teares,
As I come out; this Action I now goe on,
Is for my better grace. Adieu (my Lord)
I neuer wifh'd to fee you forry, now
I truft I fhall: my Women come, you haue leaue.

Leo. Goe, doe our bidding: hence.

Lord. Befeech your Highneffe call the Queene againe.

Antig. Be certaine what you do (Sir) leaft your Iuftice
Proue violence, in the which three great ones fuffer,
Your Selfe, your Queene, your Sonne.

Lord. For her (my Lord)
I dare my life lay downe, and will do't (Sir)
Pleafe you t'accept it, that the Queene is fpotleffe
I'th' eyes of Heauen, and to you (I meane
In this, which you accufe her.)

Antig. If it proue
Shee's otherwife, Ile keepe my Stables where
I lodge my Wife, Ile goe in couples with her:
Then when I feele, and fee her, no farther truft her:
For euery ynch of Woman in the World,
I, euery dram of Womans flefh is falfe,
If fhe be.

Leo. Hold your peaces.

Lord. Good my Lord,

Antig. It is for you we fpeake, not for our felues:
You are abus'd, and by fome putter on,
That will be damn'd for't: would I knew the Villaine,
I would

I would Land-damne him : be fhe honor-flaw'd,
I haue three daughters : the eldeft is eleuen;
The fecond, and the third, nine : and fome fiue :
If this proue true, they'l pay for't.   By mine Honor
Ile gell'd em all : fourteene they fhall not fee
To bring falfe generations : they are co-heyres,
And I had rather glib my felfe, then they
Should not produce faire iffue.

Leo. Ceafe, no more :
You fmell this bufineffe with a fence as cold
As is a dead-mans nofe : but I do fee't, and feel't,
As you feele doing thus : and fee withall
The Inftruments that feele.

Antig. If it be fo,
We neede no graue to burie honefty,
There's not a graine of it, the face to fweeten
Of the whole dungy-earth.

Leo. What? lacke I credit?

Lord. I had rather you did lacke then I (my Lord)
Vpon this ground : and more it would content me
To haue her Honor true, then your fufpition
Be blam'd for't how you might.

Leo. Why what neede we
Commune with you of this? but rather follow
Our forcefull inftigation? Our prerogatiue
Cals not your Counfailes, but our naturall goodneffe
Imparts this : which, if you, or ftupified,
Or feeming fo, in skill, cannot, or will not
Rellifh a truth, like vs : informe your felues,
We neede no more of your aduice : the matter,
The loffe, the gaine, the ord'ring on't,
Is all properly ours'

Antig. And I wifh (.my Liege)
You had onely in your filent iudgement tride it,
Without more ouerture.

Leo. How could that be ?
Either thou art moft ignorant by age,
Or thou wer't borne a foole : *Camillo's* flight
Added to their Familiarity
(Which was as groffe, as euer touch'd coniecture,
That lack'd fight onely, nought for approbation
But onely feeing, all other circumftances
Made vp to'th deed) doth pufh-on this proceeding.
Yet, for a greater confirmation
(For in an Acte of this importance, 'twere
Moft pitteous to be wilde) I haue difpatch'd in poft,
To facred *Delphos,* to *Appollo's* Temple,
Cleomines and *Dion,* whom you know
Of ftuff'd-fufficiency : Now, from the Oracle
They will bring all, whofe fpirituall counfaile had
Shall ftop, or fpurre me. Haue I done well?

Lord. Well done (my Lord.)

Leo. Though I am fatisfide, and neede no more
Then what I know, yet fhall the Oracle
Giue reft to th'mindes of others ; fuch as he
Whofe ignorant credulitie, will not
Come vp to th'truth. So haue we thought it good
From our free perfon, fhe fhould be confinde,
Leaft that the treachery of the two, fled hence,
Be left her to performe. Come follow vs,
We are to fpeake in publique : for this bufineffe
Will raife vs all.

Antig. To laughter, as I take it,
If the good truth, were knowne.   *Exeunt*

Scena Secunda.

Enter Paulina, a Gentleman, Gaoler, Emilia.

Paul. The Keeper of the prifon, call to him :
Let him haue knowledge who I am. Good Lady,
No Court in Europe is too good for thee,
What doft thou then in prifon? Now good Sir,
You know me, do you not?

Gao. For a worthy Lady,
And one, who much I honour.

Pau. Pray you then,
Conduct me to the Queene.

Gao. I may not (Madam)
To the contrary I haue expreffe commandment.

Pau. Here's a-do, to locke vp honefty & honour from
Th'acceffe of gentle vifitors. Is't lawfull pray you
To fee her Women? Any of them? *Emilia?*

Gao. So pleafe you (Madam)
To put a-part thefe your attendants, I
Shall bring *Emilia* forth.

Pau. I pray now call her :
With-draw your felues.

Gao. And Madam,
I muft be prefent at your Conference.

Pau. Well : be't fo : prethee.
Heere's fuch a-doe, to make no ftaine, a ftaine,
As paffes colouring. Deare Gentlewoman,
How fares our gtacious Lady?

Emil. As well as one fo great, and fo forlorne
May hold together : On her frights, and greefes
(Which neuer tender Lady hath borne greater)
She is, fomething before her time, deliuer'd.

Pau. A boy?

Emil. A daughter, and a goodly babe,
Lufty, and like to liue : the Queene receiues
Much comfort in't : Sayes, my poore prifoner,
I am innocent as you,

Pau. I dare be fworne:
Thefe dangerous, vnfafe Lunes i'th'King, befhrew them:
He muft be told on't, and he fhall : the office
Becomes a woman beft. Ile take't vpon me,
If I proue hony-mouth'd, let my tongue blifter.
And neuer to my red-look'd Anger bee
The Trumpet any more : pray you *(Emilia)*
Commend my beft obedience to the Queene,
If fhe dares truft me with her little babe,
I'le fhew't the King, and vndertake to bee
Her Aduocate to th'lowd'ft. We do not know
How he may foften at the fight o'th'Childe :
The filence often of pure innocence
Perfwades, when fpeaking failes.

Emil. Moft worthy Madam,
your honor, and your goodneffe is fo euident,
That your free vndertaking cannot miffe
A thriuing yffue : there is no Lady liuing
So meete for this great errand ; pleafe your Ladifhip
To vifit the next roome, Ile prefenrly
Acquaint the Queene of your moft noble offer,
Who, but to day hammered of this defigne,
But durft not tempt a minifter of honour
Leaft fhe fhould be deny'd.

                                                                    Pau

Paul. Tell her (*Emilia*)
Ile vſe that tongue I haue : If wit flow from't
As boldneſſe from my boſome, le't not be doubted
I ſhall do good,
Emil. Now be you bleſt for it.
Ile to the Queene : pleaſe you come ſomething neerer.
Gao. Madam, if't pleaſe the Queene to ſend the babe,
I know not what I ſhall incurre, to paſſe it,
Hauing no warrant.
Pau. You neede not feare it (ſir)
This Childe was priſoner to the wombe, and is
By Law and proceſſe of great Nature, thence
Free'd, and enfranchis'd, not a partie to
The anger of the King, nor guilty of
(If any be) the treſpaſſe of the Queene.
Gao. I do beleeue it.
Paul. Do not you feare : vpon mine honor, I
Will ſtand betwixt you, and danger.   *Exeunt*

Scæna Tertia.

Enter Leontes, Seruants, Paulina, Antigonus,
and Lords.

Leo. Nor night, nor day, no reſt : It is but weakneſſe
To beare the matter thus : meere weakneſſe, if
The cauſe were not in being : part o'th cauſe,
She, th'Adultreſſe : for the harlot-King
Is quite beyond mine Arme, out of the blanke
And leuell of my braine : plot-proofe : but ſhee,
I can hooke to me : ſay that ſhe were gone,
Giuen to the fire, a moity of my reſt
Might come to me againe. Whoſe there?
Ser. My Lord.
Leo. How do's the boy?
Ser. He tooke good reſt to night : 'tis hop'd
His ſickneſſe is diſcharg'd.
Leo. To ſee his Nobleneſſe,
Conceyuing the diſhonour of his Mother.
He ſtraight declin'd, droop'd, tooke it deeply,
Faſten'd, and fix'd the ſhame on't in himſelfe :
Threw-off his Spirit, his Appetite, his Sleepe,
And down-right languiſh'd. Leaue me ſolely : goe,
See how he fares : Fie, fie, no thought of him,
The very thought of my Reuenges that way
Recoyle vpon me : in himſelfe too mightie,
And in his parties, his Alliance ; Let him be,
Vntill a time may ſerue. For preſent vengeance
Take it on her : Camillo, and Polixenes
Laugh at me : make their paſtime at my ſorrow:
They ſhould not laugh, if I could reach them, nor
Shall ſhe, within my powre.
Enter Paulina.
Lord. You muſt not enter.
Paul. Nay rather (good my Lords) be ſecond to me :
Feare you his tyrannous paſsion more (alas)
Then the Queenes life ? A gracious innocent ſoule,
More free, then he is iealous.
Antig. That's enough.
Ser. Madam ; he hath not ſlept to night, commanded
None ſhould come at him.
Pau. Not ſo hot (good Sir)
I come to bring him ſleepe. 'Tis ſuch as you

That creepe like ſhadowes by him, and do ſighe
At each his needleſſe heauings : ſuch as you
Nouriſh the cauſe of his awaking.   I
Do come with words, as medicinall, as true ;
(Honeſt, as either;) to purge him of that humor,
That preſſes him from ſleepe.
Leo. Who noyſe there, hoe?
Pau. No noyſe (my Lord) but needfull conference,
About ſome Goſsips for your Highneſſe.
Leo. How?
Away with that audacious Lady. *Antigonus,*
I charg'd thee that ſhe ſhould not come about me,
I knew ſhe would.
Ant. I told her ſo (my Lord)
On your diſpleaſures perill, and on mine,
She ſhould not viſit you.
Leo. What? canſt not rule her?
Paul. From all diſhoneſtie he can : in this
(Vnleſſe he take the courſe that you haue done)
Commit me, for committing honor, truſt it,
He ſhall not rule me:
Ant. La-you now, you heare,
When ſhe will take the raine,I let her run,
But ſhee'l not ſtumble.
Paul. Good my Liege, I come :
And I beſeech you heare me, who profeſſes
My ſelfe your loyall Seruant, your Phyſitian,
Your moſt obedient Counſailor : yet that dares
Leſſe appeare ſo, in comforting your Euilles,
Then ſuch as moſt ſeeme yours. I ſay, I come
From your good Queene.
Leo. Good Queene?
Paul. Good Queene(my Lord)good Queene,
I ſay good Queene,
And would by combate, make her good ſo, were I
A man, the worſt about you.
Leo. Force her hence.
Pau. Let him that makes but trifles of his eyes
Firſt hand me : on mine owne accord, Ile off,
But firſt, Ile do my errand. The good Queene
(For ſhe is good)hath brought you forth a daughter,
Heere 'tis : Commends it to your bleſsing.
Leo. Out:
A mankinde Witch? Hence with her, out o'dore :
A moſt intelligencing bawd.
Paul. Not ſo :
I am as ignorant in that, as you,
In ſo entit'ling me : and no leſſe honeſt
Then you are mad : which is enough, Ile warrant
(As this world goes)to paſſe for honeſt:
Leo. Traitors ;
Will you not puſh her out ? Giue her the Baſtard,
Thou dotard, thou art woman-tyr'd : vnrooſted
By thy dame Partlet heere. Take vp the Baſtard,
Take't vp, I ſay : giue't to thy Croane.
Paul. For euer
Vnvenerable be thy hands, if thou
Tak'ſt vp the Princeſſe, by that forced baſeneſſe
Which he ha's put vpon't.
Leo. He dreads his Wife.
Paul. So I would you did : then 'twere paſt all doubt
You'd call your children, yours.
Leo. A neſt of Traitors.
Ant. I am none, by this good light.
Pau. Nor I : nor any
But one that's heere : and that's himſelfe : for he,

The

The facred Honor of himfelfe, his Queenes,
His hopefull Sonnes, his Babes, betrayes to Slander,
Whofe fting is fharper then the Swords; and will not
(For as the cafe now ftands, it is a Curfe
He cannot be compell'd too't) once remoue
The Root of his Opinion, which is rotten,
As euer Oake, or Stone was found.

Leo. A Callat
Of boundleffe tongue, who late hath beat her Husband,
And now bayts me : This Brat is none of mine,
It is the Iffue of *Polixenes*.
Hence with it, and together with the Dam,
Commit them to the fire.

Paul. It is yours :
And might we lay th'old Prouerb to your charge,
So like you,'tis the worfe. Behold (my Lords)
Although the Print be little, the whole Matter
And Coppy of the Father: (Eye, Nofe, Lippe,
The trick of's Frowne, his Fore-head, nay, the Valley,
The pretty dimples of his Chin, and Cheeke; his Smiles:
The very Mold, and frame of Hand, Nayle, Finger.)
And thou good Goddeffe *Nature*, which haft made it
So like to him that got it, if thou haft
The ordering of the Mind too,'mongft all Colours
No Yellow in't, leaft fhe fufpect, as he do's,
Her Children, not her Husbands.

Leo. A groffe Hagge :
And *Lozell*, thou art worthy to be hang'd,
That wilt not ftay her Tongue.

Antig. Hang all the Husbands
That cannot doe that Feat, you'le leaue your felfe
Hardly one Subiect.

Leo. Once more take her hence.

Paul. A moft vnworthy, and vnnaturall Lord
Can doe no more.

Leo. Ile ha' thee burnt.

Paul. I care not :
It is an Heretique that makes the fire,
Not fhe which burnes in't. Ile not call you Tyrant:
But this moft cruell vfage of your Queene
(Not able to produce more accufation
Then your owne weake-hindg'd Fancy) fomthing fauors
Of Tyrannie, and will ignoble make you,
Yea, fcandalous to the World.

Leo. On your Allegeance,
Out of the Chamber with her. Were I a Tyrant,
Where were her life? fhe durft not call me fo,
If fhe did know me one. Away with her.

Paul. I pray you doe not pufh me, Ile be gone.
Looke to your Babe (my Lord) 'tis yours: *Ioue* fend her
A better guiding Spirit. What needs thefe hands?
You that are thus fo tender o're his Follyes,
Will neuer doe him good, not one of you.
So, fo : Farewell, we are gone.   *Exit.*

Leo. Thou (Traytor) haft fet on thy Wife to this.
My Child? away with't? euen thou, that haft
A heart fo tender o're it, take it hence,
And fee it inftantly confum'd with fire.
Euen thou, and none but thou. Take it vp ftraight:
Within this houre bring me word 'tis done,
(And by good teftimonie) or at thy perill,
With what thou elfe call'ft thine : if thou refufe,
And wilt encounter with my Wrath, fay fo ;
The Baftard-braynes with thefe my proper hands
Shall I dafh out. Goe, take it to the fire,
For thou fett'ft on thy Wife.

Antig. I did not, Sir :
Thefe Lords, my Noble Fellowes, if they pleafe,
Can cleare me in't.

Lords. We can : my Royall Liege,
He is not guiltie of her comming hither.

Leo. You're lyers all.

Lord. Befeech your Highneffe, giue vs better credit:
We haue alwayes truly feru'd you, and befeech'
So to efteeme of vs : and on our knees we begge,
(As recompence of our deare feruices
Paft, and to come) that you doe change this purpofe,
Which being fo horrible, fo bloody, muft
Lead on to fome foule Iffue. We all kneele.

Leo. I am a Feather for each Wind that blows :
Shall I liue on, to fee this Baftard kneele,
And call me Father? better burne it now,
Then curfe it then. But be it : let it liue.
It fhall not neyther. You Sir, come you hither :
You that haue beene fo tenderly officious
With Lady *Margerie*, your Mid-wife there,
To faue this Baftards life; for 'tis a Baftard,
So fure as this Beard's gray. What will you aduenture,
To faue this Brats life?

Antig. Any thing (my Lord)
That my abilitie may vndergoe,
And Nobleneffe impofe : at leaft thus much ;
Ile pawne the little blood which I haue left,
To faue the Innocent : any thing poffible.

Leo. It fhall be poffible : Sweare by this Sword
Thou wilt performe my bidding.

Antig. I will (my Lord.)

Leo. Marke, and performe it : feeft thou? for the faile
Of any point in't, fhall not onely be
Death to thy felfe, but to thy lewd-tongu'd Wife,
(Whom for this time we pardon) We enioyne thee,
As thou art Liege-man to vs, that thou carry
This female Baftard hence, and that thou beare it
To fome remote and defart place, quite out
Of our Dominions; and that there thou leaue it
(Without more mercy) to it owne protection,
And fauour of the Climate : as by ftrange fortune
It came to vs, I doe in Iuftice charge thee,
On thy Soules perill, and thy Bodyes torture,
That thou commend it ftrangely to fome place,
Where Chance may nurfe, or end it : take it vp.

Antig. I fweare to doe this: though a prefent death
Had beene more mercifull. Come on (poore Babe)
Some powerfull Spirit inftruct the Kytes and Rauens
To be thy Nurfes. Wolues and Beares, they fay,
(Cafting their fauageneffe afide) haue done
Like offices of Pitty. Sir, be profperous
In more then this deed do's require ; and Bleffing
Againft this Crueltie, fight on thy fide
(Poore Thing, condemn'd to loffe.)   *Exit.*

Leo. No : Ile not reare
Anothers Iffue.   *Enter a Seruant.*

Seru. Pleafe ' your Highneffe, Pofts
From thofe you fent to th'Oracle, are come
An houre fince : *Cleomines* and *Dion*,
Being well arriu'd from Delphos, are both landed,
Hafting to th'Court.

Lord. So pleafe you (Sir) their fpeed
Hath beene beyond accompt.

Leo. Twentie three dayes
They haue beene abfent : 'tis good fpeed : fore-tells
The great *Apollo* fuddenly will haue

The

The truth of this appeare : Prepare you Lords,
Summon a Seffion, that we may arraigne
Our moſt diſloyall Lady : for as ſhe hath
Been publikely accus'd, ſo ſhall ſhe haue
A iuſt and open Triall. While ſhe liues,
My heart will be a burthen to me. Leaue me,
And thinke vpon my bidding.   *Exeunt.*

Actus Tertius. Scena Prima.

Enter Cleomines and Dion.

Cleo. The Clymat's delicate, the Ayre moſt ſweet,
Fertile the Iſle, the Temple much ſurpaſſing
The common prayſe it beares.
  Dion. I ſhall report,
For moſt it caught me, the Celeſtiall Habits,
(Me thinkes I ſo ſhould terme them) and the reuerence
Of the graue Wearers. O, the Sacrifice,
How ceremonious, ſolemne, and vn-earthly
It was i'th'Offring?
  Cleo. But of all, the burſt
And the eare-deaff'ning Voyce o'th'Oracle,
Kin to *Ioues* Thunder, ſo ſurpriz'd my Sence,
That I was nothing.
  Dio. If th'euent o'th'Iourney
Proue as ſucceſſefull to the Queene (O be't ſo)
As it hath beene to vs, rare, pleaſant, ſpeedie,
The time is worth the vſe on't.
  Cleo. Great *Apollo*
Turne all to th'beſt : theſe Proclamations,
So forcing faults vpon *Hermione*,
I little like.
  Dio. The violent carriage of it
Will cleare, or end the Buſineſſe, when the Oracle
(Thus by *Apollo's* great Diuine ſeal'd vp)
Shall the Contents diſcouer : ſomething rare
Euen then will ruſh to knowledge. Goe: freſh Horſes,
And gracious be the iſſue.   *Exeunt.*

Scæna Secunda.

Enter Leontes, Lords, Officers : Hermione (as to her
Triall) Ladies : Cleomines, Dion.

Leo. This Seſſions (to our great griefe we pronounce)
Euen puſhes 'gainſt our heart. The partie try'd,
The Daughter of a King, our Wife, and one
Of vs too much belou'd. Let vs be clear'd
Of being tyrannous, ſince we ſo openly
Proceed in Iuſtice, which ſhall haue due courſe,
Euen to the Guilt, or the Purgation :
Produce the Priſoner.
  Officer. It is his Highneſſe pleaſure, that the Queene
Appeare in perſon, here in Court.   *Silence.*
  Leo. Reade the Indictment.
  Officer. Hermione, *Queene to the worthy* Leontes, *King*
of Sicilia, thou art here accuſed and arraigned of High Trea-
ſon, in committing Adultery with Polixenes *King of Bohemia,*
and conſpiring with Camillo *to take away the Life of our Soue-*
raigne Lord the King, thy Royall Husband: the pretence whereof
being by circumſtances partly layd open, thou (Hermione) *con-*
trary to the Faith and Allegeance of a true Subiect, didſt coun-
ſaile and ayde them, for their better ſafetie, to flye away by
Night.
  Her. Since what I am to ſay, muſt be but that
Which contradicts my Accuſation, and
The teſtimonie on my part, no other
But what comes from my ſelfe, it ſhall ſcarce boot me
To ſay, Not guiltie : mine Integritie
Being counted Falſehood, ſhall (as I expreſſe it)
Be ſo receiu'd. But thus, if Powres Diuine
Behold our humane Actions (as they doe)
I doubt not then, but Innocence ſhall make
Falſe Accuſation bluſh, and Tyrannie
Tremble at Patience. You (my Lord) beſt know
(Whom leaſt will ſeeme to doe ſo) my paſt life
Hath beene as continent, as chaſte, as true,
As I am now vnhappy ; which is more
Then Hiſtorie can patterne, though deuis'd,
And play'd, to take Spectators. For behold me,
A Fellow of the Royall Bed, which owe
A Moitie of the Throne : a great Kings Daughter,
The Mother to a hopefull Prince, here ſtanding
To prate and talke for Life, and Honor, ſore
Who pleaſe to come, and heare. For Life, I prize it
As I weigh Griefe (which I would ſpare:) For Honor,
'Tis a deriuatiue from me to mine,
And onely that I ſtand for. I appeale
To your owne Conſcience (Sir) before *Polixenes*
Came to your Court, how I was in your grace,
How merited to be ſo : Since he came,
With what encounter ſo vncurrant, I
Haue ſtrayn'd t'appeare thus ; if one iot beyond
The bound of Honor, or in act, or will
That way enclining, hardned be the hearts
Of all that heare me, and my neer'ſt of Kin
Cry fie vpon my Graue.
  Leo. I ne're heard yet,
That any of theſe bolder Vices wanted
Leſſe Impudence to gaine-ſay what they did,
Then to performe it firſt.
  Her. That's true enough,
Though 'tis a ſaying (Sir) not due to me.
  Leo. You will not owne it.
  Her. More then Miſtreſſe of,
Which comes to me in name of Fault, I muſt not
At all acknowledge. For *Polixenes*
(With whom I am accus'd) I doe confeſſe
I lou'd him, as in Honor he requir'd :
With ſuch a kind of Loue, as might become
A Lady like me ; with a Loue, euen ſuch,
So, and no other, as your ſelfe commanded :
Which, not to haue done, I thinke had been in me
Both Diſobedience, and Ingratitude
To you, and toward your Friend, whoſe Loue had ſpoke,
Euen ſince it could ſpeake, from an Infant, freely,
That it was yours. Now for Conſpiracie,
I know not how it taſtes, though it be diſh'd
For me to try how : All I know of it,
Is, that *Camillo* was an honeſt man ;
And why he left your Court, the Gods themſelues
(Wotting no more then I) are ignorant.
  Leo. You knew of his departure, as you know
What you haue vnderta'ne to doe in's abſence.

                                        Her. Sir,

Her. Sir,
You fpeake a Language that I vnderftand not :
My Life ftands in the leuell of your Dreames,
Which Ile lay downe.

Leo. Your Aftions are my Dreames.
You had a Baftard by *Polixenes*,
And I but dream'd it : As you were paft all fhame,
(Thofe of your Faft are fo) fo paft all truth;
Which to deny,concernes more then auailes: for as
Thy Brat hath been caft out, like to it felfe,
No Father owning it(which is indeed
More criminall in thee, then it) fo thou
Shalt feele our Iuftice; in whofe eafieft paffage,
Looke for no leffe then death.

Her. Sir, fpare your Threats :
The Bugge which you would fright me with, I feeke:
To me can Life be no commoditie;
The crowne and comfort of my Life(your Fauor)
I doe giue loft, for I doe feele it gone,
But know not how it went. My fecond Ioy,
And firft Fruits of my body, from his prefence
I am bar'd, like one infeftious. My third comfort
(Star'd moft vnluckily) is from my breaft
(The innocent milke in it moft innocent mouth)
Hal'd out to murther. My felfe on euery Poft
Proclaym'd a Strumpet: With immodeft hatred
The Child-bed priuiledge deny'd, which longs
To Women of all fafhion. Laftly, hurried
Here, to this place, i'th' open ayre, before
I haue got ftrength of limit. Now(my Liege)
Tell me what bleffings I haue here aliue,
That I fhould feare to die? Therefore proceed :
But yet heare this : miftake me not : no Life,
(I prize it not a ftraw) but for mine Honor,
Which I would free: if I fhall be condemn'd
Vpon furmizes (all proofes fleeping elfe),
But what your Iealoufies awake) I tell you
'Tis Rigor, and not Law. Your Honors all,
I doe referre me to the Oracle :
Apollo be my Iudge.

Lord. This your requeft
Is altogether iuft : therefore bring forth
(And in *Apollo's* Name) his Oracle.

Her. The Emperor of Ruffia was my Father.
Oh that he were aliue, and here beholding
His Daughters Tryall : that he did but fee
The flatneffe of my miferie ; yet with eyes
Of Pitty, not Reuenge.

Officer. You here fhal fweare vpon this Sword of Iuftice,
That you (*Cleomines* and *Dion*) haue
Been both at Delphos, and from thence haue brought
This feal'd-vp Oracle, by the Hand deliuer'd
Of great *Apollo's* Prieft ; and that fince then,
You haue not dar'd to breake the holy Seale,
Nor read the Secrets in't.

Cleo Dio. All this we fweare.

Leo. Breake vp the Seales, and read.

Officer. Hermione *is chaft*, Polixenes *blameleffe*, Camillo
a true Subieft, Leontes *a iealous Tyrant, his innocent Babe
truly begotten, and the King fhall liue without an Heire, if that
which is loft, be not found.*

Lords. Now bleffed be the great *Apollo.*

Her. Prayfed.

Leo. Haft thou read truth?

Offic. I(my Lord) euen fo as it is here fet downe.

Leo. There is no truth at all i'th'Oracle :

The Seffions fhall proceed: this is meere falfehood.

Ser. My Lord the King : the King ?

Leo. What is the bufineffe ?

Ser. O Sir, I fhall be hated to report it.
The Prince your Sonne, with meere conceit, and feare
Of the Queenes fpeed, is gone.

Leo. How? gone?

Ser. Is dead.

Leo. Apollo's angry, and the Heauens themfelues
Doe ftriike at my Iniuftice. How now there ?

Paul. This newes is mortall to the Queene:Look downe
And fee what Death is doing.

Leo. Take her hence :
Her heart is but o're-charg'd : fhe will recouer.
I haue too much beleeu'd mine owne fufpition :
'Befeech you tenderly apply to her
Some remedies for life. *Apollo* pardon
My great prophaneneffe 'gainft thine Oracle.
Ile reconcile me to *Polixenes*,
New woe my Queene, recall the good *Camillo*
(Whom I proclaime a man of Truth, of Mercy:)
For being tranfported by my Iealoufies
To bloody thoughts, and to reuenge, I chofe
Camillo for the minifter, to poyfon
My friend *Polixenes*: which had been done,
But that the good mind of *Camillo* tardied
My fwift command : though I with Death, and with
Reward, did threaten and encourage him,
Not doing it, and being done : he(moft humane,
And fill'd with Honor) to my Kingly Gueft
Vnclafp'd my praftife, quit his fortunes here
(Which you knew great) and to the hazard
Of all Incertainties, himfelfe commended,
No richer then his Honor : How he glifters
Through my Ruft? and how his Pietie
Do's my deeds make the blacker ?

Paul. Woe the while !
O cut my Lace, leaft my heart(cracking it)
Breake too.

Lord. What fit is this? good Lady?

Paul. What ftudied torments(Tyrant)haft for me ?
What Wheeles?Racks? Fires? What flaying? boyling?
In Leads, or Oyles? What old, or newer Torture
Muft I receiue? whofe euery word deferues
To tafte of thy moft worft. Thy Tyranny
(Together working with thy Iealoufies,
Fancies too weake for Boyes, too greene and idle
For Girles of Nine) O thinke what they haue done,
And then run mad indeed : ftarke-mad: for all
Thy by-gone fooleries were but fpices of it.
That thou betrayed'ft *Polixenes*,'twas nothing,
(That did but fhew thee, of a Foole, inconftant,
And damnable ingratefull:) Nor was't much,
Thou would'ft haue poyfon'd good *Camillo's* Honor,
To haue him kill a King : poore Trefpaffes,
More monftrous ftanding by : whereof I reckon
The cafting forth to Crowes, thy Baby-daughter,
To be or none, or little ; though a Deuill
Would haue fhed water out of fire, ere don't :
Nor is't direftly layd to thee, the death
Of the young Prince, whofe honorable thoughts
(Thoughts high for one fo tender) cleft the heart
That could conceiue a groffe and foolifh Sire
Blemifh'd his gracious Dam : this is not, no ,
Layd to thy anfwere: but the laft: O Lords,
When I haue faid, cry woe: the Queene, the Queene,

The

The fweet'ft. deer'ft creature's dead:& vengeance for't
Not drop'd downe yet.
  Lord. The higher powres forbid.
  Pau. I fay fhe's dead : Ile fwear't. If word, nor oath
Preuaile not, go and fee : if you can bring
Tincture, or luftre in her lip, her eye
Heate outwardly, or breath within, Ile ferue you
As I would do the Gods. But, O thou Tyrant,
Do not repent thefe things, for they are beauier
Then all thy woes can ftirre : therefore betake thee
To nothing but difpaire. A thoufand knees,
Ten thoufand yeares together, naked, fafting,
Vpon a barren Mountaine, and ftill Winter
In ftorme perpetuall, could not moue the Gods
To looke that way thou wer't.
  Leo. Go on, go on :
Thou canft not fpeake too much, I haue deferu'd
All tongues to talke their bittreft.
  Lord. Say no more ;
How ere the bufineffe goes, you haue made fault
I'th boldneffe of your fpeech.
  Pau. I am forry for't ;
All faults I make, when I fhall come to know them,
I do repent : Alas, I haue fhew'd too much
The rafhneffe of a woman : he is toucht
To th'Noble heart. What's gone, and what's paft helpe
Should be paft greefe : Do not receiue affliction
At my petition ; I befeech you, rather
Let me be punifh'd, that haue minded you
Of what you fhould forget. Now (good my Liege)
Sir, Royall Sir, forgiue a foolifh woman :
The loue I bore your Queene (Lo, foole againe)
Ile fpeake of her no more, nor of your Children :
Ile not remember of my owne Lord,
(Who is loft too:) take your patience to you,
And Ile fay nothing.
  Leo. Thou didft fpeake but well,
When moft the truth : which I receyue much better,
Then to be pittied of thee. Prethee bring me
To the dead bodies of my Queene, and Sonne,
One graue fhall be for both : Vpon them fhall
The caufes of their death appeare (vnto
Our fhame perpetuall) once a day, Ile vifit
The Chappell where they lye, and teares fhed there
Shall be my recreation. So long as Nature
Will beare vp with this exercife, fo long
I dayly vow to vfe it. Come, and leade me
To thefe forrowes.   *Exeunt*

Scæna Tertia.

Enter Antigonus, a Marriner, Babe, Sheepe-
heard, and Clowne.

  Ant. Thou art perfect then, our fhip hath toucht vpon
The Defarts of *Bohemia.*
  Mar. I (my Lord) and feare
We haue Landed in ill time : the skies looke grimly,
And threaten prefent blufters. In my confcience
The heauens with that we haue in hand, are angry,
And frowne vpon's.
  Ant. Their facred wil's be done : go get a-boord,
Looke to thy barke, Ile not be long before

I call vpon thee.
  Mar. Make your beft hafte, and go not
Too-farre i'th Land : 'tis like to be lowd weather,
Befides this place is famous for the Creatures
Of prey, that keepe vpon't.
  Antig. Go thou away,
Ile follow inftantly.
  Mar. I am glad at heart
To be fo ridde o'th bufineffe.   *Exit*
  Ant. Come, poore babe ;
I haue heard (but not beleeu'd) the Spirits o'th' dead
May walke againe : if fuch thing be, thy Mother
Appear'd to me laft night : for ne're was dreame
So like a waking. To me comes a creature,
Sometimes her head on one fide, fome another,
I neuer faw a veffell of like forrow
So fill'd, and fo becomming : in pure white Robes
Like very fanctity fhe did approach
My Cabine where I lay : thrice bow'd before me,
And (gafping to begin fome fpeech) her eyes
Became two fpouts ; the furie fpent, anon
Did this breake from her. Good *Antigonus,*
Since Fate (againft thy better difpofition)
Hath made thy perfon for the Thower-out
Of my poore babe, according to thine oath,
Places remote enough are in *Bohemia,*
There weepe, and leaue it crying : and for the babe
Is counted loft for euer, *Perdita*
I prethee call't : For this vngentle bufineffe
Put on thee, by my Lord, thou ne're fhalt fee
Thy Wife *Paulina* more : and fo, with fhriekes
She melted into Ayre. Affrighted much,
I did in time collect my felfe, and thought
This was fo, and no flumber : Dreames, are toyes,
Yet for this once, yea fuperftitioufly,
I will be fquar'd by this. I do beleeue
Hermione hath fuffer'd death, and that
Apollo would (this being indeede the iffue
Of King *Polixenes*) it fhould heere be laide
(Either for life, or death) vpon the earth
Of it's right Father. Bloffome, fpeed thee well,
There lye, and there thy charracter : there thefe,
Which may if Fortune pleafe, both breed thee (pretty)
And ftill reft thine. The ftorme beginnes, poore wretch,
That for thy mothers fault, art thus expos'd
To loffe, and what may follow. Weepe I cannot,
But my heart bleedes : and moft accurft am I
To be by oath enioyn'd to this. Farewell,
The day frownes more and more : thou'rt like to haue
A lullabie too rough : I neuer faw
The heauens fo dim, by day. A fauage clamor ?
Well may I get a-boord : This is the Chace,
I am gone for euer.   *Exit purfued by a Beare.*
  Shep. I would there were no age betweene ten and
three and twenty, or that youth would fleep out the reft :
for there is nothing (in the betweene) but getting wenches with childe, wronging the Auncientry, ftealing,
fighting, hearke you now : would any but thefe boylde-
braines of nineteene, and two and twenty hunt this weather ? They haue fcarr'd away two of my beft Sheepe,
which I feare the Wolfe will fooner finde then the Maifter ; if any where I haue them, 'tis by the fea-fide, brou-
zing of Iuy. Good-lucke (and't be thy will) what haue
we heere ? Mercy on's, a Barne ? A very pretty barne ? A
boy, or a Childe I wonder ? (A pretty one, a verie prettie
one) fure fome Scape ; Though I am not bookifh, yet I
                                     can

can reade Waiting-Gentlewoman in the ſcape: this has
beene ſome ſtaire-worke, ſome Trunke-worke, ſome be-
hinde-doore worke: they were warmer that got this,
then the poore Thing is heere. Ile take it vp for pity, yet
Ile tarry till my ſonne come: he hallow'd but euen now.
Whoa-ho-hoa.

Enter Clowne.

Clo. Hilloa, loa.
Shep. What? art ſo neere? If thou'lt ſee a thing to
talke on, when thou art dead and rotten, come hither:
what ayl'ſt thou, man?
Clo. I haue ſeene two ſuch ſights, by Sea & by Land:
but I am not to ſay it is a Sea, for it is now the skie, betwixt the Firmament and it, you cannot thruſt a bodkins
point.
Shep. Why boy, how is it?
Clo. I would you did but ſee how it chafes, how it ra-
ges, how it takes vp the ſhore, but that's not to the point:
Oh, the moſt pitteous cry of the poore ſoules, ſometimes
to ſee 'em, and not to ſee 'em: Now the Shippe boaring
the Moone with her maine Maſt, and anon ſwallowed
with yeſt and froth, as you'ld thruſt a Corke into a hogſhead. And then for the Land-ſeruice, to ſee how the
Beare tore out his ſhoulder-bone, how he cride to mee
for helpe, and ſaid his name was *Antigonus*, a Nobleman:
But to make an end of the Ship, to ſee how the Sea flap-
dragon'd it: but firſt, how the poore ſoules roared, and
the ſea mock'd them: and how the poore Gentleman roared, and the Beare mock'd him, both roaring lowder
then the ſea, or weather.
Shep. Name of mercy, when was this boy?
Clo. Now, now: I haue not wink'd ſince I ſaw theſe
ſights: the men are not yet cold vnder water, nor the
Beare halfe din'd on the Gentleman: he's at it now.
Shep. Would I had bin by, to haue help'd the olde
man.
Clo. I would you had beene by the ſhip ſide, to haue
help'd her; there your charity would haue lack'd footing.
Shep. Heauy matters, heauy matters: but looke thee
heere boy. Now bleſſe thy ſelfe: thou met'ſt with things
dying, I with things new borne: Here's a ſight for thee:
Looke thee, a bearing-cloath for a Squires childe: looke
thee heere, take vp, take vp (Boy:) open't: ſo, let's ſee, it
was told me I ſhould be rich by the Fairies. This is ſome
Changeling: open't: what's within, boy?
Clo. You're a mad olde man: If the ſinnes of your
youth are forgiuen you, you're well to liue. Golde, all
Gold.
Shep. This is Fairy Gold boy, and 'twill proue ſo: vp
with't, keepe it cloſe: home, home, the next way. We
are luckie (boy) and to bee ſo ſtill requires nothing but
ſecrecie. Let my ſheepe go: Come (good boy) the next
way home.
Clo. Go you the next way with your Findings, Ile go
ſee if the Beare bee gone from the Gentleman, and how
much he hath eaten: they are neuer curſt but when they
are hungry: if there be any of him left, Ile bury him.
Shep. That's a good deed: if thou mayeſt diſcerne by
that which is left of him, what he is, fetch me to th'ſight
of him.
Clowne. 'Marry will I: and you ſhall helpe to put him
i'th'ground.
Shep. 'Tis a lucky day, boy, and wee'l do good deeds
on't *Exeunt*

Actus Quartus. Scena Prima.

Enter Time, the Chorus.

Time. I that pleaſe ſome, try all: both ioy and terror
Of good, and bad: that makes, and vnfolds error,
Now take vpon me (in the name of Time)
To vſe my wings: Impute it not a crime
To me, or my ſwift paſſage, that I ſlide
Ore ſixteene yeeres, and leaue the growth vntride
Of that wide gap, ſince it is in my powre
To orethrow Law, and in one ſelfe-borne howre
To plant, and ore-whelme Cuſtome. Let me paſſe
The ſame I am, ere ancient'ſt Order was,
Or what is now receiu'd. I witneſſe to
The times that brought them in, ſo ſhall I do
To th'freſheſt things now reigning, and make ſtale
The gliſtering of this preſent, as my Tale
Now ſeemes to it: your patience this allowing,
I turne my glaſſe, and giue my Scene ſuch growing
As you had ſlept betweene: *Leontes* leauing
Th'effects of his fond iealouſies, ſo greeuing
That he ſhuts vp himſelfe. Imagine me
(Gentle Spectators) that I now may be
In faire Bohemia, and remember well,
I mentioned a ſonne o'th'Kings, which *Florizell*
I now name to you: and with ſpeed ſo pace
To ſpeake of *Perdita*, now growne in grace
Equall with wond'ring. What of her inſues
I liſt not propheſie: but let Times newes
Be knowne when 'tis brought forth. A ſhepherds daugh-
And what to her adheres, which followes after, (ter
Is th'argument of Time: of this allow,
If euer you haue ſpent time worſe, ere now:
If neuer, yet that Time himſelfe doth ſay,
He wiſhes earneſtly, you neuer may. *Exit.*

Scena Secunda.

Enter Polixenes, and Camillo.

Pol. I pray thee (good *Camillo*) be no more importunate: 'tis a ſickneſſe denying thee any thing: a death to
grant this.
Cam. It is fifteene yeeres ſince I ſaw my Countrey:
though I haue (for the moſt part) bin ayred abroad, I deſire to lay my bones there. Beſides, the penitent King
(my Maſter) hath ſent for me, to whoſe feeling ſorrowes
I might be ſome allay, or I oreweene to thinke ſo) which
is another ſpurre to my departure.
Pol. As thou lou'ſt me (*Camillo*) wipe not out the reſt
of thy ſeruices, by leauing me now: the neede I haue of
thee, thine owne goodneſſe hath made: better not to
haue had thee, then thus to want thee, thou hauing made
me Buſineſſes, (which none (without thee) can ſuffici-
ently manage) muſt either ſtay to execute them thy ſelfe,
or take away with thee the very ſeruices thou haſt done:
which if I haue not enough conſidered (as too much I
cannot) to bee more thankefull to thee, ſhall bee my ſtudie, and my profite therein, the heaping friendſhippes.
Of that fatall Countrey Sicillia, prethee ſpeake no more,
whoſe very naming, punniſhes me with the remembrance

B b of

of that penitent (as thou calſt him) and reconciled King my brother, whoſe loſſe of his moſt precious Queene & Children, are euen now to be a-freſh lamented. Say to me, when ſaw'ſt thou the Prince *Florizell* my ſon? Kings are no leſſe vnhappy, their iſſue, not being gracious, then they are in looſing them, when they haue approued their Vertues.

Cam. Sir, it is three dayes ſince I ſaw the Prince: what his happier affayres may be, are to me vnknowne : but I haue (miſſingly) noted, he is of late much retyred from Court, and is leſſe frequent to his Princely exerciſes then formerly he hath appeared.

Pol. I haue conſidered ſo much (*Camillo*) and with ſome care, ſo farre, that I haue eyes vnder my ſeruice, which looke vpon his remouedneſſe: from whom I haue this Intelligence, that he is ſeldome from the houſe of a moſt homely ſhepheard : a man (they ſay) that from very nothing, and beyond the imagination of his neighbors, is growne into an vnſpeakable eſtate.

Cam. I haue heard (ſir) of ſuch a man , who hath a daughter of moſt rare note : the report of her is extended more, then can be thought to begin from ſuch a cottage

Pol. That's likewiſe part of my Intelligence : but(I feare) the Angle that pluckes our ſonne thither. Thou ſhalt accompany vs to the place, where we will (not appearing what we are)haue ſome queſtion with the ſhepheard ; from whoſe ſimplicity, I thinke it not vneaſie to get the cauſe of my ſonnes reſort thether. 'Prethe be my preſent partner in this buſines, and lay aſide the thoughts of Sicillia.

Cam. I willingly obey your command.

Pol. My beſt *Camillo*, we muſt diſguiſe our ſelues. *Exit*

Scena Tertia.

Enter Autolicus ſinging.
When Daffadils begin to peere,
With heigh the Doxy ouer the dale,
Why then comes in the ſweet o'the yeere,
For the red blood raigns in ỹ winters pale.

The white ſheete bleaching on the hedge,
With hey the ſweet birds, O how they ſing:
Doth ſet my pug ging tooth an edge,
For a quart of Ale is a diſh for a King.

The Larke, that tirra-Lyra chaunts,
With heigh, the Thruſh and the Iay :
Are Summer ſongs for me and my Aunts
While we lye tumbling in the hay.

I haue ſeru'd Prince *Florizell*, and in my time wore three pile, but now I am out of ſeruice.

But ſhall I go mourne for that (my deere)
the pale Moone ſhines by night :
And when I wander here, and there
I then do moſt go right.
If Tinkers may haue leaue to liue,
and beare the Sow-skin Bowget,
Then my account I well may giue,
and in the Stockes auouch-it.

My Trafficke is ſheetes : when the Kite builds, looke to leſſer Linnen. My Father nam'd me *Autolicus*, who be-

ing (as I am) lytter'd vnder Mercurie , was likewiſe a ſnapper-vp of vnconſidered trifles : With Dye and drab, I purchas'd this Capariſon, and my Reuennew is the ſilly Cheate, Gallowes, and Knocke, are too powerfull on the Highway. Beating and hanging are terrors to mee : For the life to come, I ſleepe out the thought of it. A prize, a prize.

Enter Clowne.

Clo. Let me ſee, euery Leauen-weather toddes, euery tod yeeldes pound and odde ſhilling : fifteene hundred ſhorne, what comes the wooll too ?

Aut. If the ſprindge hold, the Cocke's mine.

Clo. I cannot do't without Compters. Let mee ſee, what am I to buy for our Sheepe-ſhearing-Feaſt? Three pound of Sugar, fiue pound of Currence, Rice: What will this ſiſter of mine do with Rice ? But my father hath made her Miſtris of the Feaſt, and ſhe layes it on . Shee hath made-me four and twenty Noſe-gayes for the ſhearers (three-man ſong-men, all, and very good ones) but they are moſt of them Meanes and Baſes ; but one Puritan amongſt them, and he ſings Pſalmes to horne-pipes. I muſt haue Saffron to colour the Warden Pies, Mace : Dates, none : that's out of my note : Nutmegges, ſeuen ; a Race or two of Ginger, but that I may begge : Foure pound of Prewyns, and as many of Reyſons o'th Sun.

Aut. Oh, that euer I was borne.

Clo. I'th'name of me.

Aut. Oh helpe me, helpe mee : plucke but off theſe ragges : and then, death, death.

Clo. Alacke poore ſoule, thou haſt need of more rags to lay on thee, rather then haue theſe off.

Aut. Oh ſir, the loathſomneſſe of them offend mee, more then the ſtripes I haue receiued, which are mightie ones and millions.

Clo. Alas poore man, a million of beating may come to a great matter.

Aut. I am rob'd ſir, and beaten : my money, and apparrell tane from me, and theſe dereſtable things put vp-on me.

Clo. What, by a horſe-man, or a foot-man?

Aut. A footman (ſweet ſir) a footman.

Clo. Indeed, he ſhould be a footman, by the garments he has left with thee : If this bee a horſemans Coate , it hath ſeene very hot ſeruice. Lend me thy hand, Ile helpe thee. Come, lend me thy hand.

Aut. Oh good ſir, tenderly, oh.

Clo. Alas poore ſoule.

Aut. Oh good ſir, ſoftly, good ſir : I feare (ſir) my ſhoulder-blade is out.

Clo. How now? Canſt ſtand ?

Aut. Softly, deere ſir : good ſir, ſoftly : you ha done me a charitable office.

Clo. Doeſt lacke any mony ? I haue a little mony for thee.

Aut. No, good ſweet ſir : no, I beſeech you ſir: I haue a Kinſman not paſt three quarters of a mile hence , vnto whome I was going : I ſhall there haue money, or anie thing I want : Offer me no money I pray you, that killes my heart.

Clow. What manner of Fellow was hee that robb'd you ?

Aut. A fellow (ſir) that I haue knowne to goe about with Troll-my-dames: I knew him once a ſeruant of the Prince : I cannot tell good ſir, for which of his Vertues it was, but hee was certainely Whipt out of the Court.

Clo.

Clo. His vices you would fay : there's no vertue whipt
out of the Court : they cherifh it to make it ftay there ;
and yet it will no more but abide.

Aut. Vices I would fay (Sir.) I know this man well,
he hath bene fince an Ape-bearer, then a Proceffe-feruer
(a Bayliffe) then hee compaft a Motion of the Prodigall
fonne, and married a Tinkers wife, within a Mile where
my Land and Liuing lyes ; and (hauing flowne ouer many knauifh profeffions) he fetled onely in Rogue : fome
call him *Autolicus.*

Clo. Out vpon him : Prig, for my life Prig:he haunts
Wakes, Faires, and Beare-baitings.

Aut. Very true fir : he fir hee : that's the Rogue that
put me into this apparrell.

Clo. Not a more cowardly Rogue in all *Bohemia* ; If
you had but look'd bigge, and fpit at him, hee'ld haue
runne.

Aut. I muft confeffe to you (fir) I am no fighter : I am
falfe of heart that way, & that he knew I warrant him.

Clo. How do you now ?

Aut. Sweet fir, much better then I was : I can ftand,
and walke : I will euen take my leaue of you, & pace foftly towards my Kinfmans.

Clo. Shall I bring thee on the way ?

Aut. No, good fac'd fir, no fweet fir.

Clo. Then fartheewell, I muft go buy Spices for our
fheepe-fhearing.   *Exit.*

Aut. Profper you fweet fir, Your purfe is not hot e-
nough to purchafe your Spice : Ile be with you at your
fheepe-fhearing too : If I make not this Cheat bring out
another, and the fheerers proue fheepe, let me be vnrold,
and my name put in the booke of Vertue.

Song. *Iog-on, Iog-on, the foot-path way,*
    And merrily hent the Stile-a :
    A merry heart goes all the day,
    Your fad tyres in a Mile-a.   *Exit.*

Scena Quarta.

Enter Florizell, Perdita, Shepherd, Clowne, Polixenes, Ca-
millo, Mopfa, Dorcas, Seruants, Autolicus.

Flo. Thefe your vnvfuall weeds, to each part of you
Do's giue a life : no Shepherdeffe, but *Flora*
Peering in Aprils front. This your fheepe-fhearing,
Is as a meeting of the petty Gods,
And you the Queene on't.

Perd. Sir : my gracious Lord,
To chide at your extreames, it not becomes me :
(Oh pardon, that I name them :) your high felfe
The gracious marke o'th'Land, you haue obfcur'd
With a Swaines wearing : and me (poore lowly Maide)
Moft Goddeffe-like prank'd vp : But that our Feafts
In euery Meffe, haue folly ; and the Feeders
Digeft with a Cuftome, I fhould blufh
To fee you fo attyr'd : fworne I thinke,
To fhew my felfe a glaffe.

Flo. I bleffe the time
When my good Falcon, made her flight a-croffe
Thy Fathers ground.

Perd. Now Ioue afoord you caufe :
To me the difference forges dread (your Greatneffe

Hath not beene vs'd to feare :) euen now I tremble
To thinke your Father, by fome accident
Should paffe this way, as you did : Oh the Fates,
How would he looke, to fee his worke, fo noble,
Vildely bound vp ? What would he fay ? Or how
Should I (in thefe my borrowed Flaunts) behold
The fternneffe of his prefence ?

Flo. Apprehend
Nothing but iollity : the Goddes themfelues
(Humbling their Deities to loue) haue taken
The fhapes of Beafts vpon them. Iupiter,
Became a Bull, and bellow'd : the greene Neptune
A Ram, and bleated : and the Fire-roab'd-God
Golden Apollo, a poore humble Swaine,
As I feeme now. Their transformations,
Were neuer for a peece of beauty, rarer,
Nor in a way fo chafte : fince my defires
Run not before mine honor : nor my Lufts
Burne hotter then my Faith.

Perd. O but Sir,
Your refolution cannot hold, when 'tis
Oppos'd (as it muft be) by th'powre of the King :
One of thefe two muft be necefities,
Which then will fpeake, that you muft change this pur-
Or I my life.   (pofe,

Flo. Thou deer'ft *Perdita,*
With thefe forc'd thoughts, I prethee darken not
The Mirth o'th' Feaft : Or Ile be thine (my Faire)
Or not my Fathers. For I cannot be
Mine owne, nor any thing to any, if
I be not thine. To this I am moft conftant,
Though deftiny fay no. Be merry (Gentle)
Strangle fuch thoughts as thefe, with any thing
That you behold the while. Your guefts are comming :
Lift vp your countenance, as it were the day
Of celebration of that nuptiall, which
We two haue fworne fhall come.

Perd. O Lady Fortune,
Stand you aufpicious.

Flo. See, your Guefts approach,
Addreffe your felfe to entertaine them fprightly,
And let's be red with mirth.

Shep. Fy (daughter) when my old wife liu'd : vpon
This day, fhe was both Pantler, Butler, Cooke,
Both Dame and Seruant : Welcom'd all : feru'd all,
Would fing her fong, and dance her turne : now heere
At vpper end o'th Table; now, i'th middle :
On his fhoulder, and his : her face o'fire
With labour, and the thing fhe tooke to quench it
She would to each one fip. You are retyred,
As if you were a feafted one : and not
The Hofteffe of the meeting : Pray you bid
Thefe vnknowne friends to's welcome, for it is
A way to make vs better Friends, more knowne.
Come, quench your blufhes, and prefent your felfe
That which you are, Miftris i'th'Feaft. Come on,
And bid vs welcome to your fheepe-fhearing,
As your good flocke fhall profper.

Perd. Sir, welcome :
It is my Fathers will, I fhould take on mee
The Hofteffefhip o'th'day : you're welcome fir.
Giue me thofe Flowres there (*Dorcas.*) Reuerend Sirs,
For you, there's Rofemary, and Rue, thefe keepe
Seeming, and fauour all the Winter long :
Grace, and Remembrance be to you both,
And welcome to our Shearing.

              Bb 2   *Pol.*

Pol. Shepherdeſſe,
(A faire one are you:) well you fit our ages
With flowres of Winter.
  Perd. Sir, the yeare growing ancient,
Not yet on ſummers death, nor on the birth
Of trembling winter, the fayreſt flowres o'th ſeaſon
Are our Carnations, and ſtreak'd Gilly-vors,
(Which ſome call Natures baſtards) of that kind
Our ruſticke Gardens barren, and I care not
To get ſlips of them.
  Pol. Wherefore (gentle Maiden)
Do you negleſt them.
  Perd. For I haue heard it ſaid,
There is an Art, which in their pideneſſe ſhares
With great creating-Nature.
  Pol. Say there be :
Yet Nature is made better by no meane,
But Nature makes that Meane : ſo ouer that Art,
(Which you ſay addes to Nature) is an Art
That Nature makes : you ſee (ſweet Maid) we marry
A gentler Sien, to the wildeſt Stocke,
And make conceyue a barke of baſer kinde
By bud of Nobler race. This is an Art
Which do's mend Nature : change it rather, but
The Art it ſelfe, is Nature.
  Perd. So it is.
  Pol. Then make you Garden rich in Gilly'vors,
And do not call them baſtards.
  Perd. Ile not put
The Dible in earth, to ſet one ſlip of them :
No more then were I painted, I would wiſh
This youth ſhould ſay 'twer well : and onely therefore
Deſire to breed by me. Here's flowres for you :
Hot Lauender, Mints, Sauory, Mariorum,
The Mary-gold, that goes to bed with'Sun,
And with him riſes, weeping : Theſe are flowres
Of middle ſummer, and I thinke they are giuen
To men of middle age. Y'are very welcome.
  Cam. I ſhould leaue graſing, were I of your flocke,
And onely liue by gazing.
  Perd. Out alas:
You'ld be ſo leane, that blaſts of Ianuary   (Friend,
Would blow you through and through. Now (my fairſt
I would I had ſome Flowres o'th Spring, that might
Become your time of day : and yours, and yours,
That weare vpon your Virgin-branches yet
Your Maiden-heads growing : O *Proſerpina,*
For the Flowres now, that (frighted) thou let'ſt fall
From *Dyſſes* Waggon : Daffadils,
That come before the Swallow dares, and take
The windes of March with beauty : Violets (dim,
But ſweeter then the lids of *Iuno's* eyes,
Or *Cytherea's* breath) pale Prime-roſes,
That dye vnmarried, ere they can behold
Bright Phœbus in his ſtrength (a Maladie
Moſt incident to Maids:) bold Oxlips, and
The Crowne Imperiall : Lillies of all kinds,
(The Flowre-de-Luce being one.) O, theſe I lacke,
To make you Garlands of) and my ſweet friend,
To ſtrew him o're, and ore.
  Flo. What? like a Coarſe?
  Perd. No, like a banke, for Loue to lye, and play on:
Not like a Coarſe : or if : not to be buried,
But quicke, and in mine armes. Come, take your flours,
Me thinkes I play as I haue ſeene them do
In Whitſon-Paſtorals : Sure this Robe of mine

Do's change my diſpoſition:
  Flo. What you do,
Still betters what is done. When you ſpeake (Sweet)
I'ld haue you do it euer : When you ſing,
I'ld haue you buy, and ſell ſo : ſo giue Almes,
Pray ſo : and for the ord'ring your Affayres,
To ſing them too. When you do dance, I wiſh you
A waue o'th Sea, that you might euer do
Nothing but that : moue ſtill, ſtill ſo :
And owne no other Funſtion. Each your doing,
(So ſingular, in each particular)
Crownes what you are doing, in the preſent deeds,
That all your Aſtes, are Queenes.
  Perd. O *Doricles*,
Your praiſes are too large : but that your youth
And the true blood which peepes fairely through't,
Do plainly giue you out an vnſtain'd Sphepherd
With wiſedome, I might feare (my *Doricles*)
You woo'd me the falſe way.
  Flo. I thinke you haue
As little ſkill to feare, as I haue purpoſe
To put you to't. But come, our dance I pray,
Your hand (my *Perdita*:) ſo Turtles paire
That neuer meane to part.
  Perd. Ile ſweare for 'em.
  Po . This is the prettieſt Low-borne Laſſe, that euer
Ran on the greene-ſord : Nothing ſhe do's, or ſeemes
But ſmackes of ſomething greater then her ſelfe,
Too Noble for this place.
  Cam. He tels her ſomething
That makes her blood looke on't : Good ſooth ſhe is
The Queene of Curds and Creame.
  Clo. Come on: ſtrike vp.
  Dorcas. Mopſa muſt be your Miſtris : marry Garlick
to mend her kiſſing with.
  Mop. Now in good time.
  Clo. Not a word, a word, we ſtand vpon our manners,
Come, ſtrike vp.
     Heere a Daunce of Shepheards and
       Shepheardeſſes.
  Pol. Pray good Shepheard, what faire Swaine is this,
Which dances with your daughter ?
  Shep. They call him *Doricles*, and boaſts himſelfe
To haue a worthy Feeding ; but I haue it
Vpon his owne report, and I beleeue it :
He lookes like ſooth : he ſayes he loues my daughter,
I thinke ſo too ; for neuer gaz'd the Moone
Vpon the water, as hee'l ſtand and reade
As 'twere my daughters eyes : and to be plaine,
I thinke there is not halfe a kiſſe to chooſe
Who loues another beſt.
  Pol. She dances featly.
  Shep. So ſhe do's any thing, though I report it
That ſhould be ſilent : If yong *Doricles*
Do light vpon her, ſhe ſhall bring him that
Which he not dreames of.   *Enter Seruant.*
  Ser. O Maſter : if you did but heare the Pedler at the
doore, you would neuer daunce againe after a Tabor and
Pipe : no, the Bag-pipe could not moue you : hee ſinges
ſeuerall Tunes, faſter then you'l tell money : hee vtters
them as he had eaten ballads, and all mens eares grew to
his Tunes.
  Clo. He could neuer come better : hee ſhall come in :
I loue a ballad but euen too well, if it be dolefull matter
merrily ſet downe : or a very pleaſant thing indeede, and
ſung lamentably.
                             Ser.

Ser. He hath fongs for man, or woman, of all fizes: No Milliner can fo fit his cuftomers with Gloues: he has the prettieft Loue-fongs for Maids, fo without bawdrie (which is ftrange,) with fuch delicate burthens of Dildo's and Fadings: Iump-her, and thump-her; and where fome ftretch-mouth'd Rafcall, would (as it were) meane mifcheefe, and breake a fowle gap into the Matter, hee makes the maid to anfwere, *Whoop, doe me no harme good man* : put's him off, flights him, with *Whoop, doe mee no harme good man.*

Pol. This is a braue fellow.

Clo. Beleeee mee, thou talkeft of an admirable conceited fellow, has he any vnbraided Wares?

Ser. Hee hath Ribbons of all the colours i'th Rainebow ; Points, more then all the Lawyers in *Bohemia*, can learnedly handle, though they come to him by th'groffe: Inckles, Caddyffes, Cambrickes, Lawnes : why he fings em ouer, as they were Gods, or Goddeffes : you would thinke a Smocke were a fhee-Angell, he fo chauntes to the fleeue-hand, and the worke about the fquare on't.

Clo. Pre'thee bring him in, and let him approach finging.

Perd. Forewarne him, that he vfe no fcurrilous words in's tunes.

Clow. You haue of thefe Pedlers, that haue more in them, then youl'd thinke (Sifter.)

Perd. I, good brother, or go about to thinke.

Enter Autolicus finging.

Lawne as white as driuen Snow,
Cypreffe blacke as ere was Crow,
Gloues as fweete as Damaske Rofes,
Maskes for faces, and for nofes :
Bugle-bracelet, Necke-lace Amber,
Perfume for a Ladies Chamber :
Golden Quoifes, and Stomachers
For my Lads, to giue their deers :
Pins, and poaking-fickes of feele.
What Maids lacke from head to heele :
Come buy of me, come:come buy, come buy,
Buy Lads, or elfe your Laffes cry : Come buy.

Clo. If I were not in loue with *Mopfa*, thou fhouldft take no money of me, but being enthrall'd as I am, it will alfo be the bondage of certaine Ribbons and Gloues.

Mop. I was promis'd them againft the Feaft, but they come not too late now.

Dor. He hath promis'd you more rhen that, or there be lyars.

Mop. He hath paid you all he promis'd you: 'May be he has paid you more, which will fhame you to giue him againe.

Clo. Is there no manners left among maids? Will they weare their plackets, where they fhould bear their faces? Is there not milking-time? When you are going to bed? Or kill-hole? To whiftle of thefe fecrets, but you muft be tittle-tatling before all our guefts? 'Tis well they are whifpring:clamor your tongues, and not a word more.

Mop. I haue done ; Come you ptomis'd me a tawdrylace, and a paire of fweet Gloues.

Clo. Haue I not told thee how I was cozen'd by the way, and loft all my money.

Aut. And indeed Sir, there are Cozeners abroad, therfore it behooues men to be wary.

Clo. Feare not thou man, thou fhalt lofe nothing here.

Aut. I hope fo fir, for I haue about me many parcels of charge.

Clo. What haft heere? Ballads?

Mop. Pray now buy fome : I loue a ballet in print, a life, for then we are fure they are true.

Aut. Here's one, to a very dolefull tune, how a Vfurers wife was brought to bed of twenty money baggs at a burthen, and how fhe long'd to eate Adders heads, and Toads carbonado'd.

Mop. Is it true, thinke you?

Aut. Very true, and but a moneth old.

Dor. Bleffe me from marrying a Vfurer.

Aut. Here's the Midwiues name to't : one Mift. *Tale-Porter*, and fiue or fix honeft Wiues, that were prefent. Why fhould I carry lyes abroad?

Mop. 'Pray you now buy it.

Clo. Come-on, lay it by : and let's firft fee moe Ballads : Wee'l buy the other things anon.

Aut. Here's another ballad of a Fifh, that appeared vpon the coaft, on wenfday the fourefcore of April, fortie thoufand fadom aboue water, & fung this ballad againft the hard hearts of maids : it was thought fhe was a Woman, and was turn'd into a cold fifh, for fhe wold not exchange flefh with one that lou'd her : The Ballad is very pittifull, and as true.

Dor. Is it true too, thinke you.

Autol. Fiue Iuftices hands at it, and witneffes more then my packe will hold.

Clo. Lay it by too ; another.

Aut. This is a merry ballad, but a very pretty one.

Mop. Let's haue fome merry ones.

Aut. Why this is a paffing merry one, and goes to the tune of two maids wooing a man : there's fcarfe a Maide weftward but fhe fings it:'tis in requeft, I can tell you.

Mop. We can both fing it : if thou'lt beare a part, thou fhalt heare, 'tis in three parts.

Dor. We had the tune on't, a month agoe.

Aut. I can beare my part, you muft know 'tis my occupation : Haue at it with you.

Song	*Get you hence, for I muft goe*
Aut.	*Where it fits not you to know.*
Dor.	*Whether?*
Mop	*O whether?*
Dor.	*Whether?*
Mop.	*It becomes thy oath full well,*
	Thou to me thy fecrets tell.
Dor:	*Me too : Let me go thether :*
Mop	*Or thou goeft to th'Grange, or Mill,*
Dor:	*If to either thou doft ill,*
Aut:	*Neither.*
Dor:	*What neither?*
Aut:	*Neither :*
Dor:	*Thou haft fworne my Loue to br,*
Mop	*Thou haft fworne it more to mee.*

Then whether goeft? Say whether?

Clo. Wee'l haue this fong out anon by our felues : My Father, and the Gent.are in fad talke, & wee'll not trouble them : Come bring away thy packe after me, Wenches Ile buy for you both:Pedler let's haue the firft choice;folow me girles. *Aut:* And you fhall pay well for 'em.

Song. *Will you buy any Tape, or Lace for your Crpe?*
My dainty Ducke, my deere-a?
Any Silke, any Thred, any Toyes for your head
Of the news't, and fins't, fins't weare-a.
Come to the Pedler, Money's a medler,
That doth vtter all mens ware-a. *Exit*

Seruant. Mayfter, there is three Carters, three Shepherds, three Neat-herds, three Swine-herds y haue made them

Bb 3

themfelues all men of haire, they cal themfelues Saltiers,
and they haue a Dance, which the Wenches fay is a gal-
ly-maufrey of Gambols, becaufe they are not in't : but
they themfelues are o'th'minde (if it bee not too rough
for fome, that know little but bowling) it will pleafe
plentifully.

Shep. Away : Wee'l none on't ; heere has beene too
much homely foolery already. I know (Sir) wee wearie you.

Pol. You wearie thofe that refrefh vs : pray let's fee
thefe foure-threes of Heardfmen.

Ser. One three of them, by their owne report (Sir)
hath danc'd before the King : and not the worft of the
three, but iumpes twelue foote and a halfe by th'fquire.

Shep. Leaue your prating, fince thefe good men are
pleaf'd, let them come in ; but quickly now.

Ser. Why, they ftay at doore Sir.

Heere a Dance of twelue Satyres.

Pol. O Father, you'l know more of that heereafter:
Is it not too farre gone ?'Tis time to part them,
He's fimple, and tels much. How now(faire fhepheard)
Your neart is full of fomething, that do's take
Your minde from feafting. Sooth, when I was yong,
And handed loue, as you do ; I was wont
To load my Shee with knackes : I would haue ranfackt
The Pedlers filken Treafury, and haue powr'd it
To her acceptance : you haue let him go,
And nothing marted with him. If your Laffe
Interpretation fhould abufe, and call this
Your lacke of loue, or bounty, you were ftraited
For a reply at leaft, if you make a care
Of happie holding her.

Flo. Old Sir, I know
She prizes not fuch trifles as thefe are :
The gifts fhe lookes from me, are packt and lockt
Vp in my heart, which I haue giuen already,
But not deliuer'd. O heare me breath my life
Before this ancient Sir, whom (it fhould feeme)
Hath fometime lou'd : I take thy hand, this hand,
As foft as Doues-downe, and as white as it,
Or Ethyopians tooth, or the fan'd fnow, that's bolted
By th'Northerne blafts, twice ore.

Pol. What followes this?
How prettily th'yong Swaine feemes to wafh
The hand, was faire before? I haue put youout,
But to your proteftation : Let me heare
What you profeffe.

Flo. Do, and be witneffe too't.

Pol. And this my neighbour too?

Flo. And he, and more
Then he, and men : the earth, the heauens, and all ;
That were I crown'd the moft Imperiall Monarch
Thereof moft worthy : were I the fayreft youth
That euer made eye fwerue, had force and knowledge
More then was euer mans, I would not prize them
Without her Loue ; for her, employ them all,
Commend them, and condemne them to her feruice,
Or to their owne perdition.

Pol. Fairely offer'd.

Cam. This fhewes a found affection.

Shep. But my daughter,
Say you the like to him.

Per. I cannot fpeake
So well, (nothing fo well) no, nor meane better
By th'patterne of mine owne thoughts, I cut out
The puritie of his.

Shep. Take hands, a bargaine ;
And friends vnknowne, you fhall beare witneffe to't :
I giue my daughter to him, and will make
Her Portion, equall his.

Flo. O, that muft bee
I'th Vertue of your daughter : One being dead,
I fhall haue more then you can dreame of yet,
Enough then for your wonder : but come-on,
Contract vs fore thefe Witneffes.

Shep. Come, your hand :
And daughter, yours.

Pol. Soft Swaine a-while, befeech you,
Haue you a Father ?

Flo. I haue : but what of him ?

Pol. Knowes he of this ?

Flo. He neither do's, nor fhall.

Pol. Me-thinkes a Father,
Is at the Nuptiall of his fonne, a gueft
That beft becomes the Table : Pray you once more
Is not your Father growne incapeable
Of reafonable affayres ? Is he not ftupid
With Age, and altring Rheumes? Can he fpeake ? heare ?
Know man, from man ? Difpute his owne eftate ?
Lies he not bed-rid ? And againe, do's nothing
But what he did, being childifh?

Flo. No good Sir :
He has his health, and ampler ftrength indeede
Then moft haue of his age.

Pol. By my white beard,
You offer him (if this be fo) a wrong
Something vnfilliall : Reafon my fonne
Should choofe himfelfe a wife, but as good reafon
The Father (all whofe ioy is nothing elfe
But faire pofterity) fhould hold fome counfaile
In fuch a bufineffe.

Flo. I yeeld all this ;
But for fome other reafons(my graue Sir)
Which 'tis not fit you know, I not acquaint
My Father of this bufineffe.

Pol. Let him know't.

Flo. He fhall not.

Pol. Prethee let him.

Flo No, he muft not.

Shep. Let him (my fonne) he fhall not need to greeue
At knowing of thy choice.

Flo. Come, come, he muft not :
Marke our Contract.

Pol. Marke your diuorce (yong fir)
Whom fonne I dare not call : Thou art too bafe
To be acknowledge. Thou a Scepters heire,
That thus affects a fheepe-hooke? Thou, old Traitor,
I am forry, that by hanging thee, I can
but fhorten thy life one weeke. And thou, frefh peece
Of excellent Witchcraft, whom of force muft know
The royall Foole thou coap'ft with.

Shep. Oh my heart.

Pol. Ile haue thy beauty fcratcht with briers & made
More homely then thy ftate. For thee (fond boy)
If I may euer know thou doft but figh,
That thou no more fhalt neuer fee this knacke (as neuer
I meane thou fhalt) wee'l barre thee from fucceffion,
Not hold thee of our blood, no not our Kin,
Farre then *Deucalion* off : (marke thou my words)
Follow vs to the Court. Thou Churle, for this time
(Though full of our difpleafure) yet we free thee
From the dead blow of it. And you Enchantment,

Wor-

Worthy enough a Heardſman : yea him too,
That makes himſelfe (but for our Honor therein)
Vnworthy thee. If euer henceforth, thou
Theſe rurall Latches, to his entrance open,
Or hope his body more, with thy embracea,
I will deuiſe a death, as cruell for thee
As thou art tender to't.   *Exit.*

  Perd. Euen heere vndone :
I was not much a-fear'd : for once, or twice
I was about to ſpeake, and tell him plainely,
The ſelfe.ſame Sun, that ſhines vpon his Court,
Hides not his viſage from our Cottage, but
Lookes on alike. Wilt pleaſe you (Sir) be gone ?
I told you what would come of this : Beſeech you
Of your owne ſtate take care : This dreame of mine
Being now awake, Ile Queene it no inch farther,
But milke my Ewes, and weepe.

  Cam. Why how now Father,
Speake ere thou dyeſt.

  Shep. I cannot ſpeake, nor thinke,
Nor dare to know, that which I know : O Sir,
You haue vndone a man of foureſcore three,
That thought to fill his graue in quiet : yea,
To dye vpon the bed my father dy'de,
To lye cloſe by his honeſt bones ; but now
Some Hangman muſt put on my ſhrowd, and lay me
Where no Prieſt ſhouels-in duſt. Oh curſed wretch,
That knew'ſt this was the Prince, and wouldſt aduenture
To mingle faith with him. Vndone, vndone :
If I might dye within this houre, I haue liu'd
To die when I deſire.   *Exit.*

  Flo. Why looke you ſo vpon me ?
I am but ſorry, not affear'd : delaid,
But nothing altred : What I was, I am :
More ſtraining on, for plucking backe ; not following
My leaſh vnwillingly.

  Cam. Gracious my Lord,
You know my Fathers temper : at this time
He will allow no ſpeech : (which I do gheſſe
You do not purpoſe to him:) and as hardly
Will he endure your ſight, as yet I feare ;
Then till the fury of his Highneſſe ſettle
Come not before him.

  Flo. I not purpoſe it :
I thinke *Camillo.*

  Cam. Euen he, my Lord.

  Per. How often haue I told you 'twould be thus ?
How often ſaid my dignity would laſt
But till 'twer knowne ?

  Flo. It cannot faile, but by
The violation of my faith, and then
Let Nature cruſh the ſides o'th earth together,
And marre the ſeeds within. Lift vp thy lookes :
From my ſucceſſion wipe me (Father) I
Am heyre to my affection.

  Cam. Be aduis'd.

  Flo. I am : and by my fancie, if my Reaſon
Will thereto be obedient : I haue reaſon :
If not, my ſences better pleas'd with madneſſe,
Do bid it welcome.

  Cam. This is deſperate (ſir.)

  Flo. So call it : but it do's fulfill my vow:
I needs muſt thinke it honeſty. *Camillo,*
Not for *Bohemia,* nor the pompe that may
Be thereat gleaned : for all the Sun ſees, or
The cloſe earth wombes, or the profound ſeas, hides

In vnknowne fadomes, will I breake my oath
To this my faire belou'd : Therefore, I pray you,
As you haue euer bin my Fathers honour'd friend,
When he ſhall miſſe me, as (in faith I meane not
To ſee him any more) caſt your good counſailes
Vpon his paſsion : Let my ſelfe, and Fortune
Tug for the time to come. This you may know,
And ſo deliuer, I am put to Sea
With her, who heere I cannot hold on ſhore:
And moſt opportune to her neede, I haue
A Veſſell rides faſt by, but not prepar'd
For this deſigne. What courſe I meane to hold
Shall nothing benefit your knowledge, nor
Concerne me the reporting.

  Cam. O my Lord,
I would your ſpirit were eaſier for aduice,
Or ſtronger for your neede.

  Flo. Hearke *Perdita,*
Ile heare you by and by.

  Cam. Hee's irremoueable,
Reſolu'd for flight : Now were I happy if
His going, I could frame to ſerue my turne,
Saue him from danger, do him loue and honor,
Purchaſe the ſight againe of deere *Sicillia,*
And that vnhappy King, my Maſter, whom
I ſo much thirſt to ſee.

  Flo. Now good *Camillo,*
I am ſo fraught with curious buſineſſe, that
I leaue out ceremony.

  Cam. Sir, I thinke
You haue heard of my poore ſeruices, i'th loue
That I haue borne your Father ?

  Flo. Very nobly
Haue you deſeru'd : It is my Fathers Muſicke
To ſpeake your deeds : not little of his care
To haue them recompenc'd, as thought on.

  Cam. Well (my Lord)
If you may pleaſe to thinke I loue the King,
And through him, what's neereſt to him, which is
Your gracious ſelfe ; embrace but my direction,
If your more ponderous and ſetled proiect
May ſuffer alteration. On mine honor,
Ile point you where you ſhall haue ſuch receiuing
As ſhall become your Highneſſe, where you may
Enioy your Miſtris ; from the whom, I ſee
There's no diſiunction to be made, but by
(As heauens forefend) your ruine : Marry her,
And with my beſt endeauors, in your abſence,
Your diſcontenting Father, ſtriue to qualifie
And bring him vp to liking.

  Flo. How *Camillo*
May this (almoſt a miracle) be done ?
That I may call thee ſomething more then man,
And after that truſt to thee.

  Cam. Haue you thought on
A place whereto you'l go ?

  Flo. Not any yet :
But as th'vnthought-on accident is guiltie
To what we wildely do, ſo we profeſſe
Our ſelues to be the ſlaues of chance, and flyes
Of euery winde that blowes.

  Cam. Then liſt to me :
This followes, if you will not change your purpoſe
But vndergo this flight ; make for Sicillia,
And there preſent your ſelfe, and your fayre Princeſſe,
(For ſo I ſee ſhe muſt be) 'fore *Leontes ;*

Shee

She ſhall be habited, as it becomes
The partner of your Bed. Me thinkes I ſee
Leontes opening his free Armes, and weeping
His Welcomes forth:asks thee there Sonne forgiueneſſe,
As 'twere i'th' Fathers perſon: kiſſes the hands
Of your freſh Princeſſe; ore and ore diuides him,
'Twixt his vnkindneſſe, and his Kindneſſe : th'one
He chides to Hell, and bids the other grow
Faſter then Thought, or Time.
  Flo. Worthy *Camillo*,
What colour for my Viſitation, ſhall I
Hold vp before him ?
  Cam. Sent by the King your Father
To greet him, and to giue him comforts. Sir,
The manner of your bearing towards him, with
What you (as from your Father) ſhall deliuer,
Things knowne betwixt vs three, Ile write you downe,
The which ſhall point you forth at euery ſitting
What you muſt ſay: that he ſhall not perceiue,
But that you haue your Fathers Boſome there,
And ſpeake his very Heart.
  Flo. I am bound to you :
There is ſome ſappe in this.
  Cam. A Courſe more promiſing,
Then a wild dedication of your ſelues
To vnpath'd Waters, vndream'd Shores; moſt certaine,
To Miſeries enough : no hope to helpe you,
But as you ſhake off one, to take another :
Nothing ſo certaine, as your Anchors, who
Doe their beſt office, if they can but ſtay you,
Where you'le be loth to be : beſides you know,
Proſperitie's the very bond of Loue,
Whoſe freſh complexion, and whoſe heart together,
Affliction alters.
  Perd. One of theſe is true :
I thinke Affliction may ſubdue the Cheeke,
But not take-in the Mind.
  Cam. Yea ? ſay you ſo ?
There ſhall not, at your Fathers Houſe, theſe ſeuen yeeres
Be borne another ſuch.
  Flo. My good *Camillo*,
She's as forward, of her Breeding, as
She is i'th' reare' our Birth.
  Cam. I cannot ſay, 'tis pitty
She lacks Inſtructions, for ſhe ſeemes a Miſtreſſe
To moſt that teach.
  Perd. Your pardon Sir, for this,
Ile bluſh you Thanks.
  Flo. My prettieſt *Perdita.*
But O, the Thornes we ſtand vpon: (*Camillo*)
Preſeruer of my Father, now of me,
The Medicine of our Houſe : how ſhall we doe ?
We are not furniſh'd like *Bohemia's* Sonne,
Nor ſhall appeare in *Sicilia.*
  Cam. My Lord,
Feare none of this : I thinke you know my fortunes
Doe all lye there : it ſhall be ſo my care,
To haue you royally appointed, as if
The Scene you play, were mine. For inſtance Sir,
That you may know you ſhall not want: one word.
         Enter Autolicus.
  Aut. Ha, ha, what a Foole Honeſtie is ? and Truſt (his
ſworne brother) a very ſimple Gentleman. I haue ſold
all my Tromperie: not a counterfeit Stone, not a Ribbon,
Glaſſe, Pomander, Browch, Table-booke, Ballad, Knife,
Tape, Gloue, Shooe-tye, Bracelet, Horne-Ring, to keepe

my Pack from faſting : they throng who ſhould buy firſt,
as if my Trinkets had beene hallowed, and brought a be-
nediction to the buyer : by which meanes, I ſaw whoſe
Purſe was beſt in Picture ; and what I ſaw, to my good
vſe, I remembred. My Clowne (who wants but ſomething to be a reaſonable man) grew ſo in loue with the
Wenches Song, that hee would not ſtirre his Petty-toes,
till he had both Tune and Words, which ſo drew the reſt
of the Heard to me, that all their other Sences ſtucke in
Eares : you might haue pinch'd a Placket, it was ſenceleſſe ; 'twas nothing to gueld a Cod-peece of a Purſe : I
would haue fill'd Keyes of that hung in Chaynes : no
hearing, no feeling, but my Sirs Song, and admiring the
Nothing of it.   So that in this time of Lethargie, I pickd
and cut moſt of their Feſtiuall Purſes : And had not the
old-man come in with a Whoo-bub againſt his Daugh-
ter, and the Kings Sonne, and ſcar'd my Chowghes from
the Chaffe, I had not left a Purſe aliue in the whole
Army.
  Cam. Nay, but my Letters by this meanes being there
So ſoone as you arriue, ſhall cleare that doubt.
  Flo. And thoſe that you'le procure from King *Leontes*?
  Cam. Shall ſatisfie your Father.
  Perd. Happy be you :
All that you ſpeake, ſhewes faire.
  Cam. Who haue we here ?
Wee'le make an Inſtrument of this : omit
Nothing may giue vs aide.
  Aut. If they haue ouer-heard me now: why hanging.
  Cam. How now (good Fellow)
Why ſhak'ſt thou ſo ? Feare not (man)
Here's no harme intended to thee.
  Aut. I am a poore Fellow, Sir.
  Cam. Why, be ſo ſtill : here's no body will ſteale that
from thee : yet for the out-ſide of thy pouertie, we muſt
make an exchange; therefore diſ-caſe thee inſtantly (thou
muſt thinke there's a neceſſitie in't) and change Garments
with this Gentleman : Though the penny-worth (on his
ſide) be the worſt, yet hold thee, there's ſome boot.
  Aut. I am a poore Fellow, Sir : (I know ye well
enough.)
  Cam. Nay prethee diſpatch : the Gentleman is halfe
fled already.
  Aut. Are you in earneſt, Sir ? (I ſmell the trick on't.)
  Flo. Diſpatch, I prethee.
  Aut. Indeed I haue had Earneſt, but I cannot with
conſcience take it.
  Cam. Vnbuckle, vnbuckle.
Fortunate Miſtreſſe (let my prophecie
Come home to ye:) you muſt retire your ſelfe
Into ſome Couert ; take your ſweet-hearts Hat
And pluck it ore your Browes, muffle your face,
Diſ-mantle you, and (as you can) diſliken
The truth of your owne ſeeming, that you may
(For I doe feare eyes ouer) to Ship-boord
Get vndeſcry'd.
  Perd. I ſee the Play ſo lyes,
That I muſt beare a part.
  Cam. No remedie :
Haue you done there ?
  Flo. Should I now meet my Father,
He would not call me Sonne.
  Cam. Nay, you ſhall haue no Hat :
Come Lady, come : Farewell (my friend.)
  Aut. Adieu, Sir.
  Flo. O *Perdita*: what haue we twaine forgot?
                  'Pray

'Pray you a word.

Cam. What I doe next, fhall be to tell the King
Of this efcape, and whither they are bound;
Wherein, my hope is, I fhall fo preuaile,
To force him after: in whofe company
I fhall re-view *Sicilia*; for whofe fight,
I haue a Womans Longing.

Flo. Fortune fpeed vs:
Thus we fet on (*Camillo*) to th'Sea-fide.

Cam. The fwifter fpeed, the better.   *Exit.*

Aut. I vnderftand the bufineffe, I heare it: to haue an
open eare, a quick eye, and a nimble hand, is neceffary for
a Cut-purfe; a good Nofe is requifite alfo, to fmell out
worke for th'other Sences. I fee this is the time that the
vniuft man doth thriue. What an exchange had this been,
without boot? What a boot is here, with this exchange?
Sure the Gods doe this yeere conniue at vs, and we may
doe any thing extempore. The Prince himfelfe is about
a peece of Iniquitie (ftealing away from his Father, with
his Clog at his heeles:) if I thought it were a peece of honeftie to acquaint the King withall, I would not do't: I
hold it the more knauerie to conceale it; and therein am
I conftant to my Profeffion.

Enter Clowne and Shepheard.

Afide, afide, here is more matter for a hot braine: Euery
Lanes end, euery Shop, Church, Seffion, Hanging, yeelds
a carefull man worke.

Clowne. See, fee: what a man you are now? there is no
other way, but to tell the King fhe's a Changeling, and
none of your flefh and blood.

Shep. Nay, but heare me.

Clow. Nay; but heare me.

Shep. Goe too then.

Clow. She being none of your flefh and blood, your
flefh and blood ha's not offended the King, and fo your
flefh and blood is not to be punifh'd by him. Shew thofe
things you found about her (thofe fecret things, all but
what fhe ha's with her:) This being done, let the Law goe
whiftle: I warrant you.

Shep. I will tell the King all, euery word, yea, and his
Sonnes prancks too; who, I may fay, is no honeft man,
neither to his Father, nor to me, to goe about to make me
the Kings Brother in Law.

Clow. Indeed Brother in Law was the fartheft off you
could haue beene to him, and then your Blood had beene
the dearer, by I know how much an ounce.

Aut. Very wifely (Puppies.)

Shep. Well: let vs to the King: there is that in this
Farthell, will make him fcratch his Beard.

Aut. I know not what impediment this Complaint
may be to the flight of my Mafter.

Clo. 'Pray heartily he be at' Pallace.

Aut. Though I am not naturally honeft, I am fo fometimes by chance: Let me pocket vp my Pedlers excrement. How now (Ruftiques) whither are you bound?

Shep. To th' Pallace (and it like your Worfhip.)

Aut. Your Affaires there? what? with whom? the
Condition of that Farthell? the place of your dwelling?
your names? your ages? of what hauing? breeding, and
any thing that is fitting to be knowne, difcouer?

Clo. We are but plaine fellowes, Sir.

Aut. A Lye; you are rough, and hayrie: Let me haue
no lying; it becomes none but Tradef-men, and they often giue vs (Souldiers) the Lye, but wee pay them for it
with ftamped Coyne, not ftabbing Steele, therefore they
doe not giue vs the Lye.

Clo. Your Worfhip had like to haue giuen vs one, if
you had not taken your felfe with the manner.

Shep. Are you a Courtier, and't like you Sir?

Aut. Whether it lke me, or no, I am a Courtier. Seeft
thou not the ayre of the Court, in thefe enfoldings? Hath
not my gate in it, the meafure of the Court? Receiues not
thy Nofe Court-Odour from me? Refle&ct; I not on thy
Bafeneffe, Court-Contempt? Think'ft thou, for that I
infinuate, at toaze from thee thy Bufineffe, I am therefore no Courtier? I am Courtier *Cap-a-pe*; and one that
will eyther pufh-on, or pluck-back, thy Bufineffe there:
whereupon I command thee to open thy Affaires.

Shep. My Bufineffe, Sir, is to the King.

Aut. What Aduocate ha'ft thou to him?

Shep. I know not (and't like you.)

Clo. Aduocate's the Court-word for a Pheazant: fay
you haue none.

Shep. None, Sir: I haue no Pheazant Cock, nor Hen.

Aut. How bleffed are we, that are not fimple men?
Yet Nature might haue made me as thefe are,
Therefore I will not difdaine.

Clo. This cannot be but a great Courtier.

Shep. His Garments are rich, but he weares them not
handfomely.

Clo. He feemes to be the more Noble, in being fantafticall: A great man, Ile warrant; I know by the picking
on's Teeth.

Aut. The Farthell there? What's i'th' Farthell?
Wherefore that Box?

Shep. Sir, there lyes fuch Secrets in this Farthell and
Box, which none muft know but the King, and which hee
fhall know within this houre, if I may come to th' fpeech
of him.

Aut. Age, thou haft loft thy labour.

Shep. Why Sir?

Aut. The King is not at the Pallace, he is gone aboord
a new Ship, to purge Melancholy, and ayre himfelfe: for
if thou bee'ft capable of things ferious, thou muft know
the King is full of griefe.

Shep. So 'tis faid (Sir:) about his Sonne, that fhould
haue married a Shepheards Daughter.

Aut. If that Shepheard be not in hand-faft, let him
flye; the Curfes he fhall haue, the Tortures he fhall feele,
will breake the back of Man, the heart of Monfter.

Clo. Thinke you fo, Sir?

Aut. Not hee alone fhall fuffer what Wit can make
heauie, and Vengeance bitter; but thofe that are Iermaine
to him (though remou'd fiftie times) fhall all come vnder
the Hang-man: which, though it be great pitty, yet it is
neceffarie. An old Sheepe-whiftiing Rogue, a Ram-ten-
der, to offer to haue his Daughter come into grace? Some
fay hee fhall be fton'd: but that death is too foft for him
(fay I:) Draw our Throne into a Sheep-Coat? all deaths
are too few, the fharpeft too eafie.

Clo. Ha's the old-man ere a Sonne Sir (doe you heare)
and't like you, Sir?

Aut. Hee ha's a Sonne: who fhall be flayd aliue, then
'noynted ouer with Honey, fet on the head of a Wafpes
Neft, then ftand till he be three quarters and a dram dead:
then recouer'd againe with Aquauite, or fome other hot
Infufion: then, raw as he is (and in the hoteft day Progno-
ftication proclaymes) fhall he be fet againft a Brick-wall,
(the Sunne looking with a South-ward eye vpon him;
where hee is to behold him, with Flyes blown to death.)
But what talke we of thefe Traitorly-Rafcals, whofe miferies are to be fmil'd at, their offences being fo capitall?
          Tell

Tell me(for you feeme to be honeft plaine men)what you
haue to the King : being fomething gently confider'd,Ile
bring you where hee is aboord, tender your perfons to his
prefence, whifper him in your behalfes; and if it be in
man, befides the King, to effect your Suites, here is man
fhall doe it.

Clow. He feemes to be of great authoritie: clofe with
him, giue him Gold; and though Authoritie be a ftubborne Beare, yet hee is oft led by the Nofe with Gold :
fhew the in-fide of your Purfe to the out-fide of his
hand, and no more adoe. Remember fton'd, and flay'd
aliue.

Shep. And't pleafe you(Sir)to vndertake the Bufineffe
for vs, here is that Gold I haue : Ile make it as much
more, and leaue this young man in pawne, till I bring it
you.

Aut. After I haue done what I promifed?

Shep. I Sir.

Aut. Well, giue me the Moitie : Are you a partie in
this Bufineffe?

Clow. In fome fort, Sir : but though my cafe be a pittifull one, I hope I fhall not be flayd out of it.

Aut. Oh, that's the cafe of the Shepheards Sonne :
hang him, hee'le be made an example.

Clow. Comfort, good comfort : We muft to the King,
and fhew our ftrange fights : he muft know 'tis none of
your Daughter, nor my Sifter : wee are gone elfe. Sir, I
will giue you as much as this old man do's, when the Bufineffe is performed, and remaine(as he fayes)your pawne
till it be brought you.

Aut. I will truft you. Walke before toward the Sea-
fide, goe on the right hand, I will but looke vpon the
Hedge, and follow you.

Clow. We are blefs'd, in this man : as I may fay, euen
blefs'd.

Shep. Let's before, as he bids vs : he was prouided to
doe vs good.

Aut. If I had a mind to be honeft, I fee *Fortune* would
not fuffer mee : fhee drops Booties in my mouth. I am
courted now with a double occafion:(Gold, and a means
to doe the Prince my Mafter good; which, who knowes
how that may turne backe to my aduancement?) I will
bring thefe two Moales, thefe blind-ones, aboord him: if
he thinke it fit to fhoare them againe, and that the Complaint they haue to the King, concernes him nothing, let
him call me Rogue, for being fo farre officious, for I am
proofe againft that Title, and what fhame elfe belongs
to't : To him will I prefent them, there may be matter in
it.   *Exeunt.*

Actus Quintus. Scena Prima.

Enter Leontes, Cleomines, Dion, Paulina, Seruants :
Florizel, Perdita.

Cleo. Sir, you haue done enough, and haue perform'd
A Saint-like Sorrow : No fault could you make,
Which you haue not redeem'd; indeed pay'd downe
More penitence, then done trefpas : At the laft
Doe, as the Heauens haue done; forget your euill,
With them, forgiue your felfe.

Leo. Whileft I remember
Her, and her Vertues, I cannot forget

My blemifhes in them, and fo ftill thinke of
The wrong I did my felfe : which was fo much,
That Heire-leffe it hath made my Kingdome, and
Deftroy'd the fweet'ft Companion, that ere man
Bred his hopes out of, true.

Paul. Too true (my Lord:)
If one by one, you wedded all the World,
Or from the All that are, tooke fomething good,
To make a perfect Woman; fhe you kill'd,
Would be vnparallell'd.

Leo. I thinke fo. Kill'd?
She I kill'd? I did fo : but thou ftrik'ft me
Sorely, to fay I did : it is as bitter
Vpon thy Tongue, as in my Thought. Now, good now,
Say fo but feldome.

Cleo. Not at all, good Lady :
You might haue fpoken a thoufand things, that would
Haue done the time more benefit, and grac'd
Your kindneffe better.

Paul. You are one of thofe
Would haue him wed againe.

Dio. If you would not fo,
You pitty not the State, nor the Remembrance
Of his moft Soueraigne Name : Confider little,
What Dangers, by his Highneffe faile of Iffue,
May drop vpon his Kingdome, and deuoure
Incertaine lookers on. What were more holy,
Then to reioyce the former Queene is well?
What holyer, then for Royalties repayre,
For prefent comfort, and for future good,
To bleffe the Bed of Maieftie againe
With a fweet Fellow to't?

Paul. There is none worthy,
(Refpecting her that's gone:) befides the Gods
Will haue fulfill'd their fecret purpofes :
For ha's not the Diuine *Apollo* faid?
Is't not the tenor of his Oracle,
That King *Leontes* fhall not haue an Heire,
Till his loft Child be found? Which, that it fhall,
Is all as monftrous to our humane reafon,
As my *Antigonus* to breake his Graue,
And come againe to me: who, on my life,
Did perifh with the Infant. 'Tis your councell,
My Lord fhould to the Heauens be contrary,
Oppofe againft their wills. Care not for Iffue,
The Crowne will find an Heire. Great *Alexander*
Left his to th' Worthieft : fo his Succeffor
Was like to be the beft.

Leo. Good *Paulina*,
Who haft the memorie of *Hermione*
I know in honor : O, that euer I
Had fquar'd me to thy councell : then, euen now,
I might haue look'd vpon my Queenes full eyes,
Haue taken Treafure from her Lippes.

Paul. And left them
More rich, for what they yeelded.

Leo. Thou fpeak'ft truth :
No more fuch Wiues, therefore no Wife : one worfe,
And better vs'd, would make her Sainted Spirit
Againe poffeffe her Corps, and on this Stage
(Where we Offendors now appeare) Soule-vext,
And begin, why to me?

Paul. Had fhe fuch power,
She had juft fuch caufe.

Leo. She had, and would incenfe me
To murther her I marryed.

Paul. I fhould fo :
Were I the Ghoft that walk'd, Il'd bid you marke
Her eye, and tell me for what dull part in't
You chofe her : then Il'd fhrieke, that euen your eares
Should rift to heare me, and the words that follow'd,
Should be, Remember mine.

Leo. Starres, Starres,
And all eyes elfe, dead coales : feare thou no Wife;
Ile haue no Wife, *Paulina.*

Paul. Will you fweare
Neuer to marry, but by my free leaue?

Leo. Neuer (*Paulina*) fo be bleff'd my Spirit.

Paul. Then good my Lords, beare witneffe to his Oath.

Cleo. You tempt him ouer-much.

Paul. Vnleffe another,
As like *Hermione*, as is her Picture,
Affront his eye.

Cleo. Good Madame, I haue done.

Paul. Yet if my Lord will marry : if you will, Sir;
No remedie but you will : Giue me the Office
To chufe you a Queene : fhe fhall not be fo young
As was your former, but fhe fhall be fuch
As (walk'd your firft Queenes Ghoft) it fhould take ioy
To fee her in your armes.

Leo. My true *Paulina*,
We fhall not marry, till thou bidft vs.

Paul. That
Shall be when your firft Queene's againe in breath :
Neuer till then.

Enter a Seruant.

Ser. One that giues out himfelfe Prince *Florizell*,
Sonne of *Polixenes*, with his Princeffe (fhe
The faireft I haue yet beheld) defires acceffe
To your high prefence.

Leo. What with him? he comes not
Like to his Fathers Greatneffe : his approach
(So out of circumftance, and fuddaine) tells vs,
'Tis not a Vifitation fram'd, but forc'd
By need, and accident. What Trayne?

Ser. But few,
And thofe but meane.

Leo. His Princeffe (fay you) with him?

Ser. I : the moft peereleffe peece of Earth, I thinke,
That ere the Sunne fhone bright on.

Paul. Oh *Hermione*,
As euery prefent Time doth boaft it felfe
Aboue a better, gone ; fo muft thy Graue
Giue way to what's feene now. Sir, you your felfe
Haue faid, and writ fo ; but your writing now
Is colder then that Theame : fhe had not beene,
Nor was not to be equall'd, thus your Verfe
Flow'd with her Beautie once ; 'tis fhrewdly ebb'd,
To fay you haue feene a better.

Ser. Pardon, Madame :
The one, I haue almoft forgot (your pardon:)
The other, when fhe ha's obtayn'd your Eye,
Will haue your Tongue too. This is a Creature,
Would fhe begin a Sect, might quench the zeale
Of all Profeffors elfe ; make Profelytes
Of who fhe but bid follow.

Paul. How? not women?

Ser. Women will loue her, that fhe is a Woman
More worth then any Man : Men, that fhe is
The rareft of all Women.

Leo. Goe *Cleomines*,
Your felfe (affifted with your honor'd Friends)

Bring them to our embracement. Still 'tis ftrange,
He thus fhould fteale vpon vs.   *Exit.*

Paul. Had our Prince
(Iewell of Children) feene this houre, he had payr'd
Well with this Lord ; there was not full a moneth
Betweene their births.

Leo. 'Prethee no more ; ceafe : thou know'ft
He dyes to me againe, when talk'd-of : fure
When I fhall fee this Gentleman, thy fpeeches
Will bring me to confider that, which may
Vnfurnifh me of Reafon. They are come.

Enter Florizell, Perdita, Cleomines, and others.

Your Mother was moft true to Wedlock, Prince,
For fhe did print your Royall Father off,
Conceiuing you. Were I but twentie one,
Your Fathers Image is fo hit in you,
(His very ayre) that I fhould call you Brother,
As I did him, and fpeake of fomething wildly
By vs perform'd before. Moft dearely welcome,
And your faire Princeffe (Goddeffe) oh : alas,
I loft a couple, that 'twixt Heauen and Earth
Might thus haue ftood, begetting wonder, as
You (gracious Couple) doe : and then I loft
(All mine owne Folly) the Societie,
Amitie too of your braue Father, whom
(Though bearing Miferie) I defire my life
Once more to looke on him.

Flo. By his command
Haue I here touch'd *Sicilia*, and from him
Giue you all greetings, that a King (at friend)
Can fend his Brother : and but Infirmitie
(Which waits vpon worne times) hath fomething feiz'd
His wifh'd Abilitie, he had himfelfe
The Lands and Waters, 'twixt your Throne and his,
Meafur'd, to looke vpon you ; whom he loues
(He bad me fay fo) more then all the Scepters,
And thofe that beare them, liuing.

Leo. Oh my Brother,
(Good Gentleman) the wrongs I haue done thee, ftirre
Afrefh within me : and thefe thy offices
(So rarely kind) are as Interpreters
Of my behind-hand flackneffe. Welcome hither,
As is the Spring to th'Earth. And hath he too
Expos'd this Paragon to th'fearefull vfage
(At leaft vngentle) of the dreadfull *Neptune*,
To greet a man, not worth her paines; much leffe,
Th'aduenture of her perfon?

Flo. Good my Lord,
She came from *Libia*.

Leo. Where the Warlike *Smalus*,
That Noble honor'd Lord, is fear'd, and lou'd?

Flo. Moft Royall Sir,
From thence : from him, whofe Daughter
His Teares proclaym'd his parting with her : thence
(A profperous South-wind friendly) we haue crofs'd,
To execute the Charge my Father gaue me,
For vifiting your Highneffe : My beft Traine
I haue from your *Sicilian* Shores difmifs'd ;
Who for *Bohemia* bend, to fignifie
Not onely my fucceffe in *Libia* (Sir)
But my arriuall, and my Wifes, in fafetie
Here, where we are.

Leo. The bleffed Gods
Purge all Infection from our Ayre, whileft you
Doe Clymate here : you haue a holy Father,
A gracefull Gentleman, againft whofe perfon

(So

(So facred as it is) I haue done finne,
For which, the Heauens (taking angry note)
Haue left me Iffue-leffe : and your Father's bleff'd
(As he from Heauen merits it) with you,
Worthy his goodneffe. What might I haue been,
Might I a Sonne and Daughter now haue look'd on,
Such goodly things as you ?

        Enter a Lord.

  Lord. Moft Noble Sir,
That which I fhall report, will beare no credit,
Were not the proofe fo nigh. Pleafe you(great Sir)
Bohemia greets you from himfelfe, by me :
Defires you to attach his Sonne, who ha's
(His Dignitie, and Dutie both caft off)
Fled from his Father, from his Hopes, and with
A Shepheards Daughter.

  Leo. Where's *Bohemia?* fpeake:

  Lord. Here, in your Citie : I now came from him.
I fpeake amazedly, and it becomes
My meruaile, and my Meffage. To your Court
Whiles he was haftning (in the Chafe, it feemes,
Of this faire Couple) meetes he on the way
The Father of this feeming Lady, and
Her Brother, hauing both their Countrey quitted,
With this young Prince.

  Flo. Camillo ha's betray'd me ;
Whofe honor, and whofe honeftie till now,
Endur'd all Weathers.

  Lord. Lay't fo to his charge :
He's with the King your Father.

  Leo. Who ? *Camillo?*

  Lord. *Camillo* (Sir:) I fpake with him: who now
Ha's thefe poore men in queftion. Neuer faw I
Wretches fo quake : they kneele, they kiffe the Earth;
Forfweare themfelues as often as they fpeake:
Bohemia ftops his eares, and threatens them
With diuers deaths, in death.

  Perd. Oh my poore Father :
The Heauen fets Spyes vpon vs, will not haue
Our Contract celebrated.

  Leo. You are married ?

  Flo. We are not (Sir) nor are we like to be:
The Starres (I fee) will kiffe the Valleyes firft :
The oddes for high and low's alike.

  Leo. My Lord,
Is this the Daughter of a King?

  Flo. She is,
When once fhe is my Wife.

  Leo. That once (I fee) by your good Fathers fpeed,
Will come-on very flowly. I am forry
(Moft forry) you haue broken from his liking,
Where you were ty'd in dutie : and as forry,
Your Choife is not fo rich in Worth, as Beautie,
That you might well enioy her.

  Flo. Deare, looke vp :
Though *Fortune,* vifible an Enemie,
Should chafe vs, with my Father ; powre no iot
Hath fhe to change our Loues. Befeech you (Sir)
Remember, fince you ow'd no more to Time
Then I doe now: with thought of fuch Affe&ions,
Step forth mine Aduocate : at your requeft,
My Father will graunt precious things, as Trifles.

  Leo. Would he doe fo, I'ld beg your precious Miftris,
Which he counts but a Trifle.

  Paul. Sir (my Liege)
Your eye hath too much youth in't : not a moneth

'Fore your Queene dy'd, fhe was more worth fuch gazes,
Then what you looke on now.

  Leo. I thought of her,
Euen in thefe Lookes I made. But your Petition
Is yet vn-anfwer'd : I will to your Father :
Your Honor not o're-throwne by your defires,
I am friend to them, and you : Vpon which Errand
I now goe toward him : therefore follow me,
And marke what way I make: Come good my Lord.

        Exeunt.

Scæna Secunda.

Enter Autolicus, and a Gentleman.

  Aut. Befeech you (Sir) were you prefent at this Relation ?

  Gent. 1. I was by at the opening of the Farthell, heard
the old Shepheard deliuer the manner how he found it :
Whereupon (after a little amazedneffe) we were all commanded out of the Chamber : onely this (me thought) I
heard the Shepheard fay, he found the Child.

  Aut. I would moft gladly know the iffue of it.

  Gent. 1. I make a broken deliuerie of the Bufineffe ;
but the changes I perceiued in the King and *Camillo,* were
very Notes of admiration : they feem'd almoft, with fta-
ring on one another, to teare the Cafes of their Eyes.
There was fpeech in their dumbneffe, Language in their
very gefture : they look'd as they had heard of a World
ranfom'd, or one deftroyed : a notable paffion of Wonder appeared in them : but the wifeft beholder, that knew
no more but feeing, could not fay, if th'importance were
Ioy, or Sorrow ; but in the extremitie of the one, it muft
needs be.   *Enter another Gentleman.*
Here comes a Gentleman, that happily knowes more :
The Newes, *Rogero.*

  Gent. 2. Nothing but Bon-fires : the Oracle is fulfill'd :
the Kings Daughter is found : fuch a deale of wonder is
broken out within this houre, that Ballad-makers cannot
be able to expreffe it.   *Enter another Gentleman.*
Here comes the Lady *Paulina's* Steward, hee can deliuer
you more. How goes it now (Sir.) This Newes (which
is call'd true) is fo like an old Tale, that the veritie of it is
in ftrong fufpition : Ha's the King found his Heire ?

  Gent. 3. Moft true, if euer Truth were pregnant by
Circumftance : That which you heare, you'le fweare
you fee, there is fuch vnitie in the proofes. The Mantle
of Queene *Hermiones :* her Iewell about the Neck of it :
the Letters of *Antigonus* found with it, which they know
to be his Chara&er : the Maieftie of the Creature, in refemblance of the Mother : the Affe&ion of Nobleneffe,
which Nature fhewes aboue her Breeding, and many o-
ther Euidences, proclayme her, with all certaintie, to be
the Kings Daughter. Did you fee the meeting of the
two Kings ?

  Gent. 2. No.

  Gent. 3. Then haue you loft a Sight which was to bee
feene, cannot bee fpoken of. There might you haue beheld one Ioy crowne another, fo and in fuch manner, that
it feem'd Sorrow wept to take leaue of them : for their
Ioy waded in teares. There was cafting vp of Eyes, holding vp of Hands, with Countenance of fuch diftra&ion,
that they were to be knowne by Garment, not by Fauor.
                                    Our

Our King being ready to leape out of himselfe, for ioy of his found Daughter; as if that Ioy were now become a Loffe, cryes, Oh, thy Mother, thy Mother : then askes *Bohemia* forgiueneffe, then embraces his Sonne-in-Law: then againe worryes he his Daughter, with clipping her. Now he thanks the old Shepheard (which ftands by, like a Weather-bitten Conduit, of many Kings Reignes.) I neuer heard of fuch another Encounter; which Iames Report to follow it, and vndo's defcription to doe it.

*Gent.*2. What, 'pray you, became of *Antigonus*, that carryed hence the Child ?

*Gent.*3. Like an old Tale ftill, which will haue matter to rehearfe, though Credit be afleepe, and not an eare open; he was torne to pieces with a Beare : This auouches the Shepheards Sonne; who ha's not onely his Innocence (which feemes much) to iuftifie him, but a Hand-kerchief and Rings of his, that *Paulina* knowes.

Gent. 1. What became of his Barke, and his Followers ?

Gent. 3. Wrackt the fame inftant of their Mafters death, and in the view of the Shepheard : fo that all the Inftruments which ayded to expofe the Child, were euen then loft, when it was found. But oh the Noble Combat, that 'twixt Ioy and Sorrow was fought in *Paulina.* Shee had one Eye declin'd for the loffe of her Husband, another eleuated, that the Oracle was fulfill'd: Shee lifted the Princeffe from the Earth, and fo locks her in embracing, as if fhee would pin her to her heart, that fhee might no more be in danger of loofing.

Gent. 1. The Dignitie of this Act was worth the audience of Kings and Princes, for by fuch was it acted.

Gent. 3. One of the prettyeft touches of all, and that which angl'd for mine Eyes (caught the Water, though not the Fifh) was, when at the Relation of the Queenes death (with the manner how fhee came to't, brauely confefs'd, and lamented by the King) how attentiuneffe wounded his Daughter, till (from one figne of dolour to another) fhee did (with an *Alas*) I would faine fay, bleed Teares; for I am fure, my heart wept blood. Who was moft Marble, there changed colour : fome fwownded, all forrowed : if all the World could haue feen't, the Woe had beene vniuerfall.

Gent. 1. Are they returned to the Court ?

Gent. 3. No: The Princeffe hearing of her Mothers Statue (which is in the keeping of *Paulina*) a Peece many yeeres in doing, and now newly perform'd, by that rare Italian Mafter, *Iulio Romano*, who (had he himfelfe Eternitie, and could put Breath into his Worke) would beguile Nature of her Cuftome, fo perfectly he is her Ape: He fo neere to *Hermione*, hath done *Hermione*, that they fay one would fpeake to her, and ftand in hope of anfwer. Thither (with all greedineffe of affection) are they gone, and there they intend to Sup.

Gent. 2. I thought fhe had fome great matter there in hand, for fhee hath priuately, twice or thrice a day, euer fince the death of *Hermione*, vifited that remoued Houfe. Shall wee thither, and with our companie peece the Reioycing ?

Gent. 1. Who would be thence, that ha's the benefit of Acceffe ? euery winke of an Eye, fome new Grace will be borne : our Abfence makes vs vnthriftie to our Knowledge. Let's along. *Exit.*

Aut. Now (had I not the dafh of my former life in me) would Preferment drop on my head. I brought the old man and his Sonne aboord the Prince; told him, I heard them talke of a Farthell, and I know not what : but

he at that time ouer-fond of the Shepheards Daughter (fo he then tooke her to be) who began to be much Sea-fick, and himfelfe little better, extremitie of Weather continuing, this Myfterie remained vndifcouer'd. But 'tis all one to me : for had I beene the finder-out of this Secret, it would not haue rellifh'd among my other difcredits.

Enter Shepheard and Clowne.

Here come thofe I haue done good to againft my will, and alreadie appearing in the bloffomes of their Fortune.

Shep. Come Boy, I am paft moe Children : but thy Sonnes and Daughters will be all Gentlemen borne.

Clow. You are well met (Sir.) you deny'd to fight with mee this other day, becaufe I was no Gentleman borne. See you thefe Clothes ? fay you fee them not, and thinke me ftill no Gentleman borne : You were beft fay thefe Robes are not Gentlemen borne. Giue me the Lye : doe : and try whether I am not now a Gentleman borne.

Ant. I know you are now (Sir) a Gentleman borne.

Clow. I, and haue been fo any time thefe foure houres.

Shep. And fo haue I, Boy.

Clow. So you haue : but I was a Gentleman borne before my Father : for the Kings Sonne tooke me by the hand, and call'd mee Brother : and then the two Kings call'd my Father Brother : and then the Prince (my Brother) and the Princeffe (my Sifter) call'd my Father, Father; and fo wee wept : and there was the firft Gentleman-like teares that euer we fhed.

Shep. We may liue (Sonne) to fhed many more.

Clow. I : or elfe 'twere hard luck, being in fo prepofterous eftate as we are.

Aut. I humbly befeech you (Sir) to pardon me all the faults I haue committed to your Worfhip, and to giue me your good report to the Prince my Mafter.

Shep. 'Prethee Sonne doe: for we muft be gentle, now we are Gentlemen.

Clow. Thou wilt amend thy life ?

Aut. I, and it like your good Worfhip.

Clow. Giue me thy hand: I will fweare to the Prince, thou art as honeft a true Fellow as any is in *Bohemia.*

Shep. You may fay it, but not fweare it.

Clow. Not fweare it, now I am a Gentleman ? Let Boores and Francklins fay it, Ile fweare it.

Shep. How if it be falfe (Sonne?)

Clow. If it be ne're fo falfe, a true Gentleman may fweare it, in the behalfe of his Friend : And Ile fweare to the Prince, thou art a tall Fellow of thy hands, and that thou wilt not be drunke: but I know thou art no tall Fellow of thy hands, and that thou wilt be drunke : but Ile fweare it, and I would thou would'ft be a tall Fellow of thy hands.

Aut. I will proue fo (Sir) to my power.

Clow. I, by any meanes proue a tall Fellow: if I do not wonder, how thou dar'ft venture to be drunke, not being a tall Fellow, truft me not. Harke, the Kings and the Princes (our Kindred) are going to fee the Queenes Picture. Come, follow vs: wee'le be thy good Mafters. *Exeunt.*

Scæna Tertia.

Enter Leontes, Polixenes, Florizell, Perdita, Camillo,
Paulina: Hermione (like a Statue:) Lords, &c.

Leo. O graue and good *Paulina*, the great comfort
That I haue had of thee ?

C c   *Paul.* What

Paul. What (Soueraigne Sir)
I did not well,I meant well : all my Seruices
You haue pay'd home. But that you haue vouchfaf'd
(With your Crown'd Brother, and thefe your contracted
Heires of your Kingdomes) my poore Houfe to vifit;
It is a furplus of your Grace, which neuer
My life may laft to anfwere.

Leo. O *Paulina,*
We honor you with trouble : but we came
To fee the Statue of our Queene. Your Gallerie
Haue we pafs'd through,not without much content
In many fingularities; but we faw not
That which my Daughter came to looke vpon,
The Statue of her Mother.

Paul. As fhe liu'd peereleffe,
So her dead likeneffe I doe well beleeue
Excells what euer yet you look'd vpon,
Or hand of Man hath done : therefore I keepe it
Louely, apart. But here it is : prepare
To fee the Life as liuely mock'd,as euer
Still Sleepe mock'd Death : behold,and fay 'tis well.
I like your filence,it the more fhewes-off
Your wonder : but yet fpeake,firft you (my Liege)
Comes it not fomething neere?

Leo. Her naturall Pofture.
Chide me (deare Stone) that I may fay indeed
Thou art *Hermione*; or rather,thou art fhe,
In thy not chiding : for fhe was as tender
As Infancie,and Grace. But yet (*Paulina*)
Hermione was not fo much wrinckled,nothing
So aged as this feemes.

Pol. Oh,not by much.
Paul. So much the more our Caruers excellence,
Which lets goe-by fome fixteene yeeres,and makes her
As fhe liu'd now.

Leo. As now fhe might haue done,
So much to my good comfort, as it is
Now piercing to my Soule. Oh, thus fhe ftood,
Euen with fuch life of Maieftie(warme Life,
As now it coldly ftands) when firft I woo'd her.
I am afham'd : Do's not the Stone rebuke me,
For being more Stone then it? Oh Royall Peece :
There's Magick in thy Maieftie,which ha's
My Euils coniur'd to remembrance ; and
From thy admiring Daughter tooke the Spirits,
Standing like Stone with thee.

Perd. And doe not fay 'tis Superftition,that
I kneele,and then implore her Bleffing. Lady,
Deere Queene, that ended when I but began,
Giue me that hand of yours, to kiffe.

Paul. O, patience :
The Statue is but newly fix'd ; the Colour's
Not dry.

Cam. My Lord, your Sorrow was too fore lay'd-on,
Which fixteene Winters cannot blow away,
So many Summers dry : fcarce any Ioy
Did euer fo long liue ; no Sorrow,
But kill'd it felfe much fooner.

Pol. Deere my Brother,
Let him, that was the caufe of this, haue powre
To take-off fo much griefe from you,as he
Will peece vp in himfelfe.

Paul. Indeed my Lord,
If I had thought the fight of my poore Image
Would thus haue wrought you (for the Stone is mine)

Il'd not haue fhew'd it.
Leo. Doe not draw the Curtaine.
Paul. No longer fhall you gaze on't,leaft your Fancie
May thinke anon, it moues.
Leo. Let be, let be :
Would I were dead,but that me thinkes alreadie.
(What was he that did make it?) See (my Lord)
Would you not deeme it breath'd? and that thofe veines
Did verily beare blood?
Pol. 'Mafterly done :
The very Life feemes warme vpon her Lippe.
Leo. The fixure of her Eye ha's motion in't,
As we are mock'd with Art.
Paul. Ile draw the Curtaine :
My Lord's almoft fo farre tranfported,that
Hee'le thinke anon it liues.
Leo. Oh fweet *Paulina,*
Make me to thinke fo twentie yeeres together :
No fetled Sences of the World can match
The pleafure of that madneffe. Let't alone.
Paul. I am forry (Sir) I haue thus farre ftir'd you : but
I could afflict you farther.
Leo. Doe *Paulina* :
For this Affliction ha's a tafte as fweet
As any Cordiall comfort. Still me thinkes
There is an ayre comes from her. What fine Chizzell
Could euer yet cut breath? Let no man mock me,
For I will kiffe her.
Paul. Good my Lord, forbeare :
The ruddineffe vpon her Lippe, is wet :
You'le marre it, if you kiffe it; ftayne your owne
With Oyly Painting : fhall I draw the Curtaine.
Leo. No : not thefe twentie yeeres.
Perd. So long could I
Stand-by, a looker-on.
Paul. Either forbeare,
Quit prefently the Chappell, or refolue you
For more amazement : if you can behold it,
Ile make the Statue moue indeed; defcend,
And take you by the hand : but then you'le thinke
(Which I proteft againft) I am affifted
By wicked Powers.
Leo. What you can make her doe,
I am content to looke on : what to fpeake,
I am content to heare : for 'tis as eafie
To make her fpeake, as moue.
Paul. It is requir'd
You doe awake your Faith : then, all ftand ftill :
On : thofe that thinke it is vnlawfull Bufineffe
I am about, let them depart.
Leo. Proceed :
No foot fhall ftirre.
Paul. Mufick; awake her : Strike :
'Tis time : defcend : be Stone no more : approach :
Strike all that looke vpon with meruaile : Come :
Ile fill your Graue vp : ftirre : nay, come away :
Bequeath to Death your numneffe : (for from him,
Deare Life redeemes you) you perceiue fhe ftirres :
Start not : her Actions fhall be holy, as
You heare my Spell is lawfull : doe not fhun her,
Vntill you fee her dye againe; for then
You kill her double : Nay, prefent your Hand :
When fhe was young,you woo'd her : now, in age,
Is fhe become the Suitor?
Leo. Oh fhe's warme :
If this be Magick, let it be an Art

Lawfull as Eating.

Pol. She embraces him.

Cam. She hangs about his necke,
If she pertaine to life, let her speake too.

Pol. I, and make it manifest where she ha's liu'd,
Or how stolne from the dead?

Paul. That she is liuing,
Were it but told you, should be hooted at
Like an old Tale : but it appeares she liues,
Though yet she speake not. Marke a little while :
Please you to interpose (faire Madam) kneele,
And pray your Mothers blessing : turne good Lady,
Our *Perdita* is found.

Her. You Gods looke downe,
And from your sacred Viols poure your graces
Vpon my daughters head : Tell me (mine owne)
Where hast thou bin preseru'd? Where liu'd?How found
Thy Fathers Court? For thou shalt heare that I
Knowing by *Paulina*, that she Oracle
Gaue hope thou wast in being, haue preseru'd
My selfe, to see the yssue.

Paul. There's ttme enough for that,
Least they desire (vpon this push) to trouble
Your ioyes, with like Relation. Go together
You precious winners all : your exultation

Partake to euery one : I (an old Turtle)
Will wing me to some wither'd bough, and there
My Mate (that's neuer to be found againe)
Lament, till I am lost.

Leo. O peace *Paulina* :
Thou shouldst a husband take by my consent,
As I by thine a Wife. This is a Match,
And made betweene's by Vowes. Thou hast found mine,
But how, is to be question'd : for I saw her
(As I thought) dead : and haue (in vaine) said many
A prayer vpon her graue. Ile not seeke farre
(For him, I partly know his minde) to finde thee
An honourable husband. Come *Camillo*,
And take her by the hand : whose worth, and honesty
Is richly noted : and heere iustified
By Vs, a paire of Kings. Let's from this place.
What? looke vpon my Brother : both your pardons,
That ere I put betweene your holy lookes
My ill suspition : This your Son-in-law,
And Sonne vnto the King, whom heauens directing
Is troth-plight to your daughter. Good *Paulina*,
Leade vs from hence, where we may leysurely
Each one demand, and answere to his part
Perform'd in this wide gap of Time, since first
We were disseuer'd : Hastily lead away. *Exeunt.*

The Names of the Actors.

Leontes, King of Sicillia.
Mamillus, yong Prince of Sicillia.
Camillo.
Antigonus.   Foure
Cleomines. } Lords of Sicillia.
Dion.
Hermione, Queene to Leontes.
Perdita, Daughter to Leontes and Hermione.
Paulina, wife to Antigonus.

Emilia, a Lady.
Polixenes, King of Bohemia.
Florizell, Prince of Bohemia.
Old Shepheard, reputed Father of Perdita.
Clowne, his Sonne.
Autolicus, a Rogue.
Archidamus, a Lord of Bohemia.
Other Lords, and Gentlemen, and Seruants.
Shepheards, and Shephcarddesses.
        FINIS.